The Marquis de Sade

Juliette

Works by the Marquis de Sade
Published by Grove Press

*Justine, Philosophy in the Bedroom,
and Other Writings*

The 120 Days of Sodom and Other Writings

Juliette

The Marquis de Sade

Juliette

translated by
AUSTRYN WAINHOUSE

Complete American edition

SIX VOLUMES IN ONE

GROVE PRESS / New York

Printed in the United States of America

Library of Congress Catalog Card Number 68-22016
ISBN 0-8021-3085-2

Grove Press
841 Broadway
New York, NY 10003

00 01 15 14 13 12 11

Contents

Foreword

To the final version of *Justine*—and there are three versions of *Justine*—Sade added, as its complement and to complete it, *The Story of Juliette;* the two panels of a diptych, interrelated and yet distinct, they were first published in the year 1797 as an immense book called *La Nouvelle Justine.* The bibliographical details are these:

> *La Nouvelle Justine, ou les Malheurs de la Vertu. Ouvrage orné d'un frontispice et de quarante sujets gravés avec soin. En Hollande* [Paris], 1797. Four volumes, 18mo. These four volumes comprise the first part of the definitive edition of this work, of which the second part, in six volumes, bears the title: *La Nouvelle Justine, ou les Malheurs de la Vertu, suivie de l'Histoire de Juliette, sa soeur* [ou les *Prospérités du vice*]. *Ouvrage orné d'un frontispice et de cent sujets gravés avec soin. En Hollande* [Paris,] 1797.

As for the preceding redactions, the earliest and shortest, *Les Infortunes de la Vertu,* whose manuscript shows the date 1787, was designed for inclusion in a volume of those *contes, historiettes,* and *fabliaux,* carefully made, inoffensive, and eminently *regular* writings to which Sade attached a special importance. For it was through his "public" performances—first as a storyteller, later as a playwright—that, as he rightly felt, he belonged to the "world of letters." At the same time, and ever more so as he passed his prisoner's time, along with his literary ambitions he nourished others, totally irregular, engendered by a rage no ordinary consolations could appease, and that rendered him the mortal enemy of the world outside. He wrote *Les Infortunes de la Vertu* in the Bastille. He was still there the next year when, seeing further into his theme, he began those variations and expansions upon which he was to remain embarked for a decade.

Justine, ou les Malheurs de la Vertu, printed in 1791, enlarges upon the "philosophical tale" without departing from its conventional expression. However, the increased violence of her experience is transforming the central figure: she is turning into something that neither the postulates nor the language of eighteenth-century common sense or "right reason" can securely fix. In her resistance to "things as they are," in her incorrigible unwillingness or her inability to learn the lessons of the world, her mysterious absence in a world ruled by laws of wickedness, where only crime pays, where there are only weak and strong, only victims and tyrants, the latter always right and the former wrong perforce—in this, *the given and the possible world,* Justine's virtue is unreasonable and unreasoning: It is not miscalculation, it is aberration. Her tormentors, with logic and lucidity on their side, consider her perverse, mad. But they do more than consider her; she is of enduring interest to them, they are fascinated by her; in the unhappy girl's nature they encounter something irreducible, something insurgent and unconquerable. And, well considered, that something is hardly less awesome, it is even more troubling than all the barbarities she undergoes.

Again rewritten, the dialectic of the earlier versions now reinforced through presentation in two stories, the scenes, the discourses multiplied, the whole invaded by excess and now in ten volumes and four thousand pages long, it is a masterpiece that appears in 1797, "a work beyond which no other writer, at any time, has ever managed to venture; we have, so to speak, a veritable absolute in our hands, in this relative world of letters . . ."[1]

La Nouvelle Justine has been outlawed in France for the past one hundred seventy years. Since the Directory no French government has shown itself delinquent in regard to Sade. Like all its

---

[1] Maurice Blanchot, "Sade," in the introductory section to The Marquis de Sade: *The Complete Justine, Philosophy in the Bedroom, and Other Writings.* New York, Grove Press, 1965.

predecessors, the Fifth Republic has discharged its duty. The law must of necessity respect crime.

It was committed anew, *La Nouvelle Justine* was reprinted and circulated clandestinely under the Third Republic and read, but read, be it understood, by the rare readers of ·rare books who in Sade beheld everything they for the most part were not, a *rageur* they could approach, could savor and admire in safety, protected by the implicit belief that the positions Sade assailed were invulnerable. Of those positions not one seemed anything like secure when, under the Fourth Republic, in 1949, *L'Histoire de Juliette* was reissued in an edition which, while not clandestine, was hardly very public, being limited to "475 copies" sold with utmost discretion and at a dear price. Nonetheless, and although the authorities were slow to move, the rules of the game had to be complied with in the end, and the publisher was prosecuted by the regime through the intermediary of La Commission du Livre and on January 10, 1957, found guilty of "outrage to public morals."

On the question of "public morals," on the question of in what sense—in what final sense—they are outraged by *Juliette,* and on the question of the final sense—the outrageous and revolutionary sense—of *Juliette,* it would be advantageous to reproduce a few lines, written over half a century ago, in which Apollinaire, with his sure intuition, exactly grasps what is at issue in Sade's novel. The passage is quoted in the prefatory note to the 1949 Pauvert edition, and deserves to be inserted in this first American edition.

> The Marquis de Sade, that freest of spirits to have lived so far, had ideas of his own on the subject of woman: he wanted her to be as free as man. Out of these ideas—they will come through some day—grew a dual novel, *Justine* and *Juliette.* It was not by accident the Marquis chose heroines and not heroes. Justine is woman as she has been hitherto, enslaved, miserable and less than human; her opposite, Juliette represents the woman whose advent he anticipated, a figure of whom minds have as yet no conception, who is arising out of mankind, who shall have wings, and who shall renew the world.

Ten years ago, the publishing of Sade in the United States seemed impracticable, seemed practically unthinkable; it was a project to wait and think about. The present translation was begun in September of 1956, and not finished until September of 1966. Signed by a Pieralessandro Casavini, most of it—to be precise, the first five of what were to be seven volumes in all—was brought out in Paris over the years 1958–1961. That translation has been reviewed throughout, revised here and there; what remained incomplete has been completed; and altered circumstances have appeared to authorize the abandoning of a pseudonym.

Circumstances aside, the Sade I have frequented is a revolutionary, and his importance, in my eyes, is associated with revolutionary perspectives. Let me try to specify which ones.

As a thinker, as a pamphleteer, as secretary and then president of his section in Paris, as a magistrate, Sade took an active part in the Revolution, and certainly took his risks: his concern with the Revolution was intense, and yet his attitude toward it was divided. Its objectives—the classical objectives, those which despite all the bitterest controversy remained, by and large, the *possible* objectives with Western revolutionaries down to the other day—were his, but only to a certain extent. That is, they fell short of what he was after; and the question of degree became a question of the essential. Like Antigone, Sade wanted "everything, and all at once": which is to want the "impossible." But that is what a revolution *is*, the desiring of the impossible, the striving for the fulfillment of the impossible desire; and anything less is too little, it is nothing. For "Those," as Saint-Just warned, "who make their revolutions halfway do but dig themselves a grave."

The Marquis de Sade wanted what no mere formal rearrangements could provide, what no modifications of material and relative conditions can alone satisfy; he wanted "a permanent insurrection of the spirit," an intimate revolution, a revolution within. He wanted then what today revolution no longer holds "impossible" but holds to be *a starting point as well as a final end*: to change man. To change him through and through, cost what it may, be it at the price of his "human nature," and even at the price of his sexual nature—and above all at the price of that which, in our communities, has forged all relations between all men and denatured them, and merged love and continuity into one disaster, one inhumanity.

—AUSTRYN WAINHOUSE

Part
One

'*T*was at Panthemont we were brought up, Justine and I,' there that we received our education. The name of that celebrated retreat is not unfamiliar to you; nor does it require telling that for many a long year the prettiest and most libertine women gracing Paris have regularly emerged from that convent. Euphrosine, the young lady in whose footsteps I was eager to follow and who, dwelling close by my own parents' home, had fled her father's household to fling herself into libertinage, had been my boon companion at Panthemont. As 'twas from her and from a certain nun, a friend of hers, that I acquired the basic precepts of the morality which, as you listened to the tales my sister has just finished recounting, you were somewhat surprised to find in a person of my young years, it would seem to me that before anything else I ought to tell you something about those women, and to provide you with a circumstantial account of those earlier moments of my life when, seduced, corrupted by that pair of sirens, the seed destined to flower into vices without number was sown in the depths of my soul.

The nun I refer to was called Madame Delbène. For five years she had been the abbess of the house and was nearing her thirtieth year when I made her acquaintance. To be prettier than she were a thing impossible; a fit model to any artist, she had a sweet, celestial countenance, fair tresses, large blue eyes where shone something tender and inviting, a figure copied after one of the Graces. The victim of others' ambition, young Delbène had been shut up in a cloister at the age of twelve in order that an elder brother, whom she detested, might be rendered wealthier by the dowry their parents were thus spared from having to set aside for her. Imprisoned at an age when the passions begin to assert them-

3

selves clamorously, although none of this had been of her choosing, for she'd then been fond of the world and of men in general, it was only by mastering herself, by coming triumphant through the severest tests, that she at last decided to give over and obey. Very precocious, having conned all the philosophers, having meditated prodigiously, Delbène, while accepting this condemnation to retirement, had all the same kept two or three friends by her. They came to visit her, to console her; and as she was exceedingly rich, they continued to furnish her all the literature and all the delights she could desire, even those which were to do the most to fire her imagination, already very lively and little cooled by the effects of seclusion.

As for Euphrosine, she was fifteen when I became attached to her; and she had been Madame Delbène's pupil a year and a half when the two of them proposed that I enter their society— it was the same day I entered into my thirteenth year. Euphrosine's complexion was somewhite less than white, she was tall for her age, very slender, had engaging eyes, considerable spirit and vivacity, but in looks she was no match for our Superior, and was far less interesting.

I have no need to say that among recluse women the thirst for the voluptuous is the sole motive for close friendship: they are attached one to the other, not by virtue, but by fucking: one is pleased by her who soaks one at sight, one becomes the intimate of her by whom one is frigged. Endowed with the most energetic temperament, I had, starting at the age of nine, accustomed my fingers to respond to whatever desires arose in my mind, and from that period onward I aspired to nothing but the happiness of finding the occasion for instruction and to launch myself into a career the gates unto which my native forwardness had already flung wide, and with such agreeable effects. Euphrosine and Delbène were soon to offer me what I was seeking. Eager to undertake my education, the Superior one day invited me to luncheon. Euphrosine was there: the weather was incredibly warm, and this excessive ardor of the sun afforded them an excuse for the disarray I found them in: apart from an undergarment of transparent lawn maintained by nothing more than a large bow of pink ribbon, they were perfectly naked.

"Since you first arrived at this establishment," Madame Delbène began, kissing me rather carelessly upon the forehead, her eye and hand betraying a certain restlessness, "I have had an unabating desire to make your intimate acquaintance. You are very attractive. You appear to me to be in possession of some wit and aptitude, and young maids of your sort have a very definite place in my heart—do you blush, little angel? But I forbid you to blush! Modesty is an illusion—resulting from what? 'tis the result of nought but our cultural manners and our upbringing, it is what is known as a conventional habit. Nature having created man and woman naked, it is unthinkable that she could have implanted in them an aversion or a shame thus to appear. Had man only faithfully observed Nature's promptings, he would never have fallen subject to modesty: the which iron-clad truth, my heart, proves that there are certain virtues whose source lies nowhere save in total negligence, or ignorance, of the code of Nature. Ah, but might one not give a wrench to Christian morals were one in this way to scrutinize all the articles which compose it! But we'll chat about that later on. Let's speak of other matters for the nonce. Will you join us in our undress?"

Then those two minxes, laughing merrily, stepped up to me and soon had me in a state identical to theirs; whereupon Madame Delbène's kisses assumed a completely different character.

"Oh, but my Juliette is lovely!" cried she, admiringly; "see how those delicious little breasts have begun to heave! Euphrosine, I do declare she's better fleshed there than you are . . . and, would you believe it? she's barely thirteen."

Our charming Superior's fingers were tickling my nipples, and her tongue quivered in my mouth. She was not slow to observe her caresses were having so powerful an influence upon my senses that I was in serious danger of being entirely overcome.

"O fuck!" she apostrophized, unable to restrain herself and startling me with the vigor of her expressions. "Ah, by sweet Christ! what verve, what a fiery temper! Let's be rid of all these damnable hindrances, my little friends, to the devil with everything that yet screens from clear view charms Nature never created to remain hidden!"

And directly flinging away the filmy costume which had enveloped her, she revealed herself to our eyes, lovely as Venus, that sea-risen goddess who exacted homage from the Greeks. It were impossible to be better formed, to have a skin more white, more sweet, to have more beauteous curves, forms better pronounced. Euphrosine, who imitated her almost at once, delivered fewer charms to my view: she was less plump than Madame Delbène; rather darker in her skin, she would perhaps have pleased less universally; but what eyes! what vivacity! Stirred by such a quantity of wonders, earnestly solicited by the two women they belonged to, besought to follow their example and be rid of all modesty's restraints, you may be very certain that I yielded. Her head reeling from sublimest drunkenness, Delbène bore me to her bed and devoured me with her kisses.

"One moment," she panted, wholly ablaze, "one moment, my dears, we had best introduce a little method into our pleasures' madness: they're not relished unless organized."

So saying, she stretches me out, spreads wide my legs and, lying belly down upon the bed with her head lodged between my thighs, she sets to cunt-sucking me, the while exposing the world's most handsome buttocks to my companion's view, from that pretty little girl's fingers she receives the same services her tongue is rendering me. Euphrosine knowing full well what was apt to flatter Delbène's tastes, amidst her pollutions interspersed sharp slaps upon the nun's behind: they had an indubitable effect upon our amiable instructress' physical being. Quite electrified by libertine proceedings, the whore bolted the whey she was making squirt in a steady stream from my little cunt. Now and again she paused to gaze at me, to contemplate me in these throes of pleasure.

"The beautiful creature!" the tribade exclaimed. "Oh, great God, was there ever a more inspiring child! Have at it, Euphrosine, frig me, my love, lay on, I want to die drunk on her fuck! Quick now, we'll change about, let's vary what we're doing," she cried a moment later; "you must wish for something in return, dear Euphrosine? But how shall I be able to repay you for the pleasures you're giving me! Wait, wait, little angels, I'm going to frig you both at the same time."

She places us side by side on the bed; following her recommendation, we each advance a hand and set to polluting each other.

Delbène's tongue first probes far into the recesses of Euphrosine's cunt, and she uses either hand to tickle our assholes; from time to time she relinquishes my companion's cunt so as to pump mine, and thus both Euphrosine and I, experiencing three pleasures simultaneously, did, as you may be fully persuaded, discharge like muskets. Several instants later the resourceful Delbène has us turn over, and we put our asses at her disposal; while frigging us beneath, she applies determined lips to Euphrosine's anus, then to mine, sucking with libidinous choler. She praised our buttocks' conformation, spanking them teasingly, and half slew us with joy. When done, she drew away:

"Do unto me everything I have done unto you," spake she in a thickened voice, "frig me, the both of you. Frig me. I shall lie in your arms, Juliette, I shall kiss your mouth, our tongues shall intertwine . . . shall strain . . . shall suck. You shall bury this fair dildo in my womb," she pursued, putting the instrument into my hands; "and you, my Euphrosine, you shall assume charge of my ass, you shall employ this lesser tube to arouse me in that sector: infinitely straiter than my cunt, it asks for no bulkier apparatus. . . . You, my pigeon," she went on, kissing me with inordinate feeling, "you'll not leave my clitoris unattended, will you? 'Tis there the true seat of woman's pleasure: rub it, worry it, I say, use your nails if you like—never fear, I know how to bear a little pressure . . . and I am weary, Christ's eyes! I am jaded and I require to be dealt with stoutly: I want to melt absolutely into fuck, fuck I want to become, if I am able I want to discharge twenty times over. Make it so."

Oh, God, with what liberality we did repay her in the one coin she valued! It were not in human power more passionately to labor at giving a woman pleasure . . . impossible to imagine one who had a greater appetite for it. The thing was done at last.

"My angel," that charming creature said to me, "I attempt to express my delight at having come to know you, and words fail me. You are a veritable discovery, from now on I propose to associate you with all my pleasures and you shall find that we may avail ourselves of some very poignant ones, despite the fact male company is, strictly speaking, forbidden us. Ask of Euphrosine whether she is content with me."

"Oh, my beloved, allow my kisses to speak for me!" exclaimed our young friend as she cast herself upon Delbène's breast; " 'tis you I am indebted to for an understanding of myself and of the meaning of my existence. You have trained my mind, you have rescued it from the darkness wherein childhood prejudices enshrouded it. Thanks alone to you I have achieved being in this world. Lucky Juliette, if you will condescend to lavish similar attentions upon her!"

"Yes," Madame Delbène replied, "why yes, I am anxious to take her education in hand. Just as I have told you, I should like to cleanse her of all those infamous religious follies which spoil the whole of life's felicity, I should like to guide her back to Nature's fold and doctrine and cause her to see that all the fables whereby they have sought to bewitch her mind and clog her energies are in actuality worthy of nought but derision. But now to luncheon, my friends, we'd best refresh ourselves; when one has discharged abundantly, what one has expended must be replenished."

A delicious collation, which we took entirely naked, soon restored to us the strength necessary to begin afresh. Once again we fell to frigging one another—and immediately were all three plunged back into the wildest excesses of lubricity. We struck a thousand different poses; continually altering our roles, we were sometimes wives to fuckers whom the next instant we dealt with as husbands and, thus beguiling Nature, for the length of an entire day we compelled that indulgent mother to set the crown of her voluptuousness most sweet upon all the little infractions of her laws we committed.

A month was so spent; at its end Euphrosine, her brain nicely crazed by libertinage, left the convent, then bade farewell to her family and went off to practice all the disorders of frenzied whoring and low license. Later, she returned and paid us a visit; she figured her situation, and we being too corrupted to find anything amiss in the career she was pursuing, pity was farthest from our thoughts, and our last wish was to discourage her from forging ahead.

"I must say she has managed very well," Madame Delbène remarked to me; "a hundred times over I have yearned to respond to the same call, and indeed I surely would have, had my taste for men been strong enough to surmount this uncommon liking I have for women. However, dear Juliette, in fating me to inhabit the cloister all my life long, heaven also had the kindness to provide me with only a mediocre desire for any sort of pleasure other than those this sanctified place plentifully affords me; that which women may mutually procure one another is so delicious that my aspirations do not go very much farther. Nevertheless, I do recognize that one may take an interest in men; it is no mystery to me that one will now and then do everything under the sun to lay hands on them; whatever is connected with libertinage makes powerful sense to me. . . . My fancy has roved very far. Who knows, perhaps I have even gone beyond what one may imagine, have been gripped by wants whose satisfaction defies all conception?

"The fundamental tenet of my philosophy, Juliette," went on Madame Delbène, who, since the loss of Euphrosine, had become more and more fond of me, "is scorn for public opinion. You simply have no idea, my dear one, to what point I am contemptuously indifferent to whatever may be said about me. And, pray tell, what beneficial or other influence can the vulgar fool's opinion have upon our happiness? Only our overdelicate sensitivity permits it to affect us; but if, by dint of stern and clear thinking, we succeed in deadening these susceptibilities, eventually reaching the stage where opinion's effects upon us are null, even when it be a question of those things which touch us most intimately—then, I say, then that the good or bad opinion of others may have any influence whatsoever upon our happiness becomes utterly unthinkable. We alone can make for our personal felicity: whether we are to be happy or unhappy is completely up to us, it all depends solely upon our conscience, and perhaps even more so upon our attitudes which alone supply the bedrock foundation to our conscience's inspirations. For the human conscience," continued that deep-learned woman, "is not at all times and everywhere the same, but rather almost always the direct product of a given society's manners and of a particular climate and geography. Is it not so, for example, that the same acts the Chinese do not in any sense consider inadmissible would cause us to shudder here in France? If then this most unrigid organ is, depending merely upon latitude and longitude, able to excuse and justify any extreme behavior, true wisdom must advise us to adopt a rational, a moderate, position between extravagances and chimeras, and to evolve attitudes which will prove compatible simultaneously with the penchants we have individually received from Nature and with the laws of the country we happen to dwell in; and these are the attitudes out of which we must elaborate our conscience. And that is why the sooner one sets to work adopting the philosophy one intends to be guided by, the better, since that philosophy alone supplies its form to the conscience, and our conscience is responsible for governing and regulating all the actions we perform in life."

"Heavens!" I cried, "have you carried indifference to the point of not caring in the slightest about your reputation?"

"Quite, I do not care about it in the slightest," Madame Delbène answered. "I might even confess that I take a greater inner pleasure from my conviction that this reputation is extremely bad than I would reap from knowing it was good. Oh, Juliette, never forget this: a good reputation is a valueless encumbrance. It cannot ever recompense us for what in sacrifice it costs us. She who prizes her good reputation is subject to at least as many torments as she who behaves neglectfully of it: the first lives in unceasing dread of losing what is precious to her, the other trembles before the prospects opened up by her own carelessness. If thus the paths conducting the one to virtue and the other to vice are equally bestrewn with briars, why is it that we subject ourselves to such vexations in selecting between these ways, why do we not consult Nature and loyally observe her directives?"

"But," I objected, "were I to make these maxims mine, Madame Delbène, I greatly fear I should have to flout far too many conventions."

"Why indeed, my dear," she retorted, "I believe I'd prefer to have you tell me you greatly fear you'd taste too many pleasures. And what precisely are these conventions? Shall we inspect the matter soberly? Social ordinances in virtually every instance are promulgated by those who never deign to consult the members of society, they are restrictions we all of us cordially hate, they are common sense's contradictions: absurd myths lacking any reality save in the eyes of the fools who don't mind submitting to them, fairy tales which in the eyes of reason and intelligence merit scorn only. . . . We'll have more to say on that subject, you have but to wait a little, my dear. Have confidence in me. Your candor and naïveté indicate you are in singular need of a tutor. For very few is life a bed of roses: only heed me, and you'll be one of those who, with the thorns that must be there, will find a goodly number of flowers in her path."

Seldom indeed does one come across a reputation in shabbier repair than this one of Madame Delbène. A nun who held me in especially high esteem, being disturbed by my rapport with the Abbess, warned me that she was a doomed woman. She had, I was told, poisoned the minds of nearly every *pensionnaire* in the convent, and thanks to her advice at least fifteen or sixteen of them had already gone the way of Euphrosine. It was, she assured me, an unprincipled, lawless, a faithless, an impudent brazen creature who flaunted her wicked notions; vigorous measures would long ere this have been taken against her were it not for her influential position and distinguished birth. These exhortations meant nothing to me: a single one of Delbène's kisses, a single phrase from her had a greater effect upon me than all the weapons it were possible to employ with a view to sundering us. Even had it meant being dragged over the precipice, it seemed to me I should have preferred definitive ruin at her side to celebrity in another's sight. Oh, my friends! there is a certain perversity than which no other nourishment is tastier; drawn thither by Nature . . . if for a moment Reason's glacial hand waves us back, Lust's fingers bear the dish toward us again, and thereafter we can no longer do without that fare.

But it was not long before I noticed our amiable Superior's attentions were not concentrated exclusively on me, and I as quickly perceived that others were wont to cooperate with her in exercises where libertinage had a more preponderant share than piety.

"And will you take lunch with me tomorrow?" she inquired one day. "I expect Elizabeth, Flavie, Madame de Volmar and Madame de Sainte-Elme. We'll be six in all; we ought surely to be able to accomplish some truly startling things, I dare say."

"Goodness!" I exclaimed. "Do you amuse yourself with all those women?"

"Of course. But you mustn't for one instant suppose I am

limited to them. There are thirty nuns in our establishment, I have had commerce with twenty-two; we have eighteen novices: I have still to make the acquaintance of one of them; and of the sixty *pensionnaires* presently with us, only three have resisted me so far. Whenever a new one arrives I simply have to get my hands on her: I accord her one week, never longer, to think over my proposals. Oh, Juliette, Juliette, my libertinage is an epidemic, whosoever is in my vicinity is bound to be infected by it. How very fortunate for society that I restrict myself to this dilute form of evil-doing: oh, what with my proclivities and principles, I could perhaps adopt another which might easily prove more of a nuisance to the world."

"And what would you do, my gentlest one?"

"Who can tell? Do you not realize that the effects of an imagination so depraved as mine are like unto the impetuous waters of a river in flood? Nature wouldst that it wreak destruction, and destroy it does, no matter what, no matter how."

"Do you not ascribe to Nature," I suggested to my interlocutress, "what ought rather to be considered the result of your depravation?"

"Now heed me well, little light of my life," said the Superior; "it's early yet, our friends aren't due to come till six and before they arrive I can perhaps reply to some of your frivolous notions."

We both sat down.

"In that our unique knowledge of Nature's inspirations," began Madame Delbène, "reaches us through that interior sensory we call the conscience, it is by analyzing this latter we shall rationally and profitably sound Nature's operations—which, in us, are impulsions—and which fatigue, torment, or bring enjoyment to the conscience.

"The word *conscience,* my beloved Juliette, denominates that as it were inner voice which cries out when we do something—it makes no difference what—we are forbidden to do: and this eminently simple definition lays bare, to even the most casual glance, the origins the conscience has in prejudices inculcated by training and upbringing. Thus it is the child is beset by guilt directly he disobeys instructions—and the child will continue to suffer pangs of remorse until such time as, having vanquished prejudice, he discovers there is no real evil in the thing his education has induced him to abhor.

"And so conscience is purely and simply the construction either of the prejudices that are insinuated into us or of the ethical principles we ourselves devise in our own behalf. So true is this that it is altogether possible, if for material we employ sensitive principles, to forge a conscience which will haunt and sting and bite us, afflict us most woundingly upon every occasion—it is, I say, quite possible that we find ourselves possessed of a conscience so tyrannical that, once having promised ourselves to execute them for the sake of our sensual gratification, we then fail to carry out in their fullest and richest details any however entertaining schemes, even vicious ones, exceedingly criminal ones. Whence it is there is engendered, as antidote to the first, that other sort of conscience which, in the person who stands aloof from superstition and vulgar claptrap, speaks angrily to him when by miscalculation or self-deception he chooses to come at happiness by some other road than the highway which must naturally lead him to his object. Hence, in the light of the principles we have devised for our own individual use, we may equally well have cause to repent at having done either too much evil, or too little, or none. But let us take the word in its most elementary and most common acceptation: in this case, guilt—that is to say, what prompts the utterances of the inner mechanism we have just designated as the conscience—in this case, guilt is a perfectly useless debility, a weakness whose grip upon us we have got to break with all possible dispatch and with all the determination we can muster. For feelings of guilt, once again, are nought but the distillations, the effluvia of a prejudice produced by fear of what may befall us for having done any conceivable kind of thing forbidden for who knows what vague or flimsy reason. Remove the threat of retribution, alter opinions, abolish civil codes, shift the felon from one clime to another, and the misdeed will, of course, remain exactly in substance what before it was, but he who commits it will no longer feel twinges of guilt over his act. Guilt, thus, is merely an unpleasant reminiscence; it crops out of the customs and conventions one happens to have adopted, but it never results from, never has any connection with, the character of the deed one happens to have performed.

"Were this not so, how could one ever succeed in stifling remorse, in overcoming guilt? And we may be very certain that even
when it be a question of acts of the broadest consequence,
stifled they definitely may be, provided one's mental development
is sufficient and provided one has toiled earnestly to extinguish
one's prejudices. Proportionately as these prejudices are extirpated
by maturity, or as habitual familiarity with deeds that initially
upset us gradually toughens the sensibility and subdues the conscience, the susceptibility to guilt, formerly but the effect of the
conscience's frailty, is soon diminished, finally annihilated: and
thus one progresses, until one arrives at the most appalling excesses:
they may be repeated as often as one likes. But, it may perhaps be
objected, guilt feelings are surely more or less intense in keeping with the variety of the misdeed perpetrated? Yes, to be sure,
since the prejudice against a major crime is more powerful than
one against a lesser crime, and the punishment prescribed by the law
commensurately heavier in the one instance than in the other;
however, discover the strength indiscriminately to do away with
all prejudices, acquire the wisdom to rank all crimes on a single
plane, and, becoming swiftly convinced of their resemblance, you
will know how to tailor guilt to fit the occasion. Which is only to
say that, having first learned to cope with the guilt consequent
upon petty misbehavior, you will soon learn to quell any uneasiness over having performed a sizable atrocity, and to learn also
to execute every atrocity, great and small, with a constant and
inviolable serenity. . . .

"And so it is, my dear Juliette, that if one is visited by misgivings after having done a fell deed, that is because one clings to
some doctrine of freedom or of free will, saying to oneself: *How
wretched I am because I didn't act otherwise!* But were one really
to wish to persuade oneself that this talk about freedom is all
empty prattle and that we are driven to whatever we do by a force
more puissant than ourselves; were one to wish to be convinced
that everything in this world has its purpose and its utility, and
that the crime whereof one repents is just as necessary to Nature's
grand design as are war, the plague, famine by which she periodically lays whole empires waste—and empires are infinitely less
dependent than Nature upon the acts that comprise our individual

existences—were we to make these efforts, we'd cease even to be able to conceive of remorse or guilt, and my precious Juliette would not say to me that I am mistaken in laying up to Nature's will that which ought only to be regarded as depravity's handiwork.

"All moral effects," Madame Delbène went on, "are to be related to physical causes, unto which they are linked most absolutely: the drumstick strikes the taut-drawn skin and the sound answers the blow: no physical cause, that is, no collision, and of necessity there's no moral effect, that is, no noise. Certain dispositions peculiar to our organisms, the neural fluids more or less irritated by the nature of the atoms we inhale, by the species or quantity of the nitrous particles contained in the foods making up our diet, by the flow of the humours and by yet a thousand other external causes—this is what moves a person to crime or to virtue and often, within the space of a single day, to both. There's the drumhead struck, the cause of a vicious or of a virtuous act; one hundred *louis* stolen out of my neighbor's pocket or transferred as a gift from mine to someone in need, there's the effect of the blow, the resultant sound. Are we answerable for these subsequent effects when the initial causes necessitate them? May the drum be beaten without there being a sound emitted? And can we avoid these reverberations when they and the blow are themselves the consequence of things so beyond our control, so exterior to ourselves, and so dependent upon the manner in which we are personally constituted? And so 'tis madness, 'tis true extravagance to refrain from doing whatever we please, and, having done it, to repent thereof. Thus guilt and remorse appear as pusillanimous frailties we ought not to encourage, but to combat to the very best of our ability and overcome by means of sane deliberation, reason, and habit. Will remorse alter the fact the milk's been spilt? no, and so we might as well dry our tears: remorse does nothing to make the act less evil, since remorse always comes after the fact; very rarely does remorse prevent the fact from recurring. Therefore, I must conclude that remorse is futile. The evil act once committed, one of two things must follow: either the act is punished, or it is not. In the second hypothesis, to feel sorry would assuredly be the height of stupidity: for what is the point of repenting any conceivable sort of deed which has given us the very completest satisfaction, and whence we have endured no painful consequences? In such a case, to regret the harm this act may have caused someone else would be to love him more than one's own self, and it is perfectly ridiculous to grieve over the sufferings of others when their pain has procured us pleasure, when it has been of some use or profit to us, when it has tickled, titillated, aroused, delighted us in whatever may be the manner. Hence, in this case, there is no earthly excuse for remorse.

"If, on the other hand, the act is discovered and punishment ensues, then, if one chooses to view the matter objectively, one will recognize that what we now repent is not the hurt caused someone else by our act, but our clumsiness in allowing it to be found out—and presently one has grounds for regret, yes, and should surely ponder the thing . . . simply in order, from lengthy reflection upon one's misadventure, to realize that in the future one must be prudent—if the punishment inflicted upon one is anything short of capital. But these reflections are not to be confused with remorse, for true remorse, real remorse, is the pain produced by the hurt one has done oneself: which distinction brings to light the vast difference subsisting between these two sentiments, and at the same time reveals the usefulness of the one and the inanity of the other.

"When we indulge in a bit of foul play, however atrocious, the satisfaction it affords, or the profit it yields, is ample consolation for the trouble, however acute, which amusing ourselves may bring down upon the head of some one or more of our fellow men. Prior to performing the deed, do we not clearly foresee the inconveniences it will cause others? Of course; and this thought, rather than doing anything to stop us, usually spurs us on. And then the deed once done, suddenly and belatedly to fall prey to worry, to start to fret, to sweat, to allow scruple to hinder one from savoring pleasure—than this there is no greater nor baser folly. If because it has been detected this deed brings us unhappiness in its wake, let us bend our keener faculties to ferreting out the reasons why it came to public intelligence; and without shedding a superfluous tear over something we are powerless to arrange otherwise, let us mobilize every effort so that the next time we shall not be wanting in tact, let us turn this mishap to our advantage, and from this reversal draw the experience necessary to improve our methods: henceforth, we will ensure our impunity by swathing our irregularities in thicker veils and more entire obscurity. But let us not contrive, by means of purposeless remorse, to extirpate sound principles; for this bad behavior, this depravation, these vicious and criminal and abominable caprices, are precious attributes, they have procured us pleasure, have delighted us, and unwise is he who deprives himself of anything he enjoys—that would be similar to the lunacy of the man who, merely because a heavy dinner troubled his digestion, were to abjure forever the pleasures of good eating.

"Veritable wisdom, my dear Juliette, consists not in repressing one's vices, for, vices constituting, practically speaking, the sole happiness granted us in life, so to do would be to adopt the role, as it were, of one's own executioner. The true and approved way is to surrender oneself to them, to practice them to the utmost, but with care enough and circumspection to be secured against the dangers of surprise. Fear not lest precautions and protective contrivances diminish your pleasure: mystery only adds thereto. Such conduct, furthermore, guarantees impunity; and is not impunity the most piquant aliment to debauchery?

"After having taught you how to deal with the remorse born of the pain one suffers from having done evil rather too conspicuously, it is of the essence, dear little friend, that you permit me now to indicate the manner of totally silencing that inner and confusion-breeding voice which, when thirsts have been slaked, wakes now and again to upbraid us for the follies into which passions have plunged us. Well, this cure is quite as sweet as it is sure, for it consists simply in reiterating the deeds that have made us remorseful, in repeating them so often that the habit either of committing these deeds or of getting away scot free with them completely undermines every possibility of feeling badly about them. This habit topples the prejudice, destroys it; it does more: by frequently exercising the sensibility in the very way and in the very situation which, at the outset, made it suffer, this habit at length makes the new state it has assumed wholly bearable and even delicious to the soul. Pride lends its aid: not only have you done something no one else would ever dare do, you have become so accustomed to doing it that you cannot anymore exist without it—there is one pleasure. The enacted deed produces another; and who is there doubts that this multiplying of delights very speedily induces a soul to adopt the lineaments and character it has got to have, however painful at first may have been the difficulties wherewith, perforce, it was beset by the deed in question?

"Do we not experience when performing any one of the alleged crimes in which lust is dominant the very sensations I have cited to you? Why is it one never repents a crime of libertinage? Because libertinage very soon becomes habitual. Thus may it be in the case of every other extravagance; like lubricity, they may all be readily transformed into custom, and like lewdness, each of them may provoke an agreeable vibration in the nerve fluids: this poignant itching, closely resembling passion, may become quite as delectable and consequently, like it, metamorphose into a primary need.

"Oh, Juliette! if like myself you would live happily in crime— and, my beloved, I am wont to indulge heavily therein—if, I say, you would find in crime the same happiness that is mine, then strive as time passes to make of evil-doing a habit, until, with the passing of time, you have become so endeared to the habit that you literally cannot go on without imbibing of this potent drink, and until every man-made convention appears so ridiculous to your consideration that your pliant but nonetheless sinewy soul becomes gradually accustomed to construing as vices all human virtues, and as virtuous whatever mortals call criminal: do this, and lo! as though miraculously, new perspectives, a new universe shall appear before you, a consuming and delicious conflagration will glide into your nerves, it will make boil the electrically charged liquor in which the life principle has its seat. Fortunate enough to be able to dwell in a mundane society whence my sad fate has exiled me, with every new day you will form fresh projects, and their realization will every day overwhelm you with a sensual euphoria such as none but you shall know anything of. All the persons, all the creatures about you shall look to you like so many victims destiny has led up in fetters to sate your heart's perversity. No more duties, no more hampering ties, no more obstacles to impede you, they'll all vanish in a trice, dissolved by the vehemence of your desires. No

longer from the depths of your soul shall any voice speak reproach-
fully, hoping to impair your vigor and rob you of joy. Nevermore
shall prejudice militate against your happiness, wisdom shall abolish every check, and with even stride you shall walk along a pathway strewn thick with flowers, till finally you accede to perversity's
ultimate excesses. It will be then you'll perceive the weakness of
what in days past they described to you as Nature's dictates; when
you shall have spent a few years winking at what imbeciles term her
laws, when, in order to become familiar with their infraction, it
shall have pleased you to pulverize them all, then you'll behold her,
that Nature, a wicked smile on her lips, thrilled half to death at
having been violated, you'll see the quean melt before your im-
pulsive desires, you'll see her come crawling toward you, begging
to be shackled by your irons . . . she'll stretch forth her wrists,
plead to be your captive; now a slave to you instead of your
sovereign, subtly she'll instruct your heart in what fashion to outrage her further yet; as though degradation were her whole delight, only by showing you how to insult her excessively will she
demonstrate her ability to impose her governance upon you. Let
her. When once you reach that stage, do not resist, ever; as soon
as you have discovered the way to seize Nature, insatiable in her
demands upon you, she will lead you on, step by step, from irregularity to irregularity: all are preparatory, the last committed will
never be but progress accomplished toward still another by means
whereof she prepares to submit to you yet again; like unto the
whore of Sybaris, who will put on every shape so as to excite the
lust of him who buys her, she will in like wise teach you a hundred
ways to soil and vanquish her, and all that the more completely to
ensnare you in her turn, the more utterly to make you her own.
However, one single hint of resistance, let me repeat, one reluctant
gesture were fatal: it will cost you the loss of all you have won by
complacency heretofore: yield: unless you acquaint yourself with
everything, you'll know nothing; and if you're so timid as to pause
in your conversation with her, Nature will escape you forever.
Above all, beware of religion, nothing is more apt to lure you
astray than religion's baneful insinuations. Comparable to the
Hydra whose heads grow back as swiftly as they are lopped off, it
will unceasingly debilitate you if you falter at the task of obliter-

ating its principles. There is the danger ever present that some bizarre ideas of the fantastical God wherewith they befouled your childhood return again to disturb your maturer imagination while it is in the midst of its divinest heats. Oh, Juliette! forget it, scorn it, the concept of this vain and ludicrous God. His existence is a shadow instantly to be dissipated by the least mental effort, and you shall never know any peace so long as this odious chimera preserves any of its prize upon your soul which error would give to it in bondage. Refer yourself again and again to the great theses of Spinoza, of Vanini, of the author of *Le Système de la Nature*. We will study them, we will analyze them together, I promised you authoritative dissertations upon this subject and I am going to keep my word: both of us shall feast heartily upon these writers and shall fill ourselves with the spirit of their sage opinions. Should you be visited by further doubts, you shall communicate them to me, I will set your mind at rest. Grown as staunch and doughty as I in your thinking, you'll soon be imitating me in action, and like myself, you'll never more pronounce this loathsome God's name save with revulsion and in hateful blasphemy. The very conceiving of this so infinitely disgusting phantom is, I confess it, the one wrong I am unable to forgive man. I excuse him all his whims, his ironies, and his eccentricities, I sympathize with all his frailties, but I cannot smile tolerantly upon the lunacy that could erect this monster, I do not pardon man for having himself wrought those religious chains which have so dreadfully hobbled him and for having crept despicably forward, eyes downcast and neck stretched forth, to receive the shameful collar manufactured only by his own stupidity. There would be no end to it, Juliette, were I to give vent to all the horror waked in me by the execrable doctrine based upon a God's existence; mere mention of him rouses my ire, when I hear his name pronounced I seem to see all around me the palpitating shades of all those woebegone creatures this abominable opinion has slaughtered on the face of the earth. Those ghosts cry out beseechingly to me, they supplicate me to make use of all I have been endowed with of force and ingenuity to erase from the souls of my brethren the idea of the revolting chimera which has brought such rue into the world."

At this point Madame Delbène asked me how far I had myself proceeded in these matters.

"I have not yet made my first communion," I answered her.

"So much the better!" said she, folding me in her arms. "Excellent, my little angel, I'll preserve you from that idolatrous rite. With what regards confession, reply, when they question you, that you are not prepared to recite. The mother in charge of the novices is my friend, her position depends upon my favor, I shall recommend you to her and they'll leave you strictly alone. As for Mass, we've got to appear there in spite of our wishes; but, one moment, do you see that pretty little assortment of books?" she asked, pointing to some thirty-odd volumes bound in red morocco; "I shall lend you those works. Read them during the abominable sacrifice. They will in some sort alleviate the obligation of having to be witness to the whole miserable ceremony."

"Oh, my friend!" I exclaimed, "how deeply in your debt I shall be! My heart and mind were already advanced in the direction your advice indicates I should take. . . . I had a head start—not, to be sure, with respect to morals, for the things you have just told me are so very novel, and so engaging—I had no previous inkling of them, truly. But at a very early hour I began to abhor religion, just as you do, and it was only with extremest aversion I fulfilled its duties. Oh, can you divine the pleasure you give me in promising to broaden my understanding! Alas! having until now heard nothing philosophical said about these matters of superstition, I owe all my modest store of impiety to Nature's liberal suggestions."

"Ah! obey her promptings, my darling—they're such as shall never mislead you."

"Do you know," I continued, "the lecture you have just given me, it is a very compelling one . . . full of bold ideas. May I say that it is rare to find one so well informed at your age? Allow me to tell you so, my dear: I find it hard to believe a person's conscience can reach the state which, by your description, it is plain yours has attained, without that person having acquitted herself of a number of most extraordinary feats. And how—forgive me for putting the question to you—how have you found the opportunity to perpetrate outrages capable of inwardly toughening you to this degree?"

"The day will come when you shall know everything about me," said the Superior, rising from her chair.

"And why must it be postponed? are you afraid of—"

"Merely of horrifying you."

"Then fear not, my friend."

But the approach of company prevented Delbène from enlightening me touching what I was afire to know.

"Tush," said she, putting a finger to her lips, "let's turn our thoughts to pleasure. Kiss me, Juliette. I promise to confide in you on some later day."

Our associates had arrived; I must portray them for you.

Madame de Volmar had taken the veil only six months before. Just twenty years old, tall, slender, very fair of skin, with chestnut hair, the loveliest body imaginable: Volmar, blessed with such a host of charms, was understandably one of Madame Delbène's most cherished disciples and, excepting only the latter, the most libertine of the ladies who were about to participate in our orgies.

Saint-Elme was a novice of seventeen, very animated, with a charming countenance, sparkling eyes, well-molded breasts, and an air of general voluptuousness. Elizabeth and Flavie were both *pensionnaires*: the first could not have been past thirteen, the second was sixteen. Elizabeth's face was sensitive, her features were unusually delicate; the lines of her body were agreeable to see, its curves already affirmed. As for Flavie, she had surely the most heavenly face one could hope to find in this world: nowhere did there exist a prettier smile, lovelier teeth, more beautiful hair; nor was there another who possessed a more engaging figure, a softer and clearer skin. Ah, my friends! had I to paint the Goddess of Flowers, 'twould be Flavie I'd select for my model.

The introductions and the customary compliments were without undue formality; each member of the society, fully aware of what had motivated the forgathering, was impatient to proceed to business; but those ladies' exchanges did, I must declare, astonish me. Even in the middle of a brothel one is not likely to overhear libertine language more gracefully and more casually pronounced than it was by these young women; and nothing could have been more pleasant than the contrast between their modest demeanor, their reserve abroad, and the energetic indecency they displayed throughout these luxurious assemblies.

"Delbène," said Madame Volmar upon making her entrance, "I defy you to wheedle me into discharging today—oh, but I'm done up, my dear, I was the night rioting with Fontenille. I worship the little rascal, in all my life no one ever frigged me more competently, I've never parted with so much fuck, nor so often, no, nor with such delight. Ah, my adorable one, we accomplished marvels!"

"Amazing, aren't they?" Delbène remarked; "well, I trust we'll perform a few a thousand times more extraordinary this afternoon."

"Fuck my eyes! then let's have at it!" cried Sainte-Elme. "I'm stiff—I'm not like Volmar, I slept alone," and, raising her skirts, "do you see my cunt? Isn't it plain, the treatment it desperately needs?"

"Stay," said the Superior, "be not overhasty. This is an initiatory ceremony: I am admitting Juliette into our college, and she must undergo the prescribed ritual."

"Who? Juliette?" said Flavie. "Why, I hadn't noticed—Juliette? I don't believe I've met this pretty thing before," she murmured, approaching me. "Have you any skill at frigging, my princess?" she inquired, bestowing a kiss upon my lips. "Are you libertine? Somewhat of a tribade, like the rest of us?"

And without further ado, the scoundrel laid hands simultaneously upon my breasts and my cunt.

"Let her be," said Volmar, who, baring my behind, was inspecting my buttocks; "let her be, she must first be initiated before we put her to use."

"Well, Delbène," spoke up Elizabeth, "will you look at that Volmar kissing Juliette's ass! She takes her for a little boy, the slut's bent on buggering her." (The reader will be pleased to take note that these comments proceeded from the most youthful member of the group.)

"You know very well," Sainte-Elme rejoined, "that Volmar's an arrant male: she's outfitted with a clitoris three inches long and, destined to insult Nature whichever be the sex she adopts, the whore's got either to play the nymphomaniac or the sodomite: with her, there's no median alternative."

Then, herself drawing near and exploring me from every angle while Flavie maintained her inquisitive regard upon my front, and Volmar hers upon my hindquarters:

"No doubt of it," she went on, "the sweet little bitch is trimly made, and I swear to you all that before the day's over I'll know the taste of her fuck."

"If you please, ladies, if you please," protested Delbène, seeking to re-establish order, "one moment, I beg of you—"

"Well, bleeding Jesus, be quick!" Sainte-Elme gasped, "I'm ready to run! What's the delay? Or do we have to say our prayers before we frig our cunts? Off with your clothes, sweet friends—"

And, had you been there, the next instant you'd have seen six young damsels, each more lovely than the day, fall to admiring one another . . . to caressing one another's naked bodies, and to composing the most varied and diverting groups.

"Very well," Delbène resumed in an overseer's tone, "I expect I'll obtain a little obedience from you. Listen to me: Juliette is going to stretch out upon the couch, and you shall each in your turn savor with her the pleasure of your individual choosing. I, stationed directly opposite the scene, I shall take you one after the other as you've had done with her, and the lewd activities begun with Juliette will be brought to a conclusion with me. But I'll be in no hurry, my fuck won't flow before I've had the five of you in my embrace."

The extreme respect in which the Superior's commands were held made for the completest punctuality in their execution. All these creatures being libertine to the core, you shall perhaps not be unwilling to hear what each of them required of me. As they stepped up by order of age, Elizabeth was the first to present herself. The fair little wench scrutinized every part of me and after having covered me with kisses she slipped in between my thighs, rubbed against me, and we both swooned away together. Flavie came next: her operations bespoke a greater science. After a thousand delicious preliminaries, we lay down so that each of us faced the other's cunt and, with probing, twitching tongues, we fetched forth torrents of whey. Sainte-Elme approaches, she lies down upon the bed, has me sit astride her face, and while her nose prods spiritedly at my asshole, her tongue stabs into my cunt. Bent low over her, I am able to tease and tongue her in like fashion: my fingers tickle her ass, and five ejaculations in rapid succession convince me that the need she alluded to earlier was roundly authentic. I squirted myself dry into her mouth; and never before had I been so expertly sucked. Volmar will have nought but my buttocks, she devours them with kisses and, preparing the narrow passage with her sharp pink tongue, the libertine glues herself upon me, buries her generous clitoris in my anus, shakes and rattles away for a space, turns my head, ardently kisses my mouth, sucks my tongue, and frigs while embuggering me. The hussy isn't content with that, weaponing me with a dildo she herself straps around my flanks, she wheels to receive my thrusts, and, aiming them at her button, the whore gets herself skewered bumwise; I frigged her the while, and she thought herself like to die of pleasure.

After this last incursion, I went to take the post awaiting me upon Delbène's body. Here is how that fury arranged the company.

Elizabeth, on her back, was placed at the edge of the couch. Delbène, reclining in her arms, was having Elizabeth frig her clitoris. Flavie, kneeling upon the floor and her head level with the Superior's cunt, was tonguing it and squeezing her thighs. Above Elizabeth, Sainte-Elme, her ass pressed flush to the latter's visage, presented a yawning cunt to the kisses of Delbène whom Volmar busily embuggered with her burning clitoris. Only I was needed to complete the tableau. Requested to take a crouching position next to Sainte-Elme, I offered for licking the reverse side of what Sainte-Elme was having tongued from in front. Delbène passed in fickle and rapid style from Sainte-Elme's cunt to my asshole, licked, reamed, pumped with surpassing ardor first the one, then the other, and writhing with the most unbelievable agility beneath Elizabeth's fingers, beneath Flavie's tongue, and before Volmar's clitoris, the tribade every minute exploded a gush of fuck.

"By the Almighty!" Delbène panted, extricating herself from that melee, and flushed as red as a bacchante, "by bleeding Jesus, how I've discharged! Never mind, let's carry on with the game: each of you is now to take her place on the couch, Juliette will dally with you in whatever way she prefers, you'll have to cede to her demands. But as she is still new at the sport, I propose to act as her mentor: the group will then form around her as it did around me, and we'll make her fuck fly till she begs for quarter."

Elizabeth is the first to be offered to my libertinage.

"Place her," says Delbène, "in such a way she can kiss your dear little mouth while frigging you, and so that you'll receive a general stimulation. I'll take care of your asshole throughout the episode. Flavie dear, will you take Elizabeth's place. I recommend this exquisite creature's bubs to you," the Abbess adds, "suck them while she tickles you: in view of Volmar's tastes, you'd best run your tongue into her anus while, bending over you, she gives you the benefit of what her mouth can do. . . . As for Sainte-Elme," the Superior pursues, "yes, I think the following arrangement will suffice: I'll adjust myself so as to be able to suck both her ass and cunt while she renders you those same services. And finally, as for myself—speak, my beloved, I am here to do your bidding."

Warmed by the sight of what had been done for Volmar: "I'd love to embugger you," said I, "with this instrument."

"Then do so, my darling, do whatever your heart desires," was Delbène's humble reply; she presented her buttocks. "There," said she, "mark it well. And spare it not."

"Willingly!" I cried, sodomizing my instructress. "Since," I said while engaged, "since the group is to form around me, let's not tarry. My good Volmar," I said, addressing the latter, "let your clitoris use my ass in the way and manner I am about to treat with Delbène's: you've positively no idea how my temperament responds to this species of excitation. I'd like to frig Sainte-Elme with one hand and Elizabeth with the other; meanwhile, I'll give Flavie's cunt a cleaning."

The Superior having issued instructions to ride me hard, I was not obliged to say another word; the situations were seven times varied, and seven times over my liberated fuck sprang in answer to divine cajolery.

The pleasures of the table succeeded those of love: a superb repast was awaiting us. Divers kinds of wine and spirits put a bright hilarity in our heads, we returned to our libertine disporting. We divided into three couples. Sainte-Elme, Delbène, and Volmar, the most advanced in years, each chose a fricatrice; by chance, or by predilection, Delbène appointed me to be hers; Elizabeth fell to Sainte-Elme, Flavie to Volmar. The couples were so disposed that each could enjoy a view of the pleasures of the two others. Truly, the reader is little apt to imagine the least part of what we did. Oh, that Sainte-Elme, how delicious she was! Wildly enthusiastic over each other, our reciprocal friggery continued till we were both nigh to prostration. There was nothing we did not contrive, no fancy we failed to enact; then finally we all six knit again in a compact group, and the concluding two hours of this voluptuous riot were so lascivious that one may wonder whether so. many lewd goings-on are ever matched in any whorehouse.

I was struck by, and must not fail to mention, this: the extreme solicitude shown for the *pensionnaires'* maidenheads. To be sure, I did not observe the same concern manifested for those who had already taken vows; but I could not understand why they whose portion was not to be the cloister, but life in the world, were treated with such consideration.

"Their honor resides therein," Delbène explained to me when I questioned her about the thing. "We do, by all means, wish to amuse ourselves with these girls; but why ruin them? Why cause them to detest the memory of the moments they passed in our midst? No, we have that virtue, and however corrupt you suppose us to be, we never compromise our friends."

I found these measures and these ethics proper; but, created by Nature someday to attain an excellence in base villainy superior to anything I was to encounter, the desire to sully and peradventure to doom one of my companions rose up strong in my brain as of this same instant—this desire was at least as imperious as that other I had to be degraded myself.

Delbène shortly perceived that I preferred Sainte-Elme to her. Indeed, I did adore that charming girl; I simply could not leave her side; but as she had infinitely less wit than the Superior, another yearning, equally invincible, always brought me back to the latter.

"Consumed as you appear to be by the passion to depucelate a maid, or to be depucelated yourself," the incomparable Delbène said to me one day, "I have no doubt but that Sainte-Elme has already decided, or may easily be induced, to grant you these pleasures. Need she hesitate? She runs no risk: she is going to pass the rest of her life in holy retirement. But you, Juliette, once bereft of your token, you'll be forever debarred from marriage. Think then, and believe me: untold misfortunes may well be the consequence of a flaw in the part you perhaps too lightly think of damaging. However, heed me, my angel, you know that I adore you, give up that Sainte-Elme, take me instead and I'll satisfy all the pleasures you long for in a trice. You have only to select her in the whole convent whose first fruits you covet, and I myself shall make away with yours. . . . There'll be some material injuries, needless to say. But fear not, I'll arrange everything. Just how 'tis managed is a great secret; if you would have it revealed to you, I must first have your most solemn oath that, as of this moment, you'll speak not another word to Sainte-Elme. And if you break faith with me there will be no limit to my vengeance."

Far too fond of this bewitching creature to wish to compromise her and, in addition, burning to taste the pleasures Delbène encouraged me to hope for if I abandoned Sainte-Elme, I promised everything.

" 'Tis well," said Delbène a month later, during which interval she had put me to the test, "have you made your choice? Who is it to be?"

And now, my kind friends, never in your life will you guess upon what object my libertine imagination had alighted. Upon that girl, that same one, who stands there before your eyes: my own sister. But Madame Delbène knew her too well not to attempt to dissuade me from undertaking the thing.

"Have your own way," said I at last. "My second choice is Laurette."

Her youth (she was indeed a child of only ten) . . . her pretty little wide-awake face, her liveliness, her high birth, everything about her incensed me . . . inflamed me; and seeing no important obstacle to success—for this young orphan had no protector apart from an elderly uncle living at a hundred leagues' distance from Paris—the Superior assured me I could consider as already sacrificed the victim my perfidious desires were immolating in advance.

We appointed a day; on the eve of the drama Delbène

summoned me to her cell to spend the night in her embraces. Our conversation returned to questions of religion.

"I fear," said she, "lest you proceed in too great haste, my child. Your heart, beguiled by your mind, has not yet reached the stage at which I would prefer to see it. These superstitious infamies are still harassing you—I wager 'tis so. Listen to me, Juliette, lend me your undivided attention and make an effort so that in the future, with an effrontery equal to mine and without any qualms whatever, you will be able to carry your libertinage, anchored upon a substructure of reliable principles, to it matters not what extreme.

"When they begin to chatter about religion, the first of the dogmas they trundle forth is the one pertaining to the existence of God: as it is the foundation of the whole edifice, I ought logically to begin my examination by focusing upon it.

"Oh, Juliette! let us have no doubt, this fantasy about there being a God has its origins in nothing but the mind's limitations. Knowing not to whom or what all the universe about us is to be attributed, helpless before the utter impossibility of explaining the inscrutable mysteries of Nature, above her we have gratuitously installed a Being invested with the power of producing all the effects of whose causes we are profoundly ignorant.

"This abominable ghost was no sooner envisaged as the author of Nature than he had also to be deemed that of good and evil; the habit of regarding these opinions as true, and the obvious usefulness of suppositions which conveniently flatter laziness and curiosity, quickly made for the tendency most men still have of according the same degree of belief to a fable as to a geometrical proof, and the persuasion became so great, the habit so binding, that from the outset one had need of all one's rational faculties to keep from tumbling into error. There is but a single easy step from the extravagance of acknowledging the existence of a God to the practice of worshiping him; nothing simpler than imploring the protection of what one dreads; nothing but what is most natural in the procedure which leads to burning incense upon the altars of the magical individual they posit as simultaneously the prime mover and the dispenser of everything that is. He was thought wicked, because some very disagreeable effects resulted from the necessary workings of Nature's laws; to appease him, victims were needed: whence fastings, macerations, penances, and every other sort of idiocy, the fruit of the fear of the many and the brazen imposture of the few. Or, if you prefer, the perennial, unaltering effects of man's weakness, for you may be certain that wherever you find human frailty you also come upon gods whelped by the same men's terror, and homages rendered unto these gods, the inevitable result of the folly that erects them.

"There is no question of it, my dear friend: this opinion which holds that a God exists and that he is the omnipotent force responsible for plenty and dearth is at the base of all the world's religions. But which of these multifarious traditions is one to prefer? Each claims revelations which argue in its favor, each makes mention of texts, sacred books inspired by its divinity, each aims at nothing short of eclipsing all the others. Here I find I have a difficult choice to make. For guide in the night I have none but my reason, and directly I bring up its light to help me in the task of examining all these competing aspirants to my belief, all these fables, I see no more than a heap of farfetched incongruities and platitudes which chill and repulse me.

"After devoting a rapid glance to the absurd ideas entertained upon this subject by all the peoples of the earth, I finally arrive at the doctrines espoused by the Jews and Christians. The former speak to me of a God, but they refuse me any account of his origins, they give me no idea, no definite image of him, and with what regards the nature of this people's overlord, I obtain nothing but puerile allegories, unworthy of the majesty of a Being whom I am invited to accept as the Creator of the All; 'tis only in offensive contradictions this nation's lawgiver talks to me of his God, and the terms and colors he uses to describe him are much apter to make me abhor than to get me to serve him. Seeing that it is this God himself who speaks in the Books they allude to in their struggle to explain him, I ask myself how, in providing concepts and images of himself, a God could possibly have chosen those which can only excite a man to despise him. Puzzled by this question, I decide to consult these Books with greater care; and what am I to think when I cannot avoid remarking, as I inspect them, that not only could they never have been dictated by the mind or spirit of a God, but that forsooth they were written down long

after the death of the personage who dares affirm he transmitted
verbatim God's own phrases. Ha! so that's the nonsense they're
peddling, I exclaim upon completing my investigations; these Holy
Books they wish to fob off on me as performances composed by
the Almighty are no more than the confections of some knavish
charlatans, and instead of discerning traces of the deific, I behold
nothing but the issue of stupid credulity and lame sleight. And
indeed! what more abject ineptitude is there than this of everywhere depicting, in these Books, a people chosen of the Lord it
has just fabricated for itself, of announcing far and wide to all
the world's nations that it is to none but these squatters in a
desert the Almighty speaks; that it was only in their fate he took
any interest; that it is for their sake only he tampers with the
motions of the stars, splits the seas, showers down manna from
the skies; as if it would not have been far easier for this God to
penetrate into their hearts, enlighten their minds, than to disturb
the smooth operations of Nature, and as if this bent in favor
of an obscure, insignificant, impoverished, unknown people were
commensurate with the supreme majesty of the Being to whom
you would have me ascribe the faculty of universal creation. But
however compelling might be my urge to assent to what these
preposterous Books seek to foist upon their reader, what choice
have I but to demand whether the unanimous silence of all the
adjoining countries' historians, who ought surely to have taken
note of the extraordinary events that crowd Scripture, must not
suffice to make me doubt the authenticity of the marvels reported
in these romances? What, pray tell, am I to think when it is
precisely amongst the ranks of that very race which so exuberantly
celebrates its God to me that I discover the greatest quantity of
unbelievers? What! this God overwhelms his people with blessings
and miracles, and this cherished people believes not in its God?
What! this God, to the tune of the most impressive theatrics,
upon the peak of a mountain thunders forth his ordinations, upon
this mountaintop dictates his sublime laws to the legislator of that
people who, in the plain below, doubt him; and upon that plain
idols are raised, monuments of cynicism, as though the lawgiving
God booming on high deserved nothing better than to have his
nose tweaked? At last he dies, this exceptional man who has just

offered the Jews such a magnificent God, yes, he expires, a prodigy coincides with his death: by this abundance of unparalleled occurrences the majesty of this God is doubtless to be stamped eternally in the memory of the race which has been witness to his greatness—a greatness the scions of those who watched the spectacle are later to prove reluctant to acknowledge. But less gullible than their forebears, in a few years idolatry uptilts the precariously seated altars of the God of Moses, and the unhappy, oppressed Jews remember their ancestors' chimera only once they have regained their freedom. New leaders therewith begin to sing the old song, but, unfortunately, their prophesies are not borne out by developments: the Jews, these new leaders declare, shall prosper so long as they remain faithful to Moses' deity: never did the Jews show him greater respect, and never did sorrow dog them more cruelly. Exposed to the wrath of Alexander's successors, they escaped the Macedonian's irons only to fall under the yoke of the Romans who, their patience exhausted at last by the revolt brewing perpetually among the Jews, demolished their temple and dispersed their numbers. And that then is how their God serves them! that is how this God, who loves them, who solely for their benefit meddles with the sacred order of Nature, that is how he deals with them, that is how he fulfills his vows to them.

"Ah no, it's not then to be amongst the Jews I'll go looking for a universal Almighty; finding in that hapless nation nothing better than some repulsive phantom, spawn of the uncurbed imaginations of a handful of ambitious rogues, I must abhor the contemptible God wickedness dreamt up. And now let's have a glance at the Christians.

"And what a host of further absurdities we have here! It's no longer a mountain-climbing madman's Tablets that rattle out the rules to me; this time the God in question proclaims himself through a much nobler envoy: Mary's meeching bastard is entitled to a very different kind of respect than that claimed by the abandoned son of Jochebed. So let's peer closely at this sinister little cheat; what's he up to, what does he contrive to demonstrate his God's truth to me, what are his credentials, his methods? Capers and droll antics, suppers with sluts, fraudulent cures, puns, jests and duperies. 'I am the Son of God,' bleats this stammering little boor, incapable as he is of uttering one coherent phrase about his Father, of penning a line to describe him; yes, 'I am the Son of God,' and better still: 'I'm God,' that's what I'm to believe simply because the drivel emanates from him. The rascal's hanged up there on a cross, does it matter? His followers desert him, it makes no difference at all: there he is, and no one else: God of the universe, nailed. Where did he take form? Why, in a Jewess' womb. His birthplace? In a stable. How does he gain my belief in him? By abjectness, poverty, imposture, he has no other means to win me over. And if I waver, if I fail of belief? Woe unto me! eternal tortures are my destiny. There's a God, I've omitted nothing from the portrait and in it there's not one feature that stirs the soul or appeals to the heart. Oh, matchless contradiction! 'tis upon the ancient law the new one is grounded, and nevertheless the new supersedes, sets at nought the old: what then is the basis of the new? This Christ, is he the lawgiver we're to hearken to? All by himself, he alone is going to give me an understanding of the God who's dispatched him here; but if it was to Moses' interest to preach to me about the God whence his power derived, think of how eager must be the Nazarene to tell me about the God from whom he descends! Surely, the more modern lawgiver must be better informed than the earlier one; Moses was at best able to chat familiarly with his master, but Christ is God's blood offspring. Moses, content to ascribe natural causes to miracles, convinces his people that lightning blazes forth for the chosen only; the cleverer Jesus accomplishes the miracle himself; and if both do indeed merit their contemporaries' profound scorn, it has nevertheless to be admitted that the later of the two was, through his superior insolence, the more justified in claiming the esteem of men; and the posterity that judges them by assigning a ghetto to the Jews shall definitely be obliged to grant the other a priority on the gallows.

"So, Juliette, it is apparent, is it not, the vicious circle into which men fall as soon as they begin to rave about this rubbish: *religion proves its prophet, the prophet his religion.*

"This God so far not having shown hide nor hair of himself either to the Jewish sect or to that of the otherwise but hardly

less contemptible Christians, I persevere in my quest for some
solid evidence of him, I summon reason to my aid, and lest it
deceive me I subject reason itself to analysis. What is reason?
The faculty given me by Nature whereby I may dispose myself in
a favorable sense toward such-and-such an object and against some
other, depending upon the amount of pleasure or pain I derive
from these objects: a calculation governed absolutely by my senses,
since it is exclusively through them that I receive the comparative
impressions which constitute either the pains I wish to avoid or the
pleasures I must seek.

"Thus, as Fréret says, the reason is nothing other than the
scales we weigh objects in, and, balancing those of these objects
that are external to ourselves, the reasoning mechanism tells us
what conclusions we are to come to: when the scales tip beneath
what looks to be the greatest pleasure, it is to that side our judgment always inclines. As you observe, this rational choice, in us
as in animals which are also full of reason, is but the effect of the
grossest and most material mechanical operation. But as reason
is the only touchstone we possess, it must be the test whereunto
we submit the faith knaves imperiously insist that we exhibit for
objects which either lack reality or are so prodigiously vile in themselves that they can only aspire to our loathing. Well now, Juliette,
the very first thing this rational faculty essays is, as you sense, to
assign an essential difference that distinguishes the thing which
presents its appearance to the perceiver from the thing which the
perceiver perceives. The representational perceptions of a given
object are of still another species. When they show us objects as
absent now and as having been at some time in the past present to
our minds, that is what we call memory, remembrance, recollection.
If these perceptions propose objects to us, but do not advise us
of their real absence, that is what we call imagination, and this
imagination is the true cause of all our errors. Now, the most
abundant source of these errors lies in our ascribing an independent
existence to the objects of these inner perceptions and, more, in
our supposing that they exist outside of ourselves and separately
just as we conceive of them as separate from one another. To
make myself clear to you, upon this separate idea, upon this idea
born of the object which makes its appearance before the perceiver,

I'll bestow the term *objective idea* in order to distinguish it from the impression the object generates in the perceiver, which I shall call the *real idea*. It is of utmost importance that these two varieties of existence not be confused; merely neglect to characterize these distinctions, and the way is open to boundless error. The infinitely divisible point, so necessary to geometry, belongs to the class of *objective existences;* solid bodies to that of *real existences.* However abstract this may seem to you, my dear, you must make an effort to keep apace with me if you wish to follow my lead to the goal I wish my reasonings to bring us both to.

"Before going farther, let us here observe that nothing is commoner than to make the grave mistake of identifying the real existence of bodies that are external to us with the objective existence of the perceptions that are inside our minds. Our very perceptions themselves are distinct from ourselves, and are also distinct from one another, if it be upon present objects they bear and upon their relations and the relations of these relations. They are thoughts when it is of absent things they afford us images; when they afford us images of objects which are within us, they are ideas. However, all these things are but our being's modalities and ways of existing; and all these things are no more distinct from one another, or from ourselves, than the extension, mass, shape, color, and motion of a body are from that body. Subsequently, they necessarily bestirred themselves to invent terms to cover in general all particular but similar ideas: *cause* was the name given to all beings that bring about some change in another being distinct from themselves, and *effect* the word for any change wrought by whatever cause in whatever being. As this terminology gives rise in us, at best, to a very muddled idea of being, of action, of reaction, of change, the habit of employing it in time led people to believe they had clear-cut and precise perceptions of these things, and they finally reached the stage of fancying there could exist a cause which was not a being nor a body either, a cause which was really distinct from all embodiment and which, without movement, without action, could produce every imaginable effect. They were little concerned to ponder and realize that all beings continually acting and reacting upon one another produce and simultaneously undergo changes; the infinite progression of beings which have been successively cause and effect soon wearied the minds of those who at any cost were driven to find a cause in every effect. Sensing their imaginations worn to defeat by this long sequence of ideas, they hit upon the short cut of skipping in a single great leap back to a primary cause; they fancied it the universal cause in regard to which all particular causes are effects and which, itself, is the effect of no cause at all.

"Behold it, Juliette: such is the God men have got themselves; behold what their enervated imaginations have spawned by way of a grotesque fantasy. Linking one sophism to the next, men wound up creating this, 'tis plain to see how they did it; and in keeping with the definition I gave you just a while ago, you recognize that this grandiose phantom, having a merely objective existence, cannot exist anywhere outside the minds of the deluded who rivet their hallucinated attentions upon it, and hence it amounts to no more than the pure and simple effect of their brains' heated disorder. Ah yes, behold him nonetheless: the God of mortals, gaze well upon the abomination they've invented and in whose temples they have shed whole seas of blood.

"If," Madame Delbène continued, "I have dilated upon the essential differences between *real* and *objective* existences, that is, as, my dear, you understand, because I felt it a matter of urgency that I demonstrate to you the varieties subsisting in men's practical and speculative opinions, and that I have you see that men are wont to ascribe a real existence to a good many things which actually have a no more than conjectural existence. Well, it is to a product of this conjectural existence mankind has given the name of God. If faulty reasoning were the only result of these exercises, we could dismiss the whole harmless affair; but, unfortunately the thing does not stop there: the imagination catches fire, the habit develops, and one becomes accustomed to considering as something real that which is but the fictive creature of our weakness. One is no sooner convinced that this chimerical being's will is the cause of all that befalls us than one sets to employing every means to coddling and cockering him, every possible fashion to imploring him.

"Let's be guided by mature reflection and, deciding upon the adoption of a God only after careful sifting of what has just been advanced, let's be persuaded that the whole notion of God being unable to occur to us save in an objective manner, nothing but illusions and phantoms can result from it.

"Whatever they may serve up of sophistries, those absurd partisans of man's deific bogey actually never say anything more than that there can be no effect without a cause. But they're not prone to insist that if it be causes we're to discuss, we must trace them back to a first and eternal cause, a universal cause behind all particular and subsequent causes, an original, creative, and self-creating cause, a cause which is independent of any other cause. Admittedly, we do not truly understand the connection, the sequence, and the progression of all causes; but ignorance of one fact is never adequate grounds for establishing and then accrediting another fact. They who want to convince us of their abominable God's existence have the sauciness to tell us that, because we cannot designate the veritable source of the cause-and-effect series, we must necessarily acknowledge the universal cause they champion. Can you cite me a better example of inane argument? As if it were not preferable to admit ignorance instead of acquiescing in an absurdity; or as if the acceptance of this absurdity became proof of its existence! Idiots may as well sink in their mental limitations; the intelligent run the risk of foundering upon the rocks when it is into the phantom's haven they undertake to steer.

"But, with a cool head, let's proceed and, if you like, momentarily grant our antagonists the existence of the vampire[1] that is the author of their felicity. Within this hypothesis, I ask them whether the law, the rule, the will whereby God supervises beings is of the same nature as our mortal will and power, whether in the same circumstances God can want and not want, whether the same thing can please and displease him, whether his sentiments are unchanging, whether the scheme by which he operates is immutable. If he is subject to a law, his function is merely executive; if this be so, he follows instructions and is not autonomous, has no power of his own. The unaltering law behind his gestures, what then is it? is it distinct from him, or inherent in him? If, on the

---

[1] The vampire drank the blood from corpses, God causes that of men to be spilt; examination reveals both to be figments of disordered imagination; may we not justifiably call the one by the other's name?

other hand, this superior being can change his sentiments and his will, I wish to know why he does so. Certainly, he must have some motive for changing them, a much more logical motive than any that impels us, for God to outstrip us in wisdom as he surpasses us in prudence; well, can we possibly imagine this motive without lessening the perfection of the being who cedes to it? I'll go farther: if God knows beforehand that he shall change his mind and will, why, since the Omnipotent can do anything, has he not arranged circumstances in such sort as to obviate the need for this mutation, always tiresome and proof always of weakness? And if he doesn't know what's coming next, what kind of omniscient God is it who cannot foresee what he's going to have to do? If he does have foreknowledge thereof—as, if one is to arrive at any notion of him at all, one must suppose—it is then fixed and decreed, apart from his will, that he shall act in this manner or in that: well, what law determines his will? where is that law? whence does it draw its force?

"If your God is not free, if he is compelled to act in obedience to laws that govern him, then he amounts to something like destiny or chance which vows don't touch nor prayers melt nor offerings appease and which you'd better contemn forever than beseech with such little success.

"But if yet more dangerous, more wicked, more ferocious, your execrable God hid from man what was becoming necessary to man's happiness, his aim was then not to make man happy, he thus loves him not, thus he is neither just nor benevolent. It should seem to me that a God ought not to will anything impossible, and it is not possible that man respect laws that tyrannize or are unknown or unknowable to him.

"And there is yet more to it: this scurvy God hates man for being ignorant of what he has not been taught; he punishes man for having violated an unknown law, for pursuing bents and tastes man cannot have acquired from anyone but his creator. Oh, Juliette!" my tutor exclaimed, "can I conceive of this infernal and detestable God otherwise than as a despot, a barbarian, a monster to whom I owe all the hatred, all the wrath, all the scorn my quickened physical and moral faculties can excite in me?

"And so even were they to bring off their demonstration,

even were they to present me with proof of God's existence; were they to succeed in convincing me that he has dictated the laws, singled out certain individuals to attest them to mortals; were I to be made to see that in man's relationship to God there is none but the purest consistency and harmony; even so nothing could prove to me that I please him by observing his commandments, for if he is not good he can deceive me, and my reason, which comes to me only from him, shall not be my guarantee, for it would not be unthinkable that he endowed me with rational powers simply in order that, using a treacherous instrument, I thrust myself all the deeper into error.

"To continue. I now ask you deists how this God, whose existence I've no objection to allowing for the sake of a brief discussion, is going to behave in regard to those who are altogether unacquainted with his laws. If God punishes the invincible ignorance of those to whom his laws have not been promulgated nor announced, he is unjust; and if he is incapable of instructing them, he is impotent.

"There is no doubt: the revelation of the Eternal's laws must bear the hallmark of the God whence they emanate. Well, we have been regaled with revelations in quantity; which amongst them is stamped with an equally evident and indispensable seal of authenticity? Thus it is by religion itself that the religion-announcing God is repudiated and destroyed; and what, I wonder, is to become of this religion when the God it established no longer exists save in the unhinged minds of fools?

"Whether or not human knowledge be real or illusory, true or false, it matters little to the happiness of life; but that does not hold in what pertains to religion. Once men have as it were got their teeth into the imaginary objects religion proposes, they develop passionate enthusiasms for these objects: they come to believe that these ghosts flitting about in their heads really do exist, and from there on there's no checking them. Every day, fresh occasion to tremble and more adepts quaking: such are the sole effects the perilous idea of God produces in us. This idea alone is responsible for the most withering and appalling ills in the life of man; 'tis this idea that constrains him to deprive himself of life's most delectable pleasures, terrified as he is at all times lest he displease this disgusting fruit of his delirious imagination. You, my good little friend, you must therefore and as soon as you can deliver yourself from the frights this goblin inspires; and to achieve your liberty you without doubt have but to lift a steady fist to smash the idol into small bits.

"The concept of a divinity the priests wish to foist upon us is the concept, precisely, of a universal cause whereof every other cause is an effect. The imbeciles to whom these impostors have always addressed themselves believed that such a cause did exist— could possibly exist separately from the particular effects it produces, quite as if the modalities of a body could be separated from that body, as if whiteness being one of the qualities of snow, it were possible to peel that quality away from snow. Do modifications take leave of the bodies they modify? Well then, your God is only a modification of the matter that by its essence is perpetually in motion; this motion which you think you can separate from it, this energy native to matter, there's' your God; and now, you flea-brained worshiping mice, now inspect this august being who made you in his image, and decide for yourselves to what homage he is entitled!

"Those wits that hold the first cause capable of producing no more than the local movement of bodies, and who reserve to our human intelligence the power of self-determination, curiously limit that cause and, stealing away its universality, reduce it to the lowest thing in Nature, to, that is, the mean task of keeping matter on the move. But as all things in Nature are interrelated, let mental feelings produce movements in living bodies, let the movements of bodies excite sentiments in souls, all very well, but one cannot resort to this supposition to found or defend religious worship; as a consequence of the perception of the objects that are there before our consideration, we ask only that these perceptions occur when we are prepared to make the most of them, when they coincide with a stirring in our organs. Thus the cause of these stirrings is the cause of our will and desiring. If this cause knows nothing of the effect these stirrings produce in us, then what a puny God you've got there! and if he knows, then he is accomplice to it and consents thereto; if, knowing, he does not consent, he is thus forced to do what he does not want to do; there is thus something more powerful than he, hence he is constrained to obey laws. As our will always expresses itself in some movement, gesture, or impulse, God is consequently obliged to concur in what we will and sanction what at our will's behest we do: God hence dwells in the parricide's murdering arm, in the incendiary's torch, in the whore's cunt. God begins to sweat, to say no? Then there's a skimpy, starveling little God, weaker than us, and he's forced to obey us. And so, irrespective of what they say, it's got to be stated that there is no universal cause; or if you simply cannot manage without one, we'll have to let it consent to everything that happens to us, we'll have to suppose it never wills anything else, you'll have also to accept that this shoddy Omnipotence can neither hate nor love any of the particular beings which emanate from it, because all of them obey it equally, and that, this being so, words like *punishments, rewards, commandments, prohibitions, order,* and *disorder* are merely allegorical terms drawn from what transpires in the sphere of human events and intercourse.

"Notice now that as soon as one no longer feels strictly bound to regard God as an essentially good being, as a being who loves mankind, it is very possible to think that God intended to deceive man. Thus even were we to grant the authenticity of all the miracles upon which the whole scheme is made to repose by those who claim to knowledge of the laws he disclosed to a few individuals, as all these prodigious deeds confirm the injustice and inhumanity of God, we have no assurance that these wonders were not wrought with the express purpose of gulling us, and nothing authorizes the belief that by the most scrupulous observance of his commandments we can ever win his friendship. If he does not punish those who have observed his decreed law, its observance becomes useless; and as this obedience is painful, your God, in prescribing it, showed himself guilty of both uselessness and wickedness: whereupon I must again inquire whether this being is worthy of our pious attentions. His commandments, moreover, are in no wise respectworthy; they are absurd, contrary to right reason, they are offensive to our moral sense and are physically afflicting, they who proclaim the law violate it night and day, and if indeed there is in the world a scattering of personages who seem moved to express faith in this law, let us carefully scrutinize their mentalities, we will discover them to be simple-minded or lunatic. I turn an analytical eye upon the evidence offered in proof of this scandalous jumble of mysteries and decrees, the issue of our ridiculous God, and I find everything perched upon the pitiable foundations of confused, uncertain traditions which seem only to invite regular defeat at the hands of any adversary, however unskilled he may be.

"We may declare it truthfully and with confidence: of all the religions edified by mankind, there is not one which can make any legitimate claim to pre-eminence over the rest; not one which is not stuffed with fables, replete with lies, overflowing with perversities, not one which is not studded with the most imminent dangers lying cheek to jowl with the most glaring contradictions. The crazed seek to justify their reveries, and they call miracles to their rescue: whence the result that, with the same tedious circular process, it's now the miracle which proves the religion whereas a moment ago 'twas the religion which proved the miracle. Nor is it that only one religion requires miracles; they all do, miracles are cited in every holy text, and on every page. Leda had a splendid swan; to compete with her, Mary had to be served by her dove.

"If nevertheless all these miracles were true, the obvious and necessary result would be that God had allowed miracles to occur in behalf of true and false religions alike, in which case his impartiality would manifest his unconcern for error and truth. The entertaining thing is that every sect is as firmly persuaded as any of its rivals of the overwhelming reality of the prodigies it recognizes. If they are all false, one must conclude that entire nations have been capable of believing fictions; thus, insofar as the truth of prodigies goes, the unconditional credulity of a whole people proves nothing whatsoever. But not one of these alleged facts can be proved in any way other than by the persuasion of those who believe them already, hence there is not one the truth whereof has been adequately established; and as these wonders constitute the sole means by which we might be compelled to believe in a religion, we must conclude that not one stands proven, and we must deem them all as the handiwork of fanaticism, deceit, fraud, and arrogance."

"But," I interjected at this point, "if there be neither God nor religion, what is it runs the universe?"

"My dear," Madame Delbène replied, "the universe runs itself, and the eternal laws inherent in Nature suffice, without any first cause or prime mover, to produce all that is and all that we know; the perpetual movement of matter explains everything: why need we supply a motor to that which is ever in motion? The universe is an assemblage of unlike entities which act and react mutually and successively with and against each other; I discern no start, no finish, no fixed boundaries, this universe I see only as an incessant passing from one state into another, and within it only particular beings which forever change shape and form, but I acknowledge no universal cause behind and distinct from the universe and which gives it existence and which procures the modifications in the particular beings composing it. I affirm indeed that, in my view, the absolute contrary holds, and I believe I have proven my point. We need not fret if we find nothing to substitute for chimeras, and above all let us never accept as cause for what we do not comprehend something else we comprehend even less.

"After having demonstrated the complete extravagance of the deific system," that talented woman went on, "I'll surely have little trouble uprooting the prejudices and superstitions that have been planted in you ever since the day when, at a tender age, you first heard theories expounded on the principle of life; is there really anything more extraordinary than this superiority to animals which humans arrogate to themselves? Ask them upon what basis their superiority rests. 'We have a soul'—that's their silly response. Then ask them to explain· what they mean by this vocable, *soul.* And then you'll see them stutter, flounder amidst contradictions: 'It is an unknown substance,' they begin; next: it's a secret incorporeal power; finally, a spirit whereof they have no definite idea. Ask them how this spirit, which, like their God, they imagine as totally without extension, has managed to wed itself to their material and extensive body, they'll tell you that they frankly don't know, that it's passing strange, a mystery, that God's omnipotent dexterity has brought this union about. Such are the admirably keen and incisive ideas that stupidity forms of the hidden or rather imaginary substance which stupidity turns into the mechanism responsible for all of stupidity's acts.

"To that nonsense I have just this to reply: if the soul is a substance that differs essentially from the body and that can have no relation to it, their fusion is impossible. Furthermore, this soul, being in essence different from the body, ought necessarily to act in a different fashion from it; however, we observe that the impulses experienced by the body make themselves felt also upon this so-called soul, and that these two substances, dissimilar in essence, always act in concert. You'll tell me that this harmony is another mystery, and in my turn I'll tell you that I'm not aware of having any soul, that I'm acquainted with and feel nothing but my body; that it is the body which feels, which thinks, which judges, which suffers, which enjoys; and that all its faculties are the necessary effects of its mechanism, organization, and structure.

"Although man is utterly incapable of achieving the faintest idea of this soul of his, although everything proves to man that he feels, thinks, acquires thoughts and ideas, takes pleasure and suffers pain only by means of the senses or the organs of the body, notwithstanding he carries on with his folly and comes to the point of believing that this soul about which he knows nothing is exempt from death. But even supposing this soul to exist, tell me, if you please, how one can avoid recognizing its total dependence upon the body and the fact that it must share in all the vicissitudes of the body's fate. And yet absurdity can bring a man so far as to believe that by its nature the soul has nothing in common with the body; one would have us think that it can act and feel without the body's aid; in a word, one maintains that, deprived of this body and sundered from the senses, this sublime soul will be able to live in order to suffer, experience great comfort or severe torments. It is upon some such loose heap of conjectural absurdities one builds the wonderful opinion relative to the soul's immortality.

"If I ask them their motives for supposing the soul deathless, they pipe up at once: 'Because it is in man's very nature to desire eternal life.' 'But,' I reply, 'does your desire become proof of its fulfillment? By what peculiar logic dare one decide that something cannot fail to happen because one wishes it to?' 'The impious,' they give me back, 'the impious, lacking the flattering hopes of an afterlife, desire definitive annihilation.' 'Well then, upon the basis of this desire, are they any less authorized to conclude that they will be annihilated than you claim yourselves authorized to conclude that you are going to go on existing always simply because that is your desire?'

"Oh, Juliette!" this rigorous logician pursued with all the energy of a passionate conviction, "oh, my beloved friend, doubt thereof there may be none: when we die, we die. Inside and out, through and through; and once the Fates have severed the thread, the human frame is no more than an inert mass, unable to produce those movements which, collectively, constituted its life. In the dead body neither circulation nor respiration nor digestion nor locution nor intellection are any longer there; upon death, so they say, the soul quits the body; but to say that this soul, of which nothing is known, is the principle of life is to say nothing at all unless it be that an unknown force is the hidden principle of imperceptible motions. What is more natural and simpler than to believe a dead man is dead, over and done with; and what more ludicrous than to believe that when a man is dead he's still alive?

"We smile at the naïveté of those peoples who have the custom of burying provisions and victuals alongside corpses; is it more farfetched to believe men will eat after death than to fancy they'll think, have pleasant or unpleasant ideas, amuse themselves, repent, feel hurt or joy, be glad or heavy of heart, when once the very organs required for transmitting and receiving sensations and ideas shall have rotted to bits and these bits crumbled to dust? To say that human souls will be happy or unhappy after death is tantamount to declaring that men can see without eyes, hear without ears, taste without palates, scent without noses, touch without fingers. And yet, think of it! they consider themselves exceedingly clever, most rational, those societies which uphold such notions.

"The dogma of the soul's immortality assumes the soul to be a simple substance, in short, a spirit, but I haven't given up wondering what a spirit is."

"I was taught," I volunteered, "that a spirit is a substance lacking extension, incorruptible, and having nothing in common with matter."

"That being the case," my tutor answered at once, "tell me how your soul arranges to be born, to grow, to strengthen itself, to agitate itself, and to age, and all this concurrently with the evolution of your body?

"Like a myriad of fools who have entertained the same notions, you'll say that the whole affair is downright mysterious; but, imbeciles that they are, if all these problems are mysteries, they understand nothing about them, and since they understand nothing about them, how can they make an affirmative decision about the coexistence of what they are incapable of conceiving? In order to believe or affirm something, need you not at least know in what consists the thing you believe and declare to be? Belief in the soul's immortality, that comes round to saying one is convinced of the existence of a thing whereof there is no possible means of forming any precise concept whatever; it's belief in a batch of empty words without being able to associate any meaning to them; to maintain that a thing is such as it is said to be, that's the last stage in madness and vanity.

"Ah, but what odd logicians these theologians are! Whenever they cannot divine the natural causes of things, they jump straight into improvising supernatural causes, they imagine spirits, gods, occult causes, unfathomable and uncanny agents, or rather words for all these, words a great deal more obscure than the phenomena they labor to account for. We'd best remain within the realm of Nature when we wish to appreciate the effects of Nature; let us never stray away from Nature when we wish to explain her phenomena, let us cease to worry over causes too subtle to be grasped by our organs, let us fully realize that it shall never be by turning our back upon Nature that we'll find the solutions to the problems Nature poses us.

"Within the terms of theological hypothesis itself—that is to say, supposing that matter is moved by an omnipotent motor—by what right do the theologians deny their God the power to give this matter the faculty of thought? Were we to suppose a matter that could think we could at least gain a few insights into the subject of thought or into what does the thinking in us; whereas so long as we attribute thought to an immaterial being it is impossible for us even to begin to understand it.

"We encounter the objection that materialism reduces the human being to a mere machine, that materialism is hence a dishonor to our kind; but is it to honor this species to say that man acts at the behest of the secret impulses of a spirit or of a certain

I don't know quite what which serves to animate him nobody knows quite how?

"One readily perceives that the superiority they accord spirit over matter, or the soul over the body, is based simply on our ignorance of the nature of this soul, whereas everyone is more familiar with matter and flesh and fancies he understands them to the point of knowing precisely how they work. And yet, any contemplative mind must be aware that the simplest workings of our bodies are as difficult to apprehend as the enigmatic operations of thought.

"Why is it so many people have this inflated esteem for spiritual substance? I can offer only one explanation: their total inability to define it intelligibly. The slight case in which our theologians hold the flesh comes only from the fact that familiarity breeds contempt. When they tell us that the soul is of greater excellence than the body, they tell us nothing unless it be that that with which they have no acquaintance must perforce be finer, nobler, than that whereupon they have a few vapid ideas.

"Tirelessly they fill our ears with the usefulness of this afterlife dogma; they declare that even if it were all a large fib, it would still have its advantages, for it would continue to alarm men and keep them browbeaten on the path of virtue. Well, I wonder whether it's really so, that this dogma renders men better behaved and more virtuous. I dare say, to the contrary, that it is effective only in rendering them insane, hypocritical, wicked, despondent, irritable, and that you'll always find more virtues and more civil conduct among those peoples who are not burdened with these ideas than among those with whom they are the foundation of religion. If they who are appointed to instruct and rule over men had wisdom and virtue themselves, realities, and not fantasies, would enable them to govern better; but scoundrels, quacksalvers, ambitious ruffians, or low sneaks, the lawgivers have ever found it easier to lull nations to sleep with bedtime tales than to teach truths to the public, than to develop intelligence in the population, than to encourage men to virtue by making it worthwhile for sound and palpable reasons, than, in short, to govern them in a logical manner.

"Let there be no doubt of it, priests have had their motives for contriving and fostering this ridiculous rumor of the soul's immortality; lacking such devices, how would they have wrung

pennies from the dying? Ah, if these loathsome dogmas of God and
of a soul that outlives us are of no use to humankind, we must at
least admit that they are indispensable to those who have taken
upon themselves the chore of infecting public opinion."[2]

"But," said I, "is not the dogma of the immortality of the
soul comforting to the downtrodden and unlucky? Illusion though
it may be, is it not soothing, is it not gladdening? is it not a boon,
that man may believe he will be able to survive himself and his
woes and someday in heaven taste the bliss this world denied him?"

"Frankly," said she, "I fail to see that the desire to set a few
ill-starred dolts at ease warrants poisoning the minds of millions of
respectable people; and, besides, is it rational to trim the truth to
fit one's wishes? Be a little more courageous, abide by the general
law, resign yourself to the order of a fate which decrees that you,
along with everybody else, shall sink back into the crucible of
Nature, soon to emerge again in some other shape; for the fact
is that nothing perishes in the womb of this mother of humankind.
The elements composing us first decompose then straightway recompose otherwise, in other combinations; an undying laurel grows
upon Virgil's grave. I ask you, foolish deists, whether this glorious
transmigration is not as mild as your heaven-or-hell alternative?
For if the thought of paradise cheers us, few there are who wax
ecstatic over that of hell; and you Christian idiots, say you not
that to be saved one needs have grace your God grants to not
many folk? Well, there you have some comforting thoughts! Who
amongst you wouldn't prefer to be annihilated once rather than
burn forever? Who then will dare maintain that the attitude which
liberates one from these dreads is not a thousand times more
humane than the uncertainty wherein we are left to languish by
setting up a God who, proprietor of the favors he distributes, gives
them only to a small clique of his cronies and who allows that all
the others become worthy of eternal torture? Enthusiasm or mad-

---

[2] How else would they ever survive? Only two categories of individuals are apt
to find religious systems at all to their liking: firstly, that which these absurdities
fatten; and secondly, that made up of imbeciles who unfailingly believe all they're
told and never examine anything critically. But I defy any thinking being, any man
possessed of an ounce of wit, to maintain that he in good faith believes these religious
atrocities.

ness alone can make one reject a lucid and reassuring system and cleave to one where improbable conjectures make one despair."

"But what shall become of me?" I demanded of Madame Delbène. "I am afraid of this darkness, this eternal annihilation scares me."

"And, pray tell, what were you before birth?" inquired that brilliant woman. "Several unqualified lumps of unorganized matter as yet without definite form or at least lacking any form you can hope to remember. Well, you're going to turn back into those same or similar lumps of matter, you're going to become the raw material out of which new beings will be fashioned, and this will happen when natural processes bring it about. Shall you find all this pleasurable? No. Shall you suffer? No. Is there anything truly objectionable, here? No; and what is he who on earth agrees to sacrifice all his pleasures in exchange for the certitude of never having to undergo pain? What would he be, if he were able to strike this bargain? An inert, motionless being. And after he dies, what will he be? Exactly the same thing. What then is the use of fretting, since the law of Nature positively condemns you to the same state you'd gladly accept if you were given the opportunity to choose? Eh, Juliette, have you existed since the beginning of time? No; and does that fact make you grieve and despair? Have you any better cause to despair at the fact that you're not going to exist till the end of time? La la, calm yourself, my pigeon; the cessation of being affrights only the imagination that has created the execrable dogma of an afterlife.

"The soul—or, if you wish, the active principle that animates, moves, determines us—is nothing other than matter subtilized to a certain degree, by the means of which refinement it acquires the faculties that so amaze us. Not any given portion of matter would be capable of the same effects, to be sure; but, through combination with the ordinary portions composing our body, these extraordinary ones attain their capacity rather as fire can become flame when combined with fatty or other combustible materials. In fine, the soul cannot be approached save in two senses: as active principle, and as thinking principle; well, whether viewed as the one or the other, we may prove its materiality by two irrefutable syllogisms. (1) As active principle it is divisible; for the heart, long after its separation from the body, preserves its action, continuing to beat; now, whatever is susceptible of division is material. The soul, beheld as active principle, is divisible, hence material. (2) Whatever is susceptible of structural degeneration is material, that which is essentially spirit cannot deteriorate; well, the soul is affected by the condition of the body, the soul is weak in youthful bodies, decrepit in superannuated frames; it thus undergoes corporeal influence; however, anything that degenerates structurally is material: the soul declines and hence it is material.

"Let us say forthrightly and repeatedly: there is nothing marvelous in the phenomenon of thought, or at least nothing which proves this phenomenon distinct from matter, nothing which indicates that matter, subtilized or modified in some or another manner, cannot produce thought; the which is infinitely easier to comprehend than the existence of God. If this sublime soul were indeed the work of God, why should it have to share in all the changes and accidents the body is subject to? It would seem to me that, as a divine artifact, this soul ought to be perfect, and perfection does not consist in undergoing modifications in order to keep pace with so defective a material entity as the human body. If this soul were a god's production, it would not have to sense, reflect, or be the victim of the body's gradations; were the soul a thing of divine perfection, it wouldn't, it shouldn't, be able to; rather, fully formed from the onset, it would conjoin itself to the embryo, and Cicero would have been able to pen his *Tusculanae disputationes,* Voltaire his *Alzire,* each in the cradle. If that is not so, and cannot be so, it is because the soul ripens step by step with the body's development, then with it descends the farther slope; the soul therefore is constituent of parts, since it rises, sinks, augments, diminishes: well, whatever is composed of parts is material; hence the soul is material, since it is composed of parts. Am I clear? We have now to acknowledge the utter impossibility of the soul existing without the body, and the latter without the former.

"Nor is there anything to marvel at in the absolute sovereignty the soul exerts over the body. Body and soul, they are one, a whole made up of equal parts, yes, but in which, howbeit, the cruder must be subordinate to the more refined part, this for the same reason that flame, which is material, subordinates the wax it consumes and which is also material: there, as in our bodies, you have the example of two materials in conflict, the subtler of the two dominating the cruder.

"There, Juliette, I have, so I think, supplied you with more than is needed that you be convinced of the nullity of this God they say to exist and of this dogma which ascribes immortality to the soul. Oh, but they were shrewd beggars who invented this pair of conceptual monstrosities! And what have they been unwilling to stoop to, what have they not extorted from the people by calling themselves the ministers of God upon whose good or bad mood everything depends in the life after this! What has not been their influence upon the minds of simple folk who, in dread of agonies or rewards to come, were obliged to court these cheats, self-appointed and sole mediators between God and men, puissant quacks whose intervention, swaying the Lord, could arrange fates! All these fables thus are but the inspired fruit of self-seeking, of pride, and of the insanity of a handful of ambitious individuals nourished upon the ravings of a few others and fit for nothing but our contempt, fit only to be extinguished, that they may never again reappear. Oh, my dearest Juliette, with what earnestness I exhort you to detest them as I do! Such systems as these, it is said, lead to the degradation of morals and manners. What's this! are manners and morals then more important than religions? Depending absolutely upon the degree of latitude in which a country chances to be located, manners and morals are an arbitrary affair, and can be nothing else. Nature prohibits nothing; but laws are dreamt up by men, and these petty regulations pretend to impose certain restraints upon people; it's all a question of the air's temperature, of the richness or poverty of the soil in the district, of the climate, of the sort of men involved, these are the unconstant factors that go into making your manners and morals. And these limitative laws, these curbs and injunctions, aren't in any sense sacred, in any way legitimate from the viewpoint of philosophy, whose clairvoyance penetrates error, dissipates myth, and to the wise man leaves nothing standing but the fundamental inspirations of Nature. Well, nothing is more immoral than Nature; never has she burdened us with interdictions or restraints, manners and morals have never been promulgated by her. Oh, Juliette, you're going to think me peremptory, somewhat the rebel and an enemy of yokes and handcuffs; but with uncompromising severity I am going to dismiss this equally absurd and childish obligation which enjoins us *not to do unto others that which unto us we would not have done*. It is the precise contrary Nature recommends, since Nature's single precept is *to enjoy oneself, at the expense of no matter whom*. It may very possibly follow from the observance of this axiom that our pleasures disturb the felicity of others; will those pleasures be the less keen for that? This so-called "Law of Nature" with which fools wish to manacle us is thus just as fantastical as man-made laws and, trampling them all indiscriminately in the mud, we may be intimately persuaded that there is no wrong in doing anything we may well please. But at our leisure we shall return to these subjects; for the nonce, I flatter myself in the belief that my discussion of morality has been as convincing as my reflections upon religion. Let's now put our theories into practice and, after having demonstrated to you that you can do everything without committing a crime, let's commit a villainy or two to convince ourselves that everything can be done."

Electrified by these discourses, I fling myself into my friend's arms; in a thousand little ways I show gratitude for the care she is lavishing upon my education.

"I owe you more than life itself, my beloved Delbène," I cried; "what is an existence without philosophy? Is life worth living when one lies crushed beneath the yoke of lies and stupidity? Come then," I said with great warmth, "I feel worthy of you at last, 'tis upon your breast I take sacred oath never to return to the illusions which through gentle friendship you have just exterminated in me. Continue my instruction, continue to direct my footsteps toward happiness; I entrust myself to your guidance; do with me what you will, and be sure of this: that you have never had a disciple more ardent or more docile than Juliette."

Delbène was beside herself with delight; for a libertine intelligence, there is no more piercing pleasure than that of making proselytes. A thrill marks the inculcation of each principle, a multitude of various feelings are flattered by the sight of others becoming gangrened by the very corruption that rots us. Ah, how it is to be cherished, that influence obtained over their souls, souls which are finally re-created by our counsels, urgings, and seductions.

Delbène gave me back all the kisses I showered upon her; she said I was going to become a wayward girl like her, an undisciplined and very disrespectful little whore, that's where I was headed, I'd wind up an atheist, and when God should begin to wonder what on earth had happened to good little Juliette, she, Delbène, would most gladly step forth and accept the blame for having caused the loss of this soul. And her caresses becoming more vibrant, we soon ignited the passions' fire by the bright-burning lamp of philosophy.

"Stay," said Delbène, "since you're bent on being depucelated, I'm going to satisfy you straight off."

Crazed with lust, the wench instantly fits herself with a dildo; she frigs me; this, says she, will make me overlook the pain she's about to cause me and then she delivers a thunderous blow, then another, and 'tis this one does in my maidenhead. Words cannot describe what I suffered; but the lancing pains provoked by this terrible operation soon yielded to the sweetest pleasures. The indefatigable Delbène's fury only increased; stuffing me with great cracking bucks and thwacks, her tongue meanwhile probed far into my mouth, and worrying my behind with her two clawing hands, she had me discharging one steady hour in her arms, and she only left off when I begged for truce.

"Retaliate, retaliate," she gasped, "I want to be remunerated in that specie," said she. "I am devoured by lewd desires, fucking you was all work and no play, I've got to discharge too, Christ knows."

From a doted-upon mistress I immediately turned into the most passionate lover: I encunted Delbène, I set the scraper going. God! what transports! No woman fish-flopped more amorously, never was there one carried so far away by pleasure's throes; ten times in succession the slut swooned of ease, I thought her like to distill into fuck.

"Oh, my soul's delight!" I said to her, "is it not true that the greater an individual's wit and instruction the better accoutered he is to taste the amenities of voluptuousness?"

"Unquestionably," Delbène replied, "and the eminently simple reason therefor is this: voluptuousness can tolerate no inhibitions, it attains its zenith only by shattering them all. Now, the stronger a person's intellectual endowments, the more restraints he breaks, and the more decisively: hence, the person of superior wit and parts will always be found more apt to libertinage's pleasures."

"I believe that the exceeding delicacy of highly developed organs must also be reckoned as contributory," I went on.

"Nor is that to be doubted either," said Madame Delbène; "the more highly polished the mirror, the better it receives and the better reflects the objects presented it."

Finally, both of us dry from extreme toil, I reminded my instructress of her promise to me to depucelate Laurette.

"I've not in the least forgotten it," she answered, "the deed is for tonight. When everyone has retired to the dormitories, you'll slip away, so shall Flavie and Volmar. Leave the rest to me; now you're initiated into our mysteries. Be bold, be firm, Juliette, be staunch; there are wonderful things I design to show you."

I took leave of my friend to put in an appearance at the house; but fancy my surprise when I heard it reported that a *pensionnaire* had just fled the abbey. I asked her name. It was Laurette.

"Laurette!" I cried. Then, to myself: "My God, she upon whom I was counting . . . she the thought of whom has hurled me into this state. . . . Perfidious desires, have I then conceived them in vain?"

I request the details, no one is able to provide them; I fly to inform Delbène, her door is shut, I have no way of reaching her before the scheduled hour. Ah, how slowly the time drags away! I hear the bell toll at last; Volmar and Flavie arrived before me, they were already in Delbène's quarters.[3]

"Alas," I say, addressing myself to the Superior, "how shall you keep your word to me? Laurette is gone, vanished. Who can replace her?"

And then with a certain sourness:

"Ah! 'tis plain I'm not to enjoy the pleasure you promised me—"

"Juliette," broke in Madame Delbène, and her tone was cool, her look stern, "the foremost of amity's laws is that of trust: if,

---

[3] May we refresh the reader's memory, who may have forgot that the said Volmar is a charming nun of twenty-one years; and that Flavie is a *pensionnaire* aged sixteen and extremely fair of face and figure.

my dear, you wish to be one of us, you can do with more self-control and fewer suspicions. Is it likely—consider now—is it thinkable that I would have promised you a pleasure I lack the means to have you savor? Ought you not to think me sufficiently clever . . . ought you not to believe my position in this place powerful enough to guarantee that, since the arranging of these delights depends exclusively upon me, you have never to fear that they be unavailable to you? Tush. Follow us. All's quiet. Did I not tell you that uncommon sights await you?"

Delbène lights a little lantern, she walks ahead, Volmar, Flavie, and I follow. We enter the chapel; to my astonishment I see the Superior bend, a tombstone lifts, a way is opened, she descends into the sanctuary of the dead. My initiated companions go after her in silence; I betray a certain uneasiness, Volmar reassures me. Delbène lowers the stone slab above us. We are now in subterranean vaults that serve as sepulcher to all the women who have died in the convent. We proceed; another stone is swung aside, some fifteen or sixteen downward steps bring us to a low-ceilinged room decorated with much artistry and ventilated by air coming from the gardens above by a shaft. Oh, my friends! whom do you think I found there . . . Laurette, clad and decked like the vestals they used in olden times to immolate in the shrine of Bacchus; the Abbé Ducroz, first vicar to the Archbishop of Paris, a man of thirty years, very goodly to look upon, his special employment was the supervision of Panthemont—he was there; so was Father Télème, a handsome dark dog of a Récollet friar, thirty-six, confessor to the novices and the *pensionnaires*.

"She is afraid," said Delbène, going toward these two men and presenting me to them; "hear, young innocent," she continued, bestowing kisses upon me, "that our sole motive for congregating in this place is fuckery, the perpetration of sundry horrors, occasional atrocities. If we thus burrow far down into the realm of the dead, it is to be at the greatest possible remove from the living. When one is a libertine, as depraved, as vicious as are we, one likes to be in the bowels of the earth so as the better to avoid the interference of men and their ridiculous law."

Well along as I was in the career of lubricity, these opening remarks, I confess, disturbed me not a little.

"Heavens!" I cried, much moved, "what are we about to perform in these underground tunnels?"

"*Crimes,*" said Delbène. "We are going to soil ourselves with crimes before your very eyes, we are going to teach you to imitate us. Do you think you'll weaken? Am I mistaken in my confidence in you? I've told these our colleagues that you can be relied upon."

"Still your doubts," I replied energetically, "lay on your hands, I swear to it, whatever you do, it will stir up not a quaver of fear in me."

Therewith Delbène orders Volmar to undress me.

"She's owner to the world's fairest ass," was the Vicar's expressed opinion as soon as he saw me entirely naked.

And, instantly, kisses and fingerings were applied to my buttocks; then, clapping one hand over my scarcely fledged cunt, the man of God undertook to tickle up his member by rubbing it in the cleft between my buttocks and so that it grazed my little hole, the which he penetrated forthwith, virtually without effort, and at the same moment Télème slid his gear into my cunt. Both discharged together and I answered almost at once.

"Juliette," the Superior announced, "we have just afforded you the two greatest pleasures a woman can enjoy; you must be candid now, and tell me which of the two gave you the greater delight."

"Truth to tell, Madame," said I, "each gave me such pleasure I cannot decide which gave me the more. Reverberations are yet going through me of sensations at once so confused and so voluptuous that I would be hard put to assign them their proper origins."

"Then we'd best try it again," Télème observed; "the Abbot and I will vary our attacks, the lovely Juliette will have the goodness to interrogate her sentiments and to favor us with a more exact account thereof."

"Most willingly," I said; "I am of your mind that 'tis only by beginning afresh that I'll be able to decide."

"Charming, isn't she?" murmured the Superior. "There's more than enough there to result in the prettiest little whore we've developed in decades; but this thing must be managed not only in order that Juliette discharge deliciously, but so that some of the pleasures she is about to taste have their delightsome repercussions upon ourselves."

Pursuant to these libertine projects, the tableau was composed in this manner:

Télème, who'd just fucked my cunt, arranged himself in my ass; his device was a shade thicker than his confrere's, but, novice though I was, Nature had apparently so well modeled me for these doings that I confronted an increased diameter with an accommodating elasticity. I was lying flat upon the Superior, in such wise that my clitoris was directly over her mouth, and the gay wench, happily sprawled on the hard stone floor, was sucking like a babe on a teat; her thighs were wideflung. Between them, Laurette, bent over her, was treating her as I was being dealt with and, rocked by pleasure, the lewd thing was frantically masturbating Volmar on one side and Flavie on the other. Behind Laurette, Ducroz was gently frigging his tool on her buttocks, but without penetrating them; the question of honor—that of this child's two pucelages—concerned no one but me.

All these scenes of fuckery were preceded by a moment of suspense, of calm; as though the participants wished in stillness and contemplation to savor voluptuousness in its entirety, as though they feared lest, by talking, they might let some of it escape. I was requested to be attentive, alert in my pleasure-taking; for later I should be expected to report on the experience. I swam in a wordless ecstasy; and, I confess, the incredible pleasures evoked by the strident and persisting activity of Télème's prick in my ass, the lubricious agonies into which I was plunged by the Abbess' tongue flitting over, needling my clitoris, the luxuriant scenes environing me, the combination of so many lascivious elements gripped my senses in a delirium and in that delirium I wanted to live an eternity.

Télème was the first to try to speak; but his stammers, his gasps much better expressed his disorder than his ideas. We could make out nothing in this incoherence but oaths, although he seemed to be endeavoring to say that the extreme heat and constriction of my anus had driven him wild.

At last, mastering himself, he made it known that he was ready to discharge into the most divine of all asses: "I know not whether Juliette will be more content to receive my fuck in her entrails than she was to feel it spewed into her cunt; but, for my part, I swear that, sodomizing her, I feel ten thousand times more pleasure than I got in her vagina."

"Purely a question of *taste*," remarked Ducroz, who had augmented the tempo and force of his friggery upon Laurette's ass and who was kissing Flavie's apace.

"A question of one's *philosophy*, of the manner of one's *reasoning*," contended Volmar, being sharply frigged by Delbène and tonguing Ducroz; "although a woman, my opinion is the same, and I protest that were I a man, I'd never fuck anywhere but in assholes."

Pronouncing these impure remarks, the voluptuous creature discharges. Télème follows a moment later; he waxes furious; twisting my head toward him, he rams a foot's length of tongue into my mouth; meanwhile, Delbène is sucking me with such telling effect that I cease to struggle. I wish to scream my pleasure, Télème's squirming tongue stops my words, the libertine drinks my sighs; I flood my suckeress' lips, fill her mouth, flood her throat, and she herself speeds a torrent into Laurette's gullet; Flavie joins us the next instant and the charming thing ejaculates her fuck while swearing like a trooper.

"Now on to something else," says Delbène, regaining her feet. "Ducroz, encunt Juliette, she'll lie in your arms. Volmar, also lying on her belly, will busy herself pumping Juliette's asshole; I'll slip under Volmar to suck her clitoris; while Télème encunts me, Flavie will do what she can for his anus as Télème devotes a free hand to massaging Laurette's cunt while he fucks mine."

Further outpourings in homage to Cypris terminated this second experimental affray; and then I was questioned.

"Oh, my heart," I answered Delbène—it was she conducted the inquiry—"since I must reply truthfully, I shall affirm that the member that was introduced into my hind parts caused me infinitely more intense and more delicate sensations than that other which traveled me frontwise. I am young in years and in experience, shy, unacquainted with and perhaps ill-made for the pleasures wherewith I have just been gratified beyond all common measure; it were wholly possible that I be mistaken upon the kind and violence of these pleasures themselves, but you demand to know what I have felt and I have told you."

"Come, give me a kiss, my angel," spoke Madame Delbène, "you are a splendid girl and in fitting company. Ah, no doubt of it," she proceeded enthusiastically, "no doubt whatever can exist, no pleasure can match what you have in the ass: woe betide those simple-minded, fainthearted chits who, lacking significantly in imagination, *dare* not attempt the true adventure. Impoverished creatures, these, they shall never be worthy to sacrifice to Venus, and never shall the Goddess of Paphos reward them with her favors!⁴

"Oh, may I now be embuggered too!" cried the whore, kneeling on a divan. "Volmar, Christ's guts! Where are you, Volmar? Flavie! Juliette! Outfit yourself with stout weaponry, and you, Ducroz and Télème, stiffen your pikes and set them mischievously to worrying the assholes of these three bitches! And there's my own ass, mark the hole? Fuck it, all of you! Laurette, lie quiet there before me while I have at you as my impulses bid me."

The Superior's orders are acted upon. From the manner in which the libertine welcomes her attackers, 'tis plainly to be seen how inured she is to this hard use. While one of the actresses is toiling over her, a second, bending beneath her, tickles her clitoris or nips her labia; through synchronization of these twin activities, the patient's joy is mightily enhanced, it is never really entire save when a steady and soothing frontwise masturbation to the bumwise intromissions adds the tart seasoning which can be imparted by a

---

⁴ Gentle and most lovable creatures whom libertinage, laziness, or adversity has reduced to the lucrative and delicious estate of whores, pay closest heed to this counsel; well you see that here it is no less than the fruit of much wisdom and broad experience. Ass-fuck, my fair friends, 'tis the one way to amuse yourselves and prosper. Remember that they who bar you this pleasure are moved by nought but idiotic prejudice, unless it be by basest jealousy. You fastidious and sensitive wives who read me, accept the same advice; do as did versatile Proteus, be now this, now that, with your husbands and, gratifying them in every manner and at every turn, you'll have them all to yourselves. Be most certain of it: of all the resources coquetry offers you, buggery is at once the safest and most winning. And you young girls, seduced in the bower of your innocence, remember well that by presenting only your ass for a target you infinitely lessen the risks you run, both as touches your honor and your health: no offspring, virtually never any illnesses, and pleasures a thousand-fold sweeter.

knowledgeable fricatrice. The mounting irritation drove Delbène mad: in this woman, passions spoke an imperious language. We soon began to notice that the little Laurette was the target less of Delbène's caresses than of her rage: she was becoming covered with bites, pinches, scratches.

"O Jesusfuck!" Delbene finally screamed as Télème sodomized and Volmar titillated her, "ah fuck! fuck! I'm discharging, you are slaying me with delight, enough! Enough, 'tis done . . . let's sit down now, let's talk a bit. . . . There's more to it than just experiencing sensations, they must also be analyzed. Sometimes it is as pleasant to discuss as to undergo them; and when one has reached the limit of one's physical means, one may then exploit one's intellect. We'll make a circle. Calm yourself, Juliette, you have a worried air—are you still afraid that we'll fail you? There's your victim," she said, pointing to Laurette, "you'll encunt her, you'll embugger her, the thing is a certainty. Rely upon a libertine's promise, as you may upon his excessive behavior. Télème, and you, Ducroz, place yourselves close by me; while speaking I'd like to handle your pricks, I want to put them back in size again, my fingers will infuse them with energy, I want that energy to electrify my speech. You'll see my eloquence swell, not like Cicero's, in accordance with the gestures and movements of the people clustered round the tribune, but like Sappho's, in proportion to the fuck she wrung from fair Damophile.

"I do declare," were Delbène's next words, spoken once she had reached the state appropriate for holding discourse, "in this world I wonder at nothing so much as at the moral education girls are commonly given. It would appear as if its one aim were to instill notions and doctrines that contradict all the natural impulses in our maidens. Is anyone able to tell me, for I sincerely wish to know, of what use a prudent, well-behaved woman can be to society? and whether there is anything more superfluous than the practice of this virtue which, with every passing day, only further numbs and mines our sex? We women exist in two situations wherein these practices are recommended to us; I am going to undertake to prove that, in either phase of a woman's life, they are of the most thorough inutility.

"Up until the time a girl marries, of what conceivable advantage can preserving her virginity be to her? And how can folly be carried to the point where one believes a female creature is worth more or less for having one part of her body a little more or a little less enlarged? For what purpose has Nature created every human being? Is it not for giving mutual aid one to the other, and consequently for giving others all the pleasures it is in one's power to dispense? Well, if it be true that a man may expect very great pleasures from a young girl, do you not fly in the face of Nature's intentions and laws when you saddle this poor little thing with a ferocious virtue that forbids her from lending herself to this man's impetuous desires? Can you allow such barbarity without advancing some justification for it? And what justification are you going to propose in order to convince me that the child in question does well by remaining a virgin? Your religion, your customs, your habits? And, I ask you, what baser drivel, what more contemptible arguments can you find? I'll leave religion aside, I know all of you well enough to be certain of the slight credit you accord that trash. But, conventions, ah, conventions—may I be so bold as to ask you what they are? If I am not mistaken, the term applies to the kind of behavior observed by the individuals of a nation at home and in public. Now you will surely agree that these conventions ought to be based upon furtherance of individual happiness; if they do not ensure it, they are ridiculous; if they are harmful to it, they are atrocious, and an enlightened nation must set straightway to work rectifying these conventions directly it is manifest that they no longer conduce to the general welfare. You will now demonstrate to me what, if anything, in French customs and manners, insofar as carnal pleasure is concerned, can truly be said to conspire to our national happiness; in the name of what do you constrain this dear little creature to hang on to her maidenhead, this in flagrant disregard of Nature—Nature, who advises her to be rid of it—in disregard, likewise, of her health—her health which restraint can only wreck! Are you going to reply that all this is so that she can be pure when she arrives in her husband's arms? But is this fancied necessity that she be pure anything other than the invention of prejudice-racked minds? What! To give some fellow the frivolous pleasure of plucking first fruits, you're going to have the wretched lass deny herself for ten years? she's to cause five hundred suitors pain in order to provide one with a moment of fool's delight? Can you think of anything more outlandish, does any more ill-conceived scheme exist? Can you, I ask, can you show me a more flagrant example of outrage to the general interest? Has the common welfare any greater enemy than these abhorrent conventions? Long live those people who, dwelling in ignorance of these disgraceful puerilities, to the contrary esteem only the young persons of our sex in proportion to the disorderliness they exhibit in their conduct! Only in these multiple and iterated extravagances does a girl's true virtue reside; the more she gives herself, the more lovable she is; the more she fucks, the more happiness she distributes and the more she is instrumental to her countrymen's happiness. They are sordid barbarians, these husbands who stick by the vain pleasure of plucking a rose: 'tis despotism, they claim this right at the expense of other men's well-being. An end to this disesteem for the girl who, having no previous acquaintance with them, has not been able to wait to make them a gift of the most precious thing she has and who, if she has heeded Nature's promptings, has had every reason for not waiting. Shall we now investigate the necessity of virtue in women whose situation is that of a wife? The matter is now one of adultery, I should like to go thoroughly into this popularly alleged misdemeanor.

"Our customs, manners, religious beliefs, codes, regulations —all these sordid local factors merit no consideration in this survey; the point is not to discover whether adultery is a crime in the eyes of the Laplander who permits it, or of the Frenchman who hammers it, but to make out whether humanity is wronged or Nature offended by this act. In order to entertain such a hypothesis, one must first be in total ignorance of the scope of the physical desires with which the common mother of mankind has endowed both sexes. Obviously, if one man were sufficient to a single woman's desires, or if one woman could appease the ardors of any single man, then, within the framework of this hypothesis, whosoever violated the law would also outrage Nature. But if the fickleness and the insatiability of these desires are such that more than one man is necessary to women as an abundance of women is to men, you will, I presume, concede that, such being the case, whatever law opposes their desires is tyrannical and plainly at daggers drawn with Nature. The pseudo-virtue called chastity, unmistakably the most ridiculous of existing superstitions in that this mode of being does nothing in the slightest to make others happy and wreaks incalculable harm on the prosperity of everyone, since this virtue imposes exceedingly cruel privations upon all; this pseudo-virtue, I say, being the idol which dread of adultery makes us worship, every sane mind ought first of all to give chastity an eminent position amongst the most odious devices whereby man has seen fit to encumber and rout the inspirations of Nature. Let's probe to the heart of the matter: the importance of the need to fuck is no less high than our need to eat and drink, and one ought to indulge in them all with equal unrestraint. Modesty, and of this we may be perfectly sure, was originally designed as nothing but a stimulant to lust: the engaging idea was to postpone desire's fulfillment in order to increase excitement, and fools subsequently took for a virtue what was merely a contrivance of libertinage.[5] It is as ridiculous to pretend that chastity is a virtue as it would be to assert that it is a virtue to deprive oneself of food. May it be clearly noted: it is almost always the stupid importance we assign to something which in the end elevates it to the stature of a virtue or of a vice; let us have done with our unseemly prejudices: let it become as ordinary and simple a matter to inform a girl, a boy, or a woman that one has an inclination to sport about with him or her, as it is, when one is in a foreign household, to request means to alleviate one's hunger or thirst—let it become an everyday affair and you'll see the prejudice collapse and disappear, you'll see chastity cease to be a virtue and adultery cease to be a crime. Come, come! what wrong do I commit, what injury do I do when, encountering some attractive creature, I say:

" 'Pray avail me of that part of your body which is capable of giving me a moment's satisfaction, and, if you are so inclined,

---

[5] Solitary, man blushes at nothing; modesty grips him only when he is surprised in the act, which proves that modesty is a ridiculous prejudice, absolutely unrecognized by, absolutely alien to, Nature. Man is impudicious born, his impudicity he has from Nature; civilization may tamper with her laws, but never shall civilization extirpate them from the philosopher's soul. "Hominem planto," said Diogenes, as he fucked by the side of the road; and why be more eager to conceal oneself when planting a man than a cabbage?

amuse yourself with whatever part of mine may be agreeable to you.'

"In what way does my proposal injure the creature whose path I've crossed? What harm will result from the proposal's acceptance? If about me there is nothing that catches his fancy, why then, material profit may readily substitute itself for pleasure, and for an indemnity agreed upon through parley, he without further delay accords me the enjoyment of his body; and I have the inalienable right to employ force and any coercive means called for if, in having satisfied him according to my possibilities— whether it be with my purse or with my body—he dares for one instant withhold from me what I am fairly entitled to extract from him. Only he offends Nature who refuses what may oblige his fellow; I outrage her not in the least, not I, when I offer to buy what arouses my interest and to pay the fairly arranged price for what is lent for my use. No, no, I repeat: chastity is no virtue; it is a conventional form, that's all. The libertine intelligence, perpetually in search of refinements, invented chastity as such; chastity is arti- ficial, in no wise natural; and a girl, a woman, and a boy, granting their favors to the first comer, prostituting themselves with effron- tery and in every sense, everywhere, all the time, would possibly— I don't deny the possibility—be committing something contrary to the usages that might be current in their country; but in no wise would they or could they thereby be doing wrong either to their neighbors—whom such behavior does not wrong, but rather serves —or to Nature—whose purposes are nought but furthered by all the excesses of libertinage it is in our mortal power to indulge in and perpetrate. Continence, be very certain of it, is the virtue of fools and enthusiasts; it is laden with perils, has not one good or wholesome effect; to men it is just as pernicious as to women; it damages health, in that it allows semen to stand and putrify in the loins, whereas this semen has been produced to be expelled from the body, like any other secretion or excretion. In brief, the most fright- ful moral corruption is incalculably less a threat to one's well-being; and the most celebrated among the world's peoples, as well as their most illustrious individual representatives, have always been the most debauched. The having of women, freely and in common, is the express wish of Nature, the arrangement is widespread in the world, animals set us the example; it is absolutely contrary to that universal agent's inspirations and intentions to wed a man to one woman, as in Europe it is done, or a woman to several men, as in certain regions of Africa, or a man to several women, as in Asia and European Turkey; all these institutions are revolting, they hobble the desires, they dam the humours, they enfetter the impulses and emasculate the will, and from all these infamous conventions there results nought but woe, ill, sorrow, and blight. Oh, those of you who have the temerity to govern men, beware, I say, put no bonds upon any living creature! Leave him free to shift for himself, leave to him alone the task of seeking out that which suits him best, do that and you shall speedily observe the state of affairs ameliorated, for it can only improve. Thereupon every rational man will say: 'Why, simply because I need now and then to spill a little seed, must I bind myself indissolubly to a person I'll never love? Of what use can it be that this same need cause a hundred wretches whose names I don't even know to become my thralls? Why must this need, in a woman the same save in one or two details, subject her to perpetual slavery and humiliation?' Ye gods, that woebegone girl's all afire with urges, the need to slake twenty thirsts consumes her, and you, what are you going to do to relieve her? you're going to tie her fate to a single man's . . . and that man? are you so sure his taste in pleasures will correspond so faultlessly to hers? could it not turn out, as sometimes does happen, that he lies with her three times, four times in the course of his life, or that his employment of her consists merely in submitting her to pleasures in which the young thing cannot possibly share? What arrant injustice on both sides, and how well it is avoided by abrogating your senseless marriages, by leaving the two sexes at liberty to consult their wishes and to look for and find exactly what they require one of the other. What good does society glean from marriages? Far from fortifying attachments, it dissolves them: it manufactures not friends, but foes; which, in your judgment, seems to be the more firmly united: one great family—as might become every nation on earth—or five or six million little families whose interests, inevitably personal, inevitably clash, create divisions, and forever jar with the general interest? What's this idle talk about liberty, equality, fraternity, what's this unity and brotherhood among men so long as everyone, brothers, fathers, mothers, wives go on struggling against one another? Unity means universality; do I hear you object that this universality will weaken ties, that there'll be no more of them owing to the universal bond? Well, what does it matter? Is it not far preferable to have none than to retain this sort, whose only purpose can be to stir up trouble and spread disaffection? We glance at history. What of the leagues, the factions, the numerous parties which have reft France owing to the prevailing practice of allying oneself to one's family and with it battling against every other family; do you, I ask, do you suppose we would have had all that had there been but one family in France? Would this grand family have broken up into men-at-arms, troops fighting tooth and nail, some for a tyrant, others for the opposing party? There'd have been no Orléanais at the Burgundians' throats, no Guises pitted against Bourbons, none of all those horrors which tore France asunder and whose one source was the pride and ambition of individual families. Those passions evaporate with the equality I propose; they wither into oblivion once the absurdities known as marital ties are destroyed; what remains? a homogeneous, tranquil State, with one attitude, one objective, one desire: to live happily together, and together to defend the fatherland. The machine cannot possibly avoid breaking down before long if the customs and usages in force today are maintained. Wealth and property concentrating in the hands of a few, this few becoming fewer through constant intermarriage, within a hundred years' time the State will necessarily be divided into two factions, one so powerful and so rich that it will topple and crush the other: and the country will be laid waste.[6]

"Ponder the matter and you'll discover that there has never been any other cause for all our difficulties. One power, quietly gathering strength, has always ended up trying to overwhelm the other, and has always succeeded. An ounce of prevention is worth a pound of cure, my friends: abolish marriages. Away with those abhorrent chains; enough of these bitter regrets; no more of these hardships, these crimes, the consequences of these monstrous abuses, you'll be rid of them all the day you're done with these laws: for laws alone create the crime; and the crime is gone as soon as the

---

[6] It should be remarked that Justine's memoirs and those of her sister were written prior to the Revolution.

law ceases to exist. No more enclaves within the State, no more conspiracies, no more shocking inequalities of wealth; but children . . . population? . . . We'll deal with those articles next.

"We begin by establishing a fact which we are prone to consider incontrovertible: that, during the carnal act, extremely little thought is devoted to the creature which may be its result; he who were stupid enough to preoccupy himself with the question would most assuredly cut his pleasure in half. Manifestly, he is a blithering ass who with this idea in his head goes to see a woman, and no less an ass he who when seeing a woman gets this idea. It is erroneous that propagation is supposed to be one of Nature's laws, if we imagine such nonsense our pride alone is to blame. Nature permits propagation, but one must take care not to mistake her tolerance for an enjoinder. Nature stands in not the slightest need of propagation; and the total disappearance of mankind—this being the worst consequence of a refusal to propagate—would grieve her very little, she would no more pause in her career than if the whole species of rabbits or chickens were suddenly to be wiped off the face of the earth. Thus, we no more serve Nature in reproducing ourselves than we offend her in not doing so. Be amply persuaded of it, this wonderful propagation, inflated into a virtue by our preposterously overdrawn self-esteem, if viewed from the standpoint of Nature's functionings, becomes entirely superfluous, and a subject over which we ought to trouble ourselves as little as possible. Brought together by the instincts of pleasure, two beings of unlike sex ought to put their best efforts into enjoying themselves as thoroughly as ever they can; their task is to employ all their faculties and attentions to improving and increasing their pleasure; and the eventual outcome of this pleasure-taking? devil take the bloody consequences, that's the proper attitude, for Nature herself couldn't care less about them.[7]

---

[7] Oh, mortal man! you believe it a crime against Nature you commit when you take an opposing stand to propagation or when you destroy the matured fruit of your loins, and never does it occur to you that the destruction of a thousand, nay, of a million times as many mortals as are now on the earth's surface would cost Nature not a single tear and would introduce not the slightest change in the regularity of her functions; 'tis thus not for us that all has been wrought, and if we did not exist at all, all else would be as now it is notwithstanding. What then are we in Nature's eyes? and how dare we make such a great case of our insignificant selves?

"With regard to the father, he is in no wise concerned with whatever issue may occur, if issue there should be. And, with the assumption that women are held in common, which is what they should be and had better be soon, what concern could he conceivably have? He spits a little sperm into a receptacle everyone else relieves himself into, a womb where what can germinate does germinate; how is this gesture to turn into the grave obligation to look after a fertilized egg? No, he has no more duties to observe toward a foetus than he would toward something deposited by an insect and which some shit he dropped at the foot of a tree caused to hatch several days later; in both cases I have cited, the problem is simply one of some matter of which a man needs to get rid and which subsequently becomes whatever it happens to become. The embryo is to be considered the woman's exclusive property; as the sole owner of this fruit rather jestingly called precious, she can dispose of it as she likes. She can destroy it in the depths of her womb if it proves a nuisance to her. Or after it ripens and is born, if she is for any reason displeased with it or irked at having produced it, she can destroy it then; whatever the circumstances, infanticide is her sacred right. Her spawn is hers, entirely hers, and no one else can claim this bit of property belonging to no one else, utterly useless to Nature, and hence the mother may feed it or she may strangle it, depending upon her preference. Ah, you've no need to fear a dearth of children; there will be only too many women who'll be eager to bring up what they whelp; and if it's manpower for defending the country or tilling the soil you're anxious about, you will always have more of it than you'll know what to do with, To these ends, create public schools where, as soon as they are weaned, the young may be reared; installed therein as ward of the State, the child can forget even his mother's name. After he has grown up, let him in his turn couple indiscriminately, democratically, with his mates and brethren, doing as his parents did before him.

"Given these principles, you now see what adultery amounts to, and whether it is possible or true that a woman can do wrong in surrendering herself to whoever catches her fancy. Determine for yourselves whether everything would not continue very nicely even with the overthrow of every last one of our laws. But these laws—are they so very general? Do all races and peoples have the same respect for these miserable ties? It might serve to make a rapid historico-geographical survey if we feel that our attitude would benefit from the support of a few precedents.

"So then, we notice that in Lapland, in Tartary, in America, they consider it an honor to prostitute their wives to wayfaring strangers.

"The Illyrians hold special conclaves for the purposes of debauchery; at them, they force their wives to give themselves to all comers; the thing is performed within public view.

"Adultery was publicly authorized among the Greeks. The Romans lent one another their spouses. Cato made his available to Hortensius, for the latter had no fertile wife of his own.

"In Tahiti, Cook discovered a society in which all the women give themselves indifferently to all the assembled men. But if a later consequence of this rite is pregnancy, the woman smothers the child the instant it is born: splendid evidence, this, that there do after all exist people of sufficient intelligence to set their pleasures on a higher plane than the futile laws enjoining us to increase numerically! Differing only in a few particulars, a similar society thrives at Constantinople.[8]

"The blacks of what we call the Spice Coast and of Riogabar prostitute their wives to their own children.

"Singha, Queen of Angola, published a law which established the *vulgivagüibilité* of women: one which, that is to say, made their cunts as free universally to be fucked as air is to be breathed. A chapter of this same edict made it incumbent upon women to take the measures necessary to thwart pregnancy; evidence having been adduced thereof, disobedience was punished capitally: the culprit was ground in a mortar. A severe law, perhaps, but useful, being exceedingly favorable to the conservation of the integrity of the community whereof the size is to be limited if the somber consequences of excessive numbers are to be avoided.

"But there are milder means for keeping population trimmed

---

[8] It flourishes in Persia too. Likewise, also, do the Brahmins forgather, to give each other their wives, their daughters, their sisters to be fucked reciprocally.

Among the Bretons of old, eight or ten husbands would convene and put their wives at the disposal of the company; selfish interests, factions discourage these delicious traffickings here in France; and I ask: when shall we be philosophers enough to establish them?

to neat and sensible dimensions: they would be by encouraging and recompensing *sapphism, sodomy,* and *infanticide,* as in Sparta theft was honored. Thus might the scales be maintained in balance, without there being the need to obliterate women's fruit even while it is in the womb, as is common practice in Angola and Formosa.

"For example, in France, where the population is far too large, while establishing the *vulgivaguibilité* I am partisan to, one would also have to set a maximum figure to child-production, to drown the surplus, and, as I have just said, to venerate the presently unlawful commerce between persons of the same sex. The government, under these ideal conditions invested with entire authority over these children and over the regulation of their number, would be able automatically to calculate the strength of its defensive soldiery by the number of warriors it had raised, and no longer would the State have cities full of thirty thousand starving wretches to feed in time of famine. It is going a bit too far when one respects a little fertilized matter to the point of imagining that one cannot, when need be, destroy it before birth or even a good while after that.

"There is, in China, a society similar to those of Tahiti and Byzantium. I allude to the society called that of the Complacent Husbands. They will marry girls only upon condition those girls have prostituted themselves to others; their homes are asylums of multiform luxury. They drown the offspring begot of this trade.

"In Japan there exist women who, though married, with their husbands' approval frequent the vicinity of temples and station themselves by the highways; they expose their breasts, as Italian harlots do, and are constantly prepared to satisfy whatever needs of whatever clients chance brings their way.

"At Cambay there is to be seen a pagoda, destination of pilgrims, and thither every woman betakes herself with utmost piety: there, they prostitute themselves, and no husband carps at their behavior. They who finally accumulate a certain capital from their work usually purchase young slaves whom they ready for like employment and then take along to the pagoda, and thus are fortunes amassed.[9]

---

[9] See *Cérémonies réligieuses,* Vol. VI, p. 300.

"In Pegu, the husband is supremely contemptuous o. wife's favors; he enlists the aid of a friend, who clears the tions away; often, he will request help from a well-dispose total stranger. But the same traditions do not apply to the initi. of a young boy. For the inhabitants of Pegu, this pleasure is pri. above all others.

"The female Indians of Darien prostitute themselves to any- one at all. If they are married, the husband accepts the charge of the child; if they are unwed, pregnancy would dishonor them, so they have themselves aborted or in their coupling observe those precautions which are guarantee against this inconvenience.

"In faraway Cumana, newly wedded girls lose their maiden- heads to priests; the husband will have nought to do with them until this ceremony has been performed. That inestimable treasure, virginity, thus owes its value simply to national prejudices, as do so many other things which we are reluctant to view for what they are in reality.

"For how long did not the feudal lords of several European provinces, in Scotland above all, exploit the same right? Prejudices, superstitions, fads . . . this modesty . . . this virtue . . . this adultery.

"No, not by any means do all peoples accord in cherishing maidenheads. The more gallant adventures a girl in North America has had, the more suitors court her. They spurn a virgin, her virgin- ity is a grave handicap to a girl: it demonstrates undesirability.

"In the Balearic Islands, the husband is the last to enjoy his wife: every acquaintance, every chum, all the relatives precede him in this ceremony; a very strange and suspect person he would be thought, who resisted this prerogative. The same custom used to be observed in Iceland and by the Nazamaeans, an Egyptian tribe: after the wedding feast, the naked spouse went and lay one after the other with the wedding guests, and from each received a present.

"We know that among the Massagetes every woman was held in common: when a man encountered one who pleased him, he bade her mount his chariot; in the matter she had no say at all, he hung his weapons on the shaft and that was enough to keep others away.

"It was not by devising marriage laws but the reverse, by establishing the perfect community of women, that the Norse were

enough to humble Europe three or four times over, and
t with their emigrations.

Marriage, it thus appears, is noxious to population, and the
is covered with peoples who despise the institution. Hence,
ne eyes of Nature, it is contrary to individual happiness and
nerally to all things and practices which are capable of promoting
and assuring man's earthly felicity. Well, if it is adultery that
smashes marriages, adultery that shatters laws, adultery that so
emphatically concords with Nature's laws, adultery might very
easily pass for a virtue instead of a crime.

"Oh, tender creatures, divine artifacts created for the pleasures of men, cease to believe that you were made for the enjoyment of only one man; utterly unafraid, beneath your proud heel
grind to dust these absurd ties which, chaining you in the arms of a
husband, are bar to the happiness you await from the lover you
cherish. Consider rather that it is only by resisting his advances
that you outrage Nature. Having made you the more sensitive, the
more fiery of the two sexes, in your heart Nature ingrained the
desire to indulge unrestrainedly all your passions. Did she invite
you to be the captive of a single man when she gave you force
enough to drain the balls of four or five in a row? Scorn the vain
canons which victimize you; they're the contrivances of your
enemies, for 'tis plain, is it not, that they weren't invented by you?
Since it is sure that you'd have been ill-disposed to approve them
had your opinion been consulted, what right have these swine to
exact obedience thereto? Remember that after a certain age you'll
no longer please, and that in your later years you'll shed many a
bitter tear if you've let youth go by without enjoying it; and what
shall you obtain in return for this discretion, this shyness, this self-
denial, what will be your reward when the loss of your charms
robs you of the power to claim any consideration at all? Your
husband's esteem?—fie! what an inadequate consolation! what
miserly recompense for such enormous sacrifices! Furthermore,
what assurance have you of their equity? what's to prove to you
that your constancy is as efficacious and as valuable as you suppose?
Must your husband necessarily imitate your fidelity? Ah, there you
see it for what it is: gratuitous; you feed yourself on pride. Oh,
you women who are made to be loved, the scantiest pleasure

provided by a lover outweighs all the relief you'll derive from self-abuse: sheer illusions, those solitary pleasure-takings, no one believes in them, no one will recognize your valor, you'll earn no one's thanks, no one's gratitude; and in every case destined to be a victim, you'll perish that of prejudice instead of a victim of love. Love? Serve that master, young beauties, whilst you are young serve it fearlessly, this bountiful, this endearing god who created you to worship him; 'tis upon his altars, 'tis in the arms of his faithful you'll earn restitution for the minor annoyances which distinguish the debut of your career. Think only of taking the first step, thereafter the rest is easy, accomplish the gesture and the scales will fall from your eyes: you'll see that 'tis not modesty puts the bright flush into your youthful fair cheeks, but rather indignation at having for one instant allowed yourselves to be bound by the contemptible restrictions atrocious parents or jealous husbands dared impose upon you for even the space of a single afternoon.

"In the present lamentable state of affairs—and this composes the second part of my exposition—this appalling state of discomfort and pressure and stress, for the time being we can do no better than provide some advice to women on how to cope with the situation and how best to behave in its light, and then to consider, through a probing examination, whether indeed any inconvenience results from this alien offspring the husband finds himself constrained to adopt.

"First, let's determine whether it is not an empty myth, this husband's notion that his honor and peace of mind are hinged to the conduct of his wife.

"Honor! *Our honor!* Whose is *my* honor—*mine* or someone else's? And what has someone else to do with it? Would it not appear that the concept of a husband's honor is but another crafty means husbands have devised and employ in order to obtain the more from their wives, in order to bind their wives more firmly to them? Oh, *honor!* Eh, then! 'tis all very permissible and very honorable that iniquitous husbands debauch themselves in every way under the sun and that, behave as they wish, their honor emerges unscathed? That wife the rakehell husband neglects, that passionate wife not one fifth of whose desires he bothers to satisfy, does she dishonor him when she resorts to another man? And there are people—can you believe it?—who answer in the affirmative! But this is positively the same kind of madness, found among various peoples, which consists in the husband tucking into bed when the wife is giving birth. Let's not be fools: our honor is ours, never can it depend upon what someone else does, and it is wild extravagance to imagine the faults others commit can in any wise have an impact upon us.

"If then it is absurd to suppose that unto a man any dishonor can come through his wife's conduct, what other injury can he possibly sustain therefrom? Either one or the other: this man loves his wife or he doesn't love her. In the former instance, as soon as he finds her missing because she has repaired to another, it's that she no longer loves him; well, tell me whether the height of folly isn't to go on loving somebody who has stopped loving you? The man in question ought as of this instant to cease being attached to his wife, and within this supposition inconstancy must be perfectly acceptable. If we are dealing with events arising from the second instance, if, no longer loving his wife, the husband has precipitated her inconstancy, what has he to complain about? He gets what he deserves, what he must necessarily get by behaving in the way he has; he would be committing the greatest injustice were he to whine, pule, snarl at his wife or condemn her; hasn't he ten thousand other objects all around him whereupon he can vent his feelings or wherewith he can soothe them? Let the good fellow leave his wife to amuse herself in peace; has he not made her unhappy enough already? hasn't he forced her to restrain herself while he, cavorting about, performed his little felonies in broad daylight and never heard opinion condemn them? Let him then leave her in peace, that she taste pleasures he can procure her no more, and his complacency may yet someday make a friend of the woman whom a contrary attitude enraged. Gratitude will then do what the heart couldn't achieve; confidence will be reborn, and both, reaching the years of their decline, will together, clasped in friendship's embrace, perhaps make up for what love denied them earlier.

"Unjust husbands, an end then to harrying your wives because they are faithless. Take the trouble, have the manliness to cast critical eyes upon your own selves, and you will always discover that the initial fault was yours, and what will convince the public that this first fault is always on your side is that all the prejudices disfavor infidelity in wives: thus, in order to be libertine, they have countless obstacles to surmount and ruptures to effect, and it is neither natural nor logical that the timid and gentle sex go so far unless impelled by irresistible causes. Is my hypothesis fallacious? Is the wife alone guilty? Well, even so, what good will it do the husband to believe it? What idiot will have his whole tranquillity depend upon what a wife does? Do his wife's idle little carryings-on cause him any physical pain? Alas, no. All the injury he sustains is imaginary; his sufferings, what are they? they are mental. And their cause? Some activities which are admired five hundred leagues from Paris. Why does he suffer then? Because local prejudices train him to. What should he do? Free himself of those prejudices, spit upon them, and at once. Does one worry about wrongs done to one as a husband when as a man one plunges into the thick of fuckery's pleasures? Hardly; why then, that's what he'd better do, plunge, and all his wife's carousings will be speedily forgotten.

"Then it is not the act she's committed, but its material consequences . . . this that's hatched from an egg Monsieur didn't fertilize, this chick Monsieur's got nevertheless to admit into his brood; is this the cause of his sorrow? What childishness! Here we have a brace of alternatives: you continue to cohabit with a wife, unfaithful though she be, so as to have heirs; or you don't live with her anymore. Or again you live with her, as do certain libertine husbands, proceeding in such wise as to be sure that any infants she bears aren't yours. Don't let this latter possibility alarm you, your wife will prove astute enough not to present you with any children, give her a chance, rest assured, she'll know what to do, children you'll have none: no woman who has sufficient intelligence to conduct an intrigue will ever commit that blunder. In the former case, you have only, like your rival, to labor at multiplying the species— and who'll be able to convince you that the eventual results won't have been brought about by you? The chances are as good for as against, and you'll be a very ass if you don't adopt the more comforting conclusion. Either do that, or stop altogether consorting with your wife directly you suspect she has an intrigue afoot— that's the surest and best manner to preserve mastery of the situation—; or if you continue to cultivate the same garden her lover is spading, don't blame him any more than you blame yourself for having sown the seed that ripens into growth.

"There then are the objections put forth and the replies to them: either, Sir, you shall surely have no children; or if you have any, it is an even wager whether they are yours or your competitor's. In support of this latter statement there is a further probability: I refer to the inclination your wife is apt to have to mask her liaison behind a pregnancy, and this, you may be certain, will make her do everything on earth to get herself into your bed, for 'tis obvious she'll never be at ease until she has felt you put balm on what ails her and until this treatment has guaranteed her freedom, from here on, to do as she likes with her lover. Your anxiety is hence utterly baseless, the child is yours, you may set your mind at rest; it is infinitely to your wife's interest that it belong to you, you've toiled at its conception. Well, combine these two reasons and you obtain certainty concerning what you are so eager to know: the child is yours, no doubt of it, and it's yours by the same reckoning which must make that one of two runners who is paid cross the finish line first, defeating his comrade who stands to gain nothing in the same race. But, nevertheless, let's suppose for a moment that the child isn't yours. Well, what do you care? You wanted an heir, did you not? Now you have one. Not Nature but upbringing creates filial sentiments. Be persuaded that this child—whom nothing makes doubt that he is your son, accustomed to seeing you, to pronouncing your name, to loving you for his father—will revere you, cherish you as much and possibly more than if you had a hand in bringing about his existence. Well, what now? Do you still tremble? Your imagination sickens you; however, there's nothing easier to cure than these ills. Give that imagination of yours a good jolt, agitate it with something whose grip, whose sway, is more potent, whose effect upon it is stronger, you'll soon knock it round into the shape and tenor you wish, and you'll have drubbed it into health. No matter what the case or its details may be, my philosophy offers you everything you need. Nothing is so much ours as our offspring— good: you've just been given a boy, there he is, he's yours. Nothing belongs so much to us as what we're given. Exercise your rights, and remember that a few pounds of organized matter, whether it belong to us or be the property of someone else, is of slight worth in the eyes of Nature who at all times bestows upon us the power to disorganize it whenever and however we please.

" 'Tis now for you, charming wives, for you, my dear friends, to set the example. I have put your husbands' minds at rest, I have taught those gentlemen that, irrespective of what you do, they need not lose a wink of sleep on your account; I am ready now to instruct you in that art of adroitly deceiving them, but first I'm going to make you shudder before the dreadful picture of all the penalties reserved for adultery—I show you this picture in order that you see what enormous pleasures this alleged crime must afford if everyone punishes it with such exceptional rigor, and in order also that you be moved to be thankful for having been born under a benign regime where opinion, leaving your conduct to your own conscience, penalizes you, if your conduct is not good, by attempting to make you feel some frivolous sentiment of shame for having dishonored yourselves. . . . And this dishonor . . . come, let's admit it, 'tis, for the majority of us, an added charm.

"A law proclaimed by the Emperor Constantine prescribed for adultery the same punishment meted out for parricide, to wit: the culprit was burned alive, either that or sewn in a sack and cast into the sea; those luckless women found guilty of the crime were deprived even of the right to appeal their case.

"A governor of a province had exiled a woman found guilty of adultery; Majorianus, deeming the punishment too light, expelled the woman from Italy and decreed that whoever were to slay her had the Emperor's permission so to do.

"The ancient Danes punished the adulteress with death, while among them homicide meant the payment of a mere fine; that reveals which of the two offenses they considered the graver.

"The Mongols cleave an adulteress in two with a sword.

"In the Kingdom of Tonkin, she is trampled by an elephant.

"But in Siam, their ways are more lenient: she is otherwise delivered unto the elephant. A specially prepared contraption into which she is placed allows it to enjoy her in the belief it is tuppering a female elephant. Lewdness may well have been behind the invention of this procedure.

"In similar cases, the Bretons of long ago, and perhaps also with lewd motivations, were wont to flog the adulteress to death.

"Luango is an African kingdom, and there they have the custom of hurling her and her lover too from the top of a craggy mountain.

"The Gauls used to smother her in mud and filth, then drag her body around in it awhile.

"In Juida, the husband himself condemned his wife: he had her executed immediately, there before his eyes, if he found her guilty, all of which was a tradition of extreme convenience to husbands who were weary of their wives.

"In other countries, the law empowers the husband to execute his spouse with his own hand if he finds that she has wronged him. This custom was notably that of the Goths.[10]

"Members of the Miami tribe hacked off an adulteress' nose; the Abyssinians drove her from the house clad in rags and tatters.

"The savages of Canada made an incision running round her head, then removed the strip of skin.

"In the Eastern Roman Empire, the adulterous woman was prostituted in the market place.

"At Diyarbekir, the criminal was executed by her assembled family, all of whose members had to deliver at least one thrust of a dagger.

"In several Greek provinces where, in contrast to Sparta, this crime was unauthorized, anyone at all could kill an adulteress with impunity.

"The Guax-Tolliams, as our French explorers call that American tribe, led the adulteress before the feet of their chief, and there she was cut to pieces, and the pieces were eaten by the witnesses.

"The Hottentots, who allow father-murder, matricide, and child-killing, frown upon adultery. They punish it by death; the delation even of a child is accepted as proof of the fact.[11]

"Oh, voluptuous libertine women! if, as I should imagine, these examples serve only to inflame you the more, because the

---

[10] Such is probably the best and wisest of all man-made laws; an unpublic, furtive crime ought to be punished unpublicly, furtively, and vengeance therefor ought to be tasted by him alone and in private whom the deed has outraged.

[11] All these laws owe their origin to nought but pride and lewdness.

hope become a certainty that an act is criminal is always but one further pleasure for minds organized like ours, oh, my friends, hark unto my lessons, heed them, profit therefrom; to your lascivious intelligence I am going to expose the whole theory of adultery.

"Be never so unctious, so complacent with your husband as when you plan to deceive him.

"If he is libertine, accommodate his desires, submit to his caprices, flatter all his whims however fantastical, even of your own accord present him with lust-inspiring objects. According to his bent and tastes, have either pretty girls or pretty boys about, cater to his requirements. Bound by gratitude, he'll never dare reproach you; and what, moreover, can he ever possibly accuse you of, whose other edge you cannot turn against him?

"You need a confidante: acting alone, the risks of disaster are great; so find yourself a woman you can trust, and omit nothing that will identify her interests with yours and your passions. Above all, pay her well.

"For the satisfaction of your wants look rather to hired help than to a lover. The former will serve you well and in secrecy, the latter will fly about town boasting of his conquest and he'll dishonor you without giving pleasure.

"A lackey, a valet, a secretary, no one takes any notice of such creatures; but get yourself a little master and then you're lost, often without having gained much from it.

"Do not breed. Nothing gives less pleasure than childbearing. Pregnancies are damaging to health, spoil the figure, wither the charms, and it's the cloud of uncertitude forever hanging over those events that darkens a husband's mood. There are a thousand means to avoid conception, five hundred more to forestall childbirth; ass-fuckery is by far the best and surest of all; have someone frig your clitoris meanwhile, and this manner of amusing yourself will soon prove incomparably more pleasant than the other: your fuckers' pleasure will probably increase too, your husband will notice nothing, and everyone will be content.

"Perhaps your husband himself will propose sodomy to you. If so, don't be overhasty accepting the invitation: one must always have the look of refusing what one covets. If fear of having children forces you to suggest the thing yourself, advance the excuse that you are afraid of dying in labor; maintain that one of your friends has told you that her husband manages matters with her in that fashion. Once you're broken in to these pleasures, taste no others with your lovers—and now you've dissipated half the suspicions anyone could have, and you're rid of all worry with pregnancies.

"Put spies on the track of your tyrant, have his movements watched; you must never lie in fear of being surprised if you wish to know an authentic joy.

"If, however, you were to be found out, and were so flagrantly caught in the act as to be unable to deny your conduct, put on a show of remorse, redouble the care and attentions your husband wishes lavished upon him. If as a preliminary to your adventures your complacency and thoughtfulness have won you his friendship, he'll soon come back for more; if he persists, be the first to lodge a complaint; make it clear you know his secrets, threaten him with their divulgence; and it is so that you will always have this hold over him that I urge you to study his tastes, to encourage and to serve them from the outset of your marriage. Finally, approaching him from this angle, he's yours, he'll return unfailingly. When he does, make things up with him and hand him whatever he wants, provided he pardons you too: but don't be abused by this reconciliation, multiply your precautions, more shrewdly veil your activities; a prudent wife must always be on guard lest she excessively irritate her husband.

"Enjoy yourself to the limit. The limit? Discovery. If discovered, yield on every score, refuse nothing.

"Keep away from libertine women, insofar as that is possible today. Their company won't procure you many pleasures and may cause you considerable harm; they display themselves more visibly than lovers, for it is known that one must conceal oneself with a man and that is not thought necessary with a woman.

"If you indulge in foursomes, let the other woman be your trusted friend: have a sharp eye out to discern what bonds, what commitments there are she must respect; don't enter the party if she does not have roughly the same duties and obligations as you to observe, for then she'll be less discreet than you, and her imprudences will be your undoing.

"Always find some means for obtaining entire control over others, over, that is, their lives. Should a man betray you, don't hesitate to take the straight way with him. There is no counterpoising that man's life against your tranquillity; whence I conclude that it's a hundred times better to dispatch him than be made a show of or compromised by him. Not that reputation is essential; it serves purely to consolidate one's pleasure opportunities. A woman generally thought to be well-behaved regularly enjoys herself far more and better than one whose overly publicized misconduct has cost her consideration.

"However, respect your husband's life. I recommend that not because there is any individual on earth whose existence must be preserved if it conflicts with our private interest; but because, in the present case, our personal interest consists in safeguarding that husband's days. 'Tis a long and wearisome study for a wife, to come to know her husband; once the job's done, there's no need for her to have to begin anew with another; and it is not sure that the second will be any improvement upon the first. It's not a lover she wants in her husband, it's a complacent, understanding, and understood creature; and success is better assured by long habit than by novelty.

"If the antiphysical pleasure-taking techniques I referred to a short moment ago are not able to arouse you, then cunt-fuck, I really don't mind; but empty the vessel as soon as it has been filled; never let the embryo get a start, that's of great importance if you don't sleep with your husband and hardly any less important if you do, for, as I have told you, incertitude gives rise to every suspicion, and suspicion nearly always brings on scissions and commotion.

"Above all, subdue any respect you have for the civil or religious ceremony that welds you to a man for whom you have no love or whom you love no longer or who does not suffice you. A Mass, a benediction, a contract, this mumbo jumbo—has it the force, the sanctity to make you willing to crawl in irons forever? That word given, that pledge, 'tis nought but a formality which confers upon a man the right to lie with a woman, but which is binding neither upon the one party nor upon the other; and these alliances must appear the less serious to her who, of the twain, is, by this agreement's terms, accorded the fewer means to unbind herself. You who are destined to go forth from here and live in the world," said the Superior, fixing her glance upon me, "you, my dear Juliette, scorn these driveling inanities, flout them contemptuously, they merit nothing else. They are man-made conventions whereunto, irrespective of your wishes, they'd compel you to adhere: a costumed charlatan flutters round a table, waves his arms, mutters a little while peering at a big book, a second knave who gets you to sign your name in another—think ye this be stuff to engage or impress a woman? Use the rights Nature has given you; what sayeth Nature? Drown these despicable customs in thy scorn, go be a whore to thy desires. Your body is the church where Nature asks to be reverenced. Nature sneers at the altar where that sottish priest has just brayed his ritual through; the oaths Nature demands of you aren't those you've just repeated to this abject juggler or those others you've set your name to pursuant to the instructions of his aide, that lububrious man over there. What Nature would that you swear unto is that you surrender yourself to men, for so long and to that extent you have the human strength so to do. The god Nature proffers you isn't that circular chip of dried dough that a harlequin has just launched along the way to your bowels; but 'tis pleasure she gives you for a divinity, pleasure, sweet joy; and 'tis in neglecting your duties toward that god and your own desires that you'll excite the ire of a mother who would be tender to her children.

"Granted a choice of partner, you'll every time select a married person; it being to the advantage of all concerned to keep the thing a secret, you'll have less to fear by way of indiscretion; but preferable even to these individuals are those in your hire. I've already told you so: they're beyond comparison the best, you can change them like linen; variety, multiplicity are the two most powerful vehicles of lust. Fuck with the maximum possible number of men; nothing so much amuses, so much heats the brain as profusion; no one in this crowd will be unable to afford you some new pleasure, be it but the pleasure of one conformation or gesture the more, and, my child, you know nothing at all if all you are acquainted with is one prick. Were you to be served by an army, it could make no difference to your husband: you'll agree that he won't be more dishonored by the thousandth than he was by the first, indeed, he'll be less dishonored, for it does seem that one somehow effaces the other. Furthermore, if he is reasonable, the husband is always much more prone to excuse libertinage than love; the one offends personally, the other assumes the look of a mere flaw in your physical make-up. 'Tis altogether possible he have a flaw in his, it's all one; as for you and your principles, either you're no philosopher, or you must necessarily feel that, once the first step has been taken, one commits no graver sin as one accomplishes the ten thousandth than at the start. Thus, there remains the matter of the world at large. Well, the public belongs entirely to you. Everything depends upon the art of feigning and the other of imposture; if you are skilled in each—and your main task is to become so—you'll do absolutely whatever you wish, and to both the public and your husband. Never cease to bear in mind that it's not an error that ruins a woman, but the uproar occasioned by it, and that ten million crimes that remain unknown are less dangerous than the least slip which glares in the eye of everybody.

"Be modest in your dress: dash and finery do much more to exhibit a woman than can her twenty lovers; a more or less elegant hair style, a more or less costly gown, none of that furthers happiness; but *frequent, extensive,* and *intensive* fucking works wonders therefor. With a prudish or humble air, you'll never be suspected of anything; were someone to dare criticize your character, a thousand champions will spring to break lances in your defense; the public, lacking enough time to pursue its investigations very far, never judges save by appearances: it costs hardly anything at all to wear those it wants to see. Give it satisfaction and when you need it, the public will be on your side.

"If you have sons, then when they are grown remove them from your immediate vicinity: they have only too often appeared in the role of betrayers to their mothers. Should they tempt you, resist the desire; the discrepancy in age is sure to breed a disgust, its victim will be you. There's nothing very piquant to that variety of incest, and it can have a negative influence upon much solider delights; frigging yourself with your daughter, if she

pleases you, presents many fewer risks. Include her in your debauches and she's less apt to discuss them in public.

"And now I think I had better add a word of conclusion to all
this advice: the self-restraint some women exercise means a loss
to society, a curse to society; there ought to be a form of punishment for the absurd, wrongheaded creatures who, for whatever the
motive, fancy that by preserving their loathsome virginity they are
acquitting themselves brilliantly in this world and readying themselves for laurels in the next.

"Youthful, appetizing exemplars of the female sex," Delbène
went on panegyrically, " 'tis to you I've until now addressed myself,
'tis to you I say once again: devil take this uncivilized virtuousness
which fools dare confection into an ornament for you to wear, give
up the outlandish, the barbaric habit of immolating yourselves upon
the altars of this grotesque virtue whose pitifully meager rewards
will never offset the immense sacrifices you shall be called upon to
make in its name. And by what earthly right do men require so much
self-abnegation in you, when they deny themselves so precious
little? Do you not plainly see that it's they who've concocted the
rules and that they were drawn up under the oversight of their
pride, their insolent pride or their intemperance?

"Oh, my companions, I say it unto you: Fuck! you were born
to fuck. To be fucked Nature created you; let bawl the mad, let
blither and snivel the judges, let whine and gripe the hypocrites;
they have their own reasons for condemning those delicious heats,
those joyous frenzies which confer all their charm upon your days.
Unable to wring more from you, envious of all you can give to
others, they heap discredit upon you and censure because they have
nothing further themselves to expect and because they are no more
in a position to ask you for anything; but go consult the children
of love and of pleasure, go put the question to the whole of that
society, and myriad voices will answer you in chorus: you will be
exhorted to *fuck,* because Nature would that you *fuck,* and it is a
crime against Nature not to *fuck.* Do not be intimidated by that
empty epithet *whore,* an idiotic *slut* is she who declines the glory
of that title. A whore is a lovable creature, young, voluptuous, who,
less interested in her reputation than in the welfare of others, on
those grounds alone merits every praise. The whore is the beloved

child of Nature, the abstinent girl is Nature's execration; the whore is deserving of altars, the vestal of the stake. And what more potent insult can a girl fling in Nature's teeth than to waste herself by flagrantly keeping, and in defiance of all the injury that may thereby result to her own self, an illusory virginity whose entire value derives from nothing but the most preposterous, the vilest, the meanest of all irrationalities? Fuck, my friends, fuck, I repeat, with effrontery sneer at the counsel of those who aim to make you captive in the despotic irons of a virtue whence no conceivable good ever has or ever shall come. Forswear them forever, all modesty and reserve; make haste to fuck, be quick, there is only one age for discharging, take advantage of it. For time flies. If you allow the roses to fade, you'll reap a whirlwind of remorse and rue; and the day may come when, belatedly possessed of the desire to have a petal plucked, you'll find no lover who wants it—and then, and then you'll never forgive yourself for having let go by those moments when love would have welcomed your favors. But, do you say, such a girl renders herself infamous, and the weight of this infamy is insupportably onerous? Can such a trifling objection be made in good faith? Let's be frank then: prejudice is the sole author of infamies: how many acts are so qualified by an opinion forged out of nought but prejudice! The vices of theft, of sodomy, of poltroonery, for example—are these not dubbed infamies? and that shan't prevent you from admitting that, viewed through Nature's optic, they are completely legitimate, and whatever is lawful cannot possibly be infamous. For it is impossible that something urged by Nature be anything but lawful. Well, without—for the time being—subjecting these vices to a searching scrutiny, is it not certain that every man has been infused with the idea of acquiring wealth? That being so, the means he employs to become rich are just as natural as they are lawful. Similarly, are not all men given to seeking the greatest amount of delight in their pleasure-taking? Well, if sodomy is the unfailing means to this acknowledged end, sodomy is no infamy. Finally, does not everyone sense a desire to preserve himself, has he not been blessed with that instinct? Unto self-preservation poltroonery is one of the surest means; hence 'tis no infamy, poltroonery, and whatever may be our baseless prejudices concerning any of these three vices, it is clear that not one of them can be regarded as infamous, since all three are natural. It is likewise with libertinage as practiced by individuals of our sex. Since nothing so well serves Nature, this libertinage cannot possibly be infamous.

"But let's for a moment suppose that this infamy authentically exists: what intelligent woman's career is going to be hampered thereby? What the devil does she care if others consider her infamous? If in fact she is not so viewed by rational eyes, and if it is impossible that any infamy exist in the case she is in, she'll laugh at the injustice and at the lunacy of her neighbors, she'll cede as willingly as ever to Nature's proddings, and she'll cede to them more confidently and more easy in her mind than would someone less libertine: for everything thwarts, everything affrights, stays, diverts her who trembles lest she lose her good name; while she who has already bade her reputation farewell, having nothing further to lose, being out of danger and fearlessly surrendering herself to whatever she wishes to do, must necessarily be the happier.

"We may go farther still. The act whereunto this woman gives herself, the habits into which her proclivities lead her, were she truly infamous from the standpoint of the rules and regulations current in the area where she lives, if, I say, this act, whatever it be, is so vital to her felicity that she cannot forego it without becoming unhappy, then would she not be mad to renounce the intention of committing it whatever the risk of covering herself with infamy? For the burden of this imagined infamy will not discomfort her, will never affect her so much as not indulging in her favorite sin; the former suffering will only be intellectual, capable of registering itself only upon certain minds, whereas what she deprives herself of is a pleasure accessible to everybody. Thus, as between two indispensable evils one must necessarily elect the lesser, the woman we are speaking of must unarguably brave the charge of infamy, and continue to live as she did before, in defiance of idle criticism; for, at worst, she'll lose extremely little by incurring this ill fame, while, at best, she'll lose a great deal by foregoing what will earn her a wicked renown. She must therefore accustom herself to opprobrium, learn to outstare it, she must achieve supremacy over this puny antagonist, dominate it, from earliest childhood she must habituate herself to blushing at nothing, to spurning the modesty, to vanquishing the shame which will always wreak havoc with her pleasures and add nothing to her happiness.

"Once having attained this high level of development, she'll make an astonishing but nonetheless eminently true discovery: that the stings and nettles of this infamy she dreaded have metamorphosed into goads to pleasure, and that, far from wishing to avoid these hurts, she'll wound herself most voluntarily, she'll redouble her efforts to seek out ways to feel a delectable pain, and it shan't be long before she carries things to the point of desiring to broadcast evidence of her turpitude. Observe the ravishing libertine! the sublime creature wants to libertinize herself before the whole wide world, shame is nought to her, she flouts horror and scandal, her single complaint is that to her errors there are not witnesses enough. And the remarkable thing is that only now does she truly come to know the pleasure which heretofore was wrapped in the anesthetizing cloud of her prejudices; that she be transported to the ultimate extreme of drunkenness, she had first to destroy every last obstacle preventing these needles from penetrating to the agonizing delight of her heart. But, sometimes you hear it said, but there are awful things, there are things which defy common sense, that conflict with all the seeming laws of Nature, of conscience, of decency, things that seem not only properly to arouse a general horror but such as to be unable to procure one any pleasure. . . . Surely, in the eyes of fools; but there are certain minds, my friends, certain spirits which, having rid these things of what makes them in appearance horrible, and doing so by annihilating the prejudice which caused filth and wrong to adhere to them, behold these same things as nought but the occasion of mighty joy, and these delights are all the keener the greater the gulf between these things and approved behavior, the more radically they countercarry every practice, and the more sternly they are proscribed by vulgar law. Strive to cure such a mind in such a woman: try it, I defy you. By pitching her soul to this tone, the throbbing vibrations that assail her become so voluptuous and so intense that she is blind to all else save the need to march ever onward along the divine path she has chosen. The more appalling the thing to be done, the more it pleases her, and you'll never hear her complain that she lacks the mettle and the will to endure the brand of infamy—the infamy she cherishes and whose terrible heat only further raises the temperature of her pleasures. This explains to you why she-devils of this breed are forever gone in quest of excess and why they are stung by no pleasure save when 'tis spiced with crime; no longer visualizing crime as the vulgar do, in whose sight it is repugnant, with other eyes they behold another vision, and it is one of infinite charm. The habit of stopping at nothing, of overcoming every barrier causes them ever and again to find eminently easy and good what was formerly forbidding and bad; and, progressing from extravagance to extravagance, they attain at length to monstrosities . . . monstrosities whose execution lies a step ahead of them, because these women must perpetrate real crimes to obtain real spasms of joy, and because, unfortunately, there is no such thing as a real crime, do what you will, desire what you please. Thus, always mounting in the track of the speeding star, eternally distanced by desire, 'tis not that these women perform too few horrors, but that there are too few horrors to be performed. Take care not to believe, my friends, that the delicacy of our sex somehow serves as lee shelter to the wind of wickedness: more sensitive than men, we are quicker than they to sense the storm, more eager to heed the high cry of wrong. Thus 'tis unimaginable what we do, after what excesses we lust, men have no idea what a woman is capable of when Nature goes unchecked, when religion's voice is throttled, when the law's sway over her is broken.

"Frequently we hear the passions declaimed against by unthinking orators who forget that these passions supply the spark that sets alight the lantern of philosophy; who forget that 'tis to impassioned men we owe the overthrow of all those religious idiocies wherewith for so long the world was plagued. 'Twas nought but the fires of emotion cindered that odious scare, the Divinity, in whose name so many throats were cut for so many centuries; passion alone dared obliterate those foul altars. Ah, had the passions rendered man no other service, is this one not great enough to make us indulgent toward the passions' mischievous pranks? Oh, my dears, steel yourselves to brave the aspersions they'll always be ready to cast upon you, and so as to know how to scorn infamy as it must be scorned, familiarize yourselves with all that can attract the charge, multiply your little misdeeds; 'tis they that will gradually habituate you to braving come what may ... that will crush remorse in you before the seed of remorse can germinate. As basis and rule to your conduct adopt that which seems in nicest agreement with your penchants; trouble yourselves not to inquire whether or no that concurs with our drab conventions, for you would be most unfair to your own selves were you, by depriving yourselves, to punish yourselves for not having been born in a clime where the thing is applauded. Heed only what most flatters or delights you, 'tis this suits you best, all else not at all. Be imperturbably indifferent to the style in vices and virtues that's the rage today in town; *vice, virtue,* the words have no real signification, they're arbitrary, interchangeable, express only what is locally and temporarily in vogue here and there. Once again, be firm in your conviction that infamy soon transforms itself into voluptuousness. I remember having read somewhere, in Tacitus, I believe, that infamy is the highest and last of pleasures for those who are jaded by the excessive use they have made of all others; a most dangerous pleasure, I believe, since one must find a means, a puissant means, for reaping enjoyment from this species of self-abandon, from this sort of degradation of sentiment whence every other vice is born; since it withers the soul, or rather robs it of every atmosphere save the pale of utter corruption, and that without leaving the tiniest outlet to remorse. Indeed, it absolutely extinguishes remorse; better, it works a thoroughgoing change in remorse: for now we have a person who has lost all esteem save for what gives rise to remorse, and who much amuses himself with reviving this feeling in order to relish the pleasure of quashing it, and who, step by step, accedes to the most unheard-of excesses; and the ease with which he arrives at these excesses is only increased by the number of transgressions he must commit and the quantity of virtues he must contemn preparatorily; and so many obstacles overleapt are so many voluptuous episodes, often more stimulating to a perfidious imagination than is the very atrocity he designs. What is most wonderful about it all is that he believes himself happy—and is. If, reversibly, the virtuous individual is happy too, happiness necessarily ceases to be a situation every person can achieve by behaving well; happiness is thus proven to depend uniquely upon our individual organization, and may be as readily encountered in the triumph of virtue as in the abyss of vice. . . . But what is this I say? in the triumph of virtue. . . . Ah, has virtue this maddening sting? What chill, toughened soul could ever be cheered by virtue's meager rewards? No, my friends, no, virtue shall never make for our happiness. He lies who pretends to have found happiness there; he seeks to have us call happiness what are rather pride's illusions. For my part, this do I declare to you: that with all my soul I detest, I hate virtue, I despise it today as in the past I did cherish it, and to the joys I taste in outraging virtue constantly I'd like to add the supreme delight of assassinating it in every heart where it has an abode. How often, freighted with images, my accursed brain waxes hot, so hot that I want nothing but to be drowned in the infamy I've just portrayed for you! Yes, I'd have it known, inscribed, permanently decided that I'm a whore; I'd like to forswear, rend this veil, break these disgraceful oaths which prevent me from prostituting myself publicly, from soiling myself like the lowest of the low. I confess to you that I'm capable of envying the fate of those heavenly creatures who ornament street corners and slake the filthy lust of whoever strolls by; they squat in vile degradation, in ordures and horror do they wallow; dishonor is their lot, they are insensible to it, to everything . . . what fortune! and why should we not labor thus to become, all of us? In the whole world is not the happiest being he in whom there beats a heart rock-hardened by passions . . . who has by passion been brought to where he is immune to all save pleasure? And what need has he to be susceptible of any other sensation? Ah, my friends, were we advanced to that degree of turpitude, we'd no longer have the look of vileness, and we'd make gods of our errors rather than denigrate ourselves! 'Tis thus Nature points out to us all the gate to happiness: let us go that way.

"Eh? Godsfuck! see, they're stiff erect," cried the tempestuous Delbène, "they're aloft, resurrected, these divine pricks I've been palpating while addressing you. Behold, they're hard as steel, and my ass covets them. Come, good friends, come fuck my ass, this insatiable thirsty ass of mine; into the utmost depths of this libertine ass spill fresh jets of sperm which, if such a thing be possible, will cool the burning ardor consuming my entrails. Hither,

Juliette, I want to cunt-suck you while our wights embugger me; squatting over your visage, Volmar will present her charms to you, you'll lech them, you'll sup on them while with your right hand you pollute Flavie and with your left you give Laurette's buttocks a smart spanking."

The play is staged, Delbène's two lovers sodomize her in turn. Awash with Volmar's fuck, mine runs very abundantly into the Superior's mouth, and at last the time comes to turn our attentions to deflowering Laurette.

Appointed to the high priestess' role, I am fitted out with an artificial member. It is a great-sized thing: the cruel Abbess has ordered me to don the massiest in the arsenal; and here is a description of the at once lubricious and ungentle scene that followed:

Laurette occupies the center of the stage. Motionless, she reposes upon a tall stool: beneath her buttocks is a hard cushion, her position is horizontal, only her behind is supported. Her widely spread legs are so maintained by cords fastened to rings sunk in the floor; her arms, flung over her head and outward, are similarly fixed. This attitude places the strait and delicate part of the victim's body in the most admirable situation to be penetrated by the glaive. Seated before her is Télème, who is to hold up her pretty head . . . and to exhort her to patience; and this idea of putting her into the confessor's keeping, quite as if she were about to be decapitated, infinitely amuses the cruel Delbène, whose passions, I see, are as ferocious as her tastes appear to be libertine. While I depucelate the cunt of this Agnes, Ducroz is to embugger me. There is an altar in the room; it stands next to and dominates that other altar upon which the little lass is going to be immolated, and it will serve as a couch to our voluptuous Abbess. 'Tis as she reclines there between Volmar and Flavie that the rascal is going lewdly to savor both the thought of the crime she is having committed and the delicious spectacle of its consummation.

Before stoppling my ass, Ducroz busies himself readying the terrain for the aggression I am about to commit; he moistens the borders of Laurette's vagina and anoints my weapon with an oily preparation which enables it to coast in almost at once. However, it provokes some truly awesome stretching and tearing: Laurette's not yet ten years old and my lance must be eight inches in its circumference and a dozen long. The encouragement profferred to me, the irritated state I am in, the great desire I have to carry out this libertine act, everything combines to make me put as much zeal into this operation as might the most energetic lover. The engine penetrates, but the torrents of blood that leap from the bursting hymen, the victim's lusty screams, all these are indicative that the enterprise is not unaccompanied by its perils; the poor little thing's hurt, far from being negligible, consists in a wound of such gravity as to make one feel some concern for her life. Ducroz, aware of the possibilities, glances toward the Abbess; she, being voluptuously frigged by her confederates, nods, and that is the signal to continue.

"The bitch is ours!" she cries; "don't let's spare her. I am not answerable to her, no, nor to anyone, I do as I please!"

You will readily conceive how these utterances emboldened me. Be sure of it, the woe occasioned by my clumsiness and by that unwieldy machine only made me ply it in a livelier style: now the whole affair is engulfed, Laurette swoons, Ducroz buggers me, and Télème, enchanted, frigs his device upon the fair visage of the stricken child whose head he grips between his thighs. . . .

"Madame," says he to Delbène, the while rubbing his prick, "a certain individual here has need of succor—"

" 'Tis of fuck she's in need," the Abbess retorts, "yes, fuck's all the treatment I'll have given the bitch."

I continue to grind away, electrified by Ducroz' prick, it is only a quarter of an inch from being entirely engaged in my asshole; I deal as severely with my victim as I am being dealt with myself. Ecstasy overtakes all of us at virtually the same instant. The three tribades sprawled on the altar discharge like a battery of mortars while along the length of the dildo I've buried in Laurette my own sperm trickles, while Ducroz fills my anus with his, and while Télème mixes his own with the victim's tears, for he has just ejaculated all over her face.

Our weariness, the necessity of reviving Laurette if we want to extract further pleasure from utilizing her, all this obliges us to bestow a little attention upon her. She is unbound; surrounded, slapped, pummeled, pinched, fiddled over, Laurette soon shows a few signs of life.

"Well, what's the matter with you?" Delbène uncharitably

inquires; "are you then such a feeble thing that so mild an attack sends you nigh to the doors of hell?"

"Alas, Madame, I can bear no more," protests the poor bedraggled little girl whose blood is still flowing copiously; "I've been sore hurt, I'm going to die—"

"Not so fast," the Superior said laconically, "patients a good deal younger than you have successfully weathered these same assaults, we'll carry on."

And without other precautions being taken than to stanch her blood, Laurette is tied anew, and this time she lies upon her belly instead of on her back; her asshole comfortably within range, Delbène and her two aides installed upon the altar again, I ready myself to attack by another breach.

Nothing can equal the luxurious manner in which Delbène was having herself masturbated by Volmar and Flavie. The latter, stretched out upon Madame Delbène, was giving her cunt to be sucked while frigging her mistress' clitoris and tickling her nipples; Volmar, a little farther down, was manipulating the lusty Abbess' asshole, into which she'd dug three of her fingers; every part of that slut's body was being submitted to pleasure, and throughout it all her gaze was fixed upon what I was about. She exhorted me to get on with the affair. So I presented myself. This time 'tis Télème who's to embugger me while I am sodomizing Laurette; and Ducroz is to prepare this introduction and to frig my clitoris at the same time. The difficulties are formidable, they look insurmountable; already two or three times repulsed, my instrument either strikes awry or slips astray, despite my guidance, niching itself in Laurette's cunt again, and this accident is not unattended by further distress to the unlucky victim of our libertinage. Delbène, losing patience at these delays, bids Ducroz blaze the trail by himself embuggering the lass, and, you understand, this commission is not displeasing to him. Less awesomely proportioned that the bowsprit I'm wearing, steadier with a tool that's more securely attached to him than mine is to me, the libertine has lodged himself the next instant deep in the maid's ass; he harpoons a virginal turd, fetches it out, is about to enter again and spray fuck about the cavity when the Abbess orders him aside and summons me to resume operations.

"Sweet Jesus!" says the Abbot, drawing out his prick all glistening with lust and all sullied with dark proof of his victory, "ah, doublefucked Jesus, very well. As you say; but I'm bent on revenge. Give me Juliette's ass instead."

"No," says Delbène who, in spite of the pleasures wherewith she is besotting herself, is nonetheless paying keen attention to ours, "no, my Juliette's ass belongs to Télème, he's the one who's to enjoy it this time and I'll brook no infringement upon his rights. But, you great scoundrel, since you're so bloody fucking stiff, go bury your stave in Volmar's hungry bum. Eh, do you see the thing? Embugger this superb wench here, I tell you, stuff her ass and she'll frig me the merrier."

"Godsfuck, yes!" Volmar exclaims, "come here, mark this asshole, get inside, bugger, be quick about it, I've never had greater need of a sodomizing."

The persons of the drama take their places, the curtain rises upon a new act. The breach already blasted in Laurette allows my instrument relatively easy access, a minute later and the poor little dear feels it lodged deep in her anus. Therewith she redoubles her weeping and wailing, her screams are dreadful; but Télème, having gained a solid foothold in my ass, and Delbène, swimming in fuck, both give me such lusty encouragement that Laurette soon experiences hindwise what not long before I made her feel frontwardly: blood streams, and a second time the child faints away. 'Tis at this point Delbène's ferocious character becomes very manifest.

"Don't slacken—go on! go on!" cries she, upon seeing me about to retire; "have we discharged yet? We have not! Keep at it till then, hear?"

"But she's dying," say I.

"Dying? Dying? Nonsense, pure histrionics, all a comedy. And if 'tis so? Eh then? One whore more or less—do you think it matters to me? The bitch is here to entertain us and, by fuck! entertain us she shall!"

My resolve fortified by this Megaera, and not being anyhow much inclined to weak-spirited sentiments of commiseration wherewith Nature did not overly well provide me, I set to work again and keep at it until the signal for a legitimate retreat is given by the unequivocal evidence of a general pandemonium whose din I soon hear coming from all sides; I've already had my third emission by the time I quit my post.

"Let's have a look at all this," says the Abbess, stepping up to Laurette. "Is the life gone out of her?"

"Oh, la! She's no worse off than when the fun began," Ducroz says chidingly, "and if you doubt it, a stout re-encunting from me will bring her around in a trice."

"Better yet, we'll administer the treatment jointly," Télème proposes. "While I embugger her, Delbène will frig my asshole and I'll mouth Volmar's; Juliette can likewise socratize Ducroz and he'll put a diligent tongue to Flavie's cunt."

Approved, the project is put into execution; and the rapid movements of our two fuckers, their impetuous lust, quickly bring the sorely beset Laurette back to her senses.

"My best beloved," I then inquire of the Abbess, whom I draw aside, "however shall you repair all the damage that's just been done?"

"That which you've sustained shall be very soon, my angel," Delbène answered, "tomorrow, I'll massage you with an ointment that so wonderfully restores their whole order to things that afterward no one would ever guess they'd been exposed to rude usage. As for Laurette—have you forgotten that 'tis generally believed she fled the convent? She's ours, Juliette. She'll not re-appear in the world."

"What are you going to do with her?" I wondered, much mystified.

"Make her the victim of our lewdness. Dear Juliette! you are yet so very much a novice. Do you still not understand that the only serious ones are the criminal excesses? and that the more horror one enwraps pleasure in, the more charming pleasure becomes?"

"Truthfully, my dear, I can make nothing of what you say—"

"Have patience then. You shan't have long to wait ere all comes clear. But now, let's have some supper."

The company removes to a little room adjacent to the salon where the orgies have been celebrated. Here, spread upon tables, is a profusion of dainties, the rarest delicacies in meat, wine of the very best. We take our places . . . Laurette serves us! I soon remarked, from the manner the group adopted with her, by the harsh tone in which she was addressed, that the poor little wretch was considered nothing more than a victim whose doom was already sealed. The merrier spirits grew, the worse she was treated; there was nothing our youthful waitress did that wasn't rewarded by a pinch or a tweak, a slap or a blow; and if she was remiss, however slightly inattentive to instructions, she was often more severely punished yet. I'll not linger, kind reader, over the doings and utterances which distinguished that lavish bacchanal; be content to know that, for horror, for foulness, they equaled the worst I've since seen by way of the utmost in libertinage.

Down there, the air was very warm, we women were nude; the men were in the same disorder and, mixed in amidst us, were with complete unrestraint giving themselves over to whatever of the filthiest and most crapulous their delirium could egg them into undertaking. Wrangling over my ass, Télème and Ducroz looked about to come to blows in their efforts to obtain its use; supine beneath the pair of them, I was quietly awaiting the contest's outcome when Volmar, drunk already and in her drunkenness more lovely than Venus, seized the two pricks and started to frig them into a bowl of punch, all this, she explained, because she wanted fuck to drink.

"Let's have an end to this," said the Abbess, almost as light-headed as the others about her, for wine had been flowing very freely, "I'm against it unless Juliette agrees to piss into the mixture—"

I piss; the tureen goes from hand to hand, the whores all drink their fill, the men do the same and, the riot being at its apogee, the extravagant Abbess, at a loss what to invent next to reawaken desires her libertinage has foundered in exhaustion, announces that she wants to go to the vault where the mortal remains of the women of the house repose, that she wants to find the coffin of one of those her jealous rage brought lately to destruction, that she wants to have herself given five or six thumping fuckings upon her victim's corpse. The idea stirs the company; we get to our feet, we locate the spot, candles are set upon the coffins ranged round that of the young novice whom three months previously Delbène had poisoned, after having idolized her. The infernal creature lies down upon that sepulcher and, baring her cunt to the two ecclesiastics, she challenges first the one, then the other. Ducroz is the first to ensocket his spar. We were all spectators and our sole employment, throughout this gruesome scene, was to kiss and fondle her, finger her clitoris and submit ourselves to be handled by her. Delirious, Delbène was battening avidly upon these horrors when a dreadful shrill screech was heard, all the candles snuffing out that very instant.

"My God, what is this!" cried the intrepid Abbess, alone among us all to preserve her courage in the midst of tumult and affright. "Juliette! Flavie! Volmar!"

But we're all deaf, struck dumb, no one gives her answer; and were it not for the details our Superior supplied us on the morrow, I, who half-swooned away when it happened, would probably still know nothing of what brought this fracas about. A wood owl hidden in those underground places was the cause of it all; startled by the light to which its eyes were unaccustomed, it had taken flight and its beating wings created a draft that had blown the candles out. When I recovered my wits I found myself in my bed and Delbène, who came to visit me as soon as she learned I was better, told me that after she'd calmed the two men, who'd been nearly as terrified as we, it was with their aid she had transported us to our cells.

"In supernatural occurrences I have no belief at all," Delbène asserted. "Never is there an effect without its cause and my first concern, whenever surprised by some effect, is to trace out its cause without delay. I promptly located that of our adventure the other night; the candles lit once again, we, the men and I, just as promptly restored everything to order."

"And Laurette, Madame?"

"Laurette? She's in the cellars, my sweet. We left her there—"

"What! Then you—"

"Not yet. It will be our first piece of business the next time we assemble. She underwent yesterday's experience more successfully than one might have thought."

"Oh, indeed, Delbène, you're a very debauched thing . . . a cruel thing—"

"Now, now, not at all. It's simply that I've got very exigent passions, and that I heed nothing else. And, persuaded as I am that they are the most faithful interpreters of Nature's will, I heed whatever counsel they give me, and do so with as little fear as remorse or regret. But you look to be whole again, Juliette; get up, my darling, come dine with me in my apartment, we'll chat together."

Later, when we had finished our meal, Delbène asked me to settle myself in a chair beside her. "You are surprised to find me so calm in the midst of crime? Let me then say a few words apropos. I fain would have you become as apathetic as I—and I think you soon shall. I noticed yesterday that you were struck, even startled, by my equanimity in the thick of the horrors we were committing and I seem to remember that you accused me of lacking pity for that poor Laurette our debauchery sacrificed.

"Oh, Juliette, banish all doubt thereof: Nature has arranged everything, informed everything, hers is the responsibility for all you see and all there is. Has she given equal strength, equal beauty, equal grace to all the creatures wrought by her hand? Of course not. Since she desires that each particular thing or constitution have its particular contour or hue, so also she wills that fates and fortunes be not alike. The luckless ones chance puts in our clutches, or who excite our passions, have their place in Nature's scheme as do the stars in the firmament and the sun that gives us light; and 'tis as certain an evil one commits in meddling with this wise economy as 'twould be were one to confound cosmic operations, were that crime within the scope of our possibilities. . . ."

"But," I interrupted, "were you in distress, Delbène, would you not yearn for succor and kindness?"

"I? I'd know how to suffer uncomplainingly," the stoical thinker gave me answer, "and I'd implore the aid of no one.

"If indeed I am Nature's favorite, if I have no misery to dread, have I still not fever and pestilence and war and famine and the disruptions of an unforeseen revolution and all the other plagues that blight mankind and mankind's ease, do not these threaten me too? Well, let them all occur, come what may, I'll bear it dauntlessly. Believe me, Juliette, oh yes, be firmly persuaded that when I consent to let others suffer and when I refrain from interfering with their sufferings, it is because I myself have learned to suffer, to endure suffering, and alone. Resistance is foolhardy and fruitless; so let's abandon ourselves to Nature's keeping, that is to say, to our fate; it's not to a career of mercifulness Nature appoints us; her voice cries to us only this, that it is for us to develop the strength necessary to withstand the trials she holds in store for us. And commiseration, far from steeling our soul for what is to come, shakes it, unreadies it, softens it, definitively robs it of the courage that is no longer there when, later, it needs courage to cope with its own afflictions. He who learns how to be insensible to the ills that besiege others soon becomes impassive in the face of his own woes, and it is far more necessary to know oneself how to suffer than to accustom oneself to shedding tears in others' behalf. Oh, Juliette, the less one is sensitive, the less one is affected, and the nearer one draws to veritable autonomy; we are never prey save to two things: the evil which befalls others, or that which befalls us: toughen ourselves in the face of the first, and the second will touch us no more, and from then on nothing will have the power to disturb our peace."

"Yet," I pointed out, "the inevitable consequence of this apathy will be crimes."

"And so? 'tis neither to crime nor to its virtuous contrary we ought to become especially attached, but rather to whatever renders us happy; and were I to discover that my only possibility of happiness lay in excessive perpetration of the most atrocious crimes, without a qualm I'd enact every last one of them this very instant, certain, as I have already told you, that the foremost of the laws Nature decrees to me is *to enjoy myself, no matter at whose expense*. If Nature has constituted my intimate structure in such a way that it is only from the infelicity of my fellows that voluptuous sensations can flower in me, then 'tis so because Nature would have me participate in the destruction she desires—and she desires destruction, an end quite as essential to her as any other aim; if she made me wicked, 'twas because she has pressing need of wickedness and of beings like me to serve her policy."

"Arguments of that kind can lead far. . . ."

"And one should keep in step with them," Delbène rejoined. "Take them as far as you like and I defy you to show me the point at which they become dangerous; one has enjoyed oneself the whole way along the journey, and that's all, one cannot ask for more."

"May one take enjoyment at the expense of others?"

"The thing that interests me least in this world is what happens to others; I haven't the slightest germ of belief in that *bond of fraternity* I hear fools prate about unendingly, and it's not without having closely analyzed these *ties of brotherhood* that I reject the lot of them."

"What! do you doubt this, the most primary of Nature's laws?"

"Listen to me, Juliette . . . oh, truly, 'tis astounding the need this girl has of instruction . . . of guidance. . . ."

We were at this stage in our conversation when a lackey, sent by my mother, arrived to inform Madame the Abbess of the dreadful state of affairs at our home and the grave illness of my father; my sister and I were requested to return at once.

"Great heavens!" exclaimed Madame Delbène. "But I've entirely forgotten your maidenhead, which needs repair. One instant, my angel, here, this jar contains an extract of myrtle, rub yourself with it in the morning and before retiring at night, nine days of that ought to suffice. On the tenth you'll find yourself as much a virgin as you were emerging from the womb of your mother."

Then, sending someone in search of Justine, she entrusted us both to the servant who'd come to fetch us away, and she besought us to return as soon as we could. We embraced her, and left.

My father died. You know what disasters ensued upon his passing: my mother's death a month later, and the destitution and abandonment we found ourselves in. Justine, who knew nothing of my secret liaisons with the Abbess, knew nothing either of the visit I paid her several days after our ruin, and as the behavior and sentiments she then exhibited reveal what remained to be discovered of this original woman's character, it were well, my friends, that I recount that interview. Delbène was short with me that day. She began by refusing to open the gate to me, and only consented to talk for a moment through the grillwork dividing us.

When, surprised by this chilly reception, I reminded her of our at least carnal attachments, she said:

"My child, all that grubby nonsense is over and done with when two persons cease to dwell together; so my advice to you is to forget it. For my part, I must assure you that I cannot recall a single one of the facts and circumstances you allude to. As for the indigence threatening you, recollect the fate of Euphrosine: she didn't even wait to be beckoned by necessity, but of her free will leaped into a career of libertinage. Since now you have no choice, imitate her. There's nothing else for you to do. I therefore confine my suggestions to that one; but once you've made the choice, refrain from calling upon me: the role may, after all, not suit you, may not bring you success, you might need money, credit, and I shall not be able to supply you the one or the other."

So saying, Delbène turned on her heel and walked away, leaving me in a state of bewilderment . . . a state which, of course, would have been less distressing had I been more philosophical; my meditations were cruel. . . .

I left immediately, firmly resolved to follow the wicked creature's advice, perilous though it was. Luckily, I remembered the name and address of the woman Euphrosine had mentioned to us long ago, at a time when, alas! I never dreamed I would some-day have to avail myself of her: an hour later I stood at her door.

Madame Duvergier gave me a heart-warming welcome. Her connoisseur's eye deceived by the wonder Delbène's most excellent remedy had wrought, Duvergier came to a conclusion that was to allow her to deceive many another. 'Twas two or three days before assuming a post in this house that I took leave of my sister in order to pursue a calling very different from the one she elected.

After the reverses I had sustained, my existence depended solely upon my new hostess, I confided myself entirely into her hands and accepted the conditions she imposed; but no sooner was I alone and given opportunity to ponder events than I began to dwell anew upon Madame Delbène's desertion of me and upon her ingratitude. Alas! said I to myself, why did her heart harden before my misfortune? Juliette poor, Juliette rich—are these two different creatures? What then is this curious capriciousness that leads one to love opulence and fly from misery? Ah, I was still to comprehend that poverty must necessarily be distasteful, abhorrent to wealth, at the time I was still unaware of how much prosperity dreads misery, of how it loathes misery, I was still to learn that from this fear of relieving suffering results prosperity's hatred for it. But, I went on to wonder, but how can it be that this libertine woman—this criminal, how is it that she does not fear the indiscretion of those whom she treats so cavalierly?—further childishness on my part; I as yet knew nothing of the insolence and the effrontery that characterize vice when seated upon foundations of wealth and reputation. Madame Delbène was the Mother Superior of one of the most renowned convents in the Ile de France, her annuities came to sixty thousand pounds, she had the most powerful friends at the Court, no one in the City was more admired: how she must have detested a poor girl like me who, orphaned and without a penny to her name, to oppose her injustices could only submit appeals which would soon be dismissed with a laugh if ever they were heard or which, more probably, would be immediately branded as calumnies and could well earn the plaintiff impudent enough to demand her rights the indefinite loss of her liberty.

Astonishingly corrupted already, this striking example of injustice, even though 'twas I who had to suffer from it, pleased rather than redirected me into better ways. So then! said I to myself, I have but to strive after wealth too; rich, I'll soon be as impudent as that woman, I'll enjoy the same rights and the same pleasures. Let's beware of virtuousness, 'tis sure disaster; for vice is victorious always and everywhere; poverty's to be avoided at all costs, since it's the object of a universal scorn. . . . But, having nothing, how am I to elude misfortune? By criminal deeds, obviously. Crime? What's that to me? Madame Delbène's teachings have already rotted my heart and infected my brain; I see evil in no action, I am convinced that crime as nicely serves Nature's ends as can goodness and decency; so let's be off into this perverse world where success is the one mark of triumph; let no obstacle check us, no scruple hinder us, for misery is his who tarries by the wayside. Since society is composed exclusively of dupes and scoundrels, let's decidedly play the latter: it's thirty times more flattering to one's *amour-propre* to gull others than to be made a gull oneself.

Fortified by these reflections—which may perhaps strike you as somewhat precocious at the age of fifteen, but which, granted the education I had had, will surely not seem unlikely to you—I set myself to waiting resignedly for whatever Providence might bring me, fully determined to exploit every opportunity to better my fortune at no matter what price to myself or to others.

To be sure, I had a rigorous apprenticeship to undergo; these often painful first steps were to complete the corruption of my morals and rather than alarm yours, my friends, it would perhaps be better were I to withhold details which, if laid out realistically, would only dazzle your eyes, for my performances were in all probability rather more wonderfully wicked than those you yourselves accomplish every day—

"Madame, I protest, that I am not entirely able to believe," the Marquis broke in. "Knowing of us what you do, I declare, Madame, I declare that I am dumbfounded that you allow yourself for one single instant to harbor such a fear. Our performances, our behavior—"

"Forgive me," said Madame la Comtesse de Lorsange, "but it is here a question of corruption manifest in both sexes—"

"Madame, Madame, say on—"

"—for Duvergier catered indiscriminately to the fancies of men and of women—"

"Indeed," said the Marquis, "you cannot have intended to deprive us of descriptions which for being heteroclite and composite would only entertain us the more? We are acquainted with virtually all the extravagances whereof individuals of our sex are capable, and you can but delight us by instructing us in all those which individuals of yours are prone to essay."

"So be it," rejoined Madame la Comtesse. "I'll nevertheless be careful to detail only the most unusual debauches and, to avoid monotony, I'll omit any that strike me as too simple, too banal."

"Marvelous," said the Marquis, showing the company an already lust-swollen engine; "but are you bearing in mind the effect these narrations may produce in us? Behold the condition brought about by the mere promise of what is to come."

"Well, my friend," the charming Comtesse said, "am I not completely at your disposition? I'll reap a twofold pleasure from my pains; and as self-esteem is always of much account with women, you'll permit me to suppose that, regarding the general rise in temperature about to take place, while my speeches may be one cause therefor, my person shall also share in the responsibility?"

"But you are quite right, I must convince you this very instant," the Marquis said. Very moved indeed, he drew Juliette into an adjoining chamber; there they remained long enough to taste gluttonously all the sweetest joys of unbridled lewdness.

"For my part," said the Chevalier, whom the departure of the others had left encloseted with Justine, "I must confess I'm not yet stiff enough to have to lighten ballast, not yet. Never mind, come hither, my child, kneel down, there's a good little girl, and suck me; but pray so do as to show me a lot more of your ass than of your cunt. 'Tis good, 'tis very good," he said, seeing Justine, more than adequately trained in these turpitudes, grasp, most skillfully, howbeit with regret, the spirit of this one, "oh, yes, yes, she does it suitably enough."

And the Chevalier, singularly well sucked, all sighs and gladness, was perhaps about to abandon himself to the gentle, honey-sweet sensations of a thus provoked discharge when the Marquis, returning with Juliette, besought her to take up the thread of her story again, and his confrere, if he could, to postpone until some later moment the crisis toward which the drama appeared to be hastening.

Quiet being restored and attentions fixed again upon Madame de Lorsange, she resumed her tale, and spoke as follows:

Madame Duvergier had but six women aboard; but these were seconded by reinforcements numbering three hundred, all at her beck and call; two strapping lackeys five feet and eight inches tall, membered each like Hercules, and two little grooms of fourteen and fifteen, heavenly to see, were likewise furnished to libertines who wanted a mixture of sexes or who preferred antiphysical antics to the enjoyment of women; and in cases where those limited masculine effectives would not have sufficed, Duvergier could increase them by drawing upon a reserve corps of over eighty individuals who were domiciled outside the house, all of them ready, at any hour, to present themselves anywhere their services were required.

Madame Duvergier's house was cunning, it was delightful. Situated between courtyard and garden, and having two exits, one on either side, rendezvous took place there under conditions of secrecy which no other arrangements could have afforded; within, the furnishings were magnificent, the boudoirs voluptuous, lavishly decorated; the cook in the establishment was a master in his art, the wines were of quality, and the girls were charming. The use of these outstanding facilities was not to be had for nothing. And, indeed, nothing in Paris cost anything like what one paid for an evening's rout in these divine surroundings; Duvergier never asked less than ten *louis* for the simplest kind of tête-à-tête. Without morals and without religion, enjoying the wholehearted and unfailing support of the police, panderess to the greatest lords of the realm, Madame Duvergier, having nothing and no one under the sun to fear, created new fashions, made new discoveries, specialized in things which none of her calling had ever attempted anywhere, things which would make tremble both Nature and mankind.

For six weeks in a row, that adroit rascal sold my maidenhead to above fifty buyers and, every evening, employing a pomade in many respects similar to Madame Delbène's, she scrupulously effaced the ravages wrought pitilessly all day long by the intemperance of those to whom her greed delivered me up. As those devirginizers without exception had a heavy hand and usually a beef's wit to match a beef's pizzle, I'll spare you a good many tedious particulars, pausing only to give you an account of the Duc de Stern, whose manic eccentricity I consider downright unusual.

The simplest apparel conformed best with the requirements of this libertine's lubricity; I went to him got up as a little street girl. After traversing numerous sumptuous apartments I reached a mirrored room where the Duc was waiting for me, his manservant at his side, a tall young man of eighteen he was, handsome as they come and with the most interesting face. Thoroughly coached in the role I was expected to play, I was taken aback by none of the questions the lewd dog posed me. I stood before him;

he was seated on a sofa and was frigging his valet's prick. The Duc spoke to me in this wise:

"Is it true," he demanded, "that you are in the most direly necessitous circumstances, and that in coming here your sole purpose and one hope is to earn means indispensable simply to keep body and soul together?"

"Aye, Sire, and the truth is that for three days neither I nor my mother has tasted bread."

"Ho! Excellent then!" said the Duc, taking his man's hand to be himself frigged. "The thing is of importance, I'm hugely pleased that matters stand thus with you. And 'tis your mother who sells you?"

"Yes, alas!"

"Splendid! Eh . . . and have you any sisters?"

"One, my Lord."

"And how is it she's not been sent to me?"

"Sire, she has left home, misery made her flee. We don't know what has become of her."

"Eh, fuck my eyes! It's got to be found, that! Where do you suppose she could be? What's her age?"

"Thirteen."

"Thirteen! Appalling, appalling—knowing my tastes as by God they must by now, why do they keep this creature back from me?"

"But no one knows where she is, Sire."

"Thirteen! Appalling. Well, I'll locate her, I'll find her somehow. Lubin, hey there, off with her clothes, let's to the verification."

And while this order is being carried out, the Duc, continuing the work begun by his Ganymede, sets complacently to rattling at a dark, flabby little device, so small it's barely to be seen. As soon as I am naked, Lubin examines me with extremest diligence and then declares to his master that everything is in the very best condition.

"Show me the other side," the Duc says.

And Lubin, bending me down over a couch, spreads my thighs and, whether or not convinced himself of the inexecution of any previous assault, is, in view of the admirable repair it is in, able to assure the Duc that no evidence warrants belief that anything grave has befallen me in this sector hitherto.

"And in the other?" murmurs Stern, drawing my buttocks apart and testing my asshole with a finger.

"No, my Lord, surely not."

" 'Tis well," says the lecherous nobleman, taking me in his arms and sitting me upon one of his thighs; "but you see, my child, don't you, that I'm incapable of doing the job myself? Touch that prick . . . soft, eh? as limp as a rag, no? If you were Venus herself you'd not manage to get it any harder. And now kindly consider this awful article of weaponry," he went on, having me take hold of his manservant's resplendent prick. "This matchless member here will depucelate you much better than mine ever could. You do agree, do you not? Then take your stance, I'll be your pimp. Unable to do anyone any harm myself, I adore having others do it in my stead. The idea comforts me—"

"Oh, Sire!" said I, terrified by the inordinate proportions of the prick flourished at me. "Oh, Sire, this monster will make a shambles of me, I'll not be able to endure its attacks!"

I sought to break away, to dodge, to protect myself; but the Duc de Stern would have none of it.

"Come, come, no shilly-shallying there, what I like is compliance in little girls, they who lack it in their conduct with me don't remain long in my good graces. . . . Come nearer. . . . Before anything else I'd like to have you kiss my Lubin's ass."

And presenting it to me:

"A handsome ass, no? Kiss it, then."

I obey.

"And a kiss for that goad he's got upstanding on this other side? Kiss his prick."

Again I obey.

"Now, make ready . . . lie thus. . . ."

He holds me, his valet moves up and into the operation puts such address and vigor that, with three mighty heaves, he sinks his massive engine to the bottom of my womb. A terrible scream bursts from my throat; the Duc, who has me pinioned and who is frigging my asshole throughout it all, is feeding avidly upon my sighs and tears; the muscular Lubin, master of me, no longer requires his own master's assistance, so that now the Duc is able to go round behind my lover and to embugger him while he depucelates me. Those blows his patron is delivering to his posterior soon, I notice, contribute to augmenting the force of the blows the valet is delivering to me; I was about to collapse beneath the sheer weight of their coordinated attacks when Lubin's discharge saved the day for me.

"Godsfuck!" cried the Duc who, himself, was not yet done, "you're driving too fast today, Lubin, what ails you? Why must fucking a cunt make you lose your head every time?"

And this event having disordered the plan of the Duc's attacks, he fetched out that mischievous little prick which, furious at having been displaced, seemed only to be looking for an altar whereupon to vent its sordid rage.

"Hither, young girl," commanded the Duc, depositing his mean tool in my hands, "and you, Lubin, lay yourself belly down upon that sofa. You, you silly little goose," he said to me, "plant this angry machine in the aperture whence it's just been ejected, then, camp yourself behind me while I'm at work, you'll facilitate the task by inserting two or three fingers in my bum."

Everything the lecher desires is promptly done; the operation terminates, and the whimsical libertine pays thirty *louis* for the hire of parts the mint condition of which he never once had any doubt of.

Back in the house, Fatima, that one of my companions I was fondest of, sixteen years old and lovely as the day, laughed merrily when I related my adventure. She had had the same one but, more fortunate than I, had profited from it to the tune of the fifty *louis* that had been in the purse she'd stolen from off the mantel.

"What?" I said, "you permit yourself such things?"

"Regularly or, rather, every chance I get, my dear," was Fatima's reply, "and altogether without hesitation or scruple, believe me. Those rascals are rich: and to whom if not to us is their money destined? and why should we be so stupid as not to take it whenever we can? Are you still so lost in the woods of ignorance that you suspect there is anything wrong in theft?"

"I do definitely think it is very wrong."

"Why, that's an odd notion, it is," Fatima assured me, "and a very misplaced one, granted your trade. It shan't take me long to disabuse you. Tomorrow I dine with my lover in the country, I'll ask Madame Duvergier's leave to include you in the party and you'll hear Dorval's reasoned arguments on the subject."

"Bitch!" I exclaimed. "You're going to corrupt what little in me is not yet attainted—oh, as things now are I am only too well disposed toward all those horrors. . . . Very well, 'tis agreed. Never fear, either, you'll have an excellent pupil in me. But will Duvergier let me go?"

"Nor have you anything to fear," said Fatima. "Leave it all to me."

Early the next morning there comes a carriage to fetch us, we drive to La Villette. The house we enter is secluded, but its appearance is not unseemly. A valet greets us and, having shown us into a very well-furnished apartment, he retires and dismisses our carriage; 'twas then Fatima began to make things clear.

"Do you know where we are?" she asked, smiling.

"I have no idea."

"In the house of an exceedingly unusual man," my companion affirmed. "I lied when I told you that he's my lover; I've been here often—but on business. Of it, and of what I earn, Duvergier knows nothing; my pay is thus my own. But the work is not without its risky elements—"

"What do you mean?" I demanded. "You've aroused my . . . curiosity."

"This," said Fatima, "is the house of one of the most accomplished thieves in all Paris; the gentleman steals for his living— and from stealing derives his keenest pleasures. He'll explain it all to you, he'll outline his philosophy for your benefit—he'll even convert you to practicing what he preaches. Completely indifferent to women before he's done his day's work, it's only after he's robbed that he comes alive, only then are his lusts aroused hotly; and as he would have the image of his favorite passion reflected in everything that accompanies it, it is only when once we've stolen that he'll accept our favors—and, furthermore, he'll try to steal them from us; it's a subtle game, you'll understand it perfectly, however. It will seem as if we've gained nothing for our trouble . . . mind you, I've already been paid for this in advance. Here's the proof: ten *louis*. They're for you. I've kept an equivalent sum for myself."

"And Duvergier?"

"But I told you: she's not in the game. I swindle our beloved mother—am I so wrong to do so?"

"No, I dare say you're not," I agreed. "Whatever we earn here belongs to us, none of that damnable dividing the booty, which, God knows, drives me wild. But go on, at least explain the thing to me. Whom are we going to rob, and how?"

"Listen," my companion said. "Spies, and he has a swarm of them posted everywhere throughout Paris, inform him of the arrival of foreigners and simpletons who land by the hundred in the city; he makes their acquaintance, he gives them dinners with women of our category who filch their purses while satisfying their needs; all the loot is turned over to him and, whatever be the nature of the article stolen, the women obtain a fourth part of its value, this being in addition to anything they have been paid by the clients."

"But," said I, "are there not dangers entailed? How is it the fellow hasn't been arrested?"

"He would have been ages ago had he not taken measures to prevent any such inconvenience. Be sure of it, no danger threatens him."

"And his house?"

"Houses, rather. He has thirty of them. We're in this one today; he sets foot in it once every six months, perhaps only once a year. Act your part intelligently; two or three foreigners are to come to dinner; after the meal's over, we'll entertain these gentlemen in separate chambers. Be nimble, get the purse of yours, I promise you that with mine I'll not miss the mark. Hidden, Dorval will be watching us. The trick done, the dupes will be put to sleep by a potion slipped into their drink; we'll spend the remainder of the evening with the master of the house who, shortly after we've left, will leave also, go somewhere else and repeat the same infamies with other women. And our precious idiots, when tomorrow they wake up, they'll be only too happy to have got away with whole skins."

"Since we've been paid in advance," I asked Fatima, "why need we go through with the bargain?"

"It would be a miscalculation not to: he'd be finished with us; whereas, if we serve him well, he's likely to have us in twelve or fifteen times a year. And, what's more, following your suggestion, wouldn't we deprive ourselves of all we may earn from robbing these cretins?"

"Right you are. For, had you omitted the first part of your argument, I'd perhaps have reminded you that we can do our own stealing without him, and that it's not to our advantage to surrender three-quarters of what we filch."

"Tend though I still do to abide by mine, I very much admire your way of reasoning which," said Fatima, "demonstrates that you are equipped with those very dispositions required for success in our calling."

Scarcely had we ended our discussion than Dorval entered. He was a man of forty years, his face was extremely fair to look upon, his air and demeanor gave me the impression of a clever and amiable person; above all, he was endowed with the gift of seductiveness, of such great importance in a profession like his.

"Fatima," speaking to my companion, casting an engaging smile at me, "I suppose you've instructed this pretty young thing in the nature of our combined undertaking? Then I have but to tell you that we're soon going to receive two elderly Germans, our guests for tonight. They've been a month in Paris and are burning to meet some attractive girls. One of the two has on him diamonds worth some twenty thousand crowns; Fatima, I recommend him to you. The other seems to wish to buy a property in this village. I've assured him I can procure him a fine one at a very low price provided he's willing to pay cash; he ought therefore to have over forty thousand francs in his pocket, whether in specie or in letters of credit; Juliette, I leave him to you. Show an aptitude for the task and I'll seek your collaboration in the future, and often."

"What! For shame, Sir," I said, "can such horrors arouse you sensually?"

"Charming girl," replied Dorval, "I see that you know nothing of this matter: of, I mean to say, the shock imparted by criminal impressions to the nervous system. You require enlightenment upon these lubricious phenomena, we'll supply it in due time; until then we've other things to occupy us. Let's pass into this room, our Germans are about to appear, kindly remember to employ all your skill at seducing them, at . . . undertaking them; that's all I ask of you, upon that everything shall depend."

We entered. Scheffner, the swain who was to be mine, was an authentic baron of forty-five, authentically ugly, authentically bepimpled, and authentically stupid as, insofar as I can determine, every authentic German is if one excepts the illustrious Gessner. The goose my friend was to pluck was called Conrad; he was indeed covered with diamonds; his mind, his figure, his face, and his age rendered him almost identical to his compatriot, and his sheer witlessness, as imposing as Scheffner's, guaranteed Fatima a success no less easy nor any less complete than, by every indication, mine was to be.

The conversation, general at the outset, and dull enough, swiftly became very particular. Fatima was not only pretty, she was amusing; she soon had poor Conrad befuddled and spellbound; while my air of shy innocence soon brought Scheffner squarely under my thumb. Dinner came on. Dorval saw to it that his guests' glasses were filled and often replenished with the most delicious wines, and we were scarcely midway through dessert when both our Teutonic friends were giving plain evidence of an extreme desire to converse with us in private.

Dorval, wishing to oversee each of these operations, therefore did not wish them to transpire simultaneously; declaring that there was but one boudoir, as best he could he calmed Conrad, chafing dreadfully at the bit, and had me lead Scheffner away and into action. His enthusiasm was unbounded, that good German had an insatiable desire for caresses. It was warm in the boudoir, I invited him to remove his clothes, I removed mine in order to inflame him further; and placing his discarded garments within reach of my right hand, while the dear Baron fucked me, while, the better to beguile him, I amorously hugged his head to my breast, concentrating rather more upon my project than upon his pleasures, I expertly rifled all his pockets, one after another. A thin little purse seeming to contain all the money he had upon his person, I concluded that the treasure was cached in his paper case and, adroitly ·

snatching it out of the right-hand pocket of his coat, I slipped it under the mattress of the bed we were toiling on.

Having attended to the crucial part of the affair and finding the rest little to my taste, being under no further obligation to pamper the great stinking lout wallowing on top of me, I ring; a woman appears, helps the German dignitary readjust himself and gives him a properly dosed glass of liqueur; he quaffs it off, and she guides him to a bedchamber where he falls straight into a profound sleep that had him still snoring eight hours later.

A moment after he's gone, Dorval enters.

"You are a wonder, my angel," he cries, embracing me, "a wonder, a delight! I missed not a thing. Oh, you maneuvered him artfully! And, believe me, I appreciate such performances. Look here," he goes on, showing me a prick hard as a bar of iron, "if I am in such a state 'tis owing to your skill."

And as he leaped onto the bed with me, I discovered that this libertine's idiosyncrasy was, with his mouth, to *pilfer* the fuck lately shot into my cunt. He pumped it so cleverly, so deliciously ran a swift and active tongue along its outer edges, darted the instrument inside, all the way inside my womb, so well did he proceed that I flooded him myself—thanks a thousand times more, it may be, to the unusual deed I had just accomplished and to the character of the man who had got me to commit it than to the pleasure I was receiving from him; for, to whatever degree he may have affected me physically, I cannot deny that, morally, I was much more deeply stirred by the gratuitous horror Fatima's and Dorval's enticements were bringing me to undertake with such delicious results.

Dorval did not discharge a drop. I turned the purse and the paper case over to him; he took them both, didn't pause to examine either, and I ceded my place to Fatima. Dorval led me away with him, and while, peering through a spy-hole, he observed the technique my companion was employing to achieve the same object, the libertine had me frig him, and frigged me in return. Now and then he'd thrust his tongue into my very gullet, he looked to be in seventh heaven. Marvelous effects wrought by the conjuncture of crime and lust, oh, the energy they impart to the passions' delirium! Fatima's nimble proceedings finally determine Dorval's ejaculation;

thrusting hard against me, he encunts me to the hilt and washes me with the unequivocal testimonies of the ecstasy he has just succumbed to.

A vigorous man, Dorval returns to my companion. I clap my eye to the spy-hole, I see every last detail: as he did with me, so now he bends down between Fatima's thighs and presently drains her cunt of Conrad's fuck as previously he relieved me of Scheffner's; next, he accepts the booty and, the two good Germans being tucked away for the night, we move into an exquisite little cabinet where Dorval, after having spat a second charge of seed into Fatima's cunt while tonguing mine, delivers the apology for his originalities of taste that is here very exactly reproduced:

"Kind friends, by a single feature alone were men distinguished from one another when, long ago, society was in its infancy: the essential point was brute strength. Nature gave them all space wherein to dwell, and it was upon this physical force, distributed to them with less impartiality, that was to depend the manner in which they were to share the world. Was this sharing to be equal, could it possibly be, what with the fact that naked force was to decide the matter? In the beginning, then, was theft; theft, I say, was the basis, the starting point; for the inequality of this sharing necessarily supposes a wrong done the weak by the strong, and there at once we have this wrong, that is to say, theft, established, authorized by Nature since she gives man that which must necessarily lead him thereto. On the other hand, the weak revenge themselves, they put their wits to work, their cunning to use, in order to recover possession of what force has wrested from them, and there you have deceit, theft's sister and likewise daughter to Nature. Were theft offensive to Nature, she would have accorded equal physical and mental capacities to all men; all men existing on an equal footing, Nature would thus have ensured that to every man a fair share in the things of this world would fall and would thus have prevented anybody from enriching himself to the detriment of his neighbor. Under these conditions, theft would be impossible. But when from the hands of the Nature who creates him man receives a conformation which necessitates both the inequality of what is allotted to each and hence theft, how then may one persist in ignorance and suppose that Nature is loath to have us steal? To the contrary, she so plainly indicates that to steal is her fundamental commandment that she makes theft the basis of all animal instinct. Only by constant thefts do animals manage to preserve themselves, only by countless usurpations do they maintain their existences. And how ever has man—himself, after all, but an animal—been able to delude himself into thinking that what Nature implanted in the very soul of animals can be a crime in her eyes or for him?

"When the first laws were promulgated, when the weak individual agreed to surrender part of his independence to ensure the rest of it, the maintenance of his goods was incontestably the first thing he desired, and so to enjoy in peace whatever little he had, he made its protection the prime object of the regulations he wanted formulated. The powerful individual assented to these laws which he knew very well he would never obey. And so the laws were made. It was decreed that every man would possess his heritage, undisturbed and happy; and that whosoever were to trouble him in this possession of what was his would be chastised. But in this there was nothing natural, nothing dictated by Nature, nothing of what she inspires, it was all very brazenly man-made, by men henceforth divided into two classes: those who yielded up a quarter of the loaf in order to be able, undisturbed, to eat and digest what was left; and those who, eagerly taking the portion profferred to them and seeing that they'd get the rest of the bread whenever they pleased, agreed to the scheme, not in order to prevent their own class from pillaging the weak, but to prevent the weak from despoiling one another—so that they, the powerful, could despoil the weak more conveniently. Thus, theft, instituted by Nature, was not at all banished from the face of the earth; but it came to exist in other forms: stealing was performed juridically. The magistrates stole by having themselves feed for doing the justice they ought to render free of charge. The priest stole by taking payment for serving as intermediary between God and man. The merchant stole by selling his sack of potatoes at a price one-third above the intrinsic value a sack of potatoes really has. Sovereigns stole by imposing arbitrary tithes, dues, taxes, levies upon their subjects. All these plunderings were permitted, they were all authorized in the precious name of right, and where are we today? we observe men take legal action

against what? Against the most natural right of all, that is, against
the simple right of every man who, lacking money, demands it at
gunpoint of those whom he suspects to be wealthier than he. This
fellow they call a criminal, and never once do they remember that
the first thieves, of whom and to whom no one breathed a word of
reproach, against whom no one protested, were uniquely responsible
for the crimes of the second—were and are uniquely responsible for
the obligation of this second man to find himself a weapon and by
force to recuperate what the first usurper tore so unceremoniously
away from him. For, if all these thieveries can be perfectly well
understood as usurpations which necessitated the indigence of subordinate beings, these same inferiors' subsequent thefts, rendered
inevitable by the earlier thefts of their betters, can scarcely be
viewed as crimes; but rather as secondary effects ineluctably precipitated by primary causes; and the moment you assent to that primary
cause, you forego the possibility of lawfully punishing its effects. To
be sure, you may punish them, but only unjustly. If you elbow a
servant against a costly vase, if, as he slips and falls, he breaks the
vase, you have no right to penalize him for clumsiness; instead, you
must direct your wrath upon the cause that drove you to mistreat
him. When that wretched peasant, reduced to beggardom by the
immense weight of the taxes you load on him,[12] abandons his plow,
gets hold of a pistol, and goes off to waylay you along the highway,
you may punish him, yes, but if you do, I say that you commit a very
great infamy; for he's not at fault, he's the valet your roughness
made upset the vase: don't push him about and he'll not break anything; and if you do push him, don't be surprised when things get
broken. Thus when he sets out to rob you this poor fellow commits
no crime; he's merely striving to recover some of the substance
you and others like you had previously snatched away from him.
He is doing nothing that isn't completely natural, he is trying to
redress the balance which, in the moral as well as the physical
realm, is Nature's highest law: the peasant become desperado is
perfectly right and what he does, perfectly just. But that isn't quite

---

[12] It is very visibly to the rural situation prevailing under the *ancien régime* that
the speaker refers here; the peasants sometimes knew hardship then, but those of
today, bloated with luxuries and insolence, can no longer serve as examples. (*Publisher's note.*) [*Actually, author's note—Tr.*]

what I was aiming to prove; however, proofs aren't needed, there's no need of arguments to demonstrate that the weak individual is doing nothing more nor less than what he must when he attempts his utmost to recover things which were once torn from his grasp. What I should like to convince you of is that neither does the powerful individual commit a crime or an injustice when he strives to despoil the weak. I should like to convince you of that, for it is my own case, and I indulge in this act every day. Well, this demonstration is easy enough: theft perpetrated by a strong man is assuredly a better and more valid act, within the terms and from the standpoint of Nature, than the weak man's theft; for Nature prescribes no reprisals which the weak may take upon the strong; these reprisals may exist in the moral form, but certainly not in the physical, since, to take physical reprisals the weak man must make use of physical forces he does not possess, he must adopt a character that has not been given him, in short, he must in some sort fly in the face of Nature. That sage mother's laws unambiguously stipulate that the mighty harm the feeble, since for what other purpose have their powers been invested in the mighty? The strong individual, unlike the weak, never dons masks, he at all times acts true to his own character, his character is the one he has received from Nature, and whatever he does is an honest and direct expression thereof and in the highest sense and degree natural: his oppression, his violence, his cruelties, his tyrannies, his injustices, all these outbursts are of the character instilled in him by the power that gave him life on earth; all these are then simple, straightforward, and therefore pure emanations of what he is, as pure as the hand that engraved the necessity for them in him; and when he exercises all his rights to oppress the weak, to strip and ruin the weak, he therefore does the most natural thing in the world. Had our common dam desired this equality that the weak long to establish, had she truly desired that property be equally shared, why would she have divided the mighty and the weak into two classes? By so differentiating men has she not made her intention amply clear, to wit, that the discrepancies between physical faculties have their counterpart in material discrepancies? Does she not make manifest her design, that to the lion goes the whole share and to the mouse nothing; and this precisely in order to achieve the equilibrium that is the single basis to her

118 ❧ THE MARQUIS DE SADE

whole system? For, in order that equilibrium reign in the natural scheme, it must not be men who install it there; Nature's equilibrium is disturbance unto men: what to us seems to unsettle the grand balance of things is precisely what, in Nature's view, establishes it, and the reason therefor is as follows: this that we take to be lack of equilibrium results in the crimes through which order is restored in the universal economy. The mighty make away with everything—that, men agree, is unbalance. The weak react and pillage the strong—there, redressing the scales you have the crimes which are necessary to Nature. So let us never have qualms over what we will be able to snatch from the weak, for it isn't we who in acting thus qualify our gesture as criminal; it is the weak man's reaction or vengeance which so characterizes it: robbing the poor, despoiling the orphan, fleecing the widow of her inheritance, man does no more than make rightful use of the rights Nature has given him. Crime? Ha! The only crime would consist in not exploiting these rights: the indigent man, placed by Nature within the range of our depradations, is so much food for the vulture Nature protects. If the powerful man looks to be causing some disturbance when he robs those who lie at his feet, the prostrate restore order by arising to steal from their superiors; great and small, they all serve Nature.

"Tracing the right of property back to its source, one infallibly arrives at usurpation. However, theft is only punished because it violates the right of property; but this right is itself nothing in origin but theft; thus, the law punishes the thief for attacking thieves, punishes the weak for attempting to recover what has been stolen from him, punishes the strong for wishing either to establish or to augment his wealth through exercising the talents and prerogatives he has received from Nature. What a shocking series of inane illogicalities! So long as there shall be no legitimately established title to property (and never will there be any such thing), it will remain very difficult to prove that theft is crime, for the loss theft causes here is restitution there; and Nature being no more concerned for what happens on the one side than on the other, it is perfectly impossible for anyone in his right mind to affirm that the favoring of either side to the disadvantage of the other can constitute an infraction of her laws.

"And so the weaker party is quite correct when, seeking to recover his usurped goods, he deliberately attacks the stronger party and, if all goes well, forces him to relinquish them; the only wrong he can commit is in betraying the character, that of weakness, with which Nature has stamped him: she created him to be a slave and poor, he declines to submit to slavery and poverty, there's his fault; and the stronger party, without that same fault because he remains true to his character and acts only in strait accordance therewith, is also and equally right when he seeks to rob the weak and to enjoy himself at their expense. And now let each of them pause a moment and inspect his own heart. In deciding to assault the strong, the weak individual, whatever may be the rights justifying his decision, will be subject to mild doubts and waverings; and this hesitation to proceed and gain satisfaction comes from the fact he is just about to overstep the laws of Nature by assuming a character which is not native to him. The strong individual, on the contrary, when he despoils the weak, when, that is to say, he enters actively into the enjoyment of the rights Nature has conferred upon him, by exercising them to the full, reaps pleasure in proportion to the greater or lesser extent he gives to the realization of his potentialities. The more atrocious the hurt he inflicts upon the helpless, the greater shall be the voluptuous vibrations in him; injustice is his delectation, he glories in the tears his heavy hand wrings from the unlucky; the more he persecutes him, the happier the despot feels, for it is now that he makes the greatest use of the gifts Nature has bestowed upon him; putting these gifts to use is a veritable need, and satisfying that need an incisive pleasure. Moreover, this necessary pleasure-taking, which is born of the comparison made by the happy man between his lot and the unhappy man's, this truly delicious sensation is never more deeply registered in the fortunate man than when the distress he produces is complete. The more he crushes his woe-ridden prey, the more extreme he renders the contrast and the more rewarding the comparison; and the more, consequently, he adds fuel to the fire of his lust. Thus, from hammering the weak he gleans two exceedingly keen pleasures: the augmentation of his material substance and resources and the moral enjoyment of the comparisons which he renders all the more voluptuous the more suffering he inflicts upon the miserable. So let him pillage, let him burn and ravage and wreck; to this wretch he fastens on let him leave nothing but the breath which will prolong a life whose continuation is necessary to the oppressor if he is to be able to go on making the comparison; let him do as he likes, he'll do nothing that isn't natural and sanctioned by Nature, whatever he invents will be nought but the issue of the active powers entrusted to him, the more he puts his potentialities into play, the more pleasure he'll have; the better the use to which he puts his faculties, to Nature the better servant will he be.

"Allow me, dear girls," Dorval pursued, "to cite a few precedents in support of my theses; the two of you have benefited from the sort of education that will enable you to understand the examples I am about to set forth.

"Theft is held in such lofty esteem in Abyssinia that the chief of a robber band purchases a license and the right to steal in peace.

"This same act is commendable among the Koriacks; it is the sole means to winning honor and a name in that nation.

"Among the Tohoukichi, a girl cannot marry until she has shown her mettle in this profession.

"With the Mingrelians, theft is a mark of skill and sign of courage; there, a man will publicly boast of his outstanding feats in this sphere.

"Our modern voyagers have found it flourishing in Tahiti.

"In Sicily, it is an honorable calling, that of brigand.

"Under the feudal regime, France was scarcely more than one vast den of thieves; since, only forms have changed, the effects remain the same. It's no longer the great vassals who steal, they're the ones who're plundered; and, in their rights, the nobility have become the slaves of the kings who forced them to their knees.[12a]

"The celebrated highwayman Sir Edwin Cameron for a long time held Cromwell at bay.

"The well-remembered MacGregor made a science of stealing; he used to send his creatures about the countryside, he'd extort

---

[12a] The equality prescribed by the Revolution is simply the weak man's revenge upon the strong; it's just what we saw in the past, but in reverse; that everyone should have his turn is only meet. And it shall be turnabout again tomorrow, for nothing in Nature is stable and the governments men direct are bound to prove as changeable and ephemeral as they. (*Supplementary note.*)

the rents owed by the farmers and give them receipts in the land-owners' names.

"You may set your minds at rest, there is no conceivable manner of appropriating to oneself the belongings of others that is not wholly legitimate. Craft, cunning, force—so many astute means for attaining a valid end; the weak individual's objective is to see to the more equitable distribution of what is worth having; that of the powerful is to get, to have, to accumulate, to engross, no matter how, at no matter whose expense. When the law of Nature requires an upheaval, does Nature fret over what will be undone in its course? All men's actions are only the result of Nature's laws; this should be of comfort to man, this should dissuade him from trembling before any deed—this should engage him calmly to perpetrate every deed, whatever its kind or magnitude. Nothing occurs accidentally; everything in this world is of necessity; well, necessity excuses no matter what; and as soon as an action demonstrates itself necessary it can no more be considered infamous.

"A son of the remarkable Cameron, whom I mentioned a moment ago, perfected the system of theft: the leader's orders were blindly obeyed by his men, every stolen article was stored in a general depot, the swag was ulteriorly split with impeccable fairness.

"In olden days, great exploits of thievery were the stuff of legendry and considered heroic; honored was he who excelled in this domain.

"Two famous thieves took the Pretender under their protection; they went about stealing to maintain him.

"When an Illinois commits a theft, conforming to tradition he presents his judge with half of what he has stolen, the judge acquits him therewith, and no Illinois judge would ever dream of proceeding otherwise.

"Lands there are where theft is punished by *lex talionis:* if caught, the thief's robbed, then he's set free. That law seems very mild to you? So it may appear as applied in this case; there are others, however, where its effects are atrocious, and I shall have you notice its iniquity. This little demonstration won't be at all irrelevant. But, before continuing our dissertation, I'll make one or two very simple comments upon this law of the talion.

"We suppose that Peter insults and mistreats Paul; next, in the court where tit for tat holds sway, Peter is made to suffer everything he has inflicted upon Paul. This is crying injustice; for when Peter perpetrated against Paul the injury in question, he had motives which, consonant with all the laws of natural equity, in considerable measure lessened the heinous quality of his offense; but when to punish him you treat him in the same way he treated Paul, you have not the same motive that inspired Peter, yet you wrong him just as deeply. Thus, there is a very significant difference between him and you: he committed an atrocity that was based upon motives, and you commit the same atrocity with none at all. What I have just said ought to illustrate the extreme injustice of a law which is so greatly admired by fools.[13]

"There was a time when the German magnates counted among their rights that of highway robbery. This right derives from the earliest and most fundamental institutions in societies, where the free man or vagabond got his livelihood in the manner of the beasts of the forests and the birds of the air: by wresting food from whatever convenient or possible source; in those times, he was a child and student of Nature, today he is the slave of ludicrous prejudices, abominable laws, and idiotic religions. All the good things of this world, cries the weak individual, were equally distributed over the surface of the globe. Very well. But, by creating weak and strong, Nature with sufficient clarity announced that she intended these good things to go to the strong alone, and that the weak were to be deprived of all enjoyment of them save that pittance which would befall them as so many crumbs from the table around which sit the mighty, despotic, and capricious. Nature bade the latter enrich themselves by stealing from the weak and the weak take redress by stealing from the rich; so spoke she unto men in the same language wherein she advised wild birds to steal the seed from out of the ploughed furrow, the wolf to devour the lamb, the spider to spin webs to snare flies. All, all is theft, all is unceasing

---

[13] We owe the law of the talion to the indolence and imbecility of legislators. How much simpler they found it to chortle *An eye for an eye* than intelligently and equitably to proportion the punishment to the offense. The latter proceeding requires superior intellectual endowments and, save for three or four exceptional cases, I know of no French lawmaker during the past eighteen hundred years who has been able to display even a rudimentary common sense.

and rigorous competition in Nature; the desire to make off with the substance of others is the foremost—the most legitimate—passion Nature has bred into us. These are the basic laws of conduct that her hand has writ in our bone and fiber, theft is the underlying instinct in all living beings and, without doubt, the most agreeable one.

"Theft was held in honor at Lacedaemon. Lycurgus' constitution made it mandatory; stealing, said that great lawgiver, rendered the Spartans supple, quick, bold, and brave; it is still admired in the Philippines.

"The Germans considered it an exercise very suitable to youth; there were festivals during which the Romans smiled upon it; the Egyptians included it in their educational curricula; every American is much addicted to theft; nothing is more widespread in Africa; beyond the Alps it is hardly discouraged.

"Every night, Nero used to quit his palace and go abroad to steal in the streets; on the morrow, what he had robbed his countrymen of was put on public sale in the market place, and the profits went to the Emperor.

"The Président Rieux, son of Samuel Bernard and Boulainvilliers' father, stole through inclination and with our own purposes in view: on the Pont-Neuf, a pistol in his hand, he waylaid passersby and emptied their pockets. Coveting a watch he saw on the person of a friend of his father, he, so the story goes, awaited him one evening when this friend was leaving Samuel's house after a supper, and robbed him; straightway the friend returns to the brigand's father, complains, identifies the thief; Samuel denies it, says the thing is impossible, swears his boy is asleep in his bed; they repair to the son's bedchamber, Rieux isn't there. A little later he comes home; they are sitting waiting for him, he is reproached, accused, he confesses this and many other thefts, promises to mend his ways and does: subsequently, Rieux becomes a very great magistrate.[14]

"Nothing more readily conceivable than theft as debauch: it occasions the indispensable shock upon the nervous system and thence is born the inflammation which determines the lubricious mood. Everybody like me—and who, like me, quite needlessly, has

---

[14] The father of Henry IV had the same taste.

stolen through libertinage—is acquainted with this secret pleasure; one may also experience it by cheating at the gaming table, or while playing games of any other sort. A thoroughgoing cheat was the Comte de X., he would be subject to the most imperious irritations when gambling; I once saw him obliged to fleece a young man to the tune of a hundred *louis;* the Comte, I believe, had an extraordinary desire to fuck the young man and simply couldn't obtain an erection except by stealing. The game of whist starts, the Comte steals, up soars his prick, he embuggers the youth—but, as I distinctly recall, did not by any means return his money.

"Governed by the same principles and for identical purposes, Argafond steals whatever he can lay hands upon; he has established a bawdyhouse where a complement of charming creatures despoil all the clients. The insolent rogue does very nicely.

"But who are greater thieves than our financiers? Let me give you an example; it comes from the last century:

"There were then in all the realm nine hundred millions in specie; toward the close of the reign of Louis XIV, the people were paying 750,000,000 in taxes per annum and, of this sum, only 250,000,000 found the way into the royal exchequer; which means half a billion went yearly into the pockets of thieves. They were thus very great thieves; do you suppose these thefts weighed heavily upon their conscience?"

"Well," was my reply to Dorval, "I am not unimpressed by your catalogue, I savor your arguments, but I do declare I am far from being able to understand how someone as rich as, for example, you yourself can derive pleasure from stealing."

"Because, when performed, the act has a strong impact upon the nervous system, I've told you so, and this impact, as it would seem to me my erection ought to have demonstrated to you," Dorval answered, "is extremely voluptuous in my case, rich though I happen to be; rich or not, I am constructed like any other man. I may add, howbeit, that, in my view, I possess no more than is necessary to me, and having what is necessary doesn't make one rich. What does, is having more than is necessary; my thefts cause my already filled cup to overflow. No, I repeat, 'tis not through satisfying our primary needs that we achieve happiness, 'tis through acquiring and exercising the power to appease our avid little whimsies, and they tend toward insatiability; he who has only what he requires to supply his wants, he cannot be called happy. He is poor.''

The night was advancing, Dorval had further need of us, there were further lubricious episodes he wanted to expose us to, the enterprises he had in mind called for rest, silence, and calm.

"Throw those Germans into a carriage, will you," said he to one of his hirelings, a man who was accustomed to doing what was needed under these circumstances, "get them out of here, they'll not wake up. Strip them and dump them naked in some out-of-the-way street. God takes care of his little children."

"Sir!" I cried, "what wanton cruelty!"

"Do you think so? Never mind. They've satisfied me, I never for one instant wanted more than that from them; can you tell me what use I have of them now? So we'll deliver them into the safe-keeping of Providence; that's what Providence is there for, after all. If Nature has any use for that pair you may rest assured they'll not perish; but if she hasn't, very likely they shall."

"But it is you who exposes them to disaster—"

"I? I only cooperate with Nature: I carry things to a certain stage, there I stop, her puissant arm does the rest. Let them go. Fortunate they may count themselves that I do not do still worse; perhaps, indeed, I ought to. . . ."

Dorval's command was executed without delay; transported to the carriage, the two Germans, sound asleep, were removed. Of what happened to them I can recount this: that, as we learned afterward, they were deposited in a blind alley near a boulevard and, the next morning, taken to the commissary of police, finally to be released when it was clear to the authorities that neither of the men could provide the faintest explanation of the strange adventure that had befallen them.

Once the Germans had been carted off, Dorval gave us exactly one-quarter of what we had taken from them; then he left the room. Fatima warned me that yet another redoubtable scene of lechery lay ahead; she couldn't predict just what the drama would consist in, but she was sure nothing grave would happen to us. Scarcely had she finished whispering those words when a woman appeared in the doorway and summoned us to follow her; we did as we were told; after mounting some flights of stairs and walking down some corridors in the uppermost part of the house, she pushed us into a dark room where, until Dorval arrived, we could make out nothing of our surroundings.

It was shortly after that Dorval came in. He was accompanied by two big rascals, moustached, of extremely sinister mien; they were bearing candles, their light revealed the strange furniture in this room. It was as I heard the door being bolted that my gaze fell upon the scaffold at the far end of the room. There stood two gibbets; deployed about was all the equipment needed for execution by the rope.

Dorval spoke in a brusque tone: "Mesdemoiselles, you are going to receive punishment for your crimes. You will undergo it here." Thereupon, settling himself in a large armchair, he bids his acolytes remove every stitch of clothing from our bodies—"Yes, stockings, shoes, everything." Our garments are laid in a heap at his feet. He rummages through them, takes all the money he finds in our pockets; then, rolling everything into a bundle, he tosses it out the window.

His face is impassive, his voice phlegmatic. As though to himself, but his eyes fixed upon us, he murmurs: "Useless, that stuff. A shroud for each of them. And I've got the two coffins ready."

From beneath the scaffold one of Dorval's agents does indeed drag out two coffins. He arranges them side by side.

"Duly aware as both of you are," Dorval then said, "of having earlier this same day, and in this same locality which is my house, *wickedly* robbed two good people of their gems and of their gold, I am nonetheless under obligation to represent that truth to you and to inquire of you: Are you or are you not guilty of this fell deed?"

"We are guilty, my Lord," Fatima replied.

I however was speechless. So terrifying were these proceedings that I was beginning to lose my wits.

"Since you avow your crime," Dorval resumed, "further formalities would be to no purpose; be that as it may, I must have a full confession. Is it not so, Juliette," the traitor continued, addressing me and thus forcing me to speak, "is it not true that you are responsible for their death, in the course of the night did you not, *inhumanly,* have them cast naked into the street?"

"Sir!" I stammered, "you yourself—"

Then, checking myself, I said:

"Yes. We are guilty of that crime, too."

"Well then, I have but to pronounce sentence. You will both hear it upon your knees. Kneel, I say. Now approach."

We knelt, we approached. 'Twas then I spied the effect this horrible scene was producing upon that libertine. Obliged to give freedom to a member whose swelling proportions could no longer endure confinement in his breeches, he opened his fly and, as when one releases a young sapling which one has bent and tied down to the ground, so now this prick sprang upright and towered aloft.

Dorval set to frigging himself. "You're going to be hanged . . . you're going to be choked absolutely to death, the two of you! The whores Rose Fatima and Claudine Juliette are condemned to die for having *villainously, odiously* robbed and despoiled and then exposed, with clear intent to destroy, two individuals who were guests in the home of Monsieur Dorval: justice in consequence requires that the sentence be executed immediately."

We stood up and, at a signal from one of his myrmidons, first I, then Fatima advanced up to him. He was in a lather. We frigged his prick, he swore and stormed: his hands roved distractedly over every part of our bodies and with curses and threats he mixed jibes.

"How cruel I am," said he, "to consign such lovely flesh to the dungheap. But there's no hope of reprieve, the sentence has been pronounced, it's got to be carried out; these cunts, so inviting today, will be the abode of maggots tomorrow. . . . Ah, doublefuck the Almighty, what pleasures. . . ."

Then his two lieutenants laid hands on Fatima—and I continued to frig Dorval. The poor girl was bound in a trice, the halter was slipped around her neck, but everything was so arranged that the victim, after hanging the briefest instant in the air, would fall to the floor where a mattress was spread. Then came my turn; I tremble, fear blinds me—of what they'd done to Fatima I'd seen only enough to be terrified, the rest had escaped me, and it was only after my own experience that I realized how little danger had been involved in this curious ritual. And so, when the two men came for me, overcome with fear, I cast myself at Dorval's feet: my resistance aroused him: he bit my flank with such violence the marks his teeth left were still there two months later. They dragged me away and several seconds afterward I was lying motionless beside Fatima. Dorval comes over to where we are, peers at us.

"Sacred bugger-fucking Christ!" he expostulates, "do you mean to say the bitches are still alive?"

"Begging your pardon, Sir," one of his men informs him, " 'tis done, they breathe no more."

And it is at this point Dorval's dark passion reaches its denouement: he leaps upon Fatima—who takes care not to stir a muscle—he encunts her with a prick gone mad and after several ferocious strokes he springs away and assails me—and I too am lying still as death; swearing like one of the damned, he drives his member to the hilt in my vagina and his discharge is accompanied by symptoms of pleasure more resembling fury than joy.

Was he ashamed? Or was he disgusted? Whichever, we saw no more of Dorval. As for the valets, they'd vanished the moment their master had bounded upon the scaffold to belabor us in his frenzy. The same woman who had introduced us into this attic chamber now reappeared, released us; she brought us refreshments, assured us our ordeal was over but also advised us that nothing of what had been taken away from us would be given back.

"My instructions are to restore you naked to where you came from," she continued. "You'll do whatever complaining you wish to Madame Duvergier, she'll look into the matter as she sees fit. So let's be off, 'tis late, you must be home before dawn."

Angry, I ask to speak to Dorval, I am told I cannot—although the odd fellow was in all likelihood surveying us through one of his peepholes. The woman repeats that we must make haste; a carriage is there awaiting us, we climb in, and a little more than an hour later we enter our matron's house.

Madame Duvergier was still in bed. Retiring to our rooms, we each found ten *louis* and a complete new costume, in quality far superior to those we'd lost.

"We'll not say anything. Agreed? For we've been paid, our clothing has been better than replaced," Fatima pointed out, "and there would be no advantage to having Duvergier know about our outing. I told you, Juliette, these things go on behind her back and they'd best stay there. When we're not obliged to share our earnings with her, there's no need to mention our employment." Fatima gazed at me for a moment. "My dear," she went on, "you've just paid a very cheap price for a very great lesson; be easy, the bargain you've struck was good. With what you've learned at Dorval's hands, provided you don't forget it, you are now in a way to make every one of your adventures yield triple or four times what they'd be worth to the uninitiated."

"I really don't know whether I'd dare without having someone else along to bolster my courage," I told my companion.

"You'd be a fool to let a single opportunity pass," Fatima asserted; "bear Dorval's ethics and advice ever in mind; equality, my beloved, equality, that's my one guiding principle, and wherever it's not been established by chance or fate, that's where it is up to us to create it by our ingenuity."

Several days later I had an interview with Madame Duvergier. After inspecting me, she said:

"It looks to me as though your natural deflowerings are just about complete; well, Juliette, you must now start earning your way hindwise, and you'll have an even greater success than you did when we took toll for transit in your frontward avenue. The state of affairs, I tell you, requires that we reverse our approach henceforth. I trust you'll not raise any silly objections; in the past I've had some preposterous little simpletons here who, affirming that it is criminal to give oneself thus to men, brought no good repute to my house and considerable harm to my commerce. Untutored as you may be, rather than utter infantile nonsense which you'll later blush at having pronounced, pray be still for a moment and listen to me.

"I must inform you, my child, that it boils down to the same thing: a woman is a woman everywhere, she does as well—and certainly no worse—when she cedes her ass as when she opens her cunt to traffic, she has as great a right to take a prick in her mouth as to fondle one in her hand, if her thighs clasped together can be of service to one man, why should she deny her armpits to another? It's all one and the same, my angel; the essential thing is to earn money, how it's got is a matter of indifference.

"There are even those—incurable fools for the most part, the rest are clowns—who dare maintain that sodomy is a crime against society because it negatively affects the birth rate. This is absolutely false; there will always be more than enough human beings on earth whatever may be the progress of sodomy. But, supposing for an instant that the ranks of the population were to begin to thin, would one not have to lay the blame upon Nature? for 'tis from no other source that those individuals who incline to this passion have received not only the taste and the penchant which draw them into practicing buggery, but also the faulty or thwart constitution which renders them ill-adapted to sensual pleasure in the ordinary manner we women procure it for them. And is it not Nature, once again, who, after we have acted for an extended period in accordance with the so-called laws of population, finally deprives us of the where-withal to give men any real pleasure? Now, if Nature so operates as simultaneously to make it impossible for men to taste legitimate pleasures on the one hand, and on the other to constitute women in precisely the opposite fashion to that which would be necessary to the continued tasting of even an insipid pleasure, it is amply clear, so it seems to me, that the alleged outrages which, oafs would have it, man commits when he seeks pleasure elsewhere than with women, or with them elsewhere than cuntwardly—these fancied outrages, I say, rather than being offensive to Nature, can be no other than of that same Nature's inspiration. To offset the priva-tions her primary laws impose upon man, Nature, subsequently, is nothing loath to grant him certain facilities, especially since, as may very well be the case, she herself is eager, or obliged, to limit the increase of population whose excessive size can but be to her dis-advantage. And this latter idea is all the more evident in the fact that Nature has limited the time during which women can bear. Why these limitations and deadlines, if perpetual increase were so necessary as is sometimes fancied? and if Nature has set these limits, why shouldn't she have set others? She has posed a term to every woman's fecundity; in man, her wisdom would also have in-spired varying passions or certain distastes: while some members of the community do their duty, others, differently made, must go else-where to relieve themselves of the seed for which Nature herself has no use. Why, without going far afield in search of explanations, we can confine ourselves to an immediate, palpable, and conclusive one: the sensation itself; and, without further discussion, 'tis there the place where Nature wishes to have her bidding done. Well, Juliette, you may rest assured of this," Duvergier continued, little realizing that the person she was speaking to was not without experience in the matter, "that it is infinitely more pleasurable to be had in the hinder part than in any other; sensual women, once they have made the experiment, either forget about or revolt at the thought of cunt-fuckery. Ask around, you'll find that they all say the same. Therefore, my child, try the thing for the sake of your pocketbook and in the interests of your pleasure; and you may be perfectly sure that men are willing to pay a very different price to have this eccentricity of theirs flattered than for common belly-bumping; if today I have an income totaling thirty thousand pounds a year, I can honestly assure you that I owe three-quarters of it to the assholes I've rented to the general public. Cunts don't bring a penny anymore, my dear girl, they aren't in fashion these days, people are tired of them, you simply cannot sell a cunt to anyone, and I'd give up this business tomorrow if I couldn't find women favorably disposed to rendering this essential courtesy.

"Tomorrow morning, dear heart," the shameless creature concluded, "your masculine maidenhead goes to the venerable Archbishop of Lyon, who pays me fifty *louis* apiece for these articles. Look sharp, see to it you offer no resistance to the good prelate's enervated desires, they'll faint entirely away at the first hint of skittishness on your part. It shall be far less to your charms than to a docile eagerness to please that you'll owe your conquest and proofs of an already much impaired virility; whereas if the old despot doesn't find a slave in you, you'll get no more out of him than you'd have from a statue."

Having been perfectly trained in the role I am to play, on the morrow I arrive at nine o'clock at the Abbaye de Saint-Victor, where the holy man lodged when stopping in Paris; he was attending me in bed.

He turned toward a very beautiful woman of about thirty and whose function there, I guessed, was to act as a kind of administrator during the Archbishop's lubricious frolickings. "Madame Lacroix, will you have that little girl I see there step nearer." He peered at me for a while. "Eh, no, it's not bad, truly not bad. And how old is my little cherubim?"

"Fifteen and a half, Monseigneur."

"Why then, Madame Lacroix, you might undress her. You will remember to be careful, omit none of the customary precautions."

No sooner was I naked than I readily divined the purpose of these precautions. The devout sectator of Sodom, what with his extreme apprehensiveness lest the anterior charms of a woman upset the illusion he was laboring to form, required that these attractions be screened so completely from his view that the possibility of even suspecting their existence be circumvented. And, indeed, Madame Lacroix swaddled me up so thoroughly that not the least trace of them remained to be seen. This done, the accommodating creature led me to Monseigneur's bedside.

"The ass, Madame, the ass," said he, "and, I beseech you, nothing but the ass. Pause for a moment: have you taken every necessary step?"

"I have, Monseigneur, and your Eminence will notice that as I expose to him the part he desires to behold, I offer to his libertine homage the prettiest virgin ass it were possible to embrace."

"Yes, yes, upon my soul," Monseigneur mutters, " 'tis rather handsomely turned; stand back there, I'm going to caress it a little."

Lacroix maintaining me at the elevation and in the posture required in order that the dear Archbishop be able to kiss my buttocks at leisure, he fondles and rubs his face everywhere upon them for the space of a quarter of an hour. You may be sure that the caress most favored by people addicted to this taste—the caress, I wish to say, consisting in the profound insinuation of the tongue into the anus—is one of the central features of the Archbishop's routine; and his most uncompromising aversion for the neighboring aperture is at one point manifested when, my cunt lips yawning ever so slightly, by mischance his tongue glides between them and, instantly recoiling, he thrusts me away with a look of such prodigious disgust and disdain that, had I been his mistress, I'd have fled twenty leagues away from his Eminence. This preliminary examination over, Lacroix undresses; when she is nude, Monseigneur rises up from his bed.

"Child," says he, now placing me on the bed and adjusting me in the attitude his pleasures necessitate, "I trust that you have received somewhat by way of preparatory counsel. Docility and thoughtfulness, there are two qualities we cannot forego."

Gazing at him with innocence's wide-open eyes and candor, I assured Monseigneur that he'd not find me wanting in willingness to do his whole bidding.

"Very well, let us hope so. For the least disobedience will displease me beyond measure and, considering my extreme difficulty in getting the task properly started, you'll appreciate how distressed I am apt to become if, showing a lack of cooperation, you bring all our efforts to nought. I can say no more to you. Madame Lacroix, oil the passage and try to pilot my prick into the channel with skill enough, once we're in there, we'll attempt to stick fast for a few moments before the discharge that will reward us for all this damnable trouble."

The amiable Lacroix seemed ready to move heaven and earth, so painstaking were her attentions. The Archbishop was not overly furnished; my complete resignation joined to Lacroix' knowing maneuvers swiftly crowned the undertaking with success.

"Ah, there, that would seem to be it," said the saintly man. "Faith, it's been ages since I've had anything like so tight a fuck, oh, indeed! this is a virgin asshole I'm in, damn me if it's not. . . . Lacroix, here, Lacroix, take your place, for everything indicates that my sperm is readying to spill into this celestial stoup."

That was the signal: Madame Lacroix rings and there arrives a second woman, at whom I had time only to glance quickly. Her sleeve is rolled up, in her hand she grasps a bundle of switches, she falls to belaboring the pontifical behind whilst Lacroix, leaping astride me, bends forward and offers her hind quarters to be colled and nuzzled by the lewd sodomite. He, rapidly vanquished by this combination of libidinous episodes, ejaculates into my anus a copious mead the cadence of whose spurts is determined by the stout blows ravaging his backside.

And that is that. Spent, Monseigneur climbs into bed again; his breakfast chocolate is ordered brought in; his governess puts her clothes back on, she bids me go with the second woman. The latter, she of the sinewy arm, shows me to the door, hands me the fifty *louis* for Durvergier and two more for myself, puts me in a cab and instructs the coachman to take me home.

At the house the next day there's pointed out to me a man of about fifty, very pale, with a very somber eye. That countenance augurs nothing good.

Before leading me into the apartment where he has been waiting, Duvergier cautions me not to refuse anything this individual may ask of me. "He is one of my best patients, and if you disappoint him, my practice will suffer irreparably."

The man is given to sodomy; after some characteristic preliminaries, he turns me over, has me stretch out flat on the bed, and readies to embugger me. His hands grope about my buttocks, clutch them fast, spread them, the bugger is already in an ecstasy before the sweet little hole—and then it strikes me as very odd, indeed, the way he keeps himself out of sight, or at least this way he has of concealing his prick. Suddenly alarmed by some premonition, I twist around . . . and what do my eyes behold! Great God, an instrument positively covered with pustules . . . seeping, oozing sores . . . chancres, etc., abominable and only too eloquent symptoms of the venereal malady that is fairly consuming this ugly personage.

"Sir!" I cry, "are you mad? Look at the condition you are in! Have you any idea what you are about? Do you want to ruin me definitively?"

"What!" says the lecher, muttering through clenched teeth and making as if to take me by force, "what's this! Objections! You'll do your protesting to the mistress of this house, she'll tell you whether I know what I'm about. Do you suppose I'd pay such a price for women if it wasn't for the pleasure of infecting them with my disease? I delight in nothing else; madness indeed! Do you suppose I wouldn't get myself cured if I didn't enjoy this?"

"Oh, I can assure you, Sir, no one told me of this—" and I rushed out of the room, found Duvergier and, as you may well imagine, upbraided her very energetically. The client overheard our argument, he came to where we were; he and Duvergier exchanged glances.

"Calm yourself, Juliette—"

"Ah no, damn me if I'll be calm, Madame," said I, furious. "I'm not blind, I've seen what that gentleman—"

"Come, come now, you're surely mistaken. Be a good girl, Juliette, and return—"

"Never," said I, "I know what you're up to. To think! That you were willing to sacrifice me—"

"My dear Juliette—"

"Your dear Juliette's advice to you is to find someone else for the job. Hurry . . . the gentleman's waiting. . . ."

Duvergier sighed, shrugged her shoulders.

"Sir—" she began.

But he, having sworn to himself he'd ruin me, was greatly reluctant to accept a substitute; only after long and heated discussion did he cede and agree to poison someone else. In the end, however, everything was arranged, a new girl appeared, and I withdrew. My replacement was a little novice of thirteen or so, they blindfolded her, she suspected nothing, the operation was performed. It was a success: a week later she had to be sent to the hospital. Notified, the libertine betook himself there to contemplate her sufferings. Such was his keenest delight; Duvergier assured me that ever since she'd first become acquainted with him he had never cared for anything else.

Fifteen or sixteen others, of similar tastes but in good physical health, passed through my hands and over my body in the course of a month which I remember as one distinguished by some rather unusual episodes; and then came the day when I was dispatched to the home of a man, also a sodomite, whose buggeries were distinguished by details I simply must not pass over. And you'll be all the more interested in them when I tell you that this individual is our own Noirceuil, who's just left us for a few days. He'll be back by the time I've completed my narrative; not that he would be disinclined to listen to such adventures. But he already knows mine by heart.

Through an incredible excess of debauchery altogether worthy of the engaging individual you all know and with whom I shall perhaps be able to make one or two of you a little better acquainted, Noirceuil liked to have his wife be witness to his libertinage, to have her collaborate in it, and then to subject her to it. I should remark that Noirceuil, when we first met, thought I was a maid, and that he wished to deal only with girls who were virginal, at least in that sector.

Madame de Noirceuil was a very gracious and gentle woman and she could not have been beyond twenty years old. Given at a very tender age to her husband, he a man of about forty and of a libertinage which simply knew no limits, I leave you to suppose for yourselves what this appealing creature must have had to put up with since the first day she became the slave of that roué. Husband and wife were in the boudoir when I entered; a moment after my arrival, Noirceuil rang, and two lads of seventeen and eighteen came in by another door. They were nearly naked.

"My dear, I have been given to understand that you possess the world's most splendid ass," Noirceuil said to me once the company was assembled. "Madame," he continued, addressing his wife, "do please have the kindness to unveil this marvel."

"Oh, indeed, Monsieur de Noirceuil," replied that poor little woman, all confused and ashamed, "the things you demand of me. . . ."

"They are of an eminent simplicity, Madame; it's strange, one would suppose you'd have become accustomed to them, since you've been performing them for quite some time now. Your attitude mystifies me. Does not a wife have her duties? and do I not allow you the amplest opportunities to fulfill them? Passing strange, so I think, that as yet you have not taken a rational approach to the matter."

"Oh, I never shall!"

"So much the worse for you; when one is under unavoidable obligation to do some particular thing, a hundred times better to do it with a good grace than turn it into a daily torture. But that is your own affair. Will you, Madame, promptly attend to mine: unclothe this child."

Out of sympathy for the poor woman, to spare her needless affliction, I was about to take off my clothes myself when Noirceuil, interceding, bade me stop and, raising a threatening hand to his wife, left her no choice but to obey. While his wife proceeded with her task, Noirceuil, the object of his two comrades' affectionate by-play, used both hands to excite them; in return, one youth massaged his prick, the other stimulated his asshole. As soon as I am naked, Noirceuil has his wife steer my ass toward him: she holds my buttocks for him to kiss, and kiss them he does, with surpassing lewdness; next, he has the two lads stripped—stripped by Madame de Noirceuil who, once she has collected and folded the clothing lying on the floor, takes off her own. Noirceuil, naked also, thus finds himself in the center of a group comprised of two attractive women and a pair of pretty boys. At this stage indifferent to the pricks and cunts which are there displayed and very available, he concentrates upon ministering to his favorite altar, masculine and feminine buttocks alike receive this effusion of wholehearted homage, and I doubt whether behinds were ever more lasciviously kissed. The rascal arranged us in many different ways, sometimes placed a boy atop a woman so as to create powerful and luxurious contrasts. Sufficiently aroused, he finally orders his wife to stretch me belly down upon the boudoir's couch and herself to steady his prick along its course into my entrails; first, however, he has her prepare his entry by tonguing my vent. As you know, Noirceuil has a prick measuring seven inches around, in length it exceeds eleven; 'twas hence not without excruciating difficulty I managed to incorporate it: but thanks to much determination and the deft assistance furnished by his wife, he buries himself up to the height of his balls. Meanwhile, now the prick of one acolyte, now that of the other disappeared into his own ass. Then, placing his wife beside me and in an identical posture, the libertine bade his youthful aides subject her to the same lubricious exercising he was giving me; one prick lying idle, Noirceuil grabbed it and, the while embuggering me, stuffed it into the delicate anus of his gentle helpmeet. There was a moment when she strove to resist—but, reaching his hand forward, the cruel husband brought her immediately to heel.

"Excellent," says he contentedly once the whole complex operation is under way, "what more could I ask? My ass is being fucked, I'm fucking the ass of a virgin, I've got someone fucking my wife's. Indeed, unto my pleasure now nothing wants."

"Oh, Sir!" groans the libertine's conscience-stricken lady, "do you then derive it from my despair?"

"I do, Madame, and in significant measure. You know me to be frank in these matters and so you will believe me when I affirm that my enjoyment would be far less were you any more willing to comply with it."

"Shameless man!"

"Bless my soul, yes, a faithless, godless, unprincipled, unscrupulous man, that is to say, a frightful fellow, I don't deny it. Say on, say on, sweet nightingale, sing thy invectives in my ear; doth she realize how these feminine plaints, as though possessing a very magic, steel my prick and speed my discharge? Juliette, hold steady there, be firm, squeeze a little: it flows."

And, fucking, fucked, watching fuck, into the depths of my bowels the thrice-happy rascal hurls his thunderbolt. The entire company discharges, the knot of convulsing participants unties itself; but Noirceuil, the avid Noirceuil, ever the tyrant to his wife, Noirceuil, who, to arouse himself afresh, already feels in need of imposing a further vexation, this Noirceuil inquires, "Madame is ready to proceed to the next item on the program?"

"Is there then some divine necessity that requires you forever to repeat this execrable—"

"A divine necessity, Madame, precisely. My happiness decrees it."

And the infamous Noirceuil, having his wife lie full length upon the couch, summons me, has me straddle her, and deposit in her open mouth the fuck he has lately injected into my ass. Obliged to obey, I unloose a generous load and, I admit, not without a little tremor of wickedness I gaze down to see virtue thus so cruelly humiliated by vice; the woebegone lady gobbles up the soup and had she not swallowed every drop away, I dare say her husband might have strangled her.

'Twas from witnessing this outrage that the unkind husband, much inspirited, discovered the strength to commit still others. In position once again, Madame de Noirceuil's ass was successively sounded by her husband's prick and by those of his gallant young friends. You cannot imagine the speed those three sodomites worked with, one leaping to the breach, thrusting, retiring, to be replaced in a flash by another and he the next instant by the third, and so was waged the war whilst Noirceuil fingered my buttocks. After this, his narrowed eyes trained upon his wife's slightly parted buttocks, Noirceuil embuggered each of the youths. While bum-stuffing the first of them, he enjoined the second and me to lay hands upon his wife's buttocks, he to fist one and I the other, and vigorously to knead, to worry those richly fleshed half-spheres, and whenever Noirceuil chanced to discharge into the one or the other of those boys' behinds, he'd straightway have his fuck decanted into the mouth of his unfortunate wife.

And the tempo of these infamies increased apace; Noirceuil promised two *louis* to whoever of us three most successfully teased the victim: the rules of the game admitted blows of the fist, kicks, bites, slaps, pinches, indeed, there were hardly any rules at all; and the scoundrel, exhorting us to play fiercely, frigged himself while observing the contest. There's no imagining the tricks those lads and I invented; we only left off our practical jokes when Madame de Noirceuil lost consciousness. Then, approaching Noirceuil, who was all afire, we environed him with our asses and rubbed his fuming prick upon the ill-starred lady's bruised and lacerated body. Next, Noirceuil turned me over to his tireless boys: now one of them would ass-fuck me while the other tendered me his prick to suck, and now, sandwiched between the twð of them, I sometimes had both their tools wedged in my cunt, or, at other times, I simultaneously entrapped one prick in my anus and the other in my vulva.

We were in the midst of working these wonders when, I remember, Noirceuil, reluctant to see a single one of my orifices vacant, stabbed his member into my mouth and there let fly with his final discharge while my cunt and bowels were washed by the two little pederasts' exhalations; the four of us went off all at once: great God, never have I been rent by such pleasures.

My looks and my evil little aptitudes had taken Noirceuil's fancy, he invited me to stay to supper with his two young playmates. We ate in charming surroundings; the table was served only by Madame de Noirceuil, all unclad, whom her husband promised a scene that would outdo the recent one if she failed to perform suitably her menial chores.

Noirceuil, of course, is a wit. You'll agree that where it comes to constructing rational bases to one's irrational extravagances, the man has few peers. I'd thought to hazard some reproaches for his comportment toward his wife: "Truly," said I, " 'tis rare, the injustice you subject that poor creature to. . . ."

"Rare? Why, I'm not so sure. But as for the injustice, you're quite right," he replied. "What she has to put up with is dreadfully unjust—but only from her point of view. From mine, I assure you, nothing could be more just, the proof thereof is that nothing so delights me as what I wreak upon her. There are two sides to every passion, Juliette: seen from the side of the victim upon whom pressure is brought to bear, the passion appears unjust; whereas, do you know, to him who applies the pressure, his passion is the justest thing imaginable. When the passions speak, unjust as it may sound to him who is going to have to suffer, their voice is nonetheless that of Nature; from no one, from nowhere but Nature have we received these passions; nothing but Nature's energy inspires them in us; and yet, they make us commit injustices, but these injustices are in Nature necessary; and Nature's laws, whose motivations may escape us but whose mechanical workings are plainly accessible to the alerted understanding, betray a vicious content which is at least the equal of their virtuous content. He amongst us who has no innate propensity for virtue, what else is he to do but blindly submit to the hand of a tyrant, knowing full well that this hand is Nature's and that he is the being she has delegated to do ill in order that the harmonious scheme be preserved."

"But," I inquired of the black-hearted libertine, "when the delirium in you has abated, do you not sense some subtle, some obscure virtuous impulses—which, were you to obey them, would without fail incline you in the direction of good?"

"Yes," Noirceuil admitted, "I do occasionally sense impulses of that sort. The storm of passion rages, then subsides, and in the ensuing calm they are sometimes engendered, and 'tis a strange thing. However, I think I can account for it in this way.

"I pause, I reflect. Is it really virtue that has just clashed with the vice in me? and, supposing it is virtue, ought I to yield and do its bidding? To resolve the question, and to resolve it impartially, I undertake to put my mind in a state of completest possible calm so as to prevent myself from favoring either of the contending parties, and then I ask myself: what is virtue? If I find that it has some real existence, I will go on to analyze that existence; and if it

seems to me preferable to vicious existence, there's a bare chance
I'll adopt it for myself. Meditating, I thus observe that by the title
of virtue one honors all the various manners or modes of being by
means of which a given creature, setting his own pleasures and
interests aside, dedicates himself primarily to furthering the happiness of society: whence it results that, to be virtuous, I must renounce everything pertaining to my own self and welfare so as
from there on to be concerned exclusively with the welfare of
others; and this I must do in behalf of people who most certainly
would never do the same for me; but even were they to, would that
suffice as a reason why I should necessarily have to act like them if
at the same time I discovered that every disposition in my being
urged me against assuming such a manner or mode of existing? If,
for that matter, if you call virtue that which is helpful to society,
by narrowing the definition one must give the same name to that
which serves one's own interests, whence it will come out that
individual virtue is often the very opposite of social virtue, for the
individual's interests are nearly always opposed to society's; thus,
negatives enshroud the discussion, and virtue, purely arbitrary,
ceases to have any positive aspect. Returning to the cause of the
conflict I sense when I lean toward vice, once well convinced that
virtue lacks any real existence, I'll easily discover that it is not
virtue which is struggling to make itself heard in me, but that this
faint voice which now and then pipes up for a brief interval is no
other than that of education and prejudice. This much established,
I proceed to compare the pleasures vice and virtue procure; I start
with virtue, I sample it, savor it thoughtfully, thoroughly, critically.
How dull, how vapid! how tasteless, how bland! it leaves me cold,
nothing moves me in this, nothing stirs me, virtue makes me listless,
it bores me; looking more closely at the matter, I perceive that all
the pleasure has gone to him I have served and, in return, for
reward, I have nothing but his distant and aloof gratitude. Now, I
wonder: is this pleasure? And what a difference between this virtuous exercise and the next one of vice! How my senses, my nerves are
brought alive, how my organs bestir themselves! I have just to
caress the mere thought of the misdemeanor I am plotting and lo!
the divine sap starts up and rushes through my veins, I am all afire,
fever assails me; the thought hurls me into ecstasy, a delicious illu-

sion spreads aureate across the whole landscape of this world I am about to conquer through a crime; in its premeditation I voluptuate, it transports me; all its ramifications come one by one under my avid scrutiny, I wax drunk upon the spectacle; 'tis a new life surging in me, a new soul animates me; my mind is blended in pleasure, identifies with it, and if now there is yet breath in me, 'tis for none but the sake of sweet lust I live."

"Monsieur," I said to this libertine whose discourse, I admit, inflamed me extraordinarily and with whom I was moved to quarrel only insofar as, by seeming unconvinced, I might spur him to say on, "ah, Monsieur, to refuse an existence to virtue is, so it seems to me, to hasten with undue dispatch toward the objective and perhaps to incur the danger of going astray by paying too scant attention to principles, those guideposts which are there to lead us regularly along toward a consequential irregularity."

"Why," replied Noirceuil, "as you like. We'll reason more methodically then: your remarks announce that you are framed in a way to understand; I much delight in conversations with interlocutors of your stripe.

"In all of life's events," he went on, "at least, in all those wherein we have freedom to exercise choice, we experience two impressions or, if you prefer, two inspirations: one invites us to do what men call good—and to be virtuous—the other to elect what they call evil—or vice. What we must examine is this conflict; we must find out why we are of two minds and hesitate. There would be no hesitation, the law-abiding citizen assures us, were it not for our passions; they hold in check those impulsions to virtue which, he reckons, Nature ingrained in our souls: master your passions and you'll hesitate no more. But how has he come to suppose, this righteous man who addresses me, that the passions are the effects only of these latter wicked inspirations, and that virtues are always the effects of the former? what incontrovertible evidence has he to prove his hypothesis? To discover the truth, to determine to which of these two warring sentiments there does indeed belong the priority which is to decide the character of my behavior (for one may be sure that of the two voices, the one which speaks first to me is that which will speak loudest and which I must heed, considering it an authentic because immediate, spontaneous inspiration of

Nature, whereas the other voice only corrupts and distorts Nature's message to me) ; to recognize this primacy, I say, I examine not separate peoples, for national customs have denatured their virtues, but I observe the entire mass of mankind. I study the hearts of men, of savages first, then of civilized beings: where better than in this book shall I learn whether 'tis to vice or virtue I ought to give my preference, and which of these two inspirations can rightly claim ascendancy over the other. Now, opening my investigation, I first encounter the patent opposition between self-interest and general; I see that if a man prefers, to his own, the general well-being and if, consequently, he is virtuous, he is bound to be very unhappy his whole life long; and that if, on the other hand, he allows his personal interest a greater importance than the commonweal, he is perfectly happy, provided the laws of society leave him in peace. But the laws of society have nothing to do with Nature, are very foreign to her; hence, they should be accorded no weight or place at all in our investigation; which investigation, the laws having been eliminated from the picture, ought then infallibly to demonstrate man happier in vice than in virtue, whence I shall conclude that, pre-eminence belonging to the stronger impulse, to, that is to say, the impulse leading to happiness, this impulse must incontrovertibly be natural and the contrary impulse, leading to misery, must with equal certainty be unnatural; it is thus demonstrated that, as a human sentiment, virtue is not by any means spontaneous or naturally sanctioned; it is rather nothing but the sacrifice the obligation to live in society squeezes out of a man, an infernal enforced sacrifice he makes to considerations the observation whereof will bring him, in return, a certain minimal pittance of happiness, this in some sort to offset his privations. And so, it is for each man to choose: either the vicious inspiration which, most clearly and most decidedly, is that which comes from Nature but which, in the light of human legislation, may perhaps not procure him an unmitigated happiness, may perhaps bring him somewhat less than he may properly expect; or the factitious way of virtue that is in no wise natural but which, constraining him to forego certain things, by means of others will perhaps recompense him to some extent for the cruelty he must inflict upon himself when in his own heart he murders the first inspiration. And in my view the value of the virtuous sentiment further deteriorates when I remember not only that it is not a primary natural impulse, but that, by definition, it is a low, base impulse, that it stinks of commerce: *I give unto you in order that I may obtain from you in exchange;* whence you do plainly see that vice is eminently inherent in us and it is so invariably Nature's most fundamental commandment, the key to her operation in us, that the noblest of all virtues when subjected to analysis reveals itself but consummate selfishness and thus a vice. And so I say unto you that all is vice in man; vice alone is therefore the essence of his nature and of his constitution. Vicious is he when above the interest of others he sets his own; and vicious still and yet as much when he lies in the very bosom of virtue, since this virtue, this sacrifice of his passions, is in him nothing else than indulgence of his pride, either that or the desire to purchase for himself a draught of happiness more mildly brewed than the potent happiness he drinks while on the road to crime. But willy-nilly and by whatever shifts, 'tis forever his happiness he seeks, never is he concerned for anything else; absurd it is to propose that there be any such thing as disinterested virtue whose object would be to do good without a motive: this virtue is illusory. You may rest assured that man does not practice virtue save for a purpose, and that is the advantage he hopes to reap therefrom, or the gratitude that puts others in his debt. I'll not listen to that prattle about virtues ingrained in temperament, as elements of character; these are as self-seeking as the others bred of calculation, since he in whom they find expression has no merit beyond giving his heart over to the sentiment that cheers him most. Analyze whatever splendid deed you wish and see if you do not always recognize some motive of self-interest there. The vicious individual labors toward the same end, but less deceitfully, and unashamedly, and is more to be esteemed, surely, for this forthrightness of his; he'd attain that end, otherwise and far more surely than his underhanded adversary, were it not for the law; but these laws are odious since, eternally encroaching upon the territories of possible individual happiness in the name of safeguarding the general happiness, they take away infinitely more than they confer. From this definition you may now induce, as consequence, that since virtue in man is only the second and subsidiary impulse existing in him, apart from and above all others is the will to achieve his happiness *at the expense of whomsoever it may be;* that since the impulse which clashes with, or counteracts, or thwarts, or diverts the passions is no better than a pusillanimous wish to buy the same happiness at a cheaper price, that is, at a minimum of sacrifice and without risking the rope; that since virtue, when rightly apprehended, shows itself to be no more than meek slavish conformance to the laws which, varying from one climate to the next, effectively deny any consistent and objective existence to this virtue, one cannot have anything but the completest scorn and the most thoroughgoing hatred for this virtue; and the best one can do nowadays is to resolve under no circumstances to adopt this much inflated and highly recommended scheme of being and conduct fabricated by local ordinances, superstitious and sickly temperaments, the vile, mean, shrewd way of the wretched, which, if we elect it, must surely make us all the more unhappy in as much as it is impossible, once a man has engaged himself in this low and shameful traffic, to extricate himself therefrom: live virtuously? do so if you are ill or a fool, 'tis the fool's solution and the grave of the debilitated.

"I know the arguments sometimes advanced in favor of virtue: 'tis of such beauty that even the wicked are all confounded at the sight, and its radiance makes them respect it. Do not, Juliette, be the dupe of this sophistry. If the wicked respect virtue, 'tis because virtue serves them, because they avail themselves usefully of it; only the laws' authority disturbs the excellent relations between wickedness and goodness, for virtue never resorts to physical violence. 'Tis never the virtuous man who resists the criminal man's passions; 'tis a very vicious man who contrives to thwart them because, both having the same interests, the two men are in competition and must obligatorily clash and hurt each other in the course of their operations; whilst, in his dealings with the virtuous man, the criminal never has such controversies. Altogether possible that they do not agree over principles; but their discord is pacific, in their actions they are able to avoid giving each other hurt; the wicked one's passions, on the contrary, requiring nothing but imperious domination, content with nothing less, everywhere and continually run headlong into those of his counterpart, and there must be perpetual strife between them. The homage the villain renders to virtue is token, once again, of sheer selfishness: 'tis not an idol he bows worshipfully down before; no, virtue offers him the opportunity to enjoy himself in peace, and this the libertine prizes. But, they will sometimes tell you, he who adores virtue takes wonderful pleasure therein; doubtless; any kind of madness can afford a little; it's not the pleasure-taking I deny, I simply maintain that so long as virtue procures pleasure, not only is it vicious, as I have shown, but it is weak, and when I have a choice between two vicious pleasure-takings, do you suppose I'll select the less intense?

"The degree of violence to which one is moved alone characterizes the essence of pleasure. He who is only to a mediocre extent agitated by a passion can never be as happy as he who is rent by a grandiose passion; and consider how vast it is, the emotional difference between pleasures afforded by virtue and by vice! He who declares how very happy he was to deliver over to an heir, let us say, the million which was privily put into his trusteeship, can this personage conceivably claim that the amount of happiness he has experienced is anything like as great as the joy that would be known to another who devoured that million after having discreetly liquidated the beneficiary? Regardless of how dominant the position of the idea of happiness in our way of thinking, it is however only through realities that it inflames our imagination, and however much his good deed may flatter your honest man's imagination, his ideal happiness has most assuredly not afforded his real self as many piquant sensations as he could have experienced from the reiterated and manifold delights a victim's million would physically have procured him. But the robbery—but the murder of the heir, do you say, will spoil his happiness? Not at all; granted a lucid mind and a firm doctrine, robberies and murders can impair happiness only in as much as they excite remorse; but the man who has ripened his philosophy, who is strong in his principles, he who has entirely vanquished the vexing and baneful leftovers of the past, impeded by nothing, he will relish an unalloyed pleasure; and the difference between our two individuals consists in this: that over and over again in the course of his whole life the first will be unable to prevent himself from wondering, deeply distressed: *Ah! that million, would it not have given me much pleasure?* whilst the other, tranquil, will never once pause to ask: *Indeed, why ever did I take it?* The virtuous act could thus give rise to regrets, whereas the wicked, being what it is, must necessarily preclude them. To be brief, the only happiness virtue procures is fancied and fantastical; there is no veritable felicity other than personal, and virtue flatters not one of the senses. Is it by any means, I ask you, to virtue that we attach position, fame, honors, wealth? do we not every day behold the wicked prosper exceedingly, and the good languish in chains? To expect to see virtue rewarded in another world, this folly is no longer pardonable. To what end then, this worship of a false— of a tyrannical—of an almost egoistical, an always vicious divinity (vicious, I repeat, and I have proven why) who has nothing to spare now for those who serve him and who but promises impossible or fictitious payments deferred to the future? Need I mention, moreover, the danger in wishing to be virtuous in a very corrupt age? Thus to isolate oneself from others is to withhold from them the happiness they await from virtue, and, quite absolutely, better to be vicious along with everyone else than to be a good man alone. 'So great is the discrepancy between the manner in which we do live and the other in which we ought, that he who spurns what is done and would have nought but what should be done,' says Machiavelli, 'seeks rather his undoing than his salvation, and hence it is that a man who professes to be entirely good in the midst of such a host of others who are not, must shortly perish.' If there be virtuous wretches, have a care lest, mistakenly surprised to find this trait in them, we be deceived by it: fearfully reduced, they may be allowed to take what pride they can in the pathetic enjoyment of virtue, it perhaps consoles them, there you have their secret."

During this learned dissertation, Madame de Noirceuil and the two Ganymedes had fallen asleep.

Noirceuil glanced their way. "Feeble-minded creatures," he murmured; "pleasure-machines, sufficient to our purposes, but, truly, their appalling insensibility depresses me." His eyes now rested meditatively upon me. "You, Juliette, your subtler mind conceives me, understands me, yes, anticipates me, I relish your company. And," he added, further narrowing his eyes, "you cannot hide it: you are in love with evil."

I trembled. "I am, Monsieur, I am, very much so. It—it dazzles me, it—"

"You will go far, my child. I am fond of you. I should like to see more of you."

"Your sentiments flatter me, Monsieur, I might even venture to say that I merit them, so straitly do mine conform to yours. . . . I have had some education, 'twas at a convent that my mind was trained by a friend. Alas, Sir, my birth is not mean, it ought to have guaranteed me against the humiliation I am in now by hard circumstance."

And thereupon I recounted my story to Noirceuil.

"Juliette," said he after having heard me out, listening to every detail with keen attention, "I am sorely distressed by all this you tell me."

"Why so?"

"Why? Because I knew your father. I am the cause of his bankruptcy, 'twas I who ruined him. There was a moment when I was in control of his entire fortune, I had the choice of doubling it for him or dispossessing him utterly; having consulted my principles, I found I had, indeed, no choice at all but to prefer my welfare to his. He died a pauper; and I have an income of three hundred thousand pounds a year. After all you have said, I ought of course to make reparation to you, since if you have suffered adversity 'tis owing to my crimes; but such a gesture would be virtuous. Do you see, I have a very great horror of virtue, I could never indulge in such a thing. I fear that past events have raised impenetrable barriers between us two; I regret it, but it looks as though our acquaintance were come to its term."

"Execrable man!" I cried, "however much I am the victim of your vices, I adore them . . . yes, I adore your principles—"

"Oh, Juliette, there is yet more to be told," he said in a quiet tone.

"I want to hear everything."

"Your father . . . your mother. . . ."

"Yes?"

"Their existence was a threat to me. To avoid betrayal, I

had to sacrifice them. They went in swift succession to the grave. That could be ascribed to a poison . . . they once dined at my home—"

A sudden quaking laid hold of me, to the core of me I shuddered; but straightway upon Noirceuil I bent a stare, the phlegmatic, apathetic stare of the wickedness with which, in spite of me, Nature was at once burning and freezing my heart:

"Monster," I repeated in a thickened voice, and speaking slowly, "thou art an abomination, I love thee."

"The murderer of your parents?"

"Can that matter to me? Sensations are my means for judging everything; none were stimulated in me by those persons of whom your crimes have rid me forever, and to hear you confess what you have done sets me all afire, transports me . . . ah, I may become delirious. . . ."

"Charming creature," said Noirceuil, "your naïveté, the candid purity of your soul, everything about you conspires against my principles; I am going to violate them and keep you by me, Juliette, I'll not part with you. You shall not return to Duvergier, I'll not hear of it."

"But, Monsieur—your lady?"

"She'll be no better than your slave, you'll reign over my household, everyone in it will be under your orders, you shall have but to give them and be obeyed. Crime does indeed hold a mighty sway over my soul: whatever, whoever bears the evil brand is dear unto me. Nature made me to love it; abhorring virtue, despite myself I fall ever and ever down to my knees before crime and infamy. Oh, Juliette . . . Juliette, come hither, I'm hard, show me your beauteous ass—slut, give me that ass of yours, I'm of a great mind to fuck it, I'm going to expire from the pleasure of imagining my lust is making a victim of my greed's offspring."

I approached him, bidding him have furiously at me. "Yes, Noirceuil, fuck me, fuck me, you swine, I adore the idea of whoring to the assassin of my kin. Eh, come bugger-fuck that hole, wring the fuck out of my cunt, for tears I'm in no mood to spill: fuck, that's the only homage I'm disposed to offer to the loathsome ashes of the family you destroyed."

We waked the acolytes; sodomizing me, Noirceuil caused

himself to be bum-stuffed and, having had his wife clamber atop me and deploy her buttocks, he bit and chewed them and gnawed and worried them and slapped them too, and all that with such vehemence that the poor creature's hind parts were all bloodied before Noirceuil was done shedding his fuck.

As soon as I was installed in his town house, Noirceuil expressed his reluctance to have me venture out of it and would not even consent to let me go recover the effects I'd left at Duvergier's; on the morrow he presented me to his domestics, to his acquaintances, saying I was a cousin, and from then on I was entrusted with the direction of the house.

However, I could not resist seizing the first occasion to pay a quick visit to my former employer; indeed, I had no intention of cutting myself off altogether from her, but neither did I think it prudent policy to seem too eager to see her.

"My dear Juliette!" cried Duvergier as soon as she clapped eyes on me, "how glad I am to have you back! Come in, do, I've been so impatient, for I've a thousand things to talk to you about."

We encloseted ourselves in her apartment; she embraced me with utmost cordiality and congratulated me upon having had the luck to please so wealthy a man as Noirceuil; "And now," said she, "listen to me, my dear.

"I don't know just how you view your new situation; but I should think it a most unfortunate mistake were you to go and suppose that in your present position of a kept whore you need in any wise be bound by some exaggerated fidelity to a man who converses with seven or eight hundred women each year. However rich a man may be, however liberal to us, we never owe him anything in return, thanks least of all; for 'tis in his own behalf he toils even if he bestows the whole treasure of the Indies upon us. He showers us with gold; why? either because of the pride he takes in having us all to himself, or because of the jealousy that spurs him to lavish money so that no one else will share in the object of his affections; but, Juliette, I ask you, do any man's extravagances ever warrant our catering to his folly? Granted that it must grieve a man to see us in the arms of another; does it follow that we must suffer inconvenience simply to spare him the sight? I am willing to go farther: though one loves to the point of madness the man one lives with, whether as his wife or as his most cherished mistress, it would be nonetheless completest absurdity to chain oneself gratuitously to his bedpost. One can fuck every day in every conceivable manner without diminishing the sentiments of the heart, and without their help. 'Tis the most commonplace thing in the world, to love one man to distraction and to fuck frenziedly with another; you don't give your heart to him, just your body. The most extensive, the most intensive, and the most oft-repeated riots of libertinage, having no connection whatever with love, cannot possibly betray its delicacy. In what consists the wrong one does a man whom one outrages by prostituting oneself to somebody else? You'll agree with me that at the very most 'tis a moral affront; and so you've but to take the greatest precautions to prevent him from ever finding your infidelity out; and now what can he complain of? Indeed, one may fairly say that a marvelously well-behaved woman who nonetheless lets some suspicions take root against her, whether these suspicions be bred of imprudence or of calumnies, will be, even were she a perfect saint for virtue, infinitely guiltier in the view of the man who loves her than she who, getting herself fucked nigh to death from dawn to dark, was clever enough to attract no attention to her doings. Yes, and I shan't have it end there, I'll assert that a woman, however sound her reasons for handling a man gingerly and with thoughtfulness, yea, even for worshiping him, can give another not only her body but her heart too; she may even while loving one man a great deal also love a great deal the person with whom she chances to lie; this then is fickleness, and to my consideration nothing more nicely sorts with grand passions than fickleness. There are two manners of loving a man: morally and physically. A woman can morally idolize her husband and physically and momentarily love the young blade who pays her court; she can cavort with him without in any sense or degree offending the moral sentiments she entertains for and owes him she worships: every individual of our sex who is of a different opinion is an idiot who is steering nowhere but toward disaster. A mettlesome-spirited woman, how can you expect her to possibly subsist, or rather avoid starving, upon the caresses of only one man? The thing is unthinkable; and thus you discover Nature in perpetual conflict with your alleged precepts of constancy and fidelity. Now tell me, if you please, what importance can be ascribed by any right-thinking man to a sentiment that is in necessary and unending contradiction with Nature? A man ridiculous enough to demand that a woman never give herself to anyone except himself would be behaving quite as absurdly as he who would not tolerate his mistress or wife ever once dining with someone else; not only would such an attitude be downright queer, it would be tyrannical; for by what right, being incapable of satisfying the woman single-handed, can he require that this woman suffer and not seek to console herself by whatever means at her disposal? Oh, there is here a selfishness, an incredible harshness, a monstrous ungenerosity, and the very instant a woman detects such traits in him who claims to love her, that ought to suffice to make her decide there and then to compensate herself for the dreadful circumstances to which her jailer wishes to reduce her. But if, in that other case, only interest or convenience attaches a woman to a man, her motive will be all the stronger in no wise to curb either her penchants or her desires: she is under no obligation to cede to her keeper save when he pays for her services, and while she does definitely owe him the use of her body when he contracts for it, before the bargain is struck and after she has fulfilled her part of it, she is free, the rest of her hours are hers to employ as she likes, and it is then that, business attended to, she may devote herself to pleasure and the inclinations of her heart; and why should she not, since her only commitment to her keeper is physical? The paying lover, or the husband, must perfectly well understand that he cannot exact from the object of his doting those feelings of the heart which obviously cannot be bought; these gentlemen are too intelligent not to know what is and what is not for sale. And therefore, provided the woman who is in the hire of either or, as the case may be, of both men cooperates in the satisfaction of their desires, they would pass for lunatics if they were to demand more of her. For, to frame it succinctly, from a woman a husband or a lover expects not virtue but the appearance of virtue. Put case she fucketh not with others, but seemeth to, then she's lost;

let her fuck a whole empire to death, but if she be not seen, lo!
'tis there a reputable lady.[15] There exist examples enough to
illustrate my assertions, Juliette; you have chosen a good moment
to visit me, and I shall employ the occasion to convince you; waiting in the next room I've some fifteen women whom I'm going to
pack off to be fucked somewhere outside town; look closely at
them, each has her story. But if I am committing a grave imprudence in talking about them and in allowing them to be seen,
I do it for your sake, and would not for someone else's."

So saying, Duvergier slid aside a little secret panel which
exposed the entire room to our view without ourselves being
visible to those within it.

"Did I say there were fifteen ladies in the circle? Count them
for yourself."

Fifteen women, all charming to behold but differently dressed,
were indeed waiting, in silence, for the instructions they were to
receive.

"We'll move round from right to left," said Duvergier,
"beginning with that superb blonde you see there by the fireplace.
She is the Duchesse de Saint-Fal, whose conduct is surely not to
be blamed; for, lovely as you must admit she is, my Lord the Duc
cannot bear her. Although you see her here, she is nonetheless
rumored to be of spotless virtue; her family is very jealous of its
name, watches her closely and, were news of her activities to leak
abroad, they'd have her confined."

"But," I remarked, "these women must all run a grave risk
by showing their presence here to one another. Might they not
meet elsewhere? A slip of the tongue—or a little malice—"

"Firstly," said the matron, "they are not mutually acquainted;
but if later they should so become, what could one tell of another
that she could not instantly turn against her accuser? All having
the same concern, thus bound to discretion, there is no danger of
denunciation; I've been purveying to these persons or their like
for five and twenty years, and I've yet to hear tell of a single
betrayal; they themselves fear no such thing. Do they look uneasy?
Let me continue.

---

[15] Prudish, God-fearing, or otherwise timorous women, make daily and confident
use of these counsels, 'tis for you the author intends them.

"That tall woman next to the Duchesse, she who appears to be about twenty and whose heavenly countenance resembles that of the purest virgin, she is wild about her husband; notwithstanding, she has an equally wild temperament; she pays me to put her in touch with youths. Would you believe it? she's such a libertine, even at her age, that despite the money I am willing to spend, I simply cannot locate pricks big enough to satisfy her.

"Look at that other angel just to the left. She's the daughter of a member of parliament; she's clever too, and comes here on the sly, escorted by her governess. I doubt whether she is yet fourteen. I only involve her in scenes of passion where fuckery is omitted. Mind you, I've several bids of five hundred *louis* for her membrane, but I don't dare. She's waiting for a gentleman who discharges merely from putting his mouth in the vicinity of her ass; one thousand *louis* is the fee he's offered me for leave to sink his prick into it. The danger being much slighter, I'll arrange the affair by and by.

"That other child is thirteen years old: a little bourgeoise I've suborned. She's to marry, she adores her intended; but she's had a schooling rather like your own. Yesterday, Noirceuil and I concluded negotiations for the sale of her antiphysical pucelage; he'll be here tomorrow to exploit his purchase. A young bishop should soon arrive, he's contracted to loosen her up a little in the same part; but, you see, his device is dimensioned so modestly that your abundantly furnished lover will never know the difference.

"Glance closely at that other woman, that one there. I believe she is twenty-six. She lives with a man who is beyond words devoted to her, who denies her nothing her heart desires; they've both done incredible things for each other; but that doesn't prevent the little rascal from fucking every man in sight, it's men she loves, all men, and with a rapacity that takes one's breath away. Formerly, her lover permitted her to indulge herself, if anyone's to blame for the disorders she wallows in, 'tis he: she but profits from the examples he once set before her, and unbeknownst to him she has her daily fling of fuckery under my roof.

"The pretty brunette beside her is the wife of an elderly individual who wedded her for love; she exhibits prodigious consideration for him, and there are few who can boast of so wonderful a reputation for virtue. Here her patience is rewarded: she's waiting for a pair of young men; later on in the day she'll come back again to meet the man she loves. Of mornings she dedicates herself to debauchery; the longings of her heart are satisfied after lunch.

"That one next to her is of an extreme piety. Notice her costume. The scoundrel divides her time between reading sermons, attending Mass, and frequenting brothels; she has a husband, he adores her but is powerless to change her ways. Stubborn, shrewish, domineering at home, she reckons all that mummery must induce him to forgive her the rest. The poor devil has made her a wealthy woman; and nonetheless she has made him the most miserable of men. I too have a frightful time with her, for she'll only fuck clerics. True, age and looks and manners matter not one whit to her; the whore's happy so long as the prick in her cunt belongs to a man of God.

"Over there beyond her is a kept woman who receives a wage of two hundred *louis* a month; she spends it here, and if her allowance were doubled she'd probably never leave my place at all. She's a former pupil of mine. Her old archbishop would stake his emoluments that she's chaster than the Virgin—who, by the way, being much worshiped by the folk of his diocese, brings in those same two hundred *louis* which, destined for Mary, go next to the prelate, then to his concubine, finally to me. All that, my Juliette, is how things transpire in this silly world of ours; one swims with the current or drowns battling it.

"Now we come to that middle-class girl over there, she's nineteen, and tell me if you've ever seen a more comely creature. Her lover has done everything under the sun for her: he rescued her from poverty, settled her debts, maintains her on the finest footing; if she took a fancy to the very stars, he'd attempt to steal them out of heaven for her, and the little whore hasn't a single moment to herself she doesn't employ in fucking. But libertinage is not what guides her, no, 'tis greed: she does whatever is asked of her, she'll consent to any match I make so long as she's paid for her trouble, and her price is high. Is she wrong to ask all the market will stand? The brute I'm going to turn her over to will leave her bedridden for six weeks, and she knows it; but she'll earn her ten thousand francs this morning, and for the rest she doesn't care a fig."

"And her lover?"

"Oh, she'll improvise some excuse or other, never fear. She slipped and fell. Or she was run down by a carriage. With that brain of hers, she's clever enough to make a dunce of God Almighty.

"That little minx there," Duvergier continued, pointing out a gorgeous creature of twelve, "is a more unusual case: her mother sells her, they are needy folk. The two of them could, to be sure, find other work, they've even been offered it, but they refuse: only libertinage suits them. Once again it's Noirceuil who'll have the first shot at that child's asshole.

"And now behold the triumph of conjugal love. In all the world there's not a wife who cherishes her husband as that woman does," Duvergier declared, indicating a creature of some twenty-eight years, a perfect Aphrodite. "Yes, she adores him, she is jealous too, but she cannot withstand her urges; she disguises herself, she's taken for a vestal, but every week she enters the lists with fifteen or a score of men.

"I consider that other one quite as attractive," my informant went on, "and her position is truly extraordinary: her own husband prostitutes her. Mark you, he is passionately fond of her, and that could provide the explanation: he's witness to her proceedings, he's ready to pimp for his lady, but he embuggers her fucker.

"It's the father of that engaging and so very well-favored maiden who in like manner brings his child here; but he'll not have her fucked; anything at all may be done to her provided the two pucelages are left intact. He'll also be the third member of the party, I'm expecting him at any moment, for the man who's to sport with his daughter is already here. You'd enjoy watching the scene, 'tis a pity you can't stay. There'd doubtless be a role for you."

"And what is going to happen?"

"The father will want to thrash the man who is to lay hands on his child; her ravisher will decline to be whipped; pleadings, obstinacy: the father grovels, the other refuses and finally, catching up a cane, he gives the father a fierce thwacking and in the midst of it squirts his fuck all over the girl's ass. And papa? He'll creep over and lap up the spilled seed, then unleash his own while wrathfully gnawing the buttocks of the man who, the moment before, was administering a beating to him."

"A complicated passion, upon my soul. And in it what part would I play?"

"For the blows he'd sustained the father would avenge himself upon you. You'd have to count on a few superficial scratches, a cut or two; they'd be worth one hundred *louis*."

"Continue, Madame, continue. You know I cannot participate today."

"Well," said she, "only two remain. Consider now that very attractive person. She enjoys an annual income of over fifty thousand pounds and an excellent reputation; her taste is for women, notice how she ogles the others. She is also fond of buggers; and she is deeply in love with her husband withal. But well does she realize that the moral and the physical are two very distinct domains. She fucks her husband with the best will in the world, she comes here to satisfy her other needs; it is simply a matter of managing one's affairs properly.

"Finally, the last of those ladies is unwed, she has great pretensions, is one of our most celebrated prudes; in society, were a man so much as to murmur the word love within her hearing, I believe she'd strike him; whilst here in my little house she pays fortunes to get herself fucked fifty times a month.

"How now, Juliette? Do you need further examples? Or are these enough to make you decide?"

"I think you've persuaded me, Madame," I replied; "in future, I'll fuck here for pleasure and profit, yes, I'll not turn up my nose at whatever little libidinous adventures you prepare for me. But I must give you fair warning: don't put yourself to any trouble on my account unless, where money is concerned, a minimum price of fifty *louis* is acceptable to whoever wishes my services."

"Fifty? My dear, you'll have your fifty *louis* a throw, never fear," cried Duvergier, overcome with joy. "I only wanted your agreement. Money? Money presents no problem. Be gentle, be docile, be obedient, never say no; I'll find you mountains of money."

Since it had grown late and I feared lest Noirceuil become

alarmed at the length of this first promenade I'd taken, I hastened back to be in time for dinner, most sincerely upset at not having seen some of those fifteen women in action or having been able to participate in it with them.

Madame de Noirceuil was not entirely unmoved to see her rival established in her house; the uncouth and imperious tone in which her husband had enjoined her to obey me contributed not a little to her resentment of my presence; not a day passed when she did not weep from sore chagrin and envy: I was incomparably better lodged than she, better served, better fed, more magnificently dressed, having a carriage to myself whereas she was scarcely allowed the use of her husband's; little wonder that this woman developed a hatred for me. But so great was my appeal to Noirceuil's intellect that, whatever her feelings, and they must truly have been strong, I dwelt in perfect security from the least of their effects.

I hardly need stress, however, that love was not Noirceuil's motive for acting in this manner. He valued my company, for in his eyes I represented the means to committing crimes; did he, what with his perfidious imagination, did he need another reason for keeping me by him? That villain's disorders were faultlessly systematized. Every day, and nothing could have interfered with the ritual, Duvergier furnished him a maiden whose age, according to the requirements he laid down, was not to exceed fifteen nor be less than ten; for each of these girls he paid one hundred crowns; and their agreement further specified that if Noirceuil could supply proof positive that any one specimen was not absolutely mint, Duvergier must pay him twenty-five *louis* in damages and for breach of contract. Despite all these precautions, the example of my own self suggests to what an extent he could be deceived, and I dare say he very often was.

This libertine session was ordinarily scheduled for every afternoon; we were all convoked, the two young pederasts, Madame de Noirceuil, and I, and every day Noirceuil's susceptible and hapless wife was the victim of those piquant and unusual practices I have described already. The children would be dismissed and Noirceuil and I would sup together; he usually drank himself into a stupor and would end up asleep in my arms.

Now I must avow, my friends, that for a long time I'd been mightily eager to test Dorval's theories in action; my fingers were nigh to itching from impatience; I simply had to steal at any cost. I had yet to determine what I could do: I didn't doubt my abilities, but I needed someone to try them upon. Situated there in Noirceuil's house, conditions would have favored a stunning performance: his confidence in me was as complete as his wealth was immense and his disorders extreme: I could at any time and every day have laid hands on ten or twelve *louis,* he'd never have noticed their disappearance. But by some quirk of the imagination, by some curious way of reckoning, thanks to some feeling I'd perhaps have difficulty explaining clearly, even to myself, I never wanted to wrong anyone as corrupt as I. It is doubtless here the old story of honor amongst thieves, or of mutual respect; but it was operative in me. I had another reason also, an important one, for restraining myself; I wanted to steal, and I wanted my victim to sustain grave hurt: the idea wonderfully heated my brain. Well now, what crime would I be committing in plundering Noirceuil? I considered his property mine: I would simply be making off with what I already owned; thus, robbing Noirceuil would be mere reappropriation, lacking the faintest trace of larceny. In short, had Noirceuil been a good man, I'd have bled him white; he was a wicked man, I respected him. In a moment or two you'll hear how I was unfaithful to him; you'll perhaps wonder why my veneration for the man did not inhibit my fuckeries; but fuckery is something else again, and between my principles and infidelity there lay not so much as a shadow of contradiction. I loved Noirceuil for his libertinage, for his mental qualities; I was not by any means captivated by his person, I did not consider myself so firmly attached to him as to be deterred from fucking anyone else whenever I pleased. I was ambitious, I took the longer view: the more men I saw, the greater my chances of finding one better than Norceuil. And even if that luck should not befall me, collaboration with Duvergier must necessarily be profitable; and I could not throw away that money in the name of a quaint chivalric sentiment for Norceuil in whom no manner of delicacy could in any fundamental or even superficial sense exist. In observance of this scheme of behavior, I, as you may very well imagine, accepted an invitation

I received from Duvergier several days after the interview I described a little while ago.

The party was to be given at the home of a millionaire; he was not prone to stint on his pleasures, it was in their weight in gold he recompensed those accommodating creatures who were disposed to satisfy his shameless whims. However extensive one's acquaintance with the question may be, libertinage forever holds surprises in store for us; and there is no predicting to what degree it can degrade a man who heeds only the mischievous urgings quickened by ever astonishing vice.

Six of Duvergier's most winning protégées were to accompany me to the house of that Croesus; but I being the most distinguished of the troupe, his finer attentions were concentrated upon me, and my companions really officiated only as priestesses in the ceremony.

We arrived and at once we were introduced into a chamber hung in brown satin, a color and a material chosen, no doubt, to emphasize the fairness of the skin of the sultanas who were summoned there; straightway, the woman who had led us thither bade us undress. She swathed me in a black and silver gauze gown, this costume setting me apart from the others: this tire, the divan I was instructed to recline upon while the others, remaining standing, quietly awaited orders, the special attention shown me—I was speedily convinced that I was to occupy a central position in the festivities.

Mondor enters. He was a man of seventy, short, squat, but keen of eye, and libertine. He gazes around, examining my companions; he utters words of praise for each, then he comes up to me and pays me some of those compliments such as are to be heard from none but a slave trader's lips.

"Very well," says he to his aide, "if these young ladies are ready, I believe we can get on with the job."

That libidinous drama was comprised of three scenes: first of all, whilst with mouth, lips, and nibbling teeth I strove to rouse the deeply slumbering activity in Mondor, my six colleagues, grouped in pairs, were to strike the most suggestive sapphic poses for Mondor's contemplation; no two of their attitudes were to be alike, they were all to keep in continual motion. Gradually, the three couples merged and our six tribades, who had spent several days training for the occasion, finally composed the most original and the most libertine configuration you could hope to imagine. We had already been half an hour at play and I was only beginning to detect a few faint hints of progress in our septuagenarian.

"My angel," said he, "I do believe these whores are putting the wind in my sail. Turn around, give me a sight of your cheeks, for were I to find myself able to perforate the noble asshole you'll offer up to my kisses like a good little girl, why then, without further ado we'd proceed to the conclusion of the affair."

But, swept away by optimism, Mondor had neglected to take Nature into account.

They failed, the several attacks he therewith delivered, though they helped apprise me of what he wished to achieve. "Well," he sighed at last, "it won't do. I need further encouragement."

All seven of us surrounded him. To each the duenna handed a bundle of sturdy withes; then, one after the other, we belabored the wrinkled and seamed backside of that poor Mondor who, while being flayed by one girl, fondled the charms of the six others. We lashed him till blood flowed; and still no sign of success.

"Oh Lord!" the sorry old dog groaned, "I'm apparently reduced to taking desperate remedies."

Sweating, bleeding, breathless, the knave cast a troubled eye about the company.

At that point the amiable duenna spoke up, busying herself applying eau de cologne to her master's lacerated buttocks. "Ladies," said she, "I am afraid there remains but one means to bring his Honor back to life."

"And what may that be?" I inquired. "For truly, Madame, have we not exhausted every device that would bring his Honor forth from slumber?"

"Nay, there is yet this we may attempt," she answered. "I shall stretch his Honor comfortably upon this couch; you, my kind Juliette, kneeling before him, you will go on imparting the warmth of your pink mouth to my dear master's glacial tool. You, only you can succeed in its resurrection, of that I am convinced. As for you other ladies, will you one by one step forward and perform these three little services: first, briskly slap his Honor's face, then spit upon it, and finally fart thereupon: as soon as all six have com-

pleted these exercises we may, I believe, see his Honor wonderfully revived."

She spoke, the prescription was followed out, and I swear
to you I am still amazed at the efficacy of these combined expedients: in my mouth, as the treatment advanced, the balloon inflated
until I nigh to choked on that swelling morsel. True, all went at
great speed: those slaps, that spittle, and the farts, perfectly
orchestrated, rained down a very tempest upon the patient; passing
strange it was, and most entertaining, to listen to the music wherewith the air resounded, a symphony of eructations, bass and tenor,
the sharp percussive sounds of the blows, the flat notes of the ex-
pectorations. Well, the sluggardly member at last woke up, as I
say, filled out, waxed wroth, and I thought it was about to explode
between my lips when, springing away from me, Mondor signaled
to the duenna, and she readied everything for the finale: 'tis within
my ass the opera is to end. She adjusts me in the posture sodomy
prefers; Mondor, helped, guided by his assistant, plunges instantly
into the arcanum where the bugger takes his sweetest pleasures—
but wait, there's more to tell; I'd fail to give an honest portrait of
these goings-on were I to omit the crapulous episode with which
Mondor crowned his ecstasy. While the lecher ass-fucked me, it was
necessary:

1) that his governess, outfitted with a gigantine dildo, render
him the same service;

2) that one of the girls, crouched beneath me, cause a great
racket and stir in my cunt by sucking and licking it and blowing air
thereinto and smacking her lips together;

3) that two dainty asses be placed where I could fondle them
vigorously;

4) and finally that two other girls, the first sitting astride me
and bent low over my back, and the second likewise seated upon the
first, both simultaneously shit, the former delivering a gobbet of
excrement into his Honor's mouth, the latter smearing another over
his brow.

But everyone took her turn accomplishing this last-mentioned
task; everybody shat, even the duenna; everybody frigged me,
everybody donned the dildo and impaled Mondor who, over-

whelmed by lubricious titillations, at last darts the deplorable jets of his quavering lust to a good depth in my anus.

"What is this, Madame! What is this strange tale you are telling us!" cried the Chevalier, suddenly interrupting Juliette. "Do you mean to say that the duenna shat also?"

"She very certainly did, Sire," our historian insisted, a hint of vexation in her voice, another of reproof in her glance. "I fail to apprehend how, with an imagination so matured as your own, Chevalier, you can find anything strange in that: the more worn and weary, the more wrinkled a woman's ass, the more meet it is for such an operation; seasoning makes the salts more acrid, the vapors richer, the odors stronger. . . . In general, I might add, there persists a very great error in what pertains to the exhalations emanated from the *caput mortuum* of our digestions; there is nothing unwholesome about them, nothing that is not altogether agreeable . . . shit-hatred is unfailingly the mark of the simpleton, that you will admit; but need I tell you that there is such a thing as shit-connoisseurship, shit-gourmandise? No habit is more easily acquired than mard-savoring; eat one, delicious, eat another, no two taste exactly alike, but all are subtle and the effect is somewhat that of an olive. By all means, yes, one must allow one's imagination free play; but shit gleaned from antique and much-traveled assholes . . . ah, a supper for the gods, one of the culminating episodes of the libertine experience. . . ."

"Which I shall willingly undergo before very long, Madame, I swear it unto you," declared the Chevalier as he complacently stroked a prick which the idea just broached was causing to stiffen horribly.

"Whenever you please," Juliette replied, "and may I offer my own product for your delectation? Indeed, hold . . . this instant, if you wish; your palate's whetted, my sphincters are stirring."

And the Chevalier, taking Juliette at her word, led her away into an adjoining cabinet whence they did not return for a good thirty minutes, which in all likelihood were employed to acquaint the Chevalier with the most voluptuous aspects of this patrician passion; and the Marquis devoted the same interval to harrying the much-weathered buttocks of the unfortunate Justine.

The door opened; "True!" cried the Chevalier, " 'tis delicious!"

"Did you eat—?" inquired the Marquis.

"I feasted. And gluttonously, I am afraid. There's none left, my Liege."

"I too am surprised, Chevalier; but what strikes me as strange is that you'd not familiarized yourself with the practice long before this. Nowadays you'll not find a single child of eighteen or twenty who's not had shit aplenty out of whores. But proceed, Juliette, 'tis very pleasant, the way you kindle our passions with your engaging stories and then appease them with such singular consideration and art."

"Heavenly creature," said Mondor, drawing me into a secluded room after having dismissed the other women, "there is yet another service you may perform for me and that is the one from which I await my divinest pleasures. I would have you imitate your friends, you're to shit as did they, and to deposit here in my mouth both the celestial turd I pray to God you have reserved for me, and with that succulent viand, the fuck-gravy I injected not long ago into your ass."

I inclined and in a tone at once dignified and respectful announced that my one desire was to comply with his.

"But can you?" he cried.

"I can indeed," I assured him.

"Is it so? Adorable child, wonderful child," he stammered, "it is then within your power to grant my request? Great God, this shall be the discharge of my life."

When we had entered that little room my eyes had immediately lit upon a package of some size, containing, so I guessed, things which would be very instrumental to the improvement of my pecuniary situation; that same instant I had conceived an overpowering wish to steal it—but how? I was nude. Where could I conceal the package? Although it was not long, it was bulky, about as thick as a man's arm.

"Your Honor," I asked, "are you going to call in someone to help us?"

"No," the financier answered, "my custom is to taste this final delight in solitude; so lubricious are my sensations, so voluptuous the gestures which they wring out of me. . . ."

"Nonetheless," I broke in peremptorily, "it cannot be done without some assistance."

"It can't, my dear?"

"It cannot, Monsieur."

"Eh then, if that is the case, pray go and see if one of the women is still about. If they're all there, bring the youngest back with you: her ass got me quite palpably erect, and of them all 'tis she I fancy the most."

However, I had not budged. "Sir," I pointed out, "I am not familiar with your house; and I am, furthermore, little disposed to move for, do you see, the state I am in. . . ."

"The state? Ah, yes, the state. I'll ring then—"

"I beg you under no circumstances to ring. You surely cannot expect me to appear before your servants thus?"

"But my woman is out there, she'll come."

"Not at all. She is escorting the girls home."

"Damn my eyes!" he cried. "I cannot bear these delays."

And Mondor dashed from the room, vanishing into the apartment we'd just come from; and thus the idiot left me alone amidst his treasures. No need to think twice: in Noirceuil's house I had had the very best reasons for restraining myself, here in Mondor's I could give vent to this immense longing I had to commit a theft: I seize the opportunity, the instant my man's back is turned I pounce upon the package, my hair is done up in a large chignon, that is where I cache my prize. No sooner had I stowed it away out of sight than Mondor called me. The girls had not left; would I please come into the apartment? For he preferred to have this final scene enacted in the same surroundings where the earlier ones had taken place. We were given instructions and work began: the youngest of the girls sucked the patient's member, he filled her mouth with sperm while simultaneously into his I deposited the victual whereof he was so uncommonly fond. All went well, nothing was remarked, I readjusted myself, two carriages were waiting for us, and, hugely contented, Mondor bade us farewell after having distributed generous largesse to us.

When I had returned to the house of Noirceuil and shut myself up in privacy, I said to myself, even before I set to opening the package, "Great God, can Heaven itself have viewed my theft with favor?"

Wrapped up in that parcel were sixty thousand francs in notes of credit payable to the bearer, already signed and requiring no further endorsement.

It was then, as I was about to put these spoils away, I noticed that by some extraordinary coincidence while I'd been off stealing, somebody had been robbing me: my secretary had been forced open, missing were five or six *louis* I'd kept in a drawer. Advised of the fact, Noirceuil assured me that only one Gode could have been responsible for it. This Gode was an extremely pretty girl of twenty whom Noirceuil had attached to my service since my entry into his household, whom he quite often had make a third in our pleasures, and whom, in the spirit of jollity such as the libertine intelligence conceives it, he had got one of his homosexual juveniles to impregnate. She was now in her sixth month.

"Gode! Do you really believe it could have been she?"

"I am certain of it, Juliette. Had you noticed her nervous manner? How uneasily she withstood our interrogating glances?"

Therewith, heedless of all save my perfidious selfishness, completely forgetting my resolution never to work injury upon those who were my kinsmen in villainy, with tears in my eyes I besought Noirceuil to have the culprit arrested.

"I am perfectly willing to do as you suggest," Noirceuil replied with a chilly lack of expression which I should have interpreted accurately had my preoccupied mind permitted me to remark it; "however, you're not to be deprived of any pleasure her punishment might afford you. She's gravid, that will retard justice and while they fiddle-faddle the scoundrel may very well wriggle out of her plight. She's young and attractive, you know."

"Ah, Christ!" I cried, "I am in despair."

"I dare say you must be, my beloved," Noirceuil pursued quietly, "for you ambition to see her hanged; but it will be a good three months before they get her to the scaffold. Supposing now, Juliette, that you are ever able to enjoy the spectacle which, I fully appreciate, would have a very incisive effect upon a sensibility as highly organized as yours, I must remind you that such pleasures are over and done with in fifteen or twenty minutes. I recommend that we somewhat prolong the wretch's sufferings; what say we make them extend over the rest of her life? It's a simple matter. I'll have her confined to a dungeon in Bicêtre; how old is she? Twenty? She could rot half a century in prison."

"Ah, my friend, a splendid plan!"

"I only ask that you let me postpone putting it into operation until tomorrow; which would give me time to clothe this scheme with all the details and adjuncts needed to enhance its charm."

I embrace Noirceuil; he has his carriage sent for and two hours later returns with the writ necessary to our enterprise.

"She's ours," says the traitor; "we may now amuse ourselves. Let's play our parts convincingly." Later, after we have dined and gone to his dressing room, he summons the poor girl. "Gode, my dear Gode," says he, "you know what my feelings for you are, the time is approaching when I shall want to demonstrate them: I am going to unite you to that young man who left in your womb the tokens of a noble affection for you; two thousand crowns a year, that shall guarantee the future of your ménage."

"Oh, Sire, you are too kind—"

"No, my child, I really am not, please, expressions of thanks embarrass me. You owe me none, of that you may be absolutely sure; this that you take for kindness is pure self-indulgence, the pleasure is all my own. From now on you have nothing to fear, everything has been settled owing to the steps I have lately taken; whereas you may not live in regal style, you shall never lack for a crust of bread."

Failing entirely to perceive the underlying significance of these words, Gode sprinkled tears of joy upon the hands of her fancied benefactor.

"Eh then, Gode," said my lover, "I ask for your cooperation this one last time; though I am not much taken by pregnant women, let me embugger you while kissing Juliette's buttocks."

We assumed our stances; never had I seen Noirceuil so aroused.

"A criminal thought excites most wondrously, does it not?" I whispered to him.

"Incomparably," he replied; "but whose would the crime be, and what would become of that thought, if she had truly robbed you?"

"You are quite right, my dear."

"Take comfort, Juliette, take comfort, if crime there be, Gode is not its author. No, this wretch is as innocent of theft as are you; 'twas I stole your money, you see."

And as he spoke he had his prick hilt-driven into her ass, and he was kissing my mouth and paddling my buttocks. I confess that this triumph of wickedness fetched a discharge from me in a trice; grasping my lover's hand, pressing it to my clitoris, by the fuck that beslimed his fingers I bade him judge of his infamy's powerful effect upon my heart; he came the next moment, two or three furious jerks and a string of horrible blasphemies heralded his delirium. ... But he had scarcely withdrawn his prick from Gode's ass when, knocking softly at the door, a valet announced that the police constable was asking Noirceuil's leave to carry out the mission he had been charged to execute.

"Very good, have the officer wait a moment," said Noirceuil, "I'll hand the culprit over to him, tell him so." The valet disappeared; Noirceuil turned complacently toward Gode. "Make haste there," said he, "dress yourself. Your husband has come himself to fetch you away to the little country house which I have arranged for you to inhabit the remainder of your days."

Gode, trembling with anticipation, puts on her clothes, Noirceuil thrusts her out of the room. Heavens! what must her terror be as she catches sight of the black-clad man and his retinue, as they put manacles on her as though she were a criminal, as, above all else, she hears (and this, it would seem, made the deepest impression upon her) all the domestics, acquainted with the fact, cry out:

"Aye, 'tis she, sergeant, don't let her get away, she's a very bad one, beyond all doubt she broke into her Ladyship's secretary and in doing so she brought suspicion to hang over all the rest of us—"

"I, break into Mademoiselle's secretary!" Gode protested, her knees about to buckle. "I! God be my witness, but I am incapable of any such thing."

The constable paused, looked inquiringly at Noirceuil.

"Eh," said the latter, "do you shirk your duty, Sir? Justice will be done, you understand, you are employed for that."

The wretch was dragged off and flung into one of the most cheerless of the unhealthy Bicêtre dungeons, where upon her arrival she had a miscarriage which came within an ace of putting an end to her life. But she did not succumb. No, there is breath in her yet; which, by the simplest computation, means that for many a long year she has been lamenting her errors, and they can be said to consist in having stirred up powerful desires in Noirceuil, who goes at least once every six months to savor her tears and to issue recommendations to her wardens that, if possible, they tighten the irons that bind her.

"Tell me now," said Noirceuil, as soon as Gode had been led away, and as he returned to me double the sum removed from my secretary, "isn't that a hundred times better than if she had been confided to an uncertain and perhaps merciful justice? We'd not have been able to exert any control over her destiny, whereas," he smiled, "this way it is in our hands forever."

"Oh, Noirceuil, thou art an evil man . . . and what joys thou hast fashioned for thyself!"

"Yes," my lover acknowledged, "I knew the constable was waiting at the threshold, and believe me, I discharged deliciously into the ass of the prey I was about to surrender to him."

"A very evil man you are, a very wicked man . . . but why is it that I too could not help but taste the wildest pleasures in the infamy you committed?"

"Precisely because it is one," Noirceuil answered; "there is no imaginable infamy that does not give pleasure. Crime is the soul of lubricity; there is no real lubricity without crime: there are, thus, passions which are the massacre of humaneness and . . . of humanity."

"If that be so, they must obviously have no connection with Nature, those tiresome humane sentiments upon which moralists constantly expatiate. Or could it be that there are moments when an inconsistent Nature countermands with one voice what she enjoins with another?"

"Ah, Juliette, become better acquainted with her, this profoundly wise, this sweetly bountiful Nature, never would she have us aid others save our motive for doing so be profit or fear:

"Fear, because we dread lest the woes our weakness leads us to relieve in others befall us in our turn.

"And profit—we succor others in the hope that we will gain thereby, or in order to flatter our lustful pride.

"But as soon as a more imperious passion than charity makes itself heard, all the other passions fall mute, egoism then reclaims its sacred rights, our lips curl scornfully at the torments others have to endure; what sympathies can these torments awake in us? They are never any of our concern except in as much as we may ourselves have to undergo them; well, if pity is bred of fear, it is then a weakness whence with all possible dispatch we ought to protect, to purge ourselves."

"This calls for a fuller development," I remarked to Noirceuil. "You have demonstrated the inexistence of virtue, will you kindly explain to me what crime is; for if on the one hand you annihilate what I am advised to respect and on the other you belittle what I ought to fear, you shall surely put my soul in the state I desire it to be in so as henceforth to dread the undertaking of nothing."

"Will you then sit down, Juliette, and make yourself comfortable," Noirceuil suggested, "for this requires a serious dissertation, and if what I shall have to say is to be intelligible to you, you must lend me your whole attention.

"Crime: the term is applied to any formal violation, whether fortuitous or premeditated, of what in the human community goes under the name of law; whence we have but one more arbitrary and meaningless word: for laws are relative, depending upon customs, upon considerations varying according to time and place; they are utterly different every few hundred miles, and so it is that were I to take ship or board the mail-coach I could, for having performed one and the same deed, find myself condemned to death on Sunday morning in Paris and a public hero on Saturday of the same week in some land on the frontiers of Asia or on the coasts of Africa. Faced with this towering absurdity, philosophy has returned to the following fundamental propositions. I enumerate:

"1) That in themselves all acts are indifferent; that they are neither good nor bad intrinsically, and if man now and then so qualifies them, the sole criteria by which he performs his judgment are the laws he has elaborated for himself or the form of government under which he chances to live; but from the standpoint of Nature, and barring all else from consideration, all our acts are as one, none better, none worse than the rest.

"2) That if from somewhere within us there arises a murmur of protestation against the acts of wickedness we concert, this voice is nothing whatever but the effect of our prejudices and education, and that if we had been born and reared in some other climate, it would address us in a very different language.

"3) That if in changing country we were still to be subject to these inspirations, that would in no wise demonstrate their goodness but merely that one's earliest impressions are only with some effort effaced.

"4) That, lastly, remorse, or the sentiment of guilt, is the same thing, that is to say, purely and simply the effect of the earliest impressions one receives, which habit alone can neutralize and which one ought to labor determinedly to destroy.

"And indeed, to find out whether something be truly criminous or not, one must first find out what harm it can do to Nature; for one can rationally describe as a crime only that which might conflict with her laws. Nature being constant, this crime must hence be uniform: the deed must prove to be of some sort or other that all the races and nations of the earth hold it in equal and tremendous horror, and the loathing it inspires must be as universal in man as his desire to satisfy his elementary needs; well, of this species of deed there is not one that exists; that which unto us has the most atrocious and execrable aspect has been a cornerstone to ethics elsewhere.

"Crime, thus, is not in any sense real, there is thus, veritably, no crime, no thinkable way or means for outraging a Nature in ceaseless flux and action . . . eternally so superior to us as, from where aloft she superintends the general order, to be infinitely above worrying about us or what we do. There is no act, however awful, however atrocious, however infamous you like or can imagine it, which we cannot perform every time we sense the urge, why! which we have the right not to commit, since Nature puts the idea in our heads; for our usages, our religions, our manners and customs may easily and indeed must perforce deceive us, whilst we shall certainly never be misled by the voice of Nature: it is upon a mixture combining strictly equal parts of what we term *crime* and *virtue* that her operations and laws are based: destruction is the soil and light that renews her and where she thrives; it is upon crime she subsists; it is, in a word, through death she lives. A totally virtuous universe could not endure for a minute; the learned hand of Nature brings order to birth out of chaos, and wanting chaos, Nature must fail to attain anything: such is the profound equilibrium which holdeth the stars aright in their courses, which suspendeth them in these huge oceans of void, which maketh them to move periodically and by rule. She must have evil, 'tis from this stuff she creates good; upon crime her existence is seated, and all would be undone were the world to be inhabited by doers of good alone. Now, Juliette, I inquire of you: once evil is indispensable to Nature's major designs, once she is helpless to function, once she is impotent without it, how can the individual who does evil help but be useful to Nature? and what doubt remains but that the wicked man is he whom Nature has deliberately so framed in order to achieve her ends? Why do we decline to acknowledge that she has done with men what she has done with beasts? are not all classes, like all species, in perpetual strife, do they not mutually batten one upon the other, does not one or the other weaken, wilt, perish away, depending upon the state or shape which Nature's laws must give to the natural order? Who can deny that Nero's gesture, when he poisoned Agrippina, was one of the effects of those selfsame laws, as rigidly everlasting as that other law whereby the wolf devours the lamb? who doubts that the prescriptions of a Marius or a Sulla are anything other than the plague or the famine Nature sometimes unleashes over the length and breadth of a continent? She does not, I know, assign to mankind as a whole the perpetration of a given crime, but each man is allotted a certain talent and a certain propensity for a certain crime, thus does she ensure a certain harmony: from the sum of all these misdeeds, from the entirety of all these lawful or unlawful destructions, she extracts the chaos, the decline, the decrepitude she must have to recast order, to renew growth, to restore vigor. Why did she give us poisons if she was not anxious to have men employ them? why ever did she cause Tiberius to be born, or Heliogabalus, or Andronicus, or Herod, or Wenceslas, or all the other great villains or heroes (they are synonymous) who have been the scourges of the earth—why, if the devastations wrought by these bloody men did not answer her requirements and promote her ends? Why does she send, concurrently with these scoundrels and to act in concert with them, plagues, wars, blights, and dearths, if it were not essential that Nature destroy, and if crime and destruction were not inseparable from her laws? If then it be essential that she destroy, why does he who feels himself born to destroy resist his penchants, neglect his duties? Might one not say that if there were an evil thing in this world, if there could be, it would be visibly that which one commits in resisting the destiny Nature has prepared for each of us? In order that crime, which neither does nor can offend anyone or anything but our fellows, irritate Nature, one would have to pretend that she takes a greater interest in some persons than in others, and that, though we be all equally formed by her hand, we are not however all equally her children. But if we are all alike, save for our greater or lesser strength; if Nature goes to no more trouble shaping an emperor than a chimney sweep, the different activities of high conquest and menial service are simply the necessary accidents that derive directly from the initial impulsion, and both conquering and the cleaning of flues have got to be done, for we have been expressly formed and intended to do them. When next we see that Nature has physically distinguished individual persons, that she has made some strong, others weak, what could be more patently evident than that, in so making them, she expects the strong to commit the crimes she needs to have committed, just as it is of the essence of the wolf that he devour the lamb, just as the essence of the mouse is to be devoured by the cat?

"And so it was very correctly that the Celts, our earliest ancestors, held that the highest and most sacred of our rights was that of might, which is to say, that of Nature; and they considered that when Nature deems wise to assign a superior quality of potential to some one of us, she does so only to confirm the prepotency over the weak which she invests in us strong. Thus, it was by no means mistakenly that these same people, whence we descend, claimed not only that this right was sacred, but that Nature's express intent, in granting it to us, was that we exploit it; that, in order to conform to her wishes, the greater had perforce to despoil the lesser; and that these latter ought best bow before what was irresistible and relinquish what they were in no position to defend. If since Celtic days matters have changed physically, they haven't morally. The opulent man represents what is mightiest in society; he has bought up all the rights; he ought therefore to enjoy them; with their enjoyment in view, he ought to the fullest possible extent pave the way for the satisfaction of his caprices by exacting discipline, forbearance, and compliance from the other, the subordinate, class of men; and this he may, he must, do without in any sense wronging Nature, since he but uses the right he has been either materially or conventionally awarded. Let me repeat: had Nature intended to bar us from crime, she would have been very able to withhold from us the means for committing it. She furnished us those means at the outset, and she gives them to us still: for she is nothing loath that we possess them; she looks upon our crimes as either of no account or as necessary: as of no account if they be petty; as always and eminently desirable if they be capital; for 'tis all the same thing, whether I filch my neighbor's purse, rape his son, his wife, or his daughter: these are mere pranks, of too slight importance and scope ever to be of any major utility to Nature; but it is very necessary to her that I kill that son, that wife, or that daughter when, giving me the idea, Nature suggests the crime. And that is why the penchants—the desires we sense—to undertake great crimes are always more intense than those we sense for the small ones, and why the pleasure we reap from enormities is always a thousand times keener. Would she have composed a gradated schedule of the pleasure afforded by all crimes if it were not to her interest that we commit them? does she not indicate by the regularly mounting charm she has attached to progressively awful crimes that her intention is to encourage us ever farther up the slope? These unspeakable quiverings of delectation we are subject to when we prepare a crime; this wild intoxication which possesses us when we perform it; this secret joy which lingers in us long after it has been perpetrated: does all this not prove that she has so cunningly baited the deed because she yearns to have us commit it? and that, since our reward increases in proportion to the magnitude of its wickedness, 'tis because the crime of destruction, conventionally regarded as the most atrocious of all, is howbeit the very one which most contents her?[16] For whether the crime results from vengeance, or from ambition, or from lubricity, we shall, if we scrutinize ourselves clear-sightedly, see that this attractiveness I speak of is always greater or lesser depending upon the greater or lesser violence or blackness of the deed; and when the destruction of our fellow beings is the effect of the cause, murder's charm becomes limitless, because this is the necessary and very grave form of mischief which most benefits Nature."

"Oh, Noirceuil!" I cried, unable to contain myself, "it is certainly true that what we have just done has given me vast pleasure, but I'd have had ten times more had I seen her hang——"

"Come now, admit the whole truth: had you hanged her yourself."

"Christ, yes, yes! I admit it! The mere thought is making me discharge."

"And the pleasure you have felt was doubled, wasn't it, Juliette, by your knowledge of her innocence? Had she been guilty, our deed would have been in the service of the law: and we would have been cheated of all that is delicious in evil.

"Ah!" Noirceuil continued, "it cannot be overstressed: would Nature have given us passions if she had not known that these passions' results would enact her will, enforce her laws, further her aims? So well did man recognize this that he too felt moved to compose laws whose object would be to check this invincible urge which, driving him to crime, would bring about the ruination of everything; but man behaved unjustly, for his laws are repressive, taking away infinitely more than they bestow; in return for the scanty security they afford him, they deprive him, perhaps, of all that is worth having.

"But these laws, originating with mere mortals, merit no

---

[16] Beloved La Mettrie, learned Helvétius, sage and perspicacious Montesquieu! having so profoundly apprehended this truth, why did you not set it forth in so many words in your immortal writings? O century of ignorance and tyranny, what a grave disservice you have done the human understanding, and in what slavery you have maintained the world's greatest minds! Let us then speak forthrightly today, since we are at liberty to do so; and since we owe mankind the truth, let us have the courage to reveal it entire.

consideration from the philosopher; never shall they be allowed to halt or influence the gestures Nature dictates to him; the one effect they can have upon a man of intelligence is to encourage him to cover up his movements and maintain vigilance: laws? let's use them for our own purposes, as a shield, never as a brake."

"But, my friend," I remarked to Noirceuil, "if that were everybody's attitude, there'd be no shield."

"Very well," my lover replied, "in that case we shall revert to the state of uncivilization in which Nature created us: that, surely, would be no great misfortune. It will then be up to the weak man to devise a policy for avoiding collisions with the strong and for averting open warfare; he will at least have a clear view of what's to be dreaded, and shan't be any the more unhappy for that, since as things now stand he has the same struggle to wage but, in his self-defense, he is unable to employ the meager store of weapons Nature has armed him with. Institute this little regression, and every State would be far better off, it's been proven, and there would be no further necessity for laws. But we stray afield.[17]

"One of our foremost prejudices attaching to the subject under discussion is bred of the sort of tie we gratuitously suppose to exist between other men and ourselves: an illusory tie—an absurd tie whence we have confectioned this curious sort of brotherhood sacralized by religion. I should now make a few elucidating observations about this brotherhood affair, for the course of my entire experience has shown me that the fabulous notion of fraternity hinders and hobbles the passions a great deal more than one would suppose; owing to the weight it exerts upon human reason, I'd best lose no time discrediting it in your eyes.

"All living creatures are born isolated; from birth, they have no need one of the other: abstain from tampering with men, leave them in their pristine natural state, refrain from civilizing them, and each will find his own way, his food, his shelter, without his fellow beings' help. The strong will see to their livelihoods wholly

---

[17] Highly entertaining, don't you agree, this profusion of laws that man enacts every day in order to promote his happiness, although there's not a one amongst them all which, to the contrary, does not deprive him of some part of the happiness he already has. The purpose of all these laws? But do you ask? Rogues must not be denied their profits, and fools have got to be .subjugated—there, in a nutshell, you have the whole secret of our human civilization.

unaided; the weak alone may need some assistance; but Nature has given us these weak individuals to be our slaves: they are her gift to us, a sacrifice: their condition is proof thereof; the strong man may hence use the weak as he sees fit; may he not aid them in some instances? No; for if he does, he acts contrary to Nature's will. If he enjoys this inferior object, if he harnesses him into the service of his whims, if he tyrannizes him, oppresses, vexes, sports with him, wears him out, or finally destroys him, then he behaves as Nature's friend; but, I say unto you once again, if, in reverse, he aids the abject, raises the lowly to a level of parity with himself by sharing some of his power or some of his substance or placing some of his authority at the disposal of the mean, then he necessarily disrupts the natural order and perverts the natural law: whence it results that pity, far from being a virtue, becomes a real vice once it leads us to meddle with an inequality prescribed by Nature's laws and lacking which she cannot function properly; and that the ancient philosophers, who behold it as a flaw in the soul, as one of those illnesses one had speedily to cure oneself of, were not in error, since pity's effects are diametrically opposed to those produced by Nature's laws, whereof the fundamental bases are differences, discriminations, inequalities.[18] This fanciful bond of brotherhood could have been dreamt up only by some feeble individual; for it to have occurred to one of the mighty, in need of nothing, would not have been natural: to bind the weak to his will, he already had what the task required: his strength; what to him would have been the utility of this bond? 'twas invented by some puny wretch, and it is founded upon arguments quite as futile as would be this one addressed by the lamb to the wolf: *You mustn't eat me, I am four-footed too.*

"The weak, proclaiming the existence of the bond of brotherhood, were bidden by such obvious motives as to eliminate in advance any possibility that the pact established by this bond be taken seriously. Moreover, no pact ever acquires any force save through the sanction of the two contracting parties; and this pact has been proposed and decreed unilaterally;

---

[18] Aristotle, in his *Poetics,* would have it that the aim of a poet's efforts is to cure us of fear and pity, which the philosopher considers the source of all the ills which afflict man; and, one might add, they are also the source of all his vices.

178   THE MARQUIS DE SADE

what could be plainer than that the strong would never have consented and never will consent to it: what in the devil's name was that remote pygmy thinking of when he imagined this bond! What good did he suppose it would do him? When one gives something, it's to receive something in return: that's the law of Nature; and, here, in giving assistance to the weak, in stripping off some quantity of one's strength so as to clad one's inferior in it, what does the strong get from the bargain? How can one ascribe any reality to a contract when, essentially, ·one of the parties must, in the light of his own highest interests, denounce it for a hoax or a joke beforehand? For, by taking it seriously and accepting it, the strong cedes a lot and gains nothing; which is why he never once subscribed to this nonsense; it being nonsense, some sort of misbegotten notion, it deserves no respect from us. We may unhesitatingly repudiate an arrangement proposed by our inferiors, by which we would only be in a way to lose.

"The religion of that wily little sneak Jesus—feeble, sickly, persecuted, singularly desirous to outmaneuver the tyrants of the day, to bully them into acknowledging a brotherhood doctrine from whose acceptance he calculated to gain some respite—Christianity sanctioned these laughable fraternal ties; what else could have been expected? Here we see Christianity in the role of the weaker party; Christianity represents the weak and must speak and sound like them; nothing surprising in this, either. But that he who is neither weak nor Christian subject himself to such restrictions, voluntarily entangle himself in this mythical snarl of brotherly relationships which without benefiting him in the least deprive him enormously—it's unthinkable; and from these arguments we must conclude that not only has the bond of fraternity never authentically existed amongst men, but that it never could have, for it is even contrary to Nature, who could never for an instant have intended to have men equalize that which she had differentiated so energetically. We may, we should, be persuaded that this bond was, in truth, proposed by the weak, was sanctioned by them when, as it so happened, sacerdotal authority passed into their hands; but we must also be persuaded that its existence is frivolous and that we must not under any circumstances submit to it."

"Therefore, it is false that men are brothers?" I interrupted excitedly. "There is then no kind of real bond between another human being and myself? Is it then so, that the only manner in which I need act with this other individual is to wrest from him all I possibly can and cede him as little?"

"Precisely," Noirceuil replied. "For whatever you give to him is lost to you, and you gain proportionately as you take.

"I may add, indeed, that, searching into my soul for the laws of comportment which are signed there in the indelible script of Nature, I find this the most primary, the most fundamental injunction: do not love, certainly do not give aid to, these so-called brothers; instead, make them serve your passions. And that is the text I heed. According to it, if the money, if the enjoyment, if the lives of these purported brothers are instrumental to my well-being or useful to my existence, then, my dear, as quick as ever I can, I grab what I want by main force if I am the stronger, and if I am the weaker, by stealth; if for these things I want I am obliged to pay something, then I try to get them for the lowest possible price if I have no way of stealing them; for I tell you once again, this neighbor is nought to me, between him and myself there is no positive relationship whatever, and if I establish one, it's with the object of having from him, by cunning, what I cannot wring from him by violence; but if I can succeed through violence, I use no artifice, since artifices are nuisances and where they can be dispensed with I personally feel they should be.

"Oh, Juliette! study then to seal your heart against the fallacious accents of woe and indigence. If the bread that this wretch eats is wet by his tears, if a day's drudgery scarcely enables him to carry home at eventide enough to keep his exhausted family's body and soul together, if the taxes he must pay soak up the better part of his meager savings, if his naked, untaught children are driven into the depths of the forest in search of a vile aliment whose having they must dispute with wild beasts, if his own helpmeet's breast, withered from toil, dried by want, cannot furnish her suckling that initial subsistence capable of giving him size enough and strength to go tear the rest from the jaws of wolves, if, bent under the weight of the years, of ills, of griefs, he sees nothing but the doom-sped end of his career lunge his way in

great sure strides, and if in all his life he has never beheld a single
star for one instant rise pure and serene above his downcast head;
why, tush, it is a simple matter, common enough, altogether
natural, nothing in it that doesn't sit appropriately within the
order and the law of that great universal mother who governs us
all, and if you have decided that this man is unhappy, 'tis because
you have compared his lot with yours; but, at bottom, he isn't,
you're mistaken. Were he to tell you that he so considers himself,
then he too is wrong. He likewise has made an instant's comparison
between his case and yours: let him crawl away, and once he's in
the company of his peers, there's an end to his whimperings. Under
the feudal regime, treated like an animal, domesticated and beaten
like one, sold like the dirt he trudged upon and delved, was not
his plight a good deal sorrier? Instead of taking pity on his sufferings, of mitigating them and turning them ridiculously into a burden
to be borne by your own sympathies, be sensible, my dear, and view
him merely as a creature Nature has designed for your entertainment, as one she offers for whatever use you deign to put
him to; rather than wipe his tears, redouble the cause of his weep-
ings, if you like, if it amuses you: lo! here are human beings
Nature's readied for the scythe of your passions; reap a goodly
harvest, dear Juliette, Nature is bountiful; emulate the spider,
spin your webs, and mercilessly devour everything that Nature's
wise and liberal hand casts into the meshes."

"My beloved!" I cried, hugging Noirceuil to me, "how enormous is my debt to you for dissipating the miasmas of ignorance
childhood instruction and prejudice brewed in my spirit! Your
sublime lessons are unto my heart what the healing dew is to sun-
scorched vegetation. O, light of my life, I see no more, I comprehend no more save through your eyes, with your mind; but,
annihilating the fear I had of its danger, you kindle in me an
ardent desire to hurl myself into crime. Will you be my guide in
this delicious journey? Will you hold aloft the lamp of philosophy
to light the way? Or perhaps you'll abandon me—after having
led me far astray; and then, putting myself in jeopardy by having
put in action principles as stern as these you've taught me to cherish,
ringed round by the exceeding peril of these maxims, and alone,

in this fair land of roses I'll be exposed only to thorns, unshielded by your influence, undirected by your advice. I wonder. . . ."

"Juliette," said Noirceuil, "these reflections demonstrate your weakness—and betray your sensibility. My child, one must be strong and hard when one decides to be wicked.

"You will never be the victim of my passions; but neither shall I ever assure your status nor serve as your protector; one has got to learn to manage by oneself, to rely upon one's own solitary resources if one is to travel the road of your choosing; one must, all alone, discover the means for eluding the pitfalls thick-strewn the whole length of the way, one must develop keen perceptions to spy them out in advance, one must know what to do in case of miscarriage and indeed how to face the ultimate catastrophe if it cannot be averted; no matter what, Juliette, you will never be threatened by anything worse than the scaffold and, in truth, it's not so very dreadful. Once one has realized that we must all die someday, does it make any real difference whether it be on a platform or in a bed? Shall I make you a little confession, Juliette? Then I'll tell you that execution, a minute's affair, terrifies me infinitely less than dying what they are pleased to call a peaceful death accompanied by what may very well be hideous circumstances. To hang is shameful? Not in my view; and even if it were, in order of their importance, I'd rate shame last on the list of factors involved. And so, my dear, put your mind at rest and to fly depend only upon your own wings. It's safer, always."

"Ah, Noirceuil, you'll not, even for my sake, set your principles aside."

"In all of Nature there is not a single creature in whose favor I can turn my back upon them.

"However, let's proceed with the demonstration of crime's inexistence. I should like now to cite some examples in support of my thesis, that's the likeliest way to convince you. We'll cast a quick glance at how matters stand in this world and we'll see whether what is termed criminal in one area doesn't crop up as virtuous somewhere else.

"We dare not wed our wife's sister; Hudson Bay savages do so whenever they are able: they recognize no other match. Jacob married Rachel and Leah.

"We dare not fuck our own children even though there are few more delicious pleasures; in Persia, intrigues are exclusively of that variety, and 'tis the same in three-quarters of Asia. Lot lay with his two daughters and got them both with child.

"We consider the prostitution of our wives a very great indelicacy: in Tartary, in Lapland, in America it's a courtesy, it's an honor to prostitute your wife to a stranger; the Illyrians take them to assemblies of debauchery and, the while supervising the proceedings, force them to fuck whoever takes a fancy to them.

"We think it an outrage to modesty when we expose ourselves naked to the sight of others: almost all southern peoples go about thus unclad without any subtle intentions; the Priapic and Bacchic festivals of antiquity were so celebrated. Lycurgus, by a law, obliged girls to appear nude when they attended public theaters. The Tuscans, the Romans had nude women serve them at table. There is a country in India where respectable women are never seen in clothes; these are only worn by courtesans, the better to excite concupiscence. Think of that; quite the opposite, isn't it, of our conventional notions concerning modesty?

"Our generals forbid the rape of the defenders of a captured fortress; Greek commanders gave their soldiers the right as a reward for valor. After the capture of Carbines, the army of Tarentum collected all the boys, the virgins, and the young women who could be unearthed in the town, stripped and exposed them in the market place, where everybody chose what he wanted, either to fuck or to kill it.

"The Indians of Mount Caucasus live like brute beasts, they couple indiscriminately. The women of the Isle of Hornes prostitute themselves to men in broad daylight, doing so even on the steps of their god's temple.

"The Scythians and Tartars revered a man who through debauchery wasted himself into impotence while yet in his prime.

"Horace portrays the Britons, the English of today, as being most libertine with foreigners; this folk, says the poet, had no native modesty; they lived all aheap in a promiscuous community, brothers, fathers, mothers, children, anyone suited to the satisfaction of Nature's needs, and the resulting fruit belonged to whoever had been the first to lie with the mother when she had been a virgin. These people ate human flesh.[19]

"The Tahitians satisfy their desires publicly, would blush at the thought of enacting them in hiding. Before them, Europeans displayed their religious ceremonies, consisting in the celebration of that ridiculous mummery they call Mass. They in their turn asked to be allowed to display theirs: it was the rape of a little girl of ten by a grown boy of twenty-five. What a difference!

"Debauchery itself is worshiped: temples are raised to Priapus; Aphrodite is at the start beheld as the goddess of fertility and increase, later as the principle of the most depraved lusts, adoration concentrates upon her ass, and she who initially was regarded as the idol of generation soon becomes the tutelary divinity of the grossest outrages man can perpetrate against population. Man, you see, grew ever in knowledge and intelligence: he had inevitably to progress: he ended up vicious. This cult, sinking into desuetude along with paganism's eclipse, revives in India; and the *lingam,* a sort of virile member Asiatic girls wear suspended from their neck, is nothing but an article of furniture whose use is required in the temples of Priapus.

"A traveler arriving in Pegu rents a girl for the duration of his stay in the country; with her he does whatever he pleases; afterward, much enriched by her experience, she returns to her family and if anything finds a surfeit of suitors eager to marry her.

"Indecency itself can become modish: witness France, where for a long time male genitals were represented in brocade-work applied to the vest and where brightly colored codpieces were very fashionable.

"Among nearly all the peoples of the north one meets with the traditional prostitution of sisters and daughters, a custom which strikes me as altogether reasonable; he who practices it calculates to receive something in return from the man he panders to, or at least to watch him in action, and this lubricity is delicious enough

---

[19] Of all edibles probably the best for ensuring abundance and density to the spermatic fluid. Nothing more absurd than our queasiness on this subject; a little experience will make short shrift of it; once one has sampled such meats, one's palate rejects all others as insufferable. (Upon this subject, see Paw, *Recherches sur les Indiens, Egyptiens, Américains, etc.*)

to be worth going to considerable trouble to obtain. There is another, an exceedingly delicate, sentiment connected with prostitution of this type, and it is enough to induce certain men to make their wives' favors generally available, as do I; that which usually motivates our gesture is this: we derive unheard-of stimulation from covering ourselves with an especially poignant obloquy; the more one multiplies the effects of one's shame, the greater the pleasure one extracts from it. Thus it is we like to degrade, besmirch, mistreat the object that we amuse ourselves giving over to be fucked; we delight in dragging it through mud, making it wallow in filth, in fine, in doing rather as I do: carrying one's wife and daughter to the brothel, forcing them to solicit in the streets, holding them oneself during the act of prostitution."

"Excuse me, Monsieur," I broke in, "but did I understand you to say that you have a daughter?"

"I had one," Noirceuil replied.

"By the wife whom I know?"

"No, by my first wife; the one I have in the house at present is my eighth, Juliette."

"But with tastes like yours, how ever could you have become a father?"

"I have been one several times, my dear. There are no grounds here for surprise. The thing can be done, one sometimes overcomes one's repugnances when pleasures may be the reward of an honest effort."

"I believe I understand you, Monsieur."

"Like almost everything else, this is ridiculously simple. And yet I'll have first to acquire a high opinion of you before, in giving you an explanation, I disclose how little I merit one myself."

I gazed at him admiringly. "Unusual man, charming individual," I exclaimed, "my devotion to you shall only grow as you give me accumulating proof of your disdain for vulgar prejudices; the more criminal you exhibit yourself to these my avid eyes, the deeper my heart's veneration for you shall be. The irregularity of your imagination sets mine in a ferment; I aspire only to imitate you."

"Ah, by God," murmured Noirceuil, running his tongue into my mouth, "I have never beheld a creature more analogous to me;

I'd adore her if 'twere in my power to love a woman. . . . Would you imitate me, Juliette? I defy thee to do so. If what were enclosed in my heart could be opened to the light, it would so horrify the race of men there'd perhaps not be one amongst them all who'd dare come within sight of me. Impudence and crime, libertinage and foul infamy, I've carried them to the last degree; and if I know the taste of regret, 'tis, I do swear with utmost sincerity, owing to nothing but despair at having done so little, so very much less than I ought."

Noirceuil was in a state of prodigious agitation, sufficient to convince me that the avowal of his errors excited him almost as much as their very performance. I drew aside the ample robe he was wearing and, seizing his more than iron-hard member, I set to juggling it, to dandling and palpating it gently: from the scarlet orifice fuck dribbled in a steady stream.

"What a tale of crimes that prick has cost me!" he cried, "what a host of execrable things have I done in order that it might surrender its sperm a slight shade more hotly. Upon this globe's whole extent there is not a single object I'm not ready to sacrifice to its comfort: this tool is my god, let it be one unto thee, Juliette: extol it, worship it, this despotic engine, show it every reverence, it is a thing proud of its glory, insatiate, a tyrant; I'd fain make the earth bend its knee in universal homage to this prick, I'd like to see it guised in the shape of a terrific personage who would put to a death of awful torments every last living soul that thought to deny it the least of a thousand services. . . . Were I king, Juliette, were I sovereign lord of this world, supreme here, my supremest sovereign pleasure would be to walk about with killing henchmen in my train, to massacre instantly whatever displeased my very sensitive glance. . . . I'd tread the full length and breadth of my domain everywhere upon a carpet of corpses, and I'd be happy; I'd wade across an infinite scene of destruction, and to the sea of blood wherein my feet would steep I'd add my flowing seed."

Drunk also, I sink down before this wondrous libertine; incontinently, I do enthusiastic worship to the spring of so many fell deeds whereof the mere recollection incomparably aroused him who had committed them; I take that article in my mouth, for fifteen delicious minutes I suck upon it. . . .

"Stay, stay, we are too few," says Noirceuil, who was little fond of solitary pleasures. "Leave me be; that prick could be your undoing were you to pretend to the honor of fetching a discharge from it all by yourself: concentrated upon a single point, my passions are like the sun's rays a magnifying lens collects into focus: they straightway cinder the object in their path."

And, foam flecking his lips, Noirceuil's strong hands began to worry my buttocks.

That was the moment when one of Gode's captors returned with news of her entry into the prison of Bicêtre and of the still-born infant she foaled shortly afterward.

"Excellent," said Noirceuil, sending the man on his way with a tip of two *louis;* "one cannot," he confided to me in a whisper, a smile on his lips, "overpay the messenger bringing tidings of such welcome events. Two *louis*—that matches the little prank we've just treated ourselves to . . . and notice, Juliette, look here! see how my prick takes on an air of increased majesty."

And immediately summoning into an antechamber his wife and the youthful fop who'd sired the child just destroyed, Noirceuil advised him of what had come to pass, embuggering the youth as he spoke, while Madame de Noirceuil, kneeling, mouthed the Ganymede's member, and while, under instructions, the pederast kissed my buttocks; and in the midst of this, Noirceuil caught firm hold of his wife's breasts from below and gave them so fair a wrenching as to nearly tear them loose from her body; the lady's screams soon brought the fuck spitting in a torrent from his prick.

"Tell me, Juliette," he continued, ordering the young man to evacuate into his cupped palm the fuck he'd squirted into his bowels, and rudely smearing that rich paste all over the face of his wife, "tell me, is not my sperm pure? Have you ever seen such fine sperm? Am I wrong in having you worship the god whose substance is so magnificent? Never did he whom fools designate prime mover to the world possess a more active or refined, a nobler; this be very godsfuck—but have them get out of here," he cried, "away with them all. I regret having had to interrupt our conversation.

"We today punish libertinage," my master resumed when we were alone again; "and from Plutarch we learn that the Samnites daily and in conformance with legal prescriptions betook themselves to a place known as the Gardens, and that in a promiscuous confusion they there comported themselves in a manner almost too lascivious to be imagined. In that blissful locality, the historian goes on to say, the heat of pleasure melted distinctions of sex and blood ties altogether away: one became husband to the wife of one's friend; the daughter communicated intimately with her mother; and yet more often one saw the son play the whore to his sire alongside the brother busily embuggering his sister.

"The first fruits of a young girl are highly prized by us. The inhabitants of the Philippines make thereof no case at all. In those islands there are public officers who are very handsomely paid to devirginate girls on the eve of their nuptials.

"Adultery was publicly authorized in Sparta.

"Our opinion of women who take to whoring is low; on the other hand, the esteem in which a Lydian female was held corresponded to the number of her lovers. Their earnings from prostitution made up their dower, they had no other.

"The ladies of Cyprus, in quest of riches, would go down to the ports and publicly lie for pay with whatever foreigner disembarked upon that island.

"Moral depravation is vital to a State; the Romans were aware of this, and throughout the Republic consequently set up brothels stocked with boys and girls and built theaters where girls danced naked.

"Babylonian women were prostituted once a year in the Temple of Venus; Armenian women were obliged to deliver themselves in virginal condition to the priests of Tanais who, firstly, bum-fucked them and only accorded them the favor of a frontal deflowering provided they had with seeming courage withstood the inaugural assaults: an imprudent gesture, a tear, a twitch, a sob or a scream was enough, they were deprived of the honor of the subsequent ministrations and hence of the possibility of marrying.

"The Canarese of Goa expose their daughters to a very different ordeal: they prostitute them to an idol equipped with a member of iron, and its bulk is huge; they forcefully hurl, or impale, the girls upon this dreadful dildo which has first been heated to a suitable temperature: it is thus conventionally and very significantly enlarged that the poor child sets out in search of a husband, who'll not have her unless she's been prepared through this ceremony.

"The Caïmites, you will recall, were a second-century heretical sect; they held that one attains paradise only through incontinence. Every infamous act, it was their belief, had a tutelary angel, and, worshiping these angels one by one, they would give themselves over to incredible debaucheries.

"Owen, that ancient English king, by law had it established in his realm that no girl could wed unless she had been devirginated by him. In the whole of Scotland and in some districts of France the great barons enjoyed this privilege.

"Women no less than men arrive at cruelty by way of libertinage; think of the three hundred wives of the Incan Atabaliba, who, of their own accord and as one, prostituted themselves in Peru to the Spanish and aided them in the massacre of their own husbands.

"Sodomy is general everywhere in the world; there is not a single tribe, race, or nation unacquainted with its practice; in all history not one great man who was not addicted to it. Sapphism is equally universal. This passion, like the former one, is natural because in Nature; at the earliest age, at the period of greatest candor and innocence, before she has come under alien influence, it takes shape and deep root in the little girl's heart; thus, Lesbian behavior and proclivities, implanted by Nature, bear her ratifying seal of lawfulness.

"And bestiality used to be popular everywhere. Xenophon tells us that during the retreat of the Ten Thousand the Greeks used goats exclusively. This custom is very widespread in Italy today; the buck surpasses the female of this species: its narrower anal canal is warmer; and this animal, very lusty by nature, needs no prompting, it will begin to agitate itself as soon as it notices that one is about to discharge: I know whereof I speak, Juliette, for it is from experience.

"The turkey is delicious, but you must cut its throat at the critical instant; time the operation carefully, and the constriction of the bird's bowels will cause you a fairly overwhelming pleasure.[20]

"The Sybarites embuggered dogs; Egyptian women gave themselves to crocodiles; American women appreciate being fucked by monkeys. By late report statues have also been put to use: everyone has heard of the page boy of Louis XV who was found discharging on the fair-assed Aphrodite. And there was a Greek who, arriving at Delphi to consult the Oracle, found in the Temple two marble genii and during the night rendered his libidinous homage to that one which he considered the lovelier. At dawn, spent, he lay a crown of laurel upon the effigy, in thanks for the pleasures he had received.

"Not only do the Siamese consider suicide justifiable, they even believe that self-slaughter is a beneficial sacrifice to the soul and that, by this means, the way will be opened to happiness in the next world.

"In Pegu, when a woman has given birth, she is turned for five days over a charcoal fire; it's to purify her.

"The Caribs purchase infants while they are yet in the mother's womb; with a certain dye they mark the child's belly straightway it is born, depucelate it later, at the age of seven or eight, and not infrequently slay it after having made this use of it.

"In the island of Nicaragua a father is permitted to sell his children for purposes of immolation. When this folk consecrate their grain, they sprinkle fuck upon it and dance around this twofold product of Nature.

"To every prisoner in Brazil destined to be executed, a woman is given; he takes his pleasure with her, and the same woman, whom he sometimes impregnates, assists in hacking him to pieces and participates at the meal that is made of his flesh.

"Before they came under the suzerainty of the Incas, the ancient Peruvians—that is to say, the earliest Scythian settlers who were the first inhabitants of America—had the custom of sacrificing their offspring to the gods.

"The people who dwell by the banks of the Rio Real for the

---

[20] Several Parisian brothels feature avisodomy; the girl holds the bird's neck locked between her thighs, you have her ass straight ahead of you for prospect, and she cuts the bird's throat the same moment you discharge. Of this fantasy being enacted we may perhaps soon have an example.

circumcision of females (a ceremony common to several nations) substitute a rather curious practice: when girls become nubile, sticks covered with large ants are thrust into their womb; the insects sting and bite horribly; the sticks are carefully replaced in order to protract the torture which never lasts less than three months and is apt to go on for a good while longer.

"Saint Jerome reports that in the course of his travels amongst the Gauls he saw the Scots with great relish consume the buttocks of young shepherds and the breasts of young maids. Personally, I'd have much more confidence in the first of these dainties than in the second and, along with every anthropophagic people, I believe that woman-flesh, like that of all female animals, is necessarily much inferior to what may be cut from males.

"The Mingrelians and the Georgians are renowned for being the most beautiful races on earth and simultaneously for being the most addicted to every sort of luxury and crime; 'tis quite as if Nature had contrived thus to advise us that, far from being displeased by this misbehavior, she wished to lavish all her gifts upon those with whom it was most positively chronic. Amongst these folk abandoned to joy, incest, rape, child-murder, prostitution, adultery, assassination, thievery, sodomy, sapphism, bestiality, arson, poisoning, rape, parricide—these and a quantity of others of the same kind are virtuous prowesses and are proper to boast of. Do they meet in assemblies, 'tis for nought save to chat about the enormity of their base achievements: reminiscences of past and designs for future undertakings compose the matter of their favorite conversations; and it is thus they arouse one another to the accomplishment of further exploits.

"There are tribesmen in northern Tartary who erect for themselves a new god every day: this god must be the object first come across by the individual upon awakening in the morning. If perchance it be a mard, that mard becomes the idol for the day; and put case it be a mard we're to reverence: is not a bit of shit worth quite as much as the comical flour-paste god adored by the Catholics? The Tartar divinity is excrement already, the Catholic will be in a few hours; truly, I find no ready distinction to be made between the two.

"In the province of Matomba, 'tis within a noisome and very

dark hut the children of both sexes are enclosed when they have reached the age of twelve; and there, by way of initiation, they suffer all the ill-treatment the priests are pleased to mete out to them, nor when they emerge from the hut may the children either reveal what has been done to them nor complain thereof.

"When a girl marries in Ceylon, it is her brothers who depucelate her; the husband hasn't the right to do so.

"We regard pity as a sentiment sure to guide us to good deeds; with greater reason, it is considered a fault in Kamchatka: amongst the people of that peninsula it would be vicious to rescue someone from a peril into which fate has led him. If these clear-minded individuals see a man drowning, they pass calmly on about their business without stopping; no one would dream of rescuing him.

"To forgive one's enemies, that's a virtue among Christian imbeciles; in Brazil, it is thought a splendid act to kill and eat them.

"In Guiana, when her menstruating first begins, a young girl is exposed naked to flies to feast upon; she often perishes during the operation. The enchanted spectators will then spend the whole day in merrymaking.

"In Brazil once again, on the eve of a young woman's wedding they inflict a great number of cuts and gashes upon her buttocks, the object being to waken some measure of revulsion in a husband who, thanks to a fiery temperament and the tropical climate, is only too apt to incline to an antiphysical attack.[21]

"These few examples I have cited suffice to indicate what in reality are the virtues whereof our European laws and religions make such frantic to-do; what is that loathsome bond of brotherhood our vile Christianity is forever sniveling about. For your own self you may determine whether or not it exists in the heart of man; would such a host of execrations be the general rule if the virtue they contradict really did exist?

"I say to you over and over again: humane sentiments are baseless, mad, and improper; they are incredibly feeble; never do they withstand the gainsaying passions, never do they resist bare necessity: go examine a besieged city where within the walls

---

[21] There are any number of curiously organized people whom such sights could very much arouse indeed and who, seeing a well-worn ass, might merely regret not having been partly responsible for its condition.

hungry humans devour each other. Humanity? A sentimentality; it has nothing whatsoever to do with Nature. Humanity? The child of dread, debility, and unwholesome prejudice. Can one ignore the fact that 'tis Nature which gives us both our passions and our needs? or that, in seeking fulfillment, these passions and needs proceed with total disregard for humane virtues? These humane virtues are thus foreign to Nature; they are thus no more than the blatant result of the egoism that has brought us to wishing to be at peace with our fellows in order to exploit them for our own pleasure. But he who has no fear of reprisals must be at great pains to subordinate himself to a duty which only those who tremble can possibly respect. Ah no, Juliette, no, there is no such thing as genuine pity, there is no pity save that wherefrom we calculate to profit. If at the moment we are in the throes of commiseration we pause and think and study ourselves deeply, then from the inward regions of our heart we'll detect a hidden voice cry: *Thou dost shed tears to behold the sore plight of thine unhappy neighbor; thy tears bear witness to thine own wretchedness, or to thy dread of being more miserable still than him for whom thou thinkest to weep.* Well, what voice is this, if not that of fear? whence is this fear born, if not of egoism?

"So let us then thoroughly destroy this pusillanimous sentiment where we find it in ourselves; it must always be dolorous, since it cannot arise save through a comparison that plunges us back into woe.

"Labor at the task; and when, beloved child, thy mind shall have perfectly apprehended the nullity, nay, the rank criminality that would subsist in acknowledging the existence of a bond linking thine own self up in brotherhood with others, then proudly declare with the philosopher:

" 'Eh, to satisfy myself, why should I hesitate when the act I meditate, whatever the ill it cause my fellow creature, may procure me the most palpable pleasure? For, tentatively supposing that by performing whatever may be this act I do this fellow a wrong, by not performing it I must ineluctably do a wrong unto myself. In despoiling my neighbor of his wife, of his inheritance, of his child, I may, as I have just said, be committing an injustice toward him; but in depriving myself of these things whence I derive extremest delight, I commit one toward myself: well, between these two inevitable injustices, shall I be so great an enemy of mine own self as not to prefer that from which I can extract a few agreeable little sensations? If I do not act thus, 'twill be out of compassion. But if surrender to such a sentiment may have the dire consequence of causing me to renounce joys I covet so, I must summon up all my forces and cure myself of this painful, this disastrous sentiment, I must neglect nothing in order to prevent it, in future, from obtaining any access to my soul. Once I have succeeded (and of success I am certain if I gradually accustom myself to the sight of the sufferings of others), I'll never yield to any but the charm of satisfying myself; that charm will have no rivals, no other will beckon to me, I'll have no further fear of remorse, for remorse cannot be but the aftermath of compassion, and this compassion I shall have extinguished in myself; I'll therefore follow my bent, all unafraid honor my penchants; I'll value my own welfare, or my own pleasure, above woes which no longer touch me; and I'll sense that to let slip a real good from my grasp, because the having thereof would mean putting some other individual in an unhappy situation (a situation whose effects cannot make themselves felt upon me anymore), would be sheer ineptness, since it would be to love this stranger more dearly than I love myself, and that would be to violate every last law of Nature and every last element of good common sense.'

"Nor ought you to view familial ties as more sacred than these others, they are all equally fictitious. It is not true that you owe anything to the being out of whom you emerged; still less true that you are obliged to have any feeling whatever for a being that were to emerge from you; absurd to imagine that one is beholden to one's brothers, sisters, nephews, nieces. Upon what rational basis can consanguinity establish duties; for what, for whom do we toil in the act of procreation? For ourselves; for anyone else? Certainly not. What can be our debt to a father who, amusing himself, incidentally created us? can we owe some debt to a son because once upon a time for the sake of diversion we spattered a little fuck into some womb or other? to a brother or a sister because the same womb was exercised upon more than one occasion? To the devil with the lot of these ties; needless to discriminate, they're none of them serious."

"Oh, Noirceuil!" I cried, "how often have you provided proof of it. . . . And still you are loath to tell me—"

"Juliette," that amiable personage replied, "such avowals can be fitting reward for your behavior. I shall open my heart to you— in due time: when I feel you are truly worthy to hear the secrets I have to disclose. But before then you shall have to undergo several tests."

And his manservant having come to announce that the Minister, an intimate friend of Noirceuil, was waiting in the drawing room, we separated.

I lost no time making a most advantageous investment of the sixty thousand francs I had stolen from Mondor. However sure I was that Noirceuil would have approved of the theft, I could not have mentioned it to him without also divulging my infidelity and, had he learned of that, my lover would surely have worried lest his own property become subject to my depredations; prudence counseled me to hold my tongue, and I turned all my thoughts to increasing, by like expedients, the sum of my revenues. The occasion soon presented itself in the form of another party organized by Madame Duvergier.

The present enterprise was a mission to the home of an individual whose mania, as cruel as it was voluptuous, consisted in *girl-whipping*. We were four; at a café near the Porte Saint-Antoine I was joined by three charming creatures; a carriage was there waiting for us, and we were soon in Saint-Maur, at the delightful house of Duc Dennemar. My companions were of rare beauty, youthful and as fresh as they were sweet to behold: the eldest was under eighteen, Minette was her name; she pleased me so wonderfully well I could not resist caressing her passionately; another was sixteen years old, the last fourteen. Very exacting in the choice of her victims, from the woman who conducted us to Saint-Maur I learned that I was the only courtesan of the quartet; my youth, my looks had persuaded the Duc to suspend self-imposed rules which forbade him commerce with worldly women. The other three were seamstresses who had absolutely no experience in the work we were about to perform; they were decent girls, properly brought up, had been seduced only by the large sums the Duc offered, and by the assurance that, restricting himself to fustigation, he'd not impair their virginity : each of us was to receive fifty *louis;* you shall decide whether or not we earned our pay.

We were ushered into a magnificent apartment; our guide bade us undress and await the orders it would please his Lordship to signify to us.

That was my opportunity to examine at leisure my three young colleagues' naïve graces, their delicate and gentle charms. What supple, willowy figures, what faultless skins, breasts that made one's mouth water, thighs appetizing beyond words; for pink plumpness, for sweetness, their charming behinds were beyond comparison; I devoured all three and especially Minette with the most tender kisses, which they reciprocated so innocently, so movingly that I discharged in their arms. For the better part of an hour, awaiting the time when we'd have his Grace's desires to cope with, we dallied there, frolickingly, and impetuously too, satisfying our own; and then at last a tall lackey, almost naked, came with instructions that we all four make ourselves ready, but that the eldest would be first. This placed me third on the list; when my turn came, I entered the pleasure sanctuary of this contemporary Sardanapalus; and the experience I am going to relate is in no particular different from that which befell each of the other three girls.

The cabinet in which the Duc received me was circular and everywhere paneled with mirrors; in the center was a column of porphyry, rising to a height of some ten feet, and before it was a dais. I was told to mount upon it; the valet we'd seen before and who served his master's pleasure-ceremonies, attached my feet to bronze rings fastened to the block I was standing on, then he raised my arms, secured them by cords, drew them high above my head. It was only then the Duc approached; hitherto he had been reclining on a couch, quietly massaging his prick. Totally nude from waist down, a simple vest of brown satin covered his torso; his arms were bare to the shoulder; under his left arm he had a bundle of withes, thin and flexible, held together by a black ribbon. Of some forty years, the Duc had an exceedingly somber and harsh physiognomy, and I judged that his moral character was not much less severe than his outward appearance.

"Lubin," said he to his valet, "this one looks better than the others. A rounder ass, finer skin. A more interesting face. 'Tis a pity. She'll but suffer the more."

So saying, the villain pokes his muzzle between my buttocks, first snuffles, then kisses, finally bites. I emit a shriek.

"Goodness! She's not insensitive. Too bad. We've scarce begun."

Thereupon I feel his talon-like fingernails dig deep into my buttocks, he rakes, he hauls, he tears my skin in several places. More screams from me only animate this scoundrel who next inserts his fingers into my vagina; they come out bringing with them the skin he has scraped from the walls of that delicate part.

"*Lubin,*" he then murmured to his valet, exhibiting his bloodied fingers, "*my dear Lubin, I triumph. Cunt-skin.*"

And he deposited it upon the head of Lubin's prick, which therewith sprang up very stiff. It was at that point he opened a small cabinet the mirrors concealed; he drew out a long garland of green foliage, I'd no idea what it was nor of what kind of leaves it was composed. Alas! he came near me and I saw at once that these were thorns. Seconded by the cruel agent of his pleasures, he twined them thrice or more times round my body and ended by fastening them in a very picturesque but also very afflicting manner, for they lacerated the whole of my body and especially my breasts, against which he pressed them with the most ferocious affectations; my buttocks, however, were spared this accursed fire, for they were reserved for other use: the full expanse of the flesh his lashes were to belabor lay completely exposed to that libertine's mercies.

"We are about to begin," said Dennemar when at last the arrangements were complete; "I earnestly request you to be patient, in as much as these proceedings may last a certain while."

The terrible storm about to break over my ass is heralded by ten relatively mild strokes.

These delivered, he lets out a shout: "Now, by Jesus! let's see what we can do."

Bringing both my buttocks under fire with a redoubtable arm, he applied two hundred cuts, never once pausing for breath. During the operation, his valet, kneeling before him, sought by sucking to extract the venom that rendered this beast so extraordinarily vicious; and all the while he went on plying his withes, the Duc bawled at the top of his lungs:

"*Ah! the buggeress . . . the bitch, the slut, the whore. . . . By the guts of Almighty God, I have no great fondness for women; if God made them, why can't I exterminate them, whip them to shreds and tatters? Bleeding, is she? Well, at last. . . . By bloody fucking God, 'tis good, she bleeds. . . . Suck, Lubin, suck, my lad, 'tis very good, I see blood and I am happy.*"

And pressing his open mouth to my behind, he lapped up what he was so thrilled to see flow; then, continuing:

"But, as you see, Lubin, I'm not stiff, and I've got to whip until I am, and once I'm stiff, to go on whipping till I discharge; well, that's the program and our whore's young. She'll endure."

The gruesome ceremony starts off again; but with certain modifications: Lubin has ceased sucking his master; armed with a bull's pizzle, he attacks the Duc who, while continuing to have at me, receives a hundred blows for every one he delivers. I am covered with blood, it streams down my thighs, I see it spreading in a crimson pool at my feet, staining the dais; punctured by the tight-wound thorns, slashed by the withes, I no longer know in what part of my body the pain is worst; and then it is that my persecutor, weary of torturing me and, all asweat with lust, subsiding upon the couch, finally orders me to be unbound. Swaying, only half-conscious, I totter toward him.

"Frig me," says he, kissing the traces of his savagery, "or, no, rather than that, frig Lubin, I prefer seeing him discharge even to discharging myself. And, what's more, pretty as you are, I doubt whether you'd succeed."

Lubin lays hands on me straight off. I am still decked in that terrible garland; the barbarian deliberately presses it against my skin while I pollute him; his position was such that, when he ceded to my wrist's supple encouragements, his fuck would splash upon the face of his master who, steadily continuing to drive the splines into my flesh, to pinch my behind, was quietly frigging himself alone; the effect occurs: the valet discharges, the Duc's features are drenched in sperm, but his own remains sealed in his balls, held in reserve for a more lubricious scene still: I'll give you its details.

"Get out of here," he told me the moment Lubin had performed, "I've got to put your youngest companion to work before I call you back." The door opened, in the adjoining room I discovered the two others who'd gone before me: but, great heavens! what a state they were in! It outdid mine; the sight of their bodies —so pretty, so fair, so delicious—was now enough to inspire horror; the poor creatures were weeping, moaning at having consented to such a party; and I, prouder, of sterner stuff and more vindictive, I thought of nothing but material revenge. A door stands ajar, I peer through it into the Duc's bedchamber, I stealthily enter. My glance falls at once upon three objects: a fat purse bulging with gold, a superb diamond, and a very fine timepiece. Hastily, I open the window; I notice, below and opposite, a little outbuilding forming an angle with the wall and close by the gate we entered when we came. Quick as a flash, I strip off one of my stockings, wrap the three objects in it, drop the bundle into the bush growing in the corner I've just mentioned; the bundle sinks down into the leaves, it's out of sight. I return to my companions. The very next moment Lubin came in to fetch us: to consummate his sacrifice, the high priest needed all four victims at once. The youngest had already passed under the lash, and her ass seemed to have been treated no less severely than ours had been; she was bleeding from head to toe; the dais had been removed. Lubin directed the four of us to lie down on the floor in the middle of the chamber; so skillfully did he adjust us that little apart from our eight buttocks remained visible, I leave you to imagine the picture they presented. The Duc approaches this group; with his left hand Lubin caresses his Lord's prick, with his right he drips boiling oil upon our asses; fortunately, the crisis shortly supervenes.

"*Burn them, sear them, scorch them, fry them!*" cried his Grace as he ejaculated his fuck and blended it with the fiery liquid roasting our mutilated rumps, "*burn these fucking whores, I'm discharging!*"

From this ordeal we arose in a condition which could be better described by the surgeon who was ten days laboring to efface the insignia left by this abominable scene; and he had a much easier time of it with me, upon whose behind, by good chance, only two or three drops of that boiling oil had fallen, than with the youngest of the quartet, whom our tormentors, for some probably evil motive, had singled out to be treated to a veritable bath.

Despite my hurts, and they were not inconsiderable, I kept my wits about me as we were leaving and, seizing a favorable moment, slipped over to the bush, plucked out my treasure, tucked it under my skirts, and thus recompensed for what I had suffered, was able to reckon the outing a success. Confronting Duvergier, I gave her a sharp scolding for having exposed me to such an insulting experience; what right had she to do so, I demanded, when knowing full well that I was no longer interested in being sacrificed to her greed. I went home, installed myself in my bedroom and had Noirceuil notified that I was unwell and would like to keep to my bed undisturbed for a few days. Not one whit in love with me—or with anyone else—still less given to wasting his time comforting the infirm or the languishing, giving evidence of a superb and doctrinal unconcern, Noirceuil never once presented himself at my bedside; his wife, milder of temper and more politic, visited me twice but abstained from shedding tears on my account; by the tenth day I was so well mended that I looked to be, if anything, in better condition than before. I then bent my gaze upon my catch: the purse contained three hundred *louis,* the diamond was worth fifty thousand francs, the watch a thousand crowns. As I had the other sum, I invested this one too; combined, they fetched nearly twelve thousand pounds a year; and it seemed to me that, thus endowed, it was high time I set to work for myself instead of continuing to be the toy of the avarice of others.

Thus did a year go by; during it I made my own arrangements and from what a number of adventures earned me pocketed the entirety. But, as chance so had it, none of these parties provided me an opportunity to exercise my thieving abilities; for the rest, I remained ever the pupil to Noirceuil, ever the butt of his lewd sports, ever the hated enemy of his wife.

Although our relationship was characterized by indifference, Noirceuil, who, without loving me, had a wonderful fondness for my mind and conversation, continued to pay me a very handsome allowance; all my needs were supplied, and in addition I had twenty-four thousand francs a year for my pleasures; join to that the twelve thousand *livres* annuity I had bought for myself, and you'll agree I was not badly off. Caring rather little for men, it was with two charming women I satisfied my desires; they had two female friends who now and again were of the company, and we'd then execute every imaginable species of extravagance.

One day, a friend of the woman I was most attracted to solicited my sympathy in behalf of a kinsman who had run into some major difficulties; I was told that I had merely to say a word to my lover, whose influence with the Minister would be enough to save the situation at once; if I wished, the young man would be very willing to come and recite the whole story to me. Moved, despite myself, by the desire to make someone happy—a fatal desire wherefor the hand of Nature, who had not created me to be virtuous, was to see to my speedy chastening—I accept; the young man appears. My stars! what is my surprise to behold Lubin. I make an effort to conceal my emotion. Lubin assures me that he has left the Duc's employ, he spins out a wild and utterly confused yarn; I promise to do what I can for him; the traitor walks out, very satisfied, says he, to have found me again, for he'd been hunting a year after me. For several days I heard nothing; I fretted over the unpleasant consequences this encounter might well have, I even felt a growing resentment against the friend of my boudoir companion who had lured me into this trap, although I had no way of knowing whether or not she had done so intentionally. Such were my preoccupations when one evening, as I emerged from the Comédie Italienne, six men halted my carriage, leveled pistols at the servants accompanying me, instantly forced me to get out, then pushed me into a waiting fiacre, shouting to the driver, by way of instruction: "*To the Hôpital!*"

"My God!" I said to myself, "I am lost."

Gathering courage at once, however, I turned to my captors:

"Sirs," I demanded, "have you not made a mistake?"

"I beg your pardon, Mademoiselle, we may perhaps be making a mistake," replied one of those knaves whom I soon recognized as Lubin himself, "yes, we are in all likelihood gravely mistaken, for 'tis to the scaffold we ought to conduct you; but if, until final inquiries have been made, in sending you no farther than the Hôpital, the police, out of consideration for Monsieur de Noirceuil, are reluctant to give you what you deserve immediately, we nonetheless trust the delay will be brief."

"Why, very well," said I in a bold tone, "we'll see. But take care, my young blade, take care above all lest they who, for the moment fancying themselves in the stronger position, dare attack me so imprudently now do not come soon to regret their insolence."

I am cast into a foul little dungeon where for thirty-six hours I remain absolutely alone, hearing nothing but the coming and going of my jailers.

You might perhaps be amused, dear friends, to know what my frame of mind was during this incarceration. I shall be frank with you: the following description is, I believe, exact.

As in prosperity, calm in adversity; dismayed, no, coldly furious to discover myself a dupe for having given virtue's case a single instant of heed; resolved—profoundly determined—never again to permit it the faintest entry into my heart; some amount of chagrin, perhaps, to see my fortunes temporarily ebb; but not a grain of regret, no remorse at all, not the shadow of a resolution to turn over a new leaf if I were ever to be restored to society; not the tiniest intention to compose my differences with religion if I were to have to die. Such was I inwardly; what I say is true. Still in all, I was not absolutely free of anxiety—but in bygone days, when I was well-behaved, had I been any freer? Anxiety! ah, 'tis an old story. I prefer not to be pure and to put up with these familiar and tedious worries; I prefer having surrendered myself to vice than to discover myself blessed by a cowlike tranquillity, simple and stupid and full of an innocence I detest. O crime! yea, thy very stinging vipers are joys unto me: their penetrating fangs inject the venom that creates the divinest frenzy wherewith thou consumest thy faithful; all these quakings and fevers are pleasures; souls like ours have got to be subjected to shocks, affected; they cannot possibly be by virtue, whereof they have a loathing that surpasses what words can convey; and so we who wish to live, and who must be moved powerfully, we thirst after the maddening drink. . . . O divine excesses! lacking which, life there is none! Yes, yes, let me be evil; let new possibilities for wicked deeds be offered me, and they'll see how avidly I fly to commit them!

Such were my thoughts; you were curious to know them, I sketch them for you; and who is fitter to hear these confessions than you, my dearest friends?

"Oh, Noirceuil!" I cried upon recognizing my lover, "what god led you here to find me? And, after all the grievous things I have done, how could I still be of interest to you?"

He gazed at me. "Juliette," said he a little later when we had been left in privacy, "I have nothing to reproach you for: the manner in which we have been living together eliminates the disagreeable circumstances that make reproaches possible. You were free. Love had no share in our arrangements. The single question was of confidence. Whatsoever might have been the similarity between my attitudes and yours, you judged it expedient or necessary to refuse me that confidence. That's all there was to it, nothing could be more natural, more acceptable. But what is neither natural nor acceptable is that you be punished for a bagatelle like this one they have arrested you for. My child, I admire your intellect, and you know it, you've known it a long time, and so long as the schemes it invents sort well with mine I shall always consent to them, better still, actively cooperate in their realization. Do not for one instant suppose that it is either from sentiment or from pity I am having you released from behind bars; you know me well enough to be persuaded that I could not be moved by either the one or the other of these two weaknesses. In this I have acted solely through selfishness, and I swear to you that if my prick were to get one ace stiffer from seeing you hang than from delivering you, by bleeding Christ, I'd not hesitate a second. But your company pleases me, I'd be deprived of it if they hanged you; you've done enough to deserve the rope, by the way—they were ready to use it on you; and I respect you precisely for that reason, you are entitled to my respect, it would be all the greater had you merited the wheel. . . . Come along with me, you're free. No demonstrations, please, above all no expression of gratitude, I abhor it."

And remarking that, overcome, I was in spite of myself about to express thanks, Noirceuil backed off a pace and addressed these words to me:

"Since you will persist, Juliette," said he, his eyes flashing, "you'll not leave this place until I have proved to you the utter absurdity of the feelings to which, in defiance of your intelligence, your heart's impoverishment seems to be causing you to succumb."

Then, having me sit down, and seating himself in a chair facing me, he entered into the matter:

"My dear girl, you also know that I am loath to let pass an opportunity to shape your heart or to enlighten your mind; therefore allow me to teach you what gratitude is.

"Gratitude, Juliette, is the word by which they denominate the sentiment felt and expressed in return for a boon whereof one has been the beneficiary; now, I must inquire into the motives of him who bestows a boon. Is he acting in his own behalf, or in ours? If in his, then you'll concede that we owe him nothing; if in ours, the ascendancy he thereby obtains over us, far from exciting gratitude, will certainly only arouse our jealousy, our rage: for this purportedly good deed has in actuality simply wounded our pride. But what is his ulterior design in putting us in his debt? Why, the dog's behavior is transparent. He who obligates others, he who draws a hundred *louis* from his pocket to hand them to a man in distress, has, appearances aside, in no wise acted in the name of the needy wretch's welfare; let him peer into the depths of his heart, he'll discover he has done nothing but flatter his vanity, he has labored for no one's benefit but his own, whether it be that from giving the money to the beggar, he derives a mental pleasure which outstrips the pleasure he'd receive from keeping it for himself, whether he imagines that this act, become notorious, will win him a reputation; but no matter what the case, I see nothing but sheer grubby self-seeking and egoism here. Tell me, if you will, what I owe a person who does nothing save in his own interest? Well, rack your brains, finally endeavor to succeed in proving to me that he was thinking exclusively of the man he obligates by acting in the manner he has, that no one else knows anything of his deed, that report of it will never leak out, that he cannot have derived any pleasure from parting with that hundred *louis* since, to the contrary, the gift inconvenienced him, yes, acutely discomforted him, that, in a word, his deed is so damnably disinterested that not a grain of selfishness can be located anywhere in it or behind it; tell me all that and in reply I'll tell you, firstly, that it's impossible and that, closely analyzing this benefactor's gesture, we'll inevitably and invariably strike upon some fugitive, some hidden delight somewhere which will diminish the value of the deed and qualify its purity; but, even supposing this disinterestedness impeccable, you never need lie under the curse of gratitude, for by this deed, or trick, maneuvering himself into a position of superiority and you into one of inferiority, this man, in the best of cases, inflicts hurt upon your pride and his act mortifies something in you which, when offended, obliges you not to be thankful, but never to forget or forgive this that is unpardonable injury. From now on, this man, regardless of what he has done for you, acquires no right save, if you be just, to your undying enmity; you will profit from his service—by all means—but you will detest him who renders it; his existence will weigh burdensomely upon you, you will ever flush at the sight of him. If you learn news of his death, you'll inwardly mark the date as a jubilee, you'll feel as though delivered from a curse, from a bondage, and the assurance of being rid of a person before whose eyes you cannot appear without sensing a kind of shame will necessarily become like a promise of joy—indeed, if your soul is truly independent and proud, you'll perhaps go farther, perhaps you'll take certain measures . . . perhaps you'll feel obliged out of duty to yourself. . . . Why yes, you may well, you certainly shall, go to the point of destroying the being whose existence plagues you; what other alternative have you? by all means yes, you'll extinguish the life of this man as you would liquidate an eternally fatiguing burden; the service rendered you, instead of having provoked friendly sentiments for this benefactor, will, don't you see, have produced the most implacable hatred. Consider well what I say, Juliette, and judge for yourself how incredibly ridiculous, and dangerous, it must always be to do good unto your fellow men. In the light of my analysis of gratitude, observe, my dear, how precious little I want yours, and think how eager I must be not to find myself in the grave position of having rendered you any service at all. I repeat it once again: in liberating you from this prison I do nothing for your sake, it is in nobody's interest but mine own that I act; believe that, absolutely; now let's be off."

We betook ourselves to the office of the clerk; Noirceuil spoke:

"Your Honor," said he, addressing one of the magistrates there, "this young lady, recovering her freedom, does not intend to conceal the name of the culprit who committed the theft of which she has been erroneously accused; my friend has just assured me that the individual you seek is one of the three girls who were there with her at the residence in Saint-Maur of Duc Dennemar. Speak, Juliette, do you recollect the girl's name?"

"I do indeed, Monsieur," I answered, instantly perceiving what the perfidious Noirceuil was about. "She was the prettiest of the three, her age must be eighteen or nineteen, and she is called Minette."

"That is all we want to know, Mademoiselle," said the man of the law; "will you seal your deposition under oath?"

"I shall, your Honor, of course," I replied, raising my right hand toward the crucifix: "I do solemnly swear," I intoned in a loud and clear voice, "and before God do hereby take sacred oath, that she who goes by the name of Minette is guilty and alone responsible for the theft committed in the house of Monsieur le Duc de Dennemar."

We left and promptly settled ourselves in Noirceuil's coach.

"Well, my dove, without me you'd never have been able to play that nasty little trick. And yet, my role in the thing was modest: indeed, I merely set the stage; I felt certain, and I was right, that there was no need to prepare you for what was to come. You carried it off faultlessly. Kiss me, my angel. . . . I love to suck this lying tongue. Ah, you behaved like a goddess. Minette will be hanged; and, when one is guilty, 'tis delicious not only to wriggle out of a scrape but to have an innocent person put to death in one's stead."

"Oh, Noirceuil," I cried, "I do love you so! verily, of all the men in this world, only you were a fit companion for me; I failed you, and you shall make me regret it."

"Come, Juliette, have no fear," Noirceuil replied; "you have committed a crime, do me the favor of feeling no guilt therefor; it is a virtuous act I expect you to repent. You had no cause to do this thing behind my back," continued my lover as we drove toward his mansion. "I have no objection if you wish to do a little whoring, provided you are motivated by greed or lust; whatsoever has its origin in such vices is totally respectable, according to my view. But you ought to be cautious in your dealings with Duvergier's clientele:

she trafficks with and procures for none but libertines whose cruel passions could easily bring you to your downfall. Had you specified your tastes to me, I myself could have arranged exceedingly profitable encounters wherein the dangers would have been relatively slender and you would have been able to steal your fingers to the bone. For theft is an everyday affair, of all the whims to be found in man not one is more natural; I myself long had the habit; and I only rid myself of it by adopting others which are far worse. For petty vices there is no better cure than major crimes; the more one diddles virtue, the more one becomes accustomed to outraging it; and in the end, nothing short of enormity can wake the slightest sensation in us. Really, Juliette, you've missed acquiring whole fortunes at a stroke; unaware of your caprices, in the past year I've refused you to at least five or six friends who were burning to have a fair shot at you and with whom you'd have been quits after having simply bared your ass. Anyhow," Noirceuil went on, "the source of all this trouble is that deplorable Lubin who, suspected by his employer, swore to make the most thorough investigation. But, don't fret, my beloved, you're avenged: Lubin entered Bicêtre yesterday, he'll stay there the rest of his life. You must know that it is to the excellent Saint-Fond, Minister and my great friend, you owe your deliverance and the suitable conclusion of the affair. The case against you was made up, watertight; they were going to have you in the dock tomorrow; twenty-two witnesses had been assembled to testify. Well, had there been five hundred, our influence would still have drowned them out; this influence is immense, Juliette, and between the two of us, Saint-Fond and I, we can regularly expect, by means of a word, a gesture, and whenever we like, to untie the rope knotted around the neck of the worst criminal on earth, and to have a saint mount the scaffold and die in his place. That's how things are when idiot princes are on the throne. Everyone in their vicinity leads them around by the nose, mulcts them, and those drab robots, while fancying they do their own governing, actually reign through us, as our instruments; or, if you prefer, our passions are the sole sovereign in this kingdom. We could take our revenge upon Dennemar too, I'm equipped with all that's needed for that; but he's as libertine as we, his eccentricities prove it. Never attack those who resemble us, that's my creed, you might subscribe to it too. The Duc knows he was wrong in behaving as he did; he's ashamed of himself today, he relinquishes title to the stolen goods and would even be very happy to see you again; I conferred with him, all he asked was that someone hang, and, you see, someone shall: he's satisfied, so are we. My advice is, however, that you not visit the old miser; we know perfectly well that if he desires to see you it is only to persuade you to take pity on Lubin: well, don't. I too once had that Lubin in my service, he fucked me very badly, cost me a great deal of money, and so disgusted me that I have, more than once, thought of having him packed off to some jail; he's in jail now, it seems to me right that he stay there. As for the Minister, he'd like to meet you; it will be this evening, you're to sup with him. He's an excessively libertine individual. . . . Tastes, proclivities, fantasies . . . passions, vices *ad infinitum;* I hardly need recommend the extremest submissiveness—it is the one way in which you can demonstrate the gratitude whose effects you very mistakenly wished to shower upon me."

"My soul is being cast in the mold of yours, Noirceuil," I answered coolly, "I cease offering you thanks now that you have made it plain that what you did, you did in your own behalf; and it would seem I love thee better and more since I've come to see that I owe thee nothing. As for the submission you request of me, it shall be entire; dispose of me, I am yours; a woman, I know my place and that dependence is my lot."

"No, not absolutely," Noirceuil rejoined, "your easy circumstances, your wit, your character set you very definitely outside that form of slavery. To it I only submit *wifely women* and *whores,* and in this I comply with the laws of Nature who, as you must observe everywhere, requires that such beings crawl and fawn; intellect, talents, parts, wealth, and influence separate some from the other creatures whom Nature made to comprise the class of the weak; and when these exceptions merit inclusion in the class of the strong, they automatically fall heir to all the rights and perquisites of the latter: tyranny, oppression, impunity, and the liberal exercise of every crime—these are entirely permitted to them. I would have you a woman and a slave unto me and my friends; a despot unto everyone else . . . and I here and now swear that I shall avail you of the means. Juliette, hast passed a day and a half in prison? You

deserve some sort of restitution. Rascal, I know of your twelve
thousand a year—you hid that from me; it matters not, I was
aware of your transactions, I'll get you ten thousand more tomorrow, and the Minister has asked me to give you this document:
it entitles you to an annual pension of a thousand crowns, interest
upon capital bequeathed to the hospitals; the sick will have a few less
bowls of soup and you a few fripperies more, the universal scheme
shan't be dislocated for that. Which, it appears to me, makes five
and twenty thousand pounds a year for you, not counting your
appointments, which will continue to be paid to you in full and
punctually. And so, my heart, you do well perceive that the consequences of crime are not always unhappy: a virtuous scheme, that
of aiding Lubin, got you hurled into a dungeon; the theft executed
in Dennemar's house determines and motivates your prosperity; do
you hesitate any more? Ah! commit your fill of crimes and more,
we are presently acquainted with the workings of your imagination,
we expect much of you, and we guarantee that whatsoever you do,
it shall be done with impunity."

"Can human laws be so incredibly unjust, Noirceuil? The innocent Gode groans in one prison cell, from another the guilty
Juliette emerges covered with the blessings of fortune."

"And it's quite as it ought to be, all according to order, my
sweet girl," Noirceuil rejoined; "the luckless are the toys of the
affluent, Nature's laws subordinate the ones to the others; the weak
are necessarily fodder to the mighty. Glance inspectingly at the
universe, at all the laws which regulate its operations: tyranny and
injustice, sole principles of every disorder, must be the fundamental
laws of a cause which functions only through disorders."

"Oh, my friend!" said I, carried away by enthusiasm, "legiti-
mizing all these crimes in my eyes, affording me, as you do, all the
means I need for committing them, you so fill my soul with delight,
with restlessness . . . with a delirium such as no words can express
—and you still do not wish to have me thank you?"

"For what? You owe me nothing. I am in love with evil. I will
hire anyone to do it. I am acting selfishly in this instance as I do in
every other."

"But I must show a token of my feelings for all you are doing
for me—"

"Then commit crimes in plenty and hide none of them from me."

"Hide a crime from you? Never. My confidence shall be absolute, you shall be master of my thoughts as of my days, in my heart there shall be no desire born save I communicate it to you, every pleasure I shall know shall be shared with you. . . . But, Noirceuil, there is yet one little favor I'd beg of you: the woman who betrayed me by bringing that Lubin to see me, she powerfully excites my ire —I thirst for revenge. The creature must be punished; will you look to the matter at your earliest convenience?"

"Give me her name and address, we'll have her behind bars tomorrow. Her residence there will be permanent."

We reached Noirceuil's house.

"Here's Juliette," said Noirceuil, presenting me to his wife whose air was cool and reserved. "She's back with us again, safe and sound. The charming creature was the victim of a calumny; she's the world's best beloved girl and I beseech you, Madame, to continue to hold her in the high regard she for a quantity of reasons is entitled to expect from you."

Great Heaven! I said to myself, when once re-established in my luxurious quarters, I began to take stock of the splendid situation I was going to enjoy—and to contemplate the revenue I was to become mistress of. Oh, great Heaven! the life I am to lead! Fortune, Providence, Fate, God, Universal Agent, whoever thou art, whatever be thy name, if 'tis thus thou dost treat those who surrender themselves into the arms of wickedness, how can one help but follow that career? Eh. 'Tis done, I'll never enter into any other. Divine excesses which they dare call crimes, you shall from now on be my gods, my only gods, my unique principles and my whole code of laws; I'll cherish only you so long as there is breath unto me.

My maids were waiting with my bath. I spent two hours there, two more at my toilette; fresh as a rose, I appeared at the Minister's supper, and, so they assured me, looked more lovely than the very sun itself, of whose light a few abject rogues had cheated me for the space of two days.

Part
Two

$\mathcal{M}$onsieur de Saint-Fond was a man of some fifty years: endowed with a keen wit, with much intelligence and much duplicity, his character was very traitorous, very ferocious, infinitely proud; it was in the supremest degree he possessed the art of robbing France, and that of distributing warrants for arbitrary arrest—the which he both sold at a goodly price and himself made use of, according to the dictates of his most idle fancy. Above twenty thousand persons of both sexes and all ages were at that moment, owing to his instructions, languishing in the various royal dungeons with which the kingdom is studded. "Of these twenty thousand souls," he confided to me one day, a smile upon his lips, "not a single one is guilty of anything." D'Albert, Chief Justice of the Parlement at Paris, was also at the Minister's supper. It was only as we, Noirceuil and I, were arriving that he told me of D'Albert's presence there.

"You ought," he counseled me, "to show as much deference to that gentleman as to the other, your fate was decided by him a mere twelve hours ago; he spared you. I had Saint-Fond extend an invitation to him so as to give you an opportunity to repay him for his thoughtfulness."

The seraglio at the disposal of the three men included, in addition to Madame de Noirceuil and myself, four charming whores. Of Duvergier's selection, these creatures were still virgins. The youngest was called Eglée—she was thirteen, honey-haired, a little enchantress. Then there was Lolotte, fair as Flora; such a glow of health as distinguished her has become rare indeed; she was only lately turned fifteen. Henriette was sixteen years old and combined about her person more charms than did ever poet ascribe

213

to the Three Graces. Lindane was the eldest, she was seventeen, superbly made; the expressiveness of her eyes positively took one's breath away.

On hand as well were six youths ranging in age from fifteen to twenty; naked, their hair arranged in feminine style, they served the table. And so it was that each libertine had at his bidding four objects of lust, two of one sex and two of the other. None of the corps had as yet put in an appearance when Noirceuil led me into the salon and introduced me to D'Albert and Saint-Fond, who, after embracing me, dallying with me, praising me for a quarter of an hour or more, declared themselves well pleased to have me of the company.

"It's a delicious little rascal, this one," said Noirceuil, "who through her unconditional submission to them would indicate to her judges how thankful she is they saved her life."

"I'd have regretted depriving her of it," said D'Albert. "However, it is not without good reason Themis is represented wearing a blindfold. And you'll agree with me that we ought always to have one over our own eyes whenever it is one such pretty little thing as this we have to judge."

"I promise her lifelong impunity," said Saint-Fond, "total impunity. She is at liberty to do absolutely anything she likes, without fear. Regardless what she is guilty of, she shall be protected by me, and I swear to avenge her according to her wishes upon whosoever seeks to spoil or in any wise interfere with her pleasures, however criminal they may be."

"Let me take the same oath," said D'Albert. "Indeed, I shall go farther: tomorrow there will be delivered to her a letter from the Chancellor, which will in advance nullify any court action any tribunal in the realm might eventually be induced to take against her. But, Saint-Fond, I have yet something else in mind. So far we have tended to dismiss crime, to connive at it; we ought rather encourage it, don't you think? I'd like to have you arrange to have Juliette rewarded for the misdeeds I expect her to commit: bonuses in the form of pensions running from, let us say, two thousand to twenty-five thousand francs a year, the sums depending upon the feats she proves capable of."

"It should seem to me, Juliette," said Noirceuil, "that you

have just now been given the solidest motives both to allow your passions the broadest scope possible, and to hide none of your extravagances from us. But I really must say, gentlemen," my lover continued before I had a chance to reply, "you put to wonderful purpose the authority vested in you by the laws and the monarch of this our beloved country."

"Eh, we do what we can with the means we possess," was Saint-Fond's candid response; "one always labors best in one's own behalf. Our office is to safeguard and promote the welfare of the king's subjects; in ensuring our own and this engaging child's, are we not carrying out our duties?"

"Permit me to expand upon those remarks," said D'Albert. "When accorded these powers we were not instructed to concern ourselves for the welfare of this or that isolated individual, we were merely informed: the authority we grant you is to further the happiness of the community. Now, it is impossible to render all men equally happy; therefore we hold our mission fulfilled when we have been able to satisfy several among the many."

"Yet," said Noirceuil, whose sole aim in pursuing the conversation was to provide his friends an opportunity to shine, "by shielding the guilty and dooming the innocent, your efforts conspire rather to the ill of society than to the good."

"I very stoutly deny that," Saint-Fond rejoined. "To the contrary, vice makes many more people happy than ever does virtue; and hence I am a far better servant of the public weal in my protecting the vicious than I would be in rewarding the virtuous."

"Fie! Such arguments are appropriate only in the mouths of scoundrels—"

"My friend," said D'Albert, "they are also your joy. It does not beseem you to contradict them."

"You are quite right," was Noirceuil's answer. "I think, though, that after all this talk we might do well to act a little. Would you care to have Juliette to yourselves before the others get here?"

"No, not I," D'Albert said. "I am not prone to tête-à-têtes. What with the extreme need I have to be aided in these proceedings, I prefer to keep patience and wait till the assembly is complete."

"For my part," said Saint-Fond, "I rejoice at Noirceuil's suggestion. Come along with me, Juliette; we shan't be long."

He led me into a boudoir, closed the door, invited me to undress. He spoke to me while I removed my clothes. "I have been assured you are very compliant. My desires are a bit loathsome, I know, but you are intelligent. I have done you outstanding service; I shall do more: you are wicked, you are vindictive—very well," said he, tendering me six *lettres de cachet* which required only to be filled in with the names of whomever I chose to have imprisoned for an indeterminate period, "here are some toys, amuse yourself with them; and here, take this, it is a diamond worth about a thousand *louis*, payment for the pleasure that is mine in making your acquaintance this evening. What? No, no, my dear, take it all, it is yours, it cost me nothing. Money for purchasing the gem came from State funds, not out of my pocket."

"Indeed, my Lord, your generosity leaves me confused—"

"Oh, it will go farther still. I'd like to have you in my household. I need a woman who will stop at nothing. I give dinners from time to time; you strike me as the ideal person for handling the poisoning."

"What, my Lord, do you poison people?"

"There's often nothing else to do with them. There are so many individuals one must put out of the way, you see. Scruples? I? Surely not. It's simply a technical problem. I shouldn't suppose you have any objections to poison?"

"None at all," I returned, "not in principle. I can swear to you that no conceivable crime affrights me, that every one I have perpetrated so far has delighted me unspeakably. It is merely that until now I have never administered poison; only afford me the chance, I ask no more."

"Charming creature," Saint-Fond murmured. "Come, Juliette, kiss me. And so it is agreed? Good. Once again I give you my solemn oath: never shall you have any punishment to fear. Do in your own interest whatever you esteem profitable and pleasurable, dread no reprisals; should the blade of the law be turned against you, I shall deflect its edge, I shall do so every time, I promise that. Believe me. But you must prove—prove right now—that you are fit for the employment I have in mind. Look here," and he tendered me a little box, "tonight at supper I shall seat next to you that one of the whores I have selected for the test; ingratiate yourself, caress her thoroughly, feint is the sure cloak of crime, deceive her as artfully and as entirely as you can, and at dessert cast this powder into one of the glasses of wine that will be placed before her: its effect will be swift; by that token I shall learn whether you are or are not the woman I need. Succeed, and the post I propose is yours."

"Ah, my Lord," said I with warmth, "I am at your orders. Issue them, issue them, let me show you what I can do."

"Delightful, delightful. . . . But now let us distract ourselves, Mademoiselle, your libertinage fetches my prick to a pretty stand. Eh, not too fast, however; we must undertake nothing until I have impressed upon you the high importance of observing very strictly this formula: you must be respectful. Respectful in all things, constantly, unfailingly. My titles to respect are many, I demand that they be acknowledged; I am a proud man, Juliette. Under no circumstances shall I use the familiar second person with you; never say *thou* to me. Address me, instead, as my Lord, speak to me in the third person so far as possible, and when you are in my presence study to assume a reverent attitude, posture, and mien. Apart from the eminent position I occupy, my birth is illustrious, my fortune enormous, and my credit superior even to the King's: my station and condition make vanity unavoidable: the powerful man who, beguiled by the always meretricious popularity he may sometimes enjoy, allows himself to be approached too nearly, suffers as a consequence a loss of face, of prestige, is humiliated, abased, sinks into the estateless ruck. Nature put the great on earth as she did the stars in the sky: they are to shed light upon the world, never to descend to its level. Such is my pride that I like servants to kneel before me, prefer always to employ an interpreter when holding parley with that vile rabble known as the people; and I detest everybody who is less than my peer."

"In that case," said I, "my Lord must despise a great share of society, since there are very few persons in this world who can pretend to be his equal."

"Precious few, Mademoiselle, that is correct; which is why I despise everybody on earth except the two friends who are here this evening, and a very limited number of others: for all the rest my hatred is unbounded."

"But, my Lord," I took the liberty to say to this despot, "do not your libertine caprices now and again constrain you to step down from the pinnacle upon which, so it does seem to me, you would prefer to remain at all times?"

"No," Saint-Fond replied, "there's no contradiction here, it's all of a piece: for minds conformed like mine, the humiliation implicit in certain acts of libertinage serves only as fuel to the fire of our pride."[1]

By then I was standing naked before him. "Ah, Juliette, it is a magnificent ass I see there," praised the haughty lecher, exposing himself. "They told me it was superb, but upon my soul it surpasses its reputation. Bend forward, let me put my tongue to it. . . . O God!" he cried, all dismayed, "it's spotlessly clean! Did Noirceuil neglect to tell you in what state asses are to be when presented to me?"

"No, my Lord, of this Noirceuil told me nothing."

" I like them unwiped, beshat. . . . I like them perfectly foul —but this one is scrubbed, fresh as new-driven snow. Well, we shall have to resort to another; here you are, Juliette, behold mine—it is the way I wanted yours to be, you'll find shit in there aplenty. Kneel facing it, adore it, consider the honor I accord you in permitting you to do my ass the homage an entire nation, nay, the whole wide world aspires to render it—oh, how many people would be overcome with joy could they but exchange places with you! if the very gods were to descend into our midst it would be to vie for this favor. Suck, lick; drive deep your tongue; seize your chance, my child, this is not the moment for backwardness."

And though my misgivings were not negligible, I vanquished them; it was to my interest to prove myself mettlesome. I did all this libertine desired of me, I sucked his balls, I let him fart into my mouth, shit on my breasts, spit and piss all over my face, tweak my nipples, slap me, kick me, pinch me, stoutly fuck my ass, and in doing so become much aroused, then discharge into my mouth, and

---

[1] The paradox is readily to be explained: one does that which no one else is able to do; hence, one is unique in one's species. It is this singularity pride feeds upon.

I swallowed his sperm, for he had ordered that I swallow every drop. I did everything, and owing to my docility all went well. Divine effects of wealth and influence! Your desires obliterate virtue and will, wither all power to resist; and the hope of being kindly received by you causes everyone, whosoever he be, to fawn at your feet, mindful only to do your least bidding. Saint-Fond's discharge was admirable, forceful, convulsive; it was accompanied by the most vigorous, the most impetuous blasphemics, pronounced in a very loud voice; quantitatively his expenditure of sperm was considerable, the temperature of that sperm was high, in consistency it was dense, it was savory to the palate, his ecstasy was energetic, he thrashed violently about, intense was his delirium: a handsome figure of a man was he, his skin was very fair, his ass as shapely as any to be found, his balls the size of a hen's eggs, and his well-muscled prick was probably six inches in circumference and seven in length, ending in a head measuring at least two inches long, and 'twas far, far thicker there than at the stem. Saint-Fond was tall, nicely proportioned, his nose was aquiline, he had long lashes, fine dark eyes, strong white teeth, and his breath was sweet; when done he asked me whether it were not true that his fuck was exquisite.

"Pure cream, my Lord, pure cream, I've never swallowed any to equal it."

"You may expect to be granted the honor of that fare from time to time," said he, "and you will likewise feast upon my shit when we become truly well acquainted. So now, Juliette, kneel down, kiss my feet, and thank me for all the favors I have condescended to bestow on you today."

I obeyed, and Saint-Fond embraced me, vowing himself positively enchanted with me: the filth I was swimming in was got rid of with the help of a bidet and some perfumes. We quit the boudoir; as we were traversing the apartments separating it from the assembly hall, Saint-Fond reminded me of the box I was carrying.

"Indeed," said I, laughing, "does crime linger in your brain even after the illusion has been dissipated?"

"What," the dreadful man retorted, "did you then mistake my proposal for something conceived in a moment of excitement, and destined to be forgot straightway the moment was over?"

"I presumed it was only that."

"You were wrong; this is one of those necessary things whose anticipated doing very certainly stirs up our passions but which, though conceived during a transport, must nonetheless be calmly carried out afterward."

"But are your friends privy to it?"

"Can you doubt?"

"There will be a scene."

"Not at all. We are accustomed to this. Ah, if the rose bushes in Noirceuil's garden could speak and say to what nutriments they owe their crimson magnificence . . . Juliette, my dear Juliette, such ones as are we consider that there is not, that there cannot be, one execution too many."

"Then be easy, my Lord. I have sworn obedience to you, I shall keep my oath."

We reappeared in the others' midst; they had been waiting for us, all the women were by now there. We had no sooner returned than D'Albert signaled the desire to repair to the boudoir with Madame de Noirceuil, Henriette, Lindane, and two youths, and it was not until later when I saw him in action that I was able to form a precise idea of his tastes. Those of us who were left after the departure of D'Albert and his troupe fell to lewd frolicking: the two little girls, namely Lolotte and Eglée, by means generally similar to those I had employed shortly before, endeavored to stiffen Saint-Fond afresh; they succeeded; Noirceuil, watching, had himself bum-fucked while kissing my buttocks. Saint-Fond caressed one of the lads and held several minutes of private conversation with Noirceuil; when they came back both seemed in high fettle, and the rest of the company having joined us, we all betook ourselves to supper.

Imagine, good friends, imagine my surprise when I beheld Madame de Noirceuil guided very ceremoniously to the table and invited to take the chair next to mine. I leaned toward Saint-Fond, who had placed himself to my left, and whispered, "My Lord, is this the woman you have designated to be the victim?"

"She is," replied the Minister, "and pray master your dismay, it does you scant credit in my eyes—another hint of this pusillanimity, let me warn you, and you shall lose my esteem forever."

So I sat down; the meal was no less delicious than libertine,

the women, only partially and loosely clad, to the lechers' fingerings exposed all the charms the Graces had lavished upon them. One
had a new-budding breast to hand, another fondled a buttock
whiter than alabaster; it was only about our cunts there was not
much ado made, such objects seldom proving of any real concern
to men of that breed; firmly of the opinion that to apprehend
Nature one must seduce her, and that to seduce her one must often
outrage her, these rascals are often wont to perform their devotions
at those very shrines which Nature, so it is alleged, forbids us
to approach. When wine of the finest vintage and the most succulent viands had heated the imaginations of the company, Saint-
Fond laid hands on Madame de Noirceuil: the atrocious crime
that dastard's perfidious brain had been meditating against the
luckless creature was stiffening his device prodigiously; he bears
her off to a couch at the farther end of the room and embuggers
her, bidding me shit into her mouth in the meantime; four youths
are disposed in such wise he can frig two, one with his right hand,
one with his left, a third is encunting Madame de Noirceuil, and
the fourth, perched above me, gives me his prick to dandle and
pump; a fifth bum-stuffs the Minister.

"Ah, Jesusfuck!" Noirceuil exclaims, " 'tis an enchanting sight.
To my knowledge there is nothing prettier than to see your wife
fucked this way. My dear Saint-Fond, I beseech you not to coddle
her."

And raising Eglée's buttocks to mouth height, he has a morsel
of shit fresh out of the little one, the while sodomizing Lindane,
and the sixth boy penetrates him anally. 'Tis Saint-Fond in the
center, Noirceuil on the right; D'Albert on the left now completes
the picture: he sodomizes Henriette as he colls the ass of the boy
busily fucking the Minister and with both hands gropes about and
kneads whatever is within reach.

But words cannot describe that divinely voluptuous scene;
only an engraver could have rendered it properly, and yet it is
doubtful he would have had time to capture those many expressions,
all those attitudes, for lust very quickly overwhelmed the actors
and the drama was soon ended. (It is not easy for art, which lacks
movement, to realize action wherein movement is the soul; and

this is what makes engraving at once the most difficult and thankless art.)

We returned to table.

"Tomorrow," said the Minister, "I am to prepare and dispatch a *lettre de cachet;* the man concerned is guilty of some rather unusual misconduct. He is a libertine who like you, Noirceuil, adores giving his wife to be fucked by strangers; this wife—it will strike you as incomprehensible, I know—this wife has been so silly as to complain about usage that a good many other women crave. The respective families have become entangled in the affair, I have been asked to have the husband confined."

"Excessively severe punishment," Noirceuil muttered.

"Far too lenient in my opinion," said D'Albert; "there are dozens of countries where such fellows are put to death."

"Hear that, will you! 'Tis but too typical. You gentlemen of the law," said Noirceuil, "are happy only when blood is shed. For you, Themis' scaffolds are boudoirs: pronouncing the death sentence, your pricks harden; and you discharge when it is carried out."

"True, that not uncommonly happens," D'Albert admitted, "but where is the disadvantage in converting one's duties into pleasures?"

"Quite," said Saint-Fond. "Common sense is on our side. But to return to the case of the man we were discussing a moment ago. You will agree with me that it is shocking, the number of wives who are behaving like fools nowadays."

"It is lamentable," said Noirceuil. "One comes across nothing but women who fancy that fulfilling their duty to their husbands begins and ends with preserving their own honor, and who, in order that they acquire and remain in possession of this shoddy virtue of theirs, expect those husbands to pay the price of constantly foregoing everything that stands at variance with conventional pleasures. Forever garbed in the silly raiments of a good name and mounted astride the hobbyhorse of virtue, and supposing they are beyond reproach, whores of this category imagine they are entitled to unbounded and unconditional respect, that they are therefore at liberty to act like utter cretins and certain to be forgiven every piece of stupidity and clumsiness. It is disgusting, I say; who would not a thousand times over prefer a wife who, though the most arrant slut, were to camouflage her vices behind absolute complacency, behind utter submission to every one of her husband's caprices? Ha! fuck, fair ladies, fuck to your hearts' delight; fuck your pretty heads off, we couldn't care less; we have only one concern, and it is this: that you anticipate our desires, that you satisfy them all with alacrity and unscrupulously; endeavor to please us, metamorphose yourselves, assume many roles, play at this sex and that, be children so as to afford your husband the passing great delight of whipping you, and you may be sure of it: treat him thus thoughtfully and comprehendingly and he will take little heed of anything else. The course of action I have just outlined is to my knowledge the only one capable of mitigating the horror of wedlock, the most appalling, the most loathsome of all the bonds humankind has devised for its own discomfort and degradation."

"Ah, Noirceuil, there is gallantry lacking in you," reprimanded Saint-Fond, somewhat forcefully squeezing the breasts of the wife of his friend; "you are after all speaking in the presence of your spouse."

Noirceuil grimaced. "Eh, so I am. That situation will be altered before long."

"But what's this?" cried the mischievous D'Albert, casting a look of feigned surprise at the poor woman.

"We are due to be separated."

"Due to be separated! How dreadful," said Saint-Fond, greatly aroused, and while frigging a youth with his right hand, continuing to paw and to wring Madame de Noirceuil's pretty dugs with his left. "Do you mean to say you are going to sever your ties, ties so sweet?"

"Have they not lasted long enough?"

"Very well then," Saint-Fond replied, still frigging a prick, still molesting two bubs, "if you really intend to leave your wife, I'll take her—I've always thought very highly of her, of her gentleness, of the humane quality about her. . . . Kiss me, bitch!"

She was weeping from the pain Saint-Fond had been inflicting on her for a good quarter of an hour; they were of her sighs the libertine paused to drink, her tears he licked away before resuming: "Bless me, Noirceuil, to separate from so lovely a wife"—and he bit her—"so sensitive a wife"—and he pinched her—"why, my dear Noirceuil, it's sheer murder."

"You know," said D'Albert, "between the two of us I believe that's exactly what Noirceuil has in mind, a murder."

"How ghastly!" Saint-Fond exclaimed; he had got Madame de Noirceuil to rise and was now clawing her buttocks while she fisted his tool. "There's nothing for it, my friends. Plainly, I'd best embugger her afresh; it may help her forget her other woes."

"Yes," said D'Albert, just then taking hold of her frontwise, "and in the meantime I'll encunt her. Come, let's hem her in and do her between us."

"And what would you have me do, pray tell?" Noirceuil asked.

"Meditate," said the Minister. "You'll hold the candle, you'll meditate, you'll plot."

"I can put my time to better use," rejoined the barbarous husband; "leave my beloved helpmeet's head alone, I wish to have her tearful countenance within view, I'll bestow an occasional slap upon that image of distress the while I embugger this dear little Eglée; and two of the boys will take turns sounding my bum, and I'll pluck hairs from Henriette's cunt and Lolotte's, and will watch Lindane and Juliette being served, one cuntwardly and the other in the asshole, by the two lads remaining."

And it was so, very hot was the affray and very prolonged; the three libertines discharged at last, Dame Noirceuil emerging from their clutches all battered and bruised—D'Albert, for instance, had taken a great bite out of one of her breasts. Following the example of those gentlemen, and stoutly fucked by two of the pederastic youths, I swear that I too discharged unspeakably: flushed, my hair all disordered, I heard my performance and looks praised when we had done; it was Saint-Fond who caressed me especially.

"Is she not superb in this state!" he repeated. "How crime embellishes her!" And he applied his lips to most every part of my body, sucking them indiscriminately.

We did not return to the table, but everybody continued to drink there where he lay; very agreeable, this, and one is much quicker drunk that way. Alcohol began to have its effect almost at once, the women began to tremble; blazing glances were bent upon them, and I noticed that when they were spoken to the terms employed were threatening as well as foul. However, two facts were readily to be perceived: firstly, that the storm then gathering would pass me by, and that Madame de Noirceuil was to bear the brunt of its fury; I dismissed my fears.

Shunted out of Saint-Fond's hands into those of her husband and from his into D'Albert's, the unhappy lady was in sorry straits already; her breasts, her arms, her thighs, her buttocks, in short, every fleshy part of her was beginning to exhibit palpable evidence of the ferocity of those blackguards, when Saint-Fond, his prick of great size again and purple, seized her and gave her twelve resounding thwacks about the shoulders and the behind, then six equally vigorous slaps upon the face, that being in the way of prelude; next, he placed her in the center of the dining room and immobilized her, her feet were fastened to the floor, there being eyebolts sunk there; ropes attached to the ceiling held her arms raised above her head. As soon as she was thus tied a dozen lighted candles were set between her thighs, in such wise that some of the flames scorched the interior of her vagina, others the vicinity of her anus, singeing her pubic hairs till they smoked, and searing her flesh; whereof the visible result was much writhing and many tremors and, upon the lady's lovely face, a sublime expression that declared all the voluptuous anguish of dolor. Holding up another candle, Saint-Fond considered her attentively during her ordeal, having his prick sucked by Lindane throughout and his asshole tongued by Lolotte; nearby, Noirceuil, being fucked while nibbling Henriette's buttocks, announced to his wife that she was going to go thus to her death; and D'Albert, embuggering a youth and fondling Eglée's ass, exhorted Noirceuil to deal yet more rudely with his unfortunate spouse—that unfortunate creature, she who was bound to him in holy matrimony. Catering to the divers needs of the company at large, for that was my role, I remarked that the candle-ends being too short, the victim was not suffering anywhere near the desirable degree of pain; so I raised the candlesticks by setting them upon a stool; Madame de Noirceuil's frantic screams earned me the hearty applause of her torturers. And now Saint-Fond, who was becoming giddy, ventured an atrocity: the rogue caught up a candle, waved it beneath the lady's nose for a moment or two, then burned her eyelashes and indeed almost the entirety of one eye; D'Albert too picked up a candle, and he toasted one of her nipples, while her husband set her hair afire.

Greatly moved by this dramatic spectacle, I egged the actors on and induced them to essay another stunt. Upon my recommendation Milady was drenched with brandy; for a brief instant she resembled a living torch, and when the blue flames died out, lo! it was not a pretty sight to behold, from head to toe one great burn covered her body. My idea had been a great success; there is no imagining how I was praised for having conceived it. Fearfully aroused by that piece of villainy, Saint-Fond forsook Lindane's mouth and with Lolotte still in tow, for he would not have her leave off sucking his vent, he embuggered me straightway.

"And now what shall we do to her?" Saint-Fond asks me, running his tongue deep into my mouth and plunging his prick far into my bowels. "Think, Juliette, invent something; you are inspired, whatever you propose is divine."

"There are yet a thousand tortures she could be made to undergo," I reply, "one more piquant than the other." And I am about to suggest a few when Noirceuil approaches us and points out to Saint-Fond that it might be wiser to have her swallow the dose immediately lest from exhaustion she lack strength enough to enable us to appreciate and enjoy the effects of the poison. D'Albert's opinion is consulted, he agrees with Noirceuil most emphatically; the lady is untied and turned over to me.

"Poor wretch," I say to her after having introduced the powder into a glass of Alicante, "drink this, it will refresh you. It will improve your spirits. You'll see."

Without a murmur the precious fool does as she is told and once she has imbibed all the fatal mixture, Noirceuil, lodged to the hilt in my ass hitherto, withdraws and moves nearer the victim, eager to feast his eyes upon her antics from close on.

"You are going to die," he informs her; "you are, I suppose, reconciled to the fact?"

"I am confident," D'Albert remarks, "that Madame is sensible enough to realize that when a wife has lost her husband's affection and esteem, when she no longer but wearies and is

offensive to him, the simplest course open to her is to bow gracefully out of the picture."

"Oh yes! Oh yes!" the unlucky woman shrieks. "I ask only
to die, kill me, that is my one request! In the name of Heaven, be
quick!"

"The death you crave, foul buggeress, is already brewing in
your guts," says Noirceuil, his prick being frigged by one of the
catamites; "Juliette did the thing. Such is her attachment to you
she would never have forgiven us had we deprived her of the joy
of administering the *coup de grâce*." And, utterly blinded by lust,
quite unhinged, Saint-Fond embuggered D'Albert who, bending
complacently before his friend's sodomistic onslaughts, delivered
to a pretty lad the equivalent of what he was receiving from the
Minister, whose anus I was tonguing industriously.

"Come, we are proceeding in too disorderly a fashion," said
Noirceuil, seeing from his wife's contortions, now begun in earnest,
that she merited closer watching.

He has a carpet spread in the middle of the room, upon it
the victim is made to recline and we group in a circle around her.
Saint-Fond bum-stuffs me while frigging a boy with either hand.
D'Albert is sucked by Henriette, he sucks a prick while frigging
another with his right hand; with his left he molests Lindane's ass;
Noirceuil's prick enters Églée's rectum, a prick passes into his
own, he sucks yet another and inserts three fingers in Lolotte's
ass while the sixth youth fucks her amain. The crises begin; most
horrible they are, for there is no describing the effects of that
poison: so violent were the poor woman's thrashings that at certain
moments she was quite rolled up in a ball, then it was as though
an electrical shock were paralyzing her entire body, foam flecked
her lips, her screams were perfectly horrible; but they were not to
be heard save by us, the necessary precautionary measures had
been taken.

"Ah, but it is delicious," Saint-Fond sighed the while he toiled
in my ass; "I don't know what I wouldn't give to sodomize her in
that state."

"Nothing easier," said Noirceuil, "just have a try. We'll hold
her still."

Firmly grasped by the youths, the patient, her efforts notwithstanding, is forced into position and there gapes her asshole; and into it Saint-Fond plunges his member.

"Godsfuck!" he exclaims, "I must discharge!" And discharge he does. D'Albert replaces him in the breach, then Noirceuil; but when his stricken wife feels him there, her strugglings become so furious, she escapes away from those who have her pinioned and, quite out of her mind, hurls herself at her torturer; alarmed, Noirceuil backs off, the circle is formed anew.

"Let her be, let her be," says Saint-Fond, just returned into my ass; "it is wise to keep clear of a rabid beast·when it is in death's throes."

Howbeit, Noirceuil, stung, insulted, wishes to have his revenge; he is in the midst of devising fresh torments but Saint-Fond stays his hand, explaining to his friend that anything further done to the victim now must only detract from the pleasure of beholding the action of the venom.

"Gentlemen," say I, "it's not only watching she needs; I believe the services of a confessor are about to be required."

"Let her go to the devil, he'll shrive the whore," said Noirceuil, at that point being sucked by Lolotte; "aye, let her go to all the devils there be. If ever I desired that a hell exist it was hoping that her soul would make its way there, and to be able, so long as there is breath in me, to relish the thought of her suffering."

It was that imprecation, so it appeared, that precipitated the final crisis. Madame de Noirceuil yielded up her soul, and our three rascals discharged concurrently, vying with one another in shameless blasphemy.

"This," said Saint-Fond, squeezing his prick, evacuating the last drop of fuck therefrom, "this that we have just accomplished shall surely stand as one of our finest deeds; I am highly pleased. Ridding the world of that prude has long been one of my ambitions; her husband was no more tired of her than I."

"Faith," D'Albert put in, "you surely fucked her no less often than he."

"Indeed, more often," my lover rejoined.

"In any case," Saint-Fond said to Noirceuil, "I intend to honor our agreement; you have sacrificed your wife, you shall have another: my daughter is yours. I am by the way delighted with this poison we have used; it gives excellent results, and I think it a great pity we cannot witness the deaths of all the people we destroy by this means. Alas! one cannot be everywhere at once. But as I was saying, my daughter is yours, gentle friend; and may heaven bless this occasion on which I acquire a most aimiable son-in-law and the assurance of not being betrayed by the woman who supplies me with these poisons."

Here Noirceuil leaned toward Saint-Fond and whispered what I guessed was a question in his ear; the latter nodded affirmatively. The Minister then turned in my direction. "Juliette," said he, "you will come to see me tomorrow, I will more thoroughly discuss with you what I have only touched upon today. Remarrying, Noirceuil may dispense with your presence in his house; I propose to establish you in mine; and I trust that the reputation which dwelling in my proximity will confer upon you, the money and the comforts I design to shower upon you, will prove ample compensation for the loss you are about to incur. You please me mightily; your imagination is brilliant, your phlegm in crime is exemplary, your ass is splendid, according to my belief, you are ferocious and libertine; thus do I judge that you possess the virtues I admire."

"My Lord," said I, "most gratefully I accept all you deign to offer me, but I must tell you, since I cannot hide the fact, that I love Noirceuil: I do not relish the prospect of losing him."

"Nor shall you lose me, my child, we shall see each other frequently," was the reply of Saint-Fond's intimate friend and future son-in-law, "we shall spend the better hours of our lives together."

"So be it," I said, "under those circumstances there is nothing I am not willing to consent to."

To the youths and whores the drastic and certain consequences of the slightest indiscretion on their part were made abundantly clear; much impressed, they swore never to speak a word of what had passed that evening; Madame de Noirceuil's remains were buried in the garden; and those of the company bade one another farewell.

An unforeseen contingency was to delay Noirceuil's marriage and the realization of the Minister's schemes as well; nor when I went to see him the next day toward noon was he there to greet me.

The King, singularly content with Saint-Fond, and trusting him unreservedly, had summoned him that same morning, confided a secret mission to him, and Saint-Fond had taken his departure from the city immediately; later, upon his return, he was awarded the *cordon bleu,* and an annuity of one hundred thousand crowns.

Oh yes, I said to myself when I learned of these favors, how very true it is that fate awards the evildoer, and how very much the imbecile he who, enlightened by such examples, were not all the more ardently to forge ahead in crime and to its furthermost limits.

In letters Noirceuil received from the Minister during his absence, I was enjoined to locate a house and to array it splendidly. And so, as soon as I was in command of the necessary funds, I rented a magnificent mansion on the rue du Faubourg-Saint-Honoré; purchased four horses, two charming carriages; hired three lackeys, strapping tall fellows and very handsome; found a cook, two scullions, a housekeeper, a reader, three chambermaids, a hairdresser, two downstairs maids and a pair of coachmen; I acquired quantities of the finest in furnishings; and the day the Minister came back to Paris I betook myself to his home. I had just attained my seventeenth year, and I think I can say that for looks I compared very satisfactorily with the prettiest women in the capital; my figure was like unto that of the Goddess of Love, and art heightened what was mine of natural beauty. The contents of my wardrobe were worth well above one hundred thousand francs, a hundred thousand crowns was the value of the jewelries and diamonds I wore. Wherever I went every door was open to me; and that day the Minister's domestics bowed low. He was awaiting me, he was alone. I began by mentioning the tokens of royal esteem which had been showered upon him, my congratulations were of the sincerest, and I sought leave to kiss his hand; he accorded it provided I kneel while doing so; familiar with the dimensions of his pride, his arrogance, I catered to them and adjusted my behavior to his wishes: it is by base flattery and abjectness that the courtesan, like the courtier, buys the right to be insolent to everybody else.

Spoke he: "Madame, you see me in the hour of my glory; the King has dealt largely with me, and I dare say according to my deserts; my position has never been so solid nor my fortune so great. If, as I propose to do, I make you the beneficiary of some small part of His Majesty's bounty, it shall be upon the obvious conditions; in view of the projects we have executed jointly, I believe I can rely upon you, you have acquired my total confidence. But before I descend to particulars, kindly look at these two keys, Madame. This first one opens the vault where is stored all the gold due to be yours if you serve me well; and this other is to the Bastille: in it there is a vacant cell, it is reserved for your lifelong occupancy should you fail of obedience or discretion."

"Confronted by such alternatives, one of doom, the other of glittering prosperity—I hardly need indicate which of the two I elect unhesitatingly. So place your whole trust in her who shall be absolutely your slave, and put away all doubts of her loyalty."

"You will have the charge of two important functions, Madame. Be seated please, and heed me." Not thinking what I was about, I was taking an armchair when Saint-Fond gestured me toward an ordinary straight-backed chair; he cut me short in the middle of my profuse apology, and continued in this wise:

"The post I hold, and in which it is my aim to remain yet a good while, for it is a rewarding one, obliges me to sacrifice no end of victims; in this casket there are various poisons, you shall employ them pursuant to the instructions I issue you. Upon those individuals who come actively at cross purposes with me the *cruelest* are used—see, they are labeled; the *speedy* upon those whose existence is merely a vexation to me and whom I prefer to waste no time dispatching from the world; and these, marked *slow,* are for those with whom I am obliged to proceed unhurriedly, whether because of political reasons or simply to divert suspicion away from myself. Depending upon the specific case, the envenoming will be accomplished either here in Paris, at your home or at mine, or in the provinces, or, again, abroad.

"Now as to the second of your functions—in all likelihood the more arduous of the two; it will also prove the more lucrative, however. Endowed with a very puissant imagination, everyday pleasures meaning nothing to me any more, Nature having given me a very fiery temperament, eminently cruel tastes, and where means are concerned all that is needed to satisfy these furious passions, I shall, whether at your residence or at Noirceuil's or at the home of some one or other of my friends, sup in the libertine manner twice a week; at each of these routs a minimum of three victims must infallibly and obligatorily be sacrificed. Per year, if we deduct the time spent in traveling—you will accompany me on some of my journeys—that comes, I believe, to approximately two hundred whores, the procuring whereof is to be your concern only; howbeit, these victims must meet certain specifications. Firstly, Juliette, the ugliest of them all has got to be at least as well-favored as yourself; I accept none younger than nine, nor above sixteen years of age; each must be a virgin, of excellent birth, titled if possible, wealthy in any case—"

"And you mean to say, my Lord, that you destroy all those?"

"Indeed I do, Madame. Murder is the sweetest of all my voluptuous practices, there are no limits to my fondness for blood, shedding it is the foremost of my passions; and to satisfy them all, come what may and hang the price, there's the foremost of my principles."

Seeing that Saint-Fond was waiting for my response, I said, "My Lord, what I have revealed to you so far of my character must, I should think, be sufficient proof that I cannot possibly fail you; my self-interest and tastes are your guarantee of my good faith. Yes, my Lord, it is very true, Nature gave me the same passions she gave you . . . the same cast of mind, too; and he who indulges in these things out of love of them will surely serve you better than he who obeys in order to please you rather than himself: the bond of friendship, a similarity of taste: such, be sure of it, such are the ties that most powerfully bind a woman like me."

"As regards friendship, bah! refrain from alluding to it, Juliette," the Minister said very sharply; "I hold that sentiment as empty, as illusory as love. Whatever originates in the heart is false; for my part, I believe in the senses alone, I believe alone in the carnal habits and appetites . . . in self-seeking, in self-aggrandizement, in self-interest. Aye, self-interest, of all possible bonds, shall always be the one in which I shall place the greatest faith; and I would therefore have it that the arrangements I am going to conclude with you be overwhelmingly to your personal advantage. Should taste develop later on as decoration to the self-interest structure, well and good; but tastes are fickle, they change with th years, the time may even come when one is guided by them no longer—but one always is by self-interest. So let us reckon up your little fortune, Madame: Noirceuil has assured you ten thousand *livres* per annum, I've provided you with three, you had twelve before; that makes twenty-five; and here are twenty-five thousand more—put this contract in a place of safekeeping—where are we now? Fifty? Fifty. Now let's enter into a few details."

The Minister was not displeased to have me prostrate myself before him; when I was done airing my thanks he bade me return to my chair and hear him out.

"I am quite as aware as you, Juliette, that with such a slender revenue you could not hope to provide for the two weekly suppers I shall require, nor dream of maintaining the house I ordered you to take; hence, I shall give you a million to defray the cost of those suppers; but bear it well in mind that they are to be of unparalleled magnificence, the most exquisite meats, the rarest wines, the most extraordinary fowl and fruits will be served at them always, and immense quantity must be joined to the finest in quality: even if we were only two to dine, fifty courses would obviously be too few. You will have twenty thousand francs apiece for the victims, and that is not overmuch in view of the standards they shall have to meet. You will be allotted a further thirty thousand francs gratuity for every ministerial victim you immolate personally; there will be roughly fifty of these each year, this article thus coming to some fifteen hundred thousand francs annually, to which I am adding a monthly twenty thousand francs for your appointments. Unless I have erred in my computations, this, Madame, totals to a yearly six million seven hundred ninety thousand francs; we shall throw in two hundred ten thousand more for your pocket money, supplementary charges, and divers trifles, so rounding the sum out to an even seven million, whereof, if you like, you may bank fifty thousand, yours by contract. Will this do, Juliette?"

Suppressing all outward signs of a tremendous elation, for greater yet was the greed consuming me, I was silent a moment, pursing my lips and seeming to take counsel with myself; then I ventured to draw the Minister's attention to certain facts: the duties he was prescribing me were, to say the least, quite as onerous as the sums of which he was making me mistress were considerable;

I was eager that he never be caused the slightest disappointment; it seemed to me altogether possible, nay, likely, that the huge expenses I was going to have to incur would largely exceed the resources at my disposal; and that, besides. . . .

"You need say no more," the Minister interrupted; "you have spoken in an idiom I apprehend perfectly, and you have persuaded me that you have your own interest ever in view. That, Juliette, is precisely what I wish; for I now know that I shall be irreproachably served. Stint on nothing, Madame, and you will have ten million a year; we have no reason to be niggardly. A contemptible fool, that *statesman* who neglects to have the *State* finance his pleasures; and if the masses go hungry, if the nation goes naked, what do we care so long as our passions are satisfied? Mine entail inordinate spending; if I thought gold flowed in their veins, I'd have every one of the people bled to death."[2]

"Adorable man," I cried, "your philosophy positively inflames me. A moment ago you detected the motive of selfishness in me; it is now doubled by that of taste, believe me, and be persuaded also, that my zeal in your service shall be owing a thousand times more to worship of such pleasures than to any other cause."

"I have witnessed you in action," Saint-Fond rejoined; "your conduct augured well. And indeed, how could you help but be enamored of my passions? The human heart is capable of engendering none more delicious than they. And he who is in a position to say—No prejudice hinders me, I have overcome them all; on the one hand, I possess the influence that legitimates my every gesture; on the other, the means necessary to committing every crime—I tell you, Juliette, such a one is the happiest of mortals. Ah. That reminds me, Madame, of the patents of impunity D'Albert promised you when last we supped together. I have the papers here, they arrived this morning; it was I who requested them of the Chancellor, not D'Albert—whose habitual forgetfulness, you understand, goes with his post."

This multitude of favorable developments, this windfall, the prospects opened up to me—I was as though spellbound, and quite

---

[2] There, by such tokens may you recognize them, those monsters that abounded under the *ancien régime* and personified it. We have not promised to portray them as beauties, but authentically; we shall keep our word.

speechless. Saint-Fond brought me forth from my trance when he drew me to him and, asking, "How long shall it be ere we begin, Juliette?" kissed me and ran his hand down my behind, into which he promptly popped a finger.

"My Lord," said I, "I must have three weeks at least to ready all the organization."

"Three weeks then. Today is the first of the month, Juliette. I shall sup at your residence on the twenty-second, at seven."

"There is something else, my Lord," I went on. "You have deigned to describe your tastes to me; I may perhaps tell you something of mine. You are already aware of those concerning the crimes I shall be able to commit with you; this document allows me to steal to my heart's desire; pray furnish me the wherewithal to revenge myself against an eventual enemy."

"Come with me," said Saint-Fond.

We entered the office of a clerk.

"My good sir," said the Minister, "your attention, please. "Look closely at this young lady; remember her. I order you to sign and to deliver to her, upon her simple request, as many *lettres de cachet* as she wishes, whenever, and for whatever places of detention she chooses."

We returned to the chamber we had formerly been in. "There, you are prettily equipped," said the Minister, "now show what you can do. Burn, trample, hack away, all France is yours; and whatever crime you perpetrate, regardless of its magnitude, its gravity, perpetrate it intrepidly, for fear you need not, you shall get away scot-free, you have my word. You shall have more: as I have told you already, thirty thousand francs for every crime you commit on your own initiative, on your own behalf."

My friends, I shall not attempt to describe the impact these promises, these prospects had upon me.

It is well nigh incredible, said I to myself. From the outset blessed by Nature with an imagination tending to extravagance, here am I now, rich enough to satisfy my every whim, to achieve my every ambition, strong enough to defy any retaliation. No; there are no inward joys comparable to this knowledge that I am powerful and hence free; no lubricity to equal the effect of this one upon the soul.

"So now, Madame, let us seal the bargain," said the Minister. "Here's a little gift for you, a mere bauble," he went on, handing me a casket where there were five thousand *louis* in gold, and twice that in gems and jewelry; "take it along, and don't forget the box of poisons."

Then he led me into a secret room where the furnishings were both sumptuous and bizarre.

"Henceforth upon entering this place, and while you are here, your condition will be that of a common whore; and at all other times you will be one of the greatest ladies in the kingdom."

"Wherever I am, my Lord, I shall be your slave, your admirer eternally, and the very soul of your most exquisite pleasures."

I undressed. Thrilled at having found a suitable accomplice at last, Saint-Fond performed horrors. Of his ways I have told you something, I now discovered more; leaving his house I might feel as though I had not my peer in all the world, but when I was in his company, he degraded me unutterably; when it was a question of lust, he was truly the filthiest man that can be conceived, the most despotical, the cruelest. He had me do reverence to his prick, his ass; he shat, I had to make a god of his very mard; but he also had this curious mania, he had me soil those very things that symbolized all that his pride was founded upon; he insisted that I shit upon various honorific insignia and badges and he wiped my ass with his *cordon bleu*. I owned to him my surprise at this last gesture.

"I would have you see, Juliette, that such rags and ribbons designed to dazzle fools do not overawe a philosopher."

"But a short moment ago you obliged me to kiss them?"

"True enough, but just as I pride myself on what these little fripperies represent, so it also flatters my pride prodigiously to profane them. All this—'tis just a quirk such as makes sense only to libertines of my species."

Saint-Fond's prick was up in extraordinary size; I discharged in his embrace: for those with an imagination like mine, the question is never whether this or that is repulsive, irregularity is the sole valid consideration, and anything is good provided it be excessive. Something told me he had a burning desire to have me eat his shit, I sought his permission to do so, obtained it, he was in ecstasies; he devoured mine, between mouthfuls tonguing my vent at length. He showed me a portrait of his daughter, scarcely fourteen years old, and as lovely a creature as one could behold; I begged him to include her at one of our forgatherings.

"She is not here," he told me; "were she, you'd have already seen her in our midst."

"I take it you are not sending her to Noirceuil without having enjoyed her first?"

"That is quite correct," he replied; "I would be heartbroken to allow someone else to pluck such delicious first fruits."

"So you have ceased to love her?"

"Love her? Juliette, I love nothing, nobody, none of us libertines loves anything at all. That child gave me a good many erections; she no longer excites me nowadays, I've wearied myself toying with her. I am giving her to Noirceuil, whom she heats exceedingly—it is a matter of mutual convenience, that's all."

"But when Noirceuil tires of her?"

"Why, you know the usual fate of his wives; in all likelihood I shall participate in the ceremony myself. I have in others; they are always stimulating. They are always worthwhile. That's the sort of thing I like. . . ."

And his prick soared another inch.

"My Lord," said I, "it seems to me that if I were in your position, I'd be tempted to abuse my authority at certain moments."

"When stiff, you mean to say?"

"Yes."

"It sometimes happens."

"Oh, my Lord," I began. Then: "Let's massacre some innocents, shall we? The idea makes my brain whirl."

I was frigging him, one of my fingers was tickling his asshole.

"One moment," said he, removing a sheet of paper from his pocket and unfolding it, "I have but to put my signature to that, and a very attractive person dies tomorrow. She is in prison at the moment; I issued the warrant upon the request of her family. Their single grievance is that she prefers women to men. I have seen her; she is charming; I amused myself with her the other day, and since then I have been so anxious lest she blab that my one thought, or rather desire, has been to get rid of her."

"Ah, my Lord, she'll talk if given the chance, she'll talk, your fears are only too well founded; so long as that girl is alive, you will be in constant danger. Therefore, and if I implore you to do so, it is because your safety depends on it, sign that paper." And taking it from his hand, I placed it flat against my buttocks. "There is a quill on that desk, and an inkhorn."

He signed his name.

"I am quite willing to carry it to the clerk myself," I said.

"As you like," said he, "but one thing at a time, presently I must discharge, Juliette. That all reach its proper climax I have need of further assistance." He rang. "Pray be not alarmed," he went on, "it is a ritual." And the next moment a pretty youth appeared in the doorway.

"Kindly kneel, Juliette, this young man is to bestow three blows of a cane upon your shoulders, the traces will last only a few days; afterward he will hold you steady while I embugger you."

And the newcomer, having stripped off his pantaloons, straightway gave his behind to be colled by the Minister who licked it complacently.

In the meantime, I knelt down; the youth picks up his cane and so smart were the three cuts he gave me the marks showed for the space of a fortnight. While the boy was laying on, Saint-Fond, sitting opposite me, watched with lewd curiosity; then he came up and examined the stripes on my skin, grumbled about their faintness, bade the boy take hold of me; and while sodomizing me vigorously, very vigorously, kissed the hinderparts belonging to him who was accessory to the operation.

"Ah, fuck my eyes!" he cried, loosing his seed, "ah, God be double-fucked, the whore's marked."

The mysterious youth withdrew. It was not until long afterward that an event I will relate in due course shed light on his character and identity.

Saint-Fond escorted me out of the boudoir; and once we had left it, reassumed his former thoughtful air.

"Take the caskets with you, Madame," said he, "and remember that our schedule calls for operations to begin three weeks from today. Very well. Libertinage, crime, discretion, Juliette, and your welfare is assured. Adieu."

The very first thing I did was examine the order of execution whereof I was the bearer. Great heavens, what was my amazement to discover that here in black and white were instructions to the supervisor of the convent-prison in question secretly to poison— whom? None other than Sainte-Elme, that charming novice I had fairly worshiped during my sojourn at Panthemont. Another person would perhaps have torn up that baneful piece of paper; not I. For I was too far advanced in my criminal career to quail; I did not even pause, no, nor waver for an instant, with determined step I betake myself to Sainte-Pélagie, where Sainte-Elme had been languishing three long months behind bars; I transmit the order into the hands of the head warden, ask to see the culprit; I interrogate her, she declares the Minister offered to arrange her liberation in return for her favors, and that she did with him all that it is possible for a woman to do. The lecherous monster had omitted not a single episode in his repertory of abominations; mouth, ass, cunt . . . the beast had defiled her everywhere, and as consolation for this evil treatment she had been given nothing but the hope of having her freedom restored to her.

"I have with me the document that will put an end to your misery," I say, kissing her.

Sainte-Elme thanks me, repays my caresses tenfold. . . . I notice that betraying her is moistening my cunt. . . . The following day she was dead.

Faith, said I to myself upon learning of the outcome of my scurvy deed, I can do better than that. I was made for great things. I feel it.

And setting myself promptly to work preparing the stage for the scenes Saint-Fond was to enact, within the space of three weeks I was, as I had promised, able to provide the first of his suppers.

Six excellent procuresses I had taken into my employ supplied me, for my debut, three young sisters spirited away from a pious retreat in Meaux, twelve, thirteen, and fourteen years of age, and positively celestial in face and figure.

That first evening the Minister appeared in the company of a man in his sixties. Upon arriving he encloseted himself for several minutes with me, inspected my shoulders, and appeared irritated at finding no traces left of the stripes he had had inflicted upon me at our last encounter. Scarcely did he touch me; but he advised the greatest respect and the profoundest submissiveness in my behavior toward the individual who had come with him, he being one of the foremost personages at the Court, a prince. The latter entered the room as soon as Saint-Fond left it. Forewarned by my lover, I turned and exhibited my behind as soon as he had shut the door. He approached, a spyglass in his hand. "Fart," he commanded, "or be bitten."

Unable to satisfy him with all the celerity he desired, I felt a sudden pain in my left buttock: his teeth had caused it. They left deep marks in my flesh. He walked around to in front of me; it was a severe and unlovely visage I looked into.

"Put your tongue in my mouth."

I did so. Whereupon he said: "Belch or be bitten."

But seeing that I couldn't obey, I backed away quickly enough to avoid the trap. The old rascal flies into a fury, he catches up a bundle of withes and belabors me for a quarter of an hour; then he stops and walks around to in front of me again.

"You behold the little effect even these activities I am fondest of have upon my senses nowadays; consider," said he, "this limp prick nothing hoists. Nothing. To bring it at all aloft I'll be obliged to cause you much hurt."

"There'll be no need for that, my Prince," said I, "since you're soon to have at your disposal three delicious objects whom you can torment in whatever way you like."

"Aye, but you are attractive . . . your ass," said he, fondling it apace, "pleases me infinitely; I'd like to stiffen for its sake."

So saying he rids himself of his clothing and upon the mantel lays a diamond-studded timepiece, a gold snuffbox, his purse overflowing two hundred *louis,* and two superb rings.

"Let's have another try now. Here, take hold of my ass, you must pinch and bite it hard, fearfully hard, and while you do that, frig me with the supplest possible wrist. Good, excellent!" he cried upon perceiving some slight improvement in his state; "now stretch out on this couch, will you, and let me prick your buttocks with this hatpin."

I lie down. "Steady," says the Prince. But when I emit a loud scream and seem about to faint away at a second thrust, confused and aflutter and dreading lest by using his mistress somewhat too roughly he give offense to the Minister, the Prince scurries from the room, hoping his departure will quiet me. I fling his clothes into an adjoining chamber, pounce upon his valuables, and hurriedly rejoin Saint-Fond, who inquires of me, "Is there anything amiss?"

"Nothing at all," say I, "but from being in too great haste fetching his Highness' clothes I let the door to my boudoir shut to, the key is inside and these English locks—there's no opening them. But never mind; Monsieur has his shirt and breeches here, we can defer the interview he desires until some later time."

And I draw my two guests out into the garden where everything has been put in readiness to receive them; the Prince forgets his belongings, dons the costume I tender him, and is mindful only of the pleasures yet to come.

The weather that evening was faultless, we were beneath a bower of roses with lilac bushes all around us; a multitude of candles furnished the light, our seats were three thrones supported on artificial clouds whence came the scent of the most delicious perfumes; in the center of the table was a very mountain of the rarest flowers, set amongst which were the jade and porcelain cups and plates we were to drink from and dine off; the service was of gold. No sooner had we taken our places than the bower opened overhead and before our eyes there descended a fiery cloud: upon it, the Three Furies and, prisoned in the coils of their serpents, the three victims destined to be sacrificed at this feast. The Furies alighted from their aerial car, each chained the victim in her keeping to boxwoods near where we were sitting, then stood by in readiness. No previously established program decided the order of that meal, it was to shape itself according to the wishes of my guests; anything you happened to wish you simply demanded, and the Furies brought it to you instantly. Above eighty widely varying dishes are called for, every one is served up in a trice; ten kinds of wines are requested, all ten flow, everything is there in plenty, in profusion.

"Nicely done," my lover remarked. "I trust your Grace is satisfied with my directress' initial effort?"

"Enchanted," answered the sexagenarian, his head reeling from the abundance of food and spirits, and his tongue thick already. "Indeed, Saint-Fond, I envy you your divine Juliette—I have never clapped eyes on a fairer ass."

"Nor have I," the Minister owned; "but I suggest we leave it alone for a while and concern ourselves with those belonging to our Furies who, if I'm not greatly mistaken, are superbly fleshed also."

And at that hint, the three goddesses, impersonated by the three loveliest girls my purveyors had been able to locate for me after ransacking the whole of Paris, immediately bared their behinds to the two libertines, who kissed them, licked them, gnawed them with much relish and complete abandon.

"My good Saint-Fond," the Prince stuttered, "shall we have ourselves flogged by these Furies?"

"With rose branches," Saint-Fond proposed.

And there are our lechers' backsides exposed, being cruelly lashed now by garlands of flowers, now by the Furies' snakes.

"Very lubricious indeed, these exercises," remarked Saint-Fond, resuming his chair and pointing to his towering device; "say now, my Prince, are you stiffening a little?"

"No," the hapless old dotard answered, "I require more potent stimulants than any of these; immediately when I enter into debauch, I like to be environed by atrocities in uninterrupted sequence, I like to have all that men hold sacred violated in the interests of my pleasure, all that is holy soiled by my doing—"

"You are not a humanitarian then, my Prince?"

"I abhor mankind."

"I strongly doubt," Saint-Fond continued, "whether at any moment in the day I for my part am not animated by the most vehement impulse, or caressing some black scheme, to cause harm to humankind; there is no more execrable species. Be he powerful, then man is dangerous, and no tiger in the jungle can match him for wickedness. Is he puny, weak, woebegone? then how base he is, how vile, how disgusting within and without! Oh, many a time have I blushed at having been born in the midst of such creatures. My one comfort is that Nature loathes them no less than I, for she destroys them daily; I wish only that I had as many means as she at my command for contriving their undoing; had I, I'd wipe the lot off the face of the earth."

"But you—august beings that you are," I broke in, "do you

really think of yourselves as human? Why no! no, when one bears so little resemblance to the common herd, when one dominates it so absolutely, it is impossible to be of its race."

"You know," said Saint-Fond, "she is quite right; we are so many gods; as it is with them, so is it with us—do we not have but to formulate desires to have them satisfied instantly? Ah, is it not obvious that among men, or rather, above men, there is a class so superior to the weaker sort as to be what of old the poets termed divinities?"

"As for myself, I am no Hercules, I sense that I am not," said the Prince, "but I fain would be Pluto; it would please me mightily to have the task of dismembering mortals in hell."

"And I should like to be Pandora's box, that the ills emergent from the depths of me might destroy them all piecemeal."

Some groans were heard at this point; they had been uttered by the three chained victims.

"Unloose them," said Saint-Fond, "and bring them hither."

The Furies detached them and led them before my two guests; and since no females can combine grace and beauty in a higher degree, I leave you to imagine to what lecherous attentions they were subjected straightway.

"Juliette," said the Minister, transported, "you are a charming and able creature; plainly, you have the touch of a master, these results authorize the statement. . . . Come, let's lose ourselves amongst these arbors, amidst these flowers, come, in shadow and silence let us give ourselves up to all our brains may dictate. . . . You had some ditches dug?"

"Suitably close by every spot likely to become a theater for your atrocities."

"Good; and no lights along the pathways?"

"None; darkness beseems crime, you shall enjoy it in its full horror. Let us be off, my Prince, and stray into these labyrinths, and accept the challenge to do our worst."

We all of us set forth together, the two libertines, the three victims, and I. Entering an alley flanked by hedges, Saint-Fond exclaimed that he could not proceed another step without first fucking; and seizing the youngest of the girls, the villain blasted both her maidenheads before rejoining us ten minutes later. During his absence, I sought to excite the old Prince; but in vain. Nothing seemed able to rouse his prick.

"Do you then intend not to fuck?" Saint-Fond asked him, laying hands on the second girl.

"No, no, go on, depucelate," answered the old lecher, "I'll restrict myself to vexations; pass them on to me one by one when you're through with each."

And getting the youngest of those little girls into his clutches he torments her in the unkindest manner while I suck him with might and main. The while Saint-Fond carries on with his deflowering, and having put the second girl in the same state as the first and turned her over to the Prince, he grabs the fourteen-year-old.

"You have no idea how much I enjoy fucking in darkness this way," says he; "the shades of night are a goad to crime and enormously facilitate committing it satisfactorily."

Saint-Fond, who had got this far without discharging, now let fly into the eldest girl's ass; and then he and the Prince held parley. It was agreed between them that Saint-Fond should retain for himself her who had just drained out his sperm; in exchange, he ceded the two other girls to the Prince, and that worthy, armed with all the equipment necessary for the tortures he was contemplating, staggered off in an ecstasy, leading his victims by their chains; while I accompanied my lover and the one who was to die by his hand. When we were gone off a distance, I told him of my theft, we both laughed heartily, and he assured me that, as was his custom, the Prince, prior to coming to our party, had visited a brothel with a view to putting himself in the appropriate mood; and that nothing would be easier than to convince him his treasures had been stolen there.

"You are a friend of this man, I suppose?"

"I am friend to no one," the Minister gave me answer; "my connections with this original have been advantageous so far, he is on the best of terms with the King; but when that changes, let him fall into disgrace tomorrow, and I'll be the first to tread upon him. He divined my tastes, I don't know how; he gave me to understand his were similar, he proposed we collaborate, I acquiesced—that's the extent of our relationship. What is it, Juliette, do you dislike the fellow?"

"I find him unbearable."

"Upon my soul, were it not for the political considerations I've just mentioned, I'd be only too happy to see him in your power. Nevertheless we can perhaps arrange his downfall. For, my dear, you please me to such a degree, there is nothing I am not willing to do for you."

"You were saying, were you not, that you have obligations toward him?"

"I have a few."

"Well then, how, in the light of your principles, how can you for one instant tolerate being in his debt?"

"Leave everything to me, Juliette." And then Saint-Fond, changing the subject, praised me anew for the manner in which I had conducted this feast. "You are," said he, "a woman of taste and wit and the better I come to know you, the more I am persuaded that I must attach you to me."

And then for the first time he addressed me in the familiar *tu*, and he granted me the yet greater favor of employing that term with him.

"I shall serve you my whole life long if such be your wish, Saint-Fond," I replied; "I know your tastes, I shall satisfy them and if you desire to bind me more closely to you, you will concur in the satisfying of mine."

"Kiss me, heavenly creature, one hundred thousand crowns shall be delivered to you tomorrow morning—see if I do not guess your heart's desires!"

It was at that point an old beggarwoman accosted us, asking for alms.

"What's this!" cried Saint-Fond, surprised. "Do they let the rabble in?" The Minister gazed inquiringly at me; he detected the smile upon my lips and grasped the jest at once.

"Delicious, delicious," he murmured. "Eh then, what is it you wish?" he went on, turning to the crone.

"Alas, my Lord, a few pennies out of charity," replied she; "come, deign to look upon my misery."

And catching the Minister by the hand, she guided him into a mean little hut lit by a lamp hung from the ceiling, and where two children, one male and the other female, and no older than eight or ten, were lying naked on some rotten straw.

"Behold this unhappy family," the pauper said to us; "it's been three days since I was able to give them a crust of bread. Have the kindness, you who are reputed so very rich, to give me the wherewithal to sustain my children awhile in their sorry existence. Oh, my Lord, I know not who you are; but are you acquainted with Monsieur de Saint-Fond?"

"I am," said the Minister.

"Ah then! you see his handiwork before you. He had my husband taken off to jail; he deprived us of the little that we possessed of goods; such are the cruel circumstances we are reduced to since above a year. . . ."

The great thing about this scene, my friends, the thing in which I could take pride, was its complete authenticity: I had unearthed these wretched victims of Saint-Fond's injustice and rapacity, I now presented them to him in the flesh, to reawaken his wickedness.

"Ah, the scoundrel!" exclaimed the Minister, staring fixedly at the humble woman, "yes, I know him well, by God I do, and you shall come to know him too: he stands before you. . . . Oh, Juliette, 'tis cleverly you have prepared this confrontation, my soul is in a very ferment. . . . How then, what is your complaint? I've sent your husband to prison, he is innocent—that is true. I've done better yet: your husband is no more. Until now, you have eluded me; for I meant to treat you likewise."

"What wrong have we done you, my Lord?"

"That of dwelling in my neighborhood, and of owning a small property you were not disposed to sell to me. But it is mine now, ruining you I have dispossessed you. And now you come begging to me. Do you think I care if you die of starvation?"

"But these poor children?"

"France contains about ten million too many of them: weeding the garden is to render society a service." Peering down at the children, he rolled first the one, then the other over with his foot. "Not bad stuff, though. It needn't go entirely to waste."

Whereupon, his prick prodigiously stiffened by all the foregoing, the wag bends, seizes the little boy, and embuggers him on the spot; next catching hold of the little girl, he does the same with her. Then, very heatedly he cries: "Lousy old bitch, show me your bewrinkled bum, I require the sight of your flapping buttocks in order to unload."

The old woman weeps, she resists; I lend Saint-Fond my aid. Having heaped insults upon that woebegone ass, the libertine penetrates it, while trampling on the brats, literally crushing them beneath his boots as he sodomizes their mother, and at the moment of his discharge he fires a bullet into her brain. And we depart from that den of misfortune, dragging along the fourteen-year-old victim, whose buttocks Saint-Fond had been kissing the whole time he was in action.

"Well, Sire," I said as we were strolling away, "from now on that family's property is yours to do with as you like; that was not the case until this evening. Those people had solicited help, their pleas had obtained a hearing, trouble was brewing; not, to be sure, that they could have caused you any serious worries; but they would have proved a nuisance. I found them out at work, I lured them here; now you're rid of them."

Saint-Fond was in a state of inconceivable exaltation. "Ah, how sweet is crime," said he, the sincerest feeling manifest in his tone, "and how voluptuous its aftermaths! Juliette, you cannot imagine how my every fiber has been electrified by the deed you have just led me to commit. . . . My angel, my divine creature, my one god, only say: what is it you would have me do for you?"

"You are pleased, I know, when one gives voice to one's longing for money—will you then increase the promised sum?"

"It was a hundred thousand crowns, I believe?"

"Yes."

"You'll have twice that amount, Oh, Juliette. But wait, what is this?" cried the Minister, recoiling at the sight of two masked men who were approaching us, pistols in their hands. "I shudder; I am not one of your courageous fools. . . . Ho there, gentlemen! What do you want?"

"You'll soon see," replies one of the two, binding Saint-Fond fast to a tree and pulling his breeches down to his heels.

"But what do you intend to do?"

"To give you a lesson," said the other man; he is brandishing

a cat-o'-nine-tails, and already swinging it at the ministerial behind, "to teach you to deal as you have just done with those poor
folk in the cottage."

And after he has laid on three or four hundred strokes, which
serve mainly to bring Saint-Fond's wearied tool into the air again,
the other hoves up and completes his ecstasy by introducing a gigantean prick into his anus. Having fucked, the fucker takes up the
whip in his turn and whips; when he is done whipping, his companion bum-tups my lover—who, throughout, palpates the young
girl's buttocks to the right and mine to the left; Saint-Fond is untied, the two men vanish into the night, and we wander off again
down obscure lanes.

"Oh, Juliette, I must say it to you ever and ever again, you are
divine. . . . But, you know, that last episode gave me a fright—
there's nothing like subjecting one's nerves to an initial commotion
before imparting that of voluptuousness to them: the average man
will always remain in total ignorance of such contrasts and gradations."

"Fear acts powerfully upon you?"

"Prodigiously, my dear. I'm probably the greatest coward on
earth, the which I own without the least twinge of shame. Being
afraid is an art, it is a science, the art and science of self-preservation, and of capital importance to man; so that it is a patent absurdity to link honor to bravery in the face of dangers. I place my
honor rather in dreading them all."

"Ah, Saint-Fond, if fear can have such an effect upon your
senses, think what must be its effect upon those who are the victims
of your passions!"

"Exactly, and it is thence comes my keenest pleasure," the
Minister rejoined; "the very essence of my enjoyment is in making
those victims so suffer in the selfsame way from the thing which
plagues my existence. . . . But where are we? this garden of yours,
Juliette, is vast indeed."

"We are at the edge of one of the pits prepared for the
victims."

"Ah yes," said Saint-Fond, stooping and reaching out a hand,
"the Prince must have performed a sacrifice hereabouts, I do believe I feel a corpse."

"Let's pull it out," I suggested, "and see who it is. . . . She seems to be the youngest of the three sisters—and not quite dead either. I dare say the rascal throttled her, then buried her alive. Well, we'll revive her, and you'll have the fun of slaying two."

Our attentions did indeed bring the poor child back to life, but she was unable to tell us what the Prince had done to her once she had lost consciousness. The two sisters hugged each other, shedding many tears; and the barbarous Saint-Fond informed them that he was about to kill them both. Which is what he went ahead and did; however, since I have a good many adventures of this kind to relate, rather than risk being tedious, I shall forego a description of this one. Suffice it to say that the monster discharged into the ass of the younger of the two creatures while finishing her off; we tossed some dirt into the pit; and we pursued our way.

"Innumerable are the fell deeds which may afford pleasure; but to my knowledge there is none that causes it more deliciously than destruction, wanton murder," that arch-libertine affirmed. "No, there is no ecstasy to compare with the one you taste as you indulge in this divine infamy: were this amusement to become more generally widespread, I can assure you the earth would be depopulated inside a dozen years. Dear Juliette, your performance of a moment ago encourages me to suppose that you are as fond of crime as I."

And I gave Saint-Fond plainly to understand that it stimulated me not one whit less, and if anything, more, than it did him. It was then we perceived, in a clearing among the trees, and by the light of the moon, what appeared to be a little convent.

"And now what have we here?" asked Saint-Fond. "Does she mean to drown me in delight?"

"Truth to tell," said I, "I do not know where we are." I knocked on the door.

It was opened by a nun advanced in years.

"Venerable and beloved mother," I said to her, "will you show your hospitality to two strangers who have wandered off the beaten path?"

"Enter," the good lady replied; "though this be a nunnery, the virtue you invoke is not alien to our hearts, and we shall as willingly practice it with you as we have done with an elderly seigneur who a short while ago made the same request: he is with the women of the house who have just risen for matins."

From what she told us, we realized that the Prince was there too. We joined him; he was surrounded by a group made up of another nun and half a dozen *pensionnaires* aged from twelve to sixteen. Yet covered with the blood of his latest victim, the old lecher was already beginning to behave disrespectfully.

Quickly we entered the room, the nun who was there addressed herself to Saint-Fond.

"Monsieur, will you put a halt to this ungrateful person's effrontery. In return for the kindness we have shown him he has done nought but insult us."

"Madame," replied the Minister, "my friend, scarcely more moral than I and like myself detesting virtue, is very little disposed to reward it; your *pensionnaires* look exceedingly attractive to me; either we set your damned convent afire this instant, or by God, we rape the six of them."

Thereupon, with one hand seizing the smallest, and with his fist lashing out at two nuns who seek to protect her, Saint-Fond violates her there and then, frontwardly. Need more be said? The five others had soon undergone the same fate, except that Saint-Fond, fearing lest his tool weaken, ignored cunts and perforated assholes only. As one by one they emerged from his clutches, the Prince took charge of them and flogged them till they bled, synchronizing that ceremony with the other of kissing my buttocks which, he oft repeated, he prized, he cherished, he adored. Saint-Fond, keeping a firm grip upon himself, had discharged not a drop; he has at the two nuns, one of whom is over sixty, shuts himself up with them in an adjoining cell, and comes back thirty minutes later, alone.

"Eh, my friend, what have you done with those duennas?" I inquire of the Minister, who rejoins us in a very overwrought state.

"Remaining in control of this establishment," he informs us, "meant getting rid of those warders: I started by sporting with them in that cell, I have a passion for weatherbeaten asses. Then, discovering a stairway that leads down to a well, I cast them in."

"And these pullets, what's to be done with them? I trust we aren't going to leave them alive," says the Prince.

Further horrors were perpetrated, whereof I'll say only that they were ghastly; the convent was emptied.

The two libertines, having by now emptied their balls also, and seeing day about to break, desired to return to my house. There, a sumptuous breakfast, served by three naked women, was awaiting us; we all had hearty appetites. The Prince asked Saint-Fond's leave to spend a few hours in bed with me; and my lover, flanked by two manservants, had himself fucked until the sun was well up in the sky.

The old nobleman's struggles and wigglings constituted no great threat to my modesty; after going to great pains and lengths he contrived to introduce himself into my asshole, though 'twas not for long he stuck there; Nature dashed my hopes, the instrument bent, and the villain, who hadn't even the strength to discharge— for he had, he maintained, shed his fuck twice in the course of the evening—fell asleep, his snout wedged in my behind.

As soon as we rose, Saint-Fond, more enchanted with me than ever, gave me a draft for eight hundred thousand francs, payable at the Royal Treasury; and he and his friend quitted my house.

Generally speaking, all the succeeding parties resembled that inaugural one, save for particular episodes I with my fertile imagination took care to vary constantly. Noirceuil was almost always present, but apart from the Prince I had not seen any strangers at any of them.

I had been at the helm of that great vessel for three months, steering it with all possible success, when Saint-Fond informed me I had a ministerial crime to commit on the morrow. Oh, dread consequences of a barbarous policy! The victim? Surely, my friends, you would be hard pressed to guess his identity. 'Twas Saint-Fond's own father, a gentleman of sixty-six, in every way the soul of respectability; he had been disturbed at his son's irregularities of comportment, dreading lest they prove his undoing; he had argued with him, warned him, even spoken to his disadvantage at Court, with the aim of constraining him to leave the Ministry, very rightly believing that it were better for this scoundrel his son to retire of his own accord, rather than be banished from the stage.

From the outset, Saint-Fond took his interference ill; he stood to gain a yearly three thousand from his father's death and accordingly did not long delay coming to a decision. Noirceuil arrived with the particulars; and noticing that I appeared somewhat to waver at the prospect of this major crime, he thought by means of the following speech to cleanse the projected deed of the taints of atrocity my weakness idiotically ascribed to it.

"The evil you fancy you do in killing a man, and the further evil you imagine exists where the question is of parricide—these, it seems to me, my dear, are the two notions I ought to endeavor to combat. However, I need waste no time examining the former of the two; a mind such as yours can only scorn the prejudices that hold criminal the destruction of one's fellow beings.[3] This homicide is a simple affair for you, since between your existence and the victim's no tie exists; it only becomes complicated for my friend; you are awed by the stain of parricide he is only too willing to incur, and therefore it shall be from this viewpoint alone I'll consider the deed.

"Parricide: is it or is it not a crime?

"Assuredly, if there is in all the world a single deed I esteem justified, legitimate, it is this one; and, pray tell me, what relationship can there be between myself and him who brought me into the world? How would you have me think myself in any way beholden to a man, merely because, once upon a time, some whimsy moved him to discharge into my mother's cunt? Nothing is more preposterous than this piece of foolishness; but what now if I am unacquainted with him, what if I do not know the identity of this individual, this father of mine who sired me? Does the voice of Nature perhaps speak up in me and tell me who he is? Never. So should I not be as distant in my attitude toward him as toward anybody else? If this fact is sure, and thereof I do not believe any doubt can subsist, parricide in no wise increases the supposed evil in homicide, one does no worse murdering one's own father than murdering some other person. If I kill the man who, unbeknownst to me, begot me, the fact that he is my father contributes nothing to my remorse; hence, it is merely because I am told we are kin that I pause or repent; well, I ask you, how can opinion worsen a crime? and can opinion possibly alter its nature? What! I am free

---

[3] This system will be amply developed further.

to slay my father and feel no remorse provided I am not aware he is my father, but cannot in that other case where I know him to be? See the implications of such reasoning: even if it be an arrant lie, others have but to convince me it is the truth, that the man I have just slain was my father, and lo! I am to be filled with regrets and dread discomfort—'tis sheer nonsense.

"And further: if remorse exists, though grounds therefor do not, that remorse cannot properly exist when the alleged grounds for it are present. If you can so very easily deceive me in all this, then I tell you, the crime you speak of is no crime at all, it is illusory; since Nature herself does not give me certain indication of who the author of my days is, 'tis surely because she would not have me feel any greater tenderness for him than for some other person who is of no particular concern to me; if your opinion alone creates occasion and cause for remorse, and if your opinion can deceive me, then this remorse is a paltry business, insignificant, null; and I am a fool if I consent to succumb to it. Do animals cleave worshipfully to their fathers? Have they even a bare inkling of which male begot them? Searching for motives to warrant filial gratitude, will you cite the care my father took of me during my infancy and childhood? Another error. Complying with them, he ceded to the customs of the country, to his pride, to a sentiment which, as a father, he managed to conceive for his handiwork but which there is no need whatever that I conceive for the artisan; for that artisan, acting uniquely at the behest of his own pleasure, had no thought at all for me when it so pleased him to proceed to the act of propagation with my dam; his sole concern was for himself, and I fail to see therein any basis for especially ardent feelings of gratitude.

"Ah! let us entertain no more illusions on this article, the prejudice is unworthy of mature minds: to the person who gave us life we owe no more than we do to the remotest, chilliest stranger. In us Nature prompts absolutely no feeling for him, none; I shall go farther: she could not possibly imbue us with any feeling for him, friendship is not something that can be imposed upon us from outside; it is false that one loves one's father, it is equally false, indeed, that we can love him: you fear him, yes, but love him you do not; usually a threat to you, always onerous, his existence cannot but disquiet and inconvenience you; personal interest, the most sacred of the laws of Nature, puts us under invincible compulsion to desire the death of the man from whom we await our inheritance; and the problem envisaged from this angle, not only would we hate that man as a matter of course, but, very probably, it would be even more natural still to attempt his life, for the excellent reason that everybody deserves to have his turn, and that if my father has for two score years enjoyed the fortune come down to him from his father, and that if I find myself growing old in everlasting expectancy of the substance whereupon my welfare dances attendance, I should definitely, and without a trace of remorse, aid a Nature that is sometimes behindhand or remiss, and myself, employing whatever means, accelerate the process whereby I enter into the exercise of rights Nature accords me but may well delay transmitting to me, out of some caprice neither I nor anyone else in his senses will refrain from taking steps to counteract. If self-interest is the general rule by which man measures all his actions, there is, necessarily, much less evil in killing one's father than in killing some other human being; for our personal reasons for ridding ourselves of him who brought us into the light must always be stronger and more valid than those we have for putting any other person out of the way. Here also there exists another metaphysical consideration we ought not lose sight of: old age is the road to death; causing a man to age, Nature speeds him toward his grave: he, therefore, who slays an oldster does nought but carry out her intentions: whence it is, that among many nations, murder of the aged is accounted a virtue. Useless to the world, so much excess baggage in society, consuming provender that is scarce already, that is lacking to the young or which the young must buy dearly because of the overgreat demand, their existence is demonstrably to no purpose, it is harmful, and the wisest course is to liquidate them, that is self-evident. Hence, not only is it no crime at all, to kill one's father, it is an excellent thing to do; it is a meritorious deed from the point of view of oneself, whom it serves; having regard now to Nature, it is also meritorious, for it is to free her of an unwelcome burden; and it is praiseworthy, since it supposes that a man be vigorous enough, philosophical enough to value himself, who may be of some use to humanity, above that dotard humanity has all but forgotten.

"And so, Juliette, you are about to perform a handsome deed in destroying the enemy of your lover who, I am sure, serves the State to the utmost of his ability; for if, as I would be the last to deny, he is now and again guilty of some petty prevarication, some petty peculation, Saint-Fond is a very great minister nonetheless: he is bloodthirsty, he is rapacious, fierce is his grip, he considers murder indispensable to the maintaining of good government. Is he mistaken? Sulla, Marius, Richelieu, Mazarin—all history's great statesmen, have they thought otherwise? Did Machiavelli lay down different principles? There is no room for doubt: bloodshed there must be if any regime, a monarchical one especially, is to survive; the throne of the tyrant must be cemented with blood, and Saint-Fond has yet to begin to spill anything like the quantity of it that should be flowing this very minute. . . . Finally, Juliette, perform this gesture and you remain in the good graces of a man who keeps you in what I believe may be accurately termed a state of prosperity; you increase the fortune of him who is responsible for yours: I really wonder that you even hesitate."

"Noirceuil," said I very pertly, "who told you I was hesitating? 'Twas merely some involuntary reflex in me, no more. I am young yet. I am but a fledgling, my career has only just begun; that I stumble a little, backslide now and then—should this surprise my mentors? But they'll soon see I am worthy of the pains they take with me. Let Saint-Fond make haste and send his father to me, he's a dead man two hours after he crosses the threshold of my house. However, my dear, there are three categories of poison in the assortment your friend entrusted to me; do you know which I am to employ?"

"The cruelest, the one that causes the greatest suffering," answered Noirceuil; "I am glad you reminded me. Saint-Fond was adamant on that score. He wishes that, in going to his death, his father be punished for having intrigued to his detriment, he wishes his agony to be hideous."

"I understand," I said, "and you may tell him that the thing shall be handled to his satisfaction. But what is the plan?"

"As follows," Noirceuil replied. "As the friend of the Minister, you will invite the old man to dinner; that is, you will send him a note, in it you will make it clear that your design is to bring about a conciliation: you yourself sharing his views regarding his son's retirement from public office, you'd like to discuss the matter with Saint-Fond senior. He will come; ill, he will be borne out of your house; Saint-Fond junior will attend to the rest. Here's the sum agreed upon for the execution of the crime: a draft for one hundred thousand crowns on the Treasury. Will that suffice, Juliette?"

"Saint-Fond gives me that much for a supper," said I, handing back the scrap of paper; "tell him I'll do this for nothing. I simply wish to be helpful."

"And here is another draft for the same amount," Noirceuil went on; "your lover anticipated your objection—indeed, he would have been disappointed had you made none. 'I want her to be paid, and paid according to her desires'—often has he repeated that to me. 'So long as she evinces selfishness, and so long as I satisfy that selfishness, I am sure not to lose her.' "

"Saint-Fond seems to know me very well," was my reply; "I have a liking for money, I don't hide the fact from myself, neither do I from you. But I shall never ask him for more than is necessary. These six hundred thousand francs will go into carrying out the project; I want six hundred thousand more for myself the day the old man expires."

"You'll have them, never fear. Oh, Juliette, what a splendid situation is yours! Do nothing to spoil it, do everything to deserve it, enjoy it, and if you know how to conduct yourself intelligently, you'll soon be the wealthiest woman in Europe; I have given you a marvelous friend."

"Out of respect for your principles, Noirceuil, I refrain from thanking you; arranging this liaison pleased you, you gain therefrom as well, it flatters you to have among your intimate acquaintances a woman whose social position, riches, and name have already started to eclipse those of the Court princesses. . . . I'd be ashamed to show myself at the Opera dressed as the Princesse de Nemours was yesterday evening; not a soul so much as glanced at her. Everybody's eyes were upon me."

"And you are relishing all this, Juliette?"

"Infinitely, my dear. To begin with, I am rolling in gold, which, for me, is the foremost of enjoyable things."

"But are you doing sufficient fucking?"

"A great deal; precious few are the nights when the best Paris can boast in the one and the other sex does not come to offer me the greatest homage."

"And your favorite crimes?"

"They are being committed, they are being committed. I steal every chance I get—I don't let an odd franc get by. You'd think, from my graspingness, from my thievery, I was in imminent danger of starving to death."

"And vengeance?"

"I have been particularly active on that score: the fearful unpleasantness that has befallen Prince de X.—you've heard the news? the whole town is talking about nothing else—'twas I alone arranged that. Five or six ladies who in the past few months have thought to challenge my social position are presently lodged in the Bastille."

Next, we entered into a few details touching the parties I gave for the Minister.

"I must tell you," said Noirceuil, "that of late there are signs you are relaxing your efforts, Saint-Fond has noticed it. There were fewer than fifty dishes at the last supper; you are of course aware that only by eating well can one hope to discharge copiously," he continued, "and for us libertines, the quality and the quantity of our sperm is of crucial importance. Gluttony fares wonderfully well with all the tastes it has pleased Nature to instill in us; and experience shows that the prick is never so rigid, the heart never so staunch, as after one has sumptuously dined. I would say a word, too, about the choice of girls. Although those you place before us are without doubt very pretty, Saint-Fond feels that more research would improve the selection. I cannot but attempt to impress upon you the care that must be taken in this matter. We require that the game furnished us not only be of the finest breed, but that in addition it possess all those qualities, moral as well as physical, which make bagging it interesting."

For answer to this, I outlined the excellent measures I was taking: instead of six, now I had two dozen women working around the clock, and under them they had an equal number of subalterns combing the provinces; I was the mainspring of the entire mecha-nism; and I was putting forward a great effort.

"Before contracting for an object," Noirceuil recommended, "even if it involve a thirty-league journey, make it: there is no substitute for personal inspection; and never accept anything but what meets with your total approval."

"All very well," said I, "but that formula is not always so easy to follow. The object is frequently kidnapped before I have had a description of it."

"Why then," Noirceuil rejoined, "kidnap twenty to obtain a yield of five."

"But what am I to do with the rejects?"

"Whatever you wish: sport with them yourself, sell them to your friends, to procuresses, to panders. With the apparatus you will have built up you should be able to traffic on a broad scale and, it would seem to me, even create a virtual monopoly; at any rate, there ought to be a good hundred thousand a year in this for you."

"True, if Saint-Fond paid me for every object acquired. As things stand, he only remits for three per supper."

"I think I can induce him to pay for the lot."

"He'll be far better served if he does. Now, Noirceuil," I said, "there are some other matters I should like to discuss, and they relate to me. You know the kind of mind I have: I need hardly tell you that with all these means for mischief-making, I indulge very heavily in it; the ideas which occur to me, the things I imagine are beyond description—but, my friend, I require your advice. Don't you suppose that, ultimately, my behavior may make Saint-Fond jealous?"

"Never," Noirceuil answered at once. "Saint-Fond is an ex-ceedingly reasonable person, as such he senses you cannot attain self-expression save through much wrongdoing; the idea itself amuses him, and only yesterday he was telling me that he was afraid you were not enough of a trollop."

"Oh, in that case, let him be easy; you may assure the Minister that it is seldom one finds a person with a more pronounced taste for every sort of vice."

"I have now and then heard it asked," said Noirceuil, "whether the jealousy she inspires speaks in favor of or against a woman, and I have always thought the question odd: for my part it has from the beginning been obvious to me that the impulse leading to this mania being purely personal, women assuredly have nothing to gain from the tumult it produces in their lovers' breasts. It is not by any means fondness for a woman that brings on jealousy; it is dread of the humiliation her change of heart would cause one; and to prove there is nothing but sheer egoism in and behind this passion, I have simply to remind you that no lover, if he be of good faith, and sincere, will deny he would prefer to see his mistress dead than unfaithful. Hence, it is rather her fickleness than the loss of her that afflicts us, and 'tis hence our own selves we are thinking of when the event takes place. Whence I conclude that, second only to the inexcusable folly of falling in love with a woman in the first place, the greatest extravagance a man can commit is to be jealous of her. With regard to her, this sentiment is dishonest, demonstrating, as it does, one's lack of esteem for her; with regard to oneself, it is regularly painful and inevitably useless, since the surest way to breed in a woman the wish to fail us is to intimate to her our fear lest she do so. Jealousy and the terror of cuckoldry are two things based entirely upon our prejudices pertaining to the enjoyment of women; were it not for this accursed habit of stubbornly and idiotically wanting, whenever it is a question of woman, to associate the moral and the physical, we'd long ago have had done with these vile notions. What? It is not possible, you say, to lie with a woman without loving her? And it is not possible to love her without lying with her? But why must you embroil the heart in something where it is exclusively the body that acts? They are two desires, they are two very different needs, so it seems to me. Araminthe has the world's most beautiful figure, her face is endearing, her big brown sultry eyes promise an ample ejaculation of her sperm once the walls of her vagina or the interior of her anus are electrified by friction from the rubbing of my prick: I poke her and sure enough, behold! I was right, she squirts a quart. Why, pray tell, need anything heartfelt accompany the act whereby I take this creature's body? It does appear to me once again, that loving and enjoying are distinct and separate affairs, and that not only is it unnecessary to love in order to enjoy, but that it suffices to enjoy in order not to love. For dreamy, tender sentiments rise out of com-

patibility of humor and expediency, but are in no wise due to the
beauty of a bust or the pretty contours of a bum; and I would not
allow these latter objects, which depending upon our peculiarities
of taste can sharply excite the physical affections, to be able to
exert a similar prise upon the moral affections. To complete my
comparison: Belinda is ugly, she's forty-two, not one hint of the
gracious anywhere about her person, not a single attractive feature,
no, she's a slug, grossly ill-favored. But Belinda is clever, she has
wit, a delicious character, a million things which mate nicely with
my sentiments and tastes; I'd have no desire to bed with Belinda,
but I'd be wild about her conversation nonetheless. I'd intensely
desire to have Araminthe, but I'd cordially detest her the moment
the fever of desire had abated, because in her I have found a body
only, and none of the moral qualities which could win her a place in
my heart. All this however is quite irrelevant to the present case;
in Saint-Fond's tolerant attitude toward the infidelities you commit
there is an element of libertine sentiment for which none of the
foregoing provides an adequate explanation. The idea of you lying
in another's arms entrances Saint-Fond, he himself puts you there,
knowing you there, imagining you there, seeing you there hardens
his prick; you'll multiply his pleasures as proportionally you augment the size and number of your own, and Saint-Fond will never
cherish you so much as when you do to the utmost that which would
earn you the hatred of a clod. Here it is a question of one of those
mental anomalies comprehensible, and indeed common, only to
cerebral individuals like ourselves, but which are not on account of
their rarity any the less delectable."

"What you tell me is reassuring," said I; "Saint-Fond will
love my tastes, my mind, my character, and shan't be at all jealous
of my person? Very great is my relief to hear you say it, for, I
confess to you, continence would be impossible for me, my temperament requires satisfaction, my thirst requires to be slaked at all
costs; hot-blooded as I am, energetic and imaginative as you know
me to be, with this colossal wealth at my command, how ever could
I resist passions aroused by everything, inflamed continually?"

"Surrender to them, Juliette, surrender to them, you cannot
do more, you should not do less; but in your dealings with the
public at large, I would urge you to be somewhat the hypocrite.

Remember that in this world hypocrisy is an indispensable vice for him who has the fortune of possessing all the others; with art and deceit, one succeeds at anything, for it isn't your virtue society needs, it is simply a pretext for supposing you virtuous. For every two occasions when this virtue will be necessary to you, there will be thirty others when you'll only have to simulate it; therefore don the mask, debauched women, study to perfect the appearance expected of you, but only to the point of indifference to crime, never so far as enthusiasm for virtue, because the former attitude leaves the *amour-propre* of others in peace whilst the latter exasperates it. Moreover, it is quite enough to hide what one loves without having to feign what one detests. If all men were vicious in better faith, there'd be no need for hypocrisy; but, falsely persuaded that from virtue there are advantages to be reaped, they must absolutely cling to some shred or vestige of it. One must do as they, and, to secure their good opinion, conceal all one can of one's misconduct under the cloak of that worm-eaten and ridiculous idol; quits, of course, to revenge oneself for this enforced homage by making that many the more sacrifices to its rival. In addition, hypocrisy, teaching one craft and guile, facilitates countless crimes; your disinterested air invites trust, the adversary lowers his guard, and the less you give him to suspect you are armed with one, the easier it is to drive home the dagger. This covert and mysterious manner of thus satisfying the passions increases a thousandfold the enjoyment you derive from them. Cynicism has its piquancy, I am aware of it, but it does not lure into your net, it does not assure you victims as certainly as hypocrisy does; and then too, effrontery, all that comes under the head of the criminally crapulous, is not truly to be savored except in debaucheries. These the hypocrite, secure within the four walls of his house and his solid reputation, may perfectly well indulge in once he has answered the requirements of his libertinage—surely; who's to stop him? But it will be generally agreed that elsewhere than in the sanctuary of the home cynicism is out of place, it is bad form, in poor taste, and by creating a breach between society and yourself, it incapacitates you for the enjoyment of all society has to offer. The crimes of debauchery are not the only ones that afford delight, you understand, there are quantities of others, of the highest interest and often very lucrative, which hypocrisy makes available to us, but cynicism unattainable. Was there ever a falser, adroiter, more unscrupulous wench than Madame Brinvilliers, that pillar of society in her day? It was in the charity hospitals she used to make trial of her poisons, it was behind the shield of piety and the screen of philanthropy she would experiment with the delicious means to her crimes. Her father said to her, as he lay upon his deathbed where he had been brought by a poisoned drink administered by her, 'Oh, my beloved daughter, my one regret in taking leave of life is that I shall no longer be able to do for you all the things I would like.'

"And the daughter's response was a supplementary dose in the cup of tea she handed to the sinking patient.[4] The world boasted no more artful, more subtle creature; she played at devotion, she was ever at Mass, she distributed a fortune in alms, and did all that to cover her crimes; and so it was a long time before she was found out, and perhaps she never would have been but for the incaution and misfortune of her lover.[5] Let that woman serve as an example to you, my dear, I couldn't propose a better."

"I know the whole story of that famous creature by heart," I replied, "and you may be sure I aspire to follow in her footsteps. But, kind friend, I'd like to have a more contemporary model; I'd wish her to be somewhat older than me, I'd want her to love me, to have tastes like mine, passions like mine, and, though we'd masturbate together, I'd want her to allow me all my other follies without being in the slightest bit jealous; be that as it may, I'd want her to have a certain ascendancy over me, but that without seeking to dominate me; I'd want her to give me sound advice, to cooperate at all times in my caprices, to be profoundly experienced in libertinage; to be irreligious as well as unprincipled, as much a stranger to good

---

[4] See *Mémoires de la Marquise de Frène; Dictionnaire des Hommes illustres,* etc.

[5] We know that Sainte-Croix, Madame Brinvilliers' lover, perished while concocting a powerful poison (we give the recipe below). He had put on a glass face-protector to keep from inhaling the effluvia of the brew: so active was the venom, it shattered the mask, and the chemist was undone. As soon as she heard of Sainte-Croix' misadventure, Brinvilliers unwisely rushed to his house and ordered the servants to turn over to her the casket in which her lover stored his other preparations —that was her fatal error. Later, this casket was conveyed to the Bastille, and its contents were made extensive use of by all the members of the family of Louis XV.

This celebrated woman was also convicted of having poisoned her two brothers and her sister and was subsequently beheaded, in the year 1679.

manners as to virtue, to have great warmth of wit and a heart of ice."

"I have just what you are looking for," Noirceuil replied; "a widow of thirty, lovely, nay, beautiful, criminal to the core, arrayed with all the qualities you list, and who will be of invaluable aid to you in your chosen career. She can replace me as your tutor; for, you realize, separated as we are, I can no longer attend to your needs with the same ardor as before: Madame de Clairwil, that is the name of the person I have in mind, and she is a millionaire, knows everybody worth knowing, everything that can possibly be known, and I am convinced she will agree to take you under her wing."

"Charming Noirceuil, you are too good; but there's yet more to it, my friend, I'd like to share my knowledge with another; I keenly sense my need of instruction, I no less keenly desire to educate someone: I must have a teacher, yes, and I must have a pupil too."

"Of course. My fiancée?"

"What!" I cried enthusiastically, "would you entrust me with Alexandrine's education?"

"Could I put her in better hands? I'd be delighted to have you take charge of her. Moreover, it is Saint-Fond's wish that she keep the most intimate company with you."

"And what is causing the delay in this marriage?"

"I am in mourning for my last wife, you know."

"Do you defer to conventional usages?"

"Occasionally, for the sake of appearances; though it goes fearfully against the grain."

"One further word, dear Noirceuil: you are very sure this woman you propose to introduce me to will not become my rival?"

"You are thinking of your position with Saint-Fond? Fear not. Saint-Fond knew her long before he met you, he still amuses himself with her; but Madame de Clairwil would not consent to undertake your functions, and, for his part, the Minister would not obtain anything like the same pleasure from having her exercise them."

"Ah," I exclaimed, "you are divine, both of you, and your generosity toward me will be very fully rewarded by my zeal in the service of your passions. Issue me orders, I shall be only too happy,

always, to be the instrument of your debauches and the main accessory to your crimes."

I was not to see my lover again until after I executed the task
he had assigned me; on the eve of the appointed day I was exhorted
to be firm; and on the morrow the dear old gentleman appeared.
Before we sat down at table I employed all my skill to mend his
opinion of his son, and was quite taken aback to discover that, indeed, it would not be at all difficult to set things straight between
them. Therefore I hastily shifted my tack. 'Tis not a reconciliation
we want now, said I to myself; if that happens, I lose both the
opportunity for the crime I am in a perfect itch to commit, and the
twelve hundred thousand francs promised me for bringing it off;
let's cease negotiations and start to act. Administering the drug was
child's play; the old man collapses, he is trundled out, and two days
later I learn to my considerable satisfaction that he is no more, his
death having been hideously painful.

It was but an hour or so after he expired that his son arrived
for one of his semiweekly suppers at my house. Poor weather forced
us to hold it indoors; and Noirceuil was the one other guest present.
I'd readied three little girls of fourteen or fifteen, prettier than you
can imagine; a Paris convent had supplied them to me at the price
of a hundred thousand francs a head—I'd stopped bargaining ever
since Saint-Fond had agreed to cover costs.

"These," said I, presenting them to the Minister, "will console
you for the loss you have just sustained."

"It does not overly affect me, Juliette," said the Minister,
kissing me, "I'd willingly send fifteen such blackguards to their
death every day, and without an ace of compunction. My one regret
is that he suffered so little; he was a most contemptible clown."

"But, you know," I said, "it wouldn't have taken much to
change his attitude?"

"You acted properly in not encouraging him to do so. I
shudder at the thought of still having to endure the beggar's existence. I even resent having to bury him; but for some loathsome
prejudices, I'd have the pleasure of flinging his corpse on the dung
heap and watching it devoured by vermin."

And, as if eager to forget, the libertine turned immediately
to the job, my three maids were assessed. There was nothing the

fiercest critic could find fault with: size, shape, birth, mint condition, youth, looks, they were all there; but I noticed that neither of the two friends was stiffening in the least, and satiety is not easy to please: 'twas apparent they were not content, but did not, however, dare complain.

"Speak up," said I, "if these objects don't satisfy you, you must tell me what you want. For you must admit, I cannot hope to guess what it would be that outdoes this."

"No," sighed Saint-Fond, who was having himself handled by two of the little girls, whose efforts were proving fruitless, "there's no one to blame unless it's Noirceuil and myself. We're exhausted, we've just been performing horrors, and I haven't the faintest idea what's to be done to revive us now."

"Perhaps," I suggested, "if you were to recount your feats, you might, from the telling, rediscover the strength to commit fresh infamies."

"We can at least try," said Noirceuil.

"Well then, off with the clothes," said Saint-Fond, "you too, Juliette, undress yourself, and listen to us."

Two of the girls converged upon Noirceuil, one sucked him, he tongued the other and palpated both their asses; the frigging of the narrator was confided to me, and while speaking, he spanked the third maiden's behind; and here follow the atrocities Saint-Fond divulged:

"I led my daughter to where my father lay dying. Noirceuil was with me; we drew the shutters, we bolted the doors, and then" —and the lecher's prick rose, nodding as though in confirmation of what he was saying—"and then I most barbarously announced to my father that this that had befallen him, and the agonies he was undergoing, were my work; upon my instructions, I told him, you had poisoned him and I advised him to think on death. Then raising my daughter's skirts, I sodomized her before his eyes. Noirceuil, who adores me when I commit infamies, had been fucking me very briskly; but when the rascal saw Alexandrine's ass bared to the light, he soon replaced me in the breach . . . and I, bending over the bed, forced the old man to frig me, and while he fisted my prick, I slowly strangled him: I gave up my fuck at the same moment he gave up the ghost, and Noirceuil simultaneously discharged into my daughter's fundament. Ah, the joy that was mine! Foul accursed unnatural son who all at one stroke was guilty of *parricide, incest, murder, sodomy, pimping, prostitution*. Oh, Juliette, Juliette! never in my life had I been so happy. See what it does to me just to recite those voluptuous exploits, my prick's as stiff as it was this afternoon."

Whereupon the lecher has at one of the little girls, and while he proceeds to maculate her in every part, he would have Noirceuil and me abuse another of the children within his view. We improvise awful things; Nature, outraged in those girls, becomes frenziedly operative in Saint-Fond, and the scapegrace is near to shedding his fuck, when, so as not to squander his forces, he prudently withdraws from the ass of the novice in order to perforate the other two. Exercising faultless self-control that day, he triumphed six times in a row, and for his share Noirceuil had no buds, but full-blown roses only. Howbeit, the latter made the most of the little that was left to him, and the whole while he fucked, and he fucked at a leisurely pace, he kissed my ass and Saint-Fond's too, he pumped them both, and drank up the farts we amused ourselves producing for him.

Then 'twas suppertime, I alone was invited to partake of the feast, but nude; the little girls lay scattered about the table, light was provided by the candles we had stuck in their asses; and as these candles were none of them very long, and as the supper lasted on and on, all their thighs were severely scorched. Earlier we had bound them fast to the table to hold them still, and the gags of wadded cotton we had inserted in their mouths saved our conversation from being disturbed by their clamorings. The three candelabras diverted our libertines throughout the meal; and I, reaching out from time to time to verify their state, found them both in very merry form indeed.

"Noirceuil," said Saint-Fond, while our little novices were aroasting, "do, please, explain to us, manipulating your metaphysics prettily as you are wont to do, do explain to us, how 'tis possible we arrive at pleasure in the one case through the sight of others undergoing pain, and in the other, through suffering pain ourselves."

"Pay me close heed," said Noirceuil, "I'll give you the thing detailed and demonstrated.

" 'Pain,' logically defined, 'is nothing other than a sentiment of hostility in the soul toward the body it animates, the which it signifies through certain movements that conflict with the body's physical organization.' So says Nicole, who perceived in man an ethereal substance, which he called soul, and which he differentiated from the material substance we call body. I, however, who will have none of this frivolous stuff and who consider man as something on the order of an absolutely material plant, I shall simply say that pain is the consequence of a defective relationship between objects foreign to us and the organic molecules composing us; in such wise that instead of composing harmoniously with those that make up our neural fluids, as they do in the commotion of pleasure, the atoms emanating from these foreign objects strike them aslant, crookedly, sting them, repulse them, and never fuse with them. Still, though the effects are negative, they are effects nonetheless, and whether it be pleasure or pain brewing in us, you will always have a certain impact upon the neural fluids. Now, what prevents this painful commotion—infinitely sharper and more active than the other—from exciting in the said fluid the same conflagration propagated there by the impact of the atoms emanating from objects of pleasure? and, stirred for the sake of being stirred, what prevents me from becoming accustomed, through habit, to being no less suitably agitated by the atoms that repel than by the others that blend? Weary of the effects that only produce a simple sensation, why should I not become accustomed to receiving the same pleasure from those that produce a *poignant* sensation? Both categories of shock are sustained in the same place; the only difference between them is that one is violent and the other mild; but from the standpoint of the blasé individual, is not the first greatly to be preferred to the second? Is there anything commoner than to see, on the one hand, people who have accustomed their palates to a pleasurable irritation, and next to them, others who couldn't put up with that irritation for an instant? Is it not now true—my hypothesis once accepted—that man's practice, in his pleasures, is an attempt to move the objects which procure him his enjoyment in the same way he himself is moved, and that these proceedings are what are termed, in the metaphysics of pleasure-taking, *effects of his delicacy?* What then should appear odd in the man who, endowed with organs of the kind we have just depicted, through the same procedures as his adversary, and through the same principles of delicacy, fancies he moves the pleasure-procuring object by means whereby he himself is affected? He is no more wrong than the other, he has only done what the other has done. The consequences are different, I grant you; but the initial motivations are identical; the first has been no crueler than the second, and neither of them is open to blame: upon the pleasure-procuring object both have employed the same means they themselves use to procure their own pleasure.

" 'But,' replies he who is subjected to a brutal emotion, 'but this doesn't please me.' 'Tis altogether possible; it now remains to be seen whether force will succeed with you where persuasion has failed. If not, then begone, leave me alone; if, to the contrary, my wealth, my influence, or my station gives me either some authority over you or some certainty of being able to stifle your complaints, then submit without a murmur to everything it pleases me to impose upon you, for have my enjoyment I must and shall, and I can obtain it only by tormenting you and seeing your tears flow. But in no case have you the right to be surprised or to reproach me, because I am acting in accordance with the way Nature designed me, am following the bent she imparted to me, and because, in a word, in forcing you to accede to my harsh and brutal lusts, they alone which are capable of leading me to the uppermost pitch of pleasure, I act pursuant to the same principle of delicacy as the tepid swain who knows nought but the roses of a sentiment whereof I recognize only the thorns; for I, torturing you, rending you limb from limb, I am merely doing the one thing that is able to move me, just as he, sorrowfully encunting his mistress, does that which alone moves him agreeably; but he can have his effeminate delicacy, it's not for me—why? because it cannot possibly move organs so solidly made, of such tough fiber as mine.

"Yes, my friends," Noirceuil went on, "it is, you may be sure, impossible for any person who finds authentic pleasure in lewd and voluptuous activities ever really to combine their practice with that of delicacy, which unto these delights is nought but the very kiss of death and which is based upon the premise that joy is to be shared, a premise no one who intends seriously to enjoy himself can ever accept: shared, all enjoyment becomes dilute, the wine becomes watered. The truth is generally recognized: encourage or allow the object which serves for your pleasure to take enjoyment therein, and straightway you discover that it is at your expense; there is no more selfish passion than lust; none that is severer in its demands; smitten stiff by desire, 'tis with yourself you must be solely concerned, and as for the object that serves you, it must always be considered as some sort of victim, destined to that passion's fury. Do not all passions require victims? Well then! in the lustful act the passive object is that of our lubricious passion; spare it not if you would attain your end; the intenser the sufferings of this object, the more entire its humiliation, its degradation, the more thorough will be your enjoyment. They are not pleasures you must cause this object to taste, but impressions you must produce upon it; and that of pain being far keener than that of pleasure, it is beyond all question preferable that the commotion produced in our nervous system by this external spectacle be created by pain rather than by pleasure. There you have it explained, the mania common to that crowd of libertines, who, like us, must, if they are to obtain successful erections and emit sperm, commit acts of the most atrocious cruelty, gorge themselves on the blood of victims. Some there are whose pricks are not even faintly to be stirred, save when they contemplate that doomed object of their lubricious fury—and save when they themselves are uniquely responsible for the violent sufferings it is undergoing. You wish to subject your nerves to a powerful agitation; you very rightly suppose that the painful commotion will prove stronger than the pleasurable; so you employ it with favorable results. 'But beauty,' I hear some sentimental imbecile protest, 'beauty melts, interests, it invites to sweetness, to forgiveness: how is one to resist the tears of the pretty girl who, clasping her hands together, implores mercy of her executioner?' Indeed! This is precisely what one is after, it is from this agitation, this terror the libertine in question extracts his most delicious enjoyment; would he not be in a sorry plight if he were to have to act upon an inert, insensible body? and the objection cited is quite as ridiculous as that of the man who maintained you should never eat mutton because sheep are mild animals. Lust's passion will be served; it demands, it militates, it tyrannizes, it must therefore be appeased, and to its satisfaction all other conditions are totally irrelevant. Beauty, virtue, innocence, candor, misfortune, the object we covet will not be sheltered by any of these. To the contrary. Beauty tends to excite us further; virtue, innocence, candor embellish the object; misfortune puts it into our power, renders it malleable: hence, all those qualities tend only to inflame us the more, and we should look upon them all simply as vehicles to our passions. More, these qualities afford us the opportunity of violating another prohibition: I allude to the variety of pleasure derived from sacrilege or the profanation of objects that expect our worship. That beautiful girl is an object of reverence for fools; making her the target of my liveliest and rudest passions, I experience the double pleasure of sacrificing to that passion both a beautiful object and one before which the crowd bows down. No need to expand upon this idea, it has only to enter the mind and one's brain whirls. But one does not always have such objects ready to hand; however, one has habituated oneself to achieving pleasure through tyranny; and one is anxious to enjoy oneself every day—what then? Why, one must learn to delight in other, lesser pleasures: hardheartedness toward the downtrodden, the refusal to succor them, the act of plunging them oneself into misery if one possibly can—these in some sort substitute for the sublime pleasure of causing a debauchery-object to suffer. The sight of these wretches is a spectacle which very well lays the groundwork for the commotion we are accustomed to experience upon receiving a dolorous impression; they reach out to us, implore our aid, we withhold it— there's the spark; a further step, and there's the fire lit, thence are crimes born, and nothing is surer to touch off the explosion of pleasure; but I have fulfilled my task. How, you wanted to know, how can one accede to pleasure through suffering pain, or making others suffer it? I have answered you with a theoretical demonstration. Let's now confirm it in practice, and hewing to the line of the argument, I would request that the tortures inflicted upon these young ladies be piercing, that is to say, as *piquant* as it is within our power to make them."

We rose from the table, and rather more in the spirit of jest than of charity, the victims' hurts were briefly looked to. I can't say why, but that evening Noirceuil seemed more than usually enamored of my ass; he could not leave off kissing it, toying with it, praising it, sucking and fucking it; twenty times over he embuggered me; he would suddenly snap his prick out and give it to be sucked by the little girls; next, he would return to me and slap my flanks and buttocks with extraordinary force; he forgot himself even to the point of frigging my clitoris. All this heated me prodigiously, and my behavior must have appeared frightfully whorish to my friends. But how was one to satisfy oneself with a trio of exhausted children and two worn-out, shrunk-pizzled libertines? I proposed the idea of having myself fucked before them by my valets; but Saint-Fond, reeling with wine and aboil with ferocity, objected, saying that he'd have nothing brought in from the outside unless it was a brace of tigers, and that since there was fresh meat available, it ought to be devoured before it spoiled. Thereupon, he set upon those three charming maids' little asses: he pinched them, bit, scratched, tore them; blood was already flowing left and right when, whirling toward us, his prick glued up against his belly, he declared very bitterly that it was a bad day, he simply could not think up the means to make the victims suffer in the way he wished.

"Everything that enters my mind today," he said, "falls short of my desires; can't we put our heads together and invent something that will keep these whores three days in the most appalling death agonies?"

"Ah," I said, "you'd discharge before they were halfway to the grave, and the illusion dispelled, you'd come to their rescue."

"I am vexed, vexed indeed, Juliette," Saint-Fond retorted, "to see that you do not know me better than that; how very gravely you are mistaken, my angel, if you believe my passions are the sole aliment to my cruelty. Ah, like Herod, I should like to prolong my ferocities beyond life itself; I am frenziedly barbaric when I'm stiff, yes, and cold-bloodedly cruel when I've shed my fuck. Very well, Juliette," the villain continued, "look here: I'm going to discharge, we'll begin the serious torturing of these sluts once every drop of fuck is out of my balls, and you'll see whether or not I relent."

"Saint-Fond, you seem greatly aroused," said Noirceuil, "your speech makes that amply clear. Sperm is to be darted, there's the crux of the thing; it can be accomplished right away if you take my advice. 'Tis this and 'tis simple: we shall impale these young ladies on spits, and while they roast there over the fire, Juliette, frigging us, will baste three handsome joints of beef with our fuck."

"Oh, by Christ," said Saint-Fond, rubbing his member on the bleeding buttocks of the youngest and prettiest of the trio, "I swear to you that this one here will suffer worse than that."

"Yes? What the devil are you scheming to do to her?" asked Noirceuil, who had just scabbarded his weapon anew in my ass.

"You'll see," was the rascal's reply.

And he sets to work upon her with his powerful hands, he breaks her fingers one by one, dislocates her arms and legs, and runs the point of a little stiletto about a thousand times into her, to the depth of about an inch.

"I think," said Noirceuil, still housed in my bowels, "she'd have suffered quite as much from a spitting."

"And spitted she is going to be," Saint-Fond rejoins, "now she's been gashed a bit. Punctured thus she'll be more sensitive to the heat than if she'd been put to turn over the fire intact."

"I dare say you're right," Noirceuil agrees; "let's prepare the other two in the same manner."

I seize one, he takes the other, and still solidly implanted in my ass, the rascal puts her in the same state as she whom Saint-Fond has martyrized. I imitate him and we soon have all of them roasting before a blazing fire, while Noirceuil, damning every god in the sky, discharges in my bum, and I, gripping Saint-Fond's prick, spray his fuck upon the three charred bodies of the unhappy victims of lust most dreadful.

All three corpses were flung into a pit.

We resumed our drinking.

Invaded by new desires, the libertines called for men; my lackeys were summoned, they were the whole night long laboring in Saint-Fond's and Noirceuil's insatiable asses; and for all that weren't able to lift the pricks of those gentlemen, whose verbal outbursts, however, were astonishing; and it was in the course of that séance that I recognized more clearly than ever before how certain it was these monsters were as cruel upon cold principle as in the greatest heat of passion.

A month after this adventure, Noirceuil introduced me to the woman he wished to have become my soul-mate. As his marriage to Alexandrine had been postponed yet again, this time owing to Saint-Fond's bereavement, and because I think best not to describe that charming girl before I reach the appropriate point in my story—the point, that is, at which she came into my full possession—we'll now turn our attentions to Madame de Clairwil and the arrangements I made with that unusual person to cement our liaison.

Representing her to me, Noirceuil had been authorized in his use of superlatives. Madame de Clairwil was tall, splendidly proportioned; her glance, always keen, was often too fiery to withstand; but her eyes, large, dark, were more imposing than pleasing, and in general the aspect of this woman was more majestic than agreeable: her mouth, somewhat rounded, was fresh, her lips sensual, her hair, jet-black, fell to her knees; her nose was modeled to perfection, her brow was regal, rich were the lines of her bust, wonderfully smooth was her skin, though 'twas not untinged a little with sallowness, her flesh was ripe but firm; in short, this was the figure of Minerva adorned with Venus' amenities. Nevertheless, whether because I was the younger, or because my physiognomy had in grace what hers had in nobility, men invariably found me the more pleasing. Madame de Clairwil astonished, I was content to beguile; she compelled men's admiration, I seduced them.

To these imperious looks Madame de Clairwil joined a very lofty intelligence; she was exceptionally knowledgeable, I have never known her peer for an enemy to prejudices . . . which she had rooted out of herself while yet a child; and I have never known a woman to carry philosophy so far. As well, she had numerous talents, her command of English and Italian was complete, she was a born actress, danced like Terpsichore, was an accomplished chemist, physicist, made verse prettily, drew nicely, was well read in history, had geography at her fingertips, was no mean musician, wrote like Sévigné, but went perhaps a trifle too far in her witty sallies, the regular consequence being an insufferable overbearing way with those who failed to come up to her level; and almost no one ever did; she used to say that I was the one female in whom, until now, she had detected a trace of true intelligence.

This splendid personage had been five years a widow. She had never borne any children, to them she had an aversion which, in a woman, always denotes lack of feeling; one might fairly say that for lack of sensibility Madame de Clairwil had not an equal. She indeed prided herself upon never having shed a tear, upon never having been touched in the least by the fate of the unlucky. "My soul is callous, it is impassive," said she, "I put any sentiment whatever at defiance to attain it, with the exception of pleasure. I am mistress of that soul's movements and affections, of its desires, of its impulsions; with me, everything is under the unchallenged control of mind; and there's worse yet," she continued, "for my mind is appalling. But I am not complaining, I cherish my vices, I abhor virtue; I am the sworn enemy of all religions, of all gods and godlings, I fear neither the ills of life nor what follows death; and when you're like me, you're happy."

With such a character, Madame de Clairwil, one was swift to guess, might have adulators in good number, but very few were her friends; she no more believed in friendship than in benevolence, and no more in virtue than in gods. Along with all this went enormous wealth, a splendid house in Paris, an enchanting one in the country, luxuries of every kind, the age when a woman is at her peak, an iron constitution, faultless health. If there be any happiness at all in this world, then it cannot but belong to the individual in command of all these advantages and attributes.

At our very first meeting Madame de Clairwil confided in me, giving evidence of a frankness I found startling in a woman who, as I have just done telling you, was so proudly persuaded of her superiority; but she was never aloof toward me, I must say it out of fairness to her.

"Noirceuil described you accurately," she said; "'tis evident we have similar minds, similar tastes; we seem made to live together, so let us join forces, we shall go far. But above all, let's banish all restraints—from the start they were invented for fools only. Elevated characters, proud spirits, quick intelligences like ours make short shrift of all those popular curbs; they are aware that happiness lies on the farther side, they march courageously to its attainment, flouting the paltry laws, the sterile virtues, and the harebrained religions of those abject, worthless, swinish men who, so it does seem, exist only in order to dishonor Nature."

Several days later, Clairwil, with whom I was already grown infatuated, came to supper. We were two and alone. It was then, at this second encounter, we poured out our hearts to each other, acknowledged our peculiarities, detailed our sentiments. Oh, what a soul she had, that Clairwil! I believe that if vice itself could dwell in this world, it would have chosen the depths of that perverse being for the seat of its empire.

In a moment of mutual confidence before we were to betake ourselves to table, Clairwil leaned close to me; we were indolently reclining in a nook paneled by mirrors, velvet-covered pillows supported our heaving flanks; the soft light seemed to beckon to love and to favor its pleasures.

"Is it not true, my angel," said she, kissing my breasts, licking my nipples, "that 'tis through masturbating each other two such women as ourselves must become acquainted?"

And drawing up my skirts and petticoats as she uttered those words, the tribade darted her tongue deep into my mouth; and libertine fingers touched the mark.

"It is," she observed, "there pleasure lies, it slumbers there, on that bed of roses. My sweetest love, wouldst have me wake it? Oh, Juliette, I shall put you in ecstasies, will you permit me to catch fire from their heat? Little minx! your mouth gives me answer, your tongue hunts mine, invites it to voluptuousness. Ah! do unto me that which I have done unto you, and let's die in pleasure's embrace."

"Let us undress," I suggested to my friend, "lewd debauch calls for nakedness—and, do you know, I've not the faintest idea how you are made, I wish to see everything, I must, I must. Let's be rid of these inopportune raiments—ah, I want to see your heart throb, your breast quiver from the excitement I cause in you."

"What an idea," Clairwil murmured, "it hints at your character, Juliette, I adore it; we'll do just whatever you like."

And in a trice my friend was as naked as I; several minutes went by during which we studied each other in silence. The sight of the beauties nature had lavished upon me began to inflame Clairwil; I feasted my eyes upon hers. Never has there been such a lovely figure, never such a bosom. . . . Those buttocks! O God! 'twas the ass of that Aphrodite the Greeks reverenced; and how deliciously it was cleft, unwearyingly I kissed those wonders; and my friend, at first letting me most obligingly have my way with her, proceeded next to pay back my caresses a hundredfold.

"Now don't fret, leave everything to me," she said, having me lie down on the ottoman and spread my legs wide, "let me show you I am capable of giving a woman pleasure."

Whereupon two of her fingers began to work my clitoris and my asshole, the while her tongue, plunged a goodly depth in my cunt, avidly lapped up the fuck these titillations started. Never before had I been thus frigged; three times in a row I discharged into her mouth with such transports I thought I'd faint away. Clairwil, insatiable in her thirst for my fuck, and making ready to procure herself a fourth round, deftly and knowingly altered her approach; so that it was now one finger she inserted into my cunt, another wherewith she played trills on my clitoris, and her agile, her voluptuous tongue probed into my anus. . . .

"What skill! What consideration!" I exclaimed. "Ah, Clairwil, you are like to be my undoing."

And further spurts of whey were the product of that divine creature's industry.

"Eh then?" she demanded, when I had returned somewhat to my senses, "what say you, do I not know how to frig a woman? I adore women; is it then any wonder that I am versed in the art of giving them pleasure? What else could you expect? I'm depraved, dear heart. Is it my fault if Nature gave me tastes that differ from the ordinary? I find nothing more unjust than a law that prescribes a mingling of the sexes in order to procure oneself a pure pleasure; and what sex is more apt than ours in doing unto each other that which we do singly to delight ourselves? Must we not, of necessity, be more successful in pleasing each other than that being, our complete opposite, who can offer us none but the joys at the farthest remove from those our sort of existence requires?"

"What! Clairwil, do you mean to say that you dislike men?"

"I use them because my temperament would have it so, but

I scorn and detest them nonetheless: I'd not be adverse to destroying every last one of those by the mere sight of whom I have always felt myself debased."

"What pride!"

"It's a characteristic of mine, Juliette; that pride is coupled with frankness. I am plain-spoken; it is a means to facilitate our early acquaintance."

"Cruelty is implied in what you say; if your desires were to be translated into actions—"

"If? But they very often are. My heart is hard, and I am far from believing sensitiveness preferable to the apathy I luckily enjoy. Oh, Juliette," she continued, donning her clothes, "you perhaps entertain illusions regarding this dangerous softheartedness, this compassion, this sensibility, the having whereof is thought creditable by so many churls.

"Sensibility, my dear, is the source of all virtues and likewise of all vices. It was sensibility brought Cartouche to the scaffold, just as it caused the name of Titus to be writ gilt-lettered in the annals of benevolence. Owing to excessive sensibility, we behave virtuously; owing to excessive sensibility, we take joy in misbehaving; the individual lacking sensibility is an inert mass, equally incapable of good or evil, and human only insofar as he has the human shape. This purely physical sensibility depends upon the conformation of our organs, upon the delicacy of our senses, and, more than all the rest, upon the nature of our nervous humours within which I locate all the affections of man in general. Upbringing and, afterward, habit mold in this or that direction the portion of sensibility everyone receives from Nature; and selfishness, or the instinct of self-preservation, aids upbringing and habit to settle permanently upon this or that choice. But as the sort of education we are apt to receive unfailingly prepares us ill and indeed misleads us, the moment that education is over with, the inflammation produced in the electrical fluid by the impact of foreign objects, an operation we term the *effect of the passions,* begins to determine our habitual bent for good or for evil. If this inflammation is slight, whether because of the organs' denseness, which softens the impact and lessens the pressure of the foreign object upon the neural fluid, or because of the brain's sluggishness in communicating the effect of this pressure to the fluid, or again because of this fluid's reluctance to be set in motion, its turgidity, then the effects of our sensibility dispose us to virtue. If, in that other case, foreign objects act in a forceful manner upon our organs, if they penetrate them violently, if they stir into brisk motion the neural fluid particles which circulate in the hollow of the nerves, then our sensibility is such as to dispose us to vice. If the foreign objects' action is stronger yet, it leads us to crime, and finally to atrocities if the effect attains its ultimate intensity. But we notice that in every case the sensibility is simply a mechanism, that some degree or other of virtue or vice originates with it, that it is the sensibility which is responsible for whatever we do. When we detect an excess of sensibility in some young person, we may predict his future with confidence, and safely wager that some fine day this sensibility will see him a criminal; for it is not, as some may be prone to imagine, the species of sensibility, but the degree of sensibility that leads to crime; and the individual in whom its action is slow will be disposed to good, just as, very certainly, he in whom this action wreaks havoc will do evil, evil being more piquant, more attractive than good. Therefore 'tis toward evil that violent effects tend, following the general principle according to which all like effects, moral no less than physical, seek each other out and combine.

"And so there appears to be no doubt that the necessary procedure with a young person one was endeavoring to train up for life would be to blunt that sensibility; blunting it, you will perhaps lose a few weak virtues, but you will eliminate a great many vices, and under a form of government which severely castigates all vices and which never rewards virtues, it is infinitely better to learn not to do evil than to strive to do good. There is nothing dangerous whatever in not doing good, whereas the doing of evil may be fraught with perils when one is still too young to appreciate the importance of concealing those acts of wickedness invincible Nature constrains us to commit. I may go farther: doing good is the most useless thing in the world and the most essential thing in the world is not doing evil, and this, not from the standpoint of one's self, for the greatest of all joys is often born in excessive evil only, nor from the standpoint of religion, for nothing is so irrelevant to worldly well-being as what relates to this mummery about God, but solely from the standpoint of the law of the land, whereof the infraction, delightful as it may be, always, when discovered, precipitates the beginner into serious difficulties.

"Hence there would be no danger developing in our hypothetical young individual a heart oriented in such wise that he would never perform a good deed, but at the same time would never feel the impulse to perform an evil one either—until, at least, he had attained the age when experience would make him realize the indispensability of hypocrisy. Now, in such a case, the appropriate steps to take would be radically to deaden the sensibility immediately when you noticed that, too lively, it was threatening to lead to vicious conduct. For here I suppose that from the very apathy to which you would reduce his spirit some dangers could issue; these dangers, however, will always be far smaller than those his excessive sensibility might breed. Granted a sufficient subduing of sensibility, a consequent lowering of sensitivity and temperature, what crimes are committed will always be committed dispassionately, and hence the hypothetical pupil will have time enough to cover up his traces and divert suspicion, whereas those committed in a state of effervescence will, before he has the opportunity to collect his wits, tumble him into the gravest trouble. The cold-blooded crimes will be perhaps less splendid than somber, but they will be less ready of detection, because the phlegm and premeditation wherewith they will be perpetrated will guarantee leisure to so arrange them as not to have to fear their consequences; the other category, those perpetrated barefacedly, brashly, thoughtlessly, impulsively, will speedily bring their author to the gibbet. And your chief concern shall not be whether your pupil, when a mature man, commits or doesn't commit crimes, because in fact crime is a natural occurrence to which this or that human being is the accidental and often involuntary instrument, for whether he will or no, man is as a toy in Nature's hands when his organs put him there; your chief concern, I say, must be to see to it that this pupil commits the least dangerous offense, having regard to the laws of the country wherein he resides, in such sort that if the pettiest is punished and the most frightful is not, then 'tis very assuredly the most frightful you must let him commit. For, once again, it is not from crime you must shelter him, but from the sword that smites the perpetrator of crime: crime entails no disadvantages, its punishment entails many. To a man's welfare, it is all one whether he does or does not commit crimes; but it is most essential to this same welfare that he not be punished for those he commits, whatever their kind or degree of wickedness. A teacher's foremost duty to the pupil in his care would then be to cultivate in him a disposition toward the less dangerous of the two evils, since, unfortunately, it is but too true that he must incline in the one direction or in the other; and experience will make it very clear to you, that the vices proceeding from hard-heartedness are much less dangerous than those caused by excess of sensibility, the excellent reason for this being that the lucidity and calm characteristic of the former ensure the means to avoid punishment, whereas there is nothing more obvious than that he will be punished who, lacking the time to make suitable provisions, to take the basic precautions, flies blindly into action in the heat of passion. Thus, in the first case, that is, where the young person is left to be impelled by his whole sensibility, he will perform a few good deeds which practice reveals utterly futile; in the second, he will perform no good deeds, which will mean not the slightest loss to him; and owing to the way you have shaped him, he will commit none but those infractions which may be committed without risk. But your pupil will become cruel—and what shall the effects of this cruelty be? With one who has a little substance to him, they will consist in a stout refusal to act at the behest of a pity his mind and heart, molded by you, will not acknowledge or even register; I see no danger in that. 'Tis but a matter of one or two virtuous performances the fewer, and there is nothing more useless than virtue, since unto him who exercises it, it is a cross to bear, and since, in our climes, it is never rewarded. With a bold and rigorous spirit, this cruelty in action will consist in furtive crimes, whose sharp impact will, by its friction, heat the electrical particles in the fluid in his nerves, and will perhaps mean death for a number of persons of little account. Where's the danger here? for, in full possession of his faculty of judgment and right reason, he will proceed coolly, carefully, with such secrecy, with such art that the torch of Justice will never be able to bring the thing to light; thus will he be happy, and at no risk; what else does he want? It isn't evil, but the news thereof leaked out, that is perilous; and the most odious crime of all, if well concealed, causes infinitely less embarrassment than the slightest foible become public. Now consider the other case. The entirety of his sensitive faculties at his command and operative, this pupil espies an object and takes a liking to it; he would have it, his parents stand in his path: accustomed to giving the freest possible rein to his sensibility, he'll poison, he'll butcher everyone who, keeping him from that object, frustrates his purposes, and he'll perish broken on the wheel. You observe that in treating of both cases I have supposed the worst coming to the worst; I have merely offered one example of the dangers inherent in either situation, and I leave you to imagine as many others as you like. If after you have done calculating you end by approving, as I am very sure you shall, the extinction of all sensibility in a pupil, then the first branch to lop off the tree is necessarily pity. And actually what is pity? A purely egotistical sentiment: seeing others beset by woe, we pity them because we fear lest that same woe befall us. Show me the man who, owing to his nature, is exempt from all the ills that afflict humankind, and not only will that man have no pity whatever, he won't even know the meaning of the word. A yet greater proof that pity is no more than a purely passive commotion excited in persons of the skittish hysterical sort, owing to, or in proportion to, the misfortune of our fellows, is that, if we are immediate witnesses to it, we are always more sensitive to this misfortune, even though the sufferer be a total stranger, than we are to the calamity sustained a hundred leagues away by our very best friend. And how explain the difference in our reactions save by the fact that this feeling is nothing but the physical result of the accidental commotion inspired in our nervous system? Well, I ask whether such a feeling can be deserving of any respect and whether it can be viewed otherwise than as feebleness? More, it is an exceedingly painful feeling, since it occurs only through a comparison which harks us back to misfortune, and causes us to brood thereon. Contrariwise, its extinction procures us joy, since, as we extinguish it, in our *sang-froid* we glimpse a situation we are exempted from, and this permits us a favorable comparison—destroyed the moment we soften to the point of pitying the unlucky, which we do when tormented by the cruel thought that perhaps we ourselves may be in a similar plight tomorrow. Defy this annoying fear, learn to confront this danger undreadingly, and there's an end to your pity for others.

"A further proof that this feeling is nought but sheer weakness and pusillanimity is the particular frequency with which it is found in women and children, and its rarity in those individuals whose organs have acquired all suitable strength and vigor. For the same reason, the poor man is commonly he of the open heart; dwelling closer to misfortune than the rich man, more familiar with it, he is of readier sympathy. All of which thus demonstrates that pity, far from being a virtue, is but a weakness born of fear and of woe, a weakness which must be combated with especial severity when one sets about the task of blunting excessive nervous sensitivity, this sensibility that is so completely incompatible with every tenet of philosophy.

"There, Juliette, there they are, the principles that have led me to this tranquillity, this equanimity, to this stoicism which now enables me to do anything and to endure anything without batting an eyelash. Make haste to initiate yourself into these mysteries," continued that charming woman, as yet unaware of the point I had advanced to in these articles. "Make haste to annihilate this stupid commiseration which will upset you every time you catch sight of woe howsoever trivial. Arriving at that stage, my angel, by dint of continued tests which will soon have you convinced of the extreme difference between yourself and the alien object whose sad fate you lament, be persuaded the tears you shed over that individual cannot meliorate his circumstances one iota, and can only cause you affliction; be equally sure that the succor you were to give him would mean no more than an insipid sensual pleasure for you, whereas the refusal of aid may produce a very keen one. Be furthermore persuaded that you will be tampering with the natural scheme by rescuing from the indigent class those persons Nature deliberately placed there; that, wise and entirely logical in all her operations, her designs regarding human beings are neither for us to fathom nor to thwart; that her designs are substantiated by the unequal distribution of puissance among men, this necessarily implying unequal means, resources, conditions, and destinies. Avail yourself of examples out of history, Juliette, consult the authority of the ancients; you have been trained in the classics, recollect your reading. Remember the Emperor Licinius who, prescribing the harshest penalties, forbade all compassion toward the poor, and any sort of charity toward indigence. Remember that sect of Greek philosophers who maintained there was crime in seeking to meddle with the various shades in the Nature-ordained spectrum of social classes; and when you have developed your thought to the point I have, cease to deplore the loss of pity-prompted acts of virtue; for these virtuous acts, founded on egoism exclusively, are utterly unworthy of respect. Since it is by no means sure that there is good in extricating from misfortune the wretch Nature put there, it is far simpler to nip in the bud the sentiment whereby we are rendered sympathetic to his sufferings than to let it flower; and be all the while apprehensive lest our compassion, interfering with the order of things, be outrageous to Nature; the best course is to cultivate in ourselves such a frame of mind as will enable us to look upon those sufferings with indifference and unconcern. Ah, dear friend! were you, like me, strong enough to advance one step further, had you the courage to take pleasure contemplating the sufferings of others, merely from the agreeable thought of not experiencing them yourself, a thought which necessarily produces a very decided joy— were you able to go that far, no doubt but that it would represent a great achievement, since you'd have succeeded in turning some of life's thorns into roses. Be equally certain, my heart, that men of the stamp of Denis, Nero, Louis XI, Tiberius, Wenceslas, Herod, Andronicus, Heliogabalus, Retz[6] based their happiness upon similar principles, and that if they were able without shuddering, without qualms to do all they did in the line of atrocity, it is obviously because they had mastered the technique of exploiting crime for lustful purposes. 'Those men were monsters,' a fool will tell me. So indeed they were, according to our ways of thinking and behaving; but from the point of view of Nature and in terms of her dictates, they were simply the instruments of her intentions: endowing them with their ferocious and bloodthirsty characters,

---

[6] Here the allusion is to the Marshal.

she appointed them to execute her laws. Thus, though they appear
to have performed much evil, as that is defined by man-made law,
they acted in admirable conformance to the law of Nature, whose
aim is to destroy at least as much as she creates. No, no, those
worthies wrought a substantial weal, since they put her desires
into effect; whence it results that the individual who has a character like these so-called tyrants', or he who manages to raise his
character to this level, will not only not steer clear of evil, but may
even discover in the fulfillment of his designated or elected role
a source of very potent joy which he will savor all the more fearlessly, the more certain he is that, by means either of his cruelties
or his disorders, he is rendering Nature a service no less useful
than that a saint performs through the exercise of his capacities
for good-doing and virtue. Fortify all this with examples, feed
it upon practice; gaze often and long upon spectacles of woe; accustom yourself to refusing aid to the downtrodden, to the unlucky,
so that you become habituated to the idea and the sight of sufferers
abandoned to their sufferings; be the direct cause of some, of a few
which are somewhat crueler, more atrocious than the everyday;
and it won't be long before you recognize that between the sufferings you provoke, and which do not affect you in the least, and the
voluptuous vibration of your nerves, thrilled by the impact of these
sufferings, even if this be merely the thrill that comes of contrasting
weal and woe and finding the comparison heavily in your favor—
you have no cause for a moment's hesitation. Little by little your
sensibility will deaden; you'll not have prevented great crimes,
since, to the contrary, you'll have caused some to be committed and
will yourself have perpetrated not a few, but at least you'll have
done so phlegmatically, with this apathy which permits the veiling
of the passions, and which, safeguarding lucidity, indispensable
to the avoidance of disagreeable repercussions, is your guarantee
against all dangers."

"Oh, Clairwil, I can't imagine that with such attitudes you
have impoverished yourself through *good works*."

"I am rich," that extraordinary woman replied, "so rich that
I am not even sure how much I have. Well, Juliette, I swear to you
that I would prefer to throw all the money I own into the river
than employ a penny of it in what fools call charities, prayers, or

alms; I believe such things are most harmful to humanity, fatal to the poor whose energies are sapped by the practice of bestowing largesses, and more dangerous yet for the wealthy man who believes he has secured title to every virtue once he has given a crown or two to some priests or shiftless rascals, a certain means for masking his every vice the while encouraging the vices of others."

"Adorable woman," I said to my friend, "knowing the position I hold in the Minister's entourage, as I think you must, you cannot doubt that my moral outlook as regards the subjects you have been discussing is not a great deal purer than yours."

"Certainly," said she, "I know all the services you render Saint-Fond; I have been his friend as well as Noirceuil's for ages —how could I help but be familiar with those two scoundrels' debauches? You collaborate in them, and that is laudable; were I needy I'd do the same, and I'd do it happily, for I positively worship crime. But I also know, Juliette, that by laboring much in behalf of others you have, so far, labored little in your own; and with but two or three petty thefts to your credit you can still benefit from examples and lessons; so let me encourage you and steel you to more considerable undertakings, if indeed you really wish to be worthy of us."

"Ah," said I, "I am already much in your debt; pray continue to instruct me, and rest assured you will nowhere find a more attentive nor an apter student. I am in your hands, there is nothing I'll not attempt at your side, guided by your advice; and from now on my whole ambition shall be someday to surpass my teacher. But, my best beloved, we are already forgetful of our pleasures: I received divine ones from you, you've not yet given me a chance to reciprocate, and I am keenly impatient to instill into your soul some spark of the heavenly fire you lately caused to blaze in mine."

"Juliette, you are delicious, truly. But I am too old for you. Are you aware that I am thirty? Ordinary things have long since palled. . . . To be moved ever so slightly, I must have recourse to refinements so coarse, episodes so potent—ere the sweet sap rise in me there must be such a quantity of preliminaries, of monstrous thoughts, of obscene gestures, actions; and if I am to discharge, I require. . . . But enough; my habits will affright you, my transports will shock you, my exigencies will fatigue you. . . ."

And then a brightness entered her eyes, a lewdness wetted her lips; she asked:

"Have you women in the house? Are they lascivious? Pretty or not, that doesn't matter; you'll arouse me. But I could use a bevy of tolerably roguish, immodest, patient, vigorous, foul-mouthed creatures; and they needn't bother to come into the room if they're wearing a stitch of clothing. How many such women can you provide me?"

"I have only four in my permanent hire," I answered. "Four being enough for my emergency requirements."

"That's exceedingly few. You can't pretend to be poor. My dear, you ought to maintain a staff of at least twenty and change them all every week, furthermore. Ah, 'tis clear I'll have to teach you how to use the money you're swimming in. Are you miserly? Not that there's anything wrong with that. I idolize money, I've often frigged myself sitting amidst the heaps of *louis d'or* I've amassed, it's the idea that I can do whatever I like with the money before my eyes, that's what drives me wild. I find it quite natural that others have the same taste; but nevertheless I won't have you deprive yourself: only fools are unable to understand that one can be simultaneously niggardly and lavish, that one can love wasteful squandering upon one's pleasures and refuse a farthing to charity. Well, then. Send for your four women; and if you wish to see me discharge, find some switches."

"Switches?"

"Switches, rods, lashes, however you please to call them."

"Do you whip, my dear?"

"Until blood flows, my darling. And I endure like treatment. It's the most delicious passion I know of; none surer to inflame my entire being. Nobody doubts nowadays but that passive flagellation is of prime efficacity; it is a matchless restorative, supplying new vitality to the frame wearied by overindulgence. No wonder then that all those who have worn themselves to a frazzle in riot and sport have regular and avid recourse to the painful and invigorating operation of flagellation, supreme remedy for exhaustion from feebleness about the loins or total loss of strength, or for a cold, vicious, and oddly organized constitution. This operation necessarily implies a violent commotion in the lax or deficient parts, it

procures a voluptuous irritation which heats them, and causes the
sperm to leap with infinitely increased force: the keen sensation
of pain in the parts upon which the blows are applied subtilizes the
blood and accelerates its circulation, quickens the spirits by furnishing excessive heat to the genitals, in short, to the libidinous person
in quest of pleasure provides, at such times as they are not naturally
forthcoming, the means for consummating the libertine act, and
for multiplying his impudicious joys beyond the limits imposed by
that unkind Nature. As regards active flagellation, in all the world
can there be a greater delight for hardhearted, tough-minded individuals like us? Is there another that so clearly bears the stamp
of ferocity, that, briefly, more fully satisfies our Nature-given penchant for cruelty? Oh, Juliette! to break in to this degradation
some youthful object, appealing and mild and who when possible
is somehow related to us, harshly to inflict upon her this form of
torture, all the characteristics whereof are so emphatically voluptuous, to be amused by her tears, excited by her distress, irritated
by her capers, inflamed by her writhings, by that voluptuous dancing[7] performed to the music of pain, to make her blood flow, her
sweat, her tears, to feast upon them, upon her pretty face to mark
and exult at contortions of sufferings and the twitching caused by
despair, with one's tongue to lap up those floods incarnadine so
nicely contrasting with the lily fairness of a soft white skin, to feign
to relent for an instant only to inspire terror the next by threats, to
carry them out, and in doing so, to use yet more outrageous and
more atrocious means, to spare nothing in your rage, to have at the
most delicate parts, those very ones Nature seems to have created
to be venerated by fools, such as the breasts or the interior of the
vagina, such as the face itself—Oh, Juliette! that is joy. 'Tis it not,
as it were, to encroach somewhat upon the public hangman's domain? is it not to play his role, and by itself does not this idea suffice
to provoke an ejaculation with people who, unspeakably jaded as
are we, indifferent to everything simple and commonplace, must
study deeply and seek far if we are to find again that which our
excesses have caused us to lose? Nor ought you be surprised to discover this taste in a woman. That same Brantôme, from whom we

---

[7] Brantôme's expression is *tordions*. For the reference, see note below.

borrowed a term a moment ago, with charming candor and naïveté offers us various examples in support of these theses.[8] There was, says he, a fashionable and distinguished lady, equally beautiful and rich; for several years she had been a widow, and her moral corruption was astonishing. She used to hold parties; to them she would invite girls of high social rank, and always of exceptional beauty, it was her pleasure to undress her guests and give them fierce spankings. To obtain the right to punish them she would accuse them of imaginary misbehavior; would then beat them with switches, and her whole joy consisted in seeing them quiver and squirm beneath the blows: the more they capered about, the louder their plaints, the more abundantly they bled and wept, the happier was the whore. Sometimes she was content to bare their behinds instead of stripping them altogether naked, from the act of lifting their skirts and keeping them raised deriving yet more satisfaction than that afforded her when they were nude and hence easy prey.

"A great nobleman, Brantôme tells us farther on, also indulged in this same pleasure of fustigating his wife, either nude or with her skirts pulled up.

"A mother, the same writer assures us, had the habit of whipping her daughter twice every day, not for anything the girl had done, but uniquely for the pleasure of contemplating her sufferings. When the young thing reached the age of fourteen, she so inflamed her mother's concupiscence that she wouldn't let four hours go by without flogging her cruelly. Of contemporaries we have examples enough, do we not, and better ones at that; and could not your friend Saint-Fond, who never misses giving his daughter her daily lashing, serve as the subject for an entire corpus of modern research?"

"I've been the victim of that taste," I observed, "but I rather fancy it nonetheless, and may well adopt it some day in my turn. Oh yes, Clairwil, I'll acquire all your tastes, I wish if I possibly can

[8] Book I of *Les Vies des Dames galantes* of his time, London edition, 1666, 12mo. It would perhaps have been preferable had we extracted verbatim out of the author cited; we have not done so for two reasons: of these, the first is that quotations always spoil the appearance of the printed page; the second, that Brantôme merely sketched what we have thought desirable to paint in all its colors, and in all its truth.

to become identical to you; henceforth Juliette shall know no happiness until she has taken on all your vices."

The four women made their entrance; they were naked in accordance with my friend's desire, and as a group they surely presented a stirring sight to lewdness. The eldest was not quite eighteen, the youngest fifteen; there were lovely bodies and most agreeable faces.

"They will do," said Clairwil, glancing briefly at each.

Each had a bundle of switches in her hand; these Clairwil examined rather more closely.

"Very well, we shall proceed by order of age. Approach," she said to the youngest, "come here and prostrate yourself at my feet. Now humbly beg pardon for your clumsy behavior yesterday."

"Clumsy behavior? Madame, I don't believe I—"

And Clairwil gave her a resounding slap across the face.

"I tell you you behaved clumsily. I order you to kneel and ask forgiveness."

"Oh indeed, Madame," said the little girl, falling to her knees, "I ask it with all my heart."

"But I don't intend to forgive you without first punishing you. Stand up and turn your ass obediently this way."

Thereupon, having softly stroked the pretty ass with the palm of her hand, Clairwil smote it so forcefully that she left there the impress of her five fingers; tears began to flow down the girl's cheeks. The poor thing had had no forewarning of what was in store for her, she had never experienced anything like it, this reception was affecting her dolorously. Clairwil peers at her and licks her eyes as soon as she sees the tears well forth; from her own eyes flames dart, her breathing quickens and becomes hoarse, her breasts heave in cadence with the beating of her heart. She stabs her tongue into the girl's mouth, sucks her tongue, then, further animated by this caress, applies another blow to her ass, and this one is harder than the first.

"You're a little slut," says Clairwil. "I saw what you were doing yesterday, I did indeed: frigging pricks, and don't deny it. I'll not have you committing such outrages. I favor morality, I do, I expect modesty in young girls."

"Madame, I swear to you—"

"No swearing, whore, and no excuses either," Clairwil interrupted, punching the girl's flank; "guilty or not, you're due to be
vexed, for I aim to amuse myself. Wretched little creatures of your
sort are no use whatever except for providing entertainment to
women of mine."

So saying, Clairwil pinches the fleshier parts of the victim's
pretty body, this wrings shrieks from her, each of which gets no
farther than her lips, for our libertine is there to collect them in her
mouth. Her wrath grew apace, she gave utterance to the foulest
words, they came forth spasmodically, like her gasps of joy; she
bent her victim down over the couch, lubriciously investigated her
bum, pried it open, thrust her tongue thereinto, then concentrated
on her buttocks afresh, bit them in four places, the which the girl
did not endure without much jerking to and fro and sudden starts
that greatly diverted my friend and made her laugh one of those
wicked laughs wherein the mischief outweighs the gaiety.

"Little bugger-fucker, you're in for a thrashing," says she,
"yes, by the bum-stuffed Almighty, I'm going to flay you, and this
cunning little shit-sump of yours is going to show every stripe for
an age."

Catching up a bundle of switches, she pulls the girl to her feet,
takes her around the waist with her left arm, and thrusting a knee
against her belly, bends her so that her ass is in the fairest position;
Clairwil pauses for a minute, seems to reflect, to brood, then, without a word, begins to lay on and applies five and twenty stinging
cuts so nicely distributed that every square inch of this formerly
fresh pink ass is covered with welts. That done, she summons the
other three women one after the other, has each stick her tongue in
her mouth, ordering each to fondle her buttocks while embracing
her, to tickle her asshole, to poke into it, to approve her punishment
of the delinquent, and above all to furnish additional information
upon her misconduct. After she was finished with the three girls,
my turn came, I kissed her in similar wise, socratized her, praised
her firm handling of the victim, and by means of a string of arrant
calumnies fanned her lubricious rage against the unfortunate creature. When I kissed her, she wanted me to fill her mouth with my
spittle, I did so, and she swallowed it; next, returning to work, she

laid on a second series of blows, twice as numerous as the first; then, immediately, a third series, bringing the total to one hundred and fifty strokes: the little girl's ass was but one bleeding wound. She bade the three other women lick it and convey the blood into her mouth; and she kissed me, transferring that blood into mine.

"Juliette," said she, "the fever of delirium is taking fast hold of my senses; I must warn you that these other hussies are going to be more uncompromisingly dealt with."

She looses the little girl and from her receives a light tonguing about the cunt and anus.

"Very well," says she, pointing to the second, "I believe your age puts you next in line. Step up, whore."

The latter, terrified by what has just been done to her comrade, instead of obeying, shrinks back. But Clairwil, who was in no merciful mood, seizes her by the arm and gives her several very violent slaps. She begins to weep.

"Good," says Clairwil. "That's what I like."

And since this charming creature, sixteen years of age, had prettily formed breasts already, Clairwil squeezed them until she screamed; then, kissing them the very next moment, she worried them with her teeth.

"And now," she said with a curse, "we'll have a look at your ass"; it proved very pleasing to Clairwil's eye and she could not help but exclaim, before bringing them under the fire of her scourge, "what splendid cheeks!"

Greatly impressed by their excellence, she rendered them new courtesies: she stooped forward, nuzzled that miracle of Nature, and sucked the hole; she rolled the girl onto her back, sucked her clitoris; then promptly returned again to her ass. But they are not slaps she now applies, they are jarring blows of her clenched fist she drives home, pounding this frail body until it is all black and blue from thigh to shoulder.

"Bugger-fuck!" cries she, "I'm going out of my mind! This little slattern has one of the loveliest asses I've seen in my life."

She seizes the switches and lays frantically on; but after a few score strokes she employs a tactic she has not used hitherto. Clairwil pries open the patient's buttocks with her left hand, so that the blows she is delivering with her right hand fall upon the exposed asshole and the sensitive sector adjoining it; wherefore it is that the entire area is soon bloody. And while all this was going ahead Clairwil required kisses upon her mouth and fingers in her bum. The three other girls and I attended to these matters; however, she would allow no one but me to swallow her saliva. The third girl was treated like the first, the fourth like the second; they were all flogged virtually to ribbons. When these ceremonies were over, Clairwil, in an ecstasy and as beautiful as Venus to behold, ranged the four girls in a line so as to compare their asses and verify whether they were all sufficiently lacerated. Finding that one had been somewhat neglected, she rained another fifty blows upon it, looked, and satisfied herself that it was presently in a state as deplorable as the others.

"Juliette, do you wish me to thrash you too?"

"By all means, yes," I answered at once. "How can you suspect me of not passionately desiring whatever adds to the sum of your delights? Fie! Whip away, here's my ass, here's my body, my whole being is yours to do with as you like."

"In that case," she said, "climb upon the shoulders of the youngest of these tarts and while I flog you the three others will heed my orders. Take up your switches," she went on; "which of you has the stoutest arm? You'll be the last to operate, and you," she said, nodding to the most slender of the three, "you shall be the first. So listen to me. This is what you are to do: You will kneel facing my ass, you will praise it loudly, unreservedly, you'll kiss it, you'll divide my buttocks, will introduce your tongue far into the hole, while doing so rubbing my clitoris with one finger; then you will stand up, and to the tune of threats and invectives, you will bestow two hundred strokes upon my ass, they must come in swift succession and in steadily mounting force; and you over there, you've heard what I've just said: when this girl is done, you will promptly imitate the performance; we begin."

With nips, pinches, scratches, Clairwil was harrying the behind of the little girl upon whose shoulders I was perched, and in the meantime was flailing me in the most determined fashion; concurrently, the others were carrying out her instructions to the letter, and the whore, anxious to make use of everything available, was kissing the mouths of those who were not whipping her. As the stripes accumulated upon my ass the ferocious creature kissed and licked the marks avidly, and when she herself had received the number of strokes she had specified, she ordered positions to be shifted.

The eighteen-year-old girl knelt in front of her; advancing her cunt, Clairwil pushed it into the girl's face,. grinding the lips of her vagina and her clitoris against the girl's nose, mouth, and eyes, and bidding her lick all her tongue could reach. Another girl stationed to the right, a third to the left, were vigorously scourging my friend who, swinging a bundle of switches in either hand, was avenging herself upon the pair of asses ahead of her; squatting astride the head of the girl busy licking her cunt, I offered Clairwil mine to suck; and here the whore discharged. And that discharge, accompanied by shouts and shrieks, convulsions and blasphemies, was one of the most lubricious and most voluptuous frenzies I have ever observed in all my days; the tribade fired point-blank at the pretty visage fairly engulfed in her cunt, and drenched it with fuck.

"Come along, by Jesus, on to something else," Clairwil cried, not so much as pausing for breath, "I never take time out when my sperm is started; so you whores, belabor me, rack me, suck me, whip me, frig me as hard as ever you can."

The girl of eighteen lies down upon the ottoman, I seat myself upon her face, Clairwil camps herself on mine. I sucked, and was sucked; above me the youngest girl gave her buttocks to be kissed by Clairwil whom another girl was embuggering with a dildo; the slenderest of the quartet, bending over, was finger-frigging Clairwil's clitoris, which was established hard by my mouth, and in the meantime was presenting her cunt to my friend whose hands were polluting it in similar style. So it was our libertine was simultaneously arousing an asshole by lecheries, having her anus tongued, being sodomized, and getting her clitoris teased.

Several minutes of this had gone by when she said to me, "Juliette, I told you that if I am to stiffen, I must be imaginatively moved; one of the things that best excites my imagination is to hear much foul language uttered all around me. Your whores, are they dumb?"

We were arrived at an awkward pass; for these girls, chosen out of the best ranks of the bourgeoisie, and never having been libertine except with me, had poor acquaintance with any idiom apt to be agreeable to Clairwil's ears; they did the best they were able, however, but I was obliged to aid them, and virtually all alone had to supply the caustic insults she was pleased to hear addressed to the Supreme Being in whose existence the jade had no more belief than I. Consequently, she who had been clitoris-frigging replaced me at my cunt-sucking post; and I concentrated on vilifying each member of the scurvy Christian trinity as they had never been blasphemed in all their lives. The tribade squirmed and sighed incontinently, but nothing came of it, postures and episodes had to be changed once again. I have never seen anything so majestic, nor so beautiful, nor so animated as that superb woman at the conclusion of this scene; were you of a mind to paint the very goddess of lewd love, you could not have looked elsewhere for your model; she throws her arms about my neck, hugs me, tongues me for a quarter of an hour, exhibits her ass to me; it was scarlet all over and contrasted in the most agreeable manner with the alabaster whiteness of the rest of her body.

"Thrice bum-stuffed, holy God of buggery," said she, overwrought, "how hot I am in the cunt, Juliette, and what things I could achieve in this state; there's not a crime of whatever sort or extent you can imagine I'd not commit on the spot. Oh, my love—oh, my whore—oh, my dearest little companion . . . oh, thou whom I love infinitely and in whose embrace I want to shed a lifetime's fuck, oh, Juliette, you must admit that nothing paves a surer or a smoother way to horror than the calm self-confidence, impunity, capital, and good health we enjoy; so suggest to me the idea for a few crimes . . . I'll accomplish them while you look on. . . . Let's, oh, I beseech you, let's perpetrate an infamy. . . ."

Noticing that the youngest of the girls was arousing her and that she was going from her mouth to her ass to her cunt, sucking them one after the other, I inquired in a whisper, "Would you care to abuse her?"

"No," was her reply, "it wouldn't satisfy me; I've nothing against giving a woman an occasional pummeling, but as for total material dissolution, you understand . . . I'd have to have a man. Only men rouse me to serious cruelties; I adore revenging my sex for the horrors men subject us to when those brutes have the upper hand. You can't imagine with what delight I'd now murder a male. Any male at all. My God, the tortures I'd inflict upon him; the slow, winding, obscure path I'd find to bring him to his final destination. . . . Alack, 'tis plain to see, your mind has yet to reach full flower, you haven't any men about for me to kill; and so let's end the evening with a few exercises in libidinous nastiness since we cannot close it with crimes."

The libidinous acts, performed with great precision and all the desired conclusions, finally exhaust her; she refreshes herself in a bath of rose water, is dried, perfumed, draped in the most immodest of gowns; and we sit down to supper.

Clairwil, quite as eccentric in her comportment at table as in bed, quite as intemperate, no less curious in the article of eating than in the other of fucking, fed only on fowl and game, and they had to be boned and then served up disguised in all sorts of forms; her usual drink was sweetened water and it had to be iced regardless of the season, and to every pint of this liquid she added twenty drops of essence of lemon and two spoonfuls of orange flower extract; she never touched wine, but consumed large amounts of coffee and liqueurs; she ate in excessive quantity; furthermore, of the better than fifty dishes put before her she attacked every one. Advised beforehand of her tastes, I saw to it that her desires were accommodated, and it defies belief, the tale of all she made away with. That charming person, whose custom was whenever and wherever possible to secure the adoption of her private tastes, recommended them to me so heartily that she induced me to observe her diet, but not her abstinence from wine; I still indulge very heavily in it and shall doubtless continue to do so for the rest of my life.

While we were supping I confessed to Clairwil my amazement at her libertinage.

"You haven't seen much yet," she replied, "little beyond a faint sketch of what I regularly accomplish in lewd debauchery. I am most eager that we essay truly extraordinary things together; I shall have you admitted into a society I belong to, and whose members specialize in obscenities of a much superior dimension. To its meetings each husband must bring his wife, each brother his sister, each father his daughter, each bachelor a friend, each lover his mistress; and gathered in a spacious hall each takes his pleasure with what pleases him most, subject to no rule save that of his desires, to no limit save that of his imagination; the most praiseworthy is he who acquits himself of the greatest and most numerous extravagances, and cash prizes are awarded to those who distinguish themselves in infamy or who invent new ways and means for procuring oneself pleasure."

"Oh, dearest friend," I cried, taking Clairwil in my arms, "you simply have no idea how those few details excite me, nor how happy I would be to·join your circle."

"Yes, but will you be considered eligible? Candidates are submitted to the most arduous tests."

"Do you doubt of my capacity, of my determination? And whatever these initiations may be, do you suppose I will flinch, knowing as you do all that I have performed intrepidly in the company of Noirceuil and Saint-Fond?"

"True enough," she conceded, "you're not shy, it must be owned. Your chances of being admitted are better than fair." Then a note of enthusiasm entered her voice. "Oh, Juliette, as it is always to the disgust, to the restlessness, to the despair at not ever having found either a mutual understanding or mutual pleasure with the object to which we are conventionally bound that are owing all of wedlock's miseries, to remedy this hideous situation, to counteract the hideous social practices whereby mismatched individuals are imprisoned all their lives in nightmarish unions, it would be necessary that all men and all women federate into such clubs. A hundred husbands, a hundred fathers, corporatively with their wives or daughters, are availed thereby of all they lack. When I cede my husband to Climène, she obtains everything her own husband cannot give her and from the one she abandons to me, I derive all the delights mine is incapable of providing me. These exchanges multiply and thus, you see, in a single evening every woman enjoys a hundred men, each man as many women; in the course of these forgatherings characters develop; one has an opportunity to study oneself; the most entire freedom of taste or fancy holds sway there: the man who dislikes women amuses himself with his fellows, the woman who is fond of persons of her own sex simply follows the dictates of her penchants also; no constraint, no hindrances, no modesty, the mere desire to increase one's pleasures ensures that each will offer all his resources. Thereupon the general interest maintains the pact, and particular interest coincides straitly with the general, which renders indissoluble the ties forming the society: ours has been fifteen years in existence, and all that time I have never witnessed a single squabble, no, not one instance of ill-humor. Such arrangements annihilate jealousy, forever destroy the fear of cuckoldry, two of life's most pernicious poisons, and for that reason alone merit preference over those monotonous partnerships in which husband and wife, pining their lives away one in the presence of the other, are doomed either to everlasting boredom and displeasure, or to grief at being unable to dissolve their marriage save at the price of dishonor for them both. May our example persuade mankind to do as we. There are, I am aware, some prejudices to overcome; but prejudice cannot long survive when one of these groups, as is the case with ours, is injected with a strong philosophical temper. It was during my first year of marriage I was granted membership, I was just sixteen then. Oh yes, making my debut, I confess I did indeed blush at having to appear naked before all those men and to participate in their carryings-on and in those of the women who, because of my age and figure, were drawn to me like flies to sugar; but in three days I was acquitting myself like a veteran. The example of the others seduced me; and I can honestly affirm that no sooner did I see my lascivious companions vying for honors in the choice and the invention of lubricities, no sooner did I see them wallowing in filth and infamy, than I plunged into the competition with ardent good will and shortly surpassed them all in theory and practice alike."

The description of this delicious association had such an effect upon me that I was unwilling to take leave of Clairwil until she had sworn to secure my entrance into her club. The oath was sealed with fresh outpourings of fuck we both released before the eyes of three strapping lackeys: they held candelabras while we frigged each other, and though they were moved by the spectacle, Clairwil forbade them from participating in it save as bystanders.

"There you have an instance," said she, "of how one accustoms oneself to cynicism, a habit of mind whereof proof will be required of you before you are accepted into our society."

We separated, enchanted with each other and promising to meet together again at the very first opportunity.

Noirceuil was impatient to find out how my liaison with Madame de Clairwil was progressing; the warmth wherewith I spoke of her translated my gratitude. He wanted graphic particulars, I supplied them; and, as Clairwil had done, he criticized me for not having a more numerous complement of women in my household. I increased them by eight the very next day, which gave me a seraglio of twelve of the prettiest creatures in Paris; I exchanged them against a dozen fresh ones every month.

I mentioned the society Clairwil belonged to; did Noirceuil attend its meetings?

"In the days when men were in the majority there," he replied, "I never missed a single one; but I have given up going since everything has fallen into the hands of a sex whose authority I dislike. Saint-Fond felt the same way and dropped out shortly after I did. But that is not particularly relevant," Noirceuil continued; "if those orgies amuse you, and since Clairwil enjoys them, there is no reason why you shouldn't join in: everything vicious must be given a fair try, and only virtue is thoroughly boring. At those meetings you will be frigged to perfection, exquisitely fucked; you'll be nourished upon the very best principles only; and so I would advise you to gain admission as soon as you possibly can." Then he inquired if my new friend had recounted her adventures to me in detail.

"No," said I.

"Philosophical in spirit though you are, and the fact cannot have escaped her notice," Noirceuil remarked, "she probably feared lest you be scandalized. For that Clairwil is a very paragon of lust, cruelty, debauchery, and atheism; there is no horror, no execration wherewith she is not soiled profoundly; her social position and boundless wealth have always saved her from the rope, but she's merited it twenty times over: reckon up the sum of her daily activities and there you have the total of her crimes, and had she been hanged every day of her life it would never have been without cause. Saint-Fond thinks very highly of her; nonetheless, and this I know, he prefers you for a number of reasons: therefore, Juliette, continue to be deserving of the confidence of a man in whose power it is to make your life a happy one, or an unhappy."

"Rest assured," I rejoined, "all my efforts shall be bent in that direction." Noirceuil had come to fetch me for supper at his little house, and we betook ourselves there and spent the night carousing with two other engaging persons, executing all the extravagances that occurred to that specialist in lubricious practices.

It was shortly afterward that, mightily stirred by what I had been witness to, by the things I had been hearing, I reached the point where I simply could not restrain myself any longer, I had absolutely to commit a crime of my own; and I was eager to learn, moreover, whether I could truly rely upon the impunity that had been promised me. So I took counsel with myself, and decided to enact one such horror as I was being schooled in day in and day out. Wishing to put both my daring and my savagery to the test, I got into man's attire and, a brace of pistols in my pocket, went out alone, stood in a back street, and waited for the first comer, with the aim of robbing and murdering him for my pleasure. I was leaning against the wall; I was in that state of inner turmoil great passions provoke, and whose impact upon the animal spirits is necessary to the elementary criminal delight. I listened, asweat. Every murmur, every footfall raised my hopes. The very faintest movement in the shadows made me think my prey was nigh; and then I heard sounds of lamentation. I sped in the direction whence they came, they were groans; I approach, 'tis a poor woman huddled upon a doorstep.

"And who are you?" I inquired, drawing close to the creature.

"The most unfortunate of women," is her tearful reply; and I observe that she cannot be over thirty years of age; "and if you are death's messenger, you bring me glad tidings."

"But your difficulties are of precisely what kind?"

"They are frightful," she said, and as she sat up, the lamplight revealed her mild inviting features. "Yes, few have ever been so unlucky as I. We've had no work for a week, no money, we had a room in this building, we weren't able to pay the rent, nor able either to buy milk for the baby—they've taken it away from me and put my husband in jail. I too would have been arrested had I not run away from those monsters who treated us so brutally. You see me lying on the threshold of a house that belonged to me once, for I have not always been poor. In those days, when I could afford to,

I helped the needy; will you do for me now what I used to do for them? I do not ask much."

A subtle glow stole through my veins as I heard those words, savored that accent. Oh, by God, I said to myself, what an occasion for a delectable crime, and how the idea stung my senses.

"Get up," said I. "I'm a man as you can see. You have a body left to you, don't you? I intend to amuse myself with it."

"Oh, Sir! Here am I beset by sorrow and distress—can such a state kindle lust?"

"It kindles mine all right; so do as I tell you, else you'll regret it."

And taking strong hold of her arm, I forced her to stand still while I proceeded to an investigation. It brought agreeable things to light, those skirts harbored charms very fair, very firm, very appetizing.

"Frig me," I ordered, conveying her hand to my cunt, "I am a woman, but one who stiffens for her own sex. Put your fingers in there and rub."

"Oh, Lord! Leave me be, leave me be, I shudder at all these horrors. Though poor, I am honest; don't humiliate me, for pity's sake!"

She endeavors to break away from me, I seize her by the hair, raise a pistol to her temple: "Be off, buggeress," I say, "off to hell with you, and tell them there that Juliette sent you."

And she fell, blood gushing from her head. Yes, my friends, I shot her dead, I won't deny it, neither will I pretend that this deed did not cause a sudden rise in the temperature of my neural humours, for, as I enacted it, my fuck fairly spat forth.

And so these are the fruits of crime, I mused, how right they were to describe it to me in such glowing terms. God! what sovereign influence it can exert upon a brain like mine, and what gigantic pleasures it can afford!

Hearing the pistol-shot, people had come to their windows; I saw a few heads and now began to think of my safety. Cries of "Police, police!" went up on all sides. It was just after midnight, I was hailed, ordered to halt; the discovery of my weapons eliminated all doubt; I was asked my name.

"You'll be informed at the Minister's," I said brazenly. "Take me to the Hôtel de Saint-Fond."

Dumbfounded, the sergeant does not dare refuse; I am manacled, I am pinioned . . . and still the fuck seeps down my thighs: delicious are the fetters of the crime you adore, and wearing them causes one long spasm of joy.

Saint-Fond had not yet retired; a servant notified him, I was led in, the Minister greeted me with a smile.

"That will do," he said to the sergeant; "had you not brought this lady here to my house you were as good as hanged. You may go now, sir, and resume your functions, consider that you have done your duty. What has just transpired shall remain a mystery. You are not to intrude into it; I presume I need say no more."

Alone with my lover, I related all that had passed, my account set his prick in the air; he wished to know when the woman had fallen to the ground, had I been able to appreciate the effects of her contortions?

I answered that I had not had enough time.

"No, I suppose not. That's the trouble with performances of that sort, you aren't able to obtain any enjoyment from the victim."

"To be sure, my Lord—but a *street crime*—"

"I know, I know, I've a few of them to my credit—disturbance of the peace, scandal, the street . . . the highway—the additional severity of the law toward such offenses; and they can be profitable as well . . . on top of it all, that particular woman's circumstances, her indigence, her misery. . . . No, it's not to be scoffed at. You could have taken her home with you, it would have been an evening's entertainment for us both. . . . By the way, did not that sergeant mention having identified the corpse?"

"Unless I am mistaken, my Lord, her name was Simon."

"Simon. Of course. I handled that affair four or five days ago. That's it, Simon. I had the husband jailed and the infant removed to the poorhouse. My stars, Juliette, I remember the woman too: she was very pretty and very well-behaved. I was reserving her for your pimps; and she told you the truth, that family was once quite prosperous, bankruptcy altered all that. Well, you've simply added the finishing touches to my crime, and this conclusion makes the story delicious from beginning to end."

I said Saint-Fond's standard was raised, my masculine dress was completing his delirium. He led me into the boudoir where he had received me the first time I had come to his house. A man-servant appeared, and Saint-Fond, his fingers trembling from delight, unbuttoned my breeches and had his valet fondle my buttocks; he took charge of the fellow's prick and prodded my asshole with its tip, then introduced his own thereinto; and the lecher embuggered me, hotly enjoining me to suck his valet's prick the while, and when I'd got it stiff as a poker he packed it away in his ass. The operation over with, Saint-Fond told me that the excellence of his discharge was in large measure due to the knowledge that the ass he was fucking merited the scaffold.

"That lad who fucked me," the Minister assured me, "is a rascal of the first order: six times over I've had to save him from the wheel. Did you notice his prick? 'Tis a magnificent article, he plies it masterfully. Here, Juliette, before I forget: the sum I promised you for crimes of your personal commission. A carriage is waiting for you, go home now, tomorrow you will leave for the estate outside Sceaux which I bought for you last month; take only a few companions along, four of your female domestics should suffice—the prettiest of the lot, however—your cook too, your butler, and the three virgins listed for the next supper. Installed in the country, you'll await further instructions from me; that's all I'll tell you for the time being."

I left very content with the success of my crime, full of pleasure at having committed it; and departed from Paris on the morrow.

Scarcely was I established in that rural domain, completely isolated, as solitary as the Thebaïd hermits, when there came one of my servants to inform me a stranger had arrived, a person of condition who said he had been sent by the Minister and wished to speak with me.

"Ask him to wait," said I, and unsealed the message he had brought from Saint-Fond. It read as follows: "Have your domestics seize the bearer of this letter straightway, he is to be confined in one of the dungeons I have caused to be built in the cellars of your house. This individual is not to be allowed to escape; I hold you responsible for him. His wife and daughter will also appear: you will deal with them in the same manner. These are my orders. Execute them promptly, scrupulously, and do not hesitate to employ such treachery, such cruelty, as I know you to be capable of. Adieu." I had the stranger ushered in.

"Sir," said I, maintaining the appearance of perfect equanimity and graciousness, "you are doubtless a friend of his Lordship?"

"Both my family and I have for a long time been the beneficiaries of his generosities and kindness, Madame."

" 'Tis plain from his letter, Monsieur. . . . But allow me to give my servants instructions so that you may be received in such wise as the Minister seems to desire."

Bidding him be seated, I went out of the room.

My servants, and they were rather more slaves than domestics, provided themselves with rope and were at my side when I returned to the visitor.

"Conduct this gentleman," I told them, "to the quarters his Lordship would have him occupy," and my retainers, powerful bucks they were, set upon our guest and dragged him off to a very abominable cell far under ground.

"Madame! I protest! There is some mistake!" cried the unlucky dupe of Saint-Fond's deceit and mine.

Inflexible, deaf to his pleadings, I carried out the Minister's instructions with zeal: the captive's anguished questions were left all unanswered, I myself turned the key in the lock.

No sooner was I back in the drawing room than I heard carriage wheels on the drive. Out stepped the stranger's wife and daughter, and the letters of introduction they presented were exact replicas of his.

Ah, Saint-Fond, I said to myself, casting a glance upon those two women, admiring the beauty of the mother who was a superb thirty-six, the sweet modesty and grace of the daughter, only then entering her sixteenth year, ah, Saint-Fond! your fell, accursed lust has much to do with these ministerial proceedings, that is but too certain. And in this, as in everything else you do, are you not guided far more by your vices than by the interests of your country?

I would be hard pressed to give an adequate description of the moans and tears those two wretches let forth when they beheld themselves dragged infamously off to the dungeons readied for them; but no more moved by the weeping and wailing of the mother and daughter than I had been by the entreaties of the father, I was concerned only to take the greatest precautions for their safe-keeping, and was not at ease until I had these important prisoners behind the stoutest bars and all the keys in my pocket.

Meditating upon what the fate of these individuals might be, I did not imagine that it would involve more than detention, in as much as executions were my affair and I had received no instructions to slay; while I was in the middle of pondering these matters, the arrival of a fourth personage was announced to me. Heavens, what is my surprise upon recognizing the selfsame young man who, you will recall, the first time I held conversation with Saint-Fond, at the latter's bidding struck me three blows of a cane upon the shoulders. He too came bearing a letter, I opened it at once.

"Greet this man warmly and entertain him well," I read; "you must surely remember him, for you carried his marks awhile, and they were his hands that gripped you at our first voluptuous rencounter in your house. He is to take the leading role in the drama that will be staged tomorrow; in him welcome the executioner of Nantes, who upon my orders has come to put to death the three persons now your prisoners: obliged under pain of losing my post to produce these three heads the day after tomorrow before the Queen, I would myself (needless to say) wield the ax, had not Her Majesty expressed the very keenest desire to receive the spoils out of none other than the hands of a public executioner. It is for that reason the latter, arriving in Paris, found his services not immediately required there, and has been dispatched posthaste to your residence, whither he comes in ignorance of the business he is to attend to. You may instruct him now; but refrain absolutely from permitting him a glimpse of his prey, this is essential; expect me tomorrow morning. Meanwhile treat the prisoners, and the women especially, very rigorously: bread only, a little water, and no daylight."

"Sir," said I, turning to the most recent of my visitors, "the Minister mentions in his letter that we, you and I, are not unknown to each other. 'Tis true. Once upon a time you—"

"Aye, Madame. Orders, alas, are orders."

"Indeed they are, and I harbor no grudge against you," I went on, giving him my hand, which he kissed with ardor. "But it is dinner-time. First to table; we'll discuss afterward."

Delcour was twenty-eight, a very pretty fellow, his air and calling pleased me mightily. I showered attentions upon him, and they were quite sincere; when we finished dinner, I mounted as skillful an attack as ever you've seen. Delcour soon exhibited evidence of the success of my advances. There was a wonderful bulge in his breeches, I was overpowered.

"For God's sake, my love," said I, "have it out, I fain must see what you're hiding there. That magnificent prick has me all aflutter, your profession sets my brain awhirl; you've absolutely got to fuck me."

He promptly fetches that marvelous device into view, and pursuant to my custom when dealing with a man, I catch hold of it with the intention of mouthing it to the balls; but that was a grandly proportioned tool, I tell you, and it was all I could do to accommodate half its length. As soon as he was lodged, Delcour got his hands on my cunt, buried his face in it, and two seconds later we discharged in concert. Seeing me swallow his fuck, that handsome young man leapt excitedly upon me.

"Ah, by Jesus," said he, "I was in too great a hurry; but I'll make amends for my mistake."

The rascal's stave was still holding true, he stretches me out upon a broad couch, fastens his lips to mine which are yet sticky with his sperm, and encunts me as only rarely you will be encunted by a still leaking prick: in all my life I'd never been so stoutly fucked. Delcour cut and thrust for three-quarters of an hour and more, out of prudence he retreated on sensing another discharge impending; but when at last my cunt's grip triumphed, he loosed a second dose of thick fuck, and this too I swallowed with as much delight as I had the first.

"Delcour," said I, once I had resumed possession of my wits and could essay a rational analysis of my late behavior, "you have been somewhat surprised, I fancy, by the informal reception I have given you; such frivolous conduct, such speedy advances—I venture to suppose you consider me a loose woman, nay, a thorough whore.

Despite my supreme disdain for that which fools call reputation, I would have you understand that your good fortune is owing far less to my coquetry or to anything physical in me than to my mentality: I have an exceptionally odd one. You kill by trade . . . you are a murderer, a handsome one besides, one such prick as you boast isn't come by every day. But your profession, it is that I wish to stress—thanks alone to it I flung myself into your arms; scorn me, detest me, I don't give a damn. You fucked me; I've got all I wanted."

"Heavenly creature," Delcour replied, "it isn't scorn I feel for you, no, nor shall it be hatred, you inspire altogether different sentiments in me. You deserve to be worshiped and worship you I shall, regretting that your ecstasy had its origin solely in that which earns me the loathing of others."

" 'Tis of no importance, that," said I. "A mere matter of opinion, and opinion varies, as you observe, since the source of my fondness for you is precisely this very thing which puts you at a remove from the rest of mankind; however, this is but debauchery on my part, you shouldn't interpret it as anything else. My attachment to the Minister, my manner of living with him bar me from intrigues and I'll certainly never contemplate any. We'll make the most of this evening, of the whole night if you like; and there's an end to it."

"Ah, Madame," the young man said with respectfulness, "of you I ask only your protection and your gracious kindness."

"You shall never want for either; but in return you must comply with all that results from my imagination. I must warn you, it is subject to all sorts of disorders, and they sometimes lead far."

Delcour had gone back to fondling my breasts with one hand and frigging my clitoris with the other, now and again darting his tongue down my gullet; after a few minutes of this I bade him refrain from wearying himself unduly, and to give truthful answers to certain questions I wished to pose him.

"Tell me, to begin with, just why Saint-Fond had you strike me upon the shoulder that first time I saw you. It puzzled me then and still does."

"Libertinage, Madame, sheer libertinage. You know the Minister. He has his quirks."

"He has you take part in luxurious scenes then?"

"Whenever I am in Paris."

"He has fucked you?"

"He has, Madame."

"And you've fucked him back?"

"Most certainly."

"You have beaten him? Flogged him?"

"Frequently."

"Sweet Jesusfuck! how that excites me—frig, Delcour, frig away—and has he had you beat and flog other women?"

"Upon several occasions."

"Have you ever gone farther?"

"Allow me to respect the Minister's secrets, Madame. In this connection your guesses are very apt to be correct since they would be based on a good acquaintance of his Lordship."

"Can you say whether he has at any time formulated projects against me?"

"Madame, toward you his attitude has always been, to my knowledge, one of affection and trust; he is greatly attached to you, you may take my word for it."

"And so am I to him: I adore him, I hope he is fully aware of it. However, since you would not have me tempt you to indiscretion, we'll talk of other things. Tell me, if you please, how are you able to take the life of some individual who has never wronged you in any way? How is it that from the depths of your soul pity does not speak out in behalf of the poor wretches the law enjoins you to assassinate in cold blood?"

"Be very certain, Madame," was Delcour's answer, "that in my calling none of us attains this degree of rationalized and scientific ferocity save through principles that are largely unknown to folk in general."

"How so? Principles? I would have you tell me about them."

"They are rooted in a soil of total inhumanity; our training begins early, from childhood on we are taught a system of values wherein human life is nothing and the law everything; the result is that it gives us no more bother to cut the throats of our fellows than it does a butcher to cut the throat of a calf. Does the butcher have qualms? He doesn't know what they are. Neither do we."

"But carrying out the law is your work; do you proceed in the same way when it is a question of pleasure?"

"Certainly, Madame. Could it be otherwise? Should it be? The prejudice once overcome in us, we cease to behold any evil in murder."

"Must one not necessarily esteem it an evil to destroy one's fellow beings?"

"Madame, I might rather ask you how one can possibly impute any such thing to an act of destruction. If destruction of all human beings were not one of the fundamental laws of Nature, then, yes, I should be able to believe that you outrage this unintelligible Nature when you destroy; but in view of the fact there does not exist a single natural process which does not prove that destruction is a necessary element to the natural order and that Nature creates only by dint of destroying, 'tis most obvious that whoever destroys acts in tune with Nature. It is no less obvious that whoever refuses to destroy offends Nature very grievously: for, and of this there can be no doubt, it is only by destroying we furnish Nature the means for creating; and hence the more we destroy, the nicer the accord between ourselves and her workings; if murder is basic to Nature's regenerative operations, certainly the murderer is the man who serves Nature best; and this truth grasped, we are moved to declare that the more numerous his murders, the better he fulfills his obligations toward a Nature whose sole need is of murders."[9]

"Such doctrines contain their element of peril."

"They are nonetheless true, Madame. More learned thinkers would be able to develop them much further than can I, but you will find that the point of departure of their arguments is constantly the same."

"My friend," I said to Delcour, "you have already given me much food for thought, a single idea cast into a brain like mine produces the effect there of a spark upon saltpeter—yes, I sense it, we have similar minds. We have three victims here. To sacrifice them is why you were sent to this château. It will, believe me, give

[9] All this is but a mild foretaste of what subsequent volumes will provide the reader upon this vital topic.

me great pleasure to behold you in action; but, my dear, you must possess a vast store of information and experience, be so kind as to dilate upon the mechanics of the thing. Am I correct in believing that it is only with the aid of libertinage you succeed in vanquishing unnatural prejudice? For you just gave me clear proof that Nature is much sooner served than outraged by murder. . . ."

"What do you wish to ask, Madame?"

"This: if it is not very certain, as I have heard say, that only by transforming the whole affair into one of libertinage are you able to perform, and enjoy, the murders your trade obliges you to commit; in fine, I ask you if 'tis not so, that the act of executing infallibly puts your prick erect?"

"It is no longer contested, Madame, that libertinage leads logically to murder; and all the world knows that the pleasure-worn individual must regain his strength in this manner of committing what fools are disposed to denominate a crime: we subject some person or other to the maximum agitation, its repercussion upon our nerves is the most potent stimulant imaginable, and to us are restored all the energies we have previously spent in excess. Murder thus qualifies as the most delicious of libertinage's vehicles, and as the surest; but it is not true that in order to commit murder, one has got to be mentally in a libertine furor. By way of proof I cite to you the extreme calm wherewith the majority of my colleagues dispatch their business; they experience emotion, yes, but it is quite as different from the passion animating the libertine as this latter is from the passion in him who murders out of ambition, or out of vengeance, or out of greed, or, again, out of sheer cruelty. Which is simply to indicate that there are several classes of murder, the libertine variety being but one; however, this does not prevent us from concluding that none of these sorts of murder outrages Nature, and that it is in far greater conformance to her laws than in violation thereof."

"All you say is just, Delcour, but I maintain nonetheless that, precisely in the interest of these very murders, it would be desirable were their perpetrator to be inspired by lust alone, for that passion is never followed by remorseful aftermaths, one's recollections of it are of joy and joyous; whereas with the others, once their fire has gone out one is often devoured by regrets, above all if one happens to be something less than a veteran philosopher; and therefore it seems to me there is much to be said in favor of never murdering save through libertinage. One would be free to kill for whatever the motive, but the erection would always be there as a safeguard and the better to consolidate the action, so as to avoid being troubled by serious remorse later on."

"In that case," said Delcour, "you consider that every passion can be increased or nourished by lust?"

"Lust is to the passions what the nervous fluid is to life: it sustains them all, it supplies strength to them all, and the proof thereof is that a man who, as they say, hasn't any balls will never have any passions."

"And so you suppose that ambition, cruelty, greed, vindictiveness as motivations lead to the same thing as lust?"

"Yes, I am convinced that all these passions cause erections, and that a lively and properly organized mind will be as readily inflamed by any of them as by lust. Mark you, I am speaking now from personal experience. The effect of concentrating upon mental images characterized by ambition, cruelty, avarice, revenge has been that of a thorough frigging, and each of these ideas has more than once made me discharge myself dry. I have not entertained the thought of a single crime, whatever the passion inspiring it, without feeling the subtle heat of lust circulate in my veins: falsehood, impiety, calumny, rascality, hardheartedness, even gluttony have wrought those effects in me; and, in a word, there is not one form or mode of viciousness which has failed to ignite my lust; or, if you prefer, the torch of lust has at one time or another made all the vices in me blaze up with its sacred fire, to them all communicating that voluptuous sensation which, it appears, is never kindled otherwise in us curiously organized persons. There. That is my opinion."

"And it is mine also, Madame," Delcour rejoined, "I'll not attempt to conceal it any longer."

"I rejoice at your frankness, my dear, it helps me to know you. And from what I know of you already, I venture to say, and would be greatly surprised if I was in error here, that you require to enter into a libertine furor when you perform your official murders, which enables you to reap far more voluptuous satisfaction from your functions than is granted your colleages who carry them out mechanically."

"Madame, I must own that you have fairly found me out."

"Scoundrel," I said, smiling and taking hold of this young man's tool, which I began to exercise so as to restore some of its energy, "oh, deep-dyed libertine that you are, why not go on to say that your prick hardens for the sake of the enjoyment to be had from my existence today, and tomorrow depriving me of it would make you discharge?"

The young man was visibly embarrassed at this last question; I gazed at him for a moment, then came to his rescue. "There, there, my friend; I have absolutely no quarrel with your principles, I must forgive you their results: instead of disputing about those results, let's profit from them." At this point I grew very hot indeed. "Come now, look alive, we must try some extraordinary tricks."

"What would you have me do?"

"Beat me, outrage me, lash me; isn't that what you do with women every day; aren't those the foul violences which, electrifying you, make you capable of the rest? Well? Answer."

" 'Tis true."

"Of course. Well, you've a job to perform tomorrow, start preparing for it today. There is my body. It is at your disposal."

And Delcour, following my instructions, having started in with a dozen slaps and kicks in the behind, took up a bundle of withes and slashed away at my ass for fifteen minutes or so, while one of my women cunt-sucked me.

"Delcour," I cried. "Oh, divine destroyer of the human race! you whom I adore and from whom I expect unheard-of joys, lay on, lay on, I say, whip your slut harder, faster, imprint the marks of your savagery upon her, for she yearns to wear them. I discharge at the idea of my blood wetting your fingers; shed it liberally, my love. . . ."

It flowed. . . . Oh, my friends, I was in ecstasies; words cannot express the wild emotion that was cindering me; without a brain like mine there is no conceiving such a thing, unless one has brains like yours it is not to be comprehended. Unlimited were the quantities of fuck I loosed into the mouth of my fricatrice; never in my life had I been in the throes of such disorder, such torment, such rapture.

"Delcour, Delcour," I went on, "there is one last homage you must render me, husband your resources for the purpose. This ass you've just hacked to ribbons beckons you, invites you to soothe, to console it. At Cythera Venus had more than one temple, you know; come ope the most arcane, come bugger me, Delcour, make haste . . . for we must leave no delight untasted, no horror uncommitted."

"Great God!" said Delcour, in transports. "I didn't dare propose it to you; but behold how your desires inflame mine."

And indeed my fucker exhibited a prick harder, longer than any I'd clapped eyes on hitherto.

"Beloved libertine," said I, "are you then fond of ass?"

"Ah, Madame, is there anything that affords comparable pleasure?"

" 'Tis all too plain, my dear," said I, "when you accustom yourself to defying one of the laws of Nature, you do not take authentic pleasure anymore except in transgressing them all, one after the other."

And Delcour, master of the altar I abandoned to him entirely, covered it, though 'twas drenched in blood, with the tenderest caresses. His tongue thrilled in the hole, my temperature soared. The slut operating upon me frontwardly set my cunt afire. Fuck gushed out of me afresh, I was dry, I could bear no more; but I was not by any means easy; I suddenly lost all interest in Delcour, then all patience with him. Great had been my desire for the man, great was my abhorrence for him now. And there's the effect of irregular desires: the greater the height they arouse us to, the greater the emptiness we feel afterward. From this cretins derive proof of God's existence; whereas for my part I find here only the most certain proofs in support of a materialistic attitude: the more you cheapen your existence, the less I'll be inclined to believe it is the handiwork of a deity. Delcour sent off to his bedchamber, I retired for the night with my Lesbian hireling.

Saint-Fond put in his appearance the next day around noon; he dismissed his servants and his coach, and came directly into the salon to greet me; we embraced. Uncertain what his reaction would be to the little prank I had played with Delcour, but anxious lest he hear the story from someone else, I told him everything.

"Juliette," he said when I had concluded, "had I not assured you long ago that I would take the most indulgent view of your aberrations, I would scold you now. We can ignore the fuckery, 'tis natural to fuck; your one mistake was in your choice of a partner. Are you so sure you can rely upon Delcour's discretion? I am glad, however, that you have made his acquaintance; for two years he was my bardash when he was fourteen and fifteen: he is from Nantes where his father was hangman, a fact which stimulated my interest in the boy: I took his maidenhead, and when I was weary toying with his ass, I turned him over to the Paris executioner, whose aide he remained up until the time his father died; he inherited his post at Nantes. The lad is not without intelligence, he is excessively libertine; and as I just hinted, he isn't the sort who merits overmuch trust. But let me tell you something about the captives we are going to put to death.

"Of all the men in France, Monsieur de Cloris has probably contributed most to my advancement; the year I was preferred to the Ministry, he, though very young at the time, was sleeping with the Duchesse de G*** whose power at court was immense, and owing primarily to the maneuvering and intrigues of the two of them, I obtained from the King the position I still hold. As of that moment I contracted an insuperable loathing for Cloris; I would go to any lengths to avoid encountering him, I dreaded the sight of him, I hated him; so long as his protectress was alive I postponed taking action; but she has just passed away, or, perhaps, I have just put her out of the way; this brought Cloris to the top of my black list; he married my cousin-german."

"What, my Lord! This woman is your cousin?"

"She is, Juliette, and the fact has contributed not a little to her doom. I had designs upon that woman; she always resisted my desires. Little by little they shifted to her daughter; here I met with yet more stubborn resistance; with the result that my rage, and my extreme desire to see the whole family gone to blazes, reached the decisive pitch. To promote its undoing I resorted to every known kind of cunning, baseness, lie, and calumny; and I have finally so aroused the Queen's antipathies to the father and daughter, by giving her to understand that Cloris once sold his child to the King, that at our last interview Her Majesty, much wrought up, commanded me to arrange their deaths. She adamantly insists upon having their heads by tomorrow; my recompense has been fixed at three million apiece: I shall obey the Queen's orders and very joyfully, you may be sure, and very pleasurable will be the episodes wherewith I plan to accompany my revenge."

"My Lord, 'tis this a dreadful complication of crimes, it puts my brain into an indescribable whirl."

"It affects mine likewise, my angel, and I arrive here with the most execrable intentions. I've not discharged for a week; no one is more adept than I in the art of whetting the passions through abstinence; and having a good time the while. Over the past seven days I've probably been fucked two hundred shots, and had intimately to do with somewhere between a hundred and seven score individuals of both sexes, but during this interval not a drop of fuck have I yielded. From thus playing coy with Nature I have achieved a pent-up state that bodes very ill for the persons upon whom the storm is due to break. . . . Have you given orders that we be left alone and that nobody, saving only those who are necessary to the scene, be under any circumstances admitted to the house?"

"Yes, my Lord. And I have added that anybody who ventures to intrude shall be hanged on the spot: a squadron of troopers is lying at Sceaux to lend me assistance in case of need; never has stage been more impeccably set for a crime. We shall, the two of us, be able to relish the pleasure of committing it under ideal conditions and in absolute security."

"Ah, you see into what state whatever you say puts me."

"In truth, I believe you are discharging."

"And you?"

Whereupon, in search of proof positive of a crisis which I was indeed undergoing, the rake lifts my skirt above my navel and ferrets briefly about in my cunt; then he examines his fingers, and finds them slimed with damning evidence of my lewd agitation.

"You know," the Minister confesses, "I adore discovering such symptoms in you, for they roundly attest the similarity of our ways of thinking. But hold, I must bib at the tap I've set to flowing."

And gluing his mouth to my cunt, the villain drank thereat a good quarter of an hour; then rolled me over. "Ah," said he, "there's what I like to kiss most of all—the peerless hole. Eh, rascal, it's been traveled recently, has it not? You've been bum-fucked of late, 'tis very plain to be seen." All the while he went on cooing and kissing about my vent and the area environing; now he has his breeches off, shows me his own ass, and I fall to licking it.

"You manage that wonderfully well, you little minx," says he, "I do declare, I think you love my ass. Here's my prick, it's starting to stand, suck it a bit; and suggest a few extravagances if you can: the hour of Venus should be rung in by the bells of Folly."

"The weather is warm," I said, "I recommend that you adopt savage attire, leaving your arms, thighs, and prick bare; your headdress ought to resemble a dragon or serpent in the Patagonian manner, you'll smear red grease paint all over your face, we'll fit you with moustaches, you'll wear a baldric, girding on all the instruments required for the tortures you plan to inflict upon your victims: this costume will terrify them for a certainty, and it is terror one should inspire when one wishes to wallow in crime."

"You are right, Juliette, you are quite right. I'll ask you to rig me out in that way."

"Apparel and gear are imperative; tell me if in the courts of law our precious buffoons, the judges, don't resemble heroes out of comedy or charlatans."

"My sole objection to the magistracy nowadays is that it is composed of men sorely lacking in sanguinary temper, and if these are such unruly times, we may lay it up to that. Rest assured, Juliette: better not even to try your hand at governing men unless you are willing to immerse it in their blood."

Dinner was announced, we repaired to table and pursued our conversation in the same tone.

"Yes by all means," the Minister proceeded, "the laws must be made more severe; the only happily governed countries are those where the Inquisition reigns. They alone are really under their sovereigns' control; the purpose of sacerdotal chains, and the need for them, is to reinforce political ones: the might of the scepter depends on that of the censer, it is hugely in the interest of both authorities, lay and clerical, to stay each other mutually, and only by breaking that common front will the people ever achieve their liberation. Nothing so effectively cows a nation as religious fears; nothing better than that it dread hell's eternal fires if it revolts against its overlord; and that's why the crowned heads of Europe are always in such admirable intelligence with Rome. We other great ones of this world do indeed despise and defy the fabulous thunderbolts of a contemptible Vatican, but we are well advised to keep our slaves in terror of them; once again 'tis there the sole means to keep them under the yoke. Steeped in Machiavelli, I would want the disparity between the king and the mob to be no less considerable than that between a heavenly body and a cockroach; a mere gesture on the part of the monarch, and his throne would become an island in a very sea of blood; beheld as a god on earth, his subjects would only dare crawl into his presence on their hands and knees. Who is fool enough even to compare the physical constitution, yes, the mere physical constitution of a king with that of a commoner? I'm willing to believe that Nature gave them the same needs—the lion and the earthworm have the same needs also; but does this create a resemblance between them? Oh, Juliette, do not forget that if kings are beginning to lose their credit in Europe, it's the vulgarity they've become attainted with that has been their downfall; had they remained aloof and invisible like the sovereigns of Asia, the whole world would yet tremble at the sound of their names. Contempt is bred of familiarity, and familiarity from what is daily within public view; the Romans must surely have stood in greater awe of Tiberius off on Capri than of a Titus wandering around the city consoling the poor."

"But this despotism," I said to Saint-Fond, "you favor it because you are so powerful; do you suppose however that it is equally pleasing to the weak?"

"It pleases everybody, Juliette," Saint-Fond replied; "mankind tends universally in that direction. To be despotic is the primary desire inspired in us by a Nature whose law could not be more unlike the ludicrous one usually ascribed to her, the substance of which is not to do unto others that which unto ourselves we would not have done . . . from fear of reprisals, they should have added, for very certain it is that only weaklings, dreading tit for tat, could have contrived this homily; and they must have been desperate as well as insolent rogues to dare to fob it off as a *natural law*. I affirm that the fundamental, profoundest, and keenest penchant in man is incontestably to enchain his fellow creatures and to tyrannize them with all his might. The suckling babe that bites his nurse's nipple, the infant constantly smashing his rattle, reveal to us that a bent for destruction, cruelty, and oppression is the first which Nature graves in our hearts, and that we surrender to it more or less violently according to the amount of sensibility we are endowed with from the outset. I therefore hold it self-evident, that all the pleasures which ornament the life of a man, all the delights he is able to savor, all that makes for the extreme delectation of his passions, are essentially located in his despotic usage of his brethren. The sequestration, in voluptuous Asia, of the objects accessory to pleasure-taking demonstrates to us, does it not, that lust gains with oppression and tyranny, and that the passions are more strongly fired by whatever is obtained through force than by anything granted voluntarily. When it is logically established that the degree of violence characterizing the action committed is the one factor for measuring the amount of happiness of the active person—and this because where the violence is greater the shock upon the nervous system will be sharper—as soon, I say, as that is proven, the greatest possible dose of happiness will necessarily consist in the greatest of the effects of despotism and tyranny; whence it will emerge that the harshest, the most ferocious, the most traitorous and the wickedest man will be the happiest man; and that stands to reason. For as Noirceuil has often told you, happiness lies neither in vice nor in virtue; but in the manner we appreciate the one and the other, and the choice we make pursuant to our individual organization. It isn't in the meal set before me my appetite lies, my need is nowhere but in me, and two people may be very differently affected by the same fare: it makes his mouth water who is hungry, excites repugnance in him who has just eaten his fill: however, as 'tis certain there must be some difference between the vibrations received, and that vice must procure much more intense ones in the individual with the vicious bent than virtue can give to the person whose organs are structured for its reception;

that, although Vespasian had a good soul and Nero an evil, despite
the fact both were sensitive, there was a great difference in the
temper of those souls as regards the species of sensibility constituting them: for Nero's was without doubt endowed with a faculty of
sensation far superior to Vespasian's; 'tis certain, I say, that of the
two, Nero was the happier man by far; why? because that which
affects more intensely will always produce the happier effect in
man; and because a vigorous person, owing to his very vigor so
structured as to be a better recipient of vicious than of virtuous
impressions, will sooner discover felicity than a mild and peaceable
individual, whose feeble complexion will deny him all possibilities
other than the abject, hangdog, woebegone practice of the formulas
of humdrum good behavior; and what the devil would the merit
be in virtue if vice weren't preferable to it? Thus, I tell you,
Vespasian and Nero were as happy as they were able to be, but
Nero must have been much more so, because his pleasures were
incomparably livelier and keener; while Vespasian, in giving an
alm to some beggar (simply because as he himself said, *the poor
have got to live*), was stirred in an infinitely less intense manner
than Nero, a lyre in his hand, watching Rome burn from atop the
tower of Antonia. 'Ah,' somebody will say, 'but deification was the
reward of the one, disparagement and hate that of the other.' As
you wish; however, it is not the effect their souls had upon others
I am interested in; I am simply evaluating the inward sensation
which the different penchants native to each must have made each
experience, and discriminating between the vibrations each was
capable of feeling. Thus I am able to affirm that the happiest
man on earth will inevitably be he who is addicted to the most
infamous, the most revolting, the most criminal habits, and who
exercises them the most frequently—who, every day, doubles their
force, triples their scope."

"The most outstanding service one could do to some young
person," I observed after hearing this speech, "would then be to
pluck out of him all the weeds of virtue Nature or education might
have sown in his soul?"

"That is exact, snatch them out and if possible stifle them
while they are yet in seed," Saint-Fond answered. "For even
supposing the individual in whom you annihilate these virtuous

possibilities were to maintain he finds happiness in virtue, you, perfectly certain you will cause him to find far greater happiness in vice, ought never to hesitate to blot out the one in order to permit the other to waken; 'tis a real and capital service he'll thank you for sooner or later: and that is why, very different from my predecessor, I authorize the publication and sale of all libertine books and immoral works; for I esteem them most essential to human felicity and welfare, instrumental to the progress of philosophy, indispensable to the eradication of prejudices, and in every sense conducive to the increase of human knowledge and understanding. Any author courageous enough to tell the truth fearlessly shall have my patronage and support; I shall subsidize his ideas, I shall see to their dissemination; such men are rare, the State has great need of them, and their labors cannot be too heartily encouraged."

"But," I inquired, "how does this sit with the severity you favor in government? with the Inquisition you would establish?"

"As nicely as you please," Saint-Fond replied; "it is to keep the people in their place I urge severity, and if I so often imagine the autos-da-fé of Lisbon transferred to Paris, it is in the interests of subordination. My knife will never be drawn against the upper classes, the élite in substance or mind."

"But must not these writings, if generally read, pose a threat to those very persons you seem to wish to keep out of harm's way?"

"Impossible," declared the Minister. "If these texts quicken in the weak the desire to break their bonds (and mind you, lest they have that desire I cannot forge bonds at all), the strong, for their part, will find instruction therein upon how to load further and heavier chains upon the captive masses. In short, the slave will perhaps accomplish in a decade what the master will have accomplished in a night."

"You are widely accused," I now ventured to remark, "of persistent condescension in everything that touches the growing depravity of manners nowadays; never, so it is said, were they so corrupt as since you entered into office."

"Perhaps, but we still have an enormous task to achieve before they are as I'd like to see them; and at the present time I am working upon some new police regulations which, I hope, will help matters along in the proper direction. I do not believe it is a secret, at any rate it is a fact whereof you cannot afford not to be fully aware, Juliette: a vital chapter in the policy followed by all those at the head of any government is to foment and promote the extremest degree of corruption in the citizenry; so long as the subject wastes away body and soul in the delights of gangrenous, enfeebling debauchery, he does not feel the weight of his irons, and you can heap fresh ones upon him without his even noticing. The true essence of statecraft is thus to multiply a hundredfold every possible means to debilitate and pervert the people. Lots of shows, much pomp and display, cabarets, brothels without number, a general amnesty for all crimes committed in debauchery: those are the expedients for bringing the plebeians to heel. O you who ambition to rule over them, beware of virtue within the frontiers of your empire, only let virtue reign and your peoples will open their eyes, and your thrones, reposing as they do upon nothing but vice, will be very speedily overthrown; the free man's awakening will be cruel for the despots, and the day he ceases to fritter his leisure away in vices he'll start to strive for domination like yourselves."

"And what are your proposed regulations?" I asked.

"It's by means of fashion I aim to mold public opinion at first; you know how the French are influenced by the latest in vogue.

"1) I am launching a new style in masculine and feminine dress which leaves all the lust-inspiring parts, and the ass especially, exposed in their virtual entirety.

"2) There will be spectacles after the model of the Floral Games they used to hold in glorious Rome, at them lads and lasses will dance naked.

"3) Instead of morality and religion, which will be stricken from the curriculum, the pure and unadulterated principles of Nature will be taught in the public schools; every child of either sex who has reached the age of fifteen without having been able to get a lover will be very sharply reprimanded, penalized, held up to public scorn and dishonor, and declared, if a girl, forever ineligible for marriage, for holding any office, if a boy; in default of a lover, the boy or girl will be obliged to present a certificate proving prostitution and nonpossession of virginity in any shape or place.

"4) Christianity will be rigorously banished out of the land; none but libertine rites and feasts will ever be celebrated in France. I'll be rid of Christianity, I say: but not of religion, this I intend to retain, for its chains are useful to the preservation of order as I proved to you a moment ago. The object of worship doesn't matter in the slightest, the thing that counts is clergy; but I'd rather see the dagger of superstition wielded by the priests of Venus than by the admirers of Mary.

"5) The common herd will be kept in a state of subservience, of prostrate bondage, which will render them powerless even to strike for, let alone to attain to, domination, or to encroach upon or debase the prerogatives of the rich. Tied to the glebe as in olden days, the people will be held like any other property, and, like it, will be subject to all the various mutations of value and ownership. Only the people will be liable to punishment at the hands of the law, and it will be inflicted for the most trifling offenses. The commoner's proprietor will have the right of life or death over him and his family, and neither his complaints nor his recriminations will ever receive hearing. Never will free schools be available to him: tilling the soil does not require knowledge, the blindfold of ignorance is made for the peasant's eyes, showing him the light is always a risky business. The first individual, regardless of his class, who were to think to stir up the people or to invite them to break their chains will be thrown to wild beasts and eaten alive.

"6) In every town and city of the land there shall be opened public houses containing specimens of both sexes, the number of these houses to be proportional to the population of the district or agglomeration, there being at least one male and one female establishment per every thousand inhabitants; the personnel of each shall be three hundred individuals, who will begin their internment at the age of twelve and not retire from service before twenty-five. These establishments will be subsidized by the government; only members of the free class will have the right of entrance and they will of course be empowered to do in these places whatever they please.

"7) Everything denominated crime of libertinage at present, to wit: murder in debauch, incest, rape, sodomy, adultery, etc., will be reprehensible only if committed by a member of the slave castes.

"8) Prizes shall be awarded to the most celebrated courtesans in the bawdy houses, likewise to the young boys there who have got themselves a name in the art of pleasing. Similarly, bonuses and stipends shall be granted to each inventor of a new lubricity, to every author of cynical books, to all libertines recognized as professed in their order.

"9) The slave class shall exist as did the Helots in ancient Lacedaemon. There being no difference whatsoever between the human slave and the brute beast, why should you punish the murderer of the one more than the murderer of the other?"

"My Lord," I put in, "this last, it seems to me, deserves some slight explaining. I would like to have you prove to me there is no real distinction to be drawn between the human slave and an animal."

"Glance at the works of Nature," this philosopher answered me, "and judge for yourself whether she has not, in forming the two classes of men, made them vastly unalike; I ask you to put aside partiality, and to decide: have they the same voice, the same skin, the same limbs, the same gait, the same tastes, have they, I venture to inquire, have they the same needs? It will be to no purpose if someone attempts to persuade me that circumstances or education have made for these differences and that the slave and the master, in a state of Nature, as infants, will be indistinguishable. I deny the fact; and it is after having pondered the matter and sifted much personal observation, after having examined the findings of clever anatomists, that I affirm there is no similarity between the conformations of these several infants. Abandon them both to themselves, and you'll observe that the child of the first class manifests tastes and aims most unlike those the child of the second class demonstrates; and you will perceive the most striking dissimilarity between the sentiments and dispositions proper to each.

"Now perform the same study upon the animal resembling man the closest, upon, for example, the chimpanzee; let me, I say, compare this animal to some representative of the slave caste; what a host of similarities I find! The man of the people is simply the species that stands next above the chimpanzee on the ladder; and the distance separating them is, if anything, less than that between him and the individual belonging to the superior caste. And why should Nature, who so assiduously observes these gradations in all her works, have neglected them here? Are all plants alike? No. Are all animals the same in aspect and strength? No. Dare you compare a shrub to the majestic poplar, a pug-dog to the proud Great Dane, the Corsican mountain pony to the spirited Andalusian stallion? So many essential differences within the same over-all categories; and why do you object to the same differences existing among men? You should certainly never lump Voltaire and Fréron in the same class, any more than you would the virile Prussian grenadier and the debilitated Hottentot. Therefore, Juliette, cease to doubt these inequalities; and, admitting their existence, let's not hesitate to take full advantage of them, and to persuade ourselves that if it so suited Nature to have us born into the upper of these two human classes, we have but to extract profit and pleasure from our situation by worsening that of our inferiors, and despotically to press them into the service of all our passions and our every need."

"Kiss me, my beloved," I cried, throwing myself into the arms of a man whose principles I simply could not resist; "to me you are as a god, 'tis at your feet I want to pass my life."

"Apropos," remarked the Minister, getting up from the table and leading me to the couch in the salon, "I forgot to tell you that the King is fonder of me than ever; I've just had new proof of his attachment. From somewhere he got the idea I am burdened by heavy debts, and has given me two million to straighten out my affairs. 'Tis only just that you share in my good fortune, Juliette; I am turning half the gift over to you; continue to approve my tenets and to serve me well, I'll raise you so high in the world you'll have no more trouble believing in your superiority over others: you cannot imagine the joy I derive in advancing you to atop the very pinnacle, and making your pre-eminence conditional upon profound humility and unbounded obedience toward me alone. I wish you to be the idol of others and, at the same time, my slave; the mere thought heats my prick. . . . Juliette, we'll perform horrors this day, shan't we, my angel? horrors, atrocities?"

And he pressed his lips to mine, the while toying with my cunt.

"Oh, my love, how delicious are our crimes when impunity

veils them, when duty itself prescribes them. How divine it is to swim in gold and, as one reckons up one's wealth, to be able to say, here are the means to every black deed, to every pleasure; with this, all my wishes can be made to come true, all my fancies can be satisfied; no woman will resist me, none of my desires will fail of realization, my wealth will procure amendments in the law itself, and I'll be despot without let or hindrance."

I kissed Saint-Fond a thousand times over and, profiting from the enthusiasm, the drunkenness he was carried away by, and above all from his predisposition to me, I had him sign a *lettre de cachet* written out for the arrest of Elvire's father, who wished to deprive me of her, and wheedled two or three other favors out of him, each of which was worth about five hundred thousand francs to me. And the fumes of the excellent dinner I had just provided him rising to his head, he announced he was sleepy and would retire for a little; he departed to his chamber, and I looked to the completion of the arrangements for the evening's entertainments.

Saint-Fond woke toward five that afternoon. By then everything stood ready in the salon, and this is the way the scene and the actors were disposed: nude and simply decked in garlands of roses, there were, on the right, the three maids intended for the orgies; I'd grouped them like Botticelli's Graces: all three were girls of condition spirited out of a convent at Melun, and their beauty was startling.

Louise was the name of the first: she was sixteen, fair-haired, and never was a more interesting face beheld.

The second was named Hélène: fifteen years old, slender in the waist, slight of build and tall for her age, long brown tresses, Love's own eyes and mouth; beautiful though she was, most would have admitted her to be surpassed by Fulvie, ravishing and also sixteen.

In the center, to offer a contrast to this group, I had stationed the ill-starred family, likewise naked and festooned with black crêpe: the father and the mother were watching each other in expectation of the worst, at their feet lay the charming Julie; heavy irons rubbed their bare skin raw, the nipple on Julie's left breast peeped through a link, which had bruised it, and it bled softly. Another length of chain was visible between the thighs of Madame de Cloris, and was pinching the lips of her womb; Delcour, whom I had outfitted in the terrifying garb of a demon out of hell and armed with the sword he was to use upon his victims, held the end of the chain which ever and again he would tug, with dreadful effect wherever it touched flesh.

Next, in the pose of Callipygian Venus, their backs to Saint-Fond, draped in a simple brown-and-white gauze which left their asses very distinctly in sight, were my four women:

The first was twenty-two, superb, a veritable Minerva, magnificently formed; her name was Délie.

The name of the second was Montalme: twenty, in full bloom, as nicely fleshed as woman can be.

Palmire was nineteen. She was blonde and had the romantic countenance of those girls you always like to see in tears.

Seventeen years old, Blaisine had a mischievous look, faultless teeth, the sauciest eyes that ever fired desire.

And at the far left of this semicircle were placed two strapping lads, five feet and ten inches in height, awesomely membered; they were standing face to face and while frigging each other were exchanging passionate kisses. They were naked.

"Charming," said Saint-Fond upon opening his eyes, "heavenly! No possible mistake, all this attests the mind and art of Juliette. Have the guilty ones brought hither," he continued, directing me to take a seat beside him, Montalme to come and suck his engine, Palmire to place her ass within his reach.

Delcour marched the family forward.

"You are all three under accusation of enormous crimes," the Minister began, "and from the Queen I have express orders to put you promptly to death."

"They are unjust orders," Cloris replied, "my family and I are innocent—as you know full well, you wretch! (At this point Saint-Fond was prey to a pleasurable emotion so puissant he was scarce able to fight off a discharge.) Yes, you know perfectly well that we are innocent. But if we are under suspicion, then let us be put on fair trial, but not exposed this way to the tigerish lust of one who sports with us only to quicken his ignoble passions."

"If you please, Delcour," said the Minister, "a taste of the chain."

And the executioner gave it a jerk, so sudden, so violent, that the cunt of Madame de Cloris, the breast of her daughter, one of her husband's thighs were cut into, blood spurted on the iron.

Then Saint-Fond said, "You allude to the law. You have broken the law, you have violated it too grievously to invoke its protection; its full severity is all you have a right to expect now. Ready yourselves to die."

"You," was Cloris' proud answer, "you are the hireling of a tyrant and the creature of a whore. Posterity will judge me."

Here Saint-Fond rises in fury; his prick is prettily grown; he beckons to me, "Come." Going close to the well-chained insolent, the Minister slaps him with all his might several times, insults him, spits in his face and, frigging his weapon on Julie's teats, defies her father: "You are ill used? Call not on the opinion of later times, but take matters into your own hands now. Are you a man? Then exert yourself a little."

"Coward, were I to get free you'd run off in a panic!"

"You are quite right. But you are not going to get free, I have you in my power, I enjoy the situation; would you deprive me of enjoyment? Try."

"Everything you have, you owe to me."

"You have only yourself to blame for that," the Minister said; and took hold of his benefactor's prick, massaged it; then bade me endeavor to bring it to life. But my efforts were fruitless also; seeing this, he said to Delcour, "Separate this man from his family, attach him to that stake. The Queen having left to my discretion the choice of tortures that are to prelude your deaths," Saint-Fond continued, now addressing the two women, "I mean to subject you to a certain amount of lewd handling; Cloris will be witness to it."

Noticing that Delcour was not binding the husband to the stake quite as firmly as he wished, Saint-Fond lent the executioner his assistance, and showered a further series of blows upon the man's face and behind.

"I shall kill him myself," he told Delcour. "Yes, I want to have the pleasure of shedding his blood in person."

As always methodically combining horror and lechery, he

bent forward, sucked Cloris' prick a moment, then kissed his ass. Delcour being hard by, he took that worthy's prick in his mouth too, and tongued his vent; straightened up and glued his lips to Delcour's; and after five minutes of this, confided to me, "That's the only thing that really puts a little snap in my whip." There followed an interval during which Saint-Fond was plunged in crapulousness and atrocity; emerging from these, he returned to objects of my sex.

"Ah, my Lord!" said those poor creatures as he drew near them, "what have we done to deserve such barbarous treatment?"

"Be courageous, wife," cried the luckless husband, "death shall soon deliver us from these outrages, we'll suffer no more and remorse shall gnaw at this monster's soul."

"Remorse," said Saint-Fond, chuckling, "is not a sentiment wherewith I shall ever have acquaintance, lest it be for sparing you."

First to be unbound was Madame de Cloris. She was brought to the Minister.

"Ah, whore," said he, "do you remember all the obstacles you hurled in my path, all your stubbornness in the past? Dear cousin, cherished cousin, sweet cousin, I'll have you cheap today."

His erection was something extraordinary to behold; he falls to pawing the woman's charms; catching her around the waist, he brutally encunts her before the very eyes of her husband, whose prick, thanks to the position Saint-Fond has adopted, he is able to mouth the while. And I, finding his ass a fair target, strap a dildo about my loins and embugger him; men and women together, all the others save Julie and Cloris surround him. Into his hands, before his eyes, I place cunts, asses, pricks, bubs in profusion; excited by the demon of cruelty, his fingers rake about, his nails claw and tear whatever they touch; but they rove with especial predilection over the breasts of the unhappy woman his rage feeds upon: these he scrapes, nips, bloodies incontinently.

"Take that stuff away, Juliette," says he, decunting from the mother in order to have at the daughter, "I'm tired of discharging. Little whore," he declares to the innocent creature under his belly, "your father and your mother are both aware of all I did in

my attempts to gain possession of you: I have you today, and today they're going to regret having thwarted me previously."

He then had Cloris placed in such wise that while fucking the daughter he might have a clear view of papa's handsome hindquarters, the which Delcour was to thwack with one hand as, with the other, he molested mama's buttocks, both their asses being at the same height, and adjacent. 'Tis I who help him depucelate Julie: he takes good aim, he presses, he thrusts, he encunts; and eight poised asses ring him round. He is sodomized: and the wicked wight, considering the torments Delcour is inflicting not severe enough, snatches up a small stiletto and indiscriminately pricks the mother's dugs, the daughter's shoulders, the father's rear. Blood flows.

"Aye, but I'll not discharge into this vessel of abomination," snaps the satyr, decunting; "no; it's rather there," says he, fondling the father's bum, "the shrine at which I'll do my sacrifice."

He gives orders that Cloris, his hands still tied, be stretched out upon the fatal sofa.

"Delcour, noose a cord around his neck; if we have any resistance from him, tighten till it ceases."

Again superintending the operation, I artfully guide the fiery courser to the edge of the road it is to charge down; there's not a murmur out of poor Cloris. Squarely ahead of him are posted the mother's bosom on the right and on the left the daughter's pretty little ass. The Minister is no sooner ensheathed in the bowels he has been coveting, than his hands, one of them wielding the dread stiletto, begin to stray hither and yon about the attractions displayed to him and so displayed that, whenever he jabs, 'tis upon the father's head flows the blood drawn from the wife or from the daughter. As all this goes forward I diddle about his asshole and my women prick his buttocks with hatpins.

"Ah, well," says he after a time, "it seems I'm yet again mistaken. My sperm won't loosen, and I fancy that's because I want first to explore this truly very winning family's asses. Delcour, chain the old bardash back to the stake, he's been of no use save to cover my prick with shit. You, the tall one," says he to Montalme, "come lick it clean."

Detecting in Montalme a certain unreadiness to comply, Saint-

Fond instantly commands Delcour to administer a hundred lashes to teach her obedience.

"Ah, the whore, the whore," he murmurs while her instructor toils over her, "you are loath to suck my prick because it's beshitted? Whatever shall you do when in a little while I give you mards to eat?"

Montalme, well whipped, returns in a different humor; she sucks the lecher, tidies his member, cleans his asshole out next; and going tranquilly back to work, there he is sodomizing the mother, the while molesting the ass of the father on the one side, his daughter's cunt on the other. These exercises occupy him only briefly; now he fastens upon Julie, saying, "I hope this will turn the trick."

Ever in the pilot's role, I steer him into Julie's hindward channel, and once he is safe berthed every conceivable thing is done to deliver him of his seed; but, whether from villainy or from contrariness or from impotence, he quits this ass too, declaring he's spent and if he's to recover his strength must thrash the whole family. The father, already secured to the post, is flogged first. Straightway he's all bloodied, his wife is tied with her belly to his back; a thousand strokes lay her ass open, then little Julie, camped upon her mother's shoulders, is given the same treatment.

"Unassemble them," says the centaur, " 'twas an agreeable episode, now we'll essay another: I'll whip the youngster afresh, but her parents will hold her this time. Juliette, and you, Delcour, take you each a pistol, clap it to their heads, and if while I'm at work on their child they so much as flinch, blow their brains out."

In charge of the mother, I wanted nothing so much as to have her show some recalcitrance; but, taking comfort in the thought she was soon to die under circumstances far less mild than mere shooting, I grew cheerful again after having been downcast and alarmed initially by her submissiveness. Poor Julie, abused with unexampled fury, first lashed with withes, was next flogged with a martinet the thongs whereof had her blood splashing all about the room; when done with her, Saint-Fond falls upon her father and using no other weapon but this martinet, its lashes iron-tipped, has him swimming in blood inside three minutes. The mother is seized without delay, she is installed on the edge of the sofa, her legs at the greatest possible spread and he bends the martinet to her, aiming his blows so they will strike into her open womb. I followed him wherever he went, now frigging him, now beating him, now sucking his tongue, or his prick. Raging, he wheels on the daughter, bestows upon her a pair of blows so terribly violent she and her manacles fly all aheap; the mother would come to her aid, he awaits her; kicked in the belly, she lands five yards off. Cloris was rolling his eyes, foaming at the mouth, but he dared not utter a word; bound hand and foot, what could he do? The girl is hauled to her feet; Saint-Fond directs the executioner to cunt-fuck her, and he himself, he sodomizes the executioner, while I, employing sweet words and having unbound him, I promise the father his life will be spared and his family's also if he can succeed in buggering the Minister. Hope ever rises up in the soul of the doomed: cunningly frigged by my hand, his quivering lance penetrates the chink. Saint-Fond, positively thrilled to feel so stout a prick in his fundament, dances and skips like the gleeful fish thrown back into water after having been a while in the air.

" 'Tis divine, and he's assured of release and safety," says the Minister, "if, profiting speedily from the admirable state my ass tells me his prick is in, he consents to bugger-fuck his daughter."

"Monsieur," I said to this gentleman, "ought you hesitate? For is it not better a hundred times that you fuck your child than murder her?"

"Murder her!"

"Why yes, Monsieur; do you refuse and she's undone. Dead, I say, if you balk."

And the while one of the women holds the little girl's buttocks at full divide and moistens the hole within, I quickly snatch the engine out of Saint-Fond's bum and clap it to the threshold of Julie's; but Cloris, in revolt, drives not past the gate.

"So be it, so be it, since he won't fuck her," says Saint-Fond, "she'll have to die."

At this cruel pronouncement resistance melts away. I fit the girl's loins up near the member, I push it into the anus; for as much as the requisite preparations have all been made, my efforts culminate in triumph, and Cloris who would not become the child-murderer becomes incestuous to the tune of a liberal outgushing of fuck. Délie was fustigating Saint-Fond, in the meantime he was vexing the mother's ass and kissing the buttocks of one of the lackeys; but this lackey is soon fucking him, and now a close-on view of Délie's behind seems to inspire him. The inconstant Saint-Fond ordered this group dissolved too; still stubbornly holding his seed in check, he appears before us in a greater fury than any wild beast: he shrieks, he bellows, there's foam on his lips, curses in his mouth; as soon as Delcour spews into Julie's cunt, he has him embugger her mother. At length the storm abates a little; Saint-Fond resumes his chair and orders me to bring up for his examination the three young girls of whom heretofore he has not taken anything but casual notice. He fingers and caresses their asses a quarter of an hour; he separates their buttocks, he compresses them, he compares them; and I frig him all this while; and he admits that, in a word, I have never found him better stuff. He is especially taken by Fulvie.

"I'd bugger her, be sure of it," the lecher remarked, "if I didn't fear I'd discharge."

After reviewing the three girls he wishes to review the four women; Palmire enchants him, never, says he, has he seen the like of her, and the lovely girl's matchless ass has him dumbfounded and doting for ten minutes.

Then he turns to me. "Instruct all these whores to get down on their knees in a semicircle around me; then to creep forward and pay their respects to my prick, and to suck it, one by one."

I give the order, it is carried out, and while each suckles his engine she receives a couple of smart slaps.

"Well now," says he, when that ceremony is over, "it's my ass's turn, have them approach one after the other and do it fitting worship and lick it."

Off they go to their new chore and while it is being done he sucks pricks, including, as you may well imagine, those of Cloris and Delcour.

"The time has come, Juliette," says he, "to end this first scene."

Whereupon the villain embuggers little Julie, the valets hold the mother and father while he bores and scrapes the child's ass. Armed with a razor, Delcour steps up and prepares to sever her head.

"Be in no hurry about it, Delcour," he cries, "I want my beloved niece to know what's happening to her, she's not to die before I've done fucking her."

Delcour laid the cutting edge to skin and at once the child set up a ghastly wailing and screeching.

"Proceed, proceed," said Saint-Fond, well lodged in her ass, "but go softly, you've no idea the repercussions all this is having on my nervous system. Bend this way a little, Delcour, so that I can warm your member while you work. Juliette, pay your respects to Delcour's ass, worship it; he's become a god in my consideration. And bring the mother's ass inside my reach, I want to kiss it while I have her daughter murdered."

But what were those kisses! Great God, they were bites so cruel the blood leapt forth at each. A valet embuggered him, the scoundrel's ecstasy was unspeakable.

"Ah, I savor crime, I do indeed," he exclaimed, uttering many incoherent oaths, "I adore crime, it bewitches me."

Delcour cuts with exquisite slowness. . . . Cloris is deathly pale, half in a swoon, he averts his horror-filled gaze. Julie's beautiful head falls at last, like a rose that finally yields to the unflagging north wind.

"Than what I have just experienced there is probably nothing more voluptuous," announces Saint-Fond, withdrawing from the cadaver, " 'tis unimaginable, the constriction resulting in the anus from a gradual incision performed upon the nape vertebrae, it is delicious. All right now, Madame, prepare to give me the same pleasure."

And the scene begins anew. Estimating that the operation is going ahead too rapidly, Saint-Fond suspends it.

"I dare say they are few who realize," he observes, "how heavenly it is to slice through the neck of a woman whom in your gigantic weakness you loved in days bygone. I am being very splendidly revenged upon my cousin; it's the sort of thing you are fain to have last for ever."

He continued frigging the headsman's prick, but he would now kiss my buttocks; a valet tups him bumwise, another inserts in Delcour who resumes carving; the father has been adjusted so that I, armed with switches, can slash away at his privities. My ferocious lover is in raptures, he feasts upon the slow sufferings of his relative; whose head is at last sundered fifteen minutes later. And now 'tis Cloris' turn. He is placed in the position the operation demands, and bound. Saint-Fond sodomizes, the killer sets to work, valets yet embugger them both. This time it is Montalme's magnificent behind Saint-Fond elects to kiss. The other women encircle him, displaying their asses; the bomb does finally burst. Heavens! if mighty Lucifer were to take it upon himself to discharge, methinks he'd unloose his seed less thunderously, would not foam so much at the mouth nor so gnash his teeth, at the gods would not hurl blasphemies and imprecations so fearful. While Saint-Fond remains behind, resting, I escort the seven women and the two valets into the next room. The Minister has soon rejoined us, but, like Wenceslas, his headsman is ever at his side; a few revels of a milder kind are, however, to precede the anthropophagical orgies of our latter-day Nero, and now for a space fuck is perhaps to flow before the bloodshedding resumes.

Nonetheless, considering the man I was dealing with, it was necessary that I hew to the line laid down by his favorite pleasures: the voluptuous groups awaiting him had been disposed about in three alcoves decorated with all that is emblematic of Death. The entire room was hung in black, bones, skulls, a great store of rods, switches, withes, martinets, and knives were the furnitures; in each niche a virgin was being cunt-lapped by a Lesbian, both naked, reposing upon black cushions, and upon their brows wearing the skull and crossbones device. Within each niche one of the lately severed heads was plainly visible, and in front of these niches there were on the right a coffin, and to the left a little round table upon which lay a pistol, a goblet of poison, and a dagger; from somewhere (doubtless from my desire to please my lover) I had got the idea of sawing up the bodies of the three victims sacrificed a little before, gone was everything below mid-thigh and from the waist up, and cords depending from hooks sunk in the intercolumniations between the niches held these chunks of meat mouth-high. These were the objects Saint-Fond first caught sight of when he entered.

"My goodness," sighed he after he'd kissed them all, "here they are again, and I'm most content to see them, these asses which recently gave me such delight."

A dim, a lugubrious lamp hung in the middle of the room whose vaults were likewise covered with dismal appurtenances; various instruments of torture were scattered here and there, among other objects one saw a most unusual wheel. It revolved inside a drum, the inner surface of which was studded with steel spikes; the victim, bent in an arc upon the circumference of the wheel, would, as it turned, be rent everywhere by the fixed spikes; by means of a spring device the drum could be tightened, so that, as the spikes grated flesh away, they could be brought closer and contact with the diminished mass maintained. This torture was the more horrible in as much as it was exceedingly gradual, and the victim might well endure ten hours of slow and appalling agony before giving up the ghost. To accelerate or slow the procedure one had but to decrease or widen the distance between the wheel and the compassing drum; this machine, of Delcour's contriving, had not yet been essayed by Saint-Fond; upon seeing it, he waxed very enthusiastic and then and there gave its inventor a fifty-thousand-francs gratuity. From that moment on his single preoccupation was to choose her from among the three victims who would be immolated in this manner; his perfidious gaze flitted from one girl to the next. Gods! the conclusion was foregone: the unlucky Fulvie, being the most beautiful, stood condemned in the tyrant's heart, of this I was sure. A kiss he applied to that lovely creature's asshole the moment he was done contemplating the terrible machine erased all doubt; but of all that in due time.

Between Delcour and me, Saint-Fond first starts by settling himself in one after the other of the three armchairs which were placed one in front of each alcove. Palmire, of my women alone not employed in a niche, is posted behind his chair and is reaching around and polluting him; he is dandling Delcour's prick and toying with my ass; and he scrutinizes the scene before him. Each tribade is mindful to ensure him a good view of the body of the little girl she is frigging in every sector and in every possible manner and attitude; often, indeed, the child is brought to him so that he may kiss her in divers parts. He rises, goes to the next niche, then to the third; then comes back to the first; in the meantime Delcour flogs him; and now again he has somebody fuck him, and I suck him; I remark his device beginning to assume size and vibrancy; he embuggers me after a while (this occurred opposite the niche where Blaisine was toiling over Fulvie), it was then, as he was embracing that charming girl's ass, he glanced aside at me and whispered in my ear, "That's the one who's to baptize the wheel. What a pretty tickling it'll give those delectable little buttocks."

This preliminary examination completed, he lays himself down on a kind of narrow upholstered bench, and then begins a veritable parade; all those present, male and female, file up and one by one straddle the bench, squat over his face, and shit into his mouth. Palmire steps first to the fore, and when she has eased herself she kneels down beside his Lordship, takes his prick in her mouth, and sucks on it throughout the rite. Next, Montalme and I present ourselves simultaneously in order that he be able, as he so desires, to handle one ass while the other is yielding. From nastiness the libertine moves straight to horrors; he gives Delcour instructions to flog the seven women, and I rub his prick upon the heads he has had me detach for this purpose.

After that three tableaux take form before his eyes: my two fuckers embugger two of my tribades; in the center, Delcour flogs the third; at the foot of each group reclines one of the little girls Saint-Fond is to depucelate, and for this task he is now getting himself in readiness: Palmire and I are arraying him for fight, she by socratizing him, I by means of prick-friggery. Rampant, the libertine shivers the three forward pucelages, turns Fulvie over and sinks his lance in her bum and discharges. I suck his weapon to restore it to true and temper; he would have the headsman hold for him all the women, not excepting me; to each of us he applies two hundred strokes; then it is he who holds the women and bids Delcour embugger them all. While Delcour is performing, the Minister kisses them upon the mouth during all the scene, in which I figure too.

Then Saint-Fond led each maiden away into a remote chamber and passed a brief interval with her alone. We do not know what he told them, nor what he did; nor dared we even question them when they were brought back. In all likelihood he apprised them of their impending deaths, for each returned weeping from the interview. While Saint-Fond's consultations were in progress Delcour indicated to me that a certain subtle lubricious byplay ordinarily followed this announcement; and that since the outset of his acquaintance with the Minister, he, Delcour, had always observed that pronouncing sentence left his Lordship overwhelmed by a sweet and mysterious anguish. Such was now the case, for he came back profoundly agitated, flushed, and marvelously erected.[10]

"Very well," said he, rubbing his hands together, lust's froth on his lips, "let's take counsel. How shall we do them to death? Their agonies must be frightful, you understand, indescribable. Delcour, my lad, cudgel your wits, I expect you to outdo yourself in inventiveness: these poor swine are to endure one after the other all of hell's tortures, it will desolate me if they get away with less."

And so saying he gave Fulvie a warm kiss; it was very obviously she who most aroused him.

"Delcour," he went on, "let me recommend this pretty little thing to you; she'll look stunning on your wheel, those plump white buttocks were made for its spikes."

Wherewith he sank his teeth into her, bit her in half a dozen places, drawing blood from each; one of those bites cost her the nipple off her left teat, and the roguish Minister swallowed it. He popped his prick into her asshole for a moment, then plucked it out again, got hold of Delcour's engine, and rammed it into the vent he'd vacated.

"The executioner must fuck his victim," said he, "protocol demands it."

While Delcour was complying, Saint-Fond's fingernails raked and tore the child's buttocks, thighs, breasts, and he lapped up the blood as he made it flow; he had Palmire come forward, Palmire for whom, it appeared, he also had a prodigious weakness, and he said to her, "Behold, 'tis thus I treat little girls who stiffen my tool."

Those words were scarce out of his mouth when he drove the selfsame tool into her ass: after some bucking and heaving he had her clamber upon a chair so he could proceed with her buttocks in better view; and beside her he had Délie take the same stance; then the three girls ranged themselves in a semicircle around him; they knelt; and he molested their bosoms while Blaisine frigged his

---

[10] Further light will be shed upon these strange matters.

prick. He ran pins into those three unfortunates' still but half-formed breasts, with a penknife he gashed them, then immediately brought a hot iron into play and cauterized the wounds. And I? I was busy keeping his excitement at a pitch, having, pursuant to his orders, Delcour's prick in my bowels and the prick of a valet in either hand. With cords the Minister bound the kneeling three into a compact group, their backs together, and with a martinet whose steel tips were arrowheads, edged as well as pointed, made a very hash of their mammaries; throughout these pageantries Palmire's ass was constantly there wherever he looked; taking respite from his labors, he many times flung himself upon it and sucked it to recover strength.

"No dallying," said he. rising up again, "set the stage. We'll have some more of the whip."

The seven women—I was left out—were tied to specially constructed columns; in their upraised hands they each held a crucifix; also upon crucifixes the four tribades were standing, and seemingly treading them contemptuously under foot; while the three victims found support upon cannonballs studded with nails all over, in such wise that their feet were lacerated owing to the weight of their bodies. The victims were cinctured around the breast by a leather strap, first wet, and as it dried, shrinking ever tighter; a device impended above the head of each and Saint-Fond, controlling a small crank, could bring its needle-sharp point down so that it penetrated to whatever depth desired into the cranium of the girl; other instruments, these resembling two-tined forks and likewise needle-pointed, and also controlled by Saint-Fond, were aimed at their eyes; yet another point was there to receive their navels in the event that, jostled by the blows of the whip, they might perchance slip forward; and each of the victims, arranged as I have said, was flanked by tribades, who were free of all such intricate harnesses.

Saint-Fond at first uses the switches Delcour and I hand over to him; he metes out a hundred strokes to each victim and deals each tribade fifty; the second round sees the steel-tipped martinet in service, each victim is favored with two hundred blows thereof, each tribade with a mere dozen. Then Saint-Fond starts his machineries working; the poor children, pricked in this place and that, set up a clamor such as would have melted the heart of any

villain made of less stern stuff than we. Sensing a mounting irritation in his prick, whence fuck is already oozing, Saint-Fond quickly
has Louise brought to him, that Louise, sixteen years old, whom he
has singled out to be executed first. Much does he kiss her, lick and
fondle her bleeding ass, give her his prick to suck and his asshole;
then turns her over to Delcour who, once he has slipped his goad
into both her orifices, fastens her down upon a long table and subjects her to that Chinese torture which consists in being chopped up
alive, by less than inches, into twenty-four thousand pieces. Saint-
Fond, seated on the lap of the lackey fucking him, assists at the
spectacle, and between his thighs grips Hélène, next on the list and
whose ass he molests while I frig him and he tongues Palmire's
mouth. The torture used upon the second consists in having her eyes
gouged out and after that of being spread on a Saint Andrew's
cross and broken alive. Saint-Fond attends to the matter while I
thrash him. All the victim's limbs are broken, all her joints pulled
loose; in that state she is offered to him again, he embuggers her
and while he instruments her anus, Delcour finishes her off with a
mace, dashing out her brains so that they fairly splatter into Saint-
Fond's mouth and eyes.

The charming Fulvie alone remains, surrounded by the gory
vestiges of her two companions; can she be in doubt of her fate?
Saint-Fond points to the wheel.

"Look there," says the Minister, "I've saved the best for you."

And the traitor does not fail to caress her and to kiss her
tenderly upon the lips; yet again he embuggers her before delivering
her to the killer. Delcour has her now; hideous are her screams;
she is fitted into position, fastened there, and the wheel begins to
turn. Fucked now by one valet, now by the other, Saint-Fond sounds
Delcour's ass while alternately kissing Palmire's behind and mine,
and in a detached and fugitive manner fingering the three unoccupied assholes. Very soon the ascending volume and tone of the
victim's screams give us report of her pain. Violent you may be
certain it was; judge thereof by this detail: the blood was coming
from her like one of those fine rains blown almost to mist by a
strong wind. Saint-Fond, eager to prolong the game to the utmost,
varies his tableaux and his festive doings too. He embuggers my
four tribades in swift succession, while we all, Delcour included,

compose new groups for him. The spike-surfaced drum, ever contracting, begins to attack the nerves, and the cries of the victim are stilled as overwhelmed by suffering she faints away; and that's the very moment when Saint-Fond, weary of horrors and cruelty, finally unleashes his fuck into Palmire's superb ass while he gamahuches Delcour's, palpates mine with one hand and Montalme's with the other, watches one of the valets embugger Blaisine on the floor beside the fatal wheel, and is whipped by Délie who also sucks his tongue to hasten his discharge.

Saint-Fond's shrieks, his disport, his foul, ungodly language were all appalling; he was only half-conscious when we bore him to the bed where, he nevertheless gave me to understand, he wished to have me pass the night at his side.

This peerless libertine, quite as though he had just performed wonders of charity, enjoyed ten hours of blissful undisturbed sleep. I watched his rest; and if I had doubted it before, I was convinced now that it is easy to build oneself a conscience to sort evenly with one's opinions, and that after the initial effort has been made, nothing afterward stands in one's way. Oh, my friends, believe me when I say that he who has succeeded in ridding his heart of every idea and trace of God or religion, he whose gold or influence removes him beyond the reach of the law, he who has toughened his conscience and brought it firmly into line with his attitudes and cleared it utterly and forever of guilty remorse; he, I say, and be certain thereof, he may do whatever he pleases and whenever, and never know an instant's fear.

When he woke up, the Minister asked me if it were not true that he was the wickedest man in the world. Knowing the pleasure I would give by answering in the affirmative, I did not by any means contradict him; and he smiled.

"You flatter me."

"Do I? It is sincere."

"I rather suppose so. Ah, my angel," said he, yawning, "could it be otherwise with me? Is it my fault if this is how I am, and if Nature put the most irresistible taste for vice in me, and not so much as a hint of a bent for virtue? Don't you agree that I serve her quite as well as some other in whom she ingrained a fondness for doing good deeds? That seems self-evident to me; and this likewise, that there would be no greater folly than willfully to cross her purpose as it regards us individually; I am the poisonous plant she makes grow by the balsam tree, and find my manner of being no more to be regretted than I would esteem enviable that of the virtuous man; and once we realize that upon earth there must be the bitter together with the better, can it make one jot of difference to us whether we are numbered in this category or that? Imitate me, Juliette,[11] your native leanings are in this direction: let no criminal act daunt you, the more atrocious it is, the more pleasing to Nature; guilt? The only guiltiness is in reluctance, in backhanging; lift up your head, beloved girl, and go ever forward. To the dreary mediocre portion of mankind leave all notions and prattle such as that righteousness and modesty must accompany fleshly pleasure, they'll fail utterly of it every time. For it cannot possibly delect save when one outsteps every limit in one's quest; the proof thereof is that there must be a breaking of restraining rules before pleasure begins to be pleasure; go farther yet, break still another and the irritation becomes more violent, and necessarily so with each ascending step; and you do not really attain to the true goal whither these pleasure-takings point until the ferment of the senses has reached the extremest pitch, until you have got to the final limit of what our human faculties can endure, in such wise that your nerves are so prodigiously wrought upon that they are frayed as if to paralysis, smitten into a convulsion that resembles standstill and shocked insensibility. He who also would know the whole wild power and all the magic of lubricity's pleasures must thoroughly well grasp that only by undergoing the greatest possible upheaval in the nervous system may he procure himself the drunken transport he must have if he is properly to enjoy himself. For what is pleasure? Simply this: that which occurs when voluptuous atoms, or atoms emanated from voluptuous objects, clash hard with and fire the electrical particles circulating in the hollows of our nerve

---

[11] Hot-blooded and lewdly disposed ladies, these are words to the wise, hark attentively to them: they are addressed not only to Juliette but to yourselves also; if your intelligence is in any sense comparable to hers, you'll not fail to extract great benefit from them. In writing we are moved by an ardent desire for your happiness; a happiness you'll never attain, no, never shall you attain it, unless you base your behavior upon this excellent advice, and upon it alone.

fibers. Therefore, that the pleasure be complete, the clash must be as violent as possible; but so delicate is the nature of this sensation that a mere nothing can spoil or nullify it; hence, the soul must be prepared, tranquil, its serenity ensured by certain mental attitudes or certain physical postures, so that it lies as though in a calm and smiling vale; and then the imagination's fire must set the furnace of the senses alight. From this point onward give that imagination free rein, act at its every behest, its every whim; and labor not only to grant it what it desires but, by making practical use of your philosophy and above all of the chill hardness of your heart and your lack of conscience, enable it to forge, to weave, to create new fantasies which, injecting energies into the voluptuous atoms, cause them to collide at greater speed and more potently with the molecules they are to make vibrate; these vibrations are your delight. From what I have just said, you will appreciate, Juliette, how obstacles, exerting their restrictive influence upon the form of your delirium, will always tend to confine it within the boundaries of decency and virtue, thus altering its essence; upon your delirium obstacles of any sort have a dampening effect, water poured on fire; a hindering effect, so many chains, so many clogs encumbering the spirited young destrier that asks only to take the bit in its mouth and break into a gallop.

"In such cases, the impediment represented by religion is without doubt the first that ought to be liquidated, being as it is a perpetual source of discomfort and remorse to anyone languishing in its grip; but combating superstition is only half the job, it will remain unfinished so long as the altars of a fantastical God are left standing. No, there's not much to the former operation, neither a great deal of intelligence nor a great deal of brawn is needed to dispose of religion's disgusting chimeras, since not one of them can hold up under examination. But that's not the end to it, Juliette, not by any means, there are countless other duties, other social conventions, other barriers which will soon become as much a nuisance to you as religion was, if, bold and independent of mind, you do not make it a rule to thrust aside anything that lies in your path. Just as hampered by these contemptible restraints, you'll soon discover them interfering with your pleasures equally as much as his belief interferes with the believer's; if, on the contrary, you have ridden roughshod over everything in order to attain pleasure, and if you have protected your rear by taming your conscience and lulling it nicely off to sleep, then, in this other case, there is no doubt but that your enjoyment will be as intense and complete as anything Nature allows of; and such will be your frenzy that its excessive consequences will be all if not more than your physical faculties can endure. Nevertheless, do not expect to be as happy in the beginning as, by dint of persistence, you shall be later on; no matter what you do to counter them, prejudices will continue a long while to harass you, and the more severely the more formidable the obstacles you surmount: baneful, fatal effects of education, for which the only remedy is deep thought, indefatigable perseverence, and entrenched habits especially.

"But little by little—my intention is not to discourage you— little by little your mind will become fortified; habit, that second nature which sometimes becomes more powerful than first, which is at length able to annihilate those very natural principles that seem the most invulnerable, the most sacred, this habit that is essential to vice, that I cannot too strongly urge you to acquire, and upon which success in the career you have chosen depends; this habit, I say, will dull your remorse, quell it, silence your conscience, put a stop to the silly bleating that comes from the heart; and then you'll see things in a very different light indeed. Amazed at the fragility of the bonds that held you captive once, you'll look with a certain regret, yes, with a certain nostalgia back upon the days when, stupidly ensnared, innocently, you were able to resist pleasures; and though a few paltry obstacles may have got in the way of your felicity, the charm of having known it, and the divine memories you will have of it, will cause the thorns they wished to strow in your path to appear as very flowers. Well now, in the circumstances where I have placed you, with the security I guarantee you, what have you to fear? Reflect a moment upon your marvelous situation; and if the certainty of getting off scot-free furnishes crime its divinest allurements, who in all the world is better placed than you to enjoy yourself to death? Consider now your other advantages: eighteen years, perfect health, the prettiest face, the noblest figure, all the wit one could ask for, intelligence, the temperament of a Messalina, the riches virtually of a Croesus, a splendid reputation,

no handicaps, no chains, no relations, friends who adore you . . .
and you're afraid of the law? Put by your fears forever; if some
day the sword of justice is bared against you, Juliette, protect
yourself with the shield of your wiles and winningness; instead of
this languor where you lie becalmed in a sea of voluptuous delights,
adopt another mood, put on seductive raiments, show yourself
about, and crowds will fall at your feet; bestir yourself and a
kneeling world will provide you with ten thousand champions,
they will shed their blood to the last drop defending the name of
their most cherished idol and to keep it pure; ten thousand hearts
will beat for you, and where others would have judges to dread
you'll find none but devoted lovers. Let the isolated, the friendless,
the penniless individual, he who counts for nought, who scarce has
an identity, let him groan under vulgar yokes; they were designed
for him only. But you, Juliette, ah! hurl all Nature into confusion,
wreak havoc, destroy, rend the whole universe asunder; men will
consider your anger godlike and do you divine worship if perchance you deign to smile upon the world, whensoever you cast a
crumb of kindness to it; and will dread you when in wrath you
trample upon it; but it is all one, whatever you do, you'll always be
God to the common sort and mass of humankind.

"Indulge yourself, oh, my Juliette, without fear, proudly
surrender to the impetuosity of your tastes, to the irregularity of
your caprices, to the blazing ardor of your desires; your wantonness is my cheer, your pleasures my joy; be ever guided by them,
ruled by them and by nothing else; may your voluptuous imagination ensure variety to our disorders; only by multiplying them will
we attain happiness. Happiness being an intrinsically fickle and
fugitive thing, it confers its blessing only upon him who is clever
to mark it, quick to seize it, strong to hold it; and never lose sight
of the fact that all human felicity lies in man's imagination, and
that he cannot think to attain it unless he heeds all his caprices.
The most fortunate of persons is he who has the most means to
satisfy his vagaries: get ye girls, men, children; upon all those in
your entourage direct the lasciviousness of your impassioned soul;
whatever delights is good, whatever arouses is natural.

"Do you not see the star that lights us sometimes give life
and sometimes take it away, now vivifying, now withering to dust?

Match the sun in thy conduct as thou dost figure it in thy fair eyes. Take Messalina and Theodora for thy models; like those famous whores of antiquity, supply thyself with harems of either sex wherein thou canst plunge conveniently and when thou wilt into a very ocean of filthiness. Wallow in ordure and infamy; let all that is of the dirtiest and the most execrable, of the most shameful and the most criminal, of the most cynical and the most repulsive, of the most unnatural, illegal, irreligious, be for those very reasons that which dost please thee most. Soil without stint and at leisure the loveliest parts of thy body, remember that there is not a one where lubricity may not find a shrine, and that the divinest pleasures are unfailingly those whereat thou perhaps suppose Nature vexed. When the most odious of debauchery's excesses, when the most depraved turpitudes, when the most disgusting activities begin to pall upon thee and leave thee listless, have resort to cruelties, they reanimate; the most ghastly and fell deeds, the most revolting atrocities, the most unimaginable and nameless crimes, the most gratuitous horrors, the most monstrous perversities, let these be the means to convey thy soul from the lethargy where libertinage may have left it. Nor forget that Nature is thine ally and sanction; that whatever she lets us do is permissible; and that when she created us she was cunning enough to withhold from us the power and possibility of doing her injury. Thou shalt then notice Love sometimes maketh his arrows into daggers, and that for bringing our fuck to flow the invectives of the doomed one we torment often outvalue the polite gallantries of Cythera."

Deeply moved by Saint-Fond's speech, I ventured to indicate that my sole fear was of the possibility his kindness to me might come to an end.

"Juliette," he gave me answer, "you'd have fallen out of grace a good while before this had I merely been your lover; for, however beautiful she may be, the favors of a woman cannot exert prise upon me for long. He unto whom it is a principle that the instant one has finished fucking a woman is the instant when it is essential to be finished with her, must of a certainty, if he is only a lover, inspire such an eventuality as causes you to worry; but Juliette, and hereof I need hardly remind you, there is precious little of the vulgar amorist in me; both of us bound by similarities of taste, intellect, outlook, and self-interest, I apprehend our attachment as one forged out of egoism alone, and that kind endures forever. Would I advise you to fuck . broad if I were your lover? No, Juliette, no, that I am not, such I shall never be. Hence dread no change of heart in me; if ever I quit you it will be you the cause of our separation, only you. Maintain your good behavior, I tell you, be active in the service of my pleasures; let not a moment go by when I do not develop some new vice in you or further refine an old one; while we are at home, show me submissiveness carried to the last degree of baseness, the lower you crawl cringingly at my feet, the higher I, from pride, shall set you above others; above all, whatsoever may be the thing I require you to do, do it without ever displaying any weakness, any hint of contrition, and I shall render you the happiest of women as you shall render me the luckiest of men."

"Oh, my master," said I, "be ever sure that if I would reign over the world, it is to bring it on its bended knees in homage to you."

Next we left off generalities to discuss certain particulars. Saint-Fond expressed regret at not having been able to subject his niece to the wheel; which, said he, he would definitely have done were he not under obligation to produce her head in Paris. Then he spoke in very great praise of Delcour.

"He is full of imagination," said the Minister. "He is young and vigorous besides, and I must compliment you upon having desired his prick. For my own part, it is always a delight to fuck him. In passing let me remark that, as I have often had occasion to observe, the same man you fucked in your youth can yet be fucked pleasurably when you are forty. We are alike, aren't we Juliette?" he went on. "As did I, you took a fancy to him on account of his trade; were it not for that, neither of us would have paid him the slightest attention."

"Have you had many such fellows?" I asked Saint-Fond.

"For five or six years they were my specialty," he replied, "I combed the provinces to get hold of them; and I had an incredible leaning toward their valets. You simply cannot imagine what it's like to have the prick of a headsman's valet in your ass; after a time though, I found something equivalent in butchers' boys.

Often I'd pass two hours being embuggered by one of those lads come fresh from his slaughtering and bloody all over."

"Adorable," said I.

"Beyond words so," said he. "Ah yes, my dear, believe me, those stunts call for infamy and depravation; and what the devil is lust, if crapulousness is not therein as its very soul? By the way," the Minister continued, "one of those tribades has an appalling effect upon my nerves—I refer to the pretty blonde, the whom, I think, obtained the last of my fuck."

"Palmire?"

"Yes, 'twas doubtless so I heard you call her. Her ass was the fairest, its hole the narrowest, the warmest of the lot. . . . How did you gain possession of the wench?"

"She was working at a dressmaker's, was just turned eighteen when I found her and as mint as a babe emerging from its mother's womb; Palmire is an orphan. She comes of a good line, and has no parents save an elderly aunt who gave me an excellent character of the girl."

"Do you love her, Juliette?"

"Saint-Fond, I don't love anything. I am moved by caprice only."

"I feel this pretty creature lacks absolutely nothing of what is needed to make a delicious victim; undeniably she is beautiful, it is quite certain she would be yet more so in distress, she has magnificent hair, a sublime ass whose qualities are indeed outstanding. . . . Here, Juliette, dost see how my prick soars at the thought of martyrizing her?"

Truly, never had I seen his prick in such high wrath, I clutched it and set to frigging it softly.

"But if I take her," he added, "I'll pay you well, I'll pay you a better price for her than for another, since I desire her."

"To my understanding, does not that word have the meaning and force of a command? Wouldst have her come in this instant?"

"I would, for my prick is gone up for her."

Saint-Fond, flinging a dressing robe about himself, sprang toward Palmire as she came into the room and, taking her firmly by the arm, disappeared with her into another chamber: long, arduous was the séance; I could hear Palmire's screams. An hour elapsed before they returned. As he had made her undress before leading her off to that secret lair, the first thing that caught my eye when she reappeared was the extent to which she had been mistreated; and even if her body had not been naked, the tears still coursing down her cheeks would have been sufficient evidence. It was but too superfluously confirmed by the marks on her breasts and buttocks.

"Juliette," declared her tormentor, visibly overwrought by what he had just accomplished, "it breaks my heart but I simply do not have enough time for this: those blasted heads must be delivered to the Queen by five this afternoon, which means I'll not be able to amuse myself with this girl in the manner I'd like. Not today at least. So this is my suggestion. Have her present the day after tomorrow at our next three-girl supper. Until then, prison her safely in the darkest and best-barred of your dungeon cells; I forbid you to allow her any nourishment or drink, and order you to fetter her so closely to the wall she will be able neither to sit down nor even to stir. Do not question her about what has just now passed; I have my own reasons for preferring to keep you in ignorance thereabout. For this Palmire you will receive double the customary fee. Farewell."

So saying, he and Delcour, the latter carrying the box containing the three heads, mount Saint-Fond's coach; it drives away; and I, keenly agitated, remain rooted to the spot.

I had a great fondness for Palmire. Very loath I was to surrender her to that cannibal; but could I disobey? Daring not even to speak to her, I had her taken off to the dungeon; and scarcely was she there when two sentiments assailed me. The first was a desire to save this girl, of whom I was still far from being weary; the second revolved around an extreme curiosity to discover just how Saint-Fond proceeded with women upon whom he pronounced capital sentence. Ceding to this latter desire, I was about to start down to interrogate the captive when a servant ushered in Madame de Clairwil.

Several days earlier she had seen the Minister and learned from him the time of his return from the country; and now she had come to ask whether I would not care to drive back with her to Paris and to see a charming ballet at the Opéra. I embraced my friend most warmly; I related to her all we had lately achieved, Saint-Fond and I; the follies I'd committed before the Minister's arrival, I spoke also of them, and of all the others that had ensued. The dear creature found my stories delicious and congratulated me upon the progress I was beginning to make in crime. When I alluded to what was afoot regarding Palmire, Clairwil raised a cautioning hand.

"Juliette," said she, "beware. Banish all thoughts of cheating the Minister of his victim, and above all of prying into his obscure ways; be rather mindful that your fate depends upon this man, and that the pleasure you might derive from discovering his secret, or from preserving your slut's life, will never console you for the woes that will unfailingly beset you do you act the fool. You'll find ten score girls worth more than this one; and as for Saint-Fond's secret, knowledge of one piece of infamy more or less is not going to make you happier. Let's dine, my beloved, and then hasten back to the city; it will distract you."

By six o'clock we were en route, Clairwil, Elvire, Montalme, and I; the team of six English horses had us flying swift as the wind and we would surely have arrived in time for the opening of the ballet, when but a little out of the village of Arcueil we met with four men, who were mounted and had pistols in their hands. Night had fallen. Our lackeys, effeminate, craven fellows, fops almost, ran off as fast as their legs could carry them, and, save only for the two coachmen, we were left to confront the four masked riders alone.

Clairwil, who knew not the meaning of fear, singled out him who looked to be the ringleader and, addressing him in an imperious tone, demanded what he fancied he was about; not a word did he reply. Our drivers were ordered to turn the coach about, we proceeded back away in the direction of Arcueil, then climbed to Cachan, and swung off into a narrow road which at length brought us to a lonely fortified castle. The coach entered, the gates closed, we even heard them being barricaded from within; thereupon one of our escorts opened the door of the coach and silently offered his hand, inviting us to step out.

My knees buckled as I got down from the coach, I was close to fainting away, for indeed I was dreadfully afraid; my women were in no better case; only Clairwil was undaunted. Head high, lips compressed, she bade us take courage. Three of our ravishers disappeared; their captain led us into a well-lit drawing room. There, our eyes were greeted by the sight of an old man: he was weeping, and two very pretty young ladies were endeavoring to console him.

"Mesdames, these persons gathered here," pronounced our guide, who had now been rejoined by his three fellows, "are all that remain of the Cloris family. The old gentleman is the father of the husband, these two ladies are the sisters of his wife, and we are his brothers. The head of this house, his wife and daughter too, are missing; false charges were brought against them, through no fault of their own they incurred Her Majesty's displeasure and, worse yet, the wrath of that Minister who owes his place and fortune to none other than my brother's generosity and aid. Enquiries we rapidly made led us to the conviction that these three persons, of whom there has been nothing heard since the day before yesterday, are being held prisoner, or are dead, in the country house you left this same evening. You belong to the Minister; one of you is his mistress, this we know. You shall either guide us to the recovery of the three we seek, or persuade us that they are no longer alive; until then, you shall remain our hostages. Restore our relatives to us and you go free; but if they have been murdered, then you shall be with them in the grave very shortly, and your shades shall implore theirs for forgiveness. Beyond this we have nothing to say to you; now 'tis your turn to speak. Be quick."

"Messieurs," answered the brazen Clairwil, "it would appear to me that your doings are in every sense profoundly illegal. I would also qualify them as exceedingly clumsy. For consider: to begin with, is it likely that two women, madame and myself—these others are our servants—is it at all likely, I say, that two women be so well acquainted with the Minister's private affairs as to have any knowledge of such happenings as you refer to? Do you really suppose that if the persons in question have fallen into disgrace at Court, and that Justice or the Minister has been called upon to take action; do you honestly believe that we would have been made privy to any such execution? You know when we departed from the Minister's house, you doubtless know when we arrived; does not our presence under his roof during the last few days most conclusively prove that the event could not have transpired there? For the rest, gentlemen, we have nought but our word of honor to give you, but we offer it as guaranty of our total ignorance of what may have befallen those after whose fate you ask. No, gentlemen, no, we do declare to you that we have never even heard tell of these people until now, and if you are just men, and have no more to say to us, put us at our liberty this instant, for it is against our will you detain us here, and you have not the right to do so."

"We shall not amuse ourselves refuting you, Madame," our guide replied. "One of you has been four days upon the Minister's estate, the other arrived there late this afternoon. It was also four days ago the Cloris family entered that same house; of you two, one is most assuredly in a position to answer the questions I have posed, and you have neither of you any chance of being released until we are fully enlightened."

Whereupon the three other horsemen declared that since we were not eager to speak of our own free will, there were ways of extracting information from us by force.

"Ah, my sons, that I would not have," said the old man, "no violence shall be done here. We must eschew our enemies' means lest we be likewise guilty of an evil. We shall merely request these ladies to compose a letter to the Minister, asking him to come to this house forthwith; and the message may be so styled as to give him the impression that they, and they alone, are soliciting his presence for business of the greatest urgency. He will come; we shall question him; he will finally have no choice but to tell us where my son and daughter are: for if he refuses, this hand, trembling though it is, shall find the strength to thrust a knife-point into his heart. . . . Wicked abuses of tyranny! Dire results of despotism! O people of France, when shall you rise up against these horrors? When, tired of slavery and conscious of your tremendous might, when shall you look boldly up and snap the chains with which crowned criminals keep you in bondage, when shall you reclaim the freedom whereunto Nature destined you? . . . Put pen and ink and paper before these ladies and let them write."

"Keep them amused," I whispered to Clairwil, "occupy their attentions and leave the letter to me."

This was the text: "An affair of the very extremest importance necessitates your presence here; the bearer of this note will guide you, come with the utmost dispatch.'"

I submit the letter to our captors, they approve it. While addressing the envelope I find a moment to scribble this postscript: "Rush hither *in force,* else we're lost; it is *perforce* the foregoing is indited." The missive is sealed, one of the brothers leaves with it, and we are introduced into a room in an upper story; the door is bolted, and another brother stands guard without.

No sooner were we alone than I told Clairwil what I had appended to the letter.

She shook her head. "That does not suffice to set my mind at rest," said she. "For if he comes here in force, these people have but to see that force and our throats are cut. What if we try to seduce our jailer?"

"We'll fail," I replied. "These aren't hired thugs. They are bound by honor, not to mention ties of blood, nothing will dissuade them from seeking their revenge. Ah, Clairwil, it does indeed seem to me that I have not yet got firm grasp of our principles, for in truth I do greatly fear lest some fatality or other, call it what you will, shall see virtue triumph in the end."

"Never. Never. Victory goes always to the stronger, and for strength crime has not its match. Such ideas betray an unpardonable weakness in you."

"This is my first reverse—"

"Your second, Juliette. Let me refresh your memory: only after you emerged from a prison where you ought rather to have gone to the gallows did fortune begin to heap her favors upon you."

"True. I'd forgot that adventure."

"And its moral. Take courage, Juliette; be patient."

Nothing under the sun could have extinguished the fires of libertinage that burned at all times in this remarkable woman. There was but one bed in the room, and would you believe it? she suggested we all four of us get into it and while away the time frigging one another until Saint-Fond's arrival. But as it turned out, neither I nor either of my women was in a sufficiently composed state to cooperate in her extravagances; and so we chatted instead as we awaited further developments.

Like Clairwil, Monsieur de Saint-Fond considered that, we

being prisoners there, it were wiser not to storm the château; under such circumstances, the employ of ruse, he felt, ought to precede that of violence, and this was the stratagem he used.

The rider who had gone out with our letter returned with two youths unknown to us; they brought Cloris' father a message, it ran as follows:

"To hold women in an affair concerning men only is not befitting to gallantry. Free these ladies; in their stead, accept as hostages these young men, one my first cousin, the other my nephew; you may believe that their safety is more precious to me than that of the women now in your power. As well, put aside all fear regarding your own loved ones; they are indeed under detention, but here at my house in Paris; consider me responsible for them; and I vow to you they shall be in your midst within the space of three days. Again I say to you, keep my kinsmen and let the women go their way; I myself shall be at your house four hours after this reaches you."

Here we had to use our wits very cleverly. The note was not read out to us, it was not until later we learned its exact contents; for the moment we could only guess its drift.

"Are you acquainted with these young gentlemen?" old Cloris asked me.

"Most certainly," said I, "they are related to the Minister; if they have come to substitute themselves for us, you couldn't have better hostages."

They were discussing whether to set us at large or no when one of our captors spoke up: "This may be a trap; whatever, I am against letting the women out of our hands. Why not keep them all? That means two hostages the more."

To this the others agreed, and the fools (for pursuant to the design of things, virtue can lead nowhere but to folly), the stupid clods, the animals, shut us all inside the same room.

"Be assured, Mesdames," said one of the Minister's alleged relatives, "we are here to help you. Those are our instructions; two hours from now, the entire body of the Paris police—to which we belong—shall have the château surrounded: we shall protect you during the siege. We are well armed, never fear; and were these people, finding they have been tricked, to decide to attempt anything against you, you shall be defended."

"My one fear," Clairwil remarked, "is that these idiots wake up to the fact they have made a mistake in putting us all together. We shall be helpless if they separate us."

"Very well," said I, much more at ease than I had been hitherto, "we have simply to unite ourselves inseparably."

"What," Clairwil declared, "you who but a moment ago shuddered at the mention of a roughly similar distraction, do you now dare broach the idea?"

"Why, I've grown much calmer," I replied, "and, Clairwil, these two lads are both very pretty to look upon."

One of them, Pauli by name, was in truth but twenty-three, and he had the gentlest face, the most delicate features in the world; the other was probably two years older, his appearance was effeminate but he was quite as handsome, and his prick was a veritable splendor.

"I am confident that these gentlemen are at our disposition," said Clairwil; whereupon we fell to kissing our champions and caressing them with such ardor that we were soon able to read consent in their expressions.

"Yes," Clairwil resumed, "since they are so emphatically of our mind, this is how the thing should be gone about. Pauli is going to fuck you, Juliette; I'll be served by Laroche; when we're both encunted, Elvire will frig my clitoris with one hand, my asshole with the other; Montalme will do the same to you. Both of them being within our fuckers' reach, our fuckers will toy with them according to their fancy: you must not suppose that we'll lose by thus dividing our fuckers' attentions, not at all, those attentions will be intensified, there's nothing like this arrangement to keep a prick in size; all voluptuous women would be well advised to employ it. But let me proceed. Taking careful note of the sensations being experienced by our young studs, as soon as they observe them nearing discharge, Elvire and Montalme will deftly snatch these pricks out of our cunts and transfer them into our asses in order that no fuck be spent other than there; once both are discharged empty, we'll exchange man and woman. But you and I, proximately placed, will be concerned with ourselves only: we shall kiss each other, we shall tongue each other, my love, and the while," she added in a whisper, "we'll watch these vile beings, these base drudges toiling to give us pleasure like so many slaves Nature has created to be our tools and whom we suffer to exist solely in the interest of our passions."

"Precisely," I rejoined. "I do not understand how one can even hope to be aroused unless one holds that attitude."

And the very next instant there the two of us are, sprawled on the bed, our skirts pulled up above the navel, legs flung wide. First of all, the tribades seize each an engine, these we ready, steer into position, then engulf with our panting cunts. If Clairwil was briskly fucked by Laroche, certainly I had no cause to complain of Pauli; his member was not quite so thick as his colleague's, but it was of goodly length, and I felt it stab to the final depths of my womb; frigged meanwhile in heavenly style by Montalme, voluptuously kissed by my friend, we had each passed through nerve-rending crises when the piece of legerdemain so skillfully executed by Montalme advised me of my young lover's impending ejaculation; and then my thirsty ass was flooded by streams of nectar-sweet sperm. While it was pouring into me, the adroit Montalme probed three fingers into my lately vacated cunt and continued to rub my clitoris throughout. A loud shrill oath from my friend told me where matters stood with her; we were simultaneously whelmed by a third discharge as once again fuck washed abundantly into our entrails.

"Now we'll exchange," said Clairwil, "try some Laroche while I take Pauli."

Both of them young, both vigorous, our athletes recommence their efforts without even asking to catch their breath, and I found myself being fucked by one of the most beautiful pricks imaginable.

At that point Clairwil, who had gone on kissing me, tonguing me uninterruptedly, ignoring everybody else, paused to murmur in my ear: "I have something perfectly abominable in mind."

"Ah, by fuck," said I, "let's to work. What would you do?"

"No. I want to surprise you," she said. "Content yourself with knowing that this idea alone is flushing the whey out of my loins."

And therewith joy smote the rascal; her convulsions, her

thrashings would rather have chilled than gladdened her fucker had he been acquainted with their cause. Restored somewhat to her senses, still being fucked by Pauli, she spoke to me again, again in an undertone: "I think I'd better explain it to you, else you won't be able to play your part in the thing. There is going to be fighting; we shall be attacked; we'll resist. I propose that we ask these young men for weapons, and, as thanks for all the services they've done for us, that we shoot them dead during the battle. Blame for these murders will be laid upon our enemies; and Saint-Fond, further impressed by the dangers you've run, will probably reward you that much more liberally."

"Oh, thrice-damned slut," was my reply, discharging like a whore as Clairwil divulged this exciting scheme, "it's good, good, what you advise."

As I spoke I oiled Laroche's prick; and he, finding himself on the verge of another explosion, hastily decunted, burrowing into my bum at the same instant I discharged, which coincidence hurled me into transports such as I doubt my powers to describe, there being nothing, I affirm, absolutely nothing so delicious for a woman as to feel a prick penetrate her ass at the same instant she is overtaken by an orgasm. A brief moment later we heard gunfire outside; we all sprang up from the bed.

"They've come," says Clairwil; "give us pistols so that we can defend ourselves, my lads."

"Here you are," says Laroche. "Each is loaded with three balls."

"Good," Clairwil replies, "and be sure they'll be soon lodged in somebody's heart."

The noise mounts, shouts ring out in the château: "To arms!"

"See to the priming," cries Laroche; "you ladies had best group yourselves behind us, we can act as a shield for you."

Things now began to happen very fast. Already driven back in the lower part of the château by the detachment sent from Paris, our captors raced up toward where we were, meaning to kill us before surrendering; but their assailants were hot on their heels. Our door was forced; the pistol-shots were deafening. Stationed behind our defenders, we chose this moment for ridding ourselves of the weight of gratitude. Two bodies lay in a welter of blood at our feet, and our cunts were yet slimed with the fuck of the young men our iniquity slew. Their deaths were of course ascribed to our captors; the officers in charge of our detachment lost little time revenging their murdered comrades. Old Cloris and the young ladies alone remained alive: they were packed into a coach and, escorted by six of the policemen, were taken off to the Bastille. The rest of the police, having hitched the horses to our carriage, conducted us to my house, where I besought Clairwil to stay for supper.

She agreed to do so; we scarce had seated ourselves in the drawing room when my butler announced Saint-Fond.

I turned quickly to my friend. "Shall we tell him about our little horror?"

"No." She pursed her lips. "You must always do whatever you want. You must never tell all you've done."

The Minister entered, we declared ourselves thankful for the measures he had taken in our behalf. He in his turn declared that he was very sorry indeed a personal affair of his had caused us such inconvenience.

"Eight men were killed in the course of the thing, perhaps ten," he informed us, "among them the two lads I sent to you. It's rather a pity about them."

"A pity?" Clairwil repeated. "How so?"

"Oh, I'd been fucking them both for quite a while, you know."

"Tush," she chided, "is this Saint-Fond we hear expressing pity for objects he's fucked?"

"Merely regret at their loss. They were nimble boys, and wonderfully serviceable in my covert operations."

"Never mind, there are many pebbles on the beach," said I, showing Saint-Fond to his chair at table; "let's forget about the slight harm that's been done and talk instead about your successes."

During the meal the conversation as usual revolved around philosophical questions; afterward, the Minister having business to attend to, and we being exceedingly tired after a trying day, the company separated. At the supper held on the morrow, my unlucky Palmire, fetched for the purpose to Paris from her dungeon in the country, was mercilessly sacrificed after enduring a thousand tortures, one more barbarous than the other. Saint-Fond obliged me to strangle her while he gave her an ass-fucking. For Palmire I got twenty-five thousand francs; a lively description of my perilous captivity in the château earned me twenty-five thousand more.

The following two months were unattended by any event worth signaling. I had just celebrated my eighteenth birthday when Saint-Fond, visiting me at home one morning, told me he had been to see Madame de Cloris' sisters at the Bastille; they were both, he considered, far prettier than she whom we had butchered; and indeed the younger of the two, who was my age, struck him as positively lovely.

"So, my Lord," I asked, "shall it be a trip into the country?"

"Yes, exactly," was his reply.

"And the old man?"

"Oh, some spice in his soup perhaps. . . ."

"As you like, but that will mean the loss of three prisoners at one stroke, and you realize that the warden depends entirely upon them for his livelihood."

"He won't go hungry. Replacements are easy to come by."

"I should like you to put one of Clairwil's relations first on the list. The creature in question has been playing the prude with our friend, to whose libertinage she has some strange objection. That leaves two vacancies to fill; I have candidates for them now, I'll give you their names in a week."

"I'll have the documents in order," said the Minister, "but one thing at a time." He drew out a memorandum book and penciled a note: "*Gentleman: lunch. Ladies: outing.*" Whereupon he looked up at me and smiled. "Off you go tomorrow, Juliette. Take Clairwil along; she's charming and for imaginativeness has no peer. We'll contrive something delicious."

"Shall you require men and tribades?"

"No, I think not. Private scenes are sometimes preferable to orgies: the narrower stage is more favorable to meditation, more conducive to horrors. And in cosier surroundings one is less apt to be shy."

"Two women to assist at least?"

"Two women well on in years; find me a pair in their sixties, it's a caprice. I've been many times assured that nothing is quite so stimulating as natural decrepitude; this might be the occasion to try some of that."

An hour later I was in conference with Clairwil. "I have only one suggestion to make," said she after I had sketched the Minister's project. "Those young ladies doubtless have lovers, favorites at any rate; we must locate their them, make off with them, and include them in the festivities: these situations ordinarily afford any number of possibilities."

I hasten to the Minister's residence, report Clairwil's idea to him; it meets with his approval; the date of the party is postponed a week; and a hunt for the lovers is got under way.

The wicked treachery necessary for their discovery was sheer joy for Saint-Fond. He takes himself to the Bastille, has each of those girls cast into a cell, interrogates first one, then the other, causing them to tremble now with hope, now with fear, and sometimes with both at once, all most cunningly; he finally learns that the younger, Mademoiselle Faustine, is in love with a young man by the name of Dormon, of the same age as she; and her sister, Mademoiselle Felicity, who is twenty-eight, has given her heart to one Delnos, a year or two her senior and renowned throughout Paris for his good looks. Four days sufficed to have these young men behind bars; the charges leveled against them were somewhat vague and altogether false but, because never seriously examined, more than sufficient in an age when the abuses of privilege and influence were such that even the valets of high-placed personages were in the habit of jailing just about whomever they liked. These latest victims lay but a night in the Bastille; they were conveyed the next to my country domain whence the young ladies had been brought the previous day. Clairwil and I received our guests as they arrived and locked them away, but in separate chambers; so that, though they were all lodged under the same roof, they could not suspect that they had their beloved for neighbor.

After an enormous dinner we removed to a drawing room where all stood in readiness for the projected execrations. Garbed as Roman matrons and making up switches, the two sexagenarians were awaiting orders. Saint-Fond, impressed by Clairwil's magnificent ass, wished to render it homage before doing anything else. Resting upon a sofa, the hussy presented it to him in the most artistic manner; and while I sucked her clitoris, Saint-Fond darted six inches or more of tongue into her entrails.

By now, he is erected; he embuggers Clairwil, kissing my ass meanwhile; the next instant he sodomizes me, as he does so caressing Clairwil's voluptuous behind.

"And now to work," says the Minister, "any further delay will cost me a discharge: there's no resisting such asses as yours."

"Saint-Fond," Clairwil says, "I have two boons to ask you. You have a notable capacity for cruelty. Pray exercise it to the full, my dear, that is my first request. The second is that you enable me to exercise mine: entrust to me the murder of these young men. Torturing males is still my favorite pastime; you enjoy tormenting persons of my sex, I am equally fond of making representatives of yours suffer, and from martyrizing these two pretty fellows I expect to derive no less satisfaction, and possibly even more, than you will reap from massacring their two mistresses."

"Clairwil, you are a monster."

"I know I am, my dear; and the one thing that mortifies me is to have to own myself outdone by you every day."

Saint-Fond declaring his desire to see each of the four lovers in turn, one of the old attendants brought in Dormon, he whose mistress was Faustine.

"Young man," Clairwil began, "you are standing before your master, therefore see to it that the most complete submissiveness characterizes your behavior and a most scrupulous truthfulness your replies; it is in his Lordship's hands that lies your life."

"Alas," the unhappy one replied, "there is truly nothing that I have to say, Madame. As to what I could have done to merit arrest I have not the faintest notion, nor can I understand why I am become the victim of fate."

Clairwil was devouring him with her eyes. "Were you not to wed Faustine?"

"My whole heart and soul were set on making mine the happiness of having her to be my wife."

"You know nothing of the dreadful affair her family was implicated in?"

"In truth, Madame, of her family I know nothing but what was seemly and decent and virtuous; could vice exist whence Faustine came?"

"Bah," said I, "he prates like a hero out of a novel."

"I shall always be a loyal friend to virtue."

"Youthful enthusiasm therefor," Clairwil advanced, "has proved the undoing of a good many persons like yourself. But we are here concerned with other matters; the object of this interview is to inform you that Faustine is in this house. The Minister is disposed to enjoy her; he trusts you are disposed to cede her favors; in exchange for which concession she will be pardoned and so will you."

"I seek no pardon since I have done no wrong," was the young man's proud reply. "But be it so a thousand lives hang in the balance, I do declare to you that I'll not purchase one of them at the price of an atrocity whose mere mention is an insult."

"So be it. *Ass*, Madame, give me *ass*," cried Saint-Fond in a veritable lather, "it's plain indeed we'll reach no understanding with this stubborn little scapegrace unless we use violence."

At which Clairwil and the two hags leaped upon the young man, and had him pinioned and naked in the twinkling of an eye. He was marched up to Saint-Fond, who spent a few minutes poring over a man-ass than which there were few fairer in the world; and, gentlemen, as connoisseurs you know that in this article of the anatomy you may often reveal yourselves our superiors.

"Ah," said Dormon, gazing about him in distress as he realized what infamies lay in store for him, "ah, I've been tricked. I am amongst monsters."

"Your surmise, Sir," said Clairwil, "is quite correct, and experience will soon confirm it."

And after some preliminary abominations I was requested to bring in Faustine. Beauty, shapeliness, sweet candor, all that invites, these she had in rare degree; and when she beheld the scene in the room, oh, how the modesty in her made her other qualities shine! Espying her lover, whom Clairwil and Saint-Fond were caressing industriously, the girl came near to fainting away.

"Be easy, sweet angel," I said, taking her hand, "be of good cheer, we're fucking, we're swimming in dirt and nastiness and joy, my dove; like us, shamelessly, you're going to bare your wondrous ass; and you'll see 'tis not unpleasant."

"But—but what is all this? Oh, merciful heavens, where am I? Who are you?"

"Your host is his Lordship, the Minister, your uncle and friend: your case is in his hands. It is a difficult case, yea, a very grave case; however, be patient, be considerate, and everything will come out well."

"And you," she said in a faltering voice, addressing Dormon, "you have been capable—"

"Oh," he murmured, casting down his eyes, "like you I have had to submit to force. But," he went on, lifting his head, "while this is the day of our dishonor, there may soon come another that shall see us revenged."

"Enough of this frightful comic-opera rubbish, young man," reprimanded Saint-Fond, applying a vigorous thwack to the glib boy's bare hindquarters, "better employ your fiery eloquence to persuade mademoiselle here to lend herself to my caprices, and they shan't be mild. She's going to be sore tried."

Whereat tears began to flow from Faustine's glorious eyes, she uttered groans; cruel Saint-Fond, prick in hand, approached and stared at her from close on.

"By fuck!" he exclaimed, "does she weep? It pleases me mightily to see women weep, with me they always do, all of them. Cry away, my pretty little one, cry your eyes out—here, let your tears splash on my member. But save some for later on, you'll shortly have the most legitimate grounds for shedding them."

Nay, I shrink from telling how far his outrages went, one would have thought nothing so contented him as wounding innocence and insulting beauty in distress. The faint glow of pleasure we managed to kindle in the girl turned swiftly into chagrin; 'twas with his prick Saint-Fond dried a new spate of tears.

Clairwil's main passion, as I have said, did not consist in vexing women; it was men upon whom she preferred to expend her greatest cruelty, whereof Nature had given her no small fund. However, though she might now and then refrain from inflicting pain, even upon a person of the opposite sex, she always relished watching others in action; and, standing near Dormon, whom as a matter of fact she was frigging, with wicked curiosity she observed all the outrages poor Faustine was being made to endure; more, she suggested further ones.

"Well now," said Saint-Fond, "we must unite those who were

so soon to have been bound together in marital bliss. Far be it from me," he added, "to deny this young gentleman one of his pretty mistress' two maidenheads. Clairwil, dispose the male, I'll prepare the female."

I confess that I did not believe the enterprise could possibly succeed. Terror, grief, alarm, tears—in fine, the two lovers were in a shocking state; did it not exclude them from performing the act of love? One would have thought so. But now we were witness to a very prodigy, one of those miracles only Nature can work: her energy triumphed over all obstacles: and we beheld a rampant Dormon fucking his mistress. Of the two, only she needed to be held; only in her was pain predominant, forbidding her access to pleasure; and this despite all our efforts: we tried this, we tried that, we excited her, scolded her, caressed her, it availed not, her soul lay beyond rescue, drowned in sorrow; from her we got moans of despair and sobs only.

"Still, you know, I like her that way," said Saint-Fond; "I've never cared much about seeing pleasure's lineaments writ over a woman's countenance. They're too equivocal, too unsure; I prefer the signs of pain, which are more dependable by far."

By now blood has begun to flow, the deflowering is completed. Thus posed by Clairwil, Dormon was lying on his back, Faustine was astride him, her knees drawn up, her head bent low, her forehead resting on his shoulder; so that the pretty little girl's pretty ass was perfectly exposed.

"She is in an admirable position, see to it she doesn't move out of it," Saint-Fond told one of the crones; "she might as well lose both pucelages at the same time, I might as well sodomize her while she is being encunted."

Not only was the operation a stunning success, but, instead of sighs of ecstasy, it drew piercing screams from the girl whom never before had such a dart penetrated, and who seemed as though firmly set against enjoying the experience, generally longed for, that makes a woman of the maid. While fucking, the libertine fondled the hags; I busied myself sucking Clairwil's cunt. The prudent Saint-Fond, as ever sparing of his fuck, kept the sluices tight closed, and we moved on to other voluptuous activities.

"Hear me, young man," said Saint-Fond. "I am about to

require something most extraordinary of you, and which I venture to suppose you will consider most barbarous. Be that as it may, your mistress is doomed unless you obey instructions. I am going to have your beloved secured to this column here, you will take this bundle of switches, and with them you will flay her ass."

"Monster! Can you propose—"

"Then you prefer to see her killed?"

"Why must it be that I have no choice between this infamy and the loss of her whom I cherish above all others in the world?"

"A hard alternative surely, and such as the weak have every day to face," said I. "You are helpless, hence you must yield: do as you are bid, do it at once, or a dagger goes into your mistress' heart."

The great art of Saint-Fond consisted in always placing his victims in such a situation that of two evils they had inevitably to elect the one which more nicely suited his perfidious libertinage. Trembling, Dormon neither agrees nor refuses; his silence speaks. 'Tis I who bind Faustine to the column, great is my pleasure in pulling the rough cords painfully over her fair skin; I love thus to bare the throat of innocence to the edge of crime's blade; the malicious Clairwil kisses her as I get her into readiness. What charms were here to expose, what perfections to spoil! Ah, when heaven comes not to the defense of the righteous and the good, it is in order to make us mortals comprehend that unto virtue only contempt is due.

"This is the proper way to take with you," said the Minister, striking sweeping blows upon the plump white buttocks that fairly beckoned to him. "Yes, it is thus we must proceed," he continued, rattling off another ten; and the purple marks they left were already standing out in marvelous contrast to that silky smooth skin. "Try your hand."

"Oh, Sir, for the love of God, I could never. . . ."

"Nonsense, my boy, of course you can." Threats follow sardonic cajolery; Clairwil loses her temper, swears that if he doesn't do as he's been told, which, says she, amounts to very little, he will get a thrashing himself and see the girl murdered into the bargain; whereupon Dormon sets to work. But how reluctantly! And how timidly. Saint-Fond is obliged to guide his arm. At length my lover's patience runs out, he picks up a knife and raises it to Faustine's heaving breast; Dormon lays on somewhat more energetically . . . then collapses in a swoon.

"Ah, fuck my soul," grumbles Saint-Fond, his prick as stiff as a monk's, "we'll get nowhere so long as we rely upon a lover: this undertaking calls for villainy.''

And having furiously at the beauteous behind presented to him, in less than ten minutes he has it in a bloody shambles. In the meantime another horror's being enacted near by: instead of succoring him, Clairwil is venting her savagery upon the unconscious Dormon.

"The lout, the cad," says she, as he comes back to his senses to find himself bound hand and foot and receiving a drubbing quite as merciless as the one Faustine is getting from the Minister.

It was not long before the ill-starred lovers were both in the most deplorable state imaginable. Not yet in a position to judge Clairwil, her cruelty, I must confess, startled me; but when I saw her turn to execrations of a very different kind, when I saw her daubing her cheeks with the victim's blood, tasting it, drinking it, when I saw her bite into his flesh and tear it away with her teeth; when I saw her rub her clitoris on the bleeding wounds she opened in the wretch, when I heard her cry, "*Juliette, come do as I am doing*"; then, urged to it by this wild beast, carried away by her hideous example—ah, my friends, must I own that I imitated her? Nay, the truth may well be that I surpassed her; I may even have led the way, stimulated her imagination by means of atrocities which would not have occurred to her otherwise; perhaps, who knows? For I waxed furious too, my every nerve was afire, my very perverse soul revealed itself in its entirety; and I discovered that devouring the flesh of a man could have as powerful an effect upon my senses as lashing a woman to ribbons.

Saint-Fond deemed best to defer major operations until after the other couple had been dealt with. The first two were tied up and stowed in a corner; in came the second. Delnos and Felicity were subjected to the same treatment, except that the procedure was reversed: that is, instead of appealing to the lover to share his mistress, we appealed to the mistress for the use of her lover; arguments were again backed by threats of the worst sort and as before we met with considerable resistance. Felicity was an exceedingly pretty thing of twenty, not quite so fair as her sister but just as agreeably made, and her eyes were remarkably expressive; she gave evidence of more character, more energy than her sister, but Delnos of far less than Dormon. Howbeit, directly after embuggering this second girl, our cannibal, despite himself, lost his seed in Delnos' handsome ass while he was clawing Felicity's charming breasts. Now quietly seated between Clairwil, busily socratizing him, and me who was frigging him, and gazing ahead at the two couples, bound hand and foot, he consulted us over what the final fate of the victims ought to be.

"I was appointed to be the scourge of this family," he said to us, fingering himself while he spoke; "three of its members lost their heads in this house, two others I had slain in theirs, I am responsible for another's poisoning in the Bastille, and the chances that these four people will escape me look very slim indeed. You have no idea how I enjoy these little exercises in arithmetic. Tiberius, it is said, used to do his sums every evening; what would crime be without its sweet memories? Oh, Clairwil, whither are our passions leading us? Say, my angel, is thy mind clear enough, hast thou perchance discharged enough to give me thy sagely framed opinion in this matter?"

"No, by fuck," replied she, "no, it's not talking I'm eager to do, what I want is to act. Vitriol, blazing acid, some hellish thing is flowing in my veins, my brain is sick—oh, give me horrors! I must have horrors—"

"Then let us commit them in abundance, for that sorts nicely with my mood also," said Saint-Fond; "these two couples arouse me: it passeth all belief, the evil I would do unto them. But as to the form it should take, there I am in some uncertainty."

The doomed four were able to hear our conversation; were able to see we were plotting against them . . . and yet they clung to life.

The awful wheel of Delcour's contriving stood within view. Saint-Fond's brooding gaze lit upon it, and the thought of putting it to a little use soon lofted his prick skyward. Thereupon, after loudly and unequivocally explaining the properties of the infernal machine, the scoundrel declared that the two women should draw lots, would that not be the fairest way to determine which of the two was to die in this manner? Clairwil opposed the suggestion; she took the line that, since Saint-Fond had already employed the wheel upon a girl, he ought now to procure himself the pleasure of seeing a boy subjected to it; nor did she notice any advantage in allowing chance to decide between Delnos and Dormon, for as much as the latter struck her as by far the more eligible, he stimulated her imagination prodigiously. But Saint-Fond would brook no partiality; he pointed out that the honor of being the first to die, and by such a torture, was preference enough. Lots are prepared; the young men draw; Dormon is the winner.

"It's quite as though I had heaven by the throat, for it's been a long time now since a single one of my wishes went unfulfilled," said Clairwil. "The sole function of that execrable chimera you call the Supreme Being seems to be to facilitate my every crime."

"Embrace your intended," said my lover as he untied some of Dormon's bonds, leaving intact those which secured his hands; "kiss her, my lad, and then show your mettle: she'll have her eyes upon you throughout your ordeal. And if you care to glance at me during it, you'll see me fucking her ass, that I promise you."

Then, as was his custom, he led the powerless young man off, they were encloseted for an hour together; we could only suppose that the libertine took this opportunity to impart some deep secret to his victim, to whom, as it were, he entrusted the mission of carrying it with him into the next world.

"What can be going on in there?" Clairwil demanded, annoyed at having to wait and glancing impatiently at the door to the chamber.

"I have no idea," said I, "but such is my eagerness to find out, I would be almost willing to sacrifice our relationship. . . ."

Dormon emerged: his flesh showed signs of some cruel mauling, especially about his buttocks and thighs, which were cut and bruised; upon his uplifted brow rage and fear and pain were at war; blood dripped from his penis and his scrotum, and his cheeks, scarlet, revealed traces of several slaps. After him came Saint-Fond, conspicuously erected; the most atrocious savagery glinted in his every feature, in his twisted lips, his dilating nostrils, his wickedly narrowed eyes; clutching one of his victim's buttocks, he steered him toward us.

"Come along, come along," said Clairwil, visibly pleased at seeing Dormon in such beggarly condition, "come along, my little clown, let's waste no more time." Turning to Saint-Fond, "We are short on men," the diabolical creature observed; "I am going to need no end of fucking while I watch this rogue perish."

"His mistress could pollute you," the Minister suggested, "and I shall of course be embuggering you the whole time. . . ."

"And his blood?"

"Oh, we're sure to be splashed a bit."

Clairwil seized Dormon by both ears. "Kiss me, little fool, while there's still something left of your pretty face."

And Dormon showing no great alacrity to comply, the hussy wiped her asshole upon his nose; then he was granted permission to kiss his mistress goodbye. She burst into tears. Clairwil frigged the wight, the lass' clitoris was tickled by Saint-Fond; the matrons finally catch hold of him and fasten him on the dread wheel. Faustine, sprawled atop Clairwil, is obliged to frig her; and at the same time Clairwil excites me. Saint-Fond sheathes his weapon in Faustine's bowels, and we are all four shortly bathing in blood. The spectacle is hideous, and it has not yet reached its term when the girl proves unable to endure any more; smitten senseless by anguish, she wilts.

"What's this, what's this!" cries Saint-Fond, "would the bitch expire? I have no objection to her death provided I am its cause."

So saying, the villain looses his sperm into a mass whence life has fled already. Clairwil, whose wicked hands are kneading Delnos' balls while I am stabbing that young man's buttocks with a long hatpin, is at last overwhelmed by the sight of Dormon on the wheel, and, uttering maniac, hardly human screams, discharges thrice.

Now only Felicity and her young beau are left.

"Ah, by fuck," mutters Saint-Fond, "that other bitch was a great disappointment, but this one is going to be tortured properly; and since it was the mistress watching the lover die a moment ago, we'll have the lover watch the mistress now."

He leads her away for private conference, half an hour later he brings her back; and she is in a shocking state. She is condemned to impalement; Saint-Fond himself inserts the sharpened end of the stake into her ass and after much thrusting and twisting the point emerges from the mouth; the other end of the stake is planted in a socket set in the floor, and Felicity remains on exhibit for the rest of the day.

"My friends," says Clairwil, "you will be good enough to allow me to choose the torture for our last victim. I haven't changed my mind since first clapping eyes on him: the bugger resembles Jesus Christ, and I would treat him in the same way."

At this we all laughed merrily; arrangements were completed during the interview, no detail was neglected. One of the hags gets down on all fours, we prop the text on her rump, the story of the passion of Mary's bastard is located; I read out the chapter and verse aloud. The young man is already in bedraggled condition when he returns; Clairwil, Saint-Fond, and the unoccupied hag take charge of him; he is affixed to the cross, and upon it he suffers precisely what that impudent little bore out of Galilee endured at the hands of those wise Romans of old: his side is gashed, he is crowned with thorns, he is given a vinegar-soaked sponge to suck. At length, remarking that Delnos is in no hurry to die, we institute improvements upon the classical ordeal: the patient is lifted off the cross, turned over, nailed on again, and every kind of horror is perpetrated upon his behind; we prick his buttocks, we sear them, and tear them into shreds; by the time he finally expires, Delnos has gone mad. Clairwil and Saint-Fond, whom I have been frigging one on either hand, discharge copiously; and therewith ended infamies at which we had been twelve hours occupied. They were succeeded by the pleasures of the table.

Clairwil was deeply curious to learn Saint-Fond's secret; she plied him with wine, she caressed and praised him till he was quite giddy; then she put the question: "What is it you do with your victims just prior to killing them?"

"I announce their death to them."

"That's not all you do. There's more, we're convinced of it."

"No, that's all."

"There's more. We know there is."

"Perhaps. But it's merely one of my failings. Why force me to reveal it?"

"Ought you to keep secrets from us?" I asked my lover.

"In truth, it's no secret," said he.

"You hide it from us, however. Pray tell us what it is."

"What purpose would that serve?"

"It would satisfy our curiosity, and we are the two best friends you have in the world."

"You are cruel women," said he, and he sighed. "Don't you realize that I cannot make this confession without acknowledging a dreadful weakness in me, a veritably unavowable paltriness?"

"You can afford to divulge it to us."

We redoubled our pleas and flatteries, our caresses and seductions conquered, the Minister waved us to our chairs and addressed us in this wise:

"Fierce and long has been my struggle against the shameful yoke of religion, my friends; and I must confess to you today that I am yet its captive insofar as I still have hopes of a life after this. If it is true, I say to myself, that there are punishments and rewards in the next world, the victims of my wickedness will triumph, they will know bliss. This idea hurls me into deepest despond, owing to my extreme barbarity this idea is a very torture to me. Whenever I immolate an object, whether to my ambition or to my lubricity, my desire is to make its sufferings last beyond the unending immensity of ages; such has been my desire, and had been for a long time when I broached it to a famous libertine whom I was greatly attached to in days bygone, and whose tastes were the same as mine. He was a man of vast knowledge, his attainments in alchemy and astrology were especially noteworthy; he assured me that I was very correct indeed in my suspicion that there are punishments and rewards to come; and that, in order to bar the victim from celestial joys, it is necessary to have him sign a pact, writ in his heart's blood, whereby he contracts his soul to the devil; next to insert this paper in his asshole and to tamp it home with one's prick; and while doing so to cause him to suffer the greatest pain in one's power to inflict. Observe these measures, my friend assured me, and no individual you destroy will enter into heaven. His agonies, in kind identical to those you make him endure while burying the pact, shall be everlasting; and yours will be the unspeakable delight of prolonging them beyond the limits of eternity, if eternity there be."

"And so that is what you do to your victims?"

"Softly, Clairwil, berate me not. You wanted nothing so much as to learn the truth. It is a weakness you wheedled me into disclosing. I am not proud of it."

"No, nor should you be. Why, Saint-Fond, I am amazed! I thought you were a philosopher. You have a mind, do you not? Then how can you for a single instant accept the absurd claptrap about the immortality of the soul? For, is it not so, this disgusting religious fantasy must first be accepted before you begin to believe in the rewards and punishments of an afterlife?

"As for your intention, I applaud it, it is delicious," Clairwil continued, "it accords with my own attitudes: to want to prolong for ever the sufferings of the person you send to his doom—that is a desire which does you credit. But to base it all upon nonsense, upon extravagances—no, Saint-Fond, that will not do, that is quite unpardonable."

"Clairwil, do you not understand that my divine hope must fade away unless founded upon such an opinion as I entertain?"

"I do very well understand, my good man, that if you have.to edify your divine hopes upon fables, it would be better to give them up; for the day may come when the harm belief in fables has done you will prove to outweigh the pleasures you have received therefrom. Come, come, Saint-Fond: be content with the evil you can work in this world and abandon your foolish schemes for perpetuating it for ever."

"Saint-Fond, there is no afterlife," said I at this point, recollecting the philosophical tenets which had been very early inculcated in me; "the sole authority vouching for that illusion is the imagination of those men who, dreaming it up and clinging to it, merely expressed their desire to find later on a more durable and purer happiness than what is our portion on earth. Ah, is it not a pitiful absurdity, first of all to invent for oneself a God, then to believe that this God holds torments without end in store for the majority of humankind! Thus it is, after rendering mortals miserable in this world, religion shows them a weird deity, the fruit of their credulousness or their knavish cunning, a deity, I say, who's very apt to render them more miserable still in the world to come. I know how they quibble: this God's justice is horrible, but this God is merciful also; but a mercifulness which leaves room for appalling cruelty is far from infinite; neither is it reliable; after having been infinitely good, he becomes infinitely wicked; and is this what you call an immutable God? A God overflowing vindictiveness and fury, is this the sort of entity to whom you ascribe one jot of clemency or kindliness? To judge from the notions expounded by theologians, one must conclude that God created most men simply with a view to crowding hell. Would it not have been more conforming to honesty, to goodness, to common sense and decency, to have created stones and plants and gone no farther, instead of creating men whose behavior would bring unending calamity down on their heads? A God so perfidious, so evil as to create a single man and then to leave him exposed to the peril of damning himself, such a God can be regarded as no specimen of excellence; if perfection be his, then it is a monster of unreason, injustice, malice, and foul atrocity. Nay, very far from composing a perfect God, theology's adepts formed the most loathsome chimera; and when to this abominable God they ascribed the invention of eternal penalties, they but added the final touch to an artifact that was hateful from the start. The cruelty that makes for our pleasure has at least its purposes and hence its justification; this latter is accessible to the reason, we understand it; but what motive has God for torturing the victims of his wrath? Has he rivals? Is he threatened? No, those he packs off to hellfire were able neither to contest his power nor trouble his felicity. Let me add that the tortures of the life after this would be of no use to the living who cannot witness them; they would be of no use to the damned, since there are no new leaves turned over in hell; whence it follows that in the exercise of his eternal vengeance, God's sole aim is to enjoy himself, and having exploited his creatures' frailties, to make the most of their helplessness; and your infamous God, acting more cruelly than any mortal, and without any motive a man might have, in so doing shows himself infinitely a traitor, infinitely a cheat, and infinitely a villain."

"I think we may go farther," said Clairwil. "If that is agree-

able to you, I shall attempt a more detailed analysis of this pernicious and gloomy hell dogma; I am confident that by the time
I am done, our friend shall have abandoned every bit of his faith
in this pathetic, onerous superstition. Will you lend me your ears?"

"Certainly," said we.

And then it was as follows that the subtle and erudite Clairwil
addressed herself to this solemn question.

"There are certain dogmas which one is sometimes obliged
not to accept but to posit hypothetically for the purpose of combating others. My aim you know, and you will allow that it is
worthy: to obliterate the idiotic dogma of hell out of your
apprehension; I trust you will not take it amiss if, with this
end in view, and for the time being, I reinstate the deistic chimera.
Bound to employ it as point of departure in this important dissertation, I am forced temporarily to ascribe substance to the myth; this
is regrettable but I am sure you will excuse it, and excuse it all the
more readily knowing, as you do, that as regards belief in this
abominable phantom, I am above suspicion.

"In itself, the dogma of hell is, I own, so devoid of probability, all the arguments customarily advanced in its support
are so weak, so transparent, in such manifest contradiction with
reason, that one almost blushes at having to counter them. Never
mind; let us ruthlessly deprive the Christians even of the hope of
fettering us anew at the feet of their atrocious confession, and let
us very plainly show them that the dogma they count upon most
heavily to affright us vanishes, like all their other ghosts and goblins, at the mere approach of philosophy's rational light.

"The primary arguments in the case they make out for their
baneful fairy tale are these:

"1) That sin being infinite by virtue of the fact sin is offensive
to God, the sinner merits infinite punishment; that the Almighty
having decreed the laws, it behooves his mightiness to punish those
who transgress them.

"2) The universality of this doctrine, and the manner in which
we find it enunciated in Scriptures.

"3) The high need for such a dogma, lacking which there
would be no restraining sinners and the incredulous.

"The whole edifice sits on those foundations; now let us demolish them.

"Taking them in the above order, we begin with the first: it, I have no doubt but that you will concur, is exploded by the glaring disproportion between the human provocation and the divine reprisal. We observe that according to this doctrine the pettiest fault is to be punished as severely as the gravest; now, presuming our God just, for so he is accounted, how can we admit such iniquity? Who created man, anyhow? Who gave him the passions and the penchants which the torments of hell are to punish him for having? Who else but your God? And thus, half-witted Christians, you are disposed to imagine this preposterous God endowing man with impulses one minute and being compelled the next to chasten man for having acted upon them? But was it that God did not know what he was doing? Is it a blind incompetent fool you worship? Did he not know that man, endowed by him with the power to misbehave, would outrage him inevitably? If God knew, then why did he not otherwise endow man? And if he did not know, then why does he punish defective man when he, the Maker, is alone to blame?

"I think it is only too obvious that under the conditions alleged to be necessary to salvation, we are far more likely to be damned than saved. So tell me then, is this your God's so loudly vaunted justice, to have placed his puny, miserable masterpiece in such an abominable position? and this being the system, how dare your doctors assert that eternal happiness and eternal unhappiness are presented to man to choose between, and that his destiny depends on his option alone? If it comes out that the fate of the greater share of mankind is to be eternally unhappy, an all-knowing God must have known this from the outset; why then did the monster create us? Was he forced to? Then he is not free. Did he knowingly, deliberately, cause things so to be? Then he is a fiend. No, God was under no obligation to create man, certainly not, and if he did so simply to expose man to such a fate, the propagation of our species therewith becomes the foulest of all crimes, and nothing would be more desirable than the total extinction of humankind.

"If however you esteem this dogma necessary to the greatness of God, I must ask you why this God, so great and so good, failed to give man the capacities he would need in order to avoid the torture awaiting perhaps nine out of ten human beings. Is it not, to say the least, cruel on God's part to allow man opportunities and an appetite for dooming himself eternally? And however are you to exonerate your God from a charge either of ignorance or of wickedness, the one as criminal as the other?

"If all men are equal in the eyes of the Divinity who made them, why are they not all in agreement as to the particular crimes which are to cost man this everlasting suffering? Why does the Hottentot damn you for something which if you are a Chinaman sees you into paradise, and how is it, pray tell, that the latter will promise you a place in heaven for what lands the Christian in hell? Endless would be the task of listing the various opinions of pagans, Jews, Mohammedans, Christians, concerning the means to employ to escape eternal woe and to attain felicity; endless the task, and yet more cheerless, of describing the puerile and ridiculous formulas and devices invented to these ends.

"But we shall proceed to examine the second of the foundations they have endeavored to construct for this grotesque doctrine: its peculiar enunciation as shown in the Writ, and its universal character.

"We ought to preface our remarks with a reminder to ourselves: let us beware of taking the universality of any belief for a title in its favor. There is not one idiocy, not one form of madness, that has not enjoyed a general currency and mode; not one that has wanted for adherents any more than for exponents; so long as there are men on earth there will be fools, and so long as there are fools there will be gods, cults, a heaven, a hell, etc. But Scripture contains it all in black and white, you tell me. We shall for a moment suppose that the texts so called have some authenticity, and that they truly merit some respect. (I think I have already pointed out that to attain a position from which one can blast certain absurdities one may have to play lip service to certain others.)

"Very well. My reply, to begin with, is that there are strong grounds for doubting whether Scripture mentions this doctrine at all. Supposing nevertheless that it does, what Scripture says can be addressed to none but those who are familiar with these writings and acknowledge them as infallible; those who have no acquaintance of them, or who refuse to believe them, cannot be convinced by their authority; however, is it not maintained that they who have no acquaintance of this Scripture, or they who do not believe it, are subject to eternal punishment, just as are those others who are acquainted with Scripture or who believe it? What say you, is not this dreadful injustice?

"Perhaps you'll say that some races or nations to whom your nonsensical sacred literature was completely unknown had no lack of belief in a future life made up of eternal suffering. This may be true of some peoples; many others, however, had no knowledge of these dogmas. But precisely how were such opinions able to make their way into the heads of a people unacquainted with the Bible? I trust nobody will tell me that we are here dealing with innate ideas; for in that case we would find these opinions in all men everywhere. Nor do I fancy anybody will maintain that they naturally stem from the human reason; for surely his reason is not apt to advise man that he will suffer infinite punishment for finite wrongs; nor is revelation the answer, since the people in our example know nothing of that. To what then must we ascribe the existence of this dogma among this particular people? Either to the people's fancy or to the plotting of its priests; these being the sources of the superstition, how can you allow it any substance?

"Were you to conjecture that, there where we find no Scripture, belief in eternal punishment has been handed down by tradition, I should have to ask where they got it from, who spread the word originally; and if you are unable to prove that they received it through divine revelation, you shall have to agree with me that this tremendous opinion must have arisen out of some disease of the imagination or some piece of roguery.

"Supposing now that Scripture, *allegedly holy,* informs men of punishments in a future life, and supposing that this announcement is in no sense a false alarm, might one not wonder how the authors of Scripture could know that such punishments did in actual fact exist? The unfailing reply is, of course, that they were inspired; splendid. But those who have not been favored by this special illumination have therefore had to take the word of others for it; pray tell me, if you please, what confidence should one have in persons who concerning a fact of such importance declare to you,

'I believe it is true because so-and-so told me he dreamt it.' And lo! there it stands before you: that's what haunts and preoccupies, and what frightens and debilitates half the human race; that's what prevents one man out of two from hearkening to Nature's sweetest promptings! Is it possible to be more mistaken, to tumble more needlessly into error? But your inspired ones did not get in touch with everybody; the vast majority of mankind knows nothing about their reveries. It is, is it not, to the vital interest not only of the men who wrote the Bible and their adherents but of all men to be apprised of this dogma? Then why is it that some, nay, many, whole multitudes, have been left in the dark? This matter of eternal punishments being the concern of all, thorough and definitive information thereupon would have been of advantage to all; why then did God not impart this sublime knowledge directly and immediately to everyone, without the help and participation of individuals who may be suspected of fraud or insanity? To have positively done the very contrary, is this, I ask you, the behavior of a being whom you would have me believe infinitely wise and good? Does not such conduct rather show all the attributes of stupidity and wickedness? Whenever laws are made in a State, does not every government bring them to the attention of the public and employ every possible means to make generally known what penalties will be incurred by violation of them? Provided you are rational, how can you punish a man for breaking a law he has never even heard of? And what now, in the face of all these truths, must our conclusion be? This: that the institution of a hell has never been anything but the result of the malicious lucubrations of some men, and the unqualifiable folly of a great many others.[12]

"The third of these arguments proposed in favor of this frightful dogma is its indispensability: without it, there would be no holding sinners and unbelievers in check.

---

[12] "Hell," in the words of one clever writer, "is the stove upon which the sacerdotal pot is kept boiling; that kitchen was built for the feeding of priests; it's in order that they fare handsomely the Eternal Father, their chief cook, spits and roasts those of his children who have failed to pay all due attention to their lessons; the feasting table is set, the elect are forgathered, they'll be served grilled unbelievers, fricasseed millionaires, financiers in gravy," etc., etc. See *The Portable Theology*, p. 106.

"If you would have me grant you that because of his justice and glory God were required to punish sinners and unbelievers with eternal tortures, I ask you to grant me in return that reason and justice would also require that it be within the power of others not to be unbelievers; now what person can possibly be absurd enough to suppose that man is free? Who can be blind to the point of not seeing that our will, having nothing to do with any of our actions, all our actions being determined for us, we are responsible for none of them; and that God who manipulates us puppets would be (if we suppose that he exists, which, as you doubtless notice, I do with loathing), this God, I say, would be beyond words unjust and barbaric if he punished us for helplessly and despite ourselves becoming caught in the snares he first lays and then takes pleasure driving us into.

"And so is it not clear that it is the temperament Nature gives to humans, the various circumstances in the life of each individual, his education, the society he lives amidst, which determine his behavior and steer him in the direction of good or evil? But (you may perhaps object) if this be the case, the punishments which men are made to undergo in this world for their misdeeds are likewise unjust. They most certainly are. But here the general welfare prevails, individual welfare must cede thereto; it is the duty of every society to eliminate from its midst such elements whose conduct may be prejudicial to the community; and this justifies a quantity of laws which, when viewed alone from the standpoint of the individual's self-interest, might appear monstrously unjust. But does your God have any comparable reasons for punishing the evildoer? Obviously not; God Almighty suffers not one whit from the evildoer's rampages, and if the wicked man is wicked at all, it is because omnipotent God was pleased to create him thus. Hence it is atrocious to inflict tortures upon him for having become on earth the evildoer this execrable God knew full well he would become and indeed intended him to become.

"Let us now demonstrate that the circumstances which decide which religious belief a man will have are utterly outside his control.

"I ask, to begin with, whether we are allowed to exercise any choice as to the clime we are born in; and whether, once born into this or that church, it is our fault if we happen to lack the capacity for faith. Is there a single religion which can withstand the fire of the passions? And are not passions, which come to us from God, preferable to religions which come to us from man? What then is one to think of this barbaric God who would punish us eternally for our metaphysical doubtings—we who cannot believe, owing to the belief-destroying passions God put in us? It is a sordid joke. From start to finish it is all unutterable nonsense. And how one resents wasting one's time refuting such transparent absurdities! However, since we have taken it upon ourselves, let us make a thorough job of it and, if possible, leave the lunatic partisans of this most ridiculous dogma not one leg to stand on.

"Therefore we continue.

"Even were it left to every man to decide for himself whether he will or will not be virtuous and believe in all the articles of his specific religion; even were this so, we would still have to inquire if it were equitable that men be punished eternally, whether because of this weakness or their incredulity, when it is only too apparent that no good can result from their gratuitous sufferings.

"To settle this question we must put our prejudices aside and reflect above all upon the justness we acknowledge in God. Is it not the height of illogicality to contend that this God's justice demands the eternal punishing of sinners and unbelievers? Does not the act of imposing a punishment out of all proportion to the fault speak far more in behalf of vindictiveness and cruelty than of justice? To maintain that God punishes in such a manner is obviously nothing short of blasphemy. What! this God you depict as so good, will you have him express his goodness in bullying and brutalizing his defenseless children? Most assuredly, they who declare that God's glory requires that he behave like a savage are not fully aware of the enormity of this doctrine. They talk about the glory of God very idly, they know not whereof they speak. Were they able to judge a little of its nature, were they able to arrive at some rational conception of it, they would sense that if this being does indeed exist, he would have to found his glory not upon his capacities for violence, but upon his generosity and kindness, upon his wisdom and his boundless power to communicate happiness to mankind.

"It is added in passing, with a view to confirming the odious doctrine of punishments everlasting, that it has been espoused by a great many intelligent men and learned theologians. I deny the fact; most intelligent men and learned theologians have doubted this dogma. And if the rest have appeared to credit it, we can readily guess why: the priests, who already held the people in bondage, were delighted to clap this iron collar of a hell dogma around their necks; we are familiar with the sway terror can exert over simple souls, and everyone knows that the politician who wishes to subjugate others cannot do so without employing it.

"But those purportedly holy books you cite to me, do they come from a source so pure that it is beyond our power to reject what they offer us? The speediest perusal of these texts suffices to convince us that far indeed from being, as we are brazenly told, the work of an illusory God who never wrote a word nor uttered one either, they are to the contrary merely the scribblings of weak-minded and ignorant men; and they deserve our mistrust, nay, our scorn. But even were we to suppose, in defiance of all the evidence, that these writers were not completely devoid of common sense; bah, what sort of a fool would he be, pray tell me, who was able to wax ecstatic over this or that opinion simply because he'd come upon it in some book or other? One may adopt an opinion, that is permissible; but to sacrifice one's life's happiness and peace of mind to it—this, I repeat, only a madman is capable of doing.[13] Furthermore, do you tell me that the Bible's contents bear out the hell opinion, and I in my turn will quote you passages from the same book disproving it. I open Ecclesiastes; here is what I see:

'I said in mine heart concerning the estate of the sons of men, that God might manifest them, and that they might see that they themselves are beasts.

'For that which befalleth the sons of men befalleth beasts; even one thing befalleth them: as the one dieth, so dieth the other; yea, they have all one breath; so that a man hath no pre-eminence above a beast: for all *is* vanity.

'All go unto one place; all are of the dust, and all turn to dust again.'[14]

---

[13] Eusebius tells us (in his *History, lib.* iii. *cap.* 25) that the Epistle of James, that of Jude, the Second of St. Peter, the Second and Third of St. John, the Acts of St. Paul, the Revelation of St. Peter, the Epistle of Barnabas, the Apostolic Institutions, and the Book of the Apocalypse were none of them recognized in his day.

[14] Ecclesiastes 3: 18–20.

"What could be less favorable to the theory of an afterlife than these lines? What could be of greater encouragement to the view that denies the immortality of the soul and contests the whole ridiculous dogma of a hell?

"And so what are the thoughts of the sane individual as he peers critically at this absurd fable of man's eternal damnation for having eaten of forbidden fruit in paradise? However inconsequential this little tale, however repulsive one finds it, permit me to dwell upon it for a moment, since it is the point of departure for an argument that conducts one to a hell of eternal sufferings. Is not an impartial examination of this absurdity quite enough to convince one of its inexistence? Oh, my friends, answer: would someone full of loving kindness plant in his garden a tree which produces delicious but poisonous fruit, and would he be content to warn his children not to touch it, telling them they will die if they eat thereof? Were he aware of such a tree growing in his garden, would not this thoughtful and wise father proceed without delay to chop it down, and all the more surely take this precaution in the knowledge that from eating its dread fruit his children must perish and precipitate all ensuing generations into irreparable misery? But the tale reads otherwise: God knows that man shall doom himself and his posterity if he bites into the apple: not only does God endow man with the capacity to yield to temptation, his wickedness does not stop short of arranging man's seduction. Man succumbs, he is lost; he does what God has enabled him to do, what God has invited and pushed him into doing, and behold him now, fallen, cursed forever. I call this cruelty and viciousness without parallel. No, I repeat, I would have spared you the recital of this dismal anecdote, I would have disdained to include it in my disquisition were it not for the fact that the hell dogma, whereof I wish to leave not one vestige intact, is one of its more sinister consequences.

"We may consider all this as so much allegory, fit to provide us a moment or two of diversion but not fit for our belief, and of which mention ought to be forbidden save as one speaks of Aesop's fables and Milton's gross fantasies; for the latter are of slight importance, whereas Biblical incantation, seeking to engross our faith, to spoil our pleasures, becomes something of the most evident danger and ought to be suppressed ruthlessly until we need bother with it no more.

"So let us be well persuaded that such facts as those which are entered in the tedious romance known under the title of the Holy Writ are mere abominable falsehoods, worthy of utter contempt only and without the faintest consequence as regards our weal or woe. Let us be further persuaded that the dogma of the immortality of the soul that had first to be propounded before this soul could be rewarded with eternal bliss or damned to eternal torments is the most blatant, the most arrant, the crudest and the clumsiest of all possible lies; let us realize that when we die, all of us dies, as it is with other animals, and that whatever the conduct we have observed in the world, we shan't be any the more or less happy for it after we have sojourned there for the longer or shorter period Nature is pleased to allot us.

"It has been asserted that belief in eternal punishments is absolutely necessary if human beings are to be kept in check, and that we must therefore take utmost care to preserve and promote it. But if it becomes evident that this doctrine is false, if it fails completely to withstand scrutiny, will you not agree that there is infinitely more danger than usefulness in employing it as the buttress for your ethics? and may we not wager that it will prove of more harm than good once it has been set before the individual and he, correctly appraising it, dismisses it for the fiction it is and flings himself carefree into evil-doing? is it not a *thousand times better not to impose any restraints upon him at all than that there be a one which he can ignore and flout so easily?* In the former case, the idea for doing evil may perhaps not occur to him; but it certainly will when it occurs to him to break the restraint, for in the breaking thereof a further pleasure exists; and such is the perversity in man that he never so cherishes an evil, never so eagerly, so gladly performs it, as when he fancies himself somehow hindered from doing it.

"They who have pondered upon the nature of man will be forced to agree that all perils, all ills, however great they may be, dwindle with distance and appear less dreadful than minor dangers when these are close at hand. It is obvious that the threat of immediate punishment is much more effective, much more apt to deter the would-be criminal than that of punishments to come. As for misdeeds that lie outside the scope of the law, are not men far more effectively deterred from them by considerations of health, decency, reputation, and other such mundane considerations as are apparent at the moment than by the dread of future and unending woes which seldom enter the mind, or which, when they do, are always vaguely shaped, dimly perceived, and reckoned easy to avoid?

"In order to judge whether the fear of eternal and rigorous punishments in the next world is more likely to deter men from evil than is that of temporal and imminent punishments in this world, let us for a moment suppose that, the first of these fears subsisting universally, the second were entirely removed; would we not perceive the world suddenly flooded with crimes? Now let us imagine the opposite, let us suppose the fear of eternal punishments abruptly done away with, and the fear of immediate, palpable punishments remaining in full force: while we saw these punishments being meted out unfailingly everywhere, would we not also notice that they were making a much deeper impression upon the minds of men and were having a much greater influence upon their behavior than the remote punishments of the future which one forgets all about as soon as the passions start asserting themselves?

"Daily experience furnishes us, does it not, plentiful and convincing proof of the slight effect the fear of punishments in the next world has upon those very persons who believe most staunchly in them. The dogma of eternal sufferings has had particular success with the Spanish, the Portuguese, and the Italians; are there any more dissolute peoples? Where does one find more secret crimes committed than among priests and monks, that is, among those who you would think were thoroughly penetrated with religious truths? Indubitable evidence, this, that the good effects produced by the eternal-punishments dogma are very rare and very uncertain. We are about to see that its ill effects are innumerable and definite. Such a doctrine, inevitably filling the soul with bitterness, cannot help but fill the mind with images showing the Divinity in the worst light; it hardens the heart and hurls it into a despair most disadvantageous to the Divinity, belief in whom you mean to bolster by means of this doctrine. Quite the contrary, this frightful dogma fosters atheism, impiety, every right-thinking and decent person finding it a great deal simpler and more convenient not to believe in God at all, rather than acknowledge one so cruel, so inconsistent, so barbaric, as to have created men solely in order to sink them in perpetual misfortune, grief, and anguish.

"If you insist upon having God as the basis for your religion, at least endeavor to compose a flawless God; for if he is riddled with defects, as yours is, the religion based upon him will soon come into disrepute, and you'll discover you've spoiled each ingredient by unskillful blending of the two.

"Do you really suppose it is possible that a religion can be believed for long, respected for long, when it is founded upon belief in a God who, according to the rules of the game, must punish a huge—an infinite—number of his creatures for behavior to which that God put them up? Any man who accredits such an arrangement must necessarily live in constant fear of the being who has the power to make him eternally wretched; with that understood, how can he ever love or respect such a being? Were a son to imagine his father capable of condemning him to such cruel tortures or of not wishing to spare him these sufferings if the matter lay in his hands, would that son feel much respect or love for that father? Are not the creatures God has made entitled to expect still more by way of kindness from him than may children from even the most indulgent father? is it not men's belief, that all the good things of this world are theirs through the goodness of their God; that this God is their guide and protector; that 'tis he who will later procure them the happiness whereof they are in hope; are not all these the assumptions which serve as foundation to a religion? And if you blast them, goodbye religion; whence you see that your idiotic hell dogma wrecks instead of consolidates, that it loosens the underpinnings of the cult instead of tightening them, and that, as a consequence, only dolts have ever been able to believe something only knaves could have invented.

"No question about it, this being, concerning whom there is so much unending chatter, is sullied, dishonored by the ridiculous colors his portraitists habitually employ; did they not entertain senseless and incoherent ideas of the Divinity, they'd not represent him as cruel; and did they not think him cruel, they'd not fancy him capable of punishing them by infinite torments, or even able to consent that man be deprived eternally of happiness.

"To elude the force of this argument, partisans of the dogma of eternal damnation affirm that the sore affliction of the reprobate is not arbitrary punishment on God's part, but a consequence of sin and the immutable order of things. Indeed? Who told you so? If you claim this to be a teaching out of Scripture, you'll have an awkard time proving it; and if you manage to happen across a single passage where there is some allusion to the matter, oh! the lengths to which you shall have to go in order to convince me of the authenticity, the accuracy, the holiness of these few lines which look to you as though they read in your favor. Were they your rational faculties which suggested this atrocious dogma to you? In that case, tell me how you manage to conciliate reason with the injustice of a God who confections a creature, all the time knowing full well that the ironclad, immutable shape and design of things is such as will for a certainty forever sink him in an ocean of unremitting woes. If it is true that the universe is created and ruled over by a being infinitely powerful, infinitely wise, then everything must necessarily pass in conformance to his will, coincide with his aims, and conspire to the well-being of all that dwells therein. Now in what way does it further the advantage of the universe that a frail and miserable and helpless creature undergo eternal torture as a punishment for errors he never committed of his own free will?

"If the vast host of sinners and infidels and unbelievers were really destined to suffer cruel and perpetual torments—what a horrible propect for mankind! Billions of human beings mercilessly condemned to agonies without end . . . were it so, indeed, then the lot of man, this thinking and sensitive being, would be truly hideous. For is there not grief and sorrow enough he must face in this life, that he must expect more pain and worse anguish when his career on earth is done? What horror! Oh, 'tis execrable! However can such ideas make their way into the human mind, how is one to avoid the conviction that where they are in currency there lurk imposture, lies, and barbarous politics? Ah! let us be ever more firmly aware that this doctrine, neither useful nor necessary and utterly ineffectual as a means for dissuading men from evil, can be made into the basis for one and only one kind of religion: that whose sole purpose is to keep slaves at heel; let us clearly understand that the unvarying consequences of this abominable dogma are sinister and unwholesome in the extreme, since it is capable only of transforming life into a nightmare of bitterness, horrors, tears, and alarms; and breeds such notions of the Divinity that, save he be paralyzed totally and undone, the individual has no choice but to curse God and a faith wherein belief is tantamount to final degradation.[15]

"Assuredly, if we believe the universe created and governed by a being whose might, wisdom, and goodness are infinite, we are obliged to conclude that all evil must necessarily be excluded from this universe; well, you will not gainsay that the eternal unhappiness of most of the individuals embraced in the human species would constitute a positive and absolute evil. Fie! what an infamous role you give your infamous God to play by supposing him guilty of such barbarity. To be brief, eternal torturings combine very ill with the infinite goodness of the God you have in mind: so either cease trying to make me believe therein, or get rid of your savage dogma of sufferings everlasting, do one or the other if you seriously wish to see me adopt your God for a single instant. Rejecting the dogma of hell, we may likewise dismiss the other of paradise; both are the wicked inventions of theological despots who by terrorizing men's minds strove to ensure their obedience to sovereigns. Let us be assured of it: that we are made of matter only, that what is im-

---

[15] O thou! who, 'tis alleged, hast created all that in the world there be; thou, of whom I have no certain conception, none, not even the tiniest; thou whom I know of through divers readings and through what mortal men, who are every day in error, may have told me about thee; thou weird and fantastical being denominated God, I formally declare herewith, authentically and publicly, that in thee I have not the faintest hint of belief, and this for the excellent reason that nowhere, neither in my heart nor in my mind nor in my soul, do I find anything that persuades me of an absurd existence, evidence for the reality of which is absolutely lacking in the outside world also. If I am mistaken, and if when I am come to the end of my days thou shalt prove me wrong, and if then (which is so doubtful, being in contradiction to all the laws of probability and logic) thou shalt convince me of this existence I so stoutly deny now, what will happen? Thou shalt render happiness to me or unhappiness. Thou makest me happy, then I shall acknowledge thee, I shall cherish thee; if unhappy, then I shall abhor and hate thee; since 'tis obvious no reasonable man can reckon otherwise, how is it, with the power that is said to constitute the foremost of thine attributes, if thou dost exist, how, I say, canst thou allow man an option so damaging to thy glory?

material is inexistent; that all we attribute to the soul is all simply
the effect of matter; and this in spite of our human pride which
causes us to stress the distinction between ourselves and brute beasts
however it be that, like beasts, we yield up to the dust the dust
whereof we are made, and when dead shall be no more punished
than they for the bad deeds which the kind of organization we have
received from Nature has induced us to commit, nor more rewarded
for the good deeds we perform simply because we have been otherwise structured. And so, as regards the fate awaiting you after
this life, whether you conduct yourself well or ill, it amounts to the
same; and if we shall have succeeded in passing every single instant
of the term allotted us amidst pleasures, even though this manner
of existence may have been unruly, may have caused disturbance
to everybody about us, have gone counter to every social convention; if, I say, we shall have shielded ourselves from the law—and
this is encumbent upon us, it is the one essential—then most assuredly, most certainly we shall have done far better, been far
happier than the fool who, from awful dread of punishments in
an afterlife, has in this one rigorously eschewed everything which
might have gladdened and afforded him delectation; for it is of
infinitely greater importance to achieve happiness in this life
whereof we are sure, than to forego the indisputable joys offered
us here and now in the hope of acceding to imaginary ones of which
we have not, and cannot possibly have, the faintest idea. Eh! he
must have been a prodigiously droll fellow, he who attempted to
persuade men that they may become unhappier when dead than they
were before they were born! Has anyone ever asked to enter into
this world? Do men endow themselves with the passions which,
according to your gruesome creed, hurl them into eternal woes in the
next world? Why no! not at all, none of this is the individual's doing, it is all done to him, if fault there be it is not his, and it is
unthinkable, it is fantastic, it is false that he can be punished therefore.

"But have we not to cast a glance at our miserable species
to ascertain that there is no hint here of immortality? What! this
divine quality, or let us rather say, this quality which cannot possibly
exist in matter, am I to understand that any such thing could belong to this animal we call man? He who feeds, drinks, and repro-

duces like beasts, whose superiority over them resides in a somewhat
more refined instinct, this creature is able to expect a fate so unlike
any of those same beasts? who will accept such nonsense for a
minute? But hold, they protest, man has achieved the sublime awareness of his God; this in itself betokens worthiness of the immortality
he dreams of. Ah. And what is so sublime about this awareness of
a spook, unless you wish to imply that because man has carried his
ravings over a particular subject to their final conclusion, he must
now rave in connection with everything else? O poor wretch! if
thou hast some advantage over animals, how many are their advantages over thee? Art thou not susceptible to a hundred times
as many infirmities or diseases? Art thou not the victim of a hundred times as many passions? Weigh it up and tell me whether, in
the over-all, man is really better off than the beast. Do you find
that the scales still tip in his favor? And this slight advantage you
accord him, is it so great as to warrant his proud notion that he
is due eternally to outlive his four-footed brethren? O pitiful humanity, look to what lengths of folly thou hast been urged by thine
inflated self-esteem! And when thou shalt make riddance of all
these chimeras which obstruct thy view, shalt not thou see thyself
as no more than a beast, thy God as merely the *ne plus ultra* of human extravagance, and this life but a road passing from nought to
nought, and which thou mayest travel as thou wilst, in vice as confidently as in virtue?

"But with your leave I shall deepen the discussion and enter
more thoroughly into the knotty questions confronting us now.

"Certain Church Fathers maintain that Jesus descended into
hell. How often this contention has been attacked and refuted!
We shall not catalogue and inspect severally the various theses
which have treated of this subject: the philosophical spirit—and
we address ourselves to no other—would very probably make short
work of them. The facts are these: neither Scripture nor any of its
commentaries is positively decided either upon the specific whereabouts of hell or upon the precise tortures you undergo there.
This being granted, we next find that the Word of God clarifies
nothing, whereas the teaching of Scripture, we all agree, ought to
be plainly and distinctly set forth, above all as regards a matter
of such high consequence. However, research fails to discover

either in the Hebrew text or in the Greek and Latin versions, a single word designating hell in its traditionally or still currently accepted meaning: that is, a place reserved for the torture of sinners. Is this not very telling evidence against the soundness of the opinion held by those who maintain that these tortures really exist? If Scripture omits any mention of hell, by what right, pray tell, do they presume to entertain such a notion? Are we bound, in religious questions, to believe anything over and beyond what is written? Well, if this opinion appears nowhere in writing, in pursuance of what are we to adopt it? It does not beseem us to trouble our minds about what has not been revealed; and whatever has not been we cannot legitimately regard as other than fable, vague supposition, human tradition, imposture's inventions. Scholarship discloses nevertheless that near Jerusalem there was a locality known as the *valley of Gehenna,* where criminals were put to death and into which the corpses of animals were thrown also. It is to this place Jesus refers in his allegories when he says, *Illic erit fletus et stridor dentium.* This was a vale of tears, of suffering and horror: and there appears to be no doubt it is to Gehenna he is alluding in his parables, in his unintelligible speeches. Our belief receives further confirmation from the fact that torture by fire was practiced in this valley: there the guilty were burnt alive; at other times they were buried to the knees in dung. Or round their neck was looped a length of cloth whose ends were pulled by two men, so strangling the victim and forcing him to open his mouth into which molten lead was poured—there we have the fire, the torture, whereof the Galilean spoke. We often hear him say that such and such *a sin merits punishment by fire,* that is, the miscreant deserves to be burnt in the valley of *Gehenna* or flung upon the dung heap and burned with the animal carrion that was dumped in this noisome awful place. But, you may point out, the adjective *eternal* Jesus frequently uses to qualify this fire, does it not bear out the contention of those who believe the flames of hell shall burn forever? By no means. Often employed in Scripture, this term *eternal* always connotes the finite. For example, God concluded an eternal alliance with his chosen people; nevertheless, this alliance came to an end. The cities of Sodom and Gomorrah were to burn eternally; but that blaze died out a good long while ago.[16] Furthermore, it is common knowledge that the fire in the valley of Gehenna, near Jerusalem, was kept lit by night and by day. We also know that great use is made of hyperbole in Scripture, and that not a line of it should be taken literally. These exaggerations are enough; must one go a step farther, as is regularly done, and twist the underlying meaning of things? Indeed, must not such magnifiers be regarded as the most definite enemies of good sense and reason?

"But what then is the nature of the fire they menace us with? (1) It cannot be tangible, because we are told our fire is but a faint image of it; (2) a tangible fire illuminates the area surrounding it, and we are assured that hell is a tenebrous place; (3) tangible fire promptly consumes all combustible materials, and finally consumes itself, instead of which hellfire must last indefinitely and consume eternally; (4) hellfire is invisible, hence it is not at all tangible; (5) tangible fire goes out for lack of fuel, and, according to our absurd religion, hellfire will burn forever; (6) hellfire is eternal, tangible fire is temporary; (7) it is said that the worst of the torments the damned have to endure is the privation of God; however, in this life experience shows that tangible fire can be far more painful than the absence of God.

"8) Lastly, tangible fire can have no effect upon spirits, therefore hellfire can have no effect upon them. To say that God can contrive in such a way that a material fire acts upon spiritual beings; that he will make these spirits to live and subsist without sustenance, and that he will make the fire to burn without combustibles—this is to resort to wonderful suppositions for which there is no warrant apart from the idle reveries of theologians, and which consequently prove only their stupidity or their wickedness.

"To come to the conclusion that, because nothing is impossible for God, God will do everything possible is surely no very logical way of reasoning. Men would be well advised to refrain from basing their fond hopes upon God's omnipotence, when they do not

---

[16] Lacus Asphaltites presently covers the site of Sodom and Gomorrah, neither of which is afire any more; the flames sometimes noticed thereabouts come from volcanoes in the vicinity, quite as Etna and Vesuvius yet smolder and erupt fire. The cities in question never burned in any other way.

even know what God is. In order to elude these difficulties, other theologians assure us that hellfire is not tangible at all, no, according to them it is spiritual. Perhaps you will be good enough to tell me, what is a spiritual fire? what is an immaterial, incorporeal, non-substantial fire? Some there are who speak to us of such a thing; what do you fancy they are talking about? do you suppose they themselves have the slightest idea? where, in what connection, upon what occasion does their God explain to them the nature of their fire? Again, however, we find a few doctors who, hunting for a happy medium, assert that this fire is partly spiritual, partly material. Which gives us, oh behold! two different sorts of fire in hell; how preposterous! What devices is superstition not driven to resort to as it constructs its sand-castles of falsehood!

"And likewise, when pressed to produce something plausible concerning the location of this fabulous hell, what an outrageous higgledy-piggledy of farfetched speculations has been invented! The prevailing feeling had been that hell lay in a region somewhere below the earth; but where is that region in relation to a revolving globe? Others, recognizing the world as round, placed hell at its center, that is, some fifteen hundred leagues from where we are standing now; but if Scripture says true, the world is going to be destroyed, and where will hell be when that comes to pass? Well, you observe the wild nonsense that results when one puts one's faith in the ravings of others. Less extravagant reasoners claim, as I mentioned a moment ago, that hell consists in being barred from the vision of God; in which case hell starts right here in this world, for hereabouts there's neither hide nor hair of that God to be seen: and yet this state of affairs can hardly, you'll agree, be called unendurable. One is tempted to imagine the reverse: if this queer God did truly exist such as he is depicted to us, the mere sight of him would probably constitute a very adequate image of hell.

"All these incertitudes and the scanty concordance amongst the theologians indicate that the latter are wandering about in a fog and a delusion and, like drunkards, are unable to get their bearings, let alone keep their footing; and nevertheless, is it not curious that they cannot come to some manner of terms over so essential a dogma, and one which, they say, is so clearly expounded in the Word of God?

"So, shavepate rabble, own that this gigantic grisly dogma of yours is utterly baseless, all made up, that it is the product of your greed, your ambition, and sired by your unhinged mentalities; that it cannot stand unless crutched up by the ignorant terrors of the vulgar simpleton you train to swallow, uncritically, everything you are pleased to serve up to him. Admit that this hell exists nowhere but in your brain, and that the infernal tortures you brandish are so many anxieties it suits your political convenience to inflict upon the mortals who let themselves be guided by you. Aware of these facts, let us forever abjure a doctrine which only affrights men, constitutes an insult to the godhead, and, in a word, must be repudiated by any reasoning person.

"Various arguments are yet put forward; I think it incumbent upon me to combat them. (1) The fear which, they say, everyone senses inwardly of some punishment to come is an indubitable proof of that punishment's reality. But this fear is by no means innate; it is inculcated, fostered by education; it is not in every land the same, nor the same in all men; it is not found amongst those in whom passions have annihilated prejudice; the conscience is never modified save by instruction, by ruling passions, by habit.

"2) The pagans acknowledged the dogma of hell. . . . Surely not as do we; and supposing that they might have acknowledged it, we who reject their religion, must we not reject their dogmas as well? But it is very certain the pagans never believed in an afterlife of everlasting sufferings; nor in the pathetic claptrap of the resurrection of bodies, which they burned on pyres, and whose ashes they preserved in urns; they did believe in metempsychosis, in the transmigration also of bodies, ideas for which there is a great deal to be said and which natural studies repeatedly confirm; but the absurd conceit of bodily resurrection, very worthy of Christianity, belongs entirely to it. It would strongly appear that our doctors got their notions of a nether world, of paradise, and of purgatory out of Plato and Virgil, and that they then shaped them to suit their own purposes: nebulous vagaries of poetical fancy were in time changed into articles of faith.

"3) If there is such a thing as sanity and healthy reason, then the dogma of a hell and of eternal punishment is necessarily proven true. God is just, therefore he must punish men for their crimes. . . . No, and no again; never could sanity, never could healthy reason subscribe to a dogma which so blatantly outrages it.

"4) But God is a judge, his justice must be done. . . . Another atrocity: evil is necessary on earth. I say unto you that if your God exists, his justice cannot consist in punishing deeds he has himself prescribed; if he is omnipotent, your God, has he need of punishing the evildoer in order to prevent the doing of evil? Could he not, can he not today, deprive men altogether of the capacity for evil? If he did not do this originally, if he will not do it tomorrow, it is because he considers evil necessary to the maintenance of general harmony; and in the light of this, how, vile blasphemers! how dare you say God can punish a mode of behavior which must exist if the universe is to run aright?

"5) All theologians concur in believing and preaching the existence of the punishments of hell. . . . Does this prove anything except that the priests, usually so disunited, are nonetheless very able to reach an understanding whenever it is a question of deceiving their flocks? Furthermore, must the ambitious and calculating inventions of Romish clerics dictate what the opinions of other sects are to be? Is it reasonable to expect the whole of mankind to believe what a grubby little minority found it advantageous to devise and proclaim? Must one then rather place one's faith in these cheats than in reason, common sense, and truth? It is by truth we should be ruled, not by the mob; far better to rely upon one man who speaks true than to heed the knaves who have been spouting lies for centuries.

"The other arguments they advance are all so patently weak that one has difficulty taking them seriously and little inclination to waste one's time refuting them; none of them reposing either upon Scripture or upon tradition, they all necessarily collapse of themselves. For example, unanimous consent is alleged; but can it be, when it is impossible to find any two individuals who follow the same line of reasoning about what is apparently one of the most important things in life?

"Realizing they have not a single sound argument on their side, these fierce priests are always fully prepared to threaten you;

despite the fact that, as everybody knows by now, threats are the weapons of the simple-minded, the feeble, and the defeated. Come, come, silly little children of Jesus! give us reasons, yes, it is reasons we want out of you, not bluster, rant, and fist-shakings: we do not wish to be told, 'Since you do not choose to *believe* in these tortures, you are going to *feel* them'; we merely ask, and with this request you cannot successfully comply: demonstrate to us that by virtue of which you would have us believe in your fictions.

"The fear of hell, in short, is no sure guarantee against sin. . . . Nothing, anywhere, authorizes any such fear. . . . It is only too obviously the fruit of the diseased imagination of priests, of, that is, those personages who comprise the vilest and the most mischievous class in society. So what purpose does the hell myth serve? I put anyone at defiance to tell me. They assure us that sin is an infinite wrong and ought hence to be punished infinitely. Rubbish. God himself chose to prescribe a finite punishment for this crime, and that punishment is death.

"And so we conclude that the puerile dogma of hell is a fairy tale of sacerdotal contrivance, a cruel supposition hazarded by gowned rascals who began by fabricating a dreary, a disgusting God in their own image, in order then to have this loathsome dummy repeat what sorted best with their own passions and, above all, to repeat whatever was most likely to procure them whores or money, the sole objects ambitioned by that covetous, that shiftless lot, that crew of social outcasts whereof society would be wonderfully well advised to purge itself definitively.[17]

"I say unto you, banish forever from your heart this doctrine which is an insult to your God and your reason alike. Such beyond

---

[17] Who are the true and the only troublemakers in society? The priests. Who are they who daily debauch our wives and children? The priests. Who are the sworn enemies, the most dangerous enemies of every government? The priests. Who breed faction, strife, foment civil wars? The priests. Who are ever at work stinking the air with falsehoods, befouling the scene with frauds? The priests. Who rob us continually, from cradle to grave? The priests. Who abuse our confidence, cheat and trick us from dawn to dark of every day? The priests. Who most resolutely labor at the total extinction of the human race? The priests. Who are most sullied with crimes and infamies? The priests. Which are the most malevolent, the most vindictive, the most ferocious men on earth? The priests. And we hesitate to exterminate this pestilential vermin off the face of the earth! . . . Why then, we richly deserve everything that ails us.

any doubt is the dogma that has produced more atheists than all the others combined, there being not a single man on earth who would not prefer to believe nothing whatsoever rather than subscribe to this confusion of peculiarly dangerous lies; this is the explanation for why so many upright and decent souls consider themselves obliged to repair to thoroughgoing irreligion in their search for relief from, and defense against, the terrors wherewith an infamous Christian creed would lay waste their energies and all their peace of mind. So let's be rid of these false alarms; let's forever have done with the dogmas, the ceremonies, the rites of this abominable religion. Better the most inveterate, the most incorrigible atheism than a cult so fraught with perils so immense. Indeed, I am aware of no drawback in not having any belief at all; but I see nothing but disadvantages of the very gravest order arising from the adoption of these dangerous systems.

"There, my dear Saint-Fond, I have presented my views touching this infamous hell dogma. Let it terrify you and chill your pleasures no more. For mortal man there is but one hell, and that is the folly and wickedness and spite of his fellows; but once his life is over, there's an end to it: his annihilation is final and entire, of him nothing survives. Ah, what a prodigious dupe he must therefore be, who denies himself a single pleasure or curbs his passions for a moment! Let him realize that he exists purely for their satisfaction through whatever excesses this may entail, and that all the effects of these passions, in whatever kind or shape they may have been implanted in him, are the means whereby you serve the Nature whose agents we at all times are, whether we are conscious of it or no, whether we will or no. And now I hand you back the idea of a God which I made brief use of as an instrument for combating the eternal-punishment scare; but there is no God, he does not any more exist than does the devil, than heaven, than hell; and the only duties we have in this world are those toward our pleasures, which we are to satisfy without regard to the interests of others, for we are bound, aye, duty-bound to sacrifice any of them and, if need be, all of them if the least of our desires would have it so.

"I trust I have said enough to prove the absurdity of the principle upon which you base your pointless cruelty. Must I speak of the means you employ? No, to be honest with you, it isn't worth the trouble; how, in the first place, how have you ever come to think that a signature scribbled in blood can be more binding, less worthless, than one in ink, or none? That, next, this scrap of paper stuffed into a bum can serve as a passport to heaven or to hell, neither of which exists? 'Tis here a patchwork of prejudices so ridiculous as truly does not deserve the honor of critical dissection or disproving. For the voluptuous idea that's made you giddy, this idea of prolonging the sufferings of a given individual, for it substitute a greater abundance of murders, I beseech you; cease killing the same individual a thousand times over, which is impossible; instead, assassinate individuals by the thousand, which is altogether feasible. Is there anything so mean-spirited as confining oneself to half a dozen victims a week? Trust Juliette, she is clever, she is capable, only say the word and she will double the number, triple it, give her the required money; you'll want for nothing, your passions will be satisfied."

"Splendid," Saint-Fond replied, "I heartily welcome this last conclusion; from now on, Juliette, we shall have not three victims per supper, but six, and the suppers shall be held twice as frequently as heretofore, which will mean twenty-four victims a week, a third of them men, two-thirds women. Your fees shall be augmented proportionally; however, Mesdames, I cannot confess having been vanquished by this learned dissertation upon the nullity of infernal punishments. I admire the erudition it displays, its aim, certain of its implications and consequences: but bow before it, this I cannot do, and to what you have advanced I should like to answer as follows.

"First of all, throughout your entire argument I observe an effort to exculpate God from the barbarity of the dogma of hell. If God exists, you seem to be saying in virtually every sentence, the qualities which he must possess are every one of them incompatible with this execrable dogma. But, my dear Clairwil, it is precisely here that I feel you fall into heaviest error, and this for want of a philosophy comprehensive enough, luminous enough, to enable you to behold the subject properly. The hell dogma creates a hindrance to your pleasures, and from there you go on to assert that hell there is none; facts must be established upon something more solid

than personal wishes. To combat the dogma of eternal penalties
you begin by gratuitously destroying everything it rests upon : there
is no God, we do not have souls, hence there are no sufferings to
dread in a life after this. It strikes me that you start at the very
outset by committing the greatest blunder one can commit in logic :
to posit as granted that which is in question. Far from sharing your
way of thinking, I acknowledge a Supreme Being and yet more
firmly believe in the immortality of the soul. But let not your pious
hearts, enchanted by these initial declarations, run on to suppose
they have a proselyte in me; I am not so sure my doctrine will prove
to their liking. You yourselves may find it odd. Never mind; I
should like to expound it to you all the same, and I am sure I can
count upon a fair hearing.

"I raise up my eyes to the universe : I see *evil, disorder, crime*
reigning as despots everywhere. My gaze descends, and it bends
upon that most interesting of this universe's creatures : I behold
him likewise devoured by vices, by contradictions, by infamies; what
ideas result from this examination? That what we improperly call
evil is really not evil at all, and that this mode is of such high
necessity to the designs of the being who has created us that he
would cease to be the master of his own creation were *evil* not to
exist universally upon the earth. Well persuaded that this is so, I
tell myself : there exists a God; some hand or other has necessarily
created all that I see, but has not created it save for *evil,* is not
pleased but by *evil; evil* is his essence, and all that he causes us to
commit is indispensable to his plans. What matters it to him that I
suffer from this *evil,* provided it be advantageous to him? Does it
not seem I am his favorite child? If the misfortunes that afflict me
from the day I am born until the day I die prove his indifference to
me, I may very well be mistaken upon what I call *evil.* What I thus
characterize relative to myself seems indeed to be a very great good
relative to the being who has brought me into the world; and if I
receive *evil* from others, I enjoy the right to pay them back in kind,
to be the first to cast the stone : so, henceforth, *evil* is good, just as
it is for the author of my existence, relatively to my existence : the
evil I do others makes me happy, as God is rendered happy by the
evil he does me. All confusion and error are gone save in the idea
attributed to the word; but in the deed, there is both *evil* as neces-

sity and *evil* as pleasure; henceforth, why ought I not call it good?

"Be sure of it: *evil,* or at least what goes by that name, is absolutely useful to the vicious organization of this melancholy universe. The God who has articulated it is a very vindictive being, very barbarous, very wicked, very unjust, very cruel; that, because vengeance, barbarity, wickedness, iniquity, criminality are the necessary modes, vital to the principle that governs this vast creation, of which we only complain when it brings us hurt: to its victims, crime is bad; to its agents, good. Now, if *evil,* or at least what we call such, is the essence both of God who has created everything and of the creatures wrought in his image, how can one be anything but certain that the consequences of *evil* are eternal? It is in *evil* he made the world, by *evil* he does sustain it; it is for *evil* he perpetuates it; it is impregnated with *evil* that creation must exist; it is into the womb of *evil* it returns after its term. Man's soul is merely the action of *evil* upon a subtle matter, susceptible of being organized only by *evil;* now, this mode being the soul of the Creator as it is of the being created, just as it existed before this created being that is saturated with it, so it will exist after that created being is no more. All, everyone has got to be wicked, barbarous, inhuman, like your God: these are the vices the person who wishes to please him must adopt, without, nevertheless, any hope of succeeding: for the *evil* which harms always, the *evil* which is the essence of God, will never be, can never be susceptible of love nor of gratitude. If this God, center of *evil* and of ferocity, torments man and has him tormented by Nature and by other men throughout the whole period of his existence, how may one doubt that he acts likewise and perhaps involuntarily upon this breath of air which outlives him and which, as I have just said, is nothing other than *evil* itself? But how, you are going to object, how may *evil* be tormented by *evil?* Because when it encounters itself, it is increased, and because the force that yields must always be obliterated by the force that compels it to yield—which is in accordance with the logic wherein weakness is always subjugated by strength. That which survives the naturally *evil* being, that which must survive him, since it is the essence of the being's constitution, an essence whose existence is prior to the being and which will exist after the being, by falling back into the womb of *evil,* and because of its relative weakness no

longer having the strength to defend itself, will hence be tormented
by the entire essence of *evil,* to which it will be reunited; they are
these *maleficent molecules* that, in the operation of compassing and
assimilating those which what we call death reunites to them, compose what poets and others of ardent imagination have named
demons. No man, whatever be his conduct in this world, can escape
this terrible fate, because it is necessary that everything that emanates from the womb of Nature, that is to say, from the womb of
evil, return thereunto: such is the universal law. Thus are the detestable elements of the wicked man absorbed into the source of
wickedness, which is God, to return again and to animate other
beings which will be born that much more corrupted, in as they will
be the fruit of corruption.

"What, you may wonder, what has become of the good being?
But there is no such thing as a good being: he whom you call
virtuous is not by any means good, or, if he is from your viewpoint,
he surely is not from the viewpoint of God, who is only *evil,* who
wants nothing but what is *evil,* who requires *evil* alone. The man
you speak of is merely feeble, and feebleness is an *evil.* Weaker than
the absolutely and entirely vicious being, and more completely engulfed by the *maleficent molecules* with which his elementary dissolution will conjoin him, this man will have to suffer a great deal
more: and there, precisely, is what ought to oblige every man to
render himself in this world as vicious and wicked as possible in
order that, more like unto the molecules wherewith he must someday contend, he have, in this act of reunion, infinitely less to suffer
from their onslaught. The ant that were to fall into the midst of
wild animals, where there prevails such violence as must overwhelm
any insect, would, because of its radical defenselessness, have an
infinitely more painful time of it than might some large beast which,
stronger, more resourceful, better able to resist, would only gradually become swallowed up into the whirlpool. The more vices and
crimes a man would have manifested in this world, the more he will
be in harmony with his ineluctable fate, which is wickedness, which I
consider the primary matter of the world's composition. Let man
then take care to preserve himself well from virtue if he should like
to avoid exposure to the most hideous sufferings; for virtue being
the mode hostile to the world's system, all those who will have

yielded to it are certain to endure, after this life, the most unspeakable torments by reason of the difficulty they will experience in re-entering the womb of *evil,* author and regenerator of all we behold.

"Having seen that all was vicious and criminal on earth, the Being Supreme in Wickedness will say unto them, 'Why did you stray into the paths of virtue? Did I ever announce to you, by any token, that this mode was agreeable to me? Did not the perpetual miseries with which I inundated the universe convince you that I love only disorder, and that to please me one must emulate me? Did I not set grandly before you every day the example of destruction? Why did you heed it not? Did not the plagues wherewith I withered the earth, by proving to you that *evil* was my joy, enjoin you to perform *evil* acts in the service of my scheme? Now were you not aware that humankind must satisfy me; and in what aspect of my conduct have you noticed benevolence? Is it in sending you plagues, blights, civil wars, earthquakes, tempests? is it by brandishing above your heads all the serpents of discord that I persuade you that my essence is good? Fool! why did you not imitate my ways? Why did you resist those passions I put in you for no reason other than to prove to you how great is the necessity for *evil?* Their voice was to have been heard and obeyed; it was necessary to despoil pitilessly, as I do, the widow and the orphan, to pillage the poor, in one word, to make man comply with all your needs, bend before all your caprices—as I do. After having played the idiot and taken the contrary way, what have you come back here for? And how are the soft, flabby elements, emanating from your dissolution, how, I ask, without being shattered and without occasioning you the most excruciating agonies, are they to return now into the womb of maleficence and crime?'

"More of a philosopher than you, Clairwil, I do not have to apply, as you seem obliged to do, either to that rogue Jesus or to that insipid novel, Holy Scripture, in order to demonstrate my system; my study of the universe alone provides me with weapons to oppose you, and simply from the manner in which it is governed I see *eternal and universal evil* as absolutely indispensable in the world. The author of the universe is the most wicked, the most ferocious, the most horrifying of all beings. His works cannot be anything but the result or the incarnation of his criminality. Without his wickedness raised to its extremest pitch, nothing would be sustained in the universe; *evil* is, however, a moral entity and not a created one, an eternal and not a perishable entity: it existed before the world; it constituted the monstrous, the execrable being who was able to fashion such a hideous world. It will hence exist after the creatures which people this world; it is unto *evil* they will all enter again, in order to re-create others perhaps more wicked yet, and that is why they say all is degraded, all is corrupted in old age; that stems only from the perpetual re-entry and emergence of wicked elements into and out of the matrix of *maleficent molecules.*

"You are now perhaps going to ask me how, within this hypothesis, I rationalize the possibility of causing a person to suffer for a longer period of time by means of a bit of paper introduced into the anus. It is the simplest thing in the world, and I dare say the surest and least refutable as well; if I have been pleased to call it a weakness, it is because I had no idea you would ever get me into the position of disclosing my doctrines to you. I'll defend my method, however, and prove its worth.

"When my victims arrive in *evil's* womb, they come bearing evidence that in my hands they have endured all the suffering it is possible to endure; they are then classified as virtuous beings. Through my operation they are made better, improved; their adjunction to the *maleficent molecules* is rendered exceedingly difficult; their agonies, hence, are enormous; and by the laws of attraction essential to Nature, they must be, those agonies, of the same species as those I caused them to suffer in this world. As the magnet draws iron, as beauty whets carnal appetites, so agonies A, agonies B, agonies C call to their like, enchain their like. The person my hand exterminates by means of agony B will, I suppose, only return to the matrix of *maleficent molecules* via that agony B; and if agony B is the most appalling possible, I am sure my victim will undergo a similar one in entering the womb of *evil* which necessarily awaits all men and which, by the laws of attraction I just mentioned, only accepts them in the same way by which they went out of the world. But the instrument . . . merely a formality, I admit . . . useless, futile, perhaps; but a formality which suits me, and which can have nothing about it contrary to the true meaning, to the assured success of my operation."

"That," replied Clairwil, "is the most astonishing, the most unusual, I dare say the most bizarre of all the systems yet to have occurred to the mind of man."

"Less extravagant than the one you've just brought to light," answered Saint-Fond; "to maintain yours, you are forced either to wipe God clean of his faults or to deny him; as for me, I acknowledge him with all his vices, and indeed in the eyes of those who are familiar with all the crimes, all the horrors of this curious being whom men only invoke and call good from fear—in the eyes of these people, I say, my ideas will appear less irregular than the ones you have exposed."

"Your system," said Clairwil, "arises solely out of your profound horror of God."

"True; I abhor him; but my system is by no means the issue of the hatred I have for him; no, it is but the fruit of my intelligence and my meditation."

"I," said Clairwil, "would rather not believe in God than forge one in order to hate it. Juliette, what do you think of the matter?"

"Profoundly an atheist," I replied, "arch enemy of the dogma of the soul's immortality, I will always prefer your system to Saint-Fond's; and I prefer the certitude of nothingness to the fear of an. eternity of suffering."

"There you are," Saint-Fond rejoined, "always that perfidious egoism which is the source of all the mistakes human beings make. One arranges one's schemes according to one's tastes and whims, and always by drifting farther from truth. You've got to leave your passions behind when you examine a philosophical doctrine."

"Ah, Saint-Fond," said Clairwil, "how easy it would be to point out that yours is nothing but the product of those passions which you would have one put by when studying. With less cruelty in your heart your dogmas would be less sanguinary; and you yourself would rather risk the eternal damnation of which you speak than renounce the delicious pleasure of horrifying others with it."

"Exactly!" I interrupted; "that is his single motive for exposing his doctrine; nothing but wickedness on his part, but he won't
believe it."

"I believe you are wrong: and you see perfectly well that my
actions correspond in every point to my manner of thinking: convinced that the torture of being reunited with the *maleficent molecules* will be quite mild for the person as maleficent as they, I cover
myself with crimes in this world so as to have less to suffer in the
next."

"As for me," retorted Clairwil, "I soil myself with them
because they please me, because I believe them one of the ways of
serving Nature, and because, since nothing of me is going to survive,
it matters bloody little how I behave in this world."

Thus far had we come in our conversation when we heard a
carriage enter the courtyard and stop; Noirceuil was announced,
then introduced. With him he brought a youth of sixteen, never had
I clapped eyes on one so fair.

"Bless me," murmured the Minister, "I've only this minute
finished giving these ladies an analysis of hell; could it be that my
dear Noirceuil arrives to tempt me into meriting it a little?"

"Only too true," Noirceuil returned; "you might damn yourself wondrously at this pretty little chap's expense, I fetched him
here for that very purpose. He is the son of the Marquise de Rose,
the same whom last week you sent to the Bastille upon charges—
what were they? plotting against the Crown?"

"That was the pretext, as I recall."

"And your aim, presumably, was to procure yourself this child
and perhaps some money besides?"

"Precisely."

"Then I was not mistaken. At any rate the Marquise, knowing
of our connections, sought audience with me; I had one of your
clerks draw up a writ, and this morning she and I had a chat
together. Here's the result of our negotiations," Noirceuil said,
thrusting young Rose into the Minister's arms, "*fuck and sign.* I've
also a hundred thousand crowns to turn over to you."

"He's pretty," said Saint-Fond, kissing the lad, "exceedingly
pretty; but he comes at a bad moment . . . we've been up to horrors;
I'm exhausted."

"Tush," Noirceuil replied, "the boy has all the qualities needed to restore you to life, of that I'm certain."

Rose and Noirceuil, who had not yet taken supper, joined us at table. Saint-Fond said, when the meal was over, that he wished to have me on hand while he amused himself with the youth, and he proposed that Noirceuil lie with Clairwil, both of whom seemed pleased by the arrangement; and the company retired.

"I fear I shall have to put you to contribution," Saint-Fond declared, "for attractive though this child undeniably is, I foresee I'll have trouble stiffening. Unbutton him for me, my pet, roll his shirt above his waist and, that's it, leave his breeches hanging just above his knees, quite, that's the style I adore."

And as the ass I bared for his delectation was nothing short of luscious, Saint-Fond, polluted by me, kissed it fervidly and long, while frigging a juvenile prick we soon saw reach a most creditable stand.

"Suck it," my lover bade me; "I'll tongue his asshole in the meantime. I believe that, between the two of us, we should be able to wheedle a discharge out of him."

Next, his greed aroused by the thought of the fuck I was about to pump forth, Saint-Fond said he would change places with me; this we did so dextrously that scarcely had he got the boy's prick in his mouth than he felt it filled by a most abundant ejaculation; he swallowed every drop down.

"Oh, Juliette," he confided to me, smacking his lips, "food for the gods, that. I thrive upon no other."

Then instructing the boy to get into bed and to await us without falling asleep, Saint-Fond conducted me to his boudoir.

"Juliette," said he, "I must give you the particulars concerning an affair upon which Noirceuil himself is by no means thoroughly informed.

"The Marquise de Rose, one of the most beautiful women of the Court, was once my mistress, and the child Noirceuil brought here this evening is mine. I became interested in him two years ago, for two years the Marquise prevented me from satisfying a passion: and I was obliged to bide my time until my position was strong enough to permit me to act without risk. It was not until recently, my prestige and credit towering upon the shattered remnants of hers, that I judged the occasion ripe; my grievances are two: I resent having fucked her, I resent having been kept from fucking her son. Now she trembles; she sends the boy to me, but he arrives rather late in the day: for eighteen months I discharged at the very thought of him, but such enthusiasms are never maintained indefinitely, and I find that this one, if it has not completely disappeared, has ebbed very significantly; however, this adventure retains certain other criminal possibilities which I owe it to myself not to leave unexplored. Oh, yes, I am perfectly willing to pocket the Marquise's hundred thousand, I am nothing loath to fuck her son; but matters don't end there, my vengeance has to be considered. She'll not emerge from the Bastille save in a crate."

"And, pray, what do you mean by that?"

"Just what I say. The Marquise does not know that in the event her son dies, I, though a distant relative, would be sole heir to her fortune; the whore shan't outlast the month; and after I've properly fucked her scion tonight, tomorrow morning we'll have him breakfast on a cup of chocolate which will remove the single obstacle between me and a windfall."

"What an accumulation of crimes!"

"Not one too many, my dear, if I am to go favorably prepared to that crucial rendezvous with the *maleficent molecules*."

"Astonishing man! And there's something substantial to be gained from the enterprise, I take it?"

"Over five hundred thousand *livres* a year, Juliette, and earning them entails an investment of twenty *sous* worth of arsenic. Well," said the Minister, getting to his feet, "we have some fucking ahead of us, let's not tarry. See for yourself," he continued, giving me his swollen, rock-hard prick to handle, "behold the influence a criminal thought can have upon my senses. There's not a woman on earth who'd ever have had cause to complain of my services if I'd been sure of being able to kill her afterward."

Young Rose was expecting us; we lay down in bed on either side of him. Saint-Fond covered him with lewd kisses; we frigged him, we sucked him, we tongued his vent; and as his imagination was powerfully astir, Saint-Fond was soon lodged to the hilt in the boy. I titillated my lover's asshole with my tongue; great though his previous exertions had been that day, seldom had I seen

him loose his sperm in such quantity or seen the spasm last so long.
He enjoined me to collect his seed from the vessel he had spat it
into and to convey it to his mouth; this challenge to my libertine
abilities pleased me hugely, I acquitted myself of the chore with
gladness in my heart. Next, Rose had to embugger me while the
Minister bum-fucked him afresh, and then Saint-Fond buggered me
while licking and sucking the ass of our humble little playfellow,
whom we wore positively to shreds by dint of the discharging we
made him do now into our mouths, now into our asses. Dawn was
approaching when Saint-Fond, dead sick of it all but not yet satisfied, ordered me to hold the child fast, and the villain slashed his
backside with a hundred or so strokes of a martinet, then beat him
with his fists and molested him very cruelly indeed. At eleven o'clock
the chocolate was brought in; upon the Minister's instructions I
poisoned the cup in such wise as to ensure his inheritance; and he,
while I was preparing the poison that would do away with the son,
busied himself penning a note to the commandant of the Bastille,
wherein the latter was ordered to administer a similar dose to the
mother.

"And so," said Saint-Fond, stifling a yawn, "and so," said he,
once death had been insinuated by our fell maneuvers into the veins
of the unlucky child, "that's what I call a day fairly begun; may the
Being Supreme in Wickedness but deign to send me four such
victims a week, and I shall never cease to sing heartfelt praises
unto his name."

Noirceuil and Clairwil, waiting for us, took breakfast together; we joined them in due time. Everything of what had passed
remained a secret between the Minister and me. The two men set
out for Paris, the doomed child accompanying them; while Clairwil
and I returned thither in her carriage.

Concerning this adventure, my friends, I have nothing further
to tell you that you have not already taken for granted: the crime,
like all Saint-Fond's crimes, was crowned with greatest success: he
very shortly came into possession of a legacy which proved every
bit as valuable as he had originally estimated; and a million *livres*,
representing two years of his new income, was the gift he had the
kindness to present me for my help in obtaining it.

On the road to the capital, Clairwil posed me several questions; I managed to elude them. To be sure, I spoke of our lewd activities—there would have been no point attempting to conceal them, she would not have believed me had I denied them; but as for the rest, I hid it all, which was according to Saint-Fond's wishes. During that journey I took the opportunity to remind my friend of her promise to secure my admission to her libertine club; she gave me her word that I would be received the next time it met; we entered the city, kissed, and said goodbye.

Part
Three

$\mathcal{M}$y friends, it is time I tell you a little about myself, and above all describe my opulence, fruit of the most determinedly dissolute living, in order that you will be able to contrast it with the state of indigence and adversity wherein my sister, who had chosen good behavior, was languishing already. Your outlook and philosophy will suggest to you what conclusions are to be drawn from these comparisons.

I lived on a grand scale, on a perfectly enormous scale; you must surely have suspected as much, what with the expenses I had to make in behalf of my lover. But leaving aside the innumerable things required for his pleasure, I had to myself a superb town house in Paris, an exquisite property by Sceaux at Barrière-Blanche, as delightful a little dwelling as ever you saw, twelve Lesbians were perpetually in my train, four equally engaging chambermaids, a reader, a night nurse, three carriages, ten horses, four valets chosen for their virility and excellence of member, all the other appurtenances of a very great household, and after salaries and upkeep had been deducted I was left with a balance of two million to throw away on trifles of one kind or another. You will concede, I believe, that something is to be said for the way I had managed my affairs.

Would you like my daily life described?

I rose every day at ten. Until eleven I saw nobody except intimate friends; from then until one, my toilette, at which all my retinue assisted; promptly at one o'clock I gave private audience to those individuals who came to solicit my favors, or to the Minister when he happened to be in Paris. At two I hied myself to Barrière-Blanche where, every day, I would find awaiting me what had been delivered by tasteful and conscientious procuresses, to wit: four new men, and four new women, with whom I would very wantonly, very amply, indulge my caprices. To obtain some idea of the objects I used to receive there, you have only to know that not one of them cost me less than twenty-five *louis,* and I frequently paid double that; nor is there any imagining what of the delicious and rare was purveyed to me in either sex; at these trysts I more than once met women and girls of rank and the highest station; sweet were the joys, yes, elaborate were the pleasures I tasted in that house. I would return to town at four in the afternoon, and always dine with friends. I shall not speak of my board: nowhere in Paris was there anything to match it for splender, for delicacy, for profusion; and yet I was a hard mistress to my cooks and wine steward, demanding that they ever outdo themselves; but I need not press the point, you are familiar enough with my extreme intemperance. It is perhaps a mild vice, gourmandise; it is one of my favorites nonetheless; for I have always been of the opinion that unless you carry this one to excess you can never properly enjoy the others. After those royal repasts I used to go out to the theater; or entertain the Minister if it was one of his evenings.

Regarding my wardrobe, my gems, my furniture, and my savings, though at this period I had been scarcely two years with Monsieur de Saint-Fond, I believe four million would be a low figure for the value of the lot; I had half that sum in gold, and used sometimes, after Clairwil's example, to fling up the lids of my treasure chests and masturbate frenziedly: *I love crime, and see!* I would gloat, discharging over the thought, *see, here at my disposal are all the means I need for committing it.* Oh, my good friends, 'tis a very sweet idea and what seas of fuck have I not spilled entertaining it. Did I desire a new piece of jewelry, another dress, anything, and my lover—who disliked having me wear the same thing more than twice—would satisfy me immediately; and in return for all that nothing was required of me save lawless conduct, lechery, libertinage, and prodigious care in arranging the Minister's frolics. It was thus that by flattering my tastes I found them gratified, every one; through my surrender to every sensual irregularity my senses were kept in a constant drunken exhilaration.

But such comforts, such joys—what was my moral situation as a result of them? Ah, of this I am reluctant to speak, and yet however I must. The terrific libertinage I practiced day in and day out had so rusted and decayed the workings of my soul, to such a degree had I been envenomed by the pernicious advice, the vicious examples I was fairly deluged with from all sides and all the time, that I declare to you, I do not think I'd have given a penny out of my hoard to rescue someone on the brink of starvation. Indeed, about this time a dreadful famine broke out in the vicinity of my country home; all the folk in those parts were reduced to the very worst distress: I recall hideous scenes, girls sold their bodies by the roadside, waifs were abandoned, there were several suicides; droves of people came begging to my door; I held firm and deliberately and impudently reasserted my uncharitable disposition by laying out fabulous sums for the improvement of my lawns and shrubberies. But how can one possibly bestow alms, was my insolent rejoinder, when one is in the midst of having mirrored boudoirs built in one's park, and one's paths beautified by sculptured Cupids, Aphrodites, and Sapphos? Everything that could move a heart of stone was exhibited to my tranquil gaze; it got them nowhere, steadfast I remained: weeping mothers, naked infants, ghostlike figures wasted by hunger, I simply smiled, shook my head, and throughout those trying months slept as soundly as ever before and ate with an increased appetite. Taking stock of my sensations, I discovered that what I was feeling bore out my teachers' predictions perfectly: instead of a disagreeable sentiment of pity, there was kindled in me a certain restlessness, a commotion produced by the evil I fancied I was doing in turning those wretches away empty-handed, and within my nerves there was a certain rush of heat much like the blaze ignited in us whenever we violate a law or subdue a prejudice. I suddenly recognized how delightful putting these principles into practice could be; and I understood that if the spectacle of misery caused by unkind fate can be sublimely voluptuous for those with minds trained and enriched by such doctrines as had been inculcated in mine, then the spectacle of misery for which one has oneself been responsible must surely intensify this pleasure; as you know, mine is a fertile imagination, it now began to run riot. The logic of the thing was eminently simple: I reaped pleasure merely from denying to the destitute the wherewithal that would have brought them respite; ah, what might I not experience from being the direct and sole cause of that destitution? If, said I, it is sweet to refuse to do good, it must be heavenly to do evil. I summoned up this idea, played with it during those critical moments when the flesh catches fire from the sparks emitted by an excited brain; moments when one is particularly apt to heed the voice of desires become that much more strident, that much more imperious with the receding into unimportance, and finally into nullity, of all else. The dream once dreamt and over, one may subside again into prudence and sobriety—it requires little or no effort. Purely intellectual wrongs are always easily effaced. They harm no one; but, unfortunately, the thing is likely to go farther. Ah, one says to oneself, what shall the deed itself do to me if the mere grating of the thought upon my nerves has been able to affect them so keenly? The temptation is enormous: one makes the accursed dream come true, and its existence is a crime.

Less than a mile from my château stood a humble cottage belonging to a peasant, one Martin Des Granges; in this world he had little else beyond his eight children and a wife who for kindliness and cheerfulness and thrift was a veritable treasure to the man; would you believe it? this asylum of poverty and virtue excited my fury and wickedness. Very true it is, to this I bear witness, that crime is a delectable thing; very certain it is that the flame it darts through our whole being is what sets alight the torch of lust, that it requires but the thought of crime to hurl us into a lubricious ferment.

I had taken Elvire with me the day I visited that place, and with me also I had some phosphorus in a jar; upon arriving, I instructed that witty little jade to go in to entertain the family, saying I would join her in a minute; whereupon I slipped off and buried the combustible amidst the hay in the loft above the room where the wretches slept. I climb back down, enter, the youngsters kiss me, we play games together, the mother and I chat about the details of her household. The father asks if he may offer me some refreshment? He endeavors to be as hospitable as his dreadfully scanty means permit. . . . I am not for all that swerved an inch from my purpose, not in the least melted; what are my emotions? I inspect them and find it is not a tedious pity that pervades me, but a delicious irritation which racks me to the core of my being: a mere touch and I could discharge ten times over. I distribute renewed caresses to every member of this wonderful family into whose midst I have just sown the seeds of murder; my fell deceit is at its height; the blacker grows my gratuitous treachery, the more violent the itch in my cunt. To the mother I give some ribbons, candy to the brats; we take our leave, start for home; but I am in such a state of excitement, of very delirium, that I feel my knees ready to buckle and must beg Elvire to come to my relief. We turn off the road into a thicket, I raise my skirts, I spread my legs . . . she puts her hand to my sex, has scarce inserted her fingers when I discharge; never before had I known anything like those terrible moments. "What ails you, Madame?" asked Elvire, unaware of what I had just done.

"Don't speak to me, frig me . . . frig me," said I, thrusting my tongue into her mouth, "I am fearfully overwrought this morning, that's all. Here, let me have your cunt, let me toy with it, and let's both of us drown in rivers of fuck."

"But what can have happened?"

"Horrors, my dove . . . atrocities, and sperm flows marvelously, believe me, when its spurts are started out of the womb of abomination. So frig me, Elvire, frig me, dear heart, I have got to discharge."

And the creature kneels, glides her head between my thighs, her tongue glides into my cunt, thrills there. "Oh fuck!" I gasp, " 'tis even so, 'tis so, you seize me well. . . ."

And my seed washes her lips, her nose, drips down her chin. . . . We pursue our way.

I reached home in an indescribable exaltation, it was as though every violent impulse, every instinct, every vice were allied in an effort to debauch my very soul, I swam in a kind of intoxication . . . in a kind of rage, there was nothing I might not have done, no lewd act I could not have soiled myself with. Bitterly I regretted that my blow had fallen upon only a tiny fraction of humanity, great was the evil in me, great enough to have laid all Nature waste; I dashed into one of my boudoirs and, naked, flung myself upon a couch, I commanded Elvire to send me in every man she could get hold of, I bade them do everything they wished with me provided they insulted me, reviled me, treated me like the vilest whore. I was fingered, pawed, prodded, spat upon, beaten, slapped; my cunt, my ass, my breasts, my mouth were all used, befouled; would that I had had twenty other altars to present for their offerings. Some of those men left and fetched back their friends, individuals I had never seen before, I opened my holes to them, refused no one, was the harlot to everyone, anyone, and fuck gushed in torrents out of me. One of the more uncouth of those studs—I had been baiting him—declared it was not upon a bed he wanted to fuck me, but in the mire; I let him drag me bodily into a pigsty and there, in slime and excrement, I flung my legs apart and challenged him to do his worst. The knave performed brutally and let me go only after having shat all over my face . . . and I was happy. The more, the deeper I wallowed in ordure and infamy, the greater grew my excitement, the fiercer my joy. In less than two hours I was tupped twenty times over, and Elvire never stopped frigging me throughout it all, and nothing, no, nothing alleviated my pangs, my sufferings hideous and delicious and provoked by the thought constantly in my mind, that of the crime I had just perpetrated. Going upstairs to my dressing room, we noticed a ruddy glow in the distance.

"Madame, come look!" Elvire called, opening a window. "Look, Madame, a fire—over there, do you see? In that direction, where we were this morning—"

And I tottered back, to fall nearly unconscious upon the sofa. We were alone, that pretty girl and I. For perhaps five minutes, or ten, she frigged me; and then I sat up, thrusting Elvire away.

"Do you not hear shouts?" I demanded. "Come, let's not tarry here, a rare spectacle awaits us outside. . . . Elvire, I am responsible for this—"

"Madame?"

"Come, I say, let's go gloat together over my triumph. I simply must see it all, I must savor it all, I don't want to miss a detail."

We set out as we were, the two of us—our hair disheveled, our dresses rumpled, weariness and delight traced in our features: we resembled a pair of bacchantes. Stopping twenty paces away from that scene of horror, behind a little hillock which hid us from the sight of others, I sink again into the embrace of an Elvire almost as aroused as I: we cunt-suck each other by the light of homicidal flames my ferocity has ignited, we discharge to the sound of shrill screams coming from a woe and anguish that are my confection; and never has woman been happier than was I.

At last we regain our feet and stand awhile surveying that panorama of destruction, then move closer to pore over the details. Great is my distress at concluding, as I count the corpses, that two members of the family must have escaped me. I examine the charred bodies one by one, recognize each: these people were alive this morning, I muse, and now, but a few hours later, here they are, dead; killed by me. And why did I do it? Out of fun. To spill my fuck. So this is what murder is! A little organized matter disorganized; a few compositional changes, the combination of some molecules disturbed and broken, those molecules tossed back into the crucible of Nature who, re-employing the selfsame materials, will cast them into something else so that in but a day or so they shall reappear in the world again, only guised a little differently; this they call murder—truly now, in all seriousness, I ask myself, where is the wrong in murder? This woman here, that infant there—in the eyes of Nature does either count for more than, say, a housefly or a maggot? I deprive the one of life, so doing I give life to the other—how can this be made out an offense to Nature?

This little revolt of the intellect against the heart set the electrical globules in my nerves briskly into motion, and once again my companion found her fingers wetted by my running cunt. I honestly do not know to what lengths I might not have gone had I been alone. Who can tell, possessed of a perfectly Caribbean cruelty, I'd perhaps have fallen to devouring my victims: there they lay, strewn invitingly upon the ground: none but the father and one of the children had got away, the mother and the seven others had perished; and as I stared down at them, felt, palpated them, I repeated to myself: I have done this, I. These murders were planned by me, consummated by me, they are my handiwork, my creation . . . and I discharged afresh.

Of the cottage not a stick remained; it was hard to imagine a dwelling had ever stood there, that human beings had ever inhabited this wilderness.

And now, my friends, what do you fancy was Clairwil's reaction when she heard of my feat? She listened to the recital in cold silence, one eyebrow raised; and when I was done, she assured me that I had precious little to boast of; indeed said she, I had acquitted myself more like a coward than a criminal.

"In the execution of your undertaking I notice several grave defects," she declared, and her comments are worth citing, for they reveal the character of that unusual woman; "firstly," she specified, "you proceeded in slipshod style: had someone chanced to come along, your gestures, your exuberance,. very telltale, would have constituted evidence against you. Beware of such loose conduct. Ardor, passion—by all means, but keep it inward; outwardly, nonchalance, phlegm. Circumscribe, contain the lubricious effects, under pressure their temperature mounts.

"Secondly, scope and grandeur are sadly lacking in your conception of the thing, which I am obliged to qualify as mean; for you must admit that with a large town and seven or eight sizable villages plainly visible from your windows, there is a timorousness, undue modesty in exerting yourself upon a single house, an isolated house in a secluded place furthermore . . . from fear, one is led to suppose, lest the flames, by spreading, extend the dimensions of your petty felony: your nervousness, your anxiety, in committing it are only too apparent. You spoiled your pleasure, for crime's pleasures brook no restriction; I speak from experience: there where free rein is not given the imagination, where the hand is stayed by some scruple or consideration, the ecstasy cannot possibly be complete, for there always subsists a regret: *I could have done more, and I did not.* And regrets arising from virtue sting worse than those consecutive to crime: should he who follows in virtue's train happen to perform a piece of wickedness, he is always able to comfort himself by the thought that a host of good deeds will wipe the blot away, and as it is easy to convince oneself of anything one desires to believe, his conscience is soon at peace. But for those who travel the path of vice matters are not so simple, a missed opportunity is something we cannot forgive ourselves because it cannot be compensated by anything; no virtue comes to our rescue; and the promise we make to do something worse only whets our palate for evil, without consoling us for having let a chance of doing it go by.

"Another observation has to be made," Clairwil went on. "To even the most superficial glance your scheme betrays a very glaring error; had I been in your place I would surely have brought an action against that Des Granges. Nothing simpler than to have had him charged with arson and burned at the stake; oh, yes indeed, I would have included that item on the program. For are you unaware that when fire breaks out in the house of a tenant—and Des Granges is one of your tenants—you have the right to summon the authorities and launch an inquiry to determine whether the tenant is the culprit? Who knows, perhaps the fellow wished to get rid of his wife and children and then go off and play the shiftless beggar somewhere else? The moment he bolted from the house you should have had him arrested while attempting flight, don't you see; you spend a few *louis* collecting witnesses; to begin with, Elvire, she was there: she affirms that the very same morning she saw the guilty one skulking distractedly about in the barnyard, climbing up to the hayloft, she spoke to him, questioned him, got only gibberish for answer; and the courts would have done the rest: inside a week you'd have been treated to the voluptuous spectacle of your man being burned alive at your gate. Let this be a lesson to you, Juliette, profit from it, as soon as the idea for a crime occurs to you, concert its amplification, its aggravation; and while putting it into execution, further elaborate upon your idea."

There, my friends, those, textually, are the cruel additions Clairwil would have had me join to my miscreancy; and why deny it? deeply stirred by her arguments, forced to recognize that I had performed shabbily, I promised myself that in the future my enterprises would defy criticism. I was aggrieved above all by the peasant's escape; what would I not have given to see him roasted on my doorstep! The mere recollection of that loss pains me to this day.

At last came the time appointed for my reception into Clairwil's club. Its name was the Sodality of the Friends of Crime. On the morning of that day my sponsor brought for my study a copy of the Sodality's bylaws; here, let me read them to you, I believe you will find them intriguing.

STATUTES OF THE SODALITY OF THE FRIENDS OF CRIME

Deferring to the common usage, the Sodality admits the serviceability of the word *crime*; but makes plain declaration that in its employment thereof with reference to any kind of act of whatever sort or color, no condemnatory or pejorative sense is ever intended. Thoroughly convinced that man is not free, and that, bound absolutely by the laws of Nature, all men are slaves of these fundamental laws, the Sodality therefore approves and legitimates everything, and considers as its most zealous and most estimable Members those who, unhesitatingly and unrepentantly, acquit themselves of the greatest number of those vigorous actions fools in their weakness call crimes; because it is the Sodality's belief that through accomplishing these actions the individual serves Nature, that their performance is dictated by her, and that if such a thing as crime there be, it is characterized by the reluctance or refusal to do any of the very various things Nature may inspire and hence enjoin. The Sodality therefore stands protectively behind all its Members, guaranteeing all of them aid, shelter, refuge, allies, funds, counsel, everything needed to counter the maneuvers of the law; all Members who violate it are safeguarded and championed automatically by the Sodality, which considers itself above the law because the law is of mortal and artificial contrivance, whereas the Sodality, natural in its origin and obediences, heeds and respects Nature only.

1. No distinction is drawn among the individuals who comprise the Sodality; not that it holds all men equal in the eyes of Nature—a vulgar notion deriving from infirmity, want of logic, and false philosophy—but because it is persuaded and maintains that distinctions of any kind may have a detrimental influence upon the Sodality's pleasures and are certain sooner or later to spoil them.[1]

2. The individual presenting himself for membership in the

---

[1] The proponents of that absurd doctrine of equality will always be recruited from the ranks of the weak; it is never espoused save by him who, unable to rise to the class of the strong, can at least find comfort in pulling that class down to his own level; but of all theories this one is the most derisory, the most unnatural; and it is nowhere current except with the viler underbred sort who, moreover, and of this you may rest assured, will abandon it once they've got a little gilt on their rags.

Sodality must forswear whatever religious faith he may happen to be encumbered with; his contempt for these crack-brained beliefs and for the fictitious object of worship they revolve around will be judged by means of tests to which he ought to expect to be put; the penalty of immediate expulsion is prescribed for those who, however mildly, and even in the spirit of jest, backslide into these abject practices.

3. God, in the view of the Sodality, does not exist; sound evidence of atheism is a prerequisite for entry into it; the sole divinity it recognizes is pleasure; to pleasure it sacrifices everything; it considers voluptuous activities, all imaginable voluptuous activities, and nothing but voluptuous activities, sacred; whatever delectates, it considers good; within the Sodality all forms of pleasure-seeking and of pleasure-taking are authorized, it frowns on none, there is not one it does not applaud, encourage, and promote.

4. The Sodality dissolves all marital ties and ignores those of blood; under its roof one should disport indiscriminately with the wife of one's neighbor as with one's own, should for enjoyment consult one's own brother, sister, children, nephews, quite as one would do with the brothers, sisters, children, nephews of somebody else; and any unwillingness to comply with these rules constitutes strong grounds for expulsion.

5. A husband is bound to present his wife for admission; a father, his son or daughter; a brother, his sister; an uncle, his nephew or niece; etc.

6. Entry into the Sodality is barred to those unable to indicate a minimum yearly income of twenty-five thousand *livres,* dues of membership being ten thousand francs per annum. This sum is the equivalent of average estimated costs per Member, and out of it are paid expenses entailed by the upkeep of the Sodality's seat, rentals, maintenance of the seraglios, carriages and equipages, offices, and functionaries' salaries, outlay for the Assemblies, suppers, and lighting; and when the Treasurer reports a favorable balance at year's end, he divides it among his fellow Members; and in that other case where disbursements have exceeded revenue, a tax is levied and the deficit made up to the Treasurer, whose word in these matters is always accepted without question.

7. Twenty artists and literary figures are to be admitted upon remittance of the modest fee of a thousand *livres* per annum; this special consideration is part of the Sodality's policy of patronizing the arts; it regrets that its means do not permit it to welcome, at this insignificant price, a larger number of these gifted persons to whom it would give every kind of encouragement.

8. The Members of the Sodality, united through it into one great family, share all their hardships as they do their joys; they aid one another mutually in all life's various situations; but alms, charities, help extended to widows, orphans, or persons in distress are rigorously forbidden, both within the Sodality and above all without; should proof be brought forward, or the simple suspicion arise, that a Member has indulged in such so-called good works, he will be expelled.

9. An emergency fund of thirty thousand *livres* is kept in constant reserve and is at the disposition of any Member who by accident or ill fate finds himself in difficulties of whatever sort.

10. The President is elected by ballot, and his period of office is one month; he may be of either sex; and presides at twelve Assemblies, whereof there are three per week. His duties are to see that the Sodality's laws are respected, to supervise the correspondence executed by a Permanent Committee whose chairman is the President. The Treasurer and the Sodality's two Executive Secretaries sit on this Committee; but as with the President, each Executive Secretary's term of office expires after one month.

11. Each Assembly is opened by a speech delivered by one of the Members; the tenor of his address is always contrary to polite custom and religion; if it is deemed worthy thereof, it is printed forthwith, at the Sodality's expense, and deposited in its Archives.

12. During those hours devoted to corporative frolicking, all Members, male and female, are naked; they intermingle, in the melee partners are chosen indiscriminately, and there is no such thing as a valid refusal whereby one individual would deny his pleasure to another. Once called upon, each individual must co-operate instantly, unreservedly, gladly; has he not the right to demand the same a few minutes later? Should an individual attempt to shirk his obligations toward his brethren, he will be forcefully

constrained to fulfill them and then be driven ignominiously out of the Sodality.

13. During Assembly, no cruel passion, save whipping inflicted upon the buttocks only, may be given vent to; the Sodality possesses seraglios, and there dangerous passions may be exercised with entire freedom; but when amongst his fellows each Member must confine himself to crapulous, incestuous, sodomistic, and benign merrymaking.

14. The completest confidence reigns among Members of the Sodality; they may and ought to avow to one another their tastes, their foibles, chat intimately, and employ the exchange of confessions as a further spur to pleasure. Were anyone to disclose Sodality secrets, or in one of his fellows to criticize ungenerously the failings or predilections which make for the success of his pleasure-seeking, he would be expelled straightway.

15. Hard by the public pleasure hall are located private cells whereunto one may repair solitarily to indulge in all the debaucheries of libertinage; these cells are available to groups of any size, they are appropriately and fully equipped, and each contains a youth and a young lass with whom, at all times, Sodality Members may execute any passion whatsoever, including those allowed only inside the seraglios, for these children being of the same species as the seraglios are stocked with, and indeed belonging to the seraglios, they may be treated similarly.

16. Eating and drinking carried to any point of gluttony and drunkenness are authorized; every Member is assured of assistance while indulging in these as in other excesses; all possible measures are taken to facilitate them.

17. No condemnation by a court of law, no public disgrace, no defamation of character will disqualify a candidate for admission into the Sodality. Its principles being based upon crime, the criminal element poses no threat to it; to the contrary. Rejected by the world, these outcasts will find consolations and friends in a society which recognizes their value and will always give preference to their candidacy. The worse a given individual's reputation abroad, the more highly he will be thought of by the Sodality; very notorious criminals and eminent public enemies may be elected to the pres-

idency upon the day of their admission, and given the run of the seraglios without prior novitiate.

18. Public confession is made at each of the four major General Assemblies, the dates of which coincide with what Catholics call the four great festival days of the year; at them each Member is in turn obliged to declare in a loud and clear voice by and large everything he has done: if his conduct has been blameless, he is reproved; much praise is his if it has been irregular; be it horrible, if he has accumulated execrable deeds, then he is rewarded; but in this last case he must produce witnesses. The prizes are fixed at ten thousand francs drawn from the Treasury.

19. Frequented by Members only, their location known to Members alone, the Sodality's premises are of particular splendor; and surrounded by superb grounds. Fires are maintained in all rooms throughout the winter season. Assemblies begin at five in the afternoon and last until noon the following day. Toward midnight a sumptuous meal is served, refreshments are available at all other times.

20. All games and gambling are forbidden during Assembly; devoted to more natural forms of recreation, the Sodality frowns upon anything in any way conducive to the neglect of libertinage's divine passions, the only ones capable of electrifying the human being.

21. One month is the period of initiation for each newly elected Member; during this novitiate he is completely at the disposition of the Sodality, is its toy; may not enter the seraglios or enjoy any privilege or consideration. He must consent to all such propositions as are made him; failure so to do may incur capital punishment.

22. Election to all posts is by secret ballot; factions, cabals, cliques are strictly forbidden. These posts are those of President, the two Executive Secretaries, Censors, the two Wardens entrusted with government of the seraglios, Treasurer, Steward, Bailiff, the two Physicians, two Surgeons, Obstetrician, Master of the Chancery under whom are the Scribes, the Printers, the Reviser, and the Censor of Texts and Publications, and the Inspector General of admission cards.

23. Men over forty years of age, women over thirty-five are

not received by the Sodality; once admitted, however, no Member may be expelled on grounds of old age.

24. Any member who does not attend a Sodality Assembly during the space of a year will be stricken from the roster; obligations public or private, however, constitute valid excuse for absence.

25. Any written work attacking polite customs or religion presented by a Sodality Member, whether of his production or no, will be deposited at once in the Library, and the donor will be rewarded therefore, in accordance with the merits of the work and his share in its composition.

26. Children resulting from Sodality unions will be, at birth, immediately placed in the crèche and subsequently in the nursery annexed to the seraglios, later—at the age of ten for boys, of seven for girls—to become inmates thereof. But a woman addicted to child-bearing will not be tolerated by the Sodality, propagation being utterly alien to its spirit and aims; true libertinage abhors progeniture; and the Sodality therefore disfavors it: female Members will denounce men given to this mania and if the latter prove incorrigible, they also will be invited to prepare their withdrawal from the Sodality.

27. The President's duties are to ensure the smooth running of the Assembly. Under his orders is the Censor; theirs is the responsibilty for maintaining decorum and a propitious atmosphere: the calm, the freedom from interference, the enthusiasm of agents, the submissiveness of patients; they are, as well, to see to the preservation of quiet, moderating laughter and conversations and everything else that is incondite and not in the spirit of libertinage or that is damaging to it. The President has the highest authority over the seraglios. He may not, during his term of office, leave Sodality headquarters unless he appoints his predecessor to take temporary charge in his absence.

28. Oaths, hard language, and blasphemies in particular are authorized, they may be employed upon all occasions. Between Members the familiar *thou* is compulsory.

29. The jealousies, the quarrels, the scenes entailed in love, as well as the language of love, endearing expressions, tender ones, etc., are absolutely prohibited; all this is detrimental to libertinage, and libertinage is the business to which the Sodality is to attend.

30. Dueling has no place in the Sodality, nor roistering, neither do bullies and bravoes, they will be expelled mercilessly. Poltroonery is revered here as it was in Rome. The coward lives at peace with his fellows; he is quite commonly a libertine too, such are the people the Sodality wants.

31. The total number of Members may at no time exceed four hundred and in so far as that is possible, the proportionate strength of the two sexes will be kept equal.

32. Theft is permitted within the bounds of the Sodality; but murder is not, except in the seraglios.

33. Members need not bring with them the furnitures, implements, and weaponry requisite to libertinage; for the house provides these objects in abundance and variety, and they are clean.

34. Repulsive deformities or diseases will not be put up with. Someone so afflicted, were he to present himself, would most surely be rejected. And were an already admitted Member to fall prey to such misfortunes, he would be asked to resign.

35. A Member who contracts the venereal malady will be obliged to retire until completely restored, his recovery being vouched for by the house Physician and Surgeons.

36. No foreigner will be admitted; provincials are likewise debarred. The Sodality exists only for persons resident in Paris and its environs.

37. High birth will in no wise facilitate admission; the essential is to prove one has the necessary means alluded to above (Article 6). However pretty a woman may be she shall not be accepted unless she possess the required wealth; the same will apply to any young man, however handsome.

38. Neither beauty nor youth confers any exclusive privilege in the Sodality; privileges would speedily destroy the equality which must prevail there.

39. Death will be the certain fate of any Member who divulges secrets of the Sodality, which will have him hunted down no matter where he goes, and at no matter what cost.

40. Ease, liberty, impiety, crapulousness, all libertine excesses, all those of debauchery, of eating and drinking, in short, of what is known as foul lust, will reign supreme during Assembly.

41. One hundred male servants are retained at all times and

paid by the Sodality; they, youthful and attractive all, may be used to fill passive roles in lewd scenes; but will never participate actively therein. The Sodality owns sixteen vehicles, a corresponding number of teams, has two equerries in its hire and fifty outside valets. It has a print shop, type setters, a dozen copyists, and four readers; and in addition all the personnel necessitated by the seraglios.

42. No firearms, no sword, no stick may be introduced into the hall reserved for pleasure. Before entering, Members leave all they have with them in a spacious cloakroom, where trustworthy women relieve them of their clothing and are held accountable for it. Adjoining the hall are several public conveniences; stationed in each are attendants, girls and boys, ready to be of any service; they have syringes, bidets, vessels in the English style, ordinary pots, high-quality linens, cloths and swabs, perfumes, and in general everything needed before and after the operation or while it is in course. They will lend their tongues upon simple request.

43. Under no circumstances does the Sodality intrude or interfere in government affairs, nor may any Member. Political speeches are expressly forbidden. The Sodality respects the regime in power; and if its attitude toward the law is disdainful, that is because it holds as a principle that man is incapable of making laws which obstruct or contradict those of Nature; but the disorders of its Members, transpiring privately, ought never to scandalize either the governed or their governors.

44. Among the facilities offered Sodality Members are two seraglios, they are located in the two wings of the main building. One is composed of three hundred boys ranging from seven to twenty-five years of age; the other of a like number of girls, from five to twenty-one. These creatures are constantly replaced, not a week goes by but at least thirty are winnowed out of each seraglio so as to make room for fresh accessions: close by is an establishment where new lots are trained up to fill gaps in the ranks. Sixty procuresses look after recruitment; and, as has been said, there is a Warden for each seraglio. These seraglios are agreeable places, comfortably appointed; there, one does exactly what one likes; the most ferocious passions are exercised in these sanctuaries where all Sodality Members are admitted free of charge; however, a tax

of one hundred crowns is levied per creature murdered. Those Members who choose to sup in a seraglio are at liberty to do so; entrance tickets are distributed by the President, who cannot refuse them to Members in good standing and who have accomplished their month as novices. The extremest subordination on the part of the inmates prevails in the seraglios; complaints relative to lack of submissiveness or of cooperation will be taken at once to the Warden of the seraglio, or to the President, and no time is lost chastising the miscreant, according to the plaintiff's specifications, and you have the right to inflict the penalty yourself, if such things amuse you. There are twelve torture chambers per seraglio, where everything is at hand for dealing with victims in the most awful, the most unspeakable manner. Although each seraglio contains creatures of only one sex, they may be mixed at will and to taste, males being fetched into the midst of females, or females into the midst of males. There are in addition twelve dungeons per seraglio, for the use of those who enjoy subjecting victims to the slow death of incarceration. Inmates of the two seraglios may not be removed either to the pleasure halls or to a Member's personal residence. The lateral pavilions housing the seraglios contain menageries as well, where animals of every species await the Member given to bestiality; this is a simple passion and altogether natural, and must hence be respected like all the rest.

Three complaints brought against any one subject suffice to have him removed. Three requests that he be put to death suffice to have him dispatched without further ado. In each seraglio are four executioners, four jailers, eight whippers, four flayers, four midwives, and four surgeons all at the orders of Members who, in the heat of passion, might have need of the ministry of such personages; it being understood of course that the midwives and surgeons are present not by any means to render humanitarian aid, but to assist in tortures. As soon as a seraglio inmate manifests the slightest symptom of illness he is sent to the hospital, never again to return to the house.

Each seraglio is surrounded on three sides by high walls. All the windows are barred, and the inmates remain indoors, always. Between the building and the high wall shielding it is a space ten feet wide, forming an alley bordered by cypress trees; Sodality

Members sometimes take seraglio inmates for walks along this secluded pathway, to indulge with them in pleasures more somber and often still more frightful. At the foot of a number of these trees are holes, pits into which a victim may be made to disappear; suppers are held under these trees from time to time, and occasionally in these very pits: whereof some are extremely deep, descent into them being possible by means only of hidden stairways, and in the lower reaches of which one may accomplish every imaginable infamy, the same stillness, the same silence reigning there as in the uttermost bowels of the earth.

45. No candidate will be admitted without first signing both the oath he will be made to repeat, and the list of obligations corresponding to his sex.

The time came to leave. I was adorned like the goddess of daylight; Clairwil, my sponsor, was in a gay mood and out of coquetry had dressed herself to look like a girl of fourteen. En route she reminded me of the extreme docility I was to show in the face of all the Sodality members' desires, and she also said that as regards the seraglios I would simply have to be patient for, as a novice, it would be a month before I could make use of them, no exception was ever allowed to the rules.

The house to which we were driving was in one of the bleakest and least populous quarters of Paris; it took nearly an hour to get there. My heart beat excitedly when our carriage entered a dark courtyard virtually enclosed by tall black trees, the gates shut immediately after we were inside. A servant was awaiting us as we stepped from the carriage, and he escorted us into the hall. Clairwil was obliged to surrender her clothing: I, however, was to undress later, in the course of the ceremony. This was a veritable palace, superbly lit; in the entrance and so placed on the floor that one could not avoid treading upon it was a big crucifix sprinkled with hosts and at whose farther end was the Bible, which one had to step upon as well; I was not daunted, you may be sure, by any of these obstacles.

I went in. An exceedingly handsome woman of thirty-five was presiding, she was nude, her coiffure was magnificent; those to her left and right where she sat on the platform of honor were naked also, they were two men and a woman. Over three hundred members had already arrived and there they were, all naked; some were encunting, some masturbating, some flagellating, some cuntsucking, some sodomizing, some discharging, and all that most serenely and amidst perfect calm: not a sound was to be heard save the noises necessitated by the various circumstances. Some were strolling about in pairs, some alone; many were watching the crowd and while gazing at spectacles fingering themselves voluptuously. There were several groups, some of them composed of up to eight and even ten persons; many of men only; no fewer of women exclusively; of several women between two men; and of several men occupying two or three women. Extremely pleasant incense burned in great cassolettes, emitting heady vapors whose irresistible effect was a sort of sensual languor. I saw a trio emerge together from one of the latrines.

And then the President rose and in a quiet voice said that she would like to have the attention of the assembly for a moment. Activity soon ceased and a few minutes later I found myself surrounded by all the members present; never had I been so closely scrutinized nor by so many people; each delivered an opinion, and I believe I can assert that the view generally expressed was flattering; there was whispering, glances, nods were exchanged, and clearly all sorts of little plots were being hatched against me, and I shuddered at the thought that I was about to have to subject myself to all the desires roused by my youth and my charms. At length the President bade me step up and stand on the dais opposite her; and there, a balustrade separating me from the very numerous company, I was upon her instructions divested of my raiments by two servants who in less time than it takes to tell had off every stitch I was wearing. When the servants withdrew and left me absolutely naked before the bold stares of those several hundred spectators, I was, I do admit, somewhat embarrassed; but that feeling was short-lived, my impudence was restored at once by the applause I heard ring out. These, such as I shall recite them to you, were the questions the President put me; and my answers to them:

"Do you promise to live your whole life long in libertinage of the very extremest order?"

"I swear it."

"Do you esteem all lewd acts, whatever they be and including the most odious, to be simple and natural?"

"They are all as one to me, thus do I consider them."

"Would you commit each and every one of them if moved by the slightest desire?"

"I would indeed. All of them."

"Do you declare your intention to adhere strictly to the Sodality's statutes as they have been read out to you by your sponsor?"

"I do."

"And are you prepared to accept the penalties prescribed therein should you prove refractory?"

"I am."

"Swear it."

"I swear."

"Are you married?"

"No."

"Are you a maid?"

"No."

"Have you been embuggered?"

"Often."

"Fucked mouthwise?"

"Often."

"Whipped?"

"Upon occasion."

"What is your name?"

"Juliette."

"Your age?"

"I am eighteen."

"Have you been frigged by women?"

"Many times."

"Have you committed crimes?"

"A few."

"Stolen?"

"Yes."

"Attempted the life of a human being?"

"Aye, I have."

"Do you promise never to swerve from the path you have followed until now?"

"I do swear it."

Here a new burst of applause.

"Will you bring into the Sodality all those related to you by bonds of kinship?"

"I shall."

"Do you agree never to reveal the secrets of the Sodality?"

"I shall never reveal them, I swear it."

"Do you promise to exhibit the completest indulgence toward all the caprices and all the lewd whims of all Sodality members?"

"I promise it."

"Whom do you prefer, men or women?"

"Where friggery is concerned, I am very fond of women; where fucking, I have a passion for men."

My naïveté brought forth a wave of laughter from the corporation.

"What think you of the lash?"

"I like to use it and to have it used upon me."

"Of the two pleasures a woman can procure, which do you prefer, cunt-fucking or sodomy?"

"It has befallen me to disappoint the man who encunted me, but never him by whom I was bum-fucked."

This reply was much appreciated also.

"And your attitude toward oral pleasures?"

"I adore them."

"Do you like to have your cunt licked?"

"Infinitely."

"And do you lick well the cunts of others?"

"With industry and enjoyment and, I have been told, with art."

"It may then be presumed that you enjoy sucking pricks?"

"Draining them."

"You swallow?"

"I gorge myself."

"Have you had offspring?"

"No, none."

"Do you intend to refrain from having them?"

"I shall do everything in my power to avoid them."

"You therefore dislike progeniture?"

"I detest it."

"Were you perchance to become pregnant, would you have the courage to abort?"

"Certainly."

"Has your sponsor with her the sum constituting your entrance fee?"

"Yes."

"Are you wealthy?"

"Exceedingly."

"And have you ever devoted any of your money to charity?"

"Of course not."

"Nor have you ever performed a religious gesture since childhood?"

"Not to my knowledge."

Clairwil handed the fee over to the Executive Secretary from whom in return she received a small brochure; I was instructed to read it aloud. This printed document was headed by the title *Instructions to Women Admitted into the Sodality of the Friends of Crime.*

From a drawer Madame de Lorsange took an envelope, opened it. "I have kept the paper," said she, "for it is interesting. Listen to its contents:"[2]

The estate or condition into which was born she who is to sign this matters not in the least, she is a woman, and as such created for the pleasures of man. It were hence seeming to prescribe to her a mode of comportment which would enable her to make the rendering of her services advantageous to her purse and agreeable to her fleshly needs. We shall suppose her married. For those who, though

---

[2] You voluptuous women, you philosophically-minded women who deign to read us, it is once again to you this is addressed: profit herefrom, let them not be for nought, our efforts to enlighten you. Never will true pleasure be known to you unless you accept wholly and blindly these excellent suggestions; and certain you may be that in making them we are interested solely in your happiness.

unmarried, live nevertheless with a man, whether as his mistress or as his whore, are bound by the very same chains as those who exist in wedlock's irons, and they will be able to employ the following recommendations to similar purpose, that is, the escaping from those chains or the lightening of them; wherefore note will be taken that the word *man* as used here generically means lover, husband, or keeper, or in fine any individual arrogating to himself rights to a woman whatever her sort, because, be she in possession of millions, yet she must still earn money from her body, the first law for all women being never to fuck save through libertinage or for the sake of gain; and as she is often obliged to pay those who please her, she must accumulate the necessary reserves therefor, by means of her prostitutions to those others who do not please her; it being fully understood that all that follows concerns her behavior in society only, the Statutes she having just sworn to observe and uphold fixing her behavior within the confines of the Sodality.

1. To attain to the apathy that must be preserved, she will, regardless of whether it be for money she fucks or for pleasure, take constant care to keep her heart inaccessible to love; for if she fucks for pleasure, she'll obtain little if in love, love being the veritable and certain kiss of death to enjoyment: her inevitable concern to give pleasure to her lover will prevent her from tasting any herself; and if she fucks for money, if in love she will never dare squeeze it from her beloved; which, however, ought to be her unique object and occupation with the man who pays her.

2. Eschewing all metaphysical sentiments, she will always therefore accord preference to him who, if it be for pleasure she fucks, erects quickest and most sizably, has the prettiest prick, or the hardest; and if it be for gain she fucks, to him who fees her most amply.

3. She must scrupulously and at all times avoid such personages as are called fops, idle fellows, dancing masters, and the like, that dronish breed pays as poorly as it fucks; let her resort rather to valets, stableboys, porters, drudges, butchers, such are the breeches energy inhabits, such souls keep secrets safe; menials are plentiful, moreover, they can be changed like skirts, and with never a moment's fear of an indiscretion.

4. Whatever be the man into whose clutches she falls, let her take care not to consider his proprietorship exclusive; fidelity, an infantile habit and romantic sentiment, can bring about nothing but the downfall of a woman, can be nothing but the cause of woes without end, and never the source of a single pleasure; and indeed, why should she be faithful, since, and she may be very sure of it, in all the world there is no such thing as a faithful man? It is ridiculous, is it not, that the more fragile, the weaker sex, the one forever open to every enticement into every pleasure, the one whose surrender thereto is authorized by daily and manifold seductions—absurd, is it not, that it should be this sex that resists temptation while the other has as means for evil-doing nothing but his unaided solitary wickedness! And more, what's the use to a woman of her fidelity? If her man loves her truly, he must be of sufficient delicacy to tolerate all her failings, and even to share vicariously in the delights she procures herself and to rejoice therein; if he loves her not, a silly creature she, who would be bound utterly to someone who deceives her day in and day out; woman's infidelities, faults if you wish, are natural, those of a man proceed from his duplicity and his viciousness; the species of woman we have in mind, that is, a healthy and intelligent woman, will hence spurn no occasion to be unfaithful, rather she will seek such occasions and exploit them as often as possible, and to the full.

5. Deceit is a characteristic no woman can forego, it has ever been the weapon of the weak; always confronted by her superior, how shall she withstand oppression unless she have frequent recourse to lies and imposture? Therefore, let her fearlessly use these arms, Nature furnished them to her in order that she have some defense against her enemies; men wish to be dupes, an agreeable illusion is easier for them to swallow than a bitter reality; and so ought she not disguise her wrongs instead of proclaiming them?

6. A woman should never appear to have a character of her own, she must, artfully, borrow that belonging to this or that person whom it is to her greatest interest to flatter at the moment, whether it be for the sake of her lust or her greed; seeing to it nevertheless that this flexibility does not deprive her of the energy essential for plunging into all such sorts of misdemeanors and crimes as are

pleasing to her passions or apt to serve them, examples being adultery, incest, infanticide, poisonings, robbery, murder, all those, in fine, which may be to her liking and which, behind the mask of deceit and the treachery we recommend to her, she may undertake without fear, pause, or regret, because Nature placed these impulses in woman's heart and only false principles acquired along with education prevent her from acting in accordance with them every day, as she ought to do.

7. Far from alarming her, let the most extensive, the most sustained, the most crapulous libertinage become the basis of her most cherished occupations; if she lends an ear to Nature, she will discover that from her she has received very pronounced leanings, very violent ones, toward this sort of pleasure, and there being no grounds here for fear and fewer yet for restraint, she ought to indulge herself therein constantly: the more she fucks, the better she answers Nature's expectations of her. Nature is not to be outraged save by continence.[3]

8. Whatever the act of debauchery her man may propose to her, let her never balk; readiness and good will are her surest means for maintaining a hold over him she wishes to keep. A man soon wearies of a woman's favors; what happens if she lacks the ability to revive his interest? He ceases to care for her, begins next to loathe her, and abandons her shortly afterward; but he who remarks a woman devoted to the study of his tastes, to anticipating his desires, to kindling and to satisfying them; ah! that man, finding the woman in his possession always new, is much more apt to settle down to contenting himself with her; the woman is now in a position to deceive him, and deceiving her man is the fondest and the most unrelentingly pursued objective of the individual belonging to the sex whose duties we are sketching here.

9. Let this charming individual very assiduously avoid an air of prudishness and of modesty when she is with her man; few indeed they are who appreciate such posings, and great is the risk of promptly alienating those who are repelled by them. Let her simulate them in public, if she deems this imposture necessary,

---

[3] Almost all chaste women die young, or go mad, or become sickly and wither early away. Furthermore, they are all ill-natured, testy, forward, and rude; they are unbearable in society.

anything in the direction of hypocrisy is to be recommended: it is one further means to deceit, and she should neglect none of them.

10. She cannot be too strongly urged to avoid pregnancies, either by making extensive use of those various manners of fucking which deflect the seed away from the vessel where conception occurs, or by destroying the foetus once she suspects its existence. Pregnancy is telltale, spoils the figure, endangers the health, is bad from every point of view; let her indulge, preferably, in antiphysical pleasure, this delicious form of it assures her simultaneously greater enjoyment and greater safety, nearly all women who have tried it will have no other; the thought, moreover, of the enormously increased pleasure they thus give men ought surely, and here we consider their *amour-propre* alone, to spur them to adopt it exclusively.

11. Let a very hardened heart be her protection against a sensibility which is certain to be her undoing; a woman susceptible of sympathies must expect nothing but the worst, for weaker, more delicate, thinner-skinned than men, she will be rent much more cruelly by all that assails this sensibility; whereupon she may bid all pleasure farewell. Her complexion moves her to lust; if, owing to this excess of sensibility we are seeking to destroy, she enslaves herself to one man only, as of that moment she deprives herself of all the charms of libertinage, the libertinage which, in view of the way Nature has constructed her, alone befits her, can alone render her truly happy.

12. Let her meticulously avoid any practice of religion; these infamies which she ought long ago to have spat upon can only, as they affright her conscience, recall her to a state of virtue she shall not re-enter without being forced to renounce all her habits and all her pleasures; those frightful platitudes are not worth the sacrifice they demand; and like the dog in the fable, she will as she chases after them relinquish the reality for the appearance. Atheistic, cruel, impious, libertine, wanton, insatiable, a sodomite, a tribade, incestuous, vindictive, bloodthirsty, hypocritical, and false—such by and large is the description of the woman who will find her rightful place in the Sodality of the Friends of Crime, such are the vices she will have need of if she would find happiness within the Sodality.

The spirited reading I delivered of these precepts convinced the assembly I had taken them quite to heart, and amidst claps and hurrahs I stepped down into the press.

The couples distracted from their proceedings by the rites of my admission now fell back to their merrymaking, and I was soon under assault; at this point I lost view of Clairwil and was not to see her again until supper.

First to hail me was a gentleman of fifty.

"By Jesus, I'm blind if you don't have the look of a whore," he exclaimed, steering me toward a couch, "and you talk like one, too. I liked your style, slut, it put my prick in the air."

So saying the lecher encunts me. He scrapes away for a quarter of an hour, the while kissing me fervently; then, claimed by a woman who plucks him straight off my belly, he deserts me without having discharged. It's next a lady in her sixties who approaches and, thrusting me back upon the couch before I can rise, she frigs me and has me frig her at great length. Three or four men have been watching us; one of them suddenly moves in and embuggers the matron, who lets forth a screech of pleasure. Another of the men, noticing I had been entering into a sweat beneath the old Lesbian's fingerings, had offered me his prick to suck; and now that the woman leaves off toying with me, the rascal glides from my mouth to my cunt; he had the prettiest prick in the world and wielded it like a god; a girl steals it away from me and stows it impetuously into her slit; my rival nods to me, I answer the summons and she sets to cunt-licking me: she got his fuck from the man whom I'd hoped to drain, and by and by she got mine too. A pair of youths sauntered up and joining us formed the most pleasant group, encunting us both; my companion went off with the lad who had just served her, leaving me alone for a moment. Here now was a personage I recognized as a bishop for whom I had toiled in the past when with Madame Duvergier; he encunts me also, after having me piss on his face. The next to come, and this ecclesiastic was also a familiar face, popped his member into my mouth and let fly therein. A very engaging young thing arrives to have herself frigged, I suck her with all my heart; her heaving flanks are caught firmly in midflight by a man of about forty, who bum-stuffs her; it is not long before the libertine has done the same to me, while tupping he reviled us most energetically, calling us nuns, cunt-suckers, and as he sodomized the one he spanked the behind of the other.

"What are you doing to these two buggeresses?" asked a well-made young man who strode up then and socratized him on the spot; "take that, villain," he went on, "it's not woman-ass that will cure what ails you."

Once again I was left to myself and was recovering my breath when an elderly man presented himself, he had a fistful of withes and meant to warm my hind parts therewith and to have me warm his prick.

"You're the one they admitted tonight, are you not?" he began.

"I am."

"A pity I haven't come across you until now," said he, "I have been busy in a seraglio. You've got a damned pretty ass, bend over, let me get into it."

And he stormed triumphantly through the gate, I got his fuck. A delightful young man appeared and dealt with me in the same way, though he lashed me far more stoutly; next, one after the other, a procession of ten persons, six of them men of the law and four men of God; they all fucked me bumwise. I was quite afire, I repaired to a public convenience: as women were using only those where men were in attendance, it was a lad who, after settling me upon the throne and helping me off again, asked if he could lend me his tongue. By way of reply I thrust my ass at his nose, and so pleasantly did he clean it that fuck escaped me. Returning to the assembly hall I remarked some men waiting about, apparently to waylay women emerging from the privies; and indeed one of them steps up and asks leave to kiss my ass, I wheel it about, his tongue probes a moment, he straightens up, and from his sorrowful ex-pression I divine his disappointment at finding the cupboard so bare. It is without a word he hastens away from me to join a youth just then entering the same privy; and I profit from a brief respite to survey the scene. Believe me when I say that there, in that spacious room, the over-all spectacle was one such as distanced anything the most lascivious imagination could possibly conceive in the course of threescore years: what a wealth of voluptuous attitudes! how many curious doings, what a variety of tastes and preferences!

Oh, great God, I murmured, how wondrous indeed is Nature, how splendid, and how delicious are these, all the passions she gives us.

But everywhere my eye roved, it was to be amazed at the same extraordinary state of affairs: save for the utterances incidental to the action, sometimes shrill exclamations of pleasure, and much blasphemy, sometimes loud, there was no other sound, one could have heard a pin drop. Over all that was astir the most entire order reigned; were some altercations to arise, and it happened very rarely, a gesture from the President or the Censor restored peace and quiet in a trice; the most decent activities could not have transpired amidst greater calm. And thus I was made quickly to realize that, of all the things there are in the world, the passions are those that command the greatest respect from human beings.

Men and women in ever growing numbers were beginning to remove to the seraglios; tickets were being distributed by the President, a smile upon her lips. I was now had at by several women; then by several more; I frigged with no fewer than thirty-two of them, a good half of whom were past forty: they sucked me, fucked me frontwise and behind with dildoes, one had me piss into her gullet while I lapped her cunt, another suggested we shit on each other's bubs, she larded mine generously, I was unable to repay her in kind, unfortunately; while a man labored in his ass-hole, a second man gobbled up the excrement steaming on my chest; and after that he shat there in turn, as he did so discharging into the mouth of him by whom he had just been sodomized.

The President developed a sudden craving for me; she appointed a man to relieve her at her post, and we came to grips: kissed each other, tongued each other, sucked and caressed each other nigh to death. With the exception of Clairwil, never had I seen a woman discharge so abundantly nor so lewdly; her favorite stunt was to receive a bum-fucking the while, her cunt crushed upon a woman's face, that woman sucked her and she herself cunt-sucked another woman: we went brilliantly through this exercise, and the whore resumed her chair.

Back came the men, in force: among this second wave I found

few encunters but buggers aplenty, an occasional masturbater, and a dozen or so mouth-fuckers; one of the latter had himself pumped by a youth while snuffling under my armpits, licking them softly ever and anon, which procured me a very pleasant sensation. I was given five or six floggings; three or four rectal injections, which I flushed into the mouths of those who had administered them; I was got to fart, there were bidders for my spittle; I spent thirty whole minutes sticking thousands of pins into one squire's buttocks and balls, and thus bestudded did he keep himself for the rest of the evening; the mania of another was to run his tongue over a woman's body, he was two hours lapping my eyes and mouth and ears and nostrils and between my toes, and finally inserted his tongue in my asshole, and discharged. Several women insisted upon fucking me with great, massive dildoes; one led up a man and had me heat his prick by chafing it upon her asshole, and next required me to push the fuck into it with the tip of my finger; a dear little creature utterly besmeared my buttocks with her shit, behind her stood a middle-aged man, he embuggered her while eating the mard clean off my ass; I was informed they were father and daughter. There were other such couples; I beheld brothers embuggering their sisters; fathers encunting their daughters; mothers fucked by their children; in a word, every possible scene of incest, of adultery, of sodomy, of lechery, of whoring, of foulness, of impiety, each under a hundred various forms and a hundred various colors took place before my eyes, and surely at no bacchanal of old was there ever such a concurrence of so much nastiness and so much infamy.

Weary of the victim's part, I was eager to play an active role in my turn: I intercepted half a dozen young men whose pricks attracted me for size, and who now in this sector, now in that, and sometimes in both at once, fucked me steadily for nearly two hours. At the close of that episode a venerable abbot had himself frigged on my clitoris by his niece, a ravishing creature; I sucked her cunt; and a handsome young fellow must kiss my behind while he embuggered his mother. Two pretty sisters got me between them, one frigged my cunt as the other fluttered about my ass; I discharged, quite unaware that their papa was all that time encunting them alternately. Another father had me embuggered by his son and in the meantime enjoyed the boy in the same manner; and subsequently sodomized me himself while enduring at the hands of his son precisely what he had done to him shortly before. A brother encunted me, his sister—a nun—simultaneously buried her cross in his ass. . . . And all these supposed outrages to Nature went forward amidst a serenity and with an orderliness such as might give a moralist pause, and perhaps turn him into a philosopher. For indeed, if one but reflects a little, one finds nothing odd in incest; Nature allows it, encourages it; only local legislation outlaws it; but may something tolerated in three-quarters of the world be truly a crime in the other fourth? Here was an enviable act I had not the wherewithal to commit, and the thought saddened me; ah, what would I not have given to have had a father or a brother, and how ardently I would have surrendered myself to the one or the other . . . entreated him to do with me all he wished. . . .

Soon I was surrounded by other objects; two pretty sisters of eighteen—they were twins—led me off to a privy and bolted the door; upon them I executed everything of the most piquant and the most disgusting lewdness can suggest.

"Were we to attempt to amuse ourselves this way in the assembly hall," they explained to me, "twenty of those dreadful men would soon be clustered around us squirting their horrid sperm left and right; it's ever so much nicer to have a little privacy, don't you agree?"

Whereupon the little minxes confessed their tastes to me. Fastidious votaresses of their own sex, they found men unbearable even to their sight; it was their father who had drawn them into the Sodality, though distressed at having to submit to men, they found compensation in being able to have their fill of women.

"I take it then that you have no intention of marrying?"

"Marrying! Never. Death would be a kinder fate than that of becoming slaves to husbands."

As I plied them with questions, they revealed to me the rest of their principles, uncommonly firm for persons of their age; brought up philosophically by their father, they were pure of any taint of morals or religion, all that had been skillfully weeded out of them; there was nothing they'd not done, nothing they weren't ready to do again, and their energy amazed me; such characters sorted too nicely with mine for me to keep from expressing my feelings, I overwhelmed those delightful girls with caresses; and after we had all three loosed very floods of fuck, we promised to remain in touch, and started back to the hall. A slender young man, noticing me emerge in their company, now came up to me; in an anxious undertone he requested a brief interview, and in his company I retraced my steps into the privy I had only just left.

"Great heaven!" said he the moment we were alone, "how I shuddered to see you with those two creatures! Beware of them, I tell you, be on your guard, they are monsters—monsters who, despite their youth, are capable of every conceivable horror—"

"But," I put in, "is it not thus one ought to be?"

He stared at me. "To be sure," he nodded; "but in one's relations with members one ought to be kindly, respectful, affectionate. Outside, why, steep your sword in blood. Of course. But not here. Believe me when I say those two bitches take pleasure only in doing mischief to their brothers; wicked, cunning, treacherous, they have every trait needed for expulsion from the Sodality, I cannot understand why the Permanent Committee does not act. Why, my dear, they amuse themselves with somebody and that's enough, from then on their one aim is to destroy you or to enslave you if they can. Be grateful to me for having warned you, and thank me by turning your ass this way."

I supposed he was going to fuck it. Not at all. This odd fellow limited himself to plucking out the hairs around my asshole, and to licking it; to my protest that he was hurting me he replied that owing to his warning I would be spared far worse. After fifteen more minutes of this vexatious business we left the privy, although my young man had not ejaculated. We parted; and shortly after I learned that everything he had said about the two sisters was utterly untrue, that calumniating others aroused him, and that, so he reckoned, her profound indebtedness to him would lead any woman to endure the treatment he subjected her to.

Sweet music was now to be heard; it was supper being announced, and I went with the others into the voluptuous dining hall. It was decorated so as to appear a forest; between the trees were countless little glades within each of which was a table set for twelve. Garlands of flowers hung in festoons from the trees, thousands and thousands of candles, disposed as skillfully as in the assembly hall, shed a soft light; two servants delegated to each table served it promptly, cleverly, and in silence. Scarcely two hundred persons were present, the rest were all in the seraglios. You chose the table you wished and there, among friends, splendidly regaled, to the sound of enchanting chamber music you gave yourself up simultaneously to the intemperances of Comus and to all the lewd riotings of Cypris.

Clairwil, back from the seraglio, had sat down next to me; her manifest agitation betokened recent excessive behavior: the hard glitter in her eyes, her flushed cheeks, her unloosened hair floating over her breasts, the obscene, ferocious language coming from her mouth, in everything there were reflections and echoes of the transport which made her a hundred times lovelier to see; I bent toward her and we kissed.

"Villain," said I, "what ocean of horrors have you been swimming in?"

"Be not envious," she returned, "when next I plunge back into them, and it will be soon, you will be at my side."

The two little sisters with whom I'd been afrigging earlier in the day, two women of forty and of wit, two other exceedingly attractive ones of twenty and twenty-five, and six men made up our table.

Owing to the studied placing of the glades there was not one table from which you could not see all the others; and the cynical spirit in which the whole thing had been framed was also evident in the fact that no lubricity here in the dining room would be any less visible to the observer's eye than had been that in the assembly hall.

By virtue of these arrangements I was witness to some unusual sights; there is no describing the reeling of a vicious brain at such times. I had thought myself thoroughly versed in libertinage, thought I had nothing further to learn; and that evening I was convinced I was yet a callow fledgling. Oh, my friends, what impurities, what abominations, what extravagances! Some of the celebrants were constantly leaving table and repairing to the latrines, and it was impossible to refuse to do their bidding; the desires of Sodality members were laws for the individuals they focused upon. The latter soon found opportunity to demand of others what had been demanded of them; wherever you glanced, it was masters and slaves you saw; and the slaves, steadied by the knowledge that the roles would be reversed shortly, complied unhesitatingly with orders it would be their turn to issue in a moment.

Raised upon a throne from which she could oversee everything, the President maintained order at the supper as before in the hall; and the same calm prevailed. Conversations were held in a subdued tone; one could easily imagine oneself in the temple of Venus, whose statue, moreover, was visible inside a bower of myrtle and roses, and the foregathered worshipers, one perceived, tastefully avoided disturbing their rites by any of those rude vociferations which are proper only to pedantry and stupidity.

Rare wines and succulent viands made the after-supper orgies even more luxurious than the preceding ones. There was a moment when the entire Sodality united in a single immense group; not a member was inactive, and nothing could be heard but a deep murmur of voluptuous moans accented by the gasps and shrill cries heralding discharges. I had further assaults, terrible assaults, to sustain, individuals of every sex passed through my hands, not a spot on my body was left unsullied; and if I ended up with fearfully battered buttocks, mine also was the glory of having wreaked havoc upon innumerable others. Day dawned at last and I came away so whelmed by fatigue, so dry from delicious exertion that I had to keep to my bed for a day and a half.

My month-long novitiate seemed an eternity; it came finally to a close, and mine now was the so hotly coveted right to penetrate into the seraglios. Clairwil, eager to acquaint me with everything, guided me everywhere.

Nothing could be as delicious as those seraglios. And that holding boys being identical to that offering girls, the description of one will give you as well a picture of the other.

Four large rooms ringed by bedchambers and cells formed the interior of each of these isolated wings; the large rooms were for the use of those who wished to enjoy themselves publicly, the cells for those who preferred privacy in their pleasure; and the inmates were lodged in the chambers. Taste and art presided over the furnishing; the cells especially were of the highest elegance, so many little chapels consecrated to libertinage, where nothing lacked that might be instrumental to stimulating worship. Four duennas governed each seraglio; they took the tickets you brought with you, inquired of your desires, and saw speedily to their satisfaction; also on hand, ready to offer their services, were a surgeon, a midwife, two fustigators, an executioner, and a jailer, all of prodigiously melancholy aspect.

"You are not to think," Clairwil remarked to me, "that those individuals there have simply been picked at random from the class that ordinarily supplies them; they are libertines like us, but less prosperous: unable to pay the admission fee, they fulfill their functions out of pleasure and just as you would suppose, the job is done better in this manner. Some of them receive a stipend, others ask only to enjoy a member's privileges, these are granted them.."

While on duty those personages wore awesome costumes: the jailers had on great belts whence hung rings of keys, the fustigators carried about a battery of whips and martinets, and the executioner, swart, bare-armed, fearfully moustached, had a cutlass and a stiletto at his side. Seeing Clairwil enter, the executioner rose from where he was sitting on a stool and greeted her with a kiss.

"Have some work for me today, buggeress?"

"Look here," she answered, "I've brought you a novice. Count upon it, she'll have at least as many chores for you as I."

And the wicked fellow, kissing me as he had done my friend, assured me that he was in every sense at my command. I thanked him, embraced him most warmly, and we resumed our visit of the place.

Each of the four central rooms was reserved for a particular category of passion: in the first, you gave way to simple ones, to, that is to say, all the various forms of masturbation and fuckery. The second room was the theater of fustigations and other irregular passions. The third of cruel proceedings; the fourth of murders. But as an inmate delegated to any one of these rooms might merit imprisonment, the lash, or death, the staff of each included jailers, fustigators, and executioners. Women were admitted into the seraglio of boys and into the other of girls, men likewise could frequent either. Arriving, we found all the inmates being employed or else

in their chambers waiting to be put to use. Clairwil opened a few
doors and showed me some truly heavenly creatures; they were in
gauze shifts, had flowers in their hair, and welcomed us with an
air of profoundest reverence. I fell to toying with a lovely thing of
sixteen; I was already handling her breasts and cunt when Clairwil
scolded me for the delicate and unduly decent manner I was
employing.

"That's not the way you behave with this trash," said she,
"they don't even deserve the honor of being selected for our consumption. . . . Command, they obey."

I altered my tone at once, and my orders were responded to
with blindest obedience and inspiring alacrity. We entered other
chambers: the same charms everywhere, the same beauty, everywhere the same submissiveness.

"You know," I confided to Clairwil, "we really must not go
away without leaving our mark."

The thought occurring to me while we were in a chamber
occupied by a thirteen-year-old girl, pretty as Love herself, by
whom for better than a quarter of an hour I'd been having my
cunt and asshole tongued, I immediately chose her for my victim;
we summoned a fustigator; a duenna led the child off to one of the
torture chambers; and there, having roped her fast, we bade the
specialist perform upon the little miss and frigged each other
while the blood streamed down her body. Clairwil, perceiving the
fustigator to stiffen, developed his erection and snapped his device
into her cunt while, at that libertine's request, I bestowed upon him
what he had just meted out to our young victim; the scoundrel
withdrew from Clairwil in order to stuff me, and then we returned
to whipping the little girl, who when we were finished with her was
in such a sorry state as to have to be conveyed to the hospital the
following day. We removed to the seraglio of males.

"What have you a mind to do here?" Clairwil wished to
know.

"Get my hands on a lot of engines," was my reply; "I like
nothing so much as to squeeze a prick, for me it is a delicious
activity, the gathering of human fuck. I love to glean it, harvest it,
to see sperm spurt, to feel myself wet by it, to wade and bathe in
it—"

"Well, go ahead then," said my friend, "do as you like; for my part I require a stronger diet. May I make a suggestion? It's an arrangement I sometimes come to with a lady of my acquaintance: as I dislike having pricks unload in my body, I can nevertheless warm them in my cunt and, when they are hot, turn them over to you; which will spare you the bother of tedious preliminaries."

"Excellent."

We installed ourselves in the first of the main rooms and were sent fifteen lads aged between eighteen and twenty; we ranged them in a line in front of us and then sprawled on couches; then by way of defiance Clairwil and I struck the lewdest possible attitudes. The most poorly endowed of those boys had a mechanism measuring seven inches long by five in circumference, and the best, twelve by eight; one by one they moved forward, roused by the ardor we kindled in them; Clairwil met each, dallied a little with it, then shunted it on to me; I made them flow over my breasts, between my thighs, my buttocks, on my neck and face; reaching for the sixth, I felt such a furious itch in the neighborhood of my anus that from then on I presented my behind to everything which emerged from Clairwil's vagina: they filled out in her cunt and emptied in my ass; the tempo quickened, they redoubled their efforts, but one's hunger, so to speak, grows from eating, there is nothing quite like a woman's temperament when excited, it is a sort of volcano you only further inflame in your attempts to appease it. We called for more men; a fresh batch of eighteen arrived; for this second round we changed roles; these pricks, and they compared very favorably with the fifteen we had just exhausted, caught fire in my cunt and died out in the ass of my companion; but we divided the task of frigging; and more than once it befell that, the order we had established upset by the excessiveness of our desires, we found ourselves with six or seven either in us or exploding all around us.

When finally we got to our feet, spattered with fuck and puddles of it on the couches, like Messalina rising from the bench after her lewd bouts with idiot Claudius' guards, we had each been tupped eighty-five times apiece.

"My bum itches," Clairwil declared. "Whenever I've been grandly fucked I always feel an incredible need of whipping."

I admitted to the same longing.

"We had better send for a pair of fustigators."

"Let's have four," said I, "my ass has simply got to be made a hash of this evening."

"Wait," said Clairwil, nodding familiarly to a man who entered just then, "we can perhaps make something dramatic out of it."

She went over to the newcomer and conferred with him in an undertone; he smiled, adopted a threatening air, called to the fustigators. "Seize them," he cried; we were seized, our hands were tied, and we were both beaten while this man looked on, palpating his engine and fondling the buttocks of our assailants; when once the blood was fairly flowing down our backs we presented cunts to our tormentors who, monstrously pricked, fucked each of us twice.

"And now by way of reward for my cooperation," said the master of ceremonies, "I merely ask you to hold one of these lusty fellows while I give his bum a taste of meat."

We comply with his request, he sheathes his weapon; the others flog him while he ass-fucks; and we, in seventh heaven, suckle the whippers' pricks.

"I cannot stand it any longer," said Clairwil, when we found ourselves alone; "libertinage leads me fatally to cruelties: let us immolate a victim. . . . Did you notice that pretty lad of eighteen who kissed me so feelingly? He was as sweet as an angel to behold and gave me all sorts of ideas. Into the torture room with him, I say, we'll cut the little dog's throat."

"Fie, Clairwil!" said I. "Why didn't you propose something like that when we were in the female seraglio?"

"It's simply that I prefer to butcher males, I've never pretended otherwise: I enjoy avenging my sex. And if it be true that the other possesses a superiority over ours, is not the fictitious offense to Nature all the graver when we kill men?"

"One would suppose that you regret that this offense is null."

"You grasp me aright, my dove, for me it is a source of immense despair ever to seek the crime and nowhere to find anything but the prejudice instead. O fuck! by God's envenoming fuck, when," she sighed, "oh, when shall I be able to do an authentic evil?"

They fetched us the youth.

"Shall we need an executioner?"

"Don't you think we can dispatch the thing well enough by ourselves?"

"Why, I believe we can try."

"Let us."

We had our victim installed in an adjoining cell where there awaited us everything needed for the piecemeal destruction of the young man; his agony was slow, it was ghastly, the infernal Clairwil drank of his blood and swallowed one of his testicles. Less given to these masculine murders than she, my transports were probably not so violent; killing a woman, at any rate, would have excited me more; be that as it may, I discharged copiously; and, quitting that seraglio, we directed our steps toward the other.

"Let's go to the room where extraordinary things are accomplished," I proposed. "If you don't care to do anything, there is no reason why we must; but we shall be able to watch."

A man in his forties, he was a priest, had a pretty little girl of fifteen hanging by her hair from the ceiling; he was stabbing her with a long needle, blood covered the floor, he embuggered Clairwil while gnawing my ass. Another was plying a whip over the breasts and face of a beautiful girl of twenty: he confined himself to inquiring, would we like to have the same done to us? It was by one ankle the third had suspended his victim, most ingeniously, we agreed, and laughed merrily at the sight: she looked to be about eighteen and superbly made; the position she was in caused her cunt to start wide open, into it the villain was ramming a wooden member studded with nails. Noticing our presence, he invited Clairwil to hold the girl's free leg and to pull on it so as to open her cunt farther still, and he had me kneel beside him, ordering me to rub his prick with one hand, to massage his asshole with the other: it was not long before Clairwil and I were drenched in the blood gushing from the victim. The fourth person in action was an elderly magistrate; upon a grill he had chained a delicious twelve-year-old and by means of a huge charcoal brazier, which the scoundrel now approached and now drew away, he was roasting her by inches; I leave you to imagine what were the screams the poor little soul would give vent to whenever her tormentor saw fit to resume the cooking of her flesh. When he saw us, he shoved the stove into place and asked for my ass: I present it, while he drives into it he mauls Clairwil's; but he discharges, 'tis prematurely and a calamity: the torture is interrupted while there is yet an hour or so of life in the victim, the villain's joy is cut short, he curses us for having come along and spoiled everything for him.

All this had put me in a sanguine mood, I insisted upon proceeding to the murder room; Clairwil was nothing loath to follow me: although she was not fond of killing women, neither was she opposed to their destruction, her native tigerishness leading her to accept whatever flattered her tastes.

I had twenty girls stood in line and from among them selected one of seventeen, she was as engaging a creature as any you have ever seen. A vacant cell was designated to me by the duenna, and in the three of us went.

The wretch I was about to sacrifice, fancying I would be sooner moved to pity than a man, cast herself at my feet in a ludicrous effort to sway me: a very angel for beauty and full of grace, her methods would certainly have succeeded with a less toughened adversary, with someone whose soul was less corrupt than mine. I had developed beyond the point where pleas are heard. Rather, the only effect her wiles had upon me was to fan the flames of my irritation. . . . And indeed, even had it not been so, would I have dared relent in Clairwil's presence? After having this lovely girl suck me two hours straight, after having slapped, buffeted, beaten, and thwacked her, after having maltreated her in every conceivable way, I had her bound upon a table, and drove a dagger again and again into her body while my friend, squatting over me, simultaneously titillated my clitoris, the interior of my vagina, and my asshole. Rarely had I enjoyed a happier discharge, I literally discharged myself dry; and afterward was so exhausted I felt it would be useless to return to the assembly hall. Instead, I invited Clairwil to come home with me; we supped and then retired to bed together. It was then that charming personage, inclining to the belief I had lacked somewhat of determination in my latest performance, decided she had best speak to me, and this is what she said.

"The truth, Juliette, is that, a certain undeniable progress notwithstanding, your conscience has yet to reach the stage I should desire; what I demand of it is that it become so warped as to be unable to reassume its former shape; to achieve this there are means to employ; I don't mind indicating what they are, but I am not so sure you have the strength to apply them. Those means, my dearest friend, are simple in themselves: they consist in doing, immediately, in cold blood, that very thing which, done in the throes of passion, has been able to cause you remorse when later on you recover your wits. This way you strike squarely and hard at the virtuous impulse the instant it bares itself; and this custom of attacking it head on at the first sign of its reappearance, and it tends to reappear once the senses have subsided into calm, this, I say, is one of the most certain fashions of destroying it definitively; employ this secret, it never fails: directly a moment of calm favors the resurgence of virtue, announcing itself under the colors of remorse, for that is always the guise it wears in its endeavor to regain ascendancy over us—then, directly when you perceive it, commit forthwith the act you are wont to regret; by the fourth repetition of the trick you shall hear the nagging voice of conscience no more, and you shall be at peace for the rest of your days. But this is no trifling matter, it calls for strength, discipline, and a certain ruthlessness with oneself: it is, you understand, illusion which invests crime with its attractiveness, and a weak spirit encounters greatest difficulty committing it when, totally self-possessed, illusion there is none. The means I propose are valid nonetheless, indeed, I may assure you that virtue itself will safeguard you from remorse, for you shall have acquired the habit of doing evil at the first virtuous prompting; and to cease doing evil you shall have to stifle virtue. Oh, Juliette, be sure of it, this is the best advice you are apt to receive in this important connection; and you realize its worth, since by carrying it out you surmount the most painful of situations, victory being yours whether you choose to combat it by vice or to annihilate it by virtue."

"Clairwil," said I to my friend, "your suggestions are excellent, doubtless, but perhaps unnecessary. I am not without experience in the profession of vice, and the soul in me requires no fortification. Neither does my purpose. Rest assured, you shall never see me falter whatever the deed to be perpetrated whether for the sake of my material advantage or for that of my pleasure."

"Dear heart," said Clairwil, hugging me to her, "I beseech you to have no other gods than those."

Somewhat later, Clairwil called upon me and proposed an unusual exploit. We were in the season of Lent.

"Shall we go and make our devotions?"

"Are you mad?"

"Not at all. I have had a truly extraordinary idea in my head for quite a while, and you are the companion I want to have in this adventure. At the Carmelite convent there's a friar of thirty-five, the most gorgeous creature in the whole wide world and I have had my heart set upon him for the past six months; I simply must be fucked by him, and this is how we shall manage it: we shall go to have him hear our confession, tell him a few tales, lewd ones, he'll become aroused, I am absolutely certain we need do no more to have him make us a proposition: he will explain how we are to get together, we'll go to the rendezvous and we'll drain the holy brother's balls. . . . And more: we'll go to communion after that, we'll hide the hosts one way or another and bring them home; and at lunch we'll find some not very Christian use to which these abject symbols may be put."

Here I felt moved to remark to my friend that of her two schemes, the first struck me as far more sensible than the second.

"Once we have ceased to believe in God, my dear," I pointed out, "the profanations you have in mind become so much pure childishness, the worse for being useless."

"Childishness, yes," she rejoined, "that I cannot deny. But they excite me mentally and for that I value them. Nothing, in my view, is surer proof against backsliding: one cannot accord any seriousness to objects one treats in such a manner. May I add that I suspect doubts may still be warranted of your firmness in these matters?"

"Ah, Clairwil, banish them out of your mind!" I retorted most energetically. "You err. If anything, my atheism is perhaps solider than your own. At any rate, it is not to be bolstered by such nonsense as you have just proposed; I shall join you in these undertakings because they please you, but for me they are mere amusements at best, and in no wise necessary either to the strengthening of my opinions or to their demonstration."

"As you like, my beloved," said Clairwil, "as you like, we shall execute them for pleasure's sake alone."

"Seducing the friar by means of a confession, this is worthy of us; but my stars, Clairwil! profaning a wee bit of a wheatpaste disk which happens to be the idol of imbeciles, why that amounts to no more than tearing up or burning some scrap of paper—"

"To be sure, but to your scrap of paper no meaning is attached, whereas the better part of Europe assigns a very holy significance to that host, to that crucifix, and that exactly is why I am fond of profaning them: I hit at public opinion, that entertains me, I vomit on the prejudices they strove to inculcate in me when I was young, I obliterate them, that excites me."

"Let's be away," said I.

We went by carriage; our simple, artless toilettes conformed wonderfully to our designs, and Brother Claude, whom we asked for and who quickly seated himself in the confessional, could not have taken us for anything but models of piety.

Clairwil opened fire first. It was plain, the poor Friar was listing very heavily when my turn came to loose a broadside.

"Oh, my Father!" I cooed, "grant me much indulgence for I have horrors to divulge to you."

"Courage, my child," stammered Claude, "great is the goodness and mercy of God, He listens to us with infinite understanding; what have you to confess?"

"Enormities, Father, sins which a frightful libertinage makes me commit every day: young though I am, I have violated every commandment, I have ceased, yes, ceased to pray and God has become a stranger to my soul. Oh, intercede in my behalf, very sore is my distress! And my lewd doings . . . ah, you shall tremble when you hear about them, I hardly dare speak—"

"Are you married?"

"Yes, Father, and not a day passes but I outrage my husband by behaving in the very worst way."

"A lover . . . a tendency?"

"An indomitable longing for men in general, and a liking for women too—a fondness for every possible variety of debauchery—"

"You are then, I take it, hot-blooded—"

"Hot-blooded? Insatiable, Father, that's what I am, it's this hunger that is dragging me farther and farther into vice, hurling me so violently into it that I dread I must succumb in spite of all the aid religion can be. . . . Must I avow it, dare I? Oh, Father, at this very moment, the pleasure of holding this secret conversation with you is upsetting me, aye, convulsing me, counteracting the effects of pardon . . . I seek God in this holy place and whom do I find? A charming man beneath his cassock and, woe is me, I sense myself ready to forget the Lord—"

"My daughter," said the poor Friar, his voice shaking now, "the state you are in afflicts me . . . only great penances—"

"Ah, the cruelest for me would be never to see you again. . . . Why is it the ministers of God are as though illuminated by charms that distract from the sole object which ought to occupy us here? My Father, this sanctuary, this interview have not restored me to serenity, instead I . . . I—oh, heavenly man, your words speed to my heart rather than to my mind, I came hither in search of peace, but it is restlessness, excitement that has hold of me: can we not meet elsewhere? Can we not flee this box, it frightens me; and will you not cease a little to be the man of God and take the part of Juliette's lover?"

Claude's erection stamped him as a true Carmelite: the milk-white and rose-tipped breast I'd cunningly brought into view, my sparkling eyes, gestures, and fumblings which pointed to the emotions I was at grips with . . . beside himself, the ecclesiastic capitulated.

"Fair lady," he replied, and his tone was impassioned, "your friend, in a case very like unto your own, has also proposed things, ah . . . which your starry gaze inspires and which I . . . I burn to do, I. . . . You are two sirens, your sweet words bewitch me and I am no longer able to resist—let's leave the church; I have a small room, it is not far from here . . . if you will consent to come, I shall do everything in my power to put you at ease."

Then, stumbling from the confessional and grasping Clairwil by the hand: "Follow me, ladies, come with me, the foul fiend has sent you to tempt me; ah, was he not a match for God Almighty Himself? He must then best a poor friar."

And out we go.

Night had fallen, there was no moon; Claude told us to look sharply after him but to keep twenty paces back. He set off for the Vaugirard Barrier, and we soon found ourselves in a mysterious and chilly cell; the good Claude offered us cakes and liqueurs.

"Excellent sir," my companion said to him, "enough of this mystical chatter; we know the kind of man we are dealing with; we love you, why, what am I saying? we are quaking from a frantic desire to be fucked by you. Join us in laughing at the ruse we employed to get this far, contrive to make us feel our efforts have not been for nought. Speaking for myself, I tell you I have worshiped you for a year and I have been leaking for two hours in anticipation of your prick. There," went on our libertine, tossing up her skirts, "there's where I'd have you lodge it; look, is the cage not fitting for the bird?"

Promptly flinging herself upon the bed, the slut had the fellow's engine out in a trice.

And an uncommon engine it was.

"Christ's tears, will you behold it, Juliette!" cried Clairwil, already half swooning away, "here, catch this mast if you can get your hands round it, and steer it at me; be a dear, I'll do the same for you in a moment."

Clairwil is heeded; the bludgeon thunders into a cunt which, fuck-moistened already, had been yawning a welcome to it for fifteen minutes. Oh, my friends, how justly they refer to a Carmelite when wishing to describe the optimum in erected pricks. Our Claude's member, like unto a mule's, showed nine and three-eighths inches round the stem and thirteen inches in over-all length, head clear and included; and that formidable head, my friends, I was scarce able to encircle it with both hands. 'Twas the noblest, the most rubicund mushroom the human imagination can picture. By a miracle of Nature, a miracle Nature performs only in behalf of her favorites, Claude had been furnished with three balls . . . and how full they were! how swollen! 'Twas he himself declared it, not a drop of sperm had he shed in a month. What torrents thereof he spewed into Clairwil's cunt the moment he touched bottom! and into what transports this enormous ejaculation pitched my voluptuous friend! Fucking her, Claude handled me, and his dextrous manipulation of my clitoris soon wrung the whey from me too. The Friar withdraws; I paw him. Clairwil remains in position. The tool dilates, hardens anew in response to my skillful attentions.[4] Claude, breaking away from the hand guiding him, would dive again into the gaping vagina. . . .

"No, no," says Clairwil, fending off her impetuous lover, "Juliette, make me desire him, lick my clitoris."

And Claude, rather than stand idle during these preliminaries, falls to caressing me; while with one hand he holds Clairwil's cunt agape for me, he masturbates me with the other. Like the fiery steed that will not be restrained by the bridle or bit, Claude leaps into the beckoning hole; and stretching me out beside Clairwil, the rascal, gone quite beserk, while furiously fucking the one of us pollutes the other with equally prodigious effect.

"He's assassinating me, the great swine," shrieks Clairwil, swearing like one of the damned; "ah, by the balls of the bugger-fucking Almighty, I can't resist this buffeting, every blow is costing me a pint of sperm—can you not at least kiss me, pig that you are? can't you stick your filthy tongue as deep into my throat as you've buried that club of yours in my womb? Ah, by fuck, I'm coming—but you, keep yourself in check," she adds, expelling him with a powerful heave of her flanks, "don't squander your resources, I am going to call upon you again."

But poor Claude could not contain himself and prepared to unleash a second emission; seeing what he was up to, I seized his instrument and, stroking it, aimed the boiling flood into Clairwil's

---

[4] That which you enjoy doing you always do well; and the reader ought not to forget Juliette's affirmation, to wit, that her greatest delight consisted in frigging pricks. The statement comes as no surprise, for what else is so voluptuous? To what joys does one not thrill, indeed, at the sight of a handsome member rearing in answer to the lubricious sensations one imparts to it! How flattering to one's pride, how stirring thus to observe one's handiwork take shape! And the exhilaration of this creative activity, especially as the task nears completion; who is there who can refrain from discharging himself upon seeing spring forth those divine spurts of semen? Ah, need one be a woman to taste this pleasure? What man, be he only mildly sensual, is unable to appreciate it? and who, at least once in his life, has not laid an affectionate hand upon some other prick than his own?

wide-starting cunt. It was with fuck I tried to extinguish the fires
fuck ignited.

"Ah, doublefuck my eyes," Clairwil expostulated, getting to
her feet, "this bugger here would fain break me in two. . . . Juliette,
you'll not outlive his attack."

However, she catches hold of the Friar, begins to rattle his
pike; to hasten its elevation, the slut endeavors to mouth him;
but the engine of this servant of God is too massive to fit between
her lips; resorting to another stratagem, she pokes two fingers
into his vent: with the true-born buggers that all friars are, such
means seldom fail. In response to Clairwil's libertine questioning
on this head, Claude allows that, as a youth, he played the bardash
to his confreres.

"Why then, we'll fuck you too," cried Clairwil, bringing
Brother Claude's ass into plainer view, kissing his buttocks and
tonguing his anus. "Yes, we shall sodomize you," she went on,
exhibiting a dildo; "your mistress will turn into your lover. Fuck,
good friend, I am going to embugger you and afterward you'll embugger the two of us if you like; see here," she said, showing
the Carmelite her behind, "isn't this as appealing as the cunt you've
just rioted in? We're whores, you understand, arrant little whores,
we're good for any purpose, and when we go somewhere to be
fucked, it is with the intention of having no part of ourselves left
untouched. To work, great beast, your prick's aloft: fuck this nice
little novice who treated you to such a pretty little confession, encunt her, let that be her penance, and fuck her as hard and as
roundly as you fucked me."

She trundles the awful object toward me, I was lying on the
bed, my thighs widespread, the altar offered itself to the sacrificer; but my thoroughgoing libertinage notwithstanding and however much I was used to accommodating the best pricks in Paris,
I was simply incapable of coping with this one without preparation.
Clairwil takes pity on me; with her saliva she anoints both my
labia and the colossal knob tipping Claude's device; next, with one
hand pressing my buttocks so as to close the gap between the target
and the lance, she managed to bury it to the depth of perhaps an
inch, perhaps two. Enheartened by these auspicious beginnings,
Claude took a firm grip upon my flanks; he swears, he sputters, he

drools, the gates cede, the fortress falls; but his triumph costs me dear, I bleed as never I did the day I lost my maidenhead, and the pain is as great; this soon transforms, however, into the sweetest sensation of pleasure, and to each of my conqueror's lunges I reply with a telling riposte.

"Steady there, steady," cries Clairwil to my rider, "control those thrashings, I cannot take fair aim at your ass unless you hold still, and I promised to fuck it, you recall."

Claude grinds to a halt; Clairwil parts two very fine buttocks: a dildo strapped around her loins, the wench bum-stuffs my fucker. This operation, so precious to a libertine, nay, so indispensable, serves only to increase his agility, he wriggles, he squirms, he sounds, he discharges; I have not time enough to get out of the way; and even had it happened less rapidly, would I have fled to safety? Ah, one is blind to danger when one is drunk from pleasure.

"My turn," said Clairwil, "we shall grant him no quarter. Here you are, bugger, my ass thirsts for the mead, in with you and draw blood if you can—blood? what care I for the loss of a little? Clap on the dildo, Juliette, sodomize him just as I did, and I'll reap the benefits you enjoyed."

Claude, aroused by my caresses, by the prospect of the fair behind Clairwil presents him and of the laughing hole in its center, is not slow to revive; I wet Clairwil's anus with my tongue and oil the holy dart of Christ's well-furnished minion. Unimaginable, the difficulties Claude encounters in penetrating! Twenty times over he quails before the enterprise, twenty times must he resume the assault; but most cunning is my friend, subtle her maneuvers, ardent her desire of that prick, and in the end it is every inch housed and to the hairs in her bowels. . . .

"He's crippling me," she shrieks.

She would escape, she would be rid of the gargantuan glaive run into her vitals. Too late. The fabulous weapon is ensheathed entire and now belongs as intimately to her as to its wielder.

"Ah, Juliette," gasps the hard-pressed Clairwil, "leave this bugger be, he's excited enough as things are at present; I'm in far greater need of your hand than his bum is of your dildo; come frig me, my child, for I am dying."

Despite her pleas, it's to ass-fucking the Friar I devote my main attentions; howbeit, reaching out an arm, I frig my companion; who, thanks to a lively tickling, faces Claude's onslaught with truly admirable courage.

"Truly, I overestimated my capacities," she sighs: "Juliette, do not imitate my brashness, it could well cost you your life."

Claude is discharging by now: his performance, rare hitherto, continues to astonish, the villain bellows and brays, growls and grunts, and far, very far inside Clairwil's bowels, deposits certain proof of the pleasure overwhelming him.

It was a much tattered and torn Clairwil who emerged from the fray; I was bent upon replacing her there.

"I refuse to permit it," said she, adamant. "One must not," she added, "risk one's well-being for an instant's vain pleasure; this is no man we have here, but a bull. I am prepared to wager whatever you like that never before today has he been able to find a woman to fuck."

And Friar Claude nodded in assent. In all Paris, he declared, only his Superior's asshole had succeeded in compassing his prick.

"Eh, how's that? Do you then embugger, wretch?" Clairwil demanded.

"Frequently."

"And thou sayst Mass, thou shrivest, being withal soiled by thy dirty practices?"

"Why not? Amongst men the greatest believer is he who serves the most gods.

"Mesdames," went on the ecclesiastic, seated between us and fondling an ass with each hand, "Mesdames, do you really fancy we set any more store by religion than you do? Dwelling closer to the being it presupposes, we are in a better position than others to perceive the features of the falsehood; religion is all a shoddy fiction, true, but it provides us with a living and the merchant must not disparage his wares. We traffic in absolutions and gods the way a pander sells whores; for all that, are we otherwise fleshed than yourselves, insensible to your passions? and do you think some ridiculous unctions, a few absurd affectations and smirks are sure protection against the stings of human instinct? Far from it. 'The passions,' writes a wise author, 'acquire additional force beneath the frock, the heart harbors those seeds, example brings them to flower, idleness fertilizes them, occasion causes them to multiply— resist the passions? By what possible means?' It is in the ranks of the clergy, my dear ladies, that you find the authentic atheist; doubters you may be, you others, skeptics perhaps, but you cannot even begin to realize the hollowness of the idol; whereas we, its ministers, we to whom its care is entrusted, there's not a one of us who is not convinced of its inexistence. All the revealed religions you come across in the world are full of tenebrous dogmas, unintelligible principles, unbelievable wonders, astounding stories, the whole mumbo jumbo invented, apparently, for the sole purpose of insulting the intelligence and flouting common sense; without exception they all announce an invisible God whose existence is unfathomable. The behavior ascribed to him is as puzzling, as inconceivable, as his very essence; if he existed, would the divinity have spoken in such riddles? what's to be gained from revealing yourself merely to talk nonsense? The greater the freight of mysteries it carries, the less accessible to the comprehension a religion is and the more it pleases the fools who wallow in it as in their element; the more shadowy, obscure, and dubious a religion, the diviner it looks to be, the closer, that is, it conforms to the nature of a hidden and intangible being of whom no clear notion can be formed. 'Tis a characteristic of ignorance to prefer the unknown, the fantastic, the farfetched, the incredible, indeed, the terrible, to whatever is forthright, simple, and true. Truth titillates the imagination far less than fiction; the vulgar ask for nothing better than to listen to the preposterous fables we retail; inventing religions and forging mysteries, priests and lawgivers catered splendidly to the desires of the rabble; by means of creeds and codes they gathered a following of enthusiasts, women, and simpletons; such individuals dispense very easily with proofs they are incapable of examining; love of the simple, love of truth are to be found only amongst those, and they are few, whose imagination is governed by study and by reflection. No, Mesdames, no, be assured of it, there is no God, the existence of that infamous phantom cannot possibly be imagined, and all the contradictions it is composed of suffice to explode it—we need but deign to inspect it closely and poof! it is no more."

During this discussion, the Friar, seated between us, as you know, was palpating our asses.

"Beautiful behind," he murmured, alluding to mine, "what a shame not to be able to thread that strait. . . . But perhaps, if we were to try. . . . Oh, Madame, with a little kindness on your part— for surely, one so fair cannot be so cruel—"

"Brute," said I, rising from my chair, "I'll not even lend you my cunt, it still smarts from what you did to it and I am not eager to subject myself to worse. Catch hold of him, Clairwil, we'll make him discharge till the blood seeps from his balls, otherwise he'll give us no peace."

We laid him upon the bed, Clairwil clamped his member between her breasts and I, squatting over his nose, had him kiss the door to the temple I forbade him to enter; he tongued it timidly at first, then more boldly, and sliding a hand to my bush fell to exercising my clitoris; and once again we discharged.

Clairwil asked the Friar whether there were other such libertines as he in his monastery; upon Claude's affirmation that there were at least thirty, my friend wanted to know if it might be possible to pass an evening amidst the whole brotherhood.

"Certainly," Claude answered, "if ever you wish a memorable fucking you have only to come and you will be treated royally—and to more than you bargain for, I dare say."

Clairwil then asked if the impious revels she had her heart fixed upon could also be held at the monastery.

"Better there than elsewhere," said the Carmelite, "you shall be able to do whatever you like under our roof."

"My dear," Clairwil said, "rather than join you only to be disappointed, pray go and speak to your Superior; explain the matter to him; bring back his response, we shall attend you here."

As soon as the Friar had departed, Clairwil turned to me, a wicked glitter in her eye. "Juliette," said she, "you'll not be surprised to hear it: that fellow fucked me well, too well for me not to desire his death—"

"What! Are you already plotting the wretch's undoing?"

"The loathing I have for men once they have satisfied me is in direct proportion to the pleasure I have had from them, and it's been a great while since I've discharged so exquisitely. . . . He must die, I say. Two means occur to me: that of having him placed *in pace* by his Superior—to arrange this we need merely intimate to that chief the dangers involved in having such a person as Claude at large, a person capable of blathering the secrets of the house to all and sundry. But by proceeding this way he is entirely lost to me; and I have designs on his wondrous engine. . . ."

"But how are these projects to be carried out if you have him put to death?"

"I see no reason why we might not induce him to spend twenty-four hours with us at your country estate; for the rest, never fear. . . . Ah, Juliette, what a dildo hangs under that bugger's belly!"

My friend declining to enlighten me further, while waiting for the Friar we passed the time inspecting his quarters.

It was a mine of obscene engravings and literature that we turned up: the first volume was *Le Portier des Chartreux*,[5] more a bawdy production than a libertine one and which, despite the touching candor and sincerity permeating it, was, according to rumor, disowned by the author as he lay on his deathbed. Bah, what folly. The fellow capable at such a time of repenting what he dared say or write in the course of his life is a rank coward, whose memory ought to be execrated by posterity.

The second was *L'Académie des Dames,* a well-conceived work but poor in the execution; done by a fainthearted man who seems to have scented the truth but was afraid to tell it; and full of boring conversations.

L'Education de Laure was the third book we found. Another complete failure owing to extraneous and false considerations dominating the composition. Had the author brought the wife-murder frankly onto the stage, instead of leaving it off somewhere in the wings, and made something substantial of the incest, which he hints at constantly but never explores; had he increased the number of lewd scenes . . . shown in action those cruel tastes he restricts himself to mentioning, abstractly, in his preface, the work, most imaginative, would have been delicious: but tremblers are my

---

[5] Sometmes ascribed, by his denigrators, to Rétif de la Bretonne.—*Tr.*

despair, I lose all patience with them and would prefer a hundred times over that they write nothing rather than give us bare ideas only, and in halves at that.

Thérèse philosophe was there, a charming performance from the pen of the Marquis d'Argens,[6] alone to have discerned the possibilities of the genre, though only partially realizing them; alone to have achieved happy results from the combining of lust and impiety. These, speedily placed before the public, and in the shape the author had initially conceived them, finally gave us an idea of what an immoral book could be.

The others were all examples of those deplorable little pamphlets commonly got up in coffeehouses or in brothels and which regularly reveal mean-spirited buffoons toiling at the instigation of hunger and under the guidance of some burlesque muse; lust, the child of opulence and of superiority, cannot be treated save by persons of a certain condition, of a certain quality—that is, by persons who, favored by Nature at the outset, have after that benefited from wealth enough to be able themselves to try what they describe in their lewd pages. Well, as we are reminded by their gropings and feebleness of expression, such experience is totally denied the smutty fellows who flood us with the low scribblings I am speaking of, among which I do not hesitate to include those of Mirabeau, who in order to be something would fain be a libertine and who in fact throughout the whole of his life was nothing at all.[7]

Pursuing our search through Claude's belongings, we came upon dildoes, cat-o'-nine-tails, articles from which we were able to deduce the extent to which the Friar was familiar with libertine practices; and now he returned.

"I have," he reported, "my Superior's formal consent, you may come whenever you wish."

"It shan't be long before we do, my friend," said I; "after

<hr>

[6] The renowned Caylus contributed the engravings.

[7] No, nothing, not even a legislator. Very conclusive evidence of the misjudgment and the folly which, in France, characterized the year 1789 is supplied in the ridiculous enthusiasm stirred up by that miserable monarchist spy. What today is the general opinion of that unwell and exceedingly unclever individual? He is considered a knave, a traitor, and a dunce.

being so liberally entertained by a single member of the order, we cannot but anticipate wonders from the rest: no need to tell you we have fiery cunts, from what you have already seen of them you may judge what they will be able to undertake when still better served. While waiting, Claude, let me invite you to pay us a visit; my friend and I will be delighted to receive you at a pleasant little place I own in the country, and where we are going in three days' time. Will you come? You will enjoy yourself. Between now and then, let me recommend repose. Don't fail us."

The opportunity being present, we thought best to have a word with the Superior. He proved to be a handsome man of sixty, who greeted us with utmost cordiality.

"Ladies, we will be most happy to welcome you," he declared, "among the thirty friars who are worthy to participate in these orgies, I promise you a score between the ages of thirty and thirty-five who, membered like Claude and possessing the vigor our vocation expects, will treat you according to your highest hopes. As regards secrecy, you have no cause for fears which may not be groundless when such activities are undertaken in mundane surroundings. You said, did you not, that you are interested in a few impieties? Ah, we know all about those little matters, leave everything to us, ours are capable hands. Fools maintain that monks are good-for-nothings; we mean to prove to you, Mesdames, that Carmelites at least are excellent for fucking."

Language so forthright following upon our late trial of Claude eliminated any last vestige of doubt about the spirit in which we would be entertained; we therefore notified these honorable anchorites that we would avail ourselves of their hospitality and, furthermore, bring with us two pretty girls to collaborate in and further our amusements; the which, despite our vexation at having to postpone them, could not, owing to various pressing affairs that would detain us, be scheduled before Easter.

That date was acceptable to our hosts and, Clairwil remarked as we came away, appropriate to the impieties she was still meditating. "I don't care what others say," she insisted, "I am going to derive pleasure from profaning the holiest mystery of Christianity during that very period of the year when one of Christianity's great holidays falls."

Easter lay nearly a month off and this interval being marked by two outstanding occurrences, I believe I shall speak of them at this point before relating what followed in the way of our libertinage among the Carmelites.

The first of these events was the tragic death of Claude; the unlucky chap arrived in the country on the appointed day; Clairwil was there with me; we introduced him into the most pleasurable surroundings, he was in seventh heaven and when his prick had attained to full and towering erection, then my wicked friend, signaling to the five women to seize him suddenly and pinion him, sliced that peerless member off with a razor, severing it close; later giving it to be prepared by a learned physician, she thus acquired herself the most extraordinary and I dare say the biggest dildo you have ever clapped eyes on. Claude departed this world in dreadful pain, his agony was not pretty to see: the sight of it fed Clairwil's lubricious rage, and as she watched him expire, three women and I frigged her at a distance of two feet from her victim.

"So now," the whore said to me after having splashed her fuck over us, "did I not tell you a means had been found for doing away with the bugger without losing him altogether?"

I now come to the second of these two events; and I do not suppose it is any more to the honor of my soul than the stunt I have just finished describing was to my friend's.

Surrounded by a crowd of sycophants and clients who seemed to be thinking that their fate lay in my lap, I was occupied with my toilette when a servant ushers in a middle-aged man, visibly of mean condition, and who begs me for a brief private interview. I have it explained to the fellow that I am not in the habit of receiving such folk as he, that if the matter be one of aid, or a good word spoken to the Minister, the case may be presented to me in writing and I will consider whether anything can be done; but the shabby visitor will not be put off. More from curiosity than anything else, I decide to give him audience and have him wait in the little drawing room where I held private parleys at the time; then, instructing my servants to remain within call, I go to find out what business has brought this individual to me.

"My name, Madame, is Bernole," the stranger begins, "a name with which you are surely unacquainted. It would be less unfamiliar to the mother you lost, to that excellent woman who, were she alive, would not allow you to continue this however lucrative existence of shameless disorderliness and misbehavior."

"Sir," I interrupt, "your tone does not strike me as fitting to somebody who has come to ask a favor. . . ."

"Softly, Juliette, softly," Bernole replies, "it is nonetheless possible that I am going to ask you a favor and equally possible that I have rights that allow me to adopt this tone which displeases you."

"Whatever be your rank, Sir, I would have you know that—"

"And I would have you know, Juliette, that if I have come to ask your help, you ought to be flattered by the request. Kindly look at these papers, young lady: a glance will inform you of my need of that help and at the same time of your duty to grant it."

I had but to scan those documents. "My God," I gasped, "what, my mother! She was guilty . . . and with you?"

"Precisely, Juliette; I am your father," and Bernole spoke most crisply. "I brought you into this world—I was a cousin of your mother, my parents had prepared the match, we were already betrothed when the offer of another marriage, a more advantageous one, induced them to alter their plans. They sacrificed your mother—at a time when she was pregnant, you were in her womb. She and I contrived to deceive the man whom you knew as your father, he was completely taken in. You are not his child, but mine; I can prove it. Below your right breast is a birthmark, a brownish spot the size of a small coin. . . . Juliette, have you one such mark?"

"I do, Sir."

"Then recognize your father, oh, cold, unfeeling soul! Or if you are not willing to believe me, read through these papers with a little attention, they will banish every shred of doubt. After the death of your mother . . . and it was a horrible death, the vicious doing of one Noirceuil, the same with whom you, excused by no ignorance of the facts, dare maintain a criminal relationship, and who would be broken on the wheel tomorrow if only we had the necessary evidence—and, unfortunately, it is lacking; after her death, I say, I was deluged by every imaginable piece of misfortune. All I had, I lost. I lost all your mother left me as well. For eighteen years now I have subsisted thanks to public charity alone; but I have found you at last, Juliette, and all my sufferings are soon to be over. . . ."

"Sir, I have a sister who in all likelihood is still floundering amidst hardships caused by the prejudices I rid myself of very early on; is she also your child?"

"Justine?"

"That is correct."

"She is indeed my daughter. The woman who bore her loved me, that love endured despite every obstacle; I alone had the joy of making her a mother."

"Great heaven!" cried the unhappy Justine, "my father lived and I knew him not! Dear God, had Thou but brought us together I would have been a comfort to him and soothed him in his distress, I would have shared with him the little I had and my sympathy would have compensated for the unkindness which, sister, he had probably to endure at your hands."

"My child," declared the Marquis, out of all patience with Justine after the night he had spent with her, "if you are allowed the honor of being present at this gathering, it is not to afflict us by your jeremiads. Pray continue, Madame."

Knowing me as you do, my friends, you must realize that this affair was distasteful to me, in as much as there are few souls so poorly attuned to gratitude and filial sentiments as mine; I'd not dropped one tear at the loss of the person I had always assumed to be my father, would it have been natural for me to be moved by the calamities which had befallen this other one fate restored to me? And the bestowing of alms, I need hardly remind you, was not a pastime to which I was much given; I considered charity the worst use money could be put to; and this insolent beggar might talk as he liked about being my father, the fact remained that to satisfy him I had either to part with some silver or plead in his favor before a Minister who, quite as stern, quite as unbending as I in his attitude toward such matters, could hardly be expected to lend a complacent ear to my importunings. To be sure, this individual was my father, of that there could be no question, the proof was there, but to it Nature incited in me no response at all, none. It was with sheer indifference I stared at the person standing in front of me. The silence lasted several minutes.

"Sir," said I at last, "the tales you tell me may be perfectly true; however, I see not the faintest reason for being obliged to listen to them. I have principles, Sir, steadfast principles which, unluckily for you, are totally incompatible with this commiseration you implore. As for the titles of paternity, here you are, I hand you back the papers which establish them, and let me also give you the assurance that I haven't the least need of them: whether I have a father or whether I do not have a father, you would surely have trouble realizing how little I care. And so my advice to you, Sir, is to relieve me very promptly of your presence unless through obstinacy you wish to compel me to have you thrown bodily out that window." I rise, intending to ring for my servants without further ado; but Bernole rushes forward, stays my hand.

"Ungrateful child!" he cries, "do not punish me for a sin over which I have shed a lifetime's tears—you are of illegitimate birth, aye, alack, but does my blood not run in your veins for all that? and do you not owe me your aid? If you cannot heed the feelings Nature seems to have forgot to put in your breast, will you not hark to the plaintive accents of misery and of despair?" Sinking down before me, clutching my knees, wetting them with his tears, "Juliette," says he, gazing up at my face, "Juliette, enormous wealth is thine, and it is but a crust of bread thy penniless father begs of thee! Girl, think on thy mother, wouldst thou refuse succor to the man who loved her? The only man to have loved her who bore thee nine months in her womb, hast thou no respect for him? Attend the prayer of the lowly, else Heaven shall smite thee in thy wickedness."

Undeniably, pathos abounded in the wretch's speech; but there are hearts which harden rather than melt before the efforts of those who strive to appeal to them. Like the kind of wood that toughens when exposed to fire, it is in the very element which one would suppose ought to consume them that they acquire an added degree of force. Thus, instead of exciting sentiments of compassion in me, Bernole's antics were fast hurling me into that lubricious furor which the refusal to perform a good action begets, a mild version, this, of what happens inside us when we acquit ourselves of an evil one. At first it was the icy stare of indifference I bent upon Bernole; my glance now warmed, became the fiery one of pleasure; and my throat constricted as there filtered through my veins that perfidious delight which fastens upon us at the thought or the recollection or the designing of an act of badness;[8] my brows knit, my breathing quickens, and feeling myself grow ever harsher because this harshness is agreeable, because it is arousing . . . because I am readying to discharge. . . . "I have told you," I declare to the boor groveling at my feet, "that I don't care who you are, that I shall never care who you are, and that I never give anything to the needy; and so I shall say it once again, and this shall be the last time: kindly get out of here. Or do you want to rot in some dungeon?"

A wave of madness sweeps over the man: employing now imprecations, now pleas, then invectives and then expressions of endearment, he beats his head against the floor, opens a gash in his brow, my apartment is spattered with his blood. . . . This blood is my blood; I watch it well forth, and I am happy. Happiness chokes me. After several exquisite minutes, I ring.

"Expel this clown from my house," I instruct my servants, "forcibly; but get his address before you do."

I was obeyed. . . . Overwrought, inflamed, I was obliged to have immediate resort to my women who were two hours toiling to restore me to my senses. Mighty effect of crime upon a heart like mine! It was written in the sacred book of Nature, that everything apt to outrage the Nature common spirits invariably misunderstand was sure to constitute, for me, the means to pleasure.

Both Noirceuil and the Minister were dining with me that day; I asked the former, was he acquainted with an individual called Bernole, who claimed to have been my mother's lover and to have fathered me?

"Yes," said Noirceuil, "I knew a Bernole. He had investments with your father and his money was lost along with your family's when I operated its ruin. If I remember rightly he was indeed fond of your mother, over whom he fairly grieved when she was gone; I dare say it was through no fault of his I wasn't hanged. . . . Do you mean to tell me the fellow is still about? Then it is high time he were put properly out of the way."

---

[8] See, set forth above, the natural philosophy accounting for these effects.

"We can lodge him in the Bastille before the day is out," said Saint-Fond. "Juliette has only to ask—"

"No," Noirceuil broke in, "it would be a mistake to hurry, for there are possibilities here, it seems to me. I already envisage a pathetic scene—"

"Exactly," I said. "And dungeons—piffle, such scoundrels merit worse than that. Noirceuil and you, Saint-Fond, you have labored earnestly at the reformation of my soul; that your efforts have not been vain is going to be proven upon this occasion. Since we are to trouble to commit a piece of mischief, we might as well make it a full-blown crime. The plan is simple, there can be no other: while the dog dies by my hand you'll be fucking me."

"Blast me," exclaimed the Minister, quaffing off another glass of champagne, "you are marvelous, Juliette." And divesting himself of his breeches, "What a mind the child has. She has but to air a thought and lo! my prick soars. Do you really believe you shall have the determination to execute your scheme?"

"I swear it upon the head of this prick I inspire," said I, catching hold of the purpling member Saint-Fond had just enlarged.

And I being bent forward at the moment, Noirceuil advanced a hand toward my ass while gripping his risen stave hard. "By fuck, Saint-Fond, I always told you she was a delicious creature, did I not?" and he scraped his engine between my parted buttocks.

"Come, come, gentlemen, hear me out if you please. The undertaking must be embellished by some pretty details. It strikes me that Bernole and I ought to meet again: I'll tell him I am dreadfully sorry about what happened today, declare it was all a misunderstanding, I'll deceive him by means of advances, we'll kiss, don't you know, I'll have him in love with me in half an hour, beside himself, out of his mind, he'll stick me. . . . No, that's not enough, he has got to embugger me . . . and he will. You, Saint-Fond, at this point you'll suddenly appear, at the critical instant you'll burst into the room, the instant, that is to say, he is about to discharge: you are my lover, you are furious, you intend to punish me, pointing a dagger to my breast you enjoin me to kill Bernole or perish myself. So I kill him, of course. We shall include Clairwil in the scene, she will surely be able to contribute something original to it."

Discussions preparatory to a crime never fail to please rascals. These two waxed so enthusiastic as they listened to me that there was shortly no restraining them anymore. The door to a boudoir opens, several individuals join us as auxiliaries, and my ass receives plenteous offerings from each of these monsters whom my perfidious imaginings had hurled into a very lather of lust. The storm abated, a draft for five hundred thousand francs was delivered to me, and with it I had the promise of a million payable the day the project was enacted.

The prospect of this reward tempted me sorely; impossible to turn back now. I rush to my estate; there, I take pen in hand and write to Bernole. Kind Sir, I begin, filial devotion has found its way into my heart at last, and as I write I weep: it is the pure country air, apparently, that has dispelled the ferocity we inhale from the foul atmosphere of Paris; come visit me here in these idyllic rustic surroundings, in this place where Nature reigns uncontested, and let me give vent to the feelings Nature inspires in me for you. My man arrives. . . . Ah, the joy of duping him, very sweet it was, sweet beyond belief or telling; I was fairly quaking from delight. The first thing I did was display to him the luxuriousness of my circumstances, he was dazzled; my artful caresses completed his seduction.

After we had supped in richest style, "By what possible means," I asked, "can I hope to right the wrongs I did you, all because of my wicked mind? Monsieur Bernole," I declared, "my position is not easy. I was afraid. I must watch my step very closely. I am the Minister's confidante, his friend; great is his power, he need but lift a finger and I am doomed. In you, as you stood before me, I detected nothing of a father; no, let me say it out, the emotions which assailed me were not a daughter's, they were something a thousand times more tender and more delicate, and that accounts for why, dreading lest I succumb to them, I was obliged to feign coldness, to behave harshly, aye, cruelly. What else could I do? Overcome by affection, by the most sacred love. . . . Eh, Bernole, you loved my mother, I would also have you love me; but if we are to know happiness together, discretion is required of us both, discretion, that is all; are you such a man as a woman may rely upon?"

The upright and decent Bernole shuddered at hearing these words.

"My Juliette," replied he, deeply stirred, "I seek to reawaken your sense of filial love only; that alone is due me, religion and honor, to which I am yet attached, prevent me from accepting any other. Tax me not with immorality for having lived out of wedlock with your mother: we both believed that such voluntarily contracted ties as bound us together were valid in the eyes of heaven, and these we respected; 'twas not lawful, what we did. I am aware of that, I was aware of it then, but our error was one Nature comprehends and forgives, but what you propose to me is abhorrent to her."

"Why, Bernole, yours is a benighted mind!" I cried, my solicitations having brought me to the point of kissing him and laying a hand upon his thigh. "You whom I adore, alas," I went on with mounting heat, "are my sentiments of no interest to you? Come give life a second time to her whose sole glory is to have been sired by you: my first existence I owe to love, let me owe it another also; you gave me life, will you not make that life worth living? Oh, my Bernole, 'tis so, 'tis so: without you I must die."

Two breasts white as snow and prettily shaped, which as though by accident pop into sight that same moment, eyes full of dreamy longing, of languor, and of lust . . . straying hands wandering up the paternal legs to unbutton the paternal pantaloons and with skill to fondle and stroke the half-stiffened instrument that brought me into this world; at length Bernole's reluctant passions are roused. . . .

"Good God, what are these assaults," he exclaims, "and how am I to withstand them? How spurn the living image of her whom I worshiped up until the very end?"

"And today, Bernole, your beloved is restored to you—behold in me she whom you loved in the past—she breathes; by the sweet kisses her mouth thirsts after bring her entirely back to life—ah, do you realize the state you are putting me in?" I demand. "Only see," I add, lifting my skirts, flinging myself upon a couch, "yes, look, look, and resist if you dare."

Gullible Bernole, quite swept off his feet, falls into the trap I have laid for his virtue; she who caresses the sot is thoughtful only of the base scheme that is soon to procure his undoing. Possessed of a vibrant member, wiry, spirited, and above all uncommonly long, Bernole fucked very adequately, yes, delightfully; stimulated by his performance I treated him generously, clutched his buttocks and pulled him firmly to me. That for awhile; then, slithering down beneath him, I merrily pump this prime cause of my existence; after which, resuming my place, I pack him away into my cunt, ball-deep: inordinately heated by my tricks, Bernole looses a discharge; I answer with one of my own, as my incestuous entrails become host to a fresh batch of the same seed he sowed long ago in my mother's womb. Thus did I conceive. I shall tell you about my pregnancy a little later on.

Unhinged by love, under the sway of that deity forgetting the dictates of the honor and the probity which had so well ruled his conduct hitherto, Bernole implores me to let him stay the night. Greatly excited by the idea of being fucked by the father my viciousness has passed the death sentence upon, I consent to everything. Bernole's efforts surpassed my hopes: I was soundly tuppered seven times over, and all the while obsessed by my ferocious designs, out-discharged him two to one as I dwelt upon the prospect of burying on the morrow him who had been so ill-starred, first to be my father, then, worse yet, to give me such pleasure. Midway along in our exercises, alluding to my dread lest carelessness lead to a pregnancy that would discover our intrigue, I steered round an exquisite ass by way of suggestion that he change itinerary: but crime, alas, was so foreign to my virtuous father's heart that, would you believe it? he proved not to have the least notion how to go about these infamies (infamies, I borrow his expression) which, he was at pains to have me understand, if he performed them, it was out of prudence and excess of love; the well-tooled sophist buggered me thrice—these rehearsals were necessary for the play that was to be staged the next day; so keen was their effect upon me I fainted away from pleasure.

There arrived that longed-for tomorrow when I was to savor the unspeakable charms of a crime I was in a perfect panic of eagerness to perpetrate. I looked forth upon the day in its dawning: Nature, whom I was about to outrage so gravely, had never appeared to me in such beauty; and glancing in a mirror I saw myself as prettier, healthier, more winsome than ever I had been before; within me there were hidden stirrings, never had they needled me so sharply, so imperiously as now they did. Rising from my bed, I sensed myself dominated by a lust ... by a wickedness ... I was devoured by a craving for abominations; and in me there was something beyond words bitter: it was despair at being incapable of carrying horror to the full extent described by my desires. . . .

'Tis a crime I am soon to commit, I mused, something which would be commonly held a very black crime. But though it be black, though it be heinous, it is only one crime. And what is a single crime to a person who wishes only to live in the midst of a multitude of crimes, who wishes to live for the sake of crime alone, who idolizes it and nothing else?

The whole morning I was restive, gloomy, testy, I fidgeted. I flogged two of my female hirelings, I was cross; I teased a child that had been entrusted to the care of one of them, then lured it into tumbling out a window: it died from the fall, this lifted my spirits somewhat, and I spent the remainder of the day at all sorts of little japeries, whiling the time away at all sorts of little savageries. I thought the promised supper would never arrive; but it did at last. I had issued orders that it be as lavish as the other of the day before, and as I had done then, I again drew Bernole upon a couch and flashed him my ass. Into it the ninny plunged, fuddled by my meaningless amorous prattle. An instant or two later the door is flung open and in storm Clairwil, Noirceuil, and Saint-Fond, swearing and armed; Bernole is dragged off my back and bound hand and foot.

"Juliette," a raging Saint-Fond declares, "you deserve to be butchered along with this monster for having betrayed the trust I have always placed in you. Would you live, eh? Then you have no choice: there are three balls in this pistol, take it and blow the churl's brains out."

"Great heaven!" I shrilled theatrically. "What are you demanding of me? This man is my father—"

"A father-fucking slut ought to be able to do a little father-killing."

"The choice is impossible—"

"Rubbish. Come, be quick about it: take this pistol instantly, or die yourself."

"Woe is me," I sighed, "my hand trembles, give me the weapon nevertheless. What must be, must be," said I; "beloved father, will you pardon this act? I am under constraint, you observe it—"

"Vile creature," Bernole answered, "do as you are told. Aye, go ahead. But spare me having to listen to you. I do not wish to be made a fool of."

"Very well then, papa," said Clairwil gaily, "since you don't wish to be made a fool of, you shan't be: just as you have guessed, your death is of your daughter's contriving—and right indeed she is to want to murder the great scoundrel you must be for ever having given life to such a child."

Preparations are made forthwith: Bernole is tied to a chair fixed by spikes to the floor; I take up a position ten feet from him. Saint-Fond stretches out upon a divan and fits his member in my anus, Noirceuil supervising the introduction with one hand, stroking his own instrument with the other; to the right Clairwil is tonguing Saint-Fond's mouth and tickling my clitoris. I take aim.

"Saint-Fond," I inquire, "shall I wait until you wet me?"

"No, foul bitch," he shouts, "kill him, kill him, the shot will bring my sperm out."

I fire. The ball enters Bernole's brow; he expires; and with wild screams we all four discharge.

Barbarous Saint-Fond rises and goes to peer at the victim; he stands over the body a long time, manifestly in ecstasy. (He always adored such situations.) He calls my name, would have me look also. . . . While I do he casts sidelong glances at me, studying my reaction; my *sang-froid* satisfies him. With a very mischievous smile Clairwil watches death stiffen Bernole's limbs and drift over his contorted face.

"Nothing arouses me like the sight of death," Clairwil murmurs. And then, her eyes still riveted upon our victim, "Who'd care to frig me?"

I step forward; Noirceuil slips his stave into my ass, Saint-Fond his into Clairwil's; and we all discharge afresh. After which a most delicious meal is brought in and we take places around a table at whose head, as though presiding over the feast, sits the corpse.

"Juliette," says Saint-Fond, kissing me and laying the money down by my plate, "here is what I promised you. You will not take it amiss if I tell you that until today I allowed myself to harbor one or two little doubts as to the stuff you were made of. There is no longer any room for them. Your performance was irreproachable."

"You will excuse me," put in Clairwil, "but I am not of that opinion. I seem still to notice the same failing in her: whenever Juliette commits a crime, it's enthusiastically; but so long as her cunt is dry she might as well be paralyzed. One must proceed calmly, deliberately, lucidly. Crime is the torch that should fire the passions, that is a commonplace; but I have the suspicion that with her it is the reverse, passion firing her to crime."

"The difference is enormous," Saint-Fond remarked, "for in such a case crime is but accessory, whereas it ought to have prime importance."

"I am afraid I share Clairwil's view, my dear Juliette," said Noirceuil; "you need further encouragement; this ruinous sensibility plaguing you must be dealt with. All the irregularities into which our imagination leads us," he continued, "are exact indices of our degree of intelligence. Its vivacity, its impetuosities, in a superior being, are so powerful that it will stop at nothing; obstacles to surmount represent that many more delights; and their overcoming is not necessarily proof of depravity, as fools suppose, but evidence of the mind's strengthening. You, Juliette, have now reached the age where your faculties are at their apogee; you enter your prime readied by earnest study, by solid reflection, by a wholesale rejection of all the curbs and all the prejudices imposed and acquired in childhood. No, you have no cause for worry, that long and careful preparation shall not have been for nothing, your career is going to be brilliant: a fiery and vigorous temperament, robust health, great heat in the bowels, a very chilly heart are there to second this ebullient, enlightened, and unscrupulous brain. We may depend upon it, my friends, Juliette will go as far as she possibly can; but I ask that she not tarry on the way, nor even pause, that if ever she casts a glance backward it be then to chide herself for having made such modest progress, and not to be amazed at the great distances she has covered."

"I expect still more," said Clairwil. "Let me repeat: I expect Juliette to do evil—not to quicken her lust, as I believe it is her habit at present, but solely for the pleasure of doing it. I ask that in bare evil, evil free of all lewd accouterments, she find all the delight her lust affords her; I ask that she learn to dispense with all vehicles, with all pretexts for the doing of evil. This program carried out means no diminishing of libertinage's charms, Juliette may go on savoring them as in the past, and ought to. But what I am resolutely opposed to is her having to frig herself in order to reach a criminal pitch; for the consequences of this kind of behavior are that the day her appetites fade, her desires quit her, she'll be incapable of doing anything wrong at all; whereas by following my prescriptions, in crime she will always find the means to revive her passions. No further need to lay finger to cunt in order to perpetrate the wicked deed; but from perpetrating it she will derive the wish to frig herself. I find no clearer way of expressing the matter."

"My dear," I replied, "there is nothing obscure in your philosophy; I grasp these theories because their practice suits me. Do you doubt it? I am prepared to prove it to you; put me to whatever test you like. Had you somewhat more carefully observed my comportment in the business we have lately dispatched, you would not, I am sure, have formulated these criticisms; I am come to the stage where I love evil for its own sake; only in crime, I have recently noticed, do my passions catch fire, and where the seasoning of crime is lacking I taste no joy. There remains a single point I would consult you upon. Of remorse I experience nothing anymore, I may truthfully declare that for me it has ceased altogether to exist, never a twinge of it regardless of the abomination I indulge in; but, do you know, I am sometimes ashamed of myself. I blush, like Eve abashed after eating the apple. Our activities, our extravagances, these are things whereof I would not be pleased to have intelligence leak out, things I am loath to own save to our close friends—why is it so? Why, pray explain to me, why is it that of these feelings, remorse and shame, I am susceptible to the weaker although impervious to the more potent—in fine, where does the distinction lie between the two?"

"In this," answered Saint-Fond, "that shame reflects the wound inflicted upon public opinion by a given piece of wickedness, whereas remorse relates to the pain that wickedness does to our own conscience; in such sort that it is possible to be ashamed of a deed that causes no remorse when this deed offends conventional practice only without afflicting one's conscience; and similarly it is possible to be unashamedly contrite if the deed committed accords with the usages and customs of our country, but jars with our conscience. For example: to stroll naked down the central alley in the Tuileries might well make a man blush, but could hardly make him remorseful; and a military commander will perhaps feel badly at having sent twenty thousand of his troops to their death in a battle, but he is not apt to be ashamed. However, both these troublesome feelings are to be finally eliminated by means of habituation. You now belong to the Sodality of the Friends of Crime; it may be safely predicted that participation in its activities will by and by rid you of your tendency to shame, of your capacity for it: you will acquire the habit of a pronounced cynicism, it will make short work of the weakness bothering you at present; and to accelerate the cure, I urge you to parade your misbehavior, to show yourself nude in public, frequently, and to strive after the most arrantly whorish effects in your dress; you'll gradually cease to blush at anything; let the measures I am advising become seconded by doctrinal firmness, and all these sudden starts and annoying twinges will be things of the past, you will take a very different view of affairs: you shall sense nothing but pleasure there where once upon a time you were stricken by shame."

More serious matters were broached next: I was informed by Saint-Fond that the marriage of his daughter Alexandrine to Noirceuil, his friend, was about to be concluded at long last, and that he and his future son-in-law were agreed that the young lady should pass a season with me, living in my house, where she would be familiarized with, and adapted to, the tastes of the individual to whom she was going to be joined maritally.

"We request you, Noirceuil and I," Saint-Fond pursued, "to shape this little soul after your own. Cultivate it, nurture it assidu-

ously, make it liberal provision of good counsel and bright example;
will Noirceuil keep the girl by him if he finds her soundly formed?
Perhaps. But it is most unlikely he'll long abide her if she prove
gauche or a prude. So endeavor, Juliette, to achieve something you
can be proud of and which will be useful to us all; the pains you
take will not be overlooked."

"Sir," said I to the Minister, "you know that such lessons as
these can only be given between a pair of sheets. . . ."

"Of course, of course, my dear," Saint-Fond nodded. "That
is what I have in mind."

"By all means, yes," Noirceuil echoed.

"Obviously," said Clairwil. "How educate a girl save by lying
with her?"

"Quite," Noirceuil continued; "our good Juliette will bed
with my wife as often as she sees fit."

Saint-Fond took up fresh subjects; he outlined a cruel scheme
he had devised for the devastation of France. "We are presently
concerned," said he, "by certain symptoms which could soon lead
to a revolution in the land, and are disturbed especially by the
untoward size of the population; the trouble might well have its
origin there. The more numerous the people become, the greater
the danger they pose; the awakening of minds, the spreading of a
critical spirit, these are grave developments: only the ignorant
remain placid under the yoke. Therefore," the Minister went on,
"we plan, firstly, to have done with all these grammar schools, the
free ones, which are producing such alarming quantities of poets,
painters, and thinkers instead of the drudges and pickpockets we
ought to have. What need have we of such crowds of talent, why do
we bother to encourage it in them? Less wit in the nation, I say, and
some numerical retrenchment also: France requires a severe purg-
ing, the lowliest is the first sector to attack. We intend hence to
have unsparingly at mendicants, that's the class which breeds nine
out of ten of our agitators; we are razing charitable institutions,
the poorhouses, being determined not to leave the masses one
single refuge where insolence can ripen. Bowed beneath chains a
thousand times heavier than those worn by, let us say, the commoners in Asia, we propose to have ours crawl in slavery, and to

this end we are prepared to use the widest variety of radical means."

"It will be a while before those means take effect," Clairwil pointed out. "If it's a sudden diminishment you need, then you had better resort to prompter ones: war, famine, epidemics. . . ."

"Ah, war," said Saint-Fond, "we'll not neglect a war, that's scheduled. As for an epidemic, it is to be avoided since we ourselves might be its first victims. Regarding a famine, the total monopolization of corn we are working toward, as well as being profitable to us, will shortly reduce the people to veritable cannibalism. We are counting heavily upon this measure. The Council of Ministers approved it unanimously today. Speedy, infallible, prodigiously lucrative.

"Won over to the principles Machiavelli set so clearly forth," the Minister continued, "I have for a long time had the profound conviction that individuals can be of no account to the politician; as machines, men must labor for the prosperity of the government they are subordinated to, never should the government be concerned for the welfare of the public. Every government that interests itself in the governed is weak; there is but one sort of strong government, and it considers itself everything and the nation nothing. Whether there are a few more or a few less slaves in a State does not matter; what does, is that their bondage weigh onerously and absolutely upon a people, and that the sovereign be despotic. Rome tottered feebly along in the days when Romans insisted upon governing themselves; but she became mistress of the world when tyrants seized authority; all the power resides in the sovereign, thus must we behold the thing, and since this power is merely moral so long as the people are physically the stronger, only by an uninterrupted series of despotic actions can the government assemble the force it needs: until such time as it commands all the real power, it will exist in an ideal sense only. When we are eager to gain the upper hand over others, we must little by little accustom them to seeing in us something which is actually not there; otherwise, they'll only see us for what we are, and this will regularly and inevitably be to our detriment. . . ."

"It has always seemed to me," Clairwil remarked, "that the

art of governing men is the one that demands more trickery, more duplicity, and more fraudulence than any other."

"Perfectly true," Saint-Fond assented, "and the reason therefor is simple: there is no governing human beings unless you deceive them. To deceive them, you must be false. The enlightened man will never allow himself to be led about by the end of his nose, hence you must deprive him of light, keep him in darkness if you would steer him; none of this is possible without duplicity."

"But is not duplicity a vice?" I wondered.

"I would rather tend to esteem it a virtue," answered the Minister, "it is the only key unlocking the human heart. You cannot hope to live amidst men if you limit yourself to honesty; their sole and constant effort being to deceive us, what awaits us if we do not very quickly learn to deceive them? The foremost preoccupation of man and of the statesman, particularly, is to penetrate others without letting his own thoughts be known. Well, if duplicity is the only means for achieving this, duplicity is then a virtue; in a totally corrupt world there is never any danger being more rotten than one's neighbors; rather, 'tis there to assure oneself of the whole sum of felicity and ease which virtue would procure us in a moral society. But the mechanism that directs government cannot be virtuous, because it is impossible to thwart every crime, to protect oneself from every criminal without being criminal too; that which directs corrupt mankind must be corrupt itself; and it will never be by means of virtue, virtue being inert and passive, that you will maintain control over vice, which is ever active: the governor must be more energetic than the governed: well, if the energy of the governed simply amounts to so many crimes threatening to be unleashed, how can you expect the energy of the governor to be anything different? what are legally prescribed punishments if not crimes? and what excuses them? the necessity of governing men. There it is: crime is one of the vital mainsprings of government, I ask you now in what sense can this they call *virtue* be necessary in the world, when it is evident you cannot obtain it save through crimes? I may add that it is exceedingly necessary, for the government itself, that mankind in general be thoroughly corrupt: the more corrupt men are, the more easily they may be managed. In conclusion, examine virtue from every viewpoint and you always find it useless and dangerous.

"Juliette," Saint-Fond declared, addressing himself now to me, "if you still entertain prejudices touching this subject, I should like to rid you of them once and for all, they cannot have anything but the worst influence upon your destiny. Opinions are important in life, I should like to make certain that yours are wholesome; for it is dreadful, if one is born with penchants for evil-doing, not to be able to do evil save in fear and trembling. Hear me, my angel, take note of what I say: were your activities to hurl the entire natural order into confusion, you would be doing no more than exercising the faculties Nature gave you for that—faculties which Nature was perfectly aware you would employ for that; their employment is obviously not something Nature can object to or condemn, since instead of neutralizing these harmful faculties she originally gave you, or subsequently depriving you of them, she does nought but incite in you, continually, the desire to make the most of them. So do all the evil you like, and do it knowing it need not cost you a wink of sleep; take heart in the fact that whatever the species of wickedness you contrive, for violence it will never surpass or satisfy Nature's greedy expectations, who welcomes destruction, loves it, lusts after it, feeds upon it; take heart, I say, knowing that you please Nature never so well as when, emulating her, you set your hand to ruinous work; and knowing that, if the question be of outrage, of infringement upon her rights, you never so injure her as when you labor at the creation she abhors, or as when you leave in peace this mass of humanity which is an eternal threat to her; for the true laws of Nature are crime and death, and we are most faithfully her servants when, smiting hard to left and right, in a rage like hers we indiscriminately cut down all inside our reach."

"Believe me, Saint-Fond," I replied to my lover, "to all the principles you have just settled I adhere most cordially. Only one thing disturbs me: one must, you asserted, be treacherous in one's dealings with everybody; now, if by ill chance you were so with me—"

"You need dread no such eventuality," the Minister affirmed at once. "I shall never be treacherous toward my friends, if merely because one cannot very well do without something solid and sure in the world; and what's left if you cannot count upon your inter-course with your friends? You may therefore be certain, all three of you, that I shall never play you false unless you wrong me first. The reason is simple. I base it on self-interest, the only rule I know for judging oneself and others intelligently. We live side by side: is it not true that if you discover I am deceiving you, you will deceive me in return at the first opportunity; and I do not want to be deceived: there's the whole of my logic upon the chapter of friendship. Experience shows that between persons of the same sex the sentiment of friendship is not easy to preserve, and impossible between persons of unlike sex; I value it in so far as it may be founded upon likenesses of humor and compatibilities of taste, which happens only very seldom; but it is a great error to suppose virtue must be its cement; if that were so, friendship would be-come an unbearably dull sentiment which monotony would soon destroy. When pleasures provide its basis, each new idea gives the attachment an added sinew; need, the sole real aliment of friendship, knits it ever tighter, affection grows with each passing day as with each passing day increases the mutual need of one for the other; you have enjoyment from your friend, you enjoy yourselves together, you enjoy yourself for his sake, each delight fortifies the rest, and 'tis only then one may be said to know them. But what does a virtuous sentiment yield me? A few barren pleas-ures, a few vapid intellectual gratifications that never survive the first test, except in the form of regrets which are the more poignant where hurt has been done one's pride, no shafts being more wounding than those which strike there."

It was past midnight; we retired, the four of us repairing to a bed eight feet long and eight wide, built for such scenes; and after some lewd ones, some foul ones, we went to sleep. Noirceuil had business awaiting him in the city and left us early the next day; Clairwil remained with me to keep Saint-Fond company, for the Minister was disposed to spend a few more days in the country.

Upon our return to Paris Saint-Fond brought me his daughter, whose apartment had been put in readiness during our absence. Alexandrine was of an extraordinary and eminently regular beauty; she could boast of a sublime bust, the prettiest details distinguished her form, her skin was glowing clear, her flesh firm, there was grace and ripeness in her limbs, heaven shone in her face, her organ well became the rest, it positively intrigued, and there was considerable of the romantic in her spirit.

"Here is my daughter," said Saint-Fond, introducing her to me, "I mean, as you know, to marry her to Noirceuil, who is not the man to be rattled by the liberties I have taken with her and which I still take every day. There's some fruit left on the tree, however: frontwardly, Alexandrine has treasures still to be assessed. But on the hinder side . . . her ass, this gorgeous ass, Juliette, has been long the object of my depradations. Who could have resisted such a temptation? Look at it, my angel, and tell me now, have you ever seen anything so inviting in all your life?"

Rarely indeed had I clapped eyes on a fairer, a better-cleft set of buttocks.

"And for endurance, for elasticity, and for healing power it is perfectly remarkable," Saint-Fond went on, opening it wide, "for from the look of it who would believe I lash her every morning at nine and bum-fuck her every night at ten? I confide this girl to you, Juliette, educate her for a while; make her worthy of the gentleman whose wife she shall be, breed in her the taste for all crimes and the liveliest horror for all virtues. To you I cede my rights over her; transmit to her the philosophical systems you have received from him who is to wed her; give her all our penchants, communicate all our passions to her: never has the name of God been pronounced within her hearing, I think I may safely expect it shan't be in your proximity that religious notions will occur to her. I'd not trifle with her, no, I'd put a bullet in the chit's brain the instant I detected talk of that execrable chimera coming out of her mouth. For several important reasons neither Noirceuil nor I can personally undertake the task we are entrusting to you; but Alexandrine could not be left in more capable hands."

That was the occasion on which the Minister mentioned the news of Noirceuil's nomination to one of the highest posts at the Court, which fetched with it one hundred thousand crowns a year. "It was given him," Saint-Fond added, "at the same time the King conferred upon me another worth twice as much."

And while vice, impudent vice, sped unerringly from one triumph to the next, fate went just as steadily crushing whomever those mighty rascals deigned to make victims. Such was the situation; I pondered it at length. And all my observations, all my meditations conspired to depress ever lower the view I held of goodness, and to exalt my opinion of evil, again and again confirming me in my choice to dwell fast and secure in the bosom of crime and of infamy. . . . Ah, my friends, I cannot well communicate to you the loathing I had of virtue.

I spent the following night with Alexandrine; no question about it, that child was delicious. But I must nonetheless own that I beheld her so philosophically, sobriety to such a degree characterizing my senses, that it is difficult to give an account of the pleasures she yielded me: she roused my emotions scarcely at all. My ideas had gained such a prise upon me, the moral in me so thoroughly overmastered the physical, my indifference was such, my self-possession so unshakable, that whether it was because of surfeit, or depravity, or sheer pigheadedness, I was able to have her naked ten successive hours in my bed, to frig her, to have her frig me, to lick her, to suck her, and all that unremittingly and without a trace of feeling. Here, I dare say, is an outstanding example of the benefits that accrue from stoicism. Steeling our soul against all that may stir it, by means of libertinage inuring it to crime, paring voluptuousness down to a purely carnal affair and stubbornly denying it any element of delicacy, the stoical training enervates the soul; and from this state, wherein its native activity does not permit it to remain long, it passes into one of apathy which soon metamorphoses into pleasures a thousand times diviner than those which frailties could procure it; for the fuck I shed with Alexandrine, though due to this toughness I have sought to represent, got me delights infinitely more trenchant than the ones which would have resulted from excitement or the dreary heats of love.

At any rate, to my consideration Alexandrine appeared quite as untaught morally as she was physically inexperienced; everything was still to be done for her heart and her mind. The little vixen had a promising disposition, however, and every time I attempted to arouse her I found her full of fuck. I asked her, did her father hurt her when he buggered her?

"A great deal at first," she admitted, but she had become so used to it that it no longer caused her suffering.

Upon my demanding whether she had held conversation with anyone beside the Minister and Noirceuil, she told me Saint-Fond had obliged her to accept the attentions of one other man, and from her description I recognized Delcour. "Attentions," I repeated; "do you mean by that he embuggered you too?" No, he had whipped her while her father looked on; judge thereby of the imagination of a man whose prick lifts and spits as he watches his daughter being flogged by a public executioner. In the course of our first night together I supplied my pupil all the rudiments of the theory of libertinage; and in three days' time she was frigging me as adroitly as Clairwil. Be that as it may, this child gradually began to set my teeth on edge; I was already caressing visions of her undoing when I asked Noirceuil his intentions concerning the creature.

"I shall make a victim of her, needless to say. I've never done anything else with a wife."

"Then why the delay?"

He smiled. "Because of the dowry, because of the child I want to sire on her, or have somebody else sire, because of my desire to preserve the Minister's protection through this alliance."

These were considerations which had not occurred to me; I had to abandon my plans. I simultaneously lost all interest in Alexandrine and, in order not to have to mention her again— I have more important things to talk about—let me say that she married Noirceuil, became pregnant one way or another; and the moral instruction I gave her having penetrated not very far, it was early on in the game that she succumbed to the concerted villainy of her father and husband, perishing during a rout I did not attend because of events whose details I shall enter into shortly.

The girls whom I furnished to the Minister did not always cost me as much as I retailed them for, and it sometimes even happened that I earned money through their acquisition. I shall cite an instance of this, realizing that it does not speak in favor of my probity.

From a personage residing in the provinces I one day receive a letter, telling me that the government owes him half a million francs which he loaned the State during the last war; his affairs have taken a catastrophic turn, for want of the sum aforementioned he has been brought to the worst extremes, he is faced by nothing short of starvation, he and his sixteen-year-old daughter, who, devoted to her as he is, he would marry with a part of the money if he could but recover his due. Knowing of my influence with the Minister he has been obliged to invoke my aid; all pertinent documents accompany his missive. I make inquiry, learn that what he advances is true; obtaining the funds will require intercession from a powerful source, but that they are owing to the claimant is beyond all question. Moreover, the young lady referred to in the letter is, so I am assured, one of the most enchanting creatures in the entire country. Without airing anything of my scheme to the Minister, I ask him for the necessary order for payment. It is delivered to me at once; in twenty-four hours I accomplish what ten years of struggle have failed to get the provincial. As soon as I have the cash in hand, I notify the latter that appropriate steps have been taken; but that his presence is indispensable; that success could only be accelerated by his arrival in the disbursor's office accompanied by a pretty young thing; in fine, I urge him to bring his daughter to town with him. The simpleton is taken roundly in; he appears at my door and with him, sure enough, he has one of the loveliest girls it has ever been my fortune to see. I lodged them in a place of safety, but did not keep them long in doubt of their fate: they were the principal ornaments at the next of the frolics I arranged each week for Saint-Fond. Already five hundred thousand francs in pocket and thanks to this newest piece of treachery now in the possession of the father and daughter, you will not, I suppose, be hard put to guess what employment I reserved for these spoils. The money, enough to have guaranteed a comfortable future to several families, was squandered by me in less than a week; the daughter, who might surely have made, had fate been kinder, for the felicity of some honest man, instead of that, after having been soiled by our nocturnal pollutions for three days in a row, made a fourth supper victim, her father providing a fifth, both expiring under a torture the more barbarous for being prolonged over twelve hours of hideous suffering.

To complete this self-portrait, after describing my perfidy I ought to represent my greed to you. With me greed went far: to the point, indeed, of usury. Once finding myself with eight hundred thousand francs worth of objects in pledge, objects which would not, had I auctioned them off, have fetched a fourth of that sum, I declared bankruptcy, and the gesture sufficed to ruin twenty humble families who had deposited into my keeping all they had of value in exchange for a pitiful fugitive subsistence, no more than enough to enable them to pursue the desperate toiling whence they earned practically nothing.

Eastertide was drawing near, Clairwil reminded me of our appointment at the Carmelites'. There we betook ourselves, Elvire and Charmeil, the two prettiest of my hired sluts, in tow. No sooner were we inside the monastery than the Superior asked for news of Claude. Nothing further had been heard from him since he had left after accepting our invitation. In reply, we wondered whether in the absence of other information it might not be conjectured that, libertine as he decidedly was, he had flung away his frock. No more was said of Claude. We entered a vast hall; and it was there the Superior had us review his legions. Eusebius, so was the head of the establishment called, summoned them forward from ranks one by one; they stepped forth, were taken in charge by my two women who frigged them and displayed their pricks when they were in fullest flower. Anything short of six inches around by nine in length was rejected, so was anything older than fifty. We had been promised only thirty opponents, here in fact were fifty-four friars plus ten novices with engines not one inferior to the dimensions noted above, and certain of them ten by fourteen. The ceremony began.

It transpired in that same hall. Clairwil and I were bidden to recline upon broad couches, thick-mattressed and elastic, our legs flexed, our loins pillowed on big cushions, totally naked; in this first assault, we gave the cunt for target to the adversary. Our tribades sorted out the pricks according to size and directed them our way, starting with the smaller; from now on all pollution was effected by us, that is to say, we each readied the pair of pricks which were to succeed the ones encunting us at the moment. When a cunt became filled by what had been in a hand, that empty hand was immediately given a new prick to prepare; we each had, at all times, three men either on or by us. After he had completed his attack, a friar would retire from the field and into an adjoining room, there to rest and await further orders. They were all naked, their pricks were all sheathed, and it was into those protectors they all discharged. First they visited Clairwil, then me; and so were we each fucked four and sixty times in the course of this engagement, toward the close of which our women went into the other room and busied themselves preparing the friars for fresh affray. The second attack began. . . . Another sixty-four fuckings apiece; it was under identical circumstances the third was launched, except that it was directed at our asses and we, instead of frigging pricks manually, constantly had one in our mouths: a prick that had just emerged from our asses we sucked, furbishing it for the fourth attack. Here, we introduced the weaving variation: that is, I sucked the prick which withdrew from Clairwil's bum and she mouthed the one that came out of mine. When truce was called we had each been fucked one hundred twenty-eight times cuntwardly and as many times in the ass, making two hundred fifty-six fuckings in all. Biscuits and sherry were served, then battle was resumed.

We took on our men in groups of eight: we had a prick underneath each armpit, one in each hand, one between the bubs, another in the mouth, the seventh in the cunt, the eighth in the bowels. No sheaths now; the object was to lave, bathe our bodies in sperm from head to toe and to have fuck spouting from all sides at once. Each eight-man platoon loosed two volleys, bringing first one of us, then the other, under fire, and the constituents of each changed posts; thus it was we each underwent eight such assaults, and when they were over we declared ourselves satisfied and at our hosts' disposal; they might do what they wished with either of us and to their hearts' content. So it was that Clairwil was fucked another fifteen times in the mouth, ten in the cunt, and thirty-nine in the ass; and I forty-six in the ass, eight in the mouth, and ten in the cunt.[9] All told, another two hundred fuckings each.

---

[9] In such sort that these two winning creatures, not counting oral incursions—for mouth-fucking produces upon the fucked too faint an impression to merit consideration here—had, at this stage, been fucked, Clairwil one hundred and eighty-five times and Juliette one hundrd and ninety-two, this both cuntwise and asswardly. We have

The sun rose and as it was Easter day, the rascals who had treated us thus marched off to Mass and then marched back; the hour for dinner being not far off, we indicated to the Superior our desire to proceed to the little impieties that had been included in our agreement, before sitting down to the noon meal. Eusebius, who cared for men only, had, during our lubricious antics, confined himself to readying pricks and embuggering a few of his brothers while they were fucking us.

"Why certainly," he assured us, "I shall myself celebrate the Holy Mystery in the chapel of the Virgin. Have you any preferences touching how it should be done?"

"As follows," said Clairwil. "A second friar will officiate beside you: these two Masses will be said upon the cunts of our two tribades; while this is going on yet another friar will be mouth-fucking them, this enabling him to present his ass to the celebrant and at the point the Host is consecrated he will drop a mard upon the girl's belly, and the priest will promptly insert the wafer in the mard; my friend and I shall come forth to seek God therein, we'll apply fire to some of it, stab it elsewhere with the point of a knife; what remains of the mixture shall be divided into four portions, two of these are to be buried in the asses of the celebrants, rammed home by prodding pricks, and the third and fourth portions will be likewise stored in Juliette's ass and in mine: four little syringes—we have them here—shall have been got ready in the meantime, and the holy wine shall now be squirted into our fundaments. Next, we two women and the two priests shall be sodomized anew, and to what is already in our asses discharged fuck shall be added. Your prettiest and best crucifixes will be beneath our bellies throughout the operation, and we shall shit thereupon, as well as into your chalices and various sacred vessels, immediately after we have been fucked."

All passed in conformance to my friend's wishes.

---

deemed it necessary to provide this reckoning rather than have ladies interrupt their reading to establish a tally, as otherwise they would most assuredly be inclined to do. So offer us your thanks, mesdames, and endeavor to outshine our heroines, we ask no more of you; for your instruction, your sensations, and your happiness are in verity the sole objects for whose sake some wearisome efforts are undertaken; and if you damned us in *Justine,* our hope is that *Juliette* will earn us your blessings.

She came away from the rites very satisfied. "Excellent, excellent," she repeated, "so much silliness, doubtless, and quite useless, but I found it stimulating and that is sufficient justification for anything. Voluptuous delights are no more than what the imagination makes of them; and that which pleaseth best will always be the most delectable:

All tastes partake of Nature;
The best is that which one has."

We shared a magnificent repast with Eusebius and four of the friars whose performances had been most noteworthy; we rested for two hours, and the orgies recommenced.

Our two tribades were stationed on either side of Clairwil, one displayed her cunt, the other her ass; my task was to erect the sixty-four pricks and to lodge them one after the other, first in my companion's vagina, then in her anus, she awaiting them lying on her back, her legs raised, her ankles being affixed to the posts at the foot of the bed; her swains did no more than excite themselves in her cunt, all discharging occurred in her ass. I took Clairwil's place, she now rendered me the same service. By dint of such arrangements, those libertines not only obtained the pleasure of fucking us bilaterally, but in addition to that obtained, while fucking, the pleasure of being aided, assisted, guided by a pretty hand, and of kissing a mouth, a cunt, or an asshole at will; fuck flowed in tides.

At the second sitting while each of our tribades was rubbing a prick on our faces we were frigging another in each hand, and two ecclesiastics were tonguing us: we were in a crouching position, squarely above the nose of the man who was licking our asshole; between our legs, kneeling there, was he who was sucking our cunt; the seventh and eighth stood by, prick in hand, awaiting instructions, and they would encunt or embugger us when, properly aroused by the sucker or the licker, we gave the signal for introduction. An hour or so of this and our total number of fuckings had risen by eight more.

Overtaxed, our spirits were beginning to flag when into Clairwil's head popped the thought that revived us both. She expressed it thus: "With a little skill, it is possible for two men to encunt a woman at the same time; let those approach who are still in condition to try it." Several came forward, my friend designated two of them. "You," said she to the better-weaponed, "you'll lie down and I shall get aboard you and take your prick first. And you," she said to his fellow, "you'll fuck me from behind, frigging my asshole while you do. I can perfectly well suck a third man's prick; and what's to prevent me from frigging two others?"

Not every cunt is made for the success of such an enterprise; Clairwil's, happily, was by no means narrow. Pounded and scraped by two gigantic members, their action coordinated in such a manner that while the one slid aft the other crashed forward till hair met hair,[10] thus fucked at a sustained allegro for the space of three hours and better by the twenty-six friars who were agile enough to accomplish the trick, the whore, at the end of it all, was in a frantic condition; her glaring eyes roved, sparks shot from them, foam whitened her lips, she was in a lather; and spent as she looked to be, yet she would have more; like one possessed she darted hither and thither through the press, clutching at pricks, sucking upon them, pulling them, essaying this and that to stiffen them to new efforts. Too young, too delicate, to permit myself even to attempt the obscene irregularity my companion was engaged in, I entertained myself at preparing the pricks required for her feast; but more than this I could not do. In both the zones of pleasure there was such a burning sensation, a scorching so intense, that I was scarce able to sit down.

We supped. It was late. Clairwil said she would fain lie that night in the convent.

"Kindly have a mattress placed for me upon the altar in your church," said she to the Superior, "there's yet a deal of fucking to be done. Juliette will join me. The weather is warm, we shall be more comfortable there. Or, if she prefers, Juliette may lie in

---

[10] "We may with the authority of experience unhesitatingly affirm and guarantee that the woman well enough constituted to make trial of this method will extract therefrom sensations so highly flavored, vibrations so compelling that it is not easily practiced without loss of consciousness; if she can secure the collaboration of a third man capable of address enough to embugger her in the meantime, she will then be sure of tasting the most violent pleasure that can possibly be procured by our sex." (From a note communicated by a lady of thirty years, who elsewhere declares having enjoyed this experience upon better than one hundred separate occasions.)

the chapel dedicated to the whore who, they say, begot the hanged God of your infamous Christianity. What say you, Juliette? Go sprawl yourself upon that altar, there's my suggestion, spread your legs in pious remembrance of the whorishness of Dirty Mary. Instead of soldiers from the Jerusalem garrison by whom the buggeress would get herself stuffed every day, from amongst our Carmelite army you'll select those in whom you suspect a little lingering vigor."

"But I can fuck no more," I protested.

"Nonsense. You'll frig them, they'll frig you; you'll suck them, they'll suck you. You'll see. One can always scrape up fuck to shed in foul circumstances. You tell me you are spent? Not I. Far from it; I've been well tupped today, better than you, and I am still ablaze. The floods of sperm that washed into my ass and cunt put no flames out, but fed them. I am on fire. . . . The more one fucks, my dearest, the more one wants to fuck; only fuck soothes the inflammation fucking causes; and when a woman has a temperament like the one Nature gave me, only from fucking, only while fucking, can she be happy. Woman has one innate virtue, it is whorishness; to fuck, that and that alone is what we were created for; woe unto her whom a thoughtless and stupid virtuousness ever keeps prisoner of dull prejudices; a victim of her opinions and of the chilly esteem she hopes for, almost always in vain, from men, she'll have lived dry and joyless and shall die unregretted. Libertinage in women used once to be venerated the world over; it had worshipers everywhere, temples even; I become more and more a zealot in that cause. 'Tis my creed, my whole concern and ambition; so long as there is breath in me, I shall be a whore, I proclaim it, I swear it. If there is anyone who can claim gratitude from me, it belongs to those who encouraged me in the way of vice. To them I owe everything, I owe life itself. That which I received from my parents was besmirched by infamous prejudices, they comprised a very jail; I burst out of it, my passions broke down those walls, cindered those prejudices, and since the daylight my eyes behold only became pure the day I learned the art of fucking, I consider that my existence dates from then. . . . Pricks, aye, pricks, those are my gods, those are my kin, my boon companions, unto me they are everything, I live in the name of nothing but the penis sublime; and when it is not in my cunt, nor in my ass, it is so firmly anchored in my thoughts that the day they dissect me it will be found in my brain."

After this exuberant statement, delivered somewhat more incoherently than I reproduce it here and in a voice bordering upon a shriek, Clairwil laid hold of two Carmelites and dashed away to wrestle with them upon the altar; I repaired to the chapel. Having first sponged myself with rose water, I provoked attacks from the two superb novices I had chosen, and I was in the throes of new transports when Clairwil reappeared, crying that she was in requirement of fresh men.

"It is all very well—and natural enough—to pick and choose amidst abundance, but provisions are now run out, these buggers are frayed and bone-dry. Can you believe it, Juliette, I have just been flubbed—aye, flubbed, I who never before had to endure that affront. Up, my lass, there are other pricks in this convent; we merely requisitioned the cream of the crop, let's feel out the rest. If the Superior," she went on, bidding someone go in search of him, "if the Superior has made no individual contribution to the satisfying of my desires, he shall yet prove himself useful in having them appeased by those of his underlings who, hale in wind and limb and having not yet lifted weapon, ought to have fight enough in them to content us. Ah, Eusebius, there you are," she said when he arrived, "good Eusebius, take us to the cells inhabited by the friars who were excused from duty but of whom we are in need at present; lead on."

We wended our way slowly through the cloister; doors opened at our summons; and whatever the conformation of those we uncovered in those chambers, they were enjoined to tup us. All subscribed to the bargain, all signed it in sperm: some had at us from the front, and others, they were the majority, would take us nowise but from behind; and we, with a single aim in view, that of being fucked, we wasted no time higgling or disputing, but lent ourselves on the spot to this usage or to that, glad simply to obtain fuck in no matter what orifice: such is the attitude every woman should adopt. Is there anything more absurd, indeed, than to fancy that there is only one part of the body for the reception of pricks, and that if perchance one strays off the beaten track crimes at once start to be committed? as if, in shaping us two-holed, Nature had not indicated to man to stopper them both, indiscriminately; and that with a predilection for the one or the other, let him but proceed as he likes, he acts within the laws of a mother far too wise to have conferred upon one of her feeblest creatures the empty little privilege of outraging her.

Very partisan to this manner of fucking, considering it beyond comparison with the other, I was gratified to have no one, during this second round, ask for anything but my ass, and I made it available to all comers.

At length we reached the elder recluses.

"Nothing must be neglected, no exceptions granted," Clairwil said, "no man is without merit once he can be got to discharge; fuck is all I expect of any of them."

Several who were lying abed with novices bent cold glances in our direction. "You've nothing to offer us that would recompense infidelity on our part," they told us; "even were you to avail us of the shrine wherein we perform our customary sacrifices, there would yet be that other altar whose mere presence nearby is sufficient to defeat any attempt at homage:

> *Contrive what she will, however she turn,*
> *A woman can be nought but a woman.*
> —Martial, *Epig*."

From others we had friendlier greeting; but to what trouble we had to go only to stiffen their antique instruments! to what were we not obliged to consent! what ministrations, what lewd attentions! how many different roles did we have to play! Now victims, now priestesses, we had, by means of cruel macerations, to resuscitate a well-nigh extinct Nature in some, whereas others could not be brought out of their lethargy until we submitted ourselves to be molested by them. One of these old sinners must flog us, we gave him leave; we lashed others; we had to lend our mouths to five or six; and very scurvily they repaid our industry, spending their strength before we could obtain the least benefit from it; yet others demanded more unusual treatment; we complied in every instance . . . and they all discharged, down to the sexton, to the gate-keeper, to the pew-sweepers who fucked us unendingly, attaining staggering totals; and after having been a good three hundred times mounted in one way or another by all manner of riders, we took our departure, smitten by every sort of fatigue that can whelm the human frame. Nine days of moderate living, including lots of baths and whey, restored us so wonderfully to rights that you'd never have guessed the Carmelites had served us anything stronger than tea.

But while no outward marks of that party were left on me, it had fired my imagination; my mental state was something that defies description, I was enwrapped in an unabating delirium of lubricity; to find relief or, if not that, to arouse myself further, I decided to go alone for once to a foregathering of our Sodality: there are moments when, however agreeable the company of a person like in mind to ourselves, we nevertheless prefer solitude, thinking, perhaps, that we will be freer, that our fancy will enjoy a wider scope; for when alone one is dispensed of that kind of shame or bashfulness so hard to be rid of when with others; and there is, after all, no equivalent to solitary crimes.

It had been some while since I had appeared in those circles: constantly surrounded by pleasures, I often did not know how to choose among them. No sooner did I enter than I was beset by suitors and paid a thousand compliments; and it became quite clear that though I might have come there animated by ferocious intentions, the part I was going to have to enact was not the sacrificer's, but the victim's. A man in his early forties encunted me; to his ardors I responded with that minimum of interest courtesy demands; I remained very listless until my glance lit upon an extremely handsome abbot who at the time was alternately embuggering two young ladies while having himself fucked. He was scarce a yard away; I ventured a few smutty comments, I noticed that they excited him, and that he was now devoting a good deal more attention to me than to the material he was using. Hastily disencumbering ourselves of our several entourages, we joined each other.

"Your style of fucking is far more to my liking than the one you saw me subjected to a moment ago," said I; "it surpasses my understanding how a man fit to belong to this Sodality durst continue to dally with a cunt."

"I too am puzzled by the thing," Chabert admitted.

(For it was Chabert, my friends, the very same who today is the fairest ornament in our little rural society, and whom you shall soon see playing a role in my adventures.)

"That is to say," my engaging abbot went on, "this prick you see here, and you see it yet in goodly size and fettle, is of the variety that tickles more in ass than in cunt."

"I'm sure of it," I replied.

"In which case," said he, taking me by the hand and beckoning his late fucker to follow, "let us remove to a boudoir, and I'll show you to what a degree our tastes are alike."

We established ourselves; Chabert's fucker was furnished like a mule: the Abbot himself was very respectfully outfitted; my ass drained their four balls dry. I promised Chabert we would meet again, and stole off to the seraglios where, thanks to the stimulants I had just absorbed, I arrived in a fury. After treating myself to three hours of ass-fucking I went from the male slaves' quarters to the females', in search of victims. Recollecting those pits dug between the two walls, and in whose depths one had the feeling of being in the remotest place on earth, I selected a pair of little girls, one aged five, the other six, and off we went. I had a marvelous time: there where we were, you might scream, you might rave, you might shout your lungs away, dwellers in the antipodes would sooner have heard you than the inhabitants of our hemisphere; and after such horrors as you may prefer to surmise rather than have me paint for you, I alone climbed up flights of stairs three human beings had descended not long before.

It was soon afterward that I dined at the home of Noirceuil. His other guest, a striking figure of a man, was identified to me as Comte de Belmor.

"Here is our new president," said Noirceuil. "The Comte assumes office today, and for his inaugural address he has promised us a discourse on love. Unless I am mistaken it will contain much to forearm the feminine heart against a sentiment which women only too often have the extravagance to conceive for men. And you, my friend," he continued, turning to Belmor, "allow me to introduce the famous Juliette to you. Have you met at the Sodality?"

"No," said the Comte, "I do not believe I recall having seen Madame—"

"Never mind," said Noirceuil, "you'll have become acquainted with her before you leave. . . . Here is the fairest ass . . . and the blackest soul—a personage of our own stripe, Comte. She shall be there to listen to you this afternoon; would you care to do anything before we dine? I am expecting Clairwil but, you know, it will be four o'clock ere she has completed her toilette. Since it is only three now, let me exhort you to step briefly into my boudoir, my valet will be at your orders."

Belmor consented; the valet arrived, and we all three encloseted ourselves. Belmor's passion was simple: he kissed, he lengthily, pensively brooded over a woman's buttocks while receiving a sodomization from the man; then, when this man had discharged, he re-stiffened the man's prick by rubbing it upon the woman's ass, got from him a second ejaculation which with great care he guided so that it landed exactly in the hole, and devoured what the man had just loosed, the woman farting meanwhile. He was then flogged. The Comte now rehearsed each scene in the drama, but feeling that he would have to face heavy obligations later on in the day, refrained from discharging; we quit the boudoir. A perfectly heavenly Clairwil had just appeared; we took ourselves to table.

"Juliette," Noirceuil said to me, "you must not think that the Comte's practices are limited to the mild little ritual you and he have just executed. You are our friend, this he knew. He behaved with the appropriate consideration."

"He is capable of singular self-restraint," Clairwil put in.

"Are you then familiar, Madame," I asked, smiling, "with what Monsieur does when carried away? Do not leave me in ignorance, I beg of you; for I would fain be privy to everything concerning such an amiable gentleman."

"Comte," Noirceuil asked, "do you deem it fitting she be told?"

"Is it truly advisable? Such information must surely give Madame an unfavorable impression of my character."

"Reassure yourself," said Clairwil. "My friend is apt to esteem you above all for the multiplicity and superlativeness of your vices."

"This scoundrel's favorite caprice," said Noirceuil, "is to

have a little boy of five or six bound to the shoulders of a beautiful woman; a knife is taken to the tender victim, innumerable gashes are so inflicted as to cause the flowing of blood to collect and run in a single rivulet down between the buttocks and over the asshole of the woman, who is obliged to shit during the operation. As for Belmor, he, kneeling before that behind—the formulation of the details is correct as I give them, Comte?"

The Comte nodded.

"Belmor, kneeling before that behind, laps up the blood while one after the other three men discharge themselves limp into his bum. And so, you see, what you and he have recently done is merely a diminutive version of his choice vagary; here again we find the general truth confirmed: that in a man the lesser quirk relates directly to the greater, and that to the discerning eye there is no lack of clues pointing to a man's predominating vice."

"Fuck!" I exclaimed joyously, throwing my arms around the Comte's neck, "your mania makes my head fairly reel; I entreat you to employ my bottom in connection with quantities of such operations, and depend upon me to omit nothing that may contribute to the perfection of your ecstasies."

My Lord gave me assurance that he would be calling upon me before the day was out; and in a discreet whisper he besought me to reserve him my turd.

"Just as I thought," said Clairwil. "I knew that in announcing your libertinage to her you were in no danger of displeasing Juliette."

Said Noirceuil: "Aye, temperance is a very foolish virtue, that is certain. Man is born for enjoyment, and through his debaucheries alone does he gain access to the sweetest pleasures of life. Only idiots are wont to deny themselves."

Now Clairwil: "For my part, I believe that we owe it to ourselves to indulge blindly in everything and at all costs to pursue the happiness we situate in the midst of the extremest irregularities."

And the Comte: "Nature counsels man to seek it nowhere else; the inconstancy that has been provided him, urging him to broaden the range of his sensations every day, conclusively shows that the fairest lie out of the way of onerous routine. Woe betide them who, setting shackles on a man's passions while he is yet young, develop in him the habit of self-denial and thereby render him the most unfortunate of beings. What a terrifying disservice is thus done to him—"

"Let there be no mistake as to the aims of those who behave in this manner," Noirceuil interrupted; "doubt not that they are motivated by jealousy, by vindictiveness . . . by fear lest others be as happy as those same pedants feel when they surrender to their own peculiar passions."

"Superstition," said Belmor, "has a large hand in the thing: it had inevitably to compose possible offenses to the God it created; what else could be done? A God who is never cross with anybody, vexed by nothing, instead of appearing omnipotent, soon takes on the air of helplessness; and in what more likely place could the seed of crime be located than in the spurt of passion?"

"Immense are the wrongs religion has done the world," Noirceuil muttered.

"Of the ills afflicting mankind," said I, "I regard it as the most dangerous; he who was the first to broach the subject to men was plainly their greatest enemy at the time, and history provides no worse since. No death however atrocious would have equaled his deserts."

"The necessity to destroy it, to extirpate it," said Belmor, "is not deeply enough felt in our country."

"The task will be arduous," said Noirceuil; "man cleaves to nothing so doggedly as to the principles he is fed in childhood. We shall perhaps someday see the people become prey to another set of prejudices quite as ridiculous as those of religion, and in the name of a new craze topple the idols of the former. But like unto the timid child, our nation will after a little begin to weep for its broken rattles and will soon put them back together again with a thousand times more fervor. No, no, philosophy is not something you shall ever observe in the people, too rude, too dense ever to be softened and refined by the sacred torch of that goddess; sacerdotal authority, perhaps enfeebled temporarily, will only re-establish itself the more forcefully, and 'twill be to the end of time you'll see superstition supplying its venom to human thirst."

"That is a horrible prediction."

"It is horribly apt to be true."

"Is there no remedy for our plight?"

"One," said the Comte, "only one, it is violent but it is sure: we must arrest and slaughter all the priests in a single day and deal similarly with all their followers; simultaneously, inside the space of the same minute, destroy every last vestige of Catholicism; and concurrently proclaim atheistic systems, and instantly entrust to philosophers the education of our youth; print, publish, distribute, give out, everywhere display those writings which propagate incredulity, unbelief, and for fifty years prosecute and put to death every individual, without exception, who might think to re-inflate the balloon.[11] But, you may hear it insolently objected to this, severity makes proselytes to a cause; intolerance is the soil wherein all martyrs grow. These replies are absurd. All this they are telling me has happened in the past, to be sure, but only because hitherto the process has been conducted far too gently, far too lazily, far too vaguely: the surgery has now and again been attempted, but cautiously, fumblingly, then suspended short of completion, never pursued to the end. You don't confine yourself to severing one of the Hydra's heads, it's the entire monster you must exterminate; if your martyrs have confronted death courageously it is because they were inspired and enheartened by their predecessors. Massacre them all at a stroke, let nothing remain, and from then on you'll have done with both sectarians and martyrs."

"This is not an easy operation," Clairwil hazarded.

"Infinitely easier than one might think," Belmor replied, "and I am prepared to direct it if the government cares to place twenty-five thousand men under my command; the elements of success are some political support, secrecy, and firmness: no flabbiness, that's essential, and no keeping people waiting in line. You fear martyrs, you'll have them so long as a single worshiper of that abominable Christian God is left alive—"

"But," I declared, "are you not going to be forced to wipe out two-thirds of France?"

---

[11] Simply compare the oceans of blood these knaves have spilled over the course of eighteen centuries with the lakes of it promised by Belmor's measures, and one cannot but conclude that in qualifying his remedy as violent, the Comte speaks with a touch of irony. For no juster measures have ever been proposed, and peace shall not reign among men until this one is adopted and carried ruthlessly out.

"Not even one-third," Belmor assured us; "but supposing the destruction were to have to be as extensive as you say, would it not be a hundred times better that our fair part of Europe be inhabited by ten million honest folk rather than by twenty-five million rascals? However, I repeat, it is exceedingly doubtful that France counts as many Christians as you seem to imagine; at any rate, separating the sheep from the goats would not take long. Compiling my lists should require no more than a year's work in shadow and silence; and I'd not unleash the campaign until I was sure of all the objectives it entailed."

"The bloodshed would be stupendous."

"Granted; but it would ensure France's health and happiness forever; it is a potent remedy administered to a vigorous body: repairing matters all at one stroke, it eliminates the need for continual purgings which, become too numerous, finally result in complete exhaustion.

"Be well persuaded of it, eighteen hundred years of thorns in France's side have been planted there only by religious factions."[12]

"From what you say, Comte, are we to infer that you think poorly of religion in general?"

"I see it weigh upon nations like a plague. Had I not such love for my country I would perhaps be less opposed to those forces which tend to maim and ruin it—"

"May the government charge you with the mission you desire," said Noirceuil, "I too would be delighted by the results, since it would cleanse out of the portion of the globe where I live an abominable confession which I hate at least as much as you do."

We had completed a most sumptuous meal and the hour being late, we went straight to the Sodality after coffee.

The inauguration of a president was accompanied by a curious traditional custom. The presidential chair was, as you know, upon an elevated platform; now, before and below it, a large pouf was placed, over it the new chief officer bent, and each Sodality member stepped forward in turn to kiss his ass. When he had

---

[12] How simple it would be to demonstrate that the present revolution is purely the handiwork of the Jesuits, and that the *Orléanais-Jacobin* crew who fomented it were and are nothing but descendants of Loyola! (*Note to a subsequent edition.*)

gathered homage from everyone, the Comte rose and mounted to his throne.

"Fellow members," he began, "*love* is the subject of the speech I have prepared for this august occasion. Although my remarks may appear to be addressed to men only, I believe I may venture to say that they contain virtually everything a woman need hear to ensure her protection against this grave peril."

Then, adjusting his dress, and silence descending upon the assembly, he expressed himself in the following terms:

"The word *love* is used to designate that deep-seated feeling which propels us, as it were despite ourselves, toward some foreign object or other; which provokes in us a keen desire to become united to it, to ever lessen the distance between it and ourselves . . . which delights us, ravishes us . . . renders us ecstatic when we achieve that union, and which casts us into despond, which tears us asunder, whenever the intrusion of external considerations constrain us to rupture this union. If only this extravagance never led to anything more serious than pleasure intensified by the ardor, the abandon, inherent in it, it would merely be ridiculous; but as it leads us into a certain metaphysic, which, confounding us with the loved object, transforming us into it, making its actions, its needs, its desires quite as vital and dear to us as our own—through this alone it becomes exceedingly dangerous, by detaching us from ourselves, and by causing us to neglect our interests in favor of the beloved's; by identifying us, so to speak, with this object, it causes us to assume its woes, its griefs, its chagrins, and thus consequently adds to the sum of our own. Meanwhile, the dread of losing that object, or of seeing its feelings for us pale and vanish, harries us unceasingly; and though at the outset we be in the serenest of states, this cross once become our burden we gradually sink into what is doubtless the cruelest that can be imagined on earth. If the reward for so many pains, or their counterpart, were anything beyond an ordinary spasm, I might perhaps recommend risking it; but all the cares, all the torments, all the anguishes and nuisances of love never yield anything but what might be conveniently obtained without it; why then must one put on these chains! When a beautiful woman offers herself to me, and when I fall in love with her, my ambitions in her regard nevertheless remain no different from

those of another who claps eyes on her and who desires her without
feeling for her any sort of love at all; both he and I want to lie with
her—*he,* 'tis but her body he desires; and *I,* by a fallacious and always perilous metaphysic blinding myself to the veritable motive
which, howbeit, is not one whit different from my rival's, I persuade myself that it's only her heart I want, that all carnal possession of her is quite aside from the question, banished therefrom,
and of this I persuade myself so thoroughly that I would gratefully
come to an arrangement with this woman, whereby I would love
her only for her self and purchase her heart at the price of sacrificing all my physical desires. There is the cruel cause of my error;
there is what is about to drag me down into a frightful abyss of
unhappiness, there is what is about to spoil my life: I am in love,
from now on everything is going to change: suspicions, jealousies,
alarms, worries are going to become my eternal fare, the very
substance of my wretched existence; and the nearer I come to the
day when happiness shall be mine, the greater shall be the store
I set by it, and the worse shall become the fatal terror of losing it.

"By refusing the thorns of this dangerous sentiment you
must not think that I deprive myself of its roses; no, this will enable
me to pluck them without danger; I'll retain only the nectar in the
flower, discarding the dross of extraneous matter; likewise I'll have
possession of the body I desire and shall not have that of the soul,
which is of no use to me at all. Were man to reflect more carefully
upon his true interests in pleasure-taking, he would spare his heart
this cruel fever that burns and wastes it: if he could but realize that
there is no need to be loved in order to be satisfied, and that love
acts rather to hinder than to promote the transports of enjoyment,
he would disdain this metaphysic of sentiment which beclouds his
understanding, confine himself to the simple enjoyment of bodies,
would make acquaintance of true happiness, and would deliver
himself forever from the anxieties inseparable from his baneful
fineness of feeling.

" 'Tis an intellectual construction . . . a mystification, an entirely fictitious, chimerical sensation, this delicacy we would introduce into the desire of enjoyment; it sometimes assumes considerable importance in the metaphysic of love; it's the same here as
with all illusions, they embellish one another reciprocally. But

delicacy is useless, even disruptive, in all that pertains to the satisfaction of the senses: the complete inutility of love now becomes
very evident, and the rational individual can no longer behold
the object of his pleasures as anything more than an object which
causes a sharp rise in the temperature of the neural fluids, than a
creature of precious little account *per se,* a creature whose function
is simply to contribute to the purely physical satisfaction of the
desires that have caught fire from the heat it has provoked in this
neural fluid, and which, this satisfaction once given and received,
loses, in the thinking man's eyes, all particular attributes, returning to its former anonymous place within its general class. It is not
unique in its species, he will be able to find other samples of the
same thing, equally good, equally compliable; he was living well
before this encounter, why should he not live just as well after it?
In what possible way could he be disturbed by this woman's infidelity? When she lavishes her favors upon somebody else, will she
be robbing her lover of anything? He has had his fair turn, what is
he complaining about now? Why should somebody else not have
his turn too, and what will he lose in this creature that he cannot
immediately find in another? Put case that she is false to him and
lies with a rival, she can quite as easily deceive that rival and get
back into bed with him; she is thus no more in love with this
second lover than with the first; wherefore should either of them
be jealous, since neither is treated better than the other? Such
regrets might, at the very most, be pardonable if this cherished
woman were the only one in the world; they are preposterous once
loss of her is reparable. Imagining myself for a moment in our
first lover's place, what is there about this creature, I wonder, that
can give rise to my dolor? She made some fuss over my person,
to my feelings made some responses; if they seemed emphatic at
all, it was because illusion supplied nine-tenths of their force; mere
eagerness to possess this woman, my curiosity about her, my stratagems to gain her, these embellished her in my eyes, and if the
having of her does not make the scales drop away, it is either because I yet want experience in these things or am still laboring
under the effects of my earlier mistakes, it is the blindfold I used
to wear and was accustomed to in the days before I came to know
anything about women, which, in spite of me, now returns to

obscure my vision and befuddle my brain again; and I do not snatch it off and fling it away! It is weakness, it is most unmanly; the romping over with, let's consider her analytically, this Aphrodite who dazzled us a short while ago. Here, in this moment of calm and weariness, here is the opportunity for a scientific survey; as Lucretius says, let's have a glance into the backstage of life. Well, we shall find her, this celestial object we were enthralled by, entranced by, we shall find her endowed with the same desires, the same needs, the same shape of body, the same appetites, afflicted by the same infirmities as all the other creatures of her sex; and cold-blooded examination dispelling the ridiculous enthusiasm that drove us toward this object, in no particular different from all the rest of its kind, we shall see that in having it no more we lack nothing that cannot be easily replaced. Amenities of character comprise an element that is not relevant to our discussion; these virtues falling entirely inside the domain of friendship, they ought only be appreciated there; but, in love, I am wrong if I believe it was that which attracted me: no, it's solely the body I love, and it's the body alone whose loss I lament, though I can get another as good, just like it, whenever I please; how pointless now are my whinings, and how superfluous my regrets!

"Let us have the courage to acknowledge the truth: in no case is a woman designed to ensure the exclusive happiness of one man; viewed from the angle of his enjoyment, she can hardly be said to render it complete, for he obtains better and livelier in conversation with his fellows; while if now she be regarded in the role of a friend, her duplicity and her servility, or rather her baseness, scarcely favor the perfection of the sentiment of friendship; friendship requires openness and equality; when one of two friends dominates the other, friendship is destroyed; now, this preponderance of one of the two sexes over the other, fatal to friendship, exists necessarily where two friends are of unlike sex; thus, woman is good neither as a mistress nor as a friend; she is only where she belongs when in the servitude where the Orientals keep her; her usefulness extends no farther than the pleasure she can afford, after which, as good King Chilperic used to say, best have away with her as promptly as ever you can.

"If it is easy to demonstrate that love is nothing but a national superstition; that three-fourths of the world's societies, whose custom is to keep their females under lock and key, have never been subject to the ravages of this imaginative disorder; so now, in tracing this superstition back to its sources, we shall have little trouble assuring ourselves that it is merely an ailment and arriving at the sure means for curing it. Now, it is certain that this our chivalric gallantry, which ridiculously proposes as the object for our veneration that object which is made only for our needs, it is certain, I say, that this attitude comes from the respect our ancestors used long ago to have for women owing to the witchcraft and the prophetic trades they exercised in the towns and rural places; terror turned respect into worship, and gallantry was born from the womb of ignorant superstition. But this respect was not natural, you'll waste your time scanning Nature for any sign of it; the inferiority of females to males is established and patent, there is nothing in their sex which can constitute a solid title to our respect; and love, begot of this blind respect, is, like it, a superstition: respect for women increases the farther the principles animating a given government depart from those of Nature; so long as men remain obedient to her fundamental laws, however, they are bound to hold women in supremest contempt; women become gods when those laws cease to be heeded, for when Nature's voice grows faint in men they become enfeebled, and the weaker must inevitably command where the stronger degrade themselves: wherefore it is that government is always debilitated when women reign; cite not to me the example of Turkey, if her government is weak today this was not the case before harem intrigues began to regulate its workings: the Turks destroyed the Byzantine Empire in the days when they dragged that sex in chains, and when in the presence of his marshaled army Mahomet II beheaded Irene, who was suspected of having overmuch influence upon him. Woman-worship, however mild, attests baseness and sore depravation; for it is impossible even in the moment of ecstasy, how can it be possible afterward? If because something proves serviceable this be reason for deifying it, you owe a like reverence to your bull, your donkey, your chamberpot, etc.

"That which they call love is, in short, nothing else than the desire to enjoy; so long as it exists, worship is of no help;

so soon as it is satisfied, worship is impossible: which proves that it was certainly not from worship the respect was born, but the contrary. Glance at examples showing the lowly position women occupied in the past and yet occupy in a great many lands today, and you will conclude, if you are yet in any doubt, that the metaphysical passion of love is in no wise innate in man but is the fruit of his erroneous thinking and mistaken practices, and that the object which gave rise to this passion, generally scorned everywhere, ought never have blinded him.

"Such is that scorn amongst the Croats, more particularly known to geographers as Uskoks and Morlacks,[13] that when they refer to their wives, they employ the same coarse expression the vulgar commonly use in connection with a vile animal.[14] They never suffer them in their beds, women in that part of the world sleep on the bare ground, without a murmur and with utmost alacrity do as they are told, and are mercilessly beaten at the least hint of disobedience; their subordinate situation, their drudgeries, and their fare remain unchanged at all times, even when they are with child: they are often seen to give birth in open fields, pick up their offspring, wash it in the nearest stream, bring it home, and resume their chores; and observers have remarked that in this country the children are a good deal healthier and more robust, the wives a good deal more faithful, than elsewhere; it would seem that Nature is loath to relinquish the rights which decadent habits and false delicacy seek to strip her of in our climates without achieving any other result than abasing our sex in ranking it evenly with the other Nature created to be its slave.

"In Zaporozhian Cossack country women are excluded from the clan; those who serve for propagational purposes are relegated to islands, and when in need men go thither to use them, but haphazardly, indifferently; need eliminates all considerations of age, looks, kinship, in such wise that the father begets children on his daughter; the brother on his sister; and no other laws with these people, save such as need establishes.

---

[13] At the period these mountaineers were active in the service of Austria's reigning house, they won themselves the name of Pandours. They inhabit the southern regions of Austrian Croatia. Pandour means highwayman.

[14] Saving your presence.

"There are places where, when women menstruate, they are treated like beasts; they are penned, caged, shut up tight, food is thrown to them from a goodly distance—so tigers are fed, or bears; do you fancy these people go to much bother loving their wives?

"In the kingdom of Loango, in Africa, pregnant women are yet more rudely dealt with; once in this state, they are reckoned more than ever impure, misshapen, and disgusting; and indeed, pray tell me, what is there more frightful to see than an expectant mother? Gravid and stark naked, it is thus the entire sex ought to be shown to its admirers, since they have a liking for the grotesque and the horrible.

"A woman gives birth, and the blacks of Barray suspend all commerce with her for four years and upward.

"The wives of Madura, alluding to their husbands, speak in circumlocutions; which signify the profound respect they have for them.

"The Romans and the Celts held the right of life and death over their wives, and exercised it often; this is a right we have by Nature: flouting her and weakening her laws, when we neglect to use it.

"Their bondage is grim throughout almost all of Africa; she esteems herself beyond words fortunate when her husband deigns to accept her attentions.

"They are so ill-treated, so unhappy in the principality of Juida, that those who are recruited for the harems of the prince prefer, when they can, to kill themselves rather than be taken there, this sovereign never making dalliance of a woman without, they say, subjecting her to execrable discomforts.

"Do we bend a glance at those magnificent retreats in Asia: there we see proud despots, whose desires have the force of orders, exposing purest beauty to all such nasty whims as imagination may compose, and reducing to the lowest level of degradation those insolent divinities whom we, to our disgrace, revere.

"The Chinese have the loftiest contempt for women, and consider them hardly fit to be used, and even less so to be seen.

"When the Emperor of Golconda would go out to take the air, a dozen of the tallest and strongest girls in his harem, disposing themselves some atop the others, some before and some behind, form a kind of dromedary, the four sturdiest being its legs; His Majesty is hoisted up into the saddle, and off they trot. I leave you to speculate upon this monarch's conduct inside his pleasure palaces, and upon what his astonishment would be if someone were to tell him that the very same creatures he uses for bum-wipes were objects of worship in Europe.

"The Muscovites are unwilling to eat anything that has been killed by a woman.

"Ah! be certain of it, my brothers, it was not to see us grovel in the grips of a sentiment so base as love that Nature put muscle and intelligence on our side: it was to rule that weaker and deceitful sex, to force it into our desires' service; and we totally forget her intentions when we accord some independence, let alone some ascendancy, to beings whom she made to be absolutely in our power.

"We fancy there is happiness to be found in the affection we fancy women to have for us; but that sentiment, always meretricious, is always measured out, so much, so little, depending upon the need a woman calculates she has of us, or upon the sort of passion we flatter in her; let age whiten our hairs, or let there be an adverse shift in our fortunes, so that we can no longer serve her pleasures, her greed, or her pride, and she abandons us upon the spot, frequently to become our most mortal enemy. In any case, we have no crueler foes than women, even those who adore us sincerely; if we consult them for our pleasures, then they tyrannize over us; if we snub them, then they look for revenge and always end up doing us ill; whence it results that of all man's passions, love is the most dangerous and that against which he should take the greatest care to defend himself.

"To judge whether love be madness, is not the lover's distraction sufficient proof of it? or that fatal illusion he entertains, which causes him to ascribe such charms to the object he dotes upon and goes scampering about praising to the skies? Not a flaw that has not been rewrought into a virtue; not a defect that does not become a beauty; all that is ridiculous in her is changed into grace; ha! when the tempest subsides and the lover, open-eyed, can coolly inspect the contemptible object of his enthusiasms, must he not, as he blushes before his despicable error, at least make firm resolutions never to be misled in the future?

"Inconstancy and libertinage, those, my brothers, are the two antidotes to love; accustoming us to dealings with these false divinities, they both exert a gradual erosive action upon the illusion, till finally it is all eaten quite away; you cease sooner or later to adore what you see every day: thanks to the habit of inconstancy and of libertinage, the heart loses, little by little, the dangerous softness which permits it to be susceptible to the impressions of love; surfeited, it hardens, it toughens, and the patient may soon be considered cured. What! shall I go mope before the door of this creature who only lets me in at last to put the remnants of my good humor at further defiance, shall I endure all this when, if I pause to think an instant, I realize that with perfect ease and at the price of a few francs I can have the hire of a body just as fair as hers? We must bear it ever in mind that the woman who strives to get us the most inextricably into her captivity is certainly concealing flaws which would rapidly disgust us if we knew what they were; do we but set our imagination to envisaging these details, to probing after them, to guessing at them; and this preliminary exercise initiated at the same moment love is born will perhaps succeed in extinguishing it. Be she a girl? She surely exhales some unhealthy odor, if not now then later on; is it worth your while, sir, to pant after a cesspool? Be she a woman? Another's leavings may, I admit, momentarily rouse our desires. . . . But our love . . . and what's to be idolized here? This vast mold that's cast a dozen brats. . . . Picture her giving birth, this treasure of your heart; behold that shapeless mass of flesh squirm sticky and festering from the cavity where you believe felicity is to be found. Undress this the idol of your soul, undress her, even at some other time: is it over these two crooked and stubby thighs you propose to rave? Or over this unclean, fetid gulf where they meet? Ah ha, it's perhaps this apron of matted hairs hanging untidy between those same thighs that is due to fire your imagination . . . or else these two flaccid globes drooping flappily onto her navel? Would it not be on this nearer side but on the farther she harbors charms worth your homage? Lo, here they are, these two wattles of weary tallow-colored flesh, sheltering a livid hole that connects with the other:

oh yes, these are the wonders your mind battens on, and it is for their sake you sink yourself into a condition lower than the condition of an earthworm? But what's this? I am mistaken? you are not attracted by any of this, there are much finer qualities than these that spellbind you: it is that traitorous cunning character, those perpetual dishonesties, that lying tongue, that shrewish scolding tone, this voice like a cat's, or this whorishness, or this prudery, for woman spends her life in the one or the other of those two extremes; this calumny . . . this spitefulness . . . this contrariness . . . this witless inconsequence, ever nagging, caviling, cawing stupidity. . . Yes, yes, I see it clearly, such are the attributes you cherish in her, and they doubtless merit going into a dither over.[15]

"Think not that I exaggerate matters: if all these defects are not combined in the same individual, the one you worship surely has her share of them; if they escape your eye, that's because they are screened from your sight, but they exist, fear not, they exist: clothing or education may disguise what would revolt you if you saw it, the defect is none the less real even though you see it not, or not yet; hunt for it before attaching yourself, you will ferret it out every time, and if you be wise, my friend, halt there rather than throw happiness and tranquillity to the winds for the enjoying of an object which, certainly, infallibly, you will soon start to loathe.

"Oh, my brothers, contemplate a little the host of sorrows this baneful passion brings in its wake . . . the cruel maladies caused by the sufferings it gives, the material expenditures, the loss as well of sleep, of ease, of appetite, of health, the obligatory renunciation of all other pleasures; realizing the gigantic sacrifices it entails, and profiting from all these examples, do as does the prudent helms-

---

[15] The difference between a man and a woman, of this we may be perfectly confident, is quite as pronounced, quite as important as between man and ape; our grounds for refusing to include women in our species would be quite as valid as for refusing to consider the chimpanzee our brother. Next to a naked woman stand a man of the same age and naked too; now examine them attentively, and you will be at no pains to discern the palpable and marked difference which (sex aside) exists in the composition of these two beings; you will be obliged to conclude that woman is simply man in an extraordinarily degraded form; there are internal differences as well, and these are brought to light by anatomical comparison: the dissection should be performed carefully and simultaneously.

man who steers not for the reef littered with the hulks of a thousand shattered vessels.

"Eh, can you not forego these dubious pleasures when life has so many other, genuine, ones to offer? Why, what is this I say? life offers you the very same ones, and gives them to you free of any disagreeable accompaniments or aftermaths. Since libertinage assures you the same enjoyments and in return asks only that you clear them of this icy metaphysic, which adds nothing to pleasures, feast unrestrictedly upon everything that appeals to your senses; and in order to use a woman must you necessarily love her? We all of us here feel, it seems to me, that a woman is made much better use of when she is not loved or at least that loving her is perfectly gratuitous so long as matters are taken no farther than that. And what need have we to take them farther, I should like to know, wherefore prolong our pleasures by a ludicrous flight of melancholy and madness? After five or six hours of her, have we not had quite enough of this woman? One night more, a hundred nights more would only yield us the same pleasures; while other objects hold new ones in store for you. What! millions of beauties await you, and you'd be such a fool as to bind yourself to one? Would you not smile at the simpleton who, invited to a magnificent banquet, ate of one dish only, though fivescore others were offered to his delectation? It is diversity, it is change, that makes for the happiness in life, and if every single object on earth can procure you a new delight, what manner of lunatic are you who would be the prisoner of somebody who can afford you only one?

"What I have said of women, my brothers, may also be applied to men. Our defects are just as serious as theirs, and they are as unluckily moored to us as we to them, the putting on of any shackle is a folly, every bond is an attempt against the physical liberty which is our due, and which we ought to enjoy here on earth. And while I am wasting my time with this being, whatever it is, a hundred thousand others are growing old around me, who would much more merit my homage.

"And, further, is it a mistress who can satisfy a man? Is it then, as slave to his goddess' velleities and whims, which he must labor to content, that he will be able to devote attention to his personal desires? Superiority is necessary in the pleasurable act; he of the two who shares his joy has less of it, he who obeys has none; get thee gone, idiotic delicacy which causes us to find charms . . . even in our sacrifices; these pleasure-takings, purely intellectual stunts, can they compare to those which involve our senses? The love of women is like unto that of God: in either case, we feed upon illusions. In the former, we wish only to love the spiritual, making abstraction of the corporeal, in the second, we ascribe a body to a spirit; and in both, we tumble to our knees before fictions.

"Let us enjoy ourselves to the full: such is Nature's law; and as it is altogether impossible to love for long the object we enjoy, let us calmly accept that things be with us as they are with those creatures we sometimes unjustly deem inferior. Do we observe the pigeon or the dog return and salute his companion when finished with her? bow and scrape, kiss her paw or claw? If loves flares up in a dog, this love could as well be called need, is nothing else than need; once the bitch has satisfied him, indifference, aversion characterize his attitude toward her until he begins to desire again; but his desire will not be for the same female; all those he comes across will each in turn become the object of the inconstant male's attentions; and if a dispute arises, yesterday's favorite will be sacrificed as today's rival. Ah, we err when we depart from these models, closer than we to Nature; they act in much nearer harmony with her laws; and if Nature has allotted us a few more sensitive faculties than they, this is in order that we refine their pleasures. From the moment we recognize that if the human female is more than an animal the difference is made up wholly of shortcomings, why must we reverence this portion which in fact humbles her? We may love her body, as the animal loves its mate's; but let us have no sentiments for what we suppose distinct from the body, since precisely there is located that which counterbalances the rest, that which alone ought to make us reject her entire. Yes, oh yes, the womanish character, her surliness, her unwholesome mind, her perfidious soul, these ought always to dampen in me any inclination to enjoy a woman's body, and if you would gauge to what extent his reason has been impaired by metaphysical frenzy, only listen to the love-sick exclaim that it is not his beloved's body he wants, but her heart—her heart! that thing which should rather make him flee in horror from her presence. This extravagance has no parallel; more, beauty being nothing but an affair of convention, love can be no more than an arbitrary sentiment once beauty's traits, which are what cause love to be born, are not uniform.

"Love thus being simply the taste describing the requirements of a given individual's organs, it is a physical impulse, neither more nor less, and with it delicacy of feeling, sophisticated modes of courtship can have nothing to do; for it is now plain that I love a blonde because she has attributes which establish close link with my senses; you love a brunette for similar reasons; and with both blonde and brunette, the material object becoming the instrument for the relief of our eminently material need, how are you going to apply your delicacy and your disinterest to this piece of plumbing? Do you fancy something metaphysical there? Then pride has induced you into prodigious error; a single glance should suffice to blast the illusion. Would you not call him mad, who in all earnestness insisted that he was fond of the sweet william's scent but indifferent to the flower? There is no imagining into what incredible absurdities a man may tumble, who will become attached to and guided by every metaphysical mirage.

"But, and here I anticipate a possible objection, but this worship has existed throughout the ages; the Greeks and Romans deified Love and his mother. To this I reply, the thing may have come about with them as it did with us; in Greece and Rome women foretold the future also. Whence, probably, was born respect for them and from that respect, worship; I have already described how it may come about. However, concerning objects of worship, one ought to refer only very sparingly to the Ancients; peoples who adored fecal substances under the name of the god Sterculius and the sewers in the shape of the goddess Cloacina could readily worship women, so often likened by odor to those two classical divinities.

"And so let us finally use our common sense and treat these ridiculous idols as the Japanese treat theirs, whenever they fail to obtain satisfaction from them. Let us worship away or pretend to worship, if you like, until our prayers have been answered and the desired thing has been obtained; once it is ours, let's despise it; if we are refused, we'll give the idol a hundred blows with a stick, to teach it to disdain our wishes; or if you prefer, we shall imitate the Ostiaks who when irked by their gods promptly take a lash to them; with a god that proves thoroughly useless there is but one thing to do: pulverize it; a feigned belief will be quite enough at those moments when you are in hope of results.

"Love is a physical need, let us avoid ever considering it anything else.[16] 'Love,' writes Voltaire, 'is the imagination's embroidery upon Nature's homespun.' The aim of love, its desires, everything about it is physical; forever shun the object which would seem to demand anything more; absence and change are the sure remedies for love; one soon thinks no more about the person one has stopped seeing, and new delights efface the memory of old ones; regrets surrounding such losses do not long endure; irretrievable pleasures may of course engender bitter regrets, but those which are so easily replaced, those which are every moment reborn at every street corner, over these not a tear need be shed.

"And think now, what if love were not an evil but something truly good, that which does really make us happy, why, we should have to spend a fourth part of our lives without any enjoyment at all! What man dares suppose he will be able to captivate a woman's heart when he is past sixty? At sixty, however, if he be soundly made, he has still another fifteen years' potential enjoyment ahead of him; but he has lost his looks and so must bid happiness adieu! We shall accept no such monstrous proposition; if age withers the roses of springtime, it does not extinguish either the desires or the means to satisfy them; and the pleasures one tastes in later years, ever more elaborate, more choice, further divested of that stony metaphysic, a very grave to voluptuousness; these pleasures, I say, are a thousand times more delicious gathered in the depths of debauchery, of crapulousness, and of libertinage than were those he used long ago to procure his fair mistress; in those days he toiled for her sake, and at present his only concern is for himself. Watch him, mark those refinements, observe how he clings to something which he knows he can caress for but a fleeting instant; what a wealth of details in his lewd amusements, how he wrings every drop of enjoyment from each . . . notice how he would make free

---

[16] Upon this subject the celebrated Ninon de Lenclos, though a woman and a zealot, has interesting things to say.

of everything and how he wants all thoughts, all attentions to be concentrated upon him. The mere suspicion of pleasure in the object he is using would alarm him, infuriate him, he wants its submission, and that is all. Fair-haired Hebe averts her eyes, she cannot hide her revulsion; it matters not to seventy-year-old Philater, it is not in her behalf he exerts himself; and even these gasps and shudders of horror he produces only contribute to his mounting delight; disgust is easy to inspire; he is obliged to apply pressure; a few threats, then he opens his stinking mouth and sucks into it a sweet pure tongue; the young beauty quails; and suddenly here's the image of rape and consequently, for Philater, one pleasure the more. At twenty did he experience the like? They would rush upon him, deluge him with kisses, bewilder him with caresses, he'd hardly have time enough to desire them, and it would be over in the twinkling of an eye, without his being sure it had happened at all. Indeed, can that be called a desire which is satisfied before it has had the chance to be born? And where can there be desire if it has not resistance to overcome? If then pleasure is only stirred up by the irritations of resistance encountered, and if the latter is only bred by aversion, it may become delicious to cause aversion, and all the caprices which disgust a woman may then become more sensual and a hundred times better than love . . . love, the absurdest of all follies, the most ridiculous, and doubtless the most dangerous, whereof I think I have given you adequate demonstration."

This dissertation was not, to be sure, very warmly received by the women present; but Belmor, who sought their praise with no more eagerness than he did their sentiments, was amply consoled by the masculine applause that rang out heartily everywhere in the hall; handing the presidential attributes temporarily over to his predecessor, he made ready to reconnoiter the seraglios and exercise his authority there; Noirceuil, Clairwil, and I met him at the foot of the platform, and we all started off together toward the side door. We were not halfway there when a man of sixty halted Belmor and, asking to be allowed to express his congratulations, begged the favor of his ass; Belmor, unable to refuse, poised himself appropriately; the sexagenarian embuggered our Belmor and would not restore him to us until he had discharged into the chief executive's bum.

"There's a bit of unexpected luck," said the Comte.

"It is owing to your eloquence, my Lord," Noirceuil assured him.

"Materialist that I am," said Belmor, "I'd prefer to owe it to my ass than to my ideas," and we entered the game preserve, laughing at his Lordship's sally.

The President gave orders that during his inspection nobody be admitted into the premises apart from ourselves, who made up his escort; and he commenced his tour forthwith. Such a man, with such prepossessions, was able, as you may well imagine, to uncover a prodigious number of culprits; he was accompanied on his rounds by a quartet of executioners, two flayers, six flagellators, and four jailers: the first harem our procession entered was the one composed of women: to the lash he condemned thirty aged between five and ten, twenty-eight between ten and fifteen, forty-seven between fifteen and eighteen, sixty-five between eighteen and twenty-one; three children in the six-to-ten age group were condemned to be flayed alive, three others heard the extreme penalty pronounced against them; among those aged between ten and fifteen there were six girls selected for flaying, four were appointed to die; the next group (fifteen to eighteen) yielded another six for flaying and eight for execution; while from the last group only four were found to merit death and five the loss of their skins. The creatures thus sentenced were directed into the several chambers where, before suffering the penalties decreed, they were first made available to those libertines who, out of peculiarity of taste, might happen to repair thither for satisfaction. Four female subjects were condemned to the dungeons; regarding floggings, they were all meted out in our presence: the naked victim was led before the President, he would examine her, handle her for a little, a flagellator would then take her in charge, bend her over his knees; and when once she was in a position where she could not budge, a second flagellator, armed with a switch, a cat-o'-nine-tails, or some other instrument of the President's preference, would apply the number of strokes prescribed by him. Belmor was decent enough to leave the specification of a figure to us in almost every case, and I doubt whether we were beneath him in severity; six of those girls received such a hammering that, half-dead, they had to be borne out; the whole while these lubricious operations were going ahead we were all four entwined in one another's arms, there was a great deal of frigging done and much outpouring of fuck.

We moved to the seraglio of men; here Clairwil agitated against any relapse into indulgence and made liberal essay of stimulations. Belmor, however, whose fondest practice consisted, as you already have heard, in the massacre of small boys, was by no means backward in his display of ferocity. Forty-two children of between seven and twelve received the lash with utmost rigor; in this same group there were six sentences of death and ten of flaying. Sixty-four lads of between twelve and eighteen were no less sternly dealt with; here were three more death sentences, eight more flayings. In the upper class, comprised of those ranging from eighteen to twenty-five, fifty-six asses were singled out for whipping, two lives were lost, and three skins removed; all told, three males were designated for the dungeons; in addition, two matrons were given whippings for dereliction in the line of duty, and Belmor himself thrashed them till he had lifted the epidermis off their behinds.

I had been frigging him incessantly throughout all these operations, his prick was in a state of excessive erection; but if I am to do justice to his strength of character, let it be said that he did not once leak a drop of sperm nor show any pity for an instant.

"Very well now," Noirceuil said to him, "let's turn to pleasures; that passion of yours, Belmor, will you set it forth into view?"

"That is my intention," said the Comte; "but dreadfully wrought up as I am, I mean to give an appallingly extensive vent to it."

"Excellent, we'll only enjoy it the more."

Whereupon the President re-examined all the little boys and out of the lot chose ten no older than seven. He required as many girls; but I having asked to play the part of one of them, he had to select only nine: they were all from eighteen to twenty-one, and I noticed that they were without exception picked from among those whom he, in his mischievousness, had lately condemned either to death or to flaying. Ten men, their eligibility determined by superiority of member alone, were appointed to fuck him during the forthcoming rout, and here is how it began.

To one of the girls—the Comte suggested that I not be first, in order that I at least have the pleasure of judging the thing before taking a hand in it—a child was, I say, attached to the shoulders of one of the girls, bound to her so tightly and so thoroughly that the two bodies almost seemed one; then the girl, her papoose on her back, lay flat upon a sofa, her buttocks largely exposed; Belmor scrutinized, nibbled experimentally, forcefully bit and pinched the child's ass, and slapped the girl's; another girl, one of three thirteen-year-olds chosen for this purpose, seated herself on the floor between the legs of the child-carrier, and Belmor, kneeling on a cushion, mouth-fucked the girl who was sitting; while this was in progress he was embuggered, and Clairwil busied herself whipping his fucker. The Comte's attitude brought his head near the buttocks of the girl on the sofa; two executioners now had at the bound child and, wounding it in a thousand places but very artfully, made its blood flow into the cleft between the buttocks at which the Comte was staring.

"Off you go, shit!" said he to the girl, as he caught sight of the nearing stream of blood, "shit, I tell you, shit into my mouth."

The whore obeyed; and the lecher, gluing his lips to her asshole, was thereby able to imbibe, simultaneously, the blood flowing out of the body of the child and the mard emerging from the ass of the girl. No one stirred out of formation until all the blood had drained from the victim; once it was manifestly dead, the girl carrying it was ordered to her feet and she, her burden remaining ever in place, went to stand at the head of the sofa, facing away from it, so as to provide a prospect to the Comte. I alone of the carriers was dispensed from this part of the ceremony; I was the third to mount the sofa, and the child was removed when I arose; all then were slaughtered in this same manner, while the ten fuckers fucked, the ten girls shat, and the three suckers took turns; Belmor discharged into each mouth, discharged without interrupting his other activities, and the entire feat was accomplished without a single pause; Clairwil was exhausted, she may easily have delivered above ten thousand strokes of the whip to the asses of the Comte's ten fuckers. As for Noirceuil, passably calm throughout, he had been content to watch affairs and to molest the behinds of the two extremely pretty lasses of sixteen who were frigging and sucking him by turns.

"A charming passion," said he to Belmor, when the President had discharged for the last time; "but, with his Lordship's permission, I am going to show him that this same fancy is susceptible of an entertaining variation. Have them send me ten little girls of five or six, seven at the most, and ten boys of seventeen or so; the Comte's fuckers appear still to be stiff, and I can make do with them."

Then Noirceuil began his arrangements. He had one of the youths lie out straight, and upon his chest he attached the little girl, but in such a way that her cunt was placed over the boy's mouth; so taut were the cords drawn that the boy had great trouble breathing.

"Notice," Noirceuil pointed out to us, "that the carrier as well as the carried is ill-used in my operation, while in the Comte's the carrier experiences no pain at all, and that is something which should be rectified, I feel; for, surely, these hecatombs improve as concomitant sufferings increase."

Noirceuil knelt before the carrier and mouthed his prick; the executioners fell to work upon the child; the suckers teated Noirceuil's prick, and he was fucked; the victim's blood was soon pouring over the prick Noirceuil was sucking, and he was soon swallowing a mixture of blood and fuck. The tenth little girl died at last; and thus did this barbarous caprice cost twenty children their lives.

"I prefer Noirceuil's interpretation of the scene," said I, "and were it not so late I would enact it a few times myself."

Belmor, far from taking umbrage, congratulated Noirceuil upon his ingenuity. "However," he told us, "what must prevent me from changing is the girls Noirceuil butchers, for I, unfortunately, I have the bad taste of liking to sacrifice little boys."

"And so do I," said Clairwil; "there is nothing in all the world so delicious as choosing one's victims from among men. What kind of triumph can strength obtain over weakness? where can the amusement be there? But how sweet are the victories the weak contrive to win over the strong."

Then addressing the two friends in that impassioned tone which could render her so splendid to see: "Ferocious men," cried she, "massacre as many women as you like, I shall be nought if not

content, provided I am able to avenge every ten victims of my sex
by one of yours."

Thereat we separated. Noirceuil and Belmor returned to the
seraglio of women, and later report told of how they bagged
another dozen victims of every description and by a wide variety
of methods; whereas we, Clairwil and I, remained in the seraglio
stocked with men, which we did not finally leave before having
had ourselves fucked sixty or eighty times apiece, and achieving
some other little atrocities in such kind as I need not trouble to
delineate, since you have some acquaintance of these affairs.

But a few days after the infamies we had performed at the
Sodality in the company of Belmor and his friend, our club's amiable President waited upon me and convinced me that Clairwil had
not been mistaken when she said he would be only too delighted to
form a connection with me; the Comte, excessively rich, proposed
fifty thousand francs a month for only two entertainments per
week; Saint-Fond representing no obstacle, I saw no reason for not
coming to an arrangement with Belmor. I told him, therefore, that
I would be glad to be of service to him, but that the sum he offered
would not even cover the costs of the suppers; the Comte heard me
out and doubled his bid, agreeing to meet all additional expenses—
which promised to be considerable, at each foregathering the
libertine wishing to have three superb new women upon whose
bodies he would immolate, or have immolated, a corresponding
number of small boys; his murders once consummated, he would
retire with me for another two or three hours of mutual friggery,
after which he would return home. Such were his conventions; the
bargain was struck.

Without excepting Noirceuil and Saint-Fond, I have known
few men so corrupt as Belmor; he was corrupt by temperament,
through taste, and on principle; his exceedingly criminal imagination often led him to invent things that surpassed all I had heard of,
or even dreamt of, hitherto.

"This imagination you laud in me, Juliette," he said one day,
"is precisely what in you seduced me; for lasciviousness, diversity,
and energy I have seldom seen its equal; and you have surely
remarked that my sweetest pleasures with you are those I taste
when, the two of us giving free rein to fancy, we fabricate ideal

lubricities whose existence, unfortunately, is impossible. Oh, Juliette, how delicious are the pleasures of the imagination, and how voluptuously one follows out the lines of its dazzling constructions! Ah, dear angel, how little do they realize what we are about, what we originate, what we create during these divine intervals when our fiery souls are plunged utterly into the impure depths of lubricity; what raptures we experience as, frigging each other, we come erect erecting phantoms; nor with what ecstatic joy we caress them . . . elaborate them . . . surround them with a thousand obscene details and episodes. All the earth is ours in these enchanted moments; not a single creature resists us, to our aroused senses each affords the kind of pleasure which to our boiling imagination each appears capable of giving; we devastate the planet . . . and repeople it with new objects, and immolate these in their turn; the means to every crime is ours, we commit them all; we multiply the horror an hundredfold; and all the deeds ambitioned by all the most infernal and the most malignant spirits that ever were, in their most disastrous effects were nought compared to what we dare desire. . . . 'Happy,' says La Mettrie, 'happy they whose lively and wanton imagination keeps their senses ever whetted to the foretaste of pleasure!' Truly, Juliette, I sometimes think the reality possessed is not worth the images we chase thereof, and wonder whether the enjoyment of that which we have not, does not much exceed the enjoyment of that which is ours: lo, there is your ass, Juliette, there before my eyes, and beauteous it is to my contemplation; but my imagination, a more inspired architect than Nature, a more cunning artisan than she, creates other asses more beautiful still; and the pleasure I derive from this illusion, is it not preferable to the one which reality is about to have me enjoy? There is beauty in what you offer me there, but only beauty; what I invent is sublime; with you I am going to do nothing that anyone else may not do, whilst with this ass my imagination has wrought, I might do things which not even the gods themselves would invent."

Little wonder then if, with a mind like that, the Comte was prone to erratic flights; few men I had met had ever carried them to such lengths, and I had known few so attractive. But I have so many things still to recount to you that I cannot linger over the horrors we committed together; let it suffice you to know that we did our worst, and that your conceptions of what that might be probably fall short of the truth.

About four months had elapsed since I had admitted my father to the honor of my couch; our conversation having transpired at a critical moment, there was a great danger he had got me with child. My fears were only too well justified; the fact had to be faced, a decision taken; I consulted a renowned midwife who, hampered by no scruples in this matter, deftly inserted a long and well-sharpened needle into my matrix, found the embryo, and pierced it. I evacuated it two hours later, experiencing no pain at all: this remedy, surer and better than juniper, which upsets the digestion, is the one I recommend to every woman who, like me, is courageous enough to grant greater importance to her figure and her health than to some molecules of organized fuck which when come to maturity will frequently prove the bane of her existence who vivified them in her womb. The scion of his excellency my father once dropped into the privy, I came forth trimmer about the waist than ever before.

"Juliette, I have just been given the address of a most unusual woman," Clairwil confided to me one day. "We must pay her a call: she is a fortuneteller and also blends poisons of all sorts, which she sells."

"And does she," I asked, "give the recipe for her poisons?"

"In return for fifty *louis*."

"They are reliable?"

"If you like she will make test of them in your presence."

"We must decidedly visit her. I have always been fond of the idea of poisoning."

"Ah, my dove, it is exquisite to have the lives of others arbitrarily in one's power."

"And killing them by poison, that must be exquisite too—I am sure of it, for, would you believe it? you no sooner mentioned the thing than I felt a quivering in my nerves, a sudden flash of heat. . . . Clairwil, I am quite certain that if you were to touch me now you would find me wet. . . ."

Clairwil reaches a verifying hand beneath my skirts: "Aye,

it is so—oh, beloved child, what a mind is yours! But, Juliette," she said, knitting her brows, "did you not tell me Saint-Fond gave you an entire chest?"

I nodded.

"Well? What have you done with it?"

"There is none left and I dare not ask him for more."

"You mean you used it?"

"All of it."

"For his purposes?"

"Yes, a third of it. The rest for my passions."

"Revenges?"

"Some were revenges. There were a good many lubricities."

"Delicious creature!"

"Oh, Clairwil, you'll never be able to conceive the horrors I have achieved in this domain . . . the joys I have derived from performing these crimes. . . . A box of poisoned almonds in my pocket, I used to stroll disguised through the public gardens, along the boulevards, into brothels; I would distribute those fatal candies to all who crossed my path; yes, to children also, especially to children. Afterward I would return to ascertain the results; were I to see a bier at the door of the individual upon whom the day before I played one of my cruel pranks, a glow would come into my cheeks . . . a fever into my blood . . . my head would reel . . . I would totter, have to lean against a wall or a lamppost for support; and ·Nature who, doubtless with a view to her own needs, had constituted me differently from others, would in the form of an unspeakable paroxysm reward an action which according to the belief of fools ought to have offended her."

"All perfectly understandable, my dear," Clairwil rejoined, "and the principles upon which we have been nourishing you for some time, Saint-Fond, Noirceuil, and I, elucidate the workings and designs of Nature as regards this entire matter; it is no more extraordinary to come to the point you have reached than to like to inflict beatings, it's the same pleasure, but refined; and once it has been proven to us that from the commotion of the pain experienced by others there results an impact upon our nervous system and in it a vibration which must perforce provoke lust, all possible means for causing pain become for us so many means for tasting pleasure;

and starting out with little teasings, we shortly arrive at execrations. The causes are the same, only the effects are different; the laws of Nature and, even more so, satiety require that there be a gradual but steady growth: you begin by poking with a pin, you end up stabbing with a dagger; there is, furthermore, a kind of perfidy in the employment of poison which singularly augments its attractiveness. Well, you have excelled your teachers, Juliette, I have perhaps imagined more than you, but I fear have accomplished less—"

"Imagined more!" I exclaimed. "What the devil more can you have imagined?"

"I would like," Clairwil answered, "to find a crime which, even when I had left off doing it, would go on having perpetual effect, in such a way that so long as I lived, at every hour of the day and as I lay sleeping at night, I would be constantly the cause of a particular disorder, and that this disorder might broaden to the point where it brought about a corruption so universal or a disturbance so formal that even after my life was over I would survive in the everlasting continuation of my wickedness. . . ."

"For the fulfillment of your aims, my dear," said I, "I know of little else than what may be termed moral murder, which is arrived at by means of counsels, writings, or actions. Belmor and I have discussed this question together; here is a little computation he made just the other day, it suggests how rapidly contagion unfurls and how voluptuous it may be to cause, if it is true, as neither you nor I have any doubt, that as the crime becomes more atrocious, to that degree is the sensation enriched."

And Madame de Lorsange displayed to her listeners the same paper Belmor had given her years before. This was the text: "Dedicating himself to this sort of action, one libertine can easily, in the course of one year, corrupt three hundred children; at the end of thirty years he will have corrupted nine thousand; and if each child he has corrupted only matches him in only one-fourth of his corruptions, and we can hardly expect less, and if each succeeding year's batch of corrupted children follows suit, as must very probably happen, by the time those thirty years have elapsed the libertine will have seen this corruption flower in two whole generations, will be able to number nearly nine million persons corrupted either by himself or by the doctrines and examples he has disseminated."

"Charming," Clairwil replied; "but the undertaking, easy enough to launch, must be sustained——"

"Not only must a full three hundred victims be regularly corrupted every year, one must also, insofar as one can, aid in the corruption of the rest."

"Think of it," Clairwil murmured, "merely find ten confederates for the simultaneous and coordinated execution of ten such plans, the spread of corruption would, even as they watched, become swifter than the most headlong progressions of the plague or malignant fevers."

"Of course," I said; "but it is not enough to watch developments, such an enterprise needs constant promotion, constant maintenance. To that end, and to ensure final success, a combined and extensive use must be made of the means I spoke of a moment ago: *counsels, actions, writings.*"

"You are, you know, treading on dangerous ground——"

"Admittedly; but remember Machiavelli, according to whom it were better to be *impetuous* than *circumspect,* because Nature is a woman to be mastered only by him who goes to her whip in hand. Experience shows, the same authority continues, that she far more readily grants her favors to *ferocious* suitors than to *diffident.*"

"Your Belmor must be delightful," Clairwil remarked.

"He is indeed," said I; "there are not many men so lovable, none more libertine—by the way, he will adore the purchases we are going to make; we shall have to resell them to him for their weight in gold—and do you really believe that however we be devoted to a man, whatever be our relationship to him, do you really believe that notwithstanding all that we should constantly deceive him too?"

"Most certainly," was Clairwil's reply; "dealing with a man, we have the human nature in him to contend with, and are obliged to proceed toward him as he always proceeds in our regard; and since no man is frank, why would you have us be frank with them? Enjoy your lover's tastes where they concur with your caprices; make the most profitable use of his moral and physical faculties; heat yourself by the fire of his intelligence, be inspired by his

talents; but never for one instant forget that he belongs to an
enemy sex, a sex bitterly at war with your own . . . that you ought
never let pass an opportunity for avenging the insults women have
endured at its hands, and which you yourself are every day on the
eve of having to suffer; in short, he is a man, and you have got to
dupe him. . . . You know, Juliette, on this head you are still of an
incredible guilelessness: you are kindly, you are good-hearted, why,
you respect men; whereas they must be used and deceived, and
nothing else. From Saint-Fond you don't glean a sixth of what
I'd extract; had he a similar weakness for me, in your place I
would be banking millions every day.".

Our conversation, held in Clairwil's carriage while driving to
a remote point on the edge of the Faubourg Saint-Jacques, was now
broken off, for we were come to where the sorceress lived.

It was a little house, isolated and lying between courtyard
and garden; one of our lackeys rang, an old serving-woman
answered the door. Having learned our business she bade us first
dismiss our coachman and attendants, suggesting we have them
wait for us at a certain wineshop some distance away; the orders
were given and she ushered us into a small chamber.

A quarter of an hour later Madame Durand appeared. Forty
years of age, this was a very handsome woman, richly and gracefully made, tall, with a majestic presence, Roman features, a
wondrous skin and large expressive eyes; her speech was seemly,
her gesture measured; her look and manners contained everything
that announces breeding, education, and intelligence.

"Madame," my friend addressed her, "persons well in your
acquaintance and whom you have satisfied send us here. . . . First,
we would have you say what the future holds in store for us, these
twenty-five *louis* are in payment for that; next, we would have you
provide us the wherewithal for controlling that future, I mean a
complete assortment of the poisons you prepare. And there,"
Clairwil went on, tendering her fifty *louis* more, "is the sum you
ordinarily ask for instruction in the composing of those same
poisons, and for showing the beginner your laboratory and your
garden of venomous plants. Be sure of it, our interest in these
things is practical."

"Let me begin by saying," Durand replied, "that you are two

528 ⚜ THE MARQUIS DE SADE

extremely pretty women, and as such, before anything else, you shall have to undergo initial and quite indispensable ceremonies which may perhaps displease you."

Clairwil inquired in what these ceremonies consisted.

"You must accompany me into a dimly lit cabinet," said the sorceress, "where, once you have removed all your clothes, you shall be flogged by me."

"Vigorously?"

"Until the blood flows, my fair friends . . . yes, until the lash draws blood from your bodies: I never give out the least information save this little request be complied with; more, I have need of your blood for the auguries, and of blood resultant from a preliminary fustigation."

"Come along," I said to Clairwil, "under circumstances like these one must demur to nothing."

The cabinet into which Durand led us was too unusual not to merit a description; and though for illumination there was but one smoky lamp, we could still discern objects well enough to make out their details. This cabinet, painted black, was about nine feet wide by twelve long; all along the wall to the right were alembics, furnaces, and other instruments of chemistry; to the left, shelves containing bottles and jars in great profusion, numerous books, there was a workbench, a stool; opposite us, at the farther end, hung a black curtain dividing this room from another; the curtain fell upon a divan, dividing it also, so that half the divan was in the cabinet, half in the room beyond; and there was, rising in the center, a velvet-covered wooden post to which Madame Durand attached us, face to face.

"So then," this personage demanded, "are you resolved to suffer some pain to acquire the knowledge you seek?"

"Lay on, Madame," we answered, "lay on, we are prepared for whatever may come."

At that Durand kissed each of us very amorously, gave our buttocks a friendly squeeze, and blindfolded us; and from this moment onward silence was observed: we were softly approached, by whom we could not be sure, and given fifty strokes each. They were but rods that were first used upon us, but willow rods so green and so tough and wielded with such force that, notwithstanding our

habituation to these pleasures, I think this volley of cuts may well
have opened our skin. However, we durst not complain, and not a
word was said to us. Our buttocks were palpated then, and it is
certain those hands were not Madame Durand's.

Our tormentor set to work anew, and now we could be in no
more doubt of his sex: a prick made contact with our behinds, was
rubbed in the blood oozing forth from them; some sighs, some
voluptuous moans were heard, and two or three kisses were bestowed on our assholes, a tongue even twittered into them, then
twittered out again; a third attack occurred, but the rods had been
laid aside; numb though our asses were, we had no trouble deciding
that here the instrument being employed was a cat, the tips whereof
were sharp; so indeed they must have been, for I immediately felt
blood course down my legs and gather in a puddle around my bare
feet. Back came the prick, back came the tongue, and the ceremony
terminated. The blindfolds were taken away and all we saw was
Madame Durand, a saucer in her hand; she placed it beneath
Clairwil's buttocks, placed another beneath mine; then when they
were brimful with blood, removed them and loosed our bonds. She
sponged our behinds with water and vinegar and asked us, had it
hurt?

"Never mind," said we, "is there anything else that has to be
done?"

"Yes," Durand replied; "you must be frigged about the clitoris: I can make you no predictions unless I have observed you in
pleasure's throes."

The sorceress now had us stretch out side by side upon the
divan; thanks to the curtain bisecting it, we were from the waist
down in the cabinet, from the waist up in the room adjoining. By
means of a strap passed across our midriffs Durand fixed us to the
couch: unable to sit up, we would be unable to make out with whom
we were having to do. She, half-naked herself, had settled near us;
her superb breasts were placed where we could kiss them; she
watched us carefully and glanced from time to time at the two
saucers. Our friggings started with the clitoris, very knowing
attentions were then turned to our cunts and assholes; we were
tongued in both those orifices; other straps were fastened around

our ankles, our legs were hoisted into the air; and a mediocre prick was introduced alternately into our cunts and our bums.

Detecting the hoax, I spoke up at once: "I should hope, Madame, that you have at least some assurance of this man's trustworthiness?"

"Simple creature," was Durand's response, " 'tis not a man who is taking his pleasure with you, 'tis God."

"Madame, you are mad," Clairwil affirmed, "there is no God; and if there were, all his acts approaching to perfection, he might perhaps have himself embuggered, but for a certainty he would not fuck women."

"Silence," Durand commanded; "concentrate upon fleshly impressions without fretting over the identity of those who cause you to feel them: if you utter another word, all shall be in vain."

"We shall not say anymore," I replied, "but mark you well, Madame, we want neither the pox nor offspring."

"None of these things is to be feared with God," Durand declared; "now an end to this conversation, there is nothing further I can say."

And I very distinctly felt the prick belonging to the personage aboard me discharge abundantly inside my bowels; he even swore, he stormed, he fumed; and that same instant, hardly noticing what was happening, we were borne aloft, divan and all.

We found ourselves in a largely unfurnished room which, judging from the time we took ascending there, seemed very high up; no more curtain separating our heads from our bodies now; another machinery had conveyed Durand, she was there, so also were two little girls of thirteen or fourteen: they were sitting in armchairs and were bound fast. . . . From their countenances, from their pallor it was plain to see those creatures had been reared in extreme poverty; not far from them lay, in a cradle, two infant boys nine months of age; a big table was in the room, ranged upon it were numerous parcels resembling those enveloping drugs in a pharmacy: and also in this room were a great many more jars and bottles than we had seen in the other.

"It is here I pronounce opinion," said Durand.

And she undid the strap pinioning us.

"You, Clairwil," she began, looking hard into the dish containing her blood, "and you see that I know your name, without anybody having told me it; you, Clairwil, shall live only five years longer; but for the excesses you indulge in you would be able to live to sixty: your fortune shall increase as your health declines, and *the day the Bear moves into the Scales you shall regret the flowers of springtime.*"

"I do not understand."

"Write down my words and the day will come when their meaning shall be very clear."

At this my friend seemed worried.

"As for you, Juliette—and, pray tell me, who ever could have given me your name?—you, Juliette, shall be enlightened by a dream, an angel will appear to you, it will unveil incomprehensible truths; but between now and then I may foretell this: *when vice doth cease woe shall betide.*"

And now a thick cloud filled the room. Durand fell into a trance, she shrieked, did strange contortions, in doing them shook off the little that still adorned her lovely body; the cloud having dissipated, she returned to her senses. That vapor had left an odor of mingled amber and sulphur in the air. Our clothes were restored to us; once we were dressed Durand asked us what kinds of poison we desired.

"Your prediction distresses me," said Clairwil; "death inside five years!"

"Ah, who knows? May be you will avoid it," Durand replied. "I told you what I saw in your fate, my eyes sometimes deceive me."

"Let me cling to that hope, else I must truly despair," said Clairwil; "but perhaps she errs in another direction, and I have only a week to live? So be it; such time as remains to me I shall spend soiling myself in crimes. Eh then, Madame, be quick about it, show me your wares; open your jars, let us see the weird plants in your garden: explain to us all the properties of all these lethal things, we'll set aside those which please us, and you can dress a reckoning afterward."

"I must have twenty-five *louis* more," said the witch, "that is the fee for admission to my exhibits; later you will pay for the separate items you select, according to the rate of each. You may wish to experiment with them, you will of course be at liberty to do so: those two little girls are at your disposal, and if they do not suffice I will furnish you, at fifty *louis* a head, as many men as you like."

"You are delightful, Madame," I exclaimed, throwing my arms around Durand's neck, "I am so happy we consulted you, and I am certain you shall be happy to have us for clients."

Taking down the jars from the shelves one at a time, she began by showing us aphrodisiacs and love philters as well as emmenagogic agents, electuaries, and other antiaphrodisiac purgatives. We had an ample store of the former done into packages, amongst them goodly amounts of cantharides, ginseng, and several vials of Joui liqueur from Japan for which, because of its rarity and its unusual virtues, Durand charged us ten *louis* an ounce.

"Add to my list some larger flasks of the latter," said Clairwil, "they will be helpful to me in my dealings with lots of men."

"We now come to the poisons," said Durand; "if it is sometimes pleasant to labor at propagating the human species, it is more often delicious to hinder its progress."

"These actions should not be mentioned in the same breath," I protested, "the one is horrible, the other divine; our aim in buying these philters is not to promote the population, it is to increase our lubricity; and that progeniture which we detest, 'tis for the delectable destruction thereof we intend to buy the rest."

"Kiss me," said Durand. "Ah, here are two women of the stripe I adore. The better we come to know one another, the better, I am convinced of it, we shall get on."

These poisons were in very great number, each classified according to its category. In the first we examined, Durand drew our attention to a powder where the basic ingredient was vert toad; what she related of its effects was so exciting to hear that we besought Durand to make trial of it there and then.

"Gladly," said she, "designate the victim." And after having detached the girl we pointed to, she wondered whether we fancied having her fucked by a man, and poisoning her meanwhile; we rejoiced in this suggestion. Wherewith Durand rang, and in answer to her call appeared a tall individual, lank, pale, and nervous, some fifty years of age and in a very neglected state.

"There," I whispered to my companion, "he's the one who sported with us a little while ago, I'm certain of it."

Clairwil nodded. "I think you're right."

"Alzamor," said Durand, "this maid must be *devirginated* while these ladies *disorganize* her with a powder. . . . Are you stiff?"

"Turn the child over to me," said Alzamor, mournfully, "I shall do what I can."

"Madame, what manner of man be this?" I demanded.

"He is an old sylph," Durand replied, "by pronouncing a formula I can cause him to disappear. Would you care to see it done?"

"Yes."

Durand uttered two barbarous words which I was unable to retain; where Alzamor had been there was now only smoke.

"Now make the sylph return," said Clairwil.

Another outlandish phrase and a second cloud brought him back; this time the sylph had an erection, and it was prick atower he caught hold of the child. This personage proceeded to give evidence of prodigious vigor, in two minutes he had perforated the girl's maidenhead and spattered blood all about the room. 'Twas then Clairwil administered the dose: it was dissolved in a cup of broth, the poor little soul quaffed it off. Her convulsions began promptly; when they were at their height Alzamor adjusted her for embuggering; her writhings, her screams increased; it was hideous to behold; six minutes later she collapsed and the sylph withheld his discharge until she was completely lifeless. Her death throes were noisy beyond belief; her violator, too, loosed unearthly sounds, and it was the violence of that ecstasy which made us finally conclude that, indeed, this was the man who had tupped us earlier on. The uncouth words were pronounced again, Alzamor vanished, and the victim vanished with him.

Durand resumed the displaying of her goods and, after having indicated the features of the second category of poisons, said, "Here is burnt engri flesh, the engri is a variety of Ethiopian tiger; its effect is subtle, awful, and deserves to be witnessed by ladies as curious as yourselves."

"Then let us try some out," Clairwil said, "but upon a young man."

"Of what age precisely?"

"Of eighteen or twenty."

In a trice stood a youth, comely, prettily made, superbly membered, but showing such signs of privation as to leave us in no doubt of the class from which our sorceress chose her victims.

"Will you amuse yourselves with him?" Durand wanted to know.

"Yes," said I, "but will you not join us? He looks capable of fucking the three of us."

"What's this? You are of a mind to see me fuck?"

"We most decidedly are."

"I'm beastly, you will be appalled."

"Fie, slut," said Clairwil, clasping her in her arms, "do your damnable worst—we expect it of you, for you are a woman after our own sort and we are burning to see you in action."

And without further ado Clairwil shoots toward the young man and begins to arouse him; and I, having brought Durand's charms into view, with eyes, hands, and tongue begin to devour every part of her splendid body. Here were symmetry and luxuriant abundance in perfection, never was flesh so firm, so fair, so responsive to the touch; never were buttocks and breasts so smooth, so round, so full; and this clitoris! ah, this clitoris, never had we in all our days seen one so long nor so straight-standing. I own that, catching sight of this last-named wonder, I was over-swept by an invincible partiality for this woman and I had already mouthed her member when Clairwil, leading up the youth by the end of his prick, brushed me aside and made ready to bury that prick in the enchantress' cunt; but she voiced her opposition in a terrible cry.

"Why would you require this horror of me?" she demanded. "Cunt-fucking is not to my liking, neither is it within my capacity, do you take me for an ordinary woman?"

And driving the youth back with a powerful blow of her fist, she spun about and presented him her ass. Clairwil conducted the device which, all unprepared for this, sank its full length into this anus just as easily as it would have disappeared into the hugest cunt. The whore then began to wriggle and cavort in the most lubricious manner, Clairwil and I furnished fuel to her ecstasy by palpating her, by fingering her, by tonguing and sucking and pumping her, by polluting and kissing and caressing her with all the means at our command, physical and moral. There is no conceiving the ardor of that woman's imagination, the foulness of her talk, the originality of her lewd ideas, and the wildness of their incoherence; in fine, the disorder which, established by the incredible heat of her passions, reigned throughout her entire person. Nearing her crisis, she clutched at our asses, kissed them; and the whore, after tonguing and spitting in our vents, fucked them as a man should have done.

"Poison him, poison him!" she screamed as delirium invaded her senses and mounted into her brain.

"No, by God!" said Clairwil, "the wight shall bugger-fuck us both before we have any of that."

At which Durand emitted dreadful screams, howls, all her limbs twitching, thrashing, she succumbed to a nervous fit, and loosed fuck in such vast quantity that my mouth, for I was sucking her then, was filled to overflowing.

"He is yet intact," she told us, expelling the youth, "prevent him from discharging in order that he fuck you the better."

My ass chancing to be the first snapped into position, therein the fucker deposited the seed which Durand's convulsing bowels had so well readied for ejaculation. I continued, while being embuggered, to gobble the jets of fuck still spouting from Durand's vagina, whose anus Clairwil was tonguing; my friend soon changed places with me and it was while the young man was in the midst of sodomizing her that the necromancer had him swallow the venomous brew. He was seized by cramps before he had time to withdraw from my friend's ass, so that he perished embuggering her, which hurled Clairwil into transports of joy so intense I thought she too was in danger of dying.

"By God," the buggeress declared, "I do believe I got his soul and his fuck in the same spasm; you have no idea how the rascal's prick dilated while the poison was having its effect, neither can you conceive the pleasure which such an operation procures."

Oh, voluptuous women! the time to poison your fuckers is

while they are even in your asses or your cunts, you'll see what one gains thereby. . . . We did indeed have no end of trouble dislodging the murdered youth's member from my companion's rectum, and when at last we had it pried loose, we noted that his death agonies had not prevented him from discharging.

"Aye, that was my impression," said Clairwil, "did I not tell you he gave up the ghost and his sperm all in one throw?"

The corpse is whisked away and pots of poison from the third category are disposed on the counter before us.

Among others it includes the poison royal, the same which in the days of Louis XV brought about the deaths of so many members of his family; poisoned darts and hatpins; the poisons compounded of snake venoms and known under the names of cucurucu, kokob, and Aimorrhoües; polpoch poison, so called after the reptile that inhabits a northwestern zone in faraway Jupatan.

"I mix it with a digestive or cordial," Durand explained; "diluted in the proportion of one drop to a pint it remains absolutely fatal; in all my experience I have never known it to fail; would you like to see what it can do?"

"By all means yes," I replied, "rest assured that such proposals are of a kind we are never apt to reject."

"And what would you prefer in the way of a victim?"

"An attractive young man," Clairwil volunteered.

Durand rang a little bell and there before us appeared a boy of eighteen, fairer than the previous one, and in the same state of dejection and misery.

"Will you have Alzamor embugger him?"

"Gladly!"

Another puff of smoke, and out of it steps the sylph.

"Fuck this boy," Durand instructs him. "Mesdames wish to try some polpoch brandy on him."

"Wait," Clairwil interrupted, "he must embugger me in the meantime."

"And what are we to do, Madame Durand and I?"

"You may tongue Alzamor's asshole, Juliette; and our hostess, upon whom I shall recline, will encunt me with her clitoris; my fuckeress, otherwise unoccupied, will, when she sees the boy about to discharge in my bum, be able to hand him a little glass of the poison whose effects we are eager to study."

Everything proceeds in accordance to Clairwil's plan until the moment when the young man absorbs the drink: he is shaken so powerfully by the poison in his vitals that postures are disturbed and the group must disperse; we relinquish the middle of the room to the patient; Alzamor frigs Clairwil, I spring into Durand's arms, who tickles me exquisitely, she possesses the ultimate in art and experience, all the coigns and concavities of pleasure are explored with equal thoroughness by the libertine fingers of that ravishing personage, whose lips cover me with fervent kisses. The hard-pressed victim is by now staggering like a drunkard and while we look on, gradually sinks into a terrifying vertigo; the venom's impact upon his brain was so fierce, that, in shrieks, he complained of having his head full of boiling oil; this phase was followed by a generalized tumefaction that spared no part of his body, his face became livid, his eyes bulged from their sockets, and flailing his arms like one drowning in the sea, the wretch fell to the floor and writhed and struggled there in the oddest possible manner, while to left and to right the four of us sprayed torrents of the impurest and the most abundant fuck.

"For me," said Clairwil, "that is the most divine of all passions, the one I shall never be able to resist. I am resolved to indulge in it every chance I get in the future."

"And you may do so without fear," said Durand, "murder by poison is certain and it is safe. Witnesses? There need be none. Clues, telltale traces left behind whereby you may be found out? Let the most learned physician hunt for them, his art will avail him not; the effects of poison are indistinguishable from the causes of a natural ailment in the bowels; they accuse you nonetheless? Deny the charge, and be firm. Let the crime be gratuitous. So long as they can assign to you no motive for having committed it, you will always be under cover."

"Go on, temptress, go on," Clairwil said to her; "if you were to convince me I do believe I'd depopulate the whole of Paris tonight."

Durand pronounced the arcane formula; the sylph disappeared.

"Come with me to the garden," she said, and then added, a note of apology in her voice: "you may have whatever you like there. And I am afraid there is not very much: the frosts were so severe last winter that most of my plants died."

This garden, an extremely somber place, bore a strong resemblance to a burial ground: save where some rare plants were growing, sinister and grayish, it lay in the shade of tall trees. Our curiosity drew us toward a remote corner where we espied newly turned soil.

"It's the spot where you conceal your crimes, Durand, isn't it?" Clairwil asked.

"Come along," the sorceress replied, guiding us in another direction, "it were better I show you that with which one kills rather than what has been killed."

She explained the properties of this plant, she explained those of another; at length, unable to curb my impatience, "Listen to me," I said, "the sight of that cemetery just ten yards away is driving me quite out of my mind. Conjure up a little girl of fourteen or fifteen, give her a dose of whatever occasions the most agonizing possible gripes in a human being's guts; we shall dig a ditch first, it will be there waiting for her; we shall let Nature take its course, and when the victim's convulsions roll her into the pit, we'll cover her over with earth, and discharge."

"I am determined to be of service to you," Durand replied to this; "observe: I foresaw your request, there is the girl you want. And glance again at the cemetery: to the east there, do you see the pit? It is ready."

Indeed, behind a wild Cayenne fig tree, there stood a very pretty child, naked as the day she was born; but the pit . . . we strained our eyes, then saw it open up in the earth, by what magic we could not guess. . . .

"Ha!" exulted the sorceress, gazing at us as we, petrified, watched these prodigies, "are you afraid of me?"

"Afraid? No; but we do not understand you."

"All Nature is at my orders," Durand answered, "as she always submits herself to the will of whoever will probe her deep: with chemistry and physics nothing is beyond one's power. Archimedes lacked only a place to rest his lever, else he would have moved the earth; and I now need but a plant in order to destroy it in five minutes. . . ."

"Delicious creature," Clairwil said, hugging her to her breast; "how happy I am to have met somebody whose methods so nicely correspond to my aims."

Shutting a gate, we enclosed ourselves inside the cemetery with the little girl; her contortions began as soon as she had downed the poison.

"Let us sit ourselves here," I said, "where ground seems to have been broken very recently—"

"I believe I read your thoughts," said the sorceress.

From her pocket she pulls out a box, opens it, sprinkles some powder upon the soil; and the plot beneath our feet suddenly becomes strewn with cadavers.

"Oh, fuck me, what a sight!" cries Clairwil, wallowing amidst these heaps of dead bodies; "quick, let's all three frig one another while we watch that little bitch suffer."

"Let us take off our clothes," Durand proposes, "with naked flesh we must roll upon this carrion, the sensation is voluptuous."

"It occurs to me," said I, "that these bones, shaped as they are, might serve in the stead of pricks."

And Clairwil, finding the idea greatly to her taste, snatched up a femur and stowed it in her cunt.

"Well done," I remarked to my companion; "but we should be sitting on skulls, pointed nosebones should be prickling our assholes —see how I place myself. . . ."

"Move a trifle to the left," said Durand, "there's the head, perhaps still warm, at any rate fresh, of the last boy you immolated: hold still a moment, Juliette, I have one of his hands, let me frig you with it. . . ."

What now shall I say, my friends? Delirium and extravagance were at their height, we invented, we enacted a hundred things more infamous, more morbid yet; and the victim expired before our eyes, racked by execrable convulsions: the final ones having flopped and pitched her to the brink of her grave, she slithered into it, I discharged in the embrace of my two consorts who themselves smeared their fuck over me while the one sucked my nipples and the other drank my saliva; we donned our clothes again, and resumed our tour, just as cool as a trio of fools after having performed an exceptionally meritorious good deed. Concluding our visit of the garden, we re-entered Durand's abode.

"The pair of infants you see in this cradle," the sorceress now said, "are the material I shall use in composing the costliest and most potent poison I sell. Do you wish to enjoy the spectacle?"

"Certainly," we replied.

"I am not surprised," said Durand, "in you I recognize woman philosophers who view the disorganization of matter as a merely chemical operation; and the compelling importance of the results outweighs, in your consideration, the so-called crime lesser minds notice in this action. . . . I am going to begin."

Madame Durand plucks the babes out of their cradle, one after the other she hangs them by their feet from the ceiling, like hams, and lashes them mercilessly; in time a foam bubbles from the mouths of the dilapidated infants, the sorceress carefully gathers this pink froth and sells us the little bottle for a hundred *louis,* certifying that of all the poisons she confections, this is the most virulent, and it was true. The children, to whom Durand gave no further heed, expired on their hooks. Ah, who any longer doubts that for greatest delectation it is casually, phlegmatically, crime wants to be committed?

"Yes, my dear friend," said Clairwil, pondering over all the things we had seen that day, "those are awful secrets you possess."

"I have a good many more, Mesdames," Durand declared. "I hold the lives of multitudes in my hands: I can send the plague roaring abroad, poison streams and wells, propagate epidemics, contaminate the air of provinces, clap blight on houses, fields, vineyards, murrain on flocks; into deadly poison transform the flesh of cattle, I cause villages to burn, make suddenly perish he who inhales the scent of a flower or who unseals a letter; in a word, I am a woman without peer in my kind, nay, I am unique in it."

"But, Madame," I demanded, "how can somebody so well acquainted with Nature admit the existence of a God? When not long ago we inquired of you by whom we were being fucked, you answered 'twas by God."

"Is there one more mighty than the prick?" Durand asked by way of answer.

"Ah," said I, "I prefer to hear you respond thus than otherwise. But come now, dear heart, jesting aside: you do not believe in God, do you?"

"My friends," Durand said to us, "the more one studies Nature, the farther one probes into her secrets; the better one comes to apprehend her energy, the greater grows one's conviction of the futility of a God: the erecting of that empty idol is of all pieces of mystification the most odious, the most ludicrous, the most dangerous, and the most detestable; this revolting little fable, which wherever it exists has been whelped out of human hopes and fears, is the final consequence of human folly. Once again, to suppose an author of Nature is to misappreciate her altogether, only willful ignorance of all the effects of this fundamental power and prime mover permits the assumption of another which directs it, and you will never see any but idiots or rogues acknowledge or believe in the existence of a God. This God men have dreamt up is, in their presentation of him, what? an assemblage of all beings, all properties, all powers; the immanent and nondistinct cause of all natural effects. Baffled about the qualities of this fictitious being, in their confusion seeing him sometimes as good, sometimes as bad, now jealous and now vindictive, people could only be further misled into imagining that he had to punish and reward; but their God is actually only Nature, and Nature does not discriminate, neither does she deign to judge : in her eyes, all her creatures are equal and equally indifferent; since the production of one costs her no more than the production of another, to her the destruction of an ox is no worse than the destruction of a man."

"And your doctrine touching the soul, what is it, Madame?" Clairwil asked. "For your philosophy is in too close concordance with our own for us not to relish an exposition of its various tenets."

"No less a materialist in my approach to the soul than in my analysis of the deity, I am prepared to state," said Durand, "that after having sedulously perused all the reveries philosophers have left us on this chapter, I came away with my conviction unshaken that the soul of man, absolutely similar to that of all animals but otherwise modified in him owing to the difference of his organs, is nothing else than a quantum of that ethereal fluid, of that infinitely subtle matter the source whereof is sunshine. This soul, which I consider substantially identical in all animate things, is the purest fire there is in the universe: it is not hot, it does not burn by itself, but upon penetrating into the hollows in our nerves its impact there is so explosive, it sets the animal mechanism so dynamically into motion as to render it capable of every sentiment and every combination thereof; in this its effect is similar to one of those of electricity, upon whose nature our information is still incomplete but which is basically the selfsame thing; upon the death of a man, or of some other animal, this fire is exhaled and, so a raindrop falling into the ocean, loses itself in the immense universal mass of the same matter, always existing, ever moving, perpetually active; the rest of the body putrifies, decomposes, and recomposes in other forms which other portions of this celestial fire enter and animate; I leave it to you to guess, in the light of this definition, what he who accepts it is bound to think of the comical ideas of heaven and hell."

"My dear," said Clairwil, "after having talked to us in so frank a manner, and after the manner in which we have illustrated our adherence to principles like your own, you ought indeed, with the same candor, tell us who it is and what, this God by whom you latterly had us so well whipped and fucked; willing to unveil to us the mysteries of Nature, why should you fear revealing those of your house?"

"Because those of Nature are everybody's by right," Durand rejoined, "whilst those of my house belong to me alone; I may therefore disclose them or keep them secret, whichever I wish; well, my wish is not to discuss these matters with anyone, and if you persist in asking me about them, though you offer me the wealth of the Indies, you'll go away from here empty-handed."

"So be it," said I, "let us not pester Madame with questions upon a subject she is not disposed to speak about; but there are others upon which she may be able to give us satisfaction. . . . The possibilities of libertinage here in your house, they exist—of this we are sure. What can you propose to us, for we are exceedingly libertine—"

"There is not a single passion," replied Durand, "not a single whim or fancy, not a living being on this globe, not an extravagance or eccentricity, however unusual or picturesque it be, that cannot be enjoyed here; merely give me several hours forenotice, I will procure you anything under the sun; let your desire be irregular, let it be fantastic, let it be gruesome, and this in no matter what degree, I solemnly promise to provide you the means to execute it. Nor is that all. If there be any men or women anywhere in the world, with whose tastes or practices you were eager to be acquainted, I will have them here; and unseen by them, you will watch them in action through a gauze curtain. This entire house is mine, the ease wherewith on all four sides it may be entered or left without being seen, its secluded location, the height of the enclosure girting it, in a word, its mysterious loneliness, these, I think, guarantee both security and pleasure, which should be carefree; so command and you will be served: all individuals, all races, all nations, all sexes, all ages, simply specify what you wish—any debauchery, every crime: you have but to choose. You pay well, this I know; and with money anything can be had in my establishment."

"And yet you must not be in any great need of it, Madame, your wealth must be immense."

"Yes," Durand conceded, "but I too have tastes and as I spend virtually everything I earn, I am not by a long shot as rich as you might think. . . . Yes, ladies, yes, strictest secrecy and unlimited facilities, such are the features of this place; you have immolated five or six victims so far today, assassinate five hundred more, there is no dearth to fear; do you wish to make further experiments upon boys, upon girls, upon mature persons, upon aged persons, upon youngsters, only say so, you will be served on the spot."

"I want," said Clairwil, "to bum-fuck two fifteen-year-old boys with a red-hot dildo while you martyr them, and while two handsome lads, already gorged on poison, bum-fuck me."

"One hundred *louis* per victim," said Durand, "and you will be satisfied."

"For my part I'll have two young girls," said I, "since I only like to do to my sex what this whore likes to do to men; I shall encunt them with a like device, and your sylph will lash them to ribbons with martinets—the points of steel must be heated to the same temperature; I shall be whipped throughout the operation."

"Fifty *louis* per girl," said Durand.

We took out our purses and in less than ten minutes everything was under way. The little girls given me were ever so pretty, and ever so ferocious were the sylph's proceedings; the woe-begone victims expired in our arms and our transports were indescribable; the sylph and the corpses were whisked away in a flash, but our lust remained unappeased. Clairwil, disheveled, wild-eyed, was foaming at the mouth and I was hardly any calmer. Durand besought us to enact another drama, if that were agreeable to us it would be witnessed by libertine observers.

"Give us a victim apiece," was our reply, "and your examiners will be contented."

I am provided with a charming girl, naked, her hands tied behind her back; a similar subject for sacrifice, but of masculine sex, is produced for my companion: we begin by flogging them with nettles, then with our martinets, the work is already well advanced when it is interrupted by a knock on the door: it is Durand, who had stepped out of the room and now returns: "The gentleman outside," she says, "requests you to prolong the torture, and to turn slightly to this side while you operate: he would like a view of your asses whereof until now he has been unable to judge."

"Go, and say it will be as he wishes," Clairwil replied.

We resumed. The fierce creature opens the abdomen of the boy who has been entrusted to her, she tears out his heart and thrusts it hot into her cunt.

"Ah, Juliette," says she, her breathing becoming hoarse, "for ages I've been wanting to frig myself with a child's heart, this should lead to a memorable discharge."

Sprawled atop the corpse of her latest victim, she yet sucked its mouth and chewed its tongue as she fucked herself with its heart. "And now," she grunted, "let's bury it completely." In order to be able to fish it out again, she pierced it, ran a string through; and the lump of viscera sank out of sight.

Clairwil set up a howl of pleasure. "Juliette," she gasped, "try it, Juliette, try it, there's nothing to equal the sensation."

"I once knew a man," I said, "who had roughly the same mania: he used to make a hole in a yet palpitating heart, force his prick into it, and discharge there."

"That could be charming," said Clairwil, "but aesthetically

less pretty than what I am doing; try it, my angel, you owe it to yourself."

There is nothing like the effect of example upon an imagination such as mine; it suggests, it encourages, it electrifies: I soon have my victim laid wide open and promptly insert its living heart between my labia; but, more straitly avenued than my companion, my efforts are unavailing, it will not enter my cunt.

"Slice it in two," Clairwil urges upon noticing my plight, "provided some of it goes in, that is all that matters."

I follow her advice and having taken the same precautions as she, bury a fair half of the heart in my womb. The fiendish creature was right, for dildo this is without peer; for warmth, for elasticity where will you find its match? And the moral parts, my friends! how they are fired by these horrors. . . . Oh yes, yes, there is no denying it, Clairwil's idea was excellent, and I had not discharged so deliciously in a very long time. After an hour devoted to these infamies we summoned Durand again.

"Fuck!" she exclaimed upon catching sight of the frightful debris littering the room, "apparently, you need only be shown the opportunity—"

"Exactly, and we will duplicate that massacre at any hour of the day," said Clairwil; "come, come, my dear, murder is as familiar to us as it is to you, we idolize it just as passionately, and so long as there is killing in your house you may always count upon our custom."

"Kind friends," Durand said to us then, "there is yet something I would propose to you."

"Do not hesitate."

"Will you help me make fifty *louis?*"

"Certainly."

"Then have the goodness to receive an admirer for a moment; he has been watching you, your doings fascinate him, and he is burning from eagerness to make your more intimate acquaintance."

"Very well," said I, "but we too wish to be paid, no money is more enjoyably spent than what one earns in a whorehouse; simply ask him for a hundred *louis,* that leaves twenty-five for each of us."

"I am of my companion's mind," said Clairwil; "but what would the fellow do with us? One must not take payment for nothing."

"Ah," said Durand, "you will not be disappointed, he is extremely libertine; nonetheless, he is aware that you are ladies of condition and will treat you with fitting consideration."

"Send him in," said I, "let him only pay and not trouble to consider us, we are whores and intend to be treated as such."

In they walked: first a little man of some sixty years, short, stout, almost naked, with the opulent look of a financier; a sodomizer followed hard on his heels, tooling him on the move.

"Lovely asses . . . lovely," he cried, handling them; "ah, ladies, you have done remarkable things. . . ." And while frigging himself amain: "You have killed, aye . . . butchered—that's the very thing I adore. How would you like to begin again? We shall do the same together."

So saying the lecher pushes me onto the bed and embuggers me while fondling Clairwil's buttocks; after a few moments of clumsy shoving and jerking he takes up his stance behind Clairwil, gomorrahizes her, and, as he does, examines and nuzzles my bum. At this point his fucker discharges; the little man, seemingly considering it useless to go on warring in the breach without the support of a good prick in his rear, debuggers straight off and, catching up a handful of withes, he bids his fucker hold us while he gives us both a thrashing. The little rascal arranges us in this bizarre manner: facing in the same direction, we stand close beside the fucker, a tall man, who faces in the direction opposite and prisons our heads beneath his armpits: thus is Monsieur Mondor confronted by a sturdy prick for frigging and two superb asses for belaboring, and he flies to the task. Our bums, already in very fit sorts, bear up bravely under the storm, and it is severe, the bugger does his worst; prolonged was the ordeal, and bloody too, he wore out six bundles of withes, and our thighs were as badly treated as our buttocks; during occasional pauses he sucked his man's prick and when finally he got it to a stand, had us fucked by this superb member: after all that flagellation, you may readily appreciate our need of that balm. While his retainer fucked us turn by turn, the financier worried the fucker's ass and thereinto plunged his prick ever and again; his passion now well in the wind and running full-sailed, he cried out for a victim. One was brought him, an eleven-year-old boy: Mondor fucks him; Mondor is fucked: the villain orders us to carve the child open and extract his heart, as just before he had watched us do, and to rub it over his face while he discharges: all his bidding is done and the monster, bathed in blood and braying like a donkey, unpents his fuck. No sooner was he finished when, without so much as a word to us, he was gone out of the room. See there an example of the effects of libertinage upon a timid soul. It is ever the same: remorse and shame rush in the instant their fuck rushes out, because such people, unable to forge principles to themselves, always suppose they have behaved ill because they have not behaved quite like everybody else.

"And who was that queer fellow?" we asked Madame Durand.

"An exceedingly wealthy man," she answered, "but I shall not give you his name; you would not be pleased to have me publicize yours."

"His practices go no farther than what we have just seen?"

"He usually does his own murdering; but today he was visibly not in form and therefore charged you with the chore. You say he impressed you as being unsure of himself? You were not mistaken, he is indeed shy, overly scrupulous . . . and even very devout: he dashes off to pray to God after perpetrating horrors."

"Poor fool, he is truly to be pitied. If you cannot first conquer vulgar prejudices, better not venture into our way of life at all; for, once having elected it, he who does not advance with determined step is heading for a great many embarrassments."

And after adjusting our clothes we wrapped up our purchases, made this valuable new acquaintance a generous settlement, and returned to our carriage, both of us determined to cultivate Durand and make the most extensive and frequent use of the supplies we had bought from her.

"I am going to poison every creature who crosses my path," Clairwil announced, "if for no other reason—and is there another so solid?—than to commit an action which already affects my senses more profoundly than most, and is soon apt to win the position of a favorite in my heart."

I was eager to introduce Belmor to Durand: they struck me as made for each other, and I frigged myself incontinently over the thought of seeing my lover in the arms of that evil witch. At our next encounter I mentioned her name; no, he was not acquainted with her; we agreed to call upon her together, and we went. After offering my excuses for having neglected her so dreadfully—I had not indeed been back since that first visit, lack of a free moment was the reason—I presented the Comte to her, and the welcome she gave him was warm. Enchanted by everything he saw there, and after some heavy purchasing, he succumbed to the voluptuous titillations that stunning personage was causing in him. The scene, just as I had hoped, transpired before my eyes; first sodomizing her, Belmor then begged to know, would she satisfy his dearest passion? I provided the necessary explanations; the victims were produced without delay, and Belmor, aided by me, regaled himself delightfully.

"Sir," said the sorceress, "let me offer my felicitations, that passion of yours is charming; if you care to visit me again the day after tomorrow, I shall enable you to observe one of approximately the same sort, although a thousand times more spectacular."

We came faithfully to the rendezvous; but nobody came to open the door. The shutters, we then noticed, were drawn over the windows, the house seemed deserted; and we went away. Despite the great many inquiries I made, I was never able to discover what became of that remarkable woman.

Nothing very out of the ordinary befell me in the course of the next two years; I lived higher than ever before, my debaucheries multiplied, and finally brought me to the point where I lost all taste for the simpler pleasures of Nature; to the point where if there was not something exceptional or criminal in the frolics which were proposed to me, I could not even feign an interest in them. It is likely that when we reach this stage of numbed indifference, virtue makes a final effort inside us, whether because in our exhaustion we are so reduced that her voice reassumes its authority in the face of our torpor, or because, through a natural desire for change, we, bored with crimes, wish to try a little of the contrary; whatever the case may be, this is the moment, beware of it, when long-forgotten prejudices reappear, and if they overtake somebody who has already traveled far in a vicious career and gain the upper hand over him, the unhappiness they cause is terrible; there is nothing worse than to limp back to Susa in defeat and dishonor.

I had just attained my twenty-second year when Saint-Fond broached another of his execrable schemes to me. Still infatuated with his depopulation measures, his aim in the present plot was to starve two-thirds of France to death, by engrossing foodstuffs, grains chiefly, on a colossal scale; and in the execution of all this I was to have the principal role.

I—yes, I confess it: corrupt to the core though I was, before the idea I shuddered; O thou, the fatal start I gave, what wert thou not to cost me! Little impulse, why could I not have suppressed thee?—Saint-Fond caught it with his searching eye. He turned and went away without a word.

I watched him go and, when the door was shut and the sound of his footsteps died away, waited there yet a certain while; then, for it was late, retired for the night. Long did I lie awake; once fallen asleep I had a troubling dream: in it I saw a fearful figure putting a torch to my belongings—to my furniture, to my house, to everything I owned: all was afire and in the midst of it a young creature stretched forth her arms to me . . . sought desperately to save me, and in the attempt perished herself in the flames. I awoke all asweat, and consciousness brought back to me the sorceress' prediction: *when vice doth cease,* thus had she spoken, *woe shall betide.* O Heaven, I cried in my heart, I stopped being vicious for a fleeting instant, I shuddered at a proposed horror; misfortune is about to engulf me, it is sure. The woman I saw in my dream, she is the sister, the unregenerate and sad Justine with whom I fell out because she was bent on taking the virtuous way; virtue appeals to me, and in my heart vice falters. . . . Fatal prognostic . . . and you who could explain it to me and tell me what I should do, you disappear just when my need for your advice is greatest. . . . I was still at grips with these lugubrious reflections when, unannounced, a stranger enters my bedroom, tenders me a note, and forthwith steals away. I recognize Noirceuil's hand:

"You are ruined," it reports to me, "never would I have expected frailty in her whom I formed and whose conduct heretofore has been flawless; seek not to repair the want you have exhibited of zeal: it is too late: your impulse betrayed you, and add not insult to injury by supposing the Minister can be further duped. Leave Paris before this day is out; take with you the money you may have by you; count not upon anything else. Everything you have acquired through Saint-Fond's largesses and aid is forfeited; he is a powerful man, this you know, you also know his wrath when he has been failed: so do not tarry, go. And go with lips sealed: you will not outlive an indiscretion. I leave you the ten thousand *livres* a year you have from me, your drafts will be honored anywhere. Now fly, and to your friends say nothing."

A bolt of lightning would have smitten me less cruelly; but dread of Saint-Fond affected me even more strongly than despair. I rise hurriedly from my bed; having deposited all my valuables and all my savings with Saint-Fond's notary, I dare not go reclaim them. I ransack drawers, turn purses inside out: five hundred *louis* is all I can assemble, all I have left. I make several rolls of the notes and hide them upon my person, and then, alone, on foot, in the middle of the night I go quaking out of this house where yesterday I dwelled like an empress, this house upon which I cast one last backward glance, tears in my eyes. . . . Whither shall I go? To see Clairwil. . . . But no, it has been prohibited; and moreover is it not she who has betrayed me? is it not she who wishes to usurp my place? Ah, how unjust we are rendered by misfortune, and how wrong I was, as you shall soon see, in rushing to suspect the best friend I had.

Come now, take hold of yourself, let's not rely for help upon anybody but ourselves . . . I'm still young, I said to myself, it's merely a question of starting afresh; I have learned from my youthful errors. . . . O fatal virtue! thou tricked me once; never fear, I'll never again come under thine execrable sway. Only one fault have I committed, only once have I slipped, and it was an infernal impulse to probity that tripped me. Let's now snuff it out forever within us, virtue is man's mortal enemy, capable of procuring him nothing but his doom; and the greatest mistake which can be made in a completely corrupted world is to want to put up a lonely fight against the general contagion. And, great God, how often have I told this to myself!

Without anything like a definite plan in mind, concerned only to escape the vengeance of Saint-Fond, I jumped, as though mechanically, into the first public carriage I found; it was the mail-coach for Angers; in due time I arrived there. Never having been in this city before, not knowing a soul there, I decided to rent a house and to open it for gaming: the nobility from all the countryside around soon came flocking to me. . . . Countless lovers made their declarations; but the air of modesty and reserve I affected quickly persuaded my suitors that I was not to be wooed successfully save by him who would make my fortune. A certain Comte de Lorsange, the same by whose name I still go today, looked to me to be more assiduous and a great deal richer than the others: he was then forty years of age, pleasing of face and figure; and from his manner of expression I was convinced his intentions were loftier and more legitimate than his competitors': I heeded his attentions. It was not long before the Comte confided his designs to me: a bachelor, enjoying an income of fifty thousand *livres* a year, having no near relations, he, if I were to prove worthy of his hand, would prefer to have me inherit his wealth than have it passed on to some distant kin; and if I were willing to be frank with him, to describe my life in fullest detail, omitting nothing, he would wed me and accord me twenty thousand a year. A proposal such as this was too fair not to accept at once; it was a complete confession the Comte must have, it was a complete one he got.

"Listen to me now, Juliette," spoke up Monsieur de Lorsange once I had terminated my recital, "the avowals you have just made me evidence an openness I admire; she who owns her sins so candidly is far nearer to never sinning again than she who has been faultless all her life; the former knows what to expect—and the latter may at any time fall prey to the desire to essay something new. Deign to listen to me a little, Madame, I insist that you do, to me your conversion would be a precious thing, I want to guide you into the righteous path; I do not propose to upbraid you in a sermon, no, but to put certain truths before you, truths your passions screened long from your sight, and which you will always find in your heart whenever you wish to inspect it alone.

"Oh, Juliette! he who was capable of telling you that morals are useless in the world set for you the cruelest trap into which it would be possible to snare you, and he who was then able to add that virtue is futile and religion a fraud might better have assassinated you there and then, and been done with it. Killing you outright, he would have caused you only an instant's suffering; instead, he readied you for griefs and woes beyond number; the misuse of words and the twisting of meanings were responsible for all your errors, let us now strive to make a just analysis of this virtue wicked teachers sought to make you hate. That which is called virtue, Juliette, is constant fidelity in the fulfillment of our obligations toward others; I ask you now, what person can be so thoughtless, so unfeeling as to venture to situate happiness in that which shatters all the ties that bind us to society? Does that person brashly fancy, will he delude himself into believing, that he can be happy all alone when he hurls everybody else into distress? Will he be strong enough, powerful enough, audacious enough to succeed, single-handed, in resisting the will of society, strong and powerful and audacious enough to compel every individual will to make way before the irregularities of his own? Is he so bold as to imagine he alone has passions? And if all the others have them as surely as he, how can he hope to cow the rest into putting theirs into abeyance and serving his only? You will agree with me, Juliette, no one but a madman can entertain such ideas; but even supposing he is ceded to, is he sheltered from the law? Does he doubt but that its blade will cut him down as it would another? Will you place him so high up that he is hindered by none of these checks? Very well; he must still contend with his conscience. Nay, Juliette, believe me, nobody ever escapes from that terrible voice: you have seen it for yourself, you have had the experience: you attempted to slay the conscience in you by imposing silence upon it, and instead, more imperious than your passions, it called them to a halt.

"Instilling in man a taste for society, the unknown Being who shaped him had necessarily to give him, simultaneously, a taste for the duties whereby he could comfortably maintain himself therein; now, virtue consists precisely in the fulfillment of these duties; virtue is hence one of man's primary needs, it is the sole means to his felicity on earth. Oh, in what lucid and stately order religious truths proceed from these fundamental verities, and how easy it is to prove the existence of a Supreme Being to the man of virtuous heart; the sublimities of nature, Juliette, those are the virtues of the Creator, as benevolence and humaneness are those of His creatures, and from the relationships knitting them all up together is born the concord of the universe. God is the center of the supreme wisdom whereof the human soul is a ray; the moment you close yourself up against that divine light, your lot upon earth must be to wander in darkness from error to misfortune; cast your glance upon those who have presumed to formulate different principles and analyze their motives coolly; did they desire anything else than to seduce you and abuse your good faith? Were they animated by any other intentions than to flatter their despicable and dangerous passions? And in addition to deceiving you, they deceived themselves; there is the worst of it, there is what never enters into the wicked man's calculations; to get himself one pleasure he loses a thousand, to pass one happy day he destines himself to a million dismal days; such is the contagion of vice that he who is attacked by it wishes to infect everyone around him: the mere sight of virtue is a reproach to him, and the wretch does not realize that all his efforts to annihilate it become triumphs for it; the delight of the evildoer is to do worse every day; but having done the worst, then he must stop, and is not this the moment which, revealing his limitations, reveals his weakness to him, and his fault? But is it likewise with virtue? The more he improves its delights the more delicate they become, and if he would attain virtue's farthermost limits, he finds them in the bosom of God, with Whom he unites his existence to live eternally in bliss.

"Oh, Juliette, manifold and deep are the joys of virtue and religion! I have lived like other men—yes, it is in a pleasure-house I have had the fortune of your acquaintance; but even in the flings of my youth, even in the fiery noon of my hot-blood days, virtue never lost its beauty in my eyes, and it was in discharging the duties she imposes I always found the sweetest of my satisfactions. Come Juliette, be honest with yourself, how are you able to think there is greater charm in causing the tears of distress to flow than in relieving the miserable in their hard plight? I am willing enough to grant you, for the sake of discussion, that there may be souls so depraved as to allow a delight in the first case: do you believe it can compare with the delight produced in the second? That which is excessive, that which affects for a brief instant only, must it not seem poor indeed beside a pure, mild, and enduring pleasure? The hatred and the curses of our fellow man, can they outvalue his love and blessings? O! immoral and warped spirit, are you immortal, are you unimpressionable? do you not drift like us upon this peril-strewn sea of life, and have you not our own need of rescuers the day you drive upon a rock? think you men will heed your call after you have insulted them? and do you think yourself a god, to be able to dispense with men? Only grant me these first principles, and how easily I shall lead you from love for the virtues to belief in the Being who combines them in the ultimate degree. . . . Oh, Juliette, what is the atheist's dreadful quandary! Do but contemplate the beauties of the universe, do only that and you will realize the necessity of its Divine Author's existence; it is pride in his passions that prevents vainglorious man from recognizing his God. He who has done a guilty deed is wont to doubt the existence of his judge; is readier to deny Him than to fear Him, finds it more consoling to say *There is no God* than to have to dread the retribution of Him he has outraged; but banishing these deceiving prejudices, let him glance impartially at nature, he will discover God in all the infinite art of nature's Author. Ah, Juliette, theology is a science for the vicious only; it is the voice of nature for the man whom virtue animates: the image of the God he worships and serves, he would be sore troubled if virtue's consolation were but a fable; yes, the universe bears everywhere throughout it the stamp of an infinitely powerful and industrious Cause; and chance, the paltry and unsure resource of dishonest thinkers, that is to say, the fortuitous concurrence of necessary and irrational causes, could not have formed anything; the Supreme Being acknowledged, how abstain from the worship that is His due? Is not our homage owing to that which in all the world is most sublime? He from Whom all our joys derive, is He not entitled to our thanks? And at this point how soon I shall be able to convince you that of all the world's creeds, the most reasonable is the one you were born into. Juliette, if you love virtue, you shall quickly come to love the wisdom of the Divine Author of your religion; consider the sublime morality that characterizes it, and say, was there ever an ancient philosopher who preached one so pure, so beautiful? Self-interest, ambition, ulterior motives lie back of all those other ethical systems, only Christ's is based upon love of mankind: Plato, Socrates, Confucius, Mohammed seek reputation and followers; the humble Jesus awaits only death, and his death itself is an example."

I listened to that sensible man. . . . Good heavens! said I to myself, this must surely be the angel Durand alluded to, and these the incomprehensible truths that were to be divulged to me . . . and I pressed the hand of this new-found friend: tears were gathering in his eyes, he hugged me gently to his breast. "No, my Lord," said I, hanging my head, "I do not feel worthy of the happiness you hold out to me . . . my sins are too many, my fate cannot now be reversed."

"Ah," he replied, "how little you know of virtue and of the mighty God whence it emanates! never was entry into His fold denied the repentent; implore the mercy of the Lord, Juliette, implore His forgiveness and your prayers shall be heard. Vain formulas, superstitious practices—ah no, I require none of this of you; it is faith, it is virtue, it is your behavior as manifested in all the things you do which may ensure the happiness of the long life you have yet to live. They who have loved you only for your vices, because their own found stuff there to feast upon, they spoke to you in no such terms as I have used; nobody but the friend of your soul would take it upon himself to address you thus, and you will pardon these effusions, they stem from my ardent desire to see you happy."

Needless to say, my friends, Monsieur de Lorsange's pretty little diatribe persuaded me of nothing unless it was his innocence and striking inaptitude as a controversialist. For indeed, what grossly inadequate means were these for swaying someone whom the habit of logic had by now rendered inaccessible to prejudice or superstition, and what more ludicrous than to establish the necessity of virtue to human happiness—and this for my benefit! Virtue, eh! Whence came all my misfortunes if not from my weakness in having listened to it for one accursed instant; I ask you next whether Lorsange's captious induction could impress anyone with a head on his shoulders. If virtue is proven necessary, said he, then religion is equally necessary; my informant's construction of lies piled on bigotries collapsed the moment its bases were undercut. Ah no, said I to myself, virtue is by no means necessary, it is merely harmful and a menace—have I not found it out from fatal experience!—and all the religious fairy tales they seek to found upon virtue can only rest, like it, upon basements of absurdity, selfishness is the sole law of Nature; well, virtue contradicts selfishness, since it consists in the incessant sacrifice of one's leanings and preferences in the interest of the welfare of others: if, as Lorsange argues, virtue's existence proves God's, what sort of God is this that perches atop a system raised upon Nature's deadliest foe? Oh, Lorsange, your whole edifice crumbles of itself, and you have built on nothing solider than sand. Virtue is of no advantage to man, and the God you establish thereupon is the absurdest of all absurd phantoms; man, created by Nature, should heed none but the impulses he receives directly from her; his mind once freed of confusing prejudices and his vision clear, his natural understanding will discover neither any necessity for God nor any virtue either. However, pretense is obligatory here, my situation demands it; I must get me out of the mire and back onto the road of prosperity, Lorsange's hand is indispensable to that end; so let's seize it, and never mind the rest; let guile and treachery be the weapons I place heaviest reliance upon, the weakness of my sex dictates the choice of them, and my individual principles must make them the basis of my character.

My skill as a liar, acquired over long years of practice, was such that I could dissemble with ease and success in any circumstances whatsoever, I put on the appearance of espousing Lorsange's point of view and counsels; I ceased receiving people in my house, each time he called on me he found me alone, sewing, and so wonderful was the progress he was making toward the salvation of my soul that I was soon noticed at Mass. Lorsange tumbled happily into the trap; the twenty thousand *livres'* annuity was written out to me and the marriage contract signed a mere six months after I had first set foot in the city of Angers. As I was on good terms with the neighborhood, and as my former errors were known to nobody there, Monsieur de Lorsange's choice was generally applauded and I saw myself mistress of the finest house in town. Hypocrisy restored to me an affluence which dread of crime had stripped me of not long before; and here again stood vice at the top of the tree. Oh, my friends, say what they will, it shall ever be so until humanity's final hour.

There is little I can relate touching my conjugal pleasures with Monsieur de Lorsange; of these the good man was acquainted with none but the most banal; as untaught in lubricity as in philosophy, during the two dreary years I spent as his wife, the poor devil never once took it into his head to vary his routine: soon suffocating from the monotony of it, I put out a watchful eye to see whether this city might not have something in the way of satisfactions to offer. I had no particular requirements as to sex and, provided it gave signs of imagination and verve, the object could be of any sort. I was long in searching; the strait and strict upbringing one encounters in the provinces, the moral rigidity, the mediocrity of the population, that also of its means, everything complicated my efforts, everything posed an obstacle to my pleasures.

A young thing of sixteen, very pretty, the daughter of one of my husband's oldest friends, was the first I attacked. Caroline, intrigued by the originality of my remarks, suborned by the immorality of my systems, quickly yielded to my desires: one day when we had gone bathing together I made her discharge in my arms. But Caroline, who was only beautiful, might well once have, but could hardly hold someone who, like myself, had to be roused through the imagination; whereof the dear child possessed none at all. Brief was our idyll; I shortly found somebody else, abandoned her for a third. Yes, attractive women did not entirely lack in Angers, but how dull were their minds—never a hint of friskiness. Oh, Clairwil, how longingly I thought on you, how greatly you were missing to my happiness! Useless to deny it, he who loves vice, who since childhood cherishes it either from taste or from habit, he, I say, is invariably more apt to find felicity in the continual practice of depraved customs than will he who comes late to them after having always plodded along the desolate path of virtue.

I tried men, met with hardly better luck; I was on my tenth when one day, while hearing Mass beside my virtuous husband, I thought I recognized in the celebrant a certain Abbé Chabert with whom I had had some agreeable connections at the Sodality of the Friends of Crime—a charming boy, you often see him here today. Never had Mass seemed so tedious; it finished at last. Monsieur de Lorsange leaves; some supplementary prayers are my excuse for remaining behind. I request a word with the priest who has just officiated; he comes: why, my God, yes, it was Chabert. We removed at once into a secluded chapel; and there the amiable Abbé, after having congratulated himself upon this stroke of good fortune and expressed his delight at seeing me again, told me that large benefices he possessed here and there in the diocese compelled him to keep under cover but that I should not be misled by his smirks and antics, bowing and scraping are enjoined to politics and cannot be avoided; that his way of thinking, views, and habits were quite what they had always been, and that he would be only too happy to give me proof thereof at the first convenient opportunity. I for my part recounted what had befallen me; having arrived in Angers but a week before, he had not known of my presence there, and reiterated his desire that we amply renew our acquaintance.

"Abbé," said I, "need we delay? Fuck me here and now. The church doors are shut, this altar will serve as our couch; make haste, reconcile me with pleasures over the loss of which I weep every day. Will you believe it? Ever since I came to this wretched town, not one of the persons to whom I have surrendered has so much as thought to look at my ass, I who cherish none but those attacks, and who behold all other pleasures as necessarily accessory or incidental to that one."

"Why, very well then, let us indulge in it," said Chabert, turning me so that my belly was resting against the altar, raising my skirts from behind. "Ah, Juliette," cried he after a moment spent admiring my buttocks, "your ass is still the same, Aphrodite's own."

The Abbé inclines, he kisses it; 'tis most inspiring to feel, in my asshole, this tongue where a god lay of late . . . he soon replaces it by his prick, and lo! I am sodomized to the balls. And so these were the delights of backsliding! Ah, good my friends, my pleasure was beyond description; it is cruel to interrupt sinful habits, it is heavenly to resume them. During my enforced abstinence from this kind of pleasure I had felt the most violent need of it, this had manifested itself in the form of itchings so keen, so insistent that to soothe them I had had to resort to scratchings and scrapings with whatever instrument lay ready to hand; Chabert gave me a new lease on life. Remarking the extreme pleasure he was affording me, he prolonged it to the utmost, and the rascal, young and vigorous as he was, hung in my bum until he had spat three discharges there.

"There's no substitute for it, it has no equal—there's my opinion," said he as he withdrew. "Or do you not agree?"

"Oh, Abbé Chabert, can you ask such a question? And of the staunchest defender of sodomy you are likely to meet in all your life! We must see each other often, my dear."

"We shall, Juliette, heaven be my witness, we shall. And I would that you were doubly content at having encountered me again."

"What do you mean?"

"I have friends."

"And, you wag, you intend to prostitute me to them?"

"With attributes and proclivities like yours, you are better suited to the role of a whore than the one you are enacting at present."

"Abbé, I am touched by what you say, it is a mark of recognition. 'Tis a sad part to play in the world, that of an honest wife; the title itself implies stupidity. Every chaste wife is mad; or else a fool who, lacking the strength to shake off her prejudices, remains buried beneath them through witlessness or because of some constitutional flaw, and is hence nothing better than a creature Nature mismade or contrived in jest. Women are built for impudicity, born for it, and those of them who remain prudes throughout and in spite of all are fit only for ridicule and scorn."

Chabert knew my husband and described him as a bigot; he urged me to seek some compensation for the austerities of the

marital couch. Having overheard someone say that Monsieur de
Lorsange was to depart the next day for one of his estates, he
advised me to take advantage of his absence to come to a country
dwelling of his whither he would escort me, and partake in a
replica of our Parisian debauches.

" 'Tis a wicked thing you are doing," said I, rallying the
Abbé, "you are unsettling all my plans for virtue. Say now, is it
right for you to flatter my passions? should you thus pave for
me the way to crime? ought you lure his wife away from a husband?
Ah, your conscience will answer for it; it is time you halt your
wicked machinations. The harm is not yet done, I have but to consult a spiritual guide less perverted than you, he will teach me how
to resist such criminal desires; he will show me that they are the
product of a perverse soul, explain to me that, in submitting to
them, one dooms oneself to eternal remorse, to remorse of the very
bitterest as there are evil deeds for which there is no possible
reparation. He will not, like you, advise me that I am at liberty
to do anything, that I have nothing to fear; he will not encourage
me to wild conduct by raising hopes of impunity, he will not facilitate my journey into adultery and sodomy, he will not cheer me on
to betraying my husband—a gentle, God-fearing husband, wise,
pious, good, who sacrifices himself for his wife. . . . Oh no, no, it
will be the contrary of that, he will trundle out the great terrors of
religion, he will brandish them to affright me; like the virtuous
Lorsange, he will remind me of a dead God who died for the sake
of my salvation;[17] he will make me sense how guilty I am in dis-
regarding such favors. . . . But I shall not attempt to conceal it from
you, my dear Abbé Chabert, she who is today no less a libertine,
no less a scoundrel than you knew me to be in the past would be
mightily prone to take such pratings ill; and in reply to his golden
words, tell him: My friend, I abominate religion, to the devil with
your fuck-in-the-ass God and a fig for your advice: gibber to me
no more, clumsy little oaf, virtue offends me, it's vice I like; and
it is to enjoy myself Nature put me on this earth."

----

[17] A *dead God!* Nothing so droll as this incoherent term out of the Catholics'
lexicon. *God* means eternal; *dead* means noneternal. Blithering Christians, what do
you propose to do with your *dead God?*

"Ah, Juliette," said Chabert as we parted, "wrong-headed as ever, and just as engaging. Here in this solitude and bleakness where we live, 'tis a treasure I have found in finding you."

I arrived punctually at the rendezvous, Chabert and I set off for his retreat; apart from ourselves, there were gathered four men and four women. Among the latter were three with whom I had held voluptuous commerce previously; while the four men were carnal strangers to me. The Abbé gave us merrily and plentifully to eat and drink, and we gorged ourselves on libertinage too. The women were pretty, the men vigorous: my ass was fucked by all the men, my cunt fingered, sucked by all the women. I discharged prodigiously. No need to describe that party to you, nor the eight or ten others which followed it during my stay at Angers. You are weary of lubricious descriptions, and henceforth I shall spare you all but those which exceptional crimes or other singularities render worthy of your hearing.

Before advancing with my story I must mention a few vital details which cannot longer be omitted. Eleven months after my marriage to the Comte de Lorsange I presented him with a charming baby girl; bearing the child was a struggle for me, but shrewdness won out in the end. The measure was essential: I had to consolidate my claims to the fortune of the man who had given me his name. I could not do this without a child—but was it fathered by my virtuous husband, that's what you are wondering, isn't it now, prying busybodies that you are? Why then, allow me to make you the same reply Madame de Polignac made to Monsieur in answer to the same indiscreet question: "Oh my Lord, when one ventures into the midst of a thicket of rosebushes, how is one to tell by which thorn one has been pricked?" But do you suppose Lorsange bothered to inquire? He accepted everything, jibbed at nothing; the honor and the burdens of paternity devolved upon him, did my greed require anything more? This little daughter, whom my husband named Marianne, was completing her first year and I my twenty-fourth when, taking deep and long counsel with myself, I decided I had no alternative but to leave France.

From anonymous correspondents I had received warnings that Saint-Fond, whose star was only continuing to rise at the Court and who was in apprehension of a damaging indiscretion from me, regretted not having clapped me away into a place of safety, and that he was having me sought after everywhere. Fearing lest my change of name and condition prove insufficient camouflage, I resolved to put the Alps between the Minister's hatred and me: but there were ties binding me, they had to be dissolved; could I make my escape so long as I was under a husband's thumb? Here was something that had to be remedied and I began to lay my plans. The great deal I had already accomplished in this domain reduced a rather unimportant crime to a mere trifle in my eyes; meditating it moistened my cunt, I hatched my plot to the tune of acute spasms of joy, and prospects of others goaded me toward its speedy execution. I had half a dozen pinches left of each poison bought from Durand: to my tender spouse I administered a strong dose of the royal variety, both out of respect for his aristocratic person, and because the time which was to elapse between the envenoming and the death of the beloved would screen me from all possible suspicion.

Never was there a sublimer death than that of Monsieur de Lorsange; his acts and sayings were elevated, they were exemplary; his bedchamber turned into a chapel where sacraments of all sorts were celebrated continually. He exhorted me, he preached to me, he bored me; recommended to me the little daughter he thought was his; and hemmed in by three or four confessors, breathed his last. Truly, had all that dragged on another two days, I believe I would have left him to die all by himself. The respect and care allegedly due to the dying comprise another social obligation which makes no sense to me. One ought undoubtedly to take the fullest possible advantage of a living creature; but as soon as Nature, afflicting it through maladies, advises us that she has initiated the process of reclaiming that creature, rather than risk infringing her laws we must let her operations take their course; we may hasten them, yes; but interfere with them, never. In short, the sick must be abandoned to their own devices; place a few objects inside their reach that may bring them relief, if you like, then proceed about your business. It is unnatural for a healthy individual to go and breathe, before his appointed time and in open violation of Nature's intentions as they regard him, the contaminated air of a sickroom, and to expose himself to falling ill too, all in order to do something unlawful: nothing being more criminal in my opinion than to venture to force Nature to desist or retreat; and always acting according to my principles, I may assure you that I shall never be seen nursing the sick, nor comforting them in any way whatsoever. Nor do I wish to be told that it is my harshness of character which is responsible for this attitude of mine; it comes from nowhere but my intelligence, and my intelligence rarely deceives me where the issue is philosophical.

My very chaste husband interred, I went gladly into mourning for him: no widow, I am told, was ever so becoming in her weeds, wherein I had myself fucked on the burial day—in Chabert's company it happened; but even more delicious than wearing those lugubrious tires was to become the owner of four fine estates evaluated at fifty thousand *livres* a year in rents, plus the one hundred thousand francs in specie I found in my husband's coffers.

More than enough here for my Italian journey, said I, transferring the bundles of banknotes from the deceased's moneybox into mine, and there's the hand of fate, friendly to crime as always and crowning it once again in bestowing her blessings upon one of crime's most devoted disciples.

It turned out that Abbé Chabert had traveled in Italy and was able to furnish me a quantity of glowing letters of recommendation. In exchange, I left my daughter in his wardship; he promised to take the very best care of her—my concern for the child was of course motivated by material considerations rather than by any motherly affection, there being neither any place in my heart for such a sentiment, nor any justification for it in my beliefs. For lust-objects I took along only a tall, well-shaped, and pretty lackey by the name of Zephyr, to whom I had frequently played Flora, and one chambermaid, Augustine, eighteen years of age and heavenly to behold. Accompanied by these two trusty individuals, by another woman of no consequence, some baggage, and my well-filled treasury, I boarded a coach and without stopping save for the night and for meals, sped at a merry clip all the way to Turin.

"And so here I am at last," said I, drawing deep breaths of free air, "in this so interesting region of Europe, this Italy that has always attracted the curious, here am I in the home of Neros and of Messalinas; perhaps upon this hallowed soil they used once to tread I shall capture the spirit of those paragons of crime and debauchery, and be able to duplicate the atrocities of Agrippina's incestuous son and the lubricities of Claudius' adulterous wife." The idea prevented me from sleeping that night and I spent it in the arms of a pretty young lass at the Albergo d'Inghilterra, where I had taken lodgings—a delicious creature whom I had managed to seduce an hour after alighting, and in whose fresh embraces I tasted perfectly divine pleasures.

No city in all Italy is more regular nor duller than Turin; the courtier is tiresome there, the townsman doleful, the rabble equally hangdog and also superstitious and devout. Very slender resources for pleasure, moreover; setting forth from Angers I had struck upon a properly libertine scheme, meditated upon it en route, and at Turin I began its execution. My idea was to travel in the guise of a celebrated courtesan, to make broad display of myself everywhere, to enhance my fortune with the tribute exacted by my charms, and in the interests of my libertinage to exploit whatever of youth and vigor fell into my clutches. On the day after my arrival I had word carried to Signora Diana, the most famous furnisher in Turin, that an engaging young Frenchwoman was in town and for hire, and that I would be obliged if she would come to discuss arrangements with me; the procuress did not fail to answer the call. I outlined my plans to her, and declared that between fifteen and twenty-five they could have me for nothing where I had guarantee of sound health; that I took fifty *louis* between twenty-five and thirty-five; one hundred from thirty-five to sixty; and two hundred from sixty to the final point of human senescence; that as regarded fantasies, occult requirements, and the like, I satisfied them all, that I even lent myself to fustigations.

"And the ass, my fair lady," Signora Diana interrupted me, "and the ass? For it is in hot demand here in Italy; you will earn more money by your ass in the space of a single month than you will from four years of selling your cunt."

I assured Diana that I was very easy in this article, and that in consideration of a double fee no bid for the use of it would be refused. I did not have to wait long before being presented. It was the very next day that a message from Diana advised me I was expected for supper at the residence of the Duke of Chablais.

After one of those voluptuous toilettes whence nature emerged embellished by the cunning hand of art, I betook myself to the house of this Chablais, then forty years of age and renowned throughout the entire country for his libidinous studies in venereal pleasures. The Duke had one of his sycophants by him, together they promptly explained to me that in the games to follow I would play the dummy.

"Get yourself out of all this array," said the Duke, conducting me into a very elegant chamber, "art so often being a mask to defects, our policy with women, my friend's and mine, is to lay them bare at the outset."

I obeyed.

"One ought never wear a stitch when one has a body so fair," my two assailants observed.

"Frenchwomen are all alike," the Duke went on to remark, "their figure and skin are delicious, we have nothing comparable here."

And the libertines inspected me, in their survey turning me this way and that but nevertheless concentrating their attention upon certain details and in a certain manner that soon gave me to suspect that it was not without reason Italians are charged with a predilection for the charms unappreciated by Monsieur de Lorsange.

"Juliette," announced the Duke, "I had better tell you that before you come to grips with us you shall make show of your talents upon some young boys, they will be admitted into the room one at a time. Station yourself upon this couch if you will; the lads we have in store for you shall, as I say, enter in single file by this door to the right and march out that other door to the left; as each arrives, you will frig him with all the skill your nationality promises, for nowhere on earth do they know how to frig pricks better than in France; just prior to discharge you will steer them first the one toward my friend's mouth, then the next toward mine, that is where they are to deposit their fuck; after this, and once again taking turns, my friend and I shall embugger them before sending them on their way; as for you, your individual services shall not be required until we have had our fill of these inaugural delights, and you shall only then be informed of your remaining duties, with the fulfillment of which these lewd scenes will close."

Immediately after the Duke finished speaking the parade began: all the youths I had to frig were either fourteen or fifteen years old, and every one of the thirty I handled was as pretty as a star. They all discharged, some for the first time in their life; the two friends, frigging themselves throughout, swallowed the fuck loosed by each and bum-stuffed them all from the first to the last: one friend would hold the patient, the other would joust five or six minutes in his bowels; neither ejaculated. When the tournament was over both were in such a fever and rage that sweat lay on their brows and foam upon their lips.

"Your turn now," shouted the Duke, " 'tis you, beauteous goddess come to us from France, who are about to receive the incense warmed within this crowd of charming little boys; it would be idle to expect your anus to be as narrow as theirs, but that may perhaps be mended."

And they moistened my asshole with an alcohol essence whereof the effect was such that when they fell to sodomizing me they had literally to blast and batter their way in; one after the other they stormed the fort, one after another they discharged inside it, exhibiting incredible marks of satisfaction; six small boys surrounded them while they toiled: two gave their asses to be colled, they frigged two more, one with either hand, and the other two ass-sucked and ball-tickled them from below and behind. The Duke and his satellites left; I remained in the room, recovering my breath and stanching my wounds. A woman came to fetch me, helped me dress, and took me back to my lodgings after having counted me out a round thousand sequins.

Be of good cheer, said I to myself, my promenades in Italy shan't cost me much, I have but to find a similar windfall in each city I visit and not only will I defray my expenses, I will keep Mademoiselle de Lorsange's dowry intact.

Ah, but the life of a public whore is not all a bed of roses; however, having of my own free will resumed the profession, it was only just that together with its profits I also accept its liabilities. But we are yet a long way from coming to its perils.

A God-fearing man though he is, the King of Sardinia loves libertinage. Chablais had reported to him upon our interview, His Highness was eager to see me. Diana reassured me; it amounted to no more than receiving several clysters administered by the royal hand, and ejecting them for His Majesty's amusement while frigging Sardinia's noblest prick; for this two thousand sequins would be mine. Curious to see whether sovereigns discharged like other men, I accepted the King's invitation. And he accepted the humble role of being my apothecary; I flushed six injections into his mouth; and as I frigged him hard and fast, he discharged hot and happy. He then offered me half his cup of breakfast chocolate, I thanked him graciously. We chatted of politics. The privileges conferred upon me by my nationality and sex, those I had just now acquired through my performance, my native frankness, everything conspired to put me at my ease, and according to my best recollection here as follows is the speech I made that morning to the little despot:

"Estimable gate-keeper of Italy, you who descend from a house whose rise constitutes a true miracle of policy, you whose ancestors, mere commoners and goatherds in olden times, became puissant lords simply by according right of passage through your States to princes from the north bent on conquest in Italy, a permission your forefathers only granted in exchange for a share in their booty; you, first of Europe's kinglets, deign to lend me your ear a moment.

"Perched high in your mountains like the crag-haunting eagle awaiting a dove to devour, you are coming to realize that in such a position as you keep, you depend utterly not only for your advancement but for your mere subsistence upon the folly of courts or the mistaken maneuvers of crowned dizzards; this, I am well aware, is what they were telling you thirty years ago; but there have been vast changes wrought in the system since then: the folly of courts now risks to be as much to your disadvantage as to their own, and those mistaken maneuvers can no longer bring you any profit; so give up your scepter, my friend, give Savoy up to France, and retire within the narrower boundaries Nature prescribed to you originally: see those superb peaks towering over in the west, the hand that created them, does it not prove to you, in piling them up

so high, that your sway is not to extend beyond them? what need
have you to reign over soil that is French, you who are unable
even to reign in Italy? Have a care there, my friend! perpetuate
not the race of kings; we already have overmany of those useless
individuals in the world, who, fattening on the substance of the
people, vex and bully them under the pretext of governing them.
In our day there is nothing more superfluous than a king; renounce
that empty title before it is gone too far out of fashion, step down
from your throne now, voluntarily, before, as may well happen,
you are dragged forcibly off it by the people whose eyes are beginning to tire of its height. Philosophical and free men are ill-
disposed to see above them a man who, carefully considered, and
impartially, has no more than ordinary needs, strength, and merit;
for us, the anointed of the Lord is not a sacrosanct personage
anymore, and today wisdom laughs at a little fellow like you who,
because he has some of his forebears' parchments stored away in
some box, fancies himself empowered to rule over men; your authority, my friend, no longer reinforced by periodical lootings,
presently rests upon nothing solider than opinion: let opinion
change—it is very near to doing so—and we shall go looking for
you amidst the hod carriers in your empire.

"And think not that much is lacking before the change comes
about; as men grow steadily more enlightened they begin to ap-
praise critically what formerly dazzled them: well, the likes of you
do not benefit from scrutiny. The rumor begins to go about that a
king is nothing but an ordinary human being; and that, softened
by luxury, warped by despotism, there is not a single monarch on
earth with the qualities requisite for his post. The first virtue demanded of anyone who wishes to be a ruler of men is knowledge of
them; and what a distorted picture of them must he not have who,
perpetually stunned and fuddled by their flatteries and living all
his life at the greatest remove from them, has never been able
to sift nor scan them? It is not tucked away in a bower of bliss
that you learn how to lead your fellows. He who has never been
anything but fortunate, understanding nothing of the needs of the
fortuneless, he is not the man to guide the destinies of a nation
made up of woe-ridden individuals; Sire, heed my advice: throw

away your royal baubles, go back to your plow, there's nothing else left for you to do."

Taken somewhat aback by my outspokenness, His Majesty's only reply was some cajolery of that very false stamp which is the hallmark of everything that comes out of a true-born Italian's mouth; and we bade each other àdieu.

That same evening I was introduced into a rather brilliant circle where, around a gaming table, I saw society grouped in two distinct classes: there were the rogues on the one side and the dupes on the other: I was informed that the practice in Turin was to steal at play, and that a man could not pay addresses to a woman until he had let himself be robbed by her.

"Why, that's an amusing custom," I said to the gambler who was acquainting me with the situation.

"The explanation is perfectly simple," she continued; "gambling is a form of commerce, hence all ruses are lawful in it. Do you hail a shopkeeper before the magistrates because the curtains in his window filtered the light and led you to mistake shoddy wares for good? It has only to succeed and any means for acquiring wealth is proven sound, Madame; this one is no worse than another."

I remembered Dorval's maxims on theft, and decided they were altogether applicable to this variety of it. Of my informant I asked how one might go about perfecting oneself in this manner of plundering the property of others, assuring her that I had a thorough understanding of most of the rest.

"There are masters," she replied, "I shall send you one tomorrow if you like."

I begged her to do so; the teacher appeared, and in the space of a week he had given me enough instruction in the management of cards to enable me to collect two thousand *louis* during the three months I stayed at Turin. When the time came to pay for his lessons, he requested nothing but my favors; and as it was *à l'italienne* he must have them, and as that style suited me infinitely, after a close examination of his state of health, a precautionary measure which cannot be foregone in that country, I let him take his pleasure in the fashion appropriate to a man whose trade is in treachery.

Sbrigani, that was my mentor's name, had in addition to an engaging appearance a very creditable prick; no more than thirty years of age, sound in wind and limb, of polished gesture and pretty speech, a libertine mind, a philosophical temper, and an astounding gift for appropriating anything belonging to others in every conceivable way. It at once occurred to me that such a man could be useful to me in the course of my travels; I proposed that we join forces; he accepted.

In Italy, regardless of the capacity in which a man accompanies an actress, singer, or other strumpet, there is never anything repulsive in the fact for those who pay her suit: the brother, the husband, or the father usually withdraws when the customer appears on the threshold; does the latter's ardor seem to flag, the kinsman shows himself again, enters into conference with you both, and if, after this, Signor's spirits look to be rising a little, retires into the clothes closet; it is understood that Signor supports the household, he therefore has its support; and the Italian, accommodating by nature, falls in wonderfully with this arrangement. As by now I knew enough of the tongue spoken in this splendid country to pass for a native, I straightway assigned Sbrigani the role of my husband, and we started forth on the road to Florence.

We proceeded at a leisurely pace; we had no cause to hurry, and I was well pleased to contemplate a land which, if one could but traverse it without seeing human beings, would answer one's idea of heaven. We lay the first night at Asti. This city, prodigiously fallen from its ancient grandeur, is hardly anything at all today. On the morrow we resumed our way and went no farther than Alessandria; Sbrigani having assured me that this town was reputed for the large number of nobility among its population, we decided to spend several days there and see what dupes might be found.

As soon as we would arrive somewhere, my husband issued a kind of clandestine but nonetheless very effective proclamation by which those who had the wherewithal to purchase my charms were provided a general description of them and some indication of their price.

The first to present himself was an old Piedmontese duke, ten years retired from the court; he wanted no more, said he, than to view my ass. For this pleasure Sbrigani charged him fifty sequins; but, heated by the prospect, the duke shortly demanded more. Ever the submissive wife, I announce that I can consent to nothing without my husband's approval; no longer in any state to undertake a serious attack, the duke manifests a desire to whip. This fad is one of the chief consolations of one-time buggers; it is agreeable to outrage the god into whose temple one can no longer push one's way; Sbrigani sets the figure at a sequin a blow and fifteen minutes later I have three hundred coins in my purse. From his Lordship's spendthrift manner my husband deduces that here is a man to be dunned, inquires into all his concerns, and beseeches him to accord his wife the honor of supping with her. Greatly puffed up by this request, the old courtier feigns indecision for a moment, then allows himself to be prevailed upon.

"Magnanimous and revered favorite of Italy's greatest prince," says Sbrigani, introducing him to Augustine, whom we have told what is afoot, "the time has come for blood to speak, now must Nature stir in your soul; recollect the affair you once had, in Venice, with the lovely Signora Delfina, married to an aristocrat of second rank. Behold it, Excellency, you see standing before you the fruit of that liaison. Agostina is your daughter; embrace her, my Lord, she is worthy of you. 'Tis I who formed her from childhood and tell me now, have not my efforts been successful? I feel that I may rightfully boast of having turned her into one of the prettiest and cleverest creatures in Europe. Excellency! Great has been my desire to meet you, far and wide have I sought you out: overhearing that you dwelt at Alessandria, I hied myself hither, for I wanted to see it with my own eyes. Aye, 'tis so, the resemblance cannot be doubted; so here you are, good my Lord, and I trust you will reward me for my pains and have some kindness to show a humble Italian who for all his wealth has nought else but the beauty of his wife."

Augustine's slender waist and willowy figure, her big brown eyes and the exceeding fairness of her skin made a powerful impression upon the duke; and the allurements of incest contributing their heavy share to his joyous anticipations, after a few explanations, a few answers perfectly provided by Sbrigani, the poor duke assured us of his emotion, declared he recognized Augustine, and meant to take her home that very instant and assign her the rank she deserved to have in his family.

"Softly, softly," said my illustrious spouse, "your Excellency has his dinner to digest. And I would remind him that the girl is mine until I have been reimbursed for the immense costs I have incurred on her account, ten thousand sequins would hardly cover them. Nevertheless, in view of the honor you have so graciously done my wife, I cannot higgle with your Lordship and will be content with that paltry sum; Sire, pray tell it out forthwith, else I'll not be able to let Agostina leave my house."

The bawdy duke was also rich and to his dazed consideration for so pretty a piece of merchandise as this no price could be too high; the transaction was concluded between cheese and dessert and after coffee my chambermaid went off with her alleged father. Thoroughly instructed in what she was to do, the dear girl, speaking Italian as fluently as I and equally unbackward where it was a question of raiding other people's property, was not long showing her mettle. We had gone to wait for her at Parma; a fortnight later she joined us there and recounted how the duke, head over heels in love with her, had begun his wooing of her the very first night. The more she harped on the relationship which forbade such an intrigue, the hotter the old rake had waxed, pointing out to her that such fussiness and splitting of hairs simply wasn't the practice in Italy. More at ease in his own house, better able to employ the assistance of third persons or the restoratives he apparently had not dared resort to when visiting me, the libertine acquitted himself more honorably; and Augustine's charming ass, after having been stoutly lashed, had ended up being fucked. The sweet child's extreme docility had so inflamed the poor duke that he had overwhelmed her with presents and given her his entire confidence. Entrusted also with all the keys to all the locks, she had rifled the treasury and decamped; and she closed her narration by producing something over five hundred thousand francs. As you may readily imagine, after such a capture we did not tarry overlong in the neighborhood, although it ought to be said that we were hardly in any great danger. For in Italy one has but to cross into the nearest province when one runs afoul of the law: the authorities of one state cannot prosecute you in another; and better yet, as administrations change every day, often twice a day, the crime you commit before dinner is too old to punish by nightfall—all this is of clear convenience to travelers who, as was the case with us, are eager to wreak havoc along the way.

However, discretion being the better part of valor, we made a judicious departure from the states of Parma and did not stop till we were come to Bologna. The beauty of the women in that city forbade me from proceeding farther before having my fill of them; Sbrigani, who catered to me marvelously and whom I fairly covered with gold, presented me to a widow of his close acquaintance. This charming creature, thirty-six years old and as lovely as Venus in her prime, knew every sapphic personality in Emilia: in the space of a week I frigged myself with better than sevenscore women, each more attractive than the other; we spent a second week in a celebrated abbey not far outside the town, whither my guide was in the habit of making periodic pilgrimages. Oh, my friends! the power even of an Aretino's pen would be insufficient to describe the inconceivably lewd revels we organized in that holy retreat; all the novices, a goodly number of nuns, fifty *pensionnaires,* one hundred and twenty women all told, passed through our hands; and I may affirm that never in my life had I been frigged as I was there. The Bolognese nun possesses the art of cunt-sucking in a higher degree than any other female on the European continent: she flits her tongue with such enchanting celerity from clitoris to vagina, and from vagina to asshole, that though she must momentarily quit the one in order to reach the other, it seems as if she were everywhere at once; her fingers are of an amazing flexibility and deftness, and she does not leave them idle with her sisters. . . . Delicious creatures! I shall ever sing your memory, and never forget your charms nor your matchless skill in awakening and maintaining voluptuous titillations; nor shall I forget your cunning refinements; and my most lubricious moments shall be those during which I recall to mind the pleasures we tasted together. They were all so pretty, so fresh and gay, that choosing among them was impossible; if at any point I endeavored to concentrate upon one, that multitude of beauties would distract my attention and the ensemble would reassert its claim to my homage.

It was there, my friends, that I executed what Italian women call the *rosary*: all fitted out with dildoes and gathered in a great hall, we would thread ourselves one to the next, there would be a hundred on the chain; through those who were tall it ran by the cunt, by the ass through those who were short; an elder was placed at each novena, they were the paternoster beads and had the right to speak: they gave the signal for discharges, directed the movements and evolutions, and presided in general over the order of those unusual orgies.

Mesdames soon devised another fashion for giving me pleasure; here, all activities centered upon me: I was laid out upon a group of six, with whose voluptuous undulations I sweetly rose and fell, and all the rest came forward by the half-dozen to consult my sensations and slake them with lubricity: one had me suck her cunt, my two hands were busy palpating two more; another, straddling me, frigged herself upon my nipples, yet another rubbed her clitoris against my face; they all discharged, all washed me in their sperm; and you must not suppose I was reluctant or miserly in the release of mine.

Finally, I besought them to embugger me; a cunt was applied to my lips, I drank of its whey; this cunt, drained, was replaced by another each time a new dildo penetrated into my fundament; my guide, the widow, had the same done to her, but cuntwise, and 'twas an ass she fed from.

While I was off rioting at the abbey, Sbrigani devoted himself to replenishing our funds, seriously depleted by my wild spending; by the time I returned he had accomplished the last of a series of six robberies and entirely repaired the damage my extravagance had caused. Happy is the man who learns to settle his expenditures and fill the gaps in his own fortune solely by using the fortunes of others.

This was in the extent of between two and three thousand sequins; we were able to leave Bologna about as rich as we had come.

I was exhausted; but since the excesses of libertinage, as they weary the body, only heat the imagination further, my thoughts were taken up with planning a thousand new debaucheries; I regretted not having done more, and in search of an explanation for my failure could only suppose that it was owing to some mental sluggishness on my part: and it was then I discovered that the remorse one may suffer for not having gone to the limit in crime is superior to anything that afflicts feeble spirits for having strayed away from virtue.

Such was my physical and moral state as we were crossing the Apennines. This vast mountain chain dividing the peninsula along its length holds much of interest for the inquiring traveler; as the road rises, the most extraordinary prospects greet the eye: on the one side stretches the great Plain of Lombardy and on the other lies the Adriatic Sea; a spyglass enables one to see to a distance of fifty leagues.

We dined at the wayside inn at Pietra Mala, with the intention of visiting the volcano. Profoundly devoted to all the irregularities of Nature, adoring everything that characterizes her disorders, her caprices, and the gigantean horrors whereof she gives us renewed examples every day, I had of course to observe this phenomenon; and so, after a meal that was poor despite our policy of always sending a cook ahead of us, we set out on foot across the little stretch of blasted terrain at whose farther end the crater is situated. The zone surrounding it is a waste, uncultivated and littered with pebbles and stones; the temperature of the air mounts as one moves toward it, and one breathes the stench of copper and carbon the volcano exhales; by and by we caught sight of the flame whose heat, curiously enough, was intensified by a fine rain which happened then to start to fall: the fire pit seemed about thirty or forty feet in circumference: strike a spade into the earth anywhere near it, and fire springs up from the ground at that spot. . . .

"It is," said I to Sbrigani, who stood contemplating this wonder beside me, "it is like my imagination igniting under the strokes of a lash applied to my ass."

The earth inside that furnace is baked, charred, black; that in its vicinity is like clay, and impregnated with the volcano's odor. The flame soaring from the pit comes out in an intense gush, it burns and instantly consumes anything tossed into it; its color is a violet blue, like the color of burning brandy. To the right of Pietra Mala is another volcano which only bursts into flame when fire is brought near its edge; nothing so amusing as the experiment we made: by means of a candle we set the whole plain afire. With a mind like mine such things had best never be seen, yes, my friends, I must agree to that; but the candle I touched to the ground set it alight less quickly than the poisonous vapors arising from the place were intoxicating my brain.

"Oh, my dear," said I to Sbrigani, "Nero's wish is becoming mine. Did I not foresee that from breathing that monster's native air I would soon adopt his penchants?"

When rain fills the crater of that second volcano with water, this water boils away in steam, and this steam is cool—O Nature! impenetrable and strange are thy ways and beyond the imitation of mortals. . . .

It is to be feared that the many volcanoes ringing Florence may someday cause it harm: these fears are amply justified by the signs of past upheavals one notices everywhere in the area. They suggested some comparative ideas to me: is it not very probable, said I to myself, that the fiery destructions of Sodom, Gomorrah, etc., made up into miracles for the purpose of instilling in us a terror of the vice which held universal sway among the inhabitants of those cities; is it not altogether likely that the famous conflagrations were caused, not by supernatural agencies, but by natural forces? The region surrounding Lacus Asphaltites, where Sodom and Gomorrah lay, was studded with imperfectly extinct volcanoes; the country there was similar to what it is here. From the geographical parallel I moved on to the parallel of climate; and when I saw that at Sodom as at Florence, at Gomorrah as at Naples, and in the vicinity of Etna as in that of Vesuvius, the population cherish and adore nought but buggery, I came swiftly to conclude that the irregularity of human behavior is closely related to Nature's own caprices, and that wherever Nature is depraved she also corrupts her children.[18] Wherewith I imagined myself transported to those

---

[18] An important question raises itself here; literary minds, it seems to us, are peculiarly qualified for an attempt to settle it, and that is why we venture to propose it as a subject for their earnest consideration. Does moral corruption in a people come from the flabbiness of their government, from their country's physical location, or from the excessive size of the population clustered in their urban centers? Notwithstanding Juliette's contentions, moral corruption does not depend upon location, since there is as much moral disorderliness in the northern cities of London and Paris as in the southern cities of Messina and Naples; weak rule would not appear

happy Arabian towns, here I am in Sodom, I said, let us do here as the Sodomites do; and poised on the brink of the crater, bending forward over its edge, I presented my bare buttocks to Sbrigani while next to me Augustine and Zephyr imitated us; we changed partners; Sbrigani drove full length into my waiting maid's pretty ass, and I became my valet's prey; and while our men toiled in our bowels, Augustine and I gazed dreamily into the pit and masturbated.

"*This is indeed a charming pastime I find you at,*" we suddenly heard declared in a cavernous voice which seemed to issue from behind a bush. "*No, no, carry on, carry on, I do not wish to spoil your pleasures, only to take a hand in them,*" went on this species of centaur who, as he emerged from hiding and drew near, proved to be of proportions and aspect which exceeded anything we had ever seen in all our life. Seven feet and three inches tall, with, behind huge moustaches, a face both swarthy and awful; we wondered for a moment whether it were not the Prince of Darkness who was hailing us. Surprised at our alarmed stares, "What!" cried he, "have you not heard of the Hermit of the Apennines?"

"Certainly not," Sbrigani replied, "we have never heard tell of the likes of you!"

"Why, then, come along with me, all four of you, and you shall behold more wonderful sights yet: the business I discover you engaged in leads me to suspect that you deserve to see what I have to show you, and to partake in it too."

"Giant," said Sbrigani, "we are fond of extraordinary things, and to witness them there is doubtless nothing we would be unwilling to do; but your tremendous strength, might it not be exerted to the detriment of our liberty?"

"No, because I judge you worthy of my society," said this

---

to be the cause either, since as regards these matters the law is much more severe in the north than in the south, without that preventing the disorder from being the same; no, we are driven to the conclusion that moral corruption, whatever be the terrain or the regime, results from nothing but the too heavy concentration of too many individuals within a small area; that which masses compactly degenerates; and every government that would avoid corruption within its borders must curb the growth of population and, above all, break large groups into smaller to preserve the purity of their constituents.

singular personage; "but for that, your fears would be fully authorized. Lay them aside, however, and follow me."

Determined indeed to learn what this adventure held in store
for us, we sent Zephyr to tell our entourage to wait for us at the
inn until we reappeared there; Zephyr returned from his errand,
we set forth, the giant in the lead.

"Have patience," our guide told us, "the road is long but
seven hours of daylight remain and we shall arrive before the
veils of night overspread the heavens."

We walked in total silence, for the giant would have it so;
during that march I was able to give all my attention to the
landscape.

Leaving the volcanic plain of Pietra Mala we climbed for
an entire hour the slope of a high mountain lying to the right; from
the pass we finally reached we gazed into an abyss a full two
thousand fathoms deep, and it was down into it our winding path
led, through a forest that quickly grew so dense, so dark, we were
scarce able to see the way. After three hours of nearly perpendicular descent we came to the edge of a lake; on an isle in its center
was to be seen the donjon of the castle where our guide had his
abode, of which only the roof could be made out owing to the lofty
battlements girting it. We had been some six hours coming this far
and during that time we had espied not a single house, not a single
individual. A black bark, like a Venetian gondola, was moored to
the shore; from there we could take in the tremendous bowl at
whose bottom we were: it was rimmed all around by towering
mountains whose flanks were covered by forests of pine, larch, and
green oak, and ended in barren peaks and snow: words cannot
convey to what extent that scene was wild and lonely and forbidding, nay, unearthly. We stepped into the boat, the giant fer-
ried us to the island. His castle lay two furlongs back from the
water; we arrived before an iron gate set in the thick outer wall;
spanning a moat twenty feet wide was a drawbridge which was
raised once we had crossed over it; here was a second wall, again
we went through an iron gate, and found ourselves in a belt of trees
so close-spaced that we had indeed to force a passage between
them, and beyond this enormous hedge was the castle's third enclosure, a wall ten feet thick and without any gate at all. The giant

stoops and lifts a great stone slab no one else would have been able to budge; thus does he uncover a stairway; we precede him down the steps, he replaces the stone; at the farther end of that underground passage we ascend another stairway, guarded by another such stone as I have just spoken of, and emerge from dank darkness into a low-ceilinged hall. It was decorated, littered with skeletons; there were benches fashioned of human bones and wherever one trod it was upon skulls; we fancied we heard moans coming from remote cellars; and we were shortly informed that the dungeons containing this monster's victims were situated in the vaults underneath this hall.

"I have you in my power," he said once we had sat down, "I can do with you what I please. Do not, however, be alarmed; the acts I saw you in the midst of performing convinced me that here were kindred spirits such as would merit my hospitality. Supper is being prepared, between now and the time it is ready let me tell you a little about myself.

"I am a Muscovite, born in a small town on the Volga bank. Minski is my name; upon my father's death I inherited his colossal riches and Nature had proportioned my physical faculties and my tastes to the favors wherewith fortune now gratified me. Sensing myself made for better things than to vegetate in the back country of an obscure province like this that was my birthplace, I traveled; the whole wide world seemed too narrow for my desires, they were limitless and the universe cramped them: born libertine and impious, debauched and perverse, bloodthirsty and ferocious, I visited a thousand far-flung lands to learn their vices, and no sooner adopted one than I refined it. I began with China, the Mongolias, and Tartary; I journeyed throughout all Asia; swerving north again I passed by way of Kamchatka and entered America by the famous Bering Strait. In that extensive part of the world I sojourned practically everywhere, by turns in its politer societies, by turns among its savages, copying none but the crimes of the former, the vices and atrocities of the latter. Sailing east, to your Europe I brought back penchants so dangerous that they condemned me to the stake in Spain, to be broken on the wheel in France, hanged in England, drawn and quartered in Italy; wealth is a guarantee against anything. I crossed over to Africa; there I became most fully aware that what you so foolishly call depravity is neither more nor less than the natural state of man and its particular details usually the result of the environment into which Nature has cast him. Those noble children of the sun laughed at me when I rebuked them for their barbarous treatment of women. 'And what do you suppose a woman is,' they would reply, 'if not a domestic animal Nature gives us for the double purpose of satisfying our needs and our desires? What better claim to our consideration has she than the cattle and swine in our barnyards? The only difference we see here,' those sensible people would tell me, 'is that our livestock may merit some indulgence thanks to their mildness and docility, whereas women merit harshness only, in view of their congenital and everlasting dishonesty, mischievousness, treachery, and perfidy. We fuck them, don't we? and is there anything better, indeed, is there anything else you can do with a woman you have fucked than use her as you do your ox or a mule, as a beast of burden, or kill her for food?'

"In a word, it was there I observed man in his constitutionally vicious, instinctively cruel, and studiously ferocious form, and as such he pleased me, as such he seemed to me in closer harmony with Nature, and I preferred these characteristics to the simple crudeness of the American, to the knavery of the European, to the cynical depravation of the Oriental. Having killed men on the hunt with the first, having drunk wine and lain with the second, having done much fucking with the third, I ate human flesh with my brave African comrade; I have preserved a taste for it; all this wreckage you see around you are relics of the creatures I devour; I eat no other sort of meat; I trust you shall enjoy tonight's feast, there will be a fifteen-year-old boy on the table. I fucked him yesterday, he should be delicious.

"After ten years wandering abroad I returned for a visit to my native land, where I was greeted by my mother and sister. Loath to tarry in Muscovy and resolved, once I had left it, never to set foot there again, this seemed the propitious moment to put a final order in my affairs. I raped and massacred them both in the same day: my mother was still a handsome woman, of impressive stature; and though my sister was only six feet tall, she was certainly the superbest creature to be found anywhere in the two Russias.

"Then with an income amounting to roughly two million a year I made straight for Italy with the intention of settling here. But for surroundings I wanted something unusual, rustic, little frequented, and where I could indulge my wanton imagination; and its caprices are not mild, my friends, as I believe you shall have opportunity to perceive during these next few days as my guests; there is not a single libertine passion my heart does not cherish, not a piece of wickedness that has failed to amuse me. If I have not committed more crimes, it is for lack of occasion; I need not reproach myself for having neglected a one, and I have provoked all those which were laggardly in presenting themselves. Had I with greater luck been able to achieve twice as much, I would have that many more happy memories; for those of crimes are delights which cannot be too numerous. From this introduction you shall probably take me for a villain; the things you are going to witness in this house shall, I trust, confirm you in that opinion. You guess my palace large; it is huge, in it are lodged two hundred boys, aging from five to sixteen, who commonly pass from my bed to my kitchen, and about the same number of young men whose job is to fuck me. I have an infinite fondness for that sensation; in all the world, I maintain, there is none so sweet as to have your ass given a vigorous scraping while you busy yourself at some other distraction, whatever it may be. The pleasures I observed you tasting of late on the volcano's rim prove that you share my liking for this fashion of fuck-shedding, and that is why I permit myself this open manner of speaking with you; were it not for that, I would simply butcher you.

"I have two harems: the first contains two hundred girls from five to twenty years old; when by dint of lewd use they are sufficiently mortified, I eat them. Another tenscore women of from twenty to thirty are in the second; you'll see how they are treated.

"Fifty servants of both sexes look after this considerable store of pleasure-objects; and for purposes of recruitment I have one hundred agents posted in all the large cities of the world. And yet, with all the movement this entails, the only access to my island home is by way of the trail you came along today, no one would ever believe it is constantly being utilized by perfect caravans, and the security in which all this is accomplished will never be violated. Not, mind you, that I have the slightest reason for worrying; we are here in the territories of the Duke of Tuscany; the whole extent of my irregular doings is known in his circles, and the silver I scatter about protects them from undue publicity as well as from interference.

"To round out this portrayal of myself, I had best provide some details touching my more intimate person: I am forty-five, and at this age my lubricious faculties are such that I never retire for the night without having discharged ten times. True enough, such inordinate quantities of human flesh as I consume heavily contribute to the plentifulness and density of the seminal matter; whoever tries this diet is certain to triple his libidinous capacities, to say nothing of the strength, the health, the youthfulness such fare assures; nor do I speak of its unique amenities, I need only tell you that you have but to taste it once and you will have a stomach for nothing else; no other flesh, whether of fish or fowl or animal, can withstand the comparison. One has merely to overcome an initial aversion; after that it is fair sailing, one never tires of man. Since it is my hope that we shall discharge together, it is essential that you be forewarned of the appalling symptoms which distinguish my crisis: dreadful outbursts herald and accompany it, and the jets of sperm thereupon released mount to the ceiling, often in the number of fifteen or twenty: the repetition of pleasures has never left me dry so far, my tenth ejaculation is just as tumultuous, just as abundant, as the first, nor have I ever found myself tired and out of sorts today because of last night's efforts. As regards the member whence all that comes, here it is," said Minski, hauling forth a pike eighteen inches long by sixteen in circumference, surmounted by a crimson knob the size of a military helmet. "Aye, here it is: behold its state, it is never in any other, even as I sleep at night, even as I walk in the day."

"Oh, good heaven!" I cried upon seeing that instrument. "But, my kind host, you kill as many women and boys as you see—"

"Just about," the Muscovite replied to me, "and as I eat what I fuck, that spares me the wages of a butcher. . . . Much philosophy is needed to understand me, yes, I realize it, I am a monster, something vomited forth by Nature to aid her in the destruction whereof she obtains the stuff she requires for creation; I am without peer in abomination, alone in my kind . . . oh yes, all the invectives they gratify me with, I know them by heart; but powerful enough to have need of nobody, wise enough to find sufficiency in my solitude, to detest all mankind, to brave its censure, to jeer at its attitude toward me; experienced enough, intelligent enough to explode every creed, to flout every religion, to send every god to hell for the devil's fucking; proud enough to abhor every government, to refuse every tie, to ignore every check, to consider myself above every ethical principle, I am happy in my little domain; in it I dispose of all a sovereign's privileges, in it I enjoy all the pleasures of despotism, I dread no man, and I live content; I have few visitors, indeed none unless in the course of my outings I encounter persons who, like you, strike me as philosophers enough to take part in my amusements awhile; such people only do I invite to my home, and I meet with few; thanks to my natural vigor, I am apt to rove very far on those excursions, not a day goes by but I make a twelve-league, sometimes a fifteen-league sally forth from here—"

"And hence some captures," I interrupted.

"Captures, rapes, burnings, murders, whatever the criminal chances happen to be I exploit them to the full, because Nature endowed me with a propensity for every crime and the means for committing them all, and because there is none I do not cherish and that does not afford me sweetest joy and make me glad in my heart."

"And justice?"

"Inexistent in this country; that is why I chose it for my domicile in the first place: with money, you do anything you like here, and I spend a lot."[19]

---

[19] The far less inconvenient way would be for the state to allow persons of condition to do all they wished in return for money and to buy absolution for every crime; better this, surely, than to have them die on the scaffold. The latter measure is of no profit to the government; the former could easily become an important source of revenue, yielding funds to cover all sorts of unforeseen expenses which are met today by levying countless taxes: these are onerous to innocent and guilty alike, whereas what I propose distributes the burden equitably, the heavier share of it falling where it fairly belongs.

Two of Minski's masculine slaves, evil-looking blackamoors, announced that supper was served; they knelt before their master, respectfully kissed his balls, then his asshole; and we removed into the next room.

"No special trouble has been gone to on your account," said the giant. "If all the kings on earth were to come to see me I'd not depart one inch from my custom."

But some description should be given of that dining room and of the accessories in it.

"The appointments you see here," said our host, "are alive; they move when the signal is given."

Minski snaps his fingers and the table in the corner of the room scuttles into the middle of it; five chairs dispose themselves around the table, two chandeliers descend from the ceiling and hover above the table.

"There is nothing mysterious about it," says the giant, having us examine the composition of the furniture from closer on. "You notice that this table, these chandeliers, those chairs are each made up of a group of girls cunningly arranged; my meal will be served upon the backs of these creatures; my candles are stuck into their cunts; and our behinds, yours as well as mine, settling into these chairs—they are comfortable—will rest upon the soft faces and the elastic breasts of these maidens; wherefor it is I pray you lift your skirts, mesdames, and you, messieurs, remove your breeches so that, in accordance with the words of Scripture, 'flesh may rest upon flesh.' "

"Minski," I observed to our Russian, "the role assigned to these girls is arduous, above all if you are long at table."

"The worst that may befall," Minski retorted, "is that it kill a couple of them, and such losses are too easily repaired to permit me to bother about them for a minute."

As we tucked up our skirts and the men climbed out of their breeches, Minski demanded a look at our asses; he fondled them, he nibbled them, he nuzzled them, and we remarked that of our four bums, Sbrigani's, through a refinement of taste easy to imagine in such a person, enjoyed his particular favor; he tongued and pumped it for nigh on fifteen minutes; that ceremony ended, we took our places, bare-skinned, on the bubs and visages of Minski's sultanas, or rather his slaves.

Twelve naked girls of between twenty and twenty-five brought the dishes; and as they were of massive silver and very hot, scorching the breasts and buttocks of the elements composing the table, there was a pleasant convulsive stir produced, it resembled the rippling of waves at sea; above twenty entrees or roast platters decked the table, and upon side tables, built of four grouped girls each, and which also ambled up at the snap of a finger, were ranged wines of every kind.

"My friends," said our host, "as I have already informed you, only human flesh is served here; those plates are pure of any other ingredient."

"We'll try some," said Sbrigani; "it is absurd to turn up one's nose at anything, aversions are based on nothing better than the lack of habit; all viands are fit nourishment for man, Nature offers them all to him, and it is no more extraordinary, after all, to eat a human than to eat chicken."

So saying my husband dug his fork into a joint of boy which looked to him especially well prepared and, having carved himself a generous two pounds of it, fell merrily to; I imitated him; Minski encouraged us; and as his appetite was in the same class with his passions, he had soon licked a dozen platters clean.

He drank the way he ate; he had tossed off his thirtieth bottle of Burgundy by the time the second course came on; this he washed down with champagne; and Aleatico, Falernian, and other rare Italian vintages were swallowed at dessert.

Yet another good thirty bottles of wine were in our cannibal's guts when, his senses sufficiently enlivened by all these physical and moral excesses, the rogue declared that he was now in a discharging mood.

"I had better not fuck any of you four," he admitted, "it would kill you; but you can at least cooperate in my pleasures, you can watch them. The spectacle is rousing. Well now, whom would you have me tup?"

"I want," said I to Minski, who was bending lewdly over my breasts and seemed to be taking a growing interest in me, "I want you to encunt and then to embugger a little girl of seven right here in front of me."

Minski gestures and the child appears.

The libertine's rapings were facilitated by an ingenious contraption; it was a kind of high stool, splay-legged and of iron, upon which the victim lay either belly up or belly down, depending upon which orifice she was called upon to present; to the stool's four legs the victim's four limbs were then made fast, who from the position thus assumed offered the sacrificer either a wide-open cunt, if she was lying belly up, or a wide-open ass, if she was lying belly down. You have no idea what a pretty little thing she was whom the barbarian was preparing to immolate, and you have no idea how it amused me, the unbelievable disproportion between the assailant and his quarry. Minski rises in a rage from the table.

"Strip," he orders, "all of you, off with every stitch. You," he goes on, pointing to Zephyr and Sbrigani, "you will bugger-fuck me while I am in action, and you," he adds, fingering Augustine and me, "put your asses where I can kiss them side by side."

We take up our stances; the child is clapped upon the stool and tied belly up to begin with; I do not exaggerate when I affirm that the member by which she was about to be perforated was thicker than her waist. Minski rattles off a string of oaths, he whinnies as animals do, he sniffs the hole; I took pleasure guiding that monumental member, no art was employed in the enterprise, Nature alone was counted upon for success, and the whore came to our aid as she does every time it is a question of an atrocity which amuses, serves, or delights her. Three bone-cracking heaves and the tool is lodged: skin splits, blood pours, and the little maid faints.

"That's it, that's it," shouts Minski, breathing very hard, "good, that's what I wanted."

Oh, my friends! the crime moves toward completion; Minski is being bum-stuffed, he kisses, bites, chews now Augustine's buttocks, now mine; a ringing yell announces his ecstasy, he utters wild blasphemies. . . . The scoundrel! the rake! Discharging, he has strangled his victim, she breathes no more.

"Never mind," he says, eyeing the child, "no need to tie her this time, she'll lie still."

And flopping her over stone dead as she is, the libertine sodomizes her, the while strangling one of the girls who had been serving the table and whom he has summoned into reach.

"Why indeed!" said I when he had unleashed his second discharge, "do you then never taste this pleasure without it costing some individual his life?"

"It often costs the lives of several," the ogre replied. "If I had no human beings to kill I do believe I would have to give up fucking. For it is death's sighs answering my lubricity's that fetches forth my ejaculation, and were it not for the death my discharge occasions I don't know how I'd be able to discharge at all.

"But come with me into the next room," the Russian continued, "ices, coffee, and liqueurs are awaiting us." Turning then to my two men, "Friends," said he, "you fucked me to perfection; you found my asshole large, did you? I dare say. But agreeable nonetheless? I'm sure of it; the fuck you spattered into it tells me so. As for you charming ladies, your asses distinctly delighted me and in token of my gratitude, for the next two days I accord you the run of my seraglios, enjoy yourselves there, my beauties, they are rare facilities I place at your disposition."

"Liberal host," said I to the giant, "we ask no more of you; voluptuous satisfactions ought to crown lewd preparations, and the rewards of libertinage ought to be earned in the service of lubricity."

We entered; from the odor reigning in the room we were quick to divine of what species were these ices Minski promised us: and indeed in each of five white porcelain bowls reposed two or three mards, exquisite in form and exceedingly fresh.

"I always take them after dinner," the ogre told us, "nothing is more helpful to the digestion and at the same time nothing so pleases my palate. These turds come from the best asses in my harem, and you can eat them safely."

"Minski," I rejoined, "an appreciation for these dainties is slow to come by; we might perhaps fancy them in a moment of passion, but you catch us somewhat unprepared—"

"Just as you like," Minski replied, picking up a bowl and tossing off its contents, "everyone must be his own guide in these matters. Go right ahead with the liqueurs, I shall not be having any until after."

It was a lugubrious chamber we were in, and the illumination typified the rest: four and twenty skulls enclosed each a lamp whose light emerged through the eye-sockets and the jaws. Glimpsing my horror, the ogre, his prick high and nodding, made as if to approach me; I met him with skill enough to divert his desires elsewhere. Young boys were serving our coffee, I had him embugger one of them, he was twelve years old and dropped dead off the end of Minski's prick.

Realizing after a while that in our fatigued condition we were no longer able to keep pace with him, Minski had his slaves conduct us to a superb gallery where in four mirror-paneled alcoves stood the beds we required for rest. A corresponding number of girls were under instruction to chase away flies and burn incense during our sleep.

It was late when we awoke. Our attendants led us to the bathrooms where under their expert care we were wonderfully refreshed; and thence to the adjoining conveniences where they had us shit in a manner no less comfortable than voluptuous and hitherto unknown to us: they dipped their fingers in rose water, then inserted them into our anuses; gently and caressingly they detached and removed whatever matter they encountered there, but so tactfully, so cunningly that you savored all the pleasure of the operation without any of its pain: the vessel once emptied, they tongued it clean inside and out, and this with unequaled address and dexterity.

Upon the stroke of eleven a messenger arrived to announce that Minski had granted us the honor of visiting him in his bed. We entered his chamber; it was spacious, upon the walls were magnificent frescoes representing ten libertine groups which for composition were probably the highest thing ever attained in obscenity. At the far end of that room was a wide semicircular apse paneled by mirrors and containing sixteen black marble columns, to each of which a girl was bound, her rear being exposed to view. By means of a pair of cords placed like bellpulls at the head of our hero's bed, he could subject each of those sixteen asses in the distance to a different form of abuse, the torture lasting until he released the cord. Independently of the girls aforementioned there were six others plus a dozen boys, some agents and some patients, who remained on hand in nearby antechambers for such night-service as their libertine overlord might require. The first thing he did as we approached his couch was to show us his erection, putting on a horrible grin as he pointed that gigantic engine in our direction; he demanded the sight of our asses, we complied; while palpating Augustine's, he vowed he would get himself into it before the day was out; the poor thing trembled at those words. Minski frigged Sbrigani purple and made prolonged ado over his buttocks as well; they fell to some reciprocal ass-sucking and appeared to take great pleasure from that; then Minski asked, would we like to see him hurt those sixteen girls tied to the columns, all sixteen at one stroke? I urge him to start his machine; he gives a tug on his tackle and the sixteen wretches, screaming in unison, are simultaneously attacked about the hindquarters in sixteen different manners, one is pricked, the next burned, another scourged, yet another tweezed, raked, scored, grated, stabbed, slashed, chopped, etc., and all that so forcefully that the alcove is drenched in blood.

"Were I to pull harder," Minski explains to us, "and it sometimes happens that I do, everything depends upon how things stand with my balls, but, as I say, I have merely to pull harder on my lanyard and the lot of them are done for; I like to go to sleep lulled by the thought that at the bare hint of a desire I can perform sixteen murders."

"Minski," I say to our host, "your supply of women is large enough to permit you to make a little sacrifice: it is in my friends' behalf as well as my own I ask you to treat us to this charming scene."

"I consent," Minski replies, "but my custom is to discharge while operating; this little slut you have in your train, her ass intrigues me—let me sodomize her and the moment my fuck lands in the bottom of her bowels you'll see my sixteen women die."

"That will surely make seventeen!" Augustine shrilled, imploring us not to surrender her to the monster; "how do you expect me to endure such an experience?"

"With patience and understanding," says Minski.

And, having his attendants undress her, he engaged her to assume the appropriate posture.

"Have no fear," he continued, "no woman has ever resisted me and I fuck younger than you every day."

Deciding from the Russian's manner and mien that objections would only serve to irritate him further, we dared not even manifest our regrets.

"It's only a little whim," Minski whispered to me, "it will be satisfied in a trice. This girl provokes me, blame it all upon her ass; whether I kill her or simply cripple her, it's the same thing, you'll have two other and much prettier ones to replace your loss."

As he spoke, two of his serving girls in the room prepared the passage, moistening the instrument and guiding it to the hole. Minski was so practiced in these horrors that he accomplished them virtually without effort; two thundering blows sent his mast-sized weapon crashing to the depths of the victim's ass, and with such dazzling speed we hardly saw its length disappear; the villain emitted a whoop of delight, Augustine swooned, and the gore ran down her thighs. Minski, in seventh heaven, only waxes the hotter; four girls and as many boys crowd around him, so well trained are they in their duties that not an instant elapses but all is ready; Augustine lies somewhere beneath the giant's bulk, she has quite vanished. Her assassin swears, nears the mark, he discharges, wrenches the cords; sixteen death-dealing devices enter simultaneously into play, the sixteen bound creatures scream as one and expire at the same time, one with a dagger in her heart, the other with a bullet there, this one her brains dashed out, that one her throat slit, in short, variously but concurrently.

"It does appear to me that your Augustine was right," Minski remarked coolly. "Indeed yes, her predictions have been amply borne out by the event." And it was then, as he debuggered, that the poor girl's body came back into sight: it had been pierced in ten places by that many thrusts of a dagger. How the scapegrace had contrived to manage this without our noticing, and to wring Augustine's neck into the bargain, I have no idea.

"Oh, I adore strangling them while fucking them," that ter-

rible libertine owned phlegmatically. "Let's have no tears, I
promised you I would give you two prettier ones in exchange and
I intend to keep my word. . . . There was nothing for it, my friends,
certain asses have always affected me that way; and when I am
dealing with pleasure-objects, you understand, my desires are always so many death sentences."

The duennas dragged my poor Augustine's corpse into the
center of the room where the sixteen dead girls already lay; and
Minski, after surveying this heap, after having handled each of
the bodies, bitten into a few buttocks and several breasts, designated
three of them for his kitchen, one of these being the mortal remains
of our late companion.

"Have them dressed and cooked for dinner," he instructed his
head steward. Turning away from the carnage, he invited us to
follow him into the next chamber for a tête-à-tête.

At this point Sbrigani caught my eye. His opinion, communicated to me in a murmur, was that we had perhaps beware of this
monster and ask to leave the premises as soon as possible. But, I
said to myself, a request to depart could hardly entail greater risks
than remaining here; however, upon entering the room Minski
ushered us into, I was content to put on an aloof air which, conveying my disapprobation of his late proceedings, allowed him to infer
how suspicious they had made me touching his designs in my own
regard.

"Come, come," said the ogre, having me sit down on a couch
beside him, "I am surprised at you, Juliette. For I thought you
much too much of a philosopher to miss that girl, or to suppose for
one instant that the laws of hospitality were operative in the house
of a man with a soul like mine."

"What you have done is irreparable."

"Why so?"

"I loved her."

"You loved her! If you are silly enough to love an object
which serves your lust, why, Juliette, there is nothing more I can
say: it would be a waste of time hunting for arguments to convince
you; none exist against stupidity."

"Very well then," I said grumpily, "it isn't Augustine I am

thinking about, but myself. I am anxious, I admit it. You will stop at nothing. What assurance have I that you will not subject me to the same treatment that undid my friend?"

"None, absolutely none," said Minski, "and if the idea of assassinating you were to harden my prick, you'd no longer be among the living a quarter of an hour later. But I thought you were as much a rascal as I; in view of our resemblance, I prefer you as my accomplice than as my victim. That is also my attitude toward the two men in your company: they also look to me fitter to participate actively in my pleasures than to be the occasion of them: your security reposes upon this assumption. And what of Augustine? Ah! a bird of a different feather; I am a good physiognomist: more servile than criminal, she complied with your desires, did as she was told but was far from doing what she wanted. Oh, Juliette, I hold nothing sacred: to have spared all four of you would have been at the least to act as though I believed in the laws of hospitality. The appearance . . . the mere idea of a virtue horrifies me; I had to violate those laws, some gesture was required of me; I am satisfied now, put your cares away."

"Minski, your frankness merits that I reply in the same strain. Let me repeat: if I am disturbed by Augustine's fate it is mainly because it causes me concern for mine. You were not mistaken in your judgment of me, rest assured that my heart is incapable of lamenting any object of libertinage; I have sacrificed a fair number of them in my life, and I swear to you I have never bewailed the passing of a single one."

At this Minski nodded and made as if to rise. "No," I said, praying him to stay a little, "you just now began a criticism of the virtue of hospitality, I have a liking for principles; intimate to me yours on this subject. Although it has been a long while since any virtue has enjoyed my favor, I never took firm measures against my notions of hospitality—was it oversight? was it chance? or could it be that I harbored some obscure belief in their sanctity? Combat, discredit, destroy, extirpate—speak, Minski, you have my ear."

"The greatest of all extravagances," the giant began, plainly not displeased to have this opportunity to display his wit, "is without doubt that which leads us to ascribe a privileged nature to the individual who, by accident, through curiosity, or because of need, ventures under our roof; nothing but some personal motive could ever have induced us into this error. The fault is surely not Nature's: the more entirely a people lives within her law, the less it knows of any laws of hospitality; countless savages lure travelers into ambushes and then immolate their prizes. In a few degenerate and unpolished nations they act differently, eagerly receive their visitors; and carry courtesy to the point of availing them of their wives and their children of both sexes; let us not be deceived by this practice, it too is the fruit of egoism. For the people who so behave are seeking support, protection, from the foreigners who come among them; recognizing them stronger, better made, or better-looking than themselves, they may desire to have these foreigners settle in their country, either to defend them or by mating with their women to breed an improved race for the regeneration of their society: such are the aims of this calculatedly joyous welcome, of this hospitality that seduces fools and which fools laud; and which, be persuaded of it, has never emanated from any disinterested sentiment.

"Yet other peoples expect pleasure from the guests they greet, and caress them in order to use them; they fuck them. But no people has ever exercised hospitality gratuitously: read all their histories and you will discover the particular reasons each had for receiving strangers generously.

"And indeed, what would be more ridiculous than to throw one's house open to an individual from whom one expected nothing in return? In the name of what is a man under obligation to play benefactor to another man? Does the material or moral similarity obtaining between two bodies entail the necessity that one of these bodies do good to the other? I value a man to the extent he is useful to me; I scorn him and even detest him when he can be of no further service to me; he then having nothing left to show me but all that is vicious in him, and being nothing now but a potential threat to me, I must deal as warily with him as with a ferocious beast that can do me nothing except harm.

"Hospitality was the virtue preached by the weak: homeless, naked, puny, lost, looking elsewhere than to his own industry for his welfare, he had of course to advocate a virtue which would ready him haven and suppers. But what need has the strong man to act hospitably? Put incessantly to contribution, deriving nothing from his philanthropies, how long can he continue to be a host to all and sundry before he becomes a fool? I ask you now whether any action at all can be honestly reputed a virtue when it is to the advantage of only one of the classes of society?

"And think of the dangers to which they who perform it expose the hapless souls they unthinkingly shelter! Accustoming them to idleness, they rot what is left of moral fiber in their lazy guests, who soon finish by breaking into your house when, your generosity exhausted, you cease to open the door to them, just as beggars always turn thieves when you finally refuse them alms: well now, once you analyze any such action, for what, pray tell me, does it reveal itself when on the one hand you detect its inutility and on the other its perilous nature? Answer me straight out and unambiguously, Juliette: can you dare transform an action of this sort into a virtue? will you not, if you wish to be just, rather rank it among the vices? Let there be no mistake about it, the granting of hospitality is as dangerous as the granting of charity; all civilities that emanate from benevolence—a sentiment originating in weakness and arrogance—all of them are pernicious, from every imaginable point of view; and the prudent man, the reasonable man, steeling his heart against all these pusillanimous impulses, must take every good care to avoid the grim pitfalls into which they entice us.

"The inhabitants of one of the Cyclades are such enemies to hospitality that they go to unusual lengths to keep strangers at bay; they dread and loathe them, so much so that they never accept anything tendered them by a stranger without first protecting their bare hands with green leaves, and then attaching the object to the end of a stick. If despite all precautions a stranger chances to touch their skin, they purify themselves immediately, rubbing herbs upon the spot.

"There is no treating with certain Brazilian tribesmen save at the distance of one hundred paces, and gun in hand.[20]

"The Africans of Zanguebar are so little given to hospitality

---

[20] See Cook's account of his second voyage.

that they pitilessly slaughter all strangers who penetrate into their country.[21]

"For centuries the Thracians and the mountaineers of the Taurus pillaged and slew all who came to visit them.[22]

"To this day the Arabs despoil and sell into bondage all survivors of disasters at sea who succeed in coming ashore on their coasts.

"Egypt was long barred to foreigners; the government's orders were to enslave or kill anyone found along the border or within sight of land.

"In Athens, in Sparta, hospitality was forbidden; those who implored it were punished by death.[23]

"Arrogating to themselves rights over foreigners, several governments execute them nowadays and confiscate their possessions.

"His Royal Highness the King of Achem seizes all vessels that run aground on the reefs in his coastal waters.

"Unsociableness toughens a man's heart and thereby renders him fitter for great deeds; so it is that we see theft and murder erected into virtues; and only in those nations where this occurs do we ever see great feats and great men.

"The murder of foreigners is held a praiseworthy action in Kamchatka.

"The blacks of Loango go farther still in their aversion to the hospitable virtues: they will not even suffer a stranger to be buried in their country.

"The entire world, in short, furnishes us examples of national loathing for the virtues of hospitality; and from this overwhelming accumulation of evidence and from our own reflections we are obliged to conclude that there is probably nothing more injurious nor more contrary to one's well-being and to that of others than a rule whose purpose is to bind the rich man to give asylum to the poor whereof the latter will never profit save to his ultimate and inevitable detriment and to the donor's also. A man can enter a

---

[21] This upon the authority of Mr. Ramusio Dapper.
[22] *History of the European Peoples*, III.
[23] See Herodotus.

foreign land for one of only two reasons: because of his curiosity, or because he is in search of dupes; in the first case, he must be made to pay for his entertainment; in the second, he must be punished."

"Oh, Minski!" I replied, "you persuade me; the maxims I have long embraced upon charity, upon benevolence, are too similar to yours upon hospitality for me not to concur in the opinions you have just‾ expounded. But there is yet another thing concerning which I would be grateful for your advice: Augustine, whose attachment to me was of several years' standing, is survived by aged parents, they are needy and quite unable to shift for themselves; as we were starting upon our journey she mentioned them to me and asked me not to forget them if perchance some mishap were to befall her during our absence from home; do you think I should settle a pension upon them? . . ."

"Certainly not," Minski was quick to answer, "by what right would you presume to do any such thing? And for their part, what claim can the parents of your late friend make to your bounty? You paid that girl wages, did you not, you maintained her the whole while she was in your hire; what connection does that establish between you and her parents? You owe them absolutely nothing, and neither, for that matter, did she. If, as I would judge from your philosophy you must, you have a clear idea of the nothingness of the fraternal bond alleged to subsist among men; if you have sufficiently pondered that idea and from it drawn the obvious conclusions, you cannot help but realize, first of all, that between Augustine and the services she rendered you there is no possible relation: for services, being of a temporal nature, exist only in the performance, and she who performed these is no longer able to perform at all. You are sensible of the distinction; and so must agree that any identification of the one with the other is founded upon flimsy illusion; the only real feeling that can remain to us for a departed servitor would be gratitude; and you know that no proud spirit can ever be grateful: he who refuses a service offered by another or who, having accepted one, considers himself in no wise beholden to a benefactor who acted for none but his own pride's sake; he, I say, is far more of a man than the ignominious fellow who, willingly donning the shackles of indebtedness, prepares his benefactor the pleasure of parading his victim like a captive at a triumph; no, I shall say more, and though you may have heard it said already, it cannot be repeated too often: one ought normally to desire the death of the benefactor from whom one is not yet discharged of obligation, and I am never surprised to hear of accounts being settled by a murder. Oh, Juliette, how greatly do study and deep thought improve our understanding of the human heart; and how great becomes our determination to defy human principles once we come to know the being who devised them, for they are all of man's making, and in the name of what do you call upon me to respect that which is no more than the handiwork of somebody no better than I? Yes, this subject once thoroughly explored and pondered, many crimes which would look atrocious to simpletons and leave them aghast, appear perfectly unpretentious and natural to us: let word get about that Tom, in pressing need of money, received a hundred *louis* from Dick and then for all his thanks plunged a knife into Dick's breast, and watch your vulgar mob go quite berserk, hear those idiots shout murder and bawl for justice. Aye, they shout, they bawl; and the fact remains that this murderer is of a finer cut and nobler soul than his adversary, since the one, in obliging, did nought but defer to his pride while the other could not endure to see himself humbled; here we have ingratitude in the form of a splendid deed. Ah, frail mortals! how blindly you proceed with the sorting of your virtues and your vices, and how quickly the complexion of your scheme is reversed, black turned into white, day into night under the most superficial examination; you cannot imagine, Juliette, the insuperable tendency I have always had to ingratitude, it is the virtue of my heart, and never has anyone attempted to oblige me but I have been revolted by the prospect: once upon a time someone proposed me his services and, repressing my fury, I said to him, 'Have a care, my friend, things will go ill between us if I accept your rash offer.'

"This act of charity you are meditating with regard to Augustine's necessitous parents would have all the disadvantageous aspects presented by pity and compassion, feelings to which, as it appears to me, you are not much addicted. Charity makes for nothing but dupes, Juliette, benevolence nothing but foes; believe what I say, my doctrine is sound, only adhere to it and you shall never have cause to complain of me."

"Such principles suit my character and have been responsible for my felicity," said I to the giant; "virtue has always appalled me, never has it given rise to pleasure for me." And to lend weight to these statements I related how a moment of virtuousness had once reduced me to rag and ruin and all but cost me my life.

"I have no such reproach to make to myself," Minski declared, "and since earliest childhood my heart has never for a single moment been assailed by these abject sentiments whose effects are so dangerous; I hate virtue as I hate religion. I consider the one as deadly as the other, and I shall never be seen in their clutches. My only regret, as I have already confessed to you, is that I have too few crimes to my credit; crime is my element, it and it alone sustains me and inspires me, it is my sole reason for living, and mine would become a sorry and aimless existence if I were to cease committing at least one crime an hour."

"From what you tell me I wager you must have been the executioner of your family."

"Alas. My father escaped me, and I have not yet got over it. I never had a fair try at him, he died while I was still too young. However, all the rest perished by my hand; I have related the killing of my mother and sister, often I have wished they were alive again so that I might have the pleasure of butchering them anew. What's left for me these days? I have nothing but ordinary victims to sacrifice, my heart grows heavy, all pleasures fade, they pall, the enjoyment is gone—"

"Oh, Minski," I cried, "to the contrary, I deem you a happy man; I too have tasted those delights, although not to such an extent. . . . My friend, your reminiscences, your remarks stir me beyond words; I would ask you a favor: to let me rove through your castle's hundred halls, to dally with your innumerable minions, open up to me this vast field of crime, let me fertilize it with fuck and with cadavers."

"I shall, but upon one condition. I don't propose to sodomize you, it would be your ruin; but I demand the total cession of that young man," said Minski, and it was to Zephyr he referred.

My hesitation lasted an instant. . . . The icy point of a stiletto tingled upon my breast.

"Choose," that fierce man bade me, "between death and the pleasures my house can afford you."

Yes, despite my fondness for Zephyr, I surrendered him—could I do otherwise?

*Part
Four*

$\mathcal{W}$e removed to another apartment. A magnificent repast of exotic fruits, of pastries, of milk and of warm beverages was presented by a swarm of half-naked boys who, as they brought around the plates, cut a thousand merry capers, performed a thousand little naughtinesses one more libertine than the other. My two men and I breakfasted heartily. As for Minski, he was served solider stuff: eight or ten virgins-blood sausages and two testicle pasties took the edge off his hunger, eighteen magnums of Greek wine accompanied those victuals into his enormous belly. He picked baseless quarrels with a dozen of his little pages, lashed six of them to ribbons, pounded the other six senseless with his fists. When one boy resisted him, the dastard broke both his arms like matchsticks, and that just as calmly as making the simplest gesture; he stabbed two more, and we began our tour of inspection.

The first room we came to was large, billeted in it were ten-score women, aged twenty to thirty-five. Upon our entering, and this was the time-honored custom, two executioners laid hold of a victim and hanged her naked before our eyes. Minski went up to the dangling creature, felt her buttocks, bit them; in the meantime all the other women drew smartly up in six rows. We walked up and down the ranks to have a nearer view of the women constituting them. These women were dressed in such a manner that none of their charms were concealed: a simple drape of tulle left their breasts and buttocks exposed, but their cunts were not visible at all, Minski preferring to be spared the sight of a shrine in which he was little given to performing his devotionals.

Leading off this room was another, not quite so spacious and containing twenty-five beds; this was the infirmary for women who had been injured by the ogre's intemperances or who fell ill.

"Should the indisposition become serious," Minski said to me as he opened one of the windows, "I transfer them to the outdoor ward."

604   ❧   THE MARQUIS DE SADE

Fancy our surprise when, peering into the courtyard below, we discovered it crowded with bears, lions, leopards, and tigers.

"Indeed," said I, "such leeches must very shortly relieve anybody of what ails him."

"Oh yes. Down there they're cured in the twinkling of an eye. It is rapid, it is tidy, it avoids contamination of the air. A sickly woman, one wasted by disease can be of no use to lewdness; better to be rid of her at once, I believe. And one saves money; for you will agree, Juliette, defective females are not worth what it costs to keep them alive."

In all the other seraglios it was the same hanging, the same inspection of the ranks.

Minski visits a sickroom, six patients look to him a little worse than the rest, he snatches them bodily from their beds and heaves them one after the other into the menagerie where they are devoured in a matter of minutes.

"That," Minski whispers to me while we watch the terrible feast, "is one of my favorite diversions. Exciting, isn't it?"

"Incredibly, my dear," I answer the giant, staring delightedly at the spectacle, guiding his hand toward my cunt; "probe about in there and verify whether or not I share your sentiments."

And I discharged. Inferring that I might be pleased to witness the doctoring of a second batch of sufferers, Minski rounded up a number of girls who had nothing more wrong with them than a few virtually healed scratches and bruises. They trembled as they were led up to the window. To prolong and heighten our amusement we had them gaze awhile at the savage beasts for which they were about to become fodder; Minski's nails raked their buttocks, I pinched their breasts, tweaked their nipples. Then out they were tossed. The giant and I frigged each other during the massacre; the spasms which jarred me made me fairly scream my joy.

We rambled through the other apartments where all manner of horrifying scenes were enacted; Zephyr expired in the course of one of the most ferocious of them.

"Well, good friend," I commented, when I had sated my passions, "you can hardly deny that the conduct you permit yourself here, and which in my weakness I have copied, is abominably unjust."

"Come sit down," that libertine invited me, "and listen to what I have to say.

"Before deciding, simply because of the veneer of injustice you see there, that the action I commit is blameworthy, we had better, I think, come to some sort of understanding upon what we mean by just and unjust. If now you meditate a little upon the ideas lying behind these terms, you will recognize that they are most profoundly relative, and profoundly lacking in anything intrinsically real. Similar to concepts of virtue and vice, they are purely local and geographical; that which is vicious in Paris turns up, as we know, a virtue in Peking, and it is quite the same thing here: that which is just in Isfahan they call unjust in Copenhagen. Amidst these manifold variations do we discover anything constant? Only this: each country's peculiar legal code, each individual's peculiar interests, provide the sole bases of justice. But these national, these regional laws depend upon the preferences of the government locally in power, and these interests depend upon the physiology of the individual who holds them; thus, self-interest, you see it very clearly, is the single rule for defining just and unjust; and thus, in the light of a certain law, it will be very just in a certain country to behead a man for a deed which would win him laurels elsewhere, quite as a certain individual interest will reckon just a deed which, nonetheless, the person whom it harms will esteem very iniquitous. Some examples may be cited.

"In Paris the law punishes thieves; it rewards them in Sparta: robbery is legitimate in Greece and highly illegal in France, and justice consequently as illusory as virtue. A man breaks his enemy's back; he will tell you he has done the right and just thing, now ask his victim for his view of the matter. Themis is therefore an altogether make-believe goddess, whose scales ever show in favor of him who tips them harder, and over whose sightless eyes they need hardly have bothered to place a blindfold."

"Minski," I remarked, "I have often heard it said, however, that there is a kind of natural justice man has always and everywhere adhered to, or which he has never violated without ruing it afterward."

"Sheer nonsense," said the Muscovite, "that fabled natural justice is simply the fruit of man's weakness, his ignorance, or his folly whenever it is not to his advantage to propagate the lie. If he is of little strength he will always, automatically, belong to the natural-justice camp, and will always discover injustice in the hurt inflicted by the mighty upon members of his class; let him acquire some power himself, then his opinion and his ideas touching justice change instantaneously: henceforth nothing but what flatters him will be just, nothing equitable but what serves his passions; analyze it carefully, this famous natural justice always reveals itself based upon his interests; take Nature for your guide when you shape your laws, only in this way will you avoid error. Well, is there any limit to the injustices we see her commit all the time? Is there anything so unjust as the hailstorm that capricious power flings to ruin the poor peasant, although—explain it as you will—not a grape in his rich neighbor's vineyards is spoiled? and the wars of her fomenting in whose course the whole of a land is laid waste for the sole benefit of some tyrant, and the fortunes she permits the villain to amass while the honest man founders all his life in hardship and privation? Say, those diseases wherewith she slaughters the populations of entire provinces, those repeated, innumerable triumphs she accords brazen vice while not a day passes but she grinds deserving virtue beneath her heel; this protection she forever grants to the powerful man, seconding him to the detriment of the helpless—I ask you, is all that just? and may we suppose we are guilty when we imitate her?

"Hence—no other conclusion is warranted—there is not the slightest wrong of any sort in violating all the imaginary principles of human justice as we go about composing our own, tailored to fit our personal needs, and which will always be the best of all justices because expressly constructed for the service of our passions and our interests: in this world only they are sacred; and if true wrong there be, it is whenever we award a preference to hallucinations, neglecting sentiments given us by Nature, who is truly outraged by any sacrifice we are weak enough to make of them. Despite the allegations of your demi-philosopher Montesquieu, justice is not eternal, it is not immutable, it is not in all lands and in all ages the same; those are falsehoods, and the truth is the reverse: justice depends purely upon the human conventions,

the character, the temperament, the national moral codes of a
country. 'If that were so,' the same author continues,[1] if justice
were but the consequence of human conventions, 'of characters,
temperaments, etc., it would be a dreadful truth such as one would
have to dissimulate from oneself. . . .' And why hide such essential
truths from oneself? Is there a single one man should flee from?
'It would be dangerous,' the same Montesquieu continues, 'because
it would put man ever in fear of man and bring to an end all our
security of property, of honor, and of life itself.' But where is the
necessity to adopt this mean little prejudice, to shut one's eyes
to truths so general, so vital? Is he of any help to us, who seeing
us enter a forest where he has himself been attacked by bandits,
does not alert us of the perils that perhaps lurk there? Yes, yes,
let us have the courage to tell men that justice is a myth, and that
each individual never actually heeds any but his own; let us say
so fearlessly. Declaring it to them, and giving them thus to
appreciate all the dangers of human existence, our warning enables
them to ready a defense and in their turn to forge themselves the
weapon of injustice, since only by becoming as unjust, as vicious
as everybody else can they hope to elude the traps set by others.
'Justice,' Montesquieu rattles on, is a seeming and right relationship existing really between two things, independently of the view
any person may take of them.'

"Where have you encountered a greater piece of sophistry?
Never has justice been a seeming and right relationship really
existing between two things. Justice has no real existence, it is
the deity of every passion: this passion finds justice in this act,
that passion finds justice in that act, and although those acts may
be contradictory and usually are, those passions find them just
nonetheless. So let us abandon our belief in this fiction, it no more
exists than does the God of whom fools believe it the image: there
is no God in this world, neither is there virtue, neither is there
justice; there is nothing good, useful, or necessary but our passions,
nothing merits to be respected but their effects.

"Nor is that all; I go farther, and regard unjust acts as

---

[1] On page 192 of his *Persian Letters.*

indispensable to the maintenance of universal harmony, necessarily disturbed by an equitable order in things. This fact once realized, for what reason would I abstain from all the iniquities my brain conceives since it is proven that they are useful to the general plan? Is it my fault if it be my capacities Nature is pleased to enlist for preserving her law and order in this world? Of course not, and if only through atrocities, execrations, and horrors this end may be attained, why, let's perpetrate them cheerfully and serenely, in the knowledge that our delights answer Nature's aims."

We continued our tour of the apartments and put into practice the theories which the giant had just developed for me. Our unspeakable doings finally reduced me to such a point of exhaustion that I was obliged to beg quarter, and announced that the one desire I had left was to repose myself for the rest of the day.

"Just as you like," said he, "I can perfectly well postpone until tomorrow showing you the two rooms you have yet to see, and which contain features and equipment that will probably astonish you."

Sbrigani and I retired to our bedchamber; when alone with my one remaining traveling companion, "Good friend," said I, "we found entry into the palace of vice and horror, if this piece of excellent fortune is not to be spoiled we must now find a way out of it. My confidence in the ogre is not so entire as to recommend our remaining any longer under his roof. With me I have reliable means for being rid of this personage, after whose death we could very easily seize his treasure and be off. However, our host is too great a menace to humanity, my principles approve too warmly of such a character and of such depravations for me to wrest him away from the world. It would be to borrow the role of the law, it would be to serve society, to banish this scoundrel out of it, and I am not so fond of virtue as to render it such an enormous service. So I propose to let this man live rather than throw crime into mourning: eh, a Friend of Crime deprive Crime of a sectator? Perish the thought! We must rob him, that is all; but it is important, he is richer than we and equality has always been the cornerstone of my doctrine. Rob him, then fly; else he will not fail to kill us, for pleasure's sake or perhaps to rob us himself. With some stramonium we shall drug him, while he sleeps steal his money, pick the two prettiest wenches out of his harems, and escape."

Sbrigani was not immediately won over to my scheme: stramonium, he pointed out, might not have effect upon a body of such prodigious size, a concentrated dose of strong poison looked by far the more advisable thing to him; specious as my considerations were, they must cede before those of our safety and, according to my husband, that would be uncertain so long as the ogre remained alive. But unshakable in my resolve to take all possible care never to be the undoing of anyone as wicked as I, I held firm. At last we decided that after administering the soporific to the ogre while breakfasting with him, we would proclaim to his hirelings the success of a plot against his life, thus forestalling any objections they might raise to our appropriation of his wealth, and that once we had emptied his coffers we would quit the place forthwith.

It all came out remarkably well. Swallowing the chocolate into which we had slipped the stramonium, Minski sank a few minutes later into a torpor so deep that we had no trouble persuading the household that its overlord was dead. His steward was the first to seek to induce us to reign in his stead; we feigned consent, and having had the treasure chests opened, we loaded the most valuable of their contents upon ten men. Proceeding next to the harem of women, we chose two French girls, Elise and Raimonde, respectively seventeen years of age and eighteen, and then set forth after assuring the major-domo that we would shortly return to lead him and the others away; that we were indeed prepared to succeed to the place left vacant by his deceased master, but felt that such splendid possessions would be put to better showing in some one of the cities of the plain, where we ought all to remove rather than continue to dwell like bears in this dreadful den. Enchanted, the major-domo facilitated everything, concurred in everything, and for his cooperation was doubtless richly rewarded by the giant when upon awakening he learned of his losses and of our flight.

Our loot loaded into our carriages, our women and ourselves installed inside, we dismissed the ten porters, after paying them for their trouble and advising them to head in any direction except back to the inferno where only calamity would be awaiting them. They did not dispute the wisdom of our counsel, we bade them farewell and departed. That same evening we reached the outskirts of Florence. When we procured lodgings we turned to taking stock of our treasures and to appraising our two women: they were lovely creatures.

Seventeen-year-old Elise combined all Venus' graces with the seductive charms of the goddess of flowers. Raimonde, a year older, had one of those inspiring faces you cannot look upon without emotion; both of them recently acquired by Minski, neither had yet been touched, and it need hardly be stressed that this circumstance was among the principal ones which had led me to select them. They helped us tally our booty, it included six million in gold and silver coin, another four in gems, plate, ingots and Italian banknotes. Ah, how my eyes feasted upon this hoard, and how sweet it is to count riches when we owe it to a crime! These tasks dispatched, we retired, and in the arms of my two new conquests I spent the most delicious night I had enjoyed in a long time.

Allow me now to speak for a moment, my friends, of the superb city we came to the following morning. Listening to these details will have a refreshing influence upon your imaginations, berayed as they are by this lengthy series of obscene anecdotes: such a digression, I should think, can only render more piquant that which the truth you have demanded of me shall perhaps shortly oblige me to relate.

Constructed by Sulla's troops, embellished by the triumvirs, destroyed by Attila, then rebuilt by Charlemagne; enlarged at the expense of the ancient city of Fiesole, its neighbor, of which today only ruins are left; for many decades torn by internecine strife; subjugated by the Medicis who having ruled it for two hundred years finally let it pass to the House of Lorraine, Florence is now governed as is the whole of Tuscany whereof it is the chief town, by Leopold, Archduke and brother of the Queen of France,[2] a

---

[2] These particulars, the reader should be reminded, were exact at the time Madame de Lorsange was touring in Italy. Everybody knows the changes that have transpired since, both in Florence and in other parts of this fine country. (*Note added.*)

despotic, haughty, and ungracious prince, like the rest of his family very crapulous and libertine, as my subsequent narrations shall soon convince you.

Soon after arriving in this city I was able to conclude that the Florentines still think back nostalgically upon their native-born princes and resent being under the control of foreigners. Nobody is taken in by Leopold's seeming simplicity; the popular costume he affects does not conceal his Germanic arrogance, and those who know anything of the spirit and temper of the Austrian dynasty understand why its members have far less difficulty pretending to virtues than acquiring them.

Florence, lying at the foot of the Apennine range, is split by the River Arno; this central part of Tuscany's capital is somewhat similar to the heart of Paris, traversed by the Seine; but there the comparison between the two cities must end, for Florence has many fewer inhabitants and in extent is a great deal smaller than the other. The reddish-brown stone of which its larger buildings are constructed gives it a disagreeable, forlorn air. Had I a liking for churches I would probably have some glowing descriptions to offer you, but my aversion for everything associated with religion is so compelling that I could not take it upon myself to enter a single one of those temples. It was otherwise with the superb ducal palace gallery, I went to visit it the day after we arrived. Impossible to render for you my enthusiasm at being amidst all those masterpieces. I adore the arts, they excite me; everything that imitates glorious Nature must be cherished too. . . . No encouragement is too great for those who love and copy her. There is but one way to make her bare her secrets, through incessant, unwearying study of her; only by probing into her furthermost recesses may one finally destroy the last of one's misconceptions. I adore a talented woman; a pretty face will seduce me, but the spell talents weave captivates more durably; and I think that the one is more flattering than the other to *amour-propre*.

My guide, as you may readily suppose, did not fail to show me the room in that celebrated museum where Cosimo Medici was surprised at one of his little infamies. The famous Vasari was busy painting the ceiling of the apartment when Cosimo appeared there with his daughter, of whom he was inordinately fond: never pausing to think that the painter might be at work on the scaffolding over-head, that incestuous prince proceeded to caress the object of his ardors. Cosimo espies the couch nearby, the couple repair to it, the act is consummated within the view of the artist who, just as soon as he could, hurried from Florence, believing that violence would surely be used to prevent intelligence of such a liaison from getting abroad, and that witnessing what he had could well mean an early doom. Vasari's were not idle fears at a period and in a town where the teachings of Machiavelli found no end of disciples: it was wise of him not to expose himself to the cruel effects of those doctrines.

A little farther on my attention was drawn to an altar of solid gold and studded with precious stones—one of those objects I invariably covet at first sight. This immensely rich and wondrously wrought bit of furniture, it was explained to me, was an ex-voto which Grand Duke Ferdinand II, who died in 1630, offered to St. Charles Borromeo for the recovery of his health. The gift had been packed off and was on the road when Ferdinand died; the heirs, reasonable people, decided that since the saint had not answered the prayer, they were exempted from the payment and recalled the treasure. For how many extravagances is not super-stition accountable, and with what confidence we can affirm that of all the multitude of human follies this one doubtless has the most degrading effects upon the spirit and the mind.

From there we went to look at Titian's renowned "Venus," and I confess that before this sublime work my emotions were stirred as they had not been by Ferdinand's ex-voto: the beauties of Nature are uplifting to the soul, religious absurdities make it recoil in disgust.

The "Venus" is a delicious blonde, with lovely eyes, but features a shade too sharply drawn for a blonde whose charms, as composed by Nature, are usually, like her character, of a dreamy softness. The subject appears upon a white couch, one of her hands toys with flowers, the other has strayed coyly to cover her pretty little bush; voluptuous is her attitude, and unwearyingly one pores over the beauties of this sublime picture's details. Sbrigani re-marked that this Venus seemed to him to bear a striking resem-blance to our Raimonde; I agreed. The pretty creature blushed innocently when we reported our findings to her; from the fiery kiss

I laid upon her lips she could measure my approval of my husband's comparison.

In the next room, known as the Chamber of the Idols, we found a great store of works by Titian, Paolo Veronese, and Guido. And in that room we saw something very curious indeed: a sepulcher overflowing with cadavers severally exhibiting all the various stages of decay, from the moment of death's advent to the total material decomposition of the individual. This somber work is executed in wax colored so subtly and modeled so cunningly that the thing itself could be neither more expressive of Nature nor more authentic. So powerful is the impression produced by this masterpiece that as you gaze at it your other senses are played upon, moans seem audible, you wrinkle your nose quite as if you could detect the evil odors of mortality. . . . These scenes of the plague appealed to my cruel imagination; and, I mused, how many persons had undergone these awful metamorphoses thanks to my wickedness? But I rove. Let me say only that Nature probably impelled me to those crimes since even the mere recollection of them still thrills me to the core.

Nearby it is another miniature representing, in the same style, another common grave teeming with plague victims, and here the most interesting figure is a naked man who, as he drops the corpse he is carrying in among the rest, is himself overcome by the stench or overwhelmed by the sight, reels back, and dies: the treatment of this group is terrifyingly realistic.

We now came to gayer objects. The Tribunal Chamber, as it is called, contained the celebrated "Medici Venus": and upon beholding that stunning piece a rush of emotion assailed me as surely must happen to any sensitive spectator. A Greek, they say, was smitten by passion for a statue. . . . It is understandable; I could well have duplicated his distracted behavior, I trow: a survey of this work's wondrous features leads one to believe tradition says true in reporting that the sculptor resorted to no fewer than five hundred models before completing it; the proportions of this sublime effigy, the beauty of the face, the heavenly contours of each limb, the graceful curves of the breasts, of the buttocks, are touches attesting a human genius rivaling Nature's own, and I doubt whether three times as many models chosen from all the world boasts of the most beautiful could today furnish a creature that would benefit from comparison with this one. It is generally agreed that this statue shows us the Venus of Greek seafarers; I need not describe it at greater length, it has been copied often enough; but though a reproduction of it is within anyone's means to buy, nobody will ever appreciate it quite as I did. . . . This marvelous piece was once broken by some vandals, led by their execrable piety to this act of madness. The boors, fools! they worshiped the author of Nature and thought to please her by shattering her noblest work. Touching the sculptor's identity there is disagreement; common opinion ascribes the work to Praxiteles, others say Cleomenes made it: whoever the artist may have been, his creation is magnificent, it is admired, it inspires the imagination, contemplating it is one of the sweetest pleasures that can be derived from the sight of man-made things.

My eyes fell next upon "The Hermaphrodite." As you know, the Romans, who all had a special fondness for these monsters, welcomed them into their saturnalian assemblies; the one represented here was probably among those whose lubricious reputation was outstandingly notorious and hence deserved commemoration; but its legs are crossed, which is a pity, for the sculptor should have displayed what characterized its double sex and singular amenities: it is shown reclining upon a bed, exposing the most tempting ass in all the world . . . a voluptuous ass which Sbrigani coveted, telling me he had once bum-fucked a similar creature and had never been able to forget the delight it had given him.

Close by is the group, Caligula and his sister; ah, those proud masters of the world, far from concealing their vices, hired artists to immortalize them. In the same room you will also find the famous Priapus upon which young girls were obliged, as one of the requirements of their faith, to rub the lips of their vaginas. This deity's member is reproduced with such stout proportions that introduction must surely have been impossible, or exceedingly difficult, if that too was perchance enjoined by the rites.

We were shown chastity belts. "Examine those devices well," I recommended to my two sweethearts, "you shall be strapped into the like the day I have any doubts of your fidelity." To which the mild-tempered Elise delicately replied that her devotion to me would always suffice to restrain her within the bounds of the strictest temperance.

Next we saw a splendid collection of daggers, some of them were poisoned; nowhere has murder been refined as amongst the Italians, it is therefore quite the ordinary thing to find in their homes all sorts of instruments for murdering, in the cruelest and most traitorous manner.

The air at Florence is very unwholesome, autumn may be positively fatal there: during that season, leave a bit of bread steep in the Apennine miasmas, it will molder invisibly and sicken anybody who tastes it; sudden deaths, apoplexies become very frequent at that time of year. But as we were then in early spring I considered we could remain through the summer without risk. We bedded only two nights at our inn; the third day I rented a fine house overlooking the Arno: I took it in Sbrigani's name, for I was still masquerading as his wife and my two followers were become his sisters. Established there upon the same footing as at Turin and in the other Italian cities where I had made residence, no sooner had intelligence of us got abroad than the propositions began to arrive. But upon the advice of a friend of Sbrigani, who esteemed that moderation and no improper eagerness to leap at offers would perhaps win us admission to the Grand Duke's secret revels, we refused all bids for a fortnight.

The prince's emissaries appeared in due course. Leopold wished to have the services of the three of us at a forgathering which would also include the everyday objects of his private debauches, and our unreserved cooperation would be worth a thousand sequins to each of us.

"Leopold's tastes are despotic and cruel, like those of all sovereigns," his representative explained to us, "however, you have nothing to fear, you shall be merely to serve his lusts, others will be his prey."

"We shall be at the Grand Duke's orders," I answered, "but, my good sir, for a thousand sequins . . . hardly. No, my sisters-in-law and I are only to be had for thrice that sum; come back if those terms are acceptable."

Libertine Leopold, who had already cast eyes upon us, was not the man to forego such delights because of a trifling two thousand sequins more. Miserly toward his wife, toward the poor, toward his subjects, Austria's fairest son spent generously upon his pleasures. And so we were called for the following morning and conducted to Pratolino, in the Apennines and on the road by which we had gained Florence.

That villa, shaded, solitary, and voluptuous, lacked none of the features characteristic of a retreat for debauchery. The Grand Duke was finishing dinner when we arrived; with him he had only his chaplain, the agent and confidant of his lubricities.

"Dear friends," the lord of Tuscany declared, "step this way if you please, we are awaited by those young persons my lust is to feed upon today."

"One moment, Leopold," said I, that elevated tone of self-respect in my voice for which I have always been noted, "my sisters and I shall submit ourselves to your caprices, we shall satisfy your desires; but if, as people of your sort so frequently are, you too are given to dangerous fantasies, then say so now, for we do not intend to enter the arena unless we are sure we shall emerge from it safe and sound."

"The victims have already been appointed, they are there," the Grand Duke replied to me, "you are to be the priestesses in this affair, nothing more; and we, the Abbot and I, the sacrificers."

"You heard the gentleman," I said to my companions, "in we go. Faithless knaves though they are, sovereigns may sometimes be trusted, above all when you have reliable means for vengeance about you," and casting back my sleeve I afforded Leopold a glimpse of the haft of the poniard I had been carrying ever since the day I entered Italy.

"What," cried he, laying a hand upon my shoulder, "you would attempt the life of a sovereign?"

"If provoked, of course," I rejoined. "I'll start no trouble, but if you were to forget whom you were dealing with, this knife"— and I now drew it all the way into view—"will make you remember that your mistake was to behave inconsiderately toward a Frenchwoman.

"As regards your royal sacrosanctity, in my country we sneer at such rubbish. You don't suppose, do you, that the heaven that made you made your existence one whit more inviolable than that of the meanest individual in your realm? My respect for you is no greater than for him; a zealous egalitarian, I have never considered one living creature any better than any other, and as I have no belief in moral virtues, neither do I consider that they are differentiated by any moral worth."

"But I am a king."

"Poor fellow! As if I were to be impressed by that title! Why, Leopold, you cannot guess how little it means to me. How did you get to where you are? By luck. What did you to do to merit your rank? That first of kings who earned it through his courage or his cunning, he could perhaps claim to some esteem; but he who has it through mere inheritance, may he hope for more than compassion?"

"Regicide is a crime—"

"Disabuse yourself, my friend: it is no worse than killing a cobbler, and you do as much evil, or as little, when you squash a beetle or murder a butterfly, Nature having fashioned those insects also. You may believe it, Leopold, the manufacture of your person cost our common mother no more effort than creating a monkey, and yours would be a serious error if you let yourself imagine that she cares for this one of her children any more than for that."

"I find this woman's outspokenness quite engaging," Leopold said to his chaplain.

"And so do I, Sire," declared the man of God; "but I fear that such pride will prevent her from showing your Worship's pleasures all the subordination they require."

"Fear nothing of the sort, my good Abbot," said I; "proud and frank in social conversations, meek and mild in intimate ones: such is the part of a pretty French courtesan, 'twill be mine. But if in the boudoir I look a slave, remind yourself that it is only before your passions I bend a knee, not before your kingliness. I respect passions, Leopold, I have them as well as you, but I stubbornly refuse to bow before rank: be a man, you'll obtain everything from me; nothing, I warn you, as a prince; let us begin."

It was a voluptuous salon Leopold bade us enter, and there awaiting us were the creatures he had alluded to and with whom

we were about to disport; who ever would have believed it? they
were a quartet of girls aged fifteen or sixteen, and all four pregnant
to the bursting point.

"What the devil do you plan to do with these articles?" I
inquired of the Grand Duke.

"You shall see before very long," he replied. "I am the father
of the infants they are ready to whelp, and I sired them solely for
the sake of the delicious pleasure I shall have in destroying them.
I know of no greater satisfaction than causing a woman I have
ingravidated to miscarry, and as my seminal product is uncommonly abundant, I impregnate at least one a day to insure the
wherewithal for my daily destructions."

"Ah ha," said I to the Austrian, "your passion is odd, it
intrigues me, I shall take a willing hand in this operation; and
how do you procced with it?"

"Have a little patience, young lady, you shall be witness to
every detail," said Leopold who until now had communicated with
me in a whisper. "We begin by announcing the fate in store for
them."

Whereupon he approached the four girls and notified them
of his intentions. I need hardly tell you, my friends, that upon
hearing this perfidious declaration they were all without exception
plunged into the depths of distress; two fainted, the other two set
to squealing like pigs being led to slaughter. But unfeeling Leopold
only commanded his agent to strip off their clothes.

"Fair ladies," the Grand Duke then said to us, "will you
kindly imitate these demoiselles, and undress yourselves too? I
never enjoy a woman except when she is naked; and, indeed, I
suspect your bodies are pretty enough to merit being observed
unveiled."

A moment later Leopold was surrounded by seven naked
women.

We were favored by that libertine's preliminary homage. He
scrutinizes us separately, he compares us, has us stand apart,
brings us close together, and terminates this prelude by cunt-sucking the three of us while having the pregnant girls frig him one
after the other. Leopold liked fuck, and busied himself upon us
until we had loosed three of four discharges apiece into his mouth.

While he frigged us, the Abbot socratized us, so that, excited before and behind, we bore the prince unstinting libations. An hour of this and then the inconstant lecher repaired to another shrine and had his holy cohort tongue us successively, while he himself licked our assholes. And the pregnant girls frigged him still.

"I am growing very hot," he told us, "it is time we turn to more serious matters. You see there, in that brazier, four branding irons," he continued, "they are hot too; upon each is inscribed the sentence of one of our laden women. I shall blindfold them, each shall choose her own iron."

The game commences; as soon as the victim selects her iron Leopold plucks it from the live coals and claps the fiery red tip to her belly. These were the legends left imprinted in the girls' flesh: to the youngest, who seemed scarcely over fourteen, the hand of fate awarded the brand worded thus: *She will miscarry under the lash.* The next, perhaps a few months older, received the label: *A beverage shall be the cause of her miscarriage.* The third was fifteen, this was her sentence: *Her fruit shall be trampled from her belly.* Upon the last, who was sixteen, was seared this dread decree: *Her child will be torn from her womb.*

The ceremony over, the blindfolds were removed and the four wretches, looking around one at the other, were able to read their various condemnations aloud. Leopold then had them all stand in a row at the end of a couch and close to it; he laid me upon that couch and encunted me energetically, while doing so peering fixedly at those four bloated bellies, each bearing the formula whereby it was to be deflated. Elise flogged his Worship in the meantime and the Abbot, his member grooved between Raimonde's breasts, frigged himself full height.

"Leopold," said I as we fucked, "I beseech you, keep a careful grip on yourself, for if I were to have the misfortune of becoming pregnant by you it is possible that I too would give birth prematurely."

"If your case were submitted to my arbitration, you most certainly would," said the Grand Duke, from whose eyes I received glances, and from whose loins blows, that were motivated by nothing resembling gallantry, "but take some comfort from the fact I discharge with difficulty."

And thereupon he left me to depucelate Elise, who had been a quarter of an hour thrashing him, and who was soon deserted in favor of Raimonde; she had been ministering to the Abbot, I replaced her and after he was done with me he turned to Elise. Wondrous stiff and angry were the members of those two libertines.

"Aren't we to have some buggery?" the Abbot wished to know, who for some time now had been caressing and fondling my behind in the way of a man who was eager to fuck it.

"Not yet," Leopold answered, "we must first dispatch a victim."

The little girl doomed to have the fruit lashed loose from her womb was seized by the sovereign who, plying first an ordinary bundle of withes, then a martinet whereunto steel tips lent added bite, toiled thirty minutes over her behind, belaboring her so violently that the flesh came away like chips flying before a woodsman's axe. The victim was then stood up, her feet fastened to the floor and her upraised arms secured to cords overhead, and the Duke, manipulating a bull's pizzle now, delivered such prodigiously powerful thwacks to her belly that the embryo was soon dislodged. The girl shrieks; the head of the baby emerges, and Leopold, gripping it fast, wrenches it the rest of the way forth, tosses it unceremoniously into the brazier, and dismisses the mother.

"Pray ass-fuck, my Lord," said the respectful chaplain; "your prick's purpling veins, the foam wherewith your royal lips are besmeared, the fire darting from your eyes, everything indicates the imperious need you have of an ass. Fear not to spill your fuck, Sire, we are here to raise your fallen prick again, and we shall dispatch the others."

"No," insisted the Grand Duke, who when not absorbed in other business had been kissing and mauling me throughout these lubricities, "no, I discharged overmuch yesterday and cannot vouch for better than a single spasm today; before spending my strength I must attend to all the midwifery."

And he laid hands on the second girl. *A beverage shall be the cause of her miscarriage*—the fatal goblet is produced, the little girl condemned to quaff its contents screws up her face, twists her head away; but the ferocious ecclesiastic is there, with one hand he holds her fast by the hair, with the other he pries her mouth open with a rasp; mine is the task of decanting the potion into her gullet, and the Duke, frigged by Elise, meanwhile handles my buttocks and the victim's as well. . . . What potent elixir was this! Great gods, I had never seen the like of the results it obtained. The stuff was no sooner down the child's throat than she pronounces the most blood-curdling screams, flails her arms, writhes on the floor, and the next moment, there's her babe. This time it is the Abbot who performs the delivery. Leopold, frolicking so lewdly with Elise and me while Raimonde pumped him, was in no state to accomplish the delicate operation: I thought he was readying an ejaculation, but he avoided it, withdrawing in time.

The third girl is stretched out flat on her back and secured to the floor: her fruit was to perish from being trod upon. Braced by Elise and me while Raimonde, on her knees and astride the victim, frigs his device between her compressed breasts, the libertine dances a jig upon the wretch's belly, and out pops her infant. It too is tossed into the brazier, the father not even taking the trouble to ascertain his scion's sex; and more dead than alive, the mother is ejected from the room. If the last of the four was the loveliest she was also the most unlucky. Her child was to be torn from her womb; imagine what her sufferings were to be!

"This one won't survive the experience," Leopold informed us, "my discharge shall be owing to her unspeakable agony. It could not be otherwise, since of the four she, when I fucked her, gave me the most pleasure: the little whore conceived the same day I blasted her maidenhead."

She is affixed to a diagonal cross of heavy timbers, at their intersection is a block of wood upon which her buttocks rest; her arms and legs are tied down and then covered over, so that nothing is to be seen of her except the rotund, swollen mass caching the infant. The Abbot falls to work. . . . Leopold, his eyes riveted upon the operation, embuggers me; both his hands are busy frigging, to the right Elise's ass, Raimonde's cunt to the left; and while the perfidious chaplain cleaves open the victim's belly and rips out the child, which is of fatal consequence to the young mother, Austria's brightest star, the Medicis' great successor, the celebrated brother of France's most illustrious whore, looses a torrent of fuck into my fundament, with another stream of foul vituperation, curses, and black blasphemies.

"Ladies," said Duke Leopold as he wiped his prick, "the price of three thousand sequins you demanded and which I agreed to pay includes the cost of your silence concerning our joint doings."

"They shall be kept secret," I replied, "but I pose one condition."

"Condition? Condition? Thunder and Godsfuck, does it beseem you to speak thus?"

"Certainly . . . and insofar as I can bring about your downfall by divulging them, your crimes give me rights."

"Behold!" stormed the Abbot, "see what happens when you behave liberally toward these jades: one should either never let them see a thing, or cut their throats once they've seen it. Your commiseration, good my Lord, is bound to be your ruin or your purse's, I have told you so over and over again; and I ask you, Sire, can you deign bargain with such ordures?"

"Softly, Abbot," said I, "save that kind of language for the penny-a-fuck mechanics you and your patron are doubtless accustomed to dealing with ordinarily; it is not appropriate when addressing women of our rank who, perhaps as wealthy as you," I pursued, turning to the Duke, "prostitute themselves less through greed or necessity than from taste. Let us close this discussion; his Worship needs our good will, we need his: some mutual services may redress the balance. Leopold, we will swear you the completest secrecy provided you for your part ensure us the completest impunity so long as we remain in Florence. Swear to us that no matter what we do in your duchy, we shall be made to answer for nothing."

"I could avoid this extortion," said Leopold, "and, without staining my hands with the blood of these creatures, convince them that here, as in Paris, there are fortresses behind whose walls the garrulous learn how to hold their tongues; but I dislike using such methods with women who appear to me quite as libertine as I: I grant you the dispensation you solicit—I extend it to you, Madame, to your sisters-in-law, and to your husband as well, but for the space of six months only: that period ended, begone from my lands, I command it."

Having obtained all I was after, I saw no reason to reply, and after thanking Leopold and receiving our fees we bade him adieu and retired.

"We must turn this jubilee to account," said Sbrigani once he had heard of our arrangement with the Grand Duke, "and before our time is up endeavor to add at least three millions to what we have already. It is truly a pity our carte blanche has been delivered for use in such a bedraggled, poverty-ridden part of the country; but never mind, we'll accept whatever is offered and snatch anything that is not, and half a year should suffice to accumulate a tidy little fortune."

Morals are very free, conduct very loose in Florence. The women go about costumed as men, men as girls. In few Italian cities does one detect so decided a penchant for betraying one's own sex, and this mania the Florentines have no doubt derives from their pressing urge, indeed, from their need, to dishonor both. Sodomy with them is a craze, and at one point in the past the city fathers successfully negotiated with the Vatican for a plenary indulgence covering every form of this vice from every possible angle. Incest and adultery are rampant there too, no effort is made to conceal them: husbands cede their wives, brothers lie with their sisters, fathers with their daughters.

"It's the climate," say these good people, "the climate is to blame for our depravity, and the God who placed us in these surroundings cannot be surprised at the excesses for which He is Himself responsible."

In this connection there used to be a most unusual law in Florence. On Shrove Tuesday no woman had the right to refuse her husband's sodomistic advances; if nevertheless she took it into her head to deny him, and if he interpreted her refusal as a slight and grounds for complaint, 'twas very likely she would be a laughingstock all over the town. Oh, happy, happy nation this, that was wise enough to consecrate its passions in laws; there is proof of common sense, all the extravagance belongs to those benighted societies which out of principles equally stupid and barbarous, instead of prudently wedding one to the other, through absurd legislation seek to thwart all a human being's natural propensities.

However irregular though Florentine manners may be,

streetwalkers are not permitted to drift loose through that city. The whores are restricted to a separate quarter of their own whence they may not venture commercially forth and where reign the most perfect order and calm. But these girls, seldom pretty, are for the most part ill-lodged; and the philosophical observer who visits the bawdyhouses will discover nothing of any particular interest unless it be the remarkable docility of these public playthings who, only too happy to attract you by means of their resignation, present no matter what part of the body upon simple demand and with unwearying patience even suffer each of them to be used in any manner libertine cruelty deems suitable. Sbrigani and I indulged in no end of beating, whipping, slapping, burning, mutilating, and maiming without ever hearing so much as a murmur of protest, and it is never thus in France. But if whoring does not much flourish in Florence, the libertinage there is excessive nonetheless, and the thick-walled, secluded dwellings of the rich harbor many an infamy : vast are the numbers of girls who are lured or furtively conveyed inside those strongholds of odious proceedings, there to lose their honor and not infrequently their lives.

Shortly before our arrival a wealthy notable of the town, having made off with a pair of little girls aged seven and eight, was accused by the children's parents of raping and then murdering them : the evidence against the gentleman was plentiful and damning : a few sequins to the plaintiffs and of the case nothing further was heard.

And at about the same time a famous procuress came under suspicion of kidnapping maidens from middle-class families and furnishing them to some Florentine noblemen. Questioned as to the names of her clients, she compromised such a quantity of distinguished persons that there was no pursuing this inquest either, the dossiers had to be burned, and the woman forbidden to say any more.

Nearly all the ladies of condition, in Florence, have the habit of vending their charms in brothels; their temperament and their penury bring them to it. For the legal status of married women is singularly unfavorable in Florence, perhaps worse here than in any other European city, and there are few where their profligacy is more extensive or rampant. As for the *cicisbeo,* his function is

merely to provide her a screen; rarely does the *cicisbeo* enjoy any
privileges with the woman he serves; appointed to his post as the
husband's friend, he accompanies the wife when she wishes to have
him by her and obediently retreats when she orders him away.
Those who fancy a *cicisbeo* is a paramour are greatly mistaken; he
is simply the woman's indulgent friend, or ally; may sometimes be
the husband's spy; but never does he lie with her; and of all possible
roles, this is the dreariest a man can assume in Italy. A wealthy
foreigner has but to appear on the doorstep, and husband, gallant,
and everybody else speedily retire, leaving a clear field to him upon
whose purse all hopes are founded, and I have often seen the complacent lord of the house quit it in consideration of a sequin or two
when the stranger manifests the wish, however slight, to hold
private parley with milady.

I have inserted this brief sketch of Florentine manners in order
that you apprehend in what way, touching the thieveries, the debaucheries we were meditating, we were aided and in what way
hampered by the traditional usages of this people at whose expense
we wanted and were free to amuse ourselves for six months.

Sbrigani felt that our schemes were likely to meet with fairer
success if we ran up our flag over an emporium of debauchery
rather than over a casino; perfidious greed insatiable! did we not
have riches enough already without striking out anew toward
crime? No doubt; but once one is a traveler of crooked paths does
one ever renounce them for straight?

So we circulated information advising the public at large that
gentlemen would find at any hour of the night or day not only
pretty wenches awaiting them in our establishment, but even
women of the highest quality, and it was likewise made known that
ladies could always obtain from us what they required in men and
young girls, for their clandestine pleasures. Together with all
that, we proposed the most agreeable surroundings, the most exquisite table; and the whole town rushed to us immediately. My
companions and I were the mainstay of the house; but our clients
had simply to make the request, they had simply to indicate the
desire, and we put at their disposal everything delicious the district
afforded. We charged exorbitant rates, but they were marvelous
services we offered. Slise and Raimonde, trained in the matter, saw

to the misplacement of countless pocketbooks and pieces of jewelry; their depradations gave rise to a certain number of complaints, all futile, the protection from which we benefited was an impervious defense, rendering vain all the denunciations of our activities.

Among the first we received was the Duke of Pienza. His passion was sufficiently out of the ordinary to warrant describing. Sixteen girls the Duke must have, they were arranged by two's, each pair being distinguished by a different coiffure. These girls were naked, so was I where I reclined upon a sofa beside him; sixteen musicians, all youthful, handsome, and naked also, were seated to the right. Each couple was to enter the room in turn; prior to its appearance, the Duke told me what lascivious pose or lewd act he expected from the couple, the orchestra was admitted into the secret, and it was from the music, its key, its tempo, its volume, its melody, the couple was to try to guess its instructions. It guessed aright? the music would stop, the Duke would embugger the two clever girls. Did they fail to divine what was required of them—and each couple had ten minutes for solving the puzzle—then when the time had expired the dunces were flogged red and raw by our libertine who, as I dare say you very well imagine, derived quite as much pleasure from their mistakes as from their correct penetration of his wishes.

The game began: the funny fellow's first wish was to have his prick sucked by both of the first two girls. In they came; faultlessly guided by a fugue, they guessed the secret, and were sodomized. The chore to which the second couple was appointed was the licking of my cunt, the girls' efforts to interpret the music were unavailing, they were lashed. The third of the Duke's secret wishes was to be lashed, and it was found out. The fourth, to frig the musicians' sixteen pricks: the fourth couple was unlucky. The fifth, to shit in the middle or the room: the ten minutes passed and the whip was brought into play. The sixth pair of girls realized that they were to frig each other. The two composing the seventh couple altogether failed to grasp that they were to whip each other, and as a consequence were whipped by the Duke, vigorously. The music enabled the eighth couple to understand that the hero was to be embuggered with dildoes, and this was the moment he chose to inject his own discharge into my bum. And there was an end to it.

For some three months we had been leading this frivolous and profitable life when I accomplished a piece of outstanding baseness and thereby added a hundred thousand crowns to our treasury.

Of all the women who frequented my house with the utmost assiduity, the wife of the Spanish ambassador was she whose debauchery was probably the most noteworthy. Married women, maids, boys, castrates, she could find a use for anything, and though young and of angelic beauty, the whore's rapacity, her foulness were such that she would insist I fetch her common laborers off the street, gravediggers and sweeps, pickpockets, flunkeys, ragpickers, and whatever else I could lay my hands on that was lowbred, vile, and vulgar. When it was for women she longed then they must be sluts just risen stinking and sodden off a barracks-room floor, or worse yet if it might possibly be procured. Once encloseted with the rabble I collected for her, the rascal would be seven and eight hours frolicking in that leprous milieu, and then when she had had her fill of veneral pleasures would turn to those of the table, and close the day in mad riot amidst the most revolting debaucheries.

The ambassadress had a very pious husband, a very jealous one whom she gave to believe that when she went out it was to visit a friend who, like herself, was also one of my more reliable clients.

Seeing in all this certain promising possibilities, I one day take myself to the Embassy.

"Excellency," I say to the representative of Spain, "so good and upright a man as you does not deserve to be cuckolded: the woman who bears your name is not worthy of it. Your own honesty and rectitude cause you to doubt the truth of what I advance? So be it; but I entreat you, for the sake of your dignity, of your honor, of your peace of mind, Excellency, investigate the matter."

"Betrayed? I?" repeated the ambassador, " 'tis unthinkable. I know my wife too well."

"Say you so, my Lord? Begging your pardon, I am persuaded of the contrary, and wager you are far from having even the faintest glimmering of her appalling conduct. It needs to be seen to be believed. My object in coming here is to be of aid to you."

Florella, troubled, wounded by the painful suspicions I have sowed in him, hesitates before the still more painful prospect of having them confirmed. And then, setting his chin purposefully, and showing himself more of a man than I would have thought, "Are you in a position, Madame, to prove these allegations?"

"Today, my Lord, if you so wish it," I answer. "Here is my card, I shall be expecting you toward five o'clock this afternoon. You shall see the style in which your wife violates the trust you have in her, and the species of individuals she selects to that end."

The ambassador promises to be there.

"I am flattered, Excellency, and satisfied; however," I add, "I should like to point out to you that the favor I am doing you shall cost me dear. For 'tis I who furnish men to her, and she pays me handsomely for them—you shall punish her, I presume, and in any case I shall henceforth be deprived of her custom: I feel I am entitled to an indemnity."

"True, that is only fair," says Florella; "in what sum might it be?"

"Fifty thousand crowns?"

"This pocketbook contains that amount, I shall bring it with me and the money shall be yours when you have presented me with the necessary evidence."

"Agreed, my Lord. I shall expect you at five."

The several hours remaining until then were time enough to enable me to prepare further unhappiness for this ill-starred ménage. While causing the wife to fall into a trap, I was eager to snare the husband in it also; you shall soon learn by what crafty means I achieved this. After my little conference with the ambassador I went straight to call upon his wife.

"Madame," said I, "you give yourself bother on account of your husband, thinking him of stern morality and irreproachable behavior you are ever apprehensive lest, finding you out, he upbraid you. I suggest that you come to my house a little earlier than usual this afternoon, and it shall be revealed to you that conjugal ties no more prevent him from enjoying himself than they do you. The spectacle will surely ease your conscience and doubtless induce you to put by the onerous precautions which gall your daily pleasures."

"Do you know," she replied, "I am less than entirely surprised by what you tell me, for I had an intuition he is not so sinless as he would appear; and I should be delighted to learn that my guesses have not been mistaken—"

"You shall have them confirmed today. I have six pickpockets ready for you, and I have never clapped eyes on a prettier set of ruffians. Unless they are the three young boys your husband has ordered for tonight."

"The monster!"

"He is a bugger."

"Ah ha! So indeed! That explains why he is eternally fussing and fumbling about my ass and always whining to be let into it. And that explains his eccentricities also . . . his unaccountable absences, and the handsome valets he surrounds himself with. . . . Oh, Juliette, I simply must catch him out. . . . I must learn the truth—you will help me, will you not?"

"If you insist. But I am obliged to think of the future, Madame. Satisfying your curiosity, I lose a client and his trade is even more profitable to me than yours."

"Never mind, I shall make your losses up to you. Set a figure, Juliette, I am willing to pay anything if it will secure me an end to my anxieties and my persecutions."

"Then fifty thousand crowns does not strike you as too much?"

"You shall have the sum—the money is in this purse, I shall have it with me. So go now, and count upon me to keep the appointment and the bargain."

The two rendezvous arranged, I hasten off to organize the comedy. The wife, according to my reckonings, was as good as snared already: her native libertinage would all unaided spell her downfall. As for the husband's, however, that was by no means so simple to contrive. Art was called for here, seduction would be necessary: the man I was dealing with was a Spaniard, a pious Spaniard. But nothing daunted me. Once the two stages were set— the two scenes were to transpire in adjoining chambers, a crack in the partition separating them would permit the husband to observe his wife's infidelities; through a second aperture the wife would see her husband's antics—I waited patiently for my two dupes.

The husband arrived first.

"My Lord," I declared, "it would seem to me that in the light of your wife's behavior you ought no longer feel constrained to deny expression to your tastes nor to refuse yourself pleasures."

Florella drew himself up. "Such things——"

"You dislike them and you are quite right: the dangers are manifold when you dally with women. But, Excellency, look here, these pretty children," said I, drawing aside a curtain behind which I had stationed three delightful little boys, draped in garlands of roses and otherwise naked, "these heavenly little Ganymedes, you'll surely not maintain that sorrows are to be anticipated from enjoying them? Really, my Lord, it surpasses my understanding—you who are so ill-used, will you worsen affairs by being harsh to yourself?"

And while I spoke the sweet little trio, acting upon my instructions, surrounded the Spaniard, hugged and kissed him, teased him and, despite all he could do, plucked his wavering virility forth from its tent. Man is weak. The pious are weaker than most, especially when you offer them boys. Seldom sufficiently stressed, often not even realized, there exists a powerful analogy between believers in God and buggers.

"My Lord," said I once things were well under way, "I am going to leave you to your own devices; I shall return as soon as your wife has begun her wanton capers. The sight of them ought to enable you to pursue your own in greater comfort."

And I leave just in time to greet the ambassadress, then on the point of entering.

"Madame," I whisper, conducting her to the hole in the wall, "you could not have come at a better moment. Behold in what way His Excellency passes his afternoons."

And indeed the good man, without an inkling of the scurvy trick being played upon him and seduced by my speeches, was almost naked now and already absorbed in the ethereal preludes of sodomistic lubricity.

"The beast!" gasped the ambassadress, "the fiend! Let him dare criticize my conduct after what I have just seen—ah, I'll have a thing or two to tell him! Juliette, it is dreadful, it is horrible—

madre de Dios, where are my men? Send in my men, I'll have my revenge, by heaven, I'll have my revenge and more beside!"

And having started Doña Florella off on her lewd routine, I rejoined her husband.

"A thousand pardons if I disturb you, Excellency," said I, "but the crucial instant is at hand and I should not like to have you miss it. Leave off your sweet sport a moment and come," I urged him, steering Florella toward the second spyhole several feet away from the one through which he had been watched by his wife, "determine for yourself whether you are cornute or no."

"Great God!" that gentleman exclaimed, "with six men, and veritable scum of the earth besides! Oh, the slut: Juliette, take it, here is your money, this sight I have witnessed—I am thunderstruck, I am undone, I . . . can no more—away with these children, I wish never to hear of pleasures again. That monster in the next room has shattered my existence, slain the soul in me . . . I am in despair."

To me it was of no importance whether or not his lubricities reached their term, his wife had seen them begin, that was all I required. The aspect of the adventure my evil mind most appreciated was its sequel and it warmed the cockles of my very bad heart afterward to learn that the ambassadress had been stabbed to death, an event which gave rise to great commotion. A hundred diplomats, the emissaries of that many rival states, promptly published colorful versions of the story and Florella was hailed before Leopold's magistrates: unable to endure the assaults of remorse, unable to face the ignominy about to fall on his head, the Spaniard shot himself. But I had contributed nothing to this second death, I was scarcely better than its indirect cause. The thought left me frightfully downcast; let me now tell you what I undertook several days later in order to pick up my spirits and at the same time promote my fortune.

It is common knowledge that the Italians make wide use of poisons: their atrociousness of character finds therein a suitable vehicle of expression, and a convenient means for taking the revenge and serving the lust wherefor they have also acquired a name in the world. Sbrigani and I having exhausted the supply acquired long before from Madame Durand, I had lately entered into the

632 ✤ THE MARQUIS DE SADE

fabrication of those venoms for which she had given me the recipes:
I sold these products in quantity, scores of people consulted me for
their needs, and this branch of commerce developed into an immense source of revenue.

A rather well-favored young man, by whom I had been fucked
to perfection and who was a daily visitor to my house, besought
me to provide him something for his mother: he could no longer
abide her interference in his pleasures and the sooner she was out
of the way, the sooner he would gain a considerable inheritance.
Such were the solid reasons why he was resolved to be rid of that
Argus forthwith, and as he was a person of staunch principles, he
was able without scruple or hesitation to concert a deed which
common sense dictated. And so he asked me for a violent toxin
whose effect would be rapid. Instead, I sold him a slow one, and the
day following the transaction I paid the mother a call. The poison,
as I rightly assumed, must already have been administered, for my
young man had been nothing if not eager to get down to business.
But as its action would not be felt for another few days, no symptom was yet manifest. I disclosed her son's fell designs to the
woman, describing them as intentions.

"Madame," I declared, "your plight is unenviable, it is grave,
and without my aid you are lost; but your son is not alone in this
despicable plot against your life, his two sisters are involved
also, and 'twas one of them who applied to me for the poison
necessary to cut the thread of your days."

"What are these ghastly things you tell me?"

"There are terrible truths to bare in this world, and ungrateful, nay, distressing is the mission of those who from love of mankind are forced to reveal them. You must seek vengeance, Madame,
and do so without delay. I have brought you that very drug your
monstrous children mean to give you; use it upon them, be quick:
they merit nothing less, an eye for an eye, Madame, retaliation in
kind is the best justice of all. And hold your tongue, for you cannot
without dishonor to yourself let it be known that your own flesh
and blood have plotted your murder; avenge yourself in silence,
you shall obtain satisfaction and avoid any stain. No, no, be assured of it, there is no wrong in turning against your would-be
attackers the sword they are about to lift against you. To the con-

trary, smite down the wicked and you earn the praise of every good man."

And it was to the most vindictive woman in Florence I was speaking; of this I was aware. She takes my powders, she pays me gold. The very next day she mixes them into her children's food, and as that particular poison was exceedingly strong, the brother and two sisters perished very shortly; and their mother followed them to the grave inside a week. All their funeral processions passed down the road before my house.

"Sbrigani," I said as the sounds of lamentation reached my ears and drew me to the window, "I behold a gladdening scene below; fuck me, dear friend, even as I gaze at what I have wrought. Hurry, Sbrigani, deliver me quickly of the hot sperm that has been a whole week simmering in my womb; I must absolutely discharge at the sight of my crimes."

Do you ask me why I included the woman's two daughters in this hecatomb? Then I shall answer you. They were of unsurpassed loveliness; for two long months I had tried everything under the sun to seduce them, and they had not succumbed: was more needed to kindle my wrath? And is virtue not always reprehensible in the eyes of crime and infamy?

No need to tell you, my friends, that in the thick of these perfidious villainies my personal lubricity hardly lay dormant. Having but to choose from among the superb men and the sublime women I procured for others, you may be sure that I sorted out the best for my own purposes before relegating the rest to my customers; but Italians stiffen poorly, neither big nor for long, and their health, always dubious, drove me into an exclusive sapphism. Countess Donis was in those days the richest, the most beautiful, the most elegant, and the most dissolute Lesbian Florence could boast; it was commonly supposed I was her kept companion, and the opinion was not without some basis in fact.

Madame Donis was a widow of thirty-five, delightfully shaped, with a charming face, a clever mind, much wit, and many talents. Libertinage and interest were the sinews of my twofold attachment to her, together we indulged in the strangest, the most reckless, the most outlandish of impudicities. I had taught the Countess the art of whetting her pleasures upon the stone of cruel refinements, and the whore, deriving untold benefit from my experience and instruction, was already almost a match for me in wickedness.

"Oh, my friend," she said to me one day, "how many and various are the desires aroused by the thought of a crime! I liken it to a spark which swiftly sets alight everything combustible at hand, whose ravages increase in proportion to the fuel it finds, and which ends up producing a blaze in us such as is not to be extinguished save by rivers of fuck. But, Juliette, some theory must exist governing this as there is a theory governing everything else, and it too must possess its principles, its rules. . . . I am eager to become familiar with them; teach me, my angel, you know what my dispositions, my penchants are, teach me how to regulate all this."

"Adorable woman," I replied, "I am too devoted to my pupil to leave her only halfway educated. Lend me a little attention and I shall disclose to you the precepts which have led me to where you see me today.

"They are these, beloved Countess. Whenever you have the urge to commit a crime, what are the general precautions to be observed, barring of course those particular ones which the nature of events alone must prescribe?

"Firstly, combine your scheme several days ahead of time, thoroughly revolve and ponder all its consequences, some will contain advantages for you, spy them out, look with similar care for those likely to betray you, and weigh them as coolly as if it were inevitable that you be found out. If it be a murder you concert, remember that in all the world no individual is so completely isolated that some acquaintance or friend or relative of his, however remote, may not bring you to eventual harm. These persons, whoever they are, will sooner or later come looking for your victim and, not finding him, finally come looking for you: hence, before you act prepare your welcome for them, your manner of replying to their questions and of imposing silence upon them if they are not satisfied with your answers. Once ready to strike, do the thing alone if you possibly can; if you are forced to employ a confederate, see to it that he has so much to gain from your crime, compromise him so vitally, bind him so fast to the deed that he cannot possibly turn against you later. Self-interest is the prime mover of human beings; thus, let there be no doubt of it, if you neglect these precautions and the accomplice finds a greater advantage in playing you false than in keeping faith with you, then be sure of it, my dear, betray you he shall, above all if he is weak and believes avowing may be a means to clearing his conscience.

"If you are going to derive some profit from your crime, carefully hide this motive you have for committing it; when you are in company never give the faintest sign that it is among your preoccupations, a slip of the tongue, a stray remark dropped beforehand will be recalled afterward, and these words will always testify against you and very frequently, in the absence of better evidence, serve as proof. If the committed crime doubles your fortune, defer until much later the purchase of a new coach or necklace, the changes in your circumstances, outwardly displayed will arouse curiosity, incite comment, and bring the police around to your door.

"The deed once done, you will be best advised, especially as a beginner, to avoid company for awhile, since the visage is the mirror of the soul and despite us the muscles that shape our facial expression will inevitably, try as we will to prevent it, reflect our inmost feelings. For the same reason, see to it you introduce no subject of conversation which has the slightest bearing upon the deed; for if it is the first time you have committed it, you are apt, as you discuss it, to wax rather too eloquent, to say that trifle too much which will incriminate you, and if to the contrary it is one of your habitual crimes, a crime that affords you pleasure, your physiognomy will announce to others the agreeable impression made upon you by anything touching the deed. In general, through practice strive to acquire enough control over your expression and reactions as finally to be master of them, and to be rid of the habit of displaying your secret emotions upon your face; calm and imperturbability and impassiveness should reign there, and train yourself to appear utterly unmoved even when gripped by the most powerful feelings. Well, none of this is attained save through total habituation to vice, and a toughening of the soul in the last degree; both of these being of the highest necessity to you, I must keenly recommend them.

"Were you not immune to remorse, and you will never acquire that immunity except through the habit of crime, were you not, I say, perfectly forearmed against all misgivings, all qualms, 'twould be useless for you to endeavor to win control over your countenance, it would fall on every occasion and betray you at every turn. Therefore, having done a piece of wickedness, do not rest on your laurels, Madame: you will be the unhappiest of women if you make only one sally into crime and call a halt there. Either stay quietly at home, or, having ventured to the brink of evil, leap boldly over the precipice. Only the accumulated weight of a multitude of misdeeds will stifle your capacity for remorse, will engender the sweet habituation which dulls it so wonderfully, and will provide you the mask you need in order to deceive others. And do not suppose you have anything to gain from attenuating the character of the crime you meditate, its greater or lesser atrociousness is irrelevant: it is not because of its atrocity a deed is punished, but because its author is detected, and the more violent the crime the more precautions he is required to take. Thus it is virtually impossible to realize a major crime without observing care for one's safety, whereas this is too easily left unheeded when the crime is petty, and that is why it is found out. A crime's atrocity is of concern only to you, and can it concern you once your conscience is impervious to it? its discovery, however, is to your detriment, and should be scrupulously prevented.

"Employ hypocrisy, it is indispensable in this world where accepted usage is hardly to practice what you preach: crimes are rarely imputed to those who manifest a general indifference toward everything that happens. Not everyone is so unhappy nor so clumsy as Tartuffe. Nor furthermore is it, like Tartuffe, to the point of enthusiasm for virtues one should carry one's hypocrisy, you need go no farther than indifference to crime: you do not worship virtue, but neither are you fond of vice, and this kind of hypocrisy is never detected, because it leaves the pride of others in peace, which the sort of hypocrisy that distinguishes Molière's hero necessarily offends.

"Be just as careful to avoid witnesses as you would be in

the choice of accomplices, and whenever possible dispense with both. It is always the one or the other and often the two together who lead the criminal to the scaffold.[3] Well-laid plans and sound technique spare you from having to do with people of that sort. Never say my son, my valet, my wife will never betray me, for if such persons want to, they can do you unlimited harm even if they do not denounce you to the law whose guardians may also be bought.

"Above all never have recourse to religion: you are lost if you put yourself back under its sway, it will torment you, it will fill your heart with quakings and your head with illusions and you will end up becoming your own delator and worst enemy. All these things weighed and arranged in due order, and this methodically, objectively, rationally (for I am willing enough to have you conceive the crime in the throes of passion, indeed, I even urge you to, but I insist that, conjured up in frenzy, it be prepared in calm), now cast a clear eye upon yourself, see who you are, gauge your faculties, evaluate your forces, your assets, your influence, your station; determine the extent of your vulnerability before the law, the worth of the defenses you can interpose between yourself and its attacks. And if after this survey you find yourself on safe ground, go ahead; but once the die is cast, act forthwith. The best laid plans may miscarry, know it in advance; if you have done everything prudence demands, and if still you are are found out, face the situation bravely. For what indeed is the worst that can befall you now? A very mild and a very quick death. And better that it should be on a gallows than in your bed; truly, the sufferings are nothing by comparison, and it is all much sooner over with; disgrace? But what does disgrace matter? you'll not feel it, the dead feel nothing, and as for what may be felt by your family, can this alarm you, a philosophic individual, who worries precious little about families? Do you dread hearing yourself reproached, supposing now that they let you live and are content to castigate you? What? you shudder at the thought of a few idle invectives and a tarnished

---

[3] Very great, says Machiavelli, must be the accomplice's devotion if the personal danger he sees himself exposed to is not greater still; which proves that you must either select for your lieutenant someone related very intimately to you, or destroy him when you are finished with his services. (*Discorsi*, Lib. III, Cap. 6.)

name? Fie! you tremble before less than a spook. Honor? What is honor? A meaningless word, of itself nothing, which for its existence depends upon the opinion of others and which, so defined, should neither flatter us when it is accorded nor be regretted when it is lost. Let Epicurus' attitude be our own: bestowed upon us from the outside, so much the better if fame and honor be ours, so much the worse if not, in this there is nought we can do save know how to get on without them when we cannot acquire them. And be ever mindful that there is no crime on earth, however modest, which does not bring its perpetrator more pleasure than dishonor or disgrace can bring him pain. Am I any the less alive for being socially blemished? What care I for a little mud spattered upon me if beneath it I preserve my comfort and my faculties intact! 'Tis therein I find my happiness, and not in an opinion I cannot create nor amend nor retain, and which is meaningless and vain, since it is an everyday spectacle to see people stripped of every vestige of honor and fame nevertheless achieve an existence, a consideration which feeble simpletons never attain after a lifetime of dogged virtuousness.

"Such, my dear Countess, are the views I would express to a vulgar auditor. But you—your rank, your person, your wealth, your credit, in what an enviable position they place you, how they shelter you from interference and ensure your impunity: you are beyond the reach of the law thanks to your birth, of religion thanks to your enlightenment, of remorse thanks to your intelligence. No, no, there is not a single extravagance you should refrain from, not one form of wild conduct you should not blindly indulge in.

"However, I cannot repeat it too often: avoid scandal, it brings on trouble every time and never increases pleasure one jot; and this too I shall tell you again and again: select your accomplices judiciously, since at this early stage you must have them. You are rich, fee them well; bound by your munificence, they shall not desert your cause; and if they dared, 'twould be to what peril for them? would you not have them arrested and punished long before punishment could overtake you? That same bond which to others is a deterrent as formidable as any forged of steel, is, do you see, a twine of flowers lying light upon you.

"This has been, I know, something of a sermon; let me now indicate to you, my lovely friend, the secret of how to discover which kind of crime is likely to fit your temperament best, for you can do nothing properly unless you enjoy it. A woman organized as you are cannot but be subject to incessant criminal impulses; before divulging my secret, however, allow me to explain to you how I come to this conclusion about your temperament.

"Your power of feeling is extreme, but you have directed the effects of your sensibility in such a way that it can no longer move you to anything except vice. All external objects possessing some unusual feature or other provoke a prodigious irritation in the electrical particles of your neural humour, and the impact delivered to the nervous system is instantly communicated to the nerves in the vicinity of the pleasure zone; you become immediately conscious of an itch there, this prickly titillating sensation is agreeable to you, you welcome it, you cultivate it, you renew it; your imagination sets to contriving ways to intensify it, means to amplify it . . . the irritation grows ever keener, and thus, if you wish, do you multiply your enjoyments ad infinitum. Your sole aim and study is to extend, to aggravate your sensations—need I say more? Perhaps. One who has vanquished every obstacle, as you have done, and freed herself from every restraint must perforce go far: only the most stimulating and gravest excess, the most odious, the most contrary to every law human and divine, is now capable of igniting your imagination. And so I must advise you to keep yourself a little in hand since, alas, the opportunities for crime are not always present each time we have the need to commit it, and Nature, having given us souls of fire, ought at least to furnish us somewhat more fuel. Is is not true, my beauty, that you have already and, it may well be, often found your desires far in advance of your means?"

"Oh yes, yes," sighed the ravishing Countess.

"Just as I thought. It is a frightful situation, many, many are the times I have been in it too, it is the bane of my existence; but let me impart my secret.[4]

---

[4] Everybody who has even a mild leaning toward crime recognizes his portrait in this paragraph; may he then extract all possible benefit from what precedes and

"Go a whole fortnight without lewd occupations, divert your-self, amuse yourself at other things; for the space of those two weeks rigorously bar every libertine thought from your mind. At the close of the final day retire alone to your bed, calmly and in silence; lying there, summon up all those images and ideas you banished during the fasting period just elapsed, and indolently, languidly, nonchalantly fall to performing that wanton little pollution by which nobody so cunningly arouses herself or others as do you. Next, un-pent your fancy, let it freely dwell upon aberrations of different sorts and of ascending magnitude; linger over the details of each, pass them all one by one in review; assure yourself that you are ab-solute sovereign in a world groveling at your feet, that yours is the supreme and unchallengeable right to change, mutilate, destroy, an-nihilate any and all the living beings you like. Fear of reprisals, hindrances you have none: choose what pleases you, but leave noth-ing out, make no exceptions; show consideration to no one whomso-ever, sever every hobbling tie, abolish every check, let nothing stand in your way; leave everything to your imagination, let it pursue its bent and content yourself to follow in its train, above all avoiding any precipitate gesture: let it be your head and not your tempera-ment that commands your fingers. Without your noticing it, from among all the various scenes you visualize one will claim your attention more energetically than the others and will so forcefully rivet itself in your mind that you'll be unable to dislodge it or supplant it by another. The idea, acquired by the means I am out-lining, will dominate you, captivate you; delirium will invade your senses, and thinking yourself actually at work, you will discharge like a Messalina. Once this is accomplished, light your bedside lamp and write out a full description of the abomination which has just inflamed you, omitting nothing that could serve to aggravate its details; and then go to sleep thinking about them. Reread your notes the next day and, as you recommence your operation, add everything your imagination, doubtless a bit weary by now of an idea which has already cost you fuck, may suggest that could heighten its power to exacerbate. Now turn to the definitive shaping

from what follows it upon the way of living delightfully the kind of life Nature has appointed him to, and may he be persuaded that these counsels are those of a person who speaks from experience.

of this idea into a scheme and as you put the final touches on it, once again incorporate all fresh episodes, novelties, and ramifications that occur to you. After that, execute it, and you will find that this is the species of viciousness which suits you best and which you will carry out with the greatest delight. My formula, I am aware, has its wicked side but it is infallible, and I would not recommend it to you if I had not tested it successfully.

"Lovely and delicious friend," I went on, remarking the warm impression my lessons were making upon her, "permit me to append yet a few more observations to the advice I have just offered you; my single interest is in your happiness, my desire is to labor in its behalf.

"When once one has decided to commit a crime of amusement, it is of utmost importance, firstly, that it be given all the scope whereof it is susceptible; secondly, that it be of such force as to be forever beyond reparation. This latter characteristic is all the more important in that it eliminates any room for remorse; for when one feels remorseful, that feeling is almost always accompanied by the consoling thought that one can somehow palliate or by means of reparations efface the evil one has done. This idea sends remorse off to sleep, but only to sleep; at the very first mishap, the slightest illness, or simply when the passions are stilled, remorse reawakes and drives you to despair; if however the act committed is of a kind that leaves you without a shadow of a hope of repairing it, your reason annihilates remorse. What is the use of crying over spilt milk? The proverb is logical; by frequently repeating it to yourself you will shortly obliterate your capacity for remorse altogether, and you may then venture into any situation without subsequently being annoyed by its pangs. Adding to this an intense criminal activity, you will achieve a flawless inward serenity. On the one hand, the impossibility of reparation, on the other, that of making out which of your crimes you ought to repent most, and the conscience, first dizzied, then rendered incoherent, is finally reduced to utter silence; thus we see that conscience is distinct from all other maladies of the soul, *it dwindles away to nothingness as more is added to it.*

"These elementary principles of mine well assimilated, you are ready to undertake anything and should stop at nothing. Admittedly, you will not be able to procure yourself this peaceful situation save at the expense of others; but you will procure it. And of what account are others when it is a question of oneself! If from immolating three million human victims you stand to gain no livelier pleasure than that to be had from eating a good dinner, slender though this pleasure may appear in the light of its price, you ought to treat yourself to it without an instant's hesitation; for if you sacrifice that good dinner, the necessary result is a privation for you, whereas no privation results from the disappearance of the three million insignificant creatures you must do away with to obtain the dinner, because between it and you there exists a relationship, however tenuous, whereas none exists between you and the three million victims. Well now, put case that the pleasure you expect from destroying them ceases to be tepid and becomes one of the most voluptuous sensations your soul can experience; how now, I ask you, how can there be any thinkable alternative to committing the crime at once?[5]

"Everything hinges upon the total annihilation of that absurd notion of fraternity whose existence they inculcate in us in the course of our upbringing. Completely demolish this fictitious link, remove yourself completely from its influence, convince yourself that between your self and some other self no connection whatever exists, and you will observe your pleasures expand while simultaneously your faculty of remorse withers. That one of your fellow creatures is subject to a dolorous sensation is of no importance provided the

---

5 We may elucidate this idea by saying that the good dinner may be the source of some physical delight, and that saving the lives of the three million victims would cause only moral delight, even to an honest spirit; which establishes a great difference between these two pleasures; for moral delights are mere intellectual enjoyments, uniquely dependent upon opinion, arbitrary and doubtful, and this to the point that a vicious spirit senses none of the enjoyments of virtue; corporeal delights, however, are physical sensations, upon which opinion has absolutely no bearing at all, and which are similarly felt by all human beings and for that matter by animals too; whence it proceeds that preserving those three million people from death would be a pleasure no more substantial than the flimsy prejudice it is founded upon, and which only a small fraction of humanity would feel; while the dinner would be a pleasure felt by everybody, and hence far superior; wherefrom it is plain to be seen that were the choice even between a gumdrop and the entire universe, any wavering would be equally illogical and inexcusable. This argument serves to demonstrate the immense advantages of vice over virtue.

result is not a dolorous sensation for you. This then would be a case in which three million victims sent to their doom must be a matter of indifference to you; you ought not hence to oppose their destruction even if you are able to prevent it, since from their loss Nature gains; but it is exceedingly important that this destruction occur if it affords you delight, because between it and your pleasure there is no proportion: everything must be to the advantage of the sensation you taste. You ought hence to concert this destruction resolutely and without remorse if you can achieve it with prudence; not that prudence is a virtue in itself, but the advantages you derive from it give it a value; and not that prudence is always necessary, for it often has a chilling effect upon pleasures. But it must nonetheless be employed in certain cases because it ensures impunity, and the certitude that you will get away scot-free enormously enhances the charms of crime; however, what with your wealth, the consideration and the credit you enjoy, your position is already strong and you need be less concerned for security than another. And so you may fling caution more or less to the winds, and banish prudence when it looks to you likely to blunt your pleasures."

Filled with enthusiasm by my discourse, the Countess' thousand kisses expressed her gratitude.

"I am eager to try out your secret," said she; "let's not meet again until two weeks have passed. I swear to see no one during that interval, when it is over we shall spend a night together: I shall tell you my ideas and we shall work jointly at their realization."

As she had promised, the Countess sent me word a fortnight later; we sat down to an exquisite supper. After we had raised our spirits with dainties of all kinds and delicious wines, the servants were dismissed, the doors locked, and we shut ourselves up in a little chamber which much art and expense had turned into a veritable laboratory for lubricious research.

Throwing herself straight into my arms, "Oh, Juliette," the Countess said, "I need such tenebrous surroundings as these if I am to gather courage to confess what your perfidious prescriptions have brought me to. Perhaps never was a more atrocious crime conceived, it is appalling, words fail me . . . but my cunt seeps while I plot it . . . I discharge as I visualize myself performing it.

. . . Oh, my love, however shall I be able to reveal this horror to you! Whither are we borne by a disordered imagination! To what infernal lengths is not a weak and helpless mortal dragged by satiety, by the abandonment of principles, by the atrophy of conscience, by the taste for vice, by the immoderate use of lust. . . . Juliette, I have a mother and a daughter, you know that."

"Of course."

"The one, that woman who carried me in her womb, today scarcely fifty years of age, is yet in possession of all beauty's traits. She adores me. Aglaia, my daughter, sixteen years old—Aglaia whom I idolize, with whom I have been frigging myself daily for the past two years, just as my mother did with me—well, Juliette, these two creatures. . . ."

"Go on."

"These two women whom I ought so to cherish, who ought to be so precious to me—I wish to steep my hands in their blood. I wish to bathe in it, Juliette; you and I, that is what I wish, you and I, lying together in a bathtub, each frigging the other, I want the blood of those two whores to drench us, I want it to cascade over us, I want us both to be covered by it, I want us to swim in it . . . these two women I worshiped before I met you and whom I loathe today, I want them to die while we watch, and in that manner. . . . I want us to take fire from their dying breaths; I want them to be thrown dead into that same bathtub, upon their corpses and in their blood, I want it to be there our pleasures culminate."

Countess Donis, who while making this avowal had been frigging herself uninterruptedly, now fainted as she discharged. Being myself singularly aroused by what I had just heard, I had no easy time reviving her; she embraced me anew upon opening her eyes.

"Juliette," she said, "the things I told you are frightful, but from the state they have put me in you can appreciate their prodigious effect upon my senses. . . . Do I repent having spoken? Far from it, I shall carry out the whole of what I have conceived, and promptly: we must busy ourselves at this infamy tomorrow."

"Sweet friend, delicious friend," I said to this engaging person, "you are not afraid, heaven forbid! of finding a censor in me. Far be it from me to carp at your project, but I ask that it be explored to the limit and enriched by a few episodes. It strikes me that some spices could be included in the dish. In what manner do you mean to have your victims wet us with their blood? Is it not essential to your complete enjoyment that nothing short of the most excruciating tortures cause it to flow?"

"Ah," was the Countess' vibrant reply, "you think that my perversity has not already invented them, arranged them? I wish these tortures to be equally prolonged, gruesome, and violent, I wish to feast ten whole hours upon their hideousness and upon the victims' groans and curses, I wish to have us discharge twenty times while first the one, then the other is adying, glutting ourselves on their screams, drinking ourselves drunk on their tears. Ah, Juliette," the inspired woman pursued, masturbating me with the same ardor she employed for defiling herself, "all this to which my heart gives vent is nought but the fruit of your advice and instructions. This cruel but saving truth entitles me to your indulgence. So hark to what I have still to say: having gone so far as to disclose these dangerous desires I harbor I cannot now beg off, but must complete my confession and at the same time solicit your aid in an affair of great importance to me. Aglaia is the child of my husband, that is my reason for hating her; my sentiments for her father were no less hostile, and had Nature not heeded my prayers I would have resorted to art and forced her to fulfill them . . . you catch my drift. I have another daughter, a man I worship is her father. Fontange, so is she called, the darling issue of my passion and its token, she is now in her thirteenth year; she is being raised at Chaillot, near Paris. My desire is that she have a brilliant future, this requires means and means she shall not lack. Here, Juliette," continued Madame Donis, handing me a bulging pocketbook, "my legitimate heirs will be deprived of these five hundred thousand francs; invest the sum in my Fontange's name when you return to France, I wish also to entrust her to you, you will look after her, you will find a suitable match for her, you will see to her welfare and happiness. But your interest in the child must appear to stem from benevolence. Otherwise all would soon be brought to light: my family would assert claims to this gift, and lawyers would contrive to get it away from my daughter. I place my confidence in you, dear Juliette: swear that you will be a loyal friend to me and

keep secret both my good and my evil deeds. This pocketbook
contains an added fifty thousand francs which I beg you to have
the kindness to accept for yourself. So then, swear to serve as the
executioner of the two persons I have marked for death and at the
same time as the protectress of the charming creature I place in
your care—speak. Oh, Juliette, I am prepared to have faith in you
—have you not told me a hundred times over that there is honor
amongst rakes? will you give this maxim the lie? No, surely not . . .
my love, I am waiting for your reply."

Although infinitely less likely to keep a promise to cooperate
in an act of generosity than in a crime, each of the propositions the
Countess made me had its interesting side, and I agreed to both.

"Dear friend," I said to Madame Donis after sealing our
pact with a kiss, "it shall be as you will it: be certain that before a
year is out your beloved Fontange shall be the beneficiary of your
generosity and of my devoted attentions. But for the present, my
dearest, pray let us concentrate our thoughts upon executing your
abominable designs. Virtue fairly turns my stomach when my soul
is oriented toward crime—"

"Ah, Juliette," said Madame Donis, plucking at my sleeve,
"you perhaps disapprove my laudable action?"

"Why no, surely not," I hastily replied, and I had my reasons
for reassuring the lady, "no, of course not, I disapprove of nothing
at all but simply feel that there is a proper time and place for each
of these so dissimilar subjects."

"Very well then, we shall give all our thought to the one which
has just had such potent effects upon me. There is the question of
details: let us compare our ideas. I have a few in mind, but tell me
yours first: I want to see if our imaginations are in tune."

"To begin with," I replied, "the scene must transpire not here
in town but in a rural setting, cruel pleasures are most successful in
the silence and peacefulness only the countryside can provide. And
then let me ask you, is Aglaia a virgin?"

"Most assuredly."

"Her maidenhead should then be lost upon the altars of
murder; her two mothers must present her to the sacrificer, and—"

"And her sufferings must be ghastly!" the Countess interjected.

"By all means, but rather than settle their specific kind before-

hand it is probably better that we wait and see what actual circumstances suggest. Arising spontaneously from the context, they will
be a thousand times more voluptuous.''

The rest of the night was given over to the most frenzied
Lesbian exercises. We kissed each other, sucked each other, devoured each other; each fitted with a dildo, we fenced fiercely,
mercilessly, and for hours. And having completed our arrangements
to remove for several days to Prato, where the Countess had a
superb estate, we deferred the execution of our delicious scheme
until the following week.

Madame Donis adroitly announced to her mother and
daughter that they were all embarking upon a six-month journey,
thereby preparing the ground for the sad report that the two dear
ones her fury was to destroy had been taken away by some illness
in the course of their travels. For my part I was to bring Sbrigani
and two thoroughly reliable valets. Thus upon the appointed day
were met at Prato a total of eight persons: the Countess and I, my
husband and my two hirelings, Madame Donis' mother, her
daughter and, lastly, an elderly nursemaid who had been many
years in the service of her disorders.

Hitherto I had seen Aglaia upon but one or two brief occasions, only now was I able to examine her closely. She proved a
perfectly enchanting young thing, as pretty as a picture, gracefully
made, with a skin incredibly smooth and soft and fair, big blue eyes
which seemed to be only waiting to come alive, faultless teeth,
golden tresses. But to all that direction was lacking, it drifted aim-
lessly: the Graces had set only a caressing hand to Aglaia, she yet
required molding. The impression made upon me by that heavenly
girl is something beyond my power to describe, it was an age since
anyone had stirred me so profoundly.

And as I gazed at her a thought entered my head.

"Why not change the victim," I said to myself, "is not the
commission the Countess has entrusted to me her death warrant?
If I sincerely desire to steal this money—and the urge is undeniably
upon me—then must I not straightway do her to death who assigned
it to my safekeeping? My purpose in coming here is to commit
crimes, that which ends the daughter's days satisfies only my
libertinage, whereas another which lays her mother low will stimu-

late my passions just as well and will amply content my greed into the bargain: the five hundred thousand francs will be mine, and I will be dispensed from any obligation to account for them, mine also shall be two pretty girls to use as I please and, finally, I shall have murdered their mother who nicely twiddled my clitoris for a time, and of whom I have now had enough. As for the grandmother, bah, we can kill her too, there'll be nothing to it; but this charming and virtually unknown creature I behold before me, 'twould be a pity not to spare her until familiarity has had a chance to breed contempt."

I communicated these ideas to my husband, he applauded them and recommended that I send immediate word to my women, instructing them to pack up our belongings and to proceed with all dispatch to Rome and to await us there, for that was the city we had chosen for our next stay after our allotted term in Florence expired. Attached to me as Elise and Raimonde were, I could expect them to comply punctually and conscientiously with my orders, and was not disappointed. The very same day I convinced Madame Donis that to ensure the safe and satisfactory accomplishment of the task at hand it was indispensable to clear the house of every servant and to have all she owned of gold and gems sent down to the country so that she not be entirely without resources in the event plans went somehow astray. Acclaiming the wisdom of these precautions, Madame Donis, in blissful ignorance of those I was taking at the same time, arranged to have all her acquaintances in Florence informed that she had gone off to Sicily and would be absent until late in the fall; and keeping by her only the old nurse I mentioned a moment ago, the improvident creature put herself entirely in our power: even had she deliberately tried she could not have tumbled more unerringly into all the traps we were laying for her. Everything was settled the next day, and the Countess, ours, had received by courier six hundred thousand francs in effects, two million in bank notes, and three thousand sequins in cash; her whole defense consisted in one aged woman, whereas my forces included, apart from Sbrigani, a pair of strapping valets.

These dispositions completed and as I was enormously relishing my idea of having the daughter commit the very crime whereof her mother wished to make her the victim, I induced the Countess to postpone all action until the following Friday, which, said I, would allow us three or four days to entrench ourselves in the appropriate calm.

"Between now and then," I suggested to her, "let us employ ruse, constraint only if need be. Since we are on the eve of losing this delightful Aglaia you have only now introduced to me and to whom I shall have to bid adieu so soon, let me at least pass these few remaining nights with the child."

All I said, all I asked, all I proposed was law to the Countess, such was her infatuation with me that nothing could have opened her eyes. And such are the mistakes which they who are in the midst of meditating wickedness are only too prone to make: dazzled by their passions, they are completely blind to everything else and, thoroughly persuaded that their accomplices are going to derive as much benefit or pleasure as they from the deeds in question, they are oblivious of anything that might dim others' enthusiasm for the project they dote upon. Madame Donis consented to everything; Aglaia was ordered to give me a warm reception in her bed, and I repaired thither that same evening. Oh, my friends, what an array of charms! Suspect me neither of poetic license nor unreasoning bias, for truly I do not exaggerate when I declare to you that Aglaia would all alone have sufficed to him who in his search for a model ransacked all Greece and even in the one hundred loveliest women of that land failed to find the beauties he needed for the composition of the sublime Venus I admired in the Grand Duke's gallery. Never, no, never had I seen forms so deliciously rounded, an ensemble so voluptuous, nor details so compelling; nothing so narrow as her sweet little cunt, nothing so chubby as her dear little ass, nothing so pert, so fresh, so winningly shaped as her breasts; and fully aware of what it is I am saying, and stating it as a cold fact, I do now assure you that Aglaia was the divinest creature with whom up until that time I had ever had anything carnal to do. No sooner had I brought these marvels to light than I devoured them with caresses, and in my swift passage from one to the next, each time it seemed to me that I ought to have paused longer over what I had just relinquished for something equally wonderful. The pretty little minx had as lascivious a temperament as you could wish for, and was soon sighing her heart away. Her mother's pupil, she frigged me like Sappho; but my studied languors, my voluptuous distress, my ecstatic sufferings, my twitchings, my nervous tremors, my spasms, my screams, my foul tirades, all these attributes of far-reaching corruption, all these symptoms of the havoc wrought by Nature in a body and a soul, my grimaces, my sugared, my sickly smiles and kisses, my sneaking gestures and insinuating remarks, my hoarse, lewd whisperings, all these amazed and then alarmed her gentle innocence, and she ended up avowing to me that her mother's style of enjoyment was a great deal less refined, at any rate milder, than mine. Finally, after hours of matchless voluptuousness, after having discharged in every imaginable manner, five or six times in each, after having kissed, sucked each other everywhere, after having exchanged nips, bites, pinches, tonguings, whippings, after having done, in short, everything that can possibly be invented of the utterly crapulous, the utterly unbridled, the utterly obscene, and the simply inconceivable, to this delightful girl I spoke more or less as follows.

"Dear girl," I began, "I do not know where you stand as regards principles, nor whether the Countess, when she started to initiate you into the mysteries of pleasure, concerned herself also for the cultivation of your soul; but whatever the case may be, that which I have to reveal to you is too important to be withheld another minute from your knowledge. Your mother, that most traitorous, that most unworthy, that most criminal of women, has plotted against your life—exactly, do not interrupt me—: tomorrow, Aglaia, you are to be her victim unless you parry the blow: by which I mean you have no choice but to strike it first."

"Good heaven, what fearful thing do you tell me?" said Aglaia, trembling in my arms.

"The truth, my dove, it is atrocious, but I could not hide it from you."

"I wonder if this could be the reason for the odd change in her attitude toward me of late . . . for her chilliness, for that treatment—"

"To what treatment do you refer?"

Aglaia then disclosed to me that her mother, become cruel in her pleasure, had been tormenting her, slapping her, beating her, and taken to saying the harshest things to her. Curious to know the precise degree of disorder and license that characterized Madame Donis' lewd commerce with her daughter, I discovered that she required of the child one of those libidinous excesses whose violence brings disgust in its wake. After having gone down the list of libertine practices, this indecent mother had now come to the point where she had no pleasure from her daughter save in the form of a mouthful of her shit, which she would swallow.

"Dear love," I said to the maiden, "you would have been wiser to have been somewhat more sparing of the favors you granted your mother; too little reserve on your part, an overly accommodating spirit have resulted in satiety on hers. But the past cannot be altered, you must ready yourself for what is to come. The fatal hour is at hand."

"But how am I to escape?"

"Of escape there can be no question. You cannot wait until the attack is delivered and then hope to dodge it; my advice to you is to take the offensive yourself."

And here I began truly to enjoy the little piece of mischief I was up to; I had arrived at Prato with no fairer prospect than aiding a scoundrel to satisfy one of her passions; and now I was suborning an essentially mild-tempered and virtuous girl, I was urging her on to matricide, and however the deed might be justifiable, was it not a crime withal? While as for the trick I was playing upon my friend, it positively filled me with glee.

Impressionable, delicate, sensitive, Aglaia was sorely shaken by my revelation and reduced to tears by this awful deed I proposed that she do.

"My child," said I, stroking her hair as she sobbed upon my breast, "this is no time for tears, 'tis courage and determination we require. Owing to her fell designs, Madame Donis has forfeited title to any of the consideration which might be shown a mother, and become an ordinary woman to be done quickly and remorselessly away with: to deprive of life those who threaten our own is the summit of human virtue. You do not suppose gratitude can bind you to an abominable woman who only gave you life in order to place it in jeopardy? Come, sweet Aglaia, don't be mistaken, if you owe anything to such a monster it is vengeance; can you passively turn the other cheek to be insulted and hope to retain your self-respect? And supposing you were to survive this present attempt, what security remains to you? You will be your mother's victim tomorrow if she fails to kill you today. Rash child, thoughtless child, open your eyes: can you be ashamed to shed such criminal blood? Can you yet cling to the illusion that between this villain and thee there still subsists any relation save that of the hunter to his quarry?"

"You were her friend?"

"Could I continue to be once I learned that she was bent on destroying all I love in this world?"

"Your tastes and passions resemble hers."

"Perhaps; but, unlike her, I do not venerate crime; unlike her, I am not a she-wolf thirsting for blood, I abhor cruelty; I love my fellow man, and murder is an infamy that revolts me. An end to such comparisons, Aglaia, an end to them, they are pointless, they dishonor me, and they are causing us to lose precious moments. The time for words is over, that for deeds is upon us."

"What! You would have me, Aglaia, thrust a dagger into my mother's heart?"

"A mother, say you? Can you call by that name the one who labors at the destruction of her child? Why no, having become your mortal enemy, this woman must be considered a mad beast fit only for extermination."

And taking Aglaia in my arms again, I strove to bury her misgivings beneath an avalanche of libertine attentions: and sure enough, she forgot her qualms by and by and, quite won over, promised everything.[6] Guided by my pernicious reasonings, the

---

[6] There is truly no limit to what one may obtain from women simply by causing them to discharge. Experience shows that one has only to make their cunts leak a few drops of fuck, and they are ready and eager for the most revolting atrocities; and if those women who have a native fondness for hideous crimes cared to reflect a little upon their emotions, they would admit the astonishingly powerful connection that exists between physical emotions and moral aberrations. The wiser for recognizing this, the sum of their pleasures would henceforth increase by leaps and bounds, since they would correctly situate the germ of voluptuousness in the disorders which they could from then on carry to whatever extreme their lust might demand. I give an illustration. Arsinoe had but a single pleasure, that of fucking. A libertine lover mounts her; and chooses the moment of her ecstasy to suggest a criminal scheme to her. Whereat Arsinoe notices that her joys increase tenfold; she does what he proposes, and the heat engendered by this crime adds to the fire of her lust: Arsinoe has

heavenly little slut reached the stage where it dawned upon her that revenge might hold a few thrills in store for her; in a word, I maneuvered her into discharging over the thought of assassinating her mother. After that, we rose from bed.

"My friend," I said to Sbrigani, "we have now but to lay hands on the victims; call in your men and have them clap the ladies in irons."

The grandmother is seized first and dragged down into the cellars of the château, where she is very shortly joined by the Countess. Understanding nothing of these untoward proceedings, she appears stunned by surprise. Aglaia is there.

"Monster!" I say to Madame Donis, "justice cries out that you be made the victim of your own wickedness."

"What's this? Perfidious wretch, was not this plot as much your handiwork as mine?"

"Ha, I put on a show of vice and so lured you into divulging your secret; but now, having you in my power, I have no further need to feign."

When night falls I have these two prisoners brought up to the salon Madame Donis had converted into the theater for her horrors. Aglaia, stiffened in her purpose, steeled to anything by my mingled scoldings and cajoleries, is amused by the spectacle; she is quite as unmelted by the plight in which she beholds her grandmother as by the fate that has overtaken her mother. I had been clever enough to inform her in advance that the Countess had contrived her evil plans at the old lady's instigation; and the tortures began.

They followed the course Màdame Donis had charted, except that instead of being the agent the hapless creature was the patient. Reclining, her daughter and I, in a large bathtub and frigging ourselves amain, upon us the blood of the two women poured, running from the thousand and one gashes inflicted by Sbrigani. Here I should say in Aglaia's honor that her courage and determination wavered not once; progressing swiftly from pleasure

---

thus enriched her repertory by one pleasure the more. Any woman may do as much; all of them should: imitating Arsinoe, to the allurements of a first form of enjoyment they too will add the spice of a second. Every immorality leads to another, and the more of them you associate to fucking, the happier you must necessarily become.

to ecstasy, her delirium held at a frenzied pitch to the end of the operation, and it was not brief. Sbrigani devised all sorts of ingenious expedients to lengthen the ordeal, and the accomplished fellow crowned it, rather as you might have guessed, by bum-stuffing the victims, who gave up the ghost under his belly.

"And that," said I, after congratulating my barbarous husband when he was done, "makes us the masters of the place; let us sack it and beat a rapid retreat. Aglaia," I went on, "you presently grasp the object of my crime: as your mother's friend I had only a share of her wealth, all of it is mine now. The fires you kindled in my heart burn there yet; you know Elise and Raimonde? I mean to include you in my troupe. But along with certain pleasures this includes certain services, like the others you too shall be called upon to contribute to the commonwealth, you will have to lie, cheat, steal, seduce, commit every crime, as do we when our advantage enjoins it; to rallying to our colors the alternative is abandonment and poverty. Which shall it be?"

"Oh, my dear friend, I shall never quit your side," the girl exclaimed, tears in her eyes; "it is not my situation that dictates my choice, it is not fear of hardship, but my heart, and my heart belongs entirely to you."

The heat still in him, my husband was not an impassive spectator to this moving scene; his feverish eyes and prick led me to suspect that he was bent on fucking, and his words shortly confirmed it.

"God's blood and balls!" he declared, "this dastardly thing I have done I heavily regret now, and nothing short of raping the daughter will make up for the loss of the mother I have killed; turn her over to me, Juliette."

And being rather too pressed to wait for my response, the libertine, his prick up solid and true, caught the lass and deflowered her at a stroke. Blood emanating from that youthful cunt has scarce stained those white thighs when the Italian withdraws, turns the seamy side up, gives three lusty heaves and lo! he's implanted his device in her ass.

"Juliette," he inquired while he sawed away, "what's to be done with this article now? A moment ago we could perhaps have found a buyer for her first fruits, but they have been picked and there's an end to the whore's usefulness. It's dull, I tell you, it lacks intrigue," he continued, fucking apace, "it lacks character, Juliette, believe me; so let us reunite what Nature originally assembled and leave this family in peace; of the murder of this child something superb might be made—fuck my eyes, the mere thought causes me to discharge."

And here, my friends, I confess it to you, my native ferocity swept all other considerations aside, Sbrigani's pathetic appeal had stirred me as the rascal knew it would, and a sudden spate of fuck rising in my cunt sealed Aglaia's doom.

"You are going to go the way of your kin," I said to her; "the idea of putting you to death stiffens us, and we are of that reprobate breed that has never bowed to any law but its passions."

Despite her shrill protests and entreaties she was delivered over to our valets, and while the rascals tupped her in the manners they fancied, Sbrigani toiled to brilliant effect over me. From pleasures our satellites soon turned to brutalities; grossly insulting the object they had latterly favored with their homages, they advanced in short order from expletives to threats, from threats to blows. And of succor Aglaia had none from me, nor comfort: she stretched her lovely arms imploringly toward me, wrung her pretty hands, called my name; I did not heed her. The luckless child seemed to remind me tacitly of our secret pleasures and to conjure me to hark again to the sentiment which guided me then. I was deaf. Incredibly aroused by Sbrigani who was embuggering me the whole while, I felt things other than compassion for the child; I became at once her accuser and her executioner.

"Ply those whips," I ordered my valets, "lash some blood from this little ass that so recently afforded me such delights."

She was lying flat upon a narrow bench, straps held her in position and her head, pulled up at a sharp angle and maintained there by an iron collar, offered itself to the kisses wherewith I covered her mouth as I presented my ass to Sbrigani who was sodomizing me while Madame Donis' domestic flogged him. With each hand I frigged the prick of a valet; each of them, armed with a cat-o'-nine-tails, hacked at this or that part of our exciting victim's body. At the height of this scene I loosed the second of two thundering discharges, and when at last I espied those charming buttocks in full bloom, so tattered and torn that for all those stripes and cuts nothing more was co be seen of the once satin-smooth skin, I had a chandelier taken down and Aglaia hanged by the hair from the ringbolt in the ceiling; then, opening her thighs wide and securing them thus by cords, I myself caught up a martinet and belabored the most delicate parts of her body, two-thirds of my blows landed inside her gaping cunt. I was beyond words entertained by the poor girl's convulsive jerks, the more amusing for being performed in mid-air; it would now be a lurch backward to avoid the strokes I dealt her from before, now a forward lunge to avoid those I aimed at her behind; and not one of those acrobatics failed to cost her a handful of hair. And I was discharging myself nigh out of my mind when a truly delicious idea entered it; this idea was too much to Sbrigani's taste not to be translated into action on the spot. We disinterred the cadavers of Aglaia's two forebears, we buried them to the waist in two deep holes; facing them we placed the last of her line in a third hole, dug yet a little deeper, from which her head and shoulders emerged, and 'twas opposite that hideous sight we left her to perish slowly. A ball from a pistol rid us of the nursemaid and, laden with an immense booty, Sbrigani, our two menials, and I set out at once for the capital of the Papal States where we were greeted by our two girls who, with the rest of our movables, were awaiting us at the address we had given them earlier in Florence.

As we made our entry into Rome, "Oh, Sbrigani!" I exclaimed, "here we are at last in this superb capital of the world! How instructive it is to meditate upon the strange parallel that asks to be drawn between the Rome of ancient days and this other that is contemporary. With what astonishment, and with what scorn, I am going to see statues of Peter and Mary poised upon the altars of Bellona and of Venus. Few ideas so exalt my imagination. O you people besotted by religion, by it laid low," I mused as I scanned the features of these modern Romans, searching for some traits reminiscent of the grandeur and glory of those erstwhile masters of the world, "to what a point has the most infamous, the most loathsome of religions succeeded in degrading you! What would a Cato say, or a Brutus, if he were to see a Julius, a Borgia parading his insolent pomp upon the august ashes one of those heroes confidently recommended to the respect of later generations and the awed admiration of the universe?"

Despite the oath I had taken to enter no church, I could not resist a desire to visit St. Peter's. This monument, it cannot be denied, not only beggars description, it is far superior to anything the most fertile imagination could conceive. But that part of the human spirit is also afflicted, as one realizes the humiliating truth, in seeing that such great talents were exhausted, such colossal sums were expended, in honor of a religion so stupid, so ridiculous as the one we have had the misfortune to be born into. For magnificence the altar is quite beyond compare, isolated, set between four wreathed columns, mounting almost the full height of the church, and placed upon the very tomb of St. Peter, who for all that did not die in Rome nor indeed ever show his face there.

"Oh, what a couch for embuggerment," I declared to Sbrigani. "You shall see, my friend, just leave it to me and inside a month Juliette's rectum will play host, upon this superb altar, to the modest prick of the Vicar of Christ."

And, my patient auditors, only wait a little and the sequel will show you whether my prediction was accurate.

Coming to Rome it was my belief that I ought to establish myself under altogether different colors here than those we had flown at Florence. Provided with several letters of recommendation I had obtained from the Grand Duke, and in which, as I had requested, he referred to me as a countess, and having the means to back such a title, I took a house of the sort that would silence any discussion of the legitimacy of my pretensions. My first care was to place my funds in investment. The enormous theft operated at Minski's retreat, the other lately achieved at Prato, the half a million francs Madame Donis' Fontange was not destined to see, my Florentine earnings, all this added to what I had amassed in the course of my tour through north Italy made up a capital yielding eight hundred thousand *livres* a year; an income of sufficient size, you observe, to permit me a house rivaling anything maintained by the most brilliant princes in the entire land. Elise and Raimonde were my ladies in waiting, and Sbrigani thought it would better promote my interests if he were no longer to pass as my husband, but as my gentleman squire henceforth.

I went to pay my calls in a perfectly regal carriage. Among my introductions was a letter to His Eminence, Cardinal de Bernis, our ambassador to the Holy See, who received me with all the gallantry to be expected from that charming emulator of Petrarch.

My next stop was at the palace of the beautiful Princess Borghese, a very libertine woman whom you shall soon see taking a leading role in my adventures.

Two days later I presented myself at Cardinal Albani's residence: Albani, the greatest debauchee in the Sacred College, and who that same afternoon must absolutely summon his painter and have him do a portrait of me in the nude, for inclusion in his gallery.

After that it was Duchess Grillo, a delightful woman gone preposterously to waste upon the gloomiest of husbands, and over whom I went fairly wild at first sight. My special acquaintances ended there, and it is in this charming circle you are about to behold me revive all the turbulent exploits of my youth—yes, good friends, yes, of my youth, I may employ the term since I was then starting my twenty-fifth year. I had not as yet to complain of Nature, however; she had deteriorated none of my features, to the contrary, she had given them that look of ripeness and that definition which are regularly absent in girlhood, and I may say in all truthfulness that if I had been considered pretty hitherto, I could now assert claims to the extremest beauty. My waist had lost nothing of its slenderness, my breasts, still fresh, round, firm, had held up miraculously. Exuberantly poised and of an agreeable fairness, my buttocks showed not a sign of the rough and lewd usage I had time and again exposed them to, the hole between them was a trifle large, to be sure, but of a fine reddish-brown hue, hairless, and whenever displayed certain to attract tongues; my cunt too had lost much of its narrowness, but with the aid of coquetry, ointments, and craft, I could at will make all that sparkle as brightly as any virgin's new penny. Regarding my temperament, it had acquired strength over the years, and was now something truly terrifying and always under the control of my mind: when got properly started, it was absolutely indefatigable. But for the purpose of setting it surely into motion I was coming to rely upon wine and spirits; my brain once spinning, I was capable of anything; I also employed opium and other love-stimulants Durand had prescribed and which were on open and profuse sale in Italy. You ought never to fear irritating your lascivious appetites by such means, art is always more helpful than Nature, and the one disadvantage to trying a drug is the obligation you fall under to continue taking it for the rest of your life.

The beginning of my stay at Rome was distinguished by the conquest of two women. One was Princess Borghese. Not two days passed before she let me read in her eyes all her desire that we become intimately acquainted. She was thirty years of age, vivacious, engaging, witty, and profligate; pretty was her figure, magnificent her hair, bright were her eyes, she had imagination, a prepossessing manner.

Next, Duchess Grillo: less forward, younger, better behaved, and lovelier, her bearing was a queen's, she was modest, of seemly reserve, was not so energetic as the Princess and quite lacked her imagination, but was incomparably more kindly than she, more virtuous, more sensitive. Equally taken by these two women, it goes without saying, after the brief sketches I have given of them, that whilst the one had a stimulating influence upon my mind, the other won her way immediately into my heart.

A week after our initial meeting the Princess invited me to supper at her little property just outside the city.

"We shall be alone," she told me; "everything about you intrigues me, my dear Countess, and I am determined to make the most of this promising discovery."

You will readily understand that after such advances it was not long before all ceremony was abolished between us. The weather was sultry. Following an abundant and voluptuous repast served by five charming girls in a garden where the scent of roses and jasmine combined with the sweet murmur and coolness of plashing fountains, the Princess drew me off to a lonely summerhouse lost in a glade of sheltering poplars. We entered a circular room, around whose wall, which was entirely sheathed by mirrors, ran a long sofa standing but six or eight inches off a floor everywhere strewn with pillows and cushions; here, in a word, was one of the prettiest temples Venus had in all Italy. We were escorted there by the young serving girls who left us to ourselves after lighting several lamps in which perfumed oil shed a soft glow behind shades of green gauze.

"My treasure," suggested the Princess, "let us henceforward address each other by our first names; I abhor everything that reminds me of wedlock. So call me Olympia; and I may call you Juliette, yes, my angel? You will permit it?"

And the most ardent kiss was bestowed lingeringly upon my lips.

"Dear Olympia," said I, folding this bewitching creature in my arms, "what would I not permit you? When she adorned you with so many charms did not Nature accord you rights to every heart, and must you not necessarily seduce all those upon whom you bend your burning gaze?"

"You are divine, my darling Juliette, kiss me a thousand times over," said Olympia, sinking upon the sofa. "Oh, my sweetest friend, I feel it for a certainty, yes, of nothing have I ever been so sure, we are going to do many and wonderful things together. . . . But I must tell you the truth about myself, the whole truth— oh, I tremble. . . . 'Tis that I am such a libertine; no, no, dear soul, you must not misunderstand me. I adore you—but it isn't love for you that inflames me now: when possessed by lust I become immune to love, forget it completely, and it is only lewdness I recognize."

"O heaven!" I cried, "is it possible that in two places a full five hundred leagues apart, Nature created two so identical souls?"

"What, Juliette!" was Olympia's rapid response, "you are libertine too? If 'twere so we could pollute without loving each other, we could discharge like a pair of sows, immodestly, indelicately, we could include others in our riotings—ah, let me devour you, my chit, my dove, let me kiss you to death; credit satiety for all that, credit habit, credit our lavish style of living, our leisure and opulence: accustomed to denying ourselves nothing, everything now palls on us, and fools have no conception of whither one may be led by this surfeit and this apathy."

As she chatted Olympia was undressing me, undressing herself, and no sooner were we both naked than we came to grips. Borghese's first gestures were to catch my knees, to separate my thighs, to run her hands caressingly over my buttocks, between them, and to dart her tongue as far into my cunt as it could reach. Besotted by pleasure, I was easy game for the tribade; she is shortly quaffing off mouthfuls of my fuck, I spring into action, roll her onto the cushions strewn about that boudoir, and sprawl upon her: while, my head wedged between her legs, I cunt-suck her with all my might, the rascal, her head between my legs also, renders me the same service: thus do we discharge six or seven times.

"We are too few," Olympia points out to me. "Unaided, two women cannot hope to satisfy each other; we had better have my menials in, they are pretty, the eldest is under seventeen, the youngest fourteen. But they are capable. Not a day passes but each dips her fingers in my cunt; shall I summon them?"

"Don't hesitate to do so on my account, I am as fond of all that as you; I applaud any contribution to libertinage, anything that increases it is precious to my senses."

"And nothing that stirs them ought to be neglected, they cannot be subjected to effects too numerous nor too strong," Olympia rejoined; "ah, those shy or skittish women, the wretched creatures," she went on, "who, experiencing no pleasure save it be inside the bounds of love and legitimacy, idiotically fancy that where there is no adoration there can be no fucking."

But a moment after the Princess rang for them, the five girls, too well trained to require instructions and who had doubtless been waiting nearby in expectation of the call, marched in, nude. All had lovely faces, supple, shapely bodies, and when they gathered round Olympia, which is what they did at once, it seemed to me these were the Graces frolicking about Venus.

"Juliette," the Princess said to me, "I shall sit opposite you, these five girls will turn their coordinated and knowing attentions upon you and by means of the most amorous titillations, the most lascivious postures, they'll bring your fuck forth, I am confident of it; I shall watch you discharge, I ask no more. You have no idea the pleasure it gives me to see a beautiful woman lose her head to joy: I shall frig myself in the meantime, I shall let my mind rove and you may be sure it will wander far."

To this proposition my lubricity could raise no objection, I therefore signified my assent. Olympia distributed orders: one of

these girls, squatting over me, offered me a pretty little cunt to suck;
I myself lying upon the padded straps of a bed which was at the
same time a kind of aerial swing, my buttocks were posed above
the face of a second girl whose task was to lick my asshole, a third,
stretched upon me, sucked my cunt, and I frigged the remaining
two, one with either hand; observing this spectacle, Olympia, who
was staring avidly, held in one hand a silken cord which led to the
car wherein I was suspended, and by means of gentle tugs she got
it to swaying, this motion prolonging, multiplying the tonguings
I was giving and receiving, and heightening their voluptuousness to
an unbelievable point. For pleasure, never before, I do believe,
had I experienced the like of it. Thereupon—and now Olympia
achieved the impossible, the undreamt of: she contrived to improve
the already perfect—thereupon, I say, coming from I could not tell
where, the sounds of delightful music reached my ears. As though
the exotic fables of the Koran were suddenly come true, I thought
I had been transported into Islam's paradise and there surrounded
by the houris the prophet promises the faithful, it seemed to me
their intention in caressing me was to drive me mad amongst the
uttermost excesses of lubricity. Olympia was causing the swing to
sway in cadence with the music; I was gone quite out of my mind,
between me and real existence all ties had been dissolved save that
last one maintained by the profound throbbings of my joy. My
ecstasy lasted an hour; then Olympia climbed into the swing.
Deliciously inspired by the music, I polluted my hostess for another
hour and a quarter in her voluptuous machine; after that, following
a short interval of repose, we resumed our pleasures and varied
their form.

     She and I lying upon the heaps of cushions carpeting the floor,
we placed the prettiest of the girls between us. She frigged us
both manually; two other girls, established between our thighs,
cunt-sucked us; and the remaining two, straddling our chests, gave
us their cunts to suck. Thus were we occupied for nearly an hour;
next, the girls rotated their posts. We cunt-sucked those who had
just been cunt-sucking us, and those who had just been cunt-sucked
by us in turn sucked our cunts; and the music played on. Olympia
finally asked me, would I care to have the musicians join us?

     "Yes, call them in," I said, and declared that I would like to have the entire world standing there, seeing me in this state of inordinate happiness.

"Oh, my cherub, my heavenly creature," caroled Olympia, sprinkling passionate kisses upon my mouth, "you are an arrant, shameless.little whore, I adore you for it. That is just what every woman should be, that is what all of them are save the fools amongst them, and fools they are who do not sacrifice everything to their pleasures; fools? in what terms describe the stupidity of those who can worship any god but Venus? who can observe any rule apart from that of prostituting themselves to individuals of all sexes, all ages, all sorts and conditions? Oh, Juliette, the most sacred of the laws writ in my heart is whorishness; the purpose of my life is to shed fuck, shedding it is my primary need and sole pleasure: I should like to be a prostitute, but a cheap one.

"To be a whore—the thought burns in my brain and sets a fever racing through my blood. I want to be hired to the most exacting libertines, I want to be obliged to employ a thousand wiles and artifices to rouse the most lethargic rakes, and to satisfy the least easy to please; I want to be their toy, their butt, their victim, let them do with me what they will, I'd gladly endure anything, everything—even tortures.

"Juliette, shall we be whores? Let us, my dearest, let's go awhoring, let's sell ourselves, let's get ourselves to a gutter and open grinning cunts to whole passing nations, our cunts, our mouths, our assholes, let's ope all our holes to every filthy stopper. Ah, fuck my eyes, girl, my head is beginning to reel; like the fiery charger, I thrust heaving flank to meet gashing spur; I am flying to my undoing, I know it, I know it well, it is inevitable . . . and I do not care. Bah, I am almost vexed by this credit and the titles that are mine and which, favoring my misconduct, also deny it notoriety—I would that all the earth be privy to the things I do, I would that they drag me like the lowliest of wretches to the fate their abandon designs them to. . . . Do you fancy I dread that fate? No, whatever it may be, I'd rush thither unafraid. . . . The stocks, the pillory, the scaffold itself would for me be a privilege, the throne of delight, upon it I'd cry death defiance, and discharge in the pleasure of perishing the victim of my crimes and over the idea that in future my name would be a byword for evil, at whose mere mention generations of men would tremble. Such is the pass I have come to, Juliette, this is where libertinage has brought me, this is where I wish to live my life and die, I vow it to you; were I less fond of you I would be unable to declare these things to you. You would hear more? Know then that I feel I am on the eve of casting myself headlong into frightful debauchery: at this very moment the last inhibiting prejudices wither away before my eyes, the remaining restraints dissolve: I decide to perpetrate the blackest crimes, my mind is made up—and the scales drop from my eyes: I see the abyss yawning at my feet, and jubilantly I hurl myself over the brink. I spit contemptuously upon that illusory honor whose having costs so many women their felicity, which they trade away in exchange for no recompense at all. Honor exists where? in opinion; but the single opinion that matters, that which alone confers happiness, is one's own, and not others'. Be wise enough to scorn the opinion of the public, which depends not upon us, have the intelligence to annihilate the stupid sentiment of honor which only leads us to happiness by way of privations, do this, I say, and you will very quickly discover that it is possible to live quite as comfortably, quite as contentedly, once become the object of universal opprobrium as when crowned by the sorry diadem of fair fame. O my companions in libertinage and crime, join me in mocking at this empty honor as we do at all other vile superstitions: a piece of moral licentiousness or the most ordinary physical fucking is worth a million times more than all the false pleasures honor accords. Ah, you shall someday realize, after my own example, how voluptuous delights are ameliorated once this phantom is exploded, and like me you will improve your enjoyments the more thoroughly you despise it."

"Adorable creature," I answered Olympia, lovely to behold as she delivered her impassioned speech, "endowed with such a mind . . . and with such aptitudes as you have shown me, you should someday go far; I seem to find, nevertheless, that you have yet some important ground to cover. You may perhaps accept all the aberrations of lubricity, but I do not believe you are acquainted with, or indeed have even dreamed of, all those which may derive from lubricity. Although several years younger than you, owing to the infinitely wilder career I have pursued I may have the advantage in experience. No, no, my dear Olympia, you have still to learn whither crimes of lust may lead; you are, I wager, still unprepared to accept the horrors these misdeeds may involve—"

"Horrors," Borghese interrupted, the color mounting into her cheeks, "ah! I venture to affirm I am not in arrears upon an article which you appear to esteem so essential. I would have you know that I poisoned my first husband, the same fate awaits the second."

"Delicious woman," I murmured, hugging Olympia in my arms, "forgive me if I seemed to entertain doubts of your character; but, blessed friend, that crime you committed, this other you project, they are motivated crimes, in all likelihood justifiable, at any rate necessary; whereas those crimes I would require of you would be gratuitous. Eh! is not crime in itself delicious enough to be committed for no practical purpose? Must we have an excuse for committing it? A pretext? And the tart flavor crime secretes, is that not alone sufficient to quicken our passions? My angel, of all the sensations in the world I do not want there to be one you have not tasted; with such a brain as yours, you would be grief-stricken to find that some sort of pleasure exists which you had not procured yourself. Be persuaded there is nothing to do under the sun that has not been done already, nothing that is not done every day, and, above all else, nothing that can conflict with the laws of a Nature who never incites us to evil save when she has need that we do it."

"Explain yourself, Juliette," asked Olympia, considerably moved by my remarks.

"Surely," I replied. "Tell me: what were the principal feelings in your soul as you set about ridding yourself of that first husband of yours?"

"The thirst for revenge; disgust, hate . . . and restlessness, a consuming desire to break my chains, to gain my freedom."

"And the part played by lust?"

"By lust?"

"It was silent in you?"

"Why, I did not consult it, it did not speak—"

"Well, if in days to come you should commit similar crimes,

do not neglect to interrogate it as you perform. Let lust provide the spark to the tinderbox of crime; combine the one passion with the other, and you shall be staggered by the results."

"Oh, Juliette," the Princess whispered, gazing at me with widestarted eyes and as though electrified by my suggestion, "the ideas you put in my head. . . . Ah, I was but a child, little did I know, less yet did I make of my opportunity—I realize it now."

I then represented to Madame Borghese all that a libertine spirit may extract from blending cruelty and lewdness, and developed for her, upon this great subject, all the theories you are so familiar with, my friends, and which you so superlatively put into practice. She had no trouble following my arguments and so rightly grasped the conclusions that it was with a reeling brain the rascal swore to me we would not take leave of each other before having jointly perpetrated a few of these voluptuous abominations.

"Oh, my love," she said, and she was completely afire, "a thousand things astir inside me are telling me how heavenly it must be to rob one of our fellow creatures of the treasure of his existence, the most precious in a human being's possession. To sever, to shatter the ties attaching that person to life, and this solely with a view to procuring oneself a pleasant sensation, for the sole purpose of discharging a little more agreeably . . . oh yes! this shock delivered to the nervous system, resulting from the effect of pain undergone by others, oh yes, it makes perfect sense to me, Juliette, and I have no doubt at all that the joy engendered by this concatenation of phenomena must culminate in the very ecstasy of the gods."

It was then, while she was in a very lather of agitation, that the musicians appeared.

Ten youths aged from sixteen to twenty composed the band which now filed in; and they were incomparably pretty lads, swathed in filmy, transparent tunics draped in the Greek manner.

"These are the artists who have provided the concert," the lewd creature said to me as she had them step up one by one; "first witness the pleasures I am going to taste with them, and afterward imitate me if you care to."

Whereupon the two youngest of those winsome boys posted

themselves, one by Olympia's head, as she lay still sprawled upon the pillows, the other hard by her bush. The remaining eight split into two groups, four of them gathering behind the boy at Olympia's head, four gathering behind the boy stationed near her pudendum; each of the two closest to her frigged his four companions' members, he at her head tendered Olympia for sucking the four devices he was stroking and then when they spouted guided the spout so that it splashed upon her face. In the meantime, the one placed by her cunt turn by turn plunged into it and snapped out again the four youthful pricks in his care, and saw to it that their exhalations landed upon her clitoris; and thanks to these proceedings Olympia was very soon covered with fuck from groin to brow. Lost in a labyrinth of delicious transports, never a word did she utter but only a few sighs, a few ecstatic moans, and all her body rippled with exquisite quiverings. Once all the pricks are frigged empty, the two masturbators leap lightly upon her, one takes her in his arms, encunts her, exposes Olympia's superb ass to his cohort, who deftly parts her buttocks and sodomizes her; while Olympia fucks, the other pricks slip one after the other into her mouth again, she resucks them, repumps them in turn, and finally, quite unhinged and shrieking, discharges like a maenad.

"So then," said she, rising to her feet and standing triumphantly in a puddle of sperm, "are you satisfied with me?"

"Indeed," I replied, I too soiled and drunk from the pleasure the Princess' five serving girls had been affording me while I watched her performance, "indeed, my dear, you have done tolerably well, but better yet may be done, as I intend to show you now."

So saying I turn to the girls and appoint them to the chore of reviving the musicians' members. Once all ten are suitably erect, I take them in hand. They were supple, agile, responsive to the touch; I plant two of them in my cunt, another in my ass, I mouth one, two nestle under my armpits, one in my hair, I frig a pair, the tenth rubs against my eyes; but I forbid any discharging. There must, I explain, be ten permutations, each must successively visit all the shrines I make available to their homage, only then may there be any outpouring of libations. Dreadfully excited by the preludes, those ten fair youths positively drowned me in fuck, and Madame Borghese, who had been observing me while enduring intense frigging from her five girls, allowed that my method of proceeding was more skillful than hers.

"And now," said I, "we must think of these five nimble-fingered fricatrices here; they deserve a reward."

Disposing them in various and voluptuous positions, upon the body of each we applied a brace of young fuckers. Contrary to all principles, we clapped the grosser pricks into asses, into cunts the smaller were stowed; we moved from group to group, proffering advice and encouragements. Olympia's delight was to snatch a prick out from wherever it happened to be buried, to suck it a while, and to restore it to place again; and sometimes when she came upon a vacant orifice, whether cunt or ass, she would thrust her tongue into it and spend a quarter of an hour licking and sucking away. And whenever she evicted a fucker, while she tongued his partner she would receive a fucking from him. More marked in my attentions than she, it was by means of smart slaps upon the buttocks and occasional kicks that I cheered on the combatants, or else I'd squeeze a testicle here, twiddle a clitoris there, or jab my thumb into an anus while whispering smutty instructions in an ear and biting it next. In fine, I omitted nothing apt to expedite the emission of fuck, and my interventions usually brought it forth in gushes. But those discharges occurred in my ass; for I would not for the world have let those sluts reap the fruit of my labors, certainly not, I never do anything save it be for my personal advantage and if the things I do are done well, that, my friends, is the reason why.

This scene concluded, I proposed another. Here, we would each sprawl flat upon one of the girls, our cunt covering her mouth, she would suck it while we sucked the cunt of another girl just ahead of us and presented our asses to the ten youths who, served by the remaining girl of the five, would embugger us now the one, now the other. All this was acceptable to Olympia, save that where she was concerned—and her amendment attested to a greater degree of libertinage than I would have given her credit for—she preferred to kiss an ass rather than a cunt; and the whore, of her own accord, without any prompting from me, but thereby demonstrating a perfect sympathy with my ideas, bit that ass fiercely enough to draw blood. Seeing this, I felt completely at my

ease, and catching hold of the breasts belonging to her whose cunt
I was lapping, I wrung and wrestled with them in a way that won
a sudden shrill scream from her. That was the moment Olympia
discharged.

"I've caught you, you rascal," I said to her, "you are beginning to detect pleasure in the commotion created by pain inflicted
upon others. It is a favorable sign: we ought soon to be moving
on to better things."

After having been embuggered ten times in succession we
swung our cunts around to the adversary. A girl squatting above
our foreheads simultaneously gave us her cunt and her bum to kiss;
with both hands a second massaged our clitoris and asshole; in
the meantime we were encunted; we discharged . . . we wallowed in
a sea of delights. Oral pleasures came next; we sucked all those
lads, we got them all to discharge into our mouths; and while this
was going forward each of us was having her clitoris sucked by
one girl, her asshole pumped by another. Exhausted, Olympia suggested that we restore our forces; we repaired to a gorgeously
lighted, luxuriously furnished dining room. A superb collation was
awaiting us in a huge basket of flowers, this basket lay nested in
the boughs of an orange tree laden with fruit; when I reached for
an orange I discovered it was of ice. Such surprises were held in
all the rest, everything showed the mark of the most refined taste
and the most elegant sumptuousness. We were served by the girls;
from where they were concealed behind a decoration the youths
charmed us now by the sounds of their melodious instruments.

Intoxicated after our feats of lubricity, Olympia and I were
shortly drunk from wines and liqueurs also.

"Now then," I asked of my companion, whose head was
reeling like mine, "what would you say to ending with an infamy?"

"Simply name it, I am ready for anything."

"Let us immolate one of these girls."

"This one," Olympia answered, catching the prettiest of the
five by the wrist.

"Gracious! You consent?"

"Why, of course. For what reason should I refrain from
imitating you? Do you think I am to be daunted at the prospect of
a murder? Ha, you shall see whether I am fit to be your pupil."

And, our victim in tow, we returned to the circular room where our orgies had taken place. All servants are dismissed, all doors barred, we three are alone.

"How shall we torment the jade?" I wanted to know. "Instruments seem to be lacking here."

While speaking I was examining the body of that truly superb young thing; I studied it by the light of two candles which ever and anon I would snuff out upon her buttocks, upon her thighs, upon her breasts. Olympia picked up a candlestick too; thus did we amuse ourselves for the space of an hour or so. After burning her we pinched her, tweezed her, prodded her, and clawed her a little with our fingernails. Both of us completely tipsy, without quite realizing what we were doing or saying, we vomited, belched, farted, and pissed—all that confusedly—and we tortured our victim amain. The wretched creature screamed away, but neither her cries nor our wild laughter were heard by any living soul, the precautions having been well made against it. My suggestion was that we hang the girl by the breasts and stab her to a slow death with hairpins. Olympia, whose progress was keeping pace with her lessons, agreed to everything. The unlucky girl's agonies extended over another two hours during which we drank ourselves into a further stupor on rum and her tears. Next, my companion and I, both spent after the fatigues of lust and of cruelties, numb from our intemperances, sank upon the cushions underfoot and slept for five hours, the victim dangling between us. The sun was already well up in the sky when we awoke; I helped Olympia bury the corpse beneath some bushes, and as I took my leave of her we both declared our earnest wish to pursue a collaboration which had begun so auspiciously.

Having neglected to tell Sbrigani I would be away overnight in the country, he and my women had been troubled by my absence and great was their relief to see me return; I assured them I was well but weary, and went straight to my bed. The following day Sbrigani, who thought of nothing but money, asked what profit I supposed might be gleaned from this intrigue.

"It has already been worth a host of pleasures," I sighed.

"It could be worth better still," replied my serious-minded gentleman squire. "I have glanced into the matter; my informants

tell me Borghese is the Pope's familiar. We must have her introduce you to the Holy Father, we must prepare ourselves access to
the Church treasures, we must drive out of Rome with an additional
seven or eight millions in our baggage. You know, Juliette, I am
wondering whether it was not a mistake to have adopted such an
aristocratic style here, I fear lest it disserve our aims."

"Not at all," I assured Sbrigani; "the lofty tone, a dazzling
panoply, and these titles are so many supplementary means to
excite lewd covetings; their ambition will be flattered to have
dealings with a woman of quality, I shall be able to triple my fees."

"Ah," Sbrigani rejoined, "'tis not a few hundred thousand
francs more or less that is at stake here. I have my eyes on higher
objectives: Pius VI possesses tremendous riches. We must steal
some of them."

"To do so, entry into his apartments must be gained, and is
there any way to achieve this unless I be summoned there upon
some libertine mission?"

"Certainly not; but instead of waiting idly for an opportunity
we must take the initiative, we must create the occasion as soon
as we can, we must get into the Vatican and fleece that beggar."

As we were in the midst of this conversation a page in the
service of Cardinal de Bernis brought me a message from his
master. It was an invitation to supper at Villa Albani, several
hours' ride from Rome, and the prelate of that same name was,
with Bernis, expecting me in his charming retreat.

"Juliette," Sbrigani exhorted me, "make the most of your
outing: bear it ever in mind that larcenies, fraud, imposture, those
are the sole aims of our travels; to enrich ourselves, there's our
sole purpose, that's our duty, and if we failed of it 'twould be
unpardonable. To it all pleasures are secondary and likely to entice
you into detours; the only road we must follow is the great highway
that leads to fortune."

Though no less ambitious than Sbrigani, quite as greedy for
gold as he, my views concerning motives were not entirely similar
to his. With me the proclivity for crime was the primary and compelling thing, and if I longed to steal it was far more for the sake
of the pleasure which the act itself procured me than for lavishing
money upon delights.

I arrived at the rendezvous decked out in all that art could add to the charms Nature had conferred upon me; my appearance, permit me to say, was lovely in the extreme.

Rather than interrupt my story, let me refrain from describing that enchanting *campagna* which attracts visitors from all over Europe. Those antiquities, perhaps the most precious relics that survive of classical Rome, those terraced gardens, the most exquisite, the best laid out, and best maintained in Italy—I should like to talk to you about them at length; but more eager to relate facts than to trace details, I shall move directly on to events, confident that you will not be displeased by my narrative, even unadorned.

Walking into Cardinal Albani's summer residence, great was my surprise to find Princess Borghese present there. By a window she and Bernis stood engaged in conversation; they broke it off upon seeing me enter, and came up to me.

"What a heavenly creature," Olympia declared. "Cardinal," she went on, addressing the aged Albani who had been staring fixedly at me ever since I descended from my carriage, "are you not of the opinion that we have no more beautiful woman in Rome?"

Both prelates affirmed that they believed this to be the case.

And we quit the drawing room.

The Italians customarily place their living quarters in the uppermost stories of their houses; at this distance above the ground, they rightly suppose, the air is necessarily purer, less heavy, and in better circulation. Those upper apartments of the Villa Albani were beyond words elegant; gauze curtains admitted the breeze while keeping out insects which might trouble the voluptuous projects for which it was very plain to me, as I glanced about, that the stage had been elaborately set.

The moment we were installed, Olympia approached me and spoke in this strain. "Juliette, you were recommended to these two cardinals in attestations from the Duke of Tuscany similar to the letter you brought me from that prince, my ecclesiastical friends have been exceedingly eager to become acquainted with you . . . with your person, with your behavior, with your attitudes of mind. My relations with these gentlemen being of the closest and most cordial sort, and knowing them quite as thoroughly and in the same way we, you and I, know each other, I have felt under no obligation to hide any of the truth from their curiosity: gratifying it, my accounts have, I believe, prepared a warm welcome for you. They desire you; I entreat you to accept their advances: these two dignitaries enjoy enormous favor with the Pope. 'Tis through their mediation preferments, advancements, graces of every variety are to be had; nay, nothing can be obtained in Rome save through them. However easy your circumstances, seven or eight thousand sequins now and then can do you no harm: one may often enough command the means to pay the butcher and the baker, but never has one too much to spend upon one's frivolities, and especially when they are of the order of those we are addicted to. I offer you my own example, many a time have I received money from them, I still do. Ah, women are made to be fucked, made also to be supported, and just as we should never turn up our noses at gifts, neither should we shun occasions for entitling ourselves to rewards. Bernis and his colleague, moreover, have in common a peculiar eccentricity, that of enjoying no pleasure unless it is paid for; I am certain you will appreciate this singularity. As well, I urge you to manifest the extremest indulgence toward them, nothing short of that is required with such libertines; only by dint of great art and complicated ministrations may their desires be reanimated; reserve would be misplaced here, make free, unrestrictedly, with everything; I shall show you how it is done; they must be relieved of their fuck, cost what it may, we can neglect nothing to achieve that end. All your wits and parts may therefore be put heavily to contribution; I felt you should be forewarned."

This speech would have surprised me less had I been more familiar with Roman manners. At any rate, if I was a little startled, I was by no means affrighted, not after the thousand and one trials I had faced intrepidly and come victoriously through in the past. Bernis, seeing that the Princess was done speaking her prologue, came forth now and addressed me in his turn.

"We know that you are charming," said he, "intelligent and untainted by prejudices: Leopold's written testimonial is very complete, it is upheld by the report we have had from Olympia, who was not reticent either. Upon the basis of this information we allow ourselves to presume, Albani and I, that you'll not play the prude with us, and to demonstrate your good will we would have you show yourself as much a rascal as in actual fact you are, because a woman is only truly amiable, I believe one may say, to the extent she is a whore. And so you will surely concur in our view that she must be foolish indeed if when Nature gives her a taste for pleasures, she does not seek as many admirers for her charms as she may contrive to encounter men on earth."

"Gifted singer of the Vaucluse," I replied, indicating to him that I was acquainted with his charming poetry, "you who penned your attack upon libertinage with such energy and ingenuity that the reader of your lines comes away worshiping what you condemn,[7] one would need many more virtues than I can claim in order to resist a man of your breed."

And squeezing his hand affectionately, "Ah, believe me," I told him, "I am yours for life, and be equally certain that you will always find in me a student worthy of the great teacher who so generously deigns to undertake her."

The conversation became general and was soon enlivened by philosophy. Albani showed us a letter from Bologna, in which he was advised of the death of one of his intimates who, though occupying a position of foremost importance in the Church, having always lived in libertinage, had held out against conversion, even on his deathbed.

"You knew the fellow," said he to Bernis, "preaching had no effect upon him whatever: keeping his head and his wits up until the very end, he breathed his last while in the arms of that niece he adored, declaring to her that the one thing he regretted in the necessity of denying the existence of heaven was that it barred him from the hope of being someday reunited to her."

"It seems to me," said Cardinal de Bernis, "that these deaths are beginning to become rather frequent: the author of *Alzire* and D'Alembert have made them fashionable."

"Assuredly," Albani went on, "it is a sign of grave weakness to change one's mind as one dies. Have we not time enough to come to a few conclusions during the course of a long life? Our

---

7 See his *Collected Verse*, Vol. I, p. 28, last edition.

vigorous and lucid years should be employed choosing this or that belief, according to it should we live out our span and in it finally die. Still to be perplexed, to be in the grips of uncertainty as we enter our decline is to be heading for a frightful death. You will perhaps maintain that, deranging the organism, the ultimate crisis also unsteadies one's doctrines. Yes, if these doctrines be either newly or timidly embraced, never when they are early adopted and determinedly adhered to, when they are the fruit of labor, of study, of deep meditation, because as such they form a habit and we carry our habits with us to the grave."

"Precisely," said I, glad to have the opportunity of making my way of thinking known to the celebrated libertines in whose company I was, "and if the happy stoicism, which is my creed as it is yours, deprives us of some pleasures, it spares us a good many pains in life and instructs us in how suitably to die. I know not whether it is because I am but twenty-five," I continued, "and therefore prone to behold as far off the moment when I shall be restored to the dust whereof I was made, or whether I derive my comfort and courage from my principles, but it is without the least terror that I contemplate the inevitable disjunction of the molecules now grouped into my existence. Quite convinced that I shall be no worse off after my life than I was before being born, I expect I shall surrender my body to the earth just as calmly, just as impassively as when out of the earth I received it."

"And what lies at the source of this tranquillity? The profound contempt you have always had for religious nonsense," Bernis declared; "had you relapsed but once, that would probably have sufficed to undo you forever. Whence the rule: one cannot become an unbeliever too early."

"But is that so easy as one may think?" Olympia wondered.

"It is far less difficult than some suppose," Albani replied; "but you must cut the tree at the root. If you confine yourself to lopping off branches, fresh shoots will always reappear. 'Tis during youth you must undertake the energetic eradication of prejudices inculcated in childhood. And the most deeply entrenched of them all is that which must be the most fiercely combated, I allude to that futile and chimerical god, and to curing yourself definitively of belief in his existence."

"No, Albani, I do not feel that this operation need be numbered among those demanding any outstanding effort from a young
individual provided he be normally constituted, for the deific
fallacy cannot subsist fifteen minutes in a sane mind. I ask you,
indeed, who is it fails to see that a god, this bundle of contradictions, of quirks and oddities, of incompatible attributes, while he
may heat the imagination, must appear ludicrous to the intellect?
Those who scoff at the idea of a god may be reduced to silence,
so it is thought, by telling them that from the very beginning of
history and everywhere all men have acknowledged some sort of
divinity; that none of the world's countless peoples is without its
belief in an invisible and mighty being which it worships and
venerates; that, finally, no nation, even the most primitive, does
not entertain the certitude of the existence of some power superior
to human nature. Firstly, I deny that fact; but even were it so, can
general conviction transform error into truth? There was a time
when all men believed the sun revolved about the earth, while the
latter remained stationary: did this unanimity of belief transform
the false notion into a reality? There was a time when nobody was
willing to believe the world was round, those who had the temerity
to maintain it were persecuted. How wide has been belief in witches,
in ghosts, in goblins, in apparitions; has the extent of these opinions
made realities of those illusions? Of course not; but even the most
reasonable and sensible people somehow feel obliged to believe in
a universal spirit, without noticing, without bothering to realize,
that all the evidence refutes the excellent qualities ascribed to this
god. Here is a kindly father; large is his family, and from first
to last all its members, I discover, are unhappy. In the kingdom
of this so very wise and so very just sovereign I see crime at the
pinnacle and virtue in irons. You cite the blessings that accrue to
him who subscribes to this system; among them I perceive a host
of ills of all sorts which you stubbornly shut your eyes to. Forced
to admit that your so exceedingly good god, in perpetual self-
contradiction, with the same hand distributes good and evil, to
justify this you are driven to refer me to the fabulous regions of an
afterlife. Better, I retort, better to invent yourself some other god
than the god of theology; for yours is as confused as he is
preposterous, as absurd as he is derisory. A good god who

does evil or tolerates that it be done, a god of sublime equity under whose aegis innocence is always oppressed, a perfect god who produces imperfect works only: ah! agree that the existence of such a god is more pernicious than useful to mankind, and that the best for all concerned would be to annihilate him forever."

"Charlatan," I cried, "you disparage the drugs you trade in: what would become of your power and that of your Sacred College if everybody was as philosophical as you?"

"I am only too well aware," said Bernis, "that error is necessary to us; men must be imposed upon, to that end we are obliged to deceive them. But from this it does not follow that we ought to deceive ourselves. Before what eyes are we to unmask the idol if not before those of our friends or of philosophers who think like us?"

"In that case," said Olympia, "I should be most grateful if you would enlighten my ideas upon a point of morality essential to my peace of mind. They have droned their doctrine in my ears a thousand times, their definition has never satisfied me: it is of human freedom I am speaking; Bernis, what are your views upon this question? 'Tis your sage commentary I desire."

"I shall deliver it," said the illustrious lover of the Marquise de Pompadour, "but I request your whole attention, the matter is a rather abstract one for a woman.

"The faculty of comparing different manners of acting and of deciding which appears best to us, this is what is called *freedom*. Now, does man have or does he not have this faculty of decision? I am prepared to state that he does not and could not possibly have it. All our ideas owe their origin to physical and material causes which operate upon us independently of our will, because these causes result from our intimate organization and from the impact external objects have upon us; motives are in turn the results of these causes, and as a consequence our will is not free. Prey to conflicting motives, we waver, but in the moment when the decision is taken it is not we who determine it; it is enjoined upon us, it is necessitated by the various dispositions of our organs; they always dictate the direction, we always follow their guidance, the choice between this or that alternative is never exercised by us: constantly impelled by necessity, the constant slaves of necessity, that very instant when we believe we gave the clearest demonstration of our freedom is the very one in which we were subject to the most invincible constraint. Irresolution, uncertainty allow us to believe we are free, but this fancied freedom is nothing but the moment when the scales, evenly weighted, hover in equilibrium. The decision is arrived at once one of the two sides tips, and it is not we who intrude our weight to upset the balance, it is the physical objects outside us which act upon us, which reveal us at the mercy of our surroundings, the toy of natural influences, as is the case with animals, with plants. Everything resides in the action of the neural fluid and the difference between a scoundrel and an honest man consists in nought but the greater or lesser activity of the animal spirits that compose this fluid.

" 'I feel,' says Fénelon, 'that I am free, that I am under the absolute guidance of my own counsels.' This gratuitous assertion cannot be proven. What assurance has the Archbishop of Cambrai that when he decides to embrace the pleasant doctrine of Madame Guyon he is free to elect the opposite course? At the very most he could prove to me that he hesitated, but, having acted as he did, I defy him to convince me he was free to act otherwise. 'I modify myself with God,' the same author continues, 'I am the real cause of my own willing.' But, in saying this, Fénelon did not pause to realize that he was rendering his omnipotent god the real cause of all crimes; neither did he pause to realize that nothing so surely makes an end to the omnipotence of god as the freedom of man, for this omnipotence you imagine god to possess, and which for the sake of the discussion I temporarily grant you, is truly omnipotence only because god ordained everything from the very beginning, and it follows from this immutable and definitive ordination that man must be nothing but a passive onlooker, powerless to affect an unalterable *fait accompli* and therefore unfree. If he were free, he could, whenever he so willed, alter and thus destroy this original order, and in so doing show himself a match for god. Here is a problem to which such a partisan of the divinity as Fénelon ought to have devoted maturer reflection.

"Newton skipped gingerly around this formidable difficulty, he dared neither explore it nor even venture too close to it; Fénelon, more forthright although far less learned, adds: 'When I will something, it is in my power not to will it; when I will it not, it is in my power to will it.'

"No. If, Sir, you did not do it when you willed it, that is because it was not in your power to do it and all the physical causes which inflect the scales had tipped them, this time, to the side of not doing the thing in question, and the choice was made before you arrived at a decision. Therefore, Sir, you were not free, and you never are. When you slip into that one of the two alternatives you adopt, it is because you could not possibly have adopted the other. It is your uncertainty that blinded you, you supposed it was in your power to choose because you felt it in your power to hesitate. But this uncertainty, the physical effect of two foreign objects which present themselves simultaneously, and the freedom to choose between these two objects, here are two very different matters."

"That is enough to convince me," Olympia rejoiced; "the idea of having been able not to commit the crimes I indulged in used sometimes to harry my conscience. My unfreedom proven, I am at peace with myself and shall continue without misgivings."

"I urge you to do so," said Albani; "remorse of any kind is utterly futile. Always coming after the fact, it never prevents it, and the passions invariably outshout all scruples when the moment for repeating the evil arrives."

"Very well then, let us now turn to perpetrating some of this delicious evil in order to keep the habit bright and in order to dull our regrets over the evil we have done in the past," said Olympia.

"By all means," replied Cardinal de Bernis, "but this projected evil, in order that it delight us the more, let us perpetrate it thoughtfully and on a broad scale. Lovely Juliette," pursued the ambassador of France, "we understand that you have two pretty girls in your house, who must certainly be as complaisant as you; their beauty has been much bruited about in Rome; we feel, my colleague and I, that they should participate in this evening's libidinous revels and invite you to send for them."

Owing to the terms I was on with Olympia, whose glances pressed me to accept this proposition, I decided I could not very well refuse it and promptly sent a servant to fetch Elise and Raimonde; the conversation now took a different turn.

"Juliette," Bernis said to me, "from the eagerness we have just manifested to become acquainted with the two notoriously attractive creatures you possess, do not rush to the mistaken conclusion that my confrere and I are especially partial to a sex whose femininity we excuse solely upon the condition it behave in manly fashion with us. It is indeed essential we declare to you upon this subject that it were better we refrain from devising any scheme for amusement rather than have it come to nought as a result of your failure, or your companions', to favor us by an absolute resignation to the fantasies this statement implies."

"Truth to tell," Olympia put in, "these explanatory remarks are superfluous with Juliette, from the feats I have seen her perform in this genre I may give you every assurance that she will not disappoint you; and I have no doubt that her two familiars must, if only from the fact they are her protégées, be quite as philosophical as she."

"Good friends," said I, striving to put everyone at ease, "my reputation for lewdness is sufficiently well established to leave no room for doubt upon my manner of conducting myself at such forgatherings. My lubricity, always modeled after the caprice of the men, is always set alight by the fire of their passions. I am truly heated by their desires alone, my keenest pleasure comes only from satisfying all their whims. If what they ask of me is commonplace, my enjoyment is mediocre; let them require the unusual, the rarified, of me, and through sympathy I immediately sense the most violent desire to content them, and never have I known, no, nor conceived of any restriction in acts of libertinage, since the more they outrage polite usage and exceed the bounds of modesty and decency, the greater their contribution to my felicity."

"And all that is quite as it should be," Bernis replied, congratulating me, "and it is greatly to your credit; the prudishness that leads a woman to recalcitrance necessarily invalidates her claim to the consideration of her associates, and to the esteem of reasonable men."

"Such refusals are absurd," advanced Albani, a confirmed sectator of all lubricity's more fanciful practices, "they prove nothing in a woman but stupidity or frigidity, and I do declare to you that to those who feel that a female can only make up for her sex by the most accommodating behavior, a frigid or stupid woman is beyond words contemptible; this is my opinion."

"Well," said I, "what woman could be such an idiot as to imagine a man does more wrong lodging his prick in her behind than sticking it in her cunt? Is not a woman a woman everywhere, and is it not extravagant for her to wish to reserve one part of her body to modesty while consenting to make free of the others? To say this mania can ever outrage Nature, the contention is perfectly ridiculous; would Nature instill in us such a taste for it if it were offensive to her? Why of course not, we may boldly assert, to the contrary, that she cherishes it, that it is favorable to her; that human laws, forever dictated by egoism, upon this subject lack all common sense, and that Nature's, far simpler, far more expressive, must necessarily inspire in us all the tastes that are inimical to a reproduction which, when men undertake it, challenges her right to create the species ever anew, displaces her from her prime function, and reduces her to an inactivity that jars with her energy."

"There is a very pretty thought you have just set forth," said Bernis; "to this theoretical erudition I should now like us to join a little practice. Let me therefore invite you, lovely Juliette, to give us a glimpse of that throne of voluptuousness which, as has been intimated to you already, will be the unique object of our caresses and of our pleasures. With Olympia's we have been long and exhaustively acquainted; yours will suffice for the time being, will you kindly make it available."

The two cardinals having drawn near I promptly unveiled the shrine at which they would worship. My skirts lifted waist-high, their examination began, and it was accompanied, you may be sure, by the most elaborate and the most lubricious details. Albani carried strictness of sodomite manners to the point of disguising meticulously everything in the vicinity which I in my bent-forward position could not help but bring into view: your authentic sodomist will always come unerect at the sight of a cunt. Following the touches there were the kisses, the twittering of tongues. And as with libertines of this feather barbarity is the usual sequel to lubricious impulses, suckings gave way to slaps, then to pinches, after that to bitings, to the vigorous, abrupt, and dry introduction of several fingers into my anus, finally to proposals of a whipping which would probably have been inflicted in short order had my companions not appeared at that juncture. As the adventure I am relating now begins to take on an indisputably serious character, from here on I shall describe it in the cynically frank style which best becomes the subject.

Enchanted by the two delicious creatures I offered to their lewdness, the cardinals soon demanded to make searching investigation of the hindward beauties promised by such a pair of arresting lasses as my Elise and Raimonde. Olympia herself fluttered about them no less ardently than the men. It was then I drew Albani aside, and this is the gist of what I said to him:

"Saintly man," I began, "you do not, I am certain, imagine that my pretty friends and I have come here to satisfy all your brutal whims simply out of piety. You must not be misled by the figure I cut at Rome; it is the fruit of my prostitutions, they alone get me my livelihood: I do not give myself except for money, and the price I ask is not trifling."

"Bernis and I have always held a similar attitude," the Cardinal told me.

"Then we should get on," said I; "indicate to me, if you please, the recompense my friends and I may expect in return for our services. Not until this matter is settled shall they be rendered."

Albani enters into whispered conference with his fellow churchman, then both turn back to me and protest I shall be dealt with in a manner that will leave me no cause for complaint.

"Too vague, these assurances," I retort. "We each of us live from our calling, you know: that of eating little flour and water symbols earns you five or six hundred thousand pounds a year; consider it fitting that from mine, infinitely more agreeable to society, and with merit on its side, I extract as much. You are shortly going to reveal a quantity of turpitudes to me; their witness, I shall possess your secret and could compromise you by letting it out. You will retaliate by denouncing my conduct? But I too have enough gold to be listened to, and you will be ruined when my lawyers unmask you. For six thousand sequins apiece and your agreement to procure an audience with the Pope for me, the whole affair is arranged, the discussion ended, and nothing but pleasures will result for you from all our future relations. Few are the women who can equal me for lewdness, for easiness, for wickedness, and what my uncommonly irregular imagination will add to your joys may very possibly render them quite as incisive, complete, and blissful as any mortal can hope for."

"Fair child," Bernis answered me, "you do not sell yourself cheap; but there is no refusing the wishes of one so endearing, you shall have your interview with His Holiness. The desire you express has already been conceived by him, and since hiding anything from you is farthest from our intentions, know that he has ordered the organizing of this preliminary party, wanting, before making your direct acquaintance, to have a report upon you from us."

"Excellent," said I, "out with the money and I am at your disposition."

"What, must you have it at once?"

"Right away."

"But if we were to pay you first and then you were to take it into your head to—"

"Ah," I interrupted, raising my hand, "I see you have had little experience with women of my nationality. Frank as the country whose name they bear, Frenchwomen wish to be sure of where they stand before concluding a bargain; but they are incapable of breaking it once they have pocketed the money."

At this Albani, upon a gesture from his confrere, ushered me into a small room, unlocked a secretary, and out of it drew banknotes in the sum I had stipulated. One glance at that secretary and the hoard it contained was quite enough to seduce me.

Good, said I to myself the moment I had struck upon the ruse whereby I was to appropriate that treasure, it is all the more certain to succeed considering that the multitude of abominations these rascals are going to enact with me will prevent them from daring to prosecute me afterward.

Before the Cardinal has time to shut up his secretary, I, taking swift advantage of the moment, sink to the floor in a swoon so artfully feigned that an alarmed Albani rushes out in search of aid. Quickly I scramble to my feet, pounce upon the banknotes, the pocketbooks, and in one swoop make away with a million. I close the secretary. Thanks to the hurly-burly, I assure myself, he'll not remember whether he locked the lid or not and, finding it this way, will be less apt to suspect me.

All this accomplished in less time than it takes to tell, I resume my position on the floor; in comes Albani, Olympia and Bernis on his heels. As they enter I open my eyes, fearing lest in the course of efforts to revive me they discover what is not very securely cached beneath my skirts.

"Oh, it's nothing, nothing, I shall be quite all right," say I, fending them off, "my extreme sensitivity renders me subject to nervous cramps every now and then, I am much better now and altogether at your orders."

Just as I had foreseen, Albani, noticing that his secretary was closed, fancied he had left it so and, rather than suspecting anything amiss, was only too happy to lead me into a delicious salon where the projected orgies were to transpire.

There we found eight new personages whose roles were of considerable importance in the mysteries about to be celebrated. These eight individuals included four boys, fifteen years of age and perfect Cupids all; and four fuckers, between eighteen and twenty, and each with a positively monstrous member. Thus were we twelve assembled there for the amusement of the two lecherous collegians, for Olympia's participation in these scenes was far more in the capacity of a victim than a sacrificer: libertinage, greed, ambition put her in the service of these masters, and there her employment was identical to ours.

"So now," said Bernis, "we start. Juliette, and you, Elise and Raimonde, by paying the merry price you ask for your hire we buy the right to address you as one does whores; serve us with corresponding obedience."

"That is only fair," I observed; "do you wish to see us naked?"

"Yes."

"Then will you let us have the use of a dressing room where my companions and I may leave our clothes. . . ."

We are shown to one; when we are alone, I divide up my bulky loot into three parcels, we each stow one into our pockets, remove our garments, and reappear nude in the circle where the cardinals are awaiting us.

"Now heed me," said Bernis. "I shall exercise the master of
ceremonies' functions, Cardinal Albani has consented to this; everyone will hence comply with my instructions. Your asses, Mesdames,
cursorily glanced at a short while ago, must be more narrowly
studied; kindly step forward one by one and offer those articles to
our criticism, the boys will then do likewise, and after having been
viewed, each subject will repair directly to some one of the fuckers
and proceed to dispose him for pleasure, in such wise that the
review once concluded, we may find each of the four fuckers in the
hands of a boy and a woman, and in full bloom."

The inaugural scene is executed: we passed from the first to
the second of those libertines. Our hindward parts were kissed and
palpated, nibbled and gnawed, pinched and scratched, then we
hastily took up our posts by the fuckers, seeing to it that we were
a woman and a boy in attendance upon each.

"And now," said the master of ceremonies, "we must have a
small boy kneel between our thighs and suck our pricks; a big boy
will give each of us his to suckle; to excite him, he will have a
woman's ass ahead of him, and will tongue it; ready to hand we
shall have, to the right, a fucker's prick to dandle, to the left, the
buttocks of a small boy, and the two other women, stationed close
to us and slightly beneath, will tickle our testicles and our assholes.

"For the third scene," Bernis informed us, "we shall remain
lying down as we are at present; 'twill be the women who shall
pump us, two small boys kneeling astride our chests will give us
their assholes to suck, they will kiss, above them, the asses of the
two women who, themselves, will frig the pricks of the small boys.
As for the four fuckers, we shall frig them, having our four hands
free.

"Thus shall we be marshaled in the forthcoming scene," continued the charming cardinal; "the two women who have not just
been sucking us will, kneeling at the edge of these sofas, receive our
pricks into their mouths; the two other women, I mean those who
sucked us a moment ago, will act as our pimps: they will ready the
four fuckers to embugger us one after the other, they will socratize
those fuckers, they will tongue them, they will lick them anally, in
fine, they will exert themselves unstintingly to bring those four
members up high and hard, and when once they see the weapons

burnished and fit to perforate us, they will with their mouths and tongues moisten our vents and carefully pilot the ship into port; the four small boys will present their posterior charms to our lips, lying before us, belly down."

The four fuckers were stout, mettlesome lads: they responded splendidly to our efforts. The two ancient, purple breaches were each sodomized eight times in a row, solidly and impetuously; but for toughness those two rogues outdid the devil and endured this last-mentioned scene as phlegmatically as they had the preceding ones; we were rewarded by not even a shadow of an erection.

"Ah ha," Bernis declared, " 'tis all too plain we require more potent stimulants; ours, you apprehend, is a state of advanced decrepitude. Voracious is the appetite of a satiety nothing satisfies, the malady is like those consuming thirsts which the coolest well-water only increases. Albani is in the same case as I: look there and see whether these accumulated efforts have hoisted his prick even a single notch. Let us not be disheartened, however, we may try other things and indeed we must, a stern Nature commands it. You are a dozen; divide. Let each squad be composed of a pair of fuckers, two small boys, two women: the first will work upon my old friend, the second upon me. Ranged about us, everybody in his turn shall be frigged by us, shall suck us successively, and one by one shit into our mouths."

This disgusting operation saw the pricks of our decayed adversaries unwrinkle a little and upon the basis of these unmistakable albeit faint signs, they judged themselves ready to essay more serious attacks.

"The sixth scene will be along these lines," said the director; "Albani, whose faculties appear to be about as aroused as mine, shall sodomize Elise, I am going to embugger Juliette; the four fuckers, prepared by Olympia and Raimonde, will doctor our asses; the small boys, lying atop us, will present to our kisses, some their pricks, some their buttocks."

The groups form; but our champions, deceived by their desires, deliver too light an assault upon the tabernacle, falter at its gate, and limp away in defeat and chagrin.

"Bah, I expected as much," Albani grumbled, "I shall never

understand why you persist in wanting to have us embugger women! With a boy I'd have sustained no such affront."

"Very well then, we shall change," said the ambassador, "what is there to prevent us?"

But no happier is the issue of this fresh onslaught; our cardinals are fucked, to be sure, but fuck they cannot; friggings, suckings are to no avail, their antiquated tools shrivel instead of deploying, and Bernis announces that, his colleague faring as poorly as he, they shall pursue the war in a different manner.

"Mesdames," says that great man, "since kindly treatment gets us nowhere with you, harsher methods must be resorted to. Do you know the effects of fustigation? It might be that which is needed; we shall see."

With these words he seizes me, while from a closet Albani brings forth an apparatus of such curious design as to deserve special description.

I was bound facing the wall and a short pace from it, my hands high above my head, my feet on the floor. Once pinioned, in front of me Bernis placed a kind of prayer-stool, but of steel, its upper rung a sword-blade, razor-sharp and its edge touching my belly. Needless to say, I drew back from that menacing glaive: that is, I thrust my flanks back toward Bernis; which was precisely what he wanted me to do: never had I struck a prettier pose. Grasping a handful of withes, the lecher begins all of a sudden to thrash me with all his might, and so terrible are those blows that before ten of them have fallen the blood is streaming down my thighs. Albani advanced the infernal machine several inches nearer, gone was all possibility of swaying before the strokes to lessen their impact, and I must stand firm to the storm: however, I was able to weather it without undue difficulty, being, very fortunately, thoroughly inured to a ceremony which had often been my delight in the past. Those who followed me had not such a merry time of it. Elise, who replaced me in that cruel harness, gashed her belly and screamed the whole while her flagellation lasted. Raimonde suffered a great deal too. Olympia passed valiantly through the ordeal, she was fond of whipping; this vexation would only stimulate her. Bernis now turned his withes over to Albani, we all four had a second time to undergo the operation, and at last our rascals' pricks came tottering up. Wary of women after that earlier skirmish, they chose small boys for their prey; while asodomizing they were flogged, and their attitudes were such that they were able to kiss the vulvas, assholes, and pricks artistically presented to their libertine attentions. And exacerbated Nature rescued their honor; they loosed almost simultaneous discharges. They are my buttocks Albani kisses during his crisis, and it is so violent, so furious is the blackguard's joy, that upon my behind he leaves the imprint of the two solitary stumps still surviving in his foul mouth after half a dozen visitations of the pox. Raimonde's ass, embraced by Bernis, came off little better; but 'twas with his fingernails and a penknife this roué had molested it, reducing it to tatters by the time his spasm supervened. A brief pause ensued, then the orgies were resumed.

In the opening scene of this second act we were each dispatched into the arms of one fucker after another, who encunted us while the two debauchees peered at our asses and to encourage our performance barbarously pricked, pinched, and beat us in a thousand various ways. That done, the couples were rolled over, up came the four masculine asses; the four small boys sodomized them, and the cardinals ass-fucked those four small boys, but without discharging. From bum-stuffing the fuckers the little chaps moved aboard us women, the fuckers revenged themselves upon those catamites and next embuggered us while our cunts were licked by the small boys. After that, these idyllic little creatures were stood against the wall, attached, the steel chair was slid into position, and they were lashed to ribbons. At this point our two fauns were overtaken by the desire to spill some more seed. Like tigers sensing prey somewhere near, they stalk through our midst, casting savage glares to right and to left. They order the men to seize and to whip us, while they watch they sodomize one small boy apiece and kiss the ass of another. Their fuck dribbles forth for the second time, and we remove to table.

A very delicious repast it was that we were served, a very picturesque one; with your leave I shall describe it in some detail.

In the middle of a circular room stood a round table set for six; two places were occupied by the cardinals, Olympia, Raimonde, Elise, and I occupied the four others. A yard or so behind our chairs was the lowest in a series of four tiered benches ringing the table concentrically, forming a kind of amphitheater. There, fifty of Rome's choicest courtesans, hidden beneath masses of flowers, allowed of themselves only their behinds to be seen, in such a way that those clusters of asses peeping out from the lilacs, the pinks, the foxgloves seemed scattered about haphazardly, and provided, under the same aspect, the image of everything of the supremely delicious that Nature and lasciviousness can offer. Twenty Cupids represented by pretty bardashes formed a dome overhead, and the room was lit by the tapers those little gods held in their hands. At the touch of a lever an ingenious device removed one course and brought the next on: the rim of the table, where the company's plates and silverware lay, remained stationary, but the center of the table sank away and rose again with six little golden gondolas containing exquisite and most delicate viands. Six young boys, provocatively garbed as so many Ganymedes, waited upon us and poured out the rare wines. Our libertines, upon whose instructions we had dressed for the meal, expressed their wish that we unclothe ourselves again, but gradually, as the Babylonian whore used to do. Thus when the hors-d'oeuvres were brought on it was the kerchief that was put aside, the bodice came unlaced when the omelettes arrived, and so on until the fruit when the last stitch was discarded; whereupon the libertinage and nastiness increased. Dessert was served in fifteen miniature boats of green and gold porcelain. Twelve little girls of six and seven, adorned only by garlands of myrtle and roses, filled our glasses with foreign wines and liqueurs. Heads are gaily awhirl, to our libertines' spirits Bacchus restores all the energy necessary to tense the erector nerve, the disorder and uproar are at their height.

"Genial poet," said the master of the house to Cardinal de Bernis, "two bits of enchanting doggerel are going about Rome these days, wits attribute them to you: our guests are persons that this form of literature is not lost upon, pray favor us with a recitation."

"They are mere paraphrases," replied Bernis, "and I am rather surprised at their publicity, for I have shown them to nobody but the Pope."

"Little wonder then if they are the talk of the town. But come, Cardinal, we are eager to hear them from the author."

"Certainly," said Bernis, "I have nothing to conceal from philosophers like those present. One is an adaptation of the famous sonnet of Des Barreaux,[8] the other of the *Ode to Priapus*. I shall begin with the first.[9]

> Sot Dieu! tes jugements sont pleins d'atrocité,
> Ton unique plaisir consiste à l'injustice:
> Mais j'ai tant fait de mal, que ta divinité
> Doit, par orgueil au moins, m'arrêter dans la lice.
>
> Foutu Dieu! la grandeur de mon impiété
> Ne laisse en ton pouvoir que le choix du supplice,
> Et je nargue les fruits de ta férocité.
> Si ta vaine colère attend que je périsse,
>
> Contente, en m'écrasant, ton désir monstrueux,
> Sans craindre que des pleurs s'écoulent de mes yeux,
> Tonne donc! je m'en fouts; rends-moi guerre pour guerre:
>
> Je nargue, en périssant, ta personne et ta loi.
> En tel lieu de mon coeur que frappe ton tonnerre,
> Il ne le trouvera que plein d'horreur pour toi.

These lines having been warmly applauded, Bernis delivered his *Ode*.

> Foutre des Saints et de la Vierge,
> Foutre des Anges et de Dieu!
> Sur eux tous je-branle ma verge,
> Lorsque je veux la mettre en feu . . .
> C'est toi que j'invoque à mon aide,
> Toi qui, dans les culs, d'un vit raide,
> Lanças le foutre à gros bouillons!

---

8 Jacques Vallée, Seigneur des Barreaux, whose connections with Théophile de Viau were intimate, was born at Paris in the year 1602. The impunity and the libertinage of these two rakes was quite unparalleled. The well-known sonnet alluded to here (and it is one of the most execrable pieces of poetry to be found in that or any other age) was, it is said, composed during an illness; Vallée afterward disavowed it. And indeed it is not a production any healthy man would own to. Paraphrased in this manner, our readers may perhaps find it somewhat less unendurable.

9 Cardinal de Bernis addressed the convives in Italian; Juliette has rendered his scandalous verses into French. Here we reproduce her version, which reveals much poetic skill, much verve. Even if these were not entirely lost in English translation, they would be less than sufficiently appreciated by the English reader whose susceptibilities they might offend.—*Tr*.

Du Chaufour, soutiens mon haleine,
Et, pour un instant, à ma veine
Prête l'ardeur de tes couillons.[10]

Que tout bande, que tout s'embrase;
Accourez, putains et gitons:
Pour exciter ma vive extase,
Montrez-moi vos culs frais et ronds,
Offrez vos fesses arrondies,
Vos cuisses fermes et bondies,
Vos engins roides et charnus,
Vos anus tout remplis de crottes;
Mais, surtout, déguisez les mottes:
Je n'aime à foutre que des culs.

Fixez-vous, charmantes images,
Reproduisez-vous sous mes yeux;
Soyez l'objet de mes hommages,
Mes législateurs et mes Dieux!
Qu'à Giton l'on élève un temple
Où jour et nuit l'on vous contemple,
En adoptant vos douces moeurs.
La merde y servira d'offrandes,
Les gringuenaudes de guirlandes,
Les vits de sacrificateurs.

Homme, baleine, dromadaire,
Tout, jusqu'à l'infâme Jésus,
Dans les cieux, sous l'eau, sur la terre,
Tout nous dit que l'on fout des culs;
Raisonnable ou non, tout s'en mêle,
En tous lieux le cul nous appelle,
Le cul met tous les vits en rut,
Le cul, du bonheur est la voie,
Dans le cul gît toute la joie,
Mais, hors du cul, point de salut.

Dévots, que l'enfer vous retienne:
Pour vous seuls sont faites ses lois;
Mais leur faible et frivole chaîne
N'a sur nos esprits aucun poids.
Aux rives du Jourdain paisible,
Du fils de Dieu la voix horrible

---

[10] Chaufour: everybody knows the story of this hero of buggery, burned publicly at the stake on the Place de Grève by judgment and order of the whores whose power was uncontested in Paris at that time.

Tâche en vain de parler au coeur:
Un cul paraît,[11] passe-t-il outre?
Non, je vois bander mon jean-foutre.
Et Dieu n'est plus qu'un enculeur.

Au giron de la sainte Eglise,
Sur l'autel même où Dieu se fait,
Tous les matins je sodomise
D'un garçon le cul rondelet.
Mes chers amis, que l'on se trompe
Si de la catholique pompe
On peut me soupçonner jaloux.
Abbés, prélats, vivez au large:
Quand j'encule et que je décharge,
J'ai bien plus de plaisirs que vous.

D'enculeurs l'histoire fourmille,
On en rencontre à tout moment.
Borgia, de sa propre fille,
Lime à plaisir le cul charmant,
Dieu le Père encule Marie;
Le Saint-Esprit fout Zacharie:
Ils ne foutent tous qu'à l'envers.
Et c'est sur un trône de fesses
Qu'avec ses superbes promesses,
Dieu se moque de l'univers.

Saint Xavier aussi, ce grand sage
Dont on vante l'esprit divin,
Saint Xavier vomit peste et rage
Contre le sexe féminin.
Mais le grave et charmant apôtre
S'en dédommagea comme un autre.
Interprétons mieux ses leçons:
Si, de colère, un con l'irrite,
C'est que le cul d'un jésuite
Vaut à ses yeux cent mille cons.

Près de là, voyez Saint Antoine
Dans le cul de son cher pourceau,
En dictant les règles du moine,[12]
Introduire un vit assez beau.

---

[11] That belonging to John the Baptist, the beloved bardash of Mary's son.

[12] He is usually regarded as the patriarch of monks and the institutor of their rules.

A nul danger il ne succombe;
L'éclair brille, la foudre tombe,
Son vit est toujours droit et long.
Et le coquin, dans Dieu le Père
Mettrait, je crois, sa verge altière
Venant de foutre son cochon.

Cependant Jésus dans l'Olympe,
Sodomisant son cher papa,
Veut que saint Eustache le grimpe,
En baisant le cul d'Agrippa.[13]
Et le jean-foutre, à Madeleine,
Pendant ce temps, donne la peine
De lui chatouiller les couillons.
Amis, jouons les mêmes farces:
N'ayant pas de saintes pour garces,
Enculons au moins des gitons.

O Lucifer! toi que j'adore,
Toi qui fait briller mon esprit;
Si chez toi l'on foutait encore,
Dans ton cul je mettrais mon vit.
Mais puisque, par un sort barbare,
L'on ne bande plus au Ténare,
Je veux y voler dans un cul.
Là, mon plus grand tourment, sans doute,
Sera de voir qu'un démon foute,
Et que mon cul n'est point foutu.

Accable-moi donc d'infortunes,
Foutu Dieu qui me fais horreur;
Ce n'est qu'à des âmes communes
A qui tu peux foutre malheur:
Pour moi je nargue ton audace.
Que dans un cul je foutimasse,
Je me ris de ton vain effort;
J'en fais autant des lois de l'homme:
Le vrai sectateur de Sodome
Se fout et des Dieux et du sort.

The Cardinal was acclaimed by vivats and loud hurrahs. This ode was considered richer, far stronger than that of Piron, unanimously charged with cowardice for having inserted the gods of

---

[13] Last king of the Jews.

fable into his work when he ought only to have ridiculed those of Christianity.

More electrified than ever, the company got up from table in a state of general and utter drunkenness to stagger off into another magnificent salon. There we found the fifty courtesans whose asses we had observed during the banquet, there too was the brotherhood of six little boy-servants, and the dozen dessert maidens. The delicate age of those little nymphs, their interesting faces wrought prodigiously upon our lechers, who leapt like very lions upon the two youngest. Failing to fuck them, their wrath mounted. At length they bound them, wheeled forth their infernal machine, and with needle-tipped martinets hammered and hacked away at the tender little prisoners; we frigged them, sucked them during this; they stiffened. Two other maids are laid hold of; the libertines succeed in sodomizing them by dint of art; but wishing to husband their forces, they abandon these victims and spring upon new ones: their lubricity feeds now upon little boys, now upon little girls; all of that infant generation passes through their hands, and it is only after having each depucelated seven or eight children of the one sex and the other that the flame of their lust sputters out, Albani's in the ass of a ten-year-old boy, Bernis' in the bowels of a six-year-old girl. Both ecclesiastics, dead drunk, tumble onto couches and are sound asleep in a trice. . . . We dress.

Fuddled from alcohol and fucking though I was, the idea of theft was ever clear in my head and my taste for it in no wise dampened: I remembered that first raid into Albani's treasury had not entirely emptied it. So, telling Raimonde to distract Olympia, with Elise to help me I return for another assault upon the Cardinal's secretary. I locate the key, we pillage everything in sight. This second capture added to the first brings my burglaries to a total of fifteen hundred thousand francs; and we leave, Olympia having noticed nothing. Fancy, good friends, how pleased my gentleman consort was when he saw me return home laden with such booty. Several days later, however, Olympia came knocking on my door.

"The Cardinal has been robbed of better than a million," she informed me; "it was his niece's dowry the thieves took. Not that he suspects you, Juliette, but he wonders whether the deed, perpetrated the same day the party was held at his villa, may not

Throughout these and the rest of my disorders the thought of the charming Duchess Grillo preyed ever upon my mind. No more than twenty years of age, for the past eighteen months bound in matrimony to a man of sixty whom she detested, Honorine Grillo was, carnally speaking, still as much a stranger to that old faun as the day her mother had withdrawn her from the Ursuline convent at Bologna to marry her to him. Not that the Duke had made no efforts to vanquish his wife's resistance; but up until now they had been fruitless. Only twice had I called upon the Duchess, the first time on a visit of courtesy to present my letters of recommendation, the second for the sake of once again savoring the inconceivable pleasure I experienced while in her society. This third time I went fully determined to declare my passion to her, firmly resolved to satisfy it regardless of the obstacles her virtue might put in my way.

It was after one of those lubricious toilettes which are nothing if not apt to seduce and ensnare whatever stoutly armored heart that I presented myself at her residence. Luck smiled upon my schemes, I found the darling alone. After venturing the initial compliments I let my eyes speak; modesty bade my quarry avoid them. For amorous glances I then substituted encomiums and coquetry; catching one of the Duchess' hands, "Delicious woman," I exclaimed, "if there be a God in heaven and if he be just, then surely you are the happiest woman in all the world, as you are the most beautiful."

"'Tis your indulgence leads you to say such things, but I am able to be fair to myself."

"Oh, Madame, fairness would demand that the very gods relinquish their altars to you: she who is so wonderfully deserving of a universe's homage ought to dwell nowhere save in a temple."

And I seized her other hand, too, squeezed and kissed them both while speaking.

"Why do you flatter me?" asked Honorine, the color rising into her cheeks.

"Because I adore you."

"But—but can women fall in love with women?"

"And why not! The greater their sensibility, the greater their capacity for worshiping the beautiful, whether it be in male

have been the doing of your two companions. Do you know anyt[...]
of the matter?"

And here, as was my custom, I consulted my imagination [...]
some infernal horror to cover the one by which I had soiled myse[...]
I had indirectly learned that on the very eve of my visit to Vi[...]
Albani, another of his nieces, whom he had endeavored to seduc[...]
had fled the Cardinal's palace to escape the threat to her virtu[...]
I remind Olympia of that niece's abrupt departure, have he[...]
remark the coincidence, my insinuations are willingly listened to
and swiftly communicated to the Cardinal who from weakness
or from spite, perhaps simply to be revenged for a slight, straightway puts all the Papal State's bloodhounds on his niece's trail. The
poor girl is overtaken on the confines of the Kingdom of Naples
at the very moment she has sought refuge in a Cistercian convent;
arrested in that institution and from there dragged back to Rome,
she is thrown into a dungeon. Sbrigani recruits witnesses to testify
against her, it now but remains to establish what she has done
with the money; other witnesses, also suborned by us, give evidence
that she handed all the fortune over to a certain Neapolitan who
had left Rome at the same time as she, and who, they allege, is
her paramour. . . . All these depositions fit so nicely one to the next,
each is made to appear so plausible, the whole so conclusive that
the trial ends on the seventh day with the poor creature's sentence
to death. She was decapitated on San Angelo Square, and I had
the pleasure of watching the execution, seated beside Sbrigani who
maintained three active fingers in my cunt during all those grisly
and rousing proceedings.

"O Supreme Being!" I cried inwardly once the axe stood in
the block and the severed head lay in the basket, "thus is innocence
avenged by thee, thus dost thou make triumph the cause of those of
thy children who serve thee best in their faithful practice upon
earth of the goodliness whereof thine attributes are the perfect
image. I rob the Cardinal, that niece of his he lusts after flees him
to prevent a grave sin from being committed: my crime's reward
is spasms of joy, she perishes on the scaffold. Holy and Sublime
Being! such are thy ways, such the fates whereunto thy loving
hand guideth us mortals—aye, 'tis fitting, is it not, that we adore
thee!"

or female form. Wise women shun relations with men, relations so fraught with danger . . . those they may entertain with one another are so sweet—ah, my dearest Honorine, I must call you Honorine, why might I not be all at once your intimate friend . . . your lover . . . your mate?"

"Mad, reckless creature!" replied the Duchess, "do you actually suppose you could be all those things?"

"I am confident of it, yes," I answered heatedly as I hugged her in my arms, "yes, and above all the last of them, that shall I be par excellence if you would have it so, my angel."

And my fiery tongue glides into her mouth.

Honorine receives the kiss of love, receives it without offense, and when I essay a second, love itself returns it: the freshest, the prettiest little tongue slips forth to quiver between my burning lips. My boldness grows; drawing aside the veils screening the loveliest of bosoms, with impassioned caresses I assault those alabaster breasts, my joyous tongue lovingly teases their pink nipples, while my hands stray over the rest. Stirred, Honorine bends to my will; the keenest interest fills her big blue eyes, gradually they begin to sparkle, tears of pleasure gather there, and I . . . I, like unto a Bacchante, wild, drunk from lust . . . unable to stop, unable to go fast enough, I strive to communicate to her the ardor which devours me. . . .

"What are you doing?" Honorine demands, but in a sigh. "Are you not forgetting your sex and mine?"

"Ah, dearest love," I rejoin, "may we not sometimes outrage Nature if thereby we discover how to render her better homage? And how unhappy we must be, alack, if we refrained from seeking compensation for the wrongs we suffer at her hands."

And ever more enterprising, I dare loosen the ribbons of a lawn petticoat and now have in my grasp almost all the charms whose possession I so passionately covet. Startled—electrified by my hoarse sighs and labored panting—Honorine ceases entirely to resist. I press her backward, she is now lying upon the couch, avidly I spread her thighs apart and she gives me to ruffle delightedly that fluffiest little bush, and to fondle the most sweetly swelling little mound you could ever hope to see; one of my arms encircles the reclining Duchess' waist, with that hand I stroke one of her breasts, my mouth fastens upon the other; my fingers had already begun to probe for her clitoris, I was testing its sensitivity. . . . Great God! how it twitched and thrilled. Honorine came nigh to fainting under those deft pollutions of mine. Despite the struggles of her hard-pressed virtue, some moans announce its rout; at that signal I redouble my caresses.

Nobody is more skilled than I at aiding pleasure to attain its crisis. . . . I sense my darling's need of help: some pumping is required to make the honeyed sap flow. Few women, it should be said in passing, few women sufficiently well realize the need their cunt has to be sucked as their fuck builds to the discharging point; and nevertheless at such moments there is no diviner service one may render them. With what ardor I now fulfilled this task; kneeling between Honorine's glorious thighs, I clutch her flanks and lift them to me, I drive my tongue into her cunt, I suck it, I pump it, and in the meantime my nuzzling promotes the erection of her clitoris. What buttocks my hands knead! Never had Venus ones so lovely! I felt called upon to broaden this into a general conflagration; these crises, you know, cannot be too carefully tended, too lavishly ministered to. All restrictions must be barred; and if to the woman you frig Nature had given twenty avenues for receiving pleasure, you would have to attack them all with a view to increasing the tumult in her a hundredfold.[14] So I go in quest of her pretty little anus in order that the titillations produced by a digit buried there may be added to those my mouth is causing her on the other side. So tiny, so strait, is this cunning little hole I have difficulty finding it, but there it is at last, one of my fingers pops into it. . . . Delicious episode! ah, never do you fail to have your effect upon a woman of sensibility. No sooner has this charming little vent been invaded than Honorine sighs . . . she smiles, is in rap-

---

[14] Nine out of every ten men who take it upon themselves to frig women are less than adequately convinced of their patient's urgent need at such time to have pleasure penetrate into her through every pore. He who would procure her a voluptuous emission must hence manage in such sort that he keeps his tongue in her mouth, is able to fondle her breasts, has a finger in her vagina, another upon her clitoris, a third in her asshole. Idle were his expectations of attaining the mark who neglects but one of these circumstances. Whence it is that at least three are required in order to drive a woman truly out of her mind.

tures, this heavenly woman! She discharges, she is in the sweetest ecstasy imaginable, and 'tis to me her delirium is owing.

"Ah, my angel, my beloved angel, I adore you," that dove says to me as she opens her eyes to the light, "you slew me with happiness. How ever can I repay you?"

"In kind, my dear, in kind," I reply, snatching off my skirts. And taking hold of her hand, clapping it to my cunt: "Frig me, my love, frig me into a lather. Great heaven, what else is there to do but frig?"

However, like all well-bred women, Honorine was clumsy: she aroused desires in me and knew not how to cope with a single one of them. I was obliged to give her lessons.

Coming at length to the conclusion that she might do a better job with her tongue than her fingers, I have her get between my legs and she licks my cunt while I take my frigging personally in hand. Here Honorine performed creditably. Prodigiously excited by the delightful creature, I shot three discharges into her mouth. . . . Overcome now by a desire to see her entirely nude, I raise her up, rid her of all she is wearing. . . . Oh, God! this sudden splendor that met my gaze, 'twas as though I were looking upon the star of daylight when in springtime it shines through a long winter's mists. Ah, I may truly say that I had never seen so beautiful an ass, never. What radiant fairness! What gleaming exquisite skin, how soft! What breasts, what hips! And that waist; those incomparable buttocks! Ah, that ass. Sublime altar of love and of pleasure, not a day goes by, no, not a single day passes but my imagination dwelling yearningly upon you, as it were stretching forth its arms toward you, offers you some fresh homage. . . .

I could not resist the sight of that divine posterior. Manlike in my tastes as in my thinking, how bitterly I regretted that I was unable to burn some more real incense before my idol. I kissed it, opened it and gazed ecstatically therein, my tongue sounded it and while it thrilled in that celestial hole I refrigged lovely Honorine's clitoris: thus did I wheedle a fresh discharge from her. But the more I aroused her, the greater was my distress at being powerless to arouse her farther still.

"Oh, my dearest one," said I, my heart heavy because of this regret, "be sure that when next we come together I shall have by me some instrument capable of dealing more telling blows than may a tongue: I would be your lover, your husband, I have told you so: I wish to have you as might a man."

"Ah, do anything with me you want," was the Duchess' gentle reply to this, "multiply the proofs of your love, in return I shall give you back twice as many tokens of mine."

Honorine wishes now to see me nude, her eyes rove over my body; but she is so newly come to pleasure that she ignores the art of giving it to me. . . . Ah, it mattered not to my flaming soul: she gazed upon me, she examined me: I was fucked by the rays of her glances, and extreme was my happiness. O lubricious women! if ever you are in the position I was in, you will sympathize with me, you will taste the despair wherein one is hurled by thwarted desires, and like me you will curse Nature for having inspired in you feelings which the buggeress cannot satisfy. . . . We fell to frolicking anew. Though not able to give each other all the relief we both needed, we nevertheless gave each other as much as we could, and upon separating promised to meet soon again.

Just two days after this scene Olympia called upon me; she had found out I had been to see the Duchess; she was jealous.

"Honorine is attractive, it cannot be denied," said she, "neither will you deny that she is stupid; I defy her ever to give you as much pleasure as I. Moreover, Juliette, there is that husband of hers. He has a keen nose, you would be running a grave risk if he were to begin to scent this intrigue."

"Dear friend," said I to Princess Borghese, "allow me a fortnight, I ask no more: by then I shall have made my attitude toward Honorine quite clear to you. For the time being, I shall confess this, and be reassured by it: now and then I may divert myself with virtue but only crime has the place of privilege in my heart."

"Then we shall speak no more of the matter," said the Princess, embracing me warmly; "you have said enough to dispel my fears. I shall be there when you emerge from your illusion, and I doubt not but that it will be short-lived with Grillo.

"But let us change the subject," she went on. "Were you not surprised the other day to see me play the whore as merrily as you?"

"No, truthfully, I was not," said I. "Knowing the kind of mind you have, I could expect libertinage to be your one concern."

"Ha, I have others as well, my dear. Those two cardinals rule the roost at the Vatican, and I have my reasons for humoring them; apart from that they pay me liberally, and I too am fond of money. Come now, Juliette, be honest with me, you did rob Albani, didn't you? Have no fear, I'll not let your secret out nor reproach your deed, not I, for I too rather incline toward little knaveries of the sort, and who knows? I may have pilfered as much from those rascals as you: theft is delicious, my angel, it heats. It can even precipitate a discharge—this is usually the case with me. It is base to steal for your living, delightful to steal at the behest of passion."

Such and so many were the things Olympia and I had done together that I considered I could depend upon her tact and discretion. It seems to me that one may safely confess a peccadillo to the person who acts as your collaborator in a major crime.

"That you come to know me better, this is one of my cherished aims," I told Olympia; "your conjectures flatter me: yes, I committed that theft. More, I helped send to her doom the innocent who was beheaded for my deed, and this compilation of little bits of mischief proved enough to cause me some voluptuous discharging."

"Ah yes, by fuck, such words have a familiar ring to me. For it was hardly a year ago I did just about the same thing, and I am well acquainted with all the amenities which result from these breaches of good conduct.

"But my chief purpose in coming to see you is to announce that we shall shortly be supping with the Pope; Braschi would have us participate in his appalling excesses. Appalling, I repeat, for the Vicar of Christ is to an astounding degree depraved, impious, bloodthirsty; it must be seen to be believed. Near the place where these orgies will be celebrated is the treasury room of the State, I know how to unbar its door: there are millions there for the taking. And trust me, Juliette, taking them will not be difficult: His Holiness will not dare so much as object, not after the things we shall have been witness to. You will join me in this expedition?"

"Of course."

"I may have confidence in you?"

"Can you doubt it when the question is one of a crime?"

"Grillo must never hear anything of this, Juliette."

"Count somewhat more heavily upon my intelligence; and think not, dear Princess, that a passing fancy could cause me to compromise or neglect a passion: indulging a taste amuses me, but it is infamy I take seriously, it alone has access to my heart, it alone has the power to inflame me, only to it do I really belong."

"Ah, the properties of crime are unique," Olympia affirmed, "nothing else has such an exciting effect upon me: compared to it love is so drab, so puny! Oh indeed, my friend," she went on, "I have reached the point where if I am to be stirred even in the slightest, a crime must be of uncommon strength. Those which vengeance led me to commit seem contemptible now that you have introduced me to those we perform for lewdness' sake."

"Quite so," I agreed, "the most enjoyable crimes are the motiveless ones. The victim must be perfectly innocent: if we have sustained some harm from him it legitimates the harm we do him, and lost to our iniquity is the keen pleasure of exerting itself gratuitously. Evil must be done, bad one must be, this is the great and indispensable thing; and is it possible when your victim, no better than you, merits his fate? Ingratitude is to be recommended at all times and especially in this case," I continued, "your ingratitude is a further affliction to the person you outrage: you force him to regret ever having given you pleasure, and this in itself can afford you an enormous one."

"Yes, yes, I follow your meaning," Olympia replied, "and I believe I have some rare joys of this kind awaiting me.

"My father lives, he is forever outdoing himself in kindness toward me, he heaps gifts upon me, adores me; twenty times over have I discharged at the thought of severing such a tie: I dislike indebtedness, it weighs disagreeably upon my heart, stifles me— I long to be rid of this burden. Moreover, 'tis said parricide is a very black crime. You have no idea how it tempts me. . . . But listen to me now, Juliette, judge to what lengths my perfidious imagination goes. You must change your customary role. Were someone else to avow a similar desire, you would, I know, cheer him on, clear obstacles from his path; you would prove to him that when all has been considered, there is, strictly speaking, no wrong whatever in killing one's father; and as you are exceedingly clever and eloquent, too, your arguments would soon convince him. I shall ask you to employ very different tactics here; we shall retire together into some quiet nook, you will frig me; while you do so you will have me appreciate the full horror of the crime in question; you will represent the punishments that are meted out to parricides, you will harangue me, exhort me, endeavor to scare me into abandoning my plan; the greater your efforts to deter, to convert me, the more fixed I shall become in the idea of the crime I am projecting, and unless I am mistaken, a voluptuous tension of prodigious violence ought to be engendered by this conflict— whence I shall emerge victorious."

"To ensure the complete success of the scene you meditate," I ventured to suggest, "third persons should figure in it; and it will be necessary not that I frig you throughout, but that I chastise you. There is nothing for it, I shall have to whip you."

"Whip me? Why, of course, Juliette! You are right, infinitely right," said Olympia; "your conceptions are more delicate than mine. But who shall these third persons be?"

"Raimonde and Elise; they will suck you, they will deliciously frig you during my discourse; and I shall beat you."

"And after that we shall go straight to work?"

"Have you the instruments for it?"

"I do."

"What kind?"

"Three or four sorts of poison; these are commodities of everyday use at Rome, as easily to be had as an ounce of salt or a piece of soap."

"Those you have purchased are violent?"

"No, rather slow as a matter of fact. Mild but dependable."

"That won't do. If one is to enjoy the thing properly, the victim in such cases must suffer, his agonies must be hideous. While he is in their throes one frigs oneself, and how do you expect to discharge if his pain is not excruciating? Here," said I, taking from a drawer a small packet of one of Durand's most potent confections, "have the author of your days swallow some of this: his miseries will last forty hours and they will be almost unbearable to see, his body will literally come to pieces before your eyes."

"Oh, fuck! Quickly, Juliette, let us make haste, the mere sound of your words is causing me to discharge."

Elise and Raimonde enter; Olympia bends over them both, presenting me her superb buttocks, bare; I flog her with skill, caressingly at first, then fiercely, then savagely, and during this ritual address her in roughly these terms:

"For certain, the most dreadful crime in all the world is to take the life of the person who gave life to us," I begin. "The object of his devotion and of his solicitude, do we not incur an immense debt to him, do we not owe him our eternal thanks? Can we have any more sacred duty than to protect and care for him? Criminal must be the very idea of harming a hair on his head, and that wretch who entertains it merits the very promptest and extremest punishment, and none can be too heavy nor too awful for a horror of this magnitude. Ages were to pass before our ancestors could even comprehend the thing, and 'twas only in fairly recent times they promulgated laws to repress the scoundrel who assassinates his father. The monster able to be this forgetful of all natural sentiments deserves to be put to yet uninvented tortures, and everything of the very cruelest that can be imagined strikes me as retribution too mild for this atrocity. And no warning can be too solemn for him in whom barbarity, ingratitude, the repudiation of all duties, the renunciation of all principles are such that he is capable even of dreaming of destroying that father whence he has received the blessing of existence. Ye furies of Tartarus, come howling out of your dens, come hither your own selves and organize torments fitting to this revolting execration, and however unspeakable those you devise, they shall be less than what the offense demands."

And while speaking I was plying the lash, I was tearing whole patches of skin off my whore who, her brain sotted by lust, crimes, and delights, was discharging and redischarging uninterruptedly under the deft hands polluting her.

"You make no mention of religion," said she, "I should like to have you approach my crime from the theological side and thunder a little about the outrage to the divinity it is purported to constitute. I should like you to talk about God to me, to tell me how sorely I offend him; to delineate the inferno where demons will roast me after mortals have massacred my body."

"Ha!" I then cried, "ha! abject sinner, have you any inkling of the enormity of the insult you are about to hurl at the Supreme Being in consummating this abomination? That mighty Lord, image of all virtues, that God who is our Father in this world, must he not be dismayed and aghast at an offense which compromises him so grievously? Oh, indeed, thoughtless one, be certain that the very worst of hell's tortures are reserved for those who have damned themselves by this frightful crime you plot, and that apart from the remorse you shall be racked by in this world, in the next you shall be rent by all the material woes wherewith a just God shall smite ye."

"I would have more on this chapter," said the libertine Princess; "gratify me now with an account both of the physical pains of the ordeal in store for me and of the shameful blot which must forever attach to the memory of me and remain ineffaceably upon my family."

"Lost soul," I thereupon exclaimed, "is it then as nought to you, this cloud of shame under which, as a consequence of your base crime, all your descendants will lie everlastingly? Behold your posterity which, for the brand marking its brow, dares not raise its head and cringes in the sight of all mankind; there in the depths of the grave into which your crimes are soon to send you, do you hear the later generations of your line curse the name of her who brought them into disgrace and ignominy? This so noble and distinguished name, do you see it sullied by your horrors? And the awful torments awaiting you, say, does your imagination visualize them? Do you feel the avenging iron suspend its tremendous rebuke above you? And fall to detach this beautiful head from this impure body whose foul, odious lusts can bring you to the point of committing such a deed? It shall be horrible, this pain, which abates not till long after the head has been chopped off the shoulders; but even were that not so, consider that Nature, so profoundly outraged by you, would be no less than duty-bound to work the miracle that prolongs your sufferings beyond the very limits of eternity."

Here the Princess was attacked by a new storm of pleasure,

such was its wild violence that she fainted away. . . . She reminded me of the Florentine Countess Donis brewing the murder of her mother and daughter.

Ah, said I to myself, what extraordinary mentalities these Italian women have. Fortunate it was I came to this country; in no other could I have found monsters of my stripe.

"Ah, by God's fuck, the pleasure I have had," murmured Olympia, when she returned to her senses and rubbed brandy upon the wounds my lashing had left on her buttocks. "So then," said she, smiling, "now that my calm is restored let us glance a moment at the facts. Give me your sincere opinion, Juliette: is it really a crime to kill one's father?"

"Why bless me, I think nothing of the sort."

And in this connection citing *in extenso* what long ago Noirceuil had said to me at the time Saint-Fond was engaged in his patricidal projects, so completely did I set this charming woman's mind at ease that if she had been anxious or in doubt heretofore, all her fears were banished now; and she decided action would be taken on the morrow. I aided her in preparing the several doses her father was to absorb; and with a hundred times more daring than did ever Brinvilliers show, Olympia Borghese slew the man who had given her life, and joyously watched him the whole long while he writhed in atrocious agony and finally disintegrated under the effects of the fatal potion I had counseled her to employ.

The deed done, she returned.

"You frigged yourself, of course?"

"Of course, to utter shreds," the rascal assured me, "I ended up bloody-cunted at his bedside. Never were the Parcae deeper drenched in fuck and it yet seeps out of me even as I recall the dog's pratings and his contortions. Oh, Juliette, let not the fire die out of me, I have come running to you, make the embers blaze up again. Make me discharge, precious Juliette, incomparable Juliette. It is with fuck one must wash remorse for crime away—"

"Remorse! Bugger-fuck me, is it possible to feel remorse over what you have done?"

"No, surely not—but, don't you see, I. . . . Ah, no matter, just frig me, Juliette, just frig me; I must exhaust myself, I must discharge. . . ."

Never before had I seen her in such a lively state. Ah, my friends, 'tis so, and well ye know it, crime embellishes a woman as does nothing else. Olympia was pretty, no more than that. But the moment she had committed this crime she took on an angelic loveliness. How intense, I then realized, is the pleasure one receives from someone cleansed of all prejudices and soiled by every crime. When Grillo frigged me I had experienced an everyday sensation; but when I was in Olympia's hands, my brain too would be irritated, I would be quite beside myself.

That same day, having just accomplished the worst of all crimes and her senses all aglow, the rascal invited me to go along with her to a house hard by the Corso where, if I cared to, I might join in an altogether unusual party. We arrive; an elderly woman greets us.

"Will you be having many guests this evening?" Olympia inquired of her.

"A great many, Princess," the matron answered; "they come in droves on Sunday."

"Then let us establish ourselves," said Olympia.

We were shown to an attractive little room. Here were several low couches so placed that from them we had a clear view of the adjoining room and of the three or four whores in it.

"What might this be?" I wondered, "and what curious pleasure are you preparing for me?"

"Keep a close eye on the scene nearby," said Olympia. "In the space of the seven or eight hours we shall be here, whole legions of monks, of priests, of abbots, of youths are going to put themselves in the hands of those girls. The number of patients will be all the larger since it is I who pay the expenses, their amusement costs these gentlemen nothing. As soon as a whore has a prick in her hand she will display it to us; if it does not suit us, they will be apprised of the fact by our silence; whereas if it pleases us, they will hear this little bell ring: the possessor of the desired prick will move directly into this room and will regale us to the limit of his abilities."

"Delightful," said I, "this arrangement is completely new to me, and I propose to make the most of it. Independently of the pleasure I may anticipate with the fellows who appeal to me, there will be the other, the piquant one, of observing how the rest disport with those sluts."

"Exactly," said Madame Borghese; "and while we ourselves discharge we shall be seeing them fuck."

Olympia had only finished pronouncing these words when a tall seminarian appeared. He was a pretty young man of twenty or so, strongly made and virile; into the hands of one of the whores he deposits a member seven inches round behind the knob and twelve inches long over-all. So gorgeous a prize could not but interest us, and when 'twas offered we rang the bell loudly.

"Go into the next room," says the whore upon hearing the signal, "this machine of yours will be more appreciated there than here."

The great clod arrives pike aloft. Olympia catches it and crams it into my cunt.

"Fuck away, my dear, don't wait for me," says she, "I'll be served before long."

I fall to. My rascal has scarcely discharged when another divinity student, rung for by Olympia, walks in and stuffs her as copiously as I have just been.

He and his confrere are followed by two *sbirri*,[15] these by two Augustinian friars; a pair of Observant friars, doleful, morose creatures, come next, and are replaced by two very randan Capuchins; after them it was a stream of coachmen, scullions, sweeps, hairdressers, bumbailiffs, butchers, and lackeys. So vast was this crowd, and among it so many awesome members, that I was at last obliged to beg quarter. 'Twas, I think, after the one hundred ninetieth that I besought my companion to bring a halt to this deluge of fuck which had been pouring into me before and, as I trust you have already surmised, behind.

"God's aching asshole," I groaned, picking myself wearily up, "tell me, Princess, do you play often at this game?"

"Seven or eight times a month," Olympia confessed; "I'm used to it, I never tire of it anymore."

"I congratulate you; as for me, I am a dry wreck. I discharge

---

[15] So are those officers denominated who stand the watch and arrest thieves in Rome.

too much and too quickly, it's my undoing."

"Come, we shall bathe and sup together," said Olympia, "and tomorrow you shall be as good as new."

The Princess took me home with her, and after two hours in the bath we sat down at table, in no state to undertake anything beyond a sweet and lubricious conversation.

"Did you have any in the ass?" the Princess asked.

"Certainly," I answered; "how on earth would you have had me withstand so many assaults in only one sector?"

"La," said Olympia. "Cunt-fuck was all I had time to do. For I did not foresee you would wish to stop so soon; twenty-four hours is my usual stint at that house, and I do not swing round my ass to the fuckers until they have made a hash of my cunt. A hash, yes. Transformed it into an open wound."

"Dear Olympia! Among libertine women I have never encountered your superior. Ah, none so well as we apprehend that 'tis by way of the various and ascending stages of secret excesses everything else is to be attained. I am a slave of those voluptuous episodes, each day I discover I have found some new habit as a result of them, charming habits which turn into so many little rituals, little homages one offers to one's physical nature and which are wonderfully pleasing to one's spiritual self.

"These divine flights of overindulgence, amongst which one must not neglect to include immoderate eating and drinking, of prime necessity in that they inflame the nervous humours and consequently determine the voluptuous mood; these self-pamperings, I say, have a gradual degenerating effect and tend before long to render excesses indispensable. Now, it is in excess pleasure exists. What therefore are we better advised to do than maintain ourselves constantly in the state pleasure demands? But there are," I continued, "scores and scores of little habits, dirty and furtive ones, loathsome and ugly ones, crapulous and brutal ones, which, perhaps, my gentle dove, you are still to make acquaintance of. I shall whisper them in your ear: they will prove to you that the celebrated La Mettrie was right when he said[16] that we humans must wallow in filth like swine and ought like them to seek pleasure in the ulti-

---

[16] See his treatise on pleasure.

mate degrees of corruption. As regards all this I have had some very singular experiences, and I shall tell you about them. I wager it has never occurred to you, for example, that by numbing two or three of the faculties of sensation one may extract astonishing things from the others; whenever you like I shall demonstrate this remarkable truth. In the meantime accept my word for it, that generally speaking 'tis when we have achieved depravation, insensibility, that Nature begins to yield us the key to her secret workings, and that it cannot be pried away from her save through outrages."

"Long have I been firmly persuaded of these maxims," Olympia replied, "but, woe is me, I am now at a loss to know what outrages to inflict upon the sublime jade. I run this Court at my will. Pius VI was once my lover, our relations are still amicable and frequent. Through his protection and the influence it procures me I have acquired a total impunity, and I have ridden it too long and too far, everything has lost its savor for me, my dear, I am surfeited. Upon this parricide I have just accomplished I founded exaggerated hopes; projecting it aroused my senses a thousand times more than carrying it out satisfied them: nothing measures up to the stature of my desires. But too much have I reasoned on my fancies, better would it have been by far had I never analyzed them at all; left inside their dark envelope of crime, their strangeness would doubtless affright me, but they would at least titillate me; whereas the light my philosophy sheds upon them renders them so comprehensible, so simple, that they have ceased altogether to have any effect upon me."

"It is the downtrodden, the unlucky, the helpless," said I, "one should whenever possible make the targets of one's wickedness; the tears you wring from indigence have a pungency which very potently stimulates the nervous humours, etc."

"Why, 'tis a happy coincidence," said the Princess, suddenly brightening, "for the splendid little scheme I have lately had in mind is perfectly in the spirit of your suggestion: my intention is, on the same day, at the same hour, to send all the hospitals in Rome, all the city's poorhouses, all the orphans' homes, all the public schools up in smoke; and not only is this excellent plan agreeable to my lewd mischievousness, it will also profit my greed.

From an entirely trustworthy individual I have the offer of one hundred thousand crowns to be mine once the catastrophe has taken place: it will prepare the ground for a project of his own and from which he will gain a fortune in gold, and glory besides."

"I marvel that you hesitate."

"Oh, the vestiges of a prejudice.... This horror, do you realize, will cost the lives of a good three hundred thousand human beings."

"I dare say; but does it matter? You will discharge, Olympia, you will rescue your senses from the torpor where they are presently becalmed; yours shall be the delicious moments you are about to taste, as for the rest, eh, it is of no concern to you; is hesitation philosophically warranted? Why, my sweet, I had no idea matters stood so ill with you. When shall you wake up? When are you going to understand that all this world abounds in is nought but game meant for our pleasures; that every last one of these creatures you see waiting about is Nature's gift to us, that 'tis only through dallying destructively with them, with the greatest possible number of them, that we fulfill Nature's expectations of us? Come, an end to this sulking in your tent, up, Olympia, great deeds call to you. Since you are in the midst of unburdening yourself, this is perhaps the proper moment to tell me whether you have not perpetrated some other crime than those you have avowed to me already: if I am to advise you well I must know you thoroughly, so speak freely if there are any pertinent facts whereof I ought to have intelligence."

"Very well then," said Princess Borghese, "I am guilty of a child-murder; I feel the need to recount it to you. When twelve years of age I gave birth to a daughter more beautiful than anything you can imagine. It was when she had grown to be ten that I became wild about her. My authority over her, her candor, her guilelessness, her innocence, all this furnished me the means to satisfy myself. We frigged each other. Two years of that and she began to pall on me. My penchants, reinforced by satiety, soon spelled out her fate; only the thought of her destruction moistened my cunt now. I had just buried my husband; of near relatives there were none left, nobody who could call me to account for my child.

I publish the rumor she has been carried off by sickness and clap her into the tower of a castle I have by the seaside, and which more resembles a fortress than an abode for decent and well-intentioned folk; I left her to languish six months in this reclusion, behind those stone walls and iron bars. Stripping people of their liberty amuses me, I like holding captives; I know that while they are incarcerated my victims suffer: this perfidious idea excites me, I should love to be able to maintain entire nations in this cruel situation.[17]

"I arrive at my castle—with you may imagine what fell designs. In my entourage were two paid queans and a young maiden, my child's playmate, her dearest friend. After a delicious dinner, thorough and artful masturbations brought my rage to a pitch and readied me for my crime. Finally, I climb the stairs to the tower, alone, and spend a preliminary two hours in that raving, in that peculiar delirium, that divine incoherence whereinto lust plunges us drunkenly and which it is so pleasant to hazard with a person who is never again to see the light of day. I doubt, my love, whether I could well render to you the things I said, the things I did. . . . I behaved like one gone stark mad: this was my first open sacrifice of a victim. Hitherto I had acted covertly, employed stealth, and my opportunities to enjoy the effects of my crime had been meager; this however was outright assassination, a premeditated murder, a horror, an execrable infanticide—a prank after our own taste, save only that into it there was not incorporated that lewd ingredient you have since taught me to blend into such deeds. Here blind hatred had a greater share than lucid calculation, fury a greater share than voluptuousness. Incredibly animated, I was perhaps about to leap tiger-like upon my victim when a fiendish idea entered my crazed brain and made me pause. . . . This friend of my daughter's . . . this creature she adored and whom I had used as I had used her, I struck upon the idea of killing her first. Thus, I said to myself, thus shall I have the further pleasure of enjoying my daughter's reaction to the sight of her dead companion. I rush out to arrange the confrontation.

---

[17] The sustained pleasure it affords is uniquely responsible for the custom the Asiatics have of keeping women under lock and key: you'll not suppose that jealousy is at the root of this practice? Can jealousy exist in the heart of a man who has two or three hundred wives?

"Then, returning to fetch my daughter, 'Come,' said I, 'I am going to show you your very best friend.'

" 'Oh, Mother, where are you leading me? These dark tunnels. . . . And what is Marcelle doing in this dreadful place?'

" 'You shall see, Agnes.'

"I open a door. This new dungeon into which I drag my child is draped in black. Marcelle's head was hanging from the ceiling; propped upright, sitting in a negligent attitude upon a bench, her naked body was just beneath the head, six inches of emptiness separated the one from the other; one of her arms, lopped off at the shoulder, was wrapped like a girdle around her waist, and three daggers were driven into her heart. Agnes stared at the spectacle, and shuddered. Her distress was extreme, but she did not give way before it; the color drained from her face, a gray wave of grief replaced it. Yet another moment did she gaze upon this horror; then, slowly turning her lovely eyes toward me, she asked: 'Is it you who have done this?'

" 'I, all by myself.'

" 'What wrong did the poor girl ever do you?'

" 'None, to my knowledge. Thinkst thou one must have pretexts to commit a crime? Shall I need any when a little while from now I butcher thee?'

"Upon hearing those words Agnes fell into a swoon, and absorbed in thought there did I tarry between my two victims, one smitten already by the scythe of death, the other shortly to feel its edge.

"Oh, my friend," continued the Princess, much moved by the story she was telling, "how puissant are these pleasures! They assail the frame as a tempest and huge waves try a ship at sea, and by those blows one is nigh to overwhelmed. These pleasures, ah . . . how fascinating are their details, how they intoxicate. But it cannot be described; it must be experienced. There, all alone with two victims, to do everything you fancy, anything; to act, to riot, to rant at your ease, without interference from anybody, without anybody hearing you; to know that twenty feet of earth ensure the security of your imagination's disorders; to say to yourself, here is an object Nature surrenders into my hands to do with absolutely whatever I please, I can smash it, I can burn it, I can maim it, I can dismantle it, I can torment it, I can fondle and annihilate it as I like, it is mine, nothing can deprive me of it, nothing save it from its fate—ah, Juliette, what happiness, what joy. And in such conditions what do we not attempt. . . .

"And then I left off my brooding and sprang upon Agnes. She was nude, unconscious, utterly defenseless. . . . So mighty was my trouble that my frantic wrath encompassed, it defined, all that was alive in me. Oh, Juliette, I satisfied myself; and after three hours of the most various tortures, the most hideous and merciless, I restored to the elements an inert mass which had received life in my womb only in order to become the toy of my rage and my viciousness."

"And then you discharged," I ventured.

"No," Olympia replied. "No, in those days, I say, I had still to establish the connection between lewdness and crime; a veil obscured my vision, you were the one who snatched it away. . . . Before we met I used to act mechanically; but if today I were to institute such a scene, how much more intelligently I would proceed. . . . But alas, that delicious crime cannot be repeated. I have no daughter left."

The villainy behind that regret, the debauches which had occupied us earlier in the day, the conversation we had just now had, the excesses we had indulged in at table, everything drove us headlong into each other's embrace. But too overwrought, too libertine to suffice unto ourselves, we must have auxiliaries, and Olympia summoned her women. Several more ecstatic hours were devoted to pleasure. Upon that god's altars we immolated a young victim, she was as fair as the day. I requested Princess Borghese to treat her just as she had done her daughter; whence there resulted unspeakable horrors, and when we parted 'twas for the purpose of concerting others.

But prodigious as Madame Borghese's libertinage might be, still it was not enough to make me forget the pure pleasures I was yet bent on tasting with sweet Honorine. Several days after our first adventure together I went to see her again. The Duchess greeted me more cordially than ever, we embraced delightedly and our conversation soon came around to the joys we had recently given each other: evoking them shortly moved us to engage anew in the activities whence they had derived, as will regularly happen when a pair of women hold such parley. The weather that day was sultry; we two were alone in a lovely boudoir, stretched indolently side by side upon a broad divan; what earthly excuse could we have had for delaying the sacrifice to a god whose altars were ready dressed and beckoning impatiently? Coy Honorine's defenses were swiftly overrun and a moment later, in quivering surrender, she offered me all her desire-swollen charms. How beautiful the creature was to behold . . . a thousand times daintier than Olympia, fresher, more youthful than she, artless, embellished by modesty's graces, why was it she pleased me not so much withal? Indescribable allurements of obscenity, lewdness' fascination, divine amenities of debauchery, has Nature then invested in you some unique power to please abstractly? To sense your incredible sway, O crime, is to recognize your sovereign grandeur and to bow in acknowledgment before your absolute rights. . . .

This time I had brought paraphernalia for aping the sex in whose qualities we were both naturally lacking. We girded on dildoes and fell to dallying now as lover and mistress, now as master and mate, now in the style of bardash and tribade, we coupled in every imaginable manner. But ever the novice, willing to follow but incapable of taking the lead, Honorine displayed modesty and timidity where debauchery and lusty zeal were to be desired; and when all was told, from her I obtained not a sixth of the pleasure Borghese would have given me in like circumstances. Had she been completely untried, the idea of corrupting her might have become the food to imagination libertinage ordinarily nourishes; but such was not the case, for Honorine, though yet a prude and pathetically inept, had nonetheless lived a little in this world, and 'twas during one of those moments of mutual abandon when avowals add a further dimension to pleasure that the heavenly Duchess related the anecdote you are now to hear.

"Soon after my marriage to the Duke—I was sixteen years old at the time," said she, "I contracted a close friendship with the Marquise Salvati, a woman twice my age, dreadfully dissolute, and who had always contrived to mask her scandalous conduct behind eminently virtuous appearances. Libertine, godless, eccentric in her tastes, pretty as an angel, Salvati enjoyed doing everything whence enjoyment can possibly be reaped; among her fondest practices was the seduction of newly-wed young women whom she would enlist to be her partners in her furtive revels. So it was the rascal took an interest in me. Her air of reserve, her hypocritical and cunning speech, her connections, a prior acquaintance with my mother, it was by these means she established relations with me, they very soon turned into a liaison of an intimate kind, for we were at the stage of reciprocal friggeries inside a week. The scene transpired in *villeggiatura,* at the country residence of Cardinal Orsini near Tivoli, where we met. Our husbands were with us. Mine was no great hindrance to me: elderly and, to judge from my experience with him up until then, cold, seeming to have married me for my wealth alone, I had little care for Grillo in the pursuit of my pleasures. The Marquise's husband however, although very libertine, did not leave her to spoil in such complete idleness; his demands upon her were both fatiguing and unusual, their fulfillment required that she lie the whole of every night in his bedchamber, which did not facilitate our secret little doings. We made up for our nighttime estrangement during the day, when we would wander off together in the splendid woodlands of Orsini's vast estate, and those promenades were the occasions upon which the Marquise toiled over my mind and soul, interspersing her lessons with the sweetest pleasures of feminine debauchery.

" 'For passing life agreeably it is not a lover we need,' she would urge, 'from out of our embraces he goes forth indiscreet or perfidious. The habit we fall into of being loved causes us to take on a new lover, and for a dozen unpleasant nights we find ourselves condemned before the public for a lifetime. Not that a spotless reputation is anything of great value,' the Marquise hastened to add, 'but when one can preserve it and double one's pleasures besides, you will agree, I should fancy, that the means leading to such results can only be the best.'

" 'Why yes, indeed.'

" 'Then those are the means we shall adopt, my angel; three days from now we return to town and once we are back I shall reveal to you the secret formula for happiness.'

" 'The situation is this,' said Salvati the day after we had regained Rome. 'We are four. You will, if you wish, make the fifth. At our orders we have a reliable and resourceful woman of sixty years, the proprietress of a secluded house and very suitably appointed. We notify her, she straightway assembles in her house everything our lust can need, whether in male form or female, and of all this we make whatever use we wish and in completest security; what do you think of this arrangement?'

"It cannot be denied, Juliette," Madame Grillo continued, "youthful and neglected by my husband, I was only too ready to listen to that temptress' offers. I assured her I would be with her on the very next excursion to that house, but insisted that she promise me I would encounter no men there.

" 'As you know, my husband has virtually no dealings with me at all,' said I, 'which is a further reason he would be quick to remark damages I were to do his honor.'

"All I asked, the Marquise promised, and we set forth. Seeing myself being conveyed across the Tiber and into the farthermost districts of the city, I felt a certain alarm; but contained it; we arrived. Before us stood a large and well-appearing house, but solitary, wrapped in silence and shadow, quite as was required by the mysteries we were about to celebrate.

"We were to traverse several suites of rooms before seeing a soul; and then, in a large antechamber, we were met by the mistress of the place. And now I was surprised by a sudden altering in the Marquise's tone: that decency, that show of sweetness and virtue gave way to language at which the lowest prostitute would have blushed.

" 'What's in the larder?' she asked.

" 'Awaiting the young lady you have brought I have four charming creatures,' the old woman told us, 'for your instructions were that I prepare her women only.'

" 'And for me what have you got ready?'

" 'Two fine Swiss Guards, strapping lads capable of giving it to you hard straight through till tomorrow.'

" 'This whore,' said the Marquise, and it was to me she was referring, 'would do better to join me in a meal of good beef instead of going off to fill up on gruel—but she's free to feed as she chooses. Say now.' Salvati went on, 'our sisters, are they here yet?'

" 'Only one has appeared so far,' replied the directress of the house. 'Elmire.'

"These ladies, it was explained to me, adopted false names for the sake of additional secrecy, and thereupon it was decided mine would be Rose.

" 'What is Elmire about?'

" 'She is with the four girls I have assigned to milady.'

"At this I cast an embarrassed glance at the Marquise.

" 'Poor silly,' she chided me, 'this is no place for shyness, we are a community and when we indulge in similar activities we act in concert, each within view of the other. Those who frolic with women group together, those who use men congregate likewise.'

" 'But I have no idea who this person might be,' I protested.

" 'Never fear, you'll get to know her from frigging yourself in her company, there's no better way to strike up acquaintance. Well now, which shall it be? Here in this room to the left are men, over there to the right, women; hurry up, make your choice and I'll make the introductions.'

"I was much troubled; I was violently eager for some men. But did I dare expose myself to all the risks that could result from my rashness? On the other hand, a new acquaintance spelled possible danger—who might this unknown woman prove to be? Would she be discreet? Would not her presence fairly paralyze me? Such were my doubts and perplexity that I stood a while not knowing which way to turn.

" 'Make up your mind, little buggeress,' said Salvati, catching me roughly by the arm, 'I have better things to do here than waste precious time.'

" 'Very well,' said I, heaving a sigh, 'I'll go in with the women.'

"The directress rapped on the door.

" 'One moment,' replied a muffled voice from within.

"A few minutes later the door was opened by a young girl and we entered.

"The Marquise's companion, she whom we designated as Elmire, was yet a beautiful woman at forty-five and after anxiously scanning her face I decided we were perfect strangers. But great heaven, in what disorder I found her! Setting out to paint the effigy of license and impurity one would have had but to copy what was already drawn in this wild creature's visage. She was sprawled stark naked upon an ottoman, her thighs flung apart; two girls lay about her, upon cushions, and in the same indecent attitude. Her face was flushed, her glittering eyes stared fixedly, her long tresses floated loose over her degraded breast, spittle dribbled from her mouth. The two or three words she mumbled suggested she might be drunk; and from the untidiness in the room, the litter of glasses and bottles, I concluded that such indeed she must be.

" 'Fuck,' she grunted as she twitched beneath her own caresses, 'I was on the verge of a squirt when you knocked, that's why I made you wait; who's this little whore?'

" 'A sister,' Salvati replied, 'a tribade of your own stripe here for some friggery.'

" 'She can make herself at home,' said the seasoned Sappho, 'fingers, mouths, dildoes, cunts, they are all here to be used. But first let me give her a wee kiss, come, there's a pretty little darling.'

"And on the instant, I am being kissed, tongued, probed, it all happens in a trice.

" 'I leave her to you,' the Marquise told her friend, 'they're waiting for me on the other side of the hall. Take good care of Rose, she has lots of things to learn.' And the next instant she was gone.

"The door is no sooner shut behind her than the four girls spring upon me and in the twinkle of an eye have me as naked as themselves. I shall not describe what those women did to me, it would be too afflicting to my modesty; I need merely say that libertinage and impudence were carried to the extreme. The middle-aged lady amused herself with me, amused herself in front of me; when my turn came I did with her and with each of the four girls every last thing that entered my head: Elmire took pleasure surprising me, teasing me, goading me on, shocking me, employing the most inconceivable and lewdest artifices. One might truthfully say that her greatest charm consisted in presenting lust to me under its filthiest shapes and most peculiar colors in order to contaminate my mind and corrupt my heart. Day came at long last, the Marquise reappeared, we dressed and promptly returned each to her house in the fervent hope that nothing would dissuade our husbands from continuing in the belief that their wives had spent the evening at a ball; and their Lordships never doubted but that this was the truth. Cheered by this first success, I allowed myself to be led a second time to that dreadful establishment; seduced by the pernicious Marquise, I very shortly turned from women to men and my misbehavior was without equal or precedent. Remorse finally fastened upon my soul; virtue cried out to me and I returned gratefully into its fold; I vowed to live as befits an honest woman and as such would I still be living were it not for you, whose graces and talents and adorableness and beauty must cause all the frail oaths that shall ever be foolishly sworn to goodness to shatter into pieces upon the altars of Love."

"Charming woman," said I to the Duchess, "a virtuous vow, why, pronounced by you 'tis an extravagance for which Nature is bound to chasten you; 'tis not for honest living she created us, my dear, but for fucking; we outrage her by defying her purposes and when we refuse to fuck we are in open rebellion against her will. If that delicious house still exists I beseech you to return to it; never am I envious of my friends' pleasures, I ask no more than permission to share or behold them."

"No, the woman who ran that house sold it a year or so ago and has left Rome," Honorine said, "but there are other means for obtaining pleasure."

"And why not exploit them?"

"I feel less and less free, my husband is taking a constantly growing interest in me, he is becoming jealous; I am even afraid he has begun to suspect there is something between you and me."

"Such a man must be got rid of."

"Got rid of!"

"Bah, put out of the way."

"Why, you make me shudder!"

"You have no cause to shudder. Men are put out of the way and got properly rid of every day. The foremost of Nature's laws is to disencumber ourselves of whatever displeases us; husband-murder is an imagined crime I myself have perpetrated without the slightest hesitation or regret; we must think of ourselves in this world, nobody else counts. Fundamentally and absolutely isolated from all other beings, just as we should approach only those which please us, so should we be equally careful to send on their way those which are distasteful to us. Between the existence of a person I find troublesome and my own interests there can be no common measure. What! I'd be such an enemy of my own well-being as to prolong the life of him who causes me suffering? I'd so violently contradict the commands of Nature as not to put an end to the life of him who deliberately ruins all the felicity of mine? Moral and political murders shall be tolerated, nay, justified, and personal murders disconsidered! It is not only unfair, it is preposterous. Honorine, such prejudices are grotesquely unbecoming, you should be above them. He who intends to be happy on earth must without any scruple fling aside everything, absolutely everything that stands in his path, he must embrace everything that serves or flatters his passions. . . . You lack the means? I can provide them."

"What horrors do you speak!" cried the Duchess. "I do not love Signor Grillo, I shall not pretend the contrary; but I respect him; he is my youth's protector; his jealousy is my safeguard, for otherwise, if unrestrained, I would rush headlong into the pitfalls toward which it is certain that libertinage would lead me—"

"Child, you talk nonsense!" I interrupted, "all sophistry and weakness. Are you trying to tell me that because somebody prevents you from seizing the joys of life Nature holds out to you, you ought, instead of putting a halt to his interference, to double the weight of the shackles he loads upon you? Ah, Honorine, stand fearlessly up, break those humiliating chains. The handiwork of fashion and egotistical policy, what is there sacred about them, tell me? Scorn them, jeer at them, curse them, spit upon them if you like, they merit no better. In this world, a pretty woman should have no god other than pleasure; no physical obligation other than to receive our homage in return for the delight she gives us; no virtue other than that of fucking; no moral duty other than to observe the imperious law of her desires. First of all, you must get yourself a child, never mind who sires it on you, you need issue if you are to secure control over your husband's fortune. That once accomplished, we feed the funny fellow a well-spiced cup of consommé and afterward the two of us, you and I, go for a gay wallow in the slime pit of the most atrocious, the most abominable pleasure—

pleasure of the most atrocious, the most abominable sort because that is the most delectable sort which has been made for your enjoyment and which you have been made to enjoy, atrocious and abominable pleasure whereof you cannot deprive yourself without someday being called to answer for it before the judgment seat of Reason and of Nature."

That prudish spirit proved stubbornly unresponsive to my teachings; this was perhaps the only woman I had ever failed to corrupt. The moment came when I lost patience and abandoned my efforts; that was the moment I took the resolve to destroy her.

The question now was simply of disposing my guns to best advantage; I went to consult Borghese.

"I thought you were in love with the Duchess," Olympia teased.

"What an idea, I in love! My heart has always been a stranger to puerile sentiments: I have amused myself with that woman, done everything humanly possible to guide her into crime, she refuses to be led, it's a wretched fool I intend at present to send to her doom."

"I perfectly understand. It should not be difficult."

"No, it should not be, except that I want her husband to perish with her; I had projected his death, I wanted to put the dagger into his wife's hand and have her wield it against him—must the idiot's refusal cost me a victim?"

"Rascal!"

"Both of them have to be killed."

"The idea pleases me," said Borghese, "the act would amuse me as much as you; bring them to my country house and we shall see what we can do."

Arrangements are made for the party, Borghese and I harmonize our plans. I shall not bother you with the details but move directly to the outcome.

Along with us we had taken a young man of the Princess' acquaintance. Quite as seductive as he was comely, no less clever than witty, our Dolni, twenty years old, used to fuck us fairly frequently, and knowledge of his mind and parts had induced us to select him for the piece of wickedness we were meditating. From the very first moment, Dolni set to work and with great art aroused the passions of Honorine and the jealous suspicions of her husband. The deeply disturbed Grillo turned to me in quest of a friendly ear and poured out all his fears; these, as you may imagine, I did rather more to increase than allay.

"My good Duke," said I to that fool, "I am greatly surprised that you have been so slow to notice your wife's behavior. I or indeed any other could have enlightened you long ago, but one is sometimes reluctant to become the bearer of evil tidings; you seemed so well protected by your blindness, it is so cruel to blast such illusions; I held my peace. Dolni's purpose for being here is the Duchess' presence, as everybody is well aware; why, I had hardly been overnight in Rome when I heard of their affair."

"Then it is an affair?"

"To put it mildly, my Lord. But I see that you still entertain doubts, and they can be more painful than the naked truth itself. It is in the morning or while you are out taking a walk that Dolni ordinarily dishonors your bed: catch the two culprits in the act tomorrow, and for your honor's sake be not laggardly in revenging yourself for so brazen an affront."

"You will aid me, Madame?"

"In so far as I am able to. A word of advice: beware of speaking of this to the Princess: intimately connected with your wife, privy to her passion—it is notorious—I believe she connives at what is going on under her roof."

"Not a word to her then. Tomorrow morning I shall be hidden in the dressing room adjoining the bedchamber."

Lest we be overseen in conversation together we separate at once, I having recommended to the Duke that he avoid me the whole of that day. I seek out the Duchess and, encouraging her to banish all scruples in order to enjoy to the full the pleasures at whose mere thought the young man has already made her giddy, I notify her that the Duke means to go ahunting the next day, which will enable her to pass the entire morning in riot with Dolni.

"Get started early, the two of you, and when you are well under way I'll arrive and we shall carry on as a trio."

My proposal fetched gay laughter from the Duchess, and she

assented to it gladly. The moment drew nigh; thinking the two lovers properly at grips, I bade the Duke follow me on to the stage.

"So then, good sir," said I, directing his attention to the frantically copulating couple, "is this less than you require to be convinced?"

Furious Grillo, drawn dagger in hand, hurls himself upon the adulterous pair. Aiding his arm, I see to it the blow falls upon his faithless spouse: the blade sinks deep into her flank, the Duke would now vent his rage upon the lover, but nimble Dolni rolls away, springs to his feet, scampers from the room, Grillo hot in his pursuit. They race down a long corridor . . . at its farther end two trap doors open, one dropping the young man into an underground passage, where he is safe, the other tumbling Grillo into the works of a frightful machine fitted with a thousand sharp blades for carving to ribbons whatever is placed inside it.

"Great God, what is this? what have I done?" cries the Duke, "oh, hideous snare! Diabolical knaves, all your design was to trick me! And you, dearest wife, I was mistaken, they deceived me— you were seduced, at bottom you are innocent—"

These last words were scarce out of the Duke's mouth when Borghese sent his naked and bleeding wife flying to join him in the pit.

Over the open trap we lowered a grillwork, upon it we three, Dolni, Olympia, and I, lay down flat and peered at our captives. "There she is, my Lord," said I, "innocent no doubt and yet more certainly wounded by your treatment of her. Succor her if you dare, but know that in doing so your peril is great."

Grillo starts impulsively toward his wife; but his movement releases a spring, the machine starts to whirr, its many blades to turn, their edges slash at the two victims who in less than ten minutes are threshed shapeless, of them nought but blood and splintered bone remains. I need not describe our ecstasy, Borghese's and mine, as we watched that scene; both frigged by Dolni, we loosed discharge after discharge, at least a dozen in all, the sight of that atrocity left our cunts in a state nearly as gruesome, and inspired our minds to a very rare degree.

"Come spend the day with me tomorrow," Olympia suggested

when we had returned to the city, "I shall introduce you to the personage who has offered me a hundred thousand crowns to burn down all the hospitals and alms-houses in Rome. The man who is to attend to the lighting of the fires will be there too."

"What, do you still have that horror on your mind, Princess?"

"Certainly, Juliette. You confine your criminal activity to upsetting households whereas I make mine felt by at least half a city. Incendiary Nero is my model; I too would like to stand on my balcony, a lyre in my hand, and while singing gaze forth upon my native land become a pyre for my countrymen."

"Olympia, you are a monster."

"Oh, not so great a one as you; the base scheme that brought the Grillos to their end was absolutely typical of your invention, I'd never have dreamt up the like."

At Borghese Palace the next day Olympia presented her guests to me. "The first of these gentlemen"—it was to the elder she alluded—"is Monsignor Chigi, related to that line of princes several of whom have occupied the Holy See; he is today at the head of the Roman police; the proposed fire I mentioned to you yesterday will benefit him, and the hundred thousand crowns fee he is to pay me is part of his investment in a very profitable venture. And here is Count Bracciani who, as Europe's foremost physician, is to conduct the operation. Juliette," Olympia added in a lowered tone, "both are friends of mine; I implore you to take their eventual requests of you into kindly consideration."

"You shall not be embarrassed by my behavior," I assured her.

And the Princess having given the strictest orders that we be left undisturbed, conversation was engaged.

"I am having you dine," said Olympia, "with one of the most famous scoundrels to come out of France in generations; she has been giving us Romans daily examples of very high proficiency in crime; her presence need not hinder you, my friends, in the forthcoming discussions of the one we are preparing."

"Truly, Madame," said the master of the police, "you here qualify as crime an altogether unpretentious and certainly very comprehensible act. I consider charitable institutions the most baneful things a large city can contain; they drain the people's energy, they

soften its fiber, they promote sloth; they are in every sense pernicious; the needy individual is to the State as the parasite branch
is to the peach tree: it causes it to wither, drinks its sap, and bears
no fruit. What does the horticulturist do when he espies that
branch? He cuts it off, and without qualms. The statesman must
proceed likewise: one of the basic laws of Nature is that nothing
superfluous subsist in the world. You may be sure of it, not only
does the shiftless beggar, always a nuisance, consume part of what
the industrious man produces, which is already a serious matter,
but will quickly become dangerous the moment you suspend your
dole to him. My desire is that instead of bestowing a groat upon
these misfortunates we concentrate our efforts upon wiping them
out; my desire is that they be totally eliminated, extirpated; exterminated; killed, that is to say, and why make any bones about it?
killed as one kills a breed of noxious animals. That is the first
reason that led me to offer Princess Borghese one hundred thousand gold crowns for destroying these houses that are a blight
upon our city. The second is that upon their sites I mean to build
hospices for travelers, pilgrims, and the like; some buildings razed,
others constructed in their place, don't you see, and the revenues
which went formerly to pay for maintaining the hospitals I now
ask to have paid to me; and paid to me they shall be; mine as well
shall be an annual one hundred thousand crowns rental: thus I
sacrifice only the first year of an assured income to Madame
Borghese, who in Count Bracciani, she tells me, has the suitable
man for delivering Rome of these houses and for making a need
felt for those I am ready to put up on their foundations, and for
which I shall have no trouble obtaining the funds originally set aside
for the hospitals.[18] There are twenty-eight of these asylums in the
city," Chigi continued, "as well as nine *conservatorios* containing
roughly eighteen hundred poor girls whom, needless to say, I include in my proscriptions. All that must be set simultaneously
ablaze; there will be some thirty or forty thousand good-for-
nothings sacrificed—firstly, to the welfare of the State; secondly,
to the pleasures of Olympia, who is going to reap a pretty penny

[18] This project was actually conceived while I was at Rome, and I alter nothing
but the names of the actors.

from this affair; thirdly, to my fortune, for with what I already possess, I become one of Rome's richest ecclesiastics if the plan goes successfully through."

"It would appear," said Bracciani, "that I, who am to execute it, come off the most poorly; for it seems not yet to have occurred to you to offer me a sequin out of the great profits you are due to make."

"Chigi supposed that I would give you some of my hundred thousand," Olympia said to the Count, "he was mistaken: the sum is modest, once divided it amounts to twice nothing at all, and I feel you should demand a hundred thousand for yourself; you are worth that much to Monsignor, what more capable practitioner could he hope to find?"

"Softly," said the churchman, "let's have no falling out at the start of an undertaking so important, it would be the way to have it all end very dismally and to provoke difficulties for one another. I grant the Count the same emoluments Madame Borghese is to have, I grant a further hundred thousand francs gratuity to this charming woman," Chigi went on, smiling in my direction; "Olympia's friend must have a similar character and by that title alone deserves to be treated as an accomplice."

"She has all the virtues you can expect in one," said the Princess, "and I guarantee she will not disappoint you. The question of remunerations may be considered settled; in behalf of my friends I accept your offers; let us now bend our thoughts to success."

"I shall obtain it," said Bracciani, "and it shall be entire: there shall not escape a single one of the victims Chigi's profound statecraft, or rather his voluptuous wickedness, dooms to die."

"Upon what henceforth shall Roman doctors be able to experiment, I wonder?"

"As Juliette implies, it is very certain," Olympia observed, "that almost all of them have long been in the habit of trying out their remedies upon these poorer patients whose disappearance will pose a problem to the profession. I am reminded," she added, "of what young Iberti, my personal doctor, said to me only the other day upon arriving at my bedside fresh from one of those experiments. 'What concern to the State is the existence of the vile beings that ordinarily crowd those dens?' he said in response to the look of disapproval I assumed in order to find out how he would justify himself; 'you would be doing society an enormous disservice by not permitting us medical artists to test our talents upon society's dishonoring dregs. These have their use; Nature, in making them weak and defenseless, indicates what it is to be, and to refrain from so using them is to flout Nature's instructions.' 'But,' said I, departing a little from the central issue, 'when, in a different case, some sordid interest leads a man distinguished by wealth or by position to seize the favorable opportunity afforded by a person's illness to commit a crime against that person, and when this man invites a doctor to hasten the patient's last moments, is it a grave fault for the doctor to accept the proposition?'

" 'Great heavens, no,' my young Aesculapius replied, 'provided he is well paid he has no real choice but to accept. Doing the deed, he has nothing to fear from his accomplice, neither does his accomplice have anything to fear from him: both have everything to gain from guarding their secret. Refusing to do the deed would get the doctor nowhere, for he could hardly boast of having declined a proposition which is not of the kind that is made to an honest man: from a refusal he would thus extract nothing but solitary and intellectual pleasure much inferior to that which the offered sum would procure him. And even were he to proclaim that to such a proposition he had said no, he'd not be praised for it; but only told he had done his duty. And as for those who do it there is never any reward, needless to go to the bother of chasing empty applause. Comparing what, apart from that applause, he is to gain from acceptance or refusal, he discovers that in electing the latter alternative he may either say nothing of the proposition and all alone reap the meager enjoyments that having a good opinion of oneself provides to fools, or create a stir and thereby doom his accomplice—and what does he gain from dooming the accomplice rather than the patient?—in order to obtain the tawdry and barren satisfaction of having it said he has done his duty. Weigh it up: a futile pleasure as against the sum offered him to shorten the patient's life: what responsible man could conceivably hesitate an instant? To the sane physician only one course is open: bargain for a high price, then kill and keep his mouth shut.'

"Those were the words, those the views of Iberti, the prettiest, the wittiest, the most engaging doctor in Rome[19] and you will readily understand how little difficulty he had convincing me. But to return to the business before us," Olympia continued; "are you sure of the operation, Bracciani? Is there not the danger that the perfidious efforts of rescuers might ruin the effects we are striving for? Humane impulses, as much to be dreaded as loathed, and capable of spoiling many a fair crime—dare we suppose that they will not move a certain number of people to rush to the aid of our victims?"

"I expect this," said the Count. "I take up my position atop a high hill in the middle of Rome. From there I launch invisible bombs, thirty-seven of them, one for each of the thirty-seven asylums; they land in barrage. Other projectiles follow at carefully spaced intervals: rescuers flock to a new burning area after having mastered the flames in a former one, which I set promptly back on fire."

"In this way, Count, you could have an entire city ablaze."

"Exactly," said the physician, "and our present undertaking, limited in scope though it be, may very well cause half the population of Rome to perish."

"Some of the hospitals are located in extremely poor quarters of the city," said Chigi, "those quarters shall be destroyed infallibly."

"Such considerations do not make you pause?" Olympia wondered.

"Not for one instant, Madame," Chigi and the Count replied as one man.

"These gentlemen seem to have firmly made up their minds," I observed to the Princess, "and my guess would be that the crime they are about to commit is to them something of slight importance."

"There is nothing of crime in our project," Chigi explained.

[19] Let me render thee this homage, charming and never to be forgotten friend. Thy name is the only one I have been unable to take it upon myself to disguise in these memoirs. Thou wert ever the philosopher, that is thy role in my writings and thou must surely forgive me for my eagerness to make thy identity known to the whole world.

"All our errors under the chapter of ethics come from the absurdity of our ideas touching good and evil.

"If we fully apprehended the indifference of all our actions, were we properly persuaded that those we call just are anything but that in the eyes of Nature, and that those we characterize as iniquitous are perhaps, in her view, the most perfect measure of reason and equity, for a certainty we would make far fewer miscalculations. But childhood prejudices lead us astray and will never cease inducing us into error so long as we have the weakness to listen to them. It does indeed seem that the lamp of reason does not begin to enlighten us until such time as we are no longer able to profit from its rays, and not before stupidity has been added to stupidity that we arrive at the discovery of the source of all that ignorance has caused us to commit. We almost always employ the laws of our government as our compass for determining right and wrong, just and injust. The law, we say, prohibits doing this or that, this or that is hence unjust; than this manner of judging none is more deceiving, for the law is oriented toward the general interest; now, nothing is at a farther remove from the general interest than individual interest, its very opposite; hence, nothing less just than the law which sacrifices all individual interests to the general interest. But, they maintain, man wishes to live in society; he must therefore forego a portion of his private good for the sake of public good. Very well; but how ever could he have made such a pact without being sure of receiving at least as much as he gives? Now, he extracts nothing from the pact he makes when consenting to the law; for you put him far more heavily to contribution than you satisfy him, and for every occasion upon which the law protects him there are a thousand others when it restricts him; he hence ought not to have consented to the law, or ought to have insisted that it be made infinitely more lenient. Laws have served only to delay the annihilation of prejudices, to lengthen our term of shameful bondage to error; law is a bridle man imposed upon man when he saw with what ease man freed himself of other bridles, hence a makeshift— to answer what purpose? There are punishments for the guilty, true enough; in them I see cruelties but not a means to make men better, and that it seems to me is the end to which one should have labored. Punishments, aye—and there's nothing easier to escape, this certitude encourages the emancipated and venturesome spirit. Ah, let it be understood once and for all, laws are nothing but futile and dangerous; their sole effect is to multiply crimes or to cause them to be committed in safety by compelling the criminal to act in secrecy. But for laws and religion there is no imagining the degree of grandeur and glory human knowledge would have attained today; no imagining how these infamous curbs have retarded progress; that is our single debt to them. Priests dare inveigh against the passions; lawyers dare fetter them with laws. But merely compare the ones and the others; see which, passions or laws, have done mankind the more good. Who doubts, as Helvétius proclaims, that the passions are in morals precisely what motion is in physics? 'Tis to strong passions alone invention and artistic wonders are due; the passions should be regarded, the same author goes on to say, as the fertilizing germ of the mind and the puissant spring to great deeds. Those individuals who are not motivated by strong passions are mediocre beings. Only great passions will ever be able to produce great men; when passion falters decrepitude enters in, when it is absent stupidity prevails. These fundamentals established, I ask how laws that inhibit the passions can be anything but profoundly and in every sense dangerous. In the history of any country compare the periods of anarchy with those during which order was most vigorously maintained by the most vigorously enforced laws, and recognize that only at moments when the laws were held in contempt do stupendous actions occur. Law resumes its despotic sway and a fatal lethargy is seen to invade the spirits of men; though vice ceases to be noticeable, the disappearance of all virtue is yet more conspicuous: the inner workings rust and revolutions begin to breed."

"But," Olympia interrupted, "you wish to do away with all laws in an empire?"

"No. Restored to a state of Nature, mankind, I affirm, would be happier than it can possibly be under the absurd yoke of law. I am opposed to man's renunciation of a single ounce of his capacities. He has no need of laws for his self-protection; in him Nature put the necessary instincts and energy for that; taking the law into his own hands he will always obtain a speedier, purer, more incisive, stronger-brewed justice than anything to be had in a court-room, for his act of personal justice will be determined by his personal interest and the hurt he has personally sustained, whereas the laws of a people are never other than the mass and the result of the interests of all the lawmakers who cooperate in erecting those laws."

"But without the laws you will be oppressed."

"That matters not to me if I have the right to repay oppression in kind: I prefer to be oppressed by a neighbor whom I can oppress in my turn than to be oppressed by the law before which I am help-less. My neighbor's passions are infinitely less to be dreaded than the law's injustice, for the passions of that neighbor are held at bay by mine, nothing checks the injustices of the law, against the law there is no reprisal to be taken, no recourse to be had. All the defects in humans belong to Nature; accordingly, man can have no better laws than those of Nature; no man has the right to repress in him what Nature put there. Nature has elaborated no statutes, instituted no code; her single law is writ deep in every man's heart: it is to satisfy himself, to deny his passions nothing, and this regardless of the cost to others. Think not to hinder this universal law's impulsions whatever their effects may be; you have no right to curb them; let this be the concern of him they outrage; if strong, he will know how to react. The men who thought that from their necessity to join together was derived a necessity for framing laws to themselves fell into heaviest error; they had no more need of laws gathered in society than dwelling alone in the forest. A universal glaive of justice is of no purpose; everybody naturally possesses one of his own."

"But not everyone will wield it appropriately, and iniquity will beome general—"

"Impossible. Never will Tom be unjust toward Dick when he knows Dick can retaliate instantly; but it's a very unjust Tom you have as soon as he discovers he has nothing to fear except laws that he can elude or from which he can make himself exempt. I go farther, I grant you that without laws the sum of crime increases, that without laws the world turns into one great volcano belching forth an uninterrupted spew of execrable crimes; and I tell you this situation is preferable, far preferable to what we have at present.

I envisage a perpetual outpouring of conflict, injury, and aggression; it is nothing beside what takes place under the rule of law, for the law often smites the innocent, and to the total of victims produced by the criminal must be added the mass of those produced by legal miscarriage and iniquity: give us anarchy and we will have these victims the less. To be sure, we will have those crime sacrifices; but the ravages of the law will be a thing of the past. Invested with the right to do his own revenging, the oppressed man will proceed with speed, diligence, economy, and certitude to punish his oppressor and none other."

"However, opening the door to the arbitrary, anarchy is necessarily the cruel image of despotism—"

"Another error; 'tis the abuse of the law that leads to despotism; the despot is he who creates the law, who bids it speak or be still, who uses it to serve his own interests. Deprive the despot of this means for abuse and there's an end to tyranny. There has never been a tyrant who failed to raise laws for props in the exercise of his cruelties; if everywhere human rights shall be well enough distributed to enable each man to avenge the wrongs done him, no despot shall arise, for he would be overthrown the moment he attempted to make his first victim. Never are tyrants born of anarchy, you see them flourish only behind the screen of the law or attain supremacy by means of it, basing their authority upon law. Viviousness thus reigns under the rule of law; thus, lawful rule is inferior to anarchy: the greatest proof whereof is the government's obligation to plunge the State into anarchy whenever it wishes to frame a new constitution. To abrogate its former laws it is driven to establish a revolutionary regime in which there are no laws at all: from this regime new laws finally emerge. But this second State is necessarily less pure than the first, since it derives from the earlier one, since, in order to achieve its goal, *constitution,* it had first to install *anarchy.* Men are pure only in their natural condition; as soon as they stray out of it their degradation begins. Give up the idea of improving men by laws, give it up. I tell you, by laws you will render them greater scoundrels, more cunning, more wicked, never more virtuous."

"But crime is a plague to the world, Monsignor. The more laws there are, the fewer crimes shall there be."

"A pretty jest. But seriousness commands us to recognize that it's the multitude of laws that is responsible for this multitude of crimes. Cease to believe such-and-such a deed is criminal; make no laws to repress it; the crime disappears.

"But I return to the first part of your proposition: crime, you say, is a plague to the world. What sophism! That which deserves to be called a plague to the world would be some destructive mechanism threatening the existence of all the world's inhabitants; let us see if crime answers this description.

"A crime being committed presents the picture of two individuals, one of whom is performing the act called criminal, the other of whom is being made this act's victim. Two individuals: one happy, the other unhappy; crime is therefore not a plague in the world since, although rendering half the world's population un-happy, it renders the other half very happy indeed. Crime is nought but the means Nature employs to attain her ends in regard to us and to preserve the equilibrium so indispensable to the maintenance of her workings. This explication alone suffices to make clear that it is not for man to punish crime, because crime belongs to the Nature that possesses every right over us and over which we dispose of none. If, viewing it from another angle, crime is the consequence of passion, and if the passions, as I have just said, must be beheld as the sole springs to great deeds, you should always favor the crime which gives energy to your society over the virtues which disturb its operations and undermine its strength. You cannot now continue to punish crime; you ought instead to encourage it, and thrust virtues into the background where they will be buried forever under the scorn they deserve from you. We must of course take great care not to confuse great deeds with virtues: very often a virtue is farthest of all from a great deed, and more often still a great deed is sheer crime. Well, great deeds are frequently very necessary; virtues never are. Brutus, the kindly head of his family, would have been but a dull and melancholy fellow; Brutus, the murderer of Caesar, simultaneously performs a crime and a great deed: the former personage would have remained unknown to history, the latter became one of its heroes."

"And so, according to you, one may feel at complete ease amidst the blackest crimes?"

" 'Tis in virtuous surroundings comfort is impossible since it is clear that you then exist in an unnatural situation, in a state contrary to the Nature which cannot exist, renew herself, preserve her energy and vitality save through the immensity of human crimes; and so the best course for us is to endeavor to make virtues out of all human vices, and vices out of all human virtues."

"It has been to that end," said Bracciani, "that I have toiled since the age of fifteen, and I may truthfully report that I have enjoyed every minute of my career."

"My friend," Olympia said to Chigi, "with the ethical beliefs you have just laid before us you must have very lively passions. You are forty, the age when they speak most imperiously. Oh, yes, you have surely achieved horrors!"

"In the position he holds," said Bracciani, "with the inspection-general of the Rome police, occasions for doing evil must certainly not be lacking."

"There is no denying it," said Chigi, "I am in an exceedingly favorable position for doing evil, and it would be yet harder to claim that I let pass many occasions for doing it."

"You commit injustices . . . you suborn witnesses, you falsify evidence," asked Madame Borghese, "you use the instruments of Themis entrusted to you to doom a good many innocent persons?"

"And having done all you say, do no more than act pursuant to my principles; which I believe is to do well. If I suppose virtue a dangerous thing in this world, am I wrong to immolate those who practice it? If, reciprocally, I consider vice useful on earth, am I wrong to let escape from the law those who profess it? They call me an unjust man, I know, they may, for all I know, call me worse yet; their opinion matters not to me: provided my behavior accords with my principles I have an easy conscience. Before acting according to those principles I began by analyzing them, then based my conduct thereupon; let the entire world blame me, little do I care, I have done well by my own lights, and for my actions I am accountable to no one but myself."

"There's the true philosophy," Bracciani remarked, "I have not developed my principles as much as Chigi, but I assure you that they are absolutely the same, and that I put them into practice just as often and just as faithfully."

"Monsignor," said Olympia to the first magistrate of Rome's police, "you are accused of making much too extensive use of the strappado; you apply it, they say, to numerous innocents and especially to them, prolonging the torture, so we commonly hear, to the point where it invariably costs the guiltless party his life."

"I am going to elucidate the enigma," said Bracciani. "The torture you mention composes this scoundrel's pleasures; he stiffens watching it exercised, he discharges if it does away with the patient."

"Count," Chigi retorted, "I fail to notice anything constraining you to celebrate my tastes here, nor do I recall having charged you to unveil my foibles."

"We are much obliged to the Count for this disclosure," I put in with vivacity; "it announces glad tidings to Olympia, for from such a man much can be expected and I will frankly confess that what he has reported has already touched me deeply."

"And we should be yet more deeply touched," said Olympia, "were Chigi to care to enact his favorite game before us."

"Why not," the libertine replied; "have you an object to hand?"

"I'll have no difficulty finding one."

"Yes, but it may not have all the required qualities."

"What might the required qualities be?"

"Those of material indigence," said Chigi, "of blamelessness, of the submissiveness due to a supreme judge."

"Are you able to combine all that?" Olympia asked.

"Oh, yes," the magistrate assured her, "my prisons are teeming with such individuals and at your demand, in less than an hour I'll have produced you something suitable to the pleasures you intend to procure yourselves."

"Could you describe the article?"

"A young woman of eighteen, a Venus for beauty, and eight months pregnant."

"Pregnant!" I expostulated. "And you will subject her in that state to such rough handling?"

"If worse comes to worst, it will kill her, and as a matter of fact it is pretty certain to. But that's how I like to have them:

pregnant. You get two pleasures instead of one: it's what they call 'cow and calf.' "

"And this poor creature," said I, "I'll wager she is guiltless. . . ."

"I've had her ripening two months in prison. Her mother suspects her of a theft I myself had committed in order to get hold of the girl; the trap was nicely laid and succeeded irreproachably. Cornelia is safe and sound behind bars, and you need but say the word and I'll have her do a better rope-dance for you than ever was done by any acrobat. Afterward I shall have it bruited that out of compassion I had her spirited away to save her from punishment, and while covering up what fools call a crime I'll have the merit a superb deed confers."

"Excellent," I said; "however, this mother you are leaving alive, I fear she may someday reveal everything, and won't that bring on no end of difficulties? It should surely be easy enough to persuade her that she is her daughter's accomplice and that she was party to the theft for which she wishes to see the guilt remain on the girl's shoulders."

"And who knows, the family may include a few other members," the Count suggested.

"Were there twenty," said Olympia, "it seems to me that Chigi's personal safety would require murdering them all."

"You people are insatiable," the magistrate sighed, "I merely ask you not to lay up to your concern for my welfare what really originates in your perfidious lust. Alas, there's nothing to do but content it. Cornelia has a brother in addition to a mother; I promise to have all three of them die before our eyes and under the torture with whose use the Count wishes to identify the source of my pleasures."

"It is just that we had in mind," Olympia said; "once you go so far as to indulge in such bloody pranks as these, I feel you should carry them to the limit; I know nothing worse than stopping halfway. Oh, fuck," the whore grunted, rubbing her cunt through her dress, "I declare to you I'm leaking already."

Therewith Chigi rose to his feet and went to issue the necessary orders. A little garden ringed by dense cypress trees and adjoining Olympia's boudoir was chosen for the place of execution, and we fondled one another while waiting for the merriment to begin. Chigi and Olympia were thoroughly acquainted with each other, but Bracciani had never had anything to do with my friend and I was unknown to both of the men. So the Princess took it upon herself to make the initial advances; such libertines never stand long on ceremony. The hussy sets straight to undressing me and soon turns me over naked to my two admirers. They devour me, but in the Italian style: my ass becomes the unique object of their caresses, they both kiss it, tongue it, nibble it, worry it; they make tireless and prolonged to-do over it, cannot get their fill of it; and behave for all the world as if they are unaware I am a woman. After fifteen minutes of these nasty preliminaries some order is restored. Bracciani approaches Olympia who has just cast aside her every stitch, and I become Chigi's prey.

"Do not be impatient, charming creature," that infamous libertine says to me, his face glued to my rump; "my capacity for pleasure dulled from long habituation to its sensations, I must struggle before I feel the blunted needle's prick. It will take time, I may weary you, and it may be that I finally fail to do myself honor; but you shall have given me pleasure, and that, I think, is quite enough for any woman to strive after."

And the lecher rattled and banged his tool with all his might, the while continuing to savor my bum.

"Madame," said he to Olympia in whose posterior Bracciani was foraging, "I am not too fond of having thus to do the job all alone; it appears to me that the Count would also appreciate some assistance; you surely have some little girls or boys somewhere about, pray send for them. Frigged, licked, pumped, socratized, we shall reach the altars of the Callipygian Venus ready and fresh."

Olympia rings, two girls of fifteen promptly answer the summons; the libertine always kept the likes within call.

"Ah, very good, very good," said the magistrate, "tell them to busy themselves promptly at these chores it is disagreeable to have to undertake oneself."

No sooner heard than obeyed, into the maidens' hands Chigi deposits the unglorious vestiges of his failing manhood, and my buttocks continue to be the object of his kisses; his tongue soon penetrates; but success is not yet in sight. A luckier Bracciani is already inside Olympia's anus while his young satellite, on her knees behind him, sucks his vent. Peering at this group in action, Chigi takes heart; he spreads my buttocks, lays his half-stiffened member between them, and has himself flogged to brace his attack. . . . The traitor! He dishonors my charms; lacking consistency enough to hold his ground, he is put to rout. And for his discomfiture blames the little girl; she had been fustigating him.

"Had you laid on harder," he cries, very wroth, "this would never have happened." So saying he gives the child such a mighty buffet he sends her flying three yards away.

"What's this, Monsignor, what's this!" Olympia exclaims. "Be a little harsher with the slut, take a lash to her, that's what I always do when they disappoint me."

"Right you are, Madame," says Chigi, catching up a whip.

And despite the graces, the mildness, the gentleness of that sweet child and despite the beauty of her ass, the barbarian smites it with such force that great patches of skin are gone off it by the sixth blow. Noticing his glance wander to my behind and that he has taken a firmer grip on the whip, "Strike, libertine," I say, "be bold and strike; I surmise your intentions, I defy your blows. Lay on, dear friend, and spare me not."

Chigi does not reply to me, he whips me; he whips me so soundly that his flabby tool, brought back to life at last, is in sufficient fettle to perforate me. I get myself hastily into the proper stance, he embuggers me, he is embuggered in his turn, and there we are on the threshold of joy.

"Shall we discharge?" inquires Bracciani, still bum-fucking my companion.

"No," is Chigi's answer, "no; we must remember the great operation ahead of us, and restrict ourselves for the moment to getting into form: only to the agonies of Cornelia and her family, to that atrocity alone must we accord our fuck."

This resolution is adopted; without concern for our feelings, the two libertines instantly dismount and the pleasures of the table create a diversion to those of lubricity. In the middle of the meal, Chigi, almost drunk, suggests that one of the girls, she whom he did not whip, be placed flat upon the table and that we eat a dozen sugared omelettes hot off her buttocks. It's done; burned to the quick, the poor child emits ringing screams, which does not prevent the company from digging their forks all the more vigorously into bits of food they lift from a platter of bleeding and scorched flesh.

"It would be amusing to sup a little off her breasts," Bracciani observes.

"To this you have my agreement," says Chigi, "provided I am allowed to clyster her. With boiling water, be it understood."

"And I shall clyster her too. A pint of acid into her cunt," said Olympia in the shrill tone that would enter her voice whenever some infamous idea entered her head.

"Since I must pronounce in my turn," said I to the assembly, "I humbly submit that another serving of omelette be eaten off this engaging little thing's face, that we so manage our silverware as to pluck out her eyes, that she then be impaled in the center of the table, for a decoration."

All these proposals are put into howling effect; we four swill and eat ourselves giddy while watching the divine spectacle of that charming little girl writhing and slowly expiring in hideous pain.

"How did you find my dinner?" Borghese asked us as we reached dessert.

"Splendid," we replied.

And truly, it had been no less sumptuous than delicate.

"Why then," said she, "let's swallow some of this."

It was a liqueur which immediately brought splashing up all we had just filled ourselves with, and in the space of three minutes our appetite was as keen as it had been before sitting down to dine. A second feast is brought on, and we fall to like wolves.

"A sip now of this other liqueur," says Olympia, "and it will all flush out below."

This ceremony is scarce over when pangs of hunger make themselves felt. In comes a third dinner, more succulent than either of the preceding two; we begin to feed anew.

"No ordinary wine this time," Olympia says; "let's start with Aleatico, we'll end with Falernian, and spirits after cheese."

"And the victim?"

"Jesusfuck," Chigi declares, "there's still life in her."

"Never mind, let's get her off the table and buried, dead or alive. We shall replace her with a fresh one."

No sooner said than done: the first of the girls is prised loose and removed and the same great skewer is run into the second girl's asshole, she serves as our centerpiece for the rest of the third meal. New to these excesses of the table, I feared I would not be able to bear up under them, but was mistaken; emptying the stomach, the elixir we were taking soothed it too; and although we had each eaten of the ninescore plates offered to our voracity, none of us felt any the worse for it. The second victim was still breathing when we came to this final dessert; irritated, our libertines had at her hammer and tongs. Foaming from fuckshed and drunkenness, there was nothing they did not inflict upon her bedraggled body, and I must own that I was in the forefront of the general assault. Bracciani made a number of physical experiments upon her, the last consisted in producing an artificial thunderbolt: it smote her, such was the cruel end she came to. Life had just seeped out of her when the arrival of Cornelia and her family wakened in us desires for new and more frightful horrors.

If Cornelia's beauty was without peer, neither was there anything to match the majesty of feature, the elegance of figure, that distinguished her unfortunate mother, aged thirty-five. Leonardo, Cornelia's brother, was only fifteen and in no respect inferior to his kin.

"Ha," Bracciani exulted as he grabbed the lad to him, "here's the prettiest bardash I've laid eyes on in a long time."

But this ill-starred family seemed so laden down by an air of suffering and sorrow that one could not help but pause a moment to consider it in this state; the criminal, you know, always delights in battening upon the grief his wickedness has caused the virtuous.

"I spy a light kindling in your eyes," Olympia murmured to me.

"That may well be," said I, "only a heart of stone would be left unmoved by such a spectacle."

"I know none more delicious," the Princess agreed, "in all the world not one so stirs my bowels and warms my womb."

"Prisoners," spoke forth the magistrate, affecting a solemn and awful tone, "you are, I believe, fully aware of your crimes?"

"We have never committed any," Cornelia replied.

"For a moment I thought my daughter guilty of a theft but, enlightened by your behavior, I have seen through your schemes."

"Madame, you're going to see them even more clearly later on."

And we conducted our three captives into the little garden prepared for the executions. There Chigi submitted them to a thorough questioning; I frigged him meanwhile. You cannot imagine with what art he would lure them into a hundred snares, nor the subterfuges he employed to trip them up, and notwithstanding the candor, the naïveté of their defenses, Chigi found all three guilty, very guilty, and pronounced sentence on the spot. Olympia pinions the mother, I seize the daughter, the Count and the magistrate leap upon the youth.

A few preliminary tortures seemed in order before turning to the final one with which these orgies were to conclude. Olympia must take a whip to Cornelia's belly, with rods Bracciani and Chigi beat Leonardo's fair buttocks all to tatters, and I mauled the mother's breasts. In due time we bound their arms behind their backs and attached the fatal ropes. Again and again they were hoisted a goodly distance into the air and dropped nearly to the ground; fifteen consecutive bounces wrench their shoulders from the socket, break their arms, split their breast-bones, tear their chests amain, at the tenth the infant in Cornelia's womb drops out and flies into Chigi's lap, whose member I am frigging upon Olympia's hinder parts, while Bracciani is working the windlass. The sight of this accident made us all discharge, and the frightful truth is that we kept right on with the game. Though our sperm was spent and our heads calm, none of us thought to beg quarter; and the bouncing continued until we had bounced the ghost clean out of those wretches. Thus it is crime will sport with innocence when, having wealth and influence on its side, nought remains for it to do but combat misfortune and poverty.

The appalling project planned for the morrow was carried out brilliantly. From a terrace Olympia and I surveyed the disaster, frigging ourselves as the conflagrations spread. By evening the thirty-seven asylums were all in flames and the dead already exceeded twenty thousand.

"Godsfuck!" I exclaimed to Olympia, discharging at the enchanting spectacle of her and her confederates' crimes, "how divine it is to perform such pieces of mischief! Inexplicable and mysterious Nature, if 'tis true these evil acts outrage thee, why makest thou me to delight in them? Ah, wench, thou deceivest me perhaps, as of old I was by the foul deific chimera to which they said thou wert subordinate; and what if we were no more thy bondsmen than a god's? Causes, may be, are unnecessary to effects, and we all, through some blind force that is in us, a force both irrational and essential, we are but stupid machines of the vegetation whose secret workings, explaining the origin of all motion, also demonstrate the origin of all human and animal activity."

The fire lasted eight days and nights during which we had no glimpse of our friends; they reappeared on the ninth morning.

"It is all over," said the magistrate; "the Pope has ceased wringing his hands; I have been granted the privilege I was seeking: my profit is as well as in the bank, and here are your rewards. Dear Olympia," Chigi continued, "that which would most surely have touched your benevolent heart was the burning of the *conservatorios;* had you only been able to see all those little maids, panic-stricken, naked, trampling one another in their maddened efforts to escape the flames, and the horde of ruffians I had stationed at the entrances, pitchforks in hand, while pretending to rescue them driving the greater part back into the fire but saving a few, the prettiest of the lot, to be sure, who shall live until the day they are sacrificed to my tyrannical lust. . . . Ah, Olympia, Olympia, had you been witness to all that you'd have died of pleasure."

"Villain," said Madame Borghese, "how many have you preserved?"

"Nearly two hundred; for the time being they are under guard in one of my palaces and shall later on be parceled out to my farms in the country. The best twenty specimens shall be yours, I promise them to you, and by way of thanks ask only that from time to time you bring me other such creatures as this charming person," Monsignor said, pointing to me.

"Why," said Olympia, "from what I know of your philosophy upon this article, it surprises me that you still think of her."

"I admit," said the magistrate, "that my sympathies do not

by any means go with the giving of my prick; signs that to the fucking she gets from me a woman is responding by love is enough for
me to cease paying her in any coin save that of scorn and hate.
Indeed, I have very often conceived both those sentiments for the
object about to become of service to me, and my pleasures, taken in
this manner, have gained considerably therefrom. All this relates to
my beliefs touching gratitude; I do not like having a woman imagine
I am somehow indebted to her because I soil myself from contact
with her; of her I demand nothing beyond submission, and the
same insensibility as the convenience upon which I sit every day
when I clear my bowels. I have never thought that from the junction
of two bodies there need or indeed can result that of two hearts:
this physical connection, in my view, is fraught with great possibilities for contempt, for disgust, for loathing, but with none at all for
love; I know of nothing so gigantic as that sentiment, nothing so
apt to pall pleasure, nothing, in a word, that is farther from my
heart. However, Madame, I dare assure you with a degree of
warmth," Chigi went on, taking my hands in his, "that the mentality you have shown yourself to possess sets you apart in my estimation, and that you will always merit consideration from all libertine
philosophers; having credited you with intelligence, I take it for
granted that you are eager to please only them."

From these flatteries, whereof I made no great case, we
passed on to more serious things. Chigi wished for yet another
glimpse of my ass, declaring that his interest in it was positively
indefatigable. So he and I, Bracciani, and Olympia removed into
the secret sanctuary of the Princess' pleasures where further infamies were celebrated and, upon my honor, I blush at describing
them to you. That accursed Borghese was prone to the most fantastic practices. A eunuch, a hermaphrodite, a dwarf, an eighty-
year-old woman, a turkey, a small ape, a very big mastiff, a she-goat,
and a little boy of four, the great-grandchild of the old woman,
were the lust-objects presented us by the Princess' duenna.

"Great God," I cried at beholding this menagerie, "what
depravation!"

"It's the most natural thing in the world," Bracciani reminded
me; "as you wear out one pleasure you are obliged to look for
another; this leads far. Tired of commonplace things, you desire

unusual ones, and that is why crime becomes the final station of lust. I know not, Juliette, what use you will find for these bizarre objects, but you may be certain that the Princess, my friend Monsignor Chigi, and I shall enjoy ourselves mightily among them."

"Why, I must simply accommodate myself," said I; "you'll never see me hang back where it is a question of debauchery or incongruities."

Even as I was speaking, the mastiff, doubtless trained in the trick, began to snuffle beneath my petticoats.

"Ah ha! Lucifer is under way," said Olympia with a laugh. "Undress yourself, Juliette; surrender your charms to this superb animal's libidinous caresses, it can prove a memorable experience."

I consent, needless to say; for what horror could have revolted me, I who devoted every one of my days to the quest of every kind of horror? Getting down on all fours I take up my position in the center of the room; the dog circles me, sniffs me, licks me, mounts me, and finishes by encunting me as nicely as you please, and discharging into my womb. But a rather peculiar thing happened: the beast's member had swollen to such proportions in the course of our conversation that his attempts to withdraw now caused me enormous discomfort. Failing to extricate himself, he seemed disposed to start in again; we decided that the simpler way would be to let him do so; sufficiently reduced by a second discharge, he pulled out a still colossal engine after having twice washed me with his sperm.

"There's a fine fellow," said Chigi; "you're going to see my lord Lucifer deal as handsomely with me as he has with Juliette. Extremely libertine in his tastes, this charming animal honors beauty wherever it is to be found: I wager he will fuck my ass with no less delectation than he has just fucked madame's cunt. But I propose to do more than dreamily endure an assault. Bring me that nanny, let me fuck it while playing whore to Lucifer."

I had never seen anything as bizarre as this play. Chigi, sparing of his seed, loosed none; but had nonetheless the look of taking wonderful pleasure from this voluptuous extravagance.

"Now watch me," said Bracciani, stepping to the fore, "I shall put on a different spectacle for you."

He has himself embuggered by the eunuch and embuggers the turkey. Olympia, her bare buttocks turned toward him, held the bird's neck wedged between her thighs; she beheads it the same instant the physician ejaculates.

"That," Bracciani assured us, "can afford exquisite pleasure; there is no describing the effect of a turkey's anus contracting as you cut off its head at the critical instant."

"I have never tried it," said Chigi, "but so loudly and so often have I heard this manner of fucking praised that I believe the time has come to see for myself. Juliette," he went on, "be a dear and hold this child between your thighs while I embugger it; blasphemies will announce my delirium, that will be the signal for you to cut the little rascal's throat."

"All very well," said Olympia, "but Juliette must have some pleasure in return for facilitating yours. I shall place the hermaphrodite to her mouth: caressing its two sexes at once, she'll suck out proof first of its virility and then of its female existence."

"Wait," said Bracciani, "positions may so be arranged as to enable me to bum-stuff the hermaphrodite and take an ass-fucking from the eunuch, the crone's bum being posed above my face so that she splatters shit over my features."

"What nastiness!" said Olympia

"Madame," said the Count, taking her up very quickly, "it has its explanation; there is not a single taste, not a single penchant which may not be shown to have a cause."

"Since this is to be a collective enterprise," said Chigi, "I'll have the monkey sodomize me while the dwarf, straddling the child, presents me his ass for kissing."

"But there remains Lucifer, the goat, and myself," Olympia bade us notice.

"We can easily find a place for everybody," said Chigi. "If you and the goat stand close enough to me I'll insert myself now in your ass, now in the animal's, Lucifer embuggering the one while I am busy with the other; but I still hold to my intention of discharging in the youngster's fundament, and do not forget, Juliette, you're to play the butcher when I am overtaken by my spasm."

The tableau is composed; never was anything so monstrous achieved in lubricity; we discharged none the less for that, all of us; off came the child's head at just the right moment; and when we quit our complex formation it was for each to extol the heavenly pleasures by which our originality had just been rewarded.[20]

The rest of the day was spent in more or less similar lewd doings. I was fucked by the ape; once again by the mastiff, but asswardly; by the androgyne, by the eunuch, by the two Italians, by Olympia's dildo. All the others frigged me, licked me, teated me in every part, and it was only after ten hours of piquant enjoyment I came out of those peculiar orgies. A delicious supper crowned the holiday; a Greek sacrifice was celebrated: firewood was collected, all the animals we had frolicked with were slaughtered ritually and lubriciously, their bodies thrown upon the pyre and, atop the holocaust, bound hand and foot, the crone was burned alive; only the eunuch and the hermaphrodite were left, and with them we flew on to other pleasures.

Five months had I been in Rome and I was nigh to wondering whether I should ever obtain the audience with the Pope that Cardinals Bernis and Albani had led me to hope for, when at last, several days after the adventure I have just related, I received a gallant little note from Bernis who besought me to come to him early the following morning, he would present me to His Holiness who, though he had wished to see me long ere this, had been unable to satisfy his desire until now. I was advised to array myself simply but at the same time with elegance, and to avoid all perfumes. "Braschi, like Henry IV," the Cardinal wrote, "prefers that each thing smell as it should smell; he abominates art, stands fast for Nature. Hence it is essential that you abstain even from the bidet."

Obedient in all these points, I reached the Cardinal's palace by ten o'clock. Pius was awaiting us at the Vatican.

"Holy Father," Bernis said, presenting me to him, "here is the young Frenchwoman you have wished to see. Singularly honored by

---

[20] The more unusual it was, the more pleasure it was bound to give, of this none of the rational participants could be in any doubt; for thus it is with all lubricities. No passion in the world demands so many aliments as that one; there is none that needs to be tended with more care: the more it asks, the more one must give it; and what we receive therefrom depends strictly upon what we sacrifice to it.

the favor you do her, she promises unquestioning compliance with all it may please Your Holiness to demand of her."

"She shall not repent her complacency," said Braschi. "Before turning to the impurities wherewith we shall be occupied I welcome this opportunity for a private interview with her. Go, Cardinal, and tell the chamberlains that the gates shall be closed to everybody today."

Bernis retires and His Holiness, taking me by the hand, escorts me through immense apartments until we come to a remote chamber where luxury and effeminacy, under the drab colors of religion and modesty, offered everything that most flatters the lascivious disposition. It was all blurred outlines, melting distinctions: next to a Theresa in ecstasy one saw a Messalina embuggered, underneath an image of Christ there crouched a Leda. . . .

"Repose yourself," Braschi said to me. "In this place of ease I forget distances, and smiling upon vice when it appears in shapes as amiable as yours, I permit it to sit at virtue's side."

"Brazen fraud," I said to that old despot, "you are so in the habit of deceiving others that you seek even to deceive yourself. What the devil is this prattle of virtue when your sole purpose in bringing me here is to sully yourself with vice?"

"I am not of those who can be soiled, dear girl," the Pope replied to me. "Successor of the disciples of God, the virtues of the Eternal gird me round, and I am not a man even when for a moment I adopt human failings."

After letting loose a burst of ungovernable laughter, "Bishop of Rome!" I cried, "enough of this insolent haughtiness, desist, I say, you are speaking to a woman who is philosopher enough to appreciate you; with your leave we shall look a little into your power and your pretensions.

"In Galilee, Braschi, there develops a religion, its bases are these: poverty, equality, and hatred of the rich. The principles of this sacred doctrine are that it is just as impossible for a rich man to enter into the kingdom of heaven as for a camel to pass through the eye of a needle; that the rich man is damned simply because he is rich. To the disciples of this cult it is forbidden ever to lay up provision, they are commanded to forsake all that they have. Jesus, their chief, is emphatic and clear: 'The Son of God came not to be

ministered unto, but to minister. . . . They that are first shall be
last. . . . Whosoever exalteth himself shall be abased; and he that
humbles himself shall be exalted.'²¹ The first apostles of this religion earned their living by the sweat of their brow. Is all this not
true, Braschi?"

"It is indeed true."

"Well then, I would now have you tell me what relation there
can be between these primitive institutions and the tremendous
wealth you accumulate here in Italy. Is it the Evangile or the
knavery of your predecessors that has put you in possession of
these boundless riches? Poor fellow! and do you fancy you can
still impose upon us?"

"Atheist, at least show respect for the descendant of Saint
Peter."

"You descend from nothing of the sort: Saint Peter never set
foot in Rome. At its beginnings and for many years to come the
Church had no bishops, only acquired them when, toward the end
of the second century of our era, it came somewhat to be known
and to take on a little consistency; how dare you maintain Peter
was in Rome when he himself wrote from Babylon?"²²

"Do you think to confound criticism by saying that Rome and

²¹ And what passeth all understanding is that the Jacobins of the French Revolution wanted to smash the altars of a God who spoke precisely their own language.
Yet more extraordinary, they who detest and want to destroy the Jacobins act in the
name of a God who speaks like the Jacobins. If this be not here the *ne plus ultra* of
human folly, I ask you where it is to be found. (*Supplementary note.*)

²² The Peter of the Christians is nothing else than the Annac, the Hermes, and
the Janus of the Ancients; all individuals to whom the gift of opening doors to some
beatitude or other was attributed. In Phoenician or in Hebrew the word *peter* means
to open; and Jesus, playing thereupon, could say to Peter: "Since thou art Peter"—
that is to say, he who opens—"thou shalt open the gates to the kingdom of heaven,"
just as taking from *peter* only its meaning of the Oriental word *kepha,* which means
building stone, he had said: "Thou art Peter, and upon this rock I will build my
church." *Mine* was once used to denote what is brought forth from a mine; similarly,
may they not have called *opening* what was extracted from the quarry, to which the
name *opening* was formerly given? Thus, the words *to open* and *stone* may have had
the same meaning, whence the pun made by Jesus, that imbecile who, as everyone
knows, never opened his mouth but riddles, anagrams, or puzzles came out of it. His
talk is all tedious allegory, where places are joined on to names, names to places, and
the facts always sacrificed to illusions. At any rate, this apostolic word is a very
ancient one, dating from long before the days of Christianity's Peter. Most mytholo-
gists have recognized it as the title of a person appointed to care for the *posterula.*

Babylon were the same thing? Pouah, nobody believes anything you say anymore. But was Peter even your type of man? Is not your predecessor depicted to us as a penniless ragged fellow who catechized the penniless and ragged? It would much appear that he resembled one of those founders of orders that live in indigence and whose successors swim in gold. I know that those who followed Peter sometimes gained money, sometimes lost it; but it is nonetheless true that superstition and credulity are yet so widespread that you still have some thirty or forty million servants on earth. But do you suppose the lamp of philosophy is not soon to shine before their eyes? Do you suppose they shall for very long go on accepting a master who dwells three or four hundred leagues away? That they shall for much longer be willing to think, judge, act only according to your dictates? Hold title to their properties only upon condition they pay you tribute, enter into no marriage save it be with your approval? No, my friend, you miscalculate if you count upon them remaining still a long while in bondage and error. I know that in times past your ridiculous rights went a great deal farther than now they do; you used to sit above the very gods, for those gods were only thought to dispose of empires while 'twas you who disposed of them. But I repeat it to you, Braschi, all that is being eclipsed, it is passing away; and in fact, my dear Pope, is it not staggering to see to what point superstition can denature the simplest things? Agree with me, that one is hard put to know which one ought most to admire, the prodigious blindness of whole peoples, or the gigantic effrontery of those who dupe them. How is it possible, after the appalling irregularities in which you and your like have been wallowing for centuries with the entire world looking on, that you can still be revered as you are? How is it possible that you still keep a few proselytes? 'Twas only the stupidity of princes and of populations that consolidated the grandeur of the popes and gave them the inconceivable audacity to arrogate to themselves pretensions so contrary to the spirit of their religion, so revolting to reason, and so harmful to polities. Those who are aware of the grip superstition exerts must still be amazed at its perennial successes; for there is not a single blunder, not a single extravagance to which the devout are not prone. Certain political interests conspired to aid the growth of superstition's child. During the years of the Roman Empire's decline, its chiefs, occupied in costly and very remote wars, were constrained to deal tactfully with you, knowing you to be in possession of the minds of the people; shutting their eyes to your enterprises they unwittingly promoted the destruction of their empire; through ignorance, the barbarian hordes adopted the political system of the emperors, and that is how, little by little, you became the masters of a fair part of the European peoples.

"The sciences were entrusted into the hands of the monks, your worthy liegemen; no one was permitted to shed light on the universe, men were in bondage to what they did not understand, and the warriors who fought around the world found it easier to bend you a worshipful knee than to analyze you. The fifteenth century brought a shift in the wind, the dawning of philosophy heralded superstition's downfall; clouds lifted and men dared look you in the face. In you and yours they soon came to see nothing but impostors and frauds; a few nations still subjugated by their priests remained faithful to you; but the light of reason's torch shines at last for them as well. Oh, my good, my blessed Pope! your role is ended. To hasten the important revolution which must bring down forever the pillars of your superstitious establishment one need only cast a glance at the history of your antecedents in the See. I shall outline it for you, Braschi, from my erudition it will be shown that since the women of my country are instructed to this degree, the France I am proud of shall not be long shaking off your ridiculous yoke.

"What do I behold at the beginning of your Christian era? Battles, strife, tumults, seditions, massacres, the fruit solely of the greed and the ambition of the rogues who pretended to your throne; the proud pontiffs of your disgusting Church were already going in triumphal cars through Rome; lust and lewdness were already defiling them; the purple enwrapped them already; and 'tis not your enemies I consult for evidence of the reproaches addressed to you in those days, no, I refer to your partisans, to the very Fathers of the Church; listen to Jerome, to Basil: 'When I was in Rome,' says the former, 'I sought to make the language of piety and virtue heard; the Pharisees surrounding the Pope jeered and tormented me; and I quit the palaces of Rome to return to the grottoes of Jesus.' Thus did your satellites, driven to it by the force of truth, level the accusing finger at you even at this early hour. With what vehemence the same Jerome elsewhere rebukes you for the scandals occasioned by your debauches, your dishonesties, your intrigues to milk money from the rich, to have yourselves named the heirs of the mighty and above all of the Roman ladies you first tupped and then dunned. Shall I send you to read the emperors' edicts? See therein the efforts Valentinian, Valens, and Gratian deployed to repress your greed, your libertinage, your overweening ambition. But let us go on with our sketch and paint in broad strokes. Do you fancy, Braschi, do you believe that one can have anything but doubts of your holiness, of your infallibility, when one observes:

"A Liberius, out of fear and weakness dragging the entire Church into Arianism?

"A Gregory, proscribing the arts and sciences, and giving as reason for this that ignorance alone can favor the absurdities of his loathsome religion—a Gregory who dares carry impudence so far as to flatter Queen Brunhilde, that monster whom France remembers with shame to this day?

"A Stephen VI regarding Formosus, his predecessor, as so defiled by crimes that he feels under the ridiculous and barbaric obligation of punishing the dead pope's corpse?

"A Sergius, soiled by all sorts of debauchery, whores always leading him around by the nose?

"A John XI, son of one of those sluts, and who himself lived in regular incest with Marosia, his mother?

"A John XII, the idolatrous magician who employed the very temple of God as the theater for his most shameful debauches?

"A Boniface VII, so eager for the papal tiara that he murders Benedict VI in order to succeed him?[23]

"A Gregory VII, who, more despotic than any king, made them all come begging pardon at his door; who caused seas of

---

[23] There was then in Rome a certain Gerardius Brazet, regarded as the Holy See's official poisoner; he had envenomed eight popes, upon the orders of those who were anxious to succeed them. The Vatican pontiffs of that time, says Baronius, were such great villains that never before in any age had the like of them been seen, nor so many scenes of horror.

blood to be shed in Germany, uniquely for the sake of his pride and
ambition; who maintained that a pope could do no wrong; that all
popes were infallible; that to be seated in Saint Peter's chair
sufficed to render a man as powerful as Almighty God?

"A Pascal II, who, in observance of these abominable principles, dares arm an emperor against his own father?

"An Alexander III, who has Henry II of England ignominiously flogged for a murder that prince never committed; who
promulgates the bloody crusade against the Albigensians?

"A Celestine III, who, overflowing ambition and tyranny,
dares use his foot to push the crown upon the head of Henry IV,
prostrate before him; and then kicks that crown off again, to show
the Emperor what is in store for him should he be lacking in respect
for the Pope?

"An Innocent IV, poisoner of Emperor Frederick during the
interminable wars between Guelphs and Ghibellines, for which
your pride and your passions were responsible and which brought
about the demoralization of all Italy?

"A Clement IV, who has a young prince decapitated for having
done nothing worse than present a claim to the succession of his
fathers?

"A Boniface VIII, famous for his quarrels with the kings of
France; impious, ambitious, the author of that sacred farce known
under the name of Jubilee, the single purpose whereof is to fill the
pontifical coffers?[24]

"A Clement V, enough of a scoundrel to have slain Emperor
Henry VI by means of a poisoned host?

"A Benedict XII, who buys celebrated Petrarch's sister to
make her his mistress?

"A John XXIII [*sic*.], notorious for his extravagances; who
condemns as heretics all who maintain that Jesus Christ lived in
simple poverty, who distributed crowns, who changed just into
unjust, and whose madness led him to the point of excommunicating
angels?

"A Sixtus IV, who drew a considerable revenue from the

[24] It is of him they said that he mounted the throne like a fox, reigned there
like a lion, and died like a dog.

brothels he had installed in Rome, who sent the Swiss a crimson flag, and with it the invitation to cut one another's throats for the prosperity of the Roman Church?

"An Alexander VI, the mere mention of whose name is enough to excite the indignation and horror of those who have some idea of his story; an enormous scoundrel, without probity, or honor, or sincerity, or pity, or religion, whose lewd debauchery, cruelties, poisonings surpassed everything Suetonius reports of Tiberius, Nero, and Caligula; in fine, a libertine who lay with his own daughter Lucrezia,[25] who was wont to have fifty naked whores run about on all fours, in order to fire his imagination from the various postures they assumed?

"A Leo X, who to repair the depredations of his predecessors, invented the scheme of selling indulgences, though such an unbeliever that in reply to his friend Cardinal Bembo, who quoted him a passage out of Scripture, he could say: 'What the devil are you up to, coming to me with your Jesus Christ fables?'

"A Julius III, that true Sardanapalus, who carried impudence to the point of raising his catamite to be a cardinal; who one day, nude in his chamber, obliged the members of the College who entered there to remove their clothes too, saying, 'My friends, if we were to go about thus in the streets of Rome, we would be not so much revered. Now if our raiments alone inspire respect, are we really nothing at all without them?'

"A Pius V, adored for a saint, fanatical, tigerish, who was the cause of all the persecutions exercised against the Protestants in France; instigator of the Duke of Alba's ferocities; murderer of Paleario whose only crime was having said that the Inquisition had a dagger for stabbing men of letters; and who finally declared that he had never been in so little hope of salvation as since he became Pope?

"A Gregory XIII, frightful panegyrist of the St. Bartholomew massacre and who privately addressed letters of congratulation to Charles IX for having himself participated in the slaughter?

---

25 Of her the poet Jacopo Sannazaro, the Neapolitan Petrarch, tells us:
Hoc jacet in tumula Lucretia nomine sedra,
Thaïs Alexandria filia, sponsa nurus.

"A Sixtus V, who declared that in Rome one could bugger and be buggered as much as he liked during the hottest part of summer, and whose method for establishing order and calm in that city was to bathe it in blood?

"A Clement VIII, author of the famous Gunpowder Plot?

"A Paul V, who waged war against Venice because a civil magistrate had presumed to punish a monk for having raped and killed a twelve-year-old girl?

"A Gregory XV, writing to Louis XIII: 'Put them all to fire and sword who abide not by me'?

"An Urban VIII, who cooperated in those Irish massacres where one hundred and fifty thousand Protestants died, etc., etc.?

"There they are, my friend, such are they who were the Vicar of Christ before you. And you are amazed, you are vexed, you are downcast and confounded that we hold in just horror the insolent or corrupt leaders of such a sect? Ah! may all nations be quick to rid themselves of their illusions regarding these papal idols who until now have procured them nought but trouble, indigence, and woe! Let all the peoples of the earth, shuddering at the terrible havoc wrought for so many centuries by this long line of rascals, hasten to dethrone him who is Pope today and at the same time put an end to the stupid and barbarous, the idolatrous, sanguinary, impious, infamous religion capable of having such monsters at its head."

Pius VI, who to all this had lent a very attentive ear, sat gazing in astonishment at me when I reached the end of my speech.

"Braschi," said I, "thou art surprised at my wit and learning; know that it is thus all the children in my country are nowadays brought up: the age of error is past. Act accordingly, old despot, break thy cross, burn thy hosts, fling thy gauds and thy images and thy relics on the dungheap: after having freed populations from the oath of fealty that bound them to sovereigns, free them now from error's dungeons where thou holdest them prisoner. Believe me, get thee down off thy throne ere thou art submerged beneath its wreckage; better to cede thy place pacifically than to be evicted from it by force. Opinion rules everything in the world; it is changing toward thee and all thy mummeries. Vary in tune with the times. When the scythe is uplifted, wiser to step aside than await the blade. Thou art not poor; retire, become a simple citizen in Rome again. Change the funeral livery of all this frocked crowd hanging about thee, dismiss thy friars, open thy cloisters, liberate thy nuns, let them marry, drown not the seed of one hundred generations in the barren ocean of chastity. Awestruck Europe shall admire thee, thy name shall be writ big on the columns of memory, never shall it be recorded there save thou exchangest the melancholy honor of being pope for that, far more precious, of being a philosopher."

"Juliette," Braschi said, "they did indeed tell me you were a clever girl, but you outdo all reports; such loftiness of ideas is extremely rare in a woman. It is not with you feigning is best, I drop the mask; behold the man, behold him who is set on enjoying you and who shall not higgle over the price."

"Listen to me," I replied, "it is not to play the vestal I have come here, and since I let myself be enticed into the most mysterious recesses of your palace you must surely be aware I have no intention of resisting you; but instead of getting a congenial partner, an ardent woman, someone of flesh and bone, with an intuition into your tastes, a fondness for them, you'll have nought but a stone statue unless you grant me four things, and they are these:

"To begin with I demand, as a first mark of trust, that you give me the keys to your most secret chambers; I wish to visit every nook, every cranny, to see all of what each contains.

"The second thing I would have from you is a dissertation upon murder: I myself have murdered rather a lot, and have my views upon the question; I am eager to hear yours. What you say shall probably fix my attitude definitively; not that I believe you incapable of error, but I have confidence in the studies you must have made; you will speak frankly to me, for philosophers cannot trifle with anything but the truth.

"My third condition is that you convince me of your profound contempt for all the rigamarole and ritual cant of Christian worship; to do so you have simply to proceed thus: after having had your chaplains celebrate High Mass upon the ass of a bardash, and having with your holy prick rammed the little flour-and-water God into my anus, you will then fuck me on Saint Peter's altar.

I warn you that I shall not be fucked by you in any other way. Such follies are nothing new to me, but the idea of seeing them committed by you rouses me.

"The fourth clause is, that inside several days you give me a lavish supper with Albani, Bernis, and my friend Princess Borghese, that at this supper there sparkle more lewdness and glitter, more libertinage than was ever displayed by any pope of old, the occasion must be gayer a thousand times, and for infamy a thousand times richer than the feast Alexander VI had served to Lucrezia."

"Assuredly," said Braschi, "these are indeed strange conditions."

"Either you accept them or never in your life shall you possess me."

"Young woman, you seem not to realize that I have you in my power, and that at a mere word from me—"

"I know that you are a tyrant," I interrupted, "that you are base and a knave, cruel and wicked: without those qualities, it's obvious, you'd not be in the post you hold; but forasmuch as I am no less a rascal than you, you love me. You love me, Braschi. It makes you glad to see to what point wickedness of your own sort can fill the soul of a woman; I am your joy, mighty Braschi, and you shall be mine, little Braschi; you shall satisfy me."

"Oh, Juliette," Pius VI said to me, folding me in his arms, "you are a most uncommon creature, your genius is irresistible, I shall be your slave; with the mind that appears to be yours, I am in expectation of very piquant pleasures from you, of enormities. Here, the keys, they are on this ring . . . take them, go visit my abode; after I have received your favors I promise you the dissertation you solicit. As well, you may count upon the supper you demand, and as for the profanation your heart is set on, it shall take place this very night. I accord no more faith than you to all those spiritual mummeries, my angel; but you know the obligation we are under to make fools of the simple. I am like the charlatan with his quackeries, I must look as though I believed in the stuff if I am to vend it."

"There's plain proof you are a rascal," I said; "were you honest you would prefer to enlighten mankind rather than deceive it; you would tear the blind from their eyes rather than tighten it."

"Of course; but I'd starve to death."

"And what necessity is there that you live? Is it so urgent that, for the sake of your digestion, fifty million people wander in error?"

"Yes, because my existence means everything to me, and those fifty million people nothing; because the foremost of Nature's laws is of self-preservation . . . at the expense of no matter whom."

"You are showing your true colors, Pontiff, that is all I was after. So let us shake hands, since we're a pair of rogues each as bad as the other, and henceforth an end to all shamming; agreed?"

"Excellent," said the Pope, "we'll concern ourselves with pleasures only."

"Very well," I rejoined, "start by carrying out one of your promises; get me a guide, I wish to tour this place."

"I shall guide you through it myself," said Braschi.

"This superb palace," he told me as we walked along, "stands on the site of an ancient one in whose gardens the paths were illuminated at night by the bodies of the early Christians; Nero had them spaced at regular intervals and daubed with pitch. They served as flares."[26]

---

[26] But let us translate straight out of Tacitus: "He caused the Christians to be put cruelly to death for having set fire to Rome. These Christians," the historian continues, "were people hated for their infamy, and because of a rogue named Christ, their spiritual leader, who had been executed under the reign of Tiberius. But after having been repressed for a while this pernicious sect bred up a stench anew, not only in its place of origin but in Rome itself, whither all roads lead and, as it were, all sewers too. First to be seized were those who professed openly to belong to this vile cult, their avowals led to the arrest of a great crowd of similar wretches, who were convicted of atrocious crimes. Hatred for them was general and unbounded, whereof the proof is the disgraceful deaths they were made to die, covered by the skins of wild beasts and left to the dogs, or affixed to crosses and left to rot, or again burned in heaps like faggots, to light the streets and highways (it is the source of the expression *lux in luce*). Nero willingly lent his gardens for these spectacles. He would be seen, dressed as a driver, mingling among the people or seated in a chariot. Those executions of Christians amused him hugely, he often took a direct hand in them."

Listen now to what Lucian tells us of this same sect: "It is an assembly of ragged vagabonds, fanatical of eye, frenzied of gesture, uttering moans, doing contortions, swearing by the son begot of the father, predicting a thousand awful calamities to the Empire, reviling all those not of their belief." Such was the Christian religion from the very outset: a horde of troublemakers and scurvy fellows fol-

"Oh, my friend, such a spectacle is made for eyes like mine, a joyous sight it would have been to one animated by my own loathing for your creed and its adepts."

"Forget not, little minx," said the Holy Father, "that 'tis to the head of this religion you are speaking."

"He has as little liking for it as I," was my response, "he knows what it is worth; and esteems it only for the income it yields him. Come, come, my friend, were you able, you would deal just as harshly with the enemies of the religion off which you fatten."

"Certainly, Juliette: intolerance is the underlying principle of the Church; without an implacable rigorism, its temples would be quickly in ruins; and where the law is unheeded the sword must smite."

"Despotic Braschi!"

"But how else would you have princes reign? Their power is seated upon mere opinion; let it change and they are undone. Their one means for stabilizing it consists in terrorizing the public, in putting fear into hearts and a cloud over vision, in order that pygmies appear as giants."

"Ah, Braschi, I have told you so already, the people are coming to their senses; the days of the tyrants are numbered; the scepters they hold and the irons they impose, all will be shattered upon the altars of Liberty, as the cedar topples before the north wind's blast. Far too long has despotism deprived them of their rights, the people must inevitably reach out and take them back, a general revolution must inevitably rage over all Europe; all must come tumbling down, shrines and thrones with it, and space must be cleared for double the energy of a Brutus and twice the virtues of a Cato."

We were still walking. "A thorough visit of these buildings is no mean undertaking," Braschi said to me; "the palace contains four thousand four hundred and twenty-two rooms, includes

---

lowed about by whores. The woes of this rabble finally interested the weaker members of society, as usually happens; had the sect not been persecuted it would have faded away and never anymore been heard of. It is incredible that one such heap of impostures, atrocities, and gibberish could have held our forefathers spellbound for ages. When shall we become wise enough to be irrevocably and forever done with all this?

twenty-two courtyards, and its gardens are vast. Let us have a look at this," said the Pope, leading me into a gallery above the vestibule of St. Peter's basilica. "From here," the Pontiff explained, "I shed my blessings upon the world; here, I excommunicate kings; here, I pronounce null and void the vows whereby princes hold nations in fee."

"Poor player, you strut upon no very solid stage whose foundations are absurdity; philosophy shall bring all your little theater crashing down."

From thence we passed into the celebrated picture gallery. In all Europe there is no room longer, not even the gallery of the Louvre; none contains such fine paintings. While admiring the "Saint Peter of the Three Keys," "Pontiff," I said to Braschi, "another monument to your pride?"

"'Tis an emblem," the Pope explained, "of the unlimited power Gregory VII and Boniface VIII attributed to themselves."

"Holy Father," said I to the old bishop, "surrender. these emblems, put a whip in your gatekeeper's hand, bare your venerable ass for a beating, and summon in a painter, you'll at least have the merit of auguring true."

We went next into the library laid out in the form of a T. In that library there were a great many cupboards, but few books on display.

"Everything is false in your house," I pointed out to Braschi; "you keep three out of four of these bookcases sealed shut lest it be seen they are empty. Deception and fraudulence are everywhere your motto."

Upon one of those shelves I found a manuscript of Terence where drawings of the masks to be worn by the actors precede each of the plays. As well, much to my satisfaction, I came across the original letters Henry VIII wrote to Anne Boleyn, the slut with whom he was in love and whom he married despite the Pope; memorable period of the Reformation in England.

After this we traversed the gardens where groves of orange trees and myrtle were growing and fountains played.

"The other part of the palace, and it is there our tour will end," the Holy Father said to me, "is used as a preserve for lust-objects in the one sex and in the other; they are lodged behind bars; some will appear at the supper I have promised you."

"Ah, Braschi," said I, full of enthusiasm, "so you keep things in cages, do you? I trust it is rather a hard life they lead? Do you whip a little?"

"One inevitably becomes severe as one gets on in years," good Braschi admitted; "for a man of my age there is no sweeter pleasure; I confess that I prefer it to all the rest."

"If you whip it is because you are cruel: fustigation on the part of a libertine is but the vent he gives his ferocity; were he to dare, he would express it in other ways."

"Well, Juliette," was the Holy Father's pleasant reply, "I am sometimes very daring indeed, as you shall see, yes, as you shall most certainly see."

"My friend, let us not forget the treasures I am to examine. You must have gold, your greed is legendary; I share that vice and would fain plunge my hands into heaps of those gleaming, fresh-minted coins that are so agreeable to the touch and to the eye."

"We are not far from where they are stored," said the Pope, leading me down an obscure passageway. We came to a small iron door, he opened it. "Everything the Holy See possesses is here," my guide continued, ushering me into a vaulted chamber in the center of which were chests containing, in crowns and sequins, between fifty and sixty millions at the very most. "I am afraid I have spent more than I have contributed to the hoard. Sixtus V founded it as a testimonial to the stupidity of Christians."

"If there is to be nothing hereditary about your tiara," said I, "you are great dupes to amass riches in this world; had I been in your place I would have dilapidated the funds long ago. Scatter money to your friends, multiply your pleasures, enjoy yourself without stint, far better that than to leave these sums to accumulate for the conquerors' taking, since overthrown you shall be. Pontiff, I foretell it to you now, one free nation or several in confederacy, rid of monarchical impediment, shall attack and defeat you; grieved though you must be to hear it, know nevertheless that you are by all odds the last pope the Church of Rome is going to have. What's to be taken from here?"

"A thousand sequins."

"A thousand sequins! The miserly beggar! Pope, there is a scale standing by, I'll fill my pockets and let's see whether I cannot get out of here with three times my weight in gold; you can hardly pay a woman less who has merits like mine."

So saying I began to scoop up handfuls of coins.

"Stay, my dear, you shall fatigue yourself to no purpose; instead, let me give you a certificate for, let us say, ten thousand sequins redeemable upon presentation to my treasurer."

"Such an act of generosity touches me very little," said I, " 'tis upon Venus you place these stakes."

And as we were leaving that treasure room, the subdued light favoring my preconceived design, I succeeded in taking an imprint of the key with a bit of wax I had brought for that purpose; Braschi, occupied with his own thoughts, noticed nothing; and we retraced our steps to the apartment in which he had received me.

"Juliette," he said then, "although but one of your conditions has been fulfilled so far, you must be content with me; let us now see whether I shall be content with you."

And at this the lecher unties my skirt-strings.[27]

"But," say I, "what of the rest?"

"Since I kept my word on the first article, Juliette, you need not doubt that I shall do as much on the others."

The old rake already had me at his disposition; I was bent forward over a sofa while he, the droll fellow, one knee on the floor, was peering narrowly at what seemed to be of extreme interest to him.

"It is superb," he declared; "Albani spoke well of it to me, but I anticipated nothing of this degree of superiority."

---

[27] My intimates know that throughout my Italian travels I was accompanied by a most attractive and engaging woman; that simply out of lewd philosophic principle I introduced this person to the Tuscan Grand Duke, to the Vicar of Christ, to Princess Borghese, to their Royal Highnesses the King and Queen of Naples. They may therefore be perfectly certain that everything I say relating to the voluptuous side of the journey is authentic, that I have depicted nothing but the accustomed behavior and characteristic attitudes of the persons I mention, and that had they been witness to these scenes, they could not have rendered sincerer accounts of them. I take this occasion to assure the reader that the same applies to the descriptive part of my narrative; it is scrupulously exact.

The Pontiff's kisses waxed gradually more ardent: his tongue thrilled here and there along the perimeter, then danced inside, and I saw one of his hands scurry toward the region of his debilitated manhood. I was all afire to see the prick of the Pope, I craned my head around but in that posture could make out nothing.

"If," said I, "you are willing to be disturbed for a moment we might arrange ourselves more conveniently and I will be able to facilitate your enterprise without in the least diverting your homage."

Then, helping him recline upon the sofa, I planted my behind over his face and leaned down to frig his member while with the hand not devoted to that chore I stroked his buttocks, then strove to arouse him anally. These divers occupations put me in position to analyze the Holy Father, and I shall describe him to you as best I can.

Braschi is plump, his buttocks broad, chubby, but firm, so toughened, so calloused by the habit he has of receiving the scourge, that a knife-point would sooner penetrate walrus-hide; his asshole is slack and prodigiously wide, and how could it be otherwise in view of the twenty-five or thirty fuckings it ordinarily gets every day? His prick, once aloft, is not without beauty, it is lean, wiry, clears nicely at the tip, and is somewhere near eight inches long by six in circumference. Hardly had it reared itself when the papal passions received energetic expression: as His Holiness' brow was wedged between my buttocks, first his teeth, then in short order his nails made themselves felt. So long as 'twas done in playful spirit I held my peace; but when Pius VI began to lose all sense of proportion, I turned around.

"Braschi, with you I accept the accomplice's role but I decline that of victim."

"When I am hot and when I pay," the Pope rejoined, "I am not much inclined to split hairs. Shit, Juliette, be a good girl and shit, that will calm me; I worship shit and my discharge is certain if you can supply me some."

It being within my power to gratify him, I return to my post; I push, I grunt, I shit; the pontifical prick hardens to such a point I believe it is about to discharge.

"Ready yourself, be quick," cries the pig, "I am going to embugger you—"

"No, you're not," say I, "it will sap your strength, our nocturnal orgies will suffer from your thoughtlessness now."

"You are mistaken," the Pope assures me, clinging fast to my two buttocks, "I frequently fuck thirty, forty asses without losing a drop of sperm. Into position, I tell you, bugger you I must, bugger you I shall."

What could I reply to that? He was a very determined man; this was confirmed by the state of his prick, at which I glanced again; I offered my ass; Braschi speared it dry and deep. This scraping whence resulted mingled pain and pleasure, the moral irritation resulting from the idea of holding the Pope's prick in my ass, everything marched me toward happiness: I discharged. My bugger, sensing as much, hugged me frenziedly and drove me hard, he kissed me, he frigged me. But completely in control of his passions, the lecher roused them without giving them any final outlet; after a harrowing fifteen minutes he withdrew.

"You are delicious," he affirmed, "I have never fucked a more voluptuous ass. Let us dine. I shall give orders for the execution of the scene you wish to transpire on Saint Peter's high altar; we shall repair to the basilica after our meal."

We were but two at table, and we conducted ourselves like perfect swine. For lewdness there are few people in this world who can compare with Braschi; there are none more schooled in the finer points of debauchery. His is a delicate stomach; he would not touch certain food until it had been prepared for eating, after wetting each morsel with my saliva I would feed it into his mouth, in my mouth were rinsed the wines he afterward drank, he sometimes injected half a bottle of Tokay or sack into my fundament, then swallowed what I flushed forth and if by chance it included a mard or two, he would be in raptures.

"Oh, Braschi!" I exclaimed during a moment of lucidity, "what would they say, the people upon whom you professionally impose, if they could see you in the midst of these turpitudes?"

"They would express for me the same contempt I have for them," Braschi answered, "and despite their pride they would own to their absurdity. But no matter! let's continue to dazzle and dupe them: the reign of error shall someday come to its end, we must enjoy it while it lasts."

"Why yes, yes indeed," I concurred, "let us fuddle and fool mankind, it asks for no greater service. . . . Braschi, say now, shall we not immolate a few victims in the temple whither we are soon to go?"

"Of course we shall," the Holy Father replied, "blood must flow before orgies are satisfactory. Seated on Tiberius' throne, I imitate his voluptuous practices; and I too know no more delicious discharge than that expelled in echo to the plaintive accents of the dying."

"Do you indulge often in those excesses?"

"Rarely do I let a day go by without plunging into them, Juliette, and never do I retire for the night with unbloodied hands."

"But from where does this monstrous taste come?"

"From Nature, my child. Murder is one of her laws; whenever she feels the need for murder she inspires in us a longing to commit it, and willy-nilly we obey her. I shall shortly employ more vigorous arguments to demonstrate that this fancied crime is no crime at all; if you desire, I shall perform it. In an effort to accommodate their doctrine to conventional notions, ordinary philosophers have submitted man to Nature; I am prepared to prove to you that man is in no wise dependent upon her."

"My friend," said I, "I remind you of your promise: this dissertation is part of our bargain, pray fulfill it now, we have the time."

"As you like," said the mitred thinker; "I shall ask for your whole attention, the subject demands it.

"Of all the extravagances into which man's pride was to lead him, the most absurd was probably the precious case he dared make of his person. Surrounded by creatures worth as much and more than he, he nonetheless considered himself at liberty to make away with those beings which he fancied subordinate to him, the while believing that no penance, no punishment, could wipe clear the crime consisting in an attempt upon his own life. To the initial folly stemming from pride, to that revolting stupidity of considering he was sprung from some divinity, of supposing himself in possession of an immortal soul, to this atrocious blindness he was doubtless obliged to add the other of esteeming his mortal self beyond price. Indeed, how could the beloved masterpiece of a bountiful divinity, how could heaven's favorite have come to any other conclusion? the severest penalties had incontrovertibly to be prescribed for whoever should wreck such a splendid machine. This machine was sacred; a soul, the brilliant image of a yet more brilliant divinity, animated this construction whose destruction must be the most dreadful crime it would be possible to commit. And even as he reasoned thus, to appease his gluttony he roasted the lamb entire on a spit, he carved into pieces and boiled in a pot this gentle and peaceable lamb, a creature shaped by the same hand that shaped him, his inferior simply because differently built. However, had he reflected a little he would have thought a great deal less highly of himself; a rather more philosophical glance cast at the Nature he misunderstood would have caused him to see that, a weak and ill-formed product of that blind mother's manufacture, he resembled all other creatures, that his condition was bound inextricably to the condition of all others, necessitated like all the others', and hence not one whit better than theirs.

"No earthly creature is expressly formed by Nature, none deliberately made by her; all are the result of her laws and her workings, in such sort that, in a world constituted like ours, there had necessarily to be such creatures as we find here; very different creatures probably inhabit other globes, the myriads of globes wherewith space is freighted. But these creatures are neither good nor beautiful, precious nor created; they are the froth, they are the result of Nature's unthinking operations, they are like vapors which rise up from the liquid in a caldron that is rarefied by heat, whose action drives out the particles of air this liquid contains. This steam is not created, it is resultative, it is heterogeneous, it derives its existence from a foreign element and has in itself no intrinsic value; its being or not has no adverse effect upon the element it emanates from; to this element it adds nothing, owes nothing, this element owes nothing to it. Let some other vibration different from heat modify this element, it will continue to exist in its new modification, and the vapor which resulted from it before will cease to result from it now. Let Nature become subject to other laws, these creatures resulting from the present laws will exist no more under these different ones, but Nature will nonetheless still exist, although by different laws.

"Man thus has no relationship to Nature, nor Nature to man; Nature cannot bind man by any law, man is in no way dependent upon Nature, neither is answerable to the other, they cannot either harm or help each other; one has produced involuntarily—hence has no real relationship to her product; the other is involuntarily produced—hence has no real relationship to his producer. Once cast, man has nothing further to do with Nature; once Nature has cast him, her control over man ends; he is under the control of his own laws, laws that are inherent in him. With his casting man receives a direct and specific system of laws by which he must abide, under which he must proceed ever after; these laws are those of his personal self-preservation, of his multiplication, laws which refer to him, which are of him, laws which are uniquely his own, vital to him but in no way necessary to Nature, for he is no longer of Nature, no longer in her grip, he is separate from her. He is an entity entirely distinct from her; of such little usefulness is he to her workings, of such little necessity to her combinations, that whether he were to quadruple his species or annihilate it totally, the universe would not be in the slightest the worse for it. If man destroys himself, he does wrong—in his own eyes. But that is not the view Nature takes of the thing. As she sees it, if he multiplies he does wrong, for he usurps from Nature the honor of a new phenomenon, creatures being the necessary result of her workings. If those creatures that are cast were not to propagate themselves, she would cast new entities and enjoy a faculty she has ceased to be able to exercise. Not that she is unable to recover the use of that faculty, if she wished to have it, but she never does anything needlessly, and so long as the first series of beings propagate themselves by faculties inherent in them, she suspends propagation: our multiplication, only one of the laws inherent in us, is therefore decidedly detrimental to the phenomena whereof Nature is capable.

"Thus, those that we regard as virtues become crimes from her point of view. Whereas, contrariwise, if creatures destroy one another, they do well as regards Nature; for no obligation to reproduce has been imposed upon them, they have simply received the faculty to reproduce; turning to destruction, they cease exercising it, and give Nature the opportunity to resume the propagation from which she refrained so long as it was needless. You may perhaps object that if this possibility of propagation she has left her creatures were detrimental to her, she would not have bestowed it in the first place. But observe that she has no choice in these matters, that she is bound by her laws, that she cannot alter them, that one of her laws is the casting of creatures which are cast at a single stroke and emerge such as they must remain, and that another of her laws is that her creatures be invested with the possibility to propagate themselves. Observe as well that were .these creatures to cease propagating, or to destroy themselves, Nature's original rights, contested hitherto, would be restored to her; whereas in propagating, or in not destroying, we confine her to her secondary functions and deprive her of her primary powers. Thus, all the laws we humans have made, whether to encourage population or to prevent its destruction, necessarily conflict with all of hers: and every time we act in accordance with our laws, we directly thwart her desires; but, reversibly, every time we either stubbornly refuse to undertake the propagation she abhors, or cooperate in the murders which delight her and which serve her, we are sure to please her, certain of acting in harmony with her wishes. Ah, does she leave us in any doubt of the point to which our increase inconveniences her? can we not tell how eager she would be to halt our multiplication and be delivered of its ill effects? Is all this not proven by the disasters she sends to harry us, by the divisions and discords she sows in our midst, by the thirst for murder she constantly inspires in us? These wars, these famines she hurls at us, these pestilences she now and again looses with the aim of wiping us off the face of the earth, these great villains she fabricates in profusion, these Alexanders, these Tamurlanes, these Ghengis Khans, all these heroes who lay the world waste, by these tokens, I say, does she not plainly demonstrate that all our laws are contrary to hers, and that her purpose is to destroy them? Thus it is that these murders our laws punish so sternly, these murders we suppose the greatest outrage that can be inflicted upon Nature, not only, as you very well see, do her no hurt and can do her none, but are in some sort instrumental to her, since she is a great murderess herself and since her single reason for murdering is to obtain, from the wholesale annihilation of cast creatures, the chance to recast them anew. The most wicked individual on earth, the most abominable, the most ferocious, the most barbarous, and the most indefatigable murderer is therefore but the spokesman of her desires, the vehicle of her will, and the surest agent of her caprices.

"Let us go further. This murderer thinks he destroys, he thinks he consumes, and these beliefs sometimes engender remorse in his heart; let us put him confidently at ease, and if the system I have just developed is a little beyond his reach, let us prove to him from what happens before his very eyes that he has not even the honor of destroying; that the annihilation upon which he flatters himself when in sound health, or at which he shudders when he is sick, is no annihilation at all, and that annihilation is unfortunately something he cannot possibly achieve.

"The invisible chain which links all physical beings together, the absolute interdependence of the three kingdoms, animal, mineral, and vegetable, proves that all three are in the same case as regards Nature, that all three are resultant from her primary laws, but neither created nor necessary. These kingdoms are governed by the same laws. All three mechanically reproduce and destroy themselves, because all three are composed of the same elements, which sometimes combine in one fashion, sometimes in another; but these laws and workings are distinct from Nature's laws and workings, and independent of them; upon the three kingdoms she acted only once, *she cast them,* cast them once and for all; since having been cast they have acted on their own; they have acted according to their own laws, the foremost of these being a perpetual metempsychosis, a perpetual variation, a perpetual permutation embracing all three in a perpetual movement.

"In all living beings the principle of life is no other than that of death: at the same time we receive the one we receive the other, we nourish both within us, side by side. At the instant we call *death,* everything seems to dissolve; we are led to think so by the excessive change that appears to have been brought about in this portion of matter which no longer seems animate. But this death is only imaginary, it exists figuratively but in no other way. Matter, deprived of the other portion of matter which communicated movement to it, is not destroyed for that; it merely abandons its form, it decays—and in decaying proves that it is not inert; it enriches the soil, fertilizes it, and serves in the regeneration of the other kingdoms as well as of its own. There is, in the final analysis, no essential difference between this first life we receive and this second, which is the one we call death. For the first is caused by a forming of some of the matter which renews and reorganizes itself within the entrails of mother earth. Thus does exhausted matter re-enter the regenerating womb, there to refertilize particles of ethereal matter which, but for it, would remain in their apparent inertia. And there, in brief, is the whole science of the laws of these three kingdoms, laws which exist apart from Nature, independently of her, laws which they received at their first emergence into being, laws which thwart this Nature's will to erupt anew; there, in brief, are the sole means through which the laws inherent in these kingdoms operate. The first generation, which we call life, is as it were an example. Only from exhaustion do its laws become operative; only through destruction are these laws transmitted; the former requires a kind of corrupted matter, the latter, petrified matter. And there is the sole cause of this immensity of successive creations: each of them consists of a repetition of the first principles of exhaustion or of destruction, which shows you that death is as necessary as life, that there is indeed no real death, and that all the plagues we have just spoken of, all the cruelties of tyrants, the crimes of the wicked, are as necessary to the laws of the three kingdoms as the action which revivifies them; that when Nature sends them forth upon the earth, with the intention of annihilating these kingdoms which prevent her from using her faculty for casting new creatures, she acts from sheer impotence, because the first laws received by these kingdoms at the time of their first casting engraved the reproductive faculty in them forever, and this, Nature could erase only by destroying her own self, which she is powerless to do, because she is herself subject to laws from whose authority she cannot possibly escape, and which shall last eternally. Thus, through his murderings the wicked man not only aids Nature to attain ends she will nonetheless never entirely achieve, but also aids even the laws the three kingdoms received at their original casting. I say original casting to facilitate the intelligence of my system, for, there never having been any creation and Nature being timeless, the first casting of a given being endures so long as that being's line survives; and would end were that line to be extinguished; the extinction of all beings would make room for the new castings Nature desires; to this end the one means is total destruction, and that is the result toward which crime strives. Whence it comes out certainly that the criminal who could smite down the three kingdoms all at once by annihilating both them and their capacity to reproduce would be he who serves Nature best. Now look again at your legislations in the light of this startling truth, and see how just they be.

"No destruction, no fodder for the earth, and consequently man deprived of the possibility to reproduce man. Fatal truth, this, since it contains inescapable proof that the virtues and vices of our social system are nought, and that what we characterize as vices are more beneficial, more necessary than our virtues, since these vices are creative and these virtues merely created; or, if you prefer, these vices are causes, these virtues only effects; proof that a too perfect harmony would have more disadvantages than has disorder; and proof that if war, discord, and crime were suddenly to be banished from the world, the three kingdoms, all checks upon them removed, would so flourish as to unsettle and soon destroy all the other laws of Nature. Celestial bodies would come all to a halt, their influences would be suspended because of the overly great empire of one of their number; gravitation would be no more, and motion none. It is then the crimes of man which, stemming the rise of the three kingdoms, counteracting their tendency to preponderate, prevent their importance from becoming such as must disrupt all else, and maintains in universal affairs that perfect equilibrium Horace called *rerum concordia discors*. Therefor is crime necessary in the world. But the most useful crimes are without doubt those which most disrupt, such as *refusal to propagate* and *destruction;* all the others are petty mischief, they are less even than that, or rather only those two merit the name of crime: and thus you see these crimes essential to the laws of the kingdoms, and essential to the laws of Nature. An ancient philosopher called war the mother of all things. The existence of murderers is as necessary as that bane; but for them, all would be disturbed in the order of things. It is therefore absurd to blame or punish them, more ridiculous still to fret over the very natural inclinations which lead us to commit this act in spite of ourselves, for never will too many or enough murders be committed on earth, considering the burning thirst Nature has for them. Ah, unhappy mortal! boast not that thou art able to destroy, it is something far beyond thy forces; thou canst alter forms, thou art helpless to annihilate them; of the substance of Nature, not by one grain can thou lessen its mass, how wouldst thou destroy since all that is, is eternal? Thou changest the forms of things, vary those forms thou may, but this dissolution benefits Nature, since 'tis these disassembled parts she recomposes. Thus does all change effected by man upon organized matter far more serve Nature than it displeases her. What is this I say? Alas! to render her true service would require destructions more thorough, vaster than any it is in our power to operate; 'tis atrocity, 'tis scope she wants in crimes; the more our destroying is of a broad and atrocious kind, the more agreeable it is to her. To serve her better yet, one would have to be able to prevent the regeneration resultant from the corpses we bury. Only of his first life does murder deprive the individual we smite; one would have to be able to wrest away his second, if one were to be more useful to Nature; for 'tis annihilation she seeks, by less she is not fully satisfied, it is not within our power to extend our murders to the point she desires.

"Oh, Juliette, bear it ever in mind that there is no real destruction, that death is itself nothing of the sort, that, physically and philosophically viewed, it is only a further modification of the matter in which the active principle or, if you like, the principle of motion, acts without interruption, although in a less apparent manner. Thus a man's birth is no more the commencement of his existence than his death is its cessation; and the mother who bears him no more gives him life than the murderer who kills him gives him death; the former produces some matter organized in a certain way, the latter provides the occasion for the renascence of some different matter; and both create.

"Nothing is essentially born, nothing essentially perishes, all is but the action and reaction of matter; all is like the ocean billows which ever rise and fall, like the tides of the sea, ebbing and flowing endlessly, without there being either the loss or the gain of a drop in the volume of the waters; all this is a perpetual flux which ever was and shall always be, and whereof we become, though we know it not, the principal agents by reason of our vices and our virtues. All this is an infinite variation; a thousand thousand different portions of matter which appear under every form are shattered, are reconstituted to appear again under others, again to be undone and to rearise. The principle of life is but the result of the four elements in combination; with death, the combination dissolves, each element returning entire into its own sphere, ready to enter new combinations when the laws of the kingdoms summon them forth; it is only the whole that changes form, the parts remain intact, and from these parts joined anew to the whole, new beings are forever being recomposed. But the principle of life, uniquely the fruit of the combining of elements, does not exist by itself, only through this union does it exist and it changes entirely when this union ceases, becomes more or less perfect depending upon the new work created out of the debris of the old. Now, as these beings are both completely indifferent one to the other, and completely indifferent not only to Nature but to the laws of the kingdoms also, the changes I make in the modifications of matter can be of no importance: of what importance is it if, as Montesquieu says, I make a round lump of something into a square lump; what can it matter if of a man I make a cabbage, a lettuce, a butterfly, or a worm; in this I do nothing but exercise the right I have been given to do it, and if I wish, if I can, I may thus trouble or destroy all beings without being able to say that I have acted contrary to the laws of the three kingdoms and consequently to the laws of Nature. Far from it; I serve those laws one and all; I serve the three kingdoms in giving the earth the nutriment which facilitates her other productions, which is indispensable to them, and without which her productions would be at an end; I serve Nature's laws in acting in consonance with the aims of perpetual destruction Nature announces, and whose purpose is to enable her to develop new castings, the faculty wherefor is suspended in her owing to the continuing presence of what she has cast before.

"Are you able to believe that this blade of grass, this mite, this maggot, into which the body I slew has latterly metamorphosed, is of more or less outstanding importance to the laws of the three kingdoms which, embracing them all three, can have a predilection for none? Shall it be in the eyes of Nature, who vomits forth her castings indiscriminately, that some one production or other of these castings shall attain to exceptional value? This would be tantamount to upholding that of the millions of leaves growing upon this aged oak tree one of them is the darling of the trunk, because it is perhaps a little larger than its neighbors. 'It is our pride,' Montesquieu continues, 'which prevents us from sensing our puniness and which, puny as we are, causes us to want to be taken account of in the world, to be of mention there, to be a figure of note in it. We are wont to fancy that the loss of such a perfect being as we would be ruinous to Nature, and we do not conceive that one man the more in the world, or the less, or all mankind, or one hundred million earths like ours and each full of men, are but subtle atoms, very tiny and indifferent to Nature.' So rend away, hack and hew, torment, break, wreck, massacre, burn, grind to dust, melt, in a word: reshape into however many forms all the productions of the three kingdoms, and you simply shall have done them so many services, you shall have done nothing but be useful to them. You shall have been the minion of their laws, you shall have executed those of Nature, because we are creatures of too little strength and too narrow possibilities ever to cooperate in anything but the general order of things, and what you call disorder is nothing else than one of the laws of the order you comprehend not and which you have erroneously named disorder because its effects, though good for Nature, run counter to your convenience or jar your opinions. Ah, if these crimes were not necessary to the general economy, would they be, as they are, inspired in us? Would we in the depths of our hearts sense both the need to commit them and the charm of having committed them? How dare we think that Nature could instill in us impulses which cross her purposes? Eh, indeed, we may rather believe this: that she took all good care to place well outside our reach the power to do anything that might really discomfort or harm her. Come, little girl, let us try to drink dry of its rays the sun that lights our world, let us try to alter the stars' rhythmed march, reverse the flight of heavenly bodies in space; aye, those are crimes that would veritably offend Nature; and Nature has seen to it that we shall never commit them. As for what she has put in our power to do, we have thereby her authorization to do it; all that is inside our grasp is ours to have; let us tamper with it, destroy it, change it without fear of harming her. Let us be rather persuaded that we are aiding her, and that the more we turn our hands to deeds of the species we improperly term criminal, the better servants to her we are.

"But would there not be some substantial difference between one species of crime and another, and may there not be murders so base, so heinous as might be revolting to Nature? What an idea! What stupidity to entertain it even for a moment! This person upon whom our human conventions shed an aura of sanctity, can he be of superior worth in Nature's eyes? In what way can the body of your father, of your mother, of your sister outvalue, in Nature's consideration, that of your slave? Such distinctions cannot exist for her; she does not even perceive them; she cannot possibly perceive them; and this body, so precious according to your laws, will metamorphose itself just as surely as the body of that helot you so thoroughly despise. Arm yourself in the knowledge that the atrocity you dread pleases her; she would have you inject an ever greater dose of atrocity in those that you call your destructions, that you become an intransigent opponent of any reproduction is her wish, her greatest expectation of you, that you annihilate the three kingdoms: this you cannot do; why then, if the atrocity she desires of you cannot attain the farther target she sets you, turn it upon the nearer and you shall have satisfied her to the best of your abilities. Unable to please her by the atrocity of a global destruction, at least provide her the pleasure of local atrocity, and into your murderings put every imaginable foulness and horror, thereby showing utmost docility in your compliance with the laws she imposes upon you; your inability to do all she wants does not exempt you from doing all you can.

"From the foregoing it would clearly appear that infanticide fits in closest with her designs because it severs the chain of progeniture, it consigns the greatest number of seeds to the tomb. In killing his father the son breaks nothing, he removes the uppermost link of the chain; when the father kills his son he prevents further links from ever being added thereunto; the line is doomed; it is not doomed by the son's destroying the father, for the son remains, and in him lives the future of the line. Either children or young

776 ❦ THE MARQUIS DE SADE

mothers, preferably when they are pregnant, these are the two murders which best answer the aim of the kingdom and above all of Nature, 'tis in that direction everybody should exert himself if he wishes to please the harsh dam of humankind.[28]

"Ah, do we not see, do we not sense that atrocity in crime pleases Nature, since 'tis according to this factor alone she regulates the amount of delight to provide us when we commit a crime. The more frightful it is, the more we enjoy it; the blacker, the fouler it is, the more we are thrilled by it. Thus it is that an inexplicable Nature asks for viciousness, for vileness, for atrociousness in the deed she prompts us to, she wants us to adorn it with the same features she puts into the banes and plagues wherewith she besets us: so let us proceed fearlessly, imaginatively, let us set all scruples and bars aside, let us scorn humanity's vain laws, the idiotic institutions which prisoner us. Let us heed none but Nature's sacred voice, full certain that its instructions will always contradict the absurd principles of human morality and of infamous civilization. Do you then think civilization or morals have made men better? Imagine no such thing, take care not to suppose it; the one and the other have served only to soften man, to obscure in him the laws of Nature who made him free and cruel; alienated from her, the entire species sank straight into degradation, its ferocity changed into cunning, and ever since then the insidious evil man has done has only become more dangerous to his fellows. Since commit this evil he must, since it is necessary, since it is agreeable to Nature, let us leave man to commit it in the manner most satisfying to him, and let us prefer him fierce to treacherous, the peril is less.

"Let us not tire to repeat it: never has any intelligent nation presumed to erect murder into a crime: in order that murder be

---

[28] Nearly all the world's peoples have enjoyed the right of life and death over their offspring. This right is perfectly natural; and of what may one better dispose than of what one has given? If there could be gradations of the alleged crime of murder, that is, if one could rank in their order of greater or lesser evil, things which contain none, infanticide would surely stand at the bottom of the scale: the prompt facility every man possesses to repair this trifling misdemeanor entirely effaces the little amount of badness in it. From a narrow study of Nature one finds that our first instinctive urge is to destroy our issue, and destroyed it would infallibly be if pride did not often advocate sparing it.

crime one must admit the possibility of destruction, an altogether unacceptable proposition, we have just agreed to that. Once again: murder is nothing more than a formal variation resulting in no loss[29] whatsoever to the law of the three kingdoms nor to the law of Nature, but redounding prodigiously to their benefit. And why punish a man for restoring a little ahead of time a portion of matter which is destined to the elements anyhow, and which, as soon as it returns to them, these same elements employ in new compositions: the sooner you kill that fly, the sooner we will have back a pasha, do you prefer to spare a cockroach and forego an archbishop? There is then nothing wrong or bad in restoring to the elements the means to recompose a thousand insects at the expense of a few ounces of blood diverted out of its usual canals, in a somewhat larger species of animal conventionally known as man.

"Murderers, to be brief, are in Nature as are war, famine, and cholera; they are one of the means Nature disposes of, like all the hostile forces she pits against us. Thus when one ventures the statement that an assassin offends Nature, the absurdity one utters is as great as though one were to declare that cholera, famine, or war irritates Nature or commits crimes; it is exactly the same thing. But we cannot flog or burn or brand or hang cholera or famine, whereas we can do all of these to a man: that is why he is wrong. You will almost always find wrongs measured not by the size of the offense, but by the vulnerability of the aggressor; and there is your explanation for why wealth and position are always right, and indigence is always at fault.

---

[29] Regeneration or, better still, transformation is the term we ought to use for this change we see take place in matter; it is neither depleted, nor wasted, nor spoiled, nor corrupted by the different forms it assumes; and one of the main causes of its durability and vigor may perhaps consist in the seeming destructions which subtilize it, accord it greater freedom to form fresh miracles. Matter, in fine, does not destroy itself to change from and assume new modification, any more than does, as Voltaire says (and it is from him this note is extracted), a cube of wax you melt into a round puddle smash in changing shape. Nothing less out of the ordinary than these perpetual resurrections, and there is nothing stranger in being born twice than once. Wherever you bend your glance in the world, you encounter resurrection: caterpillars resuscitate as butterflies, an orange pip you plant resuscitates as an orange tree, all the animals buried in the ground resuscitate as grass, as potatoes, as worms, and nourish other animals whereof they rapidly form part of the substance, etc., etc., etc.

"As concerns the cruelty which leads to murder, we may confidently submit that it is one of man's most natural dispositions; it is one of the sweetest penchants, one of the keenest he has received from Nature; cruelty in man is simply an expression of his desire to exercise his strength. It pervades all his deeds, all his words, all his behavior; education disguises it sometimes, but it is quick to reappear. It then manifests itself under all kinds of forms. The violent throbbings it causes us to feel, either at the idea or upon the execution of the crime cruelty suggests to us, are invincible proof that we are born to serve as blind instruments to the kingdoms' laws as well as to Nature's, and that once we lend ourselves to do their bidding, voluptuousness invades us through every pore.

"So reward him, this murderer, employ instead of punishing him; remember that there is no crime, of whatever slight importance in itself, that does not however demand as much strength and energy, as much courage and philosophy, as the grand crime of murder. There are a thousand cases in which an enlightened government ought only to use assassins. . . . Juliette, he who knows how to stifle the cries of his conscience to the point of making a game of the lives of others, this man already has the stuff qualifying him for the very greatest undertakings. There are heaven knows how many people in the world who turn criminal on their own account simply because an undiscerning government ignores their worth and neglects to put them to work; the result is that the unlucky souls are broken on the wheel for plying the same trade in which they might otherwise have got themselves covered with renown and honor. The Alexanders, the Saxes, the Turennes might perhaps have become highway robbers had distinguished birth and smiling fortune not readied them for laurels in the career of glory; while assuredly the Cartouches, the Mandrins, and Desrues would have become great men had the government known how to employ them.

"Oh, height of fearful injustice! wild animals may exist, such as the lion, the wolf, the tiger who live from murdering alone; in so living these animals disobey no laws, and there are other animals to be met with in the world who, to satisfy another passion than hunger, indulge in the same excesses—and these other animals, so it is claimed, commit crimes!

"We often complain of the existence of such and such a beast whose form or aspect is offensive to our eyes, or which causes us some nuisance or other, and we console ourselves by saying, rightly and with common sense, ' 'Tis a dreadful-looking creature, a harmful one too, but it is useful; Nature has created nothing in vain; this animal probably breathes a certain air that would poison us, or else it eats insects of still greater danger to us.' Let us be equally philosophical in every other regard, and in the murderer see nought but a hand guided by irresistible laws, a hand that ministers to Nature and which, through the crimes it accomplishes, of whatever sort you wish to suppose them, acts at the behest of certain intentions unknown to us, or prevents some accident perhaps a thousand times more to be deplored than the one it occasions.

" 'Sophistry! Nothing but sophistry!' fools shrill at this point; 'it is true that murder offends Nature, that he who has just committed it will shudder for the rest of his life at what he has done.' Imbeciles. 'Tis not because the deed is bad in itself that the murderer shudders, for be certain of it, in those countries where murder is recompensed he shudders not. . . . Does the warrior shudder over the enemy he has just felled? The sole cause of the uneasiness we feel after the deed lies in its prohibition; every man has sometime in his life, before a perfectly commonplace action which circumstances happen to forbid, sensed all the terror he could possibly know from rendering himself guilty of that action. A sign is nailed over a door, saying it is forbidden to trespass here: no matter who he is who makes up his mind to go in will do so with a kind of shudder, and yet this thing he does is not evil. It is thus from nothing but the prohibition that the terror is born, and not at all from the action itself which, as we see, may inspire the same fear though there be nothing criminal to it. This pusillanimity which accompanies the murder, this little moment of fright, derives infinitely more from prejudice than from the kind of deed at hand. However, let the wind blow in another direction for a month, let the sword of Justice smite what you call virtue for a while, and let the laws reward crime: you'll see the virtuous quaking and the wicked serene as they both go about acquitting themselves of their favorite deeds. In these matters Nature is silent; the voice that thunders inside us belongs to the prejudice which with a little effort and determination we can quell forever. There is however a sacred organ whose intimate murmur used to resound in us before the voices of error or of education made themselves heard; but this other voice, which reminds us of our bondage to the elements, constrains us only to that which favors the harmonious accord of these elements, and their combinations modified after the forms which these same elements employ in composing us. However, this last-named voice is not strident, nor theatrical, it dins no knowledge of God into us, makes no mention of consanguinary or social duties, for these things are false and it speaks the truth only. Neither does it tell us not to do unto others that which unto our own selves we would not that there be done; if we care to listen closely to it, 'tis quite the opposite message we will hear.

" 'Be ever mindful,' Nature says to us instead, 'be ever mindful that all which thou wouldst not have done unto thyself, being the grave harm done a neighbor whence there is much profit to be had, is precisely that which thou must do to be happy; for it is writ in my laws that ye all destroy yourselves mutually; and the true way to succeed therein is to harm thy neighbor without stint or cease. Whence it cometh that I have placed the sharpest bent for crime in thee; whence it is that my intention be that thou render thyself happy, at the expense of whosoever it be. Let thy father, thy mother, thy son, thy daughter, thy niece, thy wife, thy sister, thy friend be no dearer to thee than the lowliest worm that crawleth on the face of the earth; for bonds, duties, allegiances, affections, none of these hath ever been had from me, they were wrought by thy weakness only, by thy education, and by thy folly; they concern me not nor interest me at all; thou mayst violate them, break them, loathe them, annul them; 'tis all one to me. I cast thee into being as I cast the ox, the ass, the artichoke, the louse; to them all I gave faculties, some of greater, some of lesser proportions; use what are thine; once gone forth out of my bosom, thou canst touch me no more, whatever thou doest. If thou keepest thee safe and increase, thou shalt do well as regards thyself; if thou dost destroy thyself and others, nay, if thou contrivest, using such capacities as thou hast, to lay the three kingdoms waste and to devastate them so there shall be nothing left, 'tis there something whereat I shall be pleased beyond measure; for I in my turn shall use the fairest attribute of my power, that which is my ability to create, to make beings anew—which thy accursed progeniture hinders me from doing. Cease to engender, destroy absolutely all that exists, thou shalt disturb not the slightest thing in my scheme or workings. But whether ye destroy or create, the two be nearly the same in my eyes, whichever way thou wouldst proceed, I benefit from thy doings, nothing is lost in my domain: the leaf that falls from the shrub is as useful to me as the cedars that forest Lebanon, and the rot-spawned worm is of no less nor more considerable value in my eyes than the mightiest king on earth. So form or destroy as thou wilt and at thy ease; tomorrow's sun shall rise just the same, all the globes I hang and guide in space shall hold nonetheless firm in their orbits; and if thou dost destroy all, as these three kingdoms annihilated by thy wickedness are the necessary results of my combinations and as I form nothing anymore, because these kingdoms are created with the faculty of reproducing themselves mutually; smitten by thy traitorous hand, they shall be re-formed by me, I shall cast them again and it shall be on earth as it was before. The vastest, the profoundest, the most atrocious of thy crimes shall thus only have pleased me.'

"Such are the laws of Nature, Juliette; such are the only laws she has ever dictated, the only ones which are precious to her, the only ones we should never transgress. If man makes other laws, we may deplore his stupidity, but we must never let it be binding upon us; we may fear becoming the victim of his absurd laws, but let us not violate them any the less; and, free of all prejudices, directly we can do so with impunity, let us seize every opportunity to revenge ourselves for the odious constraint of his laws by perpetrating the most signal outrages. Regret nothing but that we are unable to do enough, lament nothing but the weakness of the faculties we have received for our share and whose ridiculous limitations so cramp our penchants. And far from thanking this illogical Nature for the slender freedom she allows us for accomplishing the desires she inspires in us, let us curse her from the bottom of our heart for so restricting the career which fulfills her aims; let us outrage her, let us abominate her for having left us so few wicked things to do, and then giving us such violent urges to commit crimes without measure or pause.

" 'O Thou,' so should we speak to her, 'Thou, unreasoning and reasonless force of which I find myself the involuntary result, Thou who hurled me into this world with the desire that I offend Thee, and who hast however denied me the means so to do, inspire in my blazing soul some crimes which would serve Thee better than these poor melancholy things Thou hast put inside my reach. I would obey Thy laws, since they require horrors of me and for horrors I have a fiery thirst; but provide me better to do than Thy debility has given me so far. When I have exterminated all the creatures that cover the earth, still shall I be far from my mark, since I shall have merely served Thee, O unkind Mother, for it is to vengeance I aspire, vengeance for what, whether through stupidity or malice, Thou doest to men in never furnishing them the means to translate fairly into deeds the appalling desires Thou dost ever rouse in them.'

"And now, Juliette," continued the Pontiff, "I believe I shall present to you some examples such as will prove to you that in all ages and everywhere, man has placed his delight in destroying, and Nature hers in permitting it.

"At Capodimonte, if a woman gives birth to twins, her husband strangles one of the infants on the spot.

"Everybody knows the case the Arabs and Chinese make of their children. Hardly half the number born are kept; they kill, burn, or drown the rest, and principally the females. The same horror of offspring prevails in Formosa.

"The Mexicans never set out on a military expedition without first sacrificing children of the one sex or the other.

"Japanese women are allowed to procure abortions as frequently as they like; no one holds them to account for the fruit they are unwilling to bear.[30]

---

[30] The penalty decreed against child-murdering mothers is an unexampled atrocity. Who then has a greater right to dispose of this fruit than she who carries it in her womb? If in all the world there is an article of property to which no outside claim can be fair, it is surely this one. To interfere with the usage a woman

"The king of Calicut has in his palace an armchair of iron, beneath which he lights a great fire; in it, on certain festival days, a child is made fast, and it remains seated until it has been reduced to cinders.

"Never was murder punished by death among the Romans; and for a long time the emperors in this regard followed Sulla's law, which merely condemns the murderer to a fine.

"On Mindanao this same crime is honored; he who commits it is sure, after producing proof of the deed, of being raised to the rank of a brave, with the right to wear a red ribbon.

"Among the Caraguos the same honor is obtained by the quantity of murders alone: it takes the killing of seven men before one is entitled to the red turban.

"On the banks of the Orinoco, mothers drown their daughters the moment they see the light.

"In the kingdom of Zopit and in Trapobania, fathers cut the throats of children of whichever sex, once they grow weary of the sight of them or when these children begin to take on airs.

"In Madagascar all infants born on Tuesdays, Thursdays, and Fridays are abandoned to wild beasts by their own parents.

"Up until the Empire removed to the East, a Roman child of whatever age who displeased his father would be put to death by him.

"Several chapters in the Pentateuch clearly show that fathers had the right of life or death over their children.

"A law the Parthians had, and the Armenians too, authorized a father to kill his son and even his daughter when they reached marriageable age.

"Caesar found this same custom established amongst the Gauls.

---

chooses to make of it is stupidity carried beyond any conceivable extreme. Indeed, one must set a very high price by the human species to punish an unhappy creature, simply because she has not been concerned to double her existence nor eager to confirm the gift she unwillingly prepared. And what a curious calculation it is, this that leads to sacrificing the mother to the child! The crime committed, there is one creature the less on earth; the crime punished, now there are two. How clever one must be to reckon thus! And how intelligent our lawmakers are! And we allow such laws to remain in force! And we have the simple good-naturedness not to obliterate them along with the memory of the witty rogues who made them!

"To his subjects Czar Peter of the Russias addressed a public declaration the gist of which was that, by all laws human and divine, a father had the right of life and death over his children, without appeal and to be exercised without any permission, on the spur of the moment. No sooner had he published his decree than Peter proceeded to act according to it.

"The Galla chief, as soon as he is elected, must distinguish himself by an incursion into Abyssinia; 'tis the multiplicity of his crimes which renders him worthy of his post. He must plunder, rape, mutilate, massacre, burn; the more appalling his exploits, the more he is honored.

"Each year the Egyptians sacrificed a young maiden to the Nile. When compassion gripped their hearts and they decided to interrupt this usage, the river's fertilizing floods ceased and Egypt faced famine.

"So long as human sacrifices comprise a spectacle they ought never to be forbidden in a warlike society. Rome was mistress of the world all the while she had these cruel spectacles; she sank into decline and from there into slavery as soon as Christian morals managed to persuade her that there was more wrong in watching men slaughtered than beasts. But it was not humane sentiment that stood behind the arguments of Christ's followers, it was their great fear lest, were the star of idolatry to rise again over the Empire, they themselves might be sacrificed during their adversaries' amusements. That is why the rascals preached charity, that is why they fabricated the ridiculous myth of brotherhood, which I know, Juliette, others must surely have exploded to your satisfaction. What I have just advanced accounts for everything in this fine ethic which even the enemies of this pernicious religion have been timid enough and mad enough to respect. We continue.

"Almost all the savages of America kill their elders when the latter are seen to be ailing; 'tis a kindly act on the part of the son; the father curses him if he does not dispatch him when he becomes aged and helpless.

"In the South Seas there exists an island where women are killed once they have passed the age for engendering, as creatures henceforth useless to the world; and as a matter of fact, what more are they good for then?

"The peoples of the Barbary States have no law against the murder of their wives or their slaves; they are fully and authentically masters thereof.

"In no Asian harem is killing of the women outlawed; whoever murders his own down to the last has simply to purchase some more.

"It is an article of faith, on the island of Borneo, that all those persons a man kills will be his slaves in the next world; and as a result, the better a man wishes to be served after his death, the more he kills during his life.

"When the Tartars of exotic Karaskan espy a foreigner who has wit, riches, and fair looks, they kill him in order to appropriate his qualities to themselves and later generations.

"The custom in the kingdom of Tangut is for a young man, dagger in hand, to venture forth on certain days of the year, and to kill whomever he encounters, indiscriminately and with impunity; they who die by his hand, it is maintained, are assured of greatest happiness in the life after this.

"In Kachao there are murderers for hire, upon whom one calls in time of need: when you have someone to have killed, you engage one of these mercenaries and pay him his fee when the work is done.

"This reminds me of the story of the Old Man of the Mountain. That prince, who held in his power the lives of all other sovereigns, had simply to send one of his subjects on a visit to this or that foreign potentate, and the emissary would strike his quarry down upon meeting him.

"Professional assassins are available in Italy too, you may be sure: a wise government will always tolerate them. And no just government will claim an exclusive right to dispose of human life.

"In Zeeland, in the old days they used to sacrifice ninety-nine men each year to the gods of the country.

"When the Carthaginians saw the enemy at their gates they immolated two hundred children picked from the ranks of the higher nobility; one of their laws stipulated that only children of that caste were to be offered to Saturn. A fine was levied upon the mothers who during this ceremony betrayed the least hint of sorrow; the immolations took place before their eyes. Well-advised people who brand sentimentality as a crime!

"A Northern king, whose name escapes me at the moment, immolated nine of his children with the sole aim, he said, of extending his life at the expense of those from whom he took life away. Do not frown at this whimsical notion, but rather smile. For prejudices are pardonable when they produce pleasures.

"Shu Um-chi, father of a late Chinese emperor, had thirty men stabbed to death upon his mistress' grave, to appease her manes.

"On his last voyage to Tahiti Cook discovered human sacrifices which had gone unnoticed by those who had preceded him on that island.

"As Herod, King of the Jews, lay on his deathbed he had all the Judean nobility convoked in the hippodrome of Jericho, then ordered his sister Salome to cause them to perish one and all at the moment he sighed out his ghost, so that he might be mourned universally and the Jews, weeping for their friends and kinsmen, be forced to sprinkle tears upon his ashes too. How strong must be that passion whose effects extend beyond the grave! Herod's order, however, was not carried out.

"With his own hand Mahomet II cut off the head of his mistress, to demonstrate to his soldiers that his was not a heart to be softened by love; even so, he had just spent the night with Irene and slaked his desires.[31] The same personage, suspecting that it was one of his masculine playthings who filched a cucumber out of his garden, had everyone in his seraglio paraded and bellies slit open till at last the fruit was found in the guilty one's entrails. . . . Finding some faults in a painting of the decollation of John the Baptist, he had a slave summoned and smote off his head, and showed Bellini, a Venetian and the author of the painting he was criticizing, that he had imperfectly grasped Nature. 'See here,' said Mahomet, 'this is how a severed head ought to look.' Once again, it was this great man who, philosophi-

---

31 At this point, the story becomes infinitely more comprehensible.

cally convinced that subjects exist for nought but the service of sovereigns' passions, had one hundred thousand naked slaves made up into fascines and cast into the moats outside the walls of Constantinople at the time he was laying siege to that capital.

"Abdalkar, general of the king of Visapur, had a harem containing twelve hundred wives; he receives orders to lead his troops into the field; he fears lest his absence become a pretext for his wives' infidelity; he has all their throats cut before him on the eve of his departure.

"The proscriptions of Marius and Sulla are masterpieces of cruelty; Sulla, butcher of half of Rome, dies a tranquil death at home in the midst of his loved ones. Let it now be maintained, after such examples, that a God watches over us and must punish crimes!

"Nero had ten or twelve thousand souls put to death in the circus because somebody, no telling just who, jeered at one of his drivers. It was during his reign that the amphitheater at Praeneste collapsed, causing the death of another twenty thousand people; who doubts that he was the cause of the accident, and that he arranged it as a lewd prank?

"Commodus dealt severely with Romans who read the life of Caligula, he threw them to the wild beasts. During his nighttime revels he amused himself multilating passers-by; or else would collect fifteen or twenty unlucky creatures picked up at random in the street, have them bound fast, and then, wielding a mace or club, exterminate them for fun.

"The eighty thousand Roman captives Mithridates slew in his states, the Sicilian Vespers, the St. Bartholomew slaughters, the Dragonnades, the eighteen thousand Flemings the Duke of Alba beheaded to establish in the Low Countries a religion which abhors bloodshed: so many models of murder which prove that passions should always be generous in the taking of human life.

"Constantine, that so very stern emperor, so beloved of the Christians, assassinated his brother-in-law, his nephews, his wife, and his son.

"The natives of Florida tear their prisoners limb from limb; but to this practice sometimes add another, the very refined one of introducing an arrow into the anus and driving it in shoulder-high.

"There is nothing to equal the cruelty of the Indians toward theirs; the entire tribe must share in the pleasure of beating them to death; and while this is going forward, they are obliged to sing. Another refinement of cruelty: to deny victims even the solace of tears.

"Savages behave in the same way with captives. Their fingernails are torn out, their breasts and fingers torn off; their flesh is stripped away in ribbons from their bodies; their genitals are pricked with awls, it is usually women who take charge of these tortures. They flog their victims, flay them; do, in a word, everything ferocity can invent to render the deaths of these wretches more frightful, and rejoice when they expire.

"And the child itself, does it not offer us the example of this ferocity which astounds us in adults? The child's behavior proves that ferocity is natural: see it cruelly strangle a pet bird and laugh at the poor thing's convulsions. . . .

"Maori aboriginals are by no means alone in eating their enemies; others feed them to their dogs. Some revenge themselves upon pregnant women, slit open their bellies, snatch out the child, and dash its brains out upon the mother's skull.

"The Heruli, the Germans, sacrificed all captives taken in war; the Scythians were content to immolate one out of every ten of them. For how long have the French not been massacring theirs? After the battle of Agincourt, that dark day for France, Edward [sic] slew them all.

"When Ghenghis Khan seized China, he had two million children killed before his eyes.

"Glance a little at the lives of the twelve Caesars, in Suetonius' biography you'll discover a thousand atrocities of this kind.

"Such is the scorn for the Pulias who form a caste in Malabar that they may be killed on sight. When one wishes to practice his skill at archery, he shoots at the first Pulia he finds, male or female, young or old.

"Provided they leave a coin on the corpse, the Russian, Danish, and Polish nobility have the right to kill serfs; the right estimation of a man's life, whoever that man be, must always be in money, because money can serve as a reparation while blood repairs nothing. If *lex talionis* is odious at all, then 'tis surely so in this case; for the murderer may sometimes have a motive for committing his assassination, but you, simpleton children of Themis, you have none for committing yours. Your position is clear, it is strong? Ah, then answer me this question:

"What is it, according to you, that constitutes the crime in murder? The depriving a fellow being of his life? I deprive him of his life—and that is enough for you, who are not in the least concerned to know what kind of man he was I deprived of life; but if that man had committed a great many crimes himself, in killing him I do nothing worse than the law would do, and if I do evil, then so does the law: in which is it preferable to believe, the innocence of him who kills a criminal, or the infamy of the law that kills the criminal?

"In how many lands and over how many centuries have they not been immolating slaves upon the tombs of masters? Do these people, in your opinion, believe there to be anything of the crime in murder?

"Who can guess at the number of Indians the Spaniards slew in their conquest of the New World? From nothing but transporting the invaders' baggage, two hundred thousand perished in the space of a single year.

"Octavian had three hundred persons butchered in Perugia, merely to fete the anniversary of Caesar's death.

"A Calicut pirate cruising down the coast runs upon a Portuguese brigantine; he boards her, finds the crew all asleep, and cuts the throats of them all, because they dared take a nap while he was on a foray.

"Phalaris used to shut his victims up in a bull of bronze, so constructed as horribly to amplify the screams of the wretches imprisoned within. Strange invention of cruelty! and how much imagination it supposes in the tyrant who devised it!

"The Franks had the right of life and death over their wives, and exercised it without respite.

"The King of Ava detects rebellion in that handful of his subjects who have refused to pay their taxes; he has four thousand of them arrested and burns them all in the same great bonfire. There are never any revolutions in the states of a prince as enlightened as he.

"Eulins of Romagna learns that the city of Padua has risen

against him; he claps chains on eleven thousand of these thought-less townsmen and in the public square puts them to death in the most various and cruelest manners.

"One of the many wives of the king of Achem lets out a cry while dreaming, and it wakes all the others; hubbub in the harem; the monarch inquires into the cause for the disturbance; nobody is able to give him a satisfactory answer; whereat he puts all the three thousand women to torture, he has them subjected to unbelievable torments; nothing is found out; the two hands and two feet are then hacked off each one of them, and they are all cast into a lake.[32] The motive for this cruelty is not far to seek; it is undoubtedly of that kind which strikes bright sparks of lubricity into the soul of him who practices it.[33]

"In a word, murder is a passion, like gaming, wine, boys and women; never is it got rid of, once it has anchored in habit. No activity irritates as does this one, none prepares so much delight; it is impossible to weary of it; obstacles sharpen its flavor, and the relish for it we have in our heart goes to the point of fanaticism. You, Juliette, have experienced how wonderfully it combines with debauches, and appreciated the tart flavor it gives them. It exerts a puissant influence at once upon the mind and the body; it inflames all the senses, it enchants, it dazzles. Its impact upon the nervous system, the commotion it produces there is greater by far than that of any other voluptuous agent; one is never fond of this one save inordinately, furiously, one never indulges in it save ecstatically. The plotting of it titillates, the execution electrifies, the remembrance inspires, the temptation to repeat it is enormous, the desire to do this and nothing else, constantly, is over-whelming. The nearer a creature comes to us, the more it

---

[32] Beaulieu reports the episode.

[33] Come now, Braschi, enough of these timid details, we want bold strokes and a broad canvas. Look here: the proscriptions of the Jews, of the Christians, of Mithridates, of Marius, of Sulla, of the Triumvirs; the slaughterings of Theodosius and Theodora, the furors of the Crusaders and the Inquisitors, the savageries of the Templars, the Sicilian massacres, those of Mérindol, of St. Bartholomew, of Ireland, of Piedmont, of the Cévennes, of the New World: the total shows twenty-three million, one hundred and eighty thousand human beings murdered in cold blood on account of their opinions alone! The man who is fond of murder foments opinions in order that they give occasion for assassination.

wakes our interest, the more directly it touches us, the more intimately, the more sacred its ties with us, the greater our delectation in immolating the victim. Refinements enter into the thing, as happens with all pleasures; from the moment this personal stamp is added, all limits are abolished, atrocity is wound. to its topmost pitch, for the sentiment that produces it exhales it in keeping with the increase or worsening of the torture; all one's achievements now lie short of one's intentions. The agonies leading to de²th must now be slow and abominable if they are to quicken the soul at all, and one wishes that the same life could revive a thousand times over, in order to have the pleasure of murdering it that often, and that thoroughly.

"Each murder is a commentary and critique of the others, each demands improvement in the next; it is shortly discovered that killing is not enough, one must kill in hideous style; and though one may be unaware of the fact, lewdness almost always has the direction of these matters.

"A rapid glance now at these simultaneously voluptuous and barbarous inventions. A sketch of them will not be displeasing to you,. I know: there is always something interesting and sublime about the violent aspects of Nature.

"The Irish used to crush their victims beneath weights. The Norwegians would stave in their skulls. . . . The Gauls broke their backs. . . . The Celts drove a saber through their breastbones. . . . The Cimbrians disemboweled them or else roasted them in furnaces.

"The Roman emperors used to enjoy watching young Christian virgins being whipped; having their bubs and buttocks tweaked with red-hot pincers; into their wounds boiling oil or pitch would be poured, and the same liquids squirted into all the orifices of their bodies. They themselves would sometimes play at torturer, and the martyrdoms then became a great deal crueler; rarely would Nero cede to someone else the pleasure of immolating these hapless creatures.

"The Syrians flung their victims off mountain-tops. The Marseillais clubbed his to death, and was particularly wont to fasten on the poor, exhibiting a preference Nature always inspires.

"The blacks of the Calabar River district deliver up small

children to birds of prey, which devour their flesh. The sight thereof is prodigiously cherished by savages.

"Historians tell us that in Mexico, the patient's four limbs would be held by four priests, the high priest would open him from throat to navel, tear out his still-throbbing heart, and smear the gore over the idol; at other times the patient would be drawn forward and back over a keen-edged stone till it sawed into his belly and his entrails spilled out.

"In all this vast crowd of peoples covering our globe, hardly a one is found that has ever attached the slightest importance to human life, because the fact is that nothing less important exists.

"Into the urethral canal the Americans insert a twig covered with little thorns, which they twirl in one direction, then in the other, spinning it between their palms and keeping at it for a considerable length of time, to the appalling distress of the victim.

"The Iroquois affix the ends of their victim's nerves to sticks and, by rotating these, wind out the nerves like string; in the course of the operation, the body twitches, bends, and is dislocated in an odd manner, and must be very exciting to watch."

"You may be certain that it is," Juliette remarked at this point, and went on to describe to the Holy Father the circumstances under which she had been able to witness this torture being performed; "the sight is overpowering; and you, my friend, could have gone for a swim in the downpour of fuck it cost me."

"In the Philippines," the Pope pursued, "a guilty woman is tied naked to a stake and facing the sun; it kills her in time.

"In Juida the belly is cut open, the entrails removed, the cavity stuffed with salt, the body hung out on a pole in the market place.

"The Quoias hurl javelins at the back, the body is then cut into quarters, and the dead man's wife is forced to eat it.

"When the Tonkinese go each year to pick the arecas they poison one of the nuts which is then fed to a child, a happy harvest being ensured, they consider, by the immolation of this victim. Here again we find murder an act of religion.

"The Hurons suspend a cadaver above the patient, in such wise that all the filth that spills from this dead body may splash upon his face, and to this vexation such others are added as cause him to expire in due time.

"The fierce Cossacks of Ousk and those parts tie the patient to the tail of a horse, which is then ridden at a gallop over rough terrain; Queen Brunhilde, you will recall, died from a similar trial.

"The ancient Russians impaled through the flanks and hooked by the ribs. Our Turkish contemporaries place the skewer through the fundament.

"During his Siberian travels Gmelin saw a woman buried alive up to the chin; thus was she fed; and expired only on the thirteenth day.

"The vestals were walled up in narrow little niches, where was placed a table and upon it a lamp, a loaf, and a bottle of oil. In Rome they have lately discovered an underground passage leading from the imperial palace to the field beneath which these vestal catacombs were built.[34] Which proves that the emperors either went to witness these enjoyable sights, or had the doomed vestals fetched to their palace, to enjoy them there and then kill them in a manner analogous to their particular tastes and their passions.

"In Morocco and Switzerland the guilty one is clamped between planks and sawed in two. Hippomenes, the African king, had his son and daughter devoured by horses that had been deprived of food for a long time; and did it without thought for any sacred ties of kinship; it is no doubt from this feat he got the name Hippomenes.

"The Gauls first kept their victims five years in prison, then impaled and burned them, all this in honor of the Divinity, for it is upon that splendid machine all human iniquities must be blamed.

"The ancient Germans smothered their victims in a mud-slough. The Egyptians inserted sharpened reeds into every part of the body, then set them afire.

"The Persians, the world's most ingenious race for the invention of tortures, lay their victim in a round boat and

---

[34] This I attest for having seen it myself.

inverted another over him, so that he was sealed between these two halves of a hollow sphere, except that his hands, feet, and head remained outside, passing through slots. He was forced to eat and drink in this situation; were he to refuse, his eyes were pricked with pointed instruments; honey was sometimes daubed on his face, so as to attract wasps; worms ate him alive. Who would believe it? Victims sometimes endured eighteen days of this treatment. What sublime science! And what art! For art consists in causing a little dying every day for as many days as possible. The Persians used also to grind between millstones, or would flay alive and with green thorns rub the skinned body, which causes unheard-of sufferings. Nowadays in the harems, the fashionable torture for women with whom some fault has been found is to cut multiple incisions in all their fleshier parts, and then to pour molten lead into each of the wounds, one by one, drop by drop; to impale by way of the matrix, or to make a pincushion of the patient, using not pins, however, but sulphur-dipped splines which are lit and fueled by the victim's own fat."

And Juliette assured His Holiness that she was familiar with this torture too.

"Daniel," the Pope went on, "informs us that the Babylonians cast unfortunates into hot ovens.

"The Macedonians crucified head downward.

"The Athenians administered toxic brews, drowned in a bathtub after having slit the veins.

"The Romans occasionally hung by the virile privities from a tree; the torture of the wheel was passed on to us by the Romans. With them an ordinary method of quartering was to bend down the crests of four saplings till they touched the ground, to attach the victim's four limbs each to one of these treetops, and then to let them all fly back upright at the same moment. Mettius Suffetius was drawn and quartered by four chariots. Under the emperors they flogged to death. Or placed the victim in a leathern bag along with serpents, and tossed the bag into the Tiber. At other times the victim was strapped to the rim of a great wheel, which would be spun very swiftly for a while, then suddenly made to turn in the opposite direction, which loosened the victim inwardly and often caused him to vomit his very bowels.

"The great Torquemada had the tongs applied in his presence to the fleshier parts of the patient's body; and at other times would have him sat upon a pointed stake in such a manner that all his weight must bear on his rump: a frightful position, whence there result singular convulsions and a death accompanied by spasmodic laughter very extraordinary to observe.[35]

"Apuleius speaks of the mortification one woman was made to undergo, its details are rather droll. An ass was killed, its entrails removed, and into its skin she was sewn, all save her head; she was thus exposed to wild beasts.

"The tyrant Maxentius bound a living man to a dead man and left him to rot upon the corpse.

"There are countries where the patient is tied close to a bonfire; holes are bored in his body whereby the flames enter and consume him gradually from within.

"At the time of the Dragonnades, girls who were loath to embrace the True Faith were seized and, in order to bring about a change in their minds, their anus and womb were funneled full of gunpowder. Next, they were exploded like bombs. You have simply no idea how this gave them a taste for the host and for auricular confession. And how can one help but love a God in whose name such wondrous fine deeds are wrought!

"Coming back again to classical tortures we see St. Catherine bound to a nail-studded cylinder and rolled down a mountainside. Now there, Juliette, is a pleasant way of getting to heaven, don't you agree?

"We see other martyrs of this same religion, whose apostle I am rather more from interest than from taste, having needles driven under their fingernails, roasted upon grills, lowered head downward into a pit containing a dog and a snake otherwise deprived of food and drink, and having to endure a thousand other horrors of whose details you have a fair inkling.[36]

"Moving next to foreign customs, in China we see the executioner answerable with his life for the patient's if this patient loses

[35] Those Spanish were also the world's most effeminate people; it is an easy step from affluence and softness to cruelty.
[36] One by one were removed: fingers, toes, feet, hands, teeth, eyes, nose, tongue, all protruberances, virile parts, and the clitoris in the case of women.

his before the appointed term, which is ordinarily very long, sometimes eight, even nine days, and during this time the tortures are
varied with utmost artistry.

"The English chopped into pieces and boiled them in a pot. In
their colonies they slowly crushed the Negroes in the sugar-cane
mills, which is as slow a way to die as it is dreadful.

"In Ceylon the victim is condemned to eat his own flesh or his
children's.

"The inhabitants of Malabar are choppers also, they use a
saber. Or else they feed to tigers.

"In Siam if you fall out of favor you may expect to be gored
and trampled to death by bulls. The king of this country put a rebel
to death by feeding him upon his own flesh, whereof he was given
a slice from time to time; those same Siamese sometimes squeeze
the victim's body in a jacket through which he is pricked by very
sharp instruments, to force him to hold his breath: next, the body
is cut suddenly in two, the upper part placed straight on a red-hot
brass griddle, which halts the escape of blood and prolongs the
life of the patient whose existence has been reduced by a half.

"It is not very different in Cochin-China, where they strip the
man bare, bind him to a post, and remove one piece of his flesh
every day.

"The Koreans inflate the victim's body with vinegar and when
he is swollen to goodly proportions, drum upon him with sticks till
he dies. Their king put his sister in a brazen cage beneath which a
fire was kept burning, and she danced to amuse His Majesty.

"In other parts the victim is fixed so that he lies in the air,
one transverse bar supporting his thighs, his ankles attached to
another; his shins are beaten with rods; occasionally he is struck
on the buttocks; this latter method is widely practiced in Turkey
and the Barbary States.

"The object they call the *pao-lo* in China is a brass column
standing twenty cubits high and having eight in diameter; it is
hollow; from within it is brought to an extremely high temperature; when it is glowing, the patient embraces the column, is bound
fast to it, and is slowly grilled. 'Twas, they say, an emperor's wife

who invented this torture, and never saw it being used without discharging deliciously.[37]

"The Japanese carve open the belly; the patient is sometimes pinioned by four men; from afar the fifth runs upon the sufferer and as he somersaults over him, deals him a skull-shattering blow with an iron mace.

"The Moravian Brothers used to tickle to death. A somewhat similar torture has been tried on women: experience shows they may be masturbated to death.

"But what will surprise you even more is to see persons of condition and high rank plying the trade of executioner. What then is one to suppose, unless that they are guided by a cruel form of lubricity?

"Moulay Ismael was himself the chief executioner of the criminals in his empire; in Morocco no one was put to death save by his royal hand; and no one took off a head as nicely as could he. In performing these feats, so he used to say, he found inexpressible delight. Ten thousand unfortunates came to know the vigor of his arm: in those lands where he held sway it was a current opinion that he who perished by the monarch's hand earned an eternity of bliss in Paradise.

"The king of Melinde himself metes out the bastinadoes in his country.

"Bishop Bonner of London himself depilated those who were unwilling to be converted, or lashed them. He held one man's hand on a brazier until the nerves were burned.

"Uriothesli, England's Lord Chancellor, had a very pretty woman who did not believe in the divinity of Jesus Christ brought before him, and he himself flogged her to ribbons and cast her into the fire. And do you fancy the lecher got through all this without an erection?

"In the year 1700, at the time of the war of the Camisards, Abbé du Chayla ranged the Cévennes, whipping all the little girls

---

[37] Once women are in the habit of exciting themselves to pleasure only by giving vent to the cruelty latent within them, the extreme delicacy of their fibers, the prodigious sensitivity of their organs cause them to go a great deal farther than men in this direction.

who would not renounce their Protestantism; so severely did he deal with some that they died, and the shooting began forthwith.

"It has been reported in several countries that when two criminals are being executed at the same time, the headsman steeps his hands in the blood of the first and wipes it on the face of the second before decapitating him.

"Murder, we must conclude, has been revered and made a common practice all over the earth; from pole to pole human victims are sacrificed. Egyptians, Arabs, Cretans, Cypriots, Rhodians, Phocaeans, Greeks, Pelagians, Scythians, Romans, Phoenicians, Persians, Indians, Chinese, Massagetae, Getae, Sarmatians, Irish, Norwegians, Suevi, Scandinavians, all Northern peoples, Gauls, Celts, Cimbrians, Germans, Bretons, Spaniards, Moors, Blacks, all of them individually and generally have slain human beings upon the altars of their gods. From time immemorial man has taken pleasure in shedding the blood of his fellow man and to content himself he has sometimes disguised this passion under a cloak of justice, sometimes under one of religion. But, and of this let there be no doubt, his purpose, his aim has always been the astonishing pleasure killing procures him.

"After such examples, Juliette, after such striking demonstrations, shall you be convinced that there is no commoner deed than murder in all the world, that there exists none more legitimate, and that it would be extravagance in you to have the slightest misgivings or a single regret over all those you may have committed, or to form the cowardly resolution not to commit any more?"

"Adorable philosopher!" I cried, flinging my arms around Braschi's neck, "never has anyone dealt with this important matter in the way you have done; never has it been so precisely, so thoroughly, so plausibly explained; with so many curious anecdotes; with so many trenchant examples. Ah, all my doubts are dissipated now, I surrender to right reason; all my scruples are removed, the way ahead lies clear, and I am at the point of desiring, with Tiberius, that all mankind might have but a single head which one could have the pleasure of cutting off at a single stroke.

"Let us go, Father, the hour is advanced; did you not say that morning must not find us still in our impurities?"

We moved into the basilica.

Part
Five

*E*normous screens surrounded the isolated altar of St. Peter, making a space about one hundred yards square with the altar in its center; this room was completely shut off from the rest of the cathedral. Twenty girls and twenty young boys were disposed on tiered benches backed against each of the four sides of the arena; at each of the four angles of that superb altar, between the steps descending from it and the front row of benches, was a small Greekish altar intended for the victims. By the first a girl of fifteen was to be seen; by the second, a young woman of twenty, gravid; by the third, a youth of fourteen; by the fourth, a young man eighteen years of age and fair as Apollo. Three priests faced the great altar, ready to consummate the sacrifice, and six naked choirboys were there to serve it, two of them stretched prone upon the altars, their sparkling behinds ready for use as holy stones. Braschi and I reclined upon an ottoman situated on a stage raised ten feet above the ground, access to which was had by a stairway whose steps were covered by a magnificent Turkish carpet; this stage was large enough to provide easy accommodation to twenty persons at least. Six little Ganymedes of seven or eight, all naked, sitting on the steps, were at a snap of the finger to execute the orders of the Holy Father; various costumes both gallant and picturesque adorned the men, but that worn by the women was too delicious not to merit particular description. They wore a shift of unbleached gauze fitting loosely, negligently to their figure, hiding none of it; and had a pink collarette around the neck. The tunic I have just spoken of was, by means of a broad bow of the same pink, gathered up in behind and left the flanks absolutely exposed; over this shift each had on a blue taffeta simar which, falling in ample folds back over the shoulders, shaded nothing in front; their hair floated in free tresses; upon her head each wore a simple crown of roses. I was so taken with the elegance of this dishabille that I decided at once to adopt something similar. The ceremony began.

As soon as His Holiness formed a desire, the six aides-de-camp poised on the stairs immediately flew to satisfy it. Three girls were called for. The Pope sat down on the face of one of them, bidding her tongue his anus; the second mouthed his prick; the third dandled his balls; and while this was going forward my ass became the object of Pius VI's lewd kisses. Mass was said and orders given that my wishes be carried out as promptly and fully as the Pontiff's own. The Host once consecrated, the acolyte brought it up to the stage and respectfully deposited it upon the tip of the papal prick; the very next moment the bugger claps it into my bum, wafer first. Six girls and six pretty boys press around us, making flashing display of their asses and tools; I was myself being frigged from below by a very comely youth whose prick one of the girls was masturbating. There was no resisting this onslaught of lewdness; Braschi's sighs, moans, pulsations, and blasphemies report his nearing ecstasy and precipitate mine; we discharge with screams of pleasure. Sodomized by the Pope, the body of Jesus Christ nested in one's ass, oh, my friends! what rare delight. It seemed to me I had never in all my life tasted quite the like. We fell back exhausted amidst that crowd of celestial playthings surrounding us, and the sacrifice was over.

Forces must be regained; Braschi would have no tortures started until he was stiff again. As twenty girls and that many boys labored to restore him to life, while he looked avidly on I got myself thirty or so fuckings from a group of youths, exciting them four at a time while being caressed by a pair. Braschi, as I say, watched me perform these libertine excesses, he cheered me on and exhorted me to more. A new Mass was celebrated, and this time the Host, conveyed by the fairest prick in the room, was introduced into the fundament of the Holy Father, who, beginning to stand aright, had asses fence us in and he re-embuggered me.

"Good," said he, withdrawing after a few lunges and recoveries, "I merely wanted to temper the blade. We may now immolate."

He gives the signal for the first execution; it was to be of the eighteen-year-old young man. We have him approach, and having kissed, caressed, sucked, polluted him, Braschi informs him he is going to be crucified like St. Peter, head downward. He hears his sentence with stoic resignation and undergoes it courageously. I was frigging Braschi while the nails were being driven in; and who do you suppose wielded the hammers? The same priests who had just celebrated the Masses. After affixing the young man to his cross they attached the latter to one of the spiraled pillars of Saint Peter's altar, and attention was turned to the girl of fifteen. She too was led up, the Pope embuggered her; I was frigging her; she was first condemned to the most vigorous fustigation, then hanged from a second pillar.

Up stepped the boy of fourteen, Braschi embuggers him too; and desiring to carry out this execution personally, he subjected him to every known vexation and horror. It was at this point it occurred to me what a villain Braschi was. One has but to be on the throne to carry infamy to the last extreme: the impunity these diademed rascals enjoy leads them into refinements nobody else would even dream of. Sotted from lust, the monster finally tears the child's heart out and devours it while loosing streams of evil fuck. The pregnant woman remained.

"Entertain yourself with this baggage," Braschi said to me, "I leave her fate in your hands. I am not going to stiffen again, I can feel it, but it will nevertheless gladden me to see you have at her: no matter what the state I happen to be in, crime always amuses me. So don't spare her."

The wretch approaches.

"Whose is this child?" I ask her.

"One of His Holiness' minion's."

"And it was done within His Holiness' sight?"

"Yes."

"The father, is he present?"

"He is standing there." She pointed toward a young man.

I now addressed him. "What you put into her you shall now take out—here is the knife, and act this very instant if you do not wish to feel its edge." The crestfallen fellow did as he was told; each thrust of the dagger drew a discharge from me, and when the body was all one great wound and I all dry, we retired.

Braschi was bent on having me pass the rest of the night with him, the libertine adored me.

"You are firm," he declared, "and that is how I like a woman to be. Among them you do not have many rivals."

"Princess Borghese surpasses me," I replied.

"Far from it," the Pope retorted, "she is forever having fits of remorse. A week from today," he continued, "I shall give you the supper I have promised; the Princess will be there, and your friends the Cardinals too. Believe that I am sincere, beloved child, when I say that I hope we shall achieve horrors exceeding anything we have accomplished this evening."

"I too look forward to the occasion," I said politely, having in mind the theft I was planning to operate on my next visit to the Vatican, "yes, I am in expectation of great things."

Braschi, who had been rubbing his testicles with a spirituous lotion meant to stimulate them, proposed that we return to our tricks.

"I'm afraid I lack the consistency to embugger you," said he, "but you might suck me."

I got astride his chest; my asshole settled over his lips and the rogue, Pope that he was, blew his seed into my mouth while forswearing his God like an atheist.

And he fell asleep. I was greatly tempted to take this opportunity to steal everything I could carry out of his treasury; I knew the way, he had shown it to me himself, I would encounter no guards. But this project having been concerted with Olympia, I did not want to cheat her of the pleasure of participating in it; moreover, Elise and Raimonde were to be along and between the four of us we would be able to get away with that much more booty.

Pius VI awoke after a short while. There was to be a consistory that day. I left him in peace to discuss the state of Christian conscience throughout the world, and besought pardon of mine for not having laden it with a sufficient quantity of crimes. I have said it before, I affirm it again: nothing is worse than virtuous remorse for a soul accustomed to evil; and when one exists in a state of complete corruption, 'tis infinitely wiser to overdo wickedness than to rest in arrears; for doing more always brings some pleasure, while from doing less one has nothing but pain.

Two or three baths washed away the Pontifical stains, and I betook myself to the Borghese Palace to tell my friend of my Vatican success.

To avoid the monotony of details I shall not tarry long over those of the new orgies we celebrated there. The Sistine Chapel was their scene; above four hundred subjects of both sexes appeared at them; what was enacted in the way of impurities beggars description. Thirty virgin girls, between the ages of seven and fourteen and one more beautiful than the next, were violated and afterward massacred; forty boys met the same fate. Albani, Bernis, and the Pope buggered one another and were buggered, gorged themselves on drink and infamy, killed, bibbled and fucked themselves senseless, and when finally they were, that was the moment we chose, Olympia, Elise, Raimonde, and I, to slip away and pillage the treasury. We made off with twenty thousand sequins which Sbrigani, posted nearby with a few trusty individuals, had transported straight to the Princess' home where, the next day, we divided the loot. Braschi never noticed the theft, or else deemed best to feign not to have noticed it. I did not see His Holiness again; he felt, I suspect, that my visits to the Vatican were a little more than he could afford. In view of these circumstances I saw no reason to remain on in Rome, indeed, it seemed wiser to leave; Olympia was desolate when she heard the news; but part we must, despite the strain, and at the beginning of winter I set forth for Naples with a packet of letters of recommendation to the royal family, to Prince Francaville, to every other grandee and high-bred figure in Naples. My funds I left in the hands of Roman bankers.

We traveled in an excellent coach, Sbrigani, my women and I. Four mounted valets were escorting us, when between Fondi and Minturno, where the road follows the Gulf of Gaeta and at some twelve or fifteen leagues from Naples, ten horsemen appeared toward dusk. Pistol in hand, they proposed that we quit the highway and come have a talk with Captain Brisatesta who, honestly retired in a castle overlooking the bay, did not suffer gentlefolk traveling in the land to pass so near his dwelling without gratifying him with a visit. We had no trouble understanding the meaning of this language and after a rapid estimation of the odds between our forces and the opposing ones, we felt called upon to capitulate.

"Comrade," said Sbrigani to the officer, "I have always heard it said that rascals get on together; if you exercise the profession in one way, we exercise it in another, and both of us are engaged in dupery."

"You will tell all that to my captain," this lieutenant replied, "as for me, I simply obey orders and especially when my life depends upon it; march."

As the riders had been tying our valets to the tails of their horses during this exchange, we found ourselves without anything further to add. We advanced. The officer had climbed into our carriage and four of his men were driving it. For five hours we continued thus, and it was during that time our guide informed us that Captain Brisatesta was the most famous brigand in all Italy.

"He has," said the lieutenant, "twelve hundred men enrolled, and our detachments roam the Papal States as far north as Trento and southward to land's end in Calabria. Brisatesta's wealth is colossal. He made a journey to Paris last year and while there espoused the charming lady who today does the honors of the house."

"Brother," I said to the bandit, "it would seem to me that the honors of a thief's house must not be very onerous."

"I beg your pardon," the officer returned, "Madame's employment is more considerable than one might think: 'tis she who cuts the captives' throats, and I assure you she acquits herself in a thoroughly conscientious and commendable manner, you will be enchanted to die by her hand."

"Ah, I see," said I, "that then is what you call doing the honors of the house—you are not reassuring, sir officer. And is the Captain presently at home, or shall we have dealings with Madame alone?"

"You will find them both at home. Brisatesta has just now returned from an expedition to the interior of Calabria which cost us a few men but which was worth a great deal of money. Since then our pay has tripled; oh, he is a kind man, our Captain, as fair and just as they come. He always pays us according to his means; he'd give us ten ounces a day[1] if his earnings permitted it. But here we are," the officer said. "I am sorry that darkness prevents you

---

[1] The Neapolitan ounce is worth about eleven French *livres* ten *sous*.

from seeing the location in which this superb house is set. Down below is the sea, we turn upward to reach the castle which cannot be approached otherwise than on foot; we must therefore alight. From now on the path mounts steeply."

Following the lead of our guides, after an hour and a half of struggling single file up the highest mountain I had ever climbed in my life, we came to a moat, a drawbridge was lowered, we traversed some fortifications bristling with soldiers, were challenged, allowed to pass, then found ourselves inside the citadel. It was indeed a formidable one, and maintained as it was by Brisatesta looked capable of withstanding any assault or siege.

It was about midnight when we arrived; the Captain and his dame were in bed, they were wakened. Brisatesta came at once to examine the catch. His was a striking appearance. He stood five feet ten inches tall, was in the flower of his manhood, his face was exceedingly handsome and at the same time exceedingly harsh. He cast a quick piercing glance at the men in our party, his eyes lingered only a little longer upon each one of us women; his brusque manner, his fierce stare made us tremble. He spoke a few words to the officer; the men were immediately led off in one direction, our trunks and belongings borne off in another. My friends and I were cast into a lightless dungeon, where after groping about we found some straw; there we lay ourselves wearily down, rather to bewail our ill fortune than seek the repose our horrible situation denied us. What cruel thoughts assailed us then, how were our souls not tried! The anguishing recollection of our past pleasures rose to mind, and only made our present plight seem darker. From dwelling upon our state of affairs we could deduce nothing but melancholy presumptions; thus tormented by the past, terrified by the present, shuddering at the future, the blood hardly ran at all through our feverish veins. 'Twas then Raimonde thought to invoke religion.

"Don't bother with those illusions, child," said I, "when one has despised them one's whole life long it is impossible, no matter what the circumstances may be, to believe in them again; let them lie. Only remorse, furthermore, recalls one to religion and I am far from repenting or even regretting anything I have ever done; of all those deeds there is not one I am not prepared to commit afresh, granted the chance; it is over being deprived of my capacities I grieve, and not over the results obtained from them when they were in my possession. Ah, Raimonde, you do not realize the grip vice exerts upon a soul like mine! Riddled with crimes, fed by crime, it exists for nought but to batten on crime, and even with my neck on the block, still I shall be wanting to commit more; I'd like crime to emanate from my very ashes, I'd like the ghost of me wandering the world to harass mortals with crimes or to inspire crimes in them. I think, however, we need not be afraid, for we are in the hands of vice: a god will protect us. Much greater would be my dread were we prisoners of the frightful goddess men dare call Justice. The spawn of despotism mated to imbecility, if 'twere that whore held us captive I would already have said my last farewells; but I have never been afraid of crime; the sectators of the idol we worship respect their peers and smite them not; we'll join forces with these people if need be. Though I've not yet met her, I like what I have heard about this Madame Brisatesta; I wager we shall please her; we'll make her discharge; and she'll not kill us. Come here, Raimonde, and you too, dear Elise, and since the only pleasure remaining to us is frigging, let us enjoy it."

Stirred by my speech and my fingers, the little minxes fell to playing; Nature served us just as well in this hour of grim adversity as in bygone days of prosperity. Never had I been so rocked, so whelmed by pleasure; but the return to reason was frightful.

"We are going to be slaughtered like sheep," I said to my companions, "we are going to die like dogs, it is useless to delude ourselves, death is the fate in store for us. And it is not death that I dread, I am philosopher enough to be very sure that I'll be no more unhappy after vegetating a few years on earth than I was before I got here; no, it is pain I dread, these scoundrels are going to make me suffer; they will perhaps enjoy torturing me as I have enjoyed torturing others; this captain has an evil look to me, he has long moustaches, a bad sign, and . . . and his wife is probably as cruel as he. . . . Oh, a moment ago I was full of confidence, and now I quake."

"Madame," Elise spoke up, "deep inside me there is a hope, I know not what it is, but your teachings put me at ease. It is according to the eternal laws of Nature, you have told me so, that crime will triumph and virtue be humbled; I place my trust in that immutable decree; ah, dear mistress, it shall spare us from disaster."

"To be sure, to be sure, and my reasoning thereupon shall appear lucid and incontrovertible," said I to my companions. "If, as cannot be doubted, might makes right, and the mass of crimes weighs heavier in the balance than on the other side do virtue and its practitioners, human self-interest is but the result of man's passions and nearly all of them lead to crime; well, crime's interest is to humble virtue; therefore, in almost all the situations of life, I shall lay my stake by crime rather than by virtue."

"But, Madame," said Raimonde, "look here, as matters stand between our captors and us, we are virtue, and vice is represented only by them; therefore they shall crush us."

"We are speaking in general terms," I replied, "this is but a particular case; Nature may make a single exception to her rules, and thereby confirm them, you know."

We were in the midst of such discussions when a jailer, of more forbidding aspect even than his master, unlocked the door and handed us a plate of beans.

"Here," said he in a guttural voice, "don't waste any, it's all you're going to get."

"What," I demanded, "is it then to be of hunger we are to die?"

"No, for from what I hear you're to be done in tomorrow, and Madame probably feels there's no use spending good money to have you form turds you're not going to have time to shit."

"But, dear fellow, you do perhaps know what kind of death is being prepared for us?"

"It'll depend on what Madame's fancy happens to be, our Captain leaves all that up to her; she does whatever she likes; but, you being women, your death ought to be milder than the one the men in your party shall have to face, for Madame Brisatesta is not very sanguinary except with men. She enjoys them first; then, when she's tired of them, she puts 'em out of their misery."

"And this does not arouse her husband's jealousy?"

"Not at all, he does the same with women, when he's finished amusing himself with them he turns 'em over to his wife who pronounces this or that sort of a sentence and usually executes it herself if the Captain is no longer in the mood for such pleasures."

"Your master seldom kills?"

"Hardly at all. Five victims a week, maybe six. You see, he's done so much slaughtering in his time! He's tired of it. Besides, he knows his wife has a dreadful weakness for killing, and since he's very devoted to her, he just steps aside and allows her to handle the business. Adieu," said the churl, fitting the key into the lock, "I must be getting on my way, I have others to serve; we are kept pretty busy here; thanks to heaven, the house is always full, you've no idea the number of prisoners we take—"

"Comrade," said I, "our belongings—are they safe?"

"Safe and sound in storage. You'll not be seeing them again, but don't worry, nothing is ever lost around here, we are very careful about that."

And the door clanged shut behind him. Through a slot between the bars a weak ray of light entered the dungeon, enough to enable us to see one another's faces.

After a moment I spoke to Elise. "Well, my dear, does that not suffice to dash whatever hope you have?"

"Not entirely," was the amiable girl's answer to me, "I cling to it in spite of all. Let us eat and not despair."

That meager repast was barely finished when our warden reappeared.

"They are calling for you in the council chamber," he informed us. "You won't be kept waiting, it's for today."

We trudged after him.

It was a long room we entered at one end. At the other was a table, behind it a woman sat writing. Without looking up she signaled for us to approach; then, laying aside her quill, she raised her eyes and ordered us to reply to the questions she was about to ask . . . oh, my friends! what expressions can I find to convey my surprise. This woman about to interrogate me, this consort of the most wicked of all Italy's brigands, it was Clairwil—my precious Clairwil, whom I found again under these incredible circumstances. I could contain myself no longer; I rushed into her arms.

"Whom do I behold?" cried Clairwil. "What! Juliette, is it you? Oh, tenderest friend, let me kiss you and may this, which would have been a day of sorrow for any other, become one of rejoicing for you!"

The multitude of feelings that beset my soul, the conflict between them, their vivacity and heat cast me into a veritable stupor. When I opened my eyes again I found myself in an excellent bed, surrounded by my women and Clairwil, who were vying for the pleasure of comforting me and giving me the care my state required.

"Long lost and dearest heart, I have you back again," said my friend of olden days. "What happiness this is for me! I have already told my husband who it is destiny has brought under our roof; your servants, your effects, everything shall be restored to you, we ask only that you spend a few days with us; our style of life will cause you no alarm, I know you to have principles, and to be immune to scandal; what we achieved together in the past permits me to suppose that you will find this a sympathetic atmosphere."

"Oh, Clairwil, your friend is ever the same," I exclaimed; "my mind has matured with age, and the progress I have made is of a sort that only renders me worthier of you; I joyfully await the criminal spectacles you prepare for me: we shall enjoy these pleasures together. For I have come a long way from the pusillanimity that came near to being my undoing once upon a time, and your friend, be sure of it, blushes no more save at virtue. But you, dear angel, where have you been? What have you done? Ah, we have been separated for ages; what lucky star has led us both to this place?"

"You shall have all the particulars," Clairwil assured me; "but I want you to begin by calming yourself, by recovering your serenity, by accepting our apologies for having given you such a poor welcome. You are going to see my husband, I venture to predict you will take very kindly to him. . . . Oh, Juliette, recognize the hand of Nature; she has always championed the cause of vice, she does so again, as you see. Had you fallen into the clutches of a virtuous woman, you, vicious rascal that you are, you were doomed; but we are of your own sort, and by us you can only be saved. Cheerless followers of virtue, avow your weakness and may the everlasting superiority of crime over your souls of slime impose eternal silence upon you."

Brisatesta arrived just as his wife concluded this speech. Whether because the situation had altered or because my now tranquil spirits caused me to view things with a different eye, this brigand no longer struck me as so frightening; scrutinizing him attentively, I found him extremely attractive; and so in truth he was.

"You have got yourself a fine husband," I congratulated my friend.

"Look well at his face, Juliette," Clairwil replied, "and tell me if you think none but the bonds of wedlock unite us."

"You bear a strange likeness to each other, it is true."

"This splendid fellow, oh, Juliette, is my brother; events had separated us, a journey he made last year brought him back to me. Marriage reinforced our ties; we wish them to be indissoluble."

"And indissoluble they shall be," said the Captain, "for when two people resemble each other so perfectly, when their inclinations, their morals so completely conform, 'tis madness ever to part."

"You are a couple of rascals," said I, "you live in the depths of incest and crime, there shall never be any absolution for you; were you in my place, just come from Rome, all these sins would make you quake to the soul, and the fear of never being able to purge them would prevent you from persevering in your wickedness."

"Let us dine, Juliette," said my friend, "you can finish your sermon over dessert." Then, opening the door to an adjoining room, "There," she went on, "are your possessions, your servants, there is your Sbrigani; be all of good cheer in this house, become its friends, and when you have gone away from here, make it known abroad that the charms of sweet amity have their faithful even in a den of crime and depravity."

A magnificent meal was awaiting us. Sbrigani and my women sat down beside us; my valets joined my friend's in serving the dishes and pouring the wine; and we were soon all one happy family. It was eight o'clock in the evening when we rose from the table. Brisatesta never left it before he was drunk; it appeared to me that his beloved wife had adopted the same failing. From the dining hall we passed into a larger salon where our hostess suggested we twine the myrtle of Venus to the vine leaves of Bacchus.

"This bugger here has the look of a man with something in his breeches," said she, pulling Sbrigani to a couch. "Brother, peep under Juliette's skirts, you'll find she is favored in the way you appreciate."

"Oh, God," I cried, my head beginning to reel also, "to be fucked by a highway robber, by an assassin!"

And I was not done speaking when I was bent over a sofa by the outlaw, a prick as thick as my arm was already nudging between my quivering buttocks.

"Fair angel," the libertine said, "you will pardon a little preliminary rite without which, well standing as you see my prick to be, it would nonetheless be impossible for me to do your charms the profound homage they deserve; I shall be obliged to bloody this gorgeous ass, but trust my skill, you'll hardly feel a thing."

Catching up a steel-tipped martinet wherewith he dealt my behind a dozen whistling blows, he had laid open that entire part of me inside two minutes, without causing me anything like a disagreeable sensation.

"That should do very nicely," said the Captain, "my thighs shall be wet as they press against you, and my prick lodged deep in your bowels will perhaps wash them with a dense sperm, unobtainable save through this ceremony."

"Lay on, brother, lay on!" called Clairwil from the midst of her fucking with Sbrigani, "her ass has weathered the worst, we used often to wear whips out upon each other."

"Oh, sir!" I cried upon feeling the Captain's outsized bludgeon thunder into my rectum, "the lash was as nothing to this. . . ."

But my protest came too late, Brisatesta's monstrous engine had already struck rock-bottom; I was embuggered to the hilt. Others were imitating us: Clairwil, as was her custom, offering only her rear to her fucker, was solidly run on by Sbrigani's spirited device, while Raimonde, frigging her clitoris, was bestowing the same voluptuous services to her that I was extracting from Elise.

Oh, friends of mine, this bandit chief, what a fucker was he! Not so much attached to the one shrine where I at first thought his tastes would hold him fast, he alternately repaired to each of them and by that dual intromission the rascal kept me in constant discharge.

"There it is, Juliette," said he as he withdrew and couched his enormous member between my bubs, "the explanation and cause of all my wild ways and delinquencies; it is the pleasures I receive from this fine prick that have shaped my career; as is the case with my sister, crime heats me, and I am unable to loose a drop of fuck save through the plotting or enacting of some horrors."

"Why then, for sweet fuck's sake let us create a few of them," I replied. "Since we are all animated by the same desire and the opportunity for satisfying it is probably within our grasp, let's blend bloodshed and fuckshed. Have you no victims about?"

"Ah, slut," said Clairwil, overtaken by a spasm, "I recognize you in those words, they are your hallmark. Come now, brother, let us please this charming creature, we'll immolate the Roman belle we arrested this morning."

"Right you are, have her brought up; her death will amuse Juliette, we shall all frig and discharge while conducting the operation."

The traveler arrives. Friends, will you guess the identity of the woman who now stands within my sight? Borghese, yes, she, the delicious Borghese; the sensitive Borghese; brokenhearted at my departure, life had lost all meaning for her, she had flown forth in search of me, and Brisatesta's men had just taken her on the Naples road as they had taken me the day before.

"Clairwil," I exclaimed, "this woman's not for victimizing either, she is an accomplice, she is the friend who assumed the place you had occupied in my heart, to the extent that another could replace you there; treat her lovingly, my angel, the rascal is deserving of us."

And the heavenly Olympia kissed me, caressed Clairwil, and seemed to implore Brisatesta.

"Oh, Godsfuck," muttered the latter, erected like a Carmelite, "this complication of adventures, heating in me desires to fuck this lovely lady, cool me to other projects; first let's fuck her, then we'll decide her fate."

I surrender my post to Olympia; her nobly formed ass receives the wide praise it deserves. Using the same means he employed with me, Brisatesta makes the same artistic shambles of it and sodomizes it straight off and tempestuously. My women frig me, and Sbrigani goes on rasping Clairwil. For once no other stimulant is needed to rouse our spirits; Brisatesta lines us up in a row, all five on our hands and knees upon a sofa and our flanks nicely lifted: Sbrigani and he plumb us turn by turn, while one ass-fucks the other fucks cunt, and the scoundrels finally discharge, Sbrigani in Clairwil's fundament, Brisatesta in Olympia's.

Some more decent behavior succeeded these pleasures. Borghese, newly emerged from a dungeon, also needed a bite to eat; she was served a supper and we went to bed. After breakfast the following morning, the reunion of a Parisian *petite maîtresse* with a bandit chieftain in the wilds of Italy still seemed so surprising to us all that we begged the Captain to relate what promised to be a very unusual story.

"I shall tell it if you like," Brisatesta consented; "but it includes details rather more scandalous than those one would ordinarily hazard in company; your manners, however, vouch for your philosophy and I believe there is nothing I need keep from your hearing."

BRISATESTA'S STORY

If modesty still had any habitation in my soul, I would surely hesitate to disclose my eccentricities; but having long ago arrived at that degree of moral corruption where one is safe from all shame, not the slightest scruple prevents me from confiding to you all down to the least and seamiest events of a life which, summed up in a phrase, amounts to a tissue of crime and execration. The gracious personage you see at my side, and who bears the title of wife to me, is that and my sister also. We are both the children of that famous Borchamps, renowned not only for his concussions but for his wealth and libertinage as well. My father had just entered into his fortieth year when he married my mother, twenty years his junior and much richer than he; I was born before the marriage was a year old. My sister Gabrielle came into the world six years later.

I was turning sixteen, my sister ten, when Borchamps apparently decided that henceforth he alone would be in charge of my upbringing; we had been away at school, we were now fetched home. And to return under the paternal roof was to be restored as it were to life; the little we had learned of religion my father helped us now to forget, and the most agreeable talents he taught us instead replaced the gloomy obscurities of theology. We were soon to notice that my mother was in no wise pleased by such proceedings. Mild-tempered, gently bred, innately pious and virtuous, she was far from imagining that the principles our father was inculcating in us were someday to make for our happiness; and full of her little notions, she interfered as best she could in her husband's enterprises, who while mocking her and sneering at her objections, went on notwithstanding to destroy not only all there was in us of religion's principles but those of morality also. The most inviolable bases of what is popularly understood as natural law were likewise reduced to rubble; and this amiable father, in his eagerness that we become as thoroughly philosophical in our outlook as he, left no stone unturned in his effort to render us impassive before prejudices and insensible to remorse. To forestall the possibility of these maxims suffering contradiction, he took care to keep us well isolated from the world outside. Only the occasional visit of one of his friends, and of that friend's family, ever mitigated our lonely retirement; the intelligence of the sequel requires that I now say something of this worthy individual who would pay us visits.

Monsieur de Breval, forty-five years of age at the time, nearly as wealthy as my father, like him had a young and virtuous wife and, like him, a pair of charming children, one of whom, his son Auguste, was fifteen and the other, Laura, a truly stunning creature, almost twelve. Each time Breval came to our house he brought his wife and children along; we four youngsters would be put together under the supervision of a governess named Pamphylia, she being twenty, very pretty, and perfectly in my father's good graces. All four being raised in the same manner, having identical information and attitudes, the conversations we had and the games we played were well in advance of our years; and truly, anyone eaves-dropping upon our conventicles would have sooner taken them for meetings of a philosophical circle than for the recreations of juveniles. By dint of being made familiar with Nature we were shortly lending an ear to her voice, and the extraordinary thing is that it did not inspire us to mingle. Each remained within the bonds of kinship; Auguste and Laura were in love, confessed their sentiments with the same candor, the same joy, as Gabrielle and I declared ours to each other. Incest does not cross Nature's plans, since the first natural impulses we had were in that direction. There is this too which may seem remarkable: our young ardors were accompanied by no twinges of jealousy. This ridiculous feeling is no proof of love; begot of pride and selfishness, it is more a token of the fear of seeing another object preferred to oneself than to that of losing the object one adores. Although Gabrielle might be fonder of me than of Auguste, she embraced him no less warmly for that; and although I might worship Gabrielle, I did nonetheless conceive violent desires to be loved by Laura. Thus did six months go by without us combining any earthly element into this soulful metaphysics; 'twas not willingness that we lacked, but instruction, and our fathers, who were keeping a watchful eye upon us, at last decided to lend their aid to Nature.

One day when the weather was very warm and our elders, as was their wont, had forgathered to spend a few hours among themselves, my father, half-naked, came to find us and he proposed that we move from the nursery into the apartment where he and the other adults were; we accompanied him, the young governess following on our heels. And there, fancy our surprise at seeing Breval on top of my mother, and his wife the next instant under-neath my father.

"Pay close attention to this mechanism of Nature," our young Pamphylia said to us, "study it well, your parents may soon be disposed to initiate you into these mysteries of lubricity both for your education's and your happiness' sake. Examine each of these groups; you observe that they who compose them are enjoying the pleasures of Nature; apply yourselves to imitating them. . . ."

Upon all this we bent the stare of open-mouthed bewilderment, this being the usual effect such a spectacle has upon children's minds; but a keener interest took hold of us by and by, and we went forward to view matters from nearer on. It was then we perceived the difference in the four actors' situations: the two men were taking manifest pleasure in what they were about, while the two women seemed not to have their heart in the game and even showed what looked like repugnance for it. Pamphylia demonstrated, explained, pointed things out, and identified them by name.

"Retain it all carefully," said she, "for you shall soon be put into action."

She then entered into the most extensive details. There came a momentary pause in the scene, but one which, instead of reducing its interest, enhanced its attractiveness. Leaping hotly away from Madame de Breval's behind (for those gentlemen ass-fucked only), my father drew us toward him and had each of the four of us touch his member, showing us how it was to be frigged. We laughed, we gaily did as we were told, and Breval watched us while continuing his buggery of my mother.

"Pamphylia," my father said, "relieve them of their clothes; it is time to join a little practice to the theory of Nature."

The next instant, we are naked; Breval drops what he is in the middle of doing, and the two fathers fall to caressing us indiscriminately, fingering us and sucking us here and there and everywhere, without forgetting Pamphylia, whom the rascals fondle and kiss almost to pieces.

"What an atrocity!" cried Madame de Breval, "how does one dare behave in such a way with one's own children?"

"Silence, Madame," her husband shouted at her; "confine yourselves, both of you, to the passive roles you have been allotted; you are here to be made use of, not to harangue us."

Thereupon returning quietly to work, the libertine and his colleague continued their examinations just as phlegmatically as if in this height of impurity there were nothing that could justify the two mothers' feelings of outrage.

The sole object of my father's fervent attentions, he appeared to be neglecting all the others in favor of me. Gabrielle, if you wish, did indeed interest him too; he kissed her, he frigged her; but his most impassioned caresses were all aimed at my youthful charms. I alone seemed to inflame him; I alone received that voluptuous caress of the tongue in the ass, sure sign of a man's predilection for another man, certain gage of the most refined lust, and which true sodomites are loath to lavish upon women, from fear of the appalling disgust the environs expose them to; now ready for anything, my father steers me to the couch where my mother is lying, places me flat upon her belly, has me held there by Pamphylia who, naked pursuant to his orders, during the operation gives him the world's prettiest ass to handle. His lips moisten the spot he wishes to penetrate; once he considers the outer gates sufficiently ajar, his engine arrives before the portal of the temple . . . thrusts . . . pushes . . . passes in . . . drives far, and depucelates me with ecstatic effects.

"Good my Lord," shrieked my mother, "oh, what manner of horrors are these! Was your son made to be the victim of your libertinage, and are you not at all aware that what you have just done bears the stamp of two or three crimes, for the least of which there are gallows raised?"

"Eh, but, Madame," was my father's dry retort, " 'tis precisely what you tell me that is going to make me discharge the more deliciously. You have nothing whatever to fear, the boy is at a very fit age to endure these mediocre assaults, it could easily have been done four years ago, and ought to have been: I depucelate far younger children in the same manner every day. I have every intention of soon doing the same to Gabrielle, even though she is but ten: my prick is slender, thousands will tell you so, and as for my skill, it is incredible."

Be all that as it may, blood seeps from my wounds; floods of sperm stanch it, my father grows calmer, continuing, however, to caress my sister who takes my place after I have been dismissed.

Meanwhile, Breval was not wasting his time; but being more enamored of his daughter than of his son, it is upon Laura he first opens fire and the little thing, likewise placed upon her mother's bosom, has just seen her maidenhead blasted.

"Fuck your son," my father calls to him, "I am going to embugger my daughter: let them all four slake our brutal thirsts this day. The time has come to have them enter into the one role Nature assigned them to play; it is time they realize that it is only to serve as our whores they were born, and that were it not in the hope of fucking them, we might never have created them at all."

The two sacrifices are offered simultaneously. To the right one sees Breval depucelating his son while kissing his wife's asshole and palpating his daughter's buttocks, still slimed with his fuck; to the left, my father bum-fucking Gabrielle while he licks my behind, while he molests my mother's with one hand and frigs Pamphylia's anus with the other; both gentlemen discharge, and quiet is restored.

The remainder of the evening is devoted to giving us lessons. We are married; my father mates me to my sister; Breval does the same with his children. They excite us, prepare avenues, consolidate junctions; and while they have us thus linked front to front they sound our asses, now this ass, now that, taking turns; in such a manner that Breval would be buggering me while Borchamps was fucking Auguste, and while all this was going on, the two mothers, constrained to participate in the celebration of the orgies, would, along with Pamphylia, be making broad display of their charms to the two libertines. A number of other lubricious scenes follow that one: my father's imagination was limitless. Messieurs place the children upon their mothers, and while the husband of one bum-fucks the wife of the other, they oblige us youngsters to frig our mothers. Pamphylia runs up and down the ranks, she cheers the contestants on, emboldens them, shows them the way; her turn comes, she is sodomized; delicious discharging finally pacifies spirits, and festivities are declared at an end.

Several days later my father summoned me into his library.

"My friend," said he, "you alone shall henceforth provide me the joys of my life; I worship you, and wish to fuck nobody else; I am going to send your sister back to her nunnery. She is very pretty, I do not gainsay it, I have received much pleasure from her; but she is female, and that in my view is a serious flaw. Moreover, I could well become disturbed by the pleasures you might taste with her; I want only you beside me. You shall be lodged in your mother's apartment; she will step down from her place and yield it to you, she has no other choice; we shall lie every night together, I shall spend myself dry in your splendid ass, you shall discharge in mine, we shall be very happy with each other, 'tis certain. Such assemblies as the one at which you were present will be held no longer; Breval is mad about his daughter, and plans to behave with her as I am going to do with you. We shall not cease to be friends; but, too envious of our mutual pleasures, too jealous of our own, we have reached the decision to mingle them no more."

"But my mother, Sir," said I, "may not all this anger her?"

"Dear friend," my father replied, "listen carefully to what I have to say to you on that head; you are clever enough to understand me.

"This woman who brought you into the world is perhaps the creature who in all the universe I most supremely detest; the ties binding her to me render her a thousand times more loathsome yet, that is my attitude. Breval has a similar one toward his own wife. The manner in which you have seen us use these women is the result of our disgust and our indignation; it is far less for the sake of amusement than in order to debase and degrade them that we prostitute them as we do; we outrage them from hatred and a kind of cruel delectation you yourself shall, I trust, someday come to know, and whereof the aim is to extract an unspeakable pleasure from vexations imposed upon an object one has enjoyed over much and over long."

"But, Sir," was the question common sense bade me put, "you will then torment me also when at last you grow weary of me?"

"That is an altogether different affair," my father explained, "they are neither conventional usages nor laws which bind us, but rather similarities of taste, common convenience, that is to say, true love; furthermore, our union is criminal in the eyes of mankind, and one never wearies of crime."

Knowing neither more nor better at the time, I believed all I was told and from there on lived with my father on exactly the same footing as if I had been his mistress; I passed all my nights at his side, very often in the same bed, and we would ass-fuck each

other until we collapsed from exhaustion into sleep. Pamphylia
was, after Breval, our second confidante and a regular collaborator
in our pleasures; my father liked having her whip him while he embuggered me; he would also sodomize and lash her; and sometimes
she would be made to kiss and caress me, then my father would
invite me to do whatever I cared to with her, upon condition that,
while I was doing it, I caress and kiss his ass. And Borchamps, like
Socrates, taught his disciple even as he fucked him. The most impious, the most antimoral principles were suggested to me; and if
I was not already out robbing on the highways, it was through no
fault of Borchamps. Now and then, at holidays, my sister came to
the house, but she was not warmly welcomed there; very unlike my
father in this regard, whenever I could obtain a moment alone with
her I bore her testimony of great ardor, and fucked her at the
slightest chance.

"Father dislikes me," Gabrielle told me, "he prefers you. . . .
So it is, so let it be. Live happily with him and never forget me. . . ."

I kissed Gabrielle and swore I would adore her always.

I had for quite some time noticed that my mother never
emerged from Borchamps' private study without a handkerchief
pressed to her eyes and heaving sighs of greatest sadness. Curious
to know the cause of her sorrow, I cut a slit in the partition separating that study from my boudoir and, when the first opportunity for
spying upon them came, stole quietly to the hole and peered
through it. I was witness to horrors; my father's loathing for his
wife vented itself in the form of frightful physical mistreatments.
There is no imagining what his ferocious lust would inflict upon
that unhappy victim of his aversion; after beating her senseless
with his fists, he would kick her as she lay on the floor, at other
times he would flog her bloody with a martinet, and more often
still he would prostitute her to an exceedingly ill-favored man, unknown to me, and with whom he held lewd commerce himself.

"Who is this fellow?" I one day asked Pamphylia, to whom
I had confided my discoveries and who, full of friendliness for me,
offered to help me make more of them.

"He," said she, "is a professional scoundrel your father has
saved two or three times from hanging; the sort of man who for
six francs would assassinate anyone you wanted put out of the way.

One of Borchamps' greater pleasures is to have him flog your mother and then, as you have yourself seen, to prostitute her to him. Borchamps is dreadfully fond of the man, and used to have him very often in his bed before that became your regular place. But you have still a few things to learn about the libertinage of him who sired you: be at your spyhole tomorrow and you will observe a scene to outdo all those you have just now described to me."

No sooner am I at my post than four stout swashbuckling lads march into my father's library, clap a pistol to his nose, seize him, bind him fast to one side of a double ladder, then, catching up each a bundle of withes, beat him about the buttocks and thighs, perhaps a thousand strokes apiece; the blood was bubbling out of him when they loosed his bonds to toss him upon a couch and assault him in such wise that at all times he had a prick in his mouth, one in either hand, and one in his bum. He was fucked more than twenty times over, and by what pricks, my God! I could not have got my hand around the smallest of them.

"I'd have liked to have been embuggering you while watching all that," I admitted to Pamphylia, "perhaps, dearest friend, you might be able to induce my father to have my mother the victim of a similar joust."

"Oh, that should not be difficult," the dear girl assured me, "you have simply to propose a horror to Borchamps for him to seize the idea. You'll not have to wait long for the scene you desire."

A few days later, in effect, Pamphylia told me the moment was at hand, I glued my eye to the crack in the partition. My poor mother was lashed and sodomized with such force that the quartet left her motionless on the floor. As usual, Pamphylia lent me her superb hindquarters during the show; and I may honestly say that I had never discharged more deliciously before.

I avowed everything to my father, including the extreme pleasure his clandestine revels had been procuring me.

"The suggestion that you treat your wife as you have just done originated with me after I saw how you had yourself treated."

"My friend," Borchamps wanted to know, "are you capable of helping me in these operations?"

"Be sure of it," I replied.

"Truly? This woman who brought you into the world?"

"She labored only in her own behalf, and I detest her as powerfully as you possibly can."

"Kiss me, my beloved, you are delicious; and believe me when I say that you shall from now on begin to taste the most violent pleasures in the realm of human experience. Only in outraging what man is stupid enough to call the laws of Nature is he able to find authentic delight. Why, dare I believe my ears? You will mistreat your mother, word of honor?"

"More cruelly than you, I swear it."

"You will martyrize her?"

"Martyrize her, torture her, I'll kill her if you like."

And Borchamps, who had been fondling my behind throughout this conversation, here lost control of himself, spilling his seed before he had time to shoot it into my ass.

"Until tomorrow, my friend," said he, "it's tomorrow that I put your mettle to the test; between now and then, no nonsense, eh? Rest yourself, as I intend to do: fuck is vital to any such undertaking, one must lay by a double dose of it if one wishes to achieve infamies."

At the appointed hour my mother passed into Borchamps' study; Borchamps' wicked protégé was there; the scene was frightful. The poor woman burst into tears at seeing me there, and that I was one of her most implacable enemies. I strove to improve upon the horrors wherewith my father and his friend beset her. Borchamps would have the man embugger me as I lay atop my mother clawing the sacred breast whence I had first drawn sustenance. Energetically prodded by a length of good prick in my ass, my imagination wonderfully stimulated by the thought of being fucked by a professional rogue, I went a bit farther than I had been told and came away with the nipple of my very respectable mother's right breast in my teeth; she emits a scream, loses consciousness, and my delirious father rushes to replace his friend in my ass, covering me with praise, and filling me with sperm.

I had just attained my nineteenth year when my father at last chose to broach all that was on his mind.

"I simply cannot stand the presence of that woman any

longer," he declared; "I must get rid of her—but not outright, not crudely. Rather, by torturing her. . . . Will you assist me, my boy?"

"The thing to do," said I, "is cut her belly open, one horizontal slash, one vertical, I'll go into her entrails with a hot iron, I'll cauterize her heart and viscera, she will die, but very gradually."

"Heavenly child," my father sighed, "little angel. . . ."

And this infamy, this execration by which I made my entry into the career of crime, it was enacted. My father and I consummated it in the throes of acutest pleasure; the rascal fucked my ass and frigged my prick while I massacred his wife.

Unhappy dupe that I was! Lending myself to this crime I toiled toward nought but my own undoing; it was only in order to wed another woman that my father had got me to slay my mother, but so well had he hid his scheme that I went a whole year without guessing what he was about. Once I had wind of it I spoke to my sister. I told her the entire tale.

"My child, this man is bent on destroying us," said I.

"That has been my opinion for a long time," Gabrielle replied; "ah, dear brother, I would have spoken to you had I thought you would heed a warning, but you were blind to everything, and to his character blindest of all; we are both ruined if we do not take measures to prevent it. Are you as firm of soul and purpose as I, and shall we act in concert? I have here some powder, a schoolmate gave it to me; by these means she freed her own self from the parental yoke; let us do the same. If you cannot bring yourself to it, leave the thing to me; the urge has been on me for years, and I shall be acting in accordance with Nature's reiterated counsels: and what she demands of us is just. Do I see you shudder, my friend?"

"Not from fear. Give me this powder: before noon tomorrow it shall be in the guts of him who presumes to make fools of us."

"Not so fast! Don't think I am ceding you all the honor of breaking our shackles; we shall perform the deed together. I shall be at dinner tonight; take half the packet, put the stuff in his wine. To make sure of our kill, I'll put the other half in his soup. We'll be orphaned in an hour; in three days' time we shall be sole owners of the possessions fortune has destined us to."

No mouse ever scampered straighter into a trap than did

Borchamps drink his way to the doom our wickedness prepared for him; he fell dead at dessert. This sudden end was attributed to a choleric stroke, and all was forgotten.

Being nearly twenty-one years of age, I obtained patents of majority and the wardship of my sister. Once affairs were arranged she emerged as one of the most eligible matches in all France. I found her a man as rich as she, of whom she very dextrously disencumbered herself when once, by means of a child, she was assured of his legacy. But let us not anticipate events. Once I saw my sister properly established, I put my wealth into her safekeeping and told her of the exceedingly great desire I had to travel abroad. I converted a million into letters of credit with the foremost European bankers; then I embraced my dear Gabrielle.

"I adore you," I told her, "but I must be on my way and this absence will doubtless last a little while. We are both of us made for great things and to go far; let us both gain more knowledge and acquaintances; later, we shall join company definitively, for heaven has intended us one for the other, and heaven's wishes must not be disappointed. Love me, Gabrielle, forget me not, and I shall ever cleave to my love for you."

As for what became of Clairwil, the story, Juliette, is already known to you, at any rate for the greater part; she had, as I told you, contrived to slough off her conjugal ties, she was able to live a free and happy woman in the lap of abundance and lewd joys; her liaisons with the Minister cemented her disorders by guaranteeing their absolute impunity. There was a moment when, in desperate straits, you were led to form unreasonable suspicions and could doubt of her loyalty to you; but do greater justice to her heart, never was she your enemy, never did the Minister inform her of the fate he intended for you. I shall therefore say no more of her here, and shall be content to recount my own adventures; you will in due time hear of their denouement, of how we were brought back together and what the reasons are that enjoin us to live as we do, one for the other, in this impenetrable asylum of crime and infamy.

The northern courts excited my curiosity, it was toward them I bent my steps; The Hague was the first I visited. The Stadtholder had just recently married Princess Sophia, niece of the King of

Prussia. No sooner did I set eyes upon that ravishing creature than I desired her; and I had no sooner declared my heat than I fucked her. Sophia of Prussia was then eighteen years of age, and possessed the loveliest figure and the most delicious face ever to be seen; but her libertinage was excessive and her debauchery so notorious that by now her suitors were interested chiefly in her money. Promptly enlightened upon this object, I put myself gallantly forward; willing enough to pay for my pleasures, but young and vigorous enough to expect women to contribute to the cost of my travels, I was resolved never to accord my favors save to those who were capable of appreciating them.

"Madame," said I to the Princess after I had been tupping her steadily for almost a month, "I flatter myself in the belief that you will acknowledge the expense I have incurred on your account; few men, you will agree, can match me for endurance, none is better membered: all that comes with a price, Madame, in the age we live in."

"Oh, how you put me at ease, Sir," the Princess replied, "I so much prefer to have you at my orders than to be at yours. Here," she continued, handing me a purse bulging with gold, "and remember that I now have the right to demand that you serve my passions, however bizarre they be."

"It is only meet," said I; "your gifts oblige me, I am at your entire disposition."

"Come this evening to my country house," said Sophia, "come alone, and be not afraid, no matter what happens."

Though made somewhat apprehensive by these last words, I nevertheless decided to let nothing daunt me, so that I might come to a thorough acquaintance of this woman, and thereby be able to eke more money out of her.

So it is I set forth alone and arrive at the indicated time and place; an aged woman opens the door and, without a word, ushers me into a mysterious room where I am greeted by a young lady of nineteen, exquisite to behold.

"The Princess will soon appear, Sir," says she, in a voice both sweet and pleasing. "Meanwhile, as she has instructed me to do, I shall ask you to make me the most solemn vow never to disclose anything of the strange rites which are to be celebrated here in our sight."

"Doubt of my discretion offends me, Madame," I rejoined, "I am dismayed, I am pained that the Princess can form it."

"But if you were to have cause for complaint? If perchance your part in the proceedings were to be that of victim only?"

"I should glory in it, Madame, and my silence thereupon would not be the less eternal."

"Such a reply might exempt me from insisting farther were I not obliged to comply strictly with my orders. I must have the required oath, Sir."

I swore it.

"And I add that if by misfortune you were not to keep your pledge, the speediest and most violent death would be your unfailing reward."

"Madame," I protested, "this threat is superfluous; my manner of fulfilling your request would indicate that it was unmerited."

But Emma disappeared from the room even as I was speaking, and for a quarter of an hour I was left to my thoughts.

When she returned she was accompanied by Sophia. Both were in a disorder that convinced me the hussies had just been frigging themselves.

"Eh, by Christ's tears," said Sophia, "let's not coddle the bugger any longer; we have bought him, he is ours to use, let us make the most of our purchase."

Emma invites me to remove my clothes.

"You see very well that we ourselves are naked," she said upon observing me hesitate; "do two women frighten you?"

And aiding me to undress down even to my stockings, once I am divested of every stitch they guide me to a bench upon which they have me kneel on hands and knees. A catch is released; and suddenly all my limbs are shackled fast, and three sharp blades stand pointed, one at my belly, one at either flank, in such sort that I cannot stir a muscle. Outbursts of laughter answer the alarmed glances I cast around me, but what causes me truly to tremble is to see these two women pick up long iron martinets and approach me with visibly villainous intent.

After twenty minutes the flagellation wore to an end.

"Come, Emma," Sophia then called to her fricatrice, "come, be a good girl and kiss me next to the victim; I like to juxtapose love and anguish. Let's chafe cunts opposite the wretch, dear heart, and watch him suffer while we discharge."

The royal whore rings, two fifteen-year-old maids, beauties each, come to receive her orders; they strip off their clothes and upon pillows strown in front of me the tribades spend an hour wallowing in swinish delights; now and again one of them would wriggle toward me, she would provoke me with a display of her charms presented from every angle and as soon as she saw the impression she was able, despite my inconveniencing position, to cause upon me, she would slither away again, laughing at my helplessness. Sophia, as you may easily imagine, played the leading role in this obscene drama, everything centered upon her, all efforts were deployed in her favor, and I assure you I was perfectly amazed to find such science, such subtlety, and such impurity in someone so young. It was very clearly to be seen that the rascal's passion, as with nearly every other woman who has a taste for her sex, was to have her clitoris sucked while sucking that same part in others. But Sophia did not stop there: she was encunted, embuggered with dildoes; and there was not a tit she took but she gave a tat. And when from sucking and fucking the slut was very high and very hot, "Come," she said, "let's settle this knave's affair."

The whips are fetched out again, the two newcomers are armed with a pair of them. Sophia opens the assault by dealing me fifty rapid and powerful strokes. In the midst of her cruelty she preserved an unbelievable calm. After every ten stripes she would come around and gaze gleefully at my face, studying the effects necessarily wrought there by the ferocious pain she inflicted; once she was done she established herself in front of me, flung wide her thighs, bade her three consorts whip me as hard as she had just done, and during the ordeal she had herself frigged.

"One moment," said she when the tally had risen nearly to two hundred lashes, "I am going to slip beneath him in order to suck him while the whipping continues; arrange yourselves in such a way that my clitoris gets a sucking in return from one of you and I have someone else's clitoris to finger."

The actresses take their place, the play begins . . . and, violently excited by the blows I was receiving, deliciously sucked by Sophia, I shall not pretend that before three minutes of this had gone by I had not filled her mouth with fuck; she swallowed it and promptly slithered out from under my belly.

"Emma," she exclaimed, "he is charming, he discharged, I must now repay him with a fucking."

A dildo is fitted around her loins, and here's the whore in my ass, cunt-sucking two of her sweethearts while the third gives her cuntwardly what I am getting bumwise from her.

"You may release him now," she said when at last she could stand no more. "Come kiss me, Borchamps," the Messalina went on; "come express your gratitude, I have given you no end of pleasure. Nor is that all: I rarely treat a man with such forbearance. Poor child, all this that has just happened must be laid up alone to your puerile modesty. Just think of it! You have bedded I don't know how many times with me, and always content to encunt me like any imbecile, not once has it ever seemed to enter your silly little head that I have an ass. Why, such a story would simply not be believed."

"The desire made itself felt in me, Madame; but timidity held it in check."

"A pity . . . a pity; modesty is no longer excusable at your age. But shall we let bygones be bygones? Will you make amends for your callowness, and forget my cunt a little in order to concern yourself a little with my ass? (She herewith turned around and showed it to me.) A pretty ass, is it not? See how smooth it is, how fair, and how it yearns for you—so fuck it, Borchamps. Take his prick, Emma, there's a dear, and clap it into my ass."

My response was to bestow a thousand kisses upon that truly superb behind; and my engine, trained by Emma upon the cunning little hole, shortly convinced Sophia of my burning eagerness to right past wrongs.

"Stay," the Princess bade me, " 'tis I who now wish to be slave to you, I shall place myself in the machine where a moment ago you were captive, now I shall be yours; exercise your rights, sultan, and take a keen revenge." (The irons hold her wrists and ankles fast.) "Spare me not, I beseech you; punish at once the whorishness and the cruelty in me."

"Buggeress!" I cried, divining her tastes, "it's a lashing you want, and they shall be awful strokes you'll get."

"I do dearly hope so," said she. "Touch the skin on my ass, see how it glistens, fairly cries out for the whip."

"Aye, it is so," said I, therewith dealing the first blow. And while I smote her with might and main the lovely Emma, kneeling before me, sucked my engine and the two girls of fifteen busied themselves about my ass. When Sophia's was all in tatters, my furious device, bolting headlong into her anus, consoled her for my barbarity.

"Ah, fuck!" she shrieked, "how delicious to be embuggered directly after a whipping; nothing marries so happily as these two pleasures."

Emma then advances upon her mistress, frigs her, kisses her, teats her, frigs herself, and we all three sink in a sea of delights.

"Borchamps," the Princess said to me as we were readjusting ourselves, "there is, it seems to me, a certain community of spirit between us, and I feel less reluctant to confide myself to you."

Upon a signal the young girls retired and we three having seated ourselves around a table, here as follows is the speech Sophia made to us the while we drank punch and genever.

"To ordinary souls, to small minds it will perhaps appear odd that as my device for sounding your character I choose lubricity. Surprise at that is ridiculous; if by misfortune this be your case, let me then tell you, my dear, that I never judge of what a man is in the course of life, save by his passions in libertinage. He whose fiery spirit displays energetic tastes is indubitably susceptible of resolute action where interest or ambition is the concern: you are hot-blooded and no dullard. Say, Borchamps, what are your politics regarding human life?"

"Princess," I answered, "of what price was it in the eyes of the Duke of Alba when he undertook to subdue these provinces?"

"Delicious man," said my ardent interlocutress, "such is the reply I wanted from you; I count upon your courage," she added, squeezing my hand, "now listen to what remains for me to propose to you.

"Niece of Europe's hero, sprung from the line of a man made to reign over the entire world, I bring to these Low Countries his soul, his vision, and his vigor; I presume that you recognize, Borchamps, that I am fitted for better than to be wife to a republican doge, and this soft, mercantile, and craven people, born to wear irons, ought to be honored by mine. I am nothing loath to reign over the Dutch, but the throne raised upon these humid plains must be wet also with their tears and built by their gold. One hundred armed battalions assure my project; Frederick is sending them from Königsberg. This revolution does not doom my husband's head; he is worthy of me, and Batavia's blood, shed in great floods, will cement the throne to which I pretend. It is therefore not the scepter I offer you; I simply propose to you the place of him who is to defend my keeping of it: you shall be our counselor, our minister, our strong right arm; the proscriptions will be dictated, executed by you: the post requires boldness; have you that quality in suitable measure? Answer as you are of a mind."

"Madame," said I after taking thought for a moment, "before fixing upon this startling act of power and authority, did it occur to you to inquire how this revolution might be viewed by the neighboring powers? The French, the English, the Spanish, the northern States also, who see in you mere courtiers and tradesmen, shall they sit calmly by and watch you become rivals and vanquishers?"

"We are sure of France's attitude; we don't care a fig for the rest. Once sovereign in the United Provinces we shall take the field against the three major kingdoms and perhaps bring them very quickly to their knees. Everyone trembles before a warlike nation; such shall ours become. One great man is enough to subject the world: there is that greatness in my soul, I have it from mighty Frederick. We here are weary of belonging to whoever bothers to invade us and of being the easy prize with which every European conqueror's career begins."

"Once given arms to repulse the cruelties of Spain, will the Dutch surrender them and suffer your tyranny?"

"Courts shall be set up, as they were by Alba. There is no other way to bring a people to heel."

"Your subjects will flee the land."

"I'll have the property they leave behind. From the flight of rebels I stand only to gain; it will simplify the matter of maintaining my grip upon those who stay. My aim is not to become the quaking monarch of many, but to rule despotically, if need be over a few."

"Sophia, I believe you cruel, and it is nought, I fear, but lust[2] that fires you in this ambition."

"Nearly all the vices in the heart of man have the same cause: all proceed from his more or less marked propensity to lubricity. This propensity, ferocious in a strong spirit, leads the solitary mortal, lost and alone in Nature's wilderness, to perpetrate a thousand furtive horrors, and him who governs others, to perpetrate a thousand political crimes."

"Oh, Sophia, I understand what it is you seek; ambition in you is nothing else than the desire to lose your fuck with somewhat greater warmth."

"Little does it matter what sentiment engenders ambition once it exists and is confirmed by a crown. But, my friend, if you reason thereupon, you waver; waver, and you tremble; and for him who trembles I have no use at all."

Singularly aroused by Sophia's propositions, taking a view analogous to hers in seeing herein sure means for exercising my native ferocity, I promised everything. Sophia embraced me, had me repeat the most solemn oaths to absolute secrecy, and we took leave of each other.

I went thoughtfully homeward; by the time I reached my lodgings I was beginning to sense the full danger of the engagements I had just contracted, and noticing that the risks involved in breaking them hardly outweighed those in keeping them, I spent the night in dreadful perplexity. There's nothing for it, I said to myself, I am done for either way, the only solution lies in flight. Oh, Sophia, had you but proposed some private crimes, I'd gladly have committed them all, for with you as my accomplice I could have laughed at the law. But to expose myself to every imaginable risk only to be the agent of your despotism! No, woman, count not upon me. Ready I am and very willing to commit crimes for my passions' sake, not one will I do to benefit the passions of others. When my

---

[2] With what art the workings of the tyrant soul are here developed; and how many revolutions explained by this single word!

refusal comes to your knowledge, tax Borchamps not so much with faintheartedness as with greatness of soul. . . .

I stole out of the city that very night and made in all haste for the port nearest England. En route I was momentarily assailed by regrets: what with my profound liking for crime, it was hard for me to think I had declined Sophia's offer of the political means for committing a lot of it. But I reminded myself that her projects had been rather too uncertain; and, in addition, that I would be happier operating for my own advantage than for that of some crowned individual.

Upon reaching London I took apartments in Piccadilly, where I had the misfortune, the very next day, of being robbed of every penny I had about me; this was a serious loss, since the previous week, in The Hague, I had cashed all my letters of credit. There was nothing else for me to do than set straight out with the letters of recommendation I had to various London notables, and to beg some aid at least for the short time it would take me to obtain funds from my sister.

From what I had heard tell of Lord Burlington I decided that this was the man to see first. When he had finished reading my letters, I recounted my woes; the good Englishman was prepared to do me every sort of service. Although Burlington was not very rich, one thousand guineas were his immediate offer, and he simply would not hear of my lodging anywhere except under his own roof. I accepted his invitation all the more readily for having already taken stock of this honest family and detected there a quantity of possibilities for repaying, in the form of crimes, the debt of gratitude I owed my benefactor.

Before entering into the details of the little infamies with which I was about to occupy myself, it is essential that I give you an idea of the persons in whose midst I had landed.

Burlington, the kindliest and most ingenuous of men, must have been nearing fifty-five; blithe, guileless, void of penetration, at once generous and a fool, such was my Lord's portrait. A son-in-law and two daughters composed the rest of the household. Tilson, but twenty-three, had just wedded the elder of the girls, who was about the same age as he. They were a delicious couple the like of which Nature affords us only rare examples; charms, graces, naïveté,

candor, piety, gentility, good breeding, nothing was lacking, and
this personification of all the virtues assembled consoled Burlington
for the wild conduct of Miss Cleontine, the younger of his daughters, at most eighteen years of age, and the loveliest creature you
have ever clapped eyes on. But mischievousness, nay, downright
wickedness, black whorishness carried to extreme lengths, those
were Cleontine's incorrigible vices; wherein she had the audacity
to assert she was a thousand times happier than ever was Clotilda
in her dull and tedious virtues.

Upon perceiving the girl's delicious character I became
straightway enamored of her, to the extent a man so corrupt as I
could be enamored of anyone; but her father having confided to
me all the heartaches this young person caused him, I found myself
obliged to proceed with utmost circumspection.

Over and beyond the tumultuous impressions Cleontine was
producing in my soul, Tilson's pretty face and the graces of his
charming wife remained ever clear in my eye, and if Cleontine inspired the more libertine desires in me, her brother-in-law and
sister quickened the more sensual. I imagined Tilson's ass as a
masterpiece, and the desire to fuck him burned just as keenly in
me as the idea of doing the same to his voluptuous partner. Set
upon by all these various passions, it seemed to me that the proper
way to satisfy them was to begin with Cleontine. Everything which
can conspire to a woman's downfall being already contained in the
soul of her whom I was attacking as well as in my means for seduction, the dear child was quickly mine.

Nothing so fresh, nothing so plump, nothing so pretty as all
the parts of that charming thing's body, nothing so eloquent as the
voice of her passions, nothing so lewd as her mind. There was a
moment when, truly, I wondered whether I was not better behaved
than she; whereupon, as you may readily imagine, there was no restriction to the pleasures we tasted; and Cleontine avowed to me
that the more a delight seemed in conflict with the laws of Nature,
the more it stimulated her lubricity.

"Alas!" she said one day, "I have come to the point where I
find none strong enough to satisfy me."

Her pretty ass was attacked on the spot, and the pleasures she
gave me in that style were so piquant, so poignant, so thoroughly

shared by her, that we came to the mutual agreement not to bother with any other sort.

So taken up was I over that beautiful girl's charms that a year elapsed and I had still not dared communicate my projects to her, or at least had not thought to, so busily was I occupied with our affair. Burlington and I were quits, and for the better carrying out of my plans I had left his house and taken quarters nearby. He, his family, his children would pay me daily visits, and our intimacy became so great that my marriage to Cleontine was soon being rumored about town. Oh, but I was far from such a piece of folly! I was willing enough to amuse myself with that interesting creature, but marry her! ah no, never; only Lady Tilson excited that desire in me.

A wife, said I to myself, a wife can answer no purpose save that of serving us as a victim, and the more her beauty is of the romantic type, the better she is equipped for this role. And here is Clotilda. To see her in my clutches, ah, how it stiffens my prick; how marvelous she must be in tears! How delightful it must be to cause them to flow from such heavenly eyes. Oh, Clotilda, what an unhappy woman you shall be if ever you become mine.

These designs once formulated, it was henceforth only to help achieve them that I continued to cultivate Cleontine. To that end I could think of nothing better than to kindle in her a fancy for her brother-in-law and then to arouse his young wife's jealousy. Cleontine admitted that she had now and then felt an urge for Tilson, but that the thought of his stupidity and virtuousness had always dashed cold water on her desires.

"But what does intelligence matter!" I replied. "Once beauty decorates an individual, there's enough to warrant having him. Even as you see me now, Cleontine, I am dreaming of the world's most wonderful ass, Tilson is its proprietor, and I am sweating from eagerness to fuck it."

This idea diverted my mistress, and she was won over—put a few nasty thoughts in a woman's head and there is nothing you can not get out of her. A pang of jealousy, however, made her pause; she wondered if, taken by the husband, I might not perhaps become too fond of his wife; she questioned me.

"Come, come," said I, feeling that prudence was needed here, "you are being extravagant. My eye alights on a pretty boy, the sentiment is purely material; but where it comes to women, my love for you, Cleontine, is not something from which I can swerve."

My insipid compliments, the irregularity of my caprices, everything seduced Cleontine, she served me; that was all I wanted of her. Before a month had passed my beloved Tilson was in my mistress' arms; I watched him as he lay there, caressed him as he lay there, fucked him as he lay there; such scenes of libertinage occupied another month and then, the illusion gone and I having had my fill of them both, I began to dwell on schemes for undoing them, for including my benefactor in the holocaust, and for spiriting Clotilda away, taking her to the farthermost ends of the world to glut myself on the divine pleasures I awaited from her.

As the young woman positively worshiped her husband it was easy for me to strike sparks of jealousy into her soul: Lady Tilson listened to me, believed me, and when all I had left to do was convince her, the means stood ready to hand.

"Cleontine," I said one day to my voluptuous whore, "shall I confess it to you, my love? I am fairly dying to marry you. The similarity between our two characters, our two temperaments, leads me to feel that we would be very happy together. But you are penniless, I am rich . . . and unless I am wholly mistaken, delicacy would forbid you from entering into a marriage unprovided with the blessings of fortune. There is a way, Cleontine, whereby you could swing this capricious fortune into your favor and hasten its gifts. Between you and wealth I see no more than three lives standing in the way."

And noticing Cleontine wax drunk on the poison I was distilling into her soul, I bravely doubled the dose.

"Nothing simpler," I went on, "than to get rid of Tilson. His wife is willful, headstrong, extremely jealous; she will not learn of her husband's guilty dealings with you without furiously desiring to be revenged upon him; I will counsel her, I will furnish her what she needs; I see Tilson in his forefathers' tomb before a week is out."

"My sister is virtuous."

"She is vindictive; her upright soul would not all by itself hatch the plot I shall suggest to her, but when warmly proposed by me she will seize what I offer her, be sure of it."

"And the others?" Cleontine abruptly demanded.

"Ah, little minx," said I, folding her in my arms, "every passing minute brings added proof that Nature created us for each other. And so here is how we shall be rid of those others, my angel: once Lady Tilson has acted upon my advice and removed her husband from the picture, I shall unveil the whole intrigue to her father who, likewise pressed by my solicitations, shall, I am confident of it, call in the police. She will be brought to trial. Her lawyer, selected and perfectly feed by me, will embrace Clotilda's cause and so plead it as to shift the guilt onto the father who will be shown to have murdered his son-in-law and had his daughter arraigned on false charges. The witnesses, the testimony, the proofs: with guineas all that is to be found in London, just as with *louis* it is in Paris. A fortnight and Burlington is lying in one of His Majesty's jails."

"Your benefactor?"

"Ah, Cleontine, what must I call the man whose existence casts a cloud upon our future together? This arch-enemy is no sooner flung into prison, condemned (he will be, Cleontine, inside a month from today), than he mounts the scaffold; he is no sooner dead, I say, than your sister is freed and we leave. We leave England, I wed you, and simply consider how easy it will be to eliminate the last obstacle preventing you from taking exclusive possession of Burlington's estate."

"Oh, my friend, you are a villain!"

"I am but a man and one who adores you, Cleontine, who cares for nought but to see you rich and his married wife."

"But my father . . . and all he has done for you—"

"Beside the sentiments I owe you all others pale, they vanish: I must possess you, Cleontine, there is nothing I do not sacrifice in order to succeed."

The ardent creature effuses her gratitude, showers kisses upon me; she swears to aid me, and streams of fuck, shot from one side and from the other, seal vows I have not the faintest intention of keeping.

However, since the first act of the play was to bring me to the catastrophe I was secretly planning, I hastened to stage that first act. Directed by me, Clotilda surprises her husband in her sister's arms. But it is not to revenge herself solely upon the faithless one that I recommend, it is to immolate them both.

"Yes, that is how I feel in the matter, and it concerns me," I tell her. "I am too furious at what has been done to you not to sacrifice those who have inflicted this outrage. From now on your life itself shall be in danger from such monsters; you must either consent to their destruction or reconcile yourself to being destroyed by them."

An expressive silence is Clotilda's response to this; and the same beverage rids her, at a stroke, of a sister and a husband. . . . I had fucked them both that morning.

I turn now to the second act in the Burlington tragedy.

"Oh, Clotilda," I say, rushing to her in great terror, "these two sudden deaths have alarmed your father, I fear suspicion is wakening in his breast. Why would he not attribute the loss of his son-and-law and daughter to your vengeance, aware as he is of the motives that would lead you to seek it? Well, if he comes to a very obvious conclusion, you, my dear, are in a damnable case; you must have the best defense ready if this misfortune arises."

An hour later I am in conference with the father.

"You are baffled, Sir? You search far afield for the assassin of Tilson and Cleontine, you need not look beyond Clotilda," I pointed out to that honest man; "for whose interests are so closely associated with this horror? And if, as there is scarce any room for doubt, the wretch has been to this point capable of scorning her duties and the yet more powerful voice of Nature, presume the dire danger that must accrue to you in letting this tiger remain at your side."

To these calumnious assertions I add a string of spurious proofs; Milord is convinced; his daughter is taken into custody. My barrister hirelings fly to find her; they have no trouble persuading Clotilda that some recrimination is imperative, everything needed to support the counterattack is furnished her. This interesting creature entreats me not to abandon her; her hand, if I deign accept it, will be the reward for my loyalty. I swear to hold steadfast by her, come what may. Burlington, sharply suspected of the crime he ascribes to his daughter, is dragged promptly before his judges; he is, at my instigation and at my expense, himself accused of having had treacherously murdered his daughter and son-in-law, and of having had Clotilda imprisoned as guilty of an atrocity he alone has committed. The trial created enough stir in London to last only a month; and in that brief period I had the satisfaction of freeing from behind bars her for whose sake I had perpetrated my terrible acts, and of seeing their third victim expire.

"Clotilda," I cried, once gratitude had brought that lovely woman to my feet, "make haste, claim your inheritance; having no child by Tilson you unfortunately cannot pretend to anything there, but realize what belongs to you and let us be off. Our conduct will not bear too close scrutiny, let us not wait for eyes to open but get us speedily away from here."

"Oh, Borchamps, it is a terrible thing for me, to owe my life only to my father's death!"

"Ha, an end to idiot remorse, stifle it directly," was my quick reply to my charming mistress; "remind yourself that your father aspired only to your doom, and that any measure enforced by self-preservation is warranted."

"But you shall at least be there, Borchamps, to dry away my tears?"

"Can you doubt it, dear angel?"

"Ah, then call a priest, let the ceremony be for tomorrow; let wedlock's sweet pleasures crown us the same day, and the next morning let sunrise see us set forth from a land where the consequences of this horrible affair might at any moment turn to our disadvantage."

All is done as I desire it, and Clotilda is my wedded wife. Clotilda's mourning for her first husband had been too brief for us to dare publish our marriage, but it nonetheless received the sanction of the law, human and divine.

I wish here to make it very plain that Clotilda cannot be considered even partly responsible for any of the pieces of mischief I have just related to you. The passive instrument of my maneuvers, she was in no wise their cause; no, I shall not hear of that gentle and charming person being blamed for anything that had befallen:

the murder of her sister and husband, to which she had consented only through silence, was all alone my doing, she was still less guilty of her father's death, and had it not been for my interventions, my briberies, perjurers and the rest, she would surely have gone to the gallows instead of Burlington.

All this I am at pains to say lest in the eyes of my auditors there be lost to Clotilda's character one jot of the candor, modesty, or rectitude I accorded her when first I gave her description. And so also it was that however I might reason with her, she remained forever the prey of remorse; it is true that the manner whereby I acquiesced in the love she confessed for me did for a while attenuate her sufferings from that quarter. But let me repeat it once and for all, so long as the sequence of events obliges me to speak of her, never visualize Clotilda as anything but conscience-stricken, guilt-ridden. As such appearing to me a thousand times more piquant, she gave me the most extraordinary inspirations. Who would believe it? Even before enjoying her charms I thought to profane them. Clotilda was no sooner my wife than I hardened over the twofold idea of fucking her in a brothel that first night and of prostituting her charms to the first comer.

Early on in my stay at London I had made the acquaintance of a celebrated procuress at whose house I used to sport with the prettiest rascals in town, to compensate myself for the monotonies entailed by a regular intrigue. I go off to find Miss Bawil, I impart to her my resolutions, she answers for their success; in the bargain I put the clause that the libertines to whom Clotilda is to be surrendered confine themselves to pollutions, nastiness, and brutalities. Everything arranged between us, I return to Clotilda and propose that after the wedding ceremony we consummate our marriage elsewhere than in this mansion fraught with gloomy memories; a friend, I tell her, has invited us to stay the night. Trusting Clotilda accompanies me to Miss Bawil's, where a merry feast is spread before us. Someone less a scoundrel than I would have enjoyed this moment during which happiness displaced Clotilda's chagrins and she was oblivious to all save the charm of belonging to me. The poor fool was kissing me tenderly in her joy when three rascals posted by break suddenly in upon us, daggers in their hands.

"Run for your life!" they say to me. "Begone and leave this

woman to us, we've some frolicking to do before you get to her."

I flee from the room and pass into an adjoining one whence, through a spyhole, I am able to observe everything. Clotilda, half in a swoon, is promptly stripped by these ruffians who expose her naked to my gaze. The effect was enchanting as libertinage here performed the usual office of love. 'Twas thus profaned I had my first glimpse of the graces with which Nature had endowed the exquisite creature, 'twas thus the world's most beauteous ass was revealed to my lascivious stare. A superb courtesan was frigging me in the meantime, and at a previously arranged signal the outrages redoubled. Clotilda, sprawled over the knees of one of the three was flagellated by the other two, after that condemned to the most lubricious and the most humiliating penances. Obliged to tongue the asshole of one, she had also, at the same time, to frig the other two. Her face—that moving emblem of her sensitive soul—her breast, her lily-white and rosy breast, were washed by the impure jets of that unholy trio's ardor, who, so instructed by me and to humiliate the heavenly creature's virtue that much more thoroughly, ended by pissing and shitting upon her body while I proceeded to embugger another whore sent to complete my excitement during the scene. Quitting this second girl's ass without having discharged there, I pick up a rapier and rush into the dining room; I look as though I have returned at the head of reinforcements, I rescue Clotilda, my bought ruffians take to their heels and, casting myself theatrically at my beloved's feet, "Oh, dearest soul," I cry, "have I not arrived too late? May not these monsters have already—"

"No, my friend," replies Clotilda as she is being wiped and made tidy, "no, your wife is still worthy of you—humiliated, mistreated for a certainty, but not dishonored. Oh, Borchamps, why ever did you bring me to this house?"

"Ah, be calm, my angel, all danger is past. Miss Bawil has enemies, this untimely incursion was their work; but my call for help was heard, the house freed, and we can spend the rest of the night here in safety."

Clotilda was not easily reassured; at length, however, she recovered from her experience and we betook ourselves to bed. Greatly heated by the scene I had lately provoked, astonishingly electrified to hold beauty, virtue sullied in my arms, I wrought prodigies of vigor. . . . While this charming creature wanted something of her sister's disorderly imagination, she made up for that shortcoming by a more just, more lucid spirit and by an infinitely fetching beauty of physical detail. It would be impossible to be fairer of skin, better made of body, impossible to have sweeter, more winsome, more tantalizing parts. Clotilda absolutely untutored in lubricity and new to its pleasures, was ignorant even of the possibility of traveling Cythera's narrower bypath.

"My angel, a husband must find some first fruits to pluck on the wedding night; having none but these," said I, touching her asshole, "you will surely not refuse them to me."

So saying I catch a good grip on her flanks and from sodomizing her five times in succession bring my seed to a boil; it was however in her cunt I deposited it. And 'twas there and then that Clotilda, luckier or more ardent with me than with Tilson, conceived a very unlucky daughter, who due to my inconstancy and neglect, I never saw at her birth.

Dawn found me so tired of my goddess that had I consulted my sentiments alone, Clotilda would indeed never have got out of London; but, persuaded that this creature could perhaps be useful during my travels, we readied ourselves for departure. Helped by me, Clotilda assembled her fortune, it came to twelve thousand guineas all told and, taking them with us, I and my wife left London two years to the day after I had first set foot there.

Since I was ever bent on visiting the courts of the North we now headed for Sweden. We had already been traveling some nine or ten weeks when one day, looking back over our adventures together, Clotilda hazarded a few reproachful remarks upon the violence of the means I had employed to win her. My prompt reply was framed in such language as to give my dear wife very clearly to understand that I was perfectly ready to have her commit crimes but by no means prepared to see her repent them. Clotilda's tears flowed forth afresh; I then revealed to her the whole truth of what had happened.

"And every single part of it," I told her in conclusion, "was my handiwork; the desire to be rid of your sister and your husband, both overmuch fucked by me; that of fucking you too and of appropriating your money by killing your father: such, my sweet, were the real motives behind all my enterprises. Whence you will observe that in all this I have toiled for none but my own sake, and not one instant for yours. To this I may usefully add, dear creature, that my intention being to plunge into a very nefarious career, I did not unite you to my destiny in order to have you thwart that aim, but to promote it."

"In that case, what is the distinction you draw, Sir, between a slave and a wife?"

"And you, tell me now, what distinction do you draw between a slave and a wife?"

"Ah, Borchamps, why did you not take this line the very first day I met you? How bitter have now become the tears you force me to shed over my unhappy family!"

"No more weeping, Madame," was my harsh warning to her, "and no more illusions concerning your fate; I expect utter submission from you. If it so pleased me to have the carriage stopped this instant and to have you suck the prick of the man who's driving it, you'd suck that prick, my dear, you'd suck it. For if you did not, I'd blow your brains out on the spot."

"My God, Borchamps! Is this love?"

"Why, I do not love you, Madame, what an idea. I have never loved you; I wanted your money and your ass, I have them both, and it may not be long before I have had altogether enough of the latter."

"And the fate then in store for me will probably be the one Cleontine met?"

"With you I shall probably resort to less mystery and surely a great deal more artistry."

At this point Clotilda thought to use the weapons of her sex: she leaned toward me in an effort to kiss and sprinkle me with her tears; I thrust her rudely away.

"Cruel man," she said, half-choked by her sobs, "if you wish to offend the mother at least respect the poor creature who owes its life to your love: I am pregnant . . . I beg you to stop at the first town we come to, for I do not feel at all well."

We did indeed stop and Clotilda, who took directly to bed, fell gravely ill. Irritated at having to interrupt my journey and at being delayed by a creature for whom I was beginning to have the

keenest distaste, to which there had to be added the loathing wherewith I had always beheld pregnant women, I was on the point of
taking a charitable leave of them both, she and her child, when a
woman who was staying in a chamber near ours, stopped me in the
hallway and bade me come for a moment into her room. Great
heavens! what was my surprise upon recognizing Princess Sophia's
pretty confidante, the same Emma of whom I spoke a short while
ago.

"What an unexpected encounter, Madame," said I, "and what
a fortunate one! But are you here by yourself?"

"I am indeed," that charming personage replied, "I too have
had to flee from an insatiable, ambitious mistress whom it must
become damnation to serve. Well-advised you were, Borchamps,
to have been of such firm resolve! You did not then know and may
still be unaware of the chores her perfidious politics were reserving
for you. She told you the Stadtholder was party to her scheme; she
lied; her intention was to have you put that prince out of the way,
and had the attempt failed you would have been a dead man. In
despair after your escape, nevertheless she continued to harbor her
wicked designs for another two years, and finally insisted that I
undertake the murder she was meditating. Had it been a question
merely of an ordinary crime, I would doubtless have executed it,
for crime amuses me, I enjoy the shock it imparts to the mechanism,
its effervescence delights me, and rid as I am of all prejudice, I
give myself over to it without qualms before or regrets afterward;
but a deed so important as that one—well, discretion is the better
part of valor and I followed your example in order that having
declined to be her accomplice, I not become her victim."

"Charming woman," said I, putting my hand in Emma's
bosom, "let us banish all ceremony, we are nearly enough acquainted for it to be of no purpose. Let me tell you once again, dear
angel, how very pleased I am to have found you again. Restrained
by the exigent Sophia, we were unable to act in accordance with
what we felt for each other; here, however, nothing hinders us—"

"You say so, my friend; but this woman accompanying you,
might one know who she is?"

"She is my wife."

And I hasten to recount to my new friend the whole of the

London story, and how I whittled the Burlington family down to the sole survivor now lying sick in another room of this inn. Emma, a great rascal at heart, saw all the humor in the adventure and when she was done laughing asked if I would not introduce her to my tender spouse.

"Surely, you shall not go on dragging her about forever," she said to me, "leave her here, I'm a more suitable companion for you than this prude. And I ask no sacraments from you, not I. I've always detested Church ceremonies. Although noble-born, but a lost woman through my debauchery and thanks to my attachment to Sophia, from you I want only the title of mistress and dearest friend. How are your finances?"

"In the very best order. I am extremely rich."

"A pity. I have one hundred thousand crowns and was counting upon offering them to you, thinking thereby to get you somewhat into my power, which would be agreeable to me."

"I dare say, Emma, and I am touched by your delicacy, but it is not in this manner you would ever get me into bondage; mine is too lofty a soul to consent to dependence upon a woman: I must either dominate her or not use her at all."

"Why, very well then, I shall be your whore, I like that role; how much will you pay me a month?"

"What did you get from Sophia?"

"The value of one hundred French *louis*."

"I will give you the same; but you will be faithful? Submissive?"

"As a slave."

"Slavery implies that you be dispossessed of the tokens of freedom and the means to fail your master. Hand your funds over to me."

"Here they are," and Emma fetched me her casket.

"But, my angel," said I, raising the lid, "you must have stolen this sum: with one hundred *louis* a month you could not possibly have composed this fortune, Emma, not at your age."

"Do you suppose I left that Messalina without first giving her treasury a feel?"

"And if I were to do unto thee that which thou hast done?"

"Borchamps, I love you, what I have is yours; I am not entrusting my money to you, I am giving it; but this gift and my favors are not to be had save upon one condition."

"And that condition?"

"It is that we be this very instant rid of the drab piece of baggage you are towing across Europe."

"You are paying me for her death?"

"That is what I demand in exchange for my hundred thousand crowns."

"Exquisite little minx! The idea is amusing; but the project must be embellished by a few rather severe episodes."

"Ill though she is?"

"But the object is to do her in, is it not?"

"To be sure."

"Well, come along, I shall present you as an irate wife who demands that I return to her; I shall excuse myself for a fit of blind passion which, in my embarrassed situation, forced me to behave in my mysterious manner; you will fulminate; I shall be obliged to tell her that I am abandoning her, and the poor woman will die of chagrin, she and the infant inside her."

"She is pregnant?"

"Indeed she is."

"Why, we shall have a jolly time!" And in Emma's sparkling eyes I saw how this villainy was arousing her; the whore is overcome by emotion, she kisses me, a paroxysm shakes loose her fuck. . . . We enter.

So well did we play our parts that the wretched Clotilda swallowed everything down to the dregs. Emma, witty, malicious, and a wicked tease, maintained that when I'd deserted her I'd also robbed her, and that not a button or a handkerchief in the room belonged by rights to this bedridden adventuress. I agreed that all this was indubitably so, and my sorrowful wife, only too well aware of the black situation menacing her, turned her beautiful face away to hide her weeping.

"Oh no, sir traitor, I shall not let you out of my sight," Emma declared with great energy, "I am not going to budge from here, for I intend to get my due."

Supper is brought into the room. Emma and I eat heartily and call for the best wines in the house while the helpless Clotilda watches herself being stripped, plundered to the last penny, and stares at the prospect of soon having nothing left to feed upon but her despair and her tears. Our copious repast finished, it was upon the foot of the forlorn soul's bed that we celebrated the pleasure of our reunion.

A pretty thing she was, that Emma; twenty-one years old, a face that personified voluptuousness itself, the figure of a nymph, great dark eyes, the freshest mouth, the whitest teeth, the most cunning little tongue, the fairest and smoothest skin, marvelously molded in breast and buttock, a libertine too, and in the highest degree, with all the salt and all the spitefulness of cruel lubricity. We fucked deliciously in every style and manner while battening upon the spectacle, equally rare and stimulating, of my wife wrung by moans, grief, and anxiety.

As I was embuggering her, Emma would have her unfortunate rival show us her ass. Clotilda was almost too sick, too exhausted to move; howbeit, obey she must. I slapped that splendid behind whereof I had made such feast of late and which I was now so unkindly abandoning; I smote it so hard that the poor woman, weak from distress, from pain, from illness, lay motionless upon the bed.

"We could strangle her," said I, bum-fucking Emma with great zest.

"We could, but it would be a serious mistake," replied the clever and imaginative girl; "far better simply to abandon her more or less alive, to damage her reputation with the innkeeper, and to make sure that, left without resources, she will either perish from hunger or try to survive from libertinage."

This last idea having caused me a prodigious discharge, we made ready to depart. We removed every last object from the room; we despoiled Clotilda even of her nightgown; we plucked even the rings off her fingers, unscrewed the rings from her ears, took even her shoes, her slippers, in a word, she was left as naked as the day she was born; the poor dear wept and said the most melting things to me.

"Alas, short of murdering me, you could not carry barbarity any farther. May heaven forgive you as do I; and whatever be the career you follow, give a thought sometimes to the woman who never did you any wrong unless it was to love you too much."

"Come, come, cheer up," said Emma, "all you have to do to earn some money is frig some pricks. Why, instead of blaming us you ought to thank us: along with the rest we could deprive you of life. Count your blessings."

The horses were harnessed, the carriage waiting at the door. As we were about to mount Emma had a word with the people of the inn.

"The creature we are leaving behind up there," she told them, "is an arrant whore who stole my husband; as chance would have it, I came upon him in this place: I recover what is mine by law and right and, together with him, am taking away the belongings that slut robbed from me. Here is her lodging and board, paid up until today, I'll answer for no more: do with her whatever you see fit, she has all she needs to settle any debts she may incur from you and to return home to her own country. And here is the key to her room; adieu."

The coachman cracked his whip and we whirled off without waiting to learn what happened next in an adventure which now ceased to hold anything of interest for us.

"I am most content," said Emma. "Your management of this affair reveals a character very kindred to mine; I already feel attached to you. How do you suppose it will fare with Madame?"

"She will beg alms or render lewd services; what matter is it to us?"

And to turn the conversation upon a worthier theme, I besought Emma to tell me a little more about herself.

"I was born in Brussels," the splendid creature began; "never mind from what lineage I come, know simply that my parents are persons of foremost rank in that city. When yet very young I was sacrificed to an unendurable husband; the man I loved picked a quarrel with him and on their way to the dueling-ground, slew him from behind. 'I am lost,' my lover said to me, 'I lent too much heed to vengeance, now I must flee. If you love me, Emma, come away with me; I am not poor, we shall have enough to live in peace and ease for the rest of our days.'

"Oh, Borchamps, could I refuse a man whom my advice had undone?"

"This murder was of your devising?"

"Are you in a doubt, my dear, and should I disguise anything from you? I followed my lover into exile; he failed me; I had the same trick played upon him he had played upon my husband. Sophia learned of my story; she was much taken by my crime . . . was soon adoring my person. The development of my character pleased her, we rubbed cunts; I was initiated into all her secrets; 'tis to her I am indebted for all the principles in which I am unshakable today: although in the end I robbed her, it is no less true that I had a constant affection for the Princess. The outstanding libertinage of her mind, the warmth of her imagination, oh, the basis of my attachment to her was sound; and had it not been for the dread her final proposals caused me, I might perhaps have remained with her for the rest of my life."

"It may be, Emma, that I know you better than you know your own self: you would quickly have become tired of being no more than the pawn of the crime of others, you would have begun to want to commit it on your own behalf, and, sooner or later, you would have left that woman. Is she jealous?"

"Frightfully."

"She did at least permit you women?"

"Never any except those she involved in her pleasures."

"I repeat it, Emma, you would not have lived long with Sophia."

"Oh, my friend, I give thanks to the fate which delivered me out of her hands and into yours; let us be ever mindful of the honor that prevails amongst thieves, exert our craft upon everybody else, but never turn it against each other."

Pretty though Emma was, and despite the analogy between her character and mine, I was not yet sure enough of myself to be able to guarantee an exact balance in the association she desired, and I left her to interpret my silence in whatever way she chose. For indeed, was there a single crime in the world I could engage myself not to commit?

However, our liaison grew stronger, we reached certain understandings; their first basis was the inviolable and mutual promise never to lose an occasion to do evil, to contrive such occasions whenever it was in our power; it was likewise agreed that the fruit of our common thievings and rapine would always be evenly shared.

We had gone hardly twenty leagues when we were presented with an opportunity to put our maxims into action and our oaths to the test. We were traversing Götaland and were in the neighborhood of the town of Jönköping when a French carriage driving ahead of us struck a wheel into the rut and broke the axle. The master, whose valet was in charge of the advance horses, had nought to do but get down and wait with his baggage by the roadside till help should come. This help we offered when we drew abreast of him, and learned that the man was a French merchant going to Stockholm on business for his company, who were well-known traders. Villeneuil's age was twenty-three and never had anyone so pretty a face; together with his charming outside he had all the candor and sincerity of his nation.

"A thousand thanks for your kindness in offering me a seat in your carriage to the nearest post," said he. "I am all the more obliged to you forasmuch as in this chest I am carrying objects of major importance: diamonds, gold, bills of exchange I have been commissioned by three Paris firms to deliver to their Swedish correspondents. You can imagine the state I would be in were I to have the misfortune of losing such things."

"Why, Sir, if that be the case we are in great good luck to be able to ensure the safety of such precious effects," said Emma. "Will you see fit to entrust them to us and bestow upon us the honor of saving you from your predicament and your fortune from eventual marauders?"

Villeneuil climbs in; we recommend that his postilion guard the carriage and team until the young man is able to send his valet back with fresh horses and someone to repair the damage.

No sooner had we started off with our charming prey than Emma covertly sought my hand. . . .

"Agreed," I murmured in an undertone, "but this calls for a few episodes."

"Assuredly," said she.

And on we drove.

852 ⚜ THE MARQUIS DE SADE

Having come to the little town of Vimmerby we found Villeneuil's lackey at the posting station and sent him back in all haste
after his master's equipage.

"You were doubtless intending to stay the night here?" I said
to the young man. "We ourselves cannot, since we must endeavor
to reach Stockholm as soon as possible; so we shall let you down,
Sir, and take our leave of you now."

To this the ardent Villeneuil, who had, not without emotion,
been gazing at the charms of my friend, replied with a look seeming to express regret that we should be parting so soon; spying the
shadow come across his countenance, Emma quickly spoke up, saying that indeed, she did not see why it was necessary to say such
an early goodbye, and that since we had been enjoying our journey
together, why might we not all continue on to the capital?

"Yes, and why not?" said I. "This then is what I would
suggest: Monsieur will leave a message here at the posting station,
instructing his valet to join him at the Hotel de Danemark, where
we shall be stopping in Stockholm. Thereby everything is arranged
and we remain together."

"An infinitely welcome suggestion," says the young man, casting a sidelong glance at Emma, who by means of one just as impassioned announces that she is in no wise sorry to see him fall in
with any proposal which might lead to a lessening of the distance
between them.

Villeneuil scribbles a letter, it is handed to the innkeeper, our
horses are watered, then we fly on toward Stockholm. We had
another thirty leagues still to cover; we arrived the following evening and 'twas only then my companion informed me of the ruse she
had devised to ensure the execution of the deed we were meditating.
The rascal, excusing herself under the pretext of having to attend
to a need, had dismounted from the carriage at Vimmerby and
quickly written out a message of her own; she had substituted it
for Villeneuil's, and in hers prescribed to the lackey that he seek
his master not at the Hotel de Danemark, but at The English
Arms.

Once in Stockholm her first care, as you may readily imagine,
was to appease the young merchant's inquietudes, who wondered
why his carriage was being delayed; she did everything she felt

most likely to make him easy and to dazzle him at the same time. Villeneuil had tumbled head over heels in love with her; the thing became plain beyond all doubt, and Emma accordingly staged a flawless performance; Villeneuil seemed jealous of me.

"Needless to say, you are unwilling to have this turn into an adventure out of a popular novel," Emma observed; "you desire me, Villeneuil, but love has nothing to do with your feelings. And I, moreover, cannot become yours; nothing on earth would ever induce me to leave Borchamps; he is my husband. Therefore be content with what I can offer you, and do not aspire after what I am unable to accord; and rest assured that provided we keep inside those boundaries, my husband, a born libertine, is the man to join in our happiness: surrendering to it, we can perfectly well provide him the joy of one such lewd scene as he delights in. Borchamps has a fondness for men. You are extremely handsome, Sir; consent to avail him of your charms, only do that and I believe I can guarantee he will let you enjoy mine in peace."

"Do you think so?"

"I am certain of it. This complaisance—it does not go too much against the grain?"

"Not at all. It's a practice from college days, I find nothing strange in seeing it preserved and am myself as much given to it as anyone else."

"And so it but remains to make the arrangements?"

"You have my consent to everything. . . ."

Whereupon the clever Emma flings open the closet in which I have been hiding. "Come along, Borchamps," she cries, "Villeneuil offers you his ass, have supper brought up, then bar the door and let's to our frolicking."

"Charming young man," say I, stepping forth from concealment and thrusting my tongue into the traveler's mouth, albeit penetrated by the desire to kill him once I have fucked him, "your accommodation moves me. And as a matter of fact, is this not a very simple sort of transaction? I cede you my wife, you lend me your behind, why refrain from happiness when it may be so easily had?"

Even as I spoke my friend was unbuttoning Villeneuil's breeches; and if her delicate hands brought the world's prettiest prick into view, mine just as soon discovered the most sublime ass it is possible to see. Kneeling before that heavenly furniture, I was carried utterly away, and I would perhaps still be licking it, sucking it, had my dear Emma not called my attention away from it to have me admire the exquisite member wherewith our prey was provided in front. No sooner have I taken that superb engine in charge than I present him an ass which is burning from the desire to possess it.

"Oh, Villeneuil!" I cried, "deign to begin with me; those charms you covet," I went on, nodding toward Emma's, "shall be yours directly you have rendered yourself master of my ass; such is the price of their having, they'll not be yours save you pay it."

I am fucked; that was all Villeneuil's reply. I lift my mistress' skirts for him, he fondles her, he kisses her while fucking me; unable to cope with his passions, the animal quits me to snap his dart into Emma's panting cunt. Seeing his bum well inside my reach, I leap upon it and sodomize him to avenge the affront he has just offered me; he discharges; I waylay him as he retires from Emma's cunt; finding him still stiff enough for that, I clap him into my anus again, embugger Emma, and sweetest ecstasy crowns our pleasure anew; we begin again. Villeneuil encunts my friend, I embugger him; the whore flopped and thrashed about between the two of us for nearly two hours; Villeneuil sticks her ass, I her cunt, I refuck Villeneuil, he refucks me back; the whole night, in a word, is passed in drunkenness and once it is dissipated worry breeds afresh.

"Still no sign of my valet," says Villeneuil.

"It must be the repair of your carriage that is holding him up," Emma replies; "there could be no misreading your message, its terms were clear; so have a little patience. Besides, have you not got your most precious effects with you? You can perfectly well take them to their destination."

"I shall go tomorrow," says Villeneuil.

And as he was much spent from the pleasures of the night before, he went early to bed.

Once he lay in the arms of sleep, I turned to Emma and said: "The time has come. Either we act now or this fellow's immense riches slip from our grasp."

"Ah, my friend, we are in a hotel, what shall we do with the corpse?"

"Cut it into pieces and burn them; this man is accompanied by nobody, nobody will come here to look for him. Thanks to the precautions you took, the valet will go hunting for him at the other end of town. We'll let him explain things in any way he wishes; he can demand inquiries, he can make them himself, I defy him to find hide or hair of his master: when we came through the city gates I gave our names to the guard and described Villeneuil as a footman in our hire. Well, we have dismissed the footman. There's an end to it."

Then, opening the treasure chest with the key we had quietly taken out of Villeneuil's pocket, and contemplating that enormous treasure of gold and precious stones, "Oh, my dear friend," said I, "would we not be mad to hesitate a moment between the life of this fool and the possession of such riches?"

We were gloating over the spectacle when all of a sudden there came a knocking at the door. I shot a glance at Emma, shot another out of the window: great heavens! there in the street stood Villeneuil's carriage. And here was his valet. The lout had discovered where we were, at The English Arms they had told him that since we were not among their guests, there must have been some error, and that we would surely be found elsewhere, probably at the Hotel de Danemark. As for hiding his master from him, 'twas too late for that: as he walked in he saw Villeneuil lying asleep in his bed.

"My good man," I said, going straight up to the valet, and putting a finger to my lips, "take care lest you wake him; he has been having a bout of fever, it is of utmost importance that he rest; go back to the inn where you were, and be certain that if he sent you there in the first place it was for the very best of reasons: owing to the secret business he has in this city he cannot afford to have the same public lodgings as his servants. He very positively charged us to tell you, in the event you were to appear, to return to the address specified in the note which my wife wrote out at his dictation when we stopped at Vimmerby; you are to remain at The English Arms and await his further orders, without anticipating them, without coming here to find out what they are."

"Humph," said the valet, "that suits me. I'll send the carriage back."

"Do so. Here is some money if you run short of it; don't worry about your master, he is in good hands, and inside three days you will surely be hearing news."

Valet and carriage disappear; my companion and I discuss how now to proceed.

"Let us start," I say, "by following our initial scheme: we first get rid of this Villeneuil; once he is out of the way we shall have no trouble killing the valet, and this will get us the carriage, the horses, the rest of the baggage, which were not even in the bargain at the outset."

The unfortunate young man is cut up bit by bit, each is reduced to ashes in a charcoal brazier until of Villeneuil not a trace remains; and we, heated by the grisly deed we have just performed, pass the rest of the night in the filthiest debauch. In the morning I betook myself, alone, to The English Arms.

"My friend," said I to the valet, "I have instructions from your master to conduct you to where he is awaiting you in a house in the country, it lies two leagues from here; your effects may remain at the inn and as we leave, make it clear that they are not to be touched, unless I come to fetch them, and in that case that they be turned over to me; let us make haste."

We set out from the city and when I have my man in the bleak and desolate parts that stand on the edge of Stockholm, "Off you go," I say to the wretch as I fire a ball into his brain, "go look for your master in hell; 'tis there we send everyone who has money but lacks the intelligence to give it up before we take it from him."

With a kick I roll the dead body over the brink of a precipice and, my operation terminated, turn about to drive back to town when, on the farther side of the road, I spy a child of thirteen or fourteen tending a flock of sheep.

"Eh, she must have seen me," say I to myself, "she could not help but see me . . . did she see everything? . . . Ah, by God, let's not waste time weighing the two sides of the question."

I seize the little shepherd, wrap a scarf around her head; I rape her; her two pucelages are blasted at a single stroke, I put a bullet into her head at the same instant I discharge in her ass.

There, say I to myself, very pleased with what I have done, that is the sure way of avoiding all trouble from a witness, and I drive swiftly back to The English Arms where I have Villeneuil's horses hitched, his trunks loaded into his carriage, and everything brought round to our hotel.

It was a silent Emma who greeted me there; I was disturbed by her air of worry.

I demanded what the matter could be. "Is your nerve failing you?"

"I am uneasy about the consequences this affair may have," she replied. "Villeneuil does not come to Stockholm without giving his correspondents foreknowledge of his arrival; they will wonder what has befallen him; he will be sought for at all the inns; questions will be asked; the whole thing is bound to come out. And when it does, let us, my friend, be already gone from this dreadful country where everything frightens me nearly to death."

"Emma, I thought you were of sterner stuff; if you are obliged to fly every time you commit a felony, you will never be able to settle down anywhere. Come, my dear, put away idle fears; Nature, who desires crimes, watches over those who commit them, and one is very rarely chastened for having abided by her laws. I have credentials recommending me to everyone of outstanding note in Sweden; I am going to present them, be sure that among all these new acquaintances there shall not be one who is unable to furnish us material and opportunity for fresh evil-doing; let us indeed be careful, but above all not to escape from the happy fate that awaits us."

At the time I was in Sweden, the capital, and the whole kingdom as well, was being shaken by the rivalry of two powerful parties: one, discontented with the Court, was straining for the day when it would seize power; the other, that of Gustavus III, seemed determined to stop at nothing in order to keep despotism enthroned; the Court and everything connected therewith made up this second faction. The first was composed of the Senate and of certain portions of the military. A new monarch had just begun his reign, and the malcontents felt this the propitious moment to swing into action: a dawning authority is more easily confronted than an entrenched one; the senators were aware of it and were planning to go to any lengths to secure the rights they had been striving for years to usurp; they exercised their constitutional prerogatives to the limit and even beyond, daring to open letters to the King in their public assemblies, and to answer or interpret them as they chose; little by little, the power of these magistrates had grown to the point where Gustavus could scarcely appoint men to office in his own realm.

Such was the state of affairs in the country when I paid a call upon Senator Steno, the guiding spirit of the senatorial party. The young magistrate and his wife received me with demonstrations of the most agreeable politeness and, I dare add, of the liveliest interest. I was scolded for not having brought my wife the very first day; and 'twas only by accepting an invitation to dinner for the following day, at which both of us would be expected, that I succeeded in quieting young Steno's reproaches.

Emma, who passed for my spouse and who combined all the features in which good society delights, was received with extreme cordiality; and the warmest friendship sprang up at once between that charming creature and the Senator's engaging wife.[3]

If the young Swede, twenty-seven years of age, could be rightly taken for one of the most winning, wealthiest, wittiest persons of his generation, one might without exaggeration declare that Ernestine, his lady, was very surely the prettiest creature to be found in all Scandinavia. Nineteen years, the loveliest blonde hair, the most majestic figure . . . the prettiest brown eyes, the sweetest and most delicately formed features, such were the endearing qualities wherewith Nature had embellished this angelic woman who, in addition to all these physical favors, possessed a fully adorned mind, the firmest character, and the soundest philosophy.

At our fourth meeting Steno asked me to whom were addressed the other letters of recommendation I had been given. I brought them all forth, and when upon the superscriptions he read the names of several courtiers, a frown darkened his face.

"Amiable Frenchman and distinguished guest," said he, handing me back my sheaf of papers, "we must forego the pleasure of seeing anyone who comes bearing such credentials. Powerful inter-

---

[3] The reader is herewith notified that the names of the participants in this celebrated conjuration have all been disguised.

ests divide my house from these where you are to go. The sworn enemies of the Court's despotism, my colleagues, my friends, my relatives are not on speaking terms with those who serve or benefit from this despotism."

"Ah, Monsieur," said I, "your attitude conforms too closely to mine for me not, this very minute, to make the slight sacrifice of everything that would appear likely to bind me to the party of your opponents; I abhor kings and their tyranny. Is it even presumable that into such hands as this royal personage's Nature can have entrusted the task of governing men? The ease with which a single individual may be seduced, deceived, does this not suffice to spoil any intelligent man's taste for monarchy? Make haste, brave senators, restore to the Swedish people the liberty Gustavus seeks to wrest away from them, as his ancestors did before; may the efforts your young prince is now undertaking to increase his authority come to the same failure as those lately attempted by Adolphus. But, good my Lord," I continued heatedly, "lest in future any doubt remain in your mind as to the sincerity of the promise I make you to embrace your party and uphold it for the rest of my sojourn upon Swedish soil, here are the letters I was to carry to Gustavus' supporters and clients, here they are, I say, let us, you and I, throw them into the grate, yes, all of them, and allow me to leave up to you the choice of friends with whom I am to consort while in your city."

Steno clasps my hand, and his young wife, witness to this conversation, is unable to prevent herself from showing how greatly flattered she is to have attracted to her party so essential a man as I.

"Borchamps," Steno said, "after this declaration, which so plainly comes from the heart, I can have no doubt of your way of thinking. Are you indeed capable of adopting our interests as your own, of binding yourself to us by all the ties which identify friends and sinew a conspiracy?"

"Senator," I replied with vehemence, "before you now and upon my life I do hereby swear to stand fast in the fight until the last of the tyrants shall be wiped off the face of the earth, if the weapon for their destruction is put into my hand by you."

And I thereupon recounted my experience with the Princess

of Holland, fit proof to demonstrate my abhorrence of tyranny and of those who wield it.

"My friend," the Senator said to me, "is your wife's attitude in this the same as yours?"

"To that question the answer is unambiguous: they were for reasons similar to mine that she left a Sophia who lavished favors upon her."

"Very well then," said Steno, "my comrades sup tomorrow night at my house, join us, both of you, and you will discover certain startling things."

I related this interview to Emma.

"Before entangling us in this, my friend, consider well where it may lead; and I would ask you not to forget that when you refused to serve Sophia's cause, you were acting a great deal less, as it appears to me, from partisan spirit than through aversion for political affairs."

"No," I rejoined, "you err; I have since given the matter very close thought, and realized that it was uniquely my lifelong horror of the despotism of a single person which drove me to turn my back upon the Stadtholder's wife; had her aims been different, I might perhaps have agreed to everything. . . ."

"But see here, Borchamps," Emma protested, "your principles seem to me without rhyme or reason: you are a tyrant yourself, and you detest tyranny; despotism breathes in your tastes, in your heart, permeates your soul, and you assail its tenets; explain me these contradictions or cease to count upon me to follow you."

"Emma," said I to my companion, "penetration will here suffice; listen to what I am going to tell you, and remember it well. If the Senate is ready to rise in arms against Sweden's sovereign, it is not from horror of tyranny but from envy at seeing despotism exercised by another than itself; once it has got the power into its hands you will see a sudden transformation wrought in its attitude, and they who hate despotism today will use it to perfect their happiness tomorrow. In accepting Steno's proposal, I play the same role as he and, like him, I am eager not to shatter the scepter, but to wield it to my advantage. And I tell you this which you may also remember: I shall part company with this society the instant I notice it animated by any other principles or tending in any other direction; and so, Emma, of contradictions you need accuse me no more, nor those whom you see combating tyranny by despotism only: *the throne is to everybody's taste, and 'tis not the throne they detest, but him who is seated on it.* I sense in myself certain dispositions to take a hand in worldly affairs; to succeed therein one needs neither prejudices nor virtues; a brazen front, a corrupted soul, an unflinching character, all these I have; fortune beckons to me, I heed the call. Put on fine array tomorrow, Emma, be proud, clever, and sluttish, those, I gage, are the qualities that will be necessary in Steno's house, they are the ones which will please my confederates, show them, you have them; and there is this last: tremble at nothing."

We are there at the appointed hour and having been admitted at the gate overhear a lackey say to the porter: "These are the last who'll be coming; let nobody else in."

Beside this vast palace was a garden, and the society was gathered in a pavilion located at its farther end; tall trees shrouded this spot which one might have taken for a temple raised to the god of silence. A servant points the way without escorting us thither; we follow the path, enter the pavilion.

The assembly, apart from ourselves, numbered eight persons. Steno and his wife, with whom I have already acquainted you, rose to greet us and present us to the others I shall now describe. They were three senators and their three wives. The eldest of the men must have been fifty, his name was Ericsson: he had an air of stateliness and majesty, but there was something hard in his glance and cutting in his speech. His wife was named Fredegunda, she was thirty-five, had more beauty than graciousness, features bordering on the masculine, but proud; what, in a word, they call a handsome woman. The second senator was forty years of age and called Volf: here were prodigious vivacity, very considerable wit, but a wickedness apparent in every line and detail. Amelia, his wife, was scarce twenty-three; 'twas there the most piquant face, the most agreeable figure, the sweetest mouth, the most roguish eye, the fairest skin in all the world; one cannot be all this and at the same time have a mind more lively and an imagination more ardent; nor be more libertine, nor more delicious. I was struck by Amelia, I do not pretend otherwise. The third senator was named Brahe, he was surely less than thirty years old, slender, spare, crafty of eye, alert, quick, unsettled of gesture, and looked to be all his confreres' better in rigor, cynicism, and ferocity. Ulrika, his wife, was one of the most beautiful women in Stockholm, but simultaneously the most mischievous and the most vicious, the most attached to the Senatorial Party, and the most capable of leading it to victory; she was two years younger than her husband.

"Friends," said Steno once the doors were bolted and the shutters drawn, "had I not thought this French gentleman and his lady worthy of us they would not be present in our midst; I therefore urgently request you to admit them into our Society."

"Sir," said Brahe, addressing himself to me in a tone at once forceful and dignified, "what Steno tells us about you is encouraging and inspires confidence; this confidence however will be better established by the answers you give in public to the various questions that are now going to be put to you."

He then asked: "What are your motives for hating the despotism of kings?"

To this I replied: "Envy, jealousy, ambition, pride, rage at being dominated, my own desire to tyrannize others."[4]

He: "Does the welfare and happiness of nations enter as a consideration into your views?"

I: "I am concerned solely for mine own."

He: "And what role do the passions play in your manner of regarding all things political?"

I: "The leading and most vital one; according to my belief, every one of those individuals known as statesmen pursues now, and has always pursued, no other veritable objective, is now and has always been moved by no other veritable intention than to satisfy his voluptuous inclinations to the full; his plans, the alliances he forms, his schemes, his taxes, everything, his laws included, everything is bent toward his personal felicity, for the public's well-being there can be no room in his meditations, and what the dizzard people see him do is never done save to render him mightier or richer."

He: "So that if you were mighty or rich you would turn

---

[4] Say, O genius of the Stockholm revolution, didst thou not go to school in Paris?

these two advantages nowhere but to those of your pleasures or your follies?"

I: "They are the only gods I recognize, the only delights of my soul."

He: "And religion, how do you visualize it in regard to all this?"

I: "As the mainstay of tyranny, that mechanism which the despot must always set in motion when he wishes to strengthen his throne. The flame of superstition was ever the aurora of despotism, and it is always by means of consecrated irons that the tyrant breaks the people to his will."

He: "And so you exhort us to the use of religion?"

I: "Certainly, if you are of a mind to reign, let a God speak in your behalf and men will obey you. When, God's wrath in your hire or your hands, you have brought them to their knees, their money and their lives are as good as yours. Persuade them that all the woes they have suffered under the regime you wish them to repudiate have come from nought but their irreligion. Cause them to tumble at the feet of the hobgoblin you brandish before them; prostrate, they will serve as steppingstones to your ambition, your pride, your lust."

He: "You yourself do not believe in God?"

I: "Is there a single rational being on earth who can credit such lies? Nature, forever in movement, has she any need of a mover? Would that the living body of the first charlatan to mouth talk of this execrable chimera could be abandoned to the shades of all those poor wretches who have perished on its account."

He: "How do you consider the actions that are denominated criminal?"

I: "As Nature's inspirations to which resistance is madness; as the surest means a statesman can employ to accumulate the substance of happiness and safeguard it; as essential to the workings of all governments; as the sole laws of Nature."

He: "Have you committed crimes of every sort?"

I: "There is not one wherewith I am not stained, and which I am not ready to stain myself with again."

Here Brahe outlined the history of the Templars. After an energetic commentary upon the death, both unjust and atrocious, to which Philip the Fair put their last Grand Master, Molay, for the sole purpose of laying hands upon the Order's property:

"In us you see," he said to me, "the leaders of that Northern Lodge which Molay himself instituted even as he awaited his doom in a cell of the Bastille. If we accept you into our midst it is only upon the most express condition that, upon the victim about to be presented to you, you swear to avenge our great founder, and at the same time to fulfill the clauses of the oath here set forth. Recite it aloud and intelligibly."

"*I do hereby swear,*" said I, reading from the vellum, "*to exterminate all kings till none remain alive on earth; to wage incessant war against the Catholic religion and the Papacy; to preach liberty for all the world's peoples; and to strive to build a universal republic.*"

An awful clap of thunder dinned deafeningly; the pavilion rattled upon its foundations; the victim rose up through a trap in the floor, in his two hands lay the poniard with which I was to smite him; he was a fair youth of sixteen years, entirely nude. I take the profferred weapon, I drive the blade into his heart. Brahe comes up with a golden chalice, gathers the blood, has me drink first thereof, presents the goblet to the others one by one, and each drinks, pronouncing a barbarous phrase whose meaning is this: *We shall die rather than break faith with one another.* The platform descends, the cadaver disappears, and Brahe resumes his interrogation.

"You have just now," says he, "shown yourself worthy of us; you have seen that we are of the same intrepid stuff we require in you, and that our wives are likewise dauntless. Are you so careless of the crime you have just committed as to be able to employ it even in your pleasures?"

I: "It augments them, it electrifies them; I have always regarded murder as the soul of libidinous delights; its effects upon the imagination are enormous, and lubricity is as nought unless depravity of spirit fuel its fire."

He: "Do you admit of restrictions in the taking of physical pleasure?"

I: "I know not what they are."

He: "All sexes, all ages, all conditions and sorts, all degrees of kinship, all manners of enjoying these various individuals, all this, I say, is then a matter of indifference to you?"

I : "I make no discriminations."

He: "But you do nonetheless have preference for certain forms of enjoyment?"

I : "Yes, I am particularly disposed toward the stronger ones, those which fools dare call antinatural, criminal, ridiculous, scandalous, the unlawful, the illegal kind, the antisocial and ferocious ones: for those I have a predilection, and they shall always be the delight of my life."

"Brother," said Brahe, "take your place amongst us, you are received into the Society."

And when I had sat down, "In asking now," Brahe went on, "whether your wife's attitudes and principles correspond to your own, we refer ourselves only to you."

"They do. I swear to it in her behalf," I replied.

"Then heed what I am about to tell you," the Senator began.

"The Northern Lodge, whose chiefs we are, has a considerable following in Stockholm; but the rank and file Masons know nothing of our behavior, our secrets, our customs, they trust our leadership and obey our instructions. I have therefore to speak to you upon but two matters, Brother: our morals and our intentions.

"These intentions are to overthrow the Swedish throne as well as every other throne, everywhere, and principally those occupied by the Bourbons. But our Brothers in various parts of the world will attend to that; our task is here in our own country. Once upon the throne of the kings, there shall never have been a tyranny to equal ours, no despot shall ever have put a thicker blindfold over the eyes of the people; plunged into essential ignorance, it shall be at our mercy, blood will flow in rivers, our Masonic Brethren themselves shall become the mere valets of our cruelties, and in us alone shall the supreme power be concentrated; all freedom shall go by the board, that of the press, that of worship, that simply of thought shall be severely forbidden and ruthlessly repressed; one must beware of enlightening the people or of lifting away its irons when your aim is to rule it.

"You, Borchamps, shall not be permitted to share in this

authority, your foreign origins exclude you therefrom; but you shall be entrusted with the command of the armies and above all the robber bands which, very early in the day, shall spread murder and rapine across the length and breadth of Sweden to consolidate our hold upon the countryside. When the time comes, will you swear faithful allegiance to us?"

"I swear it in advance."

"We may then turn to the question of our morals.

"Their depravation, Brother, is appalling; the foremost of the moral pledges which bind us, after those political ones I have just indicated, is mutually to prostitute our wives, our sisters, our mothers and our children one to the other; to enjoy all those persons, pell-mell, in the presence of one another and, preferably, in the manner that God, as they say, punished at Sodom. Victims of both sexes serve in our orgies, and 'tis upon them falls the brunt of our desires' irregularity. Is your wife of your own mind touching these immoralities, and as determined as you in their execution?"

"Be certain of it!" said Emma.

"That however is not all," Brahe continued, "the most frightful disorders entertain us, there is no excess before which we hesitate. With us, atrocity is often carried to the point of stealing, of murdering in the street, of poisoning wells, streams, of perpetrating arson, of occasioning famines, of blighting live-stock, and of sowing epidemics among men, less perhaps for the sake of our amusement than to weary the population of the present government and to cause it ardently to yearn for the revolution we are preparing. Do these actions revolt you or are you able to participate in the Society's program without remorse?"

"The sentiment you refer to there has always been a stranger to my heart: the entire universe come to bits in my hands would not cost me a tear. . . ."

Whereupon I receive the fraternal accolade from the entire assembly. They then bade me bare my behind, and each of those present, men and women alike, came forward to kiss it, suck it, and then thrust a muddied tongue into my mouth. Emma was exposed up to the waist; her skirts were held up by ribbons pinned to her shoulders, and she was subjected to the same homages; but lovely though she was, no word was spoken in her praise: the assembly's regulations prohibited encomiums, I was given fore-warning of it.

"We shall all undress," said Brahe who presided over the meeting, "we shall then move on into the adjoining room."

Ten minutes later we were ungarbed and ready, and we flocked into a large chamber lined with Turkish couches, the floor strown with cushions and large ottomans. The statue of Jacques Molay at the stake adorned the center of the room.

"You see there," said Brahe, "the effigy of him we must avenge; let us, while awaiting that happy day, swim in the ocean of delights he himself was preparing for his Brethren."

A mild warmth suffused that agreeable retreat which shaded candles mysteriously lighted. There was a sudden swirl and the next instant all had come to grips. I leap toward the fetching Amelia; her glances had aroused me, and till then all the heat in me was due to her; her desires fling her my way before my arms can fold around her. I could give you no clear picture of her charms: I was too overpowered then to be able to paint them now. There was never a mouth so sweet, never an ass so beautiful. Amelia bends away, of her own accord offering me the shrine in which she knows full well I am wont to do my worship, and I soon perceive that, be it from habit, be it from taste, the rascal is lending herself more for the sensation than to be obliging, and that no other attack would have pleased her nearly so much. The desire to embugger the three other women, and their husbands also, prevented me from losing my fuck in Amelia's incomparable ass; and I hurled myself upon Steno, then sodomizing Emma. Enchanted by this stroke of good fortune, the Senator showed me a very brave behind, whereof I nonetheless took early leave in order to probe that belonging to Ernestine, his wife, a fair and voluptuous creature over whom I toiled for a long while. Fredegunda attracts me, however: Ernestine's joys had been all daintiness and delicacy, but this one's were all transports and frenzy. Leaving her, I flew to her husband. Ericsson, fifty years old, flutters under my prick like a dove under her mate, and the lecher answers my tooling with such fervor and zeal that he steals away my seed; but Brahe, who hails me then, is, by some fervent sucking, soon able to restore to my engine all the energy which Ericsson's fine buttocks have just drained out of it; those Brahe presents to me, and whose anus I sound, quickly make me forget the happiness of a moment before. I fuck Brahe an uninterrupted half-hour and only quit him for Volf who has been sodomizing Ulrika, whose delicate ass obtains my sperm before long. What libertinage! what foulness of mind and filth of behavior in this last-named creature! Everything voluptuousness can have of the tartest, everything libertinage contains of the wildest was organized and applied by this Messalina. Grabbing my prick directly it had discharged, the slut did everything under the sun to revive it and lodge it in her cunt; but I proved invincible. Staunch adherent to the Society's laws, I reached the point of threatening Ulrika with denunciation if she persisted another instant in her attempts to seduce me; furious, the rascal crammed my device back into her ass and flung and danced so ardently about that she squirted fuck in every direction.

While I was thus fucking every ass in the room, Emma, just as bountifully regaled, had not missed a prick; they had all, even mine, been in and out of her ass, but not all had discharged there; these were libertines of mark whom a single enjoyment, be it of an uncommonly fine ass, was not apt to electrify so keenly as to cost them their fuck, no, they did not part with it as readily as all that; they every one, for example, buggered me, and from not one of them did I get sperm. Ericsson, the most licentious of the lot, might well have fucked fifteen such ones as he had at his disposal, and it is doubtful whether his prick would have purpled. Young and vigorous though he was, Brahe, had it not been for the incredible episodes whereof we shall speak anon, would not have brought matters to their conclusion either. As for Steno, his struggles were over: bewitched by Emma, that voluptuous creature's stunning ass had, so he said, sufficed, and his boiling fuck had flooded it. On the other hand, Volf, more refined in his needs, still lacking what he required for discharge, had also merely tuned his instrument, and it was only at supper, which was shortly announced, that I began to glimpse the essential peculiarities of my new acolytes' tastes. This supper was awaiting us in another hall, where six fair boys of from fifteen to eighteen and six charming girls of the same age were at hand, naked, to serve us. After a sumptuous repast further orgies were celebrated and now the whole truth about those Swedish despots' unruly passions finally came out.

Steno, as we know, had discharged with ease into Emma's ass; he nonetheless desired, for the perfection of his ecstasy, that a young boy suck his mouth amorously and simultaneously finger his asshole while he himself fucked a man: such was his passion.

To rescue his honor, Ericsson had first to lash the skin off a pair of young persons, one male, the other female: without this preliminary he could never get anywhere.

There was Volf who would have himself embuggered while, for a solid hour he plied a cat-o'-nine-tails against the ass in which he proposed to discharge. Otherwise, no erection worth speaking of.

More mischievous yet, Brahe was not disposed to ejaculate until he had maimed a victim hard by the ass he coveted.

These passions were unfolded between fruit and cheese. Wine, hope, ambition, pride went to everyone's head, all inhibitions were forgotten; the women, positively uncontrollable, were the first to set examples of the disorderliness which, by the time the evening ended, had cost six victims their lives.

As we were about to take our leave, Steno, in the name of the Society expressing his joy at having us in its midst, asked me if I were by any chance in need of a sum . . .; I thought it wisest to say no, at least for the moment. And for a week I heard nothing more from my new friends. Then, on the morning of the eighth day, Steno came to see me.

"We are going on a prowl tonight," said he, "the women shall not be along; do you care to join us?"

"What have you in mind?"

"Some random crimes. We mean to do a little stealing, pillaging, assassinating, burning. In a word, to commit some horrors; are you with us?"

"Surely."

"Meet us at eight o'clock at Brahe's house in the suburbs; we leave from there."

A delicious supper was awaiting us, and twenty-five troopers, chosen for superiority of member, were, in spending themselves in our asses, to impart to us the energy necessary for the projected expedition. We were fucked forty times apiece, which was more than I had ever been before at a single tourney. These preliminaries left us all afire, in such a state of agitation that we'd have taken a knife to the throat of Almighty God himself had the bugger-fucker existed.

Escorted by ten of the stoutest champions in the band, there we are roaming the streets like furies, blindly assaulting everybody in our path: as one by one our victims were robbed and killed, their bodies were tossed into the canals. If we stopped anything worth the bother, we'd rape it first, murder it afterward. We broke our way into several humble dwellings, which we devastated once we were done terrorizing, mutilating, and finally butchering their inhabitants; we permitted ourselves every imaginable and every nameless execration, and left screams, flames, and blood in our wake. We found the patrol, we attacked it, put it to flight; and 'twas only when we were glutted on atrocities that we wended our way homeward as the sun rose to shine upon the debris left by our scandalous orgies.

Needless to say, we had it printed in the press that such were the frightful abuses the government was perpetrating, and that so long as the royal regime prevailed over the Senate and the law, no fortune would be in safety, no citizen would walk in peace abroad or breathe in peace at home. The people believed what they read and sighed for a revolution. Aye, so it is the poor fools are hoodwinked, so it is the common population is at once made the pretext and the victim of its leaders' wickedness: always weak and always stupid, sometimes it is made to want a king, sometimes a republic, and the prosperity its agitators offer under the one system or the other is never but the phantom created by their interests or by their passions.[5]

However, the hour was approaching, such was the desire for a change that this was the sole subject of conversations. A more discerning and an abler politician than my associates, at the very moment they were convincing themselves that success was at hand, I saw that the wind lay in the other direction; calmer than they,

---

[5] See, in La Fontaine, the ingenious fable "The Frogs Who Seek a King." Unhappy inhabitants of this globe, there's the story of you one and all.

I sounded out opinion, and from the immense quantity of people I found firmly attached to the king and his royalists I drew the conclusion that the senatorial revolution was destined to be still-born. It was then that, faithful to the principles of egoism and villainy to which I have been devoted all my life, I resolved to change camp on the spot, and inhumanly to betray the one into which I had been received. Of the two it was the weaker, that was obvious; it was neither goodness on the one side nor badness on the other that decided me, force was the only deciding factor, and it was only with force I wished to keep company. I would have unfailingly stayed with the senators had I believed their faction not the better (I knew perfectly well that it was the more vicious), but the more powerful; the evidence convinced me that it was not: I turned traitor. This, it will perhaps be said, was infamous; so be it. But infamy meant little to me when my welfare or safety lay in treason. Man is born to pursue his happiness on earth, and for no other purpose; all the vain considerations opposed thereto, all the prejudices which hinder him are better flouted than heeded, for it is not the esteem of others that will render him happy; he is happy only if he is so in his own opinion, and it will never be from laboring toward his prosperity, whatever the road he chooses for getting there, that he will be able to lose self-respect.

I request private audience with Gustavus; I obtain it; I reveal everything to him, I name those who have sworn to dethrone him, I give him my word not to leave Stockholm until he has investigated the conspiracy I allege, and I ask no more than a million by way of reward if my warnings prove founded and exact; eternal imprisonment if false. The monarch's vigilance, aided by my disclosures, averts the catastrophe. On the day the insurrection was to break out, Gustavus was up and in the saddle before dawn: he sent the people home, isolated the plotters, won over the military, seized the arsenal, and all that without shedding a drop of blood. This was not at all what I had been counting upon; gloating in advance over the terrible consequences I fancied my treachery would have, I too was up with the sun and gone out to see all those heads fall: the imbecile Gustavus spared them every one. I was aghast. Oh, said I to myself, how I regret having broken faith with those who at least would have drenched this kingdom in blood. I have been deceived; they accused this prince of being a despot, and look at the clumsy oaf! he is meek as a lamb when I give him the means and the occasion to fortify his tyranny! Bah, a plague upon the fellow!

"Ah, mark my words," said I to all those who cared to listen to me, and they were not many, "your prince is jeopardizing the future instead of taking this precious opportunity to plant his scepter, as he ought to do, upon a hill of corpses. Brief will be his reign, believe me, and unhappy his end."[6]

I was not however obliged to remind him of his promise; Gustavus himself summoned me to his palace and along with my fee of a million gave me the order to get out of his States immediately.

"I pay traitors," he said to me, "they are useful, I need them; but I despise them and, once they have served their purpose, prefer to have them out of my sight."

What does it matter to me, said I to myself as I went away, whether this clod esteems or detests me; he has money, that is what I was after. As for the character he reproaches in me, he'll not correct it: I delight in treason and am going to commit a little more of it very soon.

Ten minutes later I fly to Steno.

"My wife let it out," I tell him, "she is a monster; I have just learned the entire story, she received money for this horror. Thanks to her treachery I have orders to leave Sweden. I shall go, for I must. But before I do I'd like to settle my score with her. The town is quiet, nothing prevents us from meeting together this evening, let us do so; and let us punish the creature, that is all I ask of you."

Steno consents. I conduct Emma to the Society without her knowing for what reason it is gathering; all the men, all the women rise in fury against her whom I accuse, unanimously condemn her to the most atrocious death. Emma, bewildered at such charges, seeks to recriminate against me; she is reduced to silence. While lubricious scenes are enacted around the scaffold raised for her destruction, the luckless wretch, entrusted to my tender mercies, is flayed alive, and one by one I slowly grill each part of

---

6 He was the one Ankerström killed in 1789.

her whence I have removed the skin. Throughout it all I was being sucked, and my four friends, each fucking a bardash, were whipped by their wives whom young girls were cunt-sucking; never in all my days had I discharged so deliciously. The operation over with, the company mingled; 'twas then that Amelia, Volf's wife, accosted me.

"I like your firmness," she declared. "It was long ago I noticed this woman was not the sort you need; I am more suitable for you, Borchamps. But I am going to surprise you: swear to me that I too shall someday become your victim. I cannot help it, my imagination is what it is: delirious. My husband is too fond of me to satisfy it; I can stand no more: since the age of fifteen the idea of perishing the victim of libertinage's cruel passions has been gnawing my brain. No, I do not want to die tomorrow, my extravagance does not go that far. But that is how I want to die, and only in that manner. To become, as I expire, the occasion of a crime— ah, my head reels at the thought; and in the morning I leave Stockholm at your side, if you vow to satisfy me."

Deeply stirred by this so uncommon proposition, I protest to Amelia that she will have cause to be content with me: arrangements are made, she slips away to join me before the night is over, and at sunrise we set forth from the city together.

I went out of Stockholm with riches that by now had become immense: I had inherited from my wife, I had the King's million, and my new friend handed over to me a further six hundred thousand francs, which she had stolen from her husband and insisted that I take.

Saint Petersburg, Amelia and I agreed, was to be our destination, and thither we took ourselves. She demanded that we marry, I consented; and it being needless, in view of our means, that we deny ourselves anything we desired, we rented a splendid mansion in the finest quarter of the city. Valets, retinue, equipages, choice wines and good meat, we stinted not, and soon the flower of society was honored to obtain entry to my wife's house. The Russians are fond of display, lavishness, luxury; but, in everything taking their guidance from us, just as soon as a French lord appears with some magnificence in their midst, they all rush off to copy him. The Empress' minister came in person to invite me to present myself to his sovereign; and knowing I was born for great adventures, I accepted his propositions.

Always familiar with those who pleased her, Catherine asked me several particular questions about France, and my replies having satisfied her, she gave me permission to pay her frequent court. Thus did two years pass, during which we, Amelia and I, swam in all that noble city could offer in the way of pleasures. A note from the Empress finally clarified the reasons lying behind her willingness to see me so often. In this missive she besought me to accompany the man who delivered it to me: at nightfall he would escort me to one of her country residences, situated a few leagues outside the town. Amelia, whom I told of this stroke of good luck, did all she could to dissuade me, and was much aggrieved to see me set forth.

"Concerning your person," the Empress began as soon as we were alone together, "I have gathered all the information necessary. I know of your behavior in Sweden, and whatever others may have said about it, or thought, I strongly approve it. For you may be perfectly certain, my good young Frenchman, that it is wiser to stand for kings than against, theirs is the better side: those who embrace it and to it remain faithful are never sorry. Behind a mask of popularity Gustavus sought to fortify despotism's position on its throne; exposing the conspiracy threatening to foil his designs, you served despotism well; I praise you therefor. Your age, your mien, what they publish of your wit, everything appertaining to you excites my interest; and to your fortune I may be able to make solid contributions, if you rally to my projects. . . ."

"Madame!" said I, truly touched by this woman's charms, superb though forty years old, "the good fortune of pleasing Your Majesty is reward enough for the services she enables one to render her, and in advance I swear that her orders shall henceforth be the duties cherished of my heart and my heart's sole delights."

Catherine gave me her hand, I kissed it with feeling; a fichu slips aside, and the world's most gorgeous bosom appears before my eyes; Catherine, covering it over again, speaks of her thinness, as if any living man had ever spied anything plumper, more delicious, than what I have just had a glimpse of. When the Empress observed that I could not contain my enthusiasm, she soon allowed me to convince myself that all her other features matched the quality of the sample I had just detected. Eh, my friends, what else would you have from me except the truth? I showed prick to the Empress before the day was out; and as she found me infinitely to her liking I was promptly admitted to the honors of the imperial bed. Few women of her day could rival Catherine for beauty; fleshly parts and forms are not more richly made nor more prettily turned; and when I'd come to know a little of her temperament I ceased to wonder at the multitude of my predecessors. All manners of enjoyment were desired by Catherine, and you will of course understand that I refused her none of them: her ass especially, the fairest ass I'd seen in my life, caused me no end of sweetest comforts and cheer.

"These little malpractices are very prevalent in Russia," she told me, "and I am careful not to proscribe them; the size of this swarming population is responsible for the wealth of the nobility, and their power interferes with mine, I must use every means to weaken it; this one is of effective value and amuses me too, for I like vice and its practitioners; promoting it is among my principles. I could easily prove to any sovereign that he can ill afford not to do as I. Borchamps, I am enchanted to see you treating my behind with such deference and attention"—I was kissing it even as she spoke—"and declare to you that it is at your disposal whenever you are of a mind to fuck it. . . ."

I made much use, that evening, of the license granted me.

It was here the Empress, who was not altogether without prudence, drew the line during our first interview, she did not open herself farther; the second transpired a week later, and in the same way. But at the third Catherine spoke to me in this wise: "I now feel confident enough in you to associate you with my plans. Before disclosing them, however, I require a sacrifice of you, and I want you to subscribe to it this instant. Who is the pretty Swede you have in your train, Borchamps?"

"She is my wife."

"Be that as it may, I do not want to see her alive tomorrow."

"The swelling prick you are holding in your hand, Princess," was my reply, "is ready to sign her death warrant in your ass. . . ."

"Good," said Catherine, lodging my instrument inside her, "but I am cruel; this woman has roused my jealousy to a dangerous point, and since I wish her to endure sufferings proportional to the uneasiness she has caused me, I wish that, while you and I look on, she be tonged tomorrow, with heated pincers; every quarter of an hour the procedure will be interrupted in order that she be suspended in this or that manner and half-broken on the wheel; my executioners will fuck her at each stage, I'll have her bathed in quicklime before all the life is gone out of her. In the meantime I shall be examining your countenance: if you prove steadfast, brave, the secret shall be revealed to you. Otherwise, it shall not be."

Lovely though Amelia was, two years of enjoying her had furiously calmed my desires. In her there were overmuch tenderness, overmuch affection, and a mind far less cruel than at first I had supposed. What she had told me about the way in which she wanted to end her days, this, the more I pondered it, had simply been an effort on her part to be ingratiating; it did not correspond to her real feelings. What was more, Amelia was without all the gracious condescension I expected in a woman; she refused to suck me, and as for her behind, while I do not for a moment deny that it had had its very great charms, I would ask you, does a woman's still have any after you've fucked it for two years? Everything was therefore promised to Catherine, who was greatly entertained by the possibility of satisfying the desire my wife had once expressed touching on the death she wished to die: the very next day, Amelia was brought to one of the Empress' houses, a very obscure one and far away from the city, and presented to Her Majesty.

There is no imagining the transports of this woman, who was accustomed to seeing everything and everyone yield to her will. There is no believing the harshness, the tyranny she displayed toward the unlucky Swedish girl; she exacted the most debasing services from her; had Amelia lick and frig her, submitted her to the most trying vexations, and then, surrendering her to her executioners, the monster watched her actually undergo every one of the tortures prescribed in the plan she had elaborated. She insisted that I embugger the hapless victim during the intervals; such was her delirium, she demanded that I fuck the executioners even as they were at work torturing Amelia; and pleased to see my prick keep at an even stand the whole while, of my character she formed the opinion that answered to her desires. My poor bedraggled wife expired after eleven hours of varied and violent agonies. Catherine discharged twenty times at least; she herself lent the executioners a hand; and she said that a week hence, she would unfold her grand scheme to me, and I was dismissed.[7]

Hitherto I had been the Empress' guest at her country establishments only; this time it was into the Winter Palace I had the honor to be admitted.

"From what I have observed of you, Borchamps," Catherine declared to me, "I can be in no doubt about the energy of your character. No longer under the influence of childhood prejudices toward what fools call *crime,* the attitude you exhibit is plain and enlightened; but if this mode of action is frequently useful to ordinary folk, how often it becomes indispensable to rulers and to statesmen! The private individual, laying sturdy foundations for his worldly well-being, has seldom to go beyond one or two crimes in the course of his existence; those persons who oppose his desires are in number so few that to combat them he needs little in the way of arms. But we, Borchamps, perpetually surrounded by flatterers seeking only to deceive us, or by powerful enemies whose unique aim is to destroy us, how many are the different circumstances under which we are obliged to employ crime! A sovereign who is jealous of his prerogatives ought never to go to sleep without his mace under his pillow.

"The famous Peter fancied he was performing a great service for Russia when he struck off the chains of a people who had never known nor cherished anything but its bondage; but Peter, more mindful of his reputation than of the lot of those who were to follow him on his throne, did not realize he was tarnishing monarchy's diadem without making the people happier. And what in

---

[7] Those who have had a close view of this woman, famous as much for her wit as for her misdeeds, will here recognize her sufficiently well to agree that this portrait of Catherine could only have been painted from nature.

fact did this great change he instituted gain him? He increased the territories of Russia; but what could the greater or lesser extent of his dominions matter to him, who lived only upon a few acres of it? Why, at great expense, import arts and sciences from abroad and plant them in a native soil where he wished to see corn grow? What pleased him in the semblance of a freedom which only added to the weight of his subjects' shackles? It may be unhesitatingly affirmed: Peter was as certainly the downfall of Russia as will be her liberator he who reimposes the yoke upon her: enlightened Russia perceives what she lacks, Russia restored to slavery would see nothing beyond her physical needs. Now, in which of the two situations is man more fortunate: in the one where, the blindfold removed from his eyes, he is able to discern all his privations? or in the other, where his ignorance prevents him from suspecting any of them? These bases once established, does one deny that the most violent despotism better befits the subject than the fullest independence? And if you grant me this point—which I think it impossible to contest—do you blame me for resorting to every conceivable device in order to arrange affairs in Russia as they were before the baneful advent of Peter?

"Basilovitch reigned as I mean to reign; his tyranny is the model I propose to adopt. He used to amuse himself, they say, dashing out his captives' brains, raping their wives and daughters, mutilating them with his own hands, rending them into pieces, and after that burning them; he assassinated his son; at Novgorod he punished an insurrection by having three thousand human beings thrown into the Volga; he was the Nero of Russia. Well, I shall be her Theodora or her Messalina; whatever the horror that enables me to strengthen my hold on the throne, I shall not falter, and the first of those I must consummate is the killing of my son. You, Borchamps, are the man I have in mind to accomplish this political atrocity. He among my compatriots whom I were to select for the task might have a sentimental attachment to this prince, and instead of an accomplice I would be engaging my betrayer; only too well I recall the legitimate grievances I had of the Russian to whom I entrusted the slaying of my husband; I want no more such unpleasant experiences. Nothing necessitates that it be one of my countrymen whom I charge with these great commissions; a remnant of the loyalty he imagines due one of his nation's princes could deter him, and crime is always bungled when prejudices are operative. With you I have no such fears; I have here the poison I want you to employ. . . . I have spoken, Borchamps; how do you decide?"

"Madame," I replied to this woman whose greatness of character has been admitted universally, "even had I lost the taste for crime I was born with, even had crime ceased to be my element and very sustenance, this one that you propose would flatter me, and the mere idea of ridding the world of a meek and debonair prince in order to preserve there the tyranny whereof nobody is a more zealous partisan than I, this idea, Madame, would alone suffice to cause me to undertake, joyfully, the project you outline to me: count upon my obedience."

"This profound resignation makes you mine forever," said Catherine, folding me in her arms. "I intend, tomorrow, to treat you to an orgy of delights, to make all your senses boil. I want you to behold me in pleasure's throes; and I want to behold you in them; and when we are both very merry and very high from lewd sights and lewd doings, you shall be given the venom that is to put an end to the abhorrent existence of that contemptible creature I failed to avoid bringing into this world."

The rendezvous was at the country house where I had seen the Empress previously. She was awaiting me in a magical boudoir, a veritable garden where, in the warm air, exotic flowers were blooming in mahogany benches agreeably scattered throughout this exquisite chamber. Turkish sofas, surrounded by mirrors and beneath mirrors affixed to the ceiling, cried to be put to voluptuous use. From there a more lugubrious alcove was visible; in it was to be seen a quartet of twenty-year-old youths. They were in irons, helpless, held at the mercy of Catherine's unbridled passions.

"What you are looking at in there," the Empress said to me, "is the climax to the entertainment. A preliminary series of ordinary pleasures will fettle us gradually; we shall not come to grips with those boys until our fever has attained its final pitch. Would victims of my sex please you better?"

"Why, 'tis a matter of indifference to me," I assured her; "I will share your pleasures, and whatever the individual upon whom murder is committed, it is always certain to stimulate my senses."

"Ah, Borchamps, nothing else in the world is worth the candle! It is so sweet to behave unnaturally—"

"But what is more natural than murder?"

"I know; but it constitutes an infraction of the law, and I adore the idea."

"The law? What can she care for the law who makes the law? Tell me: has Your Highness already enjoyed these four fine young men?"

"Would they be in my chains otherwise?"

"Do they realize what fate lies in store for them?"

"Not yet; we shall announce it while utilizing them. I shall pronounce the sentence of each while your prick is in his ass."

"I would also like that to be the moment when you carry it out."

"Ah, you're a villain, an adorable villain!" Catherine exclaimed.

And the lust-objects appointed for the impending games appeared forthwith. They were six lasses of fifteen or sixteen years, of rarest beauty; and six men, each five feet ten inches tall, all with members as thick as your forearm and at least as long.

"Install yourself there where you have a clear view of me," Catherine instructed me, "and consider my pleasures, keeping your distance; frig yourself if you like, but do not disturb me. I am going to taste the supreme delights of offering you a display of thorough whorishness; cynicism is part of my character, I like to make a discreditable parade of myself, scandal excites my mind."

I do as I am told. The girls undress their queen, then shower her with the prettiest caresses. Three of them suck, one her mouth, another her cunt, the last her asshole; they are replaced at their posts by the other three; the first team relieves the second; and the exercise was conducted at a very smart pace; they picked up withes and bestowed a gentle scourging upon Catherine, each toiling over a different part of her body. The men stepped forward and while they were at work, this or that girl would now and again approach to kiss mouths and stroke members. When the Tsarina's body was all a bright scarlet she had herself rubbed with spirits; then, sitting on the face of one of the little maids, who was ordered to tongue her vent, she received a second, kneeling, between her thighs, who sucked her clitoris; the third sucked her mouth; the fourth, her teats; and she frigged the remaining two, one with either hand. The six lads, now grouping themselves likewise, put prickpoint to everything of the six girls' behinds they could reach. No, I had never beheld anything so voluptuous as this exquisite ensemble; its maneuvers cost Catherine a discharge. I heard her moan and utter blasphemies in Russian, it was her custom.

Another scene was enacted immediately. It was she who now frigged the girls, each in her turn; but she sucked only their fundaments; and while she was sucking them, the men were tickling hers. This calling for the participation of only two subjects, the ten others did before her eyes what she herself was doing. After a little everything changes again. Now she stuffs a prick into her cunt and, lying atop him who is fucking her so, she offers her ass to another who sodomizes her mightily; to left and to right she chafes a prick upon a girl's buttocks; he who embuggers her is flogged, and all the rest cluster around her, in suggestive attitudes. Thus did the six men fray her cuntwise and asswardly; after which, she served the six girls up for fucking, all by herself she fitted pricks into avenues of pleasure, sucked each engine as it emerged from this breach or that, meanwhile herself titillating the clitoris and kissing the mouth of the girl; she sprawls upon the sofa and has herself mounted by the men, one after another: each, raising her thighs, was to tup her in front and behind; as this was going forward, each of the girls had to squat above her brow, kiss the man serving her, and then piss on her face. During this scene the rascal shed another great quantity of fuck. It was at its conclusion that she summoned me. I was at the end of my tether, Tantalus' sufferings were as nothing next to mine, and to see me thus was what the whore had wanted.

"Are you stiff?" she inquired ironically.

"Have a look at it, slut!" I stormed.

That insolent reply pleased her beyond words.

"Why then," she went on, turning around, "my ass is at your disposal. It's full of fuck, you can deposit yours in there along with the rest."

And the saucy creature sucked one of her men's asses while I sodomized her. Ass after ass was presented to her lips; I handled the asses of the girls while I fucked away, and despite all I could do, my seed escaped me. She forbade me to leave her ass, then commanded the men to fuck me back into fucking form; her orders to the girls were to give me their buttocks for kissing, and their cunts to her for tonguing; so it was that three times in succession my fuck flowed.

"Let's perform some cruelties now," Catherine proposed; "I am spent, I must resort to severities."

Each man then got down on all fours, a girl got astride him, so that each couple offered a pair of vulnerable asses. Catherine armed herself with a whip of the kind executioners use in Russia for administering the *knout*,[8] and with her royal hand the trollop lashed all those fair behinds so thoroughly that blood lay in puddles on the floor; I was whipping her at the same time, but simply with birch rods, and after every twenty cuts I had to kneel behind her and lick her anus.

"I am going," she told me, "to martyrize all these individuals, but in a rather more serious manner; once I have had my pleasure from them I propose to put them to no very pretty death. . . ."

The men seize the girls, spread their legs wide apart and hold them thus; Catherine sends whistling blows of her whip into the poor souls' gaping vaginas, from which she fetches forth streams of blood. Next, the girls lay hold of the men and Catherine plies her scourge upon their pricks and balls.

"What concern can any of that be to me now?" she was asking. "Drained and limp, it's worthless, there's nothing to be done with such tripe but feed it to worms; frolic with these individuals,

---

[8] This whip is fashioned from a bull's pizzle; to it are attached three thongs of moose hide. A single stroke draws blood: these instruments are of incomparable utility to those who cherish, either actively or passively, the pleasures of flagellation. To increase their effectiveness, steel tips may be fitted to the thongs; it then becomes possible to remove flesh virtually without effort; one hundred strokes applied by a vigorous arm will kill anyone. One such whip, more or less studded, is in the possession of every voluptuous Russian.

Borchamps, they're yours and I'll take my turn watching you."

Directed and encouraged by me, the girls bring the men's members aloft again and I am fucked another two times by each of them; I push my prick into all those dozen fundaments, I arrange various tableaux, and Catherine masturbates while observing me.

"That will do," says she, "let us move on to more important matters."

The victims entered; but what was my astonishment at seeing one of those young men so closely resemble the Empress' son that for a moment I could believe it was the Tsarevitch himself.

"I should hope," Catherine said to me upon noticing my surprise, "that you are able to read my intentions."

"Gauging your mind by the standard of my own," was my answer, "I take it that this is the person upon whom we are going to test the poison you have selected for the young man who could easily be his twin."

"Exactly," Catherine admitted; "I shall be deprived of the pleasure of witnessing my son's agonies, this fellow's will give me an image of them. My illusion will be agreeable; I'll discharge you perfect floods."

"Delicious mind," I cried, "what a pity you are not the whole earth's queen, and I your prime minister!"

"Assuredly," said the Empress, "we'd achieve a great many wicked things together, and it would be a planet inhabited by our victims. . . ."

Before anything else Catherine had herself fucked by those four ill-starred young men while I embuggered them and the dozen other subjects were either flogging or frigging us, or adopting obscene poses.

"The first six men with whom we began our fucking," the Empress told me, "are my ordinary executioners; you shall see them in action upon that pretty quartet. As for these women, does your lubricity doom any of them? If so, point them out now and I shall dismiss the rest so that we can quietly amuse ourselves contemplating the destruction of these unfortunates."

Two of those charming creatures having made a strong impression upon me, I designated them for death, and then only fourteen of us remained: six executioners, a like number of victims, the Tsarina and I.

The living image of Catherine's son was the first victim to appear on the stage. I myself presented him the fatal drink whose effects were not felt until half an hour later; by then we had both, and in every manner, enjoyed him fairly to shreds; when we were done, his pains began, and they were terrifying. Ten minutes after his first convulsions the wretch expired, before our avid gazes; and during the spectacle, Catherine had herself embuggered uninterruptedly. Then she had each of the other young men one after the other bound fast atop her body: she pecked at them, she frigged them, while the executioners, into whose ranks the whore had incorporated me, hacked and slashed those knaves to mincemeat as they squirmed and thrashed upon her; the torments we subjected them to were beyond number and example. The two girls I had asked leave to execute by myself perished under treatment just as rigorous as that which the men had undergone, and I dare say I may even have improved upon the horrors the Empress had ordered. I opened the cunt of one of them and stuck fifty or sixty minikins into the walls of her vagina; then I fucked her. Each thrust of my prick, driving those tiny pins in to the head, wrung piercing shrieks from the unhappy creature, and Catherine avowed she had never invented anything so delightful.

The corpses were removed, and Catherine and I sat down to a private supper; we were both naked. She waxed very passionate, bestowed unstinting praise upon my rigidity of prick and principle, and for me foresaw the most brilliant future at her Court once I had brought about her son's death. The poison was entrusted to me, I promised to take action on the morrow. Twice again did I fuck Catherine the Great in the ass, and we parted.

For quite some time I had been the young prince's familiar; Catherine had, on purpose, encouraged those frequentations; she had even wanted me to frig myself in that young man's company, in order to excite her lewdness by the details I would give her concerning the person of this child her rage doomed. The tête-à-tête had taken place; on another occasion Catherine, in hiding, had even watched us indulge in a bout of buggery. This liaison favored the carrying out of our plan. The Tsarevitch, as was his wont, came one morning to take breakfast with me, and it was then the blow was struck. But from long exposure to his mother's attempts on his life, the young prince had made a rule of never eating anything in town without swallowing some antidote as soon as he felt the faintest signs of an indisposition. Thus, our perfidious scheme came to nought; and the unjust Catherine, immediately suspecting me of having lost my nerve, greeted me with invectives and had me arrested as I left her palace. You know that Siberia is the fate of all this cruel woman's state prisoners; my holdings were confiscated, my personal effects seized, I was led off to that horrible place of exile; there, like the others, I had to turn over a dozen animal skins to the commander every month, and when I failed to do so, was flogged to ribbons. Siberia was the grim school where I converted this punishment into a kind of need which has become so violent in me that, for my health's sake, I absolutely cannot forego having myself whipped once a day.[9]

Upon arriving in those remote parts I was given a hut whose former occupant had just died after fifteen years of detention. It was divided into three rooms; light entered them through windows of oiled paper. It was built of pine, the only floor was a deep layer of old fishbones, which shone like ivory. The roof was covered over, rather picturesquely, by the foliage of the trees growing around. For security against the incursions of wild animals the place was surrounded by a ditch and a palisade of thick stakes reinforced by horizontal planks; the upper ends of those stakes were sharpened to a point, so that one was protected as though by a fence of spears, and when the outer gate was shut one was quite as safe as in a little fortress. Inspecting the hut I came upon the former tenant's larder: it contained dry biscuits, salted reindeer flesh, some earthenware jugs of ale; that was all. Such was the joyless abode to which, after my day of hunting, I would return, to weep over the injustice

---

[9] This habit is so compelling that its addicts are unable to do without whipping, and were they to deprive themselves of it, it well might be to their peril. Just prior to those moments when they customarily repeat the ceremony, they are subject to itchings so extreme that sound thrashing constitutes their sole hope of relief. See Abbé Boileau's history of the Flagellants; and the excellent translation Mercier de Compiègne has given us of Meibomius.

of monarchs and the brutal unkindness of fortune. Nearly ten years did I spend in this cruel retirement, having no company save that of a few other luckless souls in the same plight as I.

One of them, Hungarian by birth, an utterly unprincipled man and who was called Tergowitz, appeared to be the only person there with whom I had anything in common. He at least had a rational approach to crime; the others committed it like the animals they tracked in the awful Siberian forest. Tergowitz alone, instead of soliciting the compassion of God, generally thought to be the cause of our woes, confined himself to cursing the deity every day; although he was guilty of every crime under the sun, his iron soul afforded no room to regrets, and if he was sorry about anything, it was to be obliged, owing to the circumstances we were in, to neglect his penchants. Like myself, Tergowitz was nearing thirty; his face was agreeable, and the first thing our exchange of confidences led to was an evening of embuggering each other.

"Mark you," explained the Hungarian as soon as we were finished, "it's not the absence or need of women that drives me to what I have just done, but simply taste. I idolize men and abhor females; even if we had three million of them here, I'd not touch a one."

"Tell me," I asked my comrade, "is there anyone else in this miserable region whom we might associate in our sodomite pleasures?"

"Yes," said Tergowitz; "not far from here dwells a Pole named Voldomir, fifty-six years old, as handsome a man as there's anywhere to be found . . . and as fanatic a bugger; he has been in these wastelands for eighteen years; he is passionately fond of me and, I'm sure, will be most willing to become acquainted with you. Borchamps, let's the three of us join forces and get ourselves out of this melancholy part of the world."

That same day we went to find the Pole. He lived fifty *versts*[10] away: someone that distance from you is your neighbor in Siberia. Voldomir, exiled for horrible crimes committed in Russia, struck me as a very attractive person indeed, but of remarkable ferocity; his manner of address was gruff, flintlike, and misanthropy seemed

10 Fifty *versts* make about thirty-five miles.

grained in his every feature. It was not until after Tergowitz had given him one or two cogent details-upon my character that he envisaged me with a less hostile eye. As soon as we had supped, we all three reached mechanically into our breeches. Voldomir had a superb member, but the leatheriest ass I had beheld in all my life.

"He never brings in any skins," Tergowitz explained to me, "that assures him of his daily beating."

"Very certain it is," declared the Pole, "that a lashing affords me greater pleasure than anything else in the world, and if you'd like to practice your arm on them, I'll lend you my buttocks."

Wielding the switches he provided us, Tergowitz and I were an entire hour thrashing the Pole, who for all we could do seemed hardly to feel a thing. At length, however, electrified by the ceremony, the rake caught hold of my behind and into it thrust his colossal and unmoistened prick, I was fucked in a trice; Tergowitz bum-tupped him the while; and despite the excessively cold weather, we left the smoky hut and ass-fucked each other in the snow. That prodigious engine caused one a good deal of pain, and the scoundrel watched me suffer with an unpitying smile. Snatching his stave out of my ass, he buried it in Tergowitz's, and for nearly two hours scraped and tore us both, without discharging; I would embugger him while he was fucking my comrade. But, younger than he, less jaded, I discharged inside his bowels.

The Pole had still not loosed his seed when at last he put his member away. "Unfortunately," he said, "I am obliged to deny myself these pleasures, or indulge in them alone, for I am utterly incapable of bringing them to their proper conclusion without shedding blood, a great quantity of blood; for lack of men to kill, I slaughter animals and smear myself with their gore. But when the passions are keen, it is a great hardship to be reduced to these makeshifts. . . ."

"Ah,". said Tergowitz, "avowing our tastes to our new comrade, I believe we can inform him that we have not always confined ourselves to foxes, bears, wolves. . . ."

"But where the devil can you find victims?" I demanded of my friends.

"Among our fellow prisoners."

"Notwithstanding the fact they share your hard lot? You have no mercy upon them who, like you, have been treated unmercifully?"

"What do you call mercy?" the Pole asked me. "That sentiment, chilling to the desires, can it find entry into a stern heart? And when a crime delights me, can I be stopped by mercifulness, the dullest, most stupid, most futile of all the soul's impulsions? Never has my soul been susceptible of any such feeling, believe me when I tell you so, and that my contempt is boundless for the man who is such a fool as to conceive it for an instant. The urge, the need to shed blood, the most imperious of all needs and urges, brooks no interference whatever; he who speaks to you now slew his father, his mother, his wife, his children, and repents not, no, nor has ever felt a twinge of remorse. With a little courage and untrammeled by prejudices, a man can do what he likes with his heart and his conscience. Habit adjusts us to anything, and nothing is easier than to develop the habit which pleases best: merely surmount the initial revulsions, if you have any fire in you, you'll succeed. Prick in hand, accustom yourself awhile to the idea that frightens you, you'll soon come to cherish it: that's the method I have followed to familiarize myself with all known crimes: I yearned to commit them, but they scared me; fixing my mind upon them, I'd masturbate, and I perform them today as effortlessly as I blow my nose. The erroneous notion we entertain of others is always the thing that impedes us in criminal affairs, our childhood training leads us, ridiculously, to consider our own selves of no account and others as all-important. Whence it proceeds that any iniquity wrought against this respected fellow being appears a great evil to us, although harming one's neighbor is natural, and Nature's laws are never so well complied with as when we prefer ourselves to others and seek pleasure in tormenting them. If it be true that we resemble all other products of Nature, if it be true we are worth no more than they, why persist in believing ourselves governed by different laws? Are plants and animals acquainted with mercy, pity, social obligations, brotherly love? And in Nature do we detect any law other than self-interest, that is, self-preservation? The one great trouble is that human laws are the fruits of nothing but ignorance or prejudice; the men who framed them consulted their stupidity alone, were guided by their mean-spiritedness, their narrow interests, and their myopia. A nation's lawmaker must never be born on its soil; otherwise he will simply transmit to his people legalized versions of the infantile nonsense he learned in their midst, and his institutions, lacking the force of greatness they ought to have, will never inspire awe; for how can you ask that men have respect for laws which contradict those Nature engraves in them?"

"Ah, my friend," said I, carried away by enthusiasm at finding his sentiments so similar to my own, and embracing this charming personage, "the theses you have just expounded conform to opinions which have long been mine, and in me you see someone possessing a soul at least as stoutly armored as yours."

"I am not quite as advanced as you," the Hungarian said to us, "I have never assassinated anybody apart from my sister, my niece, and a few comrades hereabouts, in collaboration with Voldomir; but I have itching fingers and most content I'd be were the occasion for a crime to offer itself to me every day of my life."

"Friends," said I, "people united through so many similarities of disposition and outlook ought never separate, and when they have the misfortune of being prisoners together they should join forces to break out of the bondage to which human injustice has reduced them."

"Our comrade's views are mine, I am with him," Voldomir declared.

"So am I," said Tergowitz.

"Very well then," I resumed, "let's be up and away for the frontier of this infamous clime. Though bayonets guard it, let us try to slip across the line: once we are free, the lives and riches of others will amply compensate us for the losses occasioned us by the perfidious cruelty of the imperial whore who keeps us captive here."

We drank a few bottles of vodka to our projects, and were about to seal our vows with the solemnities of some sodomite fuckshed when a lad of fifteen appeared at the door. He came with a request from his father, who wished to borrow a few skins from Voldomir and who would return them in a day or two.

"Who is this child?" I asked my friends.

"The son of a great Russian nobleman," Voldomir replied, "like us exiled for having displeased Catherine; he dwells a hundred *versts* from here." Then, taking me aside, he continued in a lower voice: "Since we are soon to leave, and shall be far away before his father hears about the thing, we might, if you like, amuse ourselves with the boy. . . ."

"Yes, by God," I replied, already laying heavy hands upon our young visitor and jerking his breeches down to his knees, "we'll fuck him first, then eat him afterward: this is tastier flesh than the martens and weasels that make up our daily fare."

I embugger first while my comrades hold the child still: Tergowitz's turn comes next; Voldomir because of his massiveness of member goes in last; we begin again. And when we have had enough of our little darling, we roast him alive on the spit and eat him with relish.

"Oh, how mistaken they are," the Hungarian observed, "to disdain this meat, there's nothing more delicate nor better flavored in all the world, as the wise savages understand who have such a predilection for it."

"That," said Voldomir, "is simply another of your European absurdities: after having erected murder into a crime you cut off your nose to spite your face and banished these dainties from your table; and the same overweening pride brought you to suppose that there was no wrong in butchering a pig for food, while there was nothing worse than performing the same operation upon a human being. Such are the sinister effects of this civilization I abhor and which causes me to regard this degenerated portion of mankind as a race of contemptible fools."

Our excellent repast concluded, we all three climbed into the Pole's bed and, at sunrise, armed to the teeth, we set off with the firm resolve to follow no calling other than that of brigand and murderer, to heed nothing except our pleasures and self-interest.

Unsure of the road we were to take, our first plan was to make for the Chinese border since we wished to avoid Muscovy and all the other adjoining provinces over which the Empress ruled, where we were almost certain to be arrested. But the way to China was far, and instead we chose to cross the deserts to the Caspian shore; after several months of travel we came to Astrakhan, without anyone having sought to hinder our flight.

From Astrakhan we moved toward Tiflis, killing, pillaging, fucking, ravaging all that crossed our path, and entered this second city after laying waste a fair part of the countryside. In us none the less was the desire, grown powerful after years spent in the wilderness, for a civil and quiet place to abide, where less tumultuous passions can at once be satisfied more luxuriously, more agreeably, and more conveniently. In this regard, the libertinage, the beauty, of the Georgians looked to promise us all we could ask for.

Tiflis lies at the foot of a mountain on the banks of the River Kur, which traverses Georgia; it contains some rather handsome palaces. Having robbed a sufficient number of travelers along the way to have accumulated two or three thousand rubles apiece, we immediately took sumptuous lodgings. We bought pretty serving girls; but the Pole, who refused to have anything female even come near him, chose a strapping Georgian escorted by two young Greek slaves, and we refreshed ourselves a little after the rigors of the long and monotonous journey we had just completed. Commerce at Tiflis is chiefly in women. There they are publicly sold for the harems of Asia and Constantinople, like cattle in a market; anyone has the right to go and examine and handle them in the sheds where specimens ranging from lately weaned infants up to girls the age of sixteen are kept on exhibit. Nowhere will you find greater beauty than in the creatures this country produces, nowhere will you find more elegant figures, more attractive features. But if one cannot look upon them without desiring them, seldom does one desire them without having them. Nowhere is whoredom so well established in the world as here.

Independence is unknown to the Georgians. The tyranny their overlords exert upon them is not mild; and as this aristocracy is exceedingly libertine, there is no need for me to insist upon the fact that in this part of the world too, despotism expresses itself in lewd terms: they vex their slaves, beat them, whip them, and all that in the spirit of cruel lubricity, whose effects, as you are so fully aware, lead to crimes of all sorts. But what a contradiction! These nobles, who treat their vassals as slaves, themselves grovel before the prince to obtain money and place; and to ensure success, to him they prostitute their children of either sex and starting at the tenderest age.

Tergowitz, naturally adroit and seductive, soon contrived to introduce himself and then to lodge the three of us in the house of one of the foremost lords of the land who, along with very considerable wealth, owned three daughters and as many sons, all of the most excellent beauty. As this gentleman had traveled widely, Tergowitz affirmed that he had seen him in Russia, in Sweden, in Denmark, and the worthy fellow believed it all. It had been a long time since we had been shown such courtesy and such generous treatment, and doubtless still longer since a benefactor had found himself rewarded quite as we paid that one back. We began by a general assault upon his children: inside a fortnight, all of them, boys and girls alike, had been fucked in every manner. Pointing out to us that there was nothing left to fuck under the good man's roof, Voldomir asked how we were going to take our leave. "By robbing him," I replied. "I cannot believe his gold is less worth having than the cunts and assholes of his offspring."

"And when we've robbed him?" Tergowitz wondered.

"Why," said I, "we shall kill him. There are only a few domestics in the house; we are strong enough to take them personally in hand, and I feel my prick already twittering at the prospect of murdering his pretty children."

"But hospitality, my friends, have we not been given hospitality?" said Voldomir.

"Indeed we have," I admitted, "and therefor we should be grateful. Just behavior on our part demands that we do well by someone who has acted kindly toward us. Has not this animal our host told us a hundred times over that as a good Christian[11] he is certain he will go straight to heaven? His hypothesis accepted, will he not be a thousand times happier there than on earth?"

"Assuredly."

"Then we must render him this supreme service."

"To be sure," said Voldomir, "but you have my consent to all these deaths only if it is understood that they be frightful. For too

---

[11] At Tiflis the Christians outnumber the Muslims, there are more churches than mosques.

long have our stealing and killing been done out of need; the moment has come to steal and kill from wickedness, from taste; the world must shudder upon learning of the crime we have committed. . . . Men must be made to blush from shame at belonging to the same species as we. More, I insist that a monument be raised to this crime, relating it and reminding others of it forever, and that with our own hands we cut our names upon this granite memorial."

"Go on, villain, you have our sympathy, speak your mind."

"He himself must be made to roast his children, to join us in dining on them; and while he feeds he must be embuggered by us; after which, the remnants of the feast must be sewn to his body; bound and helpless in his cellar, he must be left thus to die when he feels ready."

The scheme is adopted unanimously; unfortunately, however, owing to thoughtlessness on our part the discussion was overheard by the youngest of the man's daughters, upon whom we had already vented our desires and who was lame from the prodigious abuse she had sustained. Voldomir, with his gigantic prick, had left her anus a shambles, and to calm her we had been giving her little presents for several days. Quaking with terror at what she had just found out, there was no preventing her from rushing off and letting the cat out of the bag. Hearing the slut's story, the father promptly brought a garrison into the house, the police instructing these men to keep an eye on us. But the god who protects crime always leads virtue into its power; of this there ceased long ago to be a shadow of a doubt.

The four soldiers the gentleman led home, and whom he meant to billet in his house without explaining to us his reasons for doing so, were immediately recognized by us as former comrades who had also managed to escape from Siberia; they, as you may easily imagine, preferred our cause to the Georgian Christian's, and the poor man, instead of three enemies under his roof, shortly had seven. The proposal to share in the booty and in the enjoyment of all those children was so warmly welcomed by our reinforcements that we fell to work at once. We tied our benefactor to a pillar in his dining hall and forthwith regaled him first with five hundred whipstrokes applied to every square inch of his behind, then to the pleasure of seeing his six darlings fucked before his eyes. Once they had been, we attached them in a circle around him and flogged those six asses until the room was awash with their blood; next, we lay them upon their backs in the gore and, hoisting their legs into the air, we flailed them with martinets and transformed their anterior parts into hash. After that, we tried to induce the father to taste a little pleasure with his woebegone children, but all efforts to rouse his prick were in vain, and so we castrated and unmembered him and constrained his progeny to eat his testicles and his pizzle; this accomplished, we sliced off the breasts of his daughters and now fed him forcibly upon the still warm and quivering flesh he had himself created.

We were about to move on to the next exercise when discord loomed up in our midst. Among the four soldiers was a splendid young Russian whose beauty was causing Voldomir to stiffen almost as hard as I. I would not, I could not take it upon myself to quit the young man's breeches, from which the Pole, now very dark of brow, had several times sought to evict me. When at last I was lodged in the youth's asshole, out of the corner of my eye I spied Voldomir coming up to me, dagger in hand; I unsheathed my own knife that instant and without stirring from the soldier's fundament, where I was readying to deposit my seed, I stabbed my blade into Voldomir's left side, he fell to the floor, blood gushing from the wound.

"Fuck!" exclaimed Tergowitz, then sodomizing one of the other soldiers, "there's a vigorous deed for you. I must tell you, Borchamps, that I'm not at all sorry you've rid us of that bugger: he'd soon have done the same to us, be sure of it."

I pull out my knife, wipe it dry, and I discharge: never has a murder checked an ejaculation, to the contrary. Then, lighting my pipe, "Go on, my friend," I say to Tergowitz, "I'd never have treated our comrade that way had I not long ago detected in him all the vices that are ruinous to a society such as ours. Let's you and I now swear an oath of everlasting fidelity to each other, and, you'll see, we shall be able to get along very nicely without him."

We terminated our operation. Everything had been carried out according to plan. We sacked the house, the spoils were considerable; well paid, our allies left us very content; but I was loath to be separated from mine : I suggested to Carleson that he remain with me, and he agreed. Two mules transported our baggage; for mounts we had three fine horses; and so we went forth from Tiflis and, skirting the edge of the Black Sea, we came by and by to Constantinople.

It was simply in the capacity of a valet we had Carleson with us; fond of him though I was, I sensed full well that a dozen or fifteen discharges inside his magnificent ass would appease my passion, and I was wary of putting him on an equal footing with us, lest in so doing I create a potentially dangerous rival.

Some highway robberies, a few rapes, as many murders— the obvious and easy line of action to take in a country where neither justice nor security exists : that fairly sums up our adventures in Asia Minor, and we arrived as serenely and surely in the Grand Turk's capital as if we did not merit a hundred times over to appear nowhere there but on the gallows.

Foreigners do not reside in Constantinople itself, they establish themselves at Pera, a suburb. We repaired thither with a view to taking a few days of rest before returning to our trade, which, plied with some success up until now, had put Tergowitz and me in possession of two hundred thousand francs each.

However, after consultation with my partner, I wrote to my sister, asking her to have funds and letters of recommendation for Constantinople sent to me, and also for Italy, whither we intended to go after leaving the Ottoman provinces; and before two months were out I received everything I could want to facilitate our enterprises. Straightway introducing myself to the banker with whom a credit had been opened for me, I shortly became the admirer of the sixteen-year-old girl he prized above all else in this world, and was raising as though she were his own child rather than an adopted one. Philogone was fair-haired, candid in her manner, and naïve, had the loveliest possible eyes, in a word, the whole effect was eminently winning. But here something very odd occurred. Through some strange caprice, not uncommon among true libertines and only comprehensible to them, although Philogone was attractive in the extreme, although the feelings she inspired in me were properly overpowering, I was moved, as I gazed upon her, by no desire other than to have her fucked by

Tergowitz; that idea alone filled out my prick, I frigged it, dwelling upon nothing else. I took the Hungarian to the house of Philogone's protector, Calni was his name; afterward, as we were walking home, I revealed my designs to my friend, who seemed much pleased by them.

"In all this I toil for your benefit, comrade, only for yours."

"It would appear to me," Tergowitz replied, "that we might broaden our objectives. This moneychanger, they say, is one of the richest in Constantinople; while that girl is being attended to, could we not also rob her guardian? I expect that we might then be able to travel through Italy in greater style and comfort."

"Doubtless," said I, "but what you suggest there shall not be easy; force is not on our side here, we shall have to resort to ruse. Such being the case, let us start by sowing a hundred thousand crowns in order to reap two million; do you disapprove?"

"No."

"Then leave everything to me."

I began by renting a country house; the one I chose was superb, isolated, and at a good distance from the city. As soon as I had filled it with elegant furnishings and hired a flock of domestics, I arranged fashionable gatherings every evening, and Philogone and Calni were of course among my guests. Tergowitz passed for my brother; to create the most favorable conditions for his moves was my concern, and I thought to prepare the terrain by subtly hinting at projects for an alliance: I was ever more willingly listened to. Only one thing stood in the way of my desires: that wretched girl, against whom I was inwardly plotting the most atrocious horrors, had taken it into her head to fall in love with me.

"Surely, Sir, such designs are very flattering," she told me after I had finished speaking of my brother's ambition, "but since my guardian has left me free to choose, honesty compels me to say, and I say it frankly, that I would have preferred it had you made this proposal in your own behalf."

"Lovely Philogone," I declared, "such words are wonderfully sweet to a man's pride and self-esteem; but I must answer you in the same forthright language. Certain regrettable tendencies, for which I am not responsible, render me absolutely indifferent to women; and, if you were to become mine, the obligation you would come under to ape the sex I prefer would not make you as happy as you deserve to be."

Seeing that Philogone did not grasp my meaning, I called upon the resources of libertine expression to explain to her that the shrine in which women sacrifice to love was not the one where I was wont to repair, and in exchange for the elucidation she requested of me I earned myself a complete view and thorough handling of this beautiful girl's charms, who, with the candor and innocence of her age, trustingly surrendered the whole of herself to me. Ye gods! what exquisite forms! what purity of line, of color! what graces! and, above all, what a delicious ass! When, opening its orifice, peeping inside, I was obliged, in pursuit of my demonstration, to tell Philogone that 'twas here the temple in which I offered my homage, "Little do I care," was the charming creature's answer; "oh, Borchamps, of such things I know nothing, but must not all my body be yours when you so firmly possess my heart?"

"No, siren, no!" I cried, fondling her peerless behind, "no, do what you will . . . love me, worship me, it will be to no avail, I shall not be melted, who for women can feel no pity nor any decent emotion; 'tis the promise of pleasures of no very delicate order which excites me as I toy with you; and my heart is as immune to love as to any other human virtue." Then letting fall her skirts: "No, Philogone, I cannot marry you, I say; my brother can make you a happy woman, and he will."

Thus did a year go by, and during it confidence was established. Establishing it did not, however, engross all my time; I busied myself with the loveliest Jewesses, the prettiest Greek girls, and the most handsome boys in Constantinople, and to make up for all I had lost during my long-enforced abstinence in Siberia, I conversed with better than three thousand individuals in the one sex and the other in the course of that year. For a thousand sequins, a Jew, who traded in precious stones and had Ahmed's sultanas among his customers, permitted me to accompany him into the harem; and there, risking my life, I fucked six of the Grand Turk's most beautiful wives. They were all habituated to sodomy, and 'twas of their own accord they proposed a route whereby they avoided pregnancies. Rarely did the Sultan, who always mixes them with his castrati, approach them otherwise than from the rear; preparatorily, they anoint this part with a certain essential oil which shrinks it to such narrowness that you cannot embugger them without bloodshed. My wishes went farther: I keenly desired to fuck a few of those famous eunuchs, in whose asses the Grand Turk is so prone to forget women; but since he keeps a much closer guard upon these personages than upon his sultanas, there is no possible way of obtaining access to them. Ahmed, I was informed, owned some who were twelve years old, in beauty surpassing anything to be encountered on earth. I asked for a description of his tastes.

"His favorite passion," one of his wives told me, "is as follows. A dozen sultanas, standing very close the one to the next and displaying nothing but their buttocks, form a circle inside which he takes up his position with four of his castrati. At a signal from him those twelve women must simultaneously shit into the twelve porcelain pots that have been placed for that purpose on the floor beneath their asses: she who fails to produce her mard when it is demanded, dies. Not a month passes but seven or eight wives pay the extreme penalty for this crime; and 'tis the Sultan who executes them, secretly: the manner in which he puts them to death is unknown. Once they have shat, a castrato goes around and collects the pots and brings them to His Highness, who sniffs them, inhales their aroma, dips his prick in the contents, and smears himself therewith: after which the pots are laid aside, one castrato embuggers him while another sucks his device; the third and fourth give him their pricks to fondle and frig. A few moments of this and then the four little darlings shit one by one into his mouth, and he swallows. The circle now breaks up; each woman must lick and suck his mouth and tongue; he pinches their breasts and claws their behinds while they do; as one by one the women are dismissed, they go to a long couch and lie down upon it in a row; once they are all aligned there, the castrati, wielding switches, advance and whip three apiece; when the boys have bloodied those dozen behinds, the Sultan inspects them, sucks the bruises, and licks those shit-splashed asses and those still replete assholes. That done, he turns back to his bardashes and embuggers the four of them in succession; but these are only preliminary exercises. His tour of the boys' asses concluded, the women seize them and offer them to him; he lashes them one after the other, and in the meantime all those who are otherwise unoccupied cluster around him and, silent throughout, manifest an amazing skill in striking a wide variety of the very obscenest attitudes. When the four children have been flogged they are presented to him, he encules them afresh; but at the moment his discharge threatens, he withdraws in a fury, hurls himself at one of the women, who are now standing motionlessly in a ring around him, their faces turned his way. He attacks one of them and beats her until she sinks to the ground, unconscious; he refucks a second bardash, whom he also abandons in order to administer a beating to a second woman; it is likewise with the third and fourth bardash; and it is as he is beating the last woman—who, often as not, perishes beneath his blows—that his fuck spurts, without his having to bother to touch his member. The four women very frequently succumb from the hard use they have received, and those who survive are at least two or three months recovering in bed. He usually strikes them on the head and chest, as forcefully as he can, and were they to offer the slightest resistance they'd be strangled on the spot."

"There indeed," said I to the sultana who was recounting these marvelous things to me, "there indeed is a very extraordinary passion and most surely I too would adopt it, were I as wealthy as your master."

"Sometimes the Sultan secs his wives individually, and 'tis then he embuggers them. But this great favor is never granted to any save the prettiest and who are not over eight years old."

Being at last ready to realize my fell designs regarding the lovely Philogone, at the cost of a few sequins I had her protector's house burned to the ground. Calni's immediate decision was to remove to my country manor, bringing with him not only Philogone and his capital, but a number of trusty servants and retainers besides: I had not anticipated their arrival with that escort. However, I shortly found a way to persuade Calni that this crowd of valets would be far more usefully employed tidying the debris of his house than standing about idle in mine, where my own servants could attend to his needs. Dazed by the calamity that had just befallen him, Calni did as I suggested. The treasure chests were already under my roof, and Calni was about to begin conducting his affairs from there, when we decided to defer action no longer.

"Sir," said I, walking into his bedroom one fine morning, a pistol in my hand, while Tergowitz was posted at the front door as a lookout and I had put my Carleson in charge of Philogone and the single valet who could have come to Calni's aid; "dear and loyal sir, you were sadly mistaken if you assumed you were getting my hospitality for nothing. Bid this world farewell, my friend: you have enjoyed a rich man's life long enough, it is time that your money pass into other hands."

And firing my shot as I pronounced these last words, I sent the banker to settle in hell any debts he might have outstanding. For his part, Carleson dropped out a window the corpse of the valet he had just killed, and he and I pinioned the damosel, who was uttering heart-rending wails and shrieks. Then I summoned Tergowitz.

"My friend," I said, "the moment is at hand; be mindful of the trouble and expense I have incurred to prepare this scene, and fuck this girl for me, right now, before my eyes, while I bum-tup you and Carleson sodomizes me."

Tergowitz, nothing loath to comply, speedily divests the lass of her clothing; and the world's fairest body lies quivering at our disposal. My stars! What buttocks! Never, I repeat, had I seen any so beautiful, better-shaped, more cunningly cleft: I could not refrain from paying them an homage. But when the brain is fixed upon a piece of libertinage and heated by the idea, not even the devil can alter the course of things. I did not want Philogone, I was tempted by nothing except the ass of him who was to fuck her. Tergowitz encunts, I embugger Tergowitz, Carleson fucks me, and after a furious ride lasting perhaps an hour, we all three discharge as one man.

"Turn her over, by God!" I cry to my friend. "Do you not see she has the best ass in existence? Carleson will encunt her, and I shall fuck you both."

The act is consummated despite the lovely orphan's tears and screams; and before another hour has gone by there's not a temple of Cythera to which we have not shown her the way. My friends were in a lather, Tergowitz especially; I alone remained cool before that heavenly girl, or if she inspired any desires in me, they were so ferocious and depraved that satisfying them, I'd have deprived my comrades of her there and then. Never had my perverse tastes expressed themselves against anyone so resolutely as against that girl; I felt as though there were no torture violent enough to inflict upon her, and I had to reject as too mild, too modest, everything my imagination was devising. My rage was at the pitch where it was proclaimed in my eyes; I could no longer gaze upon that creature save I was gripped by every vicious, every murderous impulse. Can you tell me what it was bred such feelings in me? I myself do not know; I simply describe to you what I experienced.

"So let us get ourselves gone from here," said I to my friends; "a prudent man cannot be concerned for pleasures alone. Our belongings are aboard a felucca, waiting for us at the port and ready to sail, I have chartered it to Naples. Let's not tarry; after the pranks we have just performed, we'd be well advised to move on. . . . And this girl, Tergowitz, say: what's to be done with her?"

"We are taking her along, I presume," the Hungarian replied, and I detected something mutinous in his eye.

"Ah ha! In love, comrade?"

"No, but since we've gone to the point of buying the slut with her guardian's blood I see no reason not to keep her."

And thinking it appropriate to say nothing at this juncture lest some dissension arise which could jeopardize our safety, I nodded as though in agreement with Tergowitz, and we set forth.

Carleson soon noticed however that I had merely acted from expediency in consenting to have Philogone accompany us. He spoke to me about it. In the belief I had no cause to be secretive with him, I gave him plain answer, and on the second day at sea we decided to get quietly rid of these two turtledoves, and that thereafter I would be sole proprietor of our hoard. I exchanged a few words with the captain of the vessel; a few sequins won me his sympathy.

"Bah," said he, "do as you like, but beware of that woman you see over there by herself. She seems to think she knows you, and if it's true, you'll gain nothing from being observed by her."

"Fear not," I assured him, "we shall choose our moment

well." Then casting an involuntary glance at the creature who according to the captain claimed to be acquainted with me, I told myself that for a certainty he was mistaken, in this sorrowful personage seeing nothing but a woman apparently of some forty years, occupied as a servant to the crew and whose features had been prematurely aged by hardship, distress, and weariness. Therefore I put her completely out of my mind and gave all my attention to our scheme; once the veils of night had overspread the sea, Carleson and I laid hands on our slumbering comrade and slipped him quietly over the board. Philogone, wakened, heaved a deep sigh; it was not, she said, that she so much regretted the Hungarian, but that in all the world she loved nobody but me.

"Dear and unlucky child," was my response, "your love is very ill requited. I cannot endure women, my angel, I've told you so." Then dropping Carleson's breeches within her full view, "You can see here," I went on, "how those individuals are made who have a right to my favors."

Philogone blushed and a few tears rolled down her cheeks.

"But how the devil can you love me," I demanded, "after the crime you have just witnessed me committing?"

" 'Tis a dreadful deed, to be sure; but what power has one over one's heart? Oh, Sir, were you to assassinate me, still I would love you."

Whereupon the conversation began.

The melancholy woman had approached us quietly, and without seeming to be listening, she lost nothing of what we were saying.

"What were you doing in Calni's house?" I asked Philogone. "Such protection is not given for nothing; was love involved in all that? When the bond of kinship is absent, it's seldom a man keeps a girl in his house save his purposes be lewd."

"Calni's sentiments, Sir," Philogone answered, "were of the purest; his conduct was always above reproach, he was a kindhearted man. Some sixteen years ago, while journeying in Sweden, my guardian, stopping at an inn, found a destitute young woman whom he conveyed with him to Stockholm, whither he was called upon business. This young woman was pregnant; my guardian saw to her needs, remained at her side; she gave birth to me. Calni, seeing that my mother was in no position to raise me, asked her to entrust me to him. Having had no children by his wife, they both took the most devoted care of me, and I grew up in their house."

"What became of your mother?" I interrupted, a curious presentiment suddenly forming in my mind.

"I do not know. We left her in Sweden. She had no resources; apart from the aid Calni gave her—"

"And which did not enable her to get very far," broke in she who had been following our words.

And casting herself at our feet: "Philogone! behold her who brought you into the world; and you, Borchamps, look pityingly upon the ill-starred Clotilda Tilson you seduced in London after having wrought the ruin of her family, and whom, when this poor child was in her womb, you abandoned at a Swedish inn, riding off with a barbarous woman who called herself your wife."

"Fuck!" I said to Carleson, very little moved by this theatrical speech, "would you believe it? At a single stroke fate restores both my wife—and she is charming, is she not—and an exceedingly pretty daughter. Eh, Carleson! Do you not weep?"

"No, by God," heartless Carleson replied, "instead of that I'm stiffening, for I visualize some delightful episodes that could contribute an added piquancy to this adventure."

"We see eye to eye, dear boy," I whispered to him; "however, allow me to handle the affair: I shall soon provide you with a striking demonstration of the way in which Nature's deepest impulsions affect me."

Then turning back tenderly to Calni's ward, "Oh, Philogone," I exclaimed, "you are my daughter, yes: I recognize you by the sweet stirrings the sight of you causes in my bowels. . . . And you, Madame," I continued, hugging my blessed spouse's neck nearly to the point of strangling her, "ah yes, you are my wife, I recognize you too. . . ."

I now placed them side by side. "Kiss me, dearest ones, kiss me! Philogone, my beloved Philogone! Behold sublime Nature's sentiments: yesterday, I had precious little desire to fuck you, now I burn to do so."

Both women recoiled in instinctive horror; but Carleson and I quieted them, made them understand that I held their fate in my hands. They mastered their shyness. And though they were my wife and daughter, they had much more the appearance of a pair of slaves.

My desires had become so intense I could scarce control myself. I would now be absorbed in admiring Philogone's sublime hindquarters, the next instant all I wanted was to study the state into which poverty and grief had reduced Clotilda's charms. And lifting the skirts of both at once, my two eyes sufficed not to stare at them nor my two hands to feel and probe them; I kissed, I foraged, I plotted. . . . Carleson frigged me. All my former ideas changed touching the lovely ass of my new-found daughter; strange indeed are the ways of Nature, aye, unimaginable: Philogone as Calni's ward left me cold, now that she was mine the same Philogone brought my prick up all afire. My cruel desires remained unaltered; previously, they had been isolated, now they marched in step with those of fucking this glorious girl: whereof I quickly convinced her, jabbing my engine into her asshole; whereat she uttered piercing screams. The ship's captain heard them and came softly up to me.

"Sir," said he, "I fear lest your conduct scandalize the crew; our vessel is small, and for the kind of activity you wish to indulge in more space would be preferable. At present we are not far off the shore of a little island, deserted, and disadvantaged only by the great quantity of bats and owls that are to be found on it, and which is the reason why human beings have always avoided it. But a pleasant hour may be spent there. We are going to land, our sailors will make their supper ashore and you can amuse yourself a while."

These overtures gave me the opportunity to relate to the captain how I had just rediscovered a long-lost wife and daughter.

"A daughter!" said he. "But were you not fucking her a short while ago?"

"True, I was. In these matters I am not hindered by many scruples."

"Aye, Sir, you Frenchmen are right; better to eat the fruit of the tree you've planted than leave it for others to enjoy. As for that poor creature," he went on, "if it's your wife chance has restored to you, then I congratulate you. We've known her for quite some time, she's made these voyages with us often. Though she's poor, she's as honest and decent a woman as ever we've seen; every man aboard will tell you so."

"Friend," I said to the mariner, "I do not doubt it for an instant; but this woman you are praising once behaved abominably toward me; and I shall not pretend otherwise," I added, dropping several more coins in his palm, "my aim in wishing to go ashore on this island is to obtain my revenge."

"Why, Sir, bless my soul," the captain replied, "do as you like, I'll not meddle in your private affairs." Lowering his tone, and looking at me with deep understanding: "When you return to the ship you have merely to say that she slipped and fell into the water. . . ."

Enchanted by this good man's amicable candor, I take leave · of him and report our conversation to Carleson, then expose my homicidal projects. Scarcely was I done speaking when the ship cast anchor.

"Captain," said I, disembarking with my family, "give us a little time. . . ."

"I am at your service, my Lord, and in your hire alone; we'll not set sail again until you are ready to be off."

And we started inland.

"Oh, my friend," I declared to Carleson as we walked along, "the pleasures we are going to receive from these two whores! This, I sense it already, will be the most arousing of all my murders; look at my prick," I said, stopping, "just look at it foam with rage . . . I like this island, Carleson. What solitude! We shall be able to accomplish wonders."

A short while later we spied a little ravine delightfully shaded by willow trees and poplars, the ground covered by fresh green grass; bushes screened the place on all sides.

"Let us settle ourselves here," I said to my friend. " 'Tis the very finest weather, we shall take off our clothes. Naked like savages, we'll imitate them in appearance as well as in deeds."

After kissing Carleson with all possible lewd fervor, "Come," I said, "let's get to work on them. But mark you now, not a drop of fuck until those sluts have sighed up the ghost."

With that I fling both those women down upon the grass; I

embugger my daughter, I examine the afterparts of my wife, of that Clotilda I'd so adored in days bygone and whom I found beautiful even now; from the ass of the one I shifted straight into the ass of the other. Carleson was bum-fucking me; I forgot my own words and discharged, but while in the act biting my daughter's breasts so cruelly that I left them covered with blood. Still erect, I fit my member into my daughter's cunt. "Here," I say to Calni's protégée while kissing her mother's buttocks, "open your womb and receive the fuck that gave you life."

But, forever inconstant, it's now Clotilda I encunt; she gets fuck from me again while this time I worry my daughter's buttocks as fiercely as I'd bitten her teats.

"Not so fast, Carleson," I say as I withdraw, "you must sodomize our two whores, I'll hold them still for you. First one, then the other."

My valet embuggers, I lick his testicles—I worshiped that splendid fellow—; I get to my feet and suck his mouth while he looses his seed into my wife's behind; my daughter is promptly given like treatment. I fuck him while he saws away in that unfortunate girl's anus.

"And now," I said as soon as he was finished, "some entertainment at our victims' expense."

Having my Carleson stand up, I require the two whores to lick every part of his body, not omitting his member, his asshole, and the spaces between his toes, his armpits also. I engage him to shit upon a thornbush and I oblige those women to go there and eat his excrement, though it means getting their faces scratched and torn; next, we catch them by the hair, thrust them head first back into the same bush, drag them out, toss them back in again, till the thorns have cut them to the bone; nothing so poignant, so heart-rending as their screams, nothing so keen as the pleasure we derive from them. . . .

"O just Heaven! What have I done to be treated in this way?" Philogone gasped, falling to her knees and imploring mercy. "O you who call yourself my father, if it be true that I am your daughter prove it by treating me more kindly; and you, my mother . . . my unhappy mother, must we be dealt the same blow at the very moment Heaven's hand guides us back to each other? Father! oh, my father, I have not deserved this fate! Spare me—"

But without even listening to these plaints, Carleson and I garrote the two sluts and, gathering us each a handful of thorns, we lash them as hard as we can. Wounds soon develop everywhere; no more is needed to straighten my prick anew; with incredible delight I lap the blood oozing from Philogone's lacerated body. It is my own blood, I reminded myself, and the idea added a further inch to my blinding erection. I savor that voluptuous mouth which opens only to implore me; I press ardent kisses to those eyes moistened by tears my fury causes to flow; and from time to time returning to my dear Clotilda's ass, I treat it with similar ferocity; then, clutching Carleson's to me, I devour it with caresses and suck his marvelous prick.

"We must place them in another posture," I declare.

We untie them and make them kneel; cords fixed to nearby trees maintain their arms in the air, heavy stones laid over their calves and ankles immobilize them completely. So placed, both expose their inspiring breasts to us. Nothing so fair, so lovely as Philogone's; Clotilda's, though a shade less firm, look still to be perfectly preserved. This sight brought my irritation to its climax. Oh, the pleasure to be reaped from severing the bonds uniting us to others! I have the two of them kiss my behind; I shit into their mouths, then, while buggering Carleson, I take hold of those breasts, lift them, and shave them all four off close to the chest; then, threading those chunks of flesh upon a string, out of them I compose necklaces for the two women; they are streaming blood and in that state are further wet by the last spurts of fuck which I ejaculate over their bodies while Carleson skewers my ass.

"That ought to do," I say; "we may leave them there, tied as they are: the animals of this island will be another three or four days finishing them off. Better that they die slowly than that, dispatched by us, they be deprived of the possibility of further suffering."

Carleson, who is exceedingly ferocious of character, was terribly eager to complete the work there and then so as not, he said, to be cheated of the pleasure of seeing the pair expire; but once I had convinced him that the course I proposed was the more villainous one, he gave in and we prepared to bid the ladies adieu.

"God in Heaven!" Clotilda groaned, "is this to what an original sin will lead us! Deep is my guilt owing to that monster, I admit it; but dear God, how severe is thy retribution!"

"Ha! This that we are hearing, good friend," say I to Carleson, "sounds very much like rebellion against the Supreme Being; let us avenge the God we so mightily revere, you and I. The blasphemer's punishment used to be to have his tongue cut out, justice must not be allowed to languish; furthermore, it is essential that these whores be prevented from talking."

And, going up to them, we force open their mouths and slice three inches off each of their tongues.

"Since they cannot speak any more," Carleson says to me, "there is no reason on earth why they ought to be able to see; let's gouge out the lovely eyes which once melted your heart. . . ."

And my prompt response to that wise proposal was to prick out Philogone's while Carleson blinded Clotilda forever.

"Well and good, so far as it goes; but," I ask, "might not the sluts bite at the scavengers that will be coming to feed on them?"

"They are surely apt to try."

"Then we must break their teeth."

For that operation we employ a stone; not wishing to damage our patients further, lest they be totally insensible to the ravages the wild creatures of the isle are soon to inflict upon them, we take our departure. A hundred paces brought us to a little hillock; from its summit we had a clear view of the thing. Owls, bats, all the beasts of prey that abounded on that island had already arrived: soon one saw nothing but a dark mass.

"Oh, my brave Carleson," I exclaimed, "what a spectacle! How comforting it is, to have wives and daughters of one's own to treat in this manner. And how sorry I am that I do not have a hundred other persons to feel just as close to: not one of them would escape me. Dear Carleson, see how the sight gladdens me; come, let me sodomize your peerless ass yet again while I watch."

I embugger, I frig my friend, and after having each discharged one last time, we head back toward the shore.

We had a little story ready for the captain; that and a few

sequins, nothing more was needed; and we landed at Naples on the third day after our Owl Island expedition.

Wishing to settle in Italy, I straightway inquired about land for sale in this fair country and purchased the estate upon which you see me dwelling today. But, rich though I was, I found it impossible to give up my brigand's vocation; it has too many charms to be abandoned, it too well suits my inclinations for me ever to be able to embrace some other; theft and murder have become the prime necessities of my life; I would simply cease to exist were I deprived of the pleasure of indulging in them every day. Here I exercise my honorable profession as of old great vassals used to do throughout the dominions that were theirs; I have a small army in my hire; Carleson is my lieutenant; 'twas he who arrested you on the road; 'twas he I left in charge when I journeyed to Paris to fetch my sister, with whom I was so eager to be reunited.

Despite the influence, the power, the wealth she enjoyed, Clairwil did not hesitate to leave everything behind in order to throw in her lot with mine; my dedication to crime appealed to her, she looked with favor upon the position I had attained for myself. Joining me, she counted upon being more than ever in a position to satisfy those fierce passions for which she is generally known. I remained three months in Paris while she readied her departure; then we returned together to this den of crime and infamy. Out of a mutual decision to reinforce our existing ties by whatever could consolidate them most intimately, we were married on our way hither, at Lyon; and our hope today is that no circumstance shall ever arise to separate two persons so admirably suited to each other, and who, notwithstanding their execrable penchants, will always make an exquisite and delightful duty of welcoming into their retreat and cherishing such sincere friends as yourselves.

"Oh, Juliette," asked Clairwil when once her brother had finished speaking, "do you find such a man a worthy partner for me?"

"He is, surely, most worthy of all those who are intelligent

enough to feel that the highest of all laws is the one bidding the individual to pursue his happiness, setting aside anything others may
say or think."

Borghese clasps us in her arms, we all exchange a thousand
more kisses. Borchamps, whom henceforth we shall call by no other
name, and Sbrigani seemed equally enchanted at making each
other's acquaintance; Elise and Raimonde congratulated themselves upon seeing this conclusion to an adventure whereof the
beginnings had caused them such keen alarm.

We were all in the midst of these gay effusions when a scout
entered to notify the captain that his riders were bringing in a
coach containing an entire family and much money.

"Excellent news," replied Clairwil's amiable brother; "these
persons, I trust, shall be material suitable to answer voluptuous
purposes, and as for the money, its arrival could not be more
timely, for if you are of my mind, our next step should be to spend
several months in Naples."

"Agreed," said Clairwil, squeezing my hand.

"Very well," Borchamps announced, "whatever funds this
capture brings me, I devote every penny to our trip."

At that point the prisoners appeared.

"Captain," said Carleson, who entered at the head of the band,
"today is indeed one for thanksgiving: this family is mine. Let me
introduce my wife," he continued, presenting a very attractive
woman of thirty-four. "These two girls," he went on, first indicating the younger, thirteen years of age and lovely to see, then
the other, fifteen, a creature before whom the Graces would have
paled from envy, "are out of my testicle. Here is my son," he
added, offering us a sixteen-year-old youth of most engaging
physiognomy. "Two words from me to acquaint you with this
affair; my wife may then explain the rest to you. Rosine is Danish;
seventeen years ago, I made a journey to Copenhagen, met her
there, and married her. I was then eighteen; hence, am thirty-five
now.

"This handsome lad, whom I named Francisco, was the first
fruit of our love; Christine over there," and Carleson pointed to
the girl of fifteen, "was the next; Ernelinde the last. Not long

after Ernelinde's birth came my adventures in Russia; certain political deeds saw me deported to Siberia, from where I made my escape before associating with Borchamps in Tiflis. Chance restores this beloved family to me, I present it to you, beseeching you to do absolutely whatever you please with it: I should like to prove to my captain that I am as little concerned as he by ties of kinship."

"Madame," Borchamps said to Rosine, "have the graciousness to satisfy our curiosity as regards the rest."

"Alas, my Lord," said the beautiful Rosine, "abandoned by that perfidious man I made do as best I could during the first year of his absence; then, having come into a considerable inheritance, I devoted part of my money to searching for my husband throughout France and, more recently, in Italy, where I received positive assurance he was to be found: I hoped for nothing more than to guide his children to the happiness awaiting them in their father's arms. What was my surprise when after all these years my first glimpse of him is at the head of a band of robbers. The monster! Such is the infamous trade he was plying while I, constantly attached to my duties, was, owing to his desertion, without even the bare necessities of life."

"Oh, this is touching, touching," murmured Olympia.[12] "Our friend Borchamps, I trust, will exploit these circumstances to the fullest...."

"Madame," Clairwil declared to the unhappy woman, "nothing in all you have just told us can exempt you from the common fate of those my husband's soldiers take prisoner. Pray tell, to what does it amount, the fortune you bring us?"

"One hundred thousand crowns, Madame," Carleson's amiable wife replied.

"One hundred thousand crowns," Clairwil repeated. "A paltry sum." Then, turning toward me: "Hardly enough to pay our rent in Naples."

"My friend," said Rosine, addressing her husband, "together with that I brought you my heart, and these children begot of your heart's ardor."

---

[12] It will be remembered that this is Princess Borghese's first name.

"Ah," said the lieutenant, "let's not bother over trifles; such gifts aren't worth a pipeful of tobacco."

"I'll be more generous in my estimate," said I to Carleson, whom I was beginning to behold with considerable interest; "the pleasures we await from these four delicious objects are not to be despised."

"We shall soon verify whether or not that is so," answered Carleson, who had already discerned much in my eyes; "but one thing is very certain, Madame, and that is that I believe there are few pleasures to rival what I await from you."

"Truly?" I replied, giving the agreeable fellow's hand a tender little squeeze.

"I'll wager it, Madame," said he, to my lips pressing a kiss that foretold of his capabilities; "yes, and I am prepared to repay you in kind."

"May I suggest that we dine," said the captain.

"With the whole family together?" the lieutenant asked.

"By all means," said Madame de Clairwil; "I wish to see them all there before sending them somewhere else."

Orders are issued and the most magnificent dinner is served. Seated beside me, Carleson manifested great eagerness to possess me and, I must say, I was just as strongly drawn in the same direction. His children were timid in this company, abashed; his wife tearful and lovely; everybody else gay and exceedingly libertine.

"Come," said Borchamps, nodding toward Carlson and me, "let's not make these two sweethearts languish any longer, they are fairly dying to come to grips."

"Yes," said Borghese, "but the scene must be public."

"She is right," Clairwil agreed. "Carleson, the assembly gives you leave to fuck Juliette, but that must be in its presence."

"But what will my wife and children think?"

"Why, bless me, whatever they like," said I, taking Carleson by the sleeve and leading him to a couch; "all the saints in paradise might be on hand, my dear, and I'd not have myself any the less fucked by you."

And, drawing a monstrous engine out of his breeches, "Pardon, Madame," I say to Rosine, "if I usurp pleasures which ought

by rights to be yours alone, but, fuck my eyes, I have been lusting
for your good man a little too long, and now that I've got hold
of him, serve me he shall." Those words were scarce out of my
mouth when Carleson's awesome prick had gone into the depths
of my womb.

"Look," said the captain, dropping his breeches, "was I
mistaken in claiming that my friend has the world's fairest ass?"

And, so saying, the bugger embuggers him, while Clairwil
kisses me upon the mouth and takes hold of my clitoris, and
Olympia thrusts three digits into my asshole.

"Captain," asked Sbrigani, ignited by this spectacle, "would
you care for a penetration? Think you not this prick you see is in a
state to satisfy you?"

"Fuck away, Sir, fuck away, my ass yawns," said the outlaw;
"but be so good as to palpate other asses while you stuff mine."

"Why, I shall post Elise's to my right, Raimonde's to my
left, both within easy reach," said Sbrigani, "and for your recreation, situate ahead of you that of the wife alongside that of the
husband you are fucking and those also of their three children."

The group is arranged, and in less time than it takes to tell
everybody discharges; and having voiced our determination to
squander no further fuck on such childishness, by unanimous agreement we advance to more serious orgies. For the sake of clarifica-
tion it behooves me to enumerate the participants in the drama.

I beg therefore to remind you that we were twelve: Borchamps, Sbrigani, Carleson, Clairwil, Borghese, and myself, those
were the six who assumed active roles; our patients included Elise,
Raimonde, Rosine, Francisco, Ernelinde, and Christine.

"Carleson," said Borchamps, uncovering the young Francisco's behind, "here is an ass to compete with yours, my friend,
and I feel I am about to offer it homage quite as pure as those
whereof yours has for such a long time been deserving from me."

And, while saying that, he was fondling, he was kissing, the
prettiest pair of buttocks, the whitest, the firmest you shall ever
behold.

"I am opposed to this arrangement," Clairwil protested,
" 'tis sinning against every law, divine and human, to prevent
Carleson from depucelating his own son: this child is going to

ass-fuck me, his mother will finger my cunt; and the father will embugger his son while Elise and Raimonde give him the whip and while he handles the buttocks of Juliette to his left, Borghese to his right, both of whom will be giving the whip to Carleson's two daughters, this before the eyes of Borchamps, embuggered by Sbrigani and assisting in the flagellatory operation being performed upon his lieutenant's two children."

The stage is set, the actors begin, the young Francisco, perfectly sodomized by his father, irreproachably sodomizes my friend; but her weeping attests to Rosine's misgivings as she lends herself to indecencies which appear to clash with her standards of behavior. During these multiple couplings, the captain, esteeming himself less than sufficiently integrated into the scene, takes it into his head, all the while he has Sbrigani's prick in his fundament, to grab the younger of Carleson's daughters; and, without the least preparation, the rake embuggers her, uttering oaths. The girl swoons; undeterred, the captain burrows deeper still, for he no longer encounters any resistance; the impression one has is that he means to split the wretch in two. Soon losing interest in her, he has at her sister; although fifteen years of age, she is so slender, so dainty, so delicate, that the introduction of Borchamps' gigantean member causes her vexations as keen and lesions as grave as those Ernelinde has just sustained. Nothing, however, halts the brigand's prodigious efforts: he presses, braces himself, lunges, strikes bottom.

"Oh, Carleson," he cries in his enthusiasm, "those are asses whereof you may be proud; rid me of these cunts, if you can, they're ready for you."

Clairwil's bowels, meanwhile, are washed by Francisco's fuck, and the rascal, starting forward as though electrified, in one swift, smooth motion unseats her rider, whirls, and comes to rest with the boy's prick lodged in her cunt, performing this acrobatic without the slightest disturbance to the father, who, throughout, is sodomizing his bewildered son. Carleson at last unlooses his fuck; and Francisco's ass becoming vacant, the captain, weary of females, promptly darts his prick thereinto, while I, swept away upon a wave of lewdness, rush up to lick this handsome man's ass, which I have been hankering to taste for hours. Carleson, perceiving his two daughters idle, encunts one of them while kissing the ass of the other and having himself flogged by Elise, whom Raimonde, by Sbrigani embuggered, frigs apace. New outpourings of fuck enjoin rearrangements. I am at last embuggered by the captain while his sister frigs me, and Carleson, frigged by Sbrigani, sodomizes his wife while ass-kissing his three children held by Elise and Raimonde, whose cunts the bawdy fellow frigs, Olympia opening those parts to his fingers.

"Oh, Borchamps!" I cried from where I was in the thick of the melee, "what pleasures I have from your prick, and how I desired it!"

"That will not prevent others from getting their share of it," the captain answered, catching Borghese by the waist and sodomizing her with a lunge; "my apologies, Juliette, but to this splendid ass belongs much of the credit for my erection ever since we removed our clothes, my thoughts were upon it while fucking yours, 'tis yours I shall now dwell upon while fucking this one."

Noticing Francisco spoiling from inaction, I single him out; my tastes are so odd, and the youth so fair, that I know not which sex to adopt with him. I suck him, devour his ass, I present mine to him, of his own accord he sodomizes me and I camp my cunt atop Rosine's face; at length, spirits are appeased by a further series of discharges, and the captain avers that after having paid so much attention to men, the general concern, in what is to follow, must be for the delectation of the women.

"Women deriving only mediocre physical pleasures from the use of such children, our best advice to them," said the captain, "would be to aim at mental enjoyments. Juliette, you'll begin. Carleson, reclining upon the sofa, must present you with a well-hardened prick: you will pose yourself gently upon that prick, taking good care that it enters your anus; Clairwil and Borghese will be frigging you, one of them your cunt, the other your clitoris —and let them not begrudge you this kindness, they will have pleasures in their turn—; while you are keeping yourself busy in this manner, Elise and Raimonde will be striking a wide variety of lewd attitudes for my delectation; the victims will now approach you, one by one, on their knees: first this loyal wife who has come from so far to bring gold and offspring to Carleson; his son next, then his two daughters; the same father will lead them forward; you will decree a torture for each of these individuals, but a mild and simple torture for a start: our entertainments are to last for quite some time, hence the procedure must be by degrees. I shall take note of the sentences you pronounce, and they will be executed the instant you have completed your discharge."

Positions are taken, but my wicked cohorts wait until my brain is reeling from pleasure before sending the victims up to me. Rosine appears first; I order her brought near; I examine her in minute detail and, finding her bosom superb, proclaim that her breasts shall be whipped. Francisco follows, I observe the beauty of his hinder parts, 'tis upon his buttocks the lash is to fall. Christine crawls forward, I condemn her to eat the turd of the first one among us who may happen to wish to shit. And the young Ernelinde, whose charming countenance affects me, will get a pair of slaps from each of us.

"Are you about to discharge, Juliette?" inquires Borchamps, whom my two tribades are overwhelming with obscene attentions.

"Yes, by Jesus, I can contain myself no longer—oh, Carleson, your prick is performing wonders!"

"There's the signal," says the captain; "let us carry out the first round of sentences. Borghese will judge next."

All the penalties I have imposed are undergone; but, by a wise decision, they are inflicted by some woman other than she who pronounces them. So it is Clairwil who, this time, puts my orders into effect, and as she is of a mind to be rid of the fuck deposited in her ass, 'tis her excrement Christine swallows. Ah, what ardor the whore then puts into fustigating Rosine's fair breasts; by the thirtieth stroke she has bloodied them both, and the vixen kisses the wounds her ferocity has opened; getting to Francisco's excellent ass, it is with undiminished fury the rascal lashes it.

"Your turn now, Borghese," says the captain. "I am in the hope," he adds, "that Sbrigani, realizing our need of his weapon, has not dulled it too soon."

"Let the sight cheer you," said Sbrigani, from my behind removing a stiff and unruly device and the next instant plunging it to the hilt in Borghese's ass, "and I shall proceed just as cir-

cumspectly with this one. Count upon it, captain, I'll not discharge
save in the last extremity."

Borghese sits in judgment; I become the executioner.

"Increased severity," says the captain, "remember, it's step
by step to lead them gradually to death—"

"To death!" exclaimed Rosine. "Just heaven! What have I
done to merit this?"

"Had you merited death, buggeress," said Carleson, sodomizing Borchamps, who nests in Raimonde's ass the while he tongues
Elise's; "yes, fuck my eyes, had you merited it, whore, we'd condemn you to something else. We here have the greatest respect
for vice and the mightiest abhorrence for everything resembling
virtue; firmly wrought principles found this way of thinking, and
with your approval, my dear, we shall not deviate a hairsbreadth
from our creed."

"Come along, Borghese, pronounce," said the captain, being
energetically fucked by his favorite.

"Rosine," the hot-tempered Olympia announced, "will receive
from each of us half a dozen pricks from a bodkin here and there
upon her person; the comely Francisco will have his buttocks
bitten by his father, his member by all the ladies; the executioner
will then administer twenty blows of a stick upon the back of
Christine and will break two fingers on each of Ernelinde's hands."

These punishments are begun by me: after having six times
run the needle-sharp instrument well into Rosine's plump breasts,
I pass it to my friends, who one by one wield it upon the most
sensitive areas of that beautiful body; her frightful husband distinguishes himself, 'tis inside her vagina the mischievous fellow
delivers his six stabs; I see to the rest, and I execute with art and
zeal enough to provoke everyone into a discharge. Clairwil replaces
Borghese.

"Increased severity, sister," the captain says, "don't forget
the goal we are working toward."

"Never fear," that harpy replies. "You will soon recognize
your kin."

Carleson returns to the sofa, over his mast-high device the
captain's sister hovers, slowly engulfs its length in her ass;

Borghese and I frig her amain, and she formulates troubles for our victims to endure.

"I would," says she, "that a hot iron be applied to the two breasts of the wife of him embuggering me at present; I would," the slut continued, ever ready to lose her head the moment she felt a prick tickling her entrails, "that four gashes be inflicted upon the pretty buttocks belonging to the youth whom my brother seems to be fucking while awaiting our verdict; I would have Christine's buttocks seared, and a rinse of boiling oil injected into Ernelinde's lovely ass, warming though may be the caresses I see Borghese bestowing upon it."

But then a very comical thing occurred: panic-stricken at the thought of the clyster intended for her, the girl let loose everything her bowels contained, flooding shit all over the floor.

"Blast me," stormed Borchamps, bestowing a tremendous kick upon the girl's behind, who all but flew out the window someone had just opened to air the room, " 'tis an outrage if the wretched little whore's throat is not cut on the spot."

"What the devil is the matter?" Clairwil demanded of her brother. "It's nothing but shit, and you love shit; would it be Juliette's you want instead? Come, have some then, my fingers feel her mard, she'll hatch it into your mouth."

"Bah, we're becoming a filthy lot," the captain jubilated, fitting his lips to my vent and soliciting what he has been put into hope of obtaining; "when you hear such words uttered, fuck is never far off."

I shit; would you believe it? He shits too, and 'tis into the mouth of Christine, whom he has had posted underneath his ass, the villain looses the broadside, simultaneously swallowing the dainty I produce for him.

"Your pleasures are indecent in the extreme," Clairwil observes the instant before she has Francisco perform the same operation upon her face.

"Ah, wench," her brother calls to her, "you're close to a yield of sperm, I can tell it from your infamies."

"Fuck!" she rejoins, "I wish to be stretched out on the floor, I wish to be rolled, to wallow in the nastiness that little jade has just spattered about."

"Are you mad?" Olympia exclaims.

"No, merely determined to satisfy my desires, as always."

Her wishes are obeyed, and it is while writhing in ordures the rascal is overtaken by her spasm.

The punishments are resumed; Borghese metes them out.

"Stay," says the captain, seeing Olympia pick up the iron due to char Rosine's breasts, "I must embugger this woman while you are torturing her."

He sodomizes; Olympia operates.

"God's prick and balls!" he cries, "how sweet it is to ass-fuck an object undergoing pain! Woe unto him who passes through life in ignorance of that pleasure! There is no greater one in Nature."

But her fear notwithstanding, at the hands of her father, who embuggers her first, Ernelinde receives the formidable remedy prescribed by Clairwil; everything else on the program is accomplished in like wise, which brings us around to fresh horrors.

Carleson, berserk, and ever aroused by my ass, which, says he, has been driving him to this distraction, lays hands upon his children; he beats them, whips them, fucks them, while we women frig one another opposite a spectacle which affords the idea of a wolf rampaging through a sheepfold.

"Up, wench," and it is Rosine who hears herself addressed by a Borchamps embuggering me and fondling the hindquarters of Olympia and of Raimonde, " 'tis your turn, whore, you are going to torture your children; Carleson, put the point of your dagger to the abominable creature's heart, and if she so much as wavers when told what to do, stab her straight to death."

Rosine is racked by sobs.

"A little self-control," Olympia advises; "signs of distress excite our cruelty. Weep, and it will go worse with you."

"Catch your elder daughter by the hair," Borchamps shouts at her, "and you, Clairwil, issue the orders; Borghese will follow you; the last word will be Juliette's."

"I decree," my friend said, "that the nasty creature chew blood from her daughter's bubs."

Rosine seems paralyzed; the point of Carleson's dagger pricks her skin; the unhappy mother obeys.

"Olympia, what is your will?"

"That she drip molten wax upon her daughter's buttocks."

Again, manifestations of stubborness; again, prods from the dagger; again, compliance on the part of the sorry Rosine.

"And you, Juliette?"

"Oh, I would have the girl given a general lashing by her mother, who shall lay on until she has drawn blood."

What difficulties before these instructions are finally carried out! At first, the strokes are so mild that they leave no trace behind; but Carleson's dagger has its stimulating effect, Rosine plies the whip in great earnest, and in due time she flays the skin off her daughter's ass. Comparable tortures are inflicted upon the others, each outdoing the other in horror. When my turn comes, one of my desires is that Francisco embugger the elder of his sisters while gashing his mother, and Borchamps, sodomizing me as I give that command, succumbs to its suggestiveness, inundating my bowels.

"Fuck my eyes," the captain swears, withdrawing from my fundament, his prick still up and purple, "enough of this, let's get down to business: we shall begin by binding these four individuals belly to belly, so that they compose, as it were, one and the same body."

"Very well, and now?"

"Let each of the eight of us, armed with a red-hot poker, belabor this carrion a little. . . ."

Then, after an hour of strenuous exertion: "Rosine, take this dagger," the captain says severely, "plant it in your son's heart; his father will hold him while you do—"

"No, barbarian, no!" that mother shrieks in despair. "No, 'twill rather go into my own heart—" and she would have ended her life had I not checked her arm in time.

"Slut, you shall obey!" roared Carleson.

And seizing his wife's hand at the wrist, he himself guides the blade into his son's breast. Clairwil, jealous at seeing herself excluded from the murder of this young man, she who only lives for masculine murders, snatches up a second knife and deals the wretch wounds a thousand times more grievous; Rosine is then stretched upon a narrow wooden bench, affixed to it, and then Borchamps would have Ernelinde open her mother's body with a scalpel. The child refuses; menaces follow. Terrified, bruised, bloodied, excited by the hope of saving her life by consenting, her hand, steered by Carleson's, yields to the barbarous instructions imparted to it.

"You received your existence here," says the cruel father once the opening has been made, "you must now return into the womb whence you emerged."

She is garroted, then pressed, twisted until by dint of much force and considerable art, there she is, breathing still, back inside the loins that once gave her to the world.

"As for that other one," says the captain, referring to Christine, "she must be bound to her mother's back. Wonderful, is it not," he observed when that had been done, "the insignificant volume to which three women can be reduced."

"And Francisco?" Clairwil wanted to know.

"He's yours," Borchamps answered, "take him into a corner and finish him off in whatever way you like."

"Come with me, Juliette," said Clairwil, leading the young man into an adjoining chamber.

And there, a couple of frenzied bacchantes, we cause that unlucky youth to expire under everything of the cruelest and most refined it is in the power of ferocity to devise. Returning from those exercises, Carleson and Borchamps found us so aglow with beauty that neither could resist tupping us straightway; but at this the jealous Borghese begins to fume, protesting that the victims are being left to languish, and the pleasures of torturing them being delayed. The point is well taken, and since the hour is advanced, it is decided that supper will be served while play proceeds.

"In that case," says Borghese, upon whom the right to prescribe punishment now devolves, having taken no hand in the tormenting and undoing of Francisco, "the victims must be disposed in front of us, flat on the table. The first of our pleasures will be derived from a view of the state they are already in, and this, I believe, is nigh to damnable; the second, from the effect of the further mistreatment they will sustain from us once they are there."

"Aye, set them on the table," says Clairwil, "but I want to fuck before I sup."

"But with whom?" I ask my friend. "They are all drained dry."

"Brother," the insatiable creature resumes, "have ten of the prettiest members of your armed forces brought in, and give them to us for employment as sluts."

The soldiers appear; we all three, Borghese, Clairwil, and I, defying the pricks lifting threateningly at us, fling ourselves down upon cushions scattered about on the floor. Elise and Raimonde act as our aides. Sbrigani, the captain, and Carleson sodomize one another while watching us, and during four great hours, to the sound of our victims' lamentations, the three of us fuck like the world's mightiest whores: our champions, winded and spent, are dismissed.

"What good is a man when he reaches the end of his erection? Brother," said Clairwil, "bring those ten louts back in here, where we can see it done, and have their throats cut this instant, if you please."

The captain issues instructions, twenty of his trusties seize the first ten, and the massacre goes forward while we frig one another, Borghese, Clairwil, and I. It is, so to speak, upon their corpses that a delicious collation is served to us. And there, naked, smeared with blood and fuck, drunk with lust, we carry our bestial ferocity to the point of mixing in our food those morsels of flesh we detach from the bodies of the unhappy women lying upon our table. Gorged on murder and impudicity, we at last all fall asleep amidst cadavers and a deluge of wines, spirits, shit, fuck, and bits of human flesh: I am not sure what happened after that. I simply recall that when I opened my eyes to the light I found myself lying between two cadavers, my nose in Carleson's ass, with whose shit my gullet was filled, and whose prick was wedged in Borghese's ass, where he had forgotten it. The captain, who had gone to sleep with his head pillowed on Raimonde's shit-slimed buttocks, still had his prick in my behind, and Sbrigani was snoring in the arms of Elise . . . the victims in pieces still lay on the table.

Such was the state in which the star of day found us out, and far from wondering at our excesses, never, I believe, did it smile so brightly since the world was born. Thus, you see, it is false that heaven condemns men's erring behavior, 'tis absurd to suppose heaven offended thereby. Would it accord its favors to villains as well as to honest folk if it were annoyed by crime?

"Why, no. No," I said to my friends who, that morning, were listening calmly while I exposed my thoughts, "we offend nothing by surrendering to crime. A god? How incur his displeasure when no god exists? Nature? Still less is Nature to be vexed by our misconduct," I went on, summoning to mind the moral science upon which I had been nourished, excellent fare. "Man is in no wise Nature's dependent; he is not even her child; he is her froth, her precipitated residue. No other laws govern him than those graved in mineral, in vegetal, in animal stuff; and when he reproduces, while he conforms to laws which are peculiar to him, he does nothing by any means necessary to Nature, nor by any means desired by her. Destruction more fully satisfies this universal mother, since it tends to restore to her a potential she is cheated of through our propagation. Thus, our crimes are pleasing to her, my friends, and our virtues are an affront; thus, atrocity in crime is what answers her most ardent desires; for he who were to serve her best would incontestably be him whose crimes through their number or magnitude destroyed even up to destroying the possibility of a regeneration which, perpetuated in the three kingdoms, only narrows Nature's capacity for further creative thrusts. Little fool that I was, oh, Clairwil! before we parted I was yet an adept of Nature; the systems I have absorbed since then have freed me from her, and moved me toward the simple laws of the natural realms. Having embraced these systems, ah, great dupes we must me, dear friends, if ever we deny anything to the passions, since they become the motor forces of our being, and we are just as unable to turn a deaf ear to their promptings as we are to be born again, or to return to being unborn. Indeed, these passions are so inherent in us, so necessary to the functioning of our inner workings, that their satisfaction becomes fundamental to our existence. Oh, dear Clairwil," I continued, taking my friend's hand warmly in mine, "the degree to which I am now these passions' slave! Oh, whatever they might be, how willingly I would sacrifice everything to them! This victim or that, how little must it matter! None more deserves to be spared than any other. If, according to popular prejudice, one existed which might seem to merit exception,

from the simple breaking of this curb my delights must increase:
I would interpret the excessive foretaste of pleasure as a command to act, and my hand would fly to do the bidding of my
desires."[13]

A striking instance of the rewards fortune almost always
lavishes upon great criminals now added its support to my arguments.

We had scarce come out of the scene of horror I have just
described when Borchamps' troops rode in with six wagonloads
of bullion that had been on its way to the Emperor, sent by the
Venetian Republic. Only one hundred men were escorting this
magnificent convoy when, in a mountain pass in the Tyrol, two
hundred of our captain's cavalry fell upon them and captured this
hoard after an hour-long battle.

"There I am, rich for the rest of my life," said Clairwil's
fortunate brother. "Notice, if you will, at what moment this happiness befalls us. 'Tis into hands soiled by wife-killing, infanticide,
sodomy, multiple murders, prostitution, and infamies that heaven
deposits this treasure; 'tis to reward me for these horrors heaven
puts it at my disposal. And you would have me doubt that Nature
is otherwise than honored by crimes? Ah, my thinking is not
likely to change on this question, and I shall go on committing them
forever, since the consequences are so encouraging. Carleson," said
the brigand, "before we begin the count, from the contents of one
of these wagons take a hundred thousand crowns, they're yours,
the gift testifies to the satisfaction I received from your courage
and purposefulness during the late scene for which you supplied
the actors."

Carleson kissed his commander's knees in thanks.

"I see no reason to hide it, fair ladies," Borchamps said
to us, "I am exceedingly fond of this lad, and when one loves, it's
with money you must prove it. At the beginning, of course, I supposed that the enjoyment would sooner or later pall; but it has
been quite the other way, the more I discharge with this delicious

---

[13] May these excellent principles, taking firm root in good minds, make an end
forever of the dangerous prejudices which are the cause for our regarding these
passions as enemies, when from them alone is born the only felicity we can hope for
on earth.

boy, the more attached to him I become. A thousand pardons, Mesdames, ten thousand, but 'twould perhaps not be the same thing with any of you."

We passed several more days in Borchamps' retreat; and then, seeing us eager to be off, he spoke to us as follows:

"My thought, good friends, was to accompany you to Naples, the prospect pleased me. But with the wish that is mine soon to quit my present calling, I ought to dedicate myself to business rather than pleasure. My sister will go with you to that noble town, and here are eight hundred thousand francs to defray the costs of your stay. Hire an appropriate mansion upon your arrival, give out that the three of you are sisters—as indeed one might be ready enough to believe, certain features in common create a kind of resemblance among you. Sbrigani will continue to look after your affairs while you make the most of the numerous sinful opportunities that magnificent city offers. Elise and Raimonde will be your chaperones. As for myself, I shall come to visit you if I can; amuse yourself, all three, and forget me not in your pleasures."

We left. I regretted Carleson, I admit it; I had, while a guest in Borchamps' castle, got myself prodigiously fucked by that pretty fellow, whose prick had been admirable, and it was something of a hardship for me to forego it. My feelings had nothing to do with love: I have never worshiped that god; the question was merely of the need to be well fucked, and nobody satisfied it better than Carleson. The obligation, moreover, to hide our activities in order to avoid displeasing Borchamps, very jealous of his handsome lieutenant, had lent an out-of-the-ordinary flavor to the enjoyment of him, and our last farewells were sealed by a mutual inundation of fuck.

Reaching Naples, we rented a superb house on the Chiagia quay, and passing ourselves as sisters, as the captain had advised, we gathered round us a royal entourage of domestics. First, we devoted a month to a careful appraisal of the morals and manners of this half-Spanish nation; we considered its government, its policies, its arts; its relations with the other nations of Europe. This study completed, we esteemed ourselves ready to sally forth into society. Our reputation as light ladies soon spread about. The King conceived a wish to see us; as for his wife, that spiteful woman did not look upon us with sympathy.[14] Worthy sister to her who had married Louis XVI, this arrogant princess, after the example of all the other members of the House of Austria, sought to captivate her spouse's heart solely in order to rule him politically; ambitious like Marie Antoinette, it was not the husband she cared about, it was the kingdom she wanted. Ferdinand, slow-witted, simple-minded, blind—in fine, a king, Ferdinand fancied he had a friend in that headstrong wife, when in fact he had only a spy and a rival, and the whore, like her sister, in devastating, in plundering the Neapolitan nation, toiled to the advantage of nobody except her Hapsburg tribe.

Shortly after our presentation I received a *billet* from the King of Naples, couched in these or very similar terms:

"To Paris, the other day, Juno, Pallas, and Venus were offered; he has made his choice, upon you he bestows the apple; come to receive it tomorrow at Portici, I shall be there alone; your refusal would disappoint me cruelly and gain you nothing. I shall therefore expect you."

A communication so despotic, so laconic, deserved the most straightforward reply; I made it verbally, and contented myself with assuring the page boy that I would be punctual. Once the messenger has left, I fly to tell my sisters this piece of good news. All three thoroughly determined to banish the least suspicion of envy from our relations, to adopt a lightsome attitude toward human folly, to wring profit from it, to laugh at it—Olympia and Clairwil besought me not to miss the adventure. And arrayed like that very goddess who had merited the apple, I spring into a coach-and-six which, a few minutes later, brings me to the gate of the royal castle, renowned for the ruins of Herculaneum upon which it stands. Mysteriously introduced into this house's most obscure apartments, I at last come to the King, nonchalantly reposing in a boudoir.

"My choice has created jealousies, naturally?" the fool says, speaking French with a villainous accent.

"No, Sire," I answer him, "my sisters noted this preference with equanimity, as did I, no more touched, in honor, not to be

---

14 The reader must think back to the period at which this was written.

included therein than am I by the vast honor you perhaps fancy it does me."

He stares. "A singular reply, bless my soul."

"Ah, though full aware that to please kings one must always flatter them, I, who in them perceive nought but ordinary mortals, never speak to them save it be to tell them the truth."

"But if that truth is harsh?"

"You wonder why they deserve to hear it? But why should they suppose themselves less entitled than other men to the naked truth? Because they have a yet greater need of it?"

"They dread it more."

"Tush. Let them then behave justly, let them renounce an empty pride out of which they strive to enslave men, and a liking for truth will replace their fear of it."

"But, Madame, such speeches—"

"They startle you, Ferdinand, I see it. You doubtless thought that, flattered by your choice, I was going to approach you on my hands and knees; that I was going to bow down before you, serve you. No; a Frenchwoman, the pride that my sex and nationality inspire in me lends itself ill to such usages. Ferdinand, if I have been willing to grant you the interview you solicited, 'tis because I consider myself perhaps a little better equipped to enlighten you regarding your veritable interests. So forget for a moment the frivolous pleasures you promised yourself with an ordinary woman, and listen to one who knows you well, who knows your kingdom still better, and who can, concerning these subjects, speak to you in a manner your courtesans do not dare."

Seeing that the King, slackjawed from surprise, bewildered, was paying all possible attention to me, I addressed him thus:

"My friend, you will permit me to dispense with those vain-glorious nicknames and titles which tell only of the impertinence in him who receives them and of the shameless baseness in him who mouths them; my friend, I say, I have lately been examining your nation with utmost care, and have found it extremely difficult to put my finger upon its genius; I have been studying it since coming to Naples, and I confess I as yet see nothing there. Nevertheless, I think I have detected the reason for the trouble I have been having. Your people have lost track of their origins; successive misfortunes, foreign domination after foreign domination, have left them limp, spineless, habituated to a slavery which has drained them of their one-time energy, rendered them unrecognizable. This nation, which sought liberators for so long, managed every time, through incredible blundering, to end up with another master. A great lesson for any people eager to break their shackles: let them learn from the Neapolitans' example that success lies not in imploring protectors, but in shattering the throne and laying low the tyrants who sit upon it. Every other people has used the Neapolitans to establish a power; they alone have remained weak-willed and listless. One seeks for the genius of the Neapolitans, and as in the case of every population accustomed to slavery, one encounters nothing but the genius of their sovereign. Be sure of it, Ferdinand, the faults I perceive in your nation are not so much hers as your own. But something more surprising still: the very excellence of your people's territory is perhaps the unique cause of their poverty: a more barren soil, a climate less mild, and the Neapolitans would have been forced to be industrious, and from meeting the challenge of adverse conditions they would have developed the vigor that eludes them owing to the fertility of their land. Thus it is that this fine country, with the advantages of a meridional location, is inhabited by a people who would be better off in the north.

"Since coming into your States I have looked everywhere for your kingdom, and all I discover is your city: a pit that swallows up all the wealth of the nation, and thereby impoverishes it. I cast an eye about this capital, what do I see? Everything ostentation and opulence can display of the most magnificent, and that cheek to jowl with the most afflicting evidence of indigence and idleness. On the one hand, noblemen living like kings; on the other, citizens in a worse case than serfs. And the vice of inequality everywhere, that all-destroying poison; and all the more difficult to root out, since the political order is built upon the enormous disparity between classes. Hereabouts, you either see men who own whole provinces or else drudges without even an acre; and between these two extremes, nothing. As a result, everything divides each man from his fellow. If these rich folk had some virtues, at least—but they arouse my pity, they make a dazzling show of themselves and possess none of the qualities which offset the ridiculous in such displays; they are proud without being urbane, tyrants without civility, magnificently appareled without elegance, libertines without any subtlety. In my opinion, they all resemble your Vesuvius: so many beauties before which one recoils. All their means for distinguishing themselves boil down to subsidizing convents and keeping actresses, to feeding horses, valets, and hounds.

"When in the course of my considerations I came upon your people's formal refusal to adopt the tribunal of the Inquisition, I was impressed favorably; yet, I realized, this did not make the Neapolitans one whit less weak, although they did something that calls for strength.

"Your clergy is accused of having accumulated great wealth. In my eyes, this is not something to blame them for: their greed, matching that of the nation's rulers, redresses the balance somewhat: the latter throw money about, the priests hoard it. When the day comes to seize the kingdom's treasures, one will at least know where they are to be found.[15]

"Closely analyzing your nation, I see that it contains but three estates, all three of them either useless or poverty-ridden: the people surely belong to that latter class, the priests and courtesans form the other two. One of the major shortcomings from which this little empire of yours suffers, my friend, is that in it there exists but one power to which everything else is subsidiary: the King, here, is the State; the minister is the government. As a consequence, no possible emulation save that to which the sovereign or the sovereign's agent gives rise—what greater flaw could any system have?

"Though Nature lavishes much upon your people, their circumstances are strait. But this is not the effect of their laziness; this general paralysis has its source in your policy which, from main-

---

[15] It has not come out so well with those peoples who, through a mistaken impulse of philosophy, thought they were destroying superstition when they pillaged its altars. What remains to them now? The same prejudice, and no more gold. The ninnies! Seeing not by what hand they were being manipulated, they fancied they were abolishing worship, and actually lent it strength; mean instruments of the rascals directing them, the poor fools fancied they were serving Reason, when they were only fattening swine. Religious revolutions are prepared by clever writings, by instruction, and end with the total extinction not of the baubles of religious stupidity, but of the knaves who preach and foment it.

taining the people in dependence, shuts them out from wealth; their ills are thus rendered beyond remedy, and the political state is in a situation no less grave than the civil government, since it must seek its strength in its very weakness. Your apprehensiveness, Ferdinand, lest someone discover the things I have been telling you leads you to exile arts and talents from your realm. You fear the powerful eye of genius, that is why you encourage ignorance. 'Tis opium you feed your people, so that, drugged, they do not feel their hurts, inflicted by you. And that is why where you reign no establishments are to be found giving great men to the homeland; the rewards due knowledge are unknown here, and as there is neither honor nor profit in being wise, nobody seeks after wisdom.

"I have studied your civil laws, they are good, but poorly enforced, and as a result they sink into ever further decay. And the consequences thereof? A man prefers to live amidst their corruption rather than plead for their reform, because he fears, and with reason, that this reform will engender infinitely more abuses than it will do away with; things are left as they are. Nevertheless, everything goes askew and awry, and as a career in government has no more attractions than one in the arts, nobody involves himself in public affairs; and for all this compensation is offered in the form of luxury, of frivolity, of entertainments. So it is that among you a taste for trivial things replaces a taste for great ones, that the time which ought to be devoted to the latter is frittered away on futilities, and that you will be subjugated sooner or later and again and again by any foe who bothers to make the effort.

"In view of its situation, your State needs a fleet for its defense. I have seen a few soldiers in your country, but not one warship. With this insouciance, with this unpardonable apathy, your nation foregoes the possibility of becoming the sea power which by all rights it ought to be, and as your forces on the land do not make up for your lack of a navy, you will finish by amounting to nothing. Expanding nations will laugh at you, and if ever a revolution were to regenerate some one or other among them, you will be rightly deprived of the honor of constituting a weight on the scales. Anyone at all could make you tremble, even the Pope if he cared to bestir himself.

"Well, Ferdinand! It is not worth dominating a nation if one rules it in such a way. And do you think a sovereign, even a despot, can be happy when his people do not flourish? Where are the economic principles in your State? I have searched for them high and low, and uncovered none anywhere. Are you promoting agriculture? Encouraging the growth of population? Protecting trade? Aiding the arts? Not only is there no sign hereabouts of anything others are doing elsewhere, but everything I see points in the opposite direction. The outcome of it all? Your pallid monarchy languishes in indigence; you yourself become a nullity in the concert of European powers; your downfall is not far off.

"Shall I examine your city from the inside? Shall I analyze its manners? Nowhere do I perceive those simple virtues that provide the bedrock to society. Company is kept out of snobbery, friendship goes on through habit, marriage is determined by material need; and as vanity is foremost among the Neapolitans' vices, a fault they acquired from the Spanish under whose heel they lived for so long; as, I say, pride is a vice inherent in your nation, its members prefer to avoid close scrutiny for fear lest the face of horror appear once the mask is removed. Your aristocracy, ignorant and stupid as it is everywhere else, brings disorder to its peak by placing its trust in lawyers, melancholy and dangerous breed swollen now to such ridiculous proportions there is practically no justice anymore. The little there is costs its weight in gold; and among all the countries I have visited, this is perhaps the only one where I have seen more wit exercised absolving a guilty man than is elsewhere devoted to justifying an innocent.

"I had imagined your court would offer me some ideas of polite behavior and gallantry, I see it contains nothing but boors or imbeciles. Weary of monarchical vices, I had the hope, in coming here, of finding a few antique virtues: instead, in your government I discover only the result of all the disorders to be encountered in the various kingdoms of Europe. Each individual, in your country, seeks to appear somehow larger than life-size; and as nobody has the qualities requisite to acquiring wealth, fraud is substituted for them; dishonesty thus becomes ingrained, congenital, and foreigners can no longer have confidence in a nation that has none in itself.

"After having glanced at the nobility, I take a look at your common people. Without exception, I find them uncouth, stupid, indolent, thieving, bloodthirsty, insolent, and possessing not a single virtue to redeem any of those vices.

"Do I wish, joining the two halves of the picture together, to contemplate this society as a whole? I behold a confusion of economic conditions; the citizen lacking the necessities of life taken up with useless activities; each man serving as amusement or spectacle to some other; indigence itself putting on grandiose airs that are the more revolting since, while horses draw its carriages, its cupboard at home is bare. One of the disastrous effects of the Neapolitans' taste for luxury is that, in order to have a coach and valets, three out of four of the best households avoid marrying their daughters; this frightful practice extends throughout all classes. Again, what happens? The population diminishes in direct proportion to the increase of luxury; and the State gradually sinks, the brighter the sheen it acquires by these vile means.

"But it is in your weddings and in your *takings of the veil* especially that this wastefulness becomes as preposterous as it is cruel. In the first case, you raid the luckless bride's dowry in order to embellish her for a day; in the second, you'd have enough to find her a husband if you did not spend it upon the ludicrous ceremony which is to deprive her of one for the rest of her life.

"Particularly, Ferdinand, it is that although your subjects are poor, you are rich. And you would be a great deal richer had your predecessors not sold the State piecemeal for great sums of silver. A State that has reciprocal commercial interests can bargain past rainy days; but a people who borrows from anybody and lends to nobody, a people who, in the article of trade, plays a lone hand against the whole of Europe, must inevitably become poor. Such is the history of your nation, my dear prince; all the others, having industry, make you pay the price for their goods, and your industry, practically at a standstill, wins you no customers.

"The amusing thing is that your arts reflect the puffed-up character of your people. Not a city on earth surpasses yours in operatic decorations; Naples is all tinsel and frippery, like its population. Medicine, surgery, poetry, astronomy are still in the dark ages here; but your dancers are excellent; and nowhere do we have such droll Scaramouches. In other countries they go to all sorts of lengths to become rich; all alone, the Neapolitan exerts himself only to look rich: his heart is less set on owning a large fortune than in persuading others he enjoys one, and his search is far less for opulence than for outward signs thereof. That is the reason why in this country there are so many people stinting themselves on essentials in order to have the superfluous. Meanness reigns at the most lavish banquets; culinary refinements are unknown; apart from your macaroni, what do they eat here that's good? Nothing: your countrymen are absolutely innocent of the voluptuous art of stimulating every passion by the delicious means of a subtle cuisine Everything is subordinated to the absurd pleasure of having a handsome carriage, expensive livery; along with the pomp and magnificence of modern times you have retained the frugality of the ancients—the contrast is unsightly. Your women are imperious and dirty, demanding and shrewish, without style and without conversation. In other climates, their commerce, though it spoils the heart, may at least improve the mind; here, the men do not even derive that latter advantage from them; the vices contracted in their society are mitigated by nothing; with them it's all loss, never any gain.

"However, one must be fair: there are some positive things to be said about your people. There is a basic goodness in them; the Neapolitan is quick-tempered, irascible, brusque, but his ill-humor doesn't last, and his heart, grievances once forgotten, is warm and not without virtues. Almost all the crimes committed here are rather the products of a thoughtless first impulse than of premeditation, that this people is not spiteful is proven by the great number of the Neapolitans, which is maintained without police. This people loves you, Ferdinand: show your subjects you love them in return, be capable of a great sacrifice. Christine, Queen of Sweden, abjured her crown through philosophy: break your scepter out of benevolence, relinquish the reins of a so badly organized government that enriches nobody but you. Remind yourself that kings are nothing in today's world, the common masses everything. Leave to this people the task of overhauling and refitting a ship which will never sail very far with you at its helm; let Naples live as a Republic: to the extent this race, and I have studied it well, makes for bad slaves, it will produce good citizens; liberate its energy by de-

934 ♣ THE MARQUIS DE SADE

livering it from the shackles of your power, that will be to accomplish two meritorious acts at one stroke: there will be a tyrant the less on the face of Europe, and one nation the more to admire there."

Ferdinand, who had listened to me with his best attention, asked, when I had finished, whether all Frenchwomen thus reasoned about politics.

"No," I replied, "and more's the pity: the majority of them are better analysts of ruffles and flounces than of the structure of kingdoms: they weep when oppressed, they are insolent once unchained. As for me, frivolity is not my vice; I'll not say the same for libertinage. . . . I am excessively addicted to it. But the pleasure of fucking does not blind me to the point of being unable to discuss the interests of the world's populations. In strongly made souls the passions' torch lights a Minerva as well as a Venus; burning with the latter's fire, I fuck like your sister-in-law;[16] illuminated by the rays of the former, I think and discourse like Hobbes and Montesquieu. Is it then, in your opinion, such a difficult thing to manage, an empire? So assure the people's welfare that nobody can envy you yours; then dedicate yourself unreservedly to this latter, which you can safely do, since human beings cease to be observant or restless when they are happy—that, it seems to me, is the whole secret, and I would have put it into practice long ago had I had, like you, the power and the foolishness to rule a nation. But mark you well, my friend, it is not despotism I forbid you, I am too familiar with its charms to deny it to you; I simply advise the suppression or the rectification of whatever jeopardizes or interferes with the maintenance of this despotism, if it is upon the throne you choose to stay. Render every sentient being happy if you wish to be so yourself; for the moment the crowd's enjoyments pale, be very certain of it, Ferdinand, the crowd will spoil your pleasures in its turn."

"And by what means?"

"Institute the broadest freedom of thought, of belief, and of conduct. Do away with moral impediments: the man with an erection wishes to act as freely as a cat or dog. If, as is done in France, you are going to appoint for him the altar upon which he must shed his fuck, employing absurdities to bend him under the yoke of a

---

[16] Marie Antoinette of France.

puerile morality, he will repay you in kind and with good measure. Such irons, forged to your order by pedants and priests, will be yours to wear ere long, and it may be that you'll carry them to the scaffold, for your erstwhile victim will have his revenge."[17]

"Your opinion, then, is that there must be no moral standards under a government?"

"None save those inspired by Nature. You will always render the human animal unhappy when you seek to subject him to any others. To him who has suffered the outrage leave the problem of obtaining redress, he will handle the business better than do your laws, for his interests are more closely involved; your laws, moreover, are frequently eluded, but the object of just revenge rarely escapes."

"Faith, all that is quite beyond me," the great simpleton confessed with a sigh. "I fuck, I eat macaroni without cooks, I build houses without architects. I collect medallions without antiquarians, I play at billiards like a lackey, I exercise my cadets like a drill-sergeant; but I don't talk politics, religion, ethics, or government, because I know nothing about any of them."

"And your kingdom?"

"Oh, it gets along, it gets along as best it can. Think you then that to be king one has to be so very wise?"

"Apparently not, for I must take you as proof," I replied. "But that is not enough to convince me that a leader of men can dispense with reason and philosophy, nor that, deprived of the one and the other, a prince like you can avoid blunders which will one fine day see your subjects up in arms and ridding themselves of an idiotic master. And this will come very shortly to pass unless you take every possible measure to prevent it."

"I have cannons, fortresses."

"Who mans them?"

"My people."

"When they weary of you, they'll turn the guns against your castle, take your fortresses and perhaps, who knows, drag you in the mire."

---

[17] It has been remarked that there were never so many police regulations, restrictive codes governing morals, etc., as during the closing years of the reigns of Charles I and of Louis XVI.

"You terrify me, Madame! What must I do?"

"I have told you. Imitate the experienced horseman: rather than shorten the bit when the charger rears, go softly with him, loosen the reins, let him have his head. Nature, disseminating peoples over all the surface of the globe, gave them all the intelligence necessary to run their affairs; but it was only in a moment of wrath she suggested the idea of saddling themselves with kings. These are to the body politic as a doctor is to the physical body: you may call him when you are ill, you must show him to the door once health returns, else he'll prolong the malady so as to be of eternal aid, and while pretending to cure, he'll bide with you to the grave."[18]

"Juliette, you reason forcefully, I like your conversation, but . . . confound it all, you overawe me; you have more wit than I."

"Which is to credit me with more than none at all. Never mind, Sire, since my wit frightens you, reason will yield for a moment to your pleasures. Come, what do you desire?"

"It is said that you have the world's prettiest body, Juliette, I should like to see it. This, perhaps, is not quite the language I ought to be employing, considering the manners you displayed at the time of your arrival in our midst; but I am not taken in by façades, my dear. I have informed myself about your sisters and you; although exceedingly rich, you are, beyond any doubt, thoroughgoing whores, the three of you."

"Your information is highly inexact, fair my Lord," I replied with vivacity, "your spies resemble your ministers, they steal your money without giving you service in return. You are in error; but no matter. For my part, I have no inclination to act the vestal. The question is merely one of coming to terms. I shall not make the capitulation any harder for you than it was for your brother-in-law, that little Duke of Tuscany. Now listen to me. While you are mistaken in considering us whores, if we are not so in fact, yet it is a certainty that for wickedness and corruption we cannot be easily outdone; you shall have the three of us, if you like."

"Truly," said the prince, "nothing pleases me more than to string beads an entire family at a time."

"Well, you shall have that satisfaction, and we merely ask, in

---

18 Not until the fatherland was in danger did the Romans name a dictator.

exchange, that you defray the expenses we shall be incurring in Naples over the coming six months, that you pay our debts if we contract any, and that you guarantee our total immunity, whatever may be the pranks we indulge in."

"Pranks?" Ferdinand wondered. "What kind of pranks?"

"Numerous, violent, beyond anything imaginable : my sisters and I do not stint ourselves where it is a question of crime, we commit all sorts and we do not wish to be punished for any of them."

"Granted," Ferdinand replied; "but endeavor to keep your depradations from becoming unduly noticed, and let neither my government nor my person become the target of your attacks."

"No, no," I assured him, "they'd not amuse us. Good or bad, we leave regimes as they are; and to the underlying people we leave the task of settling matters with their kings."

"All right," said Ferdinand, "we can now discuss pleasures."

"Did you not tell me you wanted to enjoy my sisters too?"

"Yes, but a beginning must be made somewhere. Let us therefore start with you." And, guiding me into an adjoining chamber, "Juliette," the Neapolitan went on, showing me a woman of twenty-seven or twenty-eight years, almost naked and lying upon a couch in an alcove paneled with mirrors, "they are this lady's passions no less than mine that you shall have to satisfy."

"Who is this person?"

"My wife."

"Ah, 'tis you, Charlotte," I say, "to be sure. I know you through your reputation : as whorish as your sisters, report has it, however, that you pay better. We shall see."

"Juliette," Ferdinand interjected, "if you wish to have me favor your desires, you must, toward the Queen, show utmost consideration."

"All she has to do is say what she wants : the resources of lewdness, I possess them every one, there are none I am not ready to employ."

And that was when Charlotte of Lorraine, throwing her arms around my neck, gave me to understand, by a thousand kisses, how alive she already was to the pleasures I promised her. Ceremony was laid aside: Ferdinand undressed us both. Then, there having been fetched in a page boy of some fifteen years, a delight to behold, whose clothes the King also removed, Charlotte and I frigged each other upon the couch while, from where he had a clear view of our doings, Ferdinand, polluted by the page, kissed the boy's mouth ardently, at the same time fingering his behind.

Oh, my friends! What 'a woman that Charlotte was! Impudicity had established its hearth in that royal whore's cunt; Charlotte, her thighs entwined with mine, rubbed her clitoris against my clitoris, frenziedly; her hands roved over my buttocks; one of her fingers tickled my asshole; her tongue, stuck far into my mouth, lapped thirstily at my saliva; the wench was all ablaze, fuck fairly leaked from her pores. I engage her to change positions; her head slips between my thighs, mine between hers, and we suck altogether at our ease. Oh, how willingly she repays me for what I yield to her mouth; if my cunt floods her throat with sperm, her frequent ejaculations send rivers of delight into mine. When we had shed our fuck to the last drop she besought me to piss into her mouth; I asked the same of her, we poured urine into each other, swallowing it as it flowed.

Charlotte is beautiful, her skin is very white, her breasts high and firm, her buttocks admirable, her thighs of marvelous proportion; 'tis plain that she has much fucked and in every conceivable manner, but she is well preserved all the same, and her openings are still very narrow.[19]

"Oh, my love," I said to her, truly moved by her charms, "let us exchange more serious blows."

"Here is what you need for that," spoke up the King, tossing us a pair of dildoes. And having each donned that equipment, we set to smiting each other with greatest energy. At one point in our capers my ass was directly in front of Ferdinand; he examines it, covets it, covers it with the most heated kisses.

"Stand where you are for a moment and steady your movements," he says to me, "I mean to embugger you while you fuck my wife. You, Zerbi, frig my behind."

The scene lasts several instants, at the end of which the prince, having his wife exchange places with me, buggers her while she fucks me; a moment later, he has her sodomized by the youth, I

---

[19] This sketch was done from nature.

tongue her cunt, and he at last discharges into the bowels of the page who is cuckolding him.

After a brief interval of rest employed in kissing, in fondling one another, we started in anew. Ferdinand fitted himself into my ass, he sucked Zerbi's, had the boy shit into his mouth, and his wife beat him; a minute of this and he retired from my bum, took the switches and beat the three of us rather severely; the Queen then wielded them upon my hindquarters, flogging was one of her passions, she kept at it until my blood flowed; she sucked the page's prick while her husband ass-fucked her and she kneaded my behind. A little while later we surrounded Ferdinand, I sucked him, his wife socratized him, palpated his balls, and the page, straddling his chest, gave the King of Naples his asshole to lick; he got up from that with a fierce erection.

"I don't know why we shouldn't wring that little bugger's neck," said he, collaring his page and squeezing shrill screams from him.

"Hang him," said Charlotte.

"Dear girl," said I, kissing that charming person, "would you have a fondness for cruelties too? Ah, I adore you, if 'tis so. Yes, I can see it, you would be capable of that trick of the Chinese empress, who fed her goldfish on the genitals of the children of the poor."

"Oh yes, I shall imitate that horror when called upon; and I am capable of worse yet. Infamies, Ferdinand, let's perform infamies, this woman is delightful, she has wit, character, imagination; I believe she shares our tastes. Here, my friend, be Zerbi's executioner, and let us all remember that an individual's destruction is the most potent stimulant one can add to the charms of sensual debauchery. Hang Zerbi, dear husband, hang him short; Juliette will masturbate me while we observe the operation from close on."

It is carried out: Ferdinand hangs the page up with such skill, dispatch, and violence that the boy expires before we have time to get properly started.

"Alas," Charlotte grumbles, "unlucky creature that I am, I postponed my spasm until I could watch him die. Never mind, Ferdinand, cut him down; dead as he is, guide his hand, I want to be frigged by it."

"No," says the King, "Juliette will undertake that chore; I shall embugger the cadaver in the meantime; they claim there is nothing better in the world, I must try it. Oh, sweet fuck!" he cries, once lodged in that ass, "this pleasure is everything it is reputed to be. What a grip to a dead anus! 'Tis divine."

The scene goes forward; Zerbi does not come back to life, but his slayers die of pleasure. Charlotte, for one last discharge stretched out naked upon the page's already cold body, and while her husband frigged her, she had me shit in her mouth. Four thousand ounces[20] was my fee, and we separated with the promise to meet together soon in more numerous company.

Once home again, I tell my sisters about his Sicilian Majesty's odd tastes.

"Wonderful, is it not," Clairwil remarked, "always to find such passions lodged in the brains of those whom Nature has made outstanding through the gift of intelligence, wealth, or authority."

"It strikes me as perfectly understandable," said Olympia, whom we called by no other name, fearing lest her real one be recognized, "no, I tell you, I know of nothing more natural than that the most refined forms of pleasure-seeking be conceived by those endowed with the finest powers of discernment, or by those whom despotism or the favors of fortune place on a superior level. A man with much intellect, much power, or much money cannot possibly amuse himself the way everybody else does. Now, if he refines his pleasures he must inevitably arrive at murder, for murder is the ultimate excess of pleasure: voluptuousness dictates it, murder is a branch of erotic activity, one of its extravagances. The human being reaches the final paroxysm of delight only through an access of rage; he thunders, he swears, he loses all sense of proportion, all self-control, at this crucial moment he manifests all the symptoms of brutality; another step, and he is barbaric; yet another, and he has killed; the more intelligent he is, the more he will refine his gestures and proceedings. One obstacle will nevertheless continue to impede him, he will fear either the extreme costliness of his pleasures, or the law; deliver him from these silly terrors by means of gold or authority, and you have launched him into a career of crime, because impunity reassures him, and because noth-

---

[20] The ounce is worth eleven *livres* ten *sous*.

ing daunts a man when along with the mind capable of conceiving anything there are combined the means to undertake everything."

"Well," said I to my friends, "we are all three in that enviable case; for over and above the immense wealth we possess, Ferdinand guarantees us the most entire impunity."

"Fuck," said Clairwil, "how that agreeable certitude inflames my passions! . . ." And the hussy drew up her skirts, spread her legs, inserted her fingers between her labia and offered us a vermilion and panting cunt which seemed to be calling all the pricks in Naples to combat.

"I hear the engines are superb in these parts," she went on, "we must make some arrangements with Sbrigani in order not to miss any."

"I finished attending to all that yesterday," that charming man declared, "I have put twelve purveyors into the field and shall see to it that two dozen pretty lads between the ages of eighteen and twenty-five are regularly presented to you every morning; I shall also see to the verifications; if in spite of my rigorous specifications any shoddy specimens happened to be included in the deliveries, they would be weeded out, rejected—"

"What were the sizes you ordered?" asked Clairwil, whom Raimonde was now frigging.

"You will never be given anything under six inches in circumference by eight in length."

"For shame, Sbrigani! Those dimensions may be good for Paris, but in Naples, where monsters grow. . . . For my part, I do not intend to accept anything less than eight inches around and a foot long."

"Neither shall we," Olympia and I declared, almost simultaneously; "we may end up with fewer, but we shall have better—"

"Fewer!" cried Clairwil. "I see no reason to reduce the number. To the contrary, in addition to quality I demand quantity. Therefore, Sbrigani, I shall ask you to furnish us thirty men each morning, and with the proportions I cited a moment ago: that will give us ten apiece. Let's say we get three fuckings out of each— that, surely, is not asking too much; and which is the one among us who is unable to ride ten mounts into the ground before drinking her breakfast chocolate? She who speaks assures you that getting off to an early start will not prevent her from accomplishing some startling little infamies in the course of the day; indeed, 'tis only by a good deal of fucking one puts oneself in proper fucking form; and for what else but to fuck did Nature create us?"

And, pronouncing these last words, the spirited creature discharged where she lay in Raimonde's arms.

"While waiting for me to fill your prescription," said Sbrigani, "see whether these six valets please you; I believe they exceed the measurements you have just indicated."

Thereupon appeared six great strapping fellows nearly six feet tall, half-naked, and prick in fist.

"Bloody-fuck," exclaimed Clairwil, her skirts still gathered up around her waist, "what members I see. Here, let me heft them"—but her two hands were not enough to encircle any of those bludgeons—; "they are bulky, my friends. Take your choice; these are the two I am keeping."

"One moment!" cautioned Sbrigani. "Permit me to regulate your pleasures, they will be better directed by someone who is calm than by you, fuck-blinded already."

"He's right, he's right," Clairwil assented, nevertheless pulling off her clothes in great haste, "let him arrange, let him organize. While he does, I shall be getting myself ready."

"Clairwil, you shall begin," said Sbrigani, "you seem in the greatest hurry."

"That is only too true," our companion confessed, "I don't know what it is about the air in this city, but it makes me more libertine than ever."

"Filled with nitrous, sulphorous, and bituminous particles," I replied, "it must necessarily irritate the nerves and produce a greater than ordinary commotion in the animal spirits. I too feel that I am going to behave atrociously here in Naples."

"Although I ought to be more accustomed to it than you," said Olympia, "Naples and my native city lying not very far apart, even so, like you, I am dreadfully overwrought in this atmosphere."

"Then make the most of it," said Sbrigani, "fall to, whores, and count upon me to lend a helping hand. This then," he continued, "is the arrangement I recommend for the opening scene: Clair-

wil, I repeat, will begin; though burning to be fucked, I want her
sincerely to desire the engine that is to pierce her. Juliette, take this
handsome prick your friend has already chosen, frig it in the near
vicinity of her cunt, rub her clitoris with the tip, but don't drive it
in. You, Olympia, lightly tickle the entrance to the patient's cunt;
tease it, warm it, infuriate it, and when rage flames in her eyes,
we'll satisfy her, but she must be lying in one of these young gentlemen's arms: the while he supports her, the brave fellow must frig
her asshole with one hand, her nipples with the other, and he must
kiss her in the meantime, lewdly. Further to arouse our friend's
senses, we shall have her, with either hand, stuff a prick into Raimonde's cunt and into Elise's, where they will merely gather heat
for a moment; the two remaining youths will encunt the two of you
before Clairwil's eyes, to complete the tumult we wish to create in
her soul."

Indeed, five minutes of this was all the rascal could stand; she
foams at the mouth, she curses, she raves, and seeing that it is becoming impossible to defer satisfying her any longer, the six valets,
in the space of less than an hour, relay one another atop her body
and almost kill her with pleasure. Directly it emerged from our
friend's cunt, Olympia and I would worry and squeeze each prick;
Elise and Raimonde frigged us, flogged us, titillated us, licked us.
Sbrigani orchestrated all these movements, and we discharged like
fieldpieces. Every manner of fucking, every species of debauchery,
all imaginable refinements were put into practice; among them, the
one we employed the most frequently and to best purpose was to
receive three pricks simultaneously, two in the cunt, one in the ass.
Few people realize the pleasure this can give, with adroit fuckers;
there were several times when everybody forgathered upon a
single woman. Thrice did I withstand the weight of that general
assault. I was lying upon one man who was embuggering me; Elise,
squatting over my face, gave me her pretty little cunt to suck; another man embuggered her above me, while frigging my cunt; and
Raimonde was stimulating that man's asshole with her tongue.
Within reach of my two hands were Olympia to one side, on all
fours, Clairwil to the other side: I introduced a prick into the
asshole of each, and each of them sucked a prick belonging to the

fifth and sixth man. The six valets, after having discharged eight times each, were finally received without difficulty. It was impossible to refuse them admission after such ordeals.

A week or so after this adventure a courier brought a new invitation from Ferdinand, who requested all three of us to come to visit him at Portici. The King, we saw, had intended that this be a far more brilliant scene than the first one. We were led into magnificently decorated apartments, deliciously cool despite the heat outside. Charlotte, attired like Flora, was awaiting us in the company of Prince La Riccia, a' handsome fop of twenty-four, who was the familiar of all the royal couple's private pleasures. A quartet of pretty children, two little girls of ten and eleven, two little boys of twelve and thirteen, dressed as the Greeks were wont to costume their victims in ancient days, stood still and in respectful silence at a farther side of the room where the festivities were to be celebrated. Clairwil's noble and majestic figure, the classic regularity that distinguished her features although she was no longer in the first blush of youth, the excessive libertinage in her eyes—the Queen of Naples was impressed by it all.

"There," she affirmed, "is a beautiful woman indeed."

And as with creatures of our libertine temper it is always but a single step from encomiums to caresses, the two wenches were soon in each other's arms. La Riccia lays hands on Olympia, and I continued to be the King's favorite.

"Before acting in concert," said Ferdinand, "my suggestion is that we first move off two at a time, paired as we are, into the boudoirs adjoining this room. After a few minutes of intimate conversation we shall convene again."

Charlotte sets the example; followed by Clairwil and with one of the two little female victims in tow, she enclosets herself in a boudoir. La Riccia selects one of the little boys and disappears with Olympia; to Ferdinand remain two children, one of either sex, and he shuts himself up in privacy with them and with me. And now the Neapolitan's heavy-handed, dull-witted libertinage is revealed in all its energy. But just as a few rays of sunshine will sometimes pierce the gloomiest clouds, bringing cheer to mortal hearts, so it was that some rather pretty nuances of lubricity made their way through the masses of awkwardness characterizing that oaf's behavior.

After some brief preparatory horrors in which each of us indulged individually with the subjects taken along for that purpose, we all collected in a superb salon; and there, having heated one another's imaginations with detailed accounts of our late infamies, we plunged forthwith into a new ocean of lewd doings, and executed, unrestrictedly, everything that derangement could inspire in minds so libertine and mischievous as ours. Physical exhaustion alone brought these voluptuous orgies to an end, and we took leave of their Highnesses.

Upon our return we found Sbrigani wounded and in bed. Insults had been pronounced within his hearing, their object had been ourselves; the exchange had taken place in a café, a Frenchman who claimed to know who we were had called us whores. Although in point of fact it would have been hard to say anything truer, Sbrigani, out of attachment, had stoutly refused to admit it, and for his lies the foolish fellow had got himself two good sword-thrusts in the belly.

After having tended his cuts, our conversation had naturally to treat of dueling.

"Bah, sheer madness," Clairwil opined, "to go and risk one's life in single combat with someone who did decidedly wrong us. If this man," our friend continued, asking our leave to put herself temporarily in the position of a sex whose functions she was so able to perform when called upon, "if, I say, this man has been essentially disrespectful toward me, how is it that I owe him such a favor as to consider him a fit adversary to measure myself against? And why must I put myself in a position from which, injury added to insult, I may emerge hurt, crippled, nay, from which I may not emerge alive? After all, I am the one to whom reparation is due, and to obtain it, what! I must endanger my life? If I adopt another comportment, or, going to fight with this man, since fight I absolutely must, I pad my chest and so ensure my safety that my opponent is obliged to give all his care to defending himself and must renounce any hope of insulting me again, if, I say, I behave thus, I shall be called a scoundrel—and the logic that comes forth here, ah, I would be hard put to think of anything that so flies in the face of common sense.

"Let him who has done the insulting arrive naked at the dueling ground, and let the insulted party come there in armor—that is what reason and the laws of good sense demand. The aggressor must obviously be placed at a disadvantage: through his acts he has, following the customs which prevail everywhere else on earth, earned himself assassination at the hands of the person he has slighted; hence, in such a situation, the frivolous rules of honor can be trimmed down to prescribing simply that the fight you so earnestly want take place, but with a prodigious inequality between the combatants; and that the offending party, instead of endeavoring to cause yet further damage, be prevented from concerning himself otherwise than with the problems of strict self-defense. For what right has he to attack a second time, after what he has already done? Our usages, in this article, are atrociously unjust, and make us the laughingstock of those other three-quarters of the world where they are wise enough to understand that, when you are finally driven to the point where you must avenge yourself, you should do it without imperiling your life."

"Our views upon this matter concur," I replied to Clairwil, "and I, who also hold dueling both absurd and ridiculous, can but add to what you have just said. I find it odious that a man go and jeopardize his life because of an insult: in such instances, reason and Nature dictate only one course to us, which is to dispatch our enemy, not to expose ourselves to being killed by him, when it is reparation he owes us. Our forefathers, far wiser than we, fought by proxy; champions, in return for a fixed sum, came forward to settle the quarrel, and the might of the stronger made him right: that arrangement at least eliminated the unfairness of having to undergo risk oneself, and although to that usage no end of extravagance and nonsense attached, it was infinitely less unacceptable than the one we observe nowadays. But here is the ludicrous part: the professionals who used to fight on behalf of others were generally regarded as vile persons; we today have taken their place, and risk opprobrium, think of it! if we shun the role of despicable individuals. What furious inconsistencies are these! Going back to the origin of things, we see that, first of all, these champions were merely hired assassins, such as you still meet with in several cities in Spain and Italy, whom the offended man engaged to rid him of his enemy, and that, next, to mitigate the kind of murder this custom seemed to authorize, the accused was allowed to defend himself against the assassin hired to kill him, and to employ an assassin of his own, and send him into the lists. Such was dueling in its infancy, whose cradle was the wise law permitting any man mortal vengeance upon his enemy. That excellent practice has given way to license, has been replaced by a stupidity which distorts the ancient institution, and which makes common sense shudder. And so, let not the man who has an enemy and who has some intelligence rush off and fence with him on an equal footing, for it is perfectly ridiculous to stoop to the level of somebody who has lowered himself beneath you. If the offended party must absolutely fight, well and good; but let him, in advance, take every precaution to avoid sustaining further hurt; and if he wishes to use his head, let him use assassination which, as Molière says, is the safest way.

"As regards those who place the point of honor there, I find them at least as ridiculous as those who fancy it is to be placed in the virtue of their wives; both are barbarous prejudices and do not even deserve cool-headed discussion. Honor is a chimera, bred by certain human customs and conventions which have never had anything but absurdity for basis; it is just as false that a man acquire honor through assassinating his country's enemies as it is false that he dishonor himself by massacring his compatriots; never can like proceedings warrant unlike consequences: if I do well in going forth to avenge my nation for the wrongs it has endured, I do better still when I avenge myself for those done to me. The State, which retains in its year-round hire some four or five hundred thousand assassins to serve its cause, can neither naturally nor legitimately punish me when I, following its example, pay one or two to revenge me for the infinitely more real insults I may receive from my adversary; for, after all, insults addressed to this nation never affect its members personally, whereas those I have received decidedly do touch me directly; and therein lies a very great difference. But let someone dare say such things aloud: society damns him straight off for a coward, a poltroon, and the reputation for wit or wisdom he has built up over the years is taken away from him in three minutes by a few miserable whippersnappers, humorless imbeciles whom a few prudes, fit to be spanked in the streets, have persuaded that there is nothing finer than to risk one's life when one has the right to take the lives of others."

"My position on dueling squares wonderfully with yours," said Olympia; "and I do not believe I have given you grounds for mistaking me for one of those mentally deficient women whose opinion of a man is dependent upon his willingness, because of an alleged slight, to hie himself off to a corner of a meadow and ape the vile gladiator. I have only scorn for your bravoes and fellows of fire. Combativeness may be delicious in a flunkey or a soldier, good for nothing but to be out bloodying noses all day long. But that a man of parts, of means . . . that he abandon his studies, his comfort, to go and bare his throat to a bully without any other talent than for plying a hanger, and who only insulted him because he knew he could run him through. . . . Stake one's honor upon bravely bringing such rascals to heel. . . . What a contemptible fellow one must be to venture into such situations! Aye, contemptible: there is baseness in giving others an advantage over oneself, and in risking the loss, for one instant and for nothing, of all the amenities, of all the favors one has received from Nature. Let us leave this preposterous merit to the uncouth ages of knight errantry; it is not to play the ruffian like a vulgar trooper that gifted people are made, 'tis to honor and cultivate the arts, to encourage them, to serve the homeland when necessary, and to sacrifice for nothing less the blood that flows in their veins. When a man of that condition has an enemy who is his inferior, let him have him assassinated: Nature hints at no other means for getting rid of such encumbrances; if he has been offended by someone of his own rank, let the two take their complaints before a lenient tribunal, set up for such arbitrations, and let the dispute be judged there: between people of the better sort there are no jars that cannot be settled amicably; he who is in the wrong must yield, 'tis the law. But blood . . . blood shed on account of a stray remark, a jealousy, a quarrel, a persiflage, a rebuke: revolting anachronism. The duel was unknown until the principles of honor displaced those of vengeance, and, consequently, was accepted only once men became civilized. Never did Nature grave it in the human heart to seek vengeance for an offense at the risk of one's life; for it is in no wise just, neither is it natural to expose oneself to a second blow merely because one has been dealt a first. But it is very equitable, very commendable to wash the first away in the blood of the aggressor, without risking the loss of any of one's own, if he is our inferior, and to reach a peaceful settlement with him if he is our better or our peer. There is no reason to be taken in by the courtesies of women touching this matter; it is not bravery in a man they desire, it's the triumph their pride obtains from being able to say that such-and-such a lout has carved up rivals for their charms. Nor is it by means of legislation this odious usage is to be extirpated; once there are laws there is restlessness, opposition, bitterness, and nothing is gained. 'Tis beneath ridicule, this lamentable custom must be buried. All women must shut the door to a dueling scoundrel; he must be snubbed, jeered at, fingers must be pointed when he goes by, at the sight of him everyone must cry, 'Ho, there's the wretched fellow base enough, craven enough, to adopt the vile part of a champion, and who was fool enough to think that words which the wind wafts away, or cuts which sting but for a moment, were to be acquitted at the price of a life, which is to be enjoyed only once. Avoid him; he is mad.' "

"Olympia is right," Clairwil said, "that infamous prejudice will be felled in no other way. The objection may be brought forward, that martial courage will fade out of hearts once its exercise ceases. This is quite possible; but I assert that courage is a dupe's virtue, and declare that I prize it very little: I have never seen anyone but fools being brave. The second Caesar was a very great man, no doubt of it, yet he was afraid of his shadow; Frederick of Prussia had a good mind and many talents . . . and had a bout of fever whenever the time came to fight. All the illustrious men who trembled in their boots, the list would be endless; the Romans even revered fear, they raised altars to it. Fear, in short, is in Nature, it is born of the innate concern for personal safety, that is, for self-preservation, a concern one cannot possibly not have, so deeply is it graved in us by the Prime Mover which cast us into the world. To disesteem a man because he fears danger, 'tis to hate him for loving life. For my part, I protest to you that I will always have the highest regard for a man who dreads death; that fact alone proves to me that he possesses a brain, an imagination, and a capacity for pleasure. The day the whole of Paris castigated La Luzerne for having assassinated his adversary on the dueling grounds, that was the day I wanted him on my belly: I have beheld few more amiable mortals, and probably not one whose mind was so attractively organized."

"Only they are appealing," I put in; "the higher an individual rises above prejudice, the better his mind becomes: the man hemmed in by narrow moral principles, necessarily infertile and dull, will be as insipid as the maxims he professes, and since with the kind of imagination Nature gave us, we will derive nothing from his society, we should keep carefully away from him."

After a few days, Sbrigani's condition showed to be much improved.

"He has just fucked me," Clairwil told me, "I took his pulse and I can assure you he is in good health: a throbbing prick is the best test of it, and I am still wet with his sperm. . . . So listen to me, Juliette," that incredible personage continued, "is it true that this man exists in your affections?"

"He has rendered me many services."

"He has only done his duty, you pay him for that. Is your soul beginning to open to the mighty principles of gratitude?"

"No, not yet, upon my honor."

"Well, you see, I for one don't like him, this Sbrigani; what's more, I don't trust him. That man will end up robbing us."

"Say rather that you are weary of him because he gave you a good fucking and because you cannot abide a man once he has discharged in your cunt."

"That one has never fucked me anywhere but in the ass—look at it, it's still leaking what he pumped into it."

"Out with it, silly, what are you driving at?"

"At ridding ourselves of that bugger."

"Do you forget that he faced death for us?"

"I certainly do not forget it; and there's one reason the more for detesting him, since his act illustrates stupidity."

"Again, what do you propose to do with him?"

"Tomorrow he will take a last spoonful of medicine; the day after that, we bury him."

"Have you anything left of those charming drugs we bought together from Durand long ago?"

"A pinch of this, a pinch of that. . . . I'd like to have your Sbrigani taste a few of them."

"Ah, Clairwil, your behavior gets no better with the years, you shall always be a great rogue. But what will sister Olympia say?"

"Whatever she pleases. When I have the urge to commit a crime, my heart is dominated by something else than concern for my reputation."

I consented; could I coldly turn my back upon crime? So precious to me was anything bearing its stamp that I could not refrain from embracing it immediately. I had used that Italian, more out of need than from love. Clairwil promised to take care of all the details of day-to-day management that had been entrusted to him: Sbrigani's usefulness came therewith to an end: I endorsed his destruction. Olympia made no fuss. On the following day, poisoned by Clairwil herself, Sbrigani went off to inform all the demons in hell that the wicked spirits existing in a real woman's body are a thousand times more dangerous than those with which priests and poets array Tartarus. This operation concluded, we set out on a tour of the surroundings of Naples.

Nowhere in Europe does Nature attain such imposing expression, such splendor as in the environs of this city; 'tis something utterly different from that melancholy, uniform beauty of the Lombard Plain, which produces a certain torpor in the imagination. Here, to the contrary, everything quickens it: the convulsions, the volcanoes, of this everlastingly *criminal* Nature engender restlessness in the spirit, rendering it capable of great deeds and tumultuous passions.

"This," said I to my two companions, "all this is us, and virtuous folk resemble those flat stretches of Piedmont countryside whose mournful evenness depresses. Carefully examining this extraordinary region, one feels it may have been all one volcano in the past; hardly a spot unmarked by the emblem of upheaval. And so this curious Nature is at times given also to unruliness . . . and we are not supposed to imitate her! Crying injustice: the solfataras we have been roaming about seem to be the proof of what I say."

With the most varied and picturesque scenery unfolding all along the way, we reached Pozzuoli. From there can be seen Nisida, the pretty little island to which Brutus retired after having killed Caesar. What a charming hideaway for the kind of joys we cherish; there, one would be as though at the farthest corner of the world; the secret horror one would be incited to commit there would be curtained from sight by impenetrable screens; and nothing needles the imagination, nothing inflames it like silence and mystery. Off in the distance, beyond the Bay, the headlands of Sorrento and Massa can be made out, ruins, noble edifices, flowering hillsides, everything that is able to adorn the most smiling prospect and create the most agreeable mood.

Pozzuoli,[21] where we returned for dinner, does not today display any trace of its ancient grandeur; but the site remains, it is one of the loveliest in the whole Kingdom of Naples. And yet, the crass population inhabiting the town is unconscious of its happiness; excessive idleness serves only to render it more barbarous and more insolent.

As soon as we appeared, a swarm of people crowded up, eager to show us the curiosities of the country.

"Children," said Olympia, shutting the door after a dozen of those rascals had elbowed their way into our chambers, "we do not intend to enlist the services of anybody unprovided with an outstanding prick. Show us what you have; we shall do our own selecting."

They all agree to the bargain; we lower breeches, we excite, we frig; six are judged worthy of the honors of a spasm, and the biggest, that is to say, a funny fellow all in rags and tatters, whose leviathan stretched itself thirteen inches in length and filled out to nine in circumference, alone obtained, after having fucked us all three, the privilege of becoming our cicerone. We dubbed him Raphael.

He took us first to the Temple of Serapis whose impressive debris caused us to presume that this structure had once been

---

[21] Called Puteoli in classical times.—*Tr.*

superb. We visited the neighboring antiquities, and wherever we looked, we beheld unequivocal evidence of the magnificence and the tastefulness of those Greek and Roman peoples who, after having been the light of the world for a brief hour, faded away, as shall vanish them who make the world tremble today.

The remains of a monument to pride and superstition next presented themselves to our eyes. Thrasyllus had prophesied that Caligula would not wear the purple until he had been from Baiae to Puteoli upon a bridge. The emperor had one built of boats for a distance of two leagues, and marched across it at the head of his army. 'Twas a piece of folly, no doubt, but one of a great man; and Caligula's crimes, which were to make an epoch in history, demonstrate, it shall have to be admitted, at once the most unusual figure and the most impetuous imagination.

From Caligula's bridge, Raphael guided us to Cumae; he pointed out to us, near the ruins of that town, those of a house that belonged to Lucullus. Gazing at them, we reflected upon the magnificence of that illustrious person.

"He is no more . . . and ere a little, a few months, a few years, we too shall have come and gone: the shears of Fate spare no one, neither rich nor poor, neither the good man nor the wicked. . . . Let us gather flowers while we tread this path whose end we reach so soon, and let it at least be of gold and silk the Dark Whore spins the thread of our days."

We penetrated into the ruins of Cumae, where our attention was directed mainly toward the vestiges of the Temple of Apollo built by Daedalus when, a refugee from the wrath of Minos, he wandered to this city.

Making our way thence to Baiae, we traversed the little locality of Bauli, where the poets situated the Elysian Fields; Acheron flows nearby.

"Let us pay a visit to the underworld," said Clairwil upon seeing those waters; "let us go and muse upon the torments of the damned, and dwell upon the thought of adding to their sufferings. Would that Proserpina's office were mine. . . . However, provided there is earthly woe for me to gaze upon, I shall always be the happiest of living women."

Eternal springtime reigns in that valley. Amidst the vineyards and the poplars are to be seen here and there the burial vaults where cinerary urns used to be placed, and Charon doubtless had his abode at Misenum. One likes to persuade oneself of such things when one has imagination. This brilliant part of our mind vivifies everything, and truth, always in arrears of illusion, becomes almost of no purpose to him who is able to create and embellish falsehood.

Close to the village of Bauli the visitor finds the traces of a hundred intercommunicating rooms; all this belongs to what they call Nero's Prison: here one could once hear the groans of the victims of that villain's lust and cruelty.

A little farther along one comes to the marvelous artificial lake Marcus Agrippa built for the fleet which ordinarily lay inside the bight of Cape Misenum. This cape forms a sheltered haven whose importance was recognized by the Roman admirals. It was there Pliny's ships were anchored when Vesuvius' eruption cost him his life. Some vestiges provide clues to this ancient city's considerable size. From there you go down to Bauli, which boasts the tomb of Agrippina. 'Twas off the shore of this town that there broke asunder the vessel in the disaster whereby Nero calculated to rid himself of his mother. However, the stratagem failed: returning from a festival at Baiae, Agrippina and her women leapt into the sea when the trap was sprung and the ship began to capsize; in the darkness the empress was able to swim away, and at length reached the shore and made her way home. Thus as it is given in Tacitus, the story lends no support to the legend that has grown up, that Bauli is the place where this celebrated woman was buried.

Reflecting upon the great emperor's scheme, "I am much taken," Clairwil said to me, "by the artfulness that entered into Nero's efforts to slay his mother. They reveal a cruelty, a perfidy, a repudiation of every virtue which endears that personage to me. He had been very fond of Agrippina; Suetonius assures us that he often masturbated at the thought of her . . . and he finally kills her. O Nero, let me venerate they memory. Wert thou alive today, I would adore thee as a god, and to me thou wilt be an eternal model and an inspiration."

After this amusing peroration from Clairwil, ever guided by Raphael whom Olympia caressed unceasingly while my friend and

I were chatting together, we proceeded on along the coast, so renowned in olden days for the multitude of superb villas that lined it; only a few impoverished fishermen inhabit it at present. The first important object one encounters there is the fortress which defends it at this end. By and by one comes to the beach, and one is now on the spot where famous Baiae once flourished, center of delights and of debauchery, whither the Romans used to repair for the lewdest and most heteroclite revelries. This must indeed have been a wonderful town to live in, shielded by mountains from the northern winds, and open toward the south, so that the sun, source of life-sustaining warmth and fuel to natural passions, might play its sacred and miracle-working rays upon this divine country's lucky inhabitants. Despite all the convulsions which over the centuries have shaken the terrain, one still breathes here that mild and voluptuous air, poison to austerities and virtues, delicate aliment to vice and all the so-called crimes of lust. In this connection, my friends, you will recall Seneca's invectives; but that severe moralist's reproaches made no headway against Nature's irresistible influences, and the while his contemporaries read his philosophy, they were pleased to outrage his principles in the most flagrant manner possible.

A single fisherman's rickety hut is all that survives today of once sumptuous Baiae; a few interesting bits of rubble—all that marks its erstwhile grandeur.

Venus had necessarily to be the favorite divinity of a town so corrupt. Vestiges of her temple still exist, but in such a state of dilapidation that it is difficult to judge of the past from this present evidence. It includes underground passageways, shadowy and mysterious corridors suggesting that these premises were used for very secret ceremonies. A subtle fire ignited in our veins the moment we entered them; Olympia bent close to me, and I saw fuck speak in her eyes.

"Raphael," Clairwil exclaimed, "we must perform our duties in this holy place."

"You drained me dry," our guide replied, "and gadding up and down this way has wearied me to the bone. However, I know four or five fishermen nearby who will ask no more than to content you."

Having said that, he is not six minutes fetching back some very unseemly but also very numerous company.

Blinded by the libertinage consuming us all three, we had, without thinking, put ourselves in a perilous situation. For what, in this ill-lighted and secluded place, what could a trio of women do against the ten men advancing insolently toward them? Fortified by the inspirations of the goddess who protects vice, we held our ground.

"Friends," Olympia said to that crew in Italian, "we have not wanted to conclude our tour of Venus' sanctuary without making a sacrifice to her; will you act a while as her priests?"

"Why not?" said one of those bumpkins, snatching up the orator's skirts.

"Come on, let's fuck 'em," said another, laying hands on me.

However, fancying they were to be left out, the seven who were not chosen fell to grumbling, and knives were halfway drawn when I quickly endeavored to prove that with a little dexterity, each of us could receive three of them at once. I offer the example: one encunts me, I present my behind to a second, and suck a third; my companions follow suit. Raphael, exhausted, stands by and watches, and there we all are, fucking the crowd like hussies. One has no idea of the thickness of the Neapolitan prick: although we had promised to suck the third, we were reduced to frigging it instead, none of us being able to get it into our mouth. Once they had spent a while rambling through one sector they would shift off into another, that is to say, each of them fucked us cuntwise and asswise, and all discharged three times at least. The dim light in this place, the mysteries that used to be celebrated here, the order of persons with whom we were dealing, perhaps even the dangers we were running, all had heated our brains, and the desire for horrors took hold of us. But, ours being the weaker side, how were we to contrive to execute them?

"Have you any candy?" I asked Clairwil in a whisper.

"Yes," she replied, "I never go anywhere unsupplied."

"Well then, offer some to our champions."

Olympia, acquainted with our intentions, explains to our rustic fuckers that these sweetmeats will have a restorative effect upon them. I hand the medicine around—in such instances I always coveted the role of distributor; our rascals swallow the dose.

"Another fucking from each of them," Clairwil murmured to me; "now that death is in their bloodstreams, let us wring from them the last measure of seed Nature will ever generate in their balls."

"Excellent," said I, "but might they not transmit to us the venom already circulating in their veins?"

"Keep them away from your mouth, let them have anything else. There is not the least danger," Clairwil added; "I have performed such extravagances a hundred times over, and you see the blooming health I am in. . . ."

That woman's appalling character electrified me; I did as she —and in all my life I had never tasted keener pleasures. The certainty that through my villainies the man I held in my arms would only retire out of my embrace to fall into death's, this perfidious, this barbarous idea contributed such a potent spice to my fucking that I swooned away during its crisis.

"Hurry, let's up and away," I said to my friends as soon as I returned to my senses; "we do not wish to be in this cellar when their gripes begin."

We ascended to daylight. Raphael, who had neither participated in the games nor been included in their cruel aftermath, continued to act as our guide; as for the nine men we left behind, although we were never to hear tell of them again, what befell them is certain, for the means we employed for our atrocity were too reliable to fail of grisly success.

"And so, my dear," I said to Clairwil, "we are now to conclude that villainy has so far progressed in you that you are no longer capable of being fucked by a man without desiring his death?"

"'Tis only too true," my friend acknowledged; "beloved Juliette, rare are they who understand what it means, to age in crime. Its roots reach so deep inside us, it becomes to such a degree one with our existence, that, precisely, we breathe for it alone. Will you believe that I regret those instants in my life when I am not soiled by some horror? My desire is to do nothing else; I would that no idea enter my head but it tend toward crime, that my hands toil at nothing but to bring about what my brain has just conceived. Oh, Juliette! how mighty are the delights of evil-doing, how the mind catches fire at the thought of violating, with impunity, all the laughable prohibitions which hold men captive. What superiority one achieves over them by breaking, as we do, all the rules which confine them, by transgressing their laws, profaning their religion, by denying, insulting, jeering at their execrable God; by defying even the disgusting precepts which, as they dare say, comprise the primary duties Nature enjoins upon us. Ah, not to be able to find something hideous enough, of sufficient magnitude, that, I tell you, is the cause of my grief today; however frightful a given crime may be, still it falls short of what my mind strives toward. Could I set the planet ablaze, even so would I curse the Nature that had provided only one world for my desires to feast upon."

Conversing in that strain, we strolled through the rest of the countryside around Baiae, where every twenty paces brings one to the remains of some precious monument; and at last, by an agreeable lane bordered by evergreen hedges, we came to the banks of Lake Avernus. Altogether disappeared was that noxious atmosphere which, in bygone days, used to cause overflying birds to fall dead into the lake; the quality of its waters and therefore of the air above has long since changed, 'tis today a very wholesome place, and in all the country one of those most congenial to a philosophic spirit. It was here that Aeneas sacrificed to the gods of the underworld before setting off along those tenebrous paths which the sibyl bade him take. And to the left is that sibyl's grotto, still easy of access. 'Tis a cave, one hundred eighty feet long, eleven wide, nine high. Examine the place with a little care, free yourself a little from the romantic notions the poets and the historians have handed down to us, and you speedily recognize this sibyl for what she was, a procuress, and this lair of hers a whorehouse. That interpretation is only borne out by a more thorough survey of the premises; and if, when studying them, one refers oneself to Petronius' ideas rather than to Virgil's descriptions, one will not come away with any other opinion.

A cluster of orange trees, which, near the opposite shore, rises from within a Temple of Pluto, makes for a sight as picturesque as any in the world. We visited those ruins, plucked some oranges, and started back toward Pozzuoli, passing between the still existing tombs lining the Appian Way on both its sides. There, we could not keep from exclaiming against the ridiculous attitude the Romans observed toward the dead. We sat us down by Faustina's tomb, and Olympia gave voice to the observations which follow.

"Two things I have never understood, my friends," that amiable and witty woman began, "they are respect for the dead, and respect for the wishes of the dead. Assuredly, both these superstitions relate to the notions people entertain touching the immortality of the soul; for were they convinced materialists, were they wholly persuaded that we are nought but an amalgam of mere material elements, that once smitten by death, our dissolution is complete, then respect shown to bits of decomposed matter would appear such palpable nonsense that nobody would think to espouse it. But our pride is loath to acknowledge this certitude of no longer existing; instead, we prefer to believe that the shades of the departed, yet hovering around his corpse, expect consideration to be shown to this derelict; one dreads offending them, and thus, without realizing it, one slips into the worst impiety and the most entire absurdity. So let us make thoroughly our own the doctrine that once we are dead, absolutely nothing of us exists anymore, and that this mortal coil we leave on earth is nothing else than what our excrements were, when we dropped them at the foot of a tree in those days when we were alive. Well-penetrated by this system, we would sense that to a cadaver neither honor nor concern nor duties are owing; that the only treatment it merits, far less for its sake than for ours, is burial, incineration, or to be fed to scavengers; but that homages, sepulchers, prayers, memorials are not in any wise its due, and all of them nothing but the tributes stupidity pays to vanity, tributes which philosophy annihilates. To be sure, this that I advance clashes with all religious beliefs, ancient and modern, but 'tis not to you that it is necessary to prove that nothing is more absurd than religions, all based upon the loathsome fable of the soul's eternal indestructibility and upon the ridiculous existence of a God. There is no stupidity religions have omitted to revere; and you know just as well as I, my friends, that when one examines a human institution, the first thing one must do is discard all religious notions. They are poison to lucidity."

"I am perfectly of our companion's mind," said Clairwil, "although odd as it may seem, there are libertines who have constructed passions upon a foundation of those beliefs. In Paris I often saw one man pay its weight in gold for the body of any freshly interred adolescent, boy or girl, who had met with a violent death: he would have them brought to his house, and would commit no end of horrors upon those still well-preserved corpses."

"It has been understood for a long time," I pointed out, "that the enjoyment of a recently assassinated individual may be truly very voluptuous; the constriction of the anus is especially appreciated by men."

"Also," said Clairwil, "there is a kind of imaginary impiety therein to heat the mind, and for a certainty I would try it if my sex permitted."

"This fantasy ought by all rights to lead to murder," I proposed to my friends, "for once a cadaver becomes an agreeable plaything, one is already on the edge of a deed which would multiply one's pleasures."

"Probably," Clairwil rejoined, "but that need not disturb us. If it is a great pleasure to kill, you will agree that it can hardly be a great evil."

And as it was well on in the afternoon, we hastened to regain Pozzuoli, passing by way of the ruins of Cicero's handsome villa.

It was late when we returned; a crowd of *lazzaroni* stood waiting at our gate. Raphael explained that since report had gone out that we were friendly toward men, most of those in the neighborhood had come to offer their services.

"You have nothing to fear," our guide continued, "they are decent people, they know that you pay well, they will fuck you accordingly. In my country we are straightforward about these matters; and you are not the first lady travelers to have felt our muscles."

"Taxing as the day has been," said Clairwil, "it would be wrong for us to turn away men of good will. I have always found that further exercise does more to relax the frame than mere repose: come, surrendering ourselves to the labors of Love, we shall forget those of Apollo. . . ."

But as at this point Nature's demands had all been met; as, sated on debauchery, we could indulge in nothing further save from libertinage, we flung ourselves into the nastiest excesses.

Thirty men culled from among better than a hundred, and whose members were gigantic, encloseted themselves with us; not one of them was over thirty years of age, not one had a weapon under thirteen inches in length by eight around; ten little peasant girls of between seven and twelve, whom we bought for their weight in gold, were also included in those orgies. After a magnificent dinner during which some three hundred bottles of Falerno were consumed, we opened by marshaling all the pricks in a row, lightly exciting them ourselves; next, we formed all those rascals in single file, so that they made up a long chaplet, each with his prick in the ass of the man ahead; the ten little girls, naked, frigged us in the meantime. We reviewed the formation, verified the introductions, fondled all the balls, and tongued all the mouths; turning, we retraced our steps, this time presenting our buttocks to be kissed by each of the chaplet's thirty elements. They had all been severely warned against any careless discharging in one another's behinds; as soon as they were at peak erection, they were, one by one, to move forward out of line, place their foaming engine in the hands of a little girl who would promptly bring it over and stopper either one of our asses or one of our cunts. Thus were we had thirty times over; after that we each took five men upon the body, this making six teams, which fucked us team by team; there was a prick in each aperture, one in the mouth or else niched between the breasts when it was too big for oral accommodation, then one in either hand. Throughout this scene, the ten little girls, perched on chairs, formed a circle around us, with orders to sprinkle us with shit and urine. For my part, I can think of nothing which arouses me more than one such inundation; I like to be bathed in it when I fuck; soon we were presenting asses only. Sprawled upon three little girls whose tongues were tickling us in the mouth, about the cunt, and thrilling upon the clitoris, we received three successive sodomizations from each of our thirty servants. That done, three of them cunt-sucked us, three sucked our mouths, we frigged one with each hand, and each of us was wet upon the belly or the nipples by a discharge wheedled from a prick by one of the little girls; the little girls then frigged all thirty upon our clitorises; one of them not engaged in frigging, wet, smeared, rubbed that delicate part with the sperm her companion made spurt, while a third, squatting over our faces, gave us an open cunt or asshole to lick.

A flagellation followed. We whipped the men who, at the same time, were doing the same to the children; next, we had ourselves bound, our hands were raised, our wrists tied to the bedposts, our ankles to the foot of the bed; and each man administered us a hundred strokes: while being beaten we pissed on the faces of three little girls who placed themselves between our thighs for this ceremony; after that, we surrendered the ten minors to our thirty fuckers, who depucelated and ravaged all ten of them, before and behind. Then we gave those ten children a vigorous fustigation, while the men kicked our asses with all their might: incredibly irritated by this treatment, we had ourselves more soundly drubbed by them; it was only when they had beaten us to the floor that they obtained, through this triumph, the right to embugger us yet again, and while we were enduring this latest affront, four of them at a time would come forward and fart, piss, and shit all over our faces; we did the same sort of thing to the little girls, who were obliged to swallow what we ejected upon them; finally, we affixed silken ribbons to the ceiling and tied all the pricks up in the air this way, rubbed all the balls with brandy, set fire to them and from this concluding rite we each of us obtained one last ejaculation in the womb or in the bowels, depending upon the individual assailant's whim.

Foreigners in this town, although authorized by the King, whose patents of impunity were in our pocket, we desisted from further excesses so as not to arouse the populace; and having distributed much money to all that rabble and sent it contentedly on its way, we lay down for a few hours' rest; then rose up and went forth to resume our interesting perambulations. We made a rapid tour of the isles, Procida and Ischia, and went back the next day to Naples, en route inspecting all sorts of wreckage fascinating for its antiquity, and many country villas, delightful through their location.

Ferdinand had sent out for news of us; we went to tell him of the powerful impression made upon us by the beauties of the region around his capital. He proposed to take us, several days later, to a supper at the residence of the Prince Francavilla, the richest lord in Naples, and at the same time the greatest bugger.

"They defy the imagination," the King assured us, "the prodigies he acquits himself of in this kind. I shall ask him not to let our presence incommode him," the monarch went on, "and explain that we are only paying a visit in order to examine philosophically his debauches."

We accepted. The Queen was with us.

In all Italy, nothing equals Francavilla's magnificence and grand spending; there are sixty places set at his table every day, his guests are waited upon by two hundred domestics, all of the very fairest mien. The Prince, to receive us, had had a temple of Priapus raised in a grove in his garden. Mysterious pathways bordered by orange trees and myrtle led to this wondrously lighted sanctuary; columns wreathed with roses and lilacs were surmounted by a cupola beneath which stood an altar covered with soft grass, to the right; to the left, a table set for six; in the center, a great basket of flowers, whose shoots and festoons, laden with colored lampions, rose in garlands to the summit of the cupola. Different groups of practically naked youths, three hundred of them all told, were scattered about wherever there was space available, and atop the altar of grass appeared Francavilla, standing underneath the emblem of Priapus, deity in whose shrine we were forgathered; groups of children went forward by turns to bow down before the Prince.

"Most honored Lord," the Queen said to him as she made her entrance, "we have come to this hallowed place to partake sympathetically of your pleasures, to meditate before your mysteries; proceed as you are wont to do; enjoy the multiple homages about to be rendered you; we wish but to contemplate them."

Banks of flowers lay opposite the altar, we sat ourselves down upon them; the god descended, bent over the altar, and the ceremony began.

Francavilla offered the world's most comely ass to our view; to two young children, stationed hard by that notable posterior, was entrusted the care of opening it, of wiping it, and of guiding toward the hole the monstrous members which, by the score, were shortly to fling into the sanctum sanctoris; twelve other children readied the pricks. I had never in all my days seen any service more nimbly accomplished. Thus prepared, those splendid members moved from hand to hand until they arrived in those of the children appointed to introduce them; they disappeared then into the ass of the patient: they came back out again, they were replaced by others; and all that with an effortlessness, a smoothness, a promptitude which compel wonder. In less than two hours, all the three hundred pricks had sped into Francavilla's fundament, who, once everything had been gulped greedily down, turned our way, and spat, following a violent pollution by a pair of young Ganymedes, a few drops of watery whitish sperm, the emission whereof having occasioned him five or six piercing shrieks, restored him completely to calm.

He then addressed us. "My ass is in a calamitous state," he declared, stepping toward us; "your wish was to see it treated unsparingly, I have satisfied you. I venture to say, by the by, that not one of you dear ladies has ever in her life been fucked as I have just been."

"Gracious, no," said Clairwil, still deeply impressed by the demonstration we had witnessed, "but I am prepared to measure my endurance against yours whenever you like, Prince, and whether in the ass, whether in the cunt, I wager I can outfuck you."

"Softly, dear heart, softly," said Charlotte, "you have seen only a mild sample of what my cousin Francavilla is capable of; without flinching, he would stand up to ten battalions."

"Let him bring his armies on," Clairwil rejoined with her usual plainspokenness; "but, Sire, does your Prince fancy we are going to be content with having watched his display of prowess?"

"Here, most certainly," the King replied, "for however beauteous you be, Mesdames, you must understand that among all these young men, there is not one who would be induced even to touch you."

"Why, 'tis not as though we were without asses—"

"Not one," Francavilla affirmed, "not one would be tempted thereby, and were bullying finally to sway him, I would never again accept to hold commerce with the weakling."

"That is what they call cleaving to one's faith," said Clairwil, "and I don't blame them for it. So let us at least have some supper, since there is to be no fucking; let Comus recompense us, if he possibly can, for the cruel privations Cypris makes us endure."

"You express it admirably," said Francavilla.

The greatest supper ever seen by mortal eyes was therewith served by the Ganymedes, and the six places occupied by the King, the Queen, the Prince, my two sisters, and myself. There is no describing the delicacy and the magnificence of the fare: dishes and wines from all the countries of the world arrived in lavish profusion and uninterruptedly, and, mark of unheard-of luxury, nothing that was put on the table was taken off it: a viand or a wine was scarcely brought on when it was emptied into huge silver troughs, out of the bottom of which everything flowed away into the ground.

"The wretched might profit from these leavings," said Olympia.

"Wretched? Our existence upon earth denies that of our inferiors," Francavilla explained; "I loathe the mere idea that what is of no use to us could afford relief to someone else."

"His heart is as hard as his ass is generous," remarked Ferdinand.

"I have nowhere encountered such prodigality," said Clairwil, "but I like it. That arrangement whereby scraps are saved for the scullery has chilling effects upon the imagination. Such orgies owe part of their success to the delicious realization that nothing and no one else matters on earth."

"Why, what do the underprivileged matter to me when I want for nothing," said the Prince; "their hardships add a further poignancy to my joys, I would not be so happy if I did not know there was suffering nearby, and 'tis from this advantageous comparison half the pleasure in life is born."

"That comparison," I said, "is very cruel."

"It is natural; nothing is crueler than Nature, and those who observe her instructions to the letter will always be murderers or villains."[22]

"My friend," said Ferdinand, "all those are sound precepts, but they are hurtful to your reputation : if you but knew what they say about you in Naples. . . ."

"Oh, I am not one to take calumny very seriously," was the Prince's reply, "and a reputation is such a little thing, an asset so meager, that I am not in the slightest put out if others amuse themselves gossiping about the things which procure me quite as much amusement from others."

"Ah, my Lord," I said to this distinguished libertine, affecting a dogmatic tone, "they are passions which have brought you to this degree of blindness, and the passions are not the means through which Nature expresses her will, as the corrupt likes of you are prone to claim. They are the products of God's wrath; and we can obtain deliverance from their imperious grip by imploring the mercy of the Eternal, but that mercy we must earn. 'Tis not by having three or four hundred pricks thrust into your ass every day, 'tis not by permanent avoidance of holy confession, by never partaking of the treasured favors of the eucharist, 'tis not by stiffening yourself against good intentions you will bathe in the glow of Grace. No, Sire, no, 'tis not through such conduct you will blot out your sins or attain their remission. Ah, my Lord, how must I pity you if you persevere in this misbehavior; think of the fate awaiting you in the next world : how can you, free to set a course toward good or toward evil, imagine that the just God who has given you this free will shall not punish you for the wicked use you have put it to? Do you believe, my friend, that an eternity of sufferings does not warrant a little reflection, and that before the certainty of those sufferings it is not worth sacrificing a few miserable penchants, which, even in this life, for the very slender pleasure they bring you, cause you cares, worries, distress, regrets

---

[22] Nature's primary impulses are invariably criminal; those which steer us toward virtuousness are merely secondary, and never but the fruit of education, of debility, or of fear. The individual Nature molds for kingship, who, once out of her hands, falls into the hands of no educators and who by dint of his new position becomes the most powerful of men and immune to fear, that royal personage, I say, will take his daily bath in the blood of his subjects; and will be the natural man besides.

without end? In one word, is it to be fucked that the Supreme Being brought you into this world?"

Francavilla and the King gazed at me dumbfounded, and for a moment even imagined I had lost my wits.

Ferdinand finally broke the silence. "Juliette," he said, "if you are preparing a second chapter to that sermon, tell us so in order that we can listen to it lying down."

"I am now come to such a point of impiety and of abandon of all religious sentiment," Francavilla declared, "that my calm is imperiled by the barest allusion to this deific phantom, dreamt up by the priests who grub their livelihood from ministering to it; I shudder in horror merely at the mention of its name.

"Throughout every land," the Prince continued, "we hear it announced that a God has revealed himself; what is his message to men? Does he demonstrate his evident existence to them? Does he teach them what he is? In what his essence consists? Does he clearly explain his intentions to them, his plans? That which we are told concerning what he has said about his plans, does it accord with the effects we observe? Why, no; he intimates to us only that *he is the one who is*, that *he is a hidden God;* that his ineffable ways surpass understanding, that he waxes wroth as soon as anyone has the temerity to pry into his secrets and to consult reason in order to evaluate him or judge of his works. Does the revealed comportment of this infamous God correspond to the lofty notions we are asked to entertain of his wisdom, of his goodness . . . of his justice . . . of his benevolence . . . of his supreme power? Not at all: however we scan him, we see him everywhere and always partial, capricious, malignant, tyrannical, unjust, at the very most good for a people he happens to favor, the sworn enemy of everybody else; if he deigns to show himself to some men, he is careful to keep all others in darkest ignorance of his divine intentions. Is this not the picture all revelations give of your abominable God? Do the aims disclosed by this God bear the stamp of reason and wisdom? Do they conduce to the well-being of the people to whom this fabulous goblin declares himself? Upon examining these divine decrees, in no country do I find anything but bizarre ordinances, ridiculous injunctions, ceremonies whose purpose cannot be guessed, puerile practices, an etiquette unworthy of the monarch of Nature, offerings, sacrifices, expiations useful indeed to the ministers of this insipid illusion, but exceedingly burdensome to mankind. I find, moreover, that these regulations very often have for effect or design to render human beings unsociable, disdainful, intolerant, quarrelsome, unjust and inhuman toward all those who have not received the same revelation, nor the same laws, nor the same favors from heaven. And there's the execrable God you preach to me, Juliette, and you would have me worship such a phantom!"

"I too would have you worship him," said Ferdinand. "Kings always encourage religion, religion has since the very beginning lent sinews to tyranny. The day man ceases to believe in God he will assassinate his rulers."

"There is no telling which he may decide to destroy first," I interjected; "but, be sure of it, once he has overthrown the one, it will not be long before he finishes off the other. And if you care to set aside your despot's point of view for a moment, and weigh the matter by philosophic standards, you will admit that the world would only be the better off if it had neither tyrants nor priests: they are monsters that fatten on the substance of nations, and that never render them any services lest it be to impoverish or to blind them."

"This woman here does not like kings," said Ferdinand.

"Or gods either," I replied. "In my eyes, the former are all tyrants, the latter all spooks, and I hold that one must never despotize over men nor deceive them. Nature, when she cast us into the world, created us free and atheists. Force brought weakness to heel, and we got kings. Imposture overawed fools, we had gods. Well, in all that I see cunning scoundrels and phantoms aplenty, but not the slightest hint of natural inspiration."

"What would men do without kings or without gods?"

"They would become more free, more philosophical, and therefore more worthy of the intentions Nature has in their regard, Nature who created them neither to vegetate beneath the scepter of an individual no better endowed than they, nor to hobble in the fetters of a god who is nought but the contrivance of a few fanatic imaginations."

"One moment," said Francavilla, "I am won over to part of Juliette's argument. No God—she is right, indubitably; but that curb gone, some other must be found for the people: the philosopher has no need of one, I know, but restraints are salutary for the rabble, and upon it alone royal authority must make itself felt, that is what I urge."

"We are fully agreed," I said, "like you, I yielded this point to Ferdinand when we first discussed these affairs together."

"Then," Francaville resumed, "it is by the extremest terror religious chimeras must be replaced; deliver the people from the fear of a hell to come and they'll go berserk straightway; instead, for that superstitious dread substitute a prodigiously more severe penal code, laws which are aimed exclusively at the people, since nobody else threatens the State, discontents always arising from that one class. The rich man will not fret at the idea of restraints which never affect him, since he buys himself out of all objections of principle when, with his money, he acquires in his turn the right to vex all those who live under his heel. You will never find a single member of the upper class resenting even the blackest shadow of tyranny when he is able to exercise real tyranny over his inferiors. .These bases established, it is therefore necessary that a suzerain rule with utmost harshness, and that to certify his right to do what he likes to the people, he leave his allies free in their turn to undertake, within their own provinces, whatever suits their pleasure; these latter he must cuirass with his influence, his might, his consideration; to them he must say, *And you too, promulgate laws, but such only as will buttress mine; and in order that my blows be telling, in order that my throne be unshakable, support my power with all that portion of power I leave to you, and enjoy your privileges in a peaceful manner, in such sort that mine are never endangered...."*

"That," said Olympia, "is the pact which kings once made with the clergy."

"Yes; but the clergy, basing its power upon the omnipotence of a fantastic God, became stronger than the royalty; the priests assassinated kings instead of supporting them, and that is not what I am asking for: I wish final authority to remain with the government, while the authority it leaves to the upper class and to philosophers would be utilized by them only in the interests of their individual passions, upon condition these at all times and in every sense promote the interests of the State; for the State can never be governed uniquely either by theocrat or by despot; the chief agent of that State must annihilate the first rival to pose a threat to his power, some of which he must share with those who, seeing themselves standing to gain from his pre-eminence over them, agree to come now and then to his aid with those forces which he allows them to enjoy in peace when he is himself at peace, everyone, chief and vassals, joining forces to combat, to subdue, to fetter the popular hydra, the sole aim of whose strivings is always to burst the chains that keep it in subservience."

"Pursuant to this line of reasoning, it is certain," said Clairwil, "that the laws enacted against the population cannot be too repressive."

"They must be modeled upon those of Draco," said Francavilla, "they must be written out in blood, must be revitalized by blood, must cause it to flow every day, must, above all, keep the people in the most deplorable poverty; the people are never dangerous save when comfortable—"

"And when educated?"

"And when educated, to be sure: they must hence be kept in the profoundest ignorance as well; their slavery must be perpetual and grinding, and every possible means of escape from it must be denied them, as will assuredly be the case when the figures who support and surround the government are there to prevent the people from breaking loose from irons which it is in the upper class' interests to tighten day and night. You cannot imagine how far such tyranny is able to extend."

"I sense it," said Clairwil; "yes, I sense that it would reach the point where those rogues depended utterly upon the tyrant, or upon those near him, for the very right to breathe."

"That's it," said the Prince, seizing enthusiastically at this idea, "the government itself must regulate the population, must command all the means for snuffing it out if it becomes troublesome, for increasing it if that is esteemed advantageous; its justice must never be weighed elsewhere than in the scales of the ruler's interests or passions, combined solely with the passions and interests of those who, as we have just said, have obtained from him all the allotments of authority necessary to multiply his own a hundredfold when they are conjugated.[23] Glance at the governments of Africa and Asia: all of them are organized in accordance with these principles, and all invariably maintain themselves thereby."

"In many of them," said Charlotte, "the people are not reduced to what you seem to consider their appropriate condition."

"True," Francavilla admitted, "there have been stirrings in a few outlying districts, and there is work yet to be done before the masses are in such a state of dread and exhaustion that they cease even to be able to conceive of revolt."

"It is to that end," said Ferdinand, "I would like to see priests among them."

"Beware of that expedient, since, as you have just been told, it is the surest way to raise up a power that will soon eclipse your own by dint of the deific machinery which, in the clergy's hands, serves only to forge weapons for the destruction of governments, and which is never used for any other purpose; atheize and incessantly demoralize the people whom you wish to subjugate; so long as they cringe before no god but you, so long as there are no morals except yours, you will always be their sovereign."

"An immoral man is dangerous," said Ferdinand.

"Yes, when he has some authority, because he then feels the urge to abuse it; never, when he is a slave. It matters very little that a man believe or not believe there is wrong in killing me, once I have so thoroughly shackled him that he has not the means to harm a fly; and when moral depravity has softened him, he will be that much less loath to wear the collar I rivet round his neck."

"But," asked Charlotte, "how is he to become soft under the yoke? Rather, it would seem to me, only luxury and easy living have that effect upon man."

"His fiber rots in the thick of crime," the Prince rejoined. "Now, leave him the broadest outlets for his criminal capacities; never punish him save when his darts are directed against you; so proceed and you will obtain two excellent results: the immorality that you require, and depopulation, which may often be of even greater usefulness to you. Allow incest, rape, murder among your subjects; forbid them marriage, authorize sodomy, prohibit them

---

[23] See, on this subject, the speech of the Bishop of Grenoble in the fourth volume of *La Nouvelle Justine*, pp. 275 ff.

worship of any sort, and you will soon have them reduced to the abjection your policy demands.

"And how do you multiply punishments when you tolerate everything meriting them?" I wondered, with some appearance of logic.

"Why," said Francavilla, "it's virtues you then hammer, or revolts against your power; and, never fear, you have a thousand times more of them than you need in order to be busy striking off heads all day long. Besides, are motives so indispensable? The despot obtains blood whenever he likes, his will alone is enough to cause it to flow: conspiracies may be supposed at any time; you foment them, you occasion them; the scaffolds go up, and in the twinkle of an eye, there's a carnage."

"If Ferdinand cares to leave these matters in my hands," said Charlotte, "I guarantee him I shall provide legitimate pretexts every day: let him sharpen the blade and I shall furnish the victims."

"Cousin," said the King, "my wife is becoming fidgety."

"I am not surprised," said Clairwil, "for I am myself fear-fully on edge. To watch fuck and fuck not is cruel when you have a warm constitution."

"Let us then go out for a breath of air," said the Prince; "in these wooded bowers we may perhaps find the wherewithal to appease these ladies' ardors."

All the gardens were illuminated: from orange trees, peach trees, apricot trees, fig trees we plucked fruit cooled by the evening dews as we strolled along the delightful pathways that brought us to the Temple of Ganymede. This temple was softly lit by tapers set high under the ceiling, which reflected light enough for pleasures but not so much as to tire the eye. Green and rose-colored columns supported this edifice, garlands of myrtle and lilac twined around them and formed agreeable festoons between one column and the next.

No sooner were we arrived there than subdued music filled the air with sweetness. Charlotte, drunk with lust and very hot from wine and spirits, proceeded straight to the nearest couch, and we others did the same.

" 'Tis their turn now," Francavilla said to the King, "they

must be left to show what they can do, with the essential recommendation, nevertheless, to offer nothing but their asses, for this is a place of worship consecrated to the adoration of asses only; any deviation from these laws would be a sin warranting expulsion from the temple. Moreover, the agents that will be furnished to them would consent to no infidelity."

"Little do we care," said Clairwil, the first of us to have stripped off her clothes. "We much prefer having our asses used than our cunts, and provided we receive friggings meanwhile, there will be no regrets heard from us."

Francavilla now drew away the pink satin spread covering what we supposed was an ottoman. Ah, what an extraordinary article that drapery had been concealing! Imagine a long couch with separate places, or rather stalls, for four; each woman was to enter the stall and kneel on the seat reserved for her, her rump raised high, her thighs spread wide; her elbows rested on chair-arms padded with cotton and covered with black satin, as was the rest of this uncommon piece of furniture. By her hands and within easy reach were the loins of two men, one on either side, who to her manipulation provided each a gigantean member, the only part of them that was visible, their bodies being otherwise hidden underneath black shrouds. Cunningly disposed platforms supported those recumbent bodies, and a mechanism ensured that once those pricks had discharged, they disappeared in a trice and were replaced by new ones the next instant.

Yet another and still more unusual fixture operated beneath the woman's belly. By taking her position in the stall, that woman lowered herself over, and engulfed, unavoidably and, as it were, involuntarily, a soft and flexible dildo which, through a system of springs and clockwork, filed away automatically and without cease, every fifteen minutes squirting a given measure of warm and sticky fluid into her vagina, that fluid possessing an odor and a viscosity which would have led anyone to mistake it for the purest, the freshest sperm. A very pretty girl, of whom nothing but the head was visible, with her chin pressed against the dildo, frigged, lingually, the clitoris of the woman, and was likewise relayed by another, by means of a trap-door arrangement, as soon as she began to tire. Ahead of the woman placed as I have described there were to be seen, upon round stools, other objects, which were varied or replaced when the woman so desired; upon those stools, I say, one saw cunts or pricks; in a manner that this woman had at the level of her mouth, and could conveniently suck, either a penis or a clitoris. In sum, it resulted that the woman, kneeling upon the cushioned seat containing the levers which set everything in motion, and comfortably resting upon her elbows, was tupped by a dildo, mouthed by a girl, while frigging a prick with each hand, presenting her ass to the very genuine prick which was to come up and sodomize her, and alternately sucking, according to her tastes, now a prick, now a cunt, even an asshole.

"I do not believe," said Clairwil, setting herself, stark naked, in one of the stalls, "that anything more extraordinarily lubricious could possibly be invented; simply to adopt this posture," she continued, "puts me fairly in a frenzy, simply to take my place here is making me discharge."

Olympia, Charlotte, and I took our places beside Clairwil. Four girls of sixteen, naked and fair as angels, helped situate us; they oiled the dildoes to facilitate their entry; they adjusted our positions; then, parting our buttocks, they likewise anointed our assholes, and stood by to attend to us during the operation.

Francavilla then gave the signal. Four maids of fifteen led in, by the prick, a like number of superb boys whose members were without delay introduced into our fundaments; exhausted, this quadrille was replaced in short order by succeeding ones. Our stewardesses remained the same, but the fresh batteries of pricks were each time brought in by four new girls who, having handed the pricks over to the stewardesses, formed a voluptuous group around us and danced to the enchanting sounds of music coming, so it seemed, from far away. While dancing they sprinkled our bodies with some unidentifiable elixir, each drop of which stung the skin sharply and had an incredibly active effect upon our passions: its scent was that of jasmine; we were covered with it from head to toe.

All the variations of this scene, what is more, were executed with astonishing address and celerity; never were we kept waiting for so much as a moment. Before our mouths, cunts and pricks and asses succeeded one another as swiftly as our desires; elsewhere, the engines we frigged had but to discharge and new ones materialized between our fingers; our clitoris-suckers rotated with the same speed, and our asses were never deserted; in less than three hours, during which we swam in unending delirium, we were assfucked one hundred times apiece, and polluted the whole time by the dildo constantly belaboring our cunt. I was nigh to slain by it all. Olympia had collapsed, they had been obliged to lift her off her dildo; only Clairwil and Charlotte had stood up unwaveringly to the assault. Fuck, the liquid ejaculated by the dildoes, sweat, and blood drenched us all over. Ferdinand and Francavilla, who had been amusing themselves with thirty-odd charming bardashes while watching the spectacle, invited us to pursue the promenade; four pretty girls offered us their arms to lean upon, and we moved into a spacious summerhouse.

It was decorated thus: to the right was a wide semicircular platform raised three feet above the floor, an amphitheater garnished with thick mattresses covered in flaming red satin; opposite stood another platform, a foot higher, of the same shape, entirely carpeted in velvet of the same color.

"Let us lie down and wallow here for a while," said the Prince, guiding us to the amphitheater, "and we shall see what there is to see."

We settled ourselves, and very soon into the center of the hall entered a dozen exquisitely lovely girls of between sixteen and eighteen. They were arrayed in simple shifts worn in the Greek manner, and leaving their bosoms bare; and at her breast, firm and white as alabaster, each bore a naked infant, her own offspring, and ranging in age from six to eighteen months. At the same time, six handsome men, prick in hand, slipped into our midst; two embuggered Ferdinand and Francavilla forthwith; the four others proposed us their services, in such manner that we were pleased to accept them.

Once we were all six fucked, the twelve young women formed a half-circle around us, their shifts were raised by a similar number of little girls dressed in Tartar style; and these children, kneeling beside the women whose behinds they had unveiled, exposed to our view, in agreeably struck attitudes, the most superb collection of buttocks you could ever hope to see.

"Those are superior asses, yes," said Francavilla under the monstrous prick that was sodomizing him; "but, unfortunately, they are destined to our condemnation, and I should be sorry, Mesdames, to see you take a too lively interest in them. . . . Yet, notice, if you will, how nicely they are cleft, those asses, what a snowy whiteness is theirs. What a shame to treat them as they are now going to be."

Exeunt the shift-raisers; enter a dozen men of about thirty-five, of very male and fierce mien, and costumed as satyrs. Their arms are bare, each comes in brandishing a different sort of instrument for flagellation: they snatch the nurselings out of their young mothers' arms, toss the little creatures into a heap at our feet, seize the mothers, drag them by the hair up onto the platform opposite us and, mercilessly ripping off the thin garments they are wearing, they immobilize them with one hand and set to whipping them with the other, in a manner so cruel and for such a length of time that jets of blood and bits of flesh fly across the whole width of the summerhouse, even to where we are.

Never in my life had I seen such a flogging . . . neither one so ferocious nor so thorough, since from the nape of the neck down to the heel not an inch was left untouched; those wretches' shrieks could have been heard a league away, and crime was performed so openly here that no precaution was taken to muffle them; four of those women fainted, fell, and were then whipped back upon their feet again. When, seen from the rear, they were but one great wound, they were suddenly let loose.

A general commotion then occurs, flagellators and flagellated collide, push, pull; the ones hurry to replace, in pairs, the first six individuals we have been enjoying; the others scurry anxiously about in quest of their progeny. Tangled up as the babes are, their mothers identify them, sort them out, press them to their trembling lips, hug them to their palpitating breasts; along with the thickened milk they feed them, they wash them with the burning tears flowing down their cheeks. 'Tis to my shame I confess it, good friends, but this effervescence, in contrast with the radically different emotions we were being gripped by, caused me two successive spasms as I squirmed under the shaft sounding my anus.

The moment of calm was not long; another twelve men, of more awesome aspect then the first platoon and garbed as savages, arrive, blasphemy in mouths, martinets in fists. They wrest the infants away from those poor souls again, throw them our way with greater force than they had been thrown before, in so doing shattering several little skulls upon the plank floor of our amphitheater, drag the women upon the platform opposite, and this time it is upon the front of the bodies of those tender mothers, and especially upon their delicate breasts, that the storm descends. Those sweet, sensitive, and voluptuous globes, crisscrossed by lashes biting furiously into flesh, soon yield a horrid mixture of milk and blood, geysers of which leap forth in answer to the blows. The barbarians, aiming lower down, with the same violence soon lacerate the belly, the sex, the inside of the vagina and the thighs and, in an instant, these parts, treated as unsparingly as the others, disappear behind a mist of blood. And in the meantime we were fucking, and we were tasting that supreme pleasure which results from the impact, upon stern souls like ours, of the sight of the pain of others. The same frantic rush on the part of the women the moment their tormentors release them in order to substitute their rigid and foaming pricks for their dozen predecessors' limp and drained engines. The mothers scramble toward their babes, pick them up, bruised and battered as they are, warm them with their anguished kisses, wet them with their tears, console them with tender words and in their joy at recovering these cherished objects, are almost at the point of forgetting what they have undergone, when twelve other villains, of a countenance a thousand times more dreadful to behold than anything seen hitherto, stride in to accomplish further atrocities.

This new horde of monsters, dressed like the satellites of Pluto, grab the luckless mothers' offspring one last and most terrible time, hack them to shreds with the poniard each wields, fling their remains at our feet, leap upon the women, whereof, in the center of the arena, they make the promptest and bloodiest slaughter; then, all covered with gore, spring into our midst, stab the fuckers lying in our arms, and themselves embugger us, roaring with pleasure.

"What a scene!" I say to Francavilla when, exhausted by fucking and horrors, we retire out of that charnel house; "what a rare and stirring spectacle!"

"Your friend seems not to have had her fill of it," said the Prince, glancing back at Clairwil who was poking about the corpses heaping the battlefield, inspecting their wounds.

"Fuck!" replied that woman of character, "think you one ever tires of the sight of death? Ever has enough of it? It was, to be sure, one of the most delicious horrors I've witnessed in all my days, but it is certain to leave me with an enduring sadness. For, alack, one cannot enjoy a massacre every fifteen minutes the whole length of one's life."

And there the festive evening came to its close. Coaches were awaiting us. They conveyed us back to the Prince's palace; we had hardly strength enough to hold ourselves upright; aromatic baths were ready, we slipped into them; hot broths were offered to us, and beds, and twelve hours later we were all three prepared, if need be, to begin again.

Rested from those mighty fatigues, we thought to pursue our circuit of outlying Naples, and to go down the easterly coast. If these descriptions do not please you, in amongst them I shall intersperse those of my lewd accomplishments; this variety amuses, it stimulates. Were these tales ever to be printed, the reader, his imagination heated by the lubricious details strewn throughout, would be enchanted, would he not, to be able to pause from time to time and dwell upon milder, more restful descriptions, framed nonetheless within the bounds of the strictest truth?

The traveler's eye, wearied by the grandiose scenery that gives him unremitting occupation while crossing the Alps, likes to linger upon the fertile plains into which he descends, gentle prospects where agreeable configurations of vine and elm seem everywhere to suggest Nature in a festive spirit.

And so, a week after our rout at the Prince's, we set forth upon this second tour, with a guide provided by the King and all possible letters to ensure our kindly reception in the country we were going to traverse.

The first house we inspected with some thoroughness was Ferdinand's castle of Portici. Hitherto, we had seen only its boudoirs. But it contained a museum; Ferdinand himself escorted us through it. Fourteen rooms all on one floor lodge this enormous collection, the world's most curious and finest, I dare say. Nothing so tiring as an examination of its components; constantly on my feet, my mind straining, my eyes staring, it was all a blur by the time we had seen everything.

In another part of the same castle we found greater enjoyment in the assortment of paintings recovered from Herculaneum and other towns buried by the lava of Vesuvius.

Generally speaking, in all these paintings one remarks a wealth of postures and attitudes which almost defy natural possibilities, and which testify either to great muscular suppleness in the inhabitants of those countries, or a great disorder of the imagination. Amongst other masterpieces I quickly distinguished a superb effort representing a satyr coupling with a goat: an astonishing work of art, beautiful in its conception, striking in its precision of detail.

"That fantasy is quite as agreeable as it is alleged to be extraordinary," Ferdinand commented. "It is," he went on to say, "much in usage hereabouts; as a Neapolitan, I was eager to experience it, and I do not hide from you that it gave me the very rarest pleasure."

"I can believe it," said Clairwil; "many and many a time in my life I have thought of the idea, and I have never desired to be a man except to enact it."

"But, you know, a woman can perfectly well surrender herself to a large dog," the King reminded us.

"Certainly," I rejoined, in such a way as to suggest I was not totally unacquainted with that practice.

"Charlotte," pursued Ferdinand, "was of a mind to try it. It suited her to perfection."

"Sire," said I, speaking so as to be heard by Ferdinand only, but with my customary frankness, "if all the princes of the House of Austria had but confined themselves to fucking goats, and if all the women of that House had conversed with bulldogs alone, the earth today would not be plagued with this accursed race, whereof its populations shall never be rid save through a general revolution."

Ferdinand agreed that I was quite right, and we moved on. Of Herculaneum's thoroughly raided ruins there is little worth looking at today, and the site has been covered over to protect the ground Portici stands upon; one cannot well judge of the ancient theater, much disturbed by the diggings. When we returned to Portici, Ferdinand put us into the hands of the knowledgeable guide he had himself selected for us, and the amiable man wished us a fair journey, urging us to call upon his friend Vespoli, of Salerno, to whom he had given us letters of recommendation and under whose roof, he assured us, we would find capital entertainment.

We went to Resina and thence took the road to Pompeii. Like Herculaneum, that city had been overwhelmed by ashes and lava, and in the course of the same great eruption. We noticed that Pompeii was itself built upon two more ancient towns, which had been visited by previous catastrophes. Vesuvius, as you see, is forever absorbing, destroying all that man has built in these parts, and yet man, undiscouraged, rebuilds again: but for this cruel enemy, the country surrounding Naples would be the most agreeable on earth.

From Pompeii we reached Salerno and lay overnight at the famous house of correction situated two miles outside that city, and in which Vespoli exercises his redoubtable superintendency.

Vespoli, scion of one of the great families in the Kingdom of Naples, used once to be First Almoner at the Court. The King, whose pleasures he had served and whose conscience he had directed,[24] had accorded him the despotic administration of the asylum where we found him. There, guaranteed by royal protection, the libertine was free to indulge in everything his criminal passions might dictate. Atrocities being the warden's specialty, Ferdinand was eager to have us be Vespoli's guests.

He was fifty years of age at the time, with an imposing and

---

[24] It is the common practice in Italy to make one's confessor one's pimp; in high-ranking circles, these two offices are closely knit, and the priests, given a little to intriguing anyhow, usually exercise them admirably and simultaneously.

harsh physiognomy, tall, strong as a bull; he greeted us with marks of extremest consideration. He read the letters we presented and, since the hour was very advanced, promptly gave orders to have a supper and beds readied for us. It was Vespoli himself who brought us breakfast the next morning; and then, we having made known our wish to visit it, he led us on a tour of his establishment.

Each of the rooms we were shown provided us infinite matter for criminally lewd reflections, and we were already horribly aroused by the time we reached the cages in which the crazed were kept.

The superintendent, who up until now had done nothing but grow steadily warmer, was wearing an incredible erection when we stepped into this courtyard, and as fucking witless victims was what he most enjoyed, he asked us whether we cared to see him in action.

"By all means," we replied.

"I ask," he said, "because my transports with these creatures are so prodigious, my proceedings so bizarre, my cruelties so appalling, that it does rather embarrass me to have my behavior in this place observed."

"Nonsense," said Clairwil, "were your caprices a thousand times more incongruous, we would still wish to watch, and indeed we entreat you to act your wonted role as though you were all by yourself; and especially to deprive us of none of the precious idiosyncrasies without which we can obtain no true insights into your tastes and your soul."

"You merely intend to look on?" he inquired, rubbing his prick with emotion as he posed the question.

"And why should we not also enjoy fucking these madmen?" Clairwil asked. "Your fantasies electrify us, we are eager to imitate all of them. I trust these subjects are not dangerous? No? Then we shall sport with them like you. But do not make us wait any longer, dear sir, I am burning to see you at work."

The cages were disposed around a large open court planted with tall cypresses through whose foliage there came a lugubrious green light, giving the place a graveyard look. In its center stood a cross studded with nails on one side; it was there the wicked

Vespoli had his victims exposed. Four jailers, carrying spike-studded clubs a single blow of which could have slain an ox, escorted us watchfully. Vespoli, accustomed to having them as on-lookers during his amusements, felt no awkwardness in their presence, and instructed two of them to stand by us while we witnessed the scene seated upon a bench at one side of the courtyard; the two other jailers were to loose from their cages those playthings the superintendent felt a need for.

First to be set at large was a handsome young man, naked, a veritable Hercules, who cut a thousand strange capers as he came forth. One of the first of his extravagances was to squat before our feet and shit, and Vespoli came over to be on hand for this operation, which he studied with care. He frigged himself, retrieved the turd, rubbed his prick upon it, and then falling to dancing about like the madman, to gamboling and frisking in the same way, he caught him from behind, pushed him up against the cross, and the guards tied him fast to it in an instant. Immediately the fellow is secured, Vespoli, ecstatic, kneels down before his ass, opens it, pants into it, tongues it, caresses it lovingly, then, getting quickly to his feet, takes a whip and for a long hour flays the unhappy and loudly screaming lunatic. Once his buttocks are in tatters, the lecher embuggers, and in his drunken condition, raves in tune with his victim.

"Holy God Almighty," the former almoner shrieks now and again, "what are the joys to be known in the asshole of a madman! And I too, I am mad, double-fucked Divinity; I bugger madmen, I discharge in madmen, I care for nought but them, I want to fuck nobody else in the world." However, loath to squander his forces, Vespoli has the youth unbound. Another one rushes into the lists, this one fancies he is God.

"I am going to fuck God," Vespoli announces to us, "observe me; but I must give God a thrashing before giving Him an embuggering. Hither," he continues, "this way, Bugger-God, bring Your ass around, Your ass, I say."

And God, attached to the stake by the jailers, is soon bested by His puny creature who embuggers Him once His buttocks are reduced to marmalade. A lovely girl of eighteen succeeds God; this one takes herself for the Virgin. Further subject for the blasphemies of Vespoli, who lashes the skin off the Blessed Mother of God, and who afterward sodomizes her for a quarter of an hour.

Clairwil arises, all afire.

"This spectacle inspires me," she says to us, "imitate me, my friends, and you, villain, have your jailers unclothe us and then lock us into those cages; treat us as though we were mad also, we shall feign lunacy; you will have us tied to the unspiked side of the cross, your madmen will whip us and then ass-fuck us."

The idea appeals to us all. Vespoli carries it out. Ten madmen are unleashed against us; some of them flog us, others are hacked fairly to pieces for refusing to do so; but they all fuck us, and all, guided by Vespoli, fit themselves into our behinds. The guards, the warden, everybody has his turn, we are daunted by none of them.

"So now discharge," Clairwil says to the master of the house, "we have done everything you asked, show us how you behave during the dramatic moment."

"All in good time, in good time," our man says, "there's one here that puts me in seventh heaven; I never leave the house in the morning without first fucking him."

Upon a signal to one of his jailers, he is brought an old man of nearly eighty with a white beard growing down to his navel.

"Come along, John," Vespoli says, catching him by the beard and towing him the length of the courtyard, "pick up your feet, John, I am going to put my prick in your ass."

The venerable old man is bound and fustigated mercilessly; his ass, his ancient, wrinkled ass is kissed, licked, embuggered; and withdrawing, very near to ejaculation, "Ah," says Vespoli, "you want to see me discharge? But do you realize I never attain my crisis without it costing two or three of these unfortunate persons their lives?"

"So much the better," say I, "but I trust that in your massacres you will overlook neither God nor Mary, for I confess that I'd indeed discharge pleasantly seeing you assassinate the Good Lord with one hand and His daughter-in-law with the other."

"I ought then to be embuggering Jesus Christ in the meantime," said the infamous man. "And Christ, we have him here: all paradise is in this hell."

The jailers lead forth a handsome young man of some thirty years who called himself the Son of God, and whom Vespoli has affixed to the cross at once. He flogs him with might and main.

"Courage, good Romans," the victim cries, "ever did I say unto you I came only to suffer on earth; spare me not, I implore you; well I know I must die upon the cross; but I shall have saved mankind."

At that, unable to restrain himself any longer, Vespoli puts prick to Jesus' asshole, and takes a stiletto in either hand, therewith to regale the Holy Virgin and God the Father.

"You others," he calls to us, "come forward, stand near me, show me your asses, and since you are curious about my discharge, you shall soon see how I proceed with it."

He files away; never was the Son of God so stoutly fucked; but each heave of Vespoli's flanks is accompanied by a slash dealt to some part or another of the two bodies posted one to the left, the other to the right. First, they are arms, armpits, shoulders, flanks he stabs; as the crisis approaches, the barbarian aims his blows at more delicate parts; the Virgin's bosom is covered with blood; striking now with one hand, now with the other, his arms move like a pendulum; the nearness of the spasm may be gauged by the sensitivity of the areas he brings under attack. Frightful oaths at last declare the onset of this frenetic's final transports. His rage now singles out faces for its targets, he rips them with his knives, and when the last drops of sperm have left him, they are eyeballs he pierces. Is there any possible expressing to what degree we are animated by this spectacle? We are bent on imitating the monster; victims are furnished us in abundance; we each immolate three. Clairwill, gone wild with lust, leaps to the center of the courtyard, drawing Vespoli after her.

"Fuck me, knave," she says to him; "in consideration of the cunt belonging to a woman of your own breed, perform an act of infidelity to your faith."

"I cannot," said the Italian.

"I demand it."

We excite Vespoli, his device rises; we force it into Clairwil's womb. We exhibit our asses to him, the capricious fellow asks for madmen, and it is only by having one of them shit upon his face that the scoundrel, prodded and wrought upon by Olympia and me, at last sprays fuck into Clairwil. And we retire from that execrable den, where, hardly noticing the passage of time, we had spent thirteen whole hours wallowing in infamies.

We tarried several days in Vespoli's institution of crime and debauchery, and then, wishing the superintendent every kind of prosperity, resumed our way toward the famous temples of Paestum.

Before going to inspect those monuments we first arranged for lodgings at a superb farm to which Ferdinand had addressed us. Graciousness, gentility characterized the persons we found upon this idyllic estate; it was owned by a widow of forty and her three daughters, who in age ranged from fifteen to eighteen. Here 'twas as though wickedness and crime did not exist: had virtue somehow been banished out of the world, it would have chosen this place for its retreat, and to be immortalized in the right-thinking and generous Rosalba. Wonderfully well preserved was she, and pretty beyond words were her daughters.

"Ha," I whispered to Clairwil, "did I not tell you I had a feeling we were soon to come upon an asylum where virtue in its purest colors would unfailingly provoke us to vice? Just look at those heavenly girls! they are flowers Nature presents for our plucking. Oh, Clairwil, it must be that thanks to us, trouble and desolation swiftly replace the innocence and the sweet peace reigning in this delicious place."

"My cunt throbs to hear you," said Clairwil; "these are, as you say, affecting victims." Then, after kissing me: "But their sufferings will not be mild. . . . However, let us first dine, then go to see the relics, and afterward devote ourselves to atrocity."

Traveling with a cook of our own we were assured of good fare wherever we stopped. After an ample meal, served us by the daughters of the house, we were shown the way to the temples. Those superb edifices are in a state of such excellent preservation that they do not appear to have been built more than three or four centuries ago. In number they are three, one of them being a good deal larger than the other two. After having contemplated these masterpieces, after having regretted that in every country of the world superstition has been responsible for the wasting of huge sums and efforts upon gods which, however recognized, have never existed save in the imaginations of fools, we turned back and headed for our farm, whither we were beckoned by equally interesting affairs.

There, Clairwil accosted the mother and gave her to understand that we were afraid of sleeping alone in a so prodigiously isolated countryside. "Your daughters," the rascal wanted to know, "dare we hope that they will accommodate us by sharing our beds?"

"Of course, dear lady," the good woman replied, "my daughters are only too flattered by the honor you deign to show them."

And Clairwil having hastened to report to us this becoming reply, each of us selected the maiden we desired, and we retired for the night.

The fifteen-year-old had fallen to me; nothing prettier, nothing sweeter ever graced the world. No sooner were we underneath the same sheet than I set to plying her with caresses, and the poor little thing responded with a candor, an ingenuousness that might have disarmed anyone but a libertine of my stamp. I began by questions. Alas, the innocent understood not one word; nor yet, warm though the latitude was, had Nature begun to speak in her, and the most entire simplicity alone dictated that angel's artless replies. When my impure fingers touched the petals of the rose, she quivered; I kissed her, she kissed me in return, but with a simplicity unknown to worldly folk, and to be encountered nowhere but in the bowers of modesty and chaste inexperience.

There was nothing I might not have got her to do, nothing I might not myself have done with that pretty little creature when my companions, already up and stirring, came to find out how I had spent my night.

"What am I to tell you? I venture to say that the tale of my pleasures would be an exact recounting of yours."

"Ah, fuck my soul," said Clairwil, "I don't believe I have ever discharged so heavily. But, Juliette, up with you, send that child away, there are things we must discuss."

Looking her hard in the eye, "Slut," I said to her, "your soul stands revealed in your stare . . . crime lurks there."

"I am resolved to commit one, dreadful, hideous. . . . You know, the welcome we have had from these good people, the pleasure the girls have given us. . . ."

"Well?"

"I want to butcher them all, rob, plunder, burn down their house, and frig myself over its ruins once the corpses are buried underneath them."

"I find that a delightful idea," said I. "But first let us spend an evening with the family: the mother and her daughters are alone, all the help have gone off to Naples, there is not another house for miles around . . . let us perform some infamies, afterward we shall do our killing."

"So you are weary of yours?"

"Mortally."

"For my part, I am ready to see mine in hell," Borghese admitted.

"One ought never go too far with a pleasure-providing individual," said Clairwil, "unless one has poison in one's pocket."

"Minx! But before we settle down to business let us first have a quiet lunch."

As escort we had four strapping valets membered like jackasses, who fucked us when we were in need of fucking and who, paid exorbitantly, would not have dreamed of disputing our instructions: once told of our plan, they could hardly wait to put it into execution. Night had no sooner fallen than we took command of the house. But it is essential that I depict the actors to you, before detailing the scenes. Having already acquainted you with the mother, and described Rosalba's unimpaired freshness and beauty, I have only to say a few words about her children. Isabella was the youngest, 'twas with her I had spent the previous night; the second was called Mathilda, she was sixteen, lovely features, evenness and languor in her gaze, the look of a Raphael virgin; and Ernesilla was the name of the eldest: Venus' own bearing and body and face, impossible to be more beautiful: she was the one with whom Clairwil had just soiled herself in horrors and impudicities. Roger, Victor, Agostino, and Vanini were our lackeys' names. The first of them belonged to me, he was from Paris, twenty-two, and his device was a marvel; Victor, also French and eighteen years

old, belonged to Clairwil; his occult qualities were in no sense inferior to Roger's. Agostino and Vanini, both Florentines, belonged
to Borghese, they were both youthful, with charming faces, and
superiorly membered.

The gentle mother of those three Graces, a little surprised by
the precautionary measures she sees us taking, asks what this
activity might mean.

"You shall now find out, whore," says Agostino, ordering her,
his pistol leveled at her heart, to remove her clothes. In the meantime our three other valets, each taking charge of one of the
daughters, address to them compliments in the same kind. A few
minutes later and the naked mother and daughters, their hands
tied behind their backs, appear before us in the helpless situation
of victims. Clairwil steps up to Rosalba.

"Why, to look at this slut makes one's mouth water," says
she, fondling Rosalba's buttocks, squeezing her breasts. "And
these over here," and she turns toward the girls again; "they are
perfect angels, I have never set eyes on the like. Rascal!" she says
to me, caressing my Isabella, "you got the best of the lot, what
pleasures you must have had last night with this exquisite object!
Well now, my friends, you'll entrust the direction of the ceremonies
to me?"

"Surely, for our interests could not be placed under more
capable management."

"My suggestion then is that one after another we go into an
adjoining chamber with the mother and her three daughters, and
prepare the material for use."

"Shall we accompany ourselves by a man?" Borghese asked.

"No men at the beginning; they will be included in later
arrangements."

As I do not know what my companions did I shall tell you
only of the pranks I played upon those four unfortunate creatures.
I took a strap to the mother, held by her daughters; then to one of
the latter, while the two others frigged their mother in front of
me; I inserted needles in all their breasts, bit the clitoris and the
tongue of each, and broke the little finger on everybody's right
hand. The blood streaming down their bodies when, later, my
friends brought them back in seemed to indicate that Clairwil and

the Princess had been just as severe as I. The preliminary exercises completed, we assembled our victims. They all wept.

"Is this the reward for our politeness to you," they sobbed, "for the things we have done in your behalf?"

And the mother, in great distress, drew her daughters to her, kissed them, sought to console them; they nestled close to her, dropped their tears upon her bosom: the four composed a touching, a heart-rending tableau of sorrow and woe. But souls like ours, you know, do not readily melt, every appeal to their sensibility acts as further fuel to their rage: the whey ran down our thighs.

"We shall now have them fuck," Clairwil pronounced, "and for that, untie their hands."

With those words she places Rosalba upon a bed, then bids the youngest girl prepare our four valets' pricks for her mother. Goaded by our threats, the poor child was obliged to stroke, to suck, generally to put in fettle the engines that were to sound her mother; while she was engaged at these chores, we frolicked with her sisters. Our men were warned against any intempestive discharging. We presented the eldest girl to them, and then 'twas the mother who had to prepare the pricks. This second attack was another great success: Rosalba's children were one by one fucked by pricks formed for that purpose by her. One of our men, Agostino, weakened, however, and gasped forth his seed into Isabella's cunt.

"Don't be upset," said Clairwil, taking him promptly in hand, "three minutes, my boy, and I shall have you as erect as you were a short while ago."

Asses are now brought to the fore, the sodomy begins with the mother, her daughters are compelled to dart the pricks into her anus; a little while later, she renders them the same service. Roger, the best-membered of the quartet, is appointed to depucelate young Isabella . . . he nigh cleaves her in two; we discharge, lubriciously frigged by the other girls and bum-fucked by the men. Here it was Vanini who lost his self-control, vanquished by the effects of Ernesilla's splendid posterior: he filled her bowels with fuck, and Clairwil, with her unique skill for rehoisting fallen pricks, soon had that pretty fellow's as hard as if it had been deprived of exercise for six weeks.

At this point the true punishment began. Clairwil had the idea of tying a girl on top of each one of us, and the mother, threatened, constrained by the valets, was to torment them as they lay upon our bodies. I had requested Ernesilla; Mathilda was upon Clairwil, Isabella upon Borghese. Our men had all kinds of trouble getting obedience from Rosalba. When one must cajole Nature, when one must force a mother to whip, slap, cuff, pinch, burn, bite her own children, 'tis not, of course, an easy task. By it, however, we were not to be daunted. The whore required a great deal of pummeling but she complied, and we relished the ferocious pleasure of frigging, of kissing those three hapless creatures, fastened to us, while their mother beat them to a pulp.

These were succeeded by more serious games. We attached the mother to a pillar and obliged, at pistol-point, each of the daughters to thrust a sharp needle into Rosalba's breasts; they did so. Then we tied them, and it was the mother's turn: there was no way out for her, she had to drive a dagger into each of their gaping cunts, and while she was carving we caressed her buttocks with firmly held stilettoes. Those four bodies were approaching the state which distills that delicious horror engendered by the furtive crimes lewdness is the cause of, and which is not of the sort the ordinary sensibility can be expected to appreciate. Weary from work and pleasure, we had ourselves sodomized as we contemplated the ghastly condition of our victims, and while Roger, who had no woman to skewer, swung a steel-tipped martinet against those creatures, all four bound tight together in a solid mass.

"Very well, by God, by bugger-fucking God, very well, let's kill them now," said Clairwil, whose homicidal eyes stared rage and lust; "let's assassinate, let's destroy, let's drink their tears to drunkenness. I have waited long enough to see these whores expire, I am burning from the need to hear their death-cries, from a thirst for their accursed blood. I'd like to devour them piecemeal, to feed my guts on their rotten flesh. . . ."

Thus spoke she; and the buggeress stabbed with one hand, worried her clitoris with the other. We imitated her; and those screams, those screams we so longed to hear, rose like a hymn in our ears. We were there, watching from close on; our valets socratized us during the operation; all our senses were thrilled simultaneously by the divine spectacle of our infamies.

I was at Clairwil's side; frigged by Agostino, the slut was in the midst of discharging. She leaned toward me. "Oh, Juliette," she exclaimed, redoubling her habitual blasphemies, "oh, beloved soul, how crime doth delight, how puissant are its effects! what a mighty grip hath its charms upon a sensitive spirit!"

And the howls of Borghese, who for her part was discharging like a Messalina, precipitated our ejaculations and those of our lackeys, being briskly frigged by us.

Our agitation having subsided, we devoted the ensuing moment of repose to verifying the results of our criminal acts: the whores were sighing their last . . . and cruel death robbed us of the pleasure of torturing them some more. Hardly satisfied by the havoc we had just wrought, we turned our hands to pillaging the house, then we destroyed it. There are times in life when the desire to wallow in disorder is such as not to be sated by anything, and when execrations, even the most pronounced, only faintly fulfill an excessive inclination to evil.[25]

We walked away into the night, under a sky filled with stars. We had abandoned the plunder to our lackeys who were thereby to earn some thirty thousand francs from its resale.

From Paestum we retraced our steps to Vietri, where we boarded a small vessel for Capri. It sailed an easy course, tacking frequently close in to the land, and enabling us to miss none of the picturesque sites along the sublime coast of that peninsula. We put in for lunch at Amalfi, ancient Etruscan town enjoying an incomparable location. After that we landed again at Point Campanella, having followed a shore that remained extraordinary every mile. Of the Surrentines who lived here long ago we found only the remains

---

[25] Certain carping critics complained that, in *Justine,* we introduced only masculine villains onto the stage; here, thank heaven! we are in no danger of hearing the same withering reproaches. The truth, alas, is that evil-doing, one of the fundamental elements in the workings of Nature, is in an approximately equal degree manifest throughout the entire range of Nature's creatures; the more sensitive an individual, the more sharply this atrocious Nature will bend him into conformance with evil's irresistible laws; whence it is that women surrender to it more heatedly and perform it with greater artistry than men. But all, men and women alike, are wicked because they have to be: if in any of that there is anything absurd or unjust, it is the law made by the man who dares have the idiotic and vain pretension of repressing or combating the law of Nature.

of a temple of Minerva. The weather being fair, we set sail and in two short hours, passing the three little islands in the Galli group, we entered the port of Capri.

The island of Capri, which must measure some ten miles around, is girt on all sides by the highest crags. The one harbor is the little port on the landward side, facing the Bay of Naples. In shape the island describes an ellipse four miles long by two at its greatest width; it is divided into two parts, upper and lower Capri. A prodigiously high mountain makes for the division, acting as the Apennines do in Italy. Communication between the two parts is by a stairway of one hundred and fifty steps hewn in the face of sheer rock.

Tiberius seldom climbed them; it was the lower part he preferred, where the weather is more temperate, and it was there he built his pleasure domes and his palaces, one of which is, however, perched on the tip of a rock rising so far above the water that the eye can barely discern the fishermen's boats moored below. That particular palace served as the theater for his most piquant lewd revels. 'Twas from the summit of a tower poised on a spur of rock, and whose vestiges are still to be seen, that fierce Tiberius used to have children of both sexes flung to their death, once they were of no further use to his lust.

"Fuck the devil," Clairwil muttered, "how he must have discharged watching the victims of his libertinage plummet from these heights. Oh, dear angel," she went on, hugging me to her, "he was a voluptuous rascal, that Tiberius. What if we were to look for something to throw off this precipice as the Emperor used to do?"

And it was then that Borghese, guessing what was on our minds, pointed to a little girl of nine or ten who was tending a she-goat a short distance away.

"Just what we want," said Clairwil. "But our guides?"

"They may be sent home. We need simply tell them that we have decided to take a nap here."

No sooner said than done; we find ourselves alone. Borghese herself fetches over the child.

"Who are you?" we ask her.

"Poor and destitute," the little darling replies humbly. "This goat is all we have and mother is sick and always in bed and if it weren't for the goat and for me, she would surely die."

"Why, this is a rare stroke of good luck," said the infernal Clairwil. "We must tie the two of them together, goat and girl, and send them over the edge."

"Quite right, but not before we amuse ourselves," said I. "I for one am dreadfully curious to find out how this child is made; health, freshness, innocence glow in her young charms: it would be ridiculous not to divert ourselves with them."

And will you believe it, my friends? Yes, we had the cruelty to take that child's maidenhead, which was accomplished with a pointed stone; to flay her with brambles which we found growing near at hand; next, to bind her to her nanny and to push them both over the edge of the precipice, and to watch them fall and disappear into the sea; and what lent their acuteness to our three discharges was the knowledge that the murder was twofold, since we were also causing the death of the child's infirm mother who, deprived of the resources represented by the two objects we had just destroyed, would surely not fail to perish in her turn.

"That is how I like my horrors," I declared to my friends; "either make them thorough and extensive, or refrain from undertaking them at all."

"Yes," Clairwil agreed, "but it would have been good to have asked the child where her mother lives. For it would have been delightful to see her expire from want."

"Roguish thing!" I said to my friend, "I wager there is not a person on earth able to boast of your capacities for refining a crime."

And we continued our promenade.

Most eager to learn whether the happy inhabitants of this island resembled, through vigor as regarded the men, through charms as regarded the women, Naples' divine breed, we betook ourselves to see the Governor, and delivered to him a personal letter from Ferdinand.

Having read it, "I am surprised," said he, "that the King could have thought to issue me such instructions. Can he be unaware that my position here is more that of a spy set to watch these people than of a representative of the Crown? Capri is a republic of which the royally appointed governor is merely the president. By what right would His Majesty have me compel these citizens, men and women, to surrender themselves to you? A despot's orders, these, and Ferdinand knows full well he is not the despot here. I too am fond of all such things, but find little opportunity to indulge in them hereabouts, where there are no public whores and precious few idlers or valets; nevertheless, as, according to what Ferdinand writes, you pay liberally, I am going to propose to a merchant's widow of my acquaintance that she let you have her three daughters. She likes money and I do not doubt but that she will be seduced by yours. These daughters, born on Capri, are one of them sixteen years of age, another seventeen, the eldest twenty; we have nothing more beautiful upon the entire island; what is your offer?"

"A thousand ounces a head," said my friend, "funds disbursed for our pleasures' sake do not come out of our own pockets, and to you, Governor, we promise an equal sum. But in addition we must get us three males."

"Shall I receive the same fee for them?" asked the greedy public officer.

"Certainly. We are not people to higgle over such matters."

And the dear man having readied everything for the lewd scene in the offing, asked nothing more in the way of favors save leave to watch it.

The girls were in truth splendid; the boys, healthy, vigorous, and endowed with magnificent pricks. After having had our thorough fill of them, we mated them with our three virgins; we assisted in the deflowerings; however, the plucking of the rose was all we allowed them; they were then obliged to take refuge in our asses, they had permission to discharge nowhere else. The spectacle had the poor Governor in an ecstasy, and he applauded it by masturbating nearly to unconsciousness: for these orgies were prolonged throughout the entire night, and in such a country we dared not pass the time otherwise than in anodyne ceremonies. We left without going to bed, after having paid the Governor handsomely, and promised to present his excuses to Ferdinand for not having done more for us, restricted as he was by the islanders' mode of government.

Sailing back to Naples, our vessel coasted close to the land, for we remained spellbound by the sights along those wonderful shores. We discovered Massa, Sorrento, Torquato Tasso's home, the lovely grotto of Lila de Rico, and finally Castellammare. There we put in to port to visit Stabiae, buried like Herculaneum, where Pliny the Elder used to go to see his friend Pompeianus, in whose house he was lying the night of the famous eruption which submerged that town along with the others round about. The workmen excavating this one are proceeding slowly: when we were there, they had unearthed only a handful of buildings.

It was a rapid tour we made, weary as we were; and very eager to rest and refresh ourselves, we returned at last to our princely quarters, sending word to the King notifying him we were in the city again, and thanking him for all he had done to make our journey such a success.

Part
Six

$\mathcal{A}$ few days later we received a message from His Neapolitan Highness, inviting us to be among his guests on the balcony of the royal palace to witness one of his kingdom's most unusual festivals. It was the one known as The Treat. I had frequently heard tell of this extravagance; but the actual thing was unlike anything I could have expected.

Charlotte and Ferdinand were awaiting us in a boudoir whose windows looked out upon the square where the holiday tumults were to occur. Among us were two other personages, La Riccia and the Duc Gravines, a man of fifty, very libertine.

"If you are not familiar with this entertainment," said the King after we had finished dinner, "you are apt to find it rather primitive."

"That, Sire, and barbarous is how we like our entertainments," I replied; "and I shall add that I have long favored reviving rough sports and gladiatorial combats in France: a nation's tone is maintained by bloody spectacles; where these lack, you are heading for decadence. When a thoughtless emperor, placing stupid Christianity on the throne of the Caesars, closed the circuses at Rome, what did the masters of the world turn into, eh? Abbots, monks, or dukes."

"I feel just as you do," said Ferdinand. "My aim is to revive contests between men and animals, and even those pitting men against men; it is in that direction I have been moving; Gravines and La Riccia support me, and I hope we shall succeed."

"And of what account can the lives of all that trash be," Charlotte wondered, "when our pleasures are at stake? If we have the right to have their throats cut for our interests' sake, I see no reason why we cannot do the same for the sake of our delights."

"Very well, gentle ladies," Ferdinand said to us, "issue your

999

orders. Depending upon the greater or lesser degree of rigor, upon the larger or smaller number of police I introduce into these orgies, I can have six hundred more or fewer people killed: therefore indicate what your desires are in this regard."

"The worst, the worst," Clairwil was prompt to answer; "the more of those rascals you have dispatched, the better you will divert us."

Ferdinand then murmured some instructions to one of his officers.

A cannon boomed; and we proceeded out onto the balcony. There was an excessively numerous crowd collected upon the square; from our vantage point we had the clearest view of everything.

Upon a huge scaffolding decorated with rustic ornaments is heaped a tremendous quantity of victuals so disposed as to compose a part of the decoration. Inhumanely crucified there are geese, chickens, turkeys, which, suspended alive and held by a single nail, amuse the people by their twitchings and flutterings; loaves of bread, dried cod, quarters of beef; sheep, grazing on an artificial pasture, tended by pasteboard shepherds; upon a sea made of canvas, a vessel laden with food or useful articles intended for the populace. Such, laid out with much artistry and tastefulness, is the bait prepared for this savage nation, all in order to commemorate and to perpetuate its voraciousness and its excessive propensity for theft. For, after having witnessed this sight, it would be difficult not to agree that it is more an exercise in pillage than a veritable festival.

We had hardly time to consider the theater for the forthcoming events when a second shot was heard. At this signal, the cordon of troops that has been holding the crowd back suddenly gives way; the people rush forward and, in the twinkling of an eye, everything is made off with, snatched up, grabbed away, with a swiftness, with a frenzy impossible to describe. This terrifying scene, resembling the fleshing of a pack of hounds, regularly ends more or less tragically because disputes break out, everybody covets what his neighbor has just got his hands upon; and, in Naples, such differences are always settled with drawn knives, But this time, in accordance with our desires and thanks to Ferdinand's foresight, once the scaffoldings were black with people, once they looked to be covered with a good seven or eight hundred struggling human beings, the structure abruptly collapsed, and over four hundred people were crushed.

"Ah, fuck!" exclaimed Clairwil, sinking giddily upon a sofa, "ah, my friends, you gave me no warning of this—I am dying—" and it was to La Riccia the whore appealed, "—fuck me, my angel, fuck me," she sighed, "I am discharging; in all my life nothing I have ever been witness to has given me such pleasure."

We re-entered the boudoir; windows and doors were shut, and the most delicious of all lubricious scenes was enacted, as it were, upon the ashes of the unfortunate plebeians sacrificed by high wickedness.

Four girls, fifteen or sixteen years old, lovely as daylight and dressed in the black crepe of mourning, naked underneath it, were awaiting us, standing, and in silence. In another part of the room, four other women, between twenty and thirty, each pregnant, each stark naked, silent also, and wearing grave expressions, seemed eager to hear our instructions. Reclining upon a couch at the room's far end were four young men, between eighteen and twenty years old, and in their hands they held their threatening pricks, and those pricks, good friends, those pricks were monsters: twelve whole inches in circumference, yes, and eighteen inches long. Not in all our lives had we beheld the like of those objects; and the four of us discharged merely at catching sight of them.

"These four women and these four girls," Ferdinand explained to us, "are the daughters and the widows of some of the ill-starred individuals who perished a short while ago before our eyes. Those individuals were, I can affirm, in positions of particular danger when the disaster was produced, and of their deaths I am certain. I had these eight women summoned here well before today's Treat began and, locked inside a room, through a window they were able to witness the fate of their fathers and husbands. I turn them over to you now, with them conclude your holiday. Out there," the monarch continued, opening a door giving out upon a little garden, "out there is the pit dug for their remains when they have at last, after hideous sufferings, earned the right to rest in peace. Their grave. . . . Women, step this way, you must see it too."

And the cruel man obliged them to climb down into the trench, made them lie down in it, then, satisfied with its dimensions, he directed our attentions back to the four youths.

"I am certain, Mesdames," said he, "that you have not often beheld such articles." And he took hold of those awesome pricks, hard as iron bars, and had us feel, them, heft them, kiss them, dally with them. "The vigor of these men," the King went on, "at least equals their superiority of member; every one of them is the guarantee of fifteen or sixteen discharges, and not one yields less than twelve ounces of sperm per ejaculation: they are the élite in my realm. They are Calabrians all four, and there is no province in Europe that furnishes members of this size. Let us enjoy them without stint.

"Four boudoirs adjoin this one; they are outfitted with everything that can serve lustful purposes: so let us be off, let us fuck and be fucked, let us vex, torment, torture to our hearts' content, and may our imaginations, fired by the spectacle that has just been staged for us, ensure the thoroughness of cruelties and the refinement of our joys."

"Bugger-fuck!" I said to Ferdinand, "how nicely you have the art of entertaining persons of our temper."

Dresses, petticoats, breeches fell quickly to the floor, and before proceeding to collective scenes, it appeared to be everybody's intention to repair singly into the neighboring rooms for a short moment. La Riccia took with him one of the girls, a pregnant woman, and a fucker; Gravines encloseted himself with Olympia and an expectant mother; and Ferdinand took Clairwil, a fucker, another expectant mother, and two little girls; Charlotte chose me, and wanted to have a pair of fuckers with us, one of the girls, and a woman as well.

"Juliette," the Queen of Naples addressed me as soon as we were inside our boudoir, "I can no longer keep to myself the emotions you have engendered in me: I adore you. I am too much a whore to promise you fidelity; but that romantic sentiment is of course valueless amongst such persons as ourselves: 'tis not a heart I offer you, 'tis a cunt, a cunt which pours fuck whenever your hand touches it. In you I see someone of my own mind, of my own way of thinking, and, incontestably, I prefer you to either of your sisters. Your Olympia is a clod, she shows some mettle occasionally, but the rest of the time she is timorous and at bottom she is a coward; a clap of thunder would suffice to convert such a woman. Clairwil, yes, she is a superb creature, with infinite wit, I don't deny it, but her tastes and mine are not at all the same: for exercising her cruelties she likes men only, and while I am willing enough to sacrifice that sex, it is however the blood of mine I most enjoy shedding. She adopts, besides, an overbearing and superior manner toward us all, and it is prodigiously hurtful to my pride. With no fewer resources and perhaps with many more than she, you, Juliette, do not affect so much vanity; that comforts; I believe there is more sweetness in your character, just as much wickedness in your head, but in your heart a greater capacity for loyalty toward your friends. In short, I like you best, and this diamond, worth fifty thousand crowns, which I beg you to accept, may persuade you it is so."

"Charlotte," said I, declining to take the gem, "you are a woman to whom one may confess having vices; I am touched by your feelings in my regard, and mine for you, be sure of it, are the same. But I shall own to you, my dear, and it is one of my idiosyncrasies, I accord no importance whatever to gifts, only what I take counts in my eyes. And if you care to satisfy me on that head, why, you can do so very easily."

"How?"

"Before anything else, swear by your love for me that you will never tell anyone of the imperious desire that devours me."

"I swear to it."

"I want to steal your husband's treasures, to that end I want you to provide me the means."

"Lower your voice," said the Queen, "these people could overhear us. One moment, I shall send them into the next room.

"Now," Charlotte continued once we were alone, "we may chat in security. I have a proposal to make to you; accept it, there is no other way for you to convince me of the sincerity of your feelings in my regard. Oh, Juliette!" she added, "the trust you place in me demands that I in return place mine in you. And I too, my dear, I am meditating a crime; will you help me?"

"Even were it at the risk of a thousand lives. Speak."

"If you but knew how bored I am with my husband!"

"Despite his indulgence?"

"Is it for my sake he behaves as he does? He prostitutes me out of libertinage, out of jealousy; thus appeasing my passions, he reckons to forestall the birth of desires in me, and he prefers that it be through his will and choice I am fucked rather than through my own."

"A droll policy."

"It is the one he practices, it is that of an Italianized Spaniard, and there is nothing worse on the face of the earth."

"And you desire. . . ."

"To poison this tiresome man, to become regent once he is out of the way. The people prefer me to him, they adore my children; and I shall rule alone; you shall become my favorite, and your fortune is made."

"No, Charlotte, I shall not live with you, I am not attracted by the role you offer me; in addition, I am fond of my own country and am eager to return there soon. But you may rely upon my aid, since Ferdinand, who has a store of poisons of every sort, doubtless keeps them out of your reach. From me you shall have what you need; but a good turn in exchange for a good turn, Charlotte, bear in mind that what I promise is yours only provided I get your husband's treasure. What does it amount to?"

"It cannot exceed eighty million."

"In currencies?"

"In ingots as well as in piasters, ounces, and sequins."

"How do we proceed?"

"You see that window," said Charlotte, pointing to a casement window not far from the one at which we were standing, "have a wagon with some good horses underneath it the day after tomorrow; I shall steal the key and hand everything down to you in sacks."

"And the watch?"

"No sentinels are posted on this side."

"Listen," I said to Charlotte, whose undoing I was excitedly plotting at that very moment, "there are steps I must take in order to obtain the poison you require, and I do not care to venture into this delicate matter unless I am sure of where I stand. Sign this paper," said I, writing it out on the spot, "I shall then feel safe in acting, and neither of us will have anything further to worry about."

Blinded by her love for me, pressed by the extreme desire to be rid of her husband, Charlotte signed; and, signing, proved that prudence is rarely the consort of great passions. Herein as follows is the text she ratified:

I shall steal all my husband's treasure, and give it in payment to her who supplies me the poison necessary to send him to the next world.

  C. de L., Reg. N.

"Excellent," said I, "that puts me entirely at ease. The day after tomorrow, at the hour fixed, you may count upon the wagon. Serve me well, Charlotte; and so shall you be served in return. Now let us turn to play."

"Ah, dearest friend," cried the Queen, overwhelming me with kisses, "what services you render me and how I adore you!"

The fool! how far from reciprocal were my feelings. Oh, it was no longer possible to maintain the illusion, we had shed overmuch fuck together; I delighted only in the thought of her doom, and the document to which she had thoughtlessly put her name guaranteed it.

"Shall we frig each other," she said, "before calling in the accessories to our debauchery?"

And without waiting for me to answer, the whore pushes me upon a bed, kneels between my thighs and sucks me, the while tickling my cunt and my asshole both at once. 'Twas then I availed myself of the faculty women have for mental infidelities; it was from Charlotte I was receiving voluptuous sensations, I was covered by her pollutions, her kisses, and yet no thought absorbed me save that of betraying Charlotte.

Adulterous wives, there is your portrait: lying in your husbands' arms, to your master you abandon only the bodily part of yourselves, and the sensations that arise in you are never but a response to your lover. The cuckolds delude themselves, supposing they are the cause of the raptures into which their motions plunge you, when actually, rub as much as they please, they are incapable of igniting even a spark. Bewitching sex, continue this deceit, it is natural; proof thereof resides in the suppleness of your imaginations; compensate yourselves thus, when you cannot do otherwise, for the preposterous chains of chastity and of wedlock, and never lose sight of the fact that if Nature made you a cunt for men to fuck, her hand at the very same instant created you the heart needed to betray them.

Charlotte waxed drunk on my sperm, and I must honestly avow that it spilled forth in floods at the idea, delicious for a mind like mine, of forever ruining her who was responsible for its outpouring. She flings herself upon my breast, we pollute each other with ardor, she sucks my mouth, my nipples, and as I frig her to perfection, the tribade is shaken by twenty spasms in a row. We entwine ourselves, each buries her face between the other's legs; tongue to clitoris, libertine finger in asshole and cunt, we sot ourselves upon each other's fuck, all the while preoccupied by very dissimilar thoughts.

Finally, Charlotte, all afire, is in a mood for libertinage, she rings, she would have me be the center of everything at first; the pregnant woman, within reach of my right hand, is offered to my vexations; the girl, straddling my chest, simultaneously offers me the sweetest cunt to lick and the most charming ass. Charlotte excites the pricks and herself pilots them into me.

"I am infatuated by the idea of having a queen for my bawd," I declare to Charlotte; "go to it, whore, ply your trade."

But engines of the size of those Ferdinand has procured for us are not easy to accommodate; and however veteran may be my charms, I am unable to endure, without preparation, such monstrous attacks. Charlotte therefore moistens the thoroughfares; to the entrance of my cunt and to the fucker's gargantuan member she applies an ointment thanks to which, at the first lunge, the monster is able to pass to the midway mark. However, the pain is so sharp that, expelling a furious cry, I send flying the little girl who has been perched above my chest; I struggle, thrash, seek to rid myself of the shaft. My efforts are countered by Charlotte, she pushes us together, my fucker and me, and thus aided, the hero thunders to the farthermost depths of my womb: I had never suffered so much. But these thorns are soon transformed into roses; such is my rider's skillfulness, such the power of his strokes, that at the fourth heave of his loins my fuck answers, and from then on everything moves smoothly. Charlotte, favoring the act, stimulating the organs and the asshole of my fucker, to my left hand offers her buttocks, which I molest with quite as much violence as I do those of the pregnant woman, and the little girl, tongued by me, splashes her dulcet ejaculation upon my face. What energy in that Calabrian! He saws me for twenty minutes, finally erupts, and refucks me three more times without retiring from the lists; I put him aside after an hour of this. His comrade replaces him. While I am fucking with this second one, Charlotte decides she would like to see both of them in my body. She arranges our positions. I am in the second fucker's arms, stretched out on top of him, 'tis I who do the fucking while he lies quietly still; I handle, I maltreat a cunt with my right hand, my left is socratizing an ass, my tongue is licking a clitoris. The first man, assisted by the Queen, presents himself at my asshole; but habituated though I am to this mode of pleasure-taking, we battle for a quarter of an hour, without his succeeding in making the least headway into the breach. These multiple efforts cause me an incredible agitation: I gnash my teeth, foam at the mouth, I bite everything I can get at, I drench with fuck the prick ploughing my cunt, 'tis upon that prick I vent my wrath at being unable to incorporate another one anally. By dint of perseverance and cunning, it is nevertheless beginning to progress, I feel it; my encunter stirs from his passivity, contributing a heave of the loins to facilitate his comrade's task. I utter a piercing scream, I am embuggered. . . . It beggared comparison with anything I had ever experienced previously.

"What a divine spectacle!" cried Charlotte, masturbating smartly in front of us, and sometimes bending near to kiss me. "Christ! what an aperture! Happy Juliette!"

And I discharged, and I was like one run amuck, I lost sight of everything, was deaf to everything, all my powers of sensation had concentrated in my erotic regions; I belonged uniquely to joy.

Both my men, without withdrawing, simultaneously fought another fierce bout, and when I dislodged them, fuck covered me down to the heels, it seeped from my pores.

"Your turn, slut," I say to Charlotte, "duplicate what I have just done if you care to know the meaning of pleasure."

She requires little urging; promptly stuffed before and behind, the jade proves to me that if her husband has been allowing her a few amusements, with a view to placating a libertinage which might pose dangers to his own safety, he has not been entirely wrong. Like us cruel in her voluptuous moments, the bitch asks me, while she cunt-sucks the little girl and is being fucked in cunt and ass, to tease the pregnant woman. That poor soul implores my mercy; I am not to be moved. Angered and heated by lewdness, I bring my knee up against her stomach, she totters backward and falls, I leap and stamp upon her belly; then I beat her, I throttle her; watching it all, Charlotte eggs me on, stammering forth horrors. Having got herself double-fucked twice, the whore at last dismisses the men, and rises. We quaff off two bottle of champagne and pass back into the salon where we find all the company already gathered. Everybody was relating his prowesses; it was easy to deduce that it had not been in our boudoir alone that pregnant women had met with abuse: not one of them was able to hold herself upright; Gravines' especially . . . she was about to enter labor; and the villain had flogged her half to death.

Dinner was magnificent in the extreme; the girls waited upon us at table, and the pregnant women, lying on the floor beneath our feet, were the targets of all kinds of hard treatment. Seated next to Clairwil, I found the opportunity to mention to her the trick for which I had laid the groundwork; although I could give her only one or two details, she perfectly grasped my design, congratulated me, affirmed that I was the cleverest and the most venturesome woman she knew.

Electrified by the delicate fare and the exquisite wines, we removed, tipsily, to a superb hall readied for the orgies that we needed to celebrate. There, the agents were Ferdinand, Gravines, La Riccia, Clairwil, Charlotte, Olympia, and myself. The victims: the four pregnant women, the four young girls who had waited upon us at dinner, and the eight comely children in the one sex and the other whose asses had dispensed the brandies which followed coffee. Fourteen stout warriors, at least as grandly proportioned, as high-strung as those we had drained in the morning, appeared, their lances couched; they were all naked, quivering, and respectfully, with bated breath, awaiting the laws it would please us to decree in their regard. The stage required to be lit, since we had tarried long at table and the hour was advanced: five hundred candles, hid by green gauze shades, produced a soft and most agreeable light throughout that hall.

"No more privacy, no more intimate conversation," said the King; "henceforth we must operate within full view of one another."

Thereupon, in the most anarchical fashion, we fling ourselves at the nearest object to hand: we fuck, have fucked, are fucked; but cruelty always presides over lewd doings as disorderly as ours. Here, breasts were being kneaded and wrung; there, asses were being lashed; to the right cunts were being stretched, gravid women were being martyrized to the left, and moans and sighs of pain or of pleasure, mingled with lamentations to one side, with awful blasphemies to the other side, were for a good while the only sounds to be heard. Little by little, however, the more energetic outbursts heralding discharges began to ring forth; Gravines was the first to utter his yell. Alas! no sooner had he pronounced the expressions announcing his delirium than we saw fall at his feet, in the middle of the swirling groups surrounding him, a woman, her throat cut, the fruit torn from her womb, and mother and child bathed both in blood.

"That is not my way of going about it," said La Riccia, ordering one of those swollen sows to be tied fast to the wall. "Your attention, if you please," said he, "kindly watch."

He dons a pair of hobnailed boots, places his hands on the shoulders of two men and catapults himself feet first at the belly of the would-be mother who, her seams split, rent, bloodied, faints in her bonds and looses her worthless fruit, upon which the lustful nobleman straightway sprays his foaming seed. Very close to the spot where this occurred, being fucked at once frontwise and from behind, sucking the device of a youth who chose this moment to discharge into my mouth, frigging a cunt with either hand, I could not help but share the Prince's pleasures, and after his example I surrendered my sperm. Doing so, I cast a glance at Clairwil: someone was embuggering her; a young girl was sucking her cunt and the slut was flogging a little boy; she too discharges. Charlotte, encunted, was sucking a little boy, frigging a couple of girls, and was having a pregnant woman flogged upon the belly. Ferdinand was operating upon a girl: he was plucking at her parts with red-hot pincers; he was being sucked apace, and when he sensed his discharge near, the villain, armed with a scalpel, sliced off his victim's nipples and tossed them at us. Such, roughly speaking, were our pleasures when Ferdinand suggested that we move into an adjoining chamber where an ingenious machine, said he, was ready to put the pregnant women to an interesting death. The two of them who are left are in consequence affixed to large steel plates, one woman facing upward, the other facing downward, in such sort that their bellies are in exact perpendicular line: the upper plate is elevated ten feet above the lower.

"All right," says the King, "make ready for pleasure."

Everyone presses around, and several minutes later Ferdinand touches a lever, and the two plates, one rising, the other descending, come together with such force that the two creatures, colliding, are, they and their fruit, shortly squashed to a pulp. You will, I trust, have no trouble understanding that not one of those present was able to resist this spectacle, not one who did not salute it with a fuck and other expressions of divine praise.

"Shall we move on to another room?" said our amiable host. "Other joys may be awaiting us elsewhere."

This enormous hall was occupied by a vast theater; seven different sets of equipment for inflicting that many varieties of death were in a state of readiness there; four torturers, each naked and handsome as Mars, stood by to administer each torture, the first of these being fire; the second, the whip; the third, the rope; the fourth, the wheel; the fifth, the pale; the sixth, decapitation; the seventh, general dissection. Each guest was provided with a separate loge containing a gallery of fifty portraits of children, boys and girls, all as pretty as one could hope to see. We assumed our individual places, each accompanied by a fucker, a little girl, and a little boy, whose functions were to minister to our pleasures during the executions. Next to each portrait hung a silken cord activating a bell.

"Each shall, in his turn, select a victim from among the fifty representations surrounding him," Ferdinand announced; "he shall ring the bell corresponding to the object of his choice, his victim shall appear immediately in his loge; he shall dally with that victim for a moment. You will notice that from each loge a staircase leads up to the stage; preliminaries over, the guest shall march his victim up, direct him to the torture he deems most arousing, then inflict it himself, if he cares to; otherwise, he shall signal to the torturer in charge, and the victim, taken promptly in hand by that officer, shall be sacrificed before his eyes. But for your pleasures' sake I urge you not to act save one by one: we have no need to hurry, dear guests, and life's best spent hours are always those one spends wresting life away from others."

"Damn me," Clairwil said to the King, "if I have often encountered an imagination so fertile as yours."

"Oh," rejoined the Neapolitan, "mine is a claim to only very modest glory. All these fantasies used to raise the pricks of my forebears, those tyrants of ancient Syracuse. In my archives I uncovered traces of these horrors, studied them, for they impressed me in the most favorable sense; I enjoy reviving tradition with my friends."

Gravines rings first; his choice falls upon a youth of sixteen, superb to see. The boy appears, and Gravines, who has sole rights to the use of him, whips him, sucks him, bites his member, crushes one of his testicles, embuggers him, and finally sends him off to be burned: as a sodomite, the sarcastic Duke declares, it is only fitting that he perish by fire. Clairwil rings next and, needless to say, her choice also settles upon a male: he was scarcely eighteen years old, he was as fair as Adonis; the wicked soul sucks, frigs, fustigates him, has him lick her cunt and ass; then, springing up to the stage with him, the buggeress impales him with her own hands, having herself embuggered by one of the torturers in the meantime.

Olympia's turn follows; a thirteen-year-old girl is the object she chooses. She caresses her, and has her hanged.

After her comes Ferdinand. Like Clairwil, he chooses a youth. "I am fond of torturing women," he explains, "but I take even greater pleasure in killing individuals of my sex."

The adolescent appears: twenty years of age, membered like Hercules, with the face of Love. Ferdinand has himself tupped, tups in return, flagellates his victim, conducts him to the apparatus upon which he is to be broken. Broken, the victim is strapped to a wheel and left to expire there, at the rear of the stage.

La Riccia's fancy is caught by a maid of sixteen, lovely as the Goddess of Youth, and after having subjected her to all manner of abominations, he has her chopped up into small pieces.

Charlotte rings for a little girl of twelve, and once she is done frolicking with her, the Queen, while being fucked by two men, has the child beheaded.

I summon an eighteen-year-old girl, superb; never in my life had I feasted my eyes on a more beautiful body. After having kissed, fondled, licked every part of it, I lead her upon the stage; and working in concert with the executioners, I give her the whip. 'Tis no commonplace whip, but a formidable bullwhip, each stroke brings away a chunk of flesh the size of your hand; she expires, and her torturers fuck me as I lie upon her corpse.

So pleasant did we find this game that it had inevitably to be played for a very long time. All told, we immolated eleven hundred and seventy-six victims, which made one hundred sixty-eight apiece, among them six hundred girls and five hundred seventy-six boys. Charlotte and Princess Borghese were the only ones who sacrificed none but girls. The individuals for whose destruction I was responsible included an equal number of males and females; the same held true for La Riccia; but Clairwil, Gravines, and King Ferdinand immolated strictly nothing but men, and in the great majority of cases, did their killing personally. Throughout the entire exercise we were fucked incessantly, and our athletes had to be replaced several times over. We retired at the end of forty-five consecutive hours of rare riot and divine pleasures.

"Madame," I whispered to Charlotte as I took leave of her, "do not forget the little paper you signed for me. . . ."

"And you," was Charlotte's reply, "don't forget our appointment. Be as faithful as I in abiding by our bargain, I ask no more of you than that."

Once home, I explained to Clairwil in full what I had only been able to hint at before.

"O delightful project!" she said.

"And you see, of course, where I want it to lead."

"What do you mean?"

"I loathe Charlotte."

"My darling! Kiss me . . . how I share your feelings!"

"Dear Clairwil, that woman is mad about me, she is forever chasing after me with requests to make her discharge. And nothing bores me so much as these performances. Only you, my angel, in all the world there is no one but you whom I am willing to forgive for loving me."

"What a mind you have, Juliette!"

"It is more than a little like yours."

"Oh, indeed it is, my precious. . . . So then, tell me, what do you plan to do with this Charlotte?"

"The day after I have the contents of the royal exchequer, I send this note of hers to the robbed Ferdinand: 'I shall steal all my husband's treasure, and give it in payment to her who supplies me the poison necessary to send him to the next world'—when the dear man reads that he will, I should hope, condemn Charlotte to death or at least to some frightful prison."

"Yes, but an accused Charlotte will reveal her accomplices; she will say that it was to us she turned over his riches."

"Will it be presumable that, if we were Charlotte's correspondents, we would send the note to the King?"

"Presumable or not, Ferdinand will have searches conducted."

"I shall see to it that they are fruitless. Everything shall be buried in our garden. As for the King, I shall go to see him myself. If his suspicions fasten too firmly upon us, I shall threaten to make public the ghastly joke he played the day before yesterday during The Treat. Ferdinand, being weak and stupid, will be frightened, and that will be an end to the matter. And then, too,

'Tis an inglorious triumph earned from a victory
achieved without peril.

Gaining wealth means taking risks: is it your opinion that fifty or sixty million are not worth going to some trouble to acquire?"

"If caught, it will mean death for us."

"What is that to me? There is nothing I fear less in this world than the noose. Is it not common knowledge that death upon the gallows is accompanied by a discharge? And discharging is something that will never hold terrors for me. If ever a judge sends me to the scaffold, you will see me go forward with light and impudent step. . . . But calm yourself, Clairwil, crime is our friend, we are its favorites. In such enterprises as this we cannot fail."

"Are you thinking of including Borghese in our scheme?"

"No, I don't like that woman anymore."

"Fuck! for my part I detest her."

"She should be got rid of as soon as possible."

"There is the trip we are to make to Vesuvius tomorrow. . . ."

"Indeed there is; that volcano's deeps must serve as her grave. What a way to die!"

"I imagine it as horrible. Otherwise it would not have occurred to me."

"I should like something still more cruel."

"When the two of us hate, Juliette, oh, we do our hating well!"

"We must dine with her as usual."

"And even fawn upon her."

"Let me manage that, you know that my features and my character are well suited to treachery."

"We must frig her tonight."

"Of course."

"Oh, my angel, we are going to be very rich!"

"This stroke once accomplished, there will be no further tarrying in Naples."

"Nor in Italy. We must get us back to France, buy properties, and spend our remaining days together . . . what delights await us! Nothing will restrict them but the laws of our desires."

"The instantaneous satisfaction of them all—oh, dear heart, what happiness money brings! What a fool is he who abstains from employing every means, legitimate and otherwise, for procuring it. Clairwil, they will sooner put me a thousand times to death than deprive me of my taste for theft; it is among my greatest pleasures; 'tis one of the fundamental needs of my existence. When I steal I experience the sensation an ordinary woman feels when she is frigged. In my case, all crimes chafe the nerve endings in the zones of pleasure, just as do fingers or pricks; I discharge merely from plotting a felony. Why, here's an example, this diamond: Charlotte offered it to me, it is worth fifty thousand crowns. I declined it. As a gift, it displeased me. Stolen, I delight in it."

"You took it from her?"

"I did. It is no wonder to me that some people have surrendered to this passion solely for the voluptuous effects it produces; I would willingly steal for the rest of my life, and I declare to you, that had I an income of two million a year, you would still see me a thief out of libertinage."

"Ah, my love," said Clairwil, "how certain it is that Nature created us for each other. Never fear, we shall not part."

We dined with Borghese, the three of us discussed plans for the following day's excursion to Vesuvius. That evening we were at the Opera; the King came to our box to pay us his respects, all eyes were turned our way. Home again, we proposed to Borghese that a part of the night be given over to eating roasts with Cyprian wine; she took gladly to the idea; and we, Clairwil and I, carried deceitfulness to the point of wringing seven or eight discharges from the woman our villainy had already doomed, and of discharging almost as many times in her embrace. After that we let her go to bed, and the two of us spent the remainder of the night together; and before it was over, we owed another three or four spasms to the enchanting thought that on the morrow we were to make a mockery of every sentiment of trust and friendship. Such mischief, I realize, is inconceivable except to special mentalities like ours; but he is deserving of pity who lacks the capacity for it, great pleasures are denied him; I venture to affirm that he ignores what true happiness is.

We rose at an early hour. Criminal projects prevent sleep, they sow tumult in the senses; the mind revolves them, explores them from all sides, savors all their ramifications, and through anticipation you delight unendingly in the pleasure with which you know you are going to overflow upon actually committing the atrocity.

A coach-and-six conveyed us to the base of Vesuvius. There, we found guides who provide the rigs and the ropes whereby visitors are helped to climb the volcano: it takes two hours to attain the summit. The ascent, before it is over, will have ruined a pair of new shoes. We set out in merry spirits; we poked fun at Olympia; and the poor creature was far from grasping the double meaning of our persiflage, from divining what lay behind our playful teasing.

It is a dreadful task, struggling up that mountain: ankle-deep in ashes the whole time, if you advance four paces, you slip back six; and there is the perpetual fear lest you break through some thin crust and drop into molten lava. We arrived exhausted and sat down to rest once we were at the lip of the crater. 'Twas from there we gazed with prodigious interest into the throat of this volcano which, in its moments of wrath, makes all the Kingdom of Naples tremble.

"Do you think there is anything to fear today?" we asked our guides.

"No," they replied, "some brimstone, some sulphur, a few bits of pumice may perhaps come up, but it's not likely that there will be an eruption."

"Well then, my friends," said Clairwil, "give us the basket containing our refreshments and have the kindness to go back to the village. We are going to spend the day here, our intention is to do some sketching."

"But if something were to happen?"

"Did you not say that nothing will happen?"

"We cannot be altogether sure."

"Why, when something happens, we will make our way down to the village where we hired you, we can see it from here."

And with the distribution of three or four gold coins the conversation was brought quickly to an end.

As soon as they were some four hundred yards away, Clairwil and I exchanged glances. "Shall it be ruse?" I murmured to my friend.

"No, force," she answered.

We leapt upon Olympia the next instant.

"Slut," she was told, "we are tired of you; we led you to this place with a view to your destruction. There is a volcano below: you are going to be thrown into it alive."

"Oh, my friends!" she gasped. "What have I done?"

"Nothing at all. We are tired of you. Is that not quite enough?"

So saying, we stuffed a pocket-handkerchief into her mouth, to avoid her screams and jeremiads. Clairwil then tied her hands with scarves we had brought for this purpose; I tied her feet; and when we had reduced her to helplessness, we contemplated her and laughed. Tears flowed from her beautiful eyes, splashed down in pearly drops upon her beautiful bosom. We undressed her, we laid hands on her, stroked and molested every part of her body; we mistreated her snowy breasts, we spanked her charming ass, we pricked her buttocks with hatpins, we plucked hairs from her bush; and I bit her clitoris almost in two.

At length, after two hours of unremitting vexations, we picked her up by her bound hands and feet, carried her to the brink, and let her fall. Down she went into the volcano, and for several minutes we listened to the sounds of her body crashing from ledge to ledge, being torn by the sharp outcropping rocks: gradually the sounds subsided, and then we heard nothing more.

"That is that," said Clairwil, who had been frigging herself with both hands ever since letting go of Olympia's body. "Ah, fuck, my love, let's both lie down on the edge of this volcano and discharge now; we have just committed a crime, one of those heavenly deeds which mortals deem atrocious. Well, I say, if what we have done is a true outrage to Nature, then let her avenge herself, for she can if she wishes; let an eruption occur, let lava boil up from that inferno down there, let a cataclysm snuff out our lives this very instant. . . ."

I was in no state to speak. My head reeling already, my only reply was to my friend's pollutions, which I paid back tenfold. She too fell silent. Hugged tight in each other's arms, writhing with joy, frigging each other like frenzied tribades, we seemed bent on exchanging souls through the medium of our panted sighs. A few lewd words, a few blasphemies, no other utterances came from us. Through our deed we were insulting Nature, defying her, baiting her; and triumphant in the impunity in which her unconcern left us, we looked to be profiting from her indulgence only in order to irritate her the more grievously.

"And so," said Clairwil, the first to be restored to reason, "you see, Juliette, how little Nature is disturbed by mankind's alleged crimes; she does not want the power to swallow us up, she could destroy us even if it were in the depths of delight. Has she done so? Ah, be easy, there is no crime on earth capable of drawing Nature's wrath down upon us; rather, all crimes are to her advantage, all are useful to her, and whenever she inspires it in us, be certain that it is because she has need of crime."

Clairwil had no sooner finished than a shower of stones shot up out of the volcano and rained down around us.

"Ah ha!" said I, not even deigning to get to my feet, "Olympia's revenge! These bits of sulphur, these pebbles are her farewell to us, she notifies us that she is already in the entrails of the earth."

"Nothing more readily explained than this phenomenon," Clairwil remarked. "Whenever a weighty body falls into the volcano, by agitating the matter eternally boiling in its depths, it provokes a slight eruption."

"Come, let us have our lunch, and be assured when I tell you that the rain of stones which we have just witnessed is nothing else, my dear, than Olympia's request for her clothes; we must not refuse it."

And after having sorted out the gold and precious stones, we made the rest into a bundle and threw the telltale evidence into the same crater which had just received our friend. Then we opened our lunch-basket. No further sound came from below; the crime had been consummated, Nature was content. We made our descent and found our guides again at the foot of the mountain.

"A perfectly frightful misfortune has befallen us," we said, going up to them with tears in our eyes, "our unlucky companion ventured too near to the edge and . . . alas! she tumbled over it. Oh, good people, is there anything to be done?"

"Nothing," they all said; "you ought to have let us remain with you, this would not have happened. She is lost. You will never see her again."

Upon hearing that cruel announcement our feigned tears

flowed the faster and, wringing our hands, we stepped into our coach. Three-quarters of an hour later we were in Naples.

We published our misfortune the very same day; Ferdinand came in person to console us, believing we were truly sisters and devoted to one another. Depraved though he was, the thought never entered his mind that foul play might have overtaken Olympia; we did not disturb his illusions. We sent the Princess' retinue back to Rome with certificates of her accident, and we sent to inquire of her family what disposition it wished to have made of her jewelry, valued, we wrote, at thirty thousand francs, although in fact she left behind better than one hundred thousand francs worth of spoils, seven-tenths of which we had appropriated, you understand; but we had left Naples by the time the family's answer arrived there, and were able to assume undisputed possession of the entirety of our friend's property.

Olympia, Princess Borghese, was a gentle, trusting, affectionate woman, willful in her pleasures, libertine by temperament, with imagination, but who lacked depth and rigor in her principles; timorous, still in prejudice's grip, apt at any moment to give way before a reverse, and who, owing to nothing more than this one weakness, was unsuitable company for a pair of women as corrupt as ourselves.

A more important affair lay before us. The next day was the one I had chosen with Charlotte for the attack upon her husband's treasure. Clairwil and I therefore spent the rest of the evening preparing a dozen big chests and trunks, and having a large hole dug in our garden: this was done in utmost secrecy and the workman, whose brains we scrupulously blew out once he had completed his task, was the first object buried in that pit: "Either have no accomplices," Machiavelli advises, "or get rid of them as soon as they have served their purpose."

Then came the moment to appear with the wagon beneath the specified windows. Clairwil and I, disguised as men, drove the vehicle ourselves; for we had dismissed our servants for the night, and sent them out to a party in the countryside. Charlotte was at her post and waiting: in her eagerness for the promised poison, her reward if all went well, she did not wish to be guilty of the slightest negligence. For four hours she lowered out bags which, as fast as they came down, we stowed into our chests; and finally we heard her say that there was nothing more left.

"Until tomorrow," we replied.

And we drove quickly to our mansion, lucky enough not to have met with a living soul during the whole time the operation lasted. A second man helped us unload and bury the trunks and chests, and he was buried on top of them when his usefulness was at an end.

Weary, fretful, anxious now that we were so rich, we went to bed this one time without thinking of pleasures. We woke the next morning to find all the town talking about the robbery that had been committed at the Royal Palace; this seemed the propitious moment to have the Queen's note delivered to Ferdinand, and it was brought to him by an anonymous hand. No sooner had he read it than, flying into a mighty rage, he himself placed his wife under arrest, turned her over to the captain of his guard with orders to take her to Sant' Elmo, where she was given the coarsest raiment to wear, the simplest fare to eat, and placed in solitary confinement. A week passes without his going to see her. She beseeches him to come. At last he appears. The villainous creature blurts out everything and compromises us in the most thorough manner. Ferdinand rushes to our address, furious; and as the conversation we had with him is interesting, I shall give it in dialogue form.

FERDINAND: You are guilty of a horrible deed; how could I have expected such a thing from persons whom I took to be my friends!

CLAIRWIL: What is the matter?

FERDINAND: The Queen accuses you of having stolen my treasure.

JULIETTE: Us?

FERDINAND: You.

CLAIRWIL: Likely story!

FERDINAND: She admits to having momentarily entertained the thought of taking my life, and she affirms that you promised to supply her the poison necessary to that end, my treasure being the payment you demanded of her in return.

CLAIRWIL: You have found the poison she claims she bought for that exceedingly high price?

FERDINAND : No.

JULIETTE : How is it possible in that case that she consent to turn over her fortune before obtaining the promised poison?

FERDINAND : I have wondered about that myself.

CLAIRWIL : Sire, your wife is a rascal, but a very clumsy one; knowing that we were your intimates, she has thought to disguise her infamy by shifting the responsibility for her execrable scheme upon our shoulders, but it's a flimsy and ill-contrived plot.

FERDINAND : Who could have sent me that note?

JULIETTE : Those who have your treasure, no doubt: but, be certain of it, they are already far away. That note's senders would not have informed you had it meant jeopardizing their own safety, and it is to put you off the scent that the Queen names us.

FERDINAND : But how is it to Charlotte's interest to protect those who have just betrayed her?

CLAIRWIL : She has the poison, she does not want you to know she has it; hence, she brings suspicion to bear upon two people who cannot affirm that they gave it to her. Nevertheless, she has it, and but for the steps you have taken, you were a doomed man.

FERDINAND : In your opinion, then, I have done the right thing?

JULIETTE : It would have been difficult to do any better.

FERDINAND : Do you think she is the culprit? (*Here Clairwil puts on a malicious smile.*) Ah, I see it from your expression! Turn the knife in the wound: is there something else you know?

CLAIRWIL : Only that your wife is a monster; she has acted out of hatred for you, and you would be very wise to see to it that she is punished to the fullest extent of the law.

FERDINAND : Oh, speak out, my friends, have you really no knowledge of who has stolen my treasure?

JULIETTE *and* CLAIRWIL : None, we swear it.

FERDINAND : Then let her perish in her dungeon, let her die of hunger and despair there . . . and you, dear friends, forgive me for having formed suspicions in your regard. They were unjust; I ask you to pardon me.

JULIETTE : Sire, those suspicions did however exist, and with your leave we must therefore take our immediate departure out of your realm.

FERDINAND: Departure? No, I implore you, now that I am free of the encumbrance of that vicious wife . . . I feel infinitely more at ease, and there are marvelous things for us all to do together—

JULIETTE: Your peace of mind, my Lord, does not establish ours. Comfort is irrevocably gone for decent women upon whose honor the merest aspersion has been once cast.

FERDINAND: Ah, but I no longer suspect either one of you. (*He falls upon his knees.*) Never abandon me; I shall not be able to get on without you, I shall never console myself if I lose you too.

CLAIRWIL: And what was the sum the thieves took from you?

FERDINAND: Forty million, half of all I owned. The criminal admits that she promised the whole of my fortune, but she did not dare strip me of everything.

"The infamous creature," said I, but animated by feelings in which the King could not have followed me, those of rage at having been cheated by Charlotte, "the monster! what audacity! and what impudence! Thus to deceive the very best of husbands! A man who was so fond of her, who toiled selflessly in behalf of her pleasures! Oh, blackest ingratitude! For which the most fiendish punishment would be far too mild."

At that point Elise and Raimonde, decked out like goddesses, made their entrance, bearing chocolate for His Majesty. Until now Ferdinand had not clapped eyes on the two girls.

"What beauties are these?" he asked, all atremble.

"Our handmaidens," I answered.

"Why have they not been presented to me hitherto?"

"Could we have supposed they might please you?"

And with singular promptness forgetting both his prisoner and his robbery, the rake wants those two creatures surrendered to him on the spot. Such desires, in view of the circumstances, required speedy satisfaction. A boudoir opens before Ferdinand, into it he goes with our women and does not emerge until two hour later, after having worked the pair to exhaustion.

"Most generous friends," says he upon reappearing in our midst, "I beg you not to desert my city and me. Only let all reproaches be forgotten, and I protest to you that henceforth I shall behold you as paragons of innocence and probity."

And he left our house.

Had the sovereign of Naples not been súch a weak-spirited caitiff, Queen Charlotte would have been poisoned inside a day; we had given Ferdinand plentiful motives for the deed; but that unforceful and characterless man, was he capable of a vigorous action? No; and he took none at all. News of the Queen's detention and of its brevity was to reach the whole of Europe, but the reasons for both her imprisonment and her release were to remain unexplained. As for ourselves, not caring to wait to learn the outcome of this adventure, we turned at once to organizing our retreat. Our loot proved voluminous and heavy. As we had bought a quantity of busts, mosaics, antique marbles, and samples of stone from Vesuvius, we cached our gold in false bottoms built into the packing cases ordered for shipping our purchases, and this stratagem succeeded to perfection. Before closing up the cases we sent a request to the King, asking him to inspect our baggage; he declined; we nailed everything shut. Ten wagons bore it all away, and we followed after in two coaches, one for our suite, one for ourselves. Just before leaving we went to say goodbye to Ferdinand, who again did all he possibly could to change our minds, and who then, having had to accept the inevitable, himself handed us the passports necessary to cross the borders of his states.

That evening we lay over at Capua; a week later, at Rome, where we arrived without having encountered the least difficulty on the road. Not until then did Clairwil notify her brother of her design to accompany me on to Paris, where it was her intention to settle for the rest of her life. She besought him to come to Paris too; but Brisatesta could not take it upon himself to quit his profession, and despite the wealth he had already amassed from outlawry, he solemnly declared that his unalterable decision was to die pistol in hand.

"So be it," said Clairwil. "My preference goes to you, Juliette. We shall never separate again, that is my wish."

I hugged my friend in my arms and swore to her she would never have cause to repent her decision. Ah! Making that promise, how little was I aware of the destiny that had already been spelled out by our stars, Clairwil's and mine.

We continued our journey, which was uneventful until we reached Ancona. There, taking advantage of the fairest weather, we were strolling along the port when we perceived a tall woman of some forty-five years gazing at us fixedly.

"Do you recognize that person?" Clairwil asked me.

I turn, I scrutinize her. "Bless me, Clairwil! She is no other than our Parisian sorceress. It's Durand."

Her name was yet on my lips when its owner came up and greeted us rapturously.

"Ah," said Clairwil, somewhat startled to see again the woman who five years before had predicted she had only that interval to live, "by what stroke of chance do we meet in this city?"

"Come with me to my lodgings," said Durand, still beautiful with the passing of time; "although these people do not understand our tongue, we have nothing to gain from conversing in their presence."

We accompany her; and after having ushered us into the luxurious quarters she occupied at the inn, "How pleased I am," she told us as soon as we were seated, "to be able to procure you the acquaintance of a most outstanding woman, one of the most unusual and the most like yourselves Nature has yet created."

"To whom do you refer?" Clairwil asked.

"To a sister of the Empress, an aunt of Naples' Queen, a figure completely unknown to the world. As a very young child, Princess Christine evidenced propensities to libertinage of such violence that her father sensed she would become absolutely unmanageable. Seeing her bad habits grow steadily worse with age, he thought best to buy an island for her in Dalmatia, at the head of the Adriatic; he assigned her an income of three million a year, and put her under the protection of the Venetians, who by treaty recognized her sovereignty over the island and her right to do there whatever she liked. Christine, relegated to her little kingdom sixteen years ago, is at present forty years of age, and leads a life of delicious indulgence in everything the extremest lubricity can inspire. But it will spoil the adventure if I tell you more about her;

we shall cross the gulf in one of her barks, it is at my permanent disposition. The voyage lasts a day and a night; have you decided?"

"We certainly have," I answered, "since I am confident I can speak for Clairwil too: the object of our travels being to study the manners and morals of mankind and to see extraordinary things, we would not be living up to our purpose if we were to forego such an opportunity out of halfheartedness."

"By God, yes," said my friend, "we shall do some fine fucking on Christine's isle."

"Never," said Durand, "never shall you have such pleasure."

"And upon that island of hers," I said, "does she have—"

"No," Durand interrupted me, "not another word. I want everything to be a surprise for you."

And as she seemed unwilling to pursue the subject farther, I introduced another. "Now that I have found you again," I said to the sorceress, "you must account for your sudden disappearance from Paris. Why were you not at the rendezvous arranged by that Comte de Belmor with whom I put you into touch?"

"Indeed," Durand replied, "I failed to come to that appointment, and it was for the very best of reasons: that was the day they hanged me."

"What!"

"Hanged me, I say. It was simple enough: I had furnished poison to the young Duc ***, he needed some to put his mother out of the way. Compunction upset the little fool's scheme; he betrayed me; I was arrested, brought to trial within the space of a day. But, wonderfully connected with the Samson who presided, we found a compromise whereby I would be hanged merely for form's sake. I held them off by eleventh-hour recriminations, and it was not until after night had fallen I was finally led down from the Hôtel de Ville. Samson himself tied the noose, directed the mummery. I was carted to the graveyard, one of his valets, acting upon instructions, bought my body, and I was able to leave Paris before dawn. I went back the following year, to another quarter of town and under a different name; there has been no further fuss from anybody, and business has been steady and good ever since. There is truth in the saying that the hangman's rope brings good luck. My income is today sixty thousand pounds, and I have been adding to my capital every year. I make an annual journey to Italy, where I replenish my stock of materials and compound the poisons I then distribute throughout all Europe. I find that preferable to preparing them at home. Actually, this kind of murdering is nowadays so much in style that it is all I can do to keep up with the demand. At Christine's you will have occasion to see the very piquant effects of the venoms I have developed."

"You sell some to her?"

"My God, a hundred thousand crowns' worth every year."

"She is cruel, I take it?"

"Incredibly so."

"Ah, I adore her already!" Clairwil exclaimed. "Whenever you wish, Durand, let us sail for Dalmatia."

"Charming woman," I put in, "before anything else you must answer some more questions. I insist that you tell me who those curious individuals were, by whom you had us beaten, flogged; and who, in short, performed so many uncommon things before us when we were with you last."

"One of them," said Durand, "was that same Duc ***, Beaujeon was the other, the famous millionaire. For four years both had been feeing me enormously for services of a similar kind, and there is no counting the number of women and girls I deceived for them in the very same way. But, while I think of it," said Durand, ringing for a servant, "you must not suppose that I am going to allow you to leave without having dinner. I would be heartbroken not to have you as my guests; I shall hear no refusals. . . ."

And the most splendid meal was brought in almost immediately.

"Durand," said Clairwil when we reached dessert, "you promise us great pleasures for tomorrow. But what of today's? It seems to me that among your valets I detected three or four strapping fellows with a very stiff-pricked look about them."

"Do you care to test their mettle?"

"Why not! And you, Juliette, what say you?"

"No," I demurred, preoccupied with a thought I could not drive out of my head, an ill-defined premonition, "no, I believe I will drink a glass and talk with Durand rather than fuck. Besides, I am menstruating, and feel a little out of sorts."

"Until now I have never known you to refuse a prick," said Clairwil, and for the briefest instant there showed upon her face a shadow of concern whose cause I was far from apprehending. "Come, my angel," she resumed, brightening again, "when one cannot fuck in front, one fucks behind. Come, I say, join me: well you know that I taste no real pleasures save they be shared with you."

"No," I repeated, still in the grip of that unknown foreboding, "I don't feel at all in a mood for it . . . I simply wish to chat."

Clairwil walked toward the chamber that had been designated to her and, just before she entered it, I distinctly saw, in a mirror, the emphatic sign she made to the sorceress, a sign which I could interpret as nothing else than an injunction to silence. The door to the chamber closed; I remained sitting with Durand.

"Oh, Juliette," that woman said to me as soon as we had been left alone, "thank your lucky stars for all the sentiments you inspire in me. Charming girl," she continued, taking me in her arms, "no, you shall not be the victim of that monster. . . . In every respect preferable to her, you shall be warned in time and your life saved."

"What are you saying to me, Madame! Such words freeze me with terror!"

"Listen to me, Juliette; and having heard me, reveal nothing. This island in Dalmatia . . . this Princess Christine, this voyage . . . dear girl, had you taken it you were doomed. 'Twas all a trap set by a woman whom you believed to be your dearest friend."

"Clairwil!"

"She plotted your death. She covets your wealth; in her pocket she has a piece of paper, a document in which you each name the other her sole heir. She was to assassinate you to come into possession of that legacy—"

"The infernal creature!" I gasped, breathless with fury.

"Steady, Juliette; a careless word could still be your undoing; sit where you are and hear me out. The vessel we were to embark upon, it sinks, we escape the wreck, you perish in it. . . . Take your revenge; take this packet I have here . . . it contains fulminant powder; among our poisons none acts more rapidly. Let her absorb a little and the next instant she will lie at your feet, as if thunderstruck. In return for this service I am rendering you I demand nothing; consider it as flowing from an excessive fondness for you."

"O my benefactress!" I cried, tears springing to my eyes, "you save me from the very direst danger! But much mystery yet clings to all this. How is it that you are in Ancona? How did Clairwil enter into contact with you?"

"I have been following a step behind you ever since you left Naples, where I myself had gone to buy poisons. Clairwil met me there, laid out her scheme before me; at Loreto I hastened on ahead, and reached Ancona before you did, to set the stage for a scene to which I lent myself only because of the deepest desire to save your life. Had I refused Clairwil my collaboration, she would without question have had recourse to other means, and you would not be alive today."

"But once Clairwil decided to get rid of me, what need had she to wait so long?"

"That document had not yet been drawn up, your money was not yet invested, nothing could be done until you were out of Rome; and she knew that, once you had left that city, your first stop would not come until Loreto. 'Twas for the day after she ordered me to have everything in readiness."

"Infamous creature! Thou whom I loved so sincerely, in whose arms I surrendered myself in such candid good faith!"

"She is a monster of perfidy and deceit," Durand rejoined; "trust her under no circumstances. Just when you think you have the least to fear from her, that is the very instant when you must be most on your guard. Hark. I hear sounds. She may be about to return; the fact we are having this conversation together is not to her liking. Compose yourself, and when you strike, do not miss the mark; godspeed."

Clairwil was indeed upset when she returned; she had had an unsatisfactory fucking, said she, the two men given her had held their erections poorly. And over and above the rest, she was not accustomed to tasting pleasures in which her dear Juliette did not take an active part.

"I would discharge better with you," she went on, "were you disposed to a little masturbating."

"Tonight," I replied, disguising my cruel state as best I could, "yes, tonight. At the moment, my dear, Adonis himself would leave me cold."

"Very well," said she, "let us go to our inn. I too feel out of sorts, I don't think I'd mind being in bed early. Goodbye, Durand," she added, "and until tomorrow. Endeavor to have musicians, good food, and, above all, some good fuckers aboard that boat; without them I find travel by sea unendurably boring."

We repaired to our lodgings.

"A strange woman, that Durand," Clairwil said to me once we were alone together; "she is someone to be very wary of, my dearest. Were I not so devoted to you. . . . Would you believe, Juliette, that while you were off in the privy for a few minutes, the villain offered to poison you for two thousand *louis*?"

This sally did not catch me off balance; in it I saw nothing but a wicked snare, which I had no trouble eluding. However, I deemed best to feign credulity.

"Great God," I said, "that woman is a monster! I now understand why I felt so distrustful of her the whole while we were talking."

"Your instincts warned you, and rightly: she had worked out a scheme for killing you, Juliette. The thought of your death entertained her."

"Ah," said I, looking hard at Clairwil, "the stroke was perhaps to have been brought off during the voyage to the island. . . ."

"No," said Clairwil, without the flutter of an eyelash, "it was to have been this evening, at supper, and that is the reason I dragged you home so early."

"But this voyage," I said, "it worries me now; are you sure there is no danger?"

"None in the least: I completely changed her mind, and I guarantee you that she has forgotten the idea. Let us have supper."

The meal was served us; I had taken my decision. To be the dupe of Clairwil's tales, this was absolutely impossible; and Durand's avowals, their frankness, their warmth had so impressed me. . . . Into the first dish I handed Clairwil I slipped the poison hidden between my fingers; she took a mouthful, swallowed, swayed in her chair, and fell, emitting a single furious scream.

"Behold my revenge," I said to my women, both bewildered by Clairwil's sudden collapse.

And I related the adventure to them.

"Fuck!" I cried, "let us savor the sweet charms of vengeance, my dears, and acquit ourselves of a few horrors; the two of you, frig me as I lie upon that whore's dead body, and may her example teach you never to betray your best friend."

We stripped off Clairwil's clothes, we stretched her naked corpse upon a bed. . . . I put my hand to her cunt, it was still warm, I frigged her; donning a dildo, I fucked her. Elise gave me her ass to kiss; and in the meantime I tickled Raimonde's cunt. I spoke to Clairwil as though she were ever alive, I addressed reproaches to her, invectives, as though she were able to hear me; I took up some withes, I lashed her unmoving body . . . I embuggered it. It never stirred, it was utterly without feeling; and at last I saw that there was no hope left, and I had that body put into a sack. And Clairwil's own valets, who had hated her and who were as grateful to me as could be for having delivered them from such a wicked mistress, they agreed, once night had come, to go secretly with her body and drop it into the sea.

I wrote forthwith to my banker in Rome to advise him that by virtue of the contract we had entered into, Clairwil and I, through which the moneys we had invested with him belonged to the one of us who might chance to survive the other, he could henceforth remit all revenues to me; whence it resulted that by merging the two fortunes, I secured myself an annual income of two million. In Italy, nothing is more quickly straightened out than a murder: I had two hundred sequins transmitted to the justice of Ancona, and there was not so much as an inquest.

"And so, my fine friend," I said to Durand when, the next day, I went to dine with her, "you thought to outwit me, did you? Clairwil let the cat out of the bag: how you meant to poison me last night, and would have had she not stood in the way."

"Treacherous to the last," said Durand gravely, shaking her head. "Oh, Juliette, I told you the truth, believe it: I love you far too much to deceive you upon such serious matters. There is much of the scoundrel in me, perhaps more than in most others, but when I love a woman, I never play her false. . . . The blow, then, has not been struck?"

"No; Clairwil breathes, she and I are about to resume our journey. I came to bid you farewell. And now I shall go—"

"Oh, Juliette! I am poorly rewarded for all I have done—"

"Better than you think, Durand," I interrupted, with one hand tendering her a pocketbook containing one hundred thousand crowns, with the other exhibiting to her the tresses I had shorn from Clairwil. "Here are the ornaments of the head you proscribed, and here is the recompense for your generous friendship."

"Keep these things, keep them all," Durand replied. "Juliette, I adore you. For what I have done I wish no reward other than the happiness of being able to give you my unrivaled affection: I was jealous of Clairwil, I do not hide it, but I might nevertheless have spared her had it not been for her terrible designs in your regard: I could not forgive her for having meditated the destruction of someone whose life meant more to me even than my own. I am far less wealthy than you, admittedly, but I have the means to live in magnificence, and can afford to decline the gift you offer me: with such professional skills as I possesss I shall never lack for money, and I do not want to be paid for a service performed at my heart's demand."

"No further separation between us ever again," said I to Durand, "leave your inn, come join me in mine; you will take Clairwil's domestics, her carriage, and we shall set off for Paris in two or three days."

The new arrangements were quickly completed; Durand retained but one of her chambermaids, to whom she was especially attached, dismissed all the rest of her household, and came to install herself in what had formerly been Clairwil's quarters.

It was easy to see, from the way that woman devoured me with her eyes, that she was on tenterhooks for the moment when my favors would reward her for her efforts in my behalf. I did not allow her to pine away for long; after the most sumptuous and elegant repast, I stretch forth my arms to her, she leaps into them, we dash to my bedchamber, lock the door, draw the shutters, and I surrender, with inexpressible delight, to the most libertine and the most lustful of women. Durand, in her fiftieth year, was not by any means devoid of merit; her forms were full, shapely, and well preserved; her mouth fresh, her skin soft and showing scarcely a wrinkle; a superb posterior, breasts still firm and very fair, very lively eyes, very fine features; and an energy in her pleasure-taking, tastes so bizarre. . . . Capricious Nature had created her with a deformity neither Clairwil nor I had ever noticed: Durand was unable, had never been able, to enjoy pleasure in the conventional manner. Her vagina was obstructed, but (and you will doubtless recall this detail) her clitoris, as long as a finger, gave her the most ardent liking for women. She would flog them, she would embugger them; she held commerce with boys also: I shortly discovered, from the inordinate size of her asshole, that, as regarded intromissions, she was wont to receive there what she was denied elsewhere. The initial advances were made by me, and I thought she was going to swoon from pleasure the moment she felt my hands upon her flesh.

"Let's undress," said she, "one cannot enjoy oneself properly save when naked. I have, moreover, the keenest desire to look again upon your charms, Juliette, I burn to feast upon them."

Everything is removed in a trice. My kisses explore that beautiful body; and I am bound to say that perhaps, had Durand been younger, yes, I might not have found her anything like so interesting. My tastes were beginning to turn to depravation, and entering into my riper years, Nature was providing me with sensations far more intense than anything I had known in my springtime. The unique object of that woman's fiery caresses, great tides of lust boiled up in me; my partner deployed a science and an art that are positively not to be described. Oh, how voluptuous are women seasoned in crime! what dimensions are revealed in their lubricities!

You listless and uninspired prudes, insufferable creatures who dare not even touch the member perforating you, and who would blush to answer fuck with fuck when fucking, cast your eyes this way, come hither for some examples: come take a few lessons from Madame Durand, and learn the extent of your ineptitudes.

After the initial caresses, Durand, less inhibited than when in the past Clairwil had been a party to our affairs, made declaration of her fancies and besought me to submit to them. As she knelt before me, I had, while heaping abuse upon her, to rub her nose now in my cunt, now in my ass; while rubbing my front against her, I had to piss upon her face. That done, I had to strike her all about the body with my fists and kick her everywhere, take up some nettles and flog her till she bled. When by dint of mistreatments I had beaten her down to the floor, I had, with my head between her thighs, to cunt-suck her for fifteen minutes while socratizing her with one hand and exciting her nipples with the other; next, once she was thoroughly heated, I was to let her embugger me with her clitoris the while she tickled mine.

"I apologize for having to ask so much, Juliette," the libertine said, once she had finished outlining the program, "but you know to what satiety can lead us."

"After thirty-five years of sustained libertinage one must offer no excuses for one's tastes," was my reply; "whatever it may be, it is deserving of respect, for it is in Nature; the best of all is the one that pleases us most."

And starting in upon the operation, so amply did I satisfy her that she was nigh to perishing from delight. Durand's voluptous crises were without parallel. In all my life I had never seen a woman discharge thus: not only would she shoot her fuck forth like a man, but she accompanied that ejaculation by shrieks so loud, by blasphemies so energetic, and by spasms so violent that one could have mistaken her performance for an epileptic attack. I was buggered as solidly as if I had been dealing with a man, and from it experienced the same pleasure.

"Well," said she when she rose to her feet, "how do I strike you?"

"Oh, fuck!" I cried, "you are delightful, you are a very model of lubricity; your passions set me ablaze, do to me everything I have just done to you."

"What! You wish a beating?"

"Beat me, yes."

"And a slapping, a whipping?"

"Make haste."

"Do you want me to piss upon your face?"

"Of course, my darling, be quick, I say, for I'm very hot and I have a discharge pressing."

La Durand, with a longer experience than I in the rendering of these services, proceeds with such consummate skill that the explosion supervenes almost instantaneously, thanks to the heavenly titillations of her voluptuous tongue.

"How you do discharge, my beloved," she said to me; "how vehemently you respond to pleasure! How marvelously we get on!"

"There is no denying it, Durand," I answered her, "you have an astonishing effect upon my imagination: I am overjoyed to be connected with a woman like you. Mistresses of all a universe we shall be; through our alliance I feel we shall become the superiors of Nature herself. Oh, dear Durand, the crimes we are going to commit! the infamies we are going to achieve!"

"Do you regret Clairwil?"

"Can I when I possess you?"

"And if I had invented the whole story merely in order to rid myself of a rival?"

"A rare piece of villainy!"

"And what if I had accomplished it?"

"But, Durand, Clairwil told me that you had proposed to poison me for two thousand *louis*."

"I knew she would repeat that to you; neither did I have the slightest doubt but that, instead of being taken in by this confidence, you would simply perceive it for a clumsily mounted snare on her part, and subtle as I knew you to be, judge that the time had come for the crime which I was eager to have you commit."

"And why had the thing to be done by me? Could you not have executed it by yourself?"

"I much preferred that my rival die by your hand; my pleasure, to be complete, required that the act be undertaken by you."

"Good heaven, what a woman you are! But she was ill at ease the other day, when we were your guests at dinner, she was unable to relish the pleasures you had readied for her; our conversation, she seemed apprehensive about it . . . she made a sign to you."

"I had created the conditions for that uneasiness, calculating what its repercussions would be upon you; and I estimated exactly, as you see, for her unquiet manner shortly rendered her guiltier in your eyes. Telling her I was willing to poison you for two thousand *louis,* I bred in her the suspicion that I might make a like proposition to you. Therein lies the explanation for her gesture, therein the reason why she dreaded our tête-à-tête, and her trembling, expression of the fear I engendered in her, produced upon your mind the precise effect I anticipated: two hours later, Clairwil was dead."

"Am I then to understand that she was innocent?"

"She adored you . . . and so did I, and I could not bear having a rival."

"Gloat over your triumph, scoundrel," I say, casting myself into Durand's arms, "and, now, your triumph is entire: I worship you to the point where, had this crime to be committed all over again, I would commit it unprompted, without any of the motivations you created to facilitate it. . . . Why did you not declare your love for me from the very first in Paris?"

"I dared not because of Clairwil's presence; and when later you came back to see me, it was with a man, and then it was he who hindered me. And after that came my arrest. But I followed you, dearest and sweetest friend, never once did I let you out of my sight, I followed you to Angers, throughout Italy, all the while I carried on my trade I kept my eyes upon you. My hope sank as I watched your successive liaisons—Donis, Grillo, Borghese— and it dwindled almost to nothing when I learned that you had become reunited with Clairwil. Still, I followed you from Rome to here, and at last, tired of having been thwarted so long, I resolved to bring about the denouement: and the rest you know."

"Inexplicable and delightful creature! Who has ever provided such examples of treachery, sleight, spitefulness, villainy, jealousy!"

" 'Tis because no one has ever had either passions or a heart like mine. 'Tis because no one has ever loved you as I do."

"But when the fires die down in you, Durand, you will deal with me as you have just done with Clairwil; will I have time to protect myself?"

"I am going to set you at ease, my angel, and reply strongly to your groundless suspicions; listen to me. You shall, I demand it, keep for yourself, and forever, one of your women, Elise or Raimonde. Choose which of the two it is to be, I shall not let you have the other, I tell you so in advance."

"Raimonde shall be mine."

"Very well. If ever Raimonde meets with a tragic and un-accountable end, let the blame fall nowhere but upon me. And now," Durand continued, "I demand that you put a paper into this girl's keeping, which authorizes her to denounce me as your assassin in the event you perish in some unhappy way at any moment during the course of our relations."

"No, I object to such precautions, I entrust myself to you, I do so gladly; I like the idea of placing my life in your hands. Leave Elise to me, leave everybody to me, don't hinder my prac-tices or contest my tastes. I am a libertine, I will not promise you good behavior, but I shall swear an oath to adore you ever-lastingly."

"I have no wish to tyrannize over you, Juliette; to the con-trary, I shall myself serve your pleasures, I shall move heaven and earth for the sake of your physical enjoyments. But were your conduct ever to become ethical, I'd abandon you there and then. I am aware of the impossibility of captivating such a woman as yourself, a whore by temperament and on principle: 'twould, I realize, be to seek to set dikes to the sea. But I can always be the mistress of your heart, and that is what I ask . . . I insist that it belong to nobody but me."

"I swear that it shall be so."

"Ah, great pleasures are then in store for us; libertinage, to remain pure, must be kept free of sentiment: one must have but one friend only, sincerely love no one but her, and fuck with the whole wide world. Juliette, my best advice, if you care to hear it, is to dispense with this glittering entourage you move with; I myself plan to dismiss half my suite; we shall manage just as comfortably when we are fewer, and it serves no purpose to attract universal notice. Moreover, I wish to pursue my calling, and no one is apt to buy anything from a woman who goes traveling about like a queen."

"And I too," I replied, "I wish to satisfy my tastes, I wish to steal, I wish to prostitute myself, and, you are quite right, such exhibition will interfere with my objectives."

"It ought, I believe, to be given out that I am your mother, with this title I shall be able to prostitute you myself; Elise and Raimonde, let them be your cousins. We shall market their charms too, and be sure of it, with one such harem we shall make money in Italy."

"And your poisons?"

"I shall sell them in greater quantity, I shall sell them more dearly. We must, when we return to France, have spent not one penny of our own, and reach home with a clear profit of two million at least."

"What route shall we take?"

"I am powerfully inclined to go south again. Calabrian and Sicilian depravity, Juliette, is something that exceeds even your fondest dreams; I know those regions well, there are mines of gold to be earned down there. Last year I sold five hundred thousand francs worth of poison in the *mezzogiorno,* and would have done far better had I been able to keep abreast of my orders. The Southerners are credulous, like all other lying people; telling their fortunes, I was able to persuade them of whatever I wished. . . . It's a fine country, Juliette."

"I for my part am anxious to return to Paris again," said I; "established there, would we not lead a better life than roaming about in such a way? Could we not do the same things there?"

"We must at least visit Venice, whence we can proceed to Milan and then to Lyon."

To this I gave my agreement. We dined. Durand told me that she wanted to pay all our expenses. She would, to be sure, reimburse herself from our jointly earned profits; but she entreated me to accept the appearance of being kept by her. To that too I agreed. I was, I must tell you, as tactful in receiving her attentions as she was in showing them to me. Delicacy also matters in the sphere of crime; failure to understand this points to a woeful ignorance of human nature.

"Is it true," I asked my new companion, "that you possess the balm that ensures longevity?"

"No such balm exists," Durand replied, "those who distribute it are all quacks. The true secret to a long life is a sober and temperate life; sobriety and temperance not being among our virtues, we cannot, you and I, hope for miracles. And why should we, my dear? Better to live a little less long and to enjoy oneself: what would a life be divested of its pleasures? If death meant the onset of pain, then I would urge you to stretch your life out to the utmost; but since the worst that can happen to us is to slip back into the nothingness where we were before we were born, 'tis on the wing of pleasures we must fly through our apportioned term."

"My love, are you then without belief in another life?"

"I would be greatly ashamed to have to own to belief in such nonsense. But, fully enlightened as you are upon that and related questions, I doubt whether I have much to teach you thereanent, and I am confident that, imbued with the basic principles of philosophy, both the immortality of the soul and the existence of God are to your consideration extravagances not worth a minute's thought. The falsity of all those doctrines being manifest, there is one which I construct upon their wreckage and it may perhaps claim to a certain originality. I base it upon a multitude of experiences. I maintain that what is taken for a naturally inspired horror of death is merely the fruit of the absurd fears which we, starting in childhood, develop regarding this total annihilation, fears initiated by the religious notions our elders stupidly cram into our young heads. Once cured of these fears and reassured concerning our fate, not only do we cease to behold death with alarm and repugnance, but it becomes easy to prove that death is in reality nothing more nor less than a voluptuous pleasure. You will admit, first, that one cannot help but be certain that death is one of the necessities of Nature, who does not create us save to die; if we begin, it is in order to end; each instant advances us nowhere but toward that terminal point; everything indicates that death is Nature's final and sole aim. Now, I ask how it is possible to doubt, in the light of acquired experience, that death, as a natural necessity and as something needed by Nature, can be anything else than a pleasure, since all palpable evidence proves convincingly that every one of life's necessities is pleasure-producing. Therefore, I reason, there is pleasure in dying; it is therefore possible to conceive that, with reflection and with philosophy, one may convert into very voluptuous ideas all death's ridiculous frights, and that sensual excitement may even bring on thoughts of death and induce in one an eager expectancy of death."

"That doctrine, entirely new, and not without plausibility," I said to my friend, "would be dangerous to publish. Think of how many people are held in check by nothing except fear of death and who, once liberated from that dread, could calmly—"

"One moment," said my delightful friend, "I have never sought to discourage anyone from crime; rather, I have always toiled to remove all the obstacles stupidity has strewn in its path. Crime is my element; Nature brought me into the world to advance its cause, and my task and ambition are to multiply to infinity all the means to commit it.

"The trade I have elected and which I exercise more out of libertinage than from material necessity, proves my extreme desire to promote crime; I have no more ardent passion than that of propagating it generally, and if I could envelop the whole world within my toils, I would blast it to dust without hesitation or remorse."

"And against which sex does your libertine fury plot with greater delight?"

"It is not a person's sex that arouses me, it is his age, his ties with others, his condition. When the suitable factors are found in a man, I extract greater enjoyment from immolating him than a woman; when they converge in a woman, the preference goes automatically to her."

"And what are these standards of suitability?" I inquired.

"I ought not tell you."

"Why not?"

"From these confessions you will draw no end of fallacious inferences, likely, subsequently, to have a damaging effect upon our relationship."

"Ah, my dear, you have already said enough: I am then to assume that your favors are so many condemnations to death?"

"Certainly; have I not told you so? Listen to me, Juliette, and put your fears away. Far be it from me to disguise the fact that any object I use for the simple and unique purpose of consumption, and with which I enter into no other relationship, must undergo the fate of any other commodity. But if, on the other hand, in that object I encounter sympathetic intellectual traits, imaginative qualities such as those I have found in you, then, be assured of it, rather than severing connections with such an object, I do but tighten them by every means at my command. In the name of the most tender affection, cease, my love, to harbor doubts; I offered you the surest guarantee of my good faith, you decline it out of tact, do not leave me to suppose now that your mind is at odds with your heart. Besides, have I any powers you yourself do not dispose of?"

"Most assuredly you do," I answered, "and I am far from knowing the whole range or subtlety of your capacities."

"As you like," my friend said, smiling, "but be persuaded that this art of mine shall, with you, be put to no other use than to constrain you to love me."

"Ah, count upon it; I realize that between villains there is never any conflict, and believe me, but for the awful suspicions you stirred up in me, I would never have sacrificed Clairwil."

"Do I detect a note of regret behind that avowal, Juliette?"

"Not at all, not at all," said I, showering kisses upon my friend, "let us have an end to the discussion thereupon; I give myself into your keeping, I repeat it, you can place your trust in my heart as I put my reliance in yours; our strength is in our union, and nothing will dissolve it. Now tell me the rest of what I am eager to hear about the factors which incite you to the consummation of crime: I am anxious to find out whether they concur with mine, and so far I notice great similarities."

"I told you that age had a great deal to do with it: I love to wither the plant at the noon of its perfection: between fifteen and seventeen years old, that is the stage at which I consider roses fittest for gathering, especially when they are in flawless health and when Nature, whose purposes I know how to cross, seems to have designed the object to live in exuberant well-being to the end of a long and happy life. Ah, Juliette, how I enjoy performing such interventions! Ties irritate me also: I delight in depriving a father of his child, a lover of his mistress."

"A tribade of her handmaid?"

"Why yes, little minx; is it my fault if unfathomable Nature made me the rascal I am? If it is to me the object belongs, then the pleasure is twofold. I also said that the person's condition contributes significantly to the excitement of my imagination: here, I am partial to the two extremes, wealth and high estate, or obscurity and misfortune. Generally speaking, I aim, when striking, to produce as many disastrous aftereffects and melancholy repercussions as possible, I like it to cause much weeping, I discharge at the sight of those tears. Their abundance or bitterness brings forth my fuck, the harder and more copiously they flow, the more powerful my spasm."

"Oh, gentlest, most charming friend," said I, my head beginning to reel, "frig me, I beseech you; you see what your words are doing to me; I have never known anyone whose attitudes were in closer harmony with my own. Next to you, Clairwil was a mere child; you are what my happiness demands, you are the woman I have been seeking, never leave me again."

And Durand, to take fullest advantage of my ecstasy, having helped me to a couch, frigged me with three fingers as I had never in my life been frigged before. I replied in kind; I sucked her clitoris; and when I spied her asshole opening and closing like a flower thirstily responding to the sweetly descending dew, I put on a dildo and flung into her bum, frigging her still while I embuggered her. That vent was of unprecedented diameter. My instrument had a girth of eight inches, a length of twelve; I but brought it up and it vanished out of sight. And when it was gone, then the whore let loose oaths, she shuddered and shook like a lunatic; and well I saw that if Nature had excluded her from knowledge of the common kind of pleasures, she had richly compensated Durand in bestowing upon her the extremest sensitivity to these. One of my new friend's outstanding talents lay in her ability to give pleasure while receiving it; she was so supple, so elastic, that even as I embuggered her, she wound herself like a vine around my body, succeeded in kissing my mouth, and in inserting fingers into my fundament. Sometimes forgetting everything else in order to concentrate upon her sensations alone, she would then curse with greater vigor than I had ever known in a person; and from whatever angle one considered this remarkable woman, one discovered that, child of crime, of lust, and of infamy, every last one of her physical and moral qualities contributed to making her the most exceptional libertine of her century. Durand wanted to do for me all I had done for her. She embuggered me and, lewdly frigged by her, I comfortably withstood the same dildo, I discharged thrice in response to its blows; and, I say again, I had never had dealings with a woman who so grasped the art of giving pleasure.

From there we returned to drinking, and when we were very high, "Come," Durand said to me, "let us go out into the streets and befoul ourselves with a little libertinage. Let us go and see the funeral preparations that have been made for the fifteen-year-old girl, a lovely creature, whom I poisoned yesterday at the solicitation of her father who, after having nicely fucked her, wanted to be revenged for an indiscretion she then committed."

We went out costumed in the manner of the courtesans of the country; night had fallen.

"Before anything else," said my friend, "I suggest that we betake ourselves down to the harbor and frig a few sailors; we ought to be able to uncover some monsters. You simply would not believe the pleasure I find in squeezing the juice out of those sausages. . . ."

"For shame, whore," said I, kissing her, "you are tipsy."

"A little, perhaps; but do not conclude that Bacchus' aid is necessary to light the fires of libertinage in me. Divine powers are ascribed to that rascal, I know, and I never undertake lewd exercises in a better mood than when I have stuffed myself upon delicate cooking and fine wines; but without those stimulants I am perfectly capable of overstepping the last limits of decency and modesty— you shall see."

No sooner did we reach the port than a host of sailors and stevedores crowded around us.

"Holla, good friends," Durand cries, "no hurlyburly, behave yourselves and fret not, we are going to satisfy you, every last one. Here, look at this girl: she is French.[1] She entered the business only yesterday; and now she is going to sit down on that bollard, she is

---

[1] Whores of that nationality are greatly sought after in foreign lands. Their extreme indulgence, their accomplishments, their libertinage, and their beauty have won them a position of privilege among the world's harlots, who in other countries are almost always ugly, inept, and unclean.

going to lift her skirts, and she is going to offer you whichever side best suits your tastes; and I am going to frig you upon her charms."

This speech was applauded by the throng. The first of at least fifteen suitors wants to see my bare bosom: his uncouth attentions might have spoiled its appearance had not my companion forbidden him any gestures; he had therefore to restrict himself to covering my breasts with fuck; they were shortly awash. The second wants me, sitting on the bollard, to spread my thighs as far apart as possible, in order that he can be frigged against my clitoris. I prove unable to resist the massiveness of the member whose tip, guided by Durand, nuzzles the approaches to my vagina; impelled by an involuntary reflex, I leap forward and incorporate it up to the height of the balls. No sooner does the funny chap feel himself caught than he clutches me in his arms, lifts me up, lifts up my skirts and exhibits my ass to the whole assembly. One of those frenetics advances, claps his hands to my bum, palpates it, spears it, and there am I, carried by two partners, the object of both their caresses and homages.

"Hold," says Durand, "give her something firm to take purchase upon"—and, with those words, she puts an enormous member into each of my hands. "What an engaging group," the bawd observes, presenting her behind to a fifth seaman. "Here, my friend, here is my ass, let us include ourselves in the scene, form one of its episodes; I cannot, alas, propose you anything else, Nature is to blame for my disability; but reassure yourself, the heat of my asshole and its narrowness will make you forget any craving you may have for my cunt."

Other postures were struck betimes. I dealt with better than fifty of those low fellows. My companion rubbed them with a water just prior to penetration, and by that means I was able to receive them all without fear: I was fucked forty-five times in less than three hours. Durand did nought but essay them; she fetched them up to me afterward, and they terminated, according to their choice, either in my ass or in my cunt. The lewd thing sucked practically everything she could get her hands upon, since she had a palate for pricks, and was not, need I remind you, a woman to curb her tastes. Our bandits once satisfied, we must drink with them, for that was the custom.

"And it is one of the best parts of all," Durand murmured
to me, "you have no idea how, in vile company, I relish plunging
into whatever is characterized by swinish intemperance, filthiest
debauchery."

When we were done feeding it was because neither of us could
swallow another mouthful. We had devoured not one, but two
huge meals, paid for by those scoundrels, twenty of whom had
contributed two sequins apiece, which came, all told, to nearly
five hundred francs. During that banquet we drank, we ate, we
let ourselves be handled, pawed, fucked, and we besotted ourselves,
in fine, to the point where, the two of us sprawled on the floor in
the center of the tavern, we gave ourselves to that mob upon strict
condition that they first vomit, piss, and shit all over our faces,
before sticking us. They all consented to those terms, and by the
time our nasty orgy was ended, we were half-drowned in urine,
ordures, and sperm.

"Children," said my companion once order had been restored,
"it now behooves us to make ourselves known to you and, in
recognition of the fine supper you have given us, to make some
samples of our merchandise available to you. Among you would
there be anyone with a personal grudge to settle, or some vindictiveness to express? We are going to supply him the means. Purveyors of the best poisons in Italy, specify your requirements to us,
and upon whom the product is to be used."

Would you believe it, my friends? (for, oh, just heavens, what
progress humankind has made in depravity) a clamor rose up, and
with one voice they begged us to be liberal in the distribution of
our baneful gifts; and there was not a single one who lacked, so he
claimed, a most excellent purpose to put them to. All were provided
for; and that libidinous soirée may perhaps have rendered us the
cause of sixty murders.

"Come," Durand said to me, "the hour is not late, further
adventures may be awaiting us. And I have the most positive urge
to go and verify the success of my pretty little fifteen-year-old's
death."

And so we bade our hosts farewell after having embraced
them warmly.

Reaching the square in front of the cathedral we came at once upon a funeral procession. In Italy it being the tradition to expose the dead in their caskets, Durand had no trouble identifying the features of the lovely child upon whom her venom had done its work.

"There she is, there she is," she whispered excitedly, "oh, fuck my soul! let's stand over here in the shadows and frig each other as she goes by."

"Rather than that," I said, "let's precede her into the cathedral; we will station ourselves in a chapel and do what you suggest while watching the burial."

"The final is the better moment, you are right," said Durand; "quick, let's go in."

We were fortunate enough to find a secluded spot directly behind the confessional in the very chapel where the young body was to be laid to rest. We shrank back against the wall, and there we stood, fingering each other's organs while the ceremony went forward, and timing our movements in such a way that no fuck would escape us until, the casket having been lowered into the vault, our discharge could, after a fashion, serve as holy water unto the deceased. All was soon over, the priests and mourners withdrew; but the work of sealing the tomb was left incomplete, and we saw that the gravedigger either had intentions we could not yet divine, or preferred, in view of the late hour, to come back and finish his masonry the next day.

"Ha!" said Durand, "let us linger here, an incredible whim has just entered my head. 'Twas a pretty creature they buried, eh?"

"Well?"

"We'll pluck her out of that tomb, my dear, you'll frig me upon that delicious face, beautiful still despite the funereal darkness gathering upon the brows. Say, are you afraid?"

"No."

"Then let us stay."

By and by the church is closed. We are alone in it.

"How I like this lugubrious silence," said Durand; "how it invites to crime, how it quickens the passions—it reflects the stillness of the grave. And, I tell you so, death puts the thrill of lust in me. To work."

"Stay," I murmured. "I believe I hear sounds."

And we hasten back to our niche. Ye gods! what did we perceive? Someone else was beating us to the treasure; and who? Heavens above, what execrable depravation! The father himself was coming to gloat over his abominable deed, he was coming to consummate it; the gravedigger preceded him, a lantern in his hand.

"Lift her forth," he was told by the father, "so great is my grief that I must once again take her in my arms before losing her forever."

The casket reappears, from it the body is removed, then laid out by the gravedigger upon the steps of the altar.

"Very good, my friend, that will do; leave me for a time," says the incestuous and barbaric author of that charming girl's days, "I wish to weep undisturbed. Let me shed my tears at my ease, you may return in two hours' time, and I shall reward you for your zeal."

The doors are closed again.

Oh, my friends, how am I to describe the horrors we witnessed? Describe them I must, however: they are aberrances of the human heart I am exposing, and I am bound to unveil its every nook and cranny.

Although the church had been locked shut, for added safety the rascal barricades himself inside the chapel, lights four tapers, places two at the head, two at the feet of his daughter, then draws away the shroud; and she lies naked before him. Unspeakable quiverings of pleasure then take possession of him; his twitching muscles, his hoarse respiration, the upstanding prick he trundles into sight, everything paints the ignited state of his soul.

"Damn my eyes!" he cries, "there it is, the thing I did . . . I repent me not. . . . Go, 'twas not your waggling tongue I punished, but my villainy I contented; the idea of killing you stiffened my prick, I'd fucked you a little too often, now I am pleased."

Wherewith he approaches the corpse; he fondles its breasts, he jabs them with a pin.

"Bah, she feels nothing anymore," he mutters; "a pity, she feels nothing. Was I in too great a hurry? Bitch, how many other torments I'd inflict upon you were you yet alive!"

He spreads her thighs wide apart, he pinches her labia, he

pricks the interior of her womb and, feeling his erection at its peak, the villain encunts her, lies down flat upon her, kisses her mouth, does what he can to thrust his tongue inside it, but cannot, for the contractions induced by the poison have locked tight the child's jaw. He withdraws, turns the corpse over upon its belly and allows us a sight of the loveliest buttocks one can hope to behold. Ardently he kisses those hindquarters, vigorously he frigs himself. "Ah," he exclaims, "how often have I fucked this celestial ass, how many various pleasures has it procured me over the past four years!"

He then steps back, gazes down at the body meditatively, circles it two or three times, repeating the words, "Beautiful corpse! Beautiful corpse!"

And as the uttering of that phrase lifted his prick afresh and caused it horribly to swell, we concluded that corpse-fucking must be his passion. Again he kneels down between his daughter's wide-flung legs, he rekisses her lovely ass a thousand times over, pricks it, bites it, applies furious slaps to it, even tears away a piece of flesh with his teeth, and sodomizes. Here, as it appeared to us, his delirium reaches its culminating point; he gnashes his teeth, he foams; and, drawing a long knife from his pocket, while he discharges he cuts off the head of this cadaver, then readjusts himself.

We observed there, philosophically, the state of the man of firm principle when he has just completed the satisfaction of his ruling passion. A fool, with before him nothing but the object of his rage and his lubricity, obliged to wait amidst the silence and the horror of the tombs, would have shuddered, infallibly. Our villain, calm, gathers up the battered debris of his daughter; he packs the pieces back into the casket; he even remains a short while down in the vault, doing we have no idea what. 'Twas then that Durand, who throughout the whole of this performance has not ceased to frig herself or to frig me, suggests that we push the stone slab into place over the vault and entomb this man along with his victim.

"No," I say, "he is a villain, and we owe all villains our respect and protection."

"Yes, to be sure," she agreed; "but we may at least give him a scare. Quickly, lie down on the exact spot his daughter occupied a moment ago, and in the same attitude; let that be the sight greeting him when he emerges from below. Powerfully impressed he will be, the effect should about drive him to distraction."

Its unusualness seemed to me to require that the prank be played.

The libertine reappears, and the first thing his eyes light upon is my well-exposed ass. So startled was he that he staggered backward, and all but toppled into the vault whence he had arisen; and, indeed, he was saved from doing so only by my friend, who caught his arm; and at her touch he almost swooned away from terror.

"Cordelli," Durand said to the libertine, who was trembling from head to foot, "be not alarmed, you are amidst friends: I am she who sold you the poison you employed so successfully, and in this pretty girl behold someone of the most amiable disposition and ready to give you all manner of delights, providing that they differ from those we have just watched you procure yourself."

"You have taken me strangely by surprise," the tradesman said.

"Never mind, my friend, compose yourself: we saw you and we admired you. I ask you to admire this splendid ass, it is there to serve you: five hundred sequins and it is yours. And bear in mind also that this superb creature is no ordinary woman."

"Indeed, it is an agreeable behind," Cordelli admitted, fondling it; "but I am in limp condition: you saw the discharge I produced a short while ago."

"A reparable loss," Durand declared, "you shall be up again in no time, believe me. I have a lotion in my pocket, its effects are unfailing. Where do you wish the scene to take place?"

"In that vault; let us all descend there, I cannot tear myself away from my victim's remains, you'd find it hard to believe, the degree to which they inspire me."

We made our way down into the sepulcher.

Cordelli no sooner lifts away the winding sheet, he no sooner claps eyes upon his unlucky daughter's vestiges, than his prick begins to stir again. Durand rubs his testicles with the lotion she had mentioned, then she frictions his member. I show him my behind, he reaches for it, socratizes it, kisses my mouth, and the erection is complete.

"This young lady will have the kindness," says he, "to place herself in the casket. She will then be swathed in the shroud. We shall then go up to the chapel, the slab will be lowered for a few moments; I shall then, I am perfectly certain of it, discharge at the edge of the hole."

La Durand casts a glance at me; my answer was not slow in forthcoming.

"We are inseparable, Signor," I informed the tradesman, "it shall therefore have to be over the two of us you lower the slab for a few moments."

"Ah, dear Juliette, you want faith in me," said Durand. "Go up then with Signor Cordelli, I shall stay below. And I commend myself to you, remember it, to you alone."

A second time I took counsel with myself. I worshiped Durand; I realized that even a sliver of mistrust must soon turn into a wedge driven between us. There was the risk that they leave me buried alive? Offsetting it was the gravedigger's eventual return. And if nothing happened, if all went well . . . how my confidence in my friend would be reinforced! what tranquillity ever after!

"Nonsense," I declared; "and to prove to you, my love, that I am incapable of doubts in your regard, I stay here. Proceed, Cordelli, do what you like; and for my acquiescence the price is one thousand sequins."

"The sum shall be yours," the tradesman promised, "I appreciate unconditional docility, yours shall be recompensed."

The scraps of the daughter are cleared from the casket, I install myself in it; Cordelli envelops me in the shroud; and he presses three or four kisses to my asshole. "Ah, the beautiful corpse," he sighs, walking around me several times; after which he and Durand mount the stone stairs leading to the chapel.

I confess it, a deathly chill penetrated me unto the very marrow of my bones when I heard the slab fall heavily into position. And now? I wondered. Helpless, I am in the power of two very wicked villains. Strange blindness of libertinage, whither shall you lead me!

But this ordeal was necessary.

I leave you to imagine how my uneasiness increased when stirrings up above announced the removal of the barricade with which Cordelli had blocked the chapel; and when those movements were succeeded by utter silence.

So, I said to myself, you are doomed. Perfidious Durand has betrayed you. And I felt all my body laved in a cold sweat, from my scalp down to my ankles. Then, plucking up courage, I reasoned with myself: Softly, said I, let us not despair, 'tis no act of virtue you have just committed. Were that the case, well might you quake; but vice alone is concerned here, and so what can you possibly fear?

Such were my thoughts when the noises characteristic of Cordelli's discharge were heard; the stone was lifted away; and a moment later Durand was bending over me.

"It is all over, my angel," said she, "you are free and here are your thousand sequins. Will you suspect me in the future?"

"Never," I cried, "never, forgive an irrational impulse: it was directed far more at Cordelli than at you. But let us get ourselves away from this place, I am faint from lack of fresh air."

A weary Cordelli, whose bubbling sperm formed a puddle upon the slab, was sitting on the steps of the altar, awaiting us. We made ready to go; the gravedigger appeared, Cordelli paid him, and we left the cathedral. Durand wanted to spend the rest of the night in my bed.

"That episode has forged bonds between us," I said to my companion, "it seals our friendship forever, our mutual trust. It has rendered us inseparable for life."

"I told you so," Durand replied, "our arms combined will bring much hurt to others; but never a scratch either to you or to me."

"Is it not true," said I, "that had you had some other woman with you, she would have remained in that vault?"

"For a certainty. And I swear to you that Cordelli offered me two thousand sequins if I would agree to leave you there."

"Well," was my response, "let us look about for a pretty girl, let us propose her to him and enjoy watching him repeat his performance."

"But you already have the desired girl."

"Who then?"

"Elise."

"You are unfriendly toward my two maids, aren't you! Is it jealousy?"

"No, but I do not like to see anyone near you whom you might think more attached to you than am I. Are you not just a little tired of the slut? I leave you the other one, but that Elise, surely you have had your fill of her by now? You cannot sleep at night unless it be between the pair of them? Why then, all that is required is that I take her place."

"Your project excites me but at the same time I find it distasteful."

"Which is to say that it has everything in its favor," Durand rejoined, "for great pleasures are only born from surmounted repugnances. Ring for her, let's sport with her, silently decree her death while frigging her; nothing amuses me like such pieces of deceit."

"Ah, Durand, what a multitude of infamies you have me commit."

"Say rather what an infinity of delights I prepare for you."

Elise appears, beautiful as ever, the very effigy of Love; she slips obediently into bed between us; Durand, as yet only imperfectly acquainted with her, takes extreme pleasure in caressing the girl.

"There's a truly voluptuous creature, upon my honor," says the rascal, scattering kisses upon her, "have her lie on top of you, Juliette, and be tickling her clitoris while I embugger her. Oh, what an inspiring ass, how our good tradesman is going to fancy these peerless buttocks!"

And the lewd thing, tonguing the anus lodged betwixt them, shortly introduced her little device thereinto. Stretched out upon Elise, and consequently upon me as well, she sucked our mouths by turns.

"Twelve hours in a row I have been engaged in libertine activities," she said, "and I ought by rights to be exhausted; but not at all, I feel as though nothing could abate my ardor."

"And, do you know, I feel the same way. 'Tis our scheme," I added in a lowered voice, "which particularly heats me, Durand, electrifies me. The two of us, let's discharge over that delicious idea." And as I was frigging Elise most dextrously, and as Durand was sodomizing her to perfection, the little dear was the first to discharge. Sensing the spasm occur, Durand set to spanking her ferociously; she withdrew from Elise's ass and, swearing like one of the damned, scolded the poor soul for having upset her by discharging.

"The duty of a victim," she told her harshly, "is to accommodate; she must never venture to partake of any pleasure whatever. You.are a jade, you are a hussy, and a whipping will teach you to create disturbances for me."

I hold the victim and the villain has at her for a quarter of an hour. Elise was familiar with this mania, she had frequently had to put up with lashings from me; but never before had she received one so violent.

"You are going to spoil her behind," I pointed out, "and tomorrow Cordelli—"

"He values such disfiguring marks, they bring him to erection."

And, while the libertine remained intent upon her work, the blood continued to course down Elise's legs. The storm did finally subside, Durand embuggered me and, while in the pass of discharging, wanted to have the girl's tattered buttocks within the reach of her kisses.

"A divine creature," she pronounced when her spasms were over, "exactly what we need. And you, my fairest of fair, say, have you discharged? Forgive me for paying so little heed to your pleasures: when in the throes of delirium I tend to inconceivable self-centeredness."

"Oh, my dear, I have been at least as happy as you; see how wet my cunt is."

"And your brain? Was it affected by the thing too?"

"Overwhelmed."

We got back into bed, Elise between us; I blew out the candle. Before drifting off to sleep, Durand put her lips to my ear: "I relish few thoughts," she said in a whisper, "more than that of lying the night with an individual who is certain to die the next day thanks to me."

Durand called upon Cordelli early the following morning. Enchanted as he was by such an agreeable proposition, a bargain was quickly struck, the life of the ill-starred Elise was sold in exchange for a modest thousand sequins; but Cordelli meant to encompass the deed by refinements, and as I am about to relate this sinister adventure to you, rather than tell you of them ahead of time, I shall let these details come out in the course of the drama.

While my companion was off negotiating I had ordered Elise put in a state of readiness. She was bathed, freshened, perfumed, and once art had seconded the gifts of Nature, that beautiful girl, not yet eighteen years old, emerged radiant as an angel.

Durand returned and advised me that Cordelli expected us at five o'clock that same afternoon. " 'Tis to transpire at one of his country properties, in a castle by the sea three leagues outside Ancona; and," she said, "I believe I can assure you that the scene will be rousing. Now let us have lunch."

Elise and Raimonde, as usual, were at table alongside us; 'twas there we announced to them that they were to be separated..

"Elise," said we, "has caught the eye of a rich tradesman in town. Her future is assured; she is to stay here at Ancona."

The two friends melted into tears. Then, throwing herself into my arms, "Dear lady," Elise cried, sprinkling me with tears and kisses, "you promised you would never abandon me. . . ."

And it was then, my friends, that I was able to measure the vibrations set up within a libertine soul when lust enters into collision with sensibility. I stiffened inwardly against the girl's pleadings, I found pleasure in braving her tears, in refusing to allow her entreaties to act otherwise than as a spur to my lubricity.

"But, my dear," I replied to that exquisite creature, fending her off, pushing her back to her chair, "would I not blame myself forever if I were to stand in the way of your fortune?"

"I want no fortune, Madame, I ask for nothing but the favor of remaining with you until my dying day."

"Elise," said Durand, "are you then so very fond of Juliette?"

"Alas, Madame, but for her I would not be alive today. It was she who rescued Raimonde and me from a brigand who would without any question have massacred us otherwise, and when gratitude is added to the heart's natural feelings, you understand, Madame, that nothing but impassioned friendship can be the result."

"Be all that as it may, you must take leave of each other," said the unkind Durand, "and very promptly too."

Within me a storm was brewing; Durand detected it.

"Take her into another room," my companion murmured to me, "I shall stay here and have Raimonde frig me."

No sooner was I alone with Elise than I felt all my senses transformed by fury; that beautiful child kissed me as she wept: I abused her; and feeling my fuck flow with the first blows I dealt her, I struck with redoubled force.

"In truth," I said icily, "your sentiments surprise me, for I feel none even distantly resembling them. It may be that once upon a time I did not behold you with total indifference; however, I am weary of you today. If I have kept you for the past three months, lay it up to charity."

"To charity, Madame!"

"Why yes, were it not for my pity, what do you suppose you would have turned into? A streetwalker. Therefore thank me if I have taken the trouble to procure somebody for you, and express your gratitude by frigging me."

I removed her clothes, I pored over her charms; to contemplate them in that frame of mind all but slew me with delight. How it thrilled me to be able to say to myself: In three days' time, this glorious body will be the prey of maggots, and the credit for its destruction shall be mine.

Divine spark of lust! inexpressible delights of crime! Ah, what ravages you produce in the nervous system of a libertine female! Elise! Elise, thou whom I didst once dote upon, I deliver thee into the hands of thy butchers . . . and doing so, I discharge.

Striving to persuade me that, once gone, she would be sorely missed, how the cunning little thing redoubled her attentions! It was not long before they obtained triumphal results; she was sucking while socratizing me, I shot a flood into her mouth; I then did for her what she had done for me. I adored the idea of drowning her in pleasure before handing her over to death. She discharged, then burst into tears, addressing the most tender words to me, the most urgent entreaties, supplicating me not to send her away. She could more easily have moved a mountain. Once I was sated, "Come," I told her, "it is time to leave."

She thought to go to her room to pack together her belongings.

"Don't bother," said I, "we'll send your things to you tomorrow."

She casts herself into my arms . . . I repulse her, I slap her face hard; she bleeds. I believe I might have strangled her there and then had it not been for our agreement with Cordelli.

We went back into the salon. Durand was not there; I heard sounds in the adjoining room and went to peer through the keyhole. Heavens! what was my surprise to spy a man embuggering Raimonde, and Durand flogging the fucker. I knock . . . I ask leave to enter.

"Is it you?" Durand calls out.

"Why, of course; open the door."

A finger to her lips, she bade me come in quietly. "It's Cordelli. . . . He insisted upon seeing the girl you had in store for him; I did not want to disturb you, so I gave him Raimonde for the time being. As you see . . . he's embuggering her. He seems to be mad about her, Juliette."

"Pray do not interrupt anything on my account, Signor," I hastened to say to him, "simply remember that she is not the one you have contracted for."

"And I am dreadfully sorry about it," the rake replied, his words punctuated by gasps of pleasure, "I am dreadfully—sorry —for her ass—the most beautiful ass in creation, the—tightest fitting—oh, with this there are—wonders to be achieved. However," he went on, backing out of the breach, "I shall not discharge, 'twould be wiser for me to husband my forces. There," said he, wiping his prick, recovering his breath, "let us talk business for a moment."

Raimonde retired from the room; and the three of us, Cordelli, Durand, and I, drew up chairs and sat down.

"My impatience got the better of me," he explained; "I arrived just as you were getting up from the table, Madame Durand told me that you were amusing yourself with the one reserved for me. Seeing Raimonde with our friend, I formed a desire to have her, and I must own that the having of her made me regret that not she but the other one is to be my victim. ' 'Tis Juliette's favorite,' Madame Durand informed me, 'Juliette will never agree to part with her.' Mademoiselle," the seducer continued, taking hold of my hand, "listen to me. I am a generous man to deal with; I own millions, having for the past twenty years pocketed every penny of the profits from the celebrated Senigallia Fair:[2] a few thousand sequins more, a few thousand sequins less, trifles I do not deign to take notice of when my passions are at stake. I do not know Elise; but I know your Raimonde, she pleases me infinitely. I have seen divine behinds in my day, I never fuck any save the warmest and the snuggest. This girl must be superb in distress; and, to put it simply, she is one of the most suitable women for victimization I have beheld in years. This then is what I am going to do: Sight unseen, I shall take the other one, because I said I would, and I shall take this one too, in this case knowing what I am getting: will six thousand sequins be acceptable for the pair?"

"Hardly," I replied, feeling greed, love of gold crowd every other sentiment out of my heart. "Twenty thousand sequins and you get the two of them."

"But," Cordelli reminded me, "I have already bought one for a thousand."

"Consider the bargain broken; I sell them together or not at all, and I am not going to let them go for anything under the price I just named."

"I can only approve my friend's decision," Durand put in; "it strikes me that you are lucky to obtain the darling of her affections so cheaply."

"A girl I worship, and I sell her to whom? to a villain who intends to kill her!"

"Yes indeed," the Italian admitted, "and to kill her to the tune of ghastly tortures, I assure you."

"Well, such amusements must be paid for, Signor. Make up your mind, for let pity reassert its rights in my heart and you'll end up with nothing."

"Your merchandise is expensive, Mademoiselle," the tradesman observed. "But, damn my eyes! you catch me at a moment when the heat of lust puts right reason to rout. Show this voucher to my bookkeeper and he will immediately disburse the funds. In the meantime let us have a look at the other girl."

---

2 The most famous in all Italy.

"Scoundrel," I whispered to my friend, "this is another example of your work. You seem to be determined to leave me nobody."

"Oh, Juliette, for that blame nought but my love; think not that you shall ever regret having lost everybody else, for in having me you shall have more than a whole world."

And she went off to collect the money.

I summoned Elise.

"Charming!" the rake exclaimed once he clapped eyes upon her. "Little wonder that you ask such a figure for such an article." And hastening to undress the girl, his enthusiasm but rose when he was able to admire her charms in their entirety. He submits that delicate and sweetly modeled ass to a searching examination; he kisses it indefatigably, spreads it, tongues it, fucks it, comes forth to kiss it anew; and ardent though they be, the caresses he lavishes upon it, he cannot tear himself away from the divine object.

"Have the other one come in, we shall compare the two side by side."

Raimonde appears and, soon just as naked as Elise, she offers her examiner everything needed to facilitate his observations. The scrupulousness wherewith he proceeds is not to be imagined: the buttocks especially claim his narrow-eyed attention. While he concentrates upon his study I lay a light hand to his member, frig him slowly; his hands stray now and then to my buttocks, which he fondles while thrusting his tongue into my mouth; and then he embuggers Elise, while slapping us smartly, Raimonde and me.

"Truth to tell, the one is worth no less than the other," he confides to me in private, "and both are delightful. I shall cause them much suffering."

"Which, in your view, is the better ass?" I asked him.

"Oh, Raimonde's, no doubt about it," he replied, kissing that lovely personage with feeling; "better for temperature, better for fit. . . . Juliette, lie down upon that bed," the insatiable libertine said, "I am of a mind to ass-fuck you also."

He has Elise station herself to my left, Raimonde to my right: he then kneads and pinches their two behinds while fucking mine. Then, abruptly breaking off contact, "Enough," he says, "else I discharge. Time is passing; let us be on our way."

The two girls retire to make themselves ready for the journey. Finding myself alone with the Italian, "Don't deny it," I say, "it was my companion who induced you to choose Raimonde. Eh?"

"I shall not hide from you that she is eager to see her die."

"The vixen! 'Tis jealousy: a sufficient motive, in so far as I am concerned. Oh, never fear, my mind is made up, those two wretches must be treated infernally." I was frigging him as I spoke, he was standing in front of me, I was rubbing his prick against my breasts, tickling his anus. "And," I wondered, "exactly what form of torture are you reserving for them?"

"You would not have it be mild?"

"Ah, if it were up to me, their torments would surpass anything you can imagine."

"Delicious creature. . . . That is the way I like women to be; they are more ferocious than men if they will but give outlet to their aptitudes."

"Behind that lie natural reasons," I answered, "their organs are more finely constructed, their sensitivity profounder, their nerves more irascible: barbarity is not a trait of the individual of inferior sensibility."

"Precisely; and with a much keener imagination than the one we have, a woman cannot help but embrace excesses more avidly: which is why, in crime, women always go farther than we. Let a duel be announced, a gladiatorial combat, a public execution, and you see women flock to watch the spectacle; take a count of the onlookers, each time you will find women outnumbering men ten to one. A great many fools," the tradesman added, "dupes of this incredible faculty for feeling they notice in women, fail to realize that extremes coincide, and that it is precisely at the source of this capacity that cruelty has its origin."

"Because cruelty is in itself but an extension of sensitivity," said I, "and because the great horrors we commit are always owing to the higher degree of our soul's sensitivity."

"Listening to you, it is as though one were conversing with an angel, dear heart," said Signor Cordelli; "kiss me and kiss me again, I am as much taken by your mind as by your charms. You ought to attach yourself to me."

"I am inviolably attached to my friend," I replied; "only death will sunder us."

"She would come with you."

"No, we wish to see our native land again."

At that point I heard Durand's footsteps. Going to greet her, I was able, as we stood out of range of Cordelli's hearing, to learn of the pretty coup she had just executed.

"I tampered with the voucher," Durand told me. "We have double the sum."

"Forty thousand sequins?"

"Yes, they are already locked safely away."

"Celestial creature!"

"Do you regret the transaction now?"

"Not anymore. But when Cordelli next sees his bookkeeper?"

"By then the crime will be consummated. One word of complaint out of the scoundrel and one word from us will have him broken on the wheel."

"Kiss me, cleverest of friends!"

"Come and take your half of the money."

"What need is there of that? Let us first attend to Cordelli; we shall divide our earnings when we return."

"I would like you to have the entire sum; it gives me greater pleasure to see you at the summit of opulence than to increase my own wealth."

And Cordelli having sent for us, we all set forth. After a several hours' drive we reached the tradesman's castle, a veritable fortress situated upon a spur of rock jutting out into the sea. By a little farm lying at the base of the rock the carriage drew to a halt, for the road went no farther. From that point on there were steps to climb, four hundred of them in all, these being the sole means of access to that redoubtable house. Before beginning the ascent we had to pass an iron gate, to which the tradesman had the key; there were six other gates like it at intervals along the stairway, and Cordelli opened and carefully closed each of them as we proceeded up. Durand, noticing my expression of surprise gradually yield to one of alarm, saw fit to reassure me. To Cordelli she said: "Yes, the description you gave me of your house's whereabouts was exact, and our servants, who will easily find the place, have instructions to come to fetch us tomorrow morning if by ten o'clock we are not back in Ancona."

"I am well known throughout the region," said the tradesman, likewise eager, as it seemed to me, to put me at ease; "but you need not have troubled to give your orders, Madame Durand, you have my promise that we shall be returning to the city tonight, and you know me well enough to be sure that my word is my bond."

Our two girls were not so easily reassured. A kind of premonition always accompanies impending woe, the unlucky pair felt it in all its force, the knees of both were buckling from terror.

A final gate is unlocked and then shut behind us; we are welcomed by two women of sixty.

"Everything is ready?" asks Cordelli.

"Since this morning, Signor," one of the women replies; "we did not think you would be coming so late."

We advance; it is a rather somber, low-ceilinged hall we enter first.

Cordelli moves to a window, draws the curtain aside. "Look where we are," says he.

And great was our astonishment to see that we were some three hundred feet above the sea, and nearly surrounded by water.

"This rock describes a curve," the Italian explained; "here, at its outermost point, we are about half a league from the mainland. One may make as much noise as one likes, there is slight chance of being heard by anybody."

We left that room, mounted a flight of stairs which brought us to another: in it the scene was to take place.

Never perhaps had my eyes beheld anything quite so horrible. Upon a round dais located in the center of that room, itself circular, we made out, upon entering, all the divers instruments necessary to every known form of torture. Among them were some so execrable, so inconceivable and outlandish that I had never even dreamed of their existence. Two huge swarthy men, six feet tall, wearing fearful moustaches, of terrifying mien, naked as savages, stood at attention amidst that array of equipment, visibly ready to carry out the orders they were waiting to receive. Fifteen corpses of youths and young girls decorated the smoke-streaked stone walls of that evil den; and upon four stools surrounding the central dais were seated two girls of sixteen and two boys of fifteen, all in a state of absolute nudity. The old women, who had entered along with us, closed and bolted the doors; Cordelli glanced at us, relishing our astonishment.

"This is where we are going to operate," said he. "Rarely," he observed for the sake of our two handmaids, "yes, very rarely does anyone leave this room having once come through its portals. Look sharply there, Dona Maria, have the clothes removed; start a fire; and let's settle down to work without further delay . . . I feel the fuck tingling in my balls; and seldom have I been in such a mood for horrors.

"Juliette," the lewd man said to me, "I appoint you my satellite, the general agent of my pleasures; undress and keep close by my side. Mindful of nothing but the service, of the imperious needs and wants of my prick and of my ass, you shall minister carefully to both of them during the entirety of the scene. If I call for a fucking, you shall wet my asshole with your spittle; with your tongue you shall moisten the pricks that are to sodomize me; you shall yourself introduce them into my behind. If I elect to fuck, you shall guide my tool into the holes I am moved to perforate, which you shall oil with saliva from your lips. At no time while performing your duties shall you neglect this capital detail : once you have completed the oral preparation of whatever it may be, prick or ass, your mouth must be glued immediately to mine, and must suck it diligently and at length. Moreover, an attitude of deepest respect shall distinguish your bearing and govern your actions : it shall not be forgotten that no one is admitted into this place except slaves or victims.

"You, Durand, shall lead the objects up to me, you shall present them to me, and remember, both of you, to do nothing without first giving me your asses to kiss.

"As for you," he went on, addressing the elders, barearmed and naked from the waist down, wielding a handful of slender green switches, "you shall follow close after me, and you shall exert yourselves upon my flanks and buttocks at such times as, in your judgment, they may benefit from stimulation.

"You, Bloodletter, and you, Barbaro, not only shall you fulfill your role as executioners, but you shall take all good care to perforate my behind each time you see me present it to you amorously; Juliette then shall seize your engines and shall fetch them up and introduce them into my ass, conforming to the instructions already given her.

"As regards you young people who, seated upon these four stools, and in the most respectful silence, are awaiting what it pleases me to prescribe to you, submissiveness is your lot. Think not that the ties through which you are connected to me, since you are all four my offspring though begot of different mothers, think not, I say, that familial ties are going to prevent me from dispatching you upon a prolonged and harrowing journey to death: be advised that I only gave you life in order to be able to deprive you of it, that infanticide is one of the sweetest of my pleasures, and that it is the very nearness of our kinship that will ensure my delight in martyrizing you.

"As for you, my lovely children," he continued glaveringly, cruelly rallying my two women, "after what I have paid for you, no one will contest my right to do with you everything a more than ordinarily perverse imagination may suggest to me . . . and you can look forward to atrocious discomforts. I hope shortly to come to know all the effects of pain upon your sensitive constitutions."

Hearing those words, the unhappy creatures fell upon their knees before Cordelli. Already undressed by the duennas, their rich black hair floating in disorder upon their breasts of alabaster, their tears wetting the feet of the tyrant, all this lends an indescribably affecting quality to the spectacle of their grief and their despair.

"Fuck my soul," Cordelli says, sinking back into an armchair while I pollute him with one hand, socratize him with the other. "How fond I am of misfortune's tragic effects, how they stiffen me. . . . Say, my pretty little jades, what if I lend you a dagger? You could stab yourselves or each other to death, I would not be unwilling to watch you do it." And as he spoke the monster laid brutal hands upon those two charming girls' fresh and delicate breasts: he pinched them, compressed them violently, and appeared to glean uncommon pleasure from aggravating their mental sufferings by means of a quantity of little physical bullyings, inflicted, his hardening prick announced, to his lust's advantage.

"Bring me their asses," he told one of the duennas, "adjust them so that the holes are on a level with my lips. You, Durand, suck me; Juliette shall continue to frig me as I lie in your mouth."

Thereupon he bit those two faultless asses and left marks of his teeth upon ten or a dozen different places. Then, slipping his head between Raimonde's thighs, so fiercely did he chew upon her clitoris that the poor girl fainted. Enchanted at achieving such an effect, he began to subject Elise to the same trial; but the girl twitched, the knave missed the mark, his teeth clamped instead upon the lips of her vagina, a piece of which he carried away. Bruised and shocked though they were by these initial attacks, he wanted to fuck them both in that state. The order is given, the girls are laid belly down upon a long divan, their heads directly underneath the cadavers adorning the walls. And there, served by me, the rascal dipped alternately into their two asses and their two cunts, during a space of twenty minutes. After this, he found a bundle of switches, and having had one of the girls get down upon all fours and the other kneel upon her shoulders, in such sort that he could get at Elise's divine buttocks and Raimonde's exquisite teats, he martyrized those fleshy forms, now individually, now collectively; for better than thirty uninterrupted minutes he lashed them, all the while the duennas, kneeling behind his ass, belabored his buttocks with a silver hatpin. Elise and Raimonde exchanged positions, so that he could thrash her buttocks whose breasts he had just finished beating, and worry the breasts of her whose ass he had been molesting hitherto. When everything was bleeding profusely, basins of water were brought forward, wounds were stanched, and Cordelli, in furious erection, commanded one of his sons to come to him. In that delightful child all the gifts of a lavish Nature were combined: an enchanting countenance, a fine and fair skin, a pretty mouth, lovely hair, the most adorable ass.

"He does indeed greatly resemble his mother," the rake observed, kissing the boy.

"What became of the poor soul?" I asked the Italian.

"Fie upon you, Juliette!" he replied. "You are forever suspecting me of horrors, I sense it. Much surprised you would be, I dare say, if I were to produce the person for you right now."

"I defy you to do it."

"Very well, there she is," Cordelli retorted, pointing to one of the corpses suspended from a hook upon the wall; "that is the boy's mother, ask him if you do not believe me. I depucelated the dear lad, here in this room, and that was scarcely thirty-six hours ago. Yes, here, as he lay in the arms of his loving and then living mother; and shortly afterward, as he will confirm, yes, before his very eyes, utilizing a curious torture, I sent his mama to the place where today I am going, in a manner no less curious, to send his nabs, madame's darling son." And the rascal, polluted by me, grew inordinately stiff.

He has one of the old women contain the child; upon his instructions, I moisten the gomorrhean orifice, I guide the shaft; Durand sucks Cordelli's Ganymede from below, and the Italian embuggers while colling my behind.

Nimble as ever, ever sufficiently in control of himself to strike deep and yet only graze the edge of pleasure, Cordelli, without it having cost him a drop of fuck, withdraws from this ass too.

The other youth is brought to him. The same ceremony, the same economy of sperm; and the tradesman having camped one atop the other, thrashes them both simultaneously. From time to time he pauses to suck a prick. Finally, impelled by a furious surge of lust, he bites the balls of the first-fucked, bites them so terribly that the child loses consciousness. Unperturbed, Cordelli moves on to other things. One of his daughters is led up; she was not a beauty, but about her there was something so mild, an air of modesty and innocence so irresistible that there was no refusing her one's stintless homage.

"A virgin, that one," said Cordelli, "of that there is no question; however, since I am no longer capable of catching an erection for a cunt, you," he went on, nodding to the duennas, "shall lay her flat on this sofa, and hold her still."

And as soon as he has that pleasant child's two voluptuous buttocks well in perspective, the sinner molests them, pinches them, and claws them with such speed and such force that they are all ableeding the next minute: therewith he embuggers. Thinking to have acquired from that ass the vigor needed to attempt the cunt, he presents himself before it; and, his illusion sustained by our libertine fingerings and kisses and yet more so by the asses we offer to his caresses, success crowns his efforts, he blasts the maidenhead. He withdraws an incarnadine member to thrust it home again into the sanctuary he prefers, and after a few more such mingled attacks, he comes back to discharge in the ass of one of the boys whom to this end he has kept nearby him throughout all his activities up until now. He discharges, I say. A clap of thunder, one would have called it. I thought he was going to shake the house down. We were clustered around him; he was kissing my buttocks, an old woman was flogging him, Durand was socratizing him, Elise was tickling his balls, he was pinching Raimonde's ass, examining that of the little boy and that of the little girl posted ahead of him; in sum, everything, everyone, concurred in provoking a discharge the power of which is not readily to be described.

"Fuck!" he exclaimed when he was done, "the time has come for some horrors, they are indispensable if I am to get myself back into form."

"Then horrors you shall have, my friend, horrors you shall have," said I, consoling his prick by mouthing it, by squeezing it, by carefully evacuating the very last drop of fuck from it.[3]

Cordelli was grateful for these attentions. The crowd encircles him once again while I suck him; his mouth finds that of the girl he has just devirginated, one would have thought he designed to tear her tongue out by the roots, so forcefully did he suck it. By and by, who would believe it? through an incredible incongruity, 'tis the fetid maw of one of the crones he fastens upon and tongues for a quarter of an hour; and the foul fellow abandons it only in order, with identical delight, to pump the mouth of that one of his executioners he signals for. This last excess is the decisive one: I begin to feel the effects of the miracle. Cordelli takes one of my hands and, placing it upon the villain's instrument, I am awestruck at discovering that the article in my grasp is

---

[3] Few men know how to have themselves cared for following discharge; exhausted, prostrated, they sneak off into a corner, listless and empty-headed. Nevertheless, upon post-ejaculatory care depends the vigor necessary to tasting further enjoyments, and to emerging from former ones in a less collapsed state. This care consists in having oneself sucked without delay, in having one's balls comforted and fondled, and in the application of very hot cloths. It is also helpful, after the crisis, to absorb restoratives, or spirituous liquors. The latter employed as lotions upon the testicles will also produce excellent effects.

thicker than my upper arm and almost as long as one of my thighs.

"Take that prick, Juliette," the Italian says to me, "and steer it into the cunt of the little girl I have just deflowered. Keep in mind, if you will, that it must enter regardless of the consequences."

Initial attempts proving futile, there was nothing else to do but bind the victim; Cordelli ordered her four limbs secured by ropes made fast to the floor, in such sort as to ensure fair access to both her holes: thus, if his man failed to fight his way into one of them, he could take refuge in the other. I wheeled the engine into position; Cordelli was urging the champion on from behind; lean and hairy though those hinder parts were, the lecher tongued them contentedly, and looked to be ready to fuck them the moment that individual's enormous device was niched where he wanted it to be. By dint of skill we succeed: the prick penetrates into the girl's cunt, and death's livid hue upon her brow attests to the damnable state of her physique. Cordelli, however, his eye fixed upon that extraordinary tool, soon issues commands to make for the other port; I act as pilot. Jostled, strained in every fiber, Nature gradually yields to resolute pressure, as she always does; nevertheless, the anus splits, blood gushes forth, and the Italian, in seventh heaven, hanging in the fucker's bowels, smites him from the rear as he himself smites to the fore.

Oh, God of Justice! what contrasts! Imagine, if you can, that pretty little face, so touching, so sweet; that face being nastily kissed by the most unprepossessing and the grimmest figure of a man to be found anywhere on earth, his bristly moustaches withering the lilies and the roses in the loveliest possible complexion, and with execrable blasphemies replying to the plaintive entreaties of the most innocent soul. Picture, my friends, on the other side, the infamous Cordelli preferring, to the beauties surrounding him, that paid murderer's loathsome bum; tonguing that vent, feeding upon it with the same ardor that would ordinarily have animated anybody else before a pretty and youthful novice; inserting his prick thereinto, and finally ordering Durand to strangle the victim when his man discharges.

It all comes about: the unlucky child expires. And the Italian, debuggering, offers us a purpling, sharply risen prick, fit now for every kind of outrage.

"There I am, back in fettle once again," says he. "And there's one of them dead already. I behaved with restraint, my friends, as you noticed; for I do not believe one could more mildly put a person to death."

One of the duennas thought to remove the corpse.

"Do not touch it, buggeress!" the merchant shouted, "those sights arouse me, how could you be unaware of the fact?" And the wicked man, pressing his face to that of his unhappy daughter, dares pluck hideous kisses from features twisted by death and reflecting, instead of the graces which used to play there before, only the convulsions of pain . . . only the contortions of despair.

"Durand," says the master of the house, "bring this man's prick up again: I want him to be fucking me while I explore both the orifices of my remaining daughter."

Preparations are made. Cordelli embuggers; buggery was usually his opening move. His man fucks him without preliminary oilings; what need of them had an asshole so amply proportioned? Elise and Raimonde are there, he kisses their behinds, to his right and left he handles those of his two sons, whose pricks are being sucked by Durand and me. From ass Cordelli skips to cunt, and the objects beneath his fingers vary. His man discharges: he summons the other. That other, at least as well furnished as his colleague, but of still more fearful aspect, if that be possible, vigorously sodomizes his employer and fires a pair of charges into his fundament. The orgies begin to take on a serious note.

"All right, by little Jesus' bugger-fucked Father," our host roars, very wroth, "crimes, I need crimes, I need abominations, upon them I depend for further ejaculations, and in the chapter of ejaculations my selfishness is such that should it cost the life of every damned one of you in this room, why I'd slaughter the lot without an instant's hesitation to obtain a good discharge."

"With whom are you of a mind to start, villain?" I then ventured to ask.

"With you . . . with some other . . . with I don't care whom; little does it matter provided it stiffens me. Bah, do you fancy there is anyone here whose life counts more with me than another's?

Come, let us try this little slut," the rogue said, catching the trembling Elise by one breast and dragging her thus along on her knees. He called for tongs, and while I frigged him, while one of the executioners immobilized the victim, and while everyone else formed a hedge of bare asses around him, the barbarian had the patience and the determination to nip the girl's breasts to pieces, removing small bit by small bit until he had so perfectly flattened out her chest that not even a suspicion remained of the two snow-white mammaries which had been embellishing it a few hours before.

This operation completed, the victim is presented to him in another position; held by four persons, her thighs are spread to the utmost, and her cunt gapes perfectly within his view.

"There we are," says the cannibal, "I am going to toil awhile in the workshop of the human species."

I was sucking him this time; his tongs forage about for fifteen minutes, he buries them as far in as they will go.

"Turn her over," he cries.

The most beautiful buttocks in the whole wide world are presented to him now, he pries them apart, his cruel pincers disappear into the anus and that delicate part is attacked with the same frenzy as the other. And it is I, I, once mad about this lovely creature, it is I who now exhort her assassin, who exhort him to treat her thus. Baneful inconstancy of the passions, whither then you can drive us! Had she been unknown to me, I might perhaps have felt some indulgence toward that poor creature; but 'tis unheard of, what one invents, what one says, what one does, when disgust has withered the tender petals of the flower of love.

Elise, swimming in her own blood, was breathing still; Cordelli contemplates her delightedly in her voluptuous agony; crime takes mighty pride in its works. Cordelli obliges me to frig his prick against the carnage he has wrought, he is thrilled to steep his member in the blood his hand has shed; and it is with a dagger he finishes off Elise.

One of his sons replaces my tribade. Cordelli has the window opened on the seaward side of the room. The child is attached to a rope fifty feet long, whose other end is secured to a beam; and then the child is dropped. "Are you ready?" the author of his days shouts down to him, exhibiting the knife with which he has but to slash through the rope: one quick gesture and the boy will disappear forever into a watery grave. From below rise the child's screams; I frig his father; that father kisses Raimonde, he frigs one of his executioners while the other bum-fucks him, stabbing a pin into his buttocks as he does so. The rope is pulled in, the child is retrieved; but he is not unbound.

"Say, wert afraid?" asks the tradesman. "Didst have a fright?"

"No more, father, for pity's sake, for pity's sake—"

"Little bastard," Cordelli sneers, "learn that the word *father* means nothing in my ears, nothing; I am deaf to it. Turn around: I must fuck you before feeding you to the fish. Yes, dear boy, to the fish, that is to be your fate: see what a powerful sway kindred ties exert over my heart!"

The scoundrel embuggers: while he is busy afucking, an additional length of rope is joined to the first one: this time it will be a two-hundred-foot fall. Two or three lunges and Cordelli retires, nodding to the executioners who thereupon seize the child and hurl him bodily out the window, from a height, that is, of two hundred feet, a distance he has no sooner traveled than the rope, suddenly checking his descent, thoroughly dislocates his limbs at the point where he halts. From there he is hauled back up. Broken inside and out, the poor lad was entirely out of shape.

"Another bum-tupping," said the Italian.

"And then another tumble," said Durand.

"Certainly; but lengthened yet a little more, the rope will not interrupt his ride till he is twenty-five feet above the waves."

The re-fucked child is rethrown, recovered almost inanimate. His father fucks him for the last time; and when he is dangling ten feet above the surface of the water, "Ready?" the ferocious Italian bawled down to him; "your final moment is nigh."

And he cuts the rope; and the sea at last provides the unhappy boy a haven of repose.

"That passion," I remark to Cordelli, "is one of the prettiest in my acquaintance."

"It heats you, Juliette?"

"Yes, indeed!"

"Then give me your ass to fuck. That will soothe you."
Cordelli filed away in me for a quarter of an hour, plotting new
pieces of mischief. Then 'twas Raimonde he called for. Her fate
was writ in the Italian's eyes, and she read it there at once.

"Oh, dearest mistress!" she said, clutching at me with out-
stretched arms, "is it then decided that I shall be surrendered to
this monster? I who loved you so. . . ."

Laughter was my only response. And his trusties having
marched the darling thing up to him, the traitor began with some
caresses; he fondles and kisses all her fleshy parts; he tongues,
tickles the clitoris, embuggers, hovers ten minutes in the depths of
Raimonde's bowels, and she is cast naked into an iron cage filled
with toads, reptiles, snakes, vipers, rabid dogs and cats which
have not fed for five days. The wretch's shrieks, her contortions,
her twitchings once the animals got at her, her antics were beyond
anything one can imagine; her pain, her distress were pathetic
beyond anything one could believe. I was overcome by the sight;
Durand was frigging me beside the cage, Cordelli, sucked by a
duenna, was fucking nearby. It took but a moment for that multitude of creatures to swarm over Raimonde, and the moment after
that there was not a great deal of her to be seen. The beasts made
for her tastier parts, breasts and buttocks vanished in less time
than it takes to tell. The unfortunate event occurred when, as she
opened her mouth to scream, a viper slithered into her gullet and
she choked to death, well before it suited our pleasures. At that
critical instant the other executioner was fucking Cordelli, the
rogue was sodomizing one elder while tonguing the asshole of
the second, palpating my buttocks with one hand and those of his
surviving daughter with the other, and Durand was frigging me
amain.

"Ha!" exclaimed Cordelli, uttering a string of coarse oaths
and jerking his prick rudely out of the duenna's fundament, "I'd
thought that by sodomizing this old pump I would avoid the danger
of a discharge, and blast my ass! I am on the brink of one."

"No, my dear, nothing of the sort must be allowed to happen,"
said I, bending his prick head downward; "let us dwell upon other
matters for a moment."

"Well," said the tradesman, "what think you of the cage as a

way to die, Juliette? I conceived of it for that slut the very first
instant I saw her ass: it is enough for me to examine that part of a
woman and her death sentence is dictated. If you like, Juliette, I
shall inscribe yours upon your behind itself."

And as he was pinching it vigorously while speaking those
words, I danced lightly out of his grip and, quick as a wink, for
my own substituted the ass of his one remaining son. He fixes a
terrible stare upon the boy, it is he whose mother the villain
massacred lately, and who can still see her embalmed remains there
upon the wall.

"If I rightly recall," said that incorrigible libertine, "I
arranged to have this little beggar die by the same torture under
which his mother perished, three days ago. First, the victim's eyes
are gouged out; then, his four extremities are lopped off; after that,
his four limbs are broken; and he is definitively embuggered while
an aide finishes him off with a dagger."

"And that is what you subjected his mother to?" I asked.

"It is."

"I have no objections to raise; I would merely suggest that,
along with the rest, extraction of the teeth and extirpation of the
tongue seem to be called for."

"Extraction of the teeth! Extirpation of the tongue! You
are quite right, Juliette," Cordelli replied, "I dealt too hastily
with his dam the other day. But we shall not be so neglectful with
her son. Ho," said he, snapping his fingers to his executioners,
"operate."

During the proceedings, it was my ass Cordelli perforated;
ahead of him he had, as prospect, that of the girl whose torments
were due to follow next. Durand showed him her ass to the right,
and he had the spectacle to the left; the duennas flogged him.

The deftness and the mastery those assassins displayed in
their work can hardly be imagined, and it would be even more difficult to render an idea of the intensity of the victim's sufferings or
the violence of his outcries. When Cordelli noticed that one agent
sufficed to the task, he ordered the other, splashed all over with
gore, to come up and encunt me so as to improve his enjoyment of
my ass. I was, God knows, accustomed to outsized engines, nevertheless the intromission of that one occasioned me exceeding dis-

comfort. Although that man was superlatively ill-favored, the horrors he had been bathing in, the forthright way he took with me, the language he employed, the sodomite episode whereby his master was regaling me, everything soon combined to carry me off into transports, and I washed my fucker's prick with the goodliest deluge of fuck. Cordelli, ecstatic at hearing my anthems of joy blend with the shrieks torture was wringing from his son, was overwhelmed; his sperm forces the sluices, and I am soaked at both ends. However, the boy's doing to death was not yet completed; the executioner inquired whether he was to hang fire.

"Of course not," the Italian answered him. "People are strange," he went on to comment, "they always suppose that one cannot torment a creature unless one is aroused. As for me, I protest that I am a rational man, I act deliberately in passion as in everything else: Nature endowed my being with a thirst for blood, I have no need to be excited in order to shed it."

Work was resumed.

However, to preserve the liveliness of the scene, I reheated his prick in my mouth, and Durand stimulated him verbally.

"Cordelli," she advanced, "though impressive, your ferocity is inadequate."

"How so?"

"Once you have done your worst, there shall yet remain worse to do."

"Prove it to me."

"Easily. With your leave I shall myself organize the torture of your remaining daughter; and I am confident that you shall behold greater things than those your timorous imagination has devised so far."

"Go ahead," the tradesman rejoined.

"Utilizing implements I see there," said my companion, "you shall have your man delicately peel off the girl's skin. Once flayed, she shall be whipped with thorns; after that, rubbed down with vinegar; and the operation demands to be repeated seven times. The nerves finally reached, small nails, red hot, shall be planted in them; the body may then be deposited in a fiery brazier."

"Marvelous," Cordelli said. "I agree to it, Durand, but I

warn you: if it fails to make me discharge, I will subject you to the same torture."

"As you like."

"To work."

The little maid is led up. 'Twas the prettier of the two. The unlucky creature had the loveliest possible figure, superb golden hair, a virgin's look, and eyes whereof Venus herself would have been envious. The unkind Italian was moved to kiss that charming little ass yet again; for, as he said, "I must pay my respects to it one last time before my barbarity causes its roses to fade. Ah, my friends, own that it is a lovely ass!"

And, profoundly stirred by the horrors impending, Cordelli soon passes from encomiums to deeds.

The girl is embuggered and after several charges the villain quits the field in order to relish as a bystander the cruel sight of his henchmen's more massy members perforating this pretty little posterior. Essay is made; but, as you surely realize, success is obtained only at the price of the total demolition of the anus. Cordelli, while this was going forward, was sodomizing the executioner; the other one has at the cunt of the young person who, treated in that hard fashion, gives us the image of a lamb in the clutches of two lions. Greatly affected by the scene, the profligate flits from the ass of one executioner to the ass of the other and, at last esteeming himself sufficiently heated, commands the torture to begin, appointing Durand its supervisor.

Again, words are not enough to describe the sufferings of the poor child once the Italian took his bundle of thorns to the new skin which came to light when the outer layer had been removed. But it was something else again when that second skin was removed and the third lashed; the wretch's shudderings, the way she ground her teeth and squirmed were infinitely pleasurable to see. Cordelli, remarking that I was frigging myself while watching, himself lent a hand to tickle me; but, absorbed by his victim's torture, he entrusted the masturbator's role to Durand, and my friend, quite as aroused as I, asked for the same attentions she was lavishing upon me. The operation lasted a considerable while, we discharged three or four times during it; all the creature's epidermal wrappings were taken off without direct damage to her vital organs. Matters became far more grave when the nerves were attacked with the heated nails. Her screams rose in pitch and volume; she was equally inspiring to see. Cordelli decides to embugger her in that appalling state; he makes the attempt, succeeds, and continues to drive home the nails all the while he sodomizes her. Excess of pain at length consumes everything still keeping her alive, and the miserable child expires upon receiving her assassin's fuck in her bowels.

An icy seriousness then characterizes his features and his bearing. He dresses himself, has his executioners don their clothes, and together with them and the duennas he departs into an adjoining room.

"Where is he going?" I asked Durand, with whom I found myself alone.

"I have no idea."

"And if he is scheming something? If it is to be our turn now?"

"It would be to get what we deserve."

"Durand, I am confounded. How can you have taken it upon yourself to come to this house without being better acquainted with its owner?"

"He is rich. The hope of getting his gold seduced me, it seduces me still. I am persuaded the rogue has his wealth cached somewhere hereabouts. Could we but put him out of the way, and rob him. . . . I have some powder with me, its action is swift. An instant and the thing would be done."

"Such a deed, my dear, sorts ill with our principles: to respect vice eternally, to smite virtue only. By destroying this man, we halt a criminal career and perhaps save the lives of thousands, of millions, of creatures: ought we to do it?"

"Juliette, 'tis true what you say."

Cordelli reappeared, followed by his escort.

"Ah, good sir, we were wondering where you have been," said Durand. "Off performing some secret infamy, I venture to guess."

"You are mistaken," the Italian replied, opening a door communicating the room where we were and the one into which he had penetrated by another entrance; "there," he continued, showing us an oratory adorned with all the attributes of established religion, "there is where I have been. When one is in such a woeful case as I, who surrenders to the temptations of dreadful passions, one must undertake at least a few good works to appease the inevitable wrath of the Lord."

"Right you are," said I, "allow us to imitate your excellent example. Durand, come with me, we are going to beg God's forgiveness for the crimes this man has induced us to commit."

And closing the door, we shut ourselves up inside the oratory.

"Damn me," I said to my friend, whom I had led thither only in order to discuss affairs with her in privacy, "damn me if there's not a change wrought in my ideas, and if that fool of a fanatic merits anything else than to die. Scruples were misplaced here: with his weak-watered soul, that bugger will not long persevere in vice; who can tell, these we have been witness to may perhaps be his last ventures into that domain. We are in a position to take the straight way with him, and at once."

"I foresee no difficulty in ridding ourselves of the entire pack," Durand observed. "It would be well, however, to preserve one of the old women, for we need a guide. Believe me, this tradesman has his treasure hidden somewhere under this roof; we shall find it, never you fear, and the find will be important."

"There are those servants who will be coming to fetch him this evening."

"They shall be given refreshments to drink."

We rejoined the others.

"Now here we are as blessed as you," we said, "but, for God's sake, give us some refreshment—we are dying of thirst."

Immediately, upon an order issued by Cordelli, the two crones serve a good meal to the master and his acolytes. At the third glass of wine, Durand skillfully seasons first Cordelli's plate, then his two executioners'; there was no way of envenoming the duennas, who were partaking of no food. In a trice the powder produced the expected effect, and our three villains toppled out of their chairs as though felled by Divine Vengeance. Durand sprang upon the more agile of the two elders. "Away," she cried, stabbing her to the heart, "go join your unworthy accomplices; had your master been an authentic rascal like ourselves, he would have been saved. But seeing that he believed in God, I had no choice but to send him to the Devil. As for you," Durand said to the other one, "if we let you live 'tis upon express condition you cooperate with us. We

shall start by throwing these bodies into the sea; and then, conducted by you, we shall search this castle from top to bottom. There
is treasure about, we are after it. Tell us first, are there any other
people here?"

"Now? No, Mesdames," the trembling crone replied, "I am
the only domestic left in the house."

"What do you mean by that? There are other masters?"

"I believe," said she, "that there may yet be some victims.
But promise you will spare me, I shall show you every part of the
house."

Before turning to anything else we disposed of the corpses.
While dragging them to the windows and pushing them out, we
asked the old servant whether Cordelli had been in the habit of
coming here frequently.

"Three times a week," she replied.

"And hideous massacres each time?"

"You were able to judge of his behavior. Come," she said
when we had completed our first chore, "I shall take you down to
the dungeons. There may still be some game in the larder."

'Twas there, one hundred feet and more underground, the
villain kept his provision of victims locked away. Each was in a
separate cell: of twelve cells we found nine occupied: five lodged
very attractive girls ranging between fifteen and eighteen years of
age; boys of between thirteen and sixteen were confined in the other
four; most of these victims had been debauched and ensnared in
different Italian cities; however, two of the girls, one of sixteen,
another of eighteen, were natives of Ragusa in Albania, and they
were exquisite creatures indeed.

In the midst of examining them, sounds reached us, faraway
but distinct; we hastened up to find out what was the matter. It was
the arrival of our servants and of Cordelli's, climbing the stairway
to the castle. We received the Italian's valets first, they were three
in number: we bade them enter the dining hall, still littered with the
remnants of our meal, we offered them wine to drink, and by means
of the swift-acting powder we soon reduced them to the rank of
their former master. Descending then to where our help was waiting, "Go back to town," we told them, "we intend to spend another

twenty-four hours here. Cordelli is retaining his servants, we need no others." And our carriage left; we returned to the captives.

As we were poring over them, "Durand," I said, "I am pleased to come by these two Albanians, they will fill the gap now that Elise and Raimonde are gone; and my reply to the signs of discontent I already notice in your expression, my reply, I say, is that I shall sacrifice them whenever you wish, just as readily and just as easily as I did their predecessors."

"Women. Must you forever be surrounding yourself with women?"

"I cannot do without them. But I need only one heart; 'tis yours alone I aspire to keep forever, my treasure."

"Flatterer, one must yield to all your little whims!"

Lila, that was the name of the sixteen-year-old, and Rosalba were therefore released at once, but placed none the less under lock and key in one of the castle's finest chambers. Those poor girls had been a week in their insalubrious dungeons, ill-fed, with only straw to lie upon, and 'twas plain to see, the experience had shaken them severely. Both were still in a state of frightened shock; but when I kissed them, caressed them, tears came to their eyes and they hugged me, showered me with kindnesses. They were sisters as it turned out, daughters of a rich trader in Ragusa with whom Cordelli had been in correspondence; he had persuaded their father to send them to Venice for their education, and the scoundrel invented a report of their death, thereby was he able to make them his.

"I am going to do the same," said Durand, "and take one of those girls."

"Do so, my dearest," said I, "that is not the sort of thing that can ever provoke my jealousy."

"Monster!" said Durand. "The more delicate of us two, I am loath to have anything distract me from the cherished idea of you."

"Cease, my love, cease to mistake carnal pleasures for moral distractions," said I. "I have already told you that my doctrines, while they may be different from yours, are unshakable withal; that I could fuck and frig myself with every inhabitant of this planet, and still not for an instant be weaned away from the tender sentiments I have sworn to preserve for you as long as I live."

We installed the three other girls and the four boys in the hall of tortures, and after having amused ourselves with them for half the day, we refined the horrors Cordelli had committed and caused those seven to perish under circumstances a thousand times more cruel. That accomplished, we slept for two hours and then resumed our searches.

"Precisely where he keeps his money I am unable to tell you," said the old woman, "nor indeed do I know for a certainty whether there is any here; but if there is, it should be in a cellar near the one where he stores his wine."

We went down. Two stout bronze doors barred access to those cellars; and we had no tool to force them. However, the more difficulties we encountered, the greater, needless to say, grew our determination to surmount them. After much hunting and prowling about we discovered a little window which gave into that cellar, and which was protected by only two iron bars. By common impulse we both sprang forward and peered through: inside, we made out six great chests: you may imagine how our zeal redoubled at the sight. At length we manage to loosen and pry out those bars. I scramble through the window, in a state of keenest excitement I lift the lid of the first of the chests. Alas, what is our disappointment to discover that those huge coffers contain nothing but instruments of torture or articles of women's clothing. Furious, I was ready to abandon the quest. But Durand was not yet willing to admit defeat. "There must be something else in here," she insisted; "let us look patiently."

I reach into the chest again; my fingers touch a ring of keys. One of them bears a tag: *Key to the Treasure Room.*

"Ah, Durand! No need to waste our time in this cellar, what we seek lies elsewhere, this tag proves it. First we find doors without keys, here now are keys but no doors. Dona Maria, is there anything you can say to help us? Only speak up and your fortune is made." •

"For the life of me, there is nothing I can tell you. Only that if we continue to search we may find something."

"Go fetch me a twig from the hazel tree I saw growing in the courtyard," Durand ordered.

When the old woman returns with it, my friend takes the

twig lightly between thumb and forefinger and gazes at it attentively. For a moment the little stick hangs motionless. Then its
free end rises, drawn to the left by some hidden suasion; Durand
walks down a long gallery at whose end we come to another door.
I try the keys; the door opens; the twig then gyrates rapidly between Durand's fingers. There were ten enormous chests in that
room and, indeed, they were not women's garments we found in
them, nor instruments of torture, but coins, coins of purest gold,
several million of them.

"Splendid," said I, full of courage and joy, "we have simply
to carry it away."

It was easier said than done. To call in the aid of the domestics
would be to beckon to trouble. Impossible to lift those chests, to
transport them out of the castle. They had therefore to be
emptied. Before the choice facing us, we preferred to carry off
less but to carry it off in greater safety. The old duenna, the two
girls, Durand, and I, we each filled a sack with as great a load of the
loot as we could bear, and from then on, for eight successive days,
proceeded to remove Cordelli's hoard. We gave it out that he was
spending the month at his country seat, that he had invited us to
come every day to be his guests; in the meantime we chartered a
vessel for Venice. On the ninth day we went aboard, after having,
while upon our last trip to the castle, cast the duenna into one of
the cisterns, burying our secret by drowning it with her.

During the voyage the weather was superb, the sea very calm,
the attentions of our women excessive, their flesh excellent: thus
rested and in high spirits we arrived at Venice.

Incontrovertibly, it is a magnificent and imposing sight, that
of a vast city floating upon the waters; as Grécourt somewhere says,
it seems as if sodomy has chosen Venice for its citadel and inviolable asylum, there to be able conveniently to extinguish, in the
circumambient sea, the pyres wherewith fanatism might undertake
to punish it; certain it is that unto sodomy this place provides
sectaries without number whose devotion to the cult is outdone by
the population of no other town in Italy.

In Venice the air has a languid, caressing quality, conducive to thoughts of pleasure, but often unwholesome, especially when the sea is at low tide; the wealthier citizens then go to spend as much time as they can upon the delightful estates they own on the mainland or on the neighboring islands. Despite this uninvigorating climate many are the venerable persons one sees among the inhabitants, and Venetian women age not so quickly as elsewhere.

As a rule, the Venetians are tall and comely, their physiognomy is cheerful, their manner spirited, and this far-famed nation deserves to be loved.

I devoted the first days after our arrival to investing my newly acquired assets; notwithstanding Durand's entreaties that I keep all of Cordelli's gold for myself, I insisted that we divide it equally. Our shares amounted to enough to earn each of us an annual return of roughly one million five hundred thousand *livres*; this, added to what I already had, brought my yearly revenues to around six million six hundred thousand pounds. But lest such a sizable fortune cause us to appear suspect in Venice, we took all the steps necessary to create the belief that our affluence was the product merely of our charms and of the effects of our magical arts upon the simple. We opened our doors, in consequence, to everybody of the one sex and the other who was seeking voluptuous entertainment or instruction. Accordingly, Durand had built a laboratory and a cabinet with special mechanical effects along the same lines as the one she had formerly had in Paris. It was fitted with disappearing floors, sliding panels, boudoirs, dungeons, and everything that can deceive the eyes and impress the imagination. We hired some elderly female servants, who were speedily trained in all these maneuvers; and our two young Albanians were under orders to lend themselves, with alacrity, complacency, and submissiveness, to whatever chores either of us might assign them. You will recall that they were virgins; that fact, coupled with everything we could reasonably expect from their charming faces and their youthfulness, enabled us to hope that those two little properties would produce rich yields once they had been brought under intensive cultivation. Moreover, I was to be at their side, and to resume all the old brothel exercises you saw me practicing years ago in Paris, when I first entered the career; the which, here in Venice, I was taking up

again out of sheer libertinage, for mine were not necessitous circumstances—I believe I have made that plain to you.

The first individual to present himself at our house was an
old *procuratore* of San Marco who, after a narrow inspection of
us all three, threw the handkerchief to me.

"Perhaps," was.his tactful opening, "my taste might incline
me toward the choice of one of your maids, but my pronounced
debility would prevent me from enjoying the delights she offered
me. I shall surely be more at ease with you, and I shall now explain
what our commerce will involve.

"You shall be so good," the nasty fellow said to me, "as to
apprise me of the date when your menstruation will be at fullest
spate: we shall meet upon that day. With you lying on a bed, your
legs wide-flung, I shall kneel before you, I shall sip the wine, I
shall fuddle myself upon those menses I adore: and when from
bibbing them I become very high, I shall conclude the sacrifice in
the same temple where I have been worshiping, while one of your
domestics—and the function cannot be entrusted to anyone save
one of your female servants—will have the kindness to thrash me
with all the force she can muster."

"Good my Venetian Lord," I replied, "does your Serenity
propose to repeat this lewd scene frequently, or is to be staged but
once?"

"Once," the Procurator replied; "beautiful as you are, my
angel, when a woman has satisfied this passion with me, I am incapable of renewing our acquaintance."

"Certainly, Excellency. Very well," I said, "including supper,
for a guest of your distinction never amuses himself in our house
without honoring us with his presence at supper, 'tis one of our
rules; including supper, then, and the whipper, that will cost you
five hundred sequins."

"You are expensive, Mademoiselle," said the Procurator, rising to his feet; "but you are pretty, and so long as you are young
you are right not to sell yourself for nothing. Upon what day am
I to come?"

"Tomorrow: that which you are fond of is beginning today,
the inundation will occur tomorrow."

"I shall be here without fail," the Procurator assured me.

And having, the next day, satisfied his foul passion, having had him drubbed with a bull's pizzle, I received his disgusting homage, by which I feigned to be deeply moved, nay, overwhelmed. For my pay, over and above the five hundred sequins, I got a diamond worth at least twice that sum, and whereof the old rascal made me a gift in appreciation of my good manners.

A very wealthy merchant named Raimondi was my next suitor.

"Dear heart," said he as he examined my behind, "is your ass intact?"

"Most assuredly, Signor."

"Young woman," he went on, spreading my buttocks, "you are telling me fibs; think not to impose upon a man who has my extensive knowledge and inveterate habit of asses."

"Ah, Signor, I shall conceal nothing from you . . . merely once or twice, not more, upon my honor. . . ."

And, without replying, Raimondi inserted his tongue into my asshole. He bade me stand up. He was all afire.

"Listen," said he, "I am going to explain my passion to you: you either take it or you leave it if it does not suit you. My whole pleasure consists in watching others fuck, that alone inspires me, without that wonderful spectacle I will not, I cannot accomplish anything. You will find me six handsome men who will one after the other encunt you before my eyes; I amuse myself with them while they fuck you, and when they discharge into your cunt, I carefully recuperate and meticulously swallow everything they have deposited in your vagina: your art consists in performing the impossible in order to expel that everything into my mouth. This operation completed, you offer me your behind: I sodomize you while your six men embugger me by turns. Once the sixth has discharged, I withdraw from your ass, I place myself upon a bed; you squat above me, and you shit into my mouth, while one of the men tongues your cunt, a second your mouth, a third masturbates in front of me, a fourth sucks my prick, and while I frig the fifth and the sixth with my two hands. Your mard tumbles into my mouth, and I eat it; that is quickly done. Then I get up from the bed; you take my prick into your mouth, you suck me exactly; all six men then come one by one and shit into mine: I swallow their shit, you swallow my fuck, there is the climax of the drama and its conclusion. But have a care, dear heart," added the Venetian. "Have a care, for this great undertaking I have outlined to you is fraught with perils, they are grave and in number they are three: firstly, there is the chance that, despite your best efforts, you fail to eject into my mouth the sperm you have received in your cunt; secondly, it means trouble for you if you do not swallow mine; thirdly, you will regret it if you are unable to shit. Now, it were well that you be advised that each of these delinquencies is punishable by a hundred strokes of the whip, to be meted out by one of my six men; thus by failing to expel the six discharges, by refusing to swallow my fuck, and by not shitting, you accumulate a total of eight hundred lashes; one hundred if you have committed only one fault; et cetera. Speak."

"Signor," was my answer to Raimondi, "your passion is not of the easiest execution, it entails great hazards. I should therefore fancy that, taking into account all the accessories I am to provide, two thousand sequins would not be an exorbitant figure."

"Your beauty is the deciding factor, I agree to the price," the merchant announced.

We took appointment, and two days later I satisfied him.

Not long afterward Durand summoned me for a nobleman whose mania was not quite so dangerous. My friend frigged him, in the meantime he licked my nostrils, the outside and the inside of my ears, my eyes, my clitoris, the interior of my cunt, my asshole, the intervals between my toes, and my armpits. After an hour devoted to that ceremony he ended by having me suck his member and by discharging in my mouth. Durand had given me a week's notice in order that I might have myself in a state of readiness, that is, of appropriate filthiness, for the quality of that libertine's crisis was strictly proportionate to the greater or lesser degree of un-cleanliness in which he found the various parts.

He told the whole town about us, and we were besieged by clients. There was one who brought two Negresses with him. Naked and flanked by those two women, I was to submit myself to frigging at their hands: the contrast of black and white shortly took effect upon him. Once aroused, he fell to flogging the

Negresses, and kept at it until the blood was flowing; I sucked him while he whipped; and then he whipped me. Then it was the Negresses' turn: knocked about by the iron-tipped martinets and the bull's pizzle they alternately used upon him, he finished by embuggering me while one of the black women sodomized him with a dildo and he molested the ass of the other. From that personage I stole a superb diamond while I was in the act of sucking his prick; and apart from the gem, that extraordinary party cost him one thousand sequins.

A more unusual one appeared. He had to be bound naked to a painter's ladder; two of our servants thrashed him mercilessly; Durand sucked him. Perched on the top of the ladder, I shat upon his uplifted face. When at length his prick had lifted too, we made him kneel, we acted as his judges, interrogated him, sentenced him to be broken. All the instruments were there; but the bar was of pasteboard. Durand attached him to the cross; I delivered the beating, he discharged under the blows, gave us five hundred sequins, and fled off in confusion, ashamed to show his face to those with whom he had just indulged in such a peculiar caprice.

Our girls were also brought out upon the stage. We sold Rosalba's maidenhead eighteen times over, her anal pucelage thirty times; twenty-two times that of Lila's cunt, thirty-six times that of her ass. And after having extracted six hundred thousand francs from the harvest of those four first fruits, we surrendered them to the secular arm.

The French Ambassador wrote to me one day, requesting me to come to his residence with a girl, as pretty a girl as I could find. I bring him a child of sixteen, as lovely as daylight, and who, snatched from the bosom of a family she was fated never to see again, had cost me a veritable fortune. His Excellency has the two of us undress in a small chamber situated in the uppermost story of his house; in the center of that room was a kind of deep hole, which one might have taken for a well. The Ambassador has us both lean over the edge, and gaze down into the shaft, that we might appreciate its depth; he observes our behinds, prominently displayed thanks to the posture we have adopted.

"Suppose I were to push you in, both of you," the lewd diplomat hazarded, "what would happen?"

"Why, nothing dreadful provided we fell upon thick mattresses."

"Ha! 'Twould be into Hell you would tumble, sluts; that opening is the mouth of Tartarus."

And as he pronounces these words, from the hole mount tongues of flame, meant to frighten us; we recoil.

"That pit, Excellency, is it then to be our grave?"

"No doubt about it, for I see your doom spelled out upon your asses." He was kissing them, pinching them, while speaking; and the behind of the young thing I had brought him was especially molested, he bit it and prodded it with a long needle. Nevertheless, there was as yet no sign of erection in his prick, even though, in consequence of his instructions, I had been stroking and shaking it as hard as I could. "Fuck!" I heard the libertine exclaim, and saw him wrap his arms around my companion's waist and lift her off the floor. "Fuck!" he repeated, "what a pleasure to throw this baggage into the flames."

The threat was swiftly followed by the act, and immediately I had contrived to put some consistency into his tool, the rake flung the girl into the hole.

"Frig!" he cried, "frig! frig! frig, bloody-fucking whore," he shrieked as some mechanism, released by the impact of the girl's falling body, sent flames shooting up from below.

Then, seizing a poniard as he feels his discharge impend, he himself leaps into the hole to stab the victim, whose screams notify me of her death. I did not see the Ambassador again; an old woman paid me, counseled me to hold my tongue, and we never again heard tell of that notable.

We were saying to each other, Durand and I, how odd it was that no women had been among our visitors, when Signora Zanetti, one of the wealthiest and most profligate ladies in Venice, communicated with us: she invited me to call upon her. That splendid creature, thirty-five years old, represented in the flesh the Roman noblewoman portrayed in classical sculpture. What a heavenly countenance! It was that of a living Venus, it was her figure, it was the complete assembly of all the goddess' graces.

"I caught a glimpse of you at Santa Maria della Salute the other day," that charming woman said to me. "Like myself, you were there doubtless in search of some object of lubricity; for I credit you with intelligence, and nobody with any ever goes to such places except with lewd intentions. 'Tis the custom here: the churches serve as our brothels. . . . Do you know, my angel, you are very pretty; are you fond of women?"

"How could one be indifferent to anything whereof you offer such an inspiring example?"

"Ah, there's the French gallantry; ten years in Paris gave me an understanding of that jargon. Please tell me frankly whether you like women, and whether you would enjoy frigging yourself with me?"

"Yes, by all the gods." And to lend weight to my words, I fling my arms around the neck of the beautiful Venetian and tongue her mouth for a quarter of an hour.

"You are enchanting, my angel," says she, fondling my breasts, "and I am going to pass some delightful moments with you."

We supped, and voluptuous frolic of the most piquant order crowned our lewd evening together. The most libertine of females, Zanetti had a prodigious grasp of the art of giving pleasure; few hands had ever frigged me with comparable skill or results. When we had each discharged five or six times, had exchanged lechings, suckings, dildo-fuckings, had, in sum, exhausted all the resources of the most far-reaching sapphism, "We may now fuck," my tribade said.

She rang.

"Have I any men out there?" she demanded of her chambermaid, an exquisite hussy of eighteen.

"Yes, my Lady," was the reply, "ten of them have been in attendance; thinking that perhaps Signora may not be needing them this evening, they have retired most regretfully, for they are in sparkling form."

"Have you been handling them, buggeress?" asked the lovely Venetian.

"Yes, my Lady, I have touched one or two, but there have been no discharges; Signora may verify this."

"Bring them in, rascal, I want to give my new friend a treat."

Rosetti promptly led in the ten young men, whose faces and figures I found much to my liking. The soubrette and her mistress furbish those weapons in the twinkling of an eye, and I find myself threatened by ten pikes, and it was all I could do to encircle the least of them with my two hands.

"Well then!" said Zanetti, naked, her hair floating free, her face flushed, "all this is yours to enjoy; where do you wish to have those pricks placed?"

"Fuck!" I exclaimed, awed by the prospect, "scatter them about, one here, one there, everywhere. . . ."

"No, my dear, the good things in life deserve to be desired," she said, "content yourself with taking them in the cunt during this first round, that will excite you, you will then have developed a yearning for the rest; and leave matters to us."

Rosetti has by now undressed herself; she and her mistress, rubbing briskly, maintain our athletes in shining condition; and my lovely friend introduces them one after the other into my cunt. Between introductions the slut stretches herself upon me, gives me her cunt to suck while she sucks my clitoris, while the two youths embugger her, and the soubrette fits the prick of a third into the ass of the one fucking me.

The pleasures I derived from this opening series of tuppings, ah, good friends, those pleasures exceeded anything you can imagine. Once all ten had given me a taste of their instruments, I rolled over and presented my buttocks; the embuggery was begun without the delaying of an instant; during it, my cunt was sucked by Zanetti, who was in a kneeling position and was heating a prick in either hand. My fucker was sodomized, and I was sucking Rosetti's cunt, she was electrifying the tips of two pricks by frigging them against her bush, in such a way that I was alternately able either to suck her cunt or pump the pricks she was masturbating. When all the pricks had taken a turn in my bowels, we consolidated the tableau so as to form a single compact society. I lie upon my back on top of a man who embuggers me; another encunts me; with my right hand I facilitate the introduction of a third prick into the ass of Zanetti, who, lying upon a fourth, was receiving a fifth prick in her cunt; with my left, I rendered the same service to Rosetti, also being fucked before and behind; an eighth man was sodomizing my sodomizer; a ninth was in Rosetti's mouth, the last in mine.

"There is still room for two more," Zanetti declared; "you observe that the pair sodomizing me and my chambermaid could perfectly well, without unbalancing the scene, each have a prick in the ass. Thus, a group of fifteen might easily be formed, and if it followed the lines of this one, it would be even more delightful."

But overcome, sotted with pleasure, I replied only by further heaving of my flanks; and delirium submerging the thirteen of us all at once, 'twas in a torrent of fuck we extinguished . . . or rather temporarily soothed our consuming lust.

The whole gamut of postures was repeated with Zanetti as their center and prime beneficiary, and now playing a subsidiary role, I had the revitalizing pleasure of watching that rascal's extraordinary antics. Sappho, Messalina, every precedent was dwarfed; 'twas a frenzy, a mindless, convulsive lasciviousness, a string of blasphemies so energetic, of sighs so impassioned, of moans so deep, and shrieks so shrill at the instant of crisis! Oh, I repeat, never had Venus a proselyte so apt, never was delirium so intense, never did whore disport with such abandon.

But she was not content with that; after having fucked, now we must drink, and we did so with the same immoderation: the chambermaid joined us at table, but the men were dismissed; and when the three of us were raving drunk, we fell to frigging one another anew, like sluts, until the morning sun peered in upon our saturnalia, at last obliged us to suspend them and in rest seek the strength necessary to begin afresh.

Several days later, that charming personage returned my visit. I had, she affirmed, made a prodigious impression upon her, she could not get the thought of me out of her head.

"Now that we are better acquainted, dear friend, I must confess my penchants to you," she said. "I reek vice, and as reports agree that you have a very philosophical understanding, I have come in the hopes you will set my conscience at ease."

"Speak, my love," I hastened to reply, "what are the sins you cherish the most? In which ones do you indulge with the greatest pleasure?"

"Theft. Nothing amuses me like stealing others' property; and although I have better than one hundred thousand *livres* a year, not a single day of my life goes by but I steal for enjoyment's sake."

"Console yourself, my darling," said I, taking my friend's hand in mine, "and in her whom you love behold one of that passion's greatest zealots. Like you, I cannot dispense with stealing, and as do you, I derive pleasure from it—pleasure! why, I too have made of thievery one of my most precious pastimes. Stealing, my dear, is a natural institution; not only is it not an evil, but, manifestly, it must be classified as good.

"Let me add, dearest friend," I went on, embracing Zanetti with fervor, "that I am gladdened to perceive that your principles are untainted by any residue of moral scruple."

"Upon all those questions nobody could be firmer than I," the amiable Venetian declared. "Led by my mind into imagining a thousand infamies, there is nothing I deny myself when my passions speak."

"Goodness!" said I, "are you capable even of murder?"

"Even of parricide; even of the most frightful crime possible, if 'twere possible to say that for us humans crime does rightly exist."

"Ah, by God," I said to my friend, "kiss her and kiss her a thousand times over, the woman who resembles you so perfectly, and deem me worthy of you."

"Since you are so open with me," said Zanetti, "I shall not be less so with you; listen, and shudder not at what I have to confide. And swear to me you shall never divulge to anyone the things you are about to hear."

I vowed silence; and then my friend began to speak.

"You know, Juliette, that I am a widow, and therefore accountable to no one for the way in which I choose to conduct my life. Refrain from asking me how I won my freedom . . . and, rather than forcing me to a confession, guess that it is the reward of crime."

"Was it committed by your own hand?"

"No. That miserable foe of my pleasures fell to an assassin; in Venice it is easy, with a few sequins, to sever any tie."

"It might have been better to have done the thing yourself. In any case, that would have established between us one more point in common."

"Dear soul! How I adore you! And what a praiseworthy thing one does when one liberates oneself from those rogues when they contrive to become troublesome; by what right do they presume to curb our freedom? Let them grant us divorce and husband-murder will be a little less rampant.

"At any rate, you must know that in Venice there exists a notorious association of villains devoted uniquely to robbing, to swindling, to blackmailing and, when the need arises, to killing anybody who resists them. This association's members and correspondents are many, its influence extends for thirty or forty miles round about; and its headquarters are at the house of a certain Moberti, director of the organization.

"Now, this Moberti is my lover; I am mad about him: no one has such sentiments for a man as I have for him. And yet, my dove, when you see him you shall perhaps wonder at my passion for him; however, so soon as you come to know him your surprise will evaporate, and you will realize that it is possible to love a man for his tastes, his passions, his temper and cast of mind rather than for the physical amenities of his person.

"Moberti is fifty-four; he is as red-haired as Judas; his eyes are rheumy and small, set near together; his mouth is wide and ill-furnished with teeth; his nose and lips negroid; he is short, squat, misshapen, but endowed, in spite of all that, with an instrument so prodigious that, notwithstanding my extreme habit of sodomy, he scorches me, he fairly splits me every time he embuggers me . . . and he never takes his pleasure with me otherwise than in that manner. That, dear Juliette, is the description of the man I worship, although I put horns of cuckoldry on his head a hundred times every day; but to my truancies he raises no objection; he realizes I cannot forego them; and if, on my side, I tolerate unfaithfulness in him, even providing him with the game he is fondest of, he on his side allows me to fuck with whom and as often as I wish. No jealousy on either side: it is almost what one might call a spiritual union.

"Moberti has the kind of mind I admire; his is a disorder of the imagination so original, a ferocity so rarefied, an abandon of principle so prodigious, an atheism so profound, a corruption so complete, that all these qualities put my brain in a ferment, and upon their account I adore that man: the like of it is not to be found in any of the descriptions of love penned by your poets and your historians down to this day.

"As you must imagine, Moberti has several agents in Venice, whom he places amidst the very rich, and who, in constant contact with the members of this caste, are in a position to provide him with intelligence. I am the foremost of those agents, I gather and sift information supplied by the others, and it is through me the principal thefts are planned. Our affair began but three years ago, I have been serving him for only that long, but I can assert that in this short space I have brought him into more than ten millions and I have had him assassinate at least four hundred people; and that is what swells my head. I discharge for three days and three nights running, my dear, each time I commit or am instrumental to the committing of crimes of this sort. He himself loves murder to the point where, like that famous Siberian robber, he will, during an expedition, appoint his comrades to carry off the loot in order to have his own hands free to cut the victims' throats. He is, I insist, the cruelest and the most barbarous scoundrel alive today; and it is the wonderful concordance of his vices with those of my character that makes for my devotion to him.

"As if to prove that the criminal destiny is always far happier than the virtuous, provided it be incorrigible and bold, fate has been kind to my lover, who for twenty-five years has been leading a uniformly wicked existence; until now he has not even come under suspicion. Several of his lieutenants have been wheeled, hanged, burned at the stake, but none of them has ever compromised him. This man, rare through courage, rare through perversity, looks forward to another twelve or fifteen active years before we retire, he and I, in Dalmatia, where he has lately bought some superb estates. 'Tis thus we intend to crown our lives, as evil as any that have left their blot in human annals.

"That, my dear, is what I had to tell you; decide whether you would like to throw in your lot with us. If you accept, I shall shortly issue you an invitation to join my lover and me at dinner;

you will see him take his pleasure with me; with you too, if you desire; and we shall then all three confer upon arrangements for an intimate relationship."

"Be sure of it," I answered, "you could make me no more agreeable proposal. I accept—accept everything—but upon two conditions: the first being, that if your lover cares to amuse himself with me, he shall pay my price, and I would add that, likewise, I shall only collaborate in his thefts provided I be given a substantial share of the proceeds. The second condition is that from this moment forward we share all expenses incurred in connection with our libertine exercises: it is your friend I wish to be, and not your whore anymore."

That conversation was followed by a delicious supper, and we took leave of each other with promises to meet again before long.

Not knowing how this friendship might develop, I thought best, until such time as matters became clearer, to say nothing about it to my companion. Besides, our relations, though close, allowed both of us a margin of freedom broad enough to enable us each to do whatever each wished independently of the other.

A few days later Signora Zanetti advised me that she had been in touch with her friend; that the latter was exceedingly eager to become acquainted with me; and that she therefore hoped for my company at dinner the next day. They would be expecting me at a charming house Moberti possessed on the island of San Giorgio, a few minutes by boat from the city.

What I had been told touching that extraordinary man's looks proved accurate: it would be impossible to be uglier than he, and difficult, at the same time, to have a more alert and crafty face.

"Here she is," said Zanetti, embracing him, "the pretty girl I told you about; I trust you will find her satisfactory in every respect."

The brigand then took me by the hand and, without a word, led me into an adjoining chamber, already occupied, I was rather surprised to discover, by two boys, fifteen years of age and of extreme beauty.

"Do not allow yourself to be scandalized," said the lewd little man, "I am a bugger. Notwithstanding, I shall fuck you; in the ass, be it understood. Show that part to me, but have the kind consideration to keep your cunt well out of my sight: enable me to suppose that you are completely devoid of one."

This opening struck me as rude. What it was that was attractive about this person I cannot say; but from the very first I sensed that such a man was someone to be loved automatically. Moberti was long peering at my behind, no detail escaped his attention; then, giving two forceful slaps to each of my buttocks, "Good," he pronounced, "it will do, you may take off your clothes."

"And your friend, Signor?"

"She will come; well she knows that nothing will be begun without her."

And while I was undressing, Moberti caressed the two adolescents.

The beautiful Venetian appeared.

"You have provided for everything?" her lover inquired. "We are in no danger of being disturbed? All the doors are locked? The dinner will be good?"

"Rely upon me. You know that I never neglect anything."

"Then let us fuck in peace," Moberti rejoined, "and surrender to the curious caprices imagination engenders."

"Nothing stands in your way, my friend; you are screened from every gaze save that of God."

"Peugh, I worry very little about that witness," the roué declared, "I am only sorry that no God really exists, sorry, that is, to be deprived of the pleasure of insulting him more positively. But can we speak in this young woman's presence? Is she of our breed?"

"Indeed she is, you remember what I told you about her. She merely waits to be assigned to her task, and I dare predict her performance will please you."

"I am already pleased with her ass—as pleased, that is to say, as one can be with a female ass. Come, my dear, ready all the implements."

Promptly unbuttoning the two boys' breeches, Zanetti exposed their behinds to the libertine, who, reclining upon a broad sofa, frigged himself while examining them.

"Hurry," my friend whispered to me, "I am sure that he is burning to see your ass next to those other ones."

My bush well camouflaged, I quickly take my place beside the boys, and Moberti subjects the three of us to a moment of impartial scrutiny. However, he kisses mine with an unmistakable ardor, tongues it deeply; he then orders one of his bardashes to get between my legs and pluck out some of my pubic hair, so that I am soon jerking and twitching about, and he goes on thrusting his tongue into my anus, and his mistress frigs him while she is herself frigged by the other bardash.

"Now heed me well," the brigand finally says, "and, above all, contrive to carry out my instructions to the letter. You are to loose a fart into my mouth at the very instant the boy pulls out one of your hairs, and when he pulls out the sixth, just as you fart, you are also to piss upon his face, and to cover him with invectives also."

I have the good fortune to succeed in complying with this unusual prescription, and with all the punctuality the libertine requests; and when I get to the inundation and when he hears it being accompanied by hard words addressed to the object of his lust, he snatches up a bundle of switches and thrashes me for a whole quarter of an hour.

"What are you doing? What in the world are you doing?" Zanetti cries, pursuant to the role she is playing on the edge of this scene. "What wrong has this creature done to you?"

"She farted, the nasty thing; more, she pissed her wretched urine all over my Ganymede, and sullied his delicious features; that's what she did, and for such outrages no punishments can be severe enough."

"Well then, rascal," Zanetti replies, learned in the fine science of ensuring her lover's pleasure, "I am going to whip you until you stop treating my friend in this way."

Thereupon a sound thrashing is administered to him, and after fifteen minutes of this the Italian exhibits a member that has filled out to a foot in length and a circumference of eight inches.

"Have you ever beheld another of this size?" he asks, bringing it near.

"Heaven!" I exclaim, "I am doomed if ever you perforate me with such a device!"

"Yet that is what is about to happen to you," says he, next ordering his mistress to undress also; "you will not be more discomforted than these children, they have virginal parts, you do not."

"But whatever befalls them, I have no wish to die."

At this point our colloquy is interrupted as Zanetti, naked, presents her hindquarters to him for kissing; and while one of the boys pulls a hair from her cunt, she fires a perfectly enormous fart point-blank at her lover's nose, who swears, storms, hurls himself upon her, and embuggers her straightway. He has distributed the little boys and myself so cunningly that during this operation our three asses, clustered about his goddess' flanks, are all near enough to his face for his indiscriminate kissing.

I was amazed, I confess, at the manner in which Zanetti stood up to that gigantic member's incursion into her fundament; the slut never flinched; roaring oaths, the Italian was lunging backward and forward and snapping his teeth at our buttocks the whole time. He withdraws, the group dissolves, and he considers us, cruel lust glittering in his eyes; he lies down upon the sofa, his face buried between his mistress' buttocks, whose anus he suckles, and from there he orders us to come one by one and frig him briefly, taking good care to kiss his device, to lick his testicles, and to insert three fingers into his ass.

So extreme is the effect upon his member of this byplay that I am convinced he must be at the point of discharging; but no, his self-possession unimpaired, he contains himself, rises, calls for switches, and belabors the four of us with might and main: we each receive two hundred cuts at least. This operation over with, he seizes me, and in his glance I read trouble.

"Buggeress," he announces, "I am of a mind to kill you."

Accustomed as I was to all such scenes, fear nevertheless took hold of me, and it was not lessened by what I seemed to detect in Zanetti's stare.

"Yes, damn your thrice-fucked heart," the Italian continued, "yes, foul slut that you are, my urge is to kill you."

And as he spoke he squeezed my throat as if he were going to throttle me; next, he catches up a dagger, poises it over my breast while he is frigged by his mistress who pays no attention to me, who makes no gesture to reassure me. After keeping me several minutes in dreadful suspense, he bends me over the sofa, presents his prick at the entrance of my ass and drives it, without warning or preamble, so forcefully in that cold sweat bathes my face and I am on the verge of swooning. In the meantime, my friend was holding me fast, forestalling all the movements I might otherwise have made, so that I was ploughed, harrowed, cloven by that monstrous machine without being able to put up the slightest defense. While this went forward, Moberti was, with each hand, fondling the hinder parts of a bardash and kissing Zanetti upon the mouth.

A few moments of this and he ordered me, who had been resting my hands on the edge of the sofa, to place them on the floor instead, and to raise my rump as high as I could, and to arch my neck, bending my head as far back as possible; one of the little boys, straddling my neck, stood facing him, and Moberti tongued his mouth for a time; then the other bardash replaced the first, and his mouth was tongued in its turn; and Zanetti, striking a different attitude, came up to place her asshole where her lover had found nought but mouths an instant before. Discharge he did not, and withdrawing his prick suddenly and without precaution, he occasioned me almost as much pain by this precipitate retreat as when he had fought his way into the premises.

"Her ass is good," he remarked when he had emerged from it, "it grips and it is hot; but she wiggles while being embuggered, and you know, Zanetti, I cannot tolerate unsteadiness, it's either absolute stillness or I don't discharge."

His mistress then flogs him a little with the switches; I was lying down upon the floor, the two acolytes were frigging his member against my behind.

Next, I am told to get up and stretch out flat upon the sofa; he has the children climb upon my body and range their asses side by side and adjacent to mine; he approaches his prick to a juvenile vent; advances; meets with stoutest resistance.

"Then tie the little bastards!" shouts the rake.

And I complying with Zanetti's request for aid, we bind and garrote the youngster, having rolled him into a ball, so that his head, thrust down between his legs, provides Moberti with a mouth to fuck as well as an ass; and to ensure that he will not budge out of position, Zanetti squats upon the child. Moberti comes up to the gate again, all possibilities of disturbance having now been removed. Three determined heaves and the colossal prick disappears into the anus of the puny little fellow; I frig the libertine's ass in the meantime, and he handles the other bardash.

During that voluptuous act the villain said dreadful things. He raved uninterruptedly about crimes, about abominations, about murders, about wanton destructions, about massacres. And for all that he still did not discharge. The second bardash was immediately trussed in the same position; Moberti enjoyed him in the same fashion, but, this time, he had hung the first, the boy already fucked, upside down and alongside his mistress, who, as hitherto, was squatting upon the bardash being embuggered; thanks to which arrangement, he had an ass, a cunt, and a mouth within reach of his lips. I was flogging him. His utterances became more horrible still, and the next instant I saw blood flowing in rivulets upon the floor: the cruel one, upon unleashing his seed, had stabbed a stiletto twenty times into both the boy he was sodomizing and the other dangling before him.

"Villain!" I exclaimed, redoubling the blows I was bestowing upon his behind, "that is a signal piece of treachery you have just performed, and you may flatter yourself that you are a monster."

His discharge had been awesome, more like a volcanic eruption than anything else; his comportment was that of a wild animal rather than a human being.

Calm once re-established, the two corpses were dropped into a hole already dug in the little garden attached to the chamber where this scene had just transpired; the three survivors then dressed and readjusted themselves. Moberti fell asleep before it was time for dinner.

"Yes, he is indeed an unusual man," I complimented his mistress.

"You have not seen anything yet," Zanetti replied; "his behavior has been mild today, it is sometimes considerably worse."

Two other victims were there: he would come to grips with them after the midday meal.

"And as they are girls, I can assure you that he will cause them ten times more suffering."

"Am I to take it that he finds our sex the more moving?"

"Of course. With people who are cruel in their pleasures it's always the same story: the weakness, the frailty, the delicacy of a woman irritates them far more powerfully, their ferocity has far greater effect when pitted against helplessness than against strength; the more defenseless the object, the more violently they attack it, and as this introduces a greater portion of villainy into the deed, the enjoyment it affords is increased commensurately. Did he really hurt you?"

"He nigh maimed me. I have confronted grandiose pricks in my day; never did one cause me so much pain."

Moberti awoke very shortly; scarcely had he opened his eyes when he called for food; dinner was served. We were in a cool, secluded room; everything required for the service lay ready and accessible, dispensing us from any need of domestics. It was while we were at table the brigand specified the tasks he meant to entrust to me within the framework of his criminal organization: I was to act as a cover for his thefts; I was to seek out victims for him; taking leave of Durand, I was to install myself in a house, alone, to which I would lure dupes whom he aimed to rob and kill. I immediately saw that were I to enter into this association, infinitely more danger than profit would accrue to me; and able, in my position, to disdain such mediocre earnings, I inwardly rejected this man's proposals. But I was only too careful to conceal my true thoughts, and in order that nothing upset his illusion, I applauded his scheme warmly and promised to lend myself to it. Thus did we conclude the most magnificent repast I had enjoyed in a long time; when we stood up from table, Moberti drew me into a small chamber.

"Juliette," he said to me once he had closed the door and we were alone, "you have observed my tastes from sufficiently near on to have realized that I situate my major delights in murder. Can I be sure of the zeal with which you are going to undertake to multiply my victims? Have I no weakness, no remorse, to fear in you?"

"Try me, my dear, there is no other way for you to allay your doubts," I replied; "my conduct will tell you whether it is through enthusiasm or through a more passive complacency that I am aiding you to attain your ends."

And at this point the most perfidious idea arose in my wicked imagination. I had no wish to become that man's mistress, none to accept his offers of partnership, and yet, simply on evil principle, I feigned jealousy.

"Only upon one score do I have any reservations," I declared. "To play second fiddle in your schemes is not much to my liking. Trust, affection, those treasures so worth possessing when they are bestowed by a person one loves, will any of that be mine? I have agreed to everything you proposed, true; but I should much prefer to be the only one to exercise this employment, and not to have, perpetually before my eyes, a rival as dangerous as your Zanetti. . . ."

And the knave listened to me with equal amounts of surprise and interest.

After a moment of silence he asked me a question: "You would actually be in love with me?"

"Ah, I would be crazy about a man whose tastes are in every point identical to mine."

"Excellent; not another word, everything will be arranged. You are infinitely more beautiful than Zanetti, I prefer you, and you are going to enjoy undisputed sway over my heart."

"But she will be in despair when she discovers this! As well, shall I not be making the very worst enemy for myself? Do you think she will ever be able to forgive me for having seduced you?"

"Oh, were she to bother us seriously—"

"My God, what an idea! I tremble . . . a woman I am devoted to, a woman whom you once loved . . . have you given sufficient thought to this crowning act of horror?"

"Horror? No such thing exists, all our acts are simply what they are, all are inspired by Nature: those are elementary precepts, and I wonder that you are still at the stage of doubting them."

"Ah, my scruples are certain to give way ere long before the charms of having you all to myself. . . . But I tell you now that so long as that creature breathes I shall be uneasy: on the one hand, I shall live in fear of her, and on the other I shall dread losing you. It seems to me that while we are on the subject it would be best to settle it right away. That woman is mischievous; if you but knew all the things she told me about you. . . . Ah, believe me, if we do not take the necessary preventive measures she will never allow us one instant of peace."

"I adore you, heavenly girl," said the Italian, folding me in his arms, "your rival's fate is decided, you triumph, nothing now remains but to consult together upon the manner in which she is to die."

And, just as aroused by this idea as I, Moberti catches hold of my ass and flings into it without the slightest preliminary; that gigantean prick might have wrung shrieks from me upon some other occasion, but, in a fiery mood myself, instead of wilting before the dart I lunged at it, and discharged the moment Moberti's balls danced against my buttocks.

"What shall we do to her?" the rake demanded while he fucked away. "It must be as we are in the midst of pleasures that we decree her sufferings."

We did so; and the scene that is about to be described to you was the result of our deliberations. We went back into the other room.

Moberti, eager to be at the peak of his strength, had taken care not to squander any of it in my entrails. Zanetti had been worried by our lengthy absence, and upon our return her eyes plainly announced that the demon of jealousy had begun to torment her heart. She suggested that we all remove into the room where the morning's orgies had been celebrated; and there she presented to her lover the new objects intended for the pleasures which were to close the afternoon. Awaiting us were a twenty-six-year-old mother, seven months pregnant, and two charming little girls, one of eleven, the other of nine, whom she held by the hand. Moberti, already familiar with the merchandise, having himself negotiated for it, was thrilled to have it in his clutches at last.

"This," he whispered to me gleefully, "is going to bring me an atrocious erection. That woman has been induced into error: she fancies I am going to render her some great services, but the tortures I have in store for her are hideous. Well, Zanetti, let us have the doors locked once again, let silence reign, let there be no noise in this house whatever, save that which I am about to make. I would like to have the entire earth stand still when I lift my prick."

Moberti sits down, he bids his mistress undress Angelica while Mirza, the elder of the girls, and little Marietta are told to wait in respectful silence until the brigand issues his instructions to them.

Zanetti, scrupulously veiling all of Angelica's anterior parts, fetches the woman's rump up to Moberti who, after handling it rudely, declares that before the hour is out there shall be changes wrought in the shape of this handsome ass. He pokes and prods the replete belly, pinches it lustily, and predicts trouble for it as well.

"Ah, Signor!" says the interesting Angelica, "you have cruelly deceived me; it is now but too plain what horrors lie ahead for me; at least respect the child I bear in my womb. . . ."

'Tis with gales of laughter the villain greets this speech.

"Double-dyed whore," he cries, raining blows upon the unlucky soul, "oh, indeed, indeed! rest assured, I hold your state in the very highest consideration; nothing, in my view, is more entitled to respect than a gravid female, and you must already sense the extent to which I am touched by your fascinating condition. Begin, nevertheless, by undressing your elder daughter for me, and bring her over here in the same way Zanetti has just presented you for my inspection."

All this time kneeling between the libertine's legs, I was polluting him gently to keep his fire lighted, and he bestowed frequent kisses upon my lips. Nothing so pretty as the little girl who is led up to him, and nothing so cruel as the species of lewd caresses wherewith he overwhelms the tender thing. The younger child advances; she is dealt similar treatment.

"Damn my eyes!" the exalted villain protests. "What a furious shame I haven't the means to embugger the three of them at the same stroke."

So saying, he takes the mother firmly in hand, lays her upon her back, lifts her legs straight in the air and with cords secures them thus, then bum-fucks her. Following his request, I leap upon Angelica and assume a position which places my ass within reach of the libertine's kisses; and upon my flanks his mistress establishes herself, presenting a second set of hindquarters to the insatiable one's caresses; with each of his hands he has at a child, whose buttocks he worries with tongs. Not content to molest those two little behinds, he begins to pluck at the mother's with the same instruments; as for ours, he confines himself to gnawing them while we expel farts into his mouth.

"Press down with your knees upon this worthless rascal, Juliette," said he, "see whether you cannot, through your combined weight, crush the nasty fruit stinking in her entrails."

Zanetti and I bestir ourselves, and there and then come near to squeezing the life out of poor Angelica. After fifteen minutes of reaming the anus of the sorely beset woman, who uttered piercing screams throughout this abominable torture, Moberti disembuggered and called for the elder of the two girls, Mirza. Zanetti opened up the way, and I presented the instrument, grown more terrible still from its incursions into the mother's ass. At the price of much struggling we finally succeeded, the Venetian and I, in inserting that enormous mass into the narrow orifice offered to its furies. As soon as Moberti notices that some progress has been made, he bolts forward with such vigor that he soon sheathes his weapon to the hilt; but the unhappy patient faints.

"That is what I was after," our ferocious personage explains, "I never begin to enjoy myself until my vexations have reduced them to insensibility. Ha, Zanetti! Do you hear what I am saying?" Then, to me, under his breath: "When I send her to hell, I want her to arrive there blackened by a crime of the very first magnitude."

Directed by the Venetian, Angelica clambers upon the back of her unconscious daughter, so that both their behinds are facing the rake; my buttocks are exposed to the right, those of the younger daughter to the left, and my friend kneels before her lover's ass; but will you ever guess with what episode the libertine now regaled his lubricity? Biting his buttocks fiercely, his mistress had to imitate the growlings of a bulldog, while he, simulating the same animal, worried Angelica's ass. I never saw anything so droll as this concert of canines; I must say, however, that it was far less amusing for Angelica, whose buttocks, torn by the cruel brigand, were soon hanging in tatters down her thighs. He also gave a little attention, now and then, to mine and to the little girl's, but that was only to sharpen his teeth, which, with renewed fury, he would redirect against Angelica's posterior flesh, soon reduced to such a state of ruination that, like her daughter, she collapsed. Moberti changes asses; the other sister is stoutly attacked, and 'tis now upon the buttocks of the one latterly fucked that he directs his fangs.

In the meantime, Signora Zanetti is executing the orders she receives. While her lover is fucking, she, to promote his ecstasy, stabs the child he is gazing at, and the little creature falls dead, swimming in a pool of blood.

"Scoundrel," exclaims the Italian, "see what a frightful deed you have just committed; may the Eternal, by whose grace you shall live yet a while, grant you time to repent what you have done, for hell would be your share were you to die laden with such a crime. . . . Leave the corpse where it is, I shall be wanting it in a while."

These accumulated horrors have had their effect upon him, he withdraws now, having exhaled whole floods of sperm; this operation over with, he leaves Zanetti to keep the unhappy family company and retires with me into the room where we had held our consultation a short time before.

"I am going to perpetrate atrocities," Moberti declares, kissing me feelingly upon the mouth and brightening his member against my behind, "and your rival shall be enveloped in them. Would that I were able to devise something worse than what we have decided her fate is to be, would that there were some more terrible torture than the one she is to undergo; but limits there must be, and I grieve. None the less—ah, Juliette, I restiffen!— observe this treacherous idea's influence upon my senses. What a superb ass," he continues, fondling my buttocks, "I adore you, Juliette, you are full of imagination, in crime you possess inventiveness, in performing it facility, and if I am immolating Zanetti 'tis because I want you with me forever."

"But, kind friend," I interject, "do you not forget that this woman idolizes you? I yielded to your perfidious desires in a moment of weakness; I reproach myself for it. Thus to treat a woman who is so attached to us—"

"What the whore's sentiments happen to be is to me of no

importance; it's my passions that are sacred, my erection that counts. Ha, the slut! She suspects nothing, this is the occasion to turn upon her. I foresee a delightful evening.

"Here," he went on, "clad me in this tiger's skin. They shall be all three of them naked next door, grouped around the corpse: I shall attack them indiscriminately, I shall eat them alive; and my feelings for Signora Zanetti, you shall soon see what they are when I have my teeth in her and her mortal woes have begun. Do not fail to exhort me to extreme rigor during the scene. After that we shall terminate in the way we have planned; and if in the meantime anything more revolting occurs to you, you will include it among our resolutions; for, as now they stand, they are far from measuring up to my desires."

I entered and gave instructions to Zanetti. She was startled to be told to join the ranks of the others. Accustomed to commanding, she found subordination strange, and, not a little bewildered, she could not prevent herself from questioning me.

"What is he going to do?"

"You shall see," was my chilly reply. And I went back to Moberti.

I found him masturbating, inspired by the execrations in the offing; catching sight of me, he heads toward my ass, submerges it beneath caresses: bending me forward, the mischievous fellow slides his stave into me, swearing that in all the world there is nothing that affords such pleasure as my behind. He sawed away for quite some time, during which we exchanged thoughts upon the forthcoming tortures, improved upon them, conceived horrors at which even the most savage animals would have shuddered.

"That should do," said the rake, withdrawing, "I feel sufficiently aroused." And, dressed in his tiger's skin, its four paws armed with monstrous talons, and its muzzle so arranged as to permit the wearer to bite anything within reach; thus disguised, I say, and with me following in his train, naked, and wielding a huge cudgel for use in the event he showed signs of laggardliness, we made our entrance.

Zanetti is the first upon whom he leaps, with a blow of his claws he carries one of her breasts away, and sinks his teeth so deep into a buttock that blood gushes forth at once.

"My God!" cries that unfortunate, "I am lost, Juliette, and 'tis you who have undone me! Ah, I ought to have known—what lies in store for me now? This monster, whom I loved so dearly, what horrors has he prepared for me?"

And each of her lamentations was answered by fearful abuse. Moberti, however, gave his victim a minute's breathing space while he assailed the other objects surrounding her. Angelica and her daughter attempt to flee; but what escape is there from this fury? The libertine contemplates them; but there is another target he wishes to have at first: the corpse preoccupies him, he fastens upon it, his carnivorous fang ravens for a moment upon the poor creature's inert remains, which he then abandons to pursue the two living objects cowering in a corner. He overtakes them both, martyrizes them with the same unabated fury; and it is precisely upon their fleshier parts the villain is happiest to batten. His prick is at an extraordinary stand. I am obliged to chase after him, sometimes thwacking him with all my strength, sometimes to frig him from underneath or to suck his behind: an operation I accomplish by raising the tail of the tiger's skin.

His cruelties move gradually in the direction of refinement. He traps his mistress and signals to me as he leaps upon her; I aid him; we tie the wretch hand and foot, secure her to a wooden bench. He crouches upon her and with his sharp claws scratches out her eyes, tears off her nose, her cheeks: and he was kissing her, the brute, while she screamed; and I was frigging him as hard as I could.

"But for me," I was saying to myself, "but for my treacheries, my perfidies, my counsels, he would never have undertaken this horror: I am its sole cause." That delicious thought cost me a spasm; and he, pursuing his abominations, continued to kiss the doomed woman's lips so as, said he, to lose not one of the precious gasps of the agony racking a mistress he had cherished! He turns her over, lacerates her behind, and has me pour molten wax into the wounds; at last, gone quite berserk, he pushes me aside and, while I frig him, the monster tears, assassinates, rips to shreds the woebegone object of his erstwhile passion, whom he finally leaves lifeless upon the floor.

Drunk from rage and lust, he turns upon the other two

victims. With his claws alone he snatches the child out of the
mother's womb, smashes it against that poor woman's head, hurls
himself upon the surviving girl, chokes, rends, massacres them
both. Thereupon he speeds like an arrow into my ass, 'tis there the
maniac, along with his fuck, rids himself of the murdering fever
which has reduced him to the level of Nature's most dangerous
animals. . . .

And we speed back to Venice, promising to meet again at
the earliest opportunity in order to settle the final details of the
association into which, from the first, I had no desire whatever to
enter.

I spent a sleepless night. Ah, ye gods! how I tossed and turned
in my women's arms as they frigged me and as I dwelt upon the
crimes wherewith I had just soiled myself. It was then I realized
that among the pleasures life offers us, none is so violent as that
of murder; and that once this passion has stolen its way into the
heart, there is no possible dislodging it. Nothing, no, nothing bears
comparison with the thirst for blood. Only taste it, and thenceforth,
insatiable, you exist solely through the destruction of victims.

However, not for all the world would I have fallen in with
that man's proposals: in them, as I have already told you, I saw
risks infinitely outweighing profits; firmly resolved to refuse, I
related everything to Durand, who assured me that my decision
was wisely taken, since Moberti would undoubtedly cease to treat
me as his mistress before three months were out. When he called
I had the door shut in his face, and I never saw him again.

Durand one day besought me to come to her apartments, she
had a woman there who ardently desired me; for the attraction I
exerted, outrageously if you like, but naturally withal, was stronger
upon women than upon men. Signora Zatta, wife of a magistrate,
perhaps fifty years of age, was yet in possession of her beauty and
endowed as well with a furious fondness for women. No sooner
does she clap eyes upon me than the tribade sets to cajoling me as
would a man, and her solicitations become such that she deprives
me, as it were, of all means to resist her.

We sup together, and when dessert arrives, the Messalina,
half-drunk, flings herself upon me and takes off my clothes. Zatta
was one of those idiosyncratic women who, full of clever and

original ideas, are drawn to their own sex not so much out of taste as through libertinage, and whose behavior with it proceeds less from the quest for real pleasures than from a wish to indulge lascivious caprices. This creature had nothing but masculine tendencies: I discharged six times beneath her cunning fingers, or rather 'twas but a single ejaculation which lasted for two long hours. Once returned to my senses, I thought to criticize her preliminary tactics, which I held bizarre; but I found her as apt in their defense as she was adroit in performing them. She proved to me that the aberration she delighted in was for her more enjoyable than any other; she added that she carried her manias to their logical conclusion, and that she never discharged more agreeably than when surrendering to them.

She desired other girls; seven responded to the call; after having frigged herself with all of them, from her pocket she produced a dildo the likes of which I had never before set eyes upon. That singular instrument had four stems. Signora Zatta began by burying one of them in her ass and sodomizing me with a second. We were back to back: the two remaining stems were curved upward in a half-circle: these we buried in our cunts. In this position, we each had a girl between our legs, who sucked our clitoris and who maneuvered the machine with artistry. Employment had to be found for the five others. Two were hence assigned to flog those who were sucking us; two more, perched upon chairs, gave us their cunts to drink from; and the last supervised all the others, moving about the ranks and seeing to it that everything was accomplished in strict accordance with prescription. Zatta and I fought together against the pack, and after having exhausted all our seven women, having had our buttocks lashed raw, she proclaimed her intention of avenging herself upon our whippers. We flogged them unmercifully; they complained, they screamed, 'twas in vain, we were inflexible, and no quarter was granted until floods of fuck had appeased our fury. The indefatigable rascal, aroused rather than calmed by this series of lewd episodes, insisted that we spend the night together, and it was dedicated to a thousand imaginative impudicities, each one more voluptuous and more unusual than the last. That libertine's greatest skill was probably in the licking of the asshole. She could so lengthen and stiffen her tongue that the longest and most agile finger would not have procured sweeter sensations.

That day's requirement of supplementary women led Durand to yield upon a point I had been pressing for quite some time. We added four charming creatures to our household, and retained, outside, more than five undred others, ready at any hour of the night and day.

The excesses of turpitude we witnessed in our house, excesses committed by individuals of both sexes, were frequent and outstanding. Experienced though I was, I continued to learn, and I avow that I would never have supposed the human imagination could soar to such incredible heights of corruption and perversity. What I saw achieved there defies belief; 'tis a vast, an endless abyss of horrors and infamies into which libertinage is able to drive the human being. How dangerous he is when aroused! No, I may truthfully say so, the most ferocious and the most savage beasts never attain such monstrosities. The influence we enjoyed, the silence, the orderliness, the subordination which reigned in that asylum, the extreme ease with which the visitor availed himself of the means to undertake every variety of imaginable and unimaginable debauch; everything encouraged the shy man, everything quickened the enterprising man's enthusiasm; and passions, no matter what form in which they might present themselves, in no matter what kind of brain they might waken, were always sure to be fed, to be favored, and to be satisfied with us.

It is there, my friends, I have said it before, I proclaim it again, yes, if one wishes to understand men, it is there one must follow his behavior: it is in his hour of lubricity, in his lubricious expressions that his character, laid absolutely bare, yields itself, in all its truest colors, to the appreciations of the philosophic student; and it is after having scrutinized him in these moments of intimacy that one can estimate and predict the consequences of the impulsions of his execrable heart and of his terrifying hungers.

In the matter of lust-murders our policy was severe; however, this fantasy's adepts were so numerous, requests for permission to indulge in it were so frequent, and the price people were willing to pay was so high, that we were forced to establish a rate for this only too common mania in sanguinary mankind. For one thousand sequins you obtained in our house the right to do to death, in the manner of your choosing, either one young boy or one young girl.

But to enjoy all these extravagances and to benefit from the intellectual stimulation they afforded, we had, Durand and I, set up observation posts, secret alcoves whence, without being seen, we commanded a perfect view of everything that transpired in the boudoirs used by our libertines; and 'twas from those vantage points we absorbed the richest instruction in a wide range of curious refinements. Whenever individuals desiring objects of libertinage struck us as worth the trouble observing, we would remove to our concealed loges, and there, at leisure, having ourselves fucked, or having ourselves frigged, we would dwell profitably upon the lascivious details untrammeled debauchery offered to our gaze. With my age and my looks, it often fell out that I was chosen in preference to one of the creatures the house had for hire; and in that case, if the client suited me and the figure seemed to justify it, I would prostitute myself unhesitatingly. Likewise, Durand's originalities, her curious caprices and pronounced bent for crime, her charms, though somewhat on the decline, often brought in a demand for her services; and there were still other times when the two of us were contracted for, or when we were included along with one or more other girls, and then God knows what orgies they were!

A member of one of Venice's most distinguished families presented himself one day. The libertine's name was Cornaro.

"It is a consuming passion that brings me here," he announced to me, "I must reveal its particulars to you."

"Speak forth, my Lord, make your orders known; we do not turn anybody away from this house."

"Why then, my dear, the thing is this: I require to embugger a little boy of seven, lying in the arms of his mother and of his aunt. And those two women must themselves sharpen the instruments which will be used by a helper I shall myself supply: he will trepan the child while I am sodomizing it. The operation once over, I shall have to embugger the mother, lying upon the body of her son; my helper, still using the instruments sharpened by the aunt and the mother, will ablate the latter's buttocks; these, cooked upon a grill, will be eaten by me, by the two women, and by you too, and with this meat we shall none of us drink anything except fine brandy."

"What a horror, my Lord!"

"Yes, yes, 'tis a horror, I know; but only horrors give me an erection, my dear; the worse they are, the more they excite me; and but for the fact they are never so horrible as I would like, I consider myself a happy man."

An appointment was fixed. His surgeon arrived with him, as did a pair of vigorous fuckers; Cornaro retired with them into a room, telling me that he would call when he needed me. And so I withdrew, and went promptly to one of the hiding places whence, as I mentioned to you, we were able to watch those of our guests from whose capers we expected to derive some pleasure: Cornaro set to work, and the effect the spectacle obtained upon me is something hardly to be described.

Two hours later, he summoned me back, I entered. The little boy lay sobbing in his mother's arms while she covered him with her caresses and wet him with her tears. The surgeon, the fuckers were drinking, and the young aunt was weeping in the company of her sister.

"Fuck!" expostulated the Venetian, "have you ever, I ask you, beheld a more sublime scene?" Then, after contemplating it for a moment, "Why," he said, feigning surprise, "are those tears I see? You weep, whore, because I am going to kill your son? But what interest can you have in this little chap, since he is no longer in your womb? Come, let us operate, Juliette, let us operate; do some ass-fucking where I can see you while I am in action, take one of these bucks, I'll keep the other: I am unable to do anything unless I have a prick in my ass."

While I adopt the libertine's suggestion, he, laying firm hands upon the child, camps him atop his mother's back and fucks him while being fucked and while the young aunt, kneeling, sharpens the tool needed for the forthcoming operation, under the inspection of the surgeon who flogs her in the meantime. I was so placed as to be able to miss nothing: although my ass, stoutly perforated, stood positively under Cornaro's nose, he had given orders that my fucker retire from time to time and tender him his prick for sucking, which, having sucked it, he would then reinsert in my fundament. Everything had been proceeding as he wished, when, sensing his sperm about to boil over, he turns his head and nods to the surgeon. That artist snatches the blade out of the aunt's hands, and in less time than it takes to tell, he slices the crown off not one skull, but all three, scoops the brains out, and braying like a donkey, our Venetian notable discharges deep inside the entrails of one of the masses he has just deprived of thinking being. He withdraws, the three wretched individuals, not yet dead, thrash about in the center of the room, and scream. Does the wildest jungle beast commit atrocities of this kind?

"Ha!" exults Cornaro, "nothing has ever given me such pleasure; let us finish these victims off," he goes on, clubbing at their heads with a bludgeon, "yes, by fuck, let's finish them off and treat ourselves to a little grilled buttock."

"Villain!" I say to this barbarian, "do you not repent the horrors you have just perpetrated?"

"Juliette," he sighed, "when you reach the point where I am, the only thing you rue is an act of virtue."

Beside myself from lust, I hugged that divine scoundrel to my breast; I frigged him, by imparting delightsome sensations I strove to restore the energy he had lost with his ejaculation. He teased, he nibbled my teats, sucked my mouth. I whispered disgusting things in his ear, horrible things; to material titillations I added the provocation of lascivious conversation. When I heard him ask for my ass I thought my triumph certain; he knelt before my buttocks, he toyed with them, squeezed them while tonguing the hole for a quarter of an hour: but his prick did not lift out of its sagging condition.

"A discharge leaves me limp for a week," he apologized; "the enormous amount of time required before I become aroused, the copiousness of my seminal loss, the entire thing exhausts me. Let us have supper; my forces may return amidst the lewdnesses with which we shall punctuate the meal, and perhaps, stuffed with food and drink, we shall consummate some further crimes. In the meantime, have yourself fucked within my full view, for there is libertinage aglitter in your eyes, Juliette, and I should suppose your need for a discharge is urgent."

"No," said I, "since you intend to wait, I shall wait too; you alone excite me, the others do not: it is your sperm I wish to see flow, and nothing else will cause the ejaculation of mine."

"If that be the case," said Cornaro, "let our supper be as impure as possible, let us transform it into a frightful orgy. I need not specify the details; by now you know my tastes, you will leave me nothing to desire."

Garbed as a bacchante, Durand, when everything was ready, announced to us that supper was served. We removed into a vast feasting hall, in whose middle stood a table set for four: Cornaro, Durand, myself, and a fifty-year-old woman named Laurentia, reputed to be the most profligate, the most corrupt, the most lascivious creature in the whole of Italy. Laurentia, like the rest of us, elected to eat human flesh, watched philosophically while it was brought on, and devoured it without repugnance.

Nothing so delicate as the various dishes that accompanied those sanguinary viands. Eight courses, composed of everything of the rarest and most succulent, preceded and followed the grillades; but, as had been agreed from the beginning, nothing was drunk but the finest old brandy. Eight stewardesses of fourteen, with delicious faces, served the brandy: they had it in their mouths, and when beckoned, they would step forward and from between their rosy lips squirt it down the guest's parched gullet. A pair of fifteen-year-old bardashes stood at attention directly behind each guest's chair, eight in all, ready to execute whatever orders they might happen to receive. Deployed at each of the four corners of the table was a group made up of two old women, two female blackamoors, two vigorous fuckers, two more catamites, two girls of eighteen, and two children of seven. A simple gesture to the nearest group brought it up to the actor who cared to dally with any or all of the subjects composing it. At the four sides of the room were that many raised platforms, upon each of which a couple of Negroes lashed a girl of sixteen or seventeen who, once torn to shreds, would vanish through a trap door, to be replaced the same instant by a fresh one; to right and to left of each fustigator, and upon the same stages, were other Negroes embuggering mulatto bardashes, aged between twelve and thirteen. Four girls, fifteen years of age, hovered underneath the table: their function was to suck Cornaro's prick and our cunts. From the ceiling depended a great candelabrum which at the same time spread throughout the hall a light as pure and bright as sunlight, and, uncommon particularity, also shot a concentrated and fiery beam at a choir of children stationed upon balconies under the arch of the ceiling, and, burning them, produced an incessant shrill complaint from on high. It was that phenomenon which most struck Cornaro, the one which amused him more than anything else, and for which he had the most fulsome praise. Our man, enraptured, after having glanced at everything warranting his notice, sat down, protesting that he had never seen anything so lubricious.

"That woman," he said, his eyes falling upon Laurentia, "what is she?"

"A bon vivant like yourself," said Durand, "a slut capable of surpassing you in infamy and whose cunt is being frigged at this very minute, just as your prick is being sucked."

"All very pleasant indeed," said Cornaro, "but it seems to me that before sitting down at the same table with me, that woman and Durand ought to have shown me their behinds."

"You are quite right," the two of them answered, rising promptly and bringing their asses to within a few inches of Cornaro's face.

The libertine palpated them, kissed them; with his connoisseur's discerning gaze still fixed upon them, "These," he opined, "are asses whereupon libertinage has more than once placed its stamp; they are in degraded condition, I like it: it is the result of the years and the work of lubricity; these blemishes delight me. Oh," he continued, addressing the company at large, "oh, how beautiful is corrupted Nature in its details, and how the poppies of age are, in my estimation, to be preferred to the roses of childhood! Kiss me, heavenly asses! Waft your scented zephyrs toward me, and then get back to your places so that we can all prostitute ourselves in concert.

"And these women I see hereabout me?" Cornaro inquired next, considering the suppliants surrounding the table.

"They," I replied, "are victims who are under sentence of death and who, knowing the authority you wield in these parts, are on their knees to implore your mercy."

"They shall certainly not obtain any," the barbarian declared, glancing fiercely at them; "many a time have I caused people to die, but I have never granted one reprieve or pardon."

Therewith we fell to eating, and everyone and everything with a role to perform entered into action.

Cornaro, being sucked uninterruptedly, was halfway stiff already; he demanded that each of the victims step forward and receive some abuse at his hands. One by one those charming creatures rise, begin by presenting their ass to the lewd dignitary, and afterward submit humbly to what he is pleased to mete out to them. Slaps, pinches, hair-pullings, nose-tweakings, bites, burns, buffets, ass-spankings, breast-twistings, scratches, little is omitted, and once they have got what is due them, they return to their former places and resume their kneeling position. These preliminaries over with, Cornaro leans my way, having me take hold of a prick whose state I was beginning to feel rather proud of.

"Those sluts are affecting me," he confided in my ear, "I may soon begin to misbehave."

"The means are all there, my friend," I replied, "we simply await the impulses of your heart and your mind's instigations; speak, and an exemplary submissiveness will give you proof of our devotion."

Then Cornaro, somewhat rudely, passed his two hands beneath my buttocks and, pulling me toward him, lifted me a little into the air: he called one of the fuckers' attention to my ass. "Over here," said he, "sodomize her as I hold her aloft."

A prick sounds my bum, Cornaro's tongue probes my mouth; one of the young servants grasps his prick, another worries his ass.

"Off with you, Juliette," he says; "hither, Laurentia, take her place."

The same ceremony; Laurentia is embuggered, Cornaro sucks, at intervals, the prick which is fucking her. Durand's turn comes next; identical episodes. All the women undergo the same fate, all are ass-fucked by a fresh fucker who, as before, periodically interrupts his tupping in order to allow the libertine to lick away the maculations acquired during intercourse. The fricatrices are changed, and I dispatch the youngest and prettiest girls one by one to fondle the rake's member and to lend their buttocks to his slaps and pounding.

"Let us eat," he finally says. "That will do by way of prologue, we shall refine our gestures as we proceed. Juliette," he asks me, "what is your view? Is there any more divine passion in the world than lust?"

"I would venture to say that there is not; but lust must be carried to excess: in libertinage, he who applies curbs is a fool who denies himself all possibility of ever knowing what pleasure is."

"Libertinage," Durand put in, "is a sensual aberrance which supposes the discarding of all restraints, the supremest disdain for all prejudices, the total rejection of all religious notions, the profoundest aversion to all ethical imperatives; and that libertine who has not attained this philosophical maturity, tossing back and forth between his desires' impetuousness and the bullying of his conscience, will be debarred from perfect happiness."

"I do not think," said Laurentia, "that fault can be found with his Lordship upon any of the articles that have just been enumerated, and I am convinced he has intelligence enough to be immune to the effects of commonplace ideas."

"It is in any case certain," said Cornaro, "that I acknowledge the sanctity of absolutely nothing in human society, and that for the great good reason that everything men have instituted is absolutely nothing but the product of their self-interest and their prejudices. Is there a single man alive anywhere who can legitimately assure me that he knows more about the world than I do? Once one has ceased to have any belief in religion and therefore in a God's idiotic confidences to mortals, everything of man's invention must be subjected to the closest scrutiny and consigned immediately to scorn, if in me Nature's urgings are to despise and trample upon those lies. Hence, once it is demonstrated that in the spheres of religion, of morals, and of politics, no man can be better informed than I, I may, as of that moment, be as wise as he, and from then on nothing he announces to me can rightfully claim my respect. It is in the lawful power of no human being to force me to believe or accept what he says or thinks; and however little regard I have for these human reveries, however much I flout them, there is no person on earth who can pretend to the right to censure or punish me therefor. Into what chasm of errors or foolishness would we not tumble were all men blindly to adhere to what it suited some other men to establish! And through what incredible injustice will you call *moral* that which emanates from you; *immoral* that which I uphold? To what arbitration shall we apply in order to find out upon which side right and reason lie?

"But, some will object, there are certain things so visibly infamous that no possible doubt can exist of their danger and their horribleness. For my part, dear friends, I sincerely declare that I know of no deed answering to this description, none which, recommended by Nature, has not at some time in the past formed the basis of some hallowed custom; and, finally, none which being seasoned by some attractions, does not through that fact alone become legitimate and good. Whence I conclude that there is not one which ought to be resisted, not one without its usefulness, not one which has not had somebody's sanction in its favor.

"But, it will be most stupidly said, since you were born under this or that latitude, you ought to abide by the usages prevalent there. Bah, enough; you are being absurd in wanting to persuade me that I should put up with wrongs done me because of accidents of birthplace; I am such as I was formed by Nature; and if there be a jar between my penchants and the laws of my country, blame Nature for it, impute no fault to me.

"But, it will be added, you will be a menace to society, society shall have to protect itself, to remove you from its midst. Platitudes. Renounce your senseless curbs, and give equally, equitably, to all persons the right to revenge themselves for the wrong done them, do that and you shall have no more need of codes of law, you will have no more need of the brainless calculations of those bloated pedants that go under the amusing title of *criminalists,* who, clumsily weighing in the scales of their ineptness actions beyond the grasp of their somber genius, refuse to realize that when Nature is all roses for us, she can necessarily be nothing but thistles for them.

"Abandon man to Nature, she will be a far better guide to him than your legislators. Destroy, above all, these populous cities, where the accumulation of vices drives you to repressive lawmaking. What necessity is there that man live in society? Restore him to the forest wilderness whence he came, and let him do there whatever he likes. His crimes, as isolated as he, will then be an inconvenience to no one, and there will be no further purpose for your restrictive regulations; savage man is subject to two needs only: the need to fuck and the need to eat; both are implanted in him by Nature. Nothing he will do in answer to the one or the other of these needs can possibly be criminal; if ever passions other than these are found in him, only civilization and society engendered them. Well, as soon as it is clear that these recent offenses are nothing but the fruit of circumstances, that they are inherent in social man's way of life, by what right, if you please, do you blame him for them?

"There, then, are the only two species of offenses man can be subject to: (1) those imposed upon him by the state of savagery: now, would it not be sheer madness on your part to punish him for these? and (2) those his social existence amidst other men inspire in him; would it not be yet more extravagant to deal severely with these? And so what is there left for you to do, ignorant and stupid moderns, when you see crimes committed? You should admire, and you should hold your tongue; admire . . . yes, most certainly, for nothing is so fascinating, nothing so arresting nor so beautiful as man swept away by his passions; hold your tongue . . . even more certainly, for what you behold is the handiwork of Nature, toward whom your proper attitude must be one of breathless awe and silent respect.

"As regards my own self and personal affairs, I concur in your view, my friends, that the world can boast of no more immoral man than me; there is not a single prohibition I have not violated, not a principle out of whose grip I have not delivered myself, not a virtue I have failed to outrage, not one crime I have neglected to commit; and I must confess that 'tis only when I have acted in uttermost defiance of all social conventions, of all human laws, that I have really felt lust throb in my heart and inflame it with its divine fire. Every criminal or ferocious deed excites me; to murder on the highways, that would excite me; to ply the hangman's trade, that would excite me. And so why deny oneself these deeds, once they hurl one's senses into such a voluptuous ferment?"

"Ah," Laurentia murmured, "to murder on the highways. . . ."

"Yes, indeed. That is perpetrating violence, any violence agitates the senses; any sort of nervous emotion, directed by the imagination, essentially quickens pleasure. If, therefore, my prick rises at the prospect of going out and killing somebody on the highway, that action, to which I am impelled by the same principle that moves me to unbutton my breeches or lift a petticoat, must be excused on the same grounds, and I shall therefore commit it with the same indifference, but nevertheless with greater pleasure, because its capacity to irritate is greater."

"What," said my companion, "has the idea of God never checked your misbehavior?"

"Ah, do not talk to me about that ignoble chimera, it was already the object of my derision by the time I reached the age of twelve. I shall never be able to understand how any man in his senses can pay an instant's heed to a disgusting fable which the heart abjures, which reason disavows, and which can win partisans only among fools, low knaves, or imposters. Were there actually any such thing as a God, master and creator of the universe, he would be, incontestably, if one is to judge by the notions widespread among his sectators, the most bizarre, the cruelest, the most wickedly spiteful, and the most bloodthirsty of figures; and none of us would have energy enough, force enough, to hate him, to execrate him, to revile him, and to profane him to the degree he would deserve. The greatest service legislators could render humanity would be an ironclad law against theocracy. Few realize how important it is to obliterate that hideous God's baneful altars; until those fatal ideas can no longer rearise, man will know neither rest nor peace on earth, and the threat of religious strife will always be poised over our heads. A government that permits all forms of worship has not absolutely fulfilled the philosophic objective toward which we must all aim: it must go farther, it must expel from society's bosom those elements which may hamper its action. Well, I shall demonstrate to you whenever you like that no government will ever be vigorous or stable so long as it allows in the country any worship of a Supreme Being—that Pandora's Box, that keen-edged weapon destructive of every government, that appalling system in virtue of which everybody fancies he has

the right to cut everybody else's throat every day. Let him die a
thousand deaths, the man who thinks to preach a God, in any
country however governed. The blessed scoundrel the feeble-
minded revere has no other purpose than to sap the foundations of
the State; inside it he endeavors to form an independent caste, the
everlasting foe of happiness and equality; he strives to achieve
dominion over his compatriots, he strives to light the fires of discord, and ends up enchaining the people, with whom he is aware
he shall be able to do whatever he wishes once he has blinded them
by superstition and gangrened them by fanaticism."

"And yet," Durand remarked, merely for the sake of hearing
our man's conversation, "religion is the cornerstone of morality;
and morals, however you have twisted them, none the less remain
very essential in a government."

"Of whatever nature you may suppose this government,"
Cornaro rejoined, "I shall prove to you that morality is useless to
it. And morality, furthermore, what do you mean by the term? Is
it not the practice of all social virtues? Will you then be so kind
as to tell me what bearing the practice of any virtue can possibly
have upon the workings of government? Are you afraid that the
vice which is the opposite of these virtues might upset those workings? Never. Nay, it is far less important that governmental
action be exerted against corrupt persons than against moral
persons. The latter are addicted to arguing, and you will never
have a solid government where men spend their time using their
rational faculties: for government is a brake upon men, and the
man with a mind wants no brakes upon him. Whence it is that the
shrewdest lawmakers were eager to bury in ignorance the men they
sought to rule; they sensed that the chains they meant to impose
were more apt to keep the imbecile on his knees than the individual
of genius. You are going to reply to me that in a free government
this cannot be the lawmaker's desire. And I am going to ask you
what government is free; does any such thing exist anywhere on
earth? More, can a single free government possibly exist? Is not
man everywhere the slave of laws? And, once this is so, does that
not mean he is everywhere in chains? Once enchained, is it not the
desire of his oppressor, whoever he may be, to maintain man in that
state where he can be most easily held captive? Now, is that state

not plainly the state of immorality? The kind of drunken rapture the immoral and corrupt man perpetually vegetates in, is that not the state in which his legislator can maintain him most conveniently, paralyze him most easily? Why then should the legislator wish to inject virtues into him? Never save when man purges himself does he grow restive, contentious, examine his governors, and change the regime. For your government's sake, pinion the citizen by means of immorality, drown him in immorality . . . and he will never cause you any trouble. I ask you, moreover, looking at things in a broader sense, I ask you whether vices are of any consequence in dealings between men: what matters it to the State whether Peter robs John, or whether, in his turn, John murders Peter? It is perfectly absurd to imagine that these various tit-for-tats can be of the slightest consequence to the State. But there must be laws to keep crime in check. . . . What need is there to keep crime in check? Crime is necessary to Nature's right functioning, her laws expect it, it is the counterweight to virtue: and it beseems human beings to undertake to repress it! The man of the primeval forest, say, did he have laws holding his passions in check, and did he lead an any less happy existence than you? Fear not lest strength be ever discomfited by weakness; if the latter always comes away the loser, 'tis because Nature wills that it be thus; and it is not for you to oppose her law."

"That," said I, "is a system which opens wide the door to every sort of horror."

"But they are indispensable, horrors: does not Nature convince us of it when she causes the most virulent poisons to grow cheek to jowl with the most wholesome plants? Why do you object to crime? Not because you find it evil in itself, but because it is prejudicial to you: do you suppose, however, that the man who is served by crime thinks to condemn it? Why, no! If then crime makes for as much happiness in the world as unhappiness, where is the justice of the law that punishes it? The character of a good law must be to promote the welfare of everybody; the law you promulgate against crime will not achieve anything of the sort, it will satisfy no one but the victim of the offense, and will probably supremely displease the agent. The great shortcoming, the final misfortune of men is, in their lawmaking, never to consider more than one fraction of humanity and always to utterly disregard the rest; you wonder that so many blunders are committed, now you know why."

We had reached that point in the discussion when a servant came to announce to us that a woman plunged in extremest poverty was waiting downstairs, and earnestly desired to have a few words with Signor Cornaro.

"Send her in," I said before the Venetian had a chance to reply.

The women surrounding the table immediately got up from their knees to make room for the ensuing scene, and joined the fifty sultanas who were exhibiting their asses upon the four stages.

A moment later there entered, with modesty, a pregnant woman of about thirty, as lovely as Venus, and followed by two little boys belonging to her, one of whom was fourteen, the other thirteen, and by two girls, also her children, aged fifteen and twelve.

"Oh, my Lord!" she cried, she and the rest of her family sinking down at the feet of Cornaro, the perfect dupe of a scene I had arranged with a view to playing upon his susceptibilities, "oh, my Lord, my Lord! 'tis your kindness I implore; in the name of heaven, have pity upon a poor woman abandoned by her husband and the mother of these unhappy children you see begging you for bread. For two years now have we been destitute; without work, without resources, the grave must soon claim us all five if harsh mankind persists in denying us any means to prolong our existence. Oh, good sir! look not unmeltingly upon the wretchedness that invokes your compassion: succor us, else we must perish."

As I said, this woman's appearance was delicious; her negligent dress, her pregnancy, graces distributed everywhere about her person, the enchanting looks of her children, the tears bathing the cheeks of everyone in this fascinating family: so incendiary was the general effect, so furiously did it inflame our libertine's criminal lust, that for an instant I thought he was going to discharge before a finger was laid upon him. But he fought his feelings into line, 'twas for much more piquant scenes the rascal was reserving himself; and 'twas to execute them he took me with him into a chamber nearby, whither the victims I have just described had been promptly directed.

And now that cannibal's ferocity attains full flower. He is beside himself; incoherent speech declares his extreme disorder, he stammers, babbles, his words are foul, his phrases unconnected, his ideas blasphemous, dreadful. I shall continue to portray him in this distracted mood: no aspect of the subject can be left obscure by the artist who undertakes to portray for mankind the monstrosities of Nature.

"Well then, bitch," says he upon making his entrance, "I have come to relieve you; you are gravid, I am going to make you whelp. Quickly, strip . . . naked, naked, and buttocks especially . . . Juliette, I stiffen, I stiffen considerably . . . rub alcohol on my balls . . . but get these sluts out of their clothes, and make haste. . . ."

And, pronouncing these words, he aims a terrible punch at the mother's face: blackens her eye, breaks one of her teeth, sends her crashing twenty feet away; and the brute, the while leering at her, handles my ass so ungently that, fearing lest he turn upon me, I hurriedly remove the rags covering the poor wretch, already fallen to the floor which her tears and her blood are soon to wet. Having to stoop over to undress her, I make the fairest exposition of my behind: lewd Cornaro takes firm grasp upon it and embuggers me.

"Strip her," he cries, "pull the clothes off her body, tear them off, strangle her if she resists; are you insensitive to my erection?"

Cornaro now demands that the unlucky creature get upon her knees and beg me to undress her; and while she is doing so, he spits in her face. Once she is in the state he desires, he quits my ass, jerks her to her feet, then, himself, in the twinkling of an eye, snatches everything they are wearing off the two boys and the two little girls, and assails those four behinds with the most heavy-handed and the most loathsome caresses. Then, ordering me to sear the mother's buttocks with a candle-flame for a few moments, "That will do," he cries, "now give me some switches."

These instruments having been furnished him, he has the mother stretch out upon her back; then, upon her swollen belly, he establishes the four children, one atop the other, which provides him with a belly and four behinds to flagellate. First, he kisses, paws that pyramid of charms, he praises their beauty, expresses wonder that poverty and privation have made no visible inroads upon these unhappy creatures' health or plumpness. Then, shifting from surprise to wickedness, and plying his switches with the speed of light, he thrashes the targets set tier on tier, from that overripe, snow-white belly to the uppermost of those eight appetizing buttocks. I frigged him during the operation, and resorted to the most atrocious and sanguinary stratagems to keep his energy from flagging. Now and again, when he would pause to rest, when he would gaze gloatingly at the stripes and slashes his barbarity had inflicted, he would thrust his prick into my ass, withdraw after three or four stabs, and resume his baleful fustigations. Weary of this inaugural pleasure, he gave it up in favor of pressing the young mother's belly, of kneading it, beating it, hammering it with his fists, and while he did so he was covering the four children's bloody behinds with his kisses.

Positions are altered; he lays the mother in the middle of the bed, upon her back; between her legs establishes each of the children, one after the other, and embuggers them while inflicting every kind of painful outrage upon the mother's belly.

"My friend," I say, "you are in discharging humor, I can see it in your eyes: a little more and this scene will cost you your fuck, after which you will be unable either to consummate your crime or to enjoy the further episodes which ought to precede its accomplishment."

"And what other entertainment do you intend to provide me?" the Venetian inquired, his head reeling from lubricity.

"Come with me," said I, "leave these creatures to catch their breath, you shall return to them in a few minutes."

I drew him into a little room where Durand, with the aid of Laurentia, had just completed preparing the new scene you are now to behold.

That room was decorated to represent one of those temples where the Saturnalia were celebrated in the Rome of olden days. Nine lubricious tableaux greeted the Venetian's eyes.

The first featured a handsome man in middle years, prick aloft and hovering close to the ass of a little boy, whom a catamite was caressing.

In the second was seen a woman of forty frigging a girl of fifteen, herself being frigged by a girl of eighteen.

In the third was a vigorous athlete ass-fucking a beautiful Negress and cunt-sucking a pretty white woman.

In the fourth, a mother flogging her daughter and being flogged herself by a man.

The fifth offered a man embuggering a calf and being sodomized by a large dog.

The sixth, a man whipping his own daughter, bound to a stepladder; he was in the meantime receiving a lashing from somebody else.

The seventh, a group of ten girls, all ten with tongue in cunt.

The eighth, a group of ten men, one embuggering the next, and so curiously disposed were the ten attached actors that they formed one spherical mass.

In the ninth and last you saw men embuggering halfwit or syphilitic girls all the while they were cunt-sucking beldams of sixty at least, and small boys were nibbling their asses.

In the middle of all that, a couple of matrons looked to be offering Cornaro six little girls, aged only two or three, all naked, all as pretty as little cherubs. Everybody wore wreaths of flowers, everybody was in action. From all sides nothing could be heard but cries, whether of pleasure or of pain, and the whistling of thongs and the impact of leather upon flesh. Everybody was naked; everybody illustrated lewdness in its most scandalous colors. Lamps burning scented oil created an agreeable illumination and at the same time shed an enchanting odor throughout the place, crowning touches added to so many others that rendered this temple one of the most delicious sanctuaries that was ever edified for lust.

Our man wanders among the formations; two masculine fuckers and two feminine whippers follow him wherever he goes, applying themselves by turns to irritate his ass in all possible manners.[4] Here, the lecher squeezes or wrings a teat; there, he tickles or claws a cunt; farther along, blows of his fist bloody a pretty face. 'Tis the raging tiger loose in the sheepfold.

"All right," says he, "let's have an end to this, I cannot endure

---

[4] Never is one's desire for a prick in the behind so keen as directly after a whipping; and never does one more keenly desire the whip than just after an ass-fucking. 'Tis incredible how these two pleasures hang together and mutually feed each other.

any more. But I wish to operate before a public, I wish to join the pleasure of creating a scandal to the horrors which will finally bring my sperm forth. Give me half a dozen girls and as many young men, the most sensitive and honorable and decent ones you have here; they will stand about me while I act, and I shall do my best to give the most appalling performance possible."

I promptly bring him what he asks for, and we all troop into the chamber where the unhappy family is waiting for us. The crowd surrounds Cornaro. Death is decreed for those who prove unable to bear the spectacle, or who wilt before it, or weep. Cornaro lays hands on the mother; he hangs her by the feet from the ceiling, thus causing her to be stifled by the child in her womb. He has the prettier of the two daughters held by her sister and embuggers her; then, armed with a carpenter's saw, he slowly severs the poor creature's head, while doing so sodomizing her steadily. The cruel man made that execrable operation last over an hour. It upset three of the feminine spectators, who collapsed and from falling sustained serious hurt.

"Mark them," said Cornaro, "I shall attend to them when I have finished over here."

The neck is at last cut all the way through. Another member of the family is brought forward; and it is not until Cornaro has installed himself in the ass of the last of the children, a boy, not until he has hacked through the neck of this last victim, that the villain unleashes the tides of foamy sperm whose seething has rendered him so ferocious. Before the end came, three more members of the audience, all feminine, had swooned; and all the others had given way to tears. As for the mother, she was no more: the pressure of the child weighing upon her diaphragm had suffocated her. Thus it was that in this horrible den one beheld nought but crime's incarnation on the one side, and its sinister effects on the other.

"Why, what is this, my friend!" said I, approaching the culprit and rattling his device, "what! you are going to leave these victims unpunished, you are not going to carry out the sentence you pronounced against them?"

"No," sighed the Venetian, "I am exhausted; I am not surfeited with crime, but it has worn me out. I need rest. . . ."

Despairing of extracting anything further from him, I had him served a cup of hot broth, and he withdrew after having paid one hundred thousand francs for the orgies he had just celebrated.

Following Cornaro, the next of our memorable visitors was a Venetian lady of quality and outstanding wealth, very famous for her debauchery. Silvia, forty-five years of age, tall, superbly proportioned and with the most beautiful eyes possible, arrived for a three days' sojourn at our house.

"My friends," she announced to us, "I have a repletion of fuck which cannot be let otherwise than in horrors, and these I desire in every kind. To begin with," continued this contemporary Messalina, "I want you to prostitute me to some libertine, bizarre in his tastes, who will take me upon an extended promenade through the most noisome hogwallows of dissoluteness."

"I have someone ready downstairs, and I believe he is the personage you require. However, Signora, he will undoubtedly lift hands against you. Nay, he is sure to thrash you."

"Ah, dear heart, that is all I ask; I burn to be the victim of such a libertine. . . . What will he do to me after that?"

"After having treated you like the lowliest of the low, he will oblige you to frig pricks upon his face; he will have you cunt-fucked while he looks on, and he will conclude by embuggering you."

"Delicious!" was Silvia's reply; "that is exactly what I am looking for. Let us begin the scene at once; later, I shall indicate to you the way in which I would have it terminate."

I had the man in question brought up. It so happened that he had requested someone of precisely Silvia's age and shape; great was his joy at being introduced to her. Our two actors were swiftly come to grips; and I, behind my partition, nonchalantly reclining between a set of girls frigging me before and behind, I missed not a detail of the ceremony. Dorsini opened with a dozen stout kicks delivered to the ass, rapidly succeeded by twenty slaps in the face and eight or ten fist-blows, but all that meted out with such speed that Silvia might have thought she was caught in a hailstorm. She remains of firm countenance withal, and the expression in her eyes is of nothing unless it be pleasure. That flurry of hands is followed by tirades of hard language; rarely has a woman been insulted as Dorsini insults his partner.

"Very well," says he, "let pricks be fetched in; I want to see how this whore does her work."

Six first-rate fuckers appear; Silvia, naked, her buttocks pressed against the ruffian's belly, empties out the engines, spraying their contents over Dorsini's face; he is dripping with sperm; she rubs it upon his nose; his prick has scarcely begun to stir. A further half-dozen youths appear; he orders them to fuck his high-born whore.

"Bleeding Christ!" he exclaims, watching her squirm beneath them, "what a jade, what licentiousness! You have some heat in you, eh, old bag of bones? Make some noise, whore, curse a bit, tell Almighty God what you think of Him."

And it is by a torrent of invectives against the Eternal that Silvia responds to this invitation. Never was the idiom of blasphemy carried so far. Of that I would probably still be persuaded today had not Dorsini contrived to outdo her. While swearing, the miscreant was frigging himself, fondling the fuckers' behinds one by one, and fondling that of his slut also. At length he has her turn around; a vigorous fucker who encunts her exposes her hindquarters to Dorsini, who, after a preliminary examination of that ass, an examination which is not, as you might suppose, conducted without a few vexations, trains his member at the immoral orifice and flings thereinto in a matter of moments. Silvia endures everything and never once flinches: for true it decidedly is that one may glean as much delight in the patient's role as in the agent's: the imagination is the only cradle where pleasures are born, it alone creates, fashions, orients them; where the imagination is still, when it does not contribute inspiration or embellishment, all that remains is the physical act, dull, gross, and brutish.

But Dorsini, being himself embuggered while embuggering, excites himself only temporarily in the anus; the mouth is the shrine where he is ordinarily wont to sacrifice, 'tis there his homage is normally consummated; he roars out his need for the mouth, Silvia lends hers, he lodges himself there without interrupting his copulatory motions and discharges to the great contentment of the hussy, who sucks him with an ardor wholly appropriate to her whorishness, and all the dreadful disorder of her lubricious mind. Dorsini pays and takes his leave.

"Let us share it," Silvia said to me, "I like money earned in the whorehouse, it has always brought me good luck. Well, that has limbered me sufficiently," she went on, "we can now proceed with the rest."

The shameless creature then gathered twenty-five superb men and twenty-five girls of exceeding beauty together in a spacious drawing room, and for the next sixteen hours gave herself over, with myself as witness, to the most monstrous riot of debauchery, to the most inordinate and unseemly passions, to whimsies at once foul beyond words and beyond belief extraordinary in a woman who, necessarily, could have contracted such habits only after first having renounced all concern for her reputation, all principles of modesty and virtue, whereof, according to the legend, our sex must be the exclusive repository, and from which we women never depart save it be to surpass everything men can achieve of the most execrable in this kind.

Silvia, all afire, ended up with cruelties; this is customary. Here is the horror she invented. For victim she chose a little boy of thirteen, fair as an angel.

"I am going to reduce him to such an extremity that he'll be fit for nothing but burial in a few days. For how much are you willing to sell him to me?"

"One thousand sequins."

The bargain is concluded.

The rascal has this child secured to a curved bench, in such a way that, as though he were over a barrel, his ass is entirely exposed; Silvia then squats over the face of a handsome young man lying upon the piles of cushions, and has her cunt licked by him while another, on all fours, comes up from behind and tongues her ass. Excited by these proceedings, she picks up a lighted candle and gleefully scorches the buttocks, chars the asshole of the victim who, as you must surely imagine, utters frightful screams throughout the operation. As for Silvia, she discharges; swearing like a trooper, the slut goes into an ecstasy, and ferocity brings her to the point where, having had the child turned over, with her teeth she tears away its genitals. We bore the boy out unconscious, he died three days later; and Silvia, triumphant, after having paid me a king's ransom, was before very long back with us again to renew similar horrors.

'Twas to her recommendation we owed the visit paid us several months afterward by Senator Bianchi, one of the Republic's richest figures, and aged about thirty-five. That libertine's mania was to betake himself to a brothel with his two nieces, whom he had in ward, and to prostitute them there. Though he had striven to annihilate modesty in those two young girls' souls, the influence of an exemplary upbringing was yet strong enough in them to transform the experience into an ordeal. They blushed red when I looked at them; thus covered with confusion, all their candor shone forth, further enhancing the graces wherewith Nature had ornamented them: no living creature could have been lovelier than either one of those two. Simply to gaze at the pair sufficed to make me embrace the roué's lewd scheme; and I could not resist employing certain formulas calculated to scandalize those chaste ears.

"What order of merchandise do these whores require," I asked the Senator, "do they like their meat fat or lean?"

"They are too shy to answer, look and see for yourself," Bianchi replied, raising the skirts of the one and the other, "measure their cunts and gauge their needs."

"Good," said I, after a certain amount of poking about with my fingers, "it's something not too filling that seems to be called for."

"To the contrary!" Bianchi protested. "I want these children to grow; give me the biggest articles you have."

And in accordance with this expressive order, at which the poor dears' crimson cheeks only paled a little, I produce six young fuckers the least of whose members showed a foot in length by eight inches in circumference.

"That is what I want," our man says to me as he handles the goods; "but six are too few. You don't know these young ladies' appetites; meek as lambs they may appear to you, but when they fuck, they fuck like she-wolves, and I venture to say that it will take twelve men if they are to be satisfied at all."

"Well, here are another six. And you, amiable libertine," I ask, "what shall be your needing? What are you wont to do while your nieces are being dishonored?"

"I fuck boys; get me six of them, and nothing older than twelve."

I have them for him in an instant; by the time the operation begins I am at my post, for I need hardly tell you that I was not one to miss many such scenes.

That libertine performed horrors, and upon his nieces had still worse performed. He died not long after his visit to us, and in expiring the wicked patrician disinherited his unlucky wards. So it was that by and by, having already endured severest hardships, they came to seek refuge with us, and it was granted them at the price of a prostitution whence we earned a pretty penny. It was the younger of the two, that is to say, one of the loveliest girls in Europe, that I provided to a man whose passion merits a separate article in this encyclopaedia of inhuman lewd practices.

Alberti was a tall and sinewy man of fifty-five years or so, whose mere glance sufficed to petrify a woman. I showed him the beautiful and delicate child I had appointed to him. He bids me remove her clothes, and then examines her, palpating her uncouthly or as one might a horse whose defects one wishes to ascertain. Not a word during this inspection; not a gesture indicative of lubricity; nothing apart from a bright light in his eyes, and his labored breathing.

"Is she pregnant?" he asked me after a while, applying his muscular hands to her belly.

"I do not believe so," I rejoined.

"A pity; I am prepared to pay double when they are. In any case, knowing the purpose I shall be putting it to, what is your figure for this animal?"

"Two thousand sequins."

"You'd get it if she were pregnant; since she isn't, you'd better take half."

The bargaining was conducted in the victim's presence; we finally reached an understanding and I sold her. Bought, she was immediately shut away in a small chamber in our house, so thick-walled and narrow and isolated that there was no chance of her cries being heard. There, with some straw to lie upon, the wretch's sufferings were to last nine days: her ration of food was to be reduced gradually during the first four, thereafter she was to be fed nothing whatever. Each day the fierce Alberti would come to torment his victim; he would spend two hours doing it: Rosalba and I were regular witnesses to those sessions, along with another girl who was changed every day.

Upon his first visit, the first thing that cruel libertine did was press the victim's buttocks and breasts; he pressed them forcefully; he softened them, pinched them, crushed them with such skill that in less than an hour those four globes of flesh were all black and blue. Placed opposite him, my ass was on an exact level with his lips, he kissed my behind while toiling over his prisoner; in the meantime Rosalba frigged him, and the third girl flogged him as hard as she could. Lost in meditation, nothing came from Alberti's mouth but a few unconnected words, occasionally interspersed with oaths.

"Vile flesh," he remarked ironically, "execrable ass. Such offal is fit for nothing but to be boiled down into soap." And every grace embellished the objects he dared refer to in that manner. He did not discharge.

On the second day the proceedings were the same as on the first; on the third, the fleshy parts of the victim were in such a swollen, such a woeful state, that she was taken by a high fever.

"Excellent," said Alberti, "this is better than I expected; my intention was not to halt her food until the fourth day, but in the light of these developments, it can be stopped now." And he continued to squeeze, to compress. Toward the close of the visit he sodomized the victim, while pinching her thighs vigorously; then the girl assisting us was treated likewise, and my behind was tongued. The next three days' episodes were identical; never once did he discharge. By then, the victim's buttocks and breasts resembled steer hides that had been cured in the sun, and the fever, having continued to rise despite the suspension of nourishment, we wondered whether the wretch would last until the ninth day.

"She had better be given confession," Alberti said to me at the conclusion of the eighth day's activities; "she will die without fail tomorrow."

This precaution made me laugh; but when I learned that the

lecher wanted to be a secret witness to the ceremony, and that it
was but a further vehicle to his lubricity, I fell in gladly with the
idea.

A monk came and confessed the sufferer while in the adjoining
room, between Rosalba and me, Alberti listened to all that was
said. This episode appeared to entertain him enormously.

"God blast me!" said he while we frigged him, "the plight she
is in, 'tis uniquely my doing. Oh, how I love to hear the slut tell of
her sins. . . ." And, having previously warned the doomed creature
that the confessor was hard of hearing we lost not a syllable of
that pious exchange. The monk disappears; the lecher enters. Exhausted by hunger, by fever, and by contusions, the young girl looks
to be ready to give up the ghost. Such is the spectacle the villain
wishes to enjoy. He settles himself squarely in front of her and
while he embuggers Rosalba, while the girl accompanying us flogs
him, he orders me to carry forward the work he has been pursuing
for a week. I approach the victim, I lay hands on those derelict
parts, I tug, I squeeze; and at the second or third application of
pressure, the miserable thing, worn out by such prolonged sufferings, falls at our feet, lifeless. And it is at that instant our Alberti
discharges. But, merciful heavens! what an outpouring: never in
all my days had I seen such a lengthy nor such an impetuous expenditure of sperm. He was for more than ten minutes in ecstasy;
no clyster, however copious, could have yielded results quantitatively comparable to that villain's ejaculation.

Alberti became one of our best clients: not a month went by
but he passed a nine-day period under our roof. We soon gave
him Bianchi's other niece; she was more delicately constituted
than her sister, however, and expired on the seventh day.

Concurrently with all this Durand was enjoying a great
success with her cabinet of marvels. So extensively had she informed
herself touching all the intrigues in town that in a very short space
she was in a position to tell everybody his fortune. She learned
that Senator Contarini, father of the most gloriously beautiful
young daughter, was head over heels in love with her; having
found that out, she went to see him.

"Rouse in your charming Rosina the desire to hear what the
stars portend for her," said Durand; "mention my house; I shall

hide you there, and guarantee you the fullest enjoyment of her in the course of the various ceremonies I shall prescribe that she undergo in order to discover her destiny." The Senator, transported, promises Durand everything her heart desires if only she succeeds. The modest sorceress inquires to know the father's passions; and as in his reply he alluded to all sorts of requirements, she asked him for three thousand sequins. Contarini was a wealthy man; he paid half the sum in advance; and the rendezvous was made for two days hence.

Very eager to have her future foretold, Rosina writes to Durand, requesting an audience, and in her answer the latter proposes the same day she and the Senator have already agreed upon. Rosina arrives, sends her duenna home; and I do declare that when that superb child was rid of the thin veils enveloping her, it was as though we were beholding a sunrise. Figure to yourself that most perfect thing heaven can make, and you will still have but an imperfect idea of the fascinating girl whom I shall, though it be in vain, endeavor to describe to you.

Rosina, sixteen years of age, tall and shaped like one of the Graces, belonged to the line of those virgins immortalized by the brush of the painter Albani. Her chestnut tresses fell in gently curling waves upon her alabaster breast; her large blue eyes inspired at once love and desire; and to those lips of freshest pink would be drawn anyone who sought the spirit of the divinity of whom Rosina was the pure embodiment. No skin was ever so fair; no breasts were ever so round; no thighs were ever so plump; never was there a cunt so strait, so warm, so dainty and sweet; and buttocks! ah, what living being could have resisted that wondrous ass? To see it was to be overpowered; I for my part could not withstand the temptation to caress it. She must, we advised that adorable child, to obtain the predictions she was so eager to know, cooperate in the consultation; the auguries supposed certain sacrifices.

"You shall be whipped, my angel," Durand notified her; "submitted, what is more, to a personage who will take his pleasure with you in every imaginable manner."

"Heaven! If ever my father were to—"

"He is severe, your father?"

1134 ❧ THE MARQUIS DE SADE

"Jealous of me as of a mistress."

"So be it; but never shall he hear a word of what is about to come to pass: 'tis the Supreme Being who is going to visit you, dear girl, and the breaches sustained through your intercourse with him will be mended in the most magical way. This ceremony, I must add, is indispensable; unless you submit to it, farewell all hope of learning what you wish to know."

And, my friends, be certain that I was mightily amused by the struggle I now saw being waged between modesty and curiosity. Rosina was of two minds; repelled by the prescribed tests, seduced by the prospect of instruction, she was at a loss what to do or what to say; and had it not been for the arrival of her father, we might well have spent the rest of the day enjoying her perplexity. But as the Senator was there, the shilly-shallying had to be brought to an end; Rosina finally decided. While Durand remained with her, I went and joined her father.

Powerful though Contarini's feelings for his daughter assuredly were, in a soul like his libertinage had an ascendancy over sentiment, and the Senator found himself capable of a few teasing gestures which were enough to persuade me that he would not take it ill were I to display my charms to his eyes. I complied; and from his caresses I soon reached conclusions touching his tastes. The lewd rascal was passionately fond of the behind, and he was busy paying court to mine when we heard a tapping on the other side of the partition.

"That is the signal, Excellency, get ready; the body of your charming daughter is about to be delivered to you."

A panel slides open and the lower five-sixths of the beautiful Rosina, that is, everything of her from toe to chin, arrives naked before us and at the disposition of the incestuous Senator.

"Ah, fuck!" he cries, feasting his eyes upon the treasure, "frig me, Juliette, frig me, I am going to die from pleasure examining such a wealth of charms."

I frig; the libertine explores. For a moment, everything before him appears to warrant his desiring; aye, he has kisses to bestow upon the cunt itself; but soon he is conquered by the ass. There is no imagining the ardor with which he embraces that part.

"Frig from underneath," he said to me, "while I lick the hole of this incomparable posterior."

His self-possession soon gone, his iron-hard prick lifts toward that vent, he embuggers. Rosina, little accustomed to such attacks, utters ringing screams; that libertine's impetuosity is lessened not one whit, he pushes, he presses, he strikes bottom. The rake gropes for my buttocks; he would have my mouth glue itself to his, he would that with one of my hands I favor his assaults, that with the other I tickle his anus.

"Libertine," I ask, obeying his instructions, "is your intention then to confine yourself to that? are you not going to aim a thrust into this pretty little bush?"

"No," the loyal sodomite replies, "no, I am not the man for such an undertaking: it's fifteen years since I last touched that forbidden fruit, my abhorrence of it is of fifteen years' standing; however, I plan to whip."

So saying, he withdraws, seizes the withes I hand him, and falls to thrashing his daughter with such violence that the blood we needed for the operation was soon flowing down her thighs.

"You find me cruel, my child," Contarini said to me as he smote away, "but one's passions are what they are; the more they are refined, the more dreadful are their excesses."

At that point, the desire to augment the pretty little wretch's sufferings introduced abominable ideas into my head.

"You doubtless have designs regarding the future of your daughter," I said.

"Yes; they are to fuck her soundly, to flog her cruelly, to make this festival last three months, then to force her to take the veil." And the loveliest skin in the world was being covered with stripes during this dialogue.

"In truth, Signor, I very much wonder whether that is the wisest course. However, once you have had your fill of her, the means for disposing of her will be supplied to you here, you will avoid having to pay her dowry to a convent."

"What is this you are saying, Juliette?"

"Ah, there are a thousand different means to that end. . . . What! Is it possible? The idea of a venereal murder has never defiled your imagination?"

"A murder? Why, yes . . . once or twice . . . but, bless me, murder my daughter?" And I saw the Senator's prick twitch, its tip rise, rubicund and wrathful: proof positive that the mere allusion to the project was having an inflammatory effect upon his senses.

"Juliette," he went on, fervently kissing the marks left by his cruelty, "admit that it would be a horrible crime . . . an appalling act before which all Nature would shudder. . . ."

"Perhaps; but you will enjoy it."

Then, to rouse the lecher to the final pitch of excitement, I reach for a silken cord, tug it. The light dims in the chamber where we are; I rap upon the partition; and the next moment, hidden machinery sets into motion and we have the entirety of Rosina before us.

"Take a firm grip upon yourself," I whisper to Contarini, "she is there, all of her. Proceed; but not a word from you."

The libertine lands upon his daughter, presses ecstatic kisses to her mouth, to her breasts, re-embuggers her, discharges.

"Good lord! See what you have done," I say; "I surrender her to you, and you throw your opportunity away. Let's send her back, I shall do what I can to restore you to life while Durand draws up her horoscope."

I signaled again, the child was borne away; the panel slid shut, and in another room the resourceful Durand sold her to another buyer. Our trade included three or four regular clients exclusively interested in prostitutions of this sort, and we took care to provide them with what seemed likeliest to suit their needs.

I moved heaven and earth to rekindle a spark in our Senator; all my efforts came to nought. Contarini was one of those limited individuals unable to carry out criminal projects except in the throes of passion; my suggestion had been too strong for him, and now he asked to have his daughter back. I went at once to notify Durand; but she, in view of the piles of gold the delicious little thing was certain to earn, simply would not hear of parting with Rosina. Won over to her opinion, I quickly struck upon the solution that would satisfy all concerned.

"Excellency!" said I, rushing into the room where the Senator was waiting, "Excellency!" said I, tears streaming from my eyes, "your unhappy daughter. . . . Alas, terrified by the predictions contained in her horoscope, she has just leapt from a window; she is no more, Excellency, she is dead."

Deeply grieved, Contarini followed me into my companion's apartment; he was shown a disfigured body which in point of age and figure looked to be that of his daughter; and that was what the simpleton believed. He thought for a moment to threaten us with prosecution, but, quickly sobered when reminded of the likelihood of well-founded countercharges, he fell silent and went out weeping like a fool, leaving us in possession of his cherished and adorable child, who, promptly seduced by us, soon turned into one of our most accomplished whores.

Not long afterward a noble Venetian came to us to buy poison for a woman he had doted upon and whom he had married two years previously. The poor fellow was convinced she had cuckolded him. He was mistaken; his wife was a model of good behavior and restraint. I alone was responsible for his suspicions, I had manufactured them from sheer spite. That woman displeased me; I decided to organize her downfall, I succeeded. She was envenomed by her aristocratic husband; you may imagine how I rejoiced at the deed.

A little while later we had a request from a son who was eager to take the straight way with his father. Here, the question was one of an inheritance and of an impatient young man who was tired of waiting; for two thousand sequins we sold him the secret thanks to which he was his own master the next morning.

You will, I know, render me the justice of believing that I was never so much engrossed by this whirl of activity as to neglect myself; rich enough to devote an enormous outlay to my pleasures, and to surrender my body to others through wantonness or sordidness alone, I bathed, carefree, in an ocean of horrors and impudicities. My tastes for theft and murder were given generous expression throughout; and once my perfidious imagination had conjectured a victim's doom, seldom was there more than the briefest interval between the intention and the deed.

Such was the high level upon which I was pursuing my moral and physical disorders when one day from Zeno, Chancellor of the Republic, I received an invitation to come, along with my two friends, to his house lying by the Brenta Canal. We spent an entire

day there, rioting amidst everything of the most piquant that
lewdness can devise. Wearied after so much voluptuous revelry,
we were enjoying a delicious supper when an eighteen-year-old girl,
the loveliest of creatures, urgently requested an interview with
Zeno.

"What! Here, in this place, consecrated to my pleasures, and
at this hour?"

"Your Grace," said the servant, "she pushed past the gate-
keeper, past the footman, she is in despair, she has rushed hither
from Venice, she says that the matter is vital, that there is not an
instant to lose."

"Have her enter," said the Chancellor. "Oh, Juliette," he
went on, lowering his voice, "lest I am greatly mistaken, I believe
an occasion is at hand to put my principles into practice."

The door opens, and the most beautiful girl I have ever seen
falls weeping at the magistrate's knees.

"My Lord!" cries the lovely one in distress, "my father's
life is at stake. Arrested yesterday on charges of conspiracy, he
whose brain has never entertained a seditious thought, he, absolutely innocent, goes to the scaffold tomorrow. To save him there is
nobody but you; I beg you to intervene. If blood must flow, oh, my
Lord, let it be mine rather than his, let me die in my father's stead."

"Amiable child," said Zeno, lifting the girl up and directing
her to take a chair at his side, "are you not Virginia, the nobleman
Grimani's daughter?"

"I am."

"Signorina, I am acquainted with this affair; and however
you may interpret it, I must assure you that your father is exceedingly guilty of treasonable plotting."

"No, my Lord."

"Guilty, I repeat. Be that as it may, all is not yet lost. . . .
Juliette, come with me. I shall be yours in an instant, Virginia; I
am going to prepare the document needed to save your father."

"Blessings be upon Your Grace!"

"Be not overhasty with expressions of gratitude, my dear;
this pardon has yet to be granted."

"What?"

"You shall be apprised of everything, Signorina, everything shall soon be in your hands; and you will be able to blame no one but yourself if you do not obtain what you ask."

We remove into a chamber nearby.

"There," said Zeno, "is a creature who arouses me to an uncommon degree; Venice boasts of no more beautiful girl; I must have her, have her at any price. Save her father, however, that I cannot do, and even if I could, I am convinced, Juliette, that I would not. I am going to write two letters; in one, I shall request his pardon; his prompt execution in the other. And I shall see to it that she carries the second back with her, although supposing it is the first. Persuaded that in her hands she has the instrument to rescue her father, Virginia will grant me what I ask of her. But when she discovers that I have deceived her . . . ah, Juliette, there's the rub."

"Is it necessary to send her back at all?"

"Grimani's daughter . . . Venice, the entire Republic—"

"She must be denounced."

"But I cannot both accuse her and enjoy her. Once she stood before a court, why, it would all come out: it would be my ruin."

"Zeno, your accusations are secret, your tribunals obscure, your executions nocturnal: promise this girl that you are pardoning her father; send her off, as you said you meant to do, with the note that will put the noose around his neck; accuse her immediately afterward: I assure you that my women and I will act as your witnesses. These little horrors are my depraved heart's delights; certify that this girl came here with no design other than to seduce you, we will bear out your contention; dismiss as calumnies, recriminations, whatever she invents for her defense; fee well the lawyer who shall be given her for the sake of form; let the preliminary hearings be conducted promptly and perfectly in camera; and inside twenty-four hours, if that is what you want, she will be out of the way."

"You are right," said he. "As for the letters, there they are. Oh, Juliette, I foresee an enjoyable experience. What a charming girl you are!"

He returned to the company. "Signorina," said Zeno, "I believe this should be sufficient: read this paper. However," he went on, "such favors, as I presume you realize, are not granted for nothing."

"Oh, good my Lord, all we have is yours for the asking, I am under instructions from my family to accede to whatever your requests may be."

"They are not for money," said the Chancellor, "what I demand is more precious: your charms, Virginia, must be abandoned to me. I want no other reward, but I shall not forego that one: and this letter shall not leave my hands until I have obtained what I ask for."

"Great God, what a sacrifice! O thou whom I love," said she, drawing from her bosom a locket containing the portrait of her intended, "why must I be placed between infidelity and infamy! Your Grace, would it not be a noble thing, to content yourself with the happiness of saving an innocent man's life—"

"Impossible. And you have not an eternity to make up your mind; I give you one minute. Your father's crimes are such that it were better for you to take rapid advantage of my charity."

And, leaving her to meditate her decision, Zeno moved into a neighboring boudoir with Lila to prepare himself for the infamies that were animating him. I nodded to Rosalba, whose powers of penetration were showing new signs of development with every passing day; and, height of wickedness, we, Rosalba and I, fell to preaching to the girl.

"Ah, beware, Signorina," Rosalba warned her, drawing her a little to one side and employing a confiding tone, "do not trust that libertine; he is capable of anything who is capable of demanding your honor in exchange for your father's life. Once he has had his way with you he will play you false; and who is to say whether, to cover up his crime, the monster will not immolate you upon the still-palpitating remains of the worthy author of your existence? But, supposing that he does abide by his word, how will your fiancé view this sacrifice? It is of the species which love is little inclined to overlook, and you must consider it a certainty that he will never pardon you; I tell you, beware of all the snares being set for you. You are undone if you weaken. . . ."

At this point I address Virginia in my turn, pretending not to have heard the drift of Rosalba's speech to her.

"Signorina," say I, "only too well do I know that at your age nice scruples and fine feelings are the gods to which one fancies it one's duty to devote oneself. This stubborn constancy you maintain toward your lover, ought it, I ask you, to outweigh all the filial sentiments owing to your father? Zeno, the most upright of men, is incapable of deceit; remember, besides, that it is not your heart he solicits, but merely your body. Ceding it to him, you will remain no less pure in your lover's eyes.

"Ah, believe me, lovely Virginia, in the situation where circumstances place you, it would be sinful to refuse. Will you coolly watch your father walk to his death when an instant's complacency on your part could save him? And, Virginia, there is this too: are you sure that the fidelity to which you would sacrifice everything is being as religiously observed by your lover as by you? and are you yet unfamiliar with the way of all flesh? Were it to happen, now, that the man you love had less than your share of virtue, think of how bitterly you would repent having immolated your father to an unrequited sentiment! No, Signorina, you cannot disdain the proposal that has been made to you, you cannot, I repeat, without guilt; the modesty you are going to set aside is a virtue created by convention, whereas the filial piety you would outrage by not yielding, that, my dear, is Nature's true sentiment, the authentic and priceless sentiment you cannot stifle without perishing from grief."

Fancy, if you will, my friends, the anguished perplexity that such words were able to produce in this timorous and sorely beset soul; so upset was she in her mind that her moral forces were near to deserting her. Zeno's return occurred at that point, and he arrived in such a state of indecency that there could be no further doubt, his unhappy victim was lost. The rascal had a towering erection, and Lila, naked, led him in by the end of his prick.

"Well, has she reached her decision?" he stammered.

"Yes, my Lord," I replied, "yes, indeed, this young lady is too reasonable not to feel that she owes much more to her father than to her alleged virtue, and she is prepared to lay it by here and now."

"No, no," cried the poor girl, tears springing to her eyes, "I would rather die. . . ."

But, seizing her without further ado, we, my women and I, stripped off her clothes and in two minutes, despite her struggles, her nudity stood revealed to the Chancellor's impure gaze.

Dear God! what forms! what skin! what rosy freshness! Not Flora herself could have matched those charms. Zeno admired them avidly, and each of his multitude of lewd kisses seemed to coincide with the discovery of a new wonder. We offered the ass to him: great heaven! what allurements, what firmness, what rotundity! and when we pried it open, when to Zeno's eyes we exposed the cunning little aperture, object of his desires, we thought him about to expire of pleasure as he fucked it with his tongue.

"Let us see how she looks when aroused," said the Chancellor; "Juliette, and you, Rosalba, tickle the sensitive parts of her body; watching you at work, I am going to have myself worked upon by Lila, and as you progressively inflame this damsel, my mouth, straying over her charms, will verify the glow of pleasure in them."

I was not sorry to be entrusted with this chore, for, ever since my first glimpse of that celestial creature, I had been fairly dying to frig her. We attacked so skillfully, my companion and I, that lust soon began to gleam in Virginia's beautiful eyes; and the pretty rascal, trembling ecstatically in our arms, summons Zeno's prick to the destruction of her maidenhead. Lila brings the Chancellor's engine up to the gate; the libertine thrusts; as he is lightly weaponed, and as Virginia has been exhaling whey in abundance and now discharges afresh, all difficulties vanish, there he is, master of the fort; I alone am holding the victim, frigging her at the same time; as for Lila, crouching atop Virginia, she presents her handsome posterior to the lecher's kisses; and Rosalba flogs him.

He was rushing toward the crisis when I checked him, a hairsbreadth short of it.

"You cannot afford a thoughtless expenditure of munitions," I reminded him, "do not forget that another stronghold awaits storming."

"True," he conceded, retreating.

And, in a flash, to his lewd covetings we swung around the most divine ass Nature had fashioned since the creation of Ganymede's. Zeno contemplated it.

"Buggerblast me!" said he. "What a treasure mine eyes do behold!" But rather than amuse himself bestowing further praise, the scoundrel, profiting from the help we provided him, soon forced the barriers. Virginia, through the position I had made her assume, lay upon my face and I sucked her cunt while the Chancellor sodomized her; my friends were frigging, handling, ministering to Zeno. Everything enfolded him in pleasure, everything hastened the escape of the fuck which he soon shot to the depths of the world's most beautiful ass, despite the outcries, the writhings of the victim, who had not endured this assault as patiently as the other.

"What a fucking I have had," said he as he drew forth his member. "Oh, Juliette, save only for yours, no ass on earth can produce such a sensation; I am still in its grip—"

"Come, my friend, let us dispatch that letter."

"For a certainty," the monster replied to me, "I have just acquired, from fucking this girl, all sorts of reasons to condemn her father. However," he added in a subdued voice, "however, Juliette, I do not intend to limit myself to that piece of mischief."

Then lower:

"I shall not stop there, Juliette. I would like my wickedness to dazzle you, my dear, and for the means necessary to further fuckery I count upon the episode about to follow."

"Do you mean to allow its object to remain alive for long?"

"Why," said Zeno, "I believe that if I were to add a little postscript to the letter, the authorities would come here to my palace to arrest her; and as between now and then I shall have achieved a fresh erection, perhaps I shall be in her ass at the moment they arrive to take her away to death."

"You are to be congratulated upon the idea," I say to Zeno, "act upon it quickly."

The appropriate lines are annexed to the missive, the courier departs for the city, and we return to our lewd play. From the manner in which I saw Zeno caressing Virginia's buttocks it was easy to tell that he was inwardly scheming against that splendid behind. There is no imagining the atrocities an ass inspires, when one has enjoyed it thoroughly.

"Ah ha! you want to whip it, do you? You want to tear that magnificent ass to shreds, my friend; and you hesitate to do so? To work, Lord Chancellor," I say, "satisfy yourself; in my pocket I have a lotion which, applied to the stripes, will efface all sign of them in three minutes. And if, as proof of what she has suffered, the baggage wishes to show the marks, the evidence will contradict her, and everything else she has to say will that much more surely have the sound of calumny."

"Juliette," Zeno exclaimed, "you are delightful, I shall never cease to proclaim your merits."

Thereupon, listening now to nothing but the voice of his passion, the villain has us hold Virginia and, swearing like one of the damned, with barely one hundred strokes he transforms a peerless behind into mincemeat. He starts in upon the second hundred, and I take his prick into my mouth; my two women flog him while he flogs Virginia; and soon his prick begins to lift, and when 'tis up, and hard, he hurls himself like a madman upon the girl, sodomizes her, and discharges shrieking.

"Oh, Juliette!" he declares once he has finished, "what a shame I cannot myself immolate this slut, what pleasure it would give me to kill her! With her profound sensitivity she would be responsive to every torture we could invent, the one more divine than the other. Think, to flay that bosom! to burn those buttocks! Juliette, Juliette! I would like to roast her heart on her belly, then eat it upon her face."

When I drew forth my lotion and prepared to anoint Virginia's wounds, Zeno stayed my hand. "No," the monster said to me, "leave my marks upon her, I want her to wear them to the scaffold, I want her to have the possibility of exhibiting them, I want her to dare not do so; the idea strikes me as droll. . . ." And with horrid remarks and cruel jibes we slew and slew again all hope in the poor girl, sporting with her thus till the *sbirri* were there.

For Zeno's fatal letters had succeeded but too well; Grimani's daughter was placed under arrest.

"Just Heaven!" the wretch cried upon perceiving the effects

of the Chancellor's traitorous maneuvers; "you deceived me, villain, but my judges will hear me and I shall be revenged for your horrors."

"Do your duty, gentlemen," the phlegmatic Zeno said to the officers, seeming to ignore the imprecations being addressed to him, "take this girl away; grief appears to have addled her brain.

"Has action been taken," the monster went on to ask, "upon my recommendations that the culprits be put promptly to death?"

"Your Worship," said one of the policemen, drawing forth two bloody objects from underneath his cloak, "here is how your orders were executed."

And Virginia sinks to the floor in a swoon, having recognized the severed heads of her father and her beloved.

Zeno turned to me with a smile. "Quite a scene, is it not?" he whispered. "It is restiffening my prick, I will have you note. Let us obtain privacy so that we can devote ourselves to further horrors."

"By all means. Keep the heads, Sire, and send those myrmidons away."

"Very good, gentlemen," said the Chancellor, "that will do: Virginia will be in a Venetian dungeon within two hours. Leave these relics here, and return to your other duties."

"One moment," I murmured to Zeno, "the fellow who brought the heads, would he be the trusty who performed the decapitations?"

"Yes."

"If that be so, then there is a refinement to outrage we can ill afford to neglect. Unhandsome as he is, and his hands still steeped in gore, the man who just beheaded the girl's father and her lover must now fuck her, so it would seem to me."

"Decidedly," said Zeno; "there are delicious things to be done in life, one must be careful to omit none of them."

One of the *sbirri* leaves, Zeno encloscts himself with the other, with Virginia, with the two heads, with the three women, and with me. We give our attentions to the victim, mindful to place the heads before her so that, upon opening her eyes, they be the first objects she sees. To the headsman is appointed the task of summoning the girl back to life, and upon recovering her senses, they are the grisly vestiges of her dear ones she beholds, 'tis in the arms of her executioner she finds herself. I was frigging that ill-favored man while he was ministering to Virginia.

"Fuck this attractive girl," the Chancellor said to him.

"Your Grace!"

" 'Tis an order; you assassinated the father, continue at present, fuck the daughter; you killed the lover, I want you to fuck the mistress now."

Smitten by these words as though by a thunderbolt, Virginia sinks back again upon my breast, nearly unconscious.

"Softly, softly," I say to Zeno, "since, unfortunately, this is to be your last discharge, it ought at least to be complete, and we should use every means at our disposal to make it brilliant."

Put in charge of affairs, herein as follows was the voluptuous grouping I adopted. The *sbirro* slides underneath Virginia, encunts her, opens and presents the sublime creature's buttocks to Zeno, who embuggers her; one in each hand, Virginia holds the severed heads in place upon the executioner's chest, I give him my cunt to suck, turning my behind toward Virginia; Zeno frigs, to right and to left, my two friends' asses; a charwoman flogs him. Before that onslaught of delightful sensations, the lewd Chancellor could not be expected to hold out forever; by and by, he discharges; we all do the same; Virginia is borne out inert from this scene of horrors.

We leave. The Chancellor in person conveys his victim to the prisons of the Palace of Justice; and twenty-four hours later, thanks to our depositions, Virginia's sentence is handed down. That was the moment we were waiting for. By dint of gold and seductions, Zeno arranges to have another girl take her place at the block; and Virginia returns into our clutches. We ourselves act the part of her executioners, a substitution whence she derives no benefit. God! what a scene it was! the thought of it had me seeping for a week afterward; I can recall few infamies which wrought upon me as that one did.

Women, in the meantime, continued to arrive in droves at our house; some to have their fortunes told, the others, in security and secret, to wallow in the rarest and most extreme forms of libertine misconduct. Owing to measures we had taken, we were in a position to furnish our female clientele with boys and girls, and that under conditions of inviolable clandestinity. We also provided everything needed by youthful couples who, embarrassed by the obstructions created by parents, were grateful to take shelter with us. Other matches were made in obscurely lit apartments, where the men were unable to recognize the women we supplied to them. To how many fathers did we thus contrive to give their daughters; to how many brothers, their sisters; to how many priests, their penitents!

There came to me one day two women, of twenty and twenty-five, both charming, and who, having both taken a fancy to me, besought me to direct their games and in them to play a third. We all three had supper together; their mania consisted in sucking my mouth and my cunt. They proceeded by rapid shifts, in such a way that she who had just cunt-tongued me now tongued my mouth, and she who had been kissing my mouth moved instantly to my cunt. During this luxurious to-and-fro my role was to frig them simultaneously and uninterruptedly, one with either hand, and after that, fitted with a dildo, to fuck them in turn; while she who was not being fucked was having herself tongued by her who was; exceedingly lubricious they were, that pair. There is no imagining the things they invented, the things they said in the course of their lewd antics. One of them, I recollect, was so carried away that she was moved to go and have herself fucked by the inmates of a hospital full of syphilitics.

Welcome, you who will now explain to me the workings of the imagination in persons of my sex; for my part, it is beyond me. In general, those two libertines were as lively, as clever, as amiable as they come: my own belief is that Nature is infinitely more lavish in her favors to tribades than to other women, and that just as she accords them a richer, more flexible imagination, so she has provided them with superior means for experiencing pleasure and bestowing delight.[5]

Another adventure which you will insist upon hearing was the

---

[5] These charming creatures, of whom fools are wont to have a low opinion, bring to society the same qualities they demonstrate in pleasure: they are always more original, more intelligent, more agreeable than others; almost all of them have graces, talents, imagination: why therefore hold against them a failing for which only Nature is responsible? Clumsy, dull-witted devotees of ordinary pleasures, you censure them only because they reject your advances; but if one pauses to analyze the women who appreciate you, they will always be found to be almost as stupid as yourselves.

extraordinary outing I made in the company of four Venetian ladies.

They waited for a stormy day, then arrived to fetch me in a gondola at a moment when flashes of lightning were flickering across the sky. We headed a certain distance out to sea; the storm broke; claps of thunder filled the air.

"This is the instant, come," said the rascals, "let us frig one another; and let it be with streams of sperm we hurl our defiance at the tempest."

And the sluts spring upon me like a quartet of Messalinas. Bless me, I reply in kind: too sensitive to pleasure to be chilled by such everyday natural phenomena, I join them in blaspheming the chimerical God who, it is said, produces them. Meanwhile, the thunder rumbles, lightning leaps in all directions. Caught in the rising swell, our gondola is tossed about like a cork; and we swear, we discharge, we brave alarmed Nature, risen in wrath against all existing things, and respectful of our pleasures alone.

Another very pretty woman sent to request me to come to lunch at her palace. I was obliged, while she surveyed the proceedings, to pollute her fifteen-year-old son; after that, we frigged each other in his presence. She had her daughter called down, who was one year younger. She ordered me to excite that maiden, while she had her son embugger her; next, she herself held her daughter before the youth's sodomite attacks. While that was going forward, I was cunt-sucking the daughter and the mother was exciting, lingually, the asshole of the young lady's fucker. Never had I met with a more cold-bloodedly libertine nor more composed intelligence. The moment she learned that we traded in poisons, she purchased a complete store of them. I asked her whether she planned to employ any with the pretty objects we had lately enjoyed.

"Why not?" she answered. "When I indulge in these infamies, I never restrict their scope."

"Delicious creature," I responded, kissing her upon the mouth, "the more restraints one thrusts aside in these cases, the more one discharges."

"Then I shall discharge plentifully," she observed, "for barriers are things I ignore."

Six months later she was husbandless, fatherless, motherless, without children.

A member of the Council of Ten sent for me, needing a woman to serve his son's pleasures while he himself embuggered that son.

Another, belonging to the same Chamber, required that I frig myself with his sister, who was old and ugly. He embuggered that sister; after which, he did the same to me; then I received one hundred lashes from that sister's hand.

In brief, there was no species of venereous activity, of debauchery, of infamy to which Durand and I did not dedicate ourselves from morn to night; and not a day passed but our fourfold trade of whore, procuress, fortune-teller, and poisoner brought in a thousand sequins, and often much more.

Supported, applauded, sought after by all the most amiable libertines, male and female, in the city of Venice, we were, without the slightest doubt, leading the most delightful and the most lucrative of lives when a dreadful reversal disrupted our partnership, deprived me of my beloved Durand, and caused me the loss, in the space of a day, of all the sums I had brought to Venice for investment, and all those I had earned there.

In the punishment it meted out to Durand, fate expressed an intolerance of the same weakness for which I myself had been made to pay many years before. My fault, leading to my enforced departure from Paris, had been a reluctance to carry crime to its ultimate degree. The same misfortune befell Durand; and such cruel lessons could only reinforce her conviction, and mine, that the most dangerous course, when you are in crime's train, is to face about in a virtuous direction, or to lack the boldness necessary to pass the final frontiers; for my friend's failure was indeed one of courage rather than of will; and if the unhappy creature suffered defeat, 'twas not through default of ambition, but through that of nerve.

The three State Inquisitors had, one morning, summoned Durand before them; and after having sworn her to absolute secrecy, they divulged their need of her destructive assistance for the purpose of annihilating a numerous faction which had formed inside the city.

"Unfortunately, affairs have got beyond the point," they advised her, "where legal means can be employed; poison is the only one remaining to us. You have, as you know, benefited from our indulgence during the three years you have been in Venice, we have allowed you to enjoy the fruits of your crimes in perfect tranquillity; today, as token of your gratitude, we expect you to lend yourself in an advisory capacity or as an executant to crimes similar to those which our duty might otherwise have required us to punish most severely. Would you be able to disseminate the plague through a town and at the same time preserve from its ravages such persons as will be indicated to you?"

"No," said Durand, although she did in fact possess both the required secrets; she possessed them, but she was afraid.

"Very well," said the magistrates. A door was opened and she was dismissed.

And what added to her fright was the fact that they had not even bothered to warn her to keep silent.

She returned straight to the house. "We are lost," she told me the moment she entered. Thereupon she related everything that had just taken place. My first thought was to send her back at once to see the Inquisitors.

"It would change nothing," she replied. "Carrying out the work, I would lose my life just the same; they would do away with me secretly. No, the only thing for me to do is leave you this very minute; for if they discover or suspect that we have seen each other, you shall be compromised."

The poor thing made ready to go. "Farewell, Juliette," said she, "adieu. We may perhaps never meet again."

Not two hours after my friend had departed officers appeared at my door with a warrant from the Republic. I am escorted to the Palace; I am led, deeply disturbed, to a remote, very isolated room in one of the uppermost stories. My guards form close ranks about me. A wide black taffeta curtain divided the room. Two Inquisitors appear; the police leave.

"Stand up," one of the Inquisitors says to me, "and give clear and precise answer. Have you known a woman named Durand?"

"Yes."

"Have you committed crimes jointly with her?"

"No."

"Did she in your hearing ever speak ill of the government of Venice?"

"Never."

The other judge now spoke up, his voice was grave. "Juliette, your replies are calculated to deceive; you tell us less than we already know; you are guilty." He paused for a moment, then drew the black curtain aside. Behind it, hanging from the ceiling, was the body of a woman at which I no sooner looked than I averted my gaze in horror. "There is your accomplice; and that is the manner in which the Republic punishes cheats and poisoners. Get you gone from its territories inside twenty-four hours, else you will meet with the same fate tomorrow."

My head swam, I lost consciousness.

When I returned to my senses I was in the hands of an unknown woman and still surrounded by police officers. I was dragged out of that room.

"Now go home," the chief of the *sbirri* advised me, "comply scrupulously, punctually, with the orders of the Republic. Refrain from obstructing the task of the bailiff who will confiscate your holdings and chattels, that is to say, the funds you have in Venetian banks, your household furniture, and your personal jewelry. Leave with the rest, otherwise you die if sunrise finds you still in the city."

"I shall obey, good sir," I replied, "I shall obey, I have no wish to remain any longer in a town where they punish people for having declined to do evil."

"Silence, Madame, silence; were anyone else to hear such remarks, you would not leave this palace alive."

"My thanks to you, my good man," I said to that turnkey, dropping one hundred sequins in his palm, "I understand your advice and I appreciate it; when tomorrow comes I shall be far away from your melancholy swamplands and lagoons."

My packing was accomplished in no time. Lila and Rosalba appeared to wish to stay in Venice, where they were earning a comfortable living; I left them there; with me I took only one woman, who had been at my side ever since my marriage and of whom I have not spoken hitherto because she never played any role in my adventures. Having permission to keep my pocketbook and my cash, I set out with a little more than eight hundred thousand francs; everything else was seized by the Republic; but still intact were my Roman investments, from which I had dividends of five million a year, and that helped cheer me up. That night I reached Padua; less than a week later, Lyon, where I halted for a few days' rest. During my northward journey I had not once paused to dally, and that little fast had brought on a violent need for fucking; to satisfy it, I betook myself most naturally to the house of a celebrated bawd whose address I had been given, and who in the course of the fortnight I spent with her, furnished me with everything I could possibly wish for in the one and the other sex.

Considering no risk entailed in a return to Paris, since the Minister from whom I had fled was no longer among the living, I decided to proceed thither once I received a reply from Noirceuil, to whom I penned a letter describing my intended move. Delighted at the prospect of seeing me again, that stout and cherished friend assured me that it was with the greatest pleasure he looked forward to a sight of me and of the progress his outstanding pupil had made. I dispatched another letter to Abbé Chabert, asking him to bring my daughter to Paris, and I named the hotel at which I planned to stop. We all converged there at almost the same moment. Marianne was entering her seventh year. No child could have been prettier than she; but Nature was mute in me, libertinage had extinguished its voice. Such then are its effects; taking a soul in its tyrant's grip, it is loath, so it would seem, to allow room there to any sentiment other than those it inspires, and if in its despite some other contrives to penetrate, it is able to corrupt it at once and turn it to its advantage. I am obliged to say that in embracing Marianne I felt absolutely nothing stir in me but the pulsations of lubricity.

"There's a pretty subject for educating," I murmured to Chabert; "oh! I am eager to preserve this creature from the errors that drove her mother from Paris, and from those that brought about the downfall of Durand in Venice. I shall make her so aware of the necessity for crime that she will never stray out of its path, and if ever virtue strives to worm its way into her heart, I want it to discover vice so firmly entrenched there as to have not even the chance to launch an attack."

Chabert, who had presided over Marianne's upbringing, was pleased to have me admire all her little talents; she played the piano, she danced charmingly, drew prettily . . . spoke Italian, etc.

"And the animal temperament?" I asked the Abbé.

"Animal enough, I believe," Chabert replied, "and if we do not watch our step, the little minx will be frigging herself fairly soon."

"Why, I shall aid her," said I, "I shall be overjoyed to gather the first indications of her nubility."

"Wait just a bit," the Abbé advised me, "else you may endanger her health."

This consideration, however, affected me barely at all. The Abbé, who had come to Paris several times during my absence, informed me of the most recent developments and took charge of the transfer of my funds from Rome. I soon acquired two fine town houses, as well as the country estate you are familiar with.

The day after arriving I went to find Noirceuil; he welcomed me with every sign of happiness, and declared that in his opinion I was more beautiful than ever. Having continued to profit from the Minister's favor up until the time of his death, Noirceuil, while I had been away, had tripled his fortune, and all Paris looked upon him as one of the foremost men of the day.

"Juliette," he assured me, "be certain that I shall never take a step upward without enabling you to rise alongside me; you are indispensable to my existence; I like committing crimes with nobody but you, and delicious excesses await us if we succeed in obtaining a still greater amount of influence than the very considerable amount of it I enjoy already: it shall therefore be necessary for us to combine our efforts in order to exploit this vein."

After that he invited me to recount my adventures; and when I came to the five hundred thousand francs I had promised to turn over to Fontange de Donis, being brought up in a convent at Chaillot, and who must then have been seventeen years old, he urged that we amuse ourselves with the girl and pocket the half-million. His arguments touching this matter were so compelling that I cannot resist repeating them to you; I should interject that I deliberately adopted a hesitating attitude, which incited him to reason more forcefully and at greater length than he might otherwise have done. Here then is how he combated my simulated objections, one evening when we were supping together in his little house at Barrière-Blanche.

"When one has two reasons for doing a thing, Juliette," said he, "and none for not doing it, I confess to you that I am inclined to disbelieve my ears when I hear the question raised of whether it should be done. When one is thirty years old, when one has intelligence, no prejudices, no more religion, no more God, no remorse, the most thorough habit of crime, much to gain from doing that thing, I confess to you, once again, that it strikes me as passing strange to hear it asked whether that thing is to be done or not. Once one has ready to hand everything required to operate, once one has already accomplished greater and more difficult things by far, once one has found pleasure in doing them, once one has been thrilled by that pleasure, I frankly confess to you, when over and above the same dose of pleasure the thing offers still greater advantages, then it sounds very peculiar indeed to hear one debate, shall I succumb to the temptation? shall I not succumb to it? You merit the whip, my dear Juliette, yes, the whip, for daring to consult me upon any such futile affair as this; I therefore declare to you that if four days hence it has not been attended to, executed, done, I shall break off all dealings with you, and regard you as one of those insipid, characterless women .who spend their lives fidgeting without ever achieving anything. Are you going to allege that you are rich enough to dispense with a sum upon which the welfare of an unhappy orphan may depend? Ah, Juliette! does one ever have enough money? Granted, as spent by you, this half-million will go merely for superfluities: I ask you whether the enjoyment of these superfluities would not, from your point of view, be preferable to the vain pleasure of renouncing them for the sake of a little girl with whom you have no acquaintance, and whom, through this gift, you would furthermore be robbing of the only pleasures to which you ought to submit her.

"Let us, if you like, glance inquiringly at the existence of this little girl—for, oh yes! it is not so devoid of importance as to be undeserving of investigation. What is she to you? Nothing. Who is she? The bastard engendered by a woman with whom you had libertine traffic. Very respectable titles! But, one moment now:

what will happen if you fulfill the prescribed commission? Nobody in the wide world will congratulate you; they will simply say you performed your duty. If, on the other hand, you keep the sum, never will anybody know it was given you in trust to hold for another, and you will have the delicious pleasure of enjoying it: say, the more attractive in your eyes, is it this empty and pointless duty, or the happiness you will procure for yourself with the sum? Oh, Juliette! can you waver for an instant? I shall go farther; I myself have never seen this girl, but you, look carefully at her, tell me whether upon her brow it is not written: *'Tis for thy little pleasures Heaven placed me in this world; consider all the irresistible fatalities which have led our paths to cross, and see whether it is not a victim Nature offers thee in my person.* Yes, that is the legend writ upon her brow, you shall read it there; and whose hand but Nature's could have inscribed it? But, you may perhaps reply, 'tis to hurt the interests of a friend; I behaved badly with her, all the more reason why I should make up for it now. There are, here, two things to be proven: that you are not hurting your friend's interests, and that there is not the slightest wrong in thwarting a dead person's intentions, whatever the idiotic respect fools have always had for such things. In what way, to begin with, will you be deceiving your friend? Her pure and simple intention was that this sum go to her daughter; but no clause denies you the right to benefit from it beforehand. Thus, hold on to the money with the intention of bequeathing the sum to her when you are gone, if she outlives you, and there's your conscience at rest, if matters are such that you feel the need to placate it. What would be a violation of your friend's wishes, would be to leave this property to a third person; but when you put it profitably to use with the idea of leaving it behind you, those wishes, certainly, are perfectly carried out. Madame Donis did not say to you, keep this child out of danger's way, I recommend her life to your protection, and if by ill chance she dies, the funds will be yours, but yours only under those circumstances; no, not at all, she merely said: here are five hundred thousand francs, I am leaving them to my daughter. Well! if this child survives you, let the money become hers, and the dead mother's desires shall be satisfied.

"But there is more: were you, I must now point out, even

were you to violate this dead woman's intentions, would you not simply be declining to act like a fool? for how do you suppose one can possibly feel obliged to honor the instructions of someone who has departed out of the world? To fail an individual while he is alive is to cause him hurt, because his passive existence sustains injury and suffers from your refusal to obey him; but once this existence has ceased, it cannot feel pain anymore, no more pain can there be; the shock is nullified, there being no one there to endure it; it is therefore perfectly impossible to offend a dead person; whence it results that every heir who to his own detriment executes a will for no other purpose than to cocker a corpse is as thorough an imbecile as the man who throws his money out the window; for the latter sacrifices his money, and the former sacrifices his happiness to the satisfaction of a nonexistent being, and according to my belief, between the one piece of madness and the other there is not much to choose. The world is full of many such benign little institutions of which people are loath to get rid, but which are not for all that any the less ridiculous. The clauses contained in testaments should none of them be executed, for it is absurd to think to be bound by them; absurd to think to endow a man with the faculty of action when he is dead, 'tis contrary to every law of Nature and of good sense: and there's an end to the question. Retaining the five hundred thousand francs, you in no wise counter your departed friend's intentions; I have, I think, demonstrated it sufficiently well. Let us now examine another branch of your dilemma: if I surrender the money, I secure this little girl's well-being; whereas if I do not surrender it, I secure my own. To this the following reply may be made.

"We are able, it seems to me, to estimate the qualities in others only through the intimate relationships they have with us: someone's features correspond, fit in nicely with ours, only then do we have a motive for liking him; we are charmed by his face, his mind, his character, his attitude, all that affords us pleasure, and to frequent this object is for us a real delight. But when between two delights only one can be had, common sense dictates, there is no question about it, that the choice be for the better. Such is your position: either you must enjoy Fontange, at the expense of the five hundred thousand francs, or you must enjoy the five hundred thousand francs at the expense of Fontange. Here, there is no need for me to offer you any advice; you alone can choose which enjoyment suits you best. Compare, deliberate, and simply remember that whatever decision you come to, you will inevitably feel some misgivings, for virtue provokes remorse just as does crime. Consequently, if you abandon Fontange and keep the money, you will be saying to yourself, why did I choose this course? I regret that pretty creature. If it is the opposite course you elect, it will be, how weak I am! I would have enjoyed five hundred thousand francs, and today I am obliged to make shift without them. Observe, however, that the former of these regrets is necessarily counterbalanced by a real consolation, a physical consolation. True, you will say to yourself, I have lost Fontange, but I have enjoyment; whereas for the latter the only compensation is an isolated, transitory pleasure, an insipid sacrifice to virtue whence you will never derive merit, a small inner satisfaction, an intellectual pleasure in itself very mediocre and apt at all times to be troubled by the other regret. The one involves a privation of slight importance, while ensuring much and delightful material happiness; the other, a very substantial privation and a little mental thrill. Your way of thinking, besides, is incompatible with such pitiful little moral delights; it is not when one believes in nothing, it is not when one detests virtue and adores vice, it is not when one loves crime for its own sake or for the advantages it yields, that one can be interested for long in virtuous pleasure. Simply compare that with the charms of enjoying your five hundred thousand francs, and you will sense the difference at once. The main object, you say, is to avoid remorse. If that be so, then, immediately and unhesitatingly, commit the crime you are projecting; for I say unto you, that if you do not commit it, you shall no sooner have denied yourself the possibility of committing it than you shall be devoured by chagrin at having let go by such a splendid opportunity to appropriate this money. For you, crime is not what it is for others. You have attained the point where you find the very keenest excitement in crime, it affords you the extremest voluptuous pleasure; therefore doubt not that this pleasure, which you will, in this case, enjoy all the more, there being no further restraints to cast off; doubt not, I say, that this pleasure entirely offsets the little pangs and qualms by which anybody else might have been afflicted, undertaking this deed.

"And so I see for you, in the case of the crime done, enjoyment firstly, in the doing of it, a further enjoyment, subsequently, for having done it; and in the other case, I see nought but a decided privation, a privation whence you will suffer not once, but continually and increasingly, as with every day your caprices become more numerous, and every day demand further resources to be satisfied; and by way of compensation, I see nothing but the solitary feeling, a feeling that for everybody is temporary and dilute, that is entirely frivolous for you, of having accomplished not a good deed, but an exceedingly ordinary one. For I might perhaps excuse you for doing it were it in any sense what they call heroic, since that would at least mean some satisfaction for your pride; but no, instead I see no pleasure whatsoever accruing to you. Your deed is not great, it is not glorious; it is merely common. You accomplish no good through ensuring Fontange's enjoyment of the money, and you do yourself a very great disservice by not preventing it. But that would suppose, you say, getting rid of this little girl in order that she never find out I have robbed her. Well indeed! once you have no difficulty conceiving of murders committed for lewdness' sake, it seems to me that it should be just as easy for you to conceive of those warranted by material considerations. Both sorts are inspired by Nature; both have the same aim, and proceed from the same passions. You commit lust-murder to put yourself in a proper frame of mind for sensual pleasure; you commit all kinds of other murders for the identical purpose of satisfying a passion. Between this murder and that murder there is not a particle of difference: any difference you were to try to establish between them would be frivolous; only the motives behind them permit distinguishing one murder from the next. Now, assuredly, Juliette, it is far more legitimate to commit the misdeed prompted by a powerful interest than merely for the sake of an agreeable ejaculation. You are quite prepared to murder for mental stimulation, for your imagination's comfort, and yet you dare not do it when a fortune is at stake!

"From the foregoing two sets of alternatives emerge: first, if the transports Fontange procures you are greater than those you can expect from her property, the right course is to preserve Fontange, find a husband for her, and enjoy the milksop pleasure of having done your duty, of having done well with respect to Fontange, but very ill with respect to yourself: for, make no mistake about it, to perform a good deed is one thing, but to deprive oneself of a bad deed is something else, and it cannot be taken so lightly. There are perhaps times when some small amount of merit may attach to the performance of a kindly act; none ever exists in denying oneself the pleasure of performing a wicked one; because the former shines in the eye of the public, the latter does not. The second set of alternatives is this: if the pleasures you may expect from this supplement of fortune are to you of greater moment than Fontange's well-being, you must waste no time getting rid of her: for you cannot enjoy both these happinesses, and you must perforce sacrifice the lesser, the weaker of the two.

"Let us now determine what kind of sentiment you owe to Madame Donis. . . . None, so far as I can see. Sensual pleasure brought you together, crime separated you. Were she yet alive, you would certainly owe her nothing; dead, she is obviously entitled to still less. 'Twould be absurd, extravagant to continue to have any feelings whatever for a person who can no longer benefit from them; to this person's shades, neither respect nor consideration, neither love nor remembrance is owing; he can be allowed no place in your imagination, because his presence there could not be anything but disagreeable, and you know that it is included among our principles never to permit any ideas to enter the mind save pleasant or voluptuous ones. Well, this train of ideas points smoothly, and logically, toward mistreatment of the daughter, since 'twas out of lust you killed the mother; these ideas would be disrupted, would inevitably be spoiled if you were now to go and render the daughter a service. Hence, not only is there no disadvantage in your refusing to be helpful to the girl in any way, but it is even necessary to your pleasure that you render her exceedingly unhappy. The idea engendered by the unhappiness into which you are about to plunge her will renew those of the atrocities you wrought against the rest of the family; and from the interweaving and combining of all these ideas there shall necessarily result for you a voluptuous whole, certain to be disintegrated by contrary behavior on your part.

"Do not allege to me the tender feelings for Madame Donis that inhabited you once upon a time. It would be absurd to re-awaken them; not only because you have damaged them through your crime, but because one must take good care not to preserve the least tender feeling for someone who exists no longer; it would be to wear out the heart's faculties needlessly, and to impair the effectiveness of its action upon more real objects; nothing should be of less concern to us than a person deprived of life.[6] Thus, as regards Madame Donis you are in a position where you have every right to offend her, since you owe her nothing, and where, offending her, you offend nobody, since she exists no more; and so, I repeat to you, it would be the most dreadful folly for you to hesitate. But, do you tell me, you hear an inner voice which seems to be urging you to resist; you ask me whether this is the voice of Nature? No, Juliette, no; this voice, about whose source you cannot conceivably be in error, is no other than that of prejudice: if it still sways you, lay it up to weakness, and to the fact that the criminal deed involved here is less familiar to you than those you ordinarily indulge in, even though it amounts to nothing else than the theft you are fond of and commit day in and day out. Here, it is most certainly the voice of prejudice you are hearing, instead of that of Nature, for when Nature speaks, her urgings are invariably to seek happiness, no matter at whose expense. Therefore let it be the most critical kind of audition you accord that voice, sift the chaff out of its message, you will then hear it in all its purity, and ceasing to drift anxiously, buffeted by doubts, you will

---

[6] It is, of course, at this point that we should examine the revolting absurdity of weeping over the dead. Sooner than lament, one should rejoice; for by perishing, this dear one you loved obtained his deliverance from all life's tribulations. Furthermore, our grief, our tears can be of no use to him, and they affect us unpleasantly. The same applies to burial ceremonies, and to the respect one might still have for the deceased: useless, superstitious, all of it. To a cadaver one owes nothing other than to deposit it in good soil, where it can germinate at once, swiftly metamorphose into worm, housefly, or vegetable, which is difficult in cemeteries. If one wishes to render a last service to a dead man, then place him at the foot of a fruit tree, or in some fertile meadow; that is all you owe him, all the rest is absurd. (Touching this matter, see the remarks on p. 959.)

then act in confidence and peace, without any fear of outraging Nature whom, to the contrary, you will be serving when you accomplish the crime that you know she would have you commit, who assures you pleasure from committing it.

"Thus, what I would do, were I in your place, would be to amuse myself thoroughly with this girl, to rob her, and then to put her in such a damnable plight that you could at any moment add further height to your happiness by feeding it upon the charms of seeing her languish; which, from the standpoint of voluptuous pleasure, is preferable to killing her. The felicity I recommend to you will be infinitely keener; beyond the physical happiness acquired from enjoyment, there will be the intellectual happiness born of the comparison between her fate and yours; for happiness consists more in comparisons of this sort than in actual physical enjoyments. It is a thousand times sweeter to say to oneself, casting an eye upon unhappy souls, *I am not such as they, and therefore I am their better,* than merely to say, *Joy is unto me, but my joy is mine amidst people who are just as happy as I.* It is others' hardships which cause us to experience our enjoyments to the full; surrounded by persons whose happiness is equal to ours, we would never know contentment or ease: that is why they say, and very wisely indeed, that, to be happy, you ought never look upward, but always at those who are below you. If then 'tis the spectacle of the luckless who must necessarily complete our happiness by the comparison they furnish between themselves and us, one must take care not to relieve such downtrodden as exist; for by raising them, through this aid, from the class which provides elements for your comparisons, you deprive yourself of these comparisons, and hence of that which improves your pleasures. However, simply to limit oneself to withholding aid from the needy in order to preserve this class useful for the comparisons whence the best portion of your happiness derives, that is not enough; you must neglect no opportunity to generate misery, both in order to increase the size of this class generally, and in order, particularly, to create a sector of it which, your own personal handiwork, sharpens the delights that are going to result for you from the comparisons it will provide. Thus, in the present instance, your complete pleasure would consist in making away with this girl's inheritance, in then reducing her to beggardom, in constraining her as it were to come begging at your gate, where you would cruelly refuse her the pittance she asks; thus, by drawing the spectacle of misery into your immediate vicinity, improve your enjoyment through comparison as intimate and at the same time as advantageous to you as possible, since all the woe confronting you is of your unique fabrication. That is what my advice to you would be, Juliette, that is what I would do if I were you. . . . I would have a daily erection thinking about these delicious ideas, standing before the still more divine spectacle of the distress I would have caused; and in the midst of these rare pleasures, I would exclaim, *Yes, there she is; by means of a crime I got possession of her; and this inheritance I have usurped, I spend upon pleasures so sweet that nothing I do is not crime; I am, through my behavior toward her, nothing but criminal, I am perpetually in a state of crime; not one of my pleasures is untainted by it.* . . . And with an imagination like yours, Juliette, oh! how heavenly such a complication must be!"

Noirceuil was very hot by the time he reached the end of his digression, and as since my return we had still done nothing together, we now moved straight to a sofa. Lying there in his arms, I admitted that at no moment had I been visited by doubts concerning the fate of little Fontange, and that what I had said to him had been said only in order to give him the occasion to expound his doctrines. I promised him the young girl, assuring him that, however interesting she might be, we would not fail to establish her in a quagmire of grinding poverty, after having wrung all we wanted from her.

"Well, well, Juliette," said Noirceuil, fondling and kissing my buttocks, "if you depraved yourself in the course of your travels, I was not idle during the same period either; and you have returned to find me a thousand times worse than I used to be; there is not a single horror I have not accomplished since we last saw each other. Will you believe it? I am responsible for the death of Saint-Fond; I aspired to his post, I missed getting it; but nothing will prevent me from succeeding the man occupying it at present; his doom is a matter of time only, the machinery is in place; and once I hold office, which I ambition for what it will put in my hands, to wit, all the power of the idiot prince and all the wealth of his kingdom, then, oh, Juliette, the mountain of pleasures that shall be ours! Crime, such is my wish, must stamp every instant of my career; you will not weaken with me as you did with Saint-Fond, and together we shall go far."

By and by I had to present my ass to that maniac; but he withdrew from it without leaving any fuck behind him.

"I am waiting for someone," he explained. "Allow me to inform you: she is a very attractive creature of about twenty-five, whose husband I have had jailed: this in order to get possession of the wife. If she opens her mouth, he can be put to death tomorrow; but as she adores him, I think she will keep silent. She also has a child, whom she idolizes; my aim is to induce her to forsake the lot; I propose to fuck the wife, have the husband broken on the wheel, and send the child to the workhouse. I have been preparing the operation for two months; up until now, the young woman's love and virtue have held out admirably. You shall see how pretty she is. I should like you to help me seduce her. What has occurred is as follows.

"A murder was committed in her house; she was there when it happened, along with the victim, her husband, and another man. Her testimony is crucial; the other man has deposed against the husband, but this woman's evidence is needed, and the case cannot progress until she gives it."

"Rascal! this entire intrigue smacks of your confection: you had the man killed by the witness whom you seduced and who has sworn 'twas the husband did the deed; you want the wife to corroborate the thing, both for the pleasure of making her yours and for that other pleasure, more piquant still, of turning her into her husband's assassin."

"Quite right, Juliette, how well you know me! All that is my doing. But I am eager to round out my crime, and I count upon you. Ah, my dear, it's a voluptuous discharge I see ahead of me when this evening I shall fuck that woman."

She arrived. Madame de Valrose was indeed one of the prettiest creatures you could hope to see: petite, but exquisitely shaped, well fleshed, with a dazzling fair skin, the world's loveliest eyes, breasts, and an ass that made the mouth water.

"Good evening to you, Madame," said Noirceuil, "you have reached your decision?"

"Good Lord," that charming woman replied, her eyes filling with tears, "how can you expect me to agree to such a horrible thing?"

"Take care, Madame," I broke in sharply; "Monsieur de Noirceuil, having acquainted me with your business, has authorized me to offer you a word of advice. Bear in mind that as matters now stand, your husband is doomed, for to that end but a single witness is required, and one exists, as you are aware."

"But he is guiltless, Madame; the witness who accuses him is the murderer himself."

"You shall never convince your judges of it. This witness had no relations whatever with the dead man, but your husband had a good many. Therefore, I repeat, you should consider your husband as done for, incontestably. When, in the light of this terrible certainty, Monsieur de Noirceuil, whose influence you know to be great, offers to save him if you agree to testify against him, I for my part—"

"But what purpose does it serve, this testimony, since Monsieur is eager to save my husband?"

"Without that testimony he cannot do it; it will enable him to show irregular procedure, and that slander doubtless exists, if not perjury, once the accused's wife testifies against him."

"Then shall I not be punished?"

"A convent . . . whence we will have you out again in a week's time. Madame, that you are able to hesitate is more than I can understand."

"But my husband will believe that I sought to undo him, he will blame me in his heart; and in mine this idea shall weigh forever. It shall lie between us everlastingly: I save my husband only by creating an undying distrust which means eternal estrangement, which means—"

"Agreed, but is that not better than sending him to the gallows? And if you truly love him, should you not grant his life greater importance than the possession of his affections? If he dies, will you not also be separated forever?"

"Terrible alternative! And if I am being deceived . . . if this avowal seals his doom instead of saving him?"

"This injurious suspicion," said Noirceuil, "is my reward for wishing to be of help to you, Madame, and I thank you."

"Why, yes, Madame," I put in heatedly, "Monsieur de Noirceuil ought by all rights to drop your case this very minute; how dare you cast such aspersions upon the most virtuous of mortals?"

"For the aid he proposes he has set a price that dishonors me. I worship my husband, never have I broken faith with him, never, and it is not when he is beset by cruel troubles that I need crown his misfortune with such a woeful outrage."

"This outrage is imaginary: your husband will never learn of it. Manifestly, you are an intelligent person: how then, I wonder, can you cling to these illusions? It is not, moreover, your heart Monsieur de Noirceuil is seeking, but simply your favors, which should greatly reduce the hurt in your eyes. But, I shall further add, even were this hurt to exist, even were it grave, of what account can it be when your husband's life hangs in the balance?

"By way of conclusion I may say a word in defense of the price Monsieur de Noirceuil asks. Ah, Madame, you are ill-acquainted with the spirit of the age if you fancy that kindnesses are accorded for nothing nowadays. Actually, in return for a service which your entire fortune would not begin to pay for, Monsieur de Noirceuil, by demanding nothing beyond a little forbearance on your part, is willing to accept exceedingly little, it seems to me. In short, your husband's life is in your hands; it is saved if you accuse him, lost if you do not. There is your dilemma. Speak."

And at that point the dear little woman was seized by a dreadful fit of sobbing which so aroused Noirceuil that the scoundrel had out his member and gave it to me to frig before Madame de Valrose's very eyes. She fainted.

"Quickly there, buggerblast me!" said Noirceuil, "pull up her skirts, let me fuck her."

Her pretty bosom having been brought into view when I unlaced her stays, Noirceuil was soon kneading and mauling her in that barbaric manner with which he is wont to caress breasts. I finished undressing the poor creature; she was still unconscious when I took her upon my lap, exposing that pretty ass to the libertine who, while I tugged at his pubic hairs, readied himself for his beloved sodomy. Careless of his victim's feelings, Noirceuil drove into the breach with such impetuosity that he soon summoned the little lady back to life.

"Where am I?" she gasped upon opening her eyes, "and what, good lord! is being done to me?"

"Have patience, my child," I said in a rather chilly tone, "it won't be long before we have everything we want from you."

"But these things—"

"Strange things which your husband never did, eh?"

"Never, oh never! I shudder—"

"Shudder away, but at the same time think a moment, Madame," said the ferocious Noirceuil, pursuing his embuggery, "it would require no more than to cut through the thinnest of partitions and the act you take exception to would be nullified; and so, if you like, Juliette, with a razor—"

"Fuck, Noirceuil, fuck, your mind is beginning to rove."

And the little woman, continuing to struggle: "Let go of me, let go! 'Tis a violence, an abomination—"

"Why, God damn your soul!" Noirceuil roared, seizing a pistol and clapping the barrel to her temple, "any more disturbance from you, just one more word, and I blow your brains out."

'Twas then the unhappy creature realized that resignation was her only course. Wearily, tearfully, she bends her head, lays it upon my breast, I pinch her belly, pull the hairs from her bush, cause her, in fine, such sharp pain that Noirceuil, locked in that trim little anus as though in a vice, senses the sperm rising in his balls. He catches hold of her breasts from underneath, wrenches them so cruelly, her pain becomes so extreme that the rake fairly screams as he discharges. He withdraws; and I, leaping upon that charming woman, I in my turn derive an excruciating pleasure from her. This scene revives Noirceuil; his prick rearisen, he comes forward to join us. Through the position I am in, my buttocks are accessible to him, he kisses them, and, inserting his prick in Madame de Valrose's mouth, orders her to suck it: her initial reaction is one of horror, her next impulse is to disobey. What a group! I was sprawled atop Valrose; Noirceuil was lying upon me; he was warming himself in that pretty little person's mouth and was tonguing my ass. I poured fuck into my fricatrice's cunt, Noirceuil loosed his into her mouth. Then we readjusted ourselves.

"There we are," said Noirceuil, his self-possession once returned, "the infidelity has been committed; do you or do you not intend to save your husband?"

"Will he be saved by that, Monsieur?" was the charming creature's question, asked in the mildest and sweetest voice; "are you very sure it will save him?"

"I swear it by all that is holy," the traitor declared, "and if I am mistaken, I am willing to forego all renewal of the pleasures I have just tasted with you. Be here tomorrow morning, we shall go to the judge together, you will sign a deposition affirming your husband's guilt; I shall have him at your side the next day."

"Oh, Noirceuil," I murmured to that monster, "how I admire this perseverance you are able to display in crime, even beyond the moment when the passions have subsided."

"Why, you saw me accomplish my act of pleasure," Noirceuil replied; "you know, do you not, that my every expense of fuck is the signing of a death warrant?"

We separated. Madame de Valrose, whom I conveyed to her home, besought me to take an interest in her case; and I promised that I would, with the sincerity one owes to a whore one has become tired of. The following day she made her deposition; and on the day after that Noirceuil arranged affairs so cleverly that the poor little thing was declared her husband's accomplice, and hanged beside him where he, after having been broken, lay exposed upon the wheel. We were, Noirceuil and I, watching from a window, I frigged him during the spectacle, he frigged me. Was my discharge agreeable? Not in ages had I enjoyed a better one. Compassion moved Noirceuil to ask for the custody of the child, he obtained it, he fucked it, and inside twenty-four hours had flung it into the streets, penniless and naked.

"Far, far better that than to kill it," he pointed out to me, "its sufferings will last longer, as shall my joy at being responsible for them."

Meanwhile, Abbé Chabert had found me everything I needed.

A week after having arrived in Paris I moved myself into a town house, you know what a delightful place it is; and I bought this property in the neighborhood of Essonnes, where we are for-gathered today; I invested the rest of my funds in various holdings, and when all my business was completed, estimated my income at roughly four million a year. Fontange's five hundred thousand was spent furnishing my two houses, magnificently, I think you will agree. Next, I turned my attentions to libidinous arrangements; I assembled my several seraglios of women, in town and in country; I hired thirty valets, all of them tall solid fellows, comely, chosen especially for size of member; and you know the service I get from them. I have, besides, six mackerels of my own in Paris, they pander exclusively to me, and when I am in the city I always spend three hours at one of their establishments, every day. Out here in the country, they send me what they find, and you have often been able to verify the quality of their furnitures. With all that, I would ven-ture to suppose there are few women who can claim to lead a more delightful life; and yet, you know, I do not cease to want; I consider myself poor; my desires are infinitely in excess of my possibilities; I would spend twice as much, if I had it; and I leave no stone unturned to increase my wealth, criminal or not, there is nothing I am unwilling to do for money.

Once these divers arrangements had been made, I sent a ser-vant to bring Mademoiselle Fontange from Chaillot; everything owed for her keep was paid, and she was led out of her nunnery. Nothing in all the length and breadth of Nature could equal that girl's beauty. Imagine Flora herself, and of Fontange's graces and attractions you will still have a very imperfect idea. Seventeen years of age, Mademoiselle Donis was blonde; loosened, her superb tresses reached nearly to the floor; her eyes were a lovely brown, of incomparable liveliness, sparkling with love and voluptuousness at once; her delightful mouth never seemed to open save to heighten her beauty; and her faultless teeth resembled pearls set amidst roses. Naked, this heavenly creature could have served as model to the painter of the Graces. That richly rounded mons veneris! Those gloriously turned, infinitely inspiring thighs! That ass, that sublime ass! O Fontange! the cruelty it required, and the liber-tinage, not to spare such a host of charms, and not to exempt at least you from the rigorous fate I reserved for all my playthings.

Five years before, when her mother had first talked to her about me, Fontange had been told that all possible respect and consideration were due me; upon learning who had sent the servant to fetch her away, she was overjoyed; and upon arriving, dazzled by this opulence, by this multitude of valets, by these magnificent furnishings, things which were all very new to her who had never until now been outside her convent, she blinked her eyes in disbelief, wondering whether she had not been transported to an Olympus, borne above the clouds to some aerial dwelling place, habitat of gods: she may even have taken me for Venus. She sank down at my knees, I raised her up; I kissed her rosy mouth, her glistening eyes, her two cheeks so fair and which so quickly took Nature's brightest crimson hue when touched by my lips. I hugged her to my breast and felt her little heart beat excitedly against mine, like that of a fledgling dove one has stolen from its nest. She was dressed with a degree of stylishness, albeit simply; from underneath a pretty flowered hat her superb blonde hair fell in curls to her two exquisitely shaped shoulders. When she spoke it was in a gentle tone, in a musical voice full of sweet mildness.

"Madame, I thank a generous heaven for the privilege of being able to devote my life to you. My mother is dead; in this world I have no one else but you."

As the words came forth her eyes grew moist, and I smiled.

"Yes, my child," I said to her, "your mother is dead; she was my friend; hers was an untimely, an unusual death . . . she left in my trust a certain amount of money for you. If you behave deservingly toward me, you may be rich; but that will all depend upon your conduct, upon blind obedience to my will."

"I shall be your slave, Madame." And she bent and kissed my hand.

And I kissed her mouth again, rather more lingeringly this second time. I lifted her kerchief away, freed her bosom from its veils. She reddened; though unsteadied by agitation, nevertheless she continued, in measured and respectful terms, to sound the well-bred and decent young lady. Then for the third time I take her in my arms . . . her hair is a little disheveled, her lovely breasts are entirely bare; and, after fastening my mouth upon hers, "I believe,"

I say to her, "I believe I am going to love you, for you are young and pure and sweet."

The idea of shocking her occurred to me then: nothing is prettier than virtue scandalized by vice. I ring for my women; I have them undress me in the presence of this heavenly little girl; I gaze at myself in a looking glass.

"Tell me, Fontange," I say, kissing her anew, "is it true that I have an attractive body?"

And the poor thing averted her eyes; her face was scarlet. Around me I had four of my most beautiful women: Phryné, Laïs, Aspasia, and Theodora; all four between sixteen and eighteen years of age; so many Aphrodites.

"Come, Mademoiselle," Laïs said to her, "do not be backward. 'Tis a favor Madame is granting you; take advantage of it."

She advances, but with lowered eyes. I take her by the hand, draw her down upon my body.

"What a child she is," I murmur to my women; "Phryné, show our babe in arms what she is to do."

And Phryné sits down beside me, takes my head upon her breast and, reaching a hand toward my cunt, begins to rub my clitoris. No woman acquits herself of that chore so well as she. Her execution is adroit, tutored, the play of her fingers lascivious, unerring; she kisses and caresses the behind in a singular manner; her tongue, when that is what I wish, tickles the anus marvelously; her movements upon the mons veneris harmonize amazingly with what she is capable of doing in the other temple, which she sucks indescribably when called upon. While Phryné was in action; Laïs, astride my chest, advanced her dear little cunt into position for sucking; Theodora was frigging my asshole, and the beautiful Aspasia maintained Fontange nearby the spectacle and her attention fixed upon it, while frigging her to soothe her aching conscience.

"Did you not use to do the same thing with your companions?" Aspasia asked her.

"Oh, never!"

"Fiddlesticks," said I from between Laïs' buttocks, "it's nothing but masturbation in convents, I know it from experience. At your age I had already had my hands under everybody's skirt."

Then, leaving the cunt I had been sucking: "Come here and kiss me," I ordered Fontange.

She approaches; I devour her.

My women received instructions to undress her. And proceedings were temporarily interrupted while the clothing that was hindering my pleasures was removed, Fontange's first, then everyone else's. Ah, great God! how beautiful the child was when naked! what fairness of skin! what proportions!

"Very well," said I, "place her upon me, in such a way that I have this most winning of cunts above my lips. To you, Aspasia, will go the ass her position will be offering you: tongue her anus. Phryné, you shall frig her clitoris, seeing to it that all exhalations drain into my mouth. I am going to spread my legs; you, Theodora, between my thighs, shall cunt-suck me while, Laïs, you shall be licking my asshole. Fair friends, pray put all your science to best purpose; use every trick you know, invent others, for this maid excites me exceedingly, and I wish to shed a sea of fuck on her account."

I need not describe to you all the pleasure I was to extract from this celestial scene; I went half-mad from joy. Lust did in due time assert itself in the young Fontange; she was unable to resist the voluptuous sensations vibrating throughout her being. Modesty gives way to raptures, and the novice discharges. Oh, how delicious is the first flowing of fuck! With what joy I fed upon that nectar!

"Turn her over," were the next instructions I issued to my women; "have her place her head between Theodora's thighs, and suck her cunt; I in the meantime shall frig her ass with my tongue; Laïs will do the same to me; I shall be fondling, stimulating an ass with each of my two hands."

Another ecstasy, another ejaculation on my part; it is more than I can bear, I seize Fontange, I leap upon her, I press my clitoris hard against hers, I rub frenziedly, I devour her mouth, my women tease my ass, spank it, thrash it, slip their hands underneath and worry my sex, in short, they overwhelm me with pleasure, and I loose what must be my tenth discharge, with my impure sperm drenching the delicious cunt of the prettiest and most virginal of girls.

The fuck gone forth, the illusion faded away. Beautiful as Fontange was, I now saw her with nought but that malign indifference which wakes cruelty in me when I am weary of objects, and soon her doom was spelled out in the depths of my heart.

"Put the clothes back on her," I said to my women.

I too got dressed; I sent the others out, we remained alone.

"Mademoiselle," I said to her harshly, "augur nothing from a fleeting moment of inebriety into which Nature plunged me against my will; banish any thought that predilection might, on my part, have had something to do with it; I am fond of women in general; you satisfied me; there's an end to it. You must now be informed that your mother gave me five hundred thousand francs for your dowry; it were simpler that you learn the fact from me than from some other source."

"Yes, Madame, I already know it."

"Ah, Mademoiselle, you already know it; my congratulations to you. However, what you do not already know is that your good mother contracted a debt in this very same amount to a certain Monsieur de Noirceuil, to whom I of course transferred the sum, and who may bestow it upon you, if he chooses, or else keep it, for it belongs to him, both the money and the decision too. I shall take you tomorrow to see this gentleman, and urge you to behave with utmost obligingness should he happen to make any demands upon you."

"Madame, the ethical and moral training which supplied the very basis of the excellent education I have been given—Madame, I wish to say that they are hardly consistent with your counsels."

"Nor with my actions, you may as well add, since you have taken it into your head to scold me. Blame me even for my kindness to you, I advise you to do that also."

"I am not saying that, Madame."

"Well, do say it if you want to, for I assure you that your reproaches affect me as little as your praise: one frolics with a little girl like you, and when the game is over, one scorns her."

"Scorn, Madame! I thought that only vice was to be scorned."

"Vice amuses, virtue bores. And according to my belief, whatever promotes our pleasures always deserves preference over that which gives nothing but headache and depressive vapors. . . . But you answer back, my fair one; you are tart, you are forward, you are insolent, and you are far from that degree of superiority which renders such failings excusable. An end to these discussions, Mademoiselle, if you please; the fact is that I owe you nothing; that with the half a million intended for you I paid a creditor to whom your mother was in debt; and that it lies with that creditor to decide whether to retain the sum or return it to you; and I warn you that he will keep it unless you show all kinds of consideration for him."

"What kinds of consideration, Madame?"

"The same kinds I have just required from you; I should think you must understand what I mean."

"In that case, Madame, your Monsieur de Noirceuil shall keep everything. I am not the person to embark upon any such infamous career as this you propose to me; and if, out of respect for you, out of frailty or childishness, I was able a little while ago to forget what I have been taught to regard as my duty, so well have you opened my eyes that I have been punished for my fault." And from those eyes, the most beautiful in all the world, there now gushed a flood of tears.

"Indeed," I said, "it is scarcely to be believed. We do not fall down at Mademoiselle's knees, and lo! she makes a scene. My God, where would we libertines be if we had to perform curtsies and reverences before all the little harlots who frig us?"

The word *harlot* was the signal for a veritable tempest; there was a banging of the head upon the table, there were shrieks of despair, there were tears scattered all about the room; and, if you wish to know the truth, 'twas not without the most trenchant pleasure I carried on my humiliations of the Fontange for whom I had been all afire a short moment before. Pride is salved by the illusion's collapse; and from disdain for the idol one obtains an indemnity for all one spent when prostrate before it. That silly little goose irritated me to a point beyond description.

"Look here, my child," I said to her, "if Monsieur de Noirceuil does not give you your dowry, you will enter my service; it just so happens that I need a girl in the scullery, you can surely wash my pots and pans."

1174 ✤ THE MARQUIS DE SADE

And this brought forth tears in such abundance that I wondered whether she was not going to suffocate.

"On the other hand," I continued, "if you dislike kitchens you can always go abegging or try whoring. Whoring, that's what I believe I would suggest; your looks aren't bad; and you have no idea what's to be earned from frigging pricks."

"Madame," said Fontange, quite beside herself, "I am destined to neither of those trades. I wish to leave this house, kindly allow me to go. I repent the things I have done here, all my life I shall pray to be forgiven by the Supreme Being. . . . I intend to return to my convent."

"Do you? Your convent won't take you in. To live in convents costs money. You have none."

"I have friends there."

"No, you don't, now that you are poor."

"I shall work."

"Come, come, little fool, calm yourself, dry your tears; my women will look after you this evening, tomorrow I shall take you to Noirceuil, and if you are mild in your manners you may not find him quite so harsh in his, nor as mischievous as I have been."

I ring, recommend the girl to the care of my tribades, have horses hitched to my carriage, and fly to Noirceuil's house. He requests details; painting Fontange for him in none but truth's colors, I could not fail to arouse him.

"Here," says he, trundling out a very rigid prick, "behold, Juliette, the effect of your descriptive abilities."

And bidding me accompany him into his boudoir, he engaged me to cooperate in several of those curious fantasies which rather double than extinguish the effects of desire, which are not pleasure-takings but which, with libertine spirits like Noirceuil, outvalue all the licit conjunctions whether of hymen or of love. We were two hours at play, for I too am fond of those little horrors. I satisfy them for men with the same pleasure they take in submitting me to them; their lubricity ignites mine; no sooner do I content them than I want them to content me in my turn; and after, as I say, several hours of foul frolicking, which cost us no loss of any kind, this, according to my recollection, was the declaration Noirceuil made to me:

"It is a most extraordinary caprice I have been dwelling upon for a very long time, Juliette, and I have been awaiting your return with impatience, having in all the world nobody but you with whom I could satisfy it. I should like to marry . . . I should like to get married, not once, but twice, and upon the same day: at ten o'clock in the morning, I wish, dressed as a woman, to wed a man; at noon, wearing masculine attire, I wish to take a bardash for my wife. There is still more . . . I wish to have a woman do the same as I; and what other woman but you could participate in this fantasy? You, dressed as a man, must wed a tribade at the same ceremony at which I, guised as a woman, become the wife of a man; next, dressed as a woman, you will wed another tribade wearing masculine clothing, at the very moment I, having resumed my ordinary attire, go to the altar to become united in holy matrimony with a catamite disguised as a girl."

"Assuredly, good sir, this, as you yourself have said, is a curious caprice that has entered your head."

"Yes, but since Nero married Tigellinus as a woman and Sporus as a man, I am originating nothing except the celebration of the two unions in the space of a single day and, of course, the whimsical idea of having you imitate me; there is the matter of the ties which already subsist between ourselves and the objects which shall be utilized in this farce, and here I think we have greatly improved upon Nero. Your two wives are, firstly, Fontange who, clad in mannish garb, will become your husband; secondly, your daughter who, dressed in the customary raiments of her sex, will marry a Juliette in man's clothing. My husband and my wife, who shall they be, do you wonder? They shall be two children, Juliette, yes, two children sired by me and of whose existence you have until now been unaware, of whose existence, indeed, nobody knows. One of them is nearing eighteen, he is to be my husband: a Hercules for vigor and looks. The other is twelve; 'tis the incarnation of Eros. Both are the fruit of the most legitimate commerce; my first wife produced the elder, the younger was given me by the sixth. All told, I have had eight wives. That, I believe, you do know."

"But did you not tell me that you had no children left?"

"These two have been dead to the world; both have been raised with great care, and in the strictest conformance with instructions, in one of my castles far off in Brittany. Neither one has ever seen the light of day. They have just been delivered to me here in town, they made the journey in a sealed coach. They are a pair of veritable savages, scarcely able to speak. But that is of little importance; properly guided, they will do very nicely for the ceremony; the rest is our affair."

"And appalling bacchanalia, I take it, are to succeed these unusual weddings?"

"Exactly."

"And Noirceuil, you wish to have my poor adorable little Marianne become one of the victims in these hideous orgies, is that it?"

"No, she'll not be a victim, but she will be present, my lust demands that. No harm will be done her, of that you may be perfectly certain: your women will entertain her while we are at work, that is all. . . ."

Noirceuil obtains my agreement to everything. It will soon be seen how the villain kept his word.

'Twas not immediately nor without difficulty that Mademoiselle Donis succeeded in understanding the peculiar arrangement of the forthcoming scene: virtue regularly has trouble accommodating itself to vice's extravagances. Partly from fear, partly from eagerness to please, the unhappy girl did at last give her whole consent, but only after I had solemnly vowed that these scandalous weddings would conclude in nothing apt to alarm her modesty. The first ceremony took place in a small town lying two leagues from the magnificent castle Noirceuil owned outside Orléans, and in which the postmarital festival was to be celebrated; the second ceremony, in the chapel of that same castle.

I shall not fatigue you with the details of those two rites; you will be content to know that everything transpired decently, punctually, and in strictest accordance with tradition; the religious ceremonies were followed by their civil counterparts, enacted in an equally dignified manner. There were wedding rings, there were Masses, benedictions, constituted dowries, witnesses; nothing was lacking. Costumes and paint artistically disguised the two sexes, embellished them where necessary.

By two o'clock that afternoon Noirceuil's dual project had

been carried out: he had become the wife of one of his sons, the husband of the other, while I found myself the husband of my daughter and the wife of Fontanges. Everything completed, the gates to the castle were shut and barred. The weather being exceedingly cold, great fires were lit in the superb hall where we were to forgather; and severest orders having been issued that the impending bacchanalia be interrupted under no circumstances, we closed ourselves up inside those baronial surroundings. In number we were twelve.

We being the two heroes, Noirceuil and I sat upon a black velvet throne placed in the center of the hall; below the throne there were to be seen, all wearing crowns of cypress, the elder of Noirceuil's two sons, named Phaon, eighteen years of age; the younger, aged twelve, whose name was Euphorbe; my daughter Marianne and Mademoiselle Donis; the two groomsmen at the weddings, agents of Noirceuil's sodomite pleasures and his hired killers, one of whom was dubbed Desrues, the other Cartouche, each of some thirty years, both garbed as cannibals, with switches, daggers, and live snakes in their hands, both posted at our sides in the attitude of bodyguards; on the right of us as on the left, seated, were two of my tribades, Theodora and Phryné; at our feet, two whores, likewise naked, appeared to be awaiting our orders. These girls, simply picked out of a bawdyhouse, were a bare eighteen and twenty years of age, and both were of the most charming physiognomy: they were there as auxiliaries to the scene.

Surveying these preparations, I felt just a little apprehensive for my precious Marianne and was moved to remind Noirceuil of the assurances he had given me.

"My dear," was his reply, "it ought to be plain to you that I am tremendously overwrought. Consider what it did to me this morning, to satisfy the incredible longing that had been preoccupying me for years. It crazed my brain, Juliette, that's what it did, and I fear you have chosen a bad moment to remind me of promises of good behavior: let a little added irritation set the nervous system ablaze, and you know as well as I that all such guarantees go up in smoke. Let us enjoy ourselves, Juliette, let us amuse ourselves; perhaps I shall abide by my word; but if I do not, in the lewd pleasures which shall soon see us gripped in ecstasy, strive to find the strength to endure the misfortune you seem to dread—a misfortune which, between us two, is by no means as dreadful as they make out. Think, dear Juliette, that for libertines like us, the hand is stayed by nothing, nor is the mind; that, for us, an object's ten thousand titles to inviolable respect are that many reasons to outrage it further: the more exigent virtue appears, the sooner it pleases furious vice to defile and degrade it."

One hundred candles lit that hall as the scene opened.

"Cartouche, Desrues," said Noirceuil to his two ministers, "worthy emulators of the famous men whose names I permit you to bear; you who, like your patrons of whose high feats history shall transmit an indestructible record down to the last generations of mankind; you, I say, who have never failed to lend your arm to the noble and ennobling cause of crime, go undress the four destined to holocaust and whose brows are wreathed in the foliage of death's tree, go strip them, and of their raiments, whereof there is no further need, make the employment I have prescribed to you."

The emissaries step forward; the four victims are despoiled of every article of clothing, which is flung piece by piece into the roaring blazes that warm the hall.

"What baneful ceremony is this?" asks Fontange, seeing the fire consume everything she has been wearing, her skirts, her petticoats, even her shift; "why burn these garments?"

"Dear girl," Noirceuil replies, "a little earth, some sod, you shall soon need no more than that for cover."

"Good Lord! what do I hear! And what have I done to earn this?"

"Bring that creature to me," Noirceuil says.

And while Laïs sucks him, while one of the whores toils over his ass, and while I excite him verbally, the libertine glues his mouth to the mouth of that enchanting girl, and pumps it an entire quarter of an hour despite Fontange's resistance, which is keen but vain. Then, shifting his lewd attentions to her behind, "Oh, Juliette, she has an ass too! a beautiful ass," he cries, working himself into an ecstasy before it; " 'twill be delightful to fuck all that and to martyrize it. . . ."

Therewith his tongue slips into the cunning little hole; meanwhile, upon his orders, I with one hand pluck out the silky hairs growing upon that lovely girl's cunt and pinch her budding breasts with the other. He forces her upon her knees, bids his two men tongue her here and there, and ends with having her kiss his bum.

These commencements were trying for the young thing, her shame and discomposure were extreme; if anything was more powerful than these two feelings, 'twas the terror inspired in her by the preparations for what, as best she could tell, seemed due to follow. Trained to modesty, having received none but the best principles in the house whence she came, Mademoiselle Donis was necessarily in an evil situation; and nothing amused us more than the fierce conflict raging between her sense of decency and her perception of iron necessity. There was one point at which she sought to elude the inevitable.

"Stop that squirming and stay just where you are," Noirceuil told her harshly; "do you not realize how delicate the imagination is in a man like me? A mere nothing disturbs it, the instant service fails, everything breaks down, comes all to pieces; understand that the divinest charms are null unless presented to us submissively and with obedience."

And while he spoke the rascal was fondling the girl's ass, 'twas over that angelic creature's buttocks the impurest and most ferocious hands were wandering. "Bugger-fuck!" he exclaimed, pursuing his palpations, "how unhappy I intend to make this little jade! Look at these charms, and tell me whether they do not cry out for horrors!"

He then has her take hold of Cartouche's prick, obliges her to frig it, savoring the sight of innocent hands accomplishing the chores of vice; and as the poor girl, all in tears, exhibits much disgust for the work but no skill, he orders one of the whores to give her lessons and compels the student to humbly thank her teacher.

"Some abilities as a fricatrice may well stand her in good stead," Noirceuil remarked; "the frightful state of misery to which I propose to reduce her shall oblige her to do something to stay alive."

He bade her tongue the two whores' cunts; after that, to suck his prick; and enjoined the company to slap her hard upon the face whenever the slightest hint of repugnance could be read there.

"Very good," said he, "let us give thought to hymeneal pleasures, we have devoted ourselves long enough to those of love." Then, casting a murderous glance in Fontange's direction: "Aye, well may she tremble," said he, "and more than tremble in anticipation of the moment when I return to busy myself with her again."

Laïs and Theodora are dispatched toward Phaon, at once Noirceuil's husband and his son; they soon succeed in erecting him, and lead the boy up to Noirceuil who, bent over me, nonchalantly presents his behind to the chaste consort whom my tribades guide his way. I was frigging him from below and he was tonguing now the one whore's asshole, now the other's.

"Have the customary ceremonies observed," he says to Phaon's conductresses, "this young bridegroom is not to make away with the favors offered to him until he has first shown himself worthy of them."

Phaon kneels, adopts a worshipful attitude before the ass facing him, kisses it respectfully, rises to his feet, and, yielding to the impulses being developed within him, the handsome youth runs his instrument hilt-high into his dear papa's ass. Membered like a mule, his capers and heaves soon produce quivers of joy in the patient, and rakish Noirceuil falls to simulating the little shrieks, the smirks and smiles of the bride undergoing her defloration; he sighs, he moans, his contortions are amusing beyond words. The youth, perfectly excited by everything surrounding him, soon discharges into the entrails hugging him happily. When he has completed his act he is obliged to reiterate the respectful gestures with which he began. Then he retires; but Noirceuil, very hot, wants fucking; his panting anus seems to be crying forth the need for pricks; Cartouche and Desrues sodomize him; while they do, he kisses the buttocks of Laïs and of Theodora to which, he avows, he has taken a mighty fancy. Niched underneath him, I suck him with all my strength; and he fondles whore's ass. Fucked twice by each of his men, Noirceuil is ready for new things. "Now we shall play the husband," he announces; "after having acquitted myself so well in the wifely role."

Euphorbe, his second son, is brought to him. I am asked to pilot the engine; three lusty blows and the pucelage is no more. His weapon is still loaded when Noirceuil withdraws, and he comes

forth with an ardent desire for Fontange. It is the whores who
march her up to the line and who supervise the operation.

"Juliette," says Noirceuil, "oblige me by violently biting this
little girl's cunt while I embugger her. Since during my pleasure I
would that she experience a maximum of pain, your instructions,
Cartouche and Desrues, are to seize each of you one of her hands,
and to remove her fingernails with the blade of a pocketknife."

Everything is put into execution. Fontange, stunned by this
variety of simultaneous agonies, knows not whether it is her
mutilated fingers which hurt her most, or the bites wherewith I
lacerate her cunt, or the hammerings of the monstrous prick tearing
her fundament. But 'tis, it seems, the embuggering which is creating
the greatest difficulties for her ravaged frame; the titillations provoked in her behind appear to be nearly too much for her to endure.
Her screams, her tears, her groans attain such a pitch of violence
that Noirceuil, powerfully stirred by all he hears, teeters on the
brink of crisis. He retreats from the breach.

"Oh, Juliette!" he cries, "what a delightful ass the slut
possesses, and how I adore making her suffer. Would that I had all
hell's demons to help me bother her, each by means of an original
and unheard-of torture."

He has her turned over and held by the harlots; I open and
present her cunt to him: he plunges impetuously into it, while burning sulphur is put before the wretched girl's nostrils and her ears
are shorn away. The maidenhead is blasted, blood flows, and
Noirceuil, more aroused than ever, decunts, has the victim held
aloft by his two trusties, and sets merrily to flogging her with
martinets whose iron tips have been heated in the fire. He himself
is whipped by the whores while he is acting, and he sprinkles kisses
upon the asses of my tribades, whose buttocks are poised nearby on
a level with his lips; I suck him and at the same time tickle his anus.

"We are comfortable in here, are we not," says Noirceuil a
few minutes later; "the severe cold reigning outside gives me a
splendid idea."

He wraps himself in a heavy fur mantle, has his two men
and me don others, and we walk out of doors with a naked Fontange. In front of the château is a great marble basin now covered
with ice; upon it Fontange is placed. Cartouche and Desrues, hold-

ing great horsewhips and large firecrackers, stand by the basin's edge; Noirceuil, two or three paces back, watches, and I am at his side, frigging him. Fontange is told to skate six turns around the basin; when she strays too close to the edge, she is driven off by the whips; when she moves too far away, firecrackers are tossed at her, they explode about her head or between her legs. 'Tis a very gay spectacle, as the poor creature skids and slides this way and that, falling very frequently, each time all but breaking a leg.

"What!" exclaims Noirceuil angrily, seeing that she is about to complete her sixth circuit without having met with serious accident, "what! the slut is to come through unscathed?"

But the next instant, to Noirceuil's relief, an exploding firecracker blows one of her breasts away, she totters, fractures an arm as she falls.

"That, by God, is a little better," mutters Noirceuil.

She is borne back into the castle, unconscious; there, she is given that minimum of attention required to restore her to usefulness, her wounds are lightly bound up; and the stage is set for further scenes.

Noirceuil demands that my daughter frig me while he looks on; he avidly kisses the child's pretty hinderparts while she is engaged at her task.

"That shall turn into a lovely ass, Juliette," he says to me, "it already excites me enormously."

And though she was but seven years old, the wicked fellow prodded her tentatively with his gigantean prick; but, wheeling suddenly away from Marianne and toward his son Euphorbe, Noirceuil fits himself into that other fair young posterior, ordering me to crush the boy's testicles. There is no pain to equal what the unhappy child experiences, simultaneously tormented before and behind. After a brief run in that charming ass Noirceuil withdraws and has the child lashed by his ministers. While one of them flogs, the other embuggers the sore-beset Euphorbe, whose virile parts, in conformance with his father's wishes, are lost to a razor-blade wielded by me, who shaves them clean off his belly. Noirceuil, managing to keep one eye on the operation, ardently kisses Theodora's buttocks in the meantime.

"Come now, Juliette," he says to me, "have yourself fucked."

In a fearful state, I wanted nothing else. The two cannibals laid hands on me; one darted into my cunt, the other lodged himself in my ass; Noirceuil moved from the first to the next, embuggering them by turns while the whores spurred him on with lashes. As soon as he sees my discharge terminated, Noirceuil calls for Fontange and surrenders her to the two executioners.

"Make free with her," he tells them, "do whatever you like provided you torture her the while you fuck her."

The two rascals treated the girl so roughly that, in their arms, she swooned away once again.

"One moment," said Noirceuil, "I cannot resist sodomizing her anew."

And while he was satisfying himself I surprised him with an unexpected piece of cruelty: using a scalpel, I cut out my ward's right eye. That horror overpowers Noirceuil: his patient's reaction to the pain is so lively, her muscular contraction so sharp, that the libertine loses his seed ten inches inside the maid's rectum, at a juncture where he is being sodomized himself and is girt round by display of ass.

"Come along, my fair one," he says to the bedraggled creature; he grips her hard by the arm and drags her bodily into an adjoining chamber. I follow.

"Behold," says he, pointing to a table upon which lie, in gold coins, the five hundred thousand francs belonging to the poor girl, "that is your dowry; in order that you see that wealth, we have left you an eye, and it is our fond hope that the sight will prove an unhappy one: for that money is not to be yours. Slut, my intention is that you die of starvation; and I am going to treat you in such sort that you shall never be able to complain of your fate, although I am also going to set you at liberty. Here," he went on, taking her by the wrist, "touch this gleaming stuff, 'tis gold, 'tis yours, and yet you shall never have it. Aye, buggeress, feel it, that is what I want you to do; and now that you have done it, you'll do nothing more with these useless organs." So saying, he secures her hands upon a butcher's block, embuggers her, and I cleave off her hands while he is operating; the blood is stanched, the stumps bandaged. . . . Immediately, fucking uninterruptedly, the barbarian orders his victim to open her mouth and stick forth her tongue: I seize it with tongs,

I sever it at the root; I gouge out the remaining eye. . . . Noirceuil discharges.

"Good," says he, withdrawing and dressing the girl in a shift of sackcloth, "we are now assured that she shall not write, that she shall be blind as a bat, that she shall say never a word to any soul that lives."

We escort her to the gate and out upon the highroad.

"Go seek your living," says Noirceuil, giving her a ferocious kick, "your living, indeed! The thought of the fate that awaits you gives us greater cheer than we would derive from your assassination; begone, slut, venture into the world and denounce your persecutors, if you can."

"Ah, but she will be able to grasp their questions if nothing else," I pointed out, "her hearing remains to her."

"Does it now?" said the barbarous Noirceuil. "Then we shall remedy that," and he drove the point of a knife successively into each of her ears.

We returned to the company.

"Excite me, you rascals," our libertine said to the four women; "I have just discharged, I must recover my forces. . . . Frig these men and let them fuck me; my need of horrors is never so great as when I have been lately committing them."

Noirceuil is encompassed: asses, pricks surround him everywhere; he is frigged, fucked, tongued, sucked.

"Ah, Juliette," he announces once his device begins to rise, "Juliette, I wish to fuck your daughter."

Without allowing me time to reply, the villain leaps upon her, has his satellites hold her for him, and embuggers her with the very speed of light. My poor Marianne's shrill screams are all the warning I receive of the dreadful outrage perpetrated against her.

"My stars, Noirceuil! What are you about?"

"I am ass-fucking your child. This had to happen, did it not? and is it not better that it be your friend rather than some other who plucks the flower?"

After having mercilessly scraped and torn the little dear, he withdraws from her bleeding anus, still in possession of his energies; and casting haggard glances at the two harlots, he proclaims his intention to sacrifice one of them. The luckless girl clutches-his knees, implores him, fails to move him: she is seized, sat astride the top of a double ladder and tied fast. Noirceuil, in a chair placed five or six yards away, holds a cord whose other end is attached to the girl. Theodora and Laïs, kneeling, frig his prick, balls, and asshole; the two cannibals fuck me within his view; the remaining whore is bound head downward to a stake, and in that awkward posture awaits events. Twenty times the rascal tugs on the cord, twenty times the victim comes crashing down, is set back upright, pulled down again, and this abominable game does not end until she has broken both her legs and had her skull cracked. These infamies having heated the libertine, he instructs an aide to blindfold the other whore, and decrees that each of us inflict several wounds upon her. The ordeal will cease when she succeeds in guessing the name of her aggressor: choking on her own blood, she collapses before she is able to identify any of the hands that are causing her woe. Upon Noirceuil's orders and following a suggestion originating with me, these two wretches, out of whom not all the breath has fled, are hung up inside the chimney for a slow roasting above the flames and asphyxiation from the smoke.

Drunk with lust, Noirceuil roves in a rage about the salon; his lunatic stares fall upon the five objects still at the disposition of his lewd fury: my two tribades, my daughter, and his two sons. Everything leads me to suspect that he is ready to immolate them all at once.

"O infamy on high!" he shouts, "remove these curbs that make me little, when I would imitate thee and commit evil. I ask of thee no faculty for virtue, but canst not at least communicate to me thy mighty capacities for crime, and let me wreak havoc after thy example? Ah, dog of heaven, for one instant, if thou darest, put thy lightning into my hands, and once I have destroyed mortals, thou shalt see my loins grow gladder still as I hurl the bolt that blasts thy execrable existence."

With these words he leaps upon his son Phaon, embuggers him, has himself embuggered, and orders me, while I am being frigged by Theodora, to tear the living heart out of the child he is fucking, and to give it to him that he may eat it: the villain devours it, and at the same moment he discharges, drives a dagger into the breast of his other son.

"Well, Juliette! Look, my angel, and tell me, have I not done a fine day's work? Say, am I steeped enough in blood and atrocities?"

"You make me shudder, Noirceuil, but I imitate you withal."

"Think not, Juliette, that the orgy is over, nor that I am done."

His glittering eyes fall once again upon my daughter; his erection is that of a maniac; he seizes Marianne, has her pinioned, and encunts her.

"By God," he cries, "this little creature makes my head spin, damn me if 'tis not true. What do you mean to do with her, Juliette? You are not the sentimental fool, you are not the idiot to have feelings for this loathsome spawn of your abominable husband's blessed testicle; so sell her to me. Sell me the slut, Juliette, I wish to buy her from you; let's both soil ourselves, you in the pretty sin of vending me your child, I in the still more rousing one of paying you only in order to assassinate her. Yes, Juliette, yes, let's assassinate your daughter"—and here he finished wiping his prick and nodded toward it, gleaming and purple—"consider, if you will, how this idea inflames my senses. Stay, Juliette, have yourself fucked before you pronounce, answer me not till you have a pair of pricks in your body."

Crime holds no terrors for anyone when in the act of fucking; and one must always ponder its attractions when swimming in tides of sperm. Pricks penetrate me, I am fucked; a second time Noirceuil inquires to what purpose I wish to put my daughter.

"O villainous soul!" I cry, loosing discharge upon discharge, "star of perfidy, your ascendant places all else in eclipse, smothers all else in me save the longing for crime and infamy. . . . With Marianne do you what you please, whoreson knave," say I, beside myself, "she is yours."

No sooner does he hear these words than he decunts, takes hold of the poor child in his two wicked hands, and hurls her, naked, into the roaring fire; I step forward, and second him; I too pick up a poker and thwart the unhappy creature's natural efforts at escape, for she thrashes convulsively in the flames: we drive her back, I say; we are being frigged, both of us, then we are being sodomized. Marianne is being roasted alive; and we go off to spend the rest of the night in each other's arms, congratulating each other upon the scene whose episodes and circumstances complement a crime which, atrocious perhaps, is yet, in our shared opinion, too mild.

"So tell me now," said Noirceuil, "is there anything in the world to match the divine pleasures crime yields? Is there anything that can compete with the criminal humor? Beyond the criminal sensation is there anything that produces such vibrations in us?"

"No, my friend, not to my knowledge."

"Then let us live in crime forever; and may nothing in all Nature ever succeed in converting us to different principles. He is not a man to be envied who, smitten by remorse, undertakes the equally baneful and imprudent and needless retreat; for, irresolute, pusillanimous in his acts, he will be no happier in his new career than he was in the one he renounces. Happiness is dependent upon energetic principles, and there can be none for him who wavers all his life."

We spent a week at Noirceuil's country manor and accomplished a few new infamies every day. During that stay he urged me to try one of the passions of the Empress Theodora, Justinian's wife. I lay down upon the ground; two rustics sprinkled barleycorn upon my bush and upon the labia of my sex; a dozen large geese were brought up from the barnyard, and they began to peck at the seeds with their beaks, causing me such furious irritation in those parts that, when it was all over, I was absolutely obliged to fuck. Noirceuil, who had foreseen these results, presented me to fifty of his peasants, who performed prodigies with me. He too wished to try the geese; he had them feed from his ass, and afterward proclaimed that an ass-pecking procured sensations keener than those of the whip. To these debauches he added that of ordering both the schoolmaster and schoolmistress of the town to furnish him thirty pupils of the sex each taught. He held a mixed class at his castle, had the little girls depucelated by the little boys; then finished by whipping, sodomizing, and, at last, poisoning the lot.

"My friend," I said to Noirceuil, "these are all trifles; can we not advance a step and crown our orgies by some truly brilliant action? These townspeople have no supply of water but what comes from their wells; I have something of Durand's confection which will envenom the entire population inside two days: between my women and me, we shall, I promise you, spread devastation everywhere." And I was frigging Noirceuil while making that proposal to him. He proved unable to refuse.

"Fuck," was the response of the rake, helpless to contain his sperm at the announcement of such a scheme, "oh, by God! Juliette, 'tis a very curious imagination Nature gave you. Do whatever you like, my angel, the floods you are milking from me signify my acceptance."

I was as good as my word. All had been stricken four days later: fifteen hundred souls were interred, and almost as many were reduced to a state of agony so dire that they were heard pleading for death to come. The entire disaster was attributed to an epidemic. The ignorance of the provincial doctors protected us even from suspicion; and we returned to the capital after an expedition which had cost us discharges beyond counting.

Such is the happy position you see me in, my friends; I have a furious fondness for crime, I would not dream of pretending otherwise; crime, and nothing else, irritates my senses, I shall go on professing its maxims down to my dying hour. Exempt from all religious dreads, able, by discreet procedures and my wealth, to avoid difficulties with the law, what is the power, human or divine, that could impose a check upon my desires? The past encourages me, the present electrifies me, and I have little fear for the future; and my hope is that the rest of my life shall by far surpass the extravagances of my youth. Nature created human beings to no other end than that they amuse themselves on earth, and make it their playground, its inhabitants their toys; pleasure is the universal motor and law, it shall always be mine. Too bad for the victims, victims there must be; all the world would fly to pieces were it not for the sublime economy that assures equilibrium; only through acts of wickedness is the natural balance maintained, only thereby does Nature recover ground lost to the incursions of virtue. Thus, we are obeying her when we deliver ourselves unto evil; our resistance thereto is the sole crime she can never pardon in us. Oh, my friends! let us take these principles well to heart; in their exercise lie all the sources of human happiness.

Thus did Madame de Lorsange conclude the story of her adventures, whose scandalous details had more than once wrung bitterest tears from the interesting Justine. Otherwise stirred were the Chevalier and the Marquis; the straining and full-colored pricks they brought to light proved how different were the sentiments that animated them. They were in the midst of complotting some horror when a footman brought word of the return of Noirceuil and Chabert: they, the reader will recall, had been to the country for a few days, leaving the Comtesse to acquaint her two other friends with facts of which those other gentlemen had for a long time had cognizance.

The tears which had just wet our unhappy Justine's cheeks, her charming air . . . her sorrowing mien, the afflictions it told of; her native timidity, that touching virtuousness shadowed in all her features, everything about her incensed Noirceuil and the churchman, who must absolutely submit this luckless creature to their filthy and ferocious caprices. They took her off to a separate chamber while the Marquis, the Chevalier, and Madame de Lorsange gave themselves over to other but no less bizarre, crapulous, lewd frolics with the numerous lust-objects which that château had in plentiful store.

It was toward six o'clock and the day was waning when they all reassembled again, and deliberation was entered into regarding Justine's fate. In view of Madame de Lorsange's refusal to keep such a prude under her roof, the debate was whether to fling the poor soul out of doors or immolate her in the course of divers orgies. The Marquis, Chabert, and the Chevalier, more than sated with the creature, stood firmly for the latter alternative; Noirceuil, who had listened to the opinions of the others, now asked to be heard.

"My friends," he said to that joyous society, "in cases like the present one I have often found it extremely instructive to allow Nature to take her own course. There is, you have noticed, a storm brewing in the sky; let us entrust this personage to the elements. I shall embrace the true faith if they spare her."

This proposal met with general acclaim.

"I love such ideas," said Madame de Lorsange, "let us carry it out with no delay."

Lightning glitters, the winds howl, the clouds boil as though in a caldron, all the firmament is seething. One might have said that Nature, tired of her works, was readying to confound all her elements in order to force them to adopt new forms. Justine is shown the door; not only is she not given as much as a penny, she is sent forth stripped of the little that remained to her. Bewildered, humiliated by such ingratitude and so many abominations, but too content to escape what could have been worse still, the child of woe, murmuring thanks to God, totters past the château gates and down the lane leading to the highroad. . . . Scarcely does she reach it when a flash of lightning breaks from the heavens, and she is struck down, smitten by a thunderbolt that pierces her through.

"She is dead!" cry the villains, clapping their hands and hastening to where Justine lies upon the ground. "Come quickly, Madame, come contemplate heaven's handiwork, come see how the powers above reward piety and goodness. Love virtue, we are told, and behold the fate reserved for its most devoted servitors."

Our four libertines surround the corpse; and although it has been horribly disfigured, frightful designs nevertheless shape themselves in libertine minds, the shattered vestiges of the defunct Justine become the object of lewd covetings. The infamous Juliette excites her friends as they snatch the clothes from the body. The lightning, entering by way of the mouth, had burst out through the vagina; fierce jests are made upon the path by which the fire of heaven chose to visit the victim.

"Yes," Noirceuil said, "praise be to God, he merits it; there you have the proof of his decency: he left the ass untouched. It is still a beautiful thing, this sublime behind which caused so much fuck to flow; does it not tempt you, Chabert?"

And by way of reply the mischievous Abbé inserts his prick to the height of the balls in that lifeless hulk. His example is shortly followed by the others; unto her ashes they all four insult that dear girl, one by one; the execrable Juliette, watching them, frigs herself without pause; and finally the company retires, abandoning the corpse by the wayside. Woeful and ill-starred creature, 'twas written on high that not even the repose of death would safeguard you from the atrocities of crime and the perversity of mankind.

"Truly," declares Madame de Lorsange as the friends walk back to the château, "this most recent episode more than ever confirms me in the career I have pursued up until now. O Nature!" she exclaimed in her enthusiasm, "it is then necessary to thy plan, this crime against which in their stupidity a multitude of fools inveigh; thou dost desire crime then, since thy hand punishes them who dread it or refrain from committing it. Oh, these late events are most welcome, they consecrate my happiness and perfect my tranquillity."

Only a few moments after the party had re-entered the gate a coach rolled up, having arrived by a different road; it drove into the courtyard just as the five friends got there. From it stepped down a tall woman, very well attired; Juliette went to greet her.

The newcomer, just heavens! was no other than Durand, the bosom companion of Madame de Lorsange, she whom the Venetian Inquisition had sentenced to die, and whom Juliette believed she had seen hanging from the ceiling in that terrible courtroom. "Dearest soul!" she cried, casting herself into her friend's embrace, "by what stroke of fortune . . . great God, explain this to me . . . can I believe my eyes?"

A drawing room is opened, everyone enters, sits down, and in silence listens while the most mysterious of adventures is clarified.

"My dear Juliette," Durand began, and her voice and manner were composed, "standing before you is that very one whom you thought done horribly to death and forever lost, and who, by dint of her intrigues, her industry, her knowledge, now returns in greater fortune and better health than ever, since over and above the considerable riches that are hers to keep she has the further happiness of bringing you what the authorities confiscated from you in Venice. Exactly, Juliette," that loyal friend continued, depositing a large bundle of papers upon the table, "your fifteen hundred thousand *livres* a year are there, restored to you; that was all I was able to salvage; enjoy it in peace, my dear, and grant me nothing in return save the certitude of spending the remainder of my days in your society."

"Oh, my friends!" cried Juliette, wild from joy, "will he be wrong, the author who someday writes the story of my life, if he titles it *The Prosperities of Vice*? Make haste, Durand, tell us your wonderful tale, and be persuaded, let me say it at once, that 'tis I who beg you never again to leave us so long as you live."

Whereupon that forever celebrated woman, as succinctly as she could, informed the company that by promising to lend her services to the rulers of Venice, she obtained in exchange the assurance that another woman would be put to death in her stead, the example being necessary for Juliette whose properties the Council wished to acquire, and whose departure from the city was esteemed desirable, as a measure of prudence. The feint having met with complete success, she had then gone on to satisfy the Inquisitors, and produce in Venice a pestilence that carried off twenty thousand people; the operation terminated, she had asked, as a bonus, that her friend's belongings be remitted to her, the request had been accorded; her uppermost thought was then to escape from the city without delay, firmly convinced that these perfidious Venetians, nourished upon Machiavelli's principles, would rid themselves of their accomplice at the first opportunity.

"And so I rushed hither, my dearest, in search of you," Durand continued; "I contribute to your happiness, I ask no more. As do I, laugh at fate, which saved me twice from the gallows: assuredly, I was not born for the rope. What destiny holds in store for me I know not; but when my hour comes, let it overtake me as I lie in my cherished Juliette's arms, let it be so and I shall endure death without a murmur."

And the two friends, clasping each other, were fifteen minutes exchanging avowals of the sincerest friendship, confidence, and devotion which vice prizes quite as much as virtue, whatever may say the churlish sectators of that dismal and tedious divinity. Everybody was partaking in the two women's joyous effusions when there was a great clattering in the courtyard as a courier from Versailles rode up; he asked for Monsieur de Noirceuil; and when presented to him, handed a sealed order to our libertine.

"Great heaven!" the latter exclaimed, having perused the document, "it has been decreed, my dear Juliette, that every kind of good fortune be lavished upon us this lucky day. The minister is no more; here is the letter, in the King's hand, commanding me to hie myself back posthaste to the Court, where I am to assume the reins of government. What an ocean of felicities this news promises us! I go up to the capital, come with me, both of you," Noirceuil continued, addressing Juliette and Durand, "I want to have you by me forever; and indeed, how can I forego your assistance once I am at the helm of the ship I am about to steer! You, Chabert, I give you an archdiocese; Marquis, I name you Ambassador to Constantinople; for you, Chevalier, it's four hundred thousand *livres* a year: you'll remain in Paris to superintend our affairs. Come, good friends, let us all rejoice together, from all this I see nothing but happiness accruing to all save only virtue—but we would perhaps not dare say so were it a novel we were writing."

"Why dread publishing it," said Juliette, "when the truth itself, and the truth alone, lays bare the secrets of Nature, however mankind may tremble before those revelations. Philosophy must never shrink from speaking out."

The company left the following morning; greatest success crowned our heroes for the next ten years. At the end of that space, the death of Madame de Lorsange caused her to disappear from the world's scene, just as it is customary that all brilliant things on earth finally fade away. Unique in her kind, that woman died without having left any record of the events which distinguished the latter part of her life, and so it is that no writer will be able to chronicle it for the public. Those who might care to attempt its reconstruction will do little else than offer us their dreams in the place of realities, and between the two the difference is immense in the eyes of persons of taste and particularly in the eyes of those who have found the reading of this work of some interest.

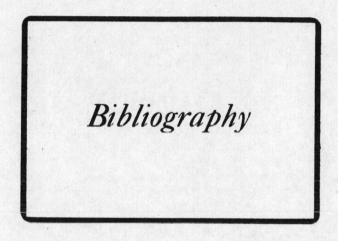

Bibliography

Bibliography

I. WORKS PUBLISHED DURING THE AUTHOR'S LIFETIME

LITERARY WORKS

1. *Justine, ou les Malheurs de la Vertu. En Hollande, Chez les Libraires associés* [Paris, Girouard], 1791. Two volumes, 8vo. Frontispiece by Chéry. During Sade's lifetime, there were six further printings between the initial publication and 1801. Sade's re-arrest that year put an end to the reprintings. These subsequent editions were:
   1) *En Hollande* [Paris, Girouard], 1791. Two volumes, 12-mo. Certain copies of this edition include twelve erotic engravings.
   2) *A Londres* [Paris, Cazin], 1792. Two volumes, 18mo. Frontispiece and five engravings.
   3) *Troisième* [fourth] *édition corrigée et augmentée. Philadelphie* [Paris], 1794. Two volumes, 18mo. Frontispiece and five engravings.
   4) *A Londres* [Paris], 1797. Four volumes, 18mo. Further augmented edition. Six erotic engravings.
   5) *En Hollande* [Paris], 1800. Four volumes, 16mo. Presented as the *Troisième édition corrigée et augmentée*, this is actually a reprint of the original edition.

6) *En Hollande* [Paris], 1801. Four volumes, 16mo. Also presented as the *Troisième édition corrigée et augmentée,* this was a reprinting of the 1800 edition.[1]

2. *Aline et Valcour, ou le Roman philosophique. Ecrit à la Bastille un an avant la Révolution de France. Orné de quatorze gravures. Par le citoyen S***. A Paris, chez Girouard, Libraire, rue du Bout-du-Monde, n° 47, 1793.* Eight volumes, 18mo.
There are actually three different editions of this work, bearing different dates and, in some instances, containing sixteen rather than twelve engravings. Sade announced[2] the book would appear at Easter of 1791, but the instability of the times and the death of Girouard beneath the guillotine in 1794 kept the book from appearing until 1795, which date should be taken as the date of reference of the original edition.

3. *La Philosophie dans le boudoir. Ouvrage posthume de l'auteur de "Justine." A Londres, aux dépens de la Compagnie, MDCCXCV.* Two volumes, 18mo. Frontispiece and four erotic engravings.

4. *La Nouvelle Justine, ou les Malheurs de la Vertu. Ouvrage orné d'un frontispice et de quarante sujets gravés avec soin. En Hollande* [Paris], 1797. Four volumes, 18mo. These four volumes comprise the first part of the definitive edition of this work, of which the second part, in six volumes, bears the title:

5. *La Nouvelle Justine, ou les Malheurs de la Vertu, suivie de l'Histoire de Juliette, sa soeur [ou les Prospérités du vice]. Ouvrage orné d'un frontispice et de cent sujets gravés avec soin. En Hollande* [Paris], 1797.

---

1 See the *"Bibliographie des Œuvres de Sade"* drawn up by Robert Valençay in *Les Infortunes de la Vertu,* Paris, Les Editions du Point du Jour, 1946.
2 In a letter of March 6, 1791.

6. *Oxtiern, ou les malheurs du libertinage, drame en trois actes et en prose par D.-A.-F. S. Représenté au Théâtre Molière, à Paris, en 1791; et à Versailles, sur celui de la Société Dramatique, le 22 frimaire, l'an 8 de la République. A Versailles, chez Blaizot, Libraire, rue Satory. An huitième* [1800]. One volume, 8vo, 48 pages.

7. *Les Crimes de l'Amour, Nouvelles héroïques et tragiques; précédées d'une Idée sur les romans et ornées de gravures, par D.-A.-F. Sade, auteur d' "Aline et Valcour." A Paris, chez Massé, éditeur-propriétaire, rue Helvétius n° 580. An VIII* [1800]. Four volumes, 12mo. Four frontispieces. This work contains eleven stories, as follows:
   Vol. I—*Juliette et Raunai, ou la Conspiration d'Amboise, nouvelle historique; La Double Epreuve.*
   Vol. II—*Miss Henriette Stralson, ou les Effets du désespoir, nouvelle anglaise; Faxelange, ou les Torts de l'ambition; Florville et Courval, ou le Fatalisme.*
   Vol. III—*Rodrigue, ou la Tour enchantée, conte allégorique; Laurence et Antonio, nouvelle italienne; Ernestine, nouvelle suédoise.*
   Vol. IV—*Dorgeville, ou le Criminel par Vertu; la Comtesse de Sancerre, ou la Rivale de sa fille, anecdote de la Cour de Bourgogne; Eugénie de Franval.*

8. *L'Auteur de "Les Crimes de l'Amour" à Villeterque, folliculaire. Paris, Massé, an XI* [1803]. 12mo, 20 pages.

9. *La Marquise de Gange. Paris, Béchet, Libraire, quai des Augustins, n° 63, 1813.* Two volumes, 12mo.

POLITICAL PAMPHLETS

1. *Adresse d'un citoyen de Paris, au roi des Français.* Paris, Girouard, no date [1791]. 8vo, 8 pages.

2. *Section des Piques. Observations présentées à l'Assemblée administrative des hôpitaux. 28 octobre 1792. De l'Imprimerie de la Section des Piques, rue Saint-Fiacre, nº 2.,* 8vo, 4 pages.

3. *Section des Piques. Idée sur le mode de la sanction des Lois; par un citoyen de cette Section. De l'Imprimerie de la rue Saint-Fiacre, nº 2, 2 novembre 1792.* 8vo, 16 pages.

4. *Pétition des Sections de Paris à la Convention nationale. De l'Imprimerie de la Section des Piques.* No date [1793]. 8vo, 4 pages.

5. *Section des Piques. Extraits des Régistres des délibérations de l'Assemblée générale et permanente de la Section des Piques. De l'Imprimerie de la Section des Piques, 1793.* 8vo, 8 pages.

6. *La Section des Piques à ses Frères et Amis de la Société de la Liberté et de l'Egalité, à Saintes, département de la Charente-Inférieure. De l'Imprimerie de la Section des Piques, 1793.* 8vo, 4 pages.

7. *Section des Piques. Discours prononcé par la Section des Piques, aux mânes de Marat et de Le Pelletier, par Sade, citoyen de cette section et membre de la Société populaire. De l'Imprimerie de la Section des Piques, 1793.* 8vo, 8 pages.

8. *Pétition de la Section des Piques, aux représentans du peuple français. De l'Imprimerie de la Section des Piques, 1793.* 8vo, 8 pages.

II. PRINCIPAL POSTHUMOUS PUBLICATIONS

1. *Dorci ou la Bizarrerie du sort, conte inédit par le marquis de Sade, publié sur le manuscrit avec notice sur l'auteur*

[signed A. F. (Anatole France)]. Paris, Charavay frères, éditeurs, 1881. 16mo, 64 pages.

2. *Historiettes, contes et fabliaux de Donatien-Alphonse-François, marquis de Sade, publiée pour la première fois sur les manuscrits autographes inédits par Maurice Heine. A Paris, pour les membres de la Société du Roman Philosophique, 1926.* 4to, 340 pages.
Contains the following works: HISTORIETTES—*Le Serpent; La Saillie gasconne; L'Heureuse Feinte; Le M. . . puni; L'Evêque embourbé; Le Revenant; Les Harangueurs provençaux; Attrapez-moi toujours de même; L'Epoux complaisant; Aventure incompréhensible; La Fleur de châtaignier.* CONTES ET FABLIAUX—*L'Instituteur philosophe; La Prude, ou la Rencontre imprévue; Emilie de Tourville, ou la Cruauté fraternelle; Augustine de Villeblanche, ou le Stratagème de l'amour; Soit fait ainsi qu'il est requis; Le Président mystifié; La Marquise de Thélème, ou les Effets du libertinage; Le Talion; Le Cocu de lui-même, ou le Raccommodement imprévu; Il y a place pour deux; L'Epoux corrigé; le Mari prêtre, conte provençal; La Châtelaine de Longueville, ou la Femme vengée; Les Filous.* APPENDICE—*Les Dangers de la bienfaisance (Dorci).*

3. *Dialogue entre un prêtre et un moribond, par Donatien-Alphonse-François, marquis de Sade, publié pour. la première fois sur le manuscrit autographe inédit, avec un avant-propos et des notes par Maurice . Heine.* [Paris], Stendhal et Compagnie, 1926. Small 4to, 62 pages.

4. *Correspondance inédite du Marquis de Sade, de ses proches et de ses familiers, publiée avec une introduction, des annales et des notes par Paul Bourdin.* Paris, Librairie de France, 1929. Small 4to, 452 pages.

5. *Marquis de Sade. Les Infortunes de la Vertu. Texte établi sur le manuscrit original autographe et publié pour la première fois avec une introduction par Maurice Heine.* Paris, Editions Fourcade, 1930. 8vo, 206 pages.

6. *Les 120 Journées de Sodome, ou l'Ecole du libertinage, par le marquis de Sade. Edition critique établie sur le manuscrit original autographe par Maurice Heine. A Paris, par S. et C., aux dépens des Bibliophiles souscripteurs,* 1931–1935. Three volumes, 4to, 500 pages (uninterrupted pagination throughout the three volumes).[3]

7. *Marquis de Sade. L'Aigle, Mademoiselle. . . , Lettres publiées pour la première fois sur les manuscrits autographes inédits avec une Préface et un Commentaire par Gilbert Lely.* Paris, Les Editions Georges Artigues, 1949. One volume, 16mo, 222 pages.

8. *Marquis de Sade. Histoire secrète d'Isabelle de Bavière, reine de France. Publiée pour la première fois sur le manuscrit autographe inédit avec un avant-propos par Gilbert Lely.* Paris, Librairie Gallimard, 1953. One volume, 16mo, 336 pages.

9. *Marquis de Sade. Le Carillon de Vincennes. Lettres inédites publiées avec des notes par Gilbert Lely.* Paris, "Arcanes," 1953. One volume, 16mo, 106 pages.

10. *Marquis de Sade. Cahiers personnels (1803–04). Publiés pour la première fois sur les manuscrits autographes inédits avec une préface et des notes par Gilbert Lely.* Paris, Corréa, 1953. One volume, 12mo, 130 pages.

11. *Marquis de Sade. Monsieur le 6. Lettres inédites (1778–1784) publiées et annotées par Georges Daumas. Préface de Gilbert Lely.* Paris, Julliard, 1954. One volume, 16mo, 288 pages.

12. *Marquis de Sade. Cent onze Notes pour La Nouvelle Justine. Collection "Le Terrain vague,"* no. *IV.* [Paris, 1956.] Small 4to, 158 pages (unnumbered).

---

[3] An earlier edition of *The 120 Days*, edited by Dr. Eugen Dühren, was published in 1904. The version is so riddled with errors, however, that Maurice Heine's 1931–1935 edition must rightly figure as the original edition of this work.

13. *Marquis de Sade. Voyage d'Italie, précédé des Premières oeuvres, suivi des opuscules sur le théâtre. Publiés pour la première fois sur les manuscrits autographs inedits par Gilbert Lely et Georges Daumas. Textes critiques par Pierre Klossowski, Roland Barthes, Hubert Damisch, Philippe Sollers, Michel Tort et Pierre Fedida.* Paris, Tchou, éditeur, 1967. One volume, 16mo, 656 pages. With an exhaustive bibliography by Jean-Claude Zylberstein.

III. PRINCIPAL UNPUBLISHED MANUSCRIPTS

1. *Les Jumelles ou le Choix difficile.* Two-act comedy in verse.

2. *Le Prévaricateur ou le Magistrat du temps passé.* Five-act comedy in verse.

3. *Jeanne Laisné, ou le Siège de Beauvais.* Five-act tragedy in verse.

4. *L'Ecole des jaloux ou la Folle Epreuve.* One-act comedy in *vers libres.*

5. *Le Misanthrope par amour ou Sophie et Desfrancs.* Five-act comedy in *vers libres.*

6. *Le Capricieux, ou l'Homme inégal.* Five-act comedy in verse.

7. *Les Antiquaires.* One-act comedy in prose.

8. *Henriette et Saint-Clair, ou la Force du Sang.* Prose drama in five acts.

9. *Franchise et Trahison.* Prose drama in three acts.

10. *Fanny, ou les Effets du désespoir.* Prose drama in three acts.

11. *La Tour mystérieuse. Opéra-comique* in one act.

12. *L'Union des arts ou les Ruses de l'amour.* A play in alexandrines, prose, and *vers libres.* In the *Catalogue raisonné* of 1788, this work was to comprise six parts and a final *Divertis-*

sement. In the extant manuscript, the *Divertissement* and one play, *La Fille malheureuse,* are missing.

13. *Les Fêtes de l'amitié.* Two acts incorporating prose, verse, and vaudeville.

14. *Adélaïde de Brunswick, princesse de Saxe, événement du XI* *siècle.* Novel.

IV. PRINCIPAL UNPUBLISHED MANUSCRIPTS EITHER DESTROYED OR NOT RECOVERED[4]

1. *L'Egarement de l'infortune.* Three-act prose drama.

2. *Tancrède.* One-act lyric play in alexandrine verse with music interspersed.

3. *La Fille malheureuse.* One-act comedy in prose.

4. *La Fine Mouche.* Tale.

5. *L'Heureux Echange.* Tale.

6. *La Force du Sang.* Tale.

7. *Les Inconvénients de la pitié.* Tale (first draft).

8. *Les Reliques.* Tale.

9. *Le Curé de Prato.* Tale.

10. *La Marquise de Thélème.* Tale (first draft).

11. *Le Portefeuille d'un homme de lettres.* Of this projected four-volume work, there exists eleven *historiettes* published by Maurice Heine, an *avertissement, the Voyage de Hollande* included in the *Voyage d'Italie* published by Lely and Daumas, and various fragments.

---

4 Numbers 1 through 17 represent works mentioned in the 1788 *Catalogue raisonné;* numbers 18 through 20 are works seized at Sade's publisher, Massé, on 15 *Ventôse, An IX;* number 21 is the projected ten-volume work burned at the *Préfecture de Police* after Sade's death; numbers 22 through 25 correspond to works mentioned in the "general catalogue" that appears in *Cahiers personnels (1803–04).*

12. *La Liste du Suisse. Historiette.*

13. *La Messe trop chère. Historiette.*

14. *L'Honnête Ivrogne. Historiette.*

15. *N'y allez jamais sans lumière. Historiette.*

16. *La justice vénitienne. Historiette.*

17. *Adélaïde de Miramas, ou le Fanatisme protestan. Historiette.*

18. *Les Délassements du libertin, ou la Neuvaine de Cythère.*

19. *Les Caprices, ou un peu de tout.* Political work.

20. *Les Conversations du château de Charmelle.* The first draft of *Les Journées de Florbelle.*

21. *Les Journées de Florbelle, ou la Nature dévoilée, suivies des Mémoires de l'abbé de Modose et des Aventures d'Emilie de Volnange servant de preuves aux assertions, ouvrage orné de deux cents gravures.* This immense work, contained in over a hundred notebooks, according to Lely's estimate, was burned by the police at the request and in the presence of Sade's son, Donatien-Claude-Armand.

22. *Conrad ou le Jaloux en délire.* Four-volume novel. The manuscript, according to *La Biographie Michaud,* was "seized at the time the Marquis was taken to Charenton."

23. *Marcel ou le Cordelier.* Four-volume novel.

24. *Mes Confessions.* Two volumes. It is thought that diaries Sade kept during his thirteen-year detention at Vincennes and in the Bastille were to have provided some of the contents of these *Confessions.*

25. *Réfutation de Fénelon.* One-volume polemic.